THE INCAS

Other Books by Daniel Peters

Border Crossings

The Luck of Huemac: A Novel About the Aztecs

Tikal: A Novel About the Maya

DANIEL PETERS

THE INCAS

A Novel

Random House New York

All rights reserved under international and Pan-American
Copyright Conventions. Published in the United States by
Random House, Inc. New York, and simultaneously by
Random House of Canada Limited, Toronto.

Grateful acknowledgement is made to University
of Oklahoma Press for permission to reprint the
"Genealogical Table of the Imperial Inca House" from
Empire of the Inca by Burr Cartwright Brundage.
Copyright © 1963 by the University of Oklahoma Press.
Reprinted by permission.

Library of Congress Cataloging-in-Publication Data
Peters, Daniel.
The Incas: a novel/by Daniel Peters.
p. cm.
ISBN 0-394-58492-9
I. Incas—Fiction. I. Title.
PS3566.E7548F68 1991 813'.54—dc20 90-44467

Manufactured in the United States of America
Typography and binding design by J. K. Lambert
24689753

To Gary

Acknowledgments

The author wishes to express his deep gratitude:

To his scholarly sources: Robert and Marcia Ascher, Louis Baudin, Garland Bills, Hiram Bingham, Pedro de Cieza de Leon, Bernabe Cobo, Kent Day, Raoul D'Harcourt, Graziano Gasparini, Victor W. von Hagen, Michael Harner, John Hemmings, Gonzalez Holguin, Edward Hyams, John Hyslop, Frederico Kauffmann-Doig, Richard Keatinge, Paul Kosok, Garcilaso de La Vega, A.R. Luria, Luise Margolies, J. Alden Mason, Craig Morris, Richard Mosely, George Ordish, Huaman Poma de Ayala, John H. Rowe, Irene Silverblatt, Donald Thompson, Margaret Towle, Rudy Troike, Gary Urton, Nathan Wachtel, Andrew Weil, Ronald Wright, R.T. Zuidema.

To his guides in Bolivia and Peru: Angel, Guido, Maarten Van de Guchte, Guillermo Reverter, Jorge Jesus Romero, Alberto Vasquez.

To those who generously shared their expertise with an amateur: Robert Ascher, Burr Cartwright Brundage, Geoffrey Conrad, Arthur Demarest, John Murra, Joseph Stirt.

To the Libraries of the University of Maryland, College Park, Rensselaer Polytechnic Institute, University of Arizona.

To my agent, Susan Lescher, for her patience and good advice.

To my friends and readers: Linda Alster, David Gregory, Judy Lindberg, and Blackburn Peters.

To my first and only wife, Annette Kolodny, who was intrepid in the Andes and her usual wise, loving self over the long haul. Let's do it all again in the next life.

Contents

Glossaries of Quechua terms, of the characters,
of the gods, of the places and tribes are to be found
in the back matter of this book.

The Sapa Inca

Manco Capac

Sinchi Roca

Lloque Yupanqui   *(no firm dates for first eight)*

Mayta Capac

Capac Yupanqui

Inca Roca

Yahuar Huacac

Viracocha

Pachacuti   A.D. 1438–1471

Topa Inca   A.D. 1471–1493

Huayna Capac   A.D. 1493–1527

Huascar   A.D. 1527–1532

Atauhuallpa   A.D. 1532–1533

Cusi's Genealogy

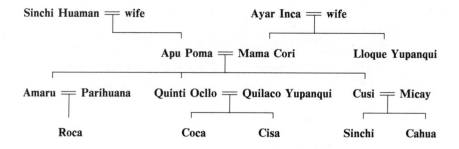

Royal Genealogy

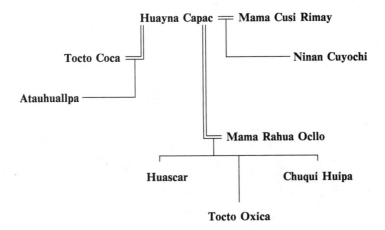

Imperial Inca House Genealogy

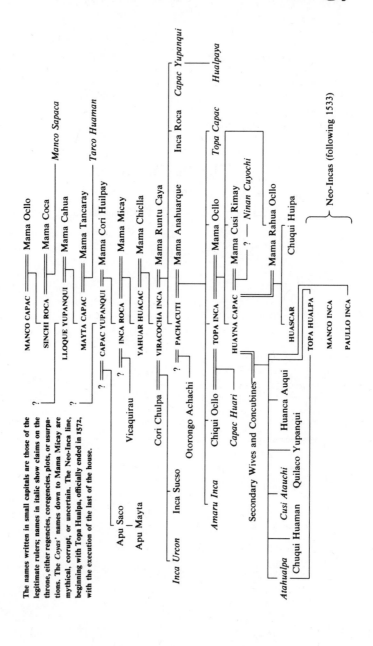

The names written in small capitals are those of the legitimate rulers; names in italic show claims on the throne, either regencies, coregencies, plots, or usurpations. The *Coyas'* names down to Mama Micay are mythical, corrupt, or uncertain. The Neo-Inca line, beginning with Topa Hualpa, officially ended in 1572, with the execution of the last of the house.

Neo-Incas (following 1533)

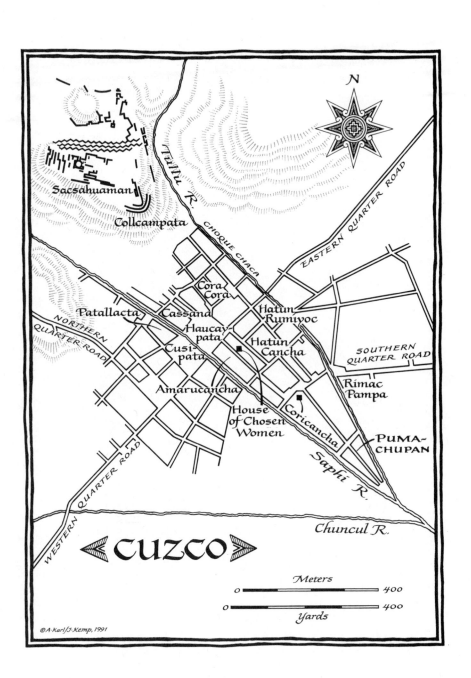

N

Sacsahuaman

Collcampata

Tullu R.

CHOQUE CHACA

EASTERN QUARTER ROAD

Cora Cora

Patallacta

Cassana

Haucay pata

Hatun Rumiyoc

Cusi pata

Hatun Cancha

NORTHERN QUARTER ROAD

SOUTHERN QUARTER ROAD

Amarucancha

Rimac Pampa

House of Chosen Women

Coricancha

PUMA-CHUPAN

WESTERN QUARTER ROAD

Saphi R.

Chuncul R.

≪CUZCO≫

Meters

0 ——————— 400

0 ——————— 400

Yards

©A·Karl/J·Kemp, 1991

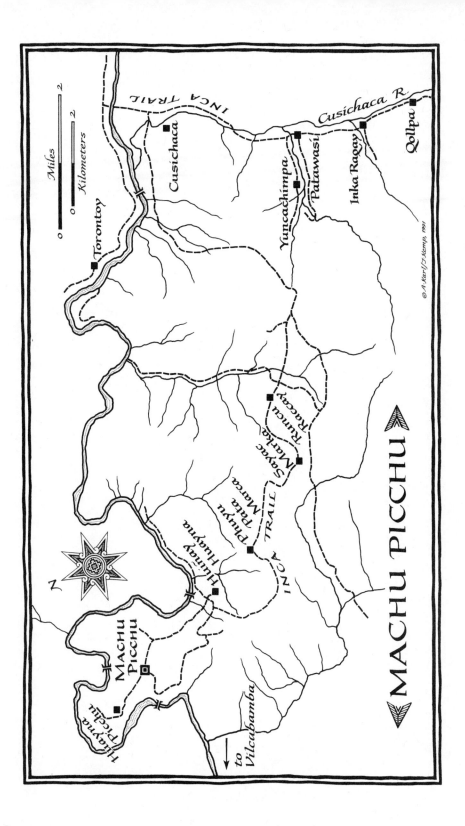

MACHU PICCHU

I

PACHACUTI:
The World Turned
Upside Down

(A.D. 1511)

O N THIS DAY Huayna Capac, the eleventh Sapa Inca, Sole Lord of the Four Quarters, was departing from Cuzco. He had called up an army of warriors from all parts of the Four Quarters, over one hundred thousand men to help him wage war upon the Quitos and the Carangui, who had destroyed the Inca garrisons on the frontier north of Tumibamba. It was the young ruler's first extended military campaign, and he was taking his entire court and most of his wives with him, along with his top administrators and their families, and a large group of artisans, stonemasons, and builders. Cuzco had been in a frenzy of preparation for months, and now the great exodus of Incas was finally about to begin.

In a short while, in the great square called Haucaypata, the most illustrious of the Inca warriors, the Old Guard, would begin forming their ranks, with their fringed shields and battle standards in their hands, their heavy golden earplugs mirroring the light of the sun. The other Incas of the blood would file out onto the terraces in front of the palaces of the past rulers, with those of Upper Cuzco on the northern side of the square and those of Lower Cuzco to the south. The Sapa Inca's litter, wreathed in gold and feathers and covered with finely embroidered gauze curtains, would already have been brought out by the Rucana bearers who would carry him and the Coya north to Tumibamba. Having completed their prayers and offerings, the Sun priests would be standing in a group around the sacred Napa, the spotless white llama who would lead the procession out of Cuzco. Men wearing the blue livery of palace servants would be leaving the square at its northwest corner, sweeping the ground as they went with grass brooms, clearing the Northern Quarter Road over which the Sapa Inca would pass. At the proper time, Huayna Capac himself, the Sole Lord, Shepherd of the Sun, would emerge from his palace, the Amarucancha, and walk toward the enormous stone dais that stood in the center of the square . . .

Cusi Auqui saw none of this with his eyes, for there were no openings in the thick stone walls of the House of Learning, and the boys were made to sit with their backs to the single doorway. Nor could he truly hear the muted shuffle of the crowd's sandaled feet, for any sound from the outside was drowned by the boys' chanting recitation, which they spoke in unison, their fingers running over the knots of the memory cords spread out on the floor in front of them. Even as he imagined the scene in the square, Cusi did likewise, his mouth and fingers possessing their own memories, independent of his attention. Yet he knew that it was wrong to let his thoughts wander when the legend of Viracocha's journey was being remembered aloud. He had been reminded many times by the teachers that his participation should not be halfhearted, no matter how easily the words came to his tongue. Remembering was not simply his personal gift but a serious form of devotion, necessary to the well-being of Cuzco and the Incas.

But only one verse later, Cusi let his eyes stray sideways to his friend Rimachi. Rimachi was a Cañari from Tumibamba, and his father, a member of the Royal Guard, was accompanying the Sapa Inca north. Most of Rimachi's family was going with him, but Rimachi himself, like Cusi, was being left in Cuzco. He was bent over his cords with a frown of concentration on his face, doing his best to resist the thoughts that threatened to pull him away. Cusi guiltily returned his attention to the recitation. Still, he was aware of his other two friends to his right: Uritu struggling as always over his cord, Tomay sitting upright with his eyes on the teacher at the front, displaying the completeness of his involvement. Both were the sons of provincial chiefs and were accustomed to being separated from their families, so the departure of the Incas did not affect them as directly as it did Cusi and Rimachi.

Cusi's fingers found the last pendant cord and his voice rose automatically, along with those of the other boys. They had come to the last verses of the legend: Viracocha and the two helpers he had created out of himself had traveled the length of the land, from Titicaca to the far north. One had gone along the coast of Mama Cocha, the Mother Water, another through the rugged jungle lands east of the Andes Mountains, and Viracocha himself along the high plateau between the mountain ranges. In each place, the Viracochas had brought the people forth from their caves in the earth and had given them the means to live, and the understanding of how they must live. Now Viracocha would depart over the waters to the north, leaving his creation behind. Cusi joined the final verse with his whole heart:

None were left to summon,
None to animate and succor;
All men stood upon the earth,
All in their places of origin;
Now he would leave them,
Now he would return
To Mama Cocha,
To the great foaming waters
From which he sprang:
Ticci Viracocha Pachayachachic
He who knows the earth
Ticci Viracocha Pachayachachic
He who disposes all things.

The boys sat upright at the conclusion of the chant, their backs straight and their eyes upon the gray-haired old man who sat at their head. But the teacher did not comment on their performance or give any sign that he was ready to dismiss them. He knows which of us have farewells to make, Cusi thought, resisting the urge to glance at Rimachi. This was the patience and demeanor the educators had been trying to teach the boys since their first day in the House of Learning: the demeanor of an Inca, who displayed none of the impatient impulses of his heart, no matter what the circumstances. The legend of Viracocha's departure had of course been chosen deliberately, in order to make those impulses even harder to control, at least for the boys whose families were leaving.

"Leave me now in an orderly fashion," the teacher said finally, his admonition causing most of the boys to sit for an additional moment before they began to wrap their cords into tight conical bundles and rise from their places. Cusi forced himself to move with the same deliberateness as Rimachi, who was in turn using Cusi as *his* standard of orderliness. As a result, Uritu and Tomay got through the doorway ahead of them and were waiting in the narrow cobblestone street outside the compound. The street was crowded with warriors, officials, and all manner of porters, some leading strings of pack llamas.

"You will be in the Haucaypata later?" Cusi asked Rimachi as the four of them huddled in a tight group outside the doorway. Rimachi adjusted the wickerwork band around his head and nodded with his usual assurance.

"Not in my customary place, though. My father is with the Sapa Inca's litter, so I will stand in the back with the families of the Guard."

"I will find you when it is over," Cusi promised, and he turned inquisitively toward Uritu and Tomay. Uritu just shrugged and shook his head, but Tomay pursed his lips resentfully and swallowed before speaking. The high color in his fleshy cheeks made Cusi sorry he had asked.

"I have to leave Cuzco immediately," Tomay said in a flat voice, his eyes going past Cusi. A moment of embarrassed silence ensued. Tomay was a Colla

from Hatuncolla, and the Collas had rebelled against the Incas too many times
ever to be fully trusted. Only one thousand of them were allowed to be in
Cuzco at any one time, which meant, on a day as important as this, that some
would have to leave before any more could enter for the departure ceremonies.

"I will walk to the turning with you," Rimachi proposed abruptly, rescuing
them all from their embarrassment by leading Tomay off down the street. Cusi
and Uritu turned to walk east, their wrapped cords in their hands, their slow
pace dictated by the crowd in the street and their proximity to the sacred heart
of Cuzco. They did not speak of the shame Tomay had to bear on behalf of
his people, since it was a matter of law and beyond questioning. Of the four
of them, Cusi was the only Inca of the blood, with full rights to Cuzco.

"You will be living in your uncle's compound after today?" Uritu suggested
as they walked, and Cusi nodded with enthusiasm.

"He has given me the room that used to belong to his eldest son. He has
always treated me more like a son than a nephew."

"You will be closer to my father's compound. You must come and visit with
me more often."

"And you must come and eat with me and Lloque Yupanqui," Cusi said
distractedly, realizing how far they had come. The broad street in front of them
was Choque Chaca, the street that covered the Tullu River. There were openings in the pavement down the middle of the street, providing a continuous
glimpse of the shiny water rushing through the channel below. Uritu suddenly
gestured with the rolled cord in his hand.

"You want to spend this time with your family. You can go faster without
me."

Cusi smiled at him, grateful for his understanding. Uritu was a Campa from
the Eastern Quarter, and it was not permitted to him to run through the streets
of Cuzco. An Inca boy like Cusi, however, might be forgiven such disrespect
on a day like this.

"The Campa do not believe in farewells, do they?" Cusi asked, glancing at
the thin lines tattooed across Uritu's cheeks, and the spray of blue-green
feathers that hung from his leather headband. Uritu replied with his customary
frankness, his face grave with received wisdom.

"No. We feel you might keep some of the departing person's spirit behind
with you and make him weak."

"But it makes you strong to remember the faces of those who love you. It
makes you less lonely."

"We do not forget. But we prefer to remember the person as he was, *here,*
not as a person who is leaving." Uritu spread his hands, apologizing for his
insistence, but Cusi just laughed and gave him a playful poke.

"I will not say farewell, then. But I will see you tomorrow," he promised,
edging out into the street as the last of a line of pack llamas passed, bobbing
their heads and bumping one another from behind. Uritu simply nodded, his
broad. tattooed face impassive, as if he were already alone and could not be
affected by Cusi's desertion.

Clutching his cord against his chest, Cusi broke into a trot and ran off down the street, picking up speed even as he wove his way through the people in front of him. He jumped over one of the open stretches of water in the center of the street, then jumped back again to avoid a column of warriors who had just come around the corner of one of the compounds. He turned left onto the steep, narrow street called Hatun Rumiyoc, which climbed the hill in terraced segments like a set of giant stairs. By habit, Cusi adopted a measured gait, taking four strides to cross each terrace before leaping up to the next. The street was lined with the walled compounds of the Incas of the blood, and through every open doorway he could see porters, llamas, and servants milling about in the courtyard within, surrounded by piles of bags and bundles. Cuzco was going to seem empty tomorrow, when all these people had departed.

His parents would be gone then, too, along with his brother and sister and most of his uncles and cousins. He knew he would miss them greatly, especially his mother and sister, but he still had his friends and his uncle Lloque Yupanqui, who had done more to raise him than Cusi's own father. And he would be joining his family soon enough, after he had completed the manhood rites and his training as a warrior. The Incas might even be marching *back* to Cuzco by then, to celebrate a swift victory over the Quitos and the Carangui. In any event, Cusi was determined to show that he was not hurt or upset at being left behind. He had already rehearsed, in his mind, what he would say to his mother to convince her not to worry, and to soothe her sorrow at their parting. He would make her feel as confident about his future as he felt himself.

Near the top of the hill, Cusi turned in through the tall trapezoidal doorway that was the only entrance to his family's compound. Within the walled enclosure, ranged around a small, central courtyard, were four stone houses, each with a single entrance and a steeply pitched roof thatched with thick, woven layers of gray and yellow ichu grass. At the far end of the courtyard, set upon a platform that compensated for the slope of the hill, was an open-sided awning house that was used as a kitchen and storage area. The head of the family servants, Runtu Caya, was inside the awning house, giving orders to a group of porters. One of the porters' llamas had strayed to the edge of the platform and was nibbling on the plants in the flower bed that lined the base of the retaining wall. The llama raised his head briefly as Cusi entered the courtyard, then went back to his eating. Let him eat, Cusi thought; there would soon be no one here to tend the garden.

He had just turned toward his mother's house when his sister, Quinti Ocllo, came through the curtained doorway, holding up her palm to make him stay where he was. She was already wearing her traveling cloak around her shoulders, and her shift was loosely belted at the waist for walking. Cusi smiled as she came up, but Quinti only bared her teeth and gave her head a slight shake, letting him know that this was no time for smiles. She was three years older than Cusi and still a whole hand taller, so he had to look up to meet her eyes.

"Father wants to see you," she told him in a voice that was raspy with tension. Cusi recognized the voice and drew back a little, since she was leaning over him protectively.

"Is he angry with me?"

"He is angry with everyone. He learned today that he will be going to Tumibamba as the micho of the province, not the governor as he wished."

"That should not make him angry with *me.*"

"He also learned that Lloque Yupanqui has been named as one of Huayna Capac's Royal Rememberers, and will be going north with us, after all. He had to find another guardian for you."

"Lloque is leaving, too?" Cusi murmured in dismay. Then he realized how childish he must sound, and tried to speak briskly. "Mother will be pleased to have her brother with her, at least."

Quinti shook her head the same way she had when he had smiled at her, though with a bit more exasperation.

"She has not made a secret of her pleasure. Nor Father of his displeasure. Be warned, Cusi. Do not let him hurt you with what he says."

"I will come and see you and Mother afterward," Cusi said bravely, but Quinti simply stared at him, as if memorizing his face, until he turned and headed for his father's house. He went through the open doorway without hesitation, trying to gain some strength from the certainty of movement. Light poured into the large single room from the windows at both ends and the two that flanked the doorway; the walls had been stripped of the helmets, shields, and cloth hangings that had formerly decorated them, making the room seem hollow and barren.

Apu Poma was standing near one of the niches in the back wall, dipping lime from a wooden container while conversing with Cusi's older brother, Amaru. They were both good-sized men, dressed in tunics and breechcloths of fine cumbi cloth, fringed bands of red cloth around their knees and ankles. Cusi felt small in their presence and inclined his head respectfully, coming to a halt beside Amaru. His brother, who would be going north in the company of the other Inca warriors, gave him a smile that seemed strained and then surprised him by laying an affectionate arm over his shoulders. The heavy round earplug fixed into the stretched lobe of Amaru's ear dangled briefly within Cusi's vision, its golden surface glinting in the light from the doorway. Their father's reaction was swift and harsh.

"Leave him be. He is too used to kindness as it is."

Amaru's handsome face sobered abruptly and he removed his arm and took a step backward, making Cusi feel small and exposed again. Apu Poma dipped his silver spatula into the carved container in his hand and lifted a rounded heap of grayish powder to his lips, adding lime to the quid of coca that was already bulging in his cheek. He chewed for a moment, making sucking sounds and reducing the bulge in his cheek. He always chewed coca when he was upset, and it always seemed to make him additionally impatient, so that Cusi thought of coca as the fuel for his anger. Apu Poma spoke abruptly, out of one side of his mouth.

"Lloque Yupanqui has relinquished his responsibility as your guardian. I spent most of the morning searching for a replacement. It was not easy to find someone who would sponsor a boy of your age and size. You are fourteen, with only one year left before your initiation group will undergo the Huarachicoy. How could I assure someone that you will be fit for the rites, when you are still so small and weak?"

"I have grown half a hand in the last year," Cusi said tightly, reminding himself that he had heard this from his father before. "And I am the fastest runner in our group," he added more forcefully, "faster even than Tomay and the other boys from the high plain."

Out of the corner of his eye, Cusi thought he saw Amaru smile at this boast. Apu Poma rubbed his chin, as if considering the merits of what he had just heard. Then his arm shot out and the flat of his hand struck Cusi on the breastbone, knocking him to the floor.

"What good is your swiftness now?" he demanded. "Would you be the first one to the enemy, only to have him slaughter you? Stand up!"

Trembling with shock, Cusi scrambled to his feet. Amaru had stepped forward with a hand raised, as if to intervene, but Apu Poma waved him back with a stern gesture.

"You are not a participant in this conversation. Attend us in silence or leave."

Nostrils flaring, Amaru stepped back but did not leave. Cusi fought to hold himself still, since the sudden fall had jarred him from the base of his spine to the top of his head. Apu Poma seemed to loom over him, making him arch his neck to meet his father's eyes.

"I spoke to some of the warriors in charge of your training. They think that you lack the desire to dominate your opponent in the drills. They say that you are immature, and more interested in keeping the friendship of the other boys than in proving your own worth."

"Immature?" Cusi echoed blankly, unable to recall ever being reprimanded for that by the warriors. "Sumac Mallqui said that I was immature?"

"It does not matter who said it. I can see it for myself. You do not *command* respect, as an Inca should—and must. You try to ingratiate yourself with smiles and kindness, like a woman."

Cusi was too stunned to speak. How could the warriors have regarded him with such contempt and not shown it to him? How could he have missed it if they had?

"You pretend that you do not know this about yourself," Apu Poma said scornfully. "That only made it more difficult to find a suitable guardian, one who could break you of your delusions. In desperation I was forced to go to Otoronco Achachi and plead with him to do me this favor. He has consented."

Cusi repressed a shiver of apprehension. Otoronco Achachi was his father's uncle and Cusi's most famous living relative, the Conquerer of the Eastern Quarter. Cusi had met him only once and remembered a scarred face and a jeweled cup made from a human skull. He had not known that his father was close enough to Otoronco Achachi to ask him such a favor.

"That is a great honor," he whispered.

"Perhaps it will inspire you to grow," Apu Poma suggested, with a pointed lack of conviction. "Because if you have not grown sufficiently by the time of next year's rites, the teachers will keep you in the House of Learning for another year, at my instruction. There is no point in risking the disgrace of failure. Otoronco Achachi will be the judge of your readiness."

Cusi felt as if he had just been knocked to the floor for a second time, though this time it gave him a voice.

"But I will be separated from my initiation brothers if I am held back. We have done everything together for three years, and we are meant to be friends and allies for as long as we live. I have no such friends among the boys who come behind us."

"An Inca who can command respect needs no friends. He can go anywhere he is sent, and live alone if he must. I had no friends with me when I commanded the garrison at Copiapo. But if you need friends so badly, it is better that you make them among Huascar and his brothers than among the sons of Chuncho savages and Colla traitors."

Apu Poma had belittled Cusi's friends before, and in similar terms. But this suggestion made no sense. Huascar was the Heir of the Sapa Inca, and he had no friends *except* his brothers. His guards would not allow anyone else to come near him. Besides, Cusi would never trade the friendship of Uritu, Rimachi, and Tomay for that of anyone else, however important in blood. If his father did not understand that, there was no way to reason with him. Cusi would simply have to grow and make himself strong, so that Otoronco Achachi would find him ready.

"I have heard you, and taken your words into my heart," he said in a determined voice. "Do I have your permission to visit with Mama Cori and Quinti Ocllo now?"

"No," Apu Poma said flatly. "That is another attachment you must break if you are ever to become a man. You will see them again when you wear the earplugs of an Inca warrior. Not before."

Cusi stood stiffly, frozen in confusion. Was he supposed to ignore his mother's departure, as if it were not happening? Where was he supposed to hide himself so he would not be seen?

"I do not understand what I am to do . . ."

"I want you to leave this room and go directly to the huaca to which you were pledged as an infant. Make an offering and ask for the strength to become a man, so that you might come to Tumibamba and see your mother again. I have already sent word to the guards at the bridge to let you pass out of the city."

"But the departure ceremonies will be over before I can return," Cusi said in a hollow voice, resisting comprehension. "You will all be gone."

"An Inca is often separated from those he loves, often without warning.

Farewells are an indulgence that will only make you weaker." Apu Poma reached back into the niche and brought forth a small woolen bag. "Your mother has agreed that this is best. She has provided you with these coca leaves as an offering to the huaca."

Cusi realized that he was still holding his cord, and he transferred it to his left hand before reaching out for the bag. It was extremely light and crackled slightly between his fingers. He looked up at his father, disbelieving him for the first time. His mother would never have agreed that this was best for him, even if she had been forced to accede to Apu Poma's wishes. She would never have denied him a proper farewell, not even as a punishment.

"Go," Apu Poma said. "You have seen enough of me, as well."

Cusi glanced once at Amaru, who was standing like a piece of stone, his eyes glazed and unseeing. Then he turned abruptly and walked out of the room, carrying the offering in one hand and the cord in the other. He walked halfway across the courtyard before he stopped. He had never disobeyed a command in his life, at least not intentionally. But he had never received one that seemed so cruel and unjust. It might be years before he would see his mother again. If he could only have a look, a parting gesture to remember her by . . .

From behind him, he heard Amaru's voice, loud and angry, then his father's, then Amaru's again, even louder. They were arguing. This is all wrong, Cusi thought, not wishing to hear what they were shouting at each other. This was not a day to be exchanging harsh and angry words, especially not between fathers and sons.

He tried to turn his body toward his mother's room, but the sight of the woolen bag in his hand arrested him in midmotion. He could not go to her with her own offering in his hand, defiling it with his disobedience. She had permitted him many liberties as a child, but disobedience had never been one of them. She would not expect to see him, and she would not wish to, now that Apu Poma had forbidden it.

Curling his fingers around the bag and the cord, he forced himself to begin moving toward the compound entrance. He had been told many times that a man who obeyed no one was a savage, doomed to live in ignorance and confusion, never knowing his proper place in the world. Yet at this moment he felt that way himself, and he had not disobeyed anyone. The feeling was even worse than he had imagined, a fearful sense of uncertainty that seemed to hollow him out from within.

Yet even in his confusion, his instinct was still to obey, so he kept on walking, putting one foot in front of the other, leaving his father's compound without looking back.

ONLY WHEN he had climbed all the way to the top of the terraced hillside northeast of his home did Cusi turn to look behind him, and then only because custom demanded it. The flat, rocky ridge on which he stood was itself a huaca, a sacred place, since it was the last vantage point from which part of the holy

center of Cuzco could be seen. Squatting near one of the blackened patches
of ground where offerings had been burned, Cusi held his palms in front of his
lips and blew kisses in the direction of Topa Cuzco, Illustrious Cuzco, the heart
of the Four Quarters and the most powerful huaca of all. The hill of Sacsahuaman thrust into his view to the west, obscuring all but a corner of the
Haucaypata, which appeared, from the slice that was visible, to be packed solid
with people. He could see all of the Amarucancha, Huayna Capac's palace,
with its many thatched roofs, and beside it the tall stone walls that enclosed
the House of Chosen Women. Further south, on a bluff overlooking the Saphi
River, was the Coricancha, the Golden Enclosure, which housed the images
of Inti, Viracocha, Illapa, and the other high gods of the Incas.

When he had finished paying his homage, Cusi remained in his crouch,
staring down the hill at the checkered pattern of terraced plots, which alternated the brown and yellow of fallowed fields with the red of turned earth and
the bright green of new maize, each section joined to those around it by the
shiny ribbons of irrigation ditches. In the time it had taken him to climb this
far, his family had probably finished their packing and gone to join the crowd
in the square. Amaru would be standing with the warriors around the dais;
his parents and Quinti in front of the Condorcancha, with the other members
of the Iñaca household. Rimachi would be there, too, in the midst of the
families of the Cañari Royal Guard. He would look for Cusi when the ceremonies were over and would wonder what had happened to him. It would never
occur to him that Cusi had been banished like their friend Tomay; such things
were not supposed to happen to Incas of the blood.

Swallowing hard, Cusi made a last mocha to his mother, plucking hairs from
his eyebrows and blowing them toward the Haucaypata, performing his farewell in silence, from afar. Then he turned and climbed up over the back of the
ridge, and was out onto the plain, the rolling, treeless grassland that was too
steep for terracing and irrigation. Here he could let himself go and just run,
leaning out over his legs in a wind of his own making, trying to outrun the
bitter thoughts that pursued him. Partridges erupted from the deep bunches
of ichu grass at his approach, but he ran on heedlessly, his breathing ragged
with emotion. Vivid images of vengeance, of spurning his father or denouncing
him publicly, sped through his mind. He would never forgive Apu Poma for
abusing him, and he would repay him in kind one day.

Soon he was among the herds of llamas and alpacas that grazed on the plain,
and the shaggy, long-necked beasts broke and scattered in alarm, huffing and
spitting as he raced through their midst. Catching sight of the commotion in
their flocks, the herd boys circled in from several directions, their slender
switches in their hands. They were all familiar with Cusi, who came this way
often, always running. Crying out in recognition, the boys tossed aside their
switches and took up the race, falling into stride with Cusi as he rushed past.
The llamas and alpacas bounded out of the way as the boys sprinted across
the sloping ground, their teeth bared in a taut grin of competition.

Usually Cusi enjoyed making a contest of it, letting the fastest stay abreast of him for a while just for the sake of the challenge. But not today, not after what his father and the warriors had said about him. Besides, the boys seemed to have strung themselves out to his left, as if they were trying to herd *him* back down the slope, away from his destination. Cusi could not imagine why they would want to keep him away from the huaca, but he was in no mood to be thwarted by anyone. Ducking his head into the wind, he ran as fast as he possibly could, reckless of balance or control, thrusting himself out in front of the pack as if he had been shot from a sling. The cord and bag of coca leaves were still in his hands, whipping up and down out of the corners of his eyes as he flew over the low clumps of grass. When he was far enough ahead of the nearest boys he cut back up the slope, heading straight for the top without regard for the incline. The boys receded behind him rapidly, shouting incoherently at his fleeing back, but still he did not slacken his pace, bending low over his digging knees, trampling his fury beneath his feet.

Once over the top of the ridge, he came gasping and lurching to a halt, incredulous at his own effort. Then he thought he was going to be sick and bent low over the grass to retch. His stomach held, though, and soon the nausea had subsided. His throat and lungs burned, and he held the woolen bag and cord against his heaving chest as he staggered across a rock-strewn depression and ascended the next ridge. As the pain in his legs eased and his breathing returned to normal, the wild anger that had propelled him up the slope began to seem like the lingering delirium of a just-broken fever. He had never experienced such violent feelings before, and they frightened him and made him feel slightly ashamed. An Inca was calm in the face of every adversity and never succumbed to his own anger. Outrunning a group of herd boys in anger only proved his father's contention that he was immature.

Yet no one who had seen him run straight up the hill could have questioned his fitness. Nor, when he was moving, would any enemy strike him as easily as his father had. Cusi Huaman, "my joyful hawk," his mother used to call him when he ran for her. She was the one who had first made him run when he was small and very sickly. She would retreat in front of him, smiling and holding out her arms in an embrace that had to be pursued. It was her way of giving him the strength to survive his premature birth, which had nearly cost both of them their lives. He was the last of Mama Cori's children, and she had nurtured him with a devotion she had not shown to Amaru or Quinti, or to her husband either. Apu Poma had been away commanding the garrison in Copiapo when Cusi was born, and he did not see his youngest son until Cusi was almost five, because Mama Cori had refused to subject such a frail child to the long, wearisome journey south.

And so he has hated me from the first day he saw me, Cusi thought bitterly. But then he caught himself and tried to put his anger aside. There was now only one grassy swale between himself and the huaca, and it would not be right to enter the holy place with rancorous feelings in his heart. The mere thought of standing in front of the stone again soothed him, making him recall all the times his mother had brought him here. He suddenly realized that it probably *had* been his mother who had suggested he go to the huaca, once Apu Poma had decided to send him away. She knew that her presence would be strongest for him here, where they had been alone together so often. He remembered the way she had humbled herself before the huaca, surrendering her dignity to the power that had saved her child. Cusi always felt loved and protected here, as grateful as his mother that he was alive.

More composed, with the bag of coca leaves in one hand and his cord in the other, Cusi walked slowly to the top of the rise. He held his breath in anticipation of his first view of the huaca: the jagged, spear-shaped stone imbedded in the barren, hollowed earth; the lightning bolt of Illapa, God of Thunder, frozen into gray rock. What he saw instead brought him up short, exhaling in surprise. There were people—people who most definitely were not Inca—standing around the huaca. When they saw him come over the ridge, they scattered and fled in the opposite direction, and Cusi, shocked though he was, instinctively began to count them as they ran away. Whoever they were, they did not belong here, and he would have to report them to the elders of the Vicaquirao household, who were the guardians of this huaca. Then he noticed that one man remained in the depression below, squatting in front of the stone, his back to the place where Cusi stood.

The man made no attempt to flee as Cusi came down the slope, scanning the perimeter of the hollow to be sure no others had stayed behind. He was astounded that these people of worthless blood would dare to profane the huaca with their presence. But he was also made wary by their boldness. People who would violate one law might violate any other, even on ground as sacred as this. Already he could feel the aura of otherness, huaca, that surrounded the crooked pillar of stone, and a peculiar, windless silence seemed to rise up around him as he stepped down into the circular hollow of well-beaten earth. The squatting man—an old man, he saw—had not moved a muscle or given any sign that he was aware of Cusi's approach. A small fire of dried grass and llama dung was burning in the blackened circle in front of the stone, and piled in a heap nearby were the offerings brought by those who had fled: tiny potatoes and pieces of rough cloth, clay cups of akha, bundles of dried flowers and sweet grasses, dark mounds of chuño flour.

Cusi shifted his grip on his own offering and his cord, realizing that his palms were sweating. He had already had too many surprises today, too many things he could not explain. He stopped a few feet away from the man, whose grayish-white hair was long and unbound, falling loosely onto his sloping shoulders. His plain brown tunic and breechcloth were made of a coarse and greasy cloth, the kind favored by the high plains dwellers. He still had not moved, and Cusi found himself unwilling to break the silence, which seemed filled with the echoes of his own breathing and thick with a smell like hot wool. Suddenly the man raised his arms and tilted his head back, as if addressing the huaca, which rose above him like a great gray finger pointed at the sky.

"What is your message?" he asked in a deep, ceremonial tone, and waited a moment. Then he slowly rose to his feet and turned around, showing his face to Cusi. A black band had been painted across his withered brown features from cheeks to temples, and out of the blackness shone two blank, clouded eyes, glowing dimly like pieces of tarnished silver. He is blind, Cusi realized. He was a small man, not much taller than Cusi himself. Yet Cusi's hands were still damp, and he could feel his heart thudding against the inside of his chest.

"What is your message?" the old man repeated, again raising his arms, and Cusi understood that the question had been intended for him all along. He could smell akha on the man's breath now, a sour, obnoxious odor that told him the akha had not been brewed from maize. Some of his outrage returned, and he remembered what his father had said about an Inca commanding respect. He spoke in the icy tone of rejection he wished he had used with his father.

"I have no message, except that you do not belong here. I will have to report your intrusion to the proper authorities."

The painted face wavered, then turned its blank eyes skyward.

"You have sent me a boy," the old man murmured, dropping his arms. Then he thrust his chin in Cusi's direction. "You must be the Running Boy, the one who was first brought here by his mother."

Cusi jerked backward in surprise, but he kept himself from demanding how the man knew that.

"I am Cusi Auqui, the son of Apu Poma Inca, of the Capac Ayllu Inca. And I tell you again that you must leave this place. You should have fled with the others."

The old man crossed his arms on his chest and blinked several times, revealing unpainted eyelids.

"They did not flee, Cusi Auqui. I sent them away."

The old man fell stubbornly silent, his wrinkled face impassive beneath the band of black paint, his silvery eyes fixed somewhere above Cusi's forehead. Though he knew it was not possible, Cusi felt himself being examined. He took a soundless step to the side and the milky eyes did not follow. But then they did, as the old man gradually shifted his whole body until he was again facing Cusi directly.

"I have never been able to see you," he said at last, "and I did not know your name until you spoke it. But I have felt your presence many times after you have been here. You and your mother always left the air warm behind you. I did not expect that you would speak with such a harsh and angry voice."

The rebuke was offered gently, but it stung Cusi into silence. He had *not* been speaking with his own voice, or in the respectful way his mother had taught him to speak here. The old man went on in the same musing tone, cocking his head to one side.

"Where is your mother now, Cusi Auqui? Have you lost her? Is it this that makes you so angry?"

"Yes!" Cusi blurted, then let out a deep sigh, relinquishing all pretense of authority. "She is going to Tumibamba with the rest of my family."

"And you are being left behind?"

"I must prepare myself for the Huarachicoy, the rites of manhood."

"But how will you become a man without your parents to guide you?"

"My father's uncle has consented to be my guardian," Cusi said after a moment's hesitation. "He is the famous war chief Otoronco Achachi."

The old man pursed his lips, appearing unimpressed by the name.

"Tell me: Does the Sapa Inca also leave his sons behind?"

"Some of them," Cusi allowed. "Huascar, the heir, is even younger than I am and must also stay behind. But what right do you have to question me?"

"I must learn why you were sent to me. Tell me: What have you brought with you?"

Cusi looked down at his hands, remembering the things he still carried.

"An offering of coca leaves, provided by my mother. And a memory cord I made myself in the House of Learning."

"What does the cord remember?" the old man asked intently, and Cusi sighed again, seeing that he was still being regarded as some kind of messenger.

"It holds a haravi, a story song," he explained. "It tells of Viracocha, the Creator. It tells of his journey across Tahuantinsuyo, awakening the people of all lands. And of his departure in the north, out over the Mother Water."

"And what of Viracocha's return? Where is that recorded?"

"I do not know what you mean. There is no legend concerning Viracocha's return."

"There was," the old man assured him, nodding his head for emphasis. "There was. And now the Sapa Inca has gone north, as well, and left his son to become a man without him. It is a powerful message you have brought, Cusi Auqui. Do you understand its meaning?"

"I have told you I am not a messenger," Cusi protested in bewilderment. "My father sent me here, and I brought the cord without thinking."

"You have a great affinity for this huaca. Why should you not be its messenger? You were the one who came when I asked the huaca for a sign, a message. It is no mistake that you came carrying this cord. Or that you came here angry, missing your mother."

Cusi raised his eyes to the leaning shaft of stone, a silhouette that was fixed in his earliest memories, from before he had ever seen his father. Perhaps the old man spoke the truth. There was no reasonable explanation for why Cusi was here now, instead of in the Haucaypata with the other Incas. He lowered his gaze to the blackened face, the pale dead eyes.

"I do not know anymore what is a mistake," he confessed. "I do not even know your name."

"I am called Raurau Illa. I am another who is dedicated to this huaca. You may tell that to those you say are authorities. But there is something I must give you first."

The old man fumbled with the woven bag hanging under his arm, finally bringing forth a hand clasped around some hidden object, extending it searchingly in Cusi's direction. Cusi hesitated, awkwardly shifting the cord to the hand holding the bag of coca leaves. He realized that he should not accept anything from this man, especially when he had nothing to give him in return.

Yet he could not stop himself from extending his free hand, opening his fingers beneath those of the old man. When they touched, Raurau Illa gently deposited a slender piece of rose-colored quartz in Cusi's palm. It was about as long as his little finger and had a crooked bend in the middle, like a serpent or a lightning bolt. The ends were still rough quartz, but the middle had been rubbed to a high polish, so that he could see into the pink-tinted depths of the crystal. The stone seemed to gather warmth very quickly when Cusi closed his fingers around it, and Raurau Illa bared his strong white teeth in a kind of smile.

"It holds the heat of Illapa's lightning," he explained. "You must keep it as your huaoqui, your spirit brother. It will be a part of your strength for as long as you live, and it will hold your spirit upon the earth after your breath is gone."

"But I am too young to have a spirit brother," Cusi said in alarm, exposing the stone on his open palm. "I must have permission, and there must be a ceremony . . ."

"I was told many years ago that one day I would know to whom the stone should be given. This is that day."

"But I cannot accept it!"

"You have already accepted it," Raurau Illa pointed out. "There is no way to dispossess yourself of it without endangering everything that is yours. Do not even think to try."

Cusi stared at the stone in his hand, thinking that it would be a simple thing to tip his palm and drop the stone at the old man's feet. He had no right to a spirit brother at his age, and the old man had tricked him into taking it. His father would have refused it outright, as an attempted bribe. Cusi closed his fingers back around it, feeling the heat where it nestled against his palm. Then he held out his memory cord to the old man.

"Here. You must have this, then."

He pushed the tightly rolled bundle of cords into Raurau Illa's groping fingers, experiencing an undeniable surge of gratification when the old man again smiled his mirthless smile.

"Perhaps someday you will sing the story song for me," he suggested, turning the cords over in his hands. "I must go now. I ask you to dispose of our offerings for me. I do not have the strength."

"I will do it," Cusi promised, and the old man turned back toward the huaca, bowing his head and making the mocha, blowing kisses over the bundle in his hands. Then he slowly walked away, his sightless gaze fixed on the horizon, his bare feet finding their own path across the circle of dirt. Cusi watched him go in silence, rolling the polished finger of stone between his own fingers. It felt somehow as if it belonged in his hand. Raurau Illa had reached the far side of the depression, and two of his people came down over the ridge to assist him up the grassy slope. They hastily averted their faces when they saw that Cusi was looking at them, and they did not look back as they guided the old man up the ridge and out of sight.

Then Cusi was alone with the huaca, and the rush of his own thoughts made him dizzy. He felt that his world had been turned upside down, emptied of all that was familiar and trustworthy. He had lost Lloque Yupanqui as his guardian and gained Otoronco Achachi, a man he knew only by reputation. His father had struck him and threatened to separate him from his friends, and then had cruelly separated him from his mother. He had come here only to find an intruder, a blind man who regarded his presence as a message from the gods. He had accepted a spirit brother he was not allowed to have in return for a memory cord he should not have given away. He wished he could run, but there was no way to flee the consequences of what had already occurred. The Inca had gone to the north, leaving his sons to find their manhood without him, as Cusi had been left by his father. That was the old man's "message." But what had he meant with his talk about Viracocha's return? Surely the Sapa Inca would return once the Quitos and Carangui had submitted to his rule. The Sapa Inca always returned to Cuzco to celebrate his victories; he would not depart over the waves as Viracocha was said to have done.

Nor could Cusi depart from here without fulfilling his promise to the old man. Squatting before the smoldering fire, he placed the bag of coca leaves on the coals and blew gently to raise a flame. The finger of stone was clasped securely in one hand, and with the other he began to add the offerings left by Raurau Illa's people to the flames. He did not hurry, exercising the same devotional care his mother had always displayed toward the huaca. Let me be with her again, he prayed wordlessly, squatting alone in the silence, sending the smoke of his hopes coiling upward into the immensity of sky.

Suta, Chachapoyas Province

T HE GIRL called Misa was making akha with her mother when one of her young cousins came running into the compound, shouting that the micho was coming. Misa spat the last of the maize she had been chewing into the akha vat and helped her mother replace the heavy wooden cover. They looked at one another across the top of the vat, Misa searching her mother's face for a response to this unexpected visit. But her mother merely shrugged and reached up to straighten one of the braids wound around Misa's head.

"The micho has been here before. But come, Casca will want us all to be waiting with him. The Inca must not think he has surprised us, even if he has."

They hastened out into the courtyard, where the rest of the family had already begun to assemble. The first wife had brought out Casca's stool and set it in the eating area between the houses, which was shaded by a row of palm trees. She and the second wife had taken their places to the left and a little behind the stool, and Misa and her mother went to join the line at that end. Casca came out of his house accompanied by his oldest remaining son and two of his nephews, who had been visiting with him. After Casca had seated himself on the stool, stretching out his scarred legs in front of him, the young men assumed their places to his right.

Misa wondered briefly where her two younger brothers were, deciding that they must have been sent to alert the rest of the clan. It was her father's custom to have as many witnesses present as possible whenever the Inca came to his compound, and the family itself was no longer so large. Misa glanced sideways at her father, who was sitting with his hands wedged against his hips, facing the entrance to the compound. She wondered if he knew why the micho was coming here today. There had been no incidents for some time, at least none for which Casca could be accused. He had been deliberately avoiding trouble.

But her father remained impassively silent, facing forward as if he had been waiting this way for days. Then the first of the warriors came into the compound, in pairs, carrying fringed shields and metal-tipped spears. They were all mitmacs, the outsiders the Inca had brought to live in Suta after the war. Twenty of them entered in advance of the micho, spreading out on both sides of the entrance. The micho strode into the courtyard between them, accompanied by Pias, the head chief of the village, and by an Inca of lesser rank who wore round silver earplugs. Even more warriors came in after them, nearly filling the compound and producing a shiver of apprehension in the women around Misa. This was an unusual show of force, especially when there had been no disputes lately between Casca and the Inca.

Even as she thought this, Misa recognized the Inca with the silver earplugs and felt the blood leave her face. It was the selector of chosen women, the man her father called the Daughter-Stealer. Misa's mother put a hand on her arm to steady her, and the other two wives moved closer in a protective gesture. Misa saw her father rise to his feet in anger as the three men came to a halt in front of him. He spoke in Quechua, the language of the Inca, addressing the micho without any of the usual amenities.

"What is the meaning of this? Why do you come here with this army of warriors? We are at peace with the Inca, are we not?"

The micho was a short, dark-skinned man by the name of Condor Tupac. He wore a tunic with a pattern of red stars and the large golden earplugs of an Inca of the blood, and he carried a painted baton as a symbol of his office. He had been the lieutenant governor of the province for the last four years, yet now he spoke to Casca as if they were complete strangers.

"There is no peace for those who violate the Inca's laws."

"And what law have I violated?" Casca demanded.

"The singing of your clan's war songs has been forbidden for many years, by decree of the Sapa Inca. Yet you sang them aloud at your last feast. We have many witnesses."

Casca sat back down on his stool, spreading his hands and glancing around in a display of utter incredulity. He held the pose for several moments, during which Misa came out of her trance sufficiently to notice that other people were joining the group around her. Her brothers had returned, and two of her father's brothers were now standing beside him. Young men from the other clans had filtered in past the warriors and were standing against the compound wall, while even younger boys hung from the branches of the trees outside. Misa realized that her father was waiting for his audience to gather, so that the micho, for all his warriors, would feel *watched.* Casca rose again from his stool, this time more slowly, straightening to his full height and pointing a finger at the man with the silver earplugs.

"If you have come to speak to me about my singing, why have you brought the selector of chosen women with you?"

"I have come to accuse you of violating the Inca's ban," the micho proclaimed, ignoring the question and the pointed finger. "Do you deny what has been said against you?"

Keeping his arm extended, Casca swung the finger toward Pias.

"Who has spoken? You, Pias?"

The chief, who was from a rival clan within the village, glanced around uneasily at the onlookers lining the wall of the compound, before making a brisk, affirmative nod.

"It is strange I did not see you there," Casca said scornfully. "You must have been hiding behind the wall with the other mitmac spies."

"I have heard the testimony of several others," the micho added, "some from your own clan."

"I will be allowed to confront them at the hearing, then."

"There will be no hearing. I have been authorized by the governor to pass judgment upon you. Do you have nothing to say in your own defense?"

Casca put his hands on his hips and stared at the micho in silence for a moment.

"You are in a great hurry to condemn me, Condor Tupac," he said at last. "I was taught in Cuzco that the Inca never makes judgments in haste, without hearing all sides. Why do you violate your own laws in order to accuse me? Can it be that you want something that is mine?"

"Do not add disrespect to your crimes," the micho warned. "I ask you for the last time: Do you deny the charges against you?"

"And I ask *you,*" Casca shot back, "if you have not already reached a judgment, why have you brought the selector of chosen women with you?"

The young men along the wall began to stir and murmur aloud, causing the warriors to tighten their ranks and face outward. The micho raised his baton and waited until it was quiet.

"Since you choose not to defend yourself, I must assume that you are guilty," he stated, raising his voice above the cries that threatened to interrupt him. "As your punishment, I hereby revoke your exemption from the levy of chosen women."

A piece of fruit sailed past the micho's head and splattered at the feet of the man with the silver earplugs, causing him to jump backward. The warriors reacted instantly, ducking behind their shields and thrusting out their spears at the young men around them, who flattened themselves against the wall.

"Do not attempt to rouse your people against me, Casca," the micho shouted angrily. "They will only be hurt."

"*You* are the one who arouses them, Micho. They have heard me sing the war songs every year at the feast that celebrates our founding as a people. It has always been illegal, but the micho has always known better than to interfere with a custom that means so much to us. You have known better yourself for four years. Yet today you would make me a criminal for it, so you can steal my daughter!"

The micho had regained his composure, though he did not signal his men to relax their vigilance. Nor did he respond to Casca's accusation. He went on as if reciting his part in a conversation he had memorized long ago.

"The governor has ordered that the ban be strictly enforced. You must present all of the eligible daughters of your secondary wives for inspection by the selector of chosen women."

Casca took a step toward him, his hands bunched into fists.

"Is this how you would please the Sapa Inca?" he demanded, his voice hoarse with outrage. "You would fill the House of Chosen Women with girls taken unjustly from their parents?"

The micho seemed to look through him, his baton held stiffly in front of his chest.

"We want to see the girl called Micay."

Casca took another step forward, as if to make it impossible for the micho to see past him. His voice was a warning growl that made the nearest warriors tighten their grips on their spears.

"We have lived together peacefully, Condor Tupac. Do not make me your enemy for life."

"Surrender the girl," the micho said flatly, giving his baton a peremptory shake in Casca's direction. In one swift motion, Casca snatched the painted stick from the micho's hand and threw it to the ground. It bounced and made a snapping sound as it split and fell into two pieces.

"*Hear me,* Inca!" Casca bellowed, so forcefully that everyone froze in their places for a moment. The micho was the first to recover, holding his hands out to his sides, palms up, to prevent his warriors from attacking. He looked straight at Casca for the first time.

"Speak, then. But you will pay for this affront to my authority."

"How will you make me pay," Casca inquired loudly, "when you have taken the last of what is precious to me? You have already taken four of my sons into your armies, and two of them have died far away from here. You have arranged marriages for my daughters with men I do not know, and you have taken the weavers and craftsmen from my clan and made them live in Cuzco and work for you. Now you would even take from me the memory of my ancestors, and you would use that as your excuse to steal my last daughter. I cannot believe the Sapa Inca needs to take so much from me, when he possesses all of the Four Quarters. I do not believe you and the governor serve him honorably by seizing my daughter. Reconsider what you do here, Condor Tupac. You may regret it until the day you die."

Casca turned and walked slowly back to his stool, seating himself with an audible sigh. One of the mitmac warriors knelt, picked up the pieces of the baton, and handed them to the micho with an apologetic bow. Condor Tupac gazed at them thoughtfully for a moment, then raised his eyes to Casca.

"I have told you that I am here at the order of the governor. I do not have the liberty to reconsider." He turned slightly to face the place where the women stood, extending his arm in a beckoning gesture. "Come forward, Micay."

Misa started at the sound of her Quechua name and immediately began to obey. Then she stopped and turned to her mother, who was blinking rapidly to hold back her tears. Without thinking, her mother reached up to straighten Misa's braids, a gesture that was arrested in midmotion and became a lingering caress as tears began to flow down her cheeks. Misa embraced her and was embraced in turn by the first and second wives. They were weeping, too, the jealousies and intrigues of the past forgotten. Misa was too stunned to weep as she stepped back from them, nodded once to each of her brothers, and walked the few steps to her father's side, turning to face the micho. The Inca summoned forward the man with the silver earplugs, the selector of chosen women.

"Do you find her worthy?"

"She is older than most," the man said slowly, trying to appear detached in his assessment. "But yes, of course . . . they will be pleased to have her in Caxamarca."

The micho beckoned to her again.

"You must surrender her, Casca. She belongs now to the Sapa Inca, Huayna Capac, Sole Lord of the Four Quarters."

Pias and the mitmac warriors bowed their heads at the name, but Misa turned for a last look at her father. His eyes were also dry, for he would never show his grief in front of the Inca. He spoke to her softly in Chacha, their own tongue.

"You are nearly a woman, my daughter. In a few more seasons, perhaps, I could have given you in marriage to a Chachapoyas man."

Misa nodded wordlessly, memorizing the lines in his face, the dark glitter in his eyes, the flecks of gray in the black braids wrapped around his head.

"Now I must be content that you are strong and able to care for yourself," Casca went on, bitterness creeping into his voice. "But I will never forget that you were taken from me against my will, and I will never forgive the men who have done this."

"Come, Micay," the micho said from behind her, and Misa turned and walked toward him with her head down. Her mother and the other wives began to keen high in their throats, making the sounds of mourning. Men fell in around her and began to lead her out of the compound.

"I will be back to deal with you another time, Casca," the micho said in parting, and as she went through the entrance to the compound, Misa just heard her father's defiant reply.

"Bring all your warriors, Micho. There is no safety here for thieves . . ."

THE GIRL called Micay lost track of the days as she and her companions journeyed westward across the province of Chachapoyas. She was now one of thirteen girls whom the selector of chosen women had collected in the villages where they stopped. All had been chosen for their beauty, and with the sole exception of Micay all were between the ages of five and nine years. Micay was some four years older than the oldest of them, and from what she could tell from their clothing and speech, the only one from a family of noble blood. This more than her age made them shy with her, so that they did not immediately turn to her as a surrogate mother.

They were marched in single file between lines of armed guards who were forbidden to speak to them, and who were replaced by new guards at regular intervals. At every stopping point, the selector of chosen women called out the girls' Quechua names one by one, waiting to hear each reply. Micay answered automatically to the name, which had been given to her by the woman who had been her Quechua teacher in Suta. It meant "round face" and though her face was not especially round, the closeness in sound to her real name had been more important to the teacher. It had not mattered to Misa, either, since the name was simply part of a disguise she put on only when the teacher or an Inca official was present. Now Misa was gone and the disguise was all that was left, moving numbly along the Inca road to Caxamarca.

The rainy season had begun, bringing a fresh green to the fields, but the landscape seemed bleak and desolate to Micay's eyes. The only distraction from her internal misery was provided by the hardships of the journey, which told on the girls despite all the selector's efforts to shelter and protect them. Descents into hot, tropical valleys were followed by steep climbs over cold mountain passes, where the altitude and thin air brought on the headaches, cramps, and dizziness of the soroche, the sickness of the heights. The selector rested them as often as possible and had them given hot food and coca tea at the wayside rest houses, but the girls had little appetite and grew increasingly tired and listless. They had bad dreams and cried out in their sleep, weeping uncontrollably in Micay's arms if she awakened them. They marched as if they had never left their dreams, making the selector and the guards extremely nervous whenever the trail narrowed or crossed one of the swaying rope bridges.

Finally, though, they came over the last pass and saw below them Caxamarca, a great city that began high up in a canyon and spread its many thatched dwellings onto a broad plain surrounded by snow-capped mountains. The procession began to move faster, shielded from the stares of passersby by the tight ranks of the guards. Micay could sense the guards' eagerness to complete this duty, and there was some of it in the girls, as well. Few had more than a vague notion of what awaited them at the House of Chosen Women, but they all welcomed the end of their time on the road. Micay could feel the same heedless euphoria in herself, the relief of having reached the destination, however unknown it might be. Though she knew the feeling was false, she did not try to deny it, because it gave her a little more strength with which to face whatever did lie ahead.

They had been in the streets of the city for some time when suddenly a high, grayish-brown stone wall loomed up beside them. It seemed sudden because it was so different from the other walls they had passed. There was no mud mortar between the stones, which were smooth and many-sided, fitted together so tightly that their joinings seemed like shadows painted over a tapestry of solid rock. The guards halted in their places, and the selector of chosen women could be seen at the head of the column, surrounded by a different set of guards. Holding a memory cord in one hand, he began to summon the girls forward one by one, explaining something about each of them to a tall, elderly woman in a black shift and mantle, with a doubled square of black cloth pinned over her gray hair. From her place near the end of the line, Micay noticed the deference the selector was paying to this woman, who listened to him without taking her eyes off of the girl in front of her.

As Micay drew closer to the front, the selector held up his hand to her, indicating that he wished to save her for last. She was not surprised by this and readily stood aside to let the girls behind move past her. She knew she was a kind of prize, due to her father's rank. Several of the girls might one day be more beautiful than she, but they would never have her blood.

When the last of the girls had been examined and sent through the high, tapering doorway beyond the guards, Micay stepped forward to present herself for the woman's inspection.

"Her name is Micay, my mother," the selector of chosen women explained. "She is from Suta, in eastern Chachapoyas. Her father has the rank of a chief, but he is a rebel and would not accept the post under our rule. He prefers conflict to accommodation, and he has clashed with the micho several times. Most recently, his exemption from the levy of chosen women was revoked and he was forced to surrender this daughter to me."

The woman's eyes had been moving all this time, studying the weave of Micay's shift and the way her hair was braided, lingering for a moment on her bare neck and shoulders. Now they came to rest on her face, appearing sympathetic, as if she did not blame Micay for her father's reputation.

"You are old to come to us, my daughter," she said, surprising Micay by speaking to her directly. "How well do you speak the high speech?"

"I was taught Quechua when I was very young," Micay offered. "By a woman who was from Caxamarca."

"And what did you learn from your father? Were you taught to scorn and disobey the laws of the Inca?"

Micay had been asked this question before, less sympathetically, so she did not flinch or try to evade it.

"My father was taken to Cuzco after the war. He was made to learn all of the Inca's laws and customs before he could return to Suta. He has been called a rebel because he expects the Inca to act like an Inca, with fairness and generosity. Instead, the micho stole me from him without a hearing. I do not belong here, my mother."

The woman raised her eyebrows slightly, then cast a fierce, sidelong glance at the selector, making *him* flinch. She drew back her head and gazed at Micay with something like bemusement, as if Micay had just changed shape in front of her. She stared so long that Micay began to feel a revival of her lost hope. Perhaps she was not such a prize, after all. But then the woman spoke, and the finality of her tone crushed all hope.

"Perhaps you did not belong in Suta, either, with a father who refuses the power that could be his. Perhaps you were meant to have a more useful life. When you have been here long enough, my daughter, you will understand what it means to be a chosen woman. That is what we teach here, and we are very patient, and very dedicated to our work. We will make you ready, and worthy of the place the Sapa Inca will find for you."

Micay lowered her eyes and bowed in resignation, but the woman simply turned and held out her hand to the selector of chosen women, who surrendered his cord with a similar bow.

"You are released from your responsibility. You must tell the micho that he demeans your office—and our work—when girls are taken as a punishment to their fathers. Remind him of that."

Taking Micay by the arm, she escorted her through the ranks of the guards, who bowed their heads over their shields. As they crossed the deep threshold of the doorway, a stout wooden door swung shut behind them, closing them off from the eyes of those outside. They entered a courtyard that seemed darkened by the high stone walls that loomed inward on two sides. At first Micay had the terrifying impression that the courtyard was filled with disembodied faces. Then she perceived that the silent figures ringing the square were other girls, all dressed in identical dark garments that covered their bodies completely from neck to ankles, so that they blended in with the walls and the façades of the buildings. Micay heard no signal, but suddenly all the girls bowed in unison, as if in response to her appearance in the courtyard.

"Your sisters greet you, Micay," the woman beside her said. "They want you to know that it is a great honor to be one of the chosen women of the Sapa Inca."

Micay shivered, strangely moved by the gesture. The woman in black turned to look down at her.

"I am the head of the mamacona, the women who will guide you here. You may call me Mamanchic. You must tell me now: Have you begun your bleeding yet?"

"No, Mamanchic."

"Cahua," the woman said, summoning one of the older girls from a group nearby. As the young woman approached, Micay saw that her face was horribly deformed, shocking to look upon. Micay quickly averted her eyes to prevent the deformity from falling on her.

"This is Micay, Cahua," the mamanchic explained. "Take her to the room you occupied when you first came here. There is clothing there for her. Show her how she is to dress herself."

Micay glanced once at the mamanchic, to see if the disfigured girl had been chosen as a kind of punishment. But the old woman's face seemed mild and composed, betraying no trace of vindictiveness. Micay bowed and allowed herself to be led toward a narrow passageway between two buildings, but she kept a careful distance from her guide and did not allow their hands or their garments to touch.

Once out of the courtyard, the girl stopped to give their eyes a moment to adjust to the murky light in the passageway, which was shaded by the over-hanging thatch of the adjacent roofs. She said something to Micay in a garbled, warbling voice that sounded like the quacking of a duck. Micay flinched and shook her head uncomprehendingly, and the older girl repeated herself more slowly, then once more, until Micay finally understood.

"You do not need to be afraid. I carry no sickness."

Micay forced herself to look at the face, which seemed only a little less awful in the half light. The tip of the nose had been severely foreshortened, as if it had been worn away by rubbing, and one nostril had collapsed into a furrow of darkened skin that split her upper lip into two unequal halves, so that her mouth seemed perpetually swollen on one side.

"I had the uta," the girl explained with great deliberateness, watching Micay's eyes to be sure she understood. "But I recovered. There is no danger to you now."

She turned and again led the way down the passage, and Micay hastened to follow, feeling slightly ashamed of her aversion. She had heard of the uta, the disease that devoured the faces of its victims and usually took their lives. It was an affliction common among the peoples who lived close to the shores of the Mother Water.

They entered a smoky anteroom where a brazier of coals burned in a doorway-sized niche in the back wall, tended by an older woman in black, no doubt another of the mamacona. A dark interior passageway took them deeper into the building, with single rooms on both sides, some with curtains over their doorways and some open but unoccupied. The girl named Cahua stopped next to an open doorway on the left and gestured for Micay to enter ahead of her. The room was all of six paces across, a tiny space that would have seemed like a tomb had the roof not been raised high overhead, slanting on its support beams. There was a narrow window where each of the side walls met the back wall, but no window to the outside. Still, it was somewhat lighter in here than in the passageway, so that Micay could see a llama-skin rug rolled up in the corner and a pile of clothing in the center of the barren stone floor.

"This is where you will sleep," Cahua told her. "And those are the clothes you will wear. You must give me the things you are wearing."

Though she understood what Cahua had said, Micay hesitated at this com-mand. She looked down at herself, fingering the string of shell beads around her neck and the fabric of her shift, which she and her mother had woven together. The soft cotton cloth was patterned with broad vertical stripes of red and yellow, separated by narrow panels of fine gauze that took on the light copper color of Micay's skin. The garments on the floor seemed to be the color of stone.

"Did you understand me?" Cahua prompted. "You must not make the mamacona ask you twice."

Micay suddenly felt very weary, so that it was an effort to nod in acquiescence. She removed the string of beads and handed it to Cahua, then untied the ends of her shift where they were knotted at her shoulder. Her fingers felt cold and inflexible, so that she inadvertently dropped the shift as she unwrapped it from around her body. Without a word Cahua stooped to pick it up, gesturing as well for Micay's sandals. Micay stepped out of them, her eyes fixed on the floor, which felt cold and unyielding beneath her feet. She began to tremble, feeling utterly naked and lost.

"Take the large piece of cloth first," Cahua instructed, reaching down for it herself when Micay did not respond. "It is called the anacu. Hold one corner over your left shoulder and wrap it down under your right arm. Hold still, and let me show you . . ."

Shaking where she stood, Micay allowed the older girl to wrap the long, blanketlike shift around her body, covering her from neck to ankles in heavy dark blue cotton. Cahua secured it at the shoulder with a copper pin and at the waist with a broad belt she referred to as a chumpi, which was white with a single blue stripe around the middle. Then a short mantle, also blue, was placed over her shoulders, and the ends were fastened together at the breast by a slender silver pin that had been flattened into the shape of a fan at its blunt end.

"That is called a tupu," Cahua said of the pin. "It is a mark of the wearer's rank and status. Only the pallas and ñustas of Cuzco can wear tupus of pure gold."

Micay stared at her indifferently, too weary to be repulsed by her face. She felt like a burial bundle, wrapped in all this heavy cloth. She did not resist as Cahua stepped behind her and began to unwind the braids in her hair.

"It will straighten out when I have combed it," Cahua said soothingly. "And I will show you how to part it correctly. You have lovely hair, Micay. It is so black against the lightness of your skin. The men of Cuzco favor women with your color, you know."

"I do not wish to be favored by the men from Cuzco," Micay said in a dull voice, yielding to Cahua's ministrations.

"You will come to think differently," Cahua assured her, raising a tortoiseshell comb above Micay's brow. Somehow Micay mustered the strength to raise a hand to stop her.

"No. Do not tell me what I will do. You do not know me so well."

Then Micay began to weep, the pent-up tears erupting from her eyes in a sudden flood. She covered her wet face with her hands, sobbing into her palms and shaking so violently that she thought she was going to fall down. There was a wailing inside her head, the noise of her own pain, a sound that alarmed her and made her cry even harder. She swayed and felt hands on her arms, then arms going around her back, pulling her against a warm, cotton-clad body. Her heart swelled and she gave herself to the embrace, remembering the tearful embraces of her mother and the other wives. All lost, she thought incoherently, weeping out her despair in Cahua's arms.

Gradually Cahua calmed her, murmuring in her ear and stroking the hair that hung down her back. Micay clung to her for a long time after her tears had stopped and her body no longer shook, refusing to comprehend what was being said to her. Finally, though, Cahua detached herself and stood back, holding on to one of Micay's hands.

"I would like to know you, Micay," she said quietly. "I would like to be your friend here."

"Is it allowed?" Micay managed.

Cahua's misshapen mouth puckered slightly. "This is not a prison. You will see that if you allow yourself to. For someone with your beauty, this is a place of great opportunity."

Micay glanced around at the close, barren walls, seeing nothing that resembled opportunity. Cahua had stepped back behind her and was once again combing out her hair, her voice and movements growing more brisk.

"It will seem hard for a while. You will feel like a jar that is too small for all that is being poured into it. Then one day you will feel full, and you will realize that you know perfectly how you should act. Then you will know you have become a chosen woman, a woman cherished by the Inca, the son of the Sun."

The comb made a slight hiss and a crackling sound as it was pulled through Micay's hair, the concerted tugging bringing warmth to her scalp. She had understood almost every one of Cahua's words, but their meaning escaped her. She did not want to know what anything meant; she no longer had the strength to care. She would do whatever they told her to, and she would be whoever they wanted her to be. The girl called Misa was dead, and the sound of her mother's mourning could not be heard through these thick stone walls.

Looking down, Micay saw the pair of sandals that had been left for her, and she reached out with a foot, keeping her head still, and drew them toward her. She slipped her toes through the thongs, putting a soft layer of woven cabuya fiber between herself and the cold floor. When Cahua had finished with her hair, it hung long and straight down her back, bound back from her forehead by a thin strip of blue cloth. Then Cahua stood back and nodded to her, and Micay followed her out into the dark corridor and went to take her place among those who dwelled in the House of Chosen Women.

II

PUSAQCONA:
Guides

Cuzco

T HE PATALLACTA, Terrace Town, had been one of the favorite retreats of the ninth Sapa Inca, Pachacuti. Its houses, gardens, and ceremonial enclosures were arranged on broad terraces that climbed the side of a large hill just northwest of Cuzco's central square. The retaining walls of the terraces were shored up by narrower terraces that acted as landings and ramps between the various levels, describing a zigzag pattern up the side of the hill. Wherever possible, the terraces were planted with shade trees and cantut bushes and flowering vines, all watered by the same irrigation channels that fed the bathing pools and fish tanks. The complex now belonged to the Iñaca household, the group of close relatives who had inherited Pachacuti's estates and who attended to his needs in death.

When Cusi was first taken to the Patallacta on the day after his family's departure, he was given lodgings in the guest quarters on the lowest level. He was told that Otoronco Achachi was very busy but would summon Cusi for an interview shortly. In the meantime he was to sleep and take his meals here, under the care of the three women who maintained the guest quarters. The women were yanacona, lifetime retainers, and they treated Cusi as if it were a great privilege to serve a relative of Otoronco Achachi. Otoronco was one of Pachacuti's sons and a high-ranking member of the Iñaca household, in addition to his fame as a war chief. He had been recalled from his duties in the provinces to serve as the lord of the Eastern Quarter, which he himself had once helped to conquer. Now he would have final responsibility for the govern-ance of the entire quarter and would act as one of the four lords who advised the regent, Auqui Topa Inca.

So Cusi understood why his guardian might be too busy to meet with him immediately, and he did his best to remain patient. It was not easy, since he was the only guest in the guest quarters, and the women, while unflagging in their diligence, were too far below him in rank to provide much companion-ship. And he was burdened by the secrets he carried, which made him feel isolated even in the company of his initiation brothers. He had told no one about his encounter with Raurau Illa at the huaca, and he had done nothing about replacing the memory cord he had given away. The longer he waited, the more his silence would seem like collaboration, and the absence of his cord like a conscious deception.

He had never had any reason to be secretive in the past, and he carried his secrets like live coals that might burn his hands at any moment. Had Otoronco summoned him upon his arrival and asked him to account for himself, Cusi would undoubtedly have told him everything. He would have been relieved to clear his conscience and ask for Otoronco's guidance.

But after having him brought to the Patallacta, Otoronco seemed to have forgotten him completely. He remained a lonely lodger, coming and going from the guest quarters but too uncertain of his status to venture any farther into the palace or to invite his friends in for a visit. Days passed, and nights spent alone in the darkness of his room, clutching the stone Raurau Illa had given him and cursing his father for abandoning him like this. When a month had gone by, he realized that it was too late to tell anyone what had happened at the huaca. So he quietly began collecting materials for a new memory cord, aware that the retainer women would have supplied him with anything he asked but unwilling to involve them in his deception. The replacement he finally fashioned was much cruder than the original, and any one of the teachers would have immediately noticed the uneven lengths of the cords and the lack of red and blue cords. But Cusi judged that it was sufficient for a song that he already knew by heart, and he managed to bury it beneath the other things in his niche in the House of Learning without being seen.

As more days passed and there was still no summons from the Apu, Cusi came to feel that his deception was justified by the neglect of his elders. He was a fatherless boy, as Raurau Illa had said, and he would have to become a man by himself. He became even more attached to his spirit brother, which felt *old* in his hand, worn smooth by the fingers of others who had brooded and suffered as he did. Only at night did he give in to self-pity, holding the stone against his heart and missing his mother and Quinti and Amaru. During the day he attended to his studies and his training, trying to act as if nothing had changed, though he found it hard to look upon Sumac Mallqui and the other warriors. He found it hard to meet the eyes of his friends, too, because he had not shared any of his secrets with them. He could not bring himself to repeat the things his father had said, especially the threat to have him held back from the initiation rites. He had always been the leader, the one who corrected their Quechua and helped them learn the ways of the Inca. He could not imagine, at this point, suddenly becoming the one who needed to be helped.

But then Aranyac, the teacher in charge of Cusi's group, had one of his assistants conduct an inspection of the boys' belongings, which were supposed to be stored in a clean and orderly fashion. The assistant was drawn to the makeshift cord because it stuck out slightly from the bottom of the pile in Cusi's niche, and as soon as he saw how it had been made, he took it to Aranyac. Aranyac, in turn, had Cusi brought before him without delay. He held out the cord without saying a word, eyeing Cusi skeptically.

Somehow Cusi had never fully thought through the consequences of being found out, but as he groped for a response, his heart sinking into his stomach, the choices seemed stark. He could tell the truth and jeopardize Raurau Illa and his spirit brother along with himself. Or he could lie and hope to be punished only for carelessness. He had had no practice at lying, and at the moment the need to protect Raurau Illa did not seem compelling. But the thought of surrendering his stone, which he would certainly be required to do if he told the truth, made the choice for him.

"I lost the original," he told Aranyac. "I dropped it somewhere on the plain and could not find it later."

"Why did you not report the loss? Why did you attempt to substitute *this*?" the teacher demanded incredulously.

"I . . . I was not thinking clearly. I was upset with myself for being so careless, and I intended to make a better copy later."

"The quality of the cord does not matter, as you should know. The deception does. Furthermore, I do not believe you were so careless you could not remember where you had been or how to find what you had dropped. No one would take a memory cord that did not belong to them."

"I searched every place I had been," Cusi insisted, feeling that both his heart and his stomach had disappeared. Aranyac stared back at him without the slightest sign of being persuaded. He had taught Cusi for three years and knew him too well; he was the one who had put Cusi together with Tomay, Rimachi, and Uritu, as much to occupy Cusi's mind as to help the foreign boys with their Quechua. He knew how good Cusi's memory was, and how seldom he misplaced anything.

"I do not believe you, Cusi Auqui," he said in a formal tone, his eyes narrowing with disappointment. "But perhaps after you have cleaned one of the rooms where our cords are stored, your memory will be refreshed."

Cusi nodded in compliance, preferring any sort of punishment to the look of judgment in the teacher's eyes. As if he sensed this, Aranyac stood staring at him for several more moments.

"There are many rooms," he said at last, "and there is no refuge from the truth in any of them. Go now, if you have nothing more to say to me."

The silence rang in Cusi's ears as he left Aranyac's chamber, and there was a reluctant strain to his every movement. He felt that he was walking away

from all of the favor he had accumulated in three years, and all the confidence
Aranyac had ever had in him. He seemed to see himself from the outside as
he crossed the courtyard toward Aranyac's assistant, who stood waiting with
a reed broom in his hands. He saw his shadow trailing after him, attached to
his heels and even smaller than he was. He wondered how he was ever going
to sweep away the shadow of the lie he had just told, which seemed much
larger than he would ever be.

Caxamarca

S INCE MICAY had already been trained by all three of her father's wives,
the practical aspects of her training as a chosen woman came to her rather
easily. She knew how to cook and clean and serve, and the mamacona
quickly recognized her talents as a weaver and began to teach her how to weave
the thick, tapestrylike cumbi cloth the Incas prized so highly. Her Quechua
pronunciation improved rapidly with use, and she had a good memory for the
many songs and prayers the girls were expected to know. She was distracted
at first by the fact that her hands were never allowed to be idle, even while
she was listening and reciting, but she learned how to watch her spindle out
of the corner of her eye, manipulating it by feel while keeping her mind
attentive to the voices of the mamacona.

Less easily, she learned the proper way to walk, moving in a straight line
without hurrying or dawdling, her head held steady and her eyes slightly
lowered, fixed on the path ahead. Micay had trouble with this because she had
not fully learned her way around the House of Chosen Women, which was a
maze of passageways and courtyards and rooms that could not be told apart.
If she did not cast her eyes around for the few landmarks she knew, she became
lost, which then forced her to hurry or dawdle in confusion. She also had a
tendency to glance up at the sky whenever she entered a courtyard and to
linger too long in the sunlight or by the side of one of the reflecting pools.

These tendencies were part of a larger failing, which Cahua and the
mamacona referred to as "dreaming." She was dreaming any time her attention was not fully absorbed in the task before her, even if that task were simply
to sit still. One day when she was weaving in a courtyard, she looked up when
a flock of redheaded finches began to sing from a nearby rooftop. Then she
realized that she was the only one who had raised her head, and that the mama
in charge of the group was frowning at her with disapproval.

"Did they simply not hear the birds," she asked Cahua later, "or did they
choose to ignore what they heard?"

"They were concentrating on their weaving," Cahua said, as if the question
were irrelevant. "They had no room in their minds for birds to fly in and
distract them."

"I was concentrating, too," Micay insisted. "But the sound surprised me."

"You are too easily surprised, then," Cahua told her bluntly. "That is what happens when you allow yourself to dream."

Cahua was very patient with her, coming to Micay's room night after night to answer her questions and discuss her mistakes. She would massage Micay's neck and shoulders and comb out her hair while they talked, the warble in her voice familiar and comforting by now, the voice Micay heard most clearly. Micay always felt encouraged afterward, reassured of her progress, or at least of her potential for improvement.

But then she would find herself in the midst of her sisters, dressed exactly as they were and doing the same work, yet feeling like a mitmac, an outsider. The fact that she was aware of herself at all was itself the difference. The other girls behaved as if they knew no other way to act, as if they had no whims, or moods, or memories to distract them. Micay felt she was the only one who noticed a change in the wind or heard the muted rumble of thunder in the distance; surely the only one who looked at the high stone walls and tried to imagine the city and the mountains beyond them. Their composure was so deep it seemed almost a kind of trance, a detachment from any source of personal impulse. Sometimes Micay had the frightening sense that they were not girls like herself, but some other kind of creature, something she had never seen before.

"I do not know how they do it," she complained to Cahua. "Maybe I have lived outside for too long, but I cannot make my ears not hear or my nose not smell or my eyes not see."

"You do exactly that whenever you concentrate on something. I have seen you when you are weaving or doing some other work you enjoy. You have no trouble shutting out distractions then. It is when the chore is tedious or trying that you begin to dream."

"But that is only natural," Micay protested. "That is why women do their chores together; the time passes more easily when you have company."

"You must stop making these useless comparisons. More is expected of a chosen woman. You speak of being a chosen woman as if it were a trick the girls had learned to perform, but it is much more than that. It is a way of being that will serve you well wherever you go. It will make you fit for the responsibilities that will be yours when you are given your place by the Sapa Inca."

"But I do not know what my place will be."

"That should not matter," Cahua said firmly. "When you are truly ready to leave, you will be able to trust yourself in any situation."

Micay could not pretend to be convinced, so Cahua suggested that she needed some time alone to think about these things and pray to Inti and Viracocha for guidance. She left Micay alone and did not return for the next two nights. During that time Micay did little praying, since the Inca gods were not familiar to her yet, and the gods of Chachapoyas, the Great Condor and the Mother of the Hills, seemed too far away to hear. Her thoughts also strayed, drawn away by the discovery that other visits were going on all around her. She heard whispering and the rustle of garments in the passageway outside her room, and closer at hand, a concerted murmuring from the room to her right. The room belonged to an older girl named Yutu, who looked to Micay as if she were also from Chachapoyas, though she had not done or said anything to confirm this impression.

Micay crept closer to the narrow window in the back corner, where the walls met. The murmuring was just loud enough that she could distinguish two separate speakers, though she could not make out any of their words. She realized how loudly she and Cahua had been speaking and wondered if they had been overheard. Then the murmuring stopped and Micay froze, standing about a foot away from the window, which was just visible in the darkness. There was a muffled sound from the next room that seemed to retreat from the window and then vanish altogether. Micay waited, turning her head once when she had the impression someone was watching her from the doorway. But it was too dark for anyone to see in this far. When she turned back, she saw a gray shape that materialized into a face as Yutu leaned forward on the windowsill between them.

"Cahua has left you alone for once," Yutu said in a Quechua that revealed no hint of her homeland.

"She wanted to give me time to think."

"Thinking will not make you a chosen woman. But then, you will not be here long enough to become a chosen woman."

"How do you know that?" Micay blurted in surprise. Yutu hesitated, as if surprised by her response, then spoke in a tone that implied that the answer was obvious.

"You are from a noble family, you are fairly pleasing to look at, and you have light skin like mine. We will surely both be taken."

"Taken where?"

"We will be chosen by the Sapa Inca. I will probably be given as a wife to one of his captains, or a chief, but you are not old enough for that. Perhaps if you are lucky you will be given to one of the women in his court, the wife of an Inca, to be her attendant or the companion to her children."

Micay felt dizzied by the older girl's certainty; Cahua had never mentioned any of this to her.

"When will this happen?"

"When the Sapa Inca arrives in Caxamarca, in another two or three months, perhaps. He travels very slowly, because of all the people he has with him. But when he gets here, he will take many of us out."

"And you think he will take *me*?"

Yutu gave a patient sigh, as if she had just realized the depths of Micay's ignorance.

"Huayna Capac came through Caxamarca twice, four years ago. But he was with his army both times, so he took only the girls old enough for marriage to his warriors. Otherwise I would have gone, because he chose all of the Chachapoyas ñustas first. This time, though, he will have all his wives and women with him, and he will want to show them his favor, too. So there will be places for the younger girls."

"Are you eager to leave here?" Micay asked curiously.

Yutu sighed again. "I have been here for a long time, and I have always known I would leave one day. I am not like Cahua, who wishes to stay here and join the Women of the Sun."

Micay had not heard *this* before, either, and she was silent for a moment, considering the implications. The mamacona were all Women of the Sun, though most of the order lived in seclusion in a separate enclosure, at the back of the House of Chosen Women. They were holy women, utterly devoted to Inti, whom they served with their prayers and fasting and purity.

"We do not have to speak through a window," Yutu prompted. "Come over to my room, if you wish."

"Is it allowed?"

"We may visit until it is time to sleep. Did you think that Cahua has privileges the rest of us do not share?"

"I did not know . . . she is the only one I have spoken to."

"Come," Yutu said succinctly, and she drew back into the darkness of her room. Micay also turned and left the window, though she hesitated in the doorway, listening to the muted sound of voices up and down the passageway. There was obviously more life here than she had suspected, certainly more than Cahua had led her to believe. Feeling both intrigued and vaguely disloyal, she slipped out into the corridor and walked the few steps to the next doorway, wondering what else she might learn from Yutu.

THOUGH THE ARRIVAL of the Sapa Inca was still two months off, as Yutu had said, the preparations for his coming began to alter the normal routine of the House of Chosen Women, just as Micay was finally becoming accustomed to it. The older girls were given more time with their weaving, so that they might finish the pieces of cumbi cloth they had begun some months before. The younger girls were organized into cleaning crews and were put to work sweeping and scrubbing every corner of the enclosure. Micay welcomed the new variety of tasks, which took her to unfamiliar parts of the house and often allowed her to work without also being made to listen and recite.

On this day she had actually been sent to work alone, in a remote courtyard that had been thoroughly cleaned several days earlier. Her task was to maintain its state of cleanliness by sweeping up any debris that might have blown in over the great outside wall that formed one side of the courtyard. There was barely any dust to be found, but she swept the gleaming flagstones slowly and conscientiously, inwardly reveling in the freedom to let her thoughts wander. Out of the corner of her eye, she studied the great wall that separated her from the world outside, a monumental edifice some fifteen feet high. It tapered and leaned inward at a slight angle as it rose, the many-sided gray-brown stones growing smaller as they went up, giving way in the top courses to rectangular adobe bricks. Despite the absence of mortar, no light came through it anywhere. It was a wall that could not be scaled without a ladder, its face smooth and perfectly even, the stones gently rounded at the edges, beveled down to the precisely shadowed lines of their joinings.

Micay had been awed and intimidated by the wall during her first days here. It seemed to deny emphatically any hope of escape; it told her that the Sapa Inca was the most powerful man in the world, and that he intended to keep everything that was his. But that was before she had heard the tales of Huayna Capac's immense generosity, and what that might mean for his chosen women. She still was not sure how much to believe of what Yutu and the other girls told her, since they spoke of places and situations none of them had ever seen. But they had all been here long enough to see other girls leave, and their dreams of the future gave her hope, which in turn allowed her to relax and accept her training as the means to a future of her own.

She suddenly realized she had been going over the same corner of the courtyard for some time; she was uncertain just how long. Needlessly stretching out a task was a form of idleness, and a sure sign that she had been dreaming. Micay knew better than to glance back over her shoulder, a movement that would only confirm her guilt for anyone watching. She swept in a circle instead, gradually turning herself around in a way that would seem natural. The first doorway to come into view was empty, and so was the second. Then panic clutched at her heart and she almost dropped her broom when she saw someone standing in the gap between buildings.

But it was Cahua. Micay let out a tremulous breath and went to meet her, sweeping the dust she had collected along with her. Cahua's misshapen lips were pressed tightly together, and her breathing whistled in her nose, as it sometimes did when the air was too dry. Micay understood for the first time that it also happened when Cahua was upset.

"The mamanchic sent me to check on you," Cahua said, her voice taut with distress. "I did not really think it was necessary."

"I am sorry, Cahua. I forgot myself for a moment."

"What if the mamanchic had come herself," Cahua persisted, "and found you staring idly at the wall?"

Micay nodded in acknowledgement, trying to summon a remorse to match Cahua's concern. But what she truly felt was annoyance at having to defend herself, and it came out clearly when she spoke.

"Then the mamanchic would be reprimanding me, instead of you doing it."

Cahua stared at her for a moment, drawing short, sibilant breaths.

"You sound as if a reprimand means nothing to you. Have you stopped caring about your conduct?"

"No, but I cannot be perfect all of the time."

"A chosen woman *must* be perfect."

"Then maybe I will never be a chosen woman," Micay said in a burst of defiance. "Maybe I will not be here long enough for that."

"What do you mean?"

"Maybe I will leave when the Sapa Inca comes."

Cahua blinked at her in astonishment, showing white around her pupils.

"Who has told you that? Micay . . . you have been here less than two months! I cannot conceive that the mamanchic would permit you to leave so soon."

"I was told that the choice belonged to Huayna Capac, and that he is very partial to Chachapoyas women."

"He will choose from the girls the mamanchic presents to him," Cahua said in a deliberate tone. "He may not even see those she feels are not ready to leave."

"Yutu said we would both be taken."

"Yutu has been here for eight years! She is well prepared to leave. But she should know that you are not."

"I have always been ready to leave here. I should never have been brought here in the first place."

"This is where you are, however. And when you leave here, you might be taken anywhere. You might have to follow a warrior to his battles, or into the jungle, or to someplace high and cold. You will not be going back to Chachapoyas, to your family and a life you know. Can you say that you are ready to live anywhere, among strangers whose ways you do not understand?"

"I live among strangers here," Micay said coldly. "You say you are my friend, but you want only to change me. You will not see that it is different for me. *I* have no reason to want to stay here for the rest of my life."

Cahua's whole face quivered and her voice flattened out and lost its warble.

"I have never told you my reasons. But there are obviously others whose judgment you trust more than mine, and perhaps they have told you. You must decide whom you wish to believe. When you are finished here, you are to go to the weaving room. I will tell the mamanchic that I found you sweeping diligently, as expected."

"I am sorry, Cahua," Micay said hastily. "I did not mean . . ."

But Cahua had already turned and was walking away, and she did not look back. Micay had an urge to call out or run after her to apologize, but she was too much of a chosen woman to do either.

"I did not mean to hurt you," she said to herself, in a voice that barely echoed off the stone walls of the empty courtyard.

Cuzco

SUMAC MALLQUI was the warrior in charge of the group on this day, and he already had the other boys wrestling by the time Cusi arrived at the field. He was a deep-chested man with long, muscular arms and a grip that no boy ever forgot once it had been applied to him in anger. The only time he had felt compelled to lay hands on Cusi, he had lifted him completely off the ground and shaken him like a bag of feathers. This was one of the reasons why Cusi had never been late for training before today, and why he expected to be roughly handled now.

But Sumac Mallqui simply gave him a disgusted look and sent him to run halfway up the small mountain the boys called Kacca Urcco, Punishment Hill.

"Warm yourself up," he commanded. "You will wrestle when you return."

Cusi set off at the brisk trot the warriors used during a forced march, a pace he could ordinarily maintain with ease for great distances. But today his muscles tightened rapidly, and he began to get winded before he had even reached the base of the hill. Aranyac had worked him particularly hard today, and he had neglected to drink water before leaving the House of Learning. His throat, already dry and prickly from all the dust he had inhaled in his cleaning, became raw and contracted itself against the painful pull of his breathing. Running up the steep, zigzagging path suddenly seemed a torture rather than a warm-up, and Cusi could feel his muscles tense even further as dread rose in his stomach. He wondered if Aranyac had spoken to Sumac Mallqui—if the two of them were working together to wear him down. He wondered if Sumac Mallqui was the one who had told his father that he was unfit and was now going to prove it.

All of his wondering, though, could not distract him from the weakness in his legs and the shortness of his breath. He should not be so tired so soon. The dust must have affected him in some way, or maybe it was how poorly he had been sleeping lately. Maybe it was just the loneliness and uncertainty of his life. Cusi was appalled to find himself thinking about being lonely, when he should have been gathering whatever strength he had for what lay ahead—the wrestling Sumac Mallqui had promised upon his return.

Reaching the stone marker at the halfway point of the hill, he circled it and started back down. The surest way to redeem himself would be to wrestle with some vigor and enthusiasm. Cusi felt neither, just the sense of his troubles gaining on him, like an avalanche he could not outrun. He felt like stopping to let it pour over him, sure that there could be only more humiliation in trying to flee. He told himself not to be a coward and kept running, but even self-hatred did not revive his courage.

When he arrived back at the circle of boys, Sumac Mallqui halted the drill and stood staring at Cusi in silence, forcing him to listen to his own ragged breathing, which sounded like an admission of guilt to Cusi's ears.

"We are honored that you have decided to join us," the warrior said at last. "Perhaps you are ready now to break a sweat with your brothers."

Despite the exertion of the run, Cusi did not feel warm, and he nodded with a corresponding lack of enthusiasm. Beyond the warrior, he saw his friend Rimachi raise his eyebrows in a gesture of support, or perhaps of warning. Sumac Mallqui simply stepped back and clapped his hands sharply.

"Tomay! Show Cusi how the Colla wrestle!"

Springing forward into the center of the circle, Tomay pulled his long woolen cap off his head and discarded it behind him, knowing that even a friend like Cusi would not hesitate to pull it down over his eyes if given the chance. He assumed a wrestler's crouch and bared his teeth in a fierce smile.

Cusi faced him grimly, still trying to recapture his breath. He and Tomay were often matched against each other, since they were both wiry and about the same height. Tomay was larger and only a little less quick, with a decided edge in strength. Cusi knew he had to get to the side or behind Tomay, just as Tomay knew that his best chance lay in keeping Cusi in front of him and wearing him down. All of this went through Cusi's mind, but slowly and without impact, as uselessly as Rimachi's raised eyebrow.

They circled for a moment, then closed and briefly locked arms, tugging and pushing for advantage before breaking free. Cusi feinted to one side and Tomay responded instantly with his whole body, shuffling crablike to keep from turning his flanks. Cusi feinted the other way and went in low, grabbing for Tomay's leg. Not fooled a bit, Tomay neatly sidestepped the charge, seizing the back of Cusi's tunic and throwing him down.

Cusi rolled and came back up to his feet, hearing the cries and whistles of the other boys. Tomay did not pursue him, since the object of this drill, as the warriors constantly reminded them, was to teach them how to outlast an opponent. That was always the Inca way: to wear down the enemy with patience and implacability, rather than going for the quick kill. So they circled some more, testing each other's reflexes with head and shoulder fakes before closing in to grapple with their arms. Cusi got a quick grip on Tomay's forearm and tried to propel himself past his friend, but again he had misjudged Tomay's readiness. Tomay pulled in his arm and swiveled sideways, planting a hand on Cusi's hip and hurling him to the ground.

"You could make Tomay sweat a little, too," Sumac Mallqui suggested, drawing derisive laughter from some of the other boys. Cusi scrambled to his feet, shaking the arm that had taken the impact of his fall. His breath hissed through his clenched teeth, and his face was hot with embarrassment. Worse, he knew that the warrior was right—that he should be using his quickness to make Tomay work harder, feinting and dodging until a true opening presented itself. He knew it, though knowing did not give him the energy and reflexes to carry it out. Tomay seemed to anticipate every fake, adjusting his stance before Cusi could make the next move. Losing patience, Cusi made a sudden lunge for Tomay's midsection, seizing him briefly around the waist—but only briefly, as Tomay jumped backward and pushed down on the top of Cusi's lowered head, knocking him flat on his face in the short grass.

Cusi lay where he was, staring past his nose at the crushed stems of bunch grass, green and yellow threads beaten into the reddish-brown texture of the earth. Three falls were all anyone was usually allowed, and even Sumac Mallqui would have to admit that he was hopeless today. There was no point in continuing such an unequal contest. Then a harsh voice shouted close to Cusi's ear, and a toe prodded him in the ribs.

"Do not lie there like a piece of llama dung! Get up, you lazy fool, and face your opponent!"

Jerking away from the toe, Cusi pushed himself onto his knees, then stood up, swaying dizzily as the blood rushed to his feet. He saw Sumac Mallqui's long arm extend itself toward him and was seized by the sudden conviction that the warrior was trying to knock him down, as his father had done. He struck out at the arm with all his might, sending it flailing back toward Sumac Mallqui's startled face.

"Cusi!" Tomay cried, stepping in to try to restrain him. Cusi whirled at the touch and pushed Tomay away with both hands, then charged him as he staggered backward, launching himself into the air before Tomay could even put up his hands in defense. He saw helplessness in his friend's eyes and wanted to wipe it out and put an end to all of this. Then his forearm struck Tomay on the chin and his shoulder slammed into his breastbone, knocking him off his feet with such force that he flew backward through the air and landed heavily on his back.

Cusi came down on all fours, seeing the circle of boys collapse inward around him as those nearest to Tomay rushed to see if he was injured. Rimachi and Uritu gingerly lifted Tomay to his feet, supporting him while he choked and gagged in an effort to recapture his breath. His eyes were unfocused and his face contorted with pain, too awful for Cusi to look upon. What have I done? he thought. Then a strong hand gripped him above the elbow and jerked him to his feet, and he was looking into the furious eyes of Sumac Mallqui.

"Have you gone mad?" the warrior demanded. "You could have injured him badly!"

Cusi stared back at him wordlessly, going limp in his grasp. Sumac Mallqui shook him so hard that Cusi's head flopped back and forth on his neck, causing him to bite his tongue. The warrior pointed toward Punishment Hill.

"You will run all the way to the top—backwards! Do not let me see you stop, or you will run it twice!"

Sumac Mallqui released him with a last shake, and Cusi turned and began to run backwards as fast as he could. He had not gone far before he tripped over a stone and fell hard onto his back. But he was up again immediately, running blindly, hoping that he might somehow run off a cliff, or fall into a hole deep enough to swallow him up.

TOMAY CANNOT *be hurting more than I am,* he thought later, as he lay in his room in the guest quarters of the Patallacta. He had soaked himself in hot water in the bathhouse, but the muscles in his legs took turns twitching and cramping, and there were still cactus spines lodged in his palms and buttocks. He could feel but not see all the scrapes and bruises on his back, and his tongue felt torn and swollen where he had bitten it.

He burrowed more deeply into the blankets, his hands clamped around his spirit brother, feeling more wretched than he had ever felt in his entire life. In the course of one day he had been punished for lying, for being late, and for attacking his friend. Soon there would be no one left to offend or disappoint;

he would have made an enemy of everyone. He remembered Raurau Illa asking how he would become a man without his parents to guide him. Cusi's answer had seemed inadequate at the time, but now it seemed like no answer at all. He had become the boy whom everyone distrusted and despised, whom no one would wish to make into a man.

Then a throat was cleared in the doorway behind him, a sound that made him jump and throw off his blankets in surprise.

"Yes?" he asked, and heard a deferential voice he did not recognize.

"The Lord Otoronco Achachi summons you, my lord."

Of course, Cusi thought wearily, he will want to punish me, too. Suppressing a groan, he got to his feet and followed the servant out into the courtyard. He was startled to find that the night air was mild; he had felt cold even in the blankets. The Great River of stars flowed across the middle of the sky, dripping a dim, silvery light onto the stone walls surrounding the guest quarters.

They left the enclosure and turned right, ascending to the next terraced level by means of a broad flight of stairs. Cusi took a deep breath and stretched his limbs, preparing himself for a long climb. Otoronco would no doubt have chosen lodgings commensurate with his rank and his relation to Pachacuti, whose unbreathing body was kept in a compound on the top of the hill. Cusi had never been anywhere near that high on the few occasions when his father had brought him to the Patallacta, but he had little chance to take note of his surroundings as he struggled to keep up with the servant. The way up alternated between long ramps and steep sets of stairs, and the paths along the main terraces twisted and turned among the buildings and garden plots, sometimes running along the outer edge of the terrace and sometimes next to the retaining wall. They passed through groves of fragrant trees and gardens that smelled of orchids and damp earth, skirting the edges of pools that shimmered in the starlight. A guard accosted them briefly outside a large feasting hall from which light and the sound of singing were emanating, but the name of Otoronco Achachi sent the man back into the shadows. Cusi trailed the servant blindly, stooping occasionally to knead his calves, which had begun to cramp from all the stairs. Several times he thought he heard the sounds of lovemaking coming from the curtained chambers they passed, but the lack of light in these passages made him concentrate instead on where he was putting his feet.

At last they came to a walled enclosure that occupied the whole eastern half of one of the terraces, which had been growing progressively narrower as they rose. A tall trapezoidal doorway with a double jamb led into a courtyard barely fifteen feet wide, with two stone buildings on either side and one at the far end of the enclosure. A large piece of dark stone with a sunken seat carved into it stood in the center of the courtyard. The servant paused to bow to the stone before leading Cusi past it toward the thatched building at the far end. Light came through the open doorway, shining on the steps leading up to it. Gesturing for Cusi to enter, the servant bowed and left him without another word.

Cusi stood for a moment, composing himself, wondering if he had the strength to absorb more harsh words. There were story songs celebrating the fierceness of Otoronco Achachi, Grandfather Jaguar, who had earned his name fighting in the dense jungles of the Eastern Quarter. Since he was the brother of Cusi's paternal grandfather, Cusi had the right to call him "grandfather," but he could not foresee that he would exercise it, given his lack of familiarity with the man. Better to call him "lord," he thought, forcing himself to climb the stairs and cross the threshold without further hesitation.

The light in the room came from rushes whose heads had been dipped in tallow before being set ablaze. They stood upright in pottery holders in all of the wall niches, casting a smoky yellow light onto the stone implements, weapons, animal skins, and cloth hangings that filled the niches and decorated the walls. Otoronco Achachi was pacing the room with a painted drinking cup clutched in one hand, muttering to himself. He was a large man whose wide shoulders strained against the black and yellow cloth of his tunic, so that the armholes stood out stiffly above his biceps. His close-cropped hair was still mostly black, bound at the forehead by a red and black headband bearing the silver insignia of the Iñaca household. His golden earplugs were studded with pieces of shining black stone, so that they looked as if they were covered with the skin of a jeweled jaguar. There was a long white scar on Otoronco's calf, just below his feathered kneeband, and another one on his opposite knee. When he stopped his pacing and lifted his blunt, powerful head, Cusi saw a star-shaped scar on his cheek and a deep cleft that divided one of his shaggy eyebrows in half. He was a man heavily marked by war, and every bit as forbidding as Cusi recalled from their only meeting.

"You are Cusi Auqui," he demanded, "the son of Apu Poma?"

"Yes, Lord."

"You look like you have lost a fight with a cactus." He came closer, so that Cusi could see his bloodshot eyes and the flecks of foam on his lips. "You do not look like someone who lies to his teachers and tries to injure his initiation brothers."

Cusi said nothing, expecting to be shaken or struck, but too tired even to brace himself. Otoronco paused to drink from his cup, which was decorated with images of monkeys.

"First Aranyac comes to speak to me. Then Sumac Mallqui. They speak to me of a boy who has suddenly become careless and deceitful and violent. I could not believe I was being told about the son of Apu Poma."

"I have no excuse for my behavior," Cusi said in a low voice, still waiting for Otoronco's free hand to descend on him. But the man stepped back instead, raising one half of his split eyebrow.

"I want an explanation, not excuses. Look at me, Cusi. Perhaps you know that for many years, I served Topa Inca as the Sapa Inca's personal inspector. I was the Tocoyricoc, He Who Sees All. You told Aranyac that you lost your memory cord. Tell *me* that you lost your cord."

Otoronco's eyes were wide and unblinking, red-rimmed but glaring at him with such concentrated force that Cusi unconsciously raised a hand to cover his heart. He felt all of his secrets crowding up under his ribs like caged birds, surely visible to that unwavering gaze. He gave in to the pressure with a kind of relief.

"I did not lose it," he confessed. "I gave it away."

Otoronco relaxed his gaze, rubbing his chin with his free hand.

"So you *did* lie to Aranyac. To whom did you give the cord?"

"A man . . . a man I found making an offering to the huaca to which I am dedicated."

"Who is this man?"

"A commoner," Cusi said evasively. "He claimed I had been sent to him by Illapa, as a messenger."

"So you did not report him," Otoronco concluded dryly. "What did he give you?"

Cusi hesitated, causing those terrible eyes to flare at him again.

"Something he said would be my spirit brother. I know I am too young to have it," Cusi added hastily. "But . . . but I kept it anyway."

"You kept it. As payment for your silence."

"No! As my spirit brother. You must believe me, Lord. I did not intend to take it. But then I could not give it up."

Otoronco's eyelids seemed to peel back even farther, so that the whites of his eyes looked like moons in a red sky, with deep black caverns in their centers. He bared his teeth and held out a large hand, speaking in a voice that seemed to shoulder the air aside.

"Give it to me."

Cusi's hands fluttered at his sides, and his heart was beating too hard to let him breathe. He stared at Otoronco's outstretched fingers, imagining them around his throat. But he could not imagine them curling around the stone, removing it forever from his sight. He would not imagine it.

"No, my lord," he heard himself say. "I must keep it with me always."

Otoronco clenched his hand into a fist that seemed as large as Cusi's whole head, and his eyes narrowed to slits. Then he suddenly threw back his head and laughed, his earplugs swinging in golden arcs beside his face. His laughter had a surprisingly pleasant sound, spontaneous and filled with appreciation.

"Then you must keep it!" he agreed, with an exuberance that made him appear intoxicated for the first time. "But you cannot be the son of Apu Poma. *He* would never have refused me what I asked. He has never understood that there are some things you do not surrender to the authority of other men." He thrust his scarred face toward Cusi, mimicking his bemusement. "You probably do not understand it yourself, even though you acted as if you did. At least your father has not destroyed your natural instincts. Tell me, do you hate him very much?"

"He is my father," Cusi said weakly, shocked to be asked to criticize his own father. Otoronco snorted in disgust.

"Do not act younger than you are. My father made *his* father drink from a filthy slop pot, and I have sons who would do the same to me if they had the courage. There is no one who can hate you more than one of your own blood. Besides, your father belittles you and tells lies about you to other people."

"Lies?" Cusi echoed, but Otoronco did not hear him. Otoronco clapped his hands, and a moment later a young serving woman glided past Cusi, carrying an akha jar and trailing an odor that reminded Cusi of the trees he had passed under earlier. Otoronco reached back into the niche behind him and came up with a drinking cup in each hand, holding them out for the woman to fill. He nodded to her, and she departed as silently as she had come.

"To Inti, our father," Otoronco intoned, raising both cups in front of his face and deliberately spilling a few drops out of each onto the floor. Then he handed one to Cusi and lifted the other to his lips. Cusi took a long swallow of the pale, foamy liquid, watching Otoronco over the rim of his cup. It was good akha, neither sweet nor sour, and Otoronco drank deeply before lowering his cup. He pulled a three-legged stool under him with one hand and sat down, gesturing with his cup for Cusi to sit on the floor across from him. Then he resumed speaking as if there had been no interruption, following his own thoughts.

"I have never liked your father, though he is brave enough. I tried not to speak to him too often, so he would not be tempted to ask me for favors. He has fewer friends in Cuzco than I do, though he has not been away as much. I agreed to help him with you only because I had failed to help him get the post he wanted in Tumibamba. That was easier than telling him I thought he was barely fit to be the micho."

"What did he tell you about me?" Cusi asked when Otoronco paused to drink. Otoronco gave him a sardonic smile.

"He said that you were small and meek, which is obviously only half true. He said that the warriors had a low opinion of your character and fitness, which is not true at all. Sumac Mallqui actually thinks quite highly of you. At least he did until you started acting like a savage."

"He did not say I was immature?"

"Not to me," Otoronco scoffed. "And I trust what he said, because he had the courage to upbraid me for ignoring you. So did Aranyac. It is not pleasant to be reminded of your duty by those below you in rank."

Cusi drank for lack of a better response, liking the way the akha warmed his insides. He felt chilled by the thought that his father had deliberately lied to him and then had punished him on the basis of the lie. Otoronco grimaced and licked his lips, looking down at Cusi and then away, as if uncertain of how to proceed. Then he went off in what seemed like another direction.

"I have been away from Cuzco for most of my life. My father, and then my brothers, saw to that. They felt that my reputation was too large and their own power too insecure, so they made me governor and inspector and kept me out in the provinces. Now I am summoned back to stay, and Huayna Capac has taken all of the Incas north. Now I must spend my time surrounded by old men, foreigners, and retainers, listening to them count on their cords while they assure me that all is well in places they have never seen. They walk around me on tiptoes and bow three times before daring to speak, and they would rush to give me their spirit brothers or anything else I asked of them. It is a position for a man whose muscles and heart want to rest."

Otoronco abruptly drained his cup and stood up, wobbling slightly on his heels as he placed the cup on his vacated stool.

"So," he said to Cusi, "I might as well make use of you. At least you are an Inca, and I have never forgotten how few of us there are."

Turning his back to Cusi, he began to examine the objects in the wall niches, obviously searching for something in particular. Cusi wondered what he would do next, and suddenly he began to feel his fatigue. Otoronco's responses seemed totally unpredictable, and his willingness to play the role of guardian was grudging at best.

Otoronco turned back with a battle-ax in his hand, his biceps bulging casually from the weight of the star-shaped stone head.

"I carried this with me to Collasuyo when I went with Topa Inca to punish the rebel Collas. The handle is light but strong and flexible, and the head is heavy enough to crush the skull of any rebel. It is a good weapon for someone fast and agile, as Sumac Mallqui tells me you are."

Cusi set down his cup and got quickly to his feet. Otoronco held out the battle-ax between them, displaying the knobbed end of the wooden handle and the taut rope wrappings that held the head in place. The head was a star of black stone with six blunt points and a round hole in its center, through which the handle fit.

"It is best employed running *at* the enemy," Otoronco said, placing the weapon into Cusi's hands. "It is yours. Treat it as you do your spirit brother. Surrender it to no man without a fight."

Cusi cradled it reverently, pulled forward onto his toes by the weight of the head. But he was too thrilled to regard it as a burden. This was an extraordinary gift: not simply a weapon, but one that had been carried into battle by Otoronco Achachi himself.

"I am honored, Grandfather," Cusi breathed, feeling flushed with gratitude. Otoronco made a sour face and cleared his throat loudly.

"You will carry that with you whenever you are in the Patallacta and whenever you come to attend me in the palace. I will arrange with Aranyac for you to be released to me on every third day. You can keep my coca bag filled, so I do not fall asleep in the middle of an accounting."

"Will you have to tell Aranyac what I told you?" Cusi asked, his voice pulled taut by the strain that holding the ax put upon his chest and stomach muscles. Otoronco reached down for Cusi's cup and drank from it. His eyes seemed to linger on Cusi's arms and midsection, which had begun to tremble.

"I do not have to account to those below me in rank. You are old enough to defend your own secrets and to live with the consequences. Deal with Aranyac in your own way, and see that he does not come to complain to me again."

Cusi nodded awkwardly, trying not to unbalance himself. The ax was much,

much heavier that it had seemed at first. Otoronco cast an amused glance at his trembling arms, and Cusi suddenly understood the purpose of this gift. It was meant to be a burden—to make him stronger.

"Tell the retainers to give you a room that receives the early light," Otoronco commanded, "and send one of them for your things. You will live here now, and you will eat the meat of the llamas we sacrifice to Inti. You will also be expected to participate in the ceremonies of the Iñaca household, and to perform whatever services are asked of you."

Cusi made a small bow, careful not to let the ax pull him over.

"I thank you for your kindness, Grandfather."

"I know nothing about kindness," Otoronco scoffed, sitting back down on his stool and waving Cusi out of the room with his free hand. Cusi went out into the darkness of the courtyard and stood for a moment, blinking in an effort to orient himself. Then he went looking for the servants, moving with some urgency, weighed down by the weapon in his hands, which made his arms ache in a most *un*kindly way.

Caxamarca

THE RAIN coming down on the thick thatch overhead made a deep, muffled sound, a heavy drumming that lulled the senses. So different, she thought dimly, from the sharp staccato it would make on the brittle palm-leaf thatch of Chachapoya houses.

"Micay, did I speak too softly for you?"

A hand gently came to rest on her bare shoulder, where her shift had slipped aside. Micay's eyes were open, but she had not seen the other girls leave or Yutu move over next to her. Her time sense told her that it was late; the conch horns would soon sound in the enclosure of the Women of the Sun, and it would be time to sleep.

"I am sorry, Yutu. I was listening to the rain."

Yutu laughed softly, caressing the side of Micay's neck.

"Was it saying something you had not heard before?" she asked in amusement.

"Perhaps," Micay murmured. "It has not rained this hard before. Often you cannot even hear it inside."

Yutu cleared her throat but did not respond. She gave Micay a tolerant pat on the shoulder, as she frequently did whenever Micay had said something she considered peculiar. Then she politely changed the subject.

"I was asking you, before, why Cahua never comes to visit you anymore."

Micay let the rain beat down on the question for a moment.

"We had a disagreement, and I said something cruel to her."

"About her face?"

"Yes. Without meaning to."

"You should apologize, Micay."

"She has not given me the chance."

Yutu's fingers gripped Micay's shoulder and gave her a slight shake, then released her altogether. Micay swayed in surprise.

"Then you should go to her," Yutu insisted. "It is very wrong to hurt someone and not try to heal the wound. It poisons your life and the lives of those around you."

Micay strained to make out the shape of Yutu's face in the darkness. Unlike Cahua, Yutu seldom corrected her or told her what to do, so that Micay had come to think of the two of them as opposites. She was not used to hearing Yutu speak with Cahua's voice.

"I am sorry I was cruel to her," she said tentatively, "but she will not let me live my life. She would have me stay here until I was perfect."

"Cahua is very strict in her beliefs," Yutu acknowledged. "She has had to be to withstand what the uta has done to her. And surely it cannot help you to be imperfect."

"I do not know what helps or what hurts," Micay complained. "You say I will be chosen, and Cahua says I will not. But the mamanchic has said nothing to me."

"Why should she say anything to you? She will decide one way or the other when the time comes."

"It is coming quickly. What if she decides to keep me here?"

"Then you will probably stay here until you are old enough to marry," Yutu said mildly. "You will surely be perfect by then."

For a brief, incredulous moment Micay thought she was being taunted. But no, Yutu was not capable of that kind of petty cruelty. She just had the patience, the unshakable equanimity of a chosen woman. She had been passed over twice herself and felt no worse for it, so how could she understand how desperately Micay wanted to leave?

"I am tired," Micay said in resignation. "I should go to my room."

Yutu found Micay's hand in the darkness and covered it with her own. The rain had diminished to gusts that seemed to march across the roof with heavy, staggering feet, and behind it rose the hoarse bellowing of conch horns.

"I do not mean to chide you, Micay," Yutu said, squeezing her hand. "But I do not understand why you are being so stubborn. You know Cahua does not mean to harm you."

"She means to make me a chosen woman," Micay said in a neutral tone, uncertain herself if she were agreeing or disagreeing. She pressed Yutu's hand between her own and rose to her feet. Then she found her way out in the darkness.

THE FOUR WOMEN who came into the enclosure one afternoon were all Incas of the blood, said to be relatives of the governor. Their garments were made of the rich, colorful cumbi cloth the chosen women wove but never wore themselves, and they fastened their mantles with golden pins that were nearly a foot long. They were accompanied by an equal number of female servants, who had their arms and carrying shawls filled with pots and jars and cloth bags that made clinking sounds when shaken. A cloud of tantalizing odors floated in with them when they entered the courtyard where the girls stood assembled in neat rows. The girls bowed and the Inca women briefly inclined their heads in recognition. Then they joined their servants in unpacking the bags and laying things out on ground cloths, talking to one another in rapid Quechua and laughing occasionally as they pulled combs and shiny mirrors and pieces of jewelry from the bags.

Micay was in the back row with the younger girls, but even at a distance the women's presence was a shock to the senses. The fragrance of their perfumes awoke memories of forest orchids and meadows of wildflowers, and their laughter and the carelessness of their voices echoed frivolously off the stone walls, a sound none of the girls had ever heard here. The mirrors and jewelry sent bright bursts of light and rainbow color ricocheting around the courtyard, dazzling their eyes. Even the mamanchic, who was standing next to the women, seemed stunned and frozen in place, rigid in the face of so much uncontrolled energy.

Finally the women finished their preparations and fell silent, waiting to be introduced. The mamanchic opened her mouth but did not speak for a moment, as if reluctant to break the silence so quickly. Her voice was hoarse with the same reluctance.

"These women have come to teach you how to make yourselves beautiful. Make them welcome and learn everything they have to teach you."

"Come, my children," one of the women coaxed, opening her arms over the display of paints, powders, implements, and scents at her feet. The girls came forward slowly, shy but fascinated. They spent most of their nightly visits discussing their beauty and admiring each other in the dark, but now, in the full light of day, confronted by these lively women and their array of paraphernalia, they assumed the humble mien of novices, squatting tentatively around the ground cloths. Micay and most of the other younger girls stayed on the outer edge of the circle, respecting the fact that this demonstration was really for the benefit of the older girls, the ñustas who had undergone the womanhood rites and were eligible for marriage. A few of the younger girls, though, had insinuated themselves into the inner circle, showing either the intensity of their interest or a desire to be noticed. Yutu had mentioned, seemingly innocently, that these women would probably remember the girls who impressed them and might convey their impressions to the members of Huayna Capac's court when they arrived.

But Micay chose not to push forward, looking over the shoulders of those in front of her as the Inca women selected a few girls as models for the rest. Yutu was one of these, and the women clicked their tongues appreciatively over her light skin, apparently admiring her Chachapoya beauty as much as their men were said to. The women were all quite dark, their skin a deep red-brown that took on an additional duskiness around the high cheekbones, which two of the women had accentuated with a sheen of powder and deft strokes of black around their eyes. Micay found their faces striking in their own way and did not wonder at the women's lack of envy. They were pallas, after all, wives of Incas, and they had the supreme self-assurance of their blood.

The girls began to murmur and ask timid questions, and the models shed some of their self-consciousness when they were given mirrors and could see how their faces were being transformed. Micay watched what was being done to Yutu very closely, imagining her own lips similarly reddened, and the same subtle rise of color in her cheeks, and her hair with that glowing bluish sheen. Mirrors had begun to circulate through the hands of the onlookers, and when Micay turned to accept one from the girl beside her, she saw Cahua standing on the other side of the courtyard, partially concealed in the shadows of an awning house. With the awkward haste of one who has been discovered, Cahua turned and disappeared around the corner of the building.

Micay took a look at herself in the polished silver plate in her hand, seeing a face that seemed pale and delicate compared to the strong faces of the Inca women. The face was marred by a sharp crease between the eyes and a downward turn to the lips, a frown she could not keep to herself. She passed the mirror on to the next girl without taking a second look. "It is a terrible thing for a chosen woman to lose her beauty," Yutu had said recently, addressing the remark to another girl in Micay's presence. Yet Yutu and the other girls were not thinking of Cahua now and would not find her absence regrettable later. Only Micay seemed to be feeling this ache of remorse that pulled her attention away from the demonstration and made it impossible for her to concentrate.

With a movement that was almost angry in its abruptness, she stepped back out of the crowd and began to walk toward the mamanchic. She realized she had never seen anyone attempt to step out of place here, and she had no idea how it was done—*if* it was ever done. The mamanchic saw her coming and turned to await her, crossing her arms on her chest. Her eyes narrowed with disapproval as Micay drew close, letting her know how irregular she found this.

"What is it, Micay? Why have you left the others?"

"I . . . noticed that Cahua was not with us. I wondered if I might be allowed to join her."

"It was Cahua's own decision not to attend the demonstration. And it was a privilege for you to be allowed to join the ñustas today. Why have you suddenly decided that you must leave?"

Micay swallowed, unable to explain the impulse, the ache, except that it did not seem sudden. It had been building in her since her first day here.

"There is something I must learn, and I do not think these women can teach it to me."

"They are not here every day. You have had ample opportunity to learn from Cahua. Why have you waited until now?"

"I was foolish and stubborn. I thought that I could learn enough by myself."

"Enough for what?" the mamanchic demanded. "There is no end to what you must learn, my daughter, beginning with the fact that *you* are not the one who decides what is worth knowing."

"Yes, Mamanchic," Micay murmured contritely, lowering her eyes. The old woman's displeasure made the air around her seem very heavy and hard to breathe, and she understood now why she had never seen anyone else try to step out of place. She must have been dreaming, or something worse.

"Return to the others," the mamanchic ordered, "and do not ever come to me like this again. *I* will be the one to determine when you have learned enough, and as I have told you, I am very patient. See that you are the same," she added dismissively, sending Micay back to the circle of flashing mirrors around the Inca women, who had not paused in their demonstration of the secrets of beauty.

CAHUA HAD an end room with a window in the back wall that actually opened to the outside, providing a view of an interior courtyard. Cahua stood framed against the trapezoid of gray light, looking back at Micay in the doorway.

"May I come in?" Micay asked. Cahua simply continued to stare at her without speaking. A draft from the window swirled past Micay, reawakening the scents the Inca women had dabbed on her wrists and throat. The paint and powder on her face made her feel as if she were wearing a mask.

"The mamanchic said you tried to come after me," Cahua said finally. "That was very foolish."

Micay leaned her shoulder against the side of the doorway and nodded bleakly. "I do not know what I was thinking. If there was a chance of my leaving with the Sapa Inca, it is probably gone now."

"Have you come to me for sympathy?" Cahua inquired, without a trace of it in her voice.

Micay shook her head. "I came to apologize for what I said. When I saw you turn away from me this afternoon, I could not stand it any longer. I never meant to spurn your friendship, Cahua."

"You told the mamanchic that you wanted to learn something from me. Was that the truth or merely something you said to cover your confusion?"

Micay straightened up, chilled by Cahua's unyielding tone. The possibility that she would not be forgiven settled in her stomach like a stone.

"Somehow I knew that learning about beauty could not help me," she said slowly. "Changing my face would not make me feel less lost. Yutu and the other girls have been kind to me, but they know, and I know, that I am not one of them. I thought . . . I felt this afternoon that you were the only one who might show me what I should be instead."

Her voice broke on the last word, and she raised a hand to her mouth to stifle a sob. The room had darkened, but a pale light infused the window behind

Cahua. Moonlight, Micay realized dimly. Then Cahua began speaking, her voice still hard.

"I lost my beauty during my first year here. One day there was a sore on my lip, a sore that grew no matter how much it was washed and treated with salves and medicines. Then there was another, inside my nose, and we knew it was the uta, and that there was no hope for my face. I wanted to die, but the mamanchic would not let me. She stayed with me and prayed to Inti and Viracocha and Mama Quilla, calling on them to heal me and let me live. She gave me coca leaves to numb the pain and boiled water to keep the air moist, because the dryness made the sores itch and sting. I could not smell the food I was made to eat, and it tasted like blood."

Micay winced at the description, again feeling the thin coating of paint and powder on her face and wishing she had washed it off.

"There was another girl," Cahua continued, "who was stricken after I was. Her name was Inquil, and she was from a village close to mine; we had been brought to the House of Chosen Women at the same time. I tried to be a friend to her in her illness, but she could not stand to look at me. She saw in my face what she would become, and she could not bear it. It did not matter to her that my sores had begun to heal and it seemed likely that I would live. That was all I wanted then—to live. It was a gift to be free of the pain and the fear that the pain would only get worse. I tried to tell that to Inquil. I sat with her in the dark and encouraged her to pray, but even my voice reminded her of what she was losing. She loved to sing, and the uta would take that from her along with her beauty."

Cahua paused to take a deep, whistling breath, silhouetted against the moonlit window. Her voice had lost its harsh declarativeness and taken on a rhythm of inevitability, of a story that told itself.

"One morning, before anyone else had awakened, Inquil left our room and went to the great feasting hall. She removed all of her clothes and folded them neatly, as we had been taught. Then she climbed as high as she could into the rafters beneath the roof and threw herself headfirst onto the floor below."

Micay took a cautious step into the room.

"You never told me any of this."

"I would have. But you did not want my encouragement, either. You did not think you had to change, so you denied the usefulness of what I had to tell you. That is what hurt the most, Micay. You assumed that my life had no purpose beyond keeping my face hidden from the world."

"You must forgive me, Cahua," Micay pleaded, taking another step forward. Cahua held up a hand to stay her, turning aside to wipe her eyes on the edge of her mantle. Her voice was muffled with tears.

"I have never forgiven Inquil. I have tried to make my life a repudiation of the choice she made and an example to the younger girls. If I, scarred and ugly as I am, can hold my life as if it were precious, should they not value their own lives even more? That is what I was trying to teach you, Micay. I had to turn your mind away from what you felt you had lost and make you believe that you had been chosen rather than stolen. Otherwise you would always be looking behind you, and you might not see the opportunities that were yours. You might end by throwing your life away, as Inquil did."

"I would never do that," Micay vowed. "Never, Cahua."

"Suppose you are kept here? Can you truly say how you will act? Perhaps your dreaming will give way to despair."

"I do not know," Micay admitted. "I do not try to dwell on the past, but it clings to me. I hear it in the rain and smell it on the wind; the people from my childhood come to me in my dreams. I have not had years to outgrow my memories, as you and the other girls have."

"Yet you want to leave here within months."

"Yes. I want to make myself ready, but I still want to leave. I cannot deny that."

Cahua shook her head sadly, letting the moonlight brush the sides of her cheeks.

"What can I tell you, then?"

"Tell me what I must do to convince you that I am ready to leave. There is another month before the Sapa Inca will be here. What can I do to prove myself worthy of his consideration?"

Cahua was silent for a long moment, then beckoned for Micay to join her at the window. She turned and put her elbows onto the deep sill, gazing up at the night sky. Micay did likewise, blinking at the brilliant luminescence of the moon, which hung round and perfect, surrounded by a nimbus of bluish light.

"Mama Quilla," Cahua breathed. "Mother Moon. When I was very ill the mamanchic used to bring me out to bathe in her light. She told me to pray to Mama Quilla and to imagine myself to be as bright and cool and perfect in all my phases. For even when she is only a sliver of her true self, she is still perfect in her constancy and devotion. That is how you must be: calm, dedicated, a light to those around you."

"I will be that," Micay promised, letting the light fill her eyes. "I will not let anything distract me."

"You must put your memories behind you and accept the life you have been given. You must embrace it with your whole heart and not try to flee from it or resist it like your father has. You must think only of the gift you have been given, and not of what has been taken from you."

Micay thought of her father and briefly saw the outline of his face in the mottled surface of the moon. But then the image vanished and there was only the moon, solitary and flawless. Cahua was looking at her, her face only a hand's breadth away.

"I will not look back," Micay said softly. "I will welcome the life that is chosen for me."

Cahua touched her on the cheek lightly, then gestured for her to squat with her before the window in an attitude of prayer.

"As Mama Quilla is the consort of Inti, so are we the chosen women of Inti's son, the Sapa Inca. Let us begin, then, with a prayer to Inti, because it is *his* world you will enter when you have made yourself ready . . ."

III

HUARI RUNA:
Origin People

(A.D. 1512)

Cuzco

THE STORY SONG that Cusi and the two old men were singing had reached its lowest point, where the melody became dark and anxious and dipped below the range of Cusi's voice. Their chanted words described the most desperate moment in the history of the Incas: A great army of Chanca warriors is bearing down on Cuzco from the west, threatening to destroy everything in its path. The legitimate ruler, Viracocha Inca, and his appointed heir, Inca Urcon, have both fled the city in terror, taking most of their warriors with them. Another son, Inca Yupanqui, has rallied the remaining Incas and gathered what allies he can to make a last stand against the Chancas.

At night, Inca Yupanqui wanders alone on the plain, seeking inspiration for the terrible struggle to come. To the west, the campfires of the Chancas spread in a great ring, just beyond the Inca barricades. On the heights to the north and east, tribesmen from the surrounding mountains stand watching, waiting to join whichever side first promises victory and easy loot. Inca Yupanqui finds himself trapped and outnumbered on all sides, the defender of a city demoralized and left helpless by the defection of its leaders. He expects to die with the knowledge that he has been the Inca who lost Holy Cuzco.

But then the song rose in pitch and became less bleak in tone, resonating with the power of the vision that came to Inca Yupanqui on the plain. Near the spring called Susurpuquio, a divine being appeared to him, having the shape of a man but with the heads of pumas attached to his shoulders and serpents twined around his arms. He wore a headband and large golden earspools, and his face was surrounded by rays of golden light. He spoke encouragingly to Inca Yupanqui, telling him that victory would be his in this and many other battles, for he and his people were destined for greatness. He had only to call to the rocks and they, too, would rise to fight for the Incas, the chosen people of Inti and Viracocha. Inspired by these revelations, Inca Yupanqui returned to Cuzco to tell his followers and ready them for battle.

At this point, a second group of three old men stood up and stepped in front of Cusi's group, raising their voices to the sudden thudding of a drum. They chanted the name that Inca Yupanqui won for himself in this battle, the name by which he would always be remembered:

> "Pachacuti, Pachacuti,
> Earth-shaker,
> World-maker,
> Chief Inca and Son of the Sun"

Cusi and his companions stepped back and sat down among the other singers. The singing went on above them, describing Pachacuti's successful defense of Cuzco. Hands patted Cusi on the back and shoulders, and the old man to his right nodded to him with veiled eyes, commending him for his participation in the song. He had not had much time to learn it, and he had hardly slept the night before, repeating the verses endlessly in his mind. He had not eaten much in the last three days, either, since he had fasted with the other singers in preparation for this ceremony. Now he felt successful and appreciated as well as enormously relieved at being finished, and the effect was distinctly intoxicating. It would not take much akha to make him drunk tonight.

He was glad now that Otoronco had put him forward for the position of story singer, one of many such posts left empty by the departure of the Incas who had gone north. There were not even enough members of the Iñaca household present to fill the narrow courtyard of the Illapa Cancha, so that the songs seemed to echo off the stone walls of the enclosure and hang dissonantly in the open air surrounding the ceremonial group. But Cusi was thrilled simply to be a part of this gathering, which celebrated the deeds of the greatest of the Incas, a man who presided over them even in death.

Not far from where Cusi sat was the canopied litter upon which Pachacuti had been carried into the courtyard. His shrunken, mummified body sat upright beneath the fringed feather canopy, wrapped in successive layers of sumptuous cumbi cloth, so that only his head was visible at the top of a pyramid of richly colored wool. His skeletal face wore a stiff covering of papery skin, and circles of beaten gold gleamed from the depths of his eye sockets. Cusi was close enough to see the wisps of white hair that still clung to his scalp and the deep furrow above his right ear, the scar left by a Cuyo assassin who had failed in an attempt on Pachacuti's life. A woman in a golden mask sat behind him, brushing the flies from his face with a jeweled whisk.

Cusi had never been so close to one of the royal mummies before, and he could feel its huaca, the strange, brooding power that could be sensed beneath the inanimate surface. His fascinated gaze slid past the singers to the ghastly, fixed features of Pachacuti, the man who had looked out at the world around Cuzco and declared that it would all belong to him. My great-grandfather, Cusi thought reverently, placing his hand over his spirit brother, which he had sewn into a little pocket in his waistband. Raurau Illa had said that the stone held the heat of Illapa's lightning, and Pachacuti's own spirit brother was a double-headed serpent of gold that was called Inti Illapa. Perhaps he was joined to Pachacuti by more than blood.

He took pleasure, as well, in the fact that he did not owe his presence here to his father's influence. Apu Poma was a member of the Iñaca, but he had never taken an active role in its affairs, and he had never bothered to introduce Cusi to those members he did know. So Cusi was known instead as the grandson of Otoronco Achachi, a designation, he had found, that could open nearly every door in the Patallacta. He had decided, recently, that he would no longer think of himself as a fatherless boy, but as a boy who had disowned his father.

A quickening of the drum beat cut short his speculations, signaling the last verse of the song, which all those present were to join in singing. The words were simple and well known to every Inca child, but as he rose with the other members of the Iñaca household, all wearing the red and black household colors, all the blood relatives of Pachacuti, Cusi felt as if he were singing the words for the first time:

> Pachacuti, Pachacuti,
> Son of the Sun,
> Foundation of the World,
> Father of us all . . .

Almost as soon as his friends walked into the courtyard, led by the servant who had met them at the gate, Cusi realized that he had made a grave miscalculation. They were wearing their finest tunics and headdresses and had gifts in their hands, but none of them smiled and there was no anticipatory eagerness in their faces. They bowed to him as if this were a duty rather than a pleasure, and they did not look around the courtyard or comment on what they had seen in coming here. Cusi had instructed the servant to take them through his favorite gardens and past the aviary and the fish tanks, hoping to impress them with the size and luxuriousness of his new surroundings. Then he would greet them in his new clothes and give them the fine food the retainers had prepared, and they would talk and relax with one another, and he would be able to apologize to Tomay and tell them all that had happened to him.

But Tomay's narrowed eyes offered no easy forgiveness, and Uritu and Rimachi had obviously taken his side, wearing the polite, impassive expressions of unfriendly witnesses. The buoyant confidence with which Cusi had arranged this meeting deserted him abruptly, and the battle-ax in his hands suddenly seemed like a boastful accoutrement, another attempt to dazzle them with his importance. He felt embarrassed yet resentful, too, because he had truly wanted to share his good fortune with his friends before he told them about his trials.

"Come with me," he said curtly, and led them through the building where he had his own room, taking them out the back entrance and down a short flight of steps to a narrow terrace landing. Two retainer women were standing next to the covered dishes of food they had laid out on a cloth on the pavement, and they bowed respectfully to the boys before squatting down to retrieve their serving spoons.

"You may leave us," Cusi said, surprising them. "We will serve ourselves when we are ready."

Recovering quickly, the women bowed again and left. Cusi stood for a moment with his back to his friends, looking down over the verdant terraces of the Patallacta, and then the streets and rooftops of Cuzco. He had wanted to share this view, too. He turned back and gestured for his friends to seat themselves on the masonry benches against the retaining wall. Then he put his battle-ax down on the cloth beside the food and came to stand in front of them.

"I had hoped that we could celebrate. These last months have been hard for me. Aranyac has been punishing me, and only stopped two days ago."

They looked back at him guardedly, as if waiting for him to say something worthy of comment. Cusi gritted his teeth.

"He punished me because he believes I lied to him. I *did,* though I had no choice. I did not tell any of you because I did not wish to make you a party to my crime."

Their impassive silence rebuked him for his lack of trust. Tomay crossed his arms on his chest and gave Cusi a direct glance, his lips pushed out in a posture of grievance.

"I know I mistreated you, Tomay," Cusi said in a low voice. "Must I beg your forgiveness?"

"You have had a long time to decide that for yourself. I would not tell an Inca what to do."

Cusi swallowed hard, feeling the same mixture of guilt and resentment. Tomay always reminded him of his rank, the only thing with which he could not compete. Cusi glanced at Uritu and Rimachi and saw that they were still on Tomay's side; he would lose their respect, too, if he took a proud stance now. Then he would always have to be the Inca and command respect as his father did, with lies and threats.

"Forgive me, then. I have been a bad friend to all of you."

Tomay nodded grudgingly, and Uritu and Rimachi let out a simultaneous breath, exchanging a relieved glance. Tomay could not resist a final thrust, though.

"We thought that you had abandoned your friends when you moved into the Patallacta."

"Enough, Tomay," Rimachi warned, but Cusi waved him off.

"No, it is all right. If you want to know all about my crimes, I will tell you. Then maybe you will understand why *I* was the one who felt abandoned. Come, let us eat this food while we talk . . ."

Cusi's confession came easily after that, eliciting grunts of appreciation from Rimachi and occasional whoops of laughter from Uritu, who expressed his amazement at both good and bad news in the traditional Campa manner. Tomay chewed stolidly with his head cocked to one side, as if weighing Cusi's words in his mind. Cusi finished on a positive note, describing how Otoronco had taken him in and given him the battle-ax, but on the whole his recital had been a somber one. The lie he had told to Aranyac seemed to hang in the air like a shadow, unresolved even if Aranyac had terminated his punishment.

Uritu was the first to break the silence that followed Cusi's conclusion, and his question took Cusi by surprise.

"Have you seen the blind man again?"

"I have been back to the huaca only once since then," Cusi admitted, "and there was no sign of him."

"It is fortunate that you did not succeed in driving him away. One must always be kind to a stranger in a holy place."

"Yes," Cusi murmured, recalling how rude he had been to Raurau Illa at first. Uritu had the humility of the forest people, who lived in a world haunted by unseen creatures, by jaguars and serpents and the spirits of the dead. He would never have regarded Raurau Illa as an ordinary man, a commoner to be shooed away and reported.

"It is fortunate, as well, that you are Inca," Tomay put in. "If Aranyac believed that any of us had lied to him, he would have made us confess to the Grass Men."

"I would have lied to the Grass Men, too," Cusi said without hesitation. The other three stopped their eating to stare at him, their faces registering various degrees of disbelief.

"No one lies to the Grass Men," Tomay said finally. "They are too skilled at detecting falsehood. I know, because I am required to confess to them every time I reenter Cuzco. As it is, you did not lie to Otoronco Achachi."

"I refused to give him my spirit brother," Cusi countered, "and he was more terrible to look upon than any Grass Man could ever be."

"The Grass Men—"

"Stop now," Rimachi interrupted, leaning forward so that his upper body was between Cusi and Tomay. Since he was half a head taller and two hands broader than either of them, he provided an effective obstacle to argument.

"You have had your apology, Tomay. And Cusi, I do not think you wish to boast about the lies you have told."

They both sat back and slowly nodded to each other, calling an unspoken truce. Rimachi reached into the bowl in front of him and tossed each of them a tiny potato as a mocking reward. Then he turned sideways and looked down his long, curving nose at Cusi, taking on an aspect that was both predatory and sly. Cusi knew he was about to be asked an uncomfortable question.

"So . . . do you think Aranyac has decided to forget your lie?"

Cusi had to think for a moment and then could only shrug.

"It has only been two days. He could make me start cleaning everything over again tomorrow, but I think he knows I will not tell him. He has not forgiven me, if that is what you mean."

"That is what I mean," Rimachi agreed. "Are you truly able to ignore his displeasure?"

"I can withstand it, anyway, certainly more easily than I could live without my spirit brother. I will tell him someday, when it is safe."

"By then he may not want to hear you."

"Then I will live with his displeasure," Cusi insisted. "There are some things you do not surrender to the authority of other men."

Rimachi stared at him with real curiosity, as if he had just discovered something different about his face. Then he grunted and ruefully shook his head.

"I did not think that choice was left to us. But then, we do not have the protection of Otoronco Achachi."

"I have to take whatever protection I can. I no longer have a father to aid me. If I ever did . . ."

Uritu let out a mournful whoop that startled Cusi, until he realized that it was Uritu's way of recognizing the seriousness of the declaration and showing his support.

"You have your spirit brother, though," Uritu pointed out encouragingly.

"Yes, and my initiation brothers. My friends. I would not give them up, either."

They were all silent for a moment, embarrassed by the earnestness of the sentiment. Then Rimachi scooped up another potato and bounded it off Cusi's chest.

"Do not ignore us, then," he said sharply, and Uritu whooped with laughter. Even Tomay smiled, ducking when Cusi threw the potato back at Rimachi and missed. They were all laughing so hard that they were not aware of Otoronco's presence until he spoke to them from the top of the steps.

"Has the dance begun without me?"

The boys hastily scrambled to their feet, brushing crumbs off the front of their tunics. Cusi picked up his battle-ax as Otoronco came down the stairs, wearing a golden Sun shield over his red and black tunic and a striped coca bag under his arm. He did not so much greet them as inspect them, looking into their faces and examining their garments and headdresses. He stopped in front of Uritu.

"You are a Campa. From where?"

"My father is the high chief of the Campas of Vitcos, Lord. His name is Ozcollo."

"I know the name. What is yours?"

"Uritu, my lord."

Otoronco stepped closer and studied the lines tattooed across Uritu's cheeks.

"You have already been initiated into your tribe, Uritu. You stood very still when you were being marked."

"I was too tired to move," Uritu said modestly, and Otoronco laughed approvingly. He next addressed himself to Rimachi, who was almost as tall as Otoronco but not nearly so thick. Otoronco sized him up carefully, eyeing the plain wickerwork band around his forehead.

"I have never been to the lands of the Cañari. Where is the home of your father?"

"Tumibamba, my lord. My father is Choque Chinchay, Captain of the Royal Guard. He has gone north with Huayna Capac."

"Along with all the other Incas," Otoronco concluded sourly. "Will they ever wish to return? I am told that Tumibamba is very beautiful."

"It is, my lord," Rimachi assured him. "But there is no place on earth that can compare to Holy Cuzco. The sons of Inti will always return here to renew themselves."

"Perhaps," Otoronco allowed, appearing impressed by the quality of the answer. "What is your name, my son?"

"Rimachi."

"You have a smooth tongue, Rimachi; you would do well in the Sapa Inca's court. Do not let yourself be trapped there while you are still young and able to fight."

Rimachi bowed as Otoronco stepped sideways to confront Tomay. There was a long moment of silence, during which Cusi was acutely conscious of the battle-ax in his hands, a weapon used in the last Colla rebellion. Tomay stood rigid as a stone, his gaze not wavering from Otoronco's face, though his eyes did not seem fully focused.

"A Colla," Otoronco mused, examining the weave of Tomay's long woolen cap. "From somewhere near the shore of the lake, I would guess."

"From Hatuncolla, Lord," Tomay announced in an unnaturally high voice. "I am Tomay Huaraca, the son of Ancoayllu, the chief of Upper Hatuncolla."

"You need not stand so stiffly," Otoronco told him. "I do not despise the Collas, like some of my people do. The Collas saved my life. If they had not rebelled, I probably would have perished somewhere in the jungles of the Eastern Quarter. I think Topa Inca had that in mind when he sent me there. But he could not put down the rebel Collas without me and my warriors."

Tomay's eyes had come into sharp, if puzzled, focus. He blinked once, as if doubting his ears.

"All I ask of any Colla," Otoronco went on, "is that he fight *for* us as fiercely as his ancestors fought against us. Can I expect that of you, Tomay Huaraca?"

"I will fight to the death for the Inca," Tomay vowed, executing a vigorous bow. A small smile played about Otoronco's lips, and he nodded to Tomay before turning to Cusi. He gestured brusquely toward the battle-ax.

"You need not carry that to the dance. I am told that your mother's father, Ayar Inca, will be present, and he would probably disapprove." Otoronco snorted, as if he found this concession to propriety necessary but fatuous. He turned back to the other boys. "You are all my guests at the dance, should anyone question your presence. Be careful, though, how you mingle with the Inca ñustas, especially you," he said to Rimachi, "with your smooth tongue. The girls might encourage your attentions, but their fathers most assuredly would not. The retainer girls might provide you with more pleasure and less complication."

The three boys bowed compliantly.

"Finish your eating," Otoronco commanded. "I will see you later at the dance, and we will drink to your success as warriors."

Waving them back to their food, he went back up the steps and disappeared into the building. The boys stared at one another in silence, as if still hearing the echoes of Otoronco's voice. Cusi was the first to regain the use of his tongue, and he gave his battle-ax a shake for emphasis.

"*Now,* let us begin our celebration!"

Caxamarca

MICAY WAS sitting in a circle with Yutu and three other girls, chewing softened maize and molle berries and spitting the residue into a large akha vat. The maize required little concentration, except to keep the throat closed against swallowing. The fat red molle berries, though, demanded more delicacy. Only the sweet outer rind of the fruit was to be gnawed off and spat into the vat; the sour flesh surrounding the inner seed had to be trapped beneath the tongue and spat out afterward into a separate bowl. The chewing helped the mixture ferment rapidly, so that in two days' time the akha would be tangy and strong, suitable for the Sapa Inca and his court.

The berries made Micay's mouth pucker and water at the same time, so she alternated them with the blander taste of maize, watching the reddish-yellow mass accumulate in the bottom of the vat. She was aware of noises from other parts of the courtyard, and of a constant din outside the enclosure's walls, but this awareness did not intrude upon her concentration or disrupt the rhythm of her chewing. The noise in the streets had begun five days before, when the forerunners of Huayna Capac's entourage had arrived in Caxamarca to the beating of drums and the bellowing of conch horns. The Sapa Inca himself had entered the city two days before, and there had not been a truly quiet moment since. Some of the sounds had been too loud and startling for even a chosen woman to ignore, causing the mamacona to enforce discipline with a strictness they had not had to employ for many years. The challenge to the girls' composure was exacerbated by the fact that they were spending most of their time making akha, a task particularly vulnerable to distraction.

Micay was one of only a few who had not been reprimanded for inattention during this time, but she was not surprised by her immunity. In the course of the past month, she had wrought a change in herself that she had not thought possible. The difference seemed to lie in her belief that she was working toward something, instead of waiting for a decision to be made about her. That alone had made it easier for her to concentrate, to dwell solely in the present moment without wishing to hold time back or have it pass more quickly. Whenever a vagrant impulse threatened to take her out of herself, she invoked the placid image of Mama Quilla to calm herself and restore control. She had felt her composure grow like a cushion beneath her skin, impenetrable from both within and without, a cushion that slowed and moderated her reactions, giving her an extra moment to decide if any reaction was called for. She heard the rain and smelled the wind as always, but her head came up only by choice, not reflex.

The something toward which she was working had also become more clear to her, defining itself despite the absence of promises from Cahua or encouragement from the mamanchic. She still did not know when she would be permitted to leave here, but she had resolved that her next life would be *hers*. She would begin it cleanly, without memories to appease or comparisons to overcome. She would not carry on her father's resistance to the Inca, which had cost her her old life and brought her here. That was firmly behind her. For the same reason, she now knew that she had to put the House of Chosen Women behind her. It was a place of transition between the old life and the new, a place meant to be left.

So Micay was now intent on using up her time as a chosen woman, consuming it slowly and thoroughly, as the moon is consumed by darkness during the course of her monthly journey. When she had taken all of its substance into herself, absorbed its muted rhythms into her flesh, then she would be changed, she would be a person ready to inhabit a new life. Her life.

"I think we have enough," Yutu said, catching Micay's eye. Micay nodded and rose without a word to follow Yutu toward the fountain in the corner of the courtyard, taking her water jar with her. As she crouched with the other girls around the sunken pool, a loud commotion started up outside the enclosure, a clashing of wood and stone and male voices shouting. One of the younger girls glanced in the direction of the sound, and Micay and Yutu clicked their tongues at her at the same time. The girl immediately lowered her eyes to her work, and Micay and Yutu exchanged a brief smile before turning to their own jars. Micay carefully dipped hers into the pool, concentrating even on this small task, aspiring to the fluid patience of a liquid, clear and untroubled.

A DELEGATION of distinguished-looking Inca women, both priestesses and wives, had come into the house that morning and had been given a tour of the enclosure by the mamanchic herself. Then they had sat down to discuss the preparations for Huayna Capac's visit, discussions that lasted well into the afternoon. It was not until after these women had left that Cahua was admitted into the mamanchic's chamber. The old woman seemed tired and distracted, unable to give her full attention to the young woman in front of her.

"What is it, my daughter?"

"I wish to speak to you about Micay, Mother."

"You have come to report her?" the mamanchic asked irritably, making no effort to show her usual concern. Cahua was taken aback by this reception and briefly contemplated a tactful retreat. But she could not count on having another chance to speak before Huayna Capac came, so she drew a breath and went on.

"No, my mother, I have come to commend her. And to ask that she be allowed into the Sapa Inca's presence."

The mamanchic raised her eyebrows and seemed about to respond with the same impatience. But then she caught herself and made a visible effort to shake off her mood, breathing deeply and rotating her head on her neck. When she was fully composed, she beckoned for Cahua to continue.

"For the past month, my mother, her conduct has been flawless. Even the excitement of Huayna Capac's coming has not distracted her. She dedicated herself to proving her readiness to me, but I think she has proven even more to herself. She knows now that she cannot evade her responsibilities or return to the life she left. She is ready to go forward and take the place the Sapa Inca finds for her, if that is his choice. I believe she is sincere in this, Mother."

"You are her friend, though. You wish to believe the best of her."

"I do," Cahua admitted. "I always have. But she did not win my approval easily. I would not ask you to trust her if any doubts remained in my own heart."

"You are willing to see her leave, then?"

"If that is the Sapa Inca's choice," Cahua said resolutely. "I will miss her company, but I will not worry that she will fail in the outside world. I am persuaded that it is where she belongs."

The mamanchic studied her with the kindly, unwavering attention to which Cahua was accustomed, though there was something sad about her eyes, a kind of resignation Cahua had never seen her display before.

"You have done my work for me, my daughter," she said, then made a weary gesture. "The decision about Micay's future, however, is no longer mine. I could not hold her back even if I wished to."

"What has happened, Mother?"

"You saw the women who came here today. My superior from Cuzco was among them, along with two of Huayna Capac's wives. I learned for the first time how many girls are desired as servants and attendants. It is more than we have. It seems that many of the Cuzco wives left their retainers behind, and Huayna Capac has acceded to all their requests for new ones. This house will soon be empty, except for those young ones who are too delicate to leave, and those few, like yourself, who wish to join the Women of the Sun."

"So Micay will be chosen," Cahua concluded. "She would have been chosen in any event."

"One of the wives asked specifically for light-skinned girls of high rank. But you need not tell this to Micay. It is better if she believes that she has earned her reward."

"She has, my mother."

"You have been more than a friend to her, Cahua. You deserve to be rewarded, as well. You will be among those who will carry akha for the Sapa Inca when he comes."

Cahua stared at her with grateful eyes, too overcome to speak.

"You deserve the chance to be close to him. *That* choice, at least, is still mine," the mamanchic added, with a trace of her earlier irritation. She shook herself wearily. "Forgive me, my daughter. I am not used to being lectured on protocol by women younger than myself. It is easier when the Sapa Inca comes alone."

"Is there any way I may help?" Cahua asked.

The mamanchic managed a small smile. "Your devotion is always helpful. Go and see that the little ones are kept calm. Tomorrow we will begin rehearsing the protocol that we will follow during the audience. As always, we will be perfect, whether it is easy or not."

Cuzco

THE IÑACA HOUSEHOLD had invited a large number of guests to its dance, successfully compensating for its own reduced membership. Some of the guests were Incas of the blood, mostly from the Vicaquirao and Capac Ayllu households, but there were also many of the Hahua Incas, the Incas by privilege, and even a few foreign chiefs. The crowd filled the huge open-sided feasting hall that occupied one of the middle terraces of the Patallacta, with additional guests filtering out into the adjacent gardens. Retainer women in red passed among them carrying two-handled akha jars, filling every cup as soon as it was empty. A band of musicians with drums, flutes, and panpipes were testing their instruments near the well-swept circle where the dancing would begin later.

After they had had their drink with Otoronco, Cusi and his friends circulated through the crowd, who were either standing with their cups in their hands or sitting on thick woven mats. Most of the people around Ayar Inca, Cusi saw, were wearing the dark blue of the Vicaquirao household, though there were also a good number of red-clad Iñaca members present, attesting to the close relations between the two groups. The Vicaquirao was the household of Inca Roca, the sixth Sapa Inca and the great-grandfather of Pachacuti, who had had a special fondness for this ancestor. Cusi did as well, since his mother and his uncle Lloque Yupanqui had been taking him to Vicaquirao ceremonies and feasts since he was a baby. He had the pleasure now of being remembered and greeted by several people as he made his way through to his grandfather.

Ayar Inca was only a few years older than Otoronco, but his hair was completely gray and he had none of Otoronco's restless, demanding energy. Instead, he had the calm eyes and deep reserve of a man who had been one of Topa Inca's Royal Rememberers, and then one of the teachers in the House of Learning. He was perhaps the most learned man Cusi knew, and the years of study had left deep creases in his forehead and a webbing of lines around his eyes. Except for the straight nose and firm chin, Cusi could see little of his mother in Ayar, at least until the old man smiled at him. Then the resemblance seemed achingly clear.

"Greetings, my son," he said, grasping Cusi lightly by the shoulders while he appraised him. "You have grown enormously since I last saw you."

Cusi laughed, realizing how long it had been since Ayar had come into Cuzco from his estate in the Yucay Valley.

"Otoronco Achachi has been giving me meat to eat and making me carry a battle-ax." Cusi glanced around politely. "Has Grandmother not come with you?"

"She is not well enough to travel, I am afraid," Ayar told him sadly, then looked past him and made an impatient gesture. "But come, you must introduce me to your companions. Welcome, my sons . . ."

Cusi presented each of his friends in turn, interrupted frequently by Ayar, who questioned the boys about their backgrounds and drew out the details of where they were from and who their parents were. Then, when Cusi had finished, Ayar called in several of the men and women in his party and introduced them to Tomay, Rimachi, and Uritu, repeating Cusi's presentation but elaborating upon it to such an extent that it almost seemed that *he* was the one who had brought the boys here. Cusi watched with admiration as Ayar matched all three with people who either knew their parents or had served in their homelands, making sure they were safely engaged in conversation before leaving them. Only then did he take Cusi aside to speak with him privately.

"You are kind to my friends," Cusi said gratefully.

Ayar shrugged as if it were nothing. "Guests should always be put at their ease. But tell me, have you received any news of your family?"

"I can only trust that they have reached Caxamarca along with the others. Have you had a message from Lloque Yupanqui?"

Ayar shook his head. Then he reached out and plucked gently at the front of Cusi's tunic.

"I was surprised to see you in red. Both Lloque and I had hoped that you would join the Vicaquirao when you are old enough to choose a household."

"That is still a year away," Cusi assured him. "But I live in the Patallacta now, so I could not refuse when Otoronco offered me as an apprentice singer."

"No, of course not," Ayar agreed. "It will not hurt you to have connections with the Iñaca, too. Has your guardian provided you with the guidance you need?"

Cusi heard the doubt in his grandfather's voice and felt a flash of resentment on Otoronco's behalf. But he paused to collect himself, aware, as he always was around Ayar or Lloque, that whatever he said might be remembered for years and might make him feel like a fool at some later date.

"Otoronco has been generous with me," he said slowly, "and honest. He treats me like a member of his regiment."

"No doubt he does," Ayar said with a rueful laugh. "He is like the warlords of long ago, the tribal war chiefs who ruled by force of arms alone. Surely he is a different sort of influence than Lloque would have been. How are you progressing in the House of Learning?"

"I do well, as always," Cusi murmured defensively, again resenting the implication of Otoronco's inadequacy.

"Just well? You should be winning the teachers' praises. You must develop *all* of your talents, Cusi. An Inca must be much more than just a warrior, if he is to serve his people fully."

Cusi had heard this many times before from both his mother and Lloque Yupanqui. It was their way of expressing the pride the Vicaquirao took in its commitment to knowledge and proper conduct, a commitment that went back to Inca Roca, who had established the first House of Learning in Cuzco. It was also their way of combating the influence of Cusi's father, who had a much narrower view of the qualities of an Inca. Cusi did not like to see this same attitude applied to Otoronco, who had done more to make Cusi feel like an Inca than anyone else.

"I must make myself a warrior first, Grandfather," Cusi said evenly, "before any other choices are mine. There is no one who knows more about that than Otoronco Achachi."

Ayar pulled back a little, reacting to the stubbornness of Cusi's tone. He stared at him the way Rimachi had earlier, as if seeing him anew.

"The dancing is beginning, so I will not detain you any longer," he said softly, not hiding his disappointment. "You should remember, though, that it is possible to have many examples. Otoronco is an impressive man, but since you do not possess his rank and reputation, it would not be wise for you to emulate him too closely."

"I have taken your words into my heart," Cusi said to mollify him, making a deep bow. But as he went to collect his friends, he thought to himself that he would rather be a warlord than a wise old man whose heart and muscles needed a rest. Certainly, he would rather have Otoronco's praises than those of the teachers. The thought made him feel both reckless and thirsty, and he had his cup filled to the rim with strong, foamy akha before heading in the direction of the dancing.

AS THE LINE of boys began to turn and double back on itself, Cusi felt a surge of anticipation, knowing that he would soon be passing her again. That knowledge put extra spring into his legs, so that he danced more lightly, and it fed the euphoria that seemed to billow up out of the akha in his stomach, filling his lungs and making his head vibrate pleasantly. The girl's name was Tocto Oxica, and she was the daughter of the Sapa Inca; Cusi had been introduced to her once at a Vicaquirao feast. He would not have expected her to remember him, but she had been staring at him ever since the dancing began. He had been disconcerted at first, because her eyes were bright and quick, like those of a bird, and they seemed to be always upon him. He could never look at her without being seen first.

But that was many dances ago. Once he had gotten over his shyness and had returned her gaze, her eyes no longer seemed so daunting. They lingered on him more casually, deliberately straying from his and then returning more slowly as they passed in line or danced across from each other. She was tiny, the top of her head coming just to his shoulder, and she had dark skin and glossy black hair that fell to the small of her back. But despite her size, she was no little girl. Her dark blue shift clung to the curves of her hips and breasts, and on the back of her head she wore a ñañaca, the cloth head covering that marked her as a ñusta.

As he came opposite her place in line, Cusi dipped a shoulder and spun himself completely around, hopping quickly from one foot to the other in order to maintain his rhythm with the other boys in his line. It was a display of agility not called for by the dance itself, and he heard Rimachi laugh behind him. But he came out of his spin just in time to see Tocto Oxica execute a similar move, and this time they exchanged smiles as well as glances. Cusi felt like laughing himself, like letting out one of Uritu's high whoops of joy, but he danced on instead, not wishing his exuberance to be mistaken for drunkenness.

The musicians stopped for a rest shortly afterward, and the dancers stood breathing heavily for a moment before dispersing into the surrounding crowd of onlookers. Cusi watched Tocto walk off toward one of the thick wooden beams that held up the roof on the hall's open side, noticing the two older women who waited to receive her. They both wore the bright blue livery of the palace retainers, and they immediately began to fuss over the girl, smoothing the hair back from her forehead and fanning her with the edges of their mantles. Cusi realized again that this was no ordinary ñusta with whom he had been flirting but then absolved himself with the thought that she had flirted with him first and was older than he was, besides.

Rimachi appeared at his side, holding a cup of akha and giving him a long, insinuating look down his nose. Cusi took the cup and drank, ignoring the look. Then he passed the cup to Tomay, who had come up to join them.

"Do you know who your dancing partner is, my friend?" Rimachi asked finally, and Cusi shrugged.

"Yes."

"Then you know that she is one of Huayna Capac's daughters."

"The daughter of the Sapa Inca?" Tomay interrupted. "By the Coya?"

"Yes," Rimachi said firmly, still eyeing Cusi. "She is Huascar's sister."

"Huascar has many sisters," Cusi said, trying to appear unimpressed.

"Yes, and he will marry all of them when he becomes the Sapa Inca himself."

"Huascar is younger than we are," Cusi said disdainfully, "and his father is still a young man. It will be many years before Huayna Capac is ready to give up the fringe."

"That may be so," Rimachi allowed. "But young as he is, Huascar is known to be jealous of his prerogatives. And he will have power over all of our lives one day."

"I would not risk offending him," Tomay averred, "even if I were an Inca of the blood."

"I only danced with her!" Cusi protested.

"I would say you were dancing *for* her," Rimachi retorted, taking the cup from Tomay and tipping it to his lips.

"It did not look so innocent, Cusi," Tomay added, and Cusi threw up his hands in a show of exasperation.

"Leave me alone," he grumbled, turning back toward the dancing area. The musicians had returned and were taking their places on the other side of the circle of open space. A slow drumbeat and a quavering flute announced a couples' dance, a courting dance traditionally reserved for the young men and women of marriageable age. Cusi had learned the steps from his sister, but he had never danced them in public, and he did not suppose he could do so now. He turned and made a sour face at his friends.

"So—I have been saved from myself. Should we go find Uritu?"

"He is out in the gardens," Tomay reported, and turned to lead the way. Cusi glanced toward the open side of the hall, seeing that the light outside was a deep orange. He did not know how it had gotten so late, and he had not noticed until now that torches had been lit inside the hall. He looked toward the pillar where he had last seen Tocto Oxica, but the people pressing in around the dancing area blocked his view. Then he realized that the dance had not yet begun, and that only three couples had entered the circle. Of course, he thought; most of the eligible men and women have gone north with Huayna Capac. Tomay and Rimachi had already begun to move off, but Cusi stopped where he was.

The musicians prolonged their wheedling announcement, and people in the crowd of onlookers began to call out for more dancers. Soon an older married

couple came out to swell the ranks, smiling and shrugging and coaxing a
bashful pair of children out with them. Then a gray-haired old man and a girl
who must have been his granddaughter joined the line of dancers, touching off
a chorus of delighted laughter in the crowd. Other such mismatched couples
began to find their way into the circle, and then Cusi saw Tocto Oxica appear
among the people across from him. She was trailed closely by the two women
in blue, who seemed to be trying to dissuade her from going any farther. But
she paid no more attention to them once she had seen Cusi on the other side
of the circle. He took a step forward, inclining his head in invitation, and she
stepped forward without hesitation. Three more steps and they were standing
side by side, facing the backs of the pair of dancers ahead of them. Cusi held
out his arm, crooked at the elbow, and she twined her arm around his, grasping
him lightly by the wrist.

"I am honored, Tocto Oxica," Cusi whispered, giving her a sidelong glance.
Up close, with her warm fingers on his arm, she seemed much older and more
substantial, daunting again. Her eyes were so dark that he could not distinguish the pupil from the iris, and she had drawn thin black lines around her
eyelids to make her eyes appear even larger. Her cheeks had also been brushed
with a fine powder that grew lighter along the high ridges of her cheekbones,
emphasizing the smooth planes of her face. He stared at her, entranced, until
finally she laughed at him.

"I am honored as well, Cusi Auqui," she said with amusement, in a voice
that was throaty and surprisingly deep. Before they could say more, the
musicians began to play in earnest, and the dancers ahead began to move in
time. Arms linked, their elbows out at their sides, they took three gliding steps
forward, then paused for a beat before hopping back one step. Since he was
taller than Tocto to begin with, Cusi was careful not to hop too high, out of
fear that he would jerk her off balance. But she was light on her feet and stayed
with him perfectly, so that he did not feel her weight on his arm as they rose
and landed together, and then glided forward again.

The line of couples moved in a circle within the circle of onlookers, some
of whom were chanting a courting song in time with the music, while others
simply swayed where they stood, smiling at the dancers and making suggestive
comments to the ones they knew. As the coordination of their movements
became instinctual and he no longer had to look at his feet, Cusi danced with
his face half turned toward Tocto, who was likewise turned toward him. It was
the way the dance was properly danced, his sister had told him, once the couple
had reached a certain level of intimacy. Cusi had not understood what that
meant at the time. Now he knew that it meant not wanting to be anywhere
else in the world but here, looking at her and being looked at, linked by more
than just their arms as they swooped through the dance.

Gradually, as the drumbeat rose in tempo, some of the older couples detached themselves from the line and dropped out of the dance. The remaining
couples began to glide faster and then hop higher, tucking their legs up under
them so that they appeared to hang suspended above the ground for a moment,

as if frozen in midair. A few attempts at this intricate maneuver eliminated the younger children, further shortening the line. Cusi cast a quick glance at the two couples ahead, gauging the height of their hops. He was as good a jumper as he was a runner, and he knew that he could soar higher than either of them.

But then he looked back at Tocto Oxica, whose eyes were radiant with the sheer pleasure of dancing, and he realized that this was not a contest. He did not have to impress her with his jumping ability, especially when he might throw them off their rhythm. We are already soaring high enough, he decided, smiling at how mature the decision made him feel. Tocto smiled back at him with some of the same amusement she had shown earlier, which convinced him that she knew what had just gone through his mind.

When the dance finally ended, the crowd of onlookers cheered the dancers lustily, raising their cups in salute. Cusi was hot and sweating and breathing hard, but he was sorry it was over, sorry that she had to let go of his arm. He did not let her walk away this time, though.

"May I walk with you?" he asked breathlessly, and she nodded, turning so he could walk beside her. They went past the two women in blue, who gave Tocto reproving looks that she totally ignored, not even deigning to greet them. Cusi was aware that the women had fallen in behind and were following him and Tocto as they wove their way through the crowd. Then they walked out onto the strip of pavement between the hall and the edge of the terrace, into the last of the day's light, which was pale pink and translucent, like still water. The terrace below was planted with rows of leafy trees that gave off a fresh green odor, and the noise of the hall seemed to have been left far behind. Cusi must have sighed, because Tocto laughed softly, glancing up at him as they began to walk down a ramp to the gardens below.

"It is very beautiful," she said, as if agreeing with something he had said aloud. He wanted to tell her that *she* was beautiful, but he suddenly felt too young to be saying such things and could not bring himself to speak at all. Tocto cocked her head slightly, her quick eyes fastening on his hesitation.

"Would you be shy with me now, Cusi? After the way we danced together?"

"I have never danced the couples' dance before, except with my sister," Cusi said lamely, struggling with his shyness. He tried to recapture the sense of maturity he had felt while dancing, and the boldness that had let him ask to walk with her.

"I know your sister well," Tocto told him, as they came down into the shadows of the trees. "And your mother and uncle, too. I thought I knew who you were, because I have seen you often enough at the Vicaquirao feasts. But you looked different today; you looked like someone I did not know, yet someone I should know."

They emerged from the shady grove into a clearing large enough to hold the light, and Tocto led him to a low stone bench surrounded by cantut bushes covered with trumpet-shaped red flowers. She seated herself cross-legged on the bench, covering her legs and feet with her long blue shift. Cusi stood awkwardly for a moment, aware that the two retainer women had crossed the clearing behind him and taken seats somewhere out of the range of his vision. He squatted on his heels in front of Tocto, finding himself at eye level with her for the first time, which necessitated another effort to master his shyness. He wondered what she saw in his face that was so fascinating.

"I was not going to come here today," she said quietly. "The rest of my family had decided not to. But something told me that I should go and see who I might find. You were the first person I noticed when I came into the hall. You were wearing the Iñaca colors and drinking akha with Otoronco Achachi, and the boys with you were all foreigners."

"They are my initiation brothers," Cusi explained. "Otoronco is my guardian now that my parents are gone. It is because of him that I wear the red and black."

Tocto nodded pertly, as if he had made her argument for her. "So you understand why you looked different to me. And then you did not flee from my glances or from the chance to dance with me."

Cusi swallowed and briefly looked away. "My friends told me I was being foolish," he confessed. "But I did not want to hear them. Not as much as I wanted to dance with you."

Tocto gave him a pained smile. "Are you afraid you have made a mistake?"

"I do not know, my lady," Cusi said truthfully. "I am glad that I danced with you. But perhaps I should know . . . what I am permitted. With you."

Tocto looked away from him for the first time, then drew a long breath. Her dark eyes glistened with emotion.

"You know who I am. I am not the first of my mother's daughters, but I have been left here with Huascar. He already acts as if he owns me. But I will never be his wife, Cusi, *never*. If I cannot be free of him in some other way, I will join the Women of the Sun."

Cusi observed a respectful moment of silence, struck by the vehemence of her refusal and how lonely it made her seem.

"What other way might there be?" he asked softly, wanting to encourage her somehow. She gave him another pained smile.

"I do not know. I can only hope and dream. My father is drawn to people who are different, people who have huaca. That is one of the reasons he chose your uncle Lloque Yupanqui to be one of his Rememberers. He knows that Lloque is your mother's twin."

"That mattered to him?" Cusi blurted in surprise.

"Of course. There are many men with excellent memories, but few who are one of twins. It is only right that everyone who serves the Sapa Inca should be unique and special. And my father is generous to those who bring him power and good fortune; he gives them great gifts. Perhaps even one of his daughters . . ."

Cusi inhaled sharply. "That is your dream?"

"It is all I have, Cusi," she said, spreading her hands wide. "Otherwise I will be saved for Huascar, however long it may take. I do not want to grow old waiting for him to either die or become the Sapa Inca. I do not want to waste what is in my heart."

A tremor went through Cusi's body so strongly that it lifted him to his feet and made his scalp tingle. He felt weak and weightless, yet strangely self-possessed. He bent down and offered his hands to Tocto, helping her to her feet. She stared at him in the failing light, still wearing the pleading expression that had touched off the tremor in him.

"You have not answered my question," he said thickly. "You have not told me how close I may come to you."

Holding onto his hands, she stepped up to him, so close that he could smell the fragrance of orchids that rose from her hair.

"You are permitted everything, and nothing," she whispered. "Whatever you have the courage to attempt and whatever fate allows us."

"I accept," Cusi murmured, wanting suddenly to touch her and hold her against him. The shadows around them had grown deep, and the two servant women did not matter to him anymore. But then Tocto stepped back from him, placing a hand lightly on his chest, over his heart. She gave him a smile that held no pain or pleading.

"You must leave me now and return to your friends. I will see that you are invited to the Vicaquirao, at a time when we will be safe. I will keep you in my heart until then, Cusi Auqui."

His chest tingling with the imprint of her hand, Cusi bowed and started back across the clearing. He wondered, as he walked through the trees and up the ramp, how a man ever knew that he had huaca . . .

Caxamarca

T HE ROPE BRIDGE stretched out in front of her, its thick support cables taut above a plaited floor that sagged slightly in the middle, describing a shallow arc across the gorge. It appeared sturdy enough, and not unfamiliar. There were two such bridges in the vicinity of Suta, and she had crossed them often, never even considering the possibility of falling off. She grasped the rope handrails and stepped out onto the walkway, her knees bent to absorb the expected give and sway.

But as she took a second step, the bridge suddenly rippled beneath her and her foot plunged down into a trough of empty air, so that she was sent to her knees and then flung back up again with the next ripple. She came down on her back and bounced off the woven floor, losing her grip on the rails and nearly slipping between the flimsy support ropes. The bridge was pitching back and forth like a live thing, and the more she struggled to steady herself, the worse the motions became. She saw the railing spring away from her hand, and her fingers groped into open space, which yawned dangerously close. Cold fear prickled her skin and she closed her eyes against the dizziness.

Then she was standing again, her hands frozen on the rails, afraid to move a muscle. Her gaze seemed to make the bridge quiver, so she took her eyes off of it, and that was when she saw the condor pass overhead. He was flying so low that the shadow of his great wings seemed to scrape the top of her head, and the wind of his passage created a hollow in the air behind him, as if the sky itself had inhaled. His feathers were a glossy slate gray, except for the ruff of white around his shriveled, featherless head, which seemed impossibly small for the size of its beak. She saw the condor's eye for only an instant, yet she was sure he knew her and had meant for her to see him.

She watched him sail down the valley, floating on the enormous canopy of his outspread wings, which coiled and occasionally lifted in a languid flap. She remembered the song of the Great Condor, the first god of the Chachapoyas, who had flown down from his home in the mountains and cleared the land with a sweep of his feathers, making a place for the first compound. The condor was far away now, but she could still see him clearly, hanging in the crack of blue sky that opened between this valley and the one beyond. The mountains shouldered in on both sides, their peaks hidden in high white clouds that split the sunlight into streaks that glinted off waterfalls and mountain streams and turned patches of forest a brilliant green. There seemed to be no limit to how far she could see, as if the condor had flown off with her vision. The vista was glorious and never ending, a view to the very end of the earth.

Then she became aware that she was moving across the bridge, walking without having willed it, her eyes still turned aside from her path. Nor could she bear to lose sight of the condor, who soared from sunlight into shadow and back again, yet somehow remained visible. Her limbs seemed to be moving expertly, causing hardly a tremor in the floor beneath her. She hung onto the condor with her eyes, but finally the fear of walking blindly overwhelmed her and she had to look down at herself. Immediately the bridge began to sway and the floor turned soft under her sandals, threatening to betray her next step.

She jerked her eyes away and found the condor, a black slash across the distant sky. The bridge became firm again and she felt herself going forward, and this time she did not resist. It was a curious sensation, walking without looking, but it was preferable to setting the bridge into motion once more.

Then she reached solid ground and suddenly realized that she could no longer see the condor, who had lost himself in the dark folds of the mountains. She felt a moment of intense grief, but it passed so quickly that soon she could not remember why she had been sad. She sat down in confusion and stopped even trying to remember . . .

Micay woke in a dim gray light, curled in a ball on her llama-skin rug, one numbed hand trapped beneath her body. Her first thought, while the images from the dream were still with her, was that she would be leaving the House of Chosen Women. The dream had been so vivid and so vast in its perspective—everything her life here was not. It had to be an omen, a sign that the Sapa Inca would find her worthy of selection and take her out of here.

She slowly pushed herself up into a sitting position, shaking and flexing her nerveless hand. Her shift and mantle lay neatly folded beside her, a pile of blue and white cloth topped by her silver pin. In her new life, she promised herself, she would have clothing of many colors again, clothing with stripes and designs and borders of embroidery. Surely, even if she were given as a servant, she would be allowed some time to weave for herself, perhaps even the freedom to choose her own patterns and colors.

But as she began to dress herself, other aspects of the dream began to assert themselves: the way the bridge had shaken and almost spilled her, the strange sensation of walking blindly, the final disappearance of the condor. Were these warnings of failure and disappointment? She had earned only the chance of being selected, not the certainty of it. Perhaps the dream was telling her that she was not ready to cross over to a life outside. Perhaps . . .

Micay stopped herself. She had not indulged in this kind of anxious speculation in a month, and she had felt stronger and healthier for it. She had put her faith in Mama Quilla, trusting that her new life would have a shining wholeness, an integrity that could not be diminished by delay or disappointment. This was not a time to be distracted by doubts rising out of a dream. She was a chosen woman, and her only concern right now was to prepare herself for the imminent arrival of the Sapa Inca.

She hung her long black hair down in front of her and began to comb it out with slow, methodical strokes, trying not to think of anything else. But one other aspect of the dream continued to gnaw at her: she had thought of herself as a Chachapoya again, remembering the bridges near Suta and the words of the song of the Great Condor. Especially in her affinity for the condor, she had felt like a Chachapoya. Yet that was the part of herself she had done away with most completely, so that it no longer entered into her waking deliberations. A return to her homeland did not even exist as a wish anymore, or so she had thought. She wondered if she truly knew her own wishes any longer, or if she knew only the wishes that others allowed her to entertain.

Again she stopped herself, steadying her gaze by staring at the finely fitted stones in the wall. If she did not know her wishes, she was certain at least of the strength of her composure, which was like a wall itself. Whatever happened today, she would not be overwhelmed by it, and she would not react impulsively or rashly. She was absolutely certain of that. The rest was in the hands of Mama Quilla and her consort Inti, who would soon be rising to light the world. Straightening her headband, Micay went out to lend her voice to the prayers and songs of welcome.

THE GIRLS saw Huayna Capac only briefly upon his entrance to the house, for he was taken immediately to visit the Women of the Sun, the priestesses who

lived in seclusion in the rear of the enclosure. They were the sacred ones of
Inti, whom they served with prayers and fasting and chastity, and Huayna
Capac came to them as the foremost of the sons of Inti and the highest of his
priests.

Before the mamanchic led him off, though, he stopped for a moment in the
courtyard where the girls had been assembled to greet him. He was a short,
stocky man who wore enormous golden earplugs and did not smile. His eyes
were hidden by the mascapaycha, the fringe of multicolored tassels hanging
from his headband that only the Sapa Inca could wear. His cape and tunic were
of the finest cumbi cloth, woven in a complex pattern of checks of many colors,
and he wore a loincloth with an embroidered apron and kneebands tufted with
green feathers bound in gold thread.

His voice, however, was the most striking thing about him: deep and resonant, the first male voice Micay had heard in months. And he spoke in a
Quechua that nearly eluded her comprehension, releasing certain words from
deep down in his throat and adding soft explosions of emphasis to others.
Micay grasped the basic message of his greeting, but she had to work at it, as
she once had done with Cahua's peculiar warble. She realized that what she
had been taught as the hatun simi, the high speech the mamanchic had found
acceptable, was not Cuzco Quechua after all.

He will think we speak like barbarians, Micay thought as she watched him
leave the courtyard. She examined her feelings closely, searching for an echo
of the excitement Cahua had expressed to her earlier. They had only had a
moment alone, and Cahua had filled it completely with the eagerness of her
anticipation, which was pure excitement, unsullied by any expectation of being
chosen. She was simply thrilled at the prospect of being near the man who
called himself Intip Michi, Herder of the Sun.

But Micay felt nothing similar; she was not *that* much of a chosen woman.
She turned her eyes to the front, to the second group that was now waiting
for the Sapa Inca's return. This group was composed of women—perhaps as
many as forty—who had come in with Huayna Capac. They were all as
handsomely attired as he was, filling their end of the courtyard with such a
profusion of bright colors that Micay was forced to squint. The sunlight glinted
off their gold and silver jewelry and gave a deep luster to their hair, which in
some cases had a blue or purple hue. In contrast to the motionless silence of
the girls, the women were talking animatedly among themselves, occasionally
gesturing toward Micay's side of the courtyard, where the girls who were not
yet ñustas were congregated. Picking their servants and attendants, Micay
realized, wondering which, if either, she would be.

She was standing at the end of the second row of girls, and a movement at
her elbow drew her attention away from the women in front. Cahua and three
other young women, all of whom were pledged to join the Women of the Sun,
had come in carrying drinking cups and jars of akha. Micay stole a glance at
her friend, who held the heavy, two-handled jar on the point of her hip while
she waited, her eyes fixed straight ahead with self-conscious dignity. Micay

studied her composure with admiration, knowing how excited Cahua was beneath the mask of calm.

Then a flat, officious voice rose up near at hand, and Micay saw that a small group of women had come forward to address the two mamacona who had escorted the akha bearers into the courtyard.

"She will not do. She will not do at all," one of the women was saying to the foremost mama, pointing with her chin at the akha bearers. Intent on deciphering the woman's difficult Quechua, Micay took an additional moment to realize that the object of her displeasure was Cahua.

"The mamanchic has chosen her, my lady," the mama replied, trying to conceal her distress with deferential gestures.

"That does not matter," the woman said. "She is an affront to the eye and unfit to serve the Sapa Inca."

The two mamacona exchanged an equivocating glance, uncertain whose authority to obey, and the awkward moment stretched on. Micay was the only one who saw Cahua's arms tremble and the jar begin to slip off her hip, and she responded without thinking, stepping out of line and wrapping her arms around the bottom of the jar before it could fall. Cahua stared at her with eyes too stricken to understand what was happening, surrendering the jar into Micay's hands without resistance.

"There," the woman said abruptly, "that one is pretty enough. Let *her* carry the jar."

Micay looked at the blank faces of the mamacona, then at the imperious features of the woman, who was actually smiling at her with satisfaction. Her full lips had been painted a deep red, and a necklace of brilliant green stones hung across her bosom, winking brightly with the movement of her breathing. But all Micay could really see was the cruelty of her intentions, which made her face seem hideous.

"No, my lady," Micay said, surprised at the firmness of her own voice. "I am even less fit. None of us is fit, if Cahua is not."

Anger flared in the woman's eyes and she turned it upon the mamacona, waving her hands in indignation.

"Will you stand by and let this child insult me? I am the Fourth Wife!"

Micay was terrified by the woman's anger, but her composure kept her from flinching. She handed the jar to one of the helpless mamacona and bowed to the woman.

"I am sorry we have displeased you, my lady. We will remove ourselves from your sight."

"Yes, go!" the woman snapped, and Micay took Cahua's limp hand and led her out of the courtyard into a dark, empty passageway where no one would hear them if they chose to weep.

MICAY SAT with her back against the retaining wall of the bathing pool, holding Cahua while she wept and moaned like a wounded animal. Micay stroked her hair and murmured sympathetically, remembering when Cahua had done this for her. They would probably be comforting each other well into the future, since there was no telling when Huayna Capac would again think of the women he owned in Caxamarca. A girl who had insulted his Fourth Wife might be forgotten forever. Micay wondered why she did not feel her regret more keenly and found her answer in the sound of Cahua's sobbing. What that woman had done was truly monstrous, a betrayal of everything Cahua had been taught to believe—worse, a betrayal of the devotion that had given meaning to her life.

Finally Cahua removed herself from Micay's embrace and squatted beside the pool, splashing handfuls of water onto her face. She patted herself dry with the underside of her mantle but remained staring out over the water, her forearms resting on the top of the low wall.

"You did not deserve this," Micay said gently. "That woman spoke for no one but herself."

Cahua looked at her with reddened eyes, blinking as if she were still trying to awaken fully.

"The mamacona did not dispute her. Only you did." Tears welled up in her eyes again. "Oh Micay, what have you done to yourself? You should not have refused her."

"She had no right to say what she did. I did not have to think about how to reply."

Cahua tried to smile but could not manage it. "Nearly all the girls will be taken; you had only to stay there and you would have been chosen. I knew this but did not tell you."

"It would not have mattered," Micay said staunchly, "and it does not matter now. I would rather stay here than leave with someone like that."

"She was not the only woman there," Cahua pointed out, but her tone was more resigned than rueful. They were silent for several moments, their presence the only consolation they could offer to one another. Micay glanced sideways at Cahua's crumpled nose and split, swollen lip, wondering if she were remembering her friend Inquil, who had chosen to die rather than be an affront to the eyes of others. Micay wondered if she were doubting her own decision, reliving all the pitying glances and scornful whispers, the fresh revulsion of each new person she met. She had borne all of that as her gift to Inti, only to hear herself reviled and pronounced unfit, her gift spurned before it could be offered.

Feeling a tenderness that made her throat ache, Micay reached for Cahua's hand. But then she saw the three women come into the courtyard and simply tapped her friend on the wrist to alert her. Two of the women were gorgeously attired, the older one wearing the long golden pin of an Inca wife. The third woman wore the dark robes of the mamacona and was one of those who had failed to defend Cahua earlier. She left the two Inca women and came forward alone, her eyes downcast as Micay and Cahua rose to meet her.

"The mamanchic sent me to find you. And to apologize, Cahua." The mama raised her eyes, blinking with shame. "She wishes to see you herself."

Cahua nodded, then cast a significant glance at the other women, who remained waiting on the other side of the courtyard.

"These ladies have asked to speak to Micay privately," the mama explained. "They are members of the Sapa Inca's court."

Micay and Cahua turned to one another, instinctively taking each other's hands.

"I will see you before you go," Cahua promised, giving Micay's hands an encouraging squeeze. Micay nodded mutely, afraid her composure would dissolve if she spoke. Cahua turned away to accompany the mama, who led her over to the two women and performed introductions that Micay could not hear. The older woman said something that caused Cahua to bow a second time, as if she had received a compliment, or perhaps an apology. Micay felt an immediate liking for them but contained it, along with her growing excitement.

Then they were coming toward her, and even at a distance, she could see that they were mother and daughter. They had the same copper-colored skin that darkened around their eyes and cheekbones, the same straight nose that was slightly flattened at the bridge and the tip. The daughter, who was perhaps three or four years older than Micay, was as tall as her mother but much thinner, still retaining the slenderness of girlhood. They were both impeccably dressed in contrasting shades of blue, and they seemed to glide across the flagstones without apparent effort, pinching the long skirts of their shifts with the fingers of one hand to hold them away from their legs. Micay was certain that she had never seen two more elegant women.

"I am Mama Cori," the older woman said, accepting Micay's bow with a gracious inclination of her head. "This is my daughter, Quinti Ocllo."

"I am honored, my ladies. I am called Micay."

Micay saw Quinti Ocllo widen her eyes at her mother, as if struck by the name. Or perhaps by the crudeness of my Quechua, Micay thought, trying to heighten her attentiveness so she would not be misled by the refinements of the woman's Cuzco dialect.

"We have been given leave by the Sapa Inca to choose a young woman to accompany us to Tumibamba. She would be my daughter's companion and a member of our household. Quinti has asked that we select you."

Micay looked back to the daughter, whose brown eyes were bright with a spontaneity her mother had tamed long ago.

"You showed great poise in the way you responded to Mama Huarcay," Quinti explained, apparently referring to the Fourth Wife. "And an admirable loyalty to your friend."

Micay lowered her eyes at the compliment but made no comment, sensing that the mother was not equally impressed. It was nothing that showed in Mama Cori's face or even in her eyes, which seemed to be examining Micay with friendly interest. But Micay had the feeling that somewhere behind her eyes, the woman was assessing her with a detachment worthy of the mamanchic herself.

"If you come with us," Mama Cori said suggestively, "you would no doubt have to face Mama Huarcay again, many times. You could not make a habit of insulting her."

"I did not intend to insult her, my lady, and I would not have refused any other request. But I could not contribute to the humiliation of my sister."

Mama Cori's expression did not change, but Micay could still feel a lingering skepticism. Finally Mama Cori looked at Quinti Ocllo, holding her daughter's eyes for a moment before turning back to Micay.

"You must see that you refuse her nothing in the future," she admonished. "My daughter and I will be responsible for your conduct, as well as your training."

"Training?" Micay repeated, wondering if she had heard correctly. She had heard that particular term used in reference only to the Inca warriors, not to their women.

"We serve in the court of Huayna Capac," Quinti told her. "One must know how to act at all times. But you will learn quickly, I am sure of it."

"I will try, my lady," Micay murmured, humbled by the realization that she had been accepted, that she was truly leaving.

"You may come with us now," Mama Cori offered, "or we can send for you tomorrow, if you prefer."

It took Micay a moment to realize that she was actually being offered a choice. She glanced around once at the blank walls of the courtyard and did not need to consider the matter further.

"I will come with you now, my lady. But I would like to say good-bye to Cahua and my other friends."

"Of course. Come, we will go with you to the mamanchic."

They separated to let her walk between them, Quinti touching her lightly behind the elbow in a subtle gesture of welcome. Micay pinched a fold of her skirt and tried to emulate their gliding walk, feeling that she was floating along between them, wafted by the gentle wind stirred by their long skirts. She kept her eyes fixed straight ahead, resisting the urge to look down at her moving feet.

IV

ICHURI:
The Grass Man

(A.D. 1512)

The Royal Road, North of Caxamarca

THE ROYAL ROAD narrowed as it climbed the gap between the mountains, rising to the top of the pass in a series of terraced segments that looked like stairs built for a giant. At the very top, it was only wide enough for two people to stand abreast between the walls of gray rock. Micay went through next to Quinti Ocllo, both of them clutching their cloaks around them against the bite of the wind. It was painfully cold at this height, and Micay felt at times as though her lungs were groping for a hold on the thin air. They moved forward one step at a time, staying an arm's length behind Apu Poma and Mama Cori, the couple directly ahead of them. Squinting into the wind, Quinti bared her teeth and pointed forward with her chin, anticipating the view.

Then Apu Poma and Mama Cori stepped down out of the way, and Micay saw the world open out in front of her, challenging her eyes to take it all in. Below them, a bowl-shaped plateau stretched out between the mountains, a rolling expanse of land checkered with squares of red, yellow, and green, which were fields of quinoa, oca, and potatoes. The multicolored plots climbed straight up the sides of the surrounding mountains, separated by terrace walls that hung like gray chains across the slopes. Brown and white flocks of llamas and alpacas could be seen feeding above the terrace line, where the ichu grass stood out in dark green tufts against the red rock crags. Beyond these mountains towered others whose peaks were totally covered with snow.

The Royal Road lay like a broad belt across the middle of the plateau, a belt that was gradually taking on the colors of the long column of people and llamas who were advancing upon it. The head of the procession sparkled with the reflection of sunlight off bronze spear points and golden earplugs, and in the midst of this vanguard of warriors was a speck of pure white that Micay knew had to be the Napa, the sacred llama of the Cuzco Incas. Close behind, looking like a lozenge of bright pink on the belt, was the Pillco Rampa, the royal litter that carried Huayna Capac and the Coya Rahua Ocllo. Other litters followed in a line, forming a raised pattern that seemed to stand out above the dense weave of people and pack llamas that surrounded the litters on all sides.

Reluctantly Micay lowered her eyes, tucking up her skirt as she and Quinti stepped down onto the first of the sloping terraces that would take them down the mountain. The steepness of the grade made her shift her weight onto her heels, leaning backward so that all she could see without straining was the back of Apu Poma's head. Quinti was craning her neck to see past her mother, risking her balance to prolong the view. Micay confined her gaze to the backs of the couple ahead and the smooth surface of the paving stones underfoot, watching Quinti out of the corner of her eye and keeping a hand cocked to catch her if she slipped. She took the precaution almost without thinking, knowing by now that it was expected of her. She owed Quinti this vigilance over small things in return for the education she was receiving in the ways of her new world.

It was a world that seemed as vast as the view she had just seen, and her education consisted of watching and listening and absorbing massive amounts of information about places she had never been and people she had yet to meet. First there was the immediate family, several of whom existed only as names for her, then the two households to which Apu Poma and Mama Cori separately belonged, then the members of Huayna Capac's court, who were stretched out for a half day's march to both the front and the rear. Since Quinti was a voluble but unsystematic teacher, Micay had found herself learning about the complicated relationship between the households before she even knew what a household was, and for several days she had thought that the yanacona, the lifetime retainers, were a tribe from a land called Yana. But she worked hard to correct her misconceptions, devising silent chants to help her memorize names, ranks, and affiliations and using the time before sleep to silently rehearse the nuances of Cuzco pronunciation and the proper forms of deference and address. Everything Quinti had learned in her seventeen years was being poured into Micay's ears, and she could only attend to it piece by piece, with a chosen woman's single-minded concentration on what was before her.

They were now ten days out of Caxamarca, on their way to Huancabamba, the next large Inca provincial center. The pace of the column was agonizingly slow, even for someone accustomed to the restrained gait of a chosen woman, but an unseemly haste did not become the dignity of the Sapa Inca. The entire procession was halted many times during each day's journey, so that Huayna Capac could greet the crowds of people who came out to bow before the Sole

Lord. These stops usually occurred near a village or in the vicinity of one of the clusters of royal storehouses, which were located at regular intervals along the road. The chiefs and clan heads would stand assembled in one place, while the common people lined the road on both sides, their feet bare and their eyes averted, wearing symbolic burdens on their backs. All carried gifts of whatever they had: sometimes flowers and fruit and fresh-caught fish from the warm valleys, sometimes only a handful of potatoes or a clay bowl of chuño flour or llama fat.

It was the duty of the members of the court to accept these humble offerings in the Sapa Inca's name and then to distribute in return the gifts that were brought from the royal storehouses by the warriors, who acted as temporary porters. Micay had participated in these exchanges only as an accessory, passing along whatever goods Mama Cori and Quinti requested, but she perceived very quickly that delicate judgments were involved. The gifts being accepted had to be received with the proper respect, examined, and praised without seeming either disdainful or overly effusive. Then the gifts to be given had to be chosen, again without the appearance of overcalculation or unconcern. Mama Cori was especially skillful at this, able to tell a family's status from their clothing and speech and to learn their needs and desires by asking a few simple questions about their lives. There was an appropriate limit to generosity, depending on the rank and disposition of the recipient, and Mama Cori could determine both while smiling and complimenting the children on their beauty. Then she would calmly fill their arms with blankets and belts and sandals, wooden spoons and drinking cups and copper knives, and bags of salt, uchu peppers, or dried meat. She attempted, Micay was told, to give them the things they could not easily obtain themselves—things they would remember receiving—and to reward most highly those whose loyalty to the Inca seemed most genuine. They were meant to go away impressed and gratified by Huayna Capac's generosity, though not enriched beyond their place in their own tribe.

Halfway down the mountainside, Micay grasped Quinti by the elbow and deftly guided her past a pile of llama droppings. Quinti nodded absently but stopped trying to see past her mother, allowing Micay to relax her vigilance. The air had also grown somewhat warmer as they descended, allowing her to loosen her cloak.

"Perhaps Amaru will come to see us in Huancabamba," Quinti suggested after a moment.

Micay glanced at her in mild surprise. "I thought your brother had gone ahead with the other warriors."

"No, he is still with us, somewhere. He is assisting Sinchi Roca in assessing the state of the road and the wayside rest houses."

Sinchi Roca. Micay had heard that name before, and she strained to recall the reference. Inca Roca had been the sixth Sapa Inca, and Sinchi Huaman was the name of Apu Poma's deceased father. But Sinchi Roca escaped her. She spread her hands helplessly, opening her cloak to a swelling gust of wind.

"Sinchi Roca is the famous builder," Quinti explained. "He designed the

Amarucancha, Huayna Capac's palace in Cuzco. He is the son of Topa Inca by a woman who was never made a wife."

Micay nodded in acknowledgement, even though Quinti, unlike her mother, seldom looked for proof that she had been properly understood. She did not look at Micay now, assuming as always that she had her companion's complete attention.

"Does Amaru wish to be a builder himself?" Micay asked.

"Perhaps," Quinti shrugged. "It is hard to tell what he wants to be. He has already spent two seasons with the garrison outside of Cochabamba and will soon earn the right to be called 'huaminca,' veteran warrior. Then a position in the command of the army would be open to him, if he wants it. But he has not shared his plans with us."

"Is he married?"

"No, though I know any number of ñustas who would like him to be. He is very handsome, and he knows how to talk to women. But he has never been serious in his attentions to any one woman; my mother says he wastes his life in pointless flirtations."

"And your other brother?" Micay asked curiously. "The one who is still in Cuzco?"

"Cusi," Quinti supplied, then glanced ahead at her parents and seemed to change her mind about going on. "Yes, he is still in Cuzco, awaiting the manhood rites."

The road had widened as they neared the bottom of the slope, and suddenly Mama Cori looked back over her shoulder and beckoned for them to move up and join her and Apu Poma. Quinti hastened to obey, seeming relieved by the excuse to leave Micay's question unanswered. Though puzzled by this sudden reticence, Micay followed without complaint. She wanted to learn as much about the family as she could, but perhaps Quinti felt that she had spoken too freely about Amaru. Micay decided that she could wait to hear about this other brother, since there was little chance that she would meet him any time soon. At present, there was no room in her life for idle curiosity, not when each day brought new faces to be memorized, not when even her dreams took the form of parades and she went on learning as she slept.

Cuzco

ON THE FIRST of his three days alone on the mountain, Cusi devoted all of his energy to gathering materials, rather than looking for food. He would eat tomorrow, if he were lucky and as well prepared as he planned to be. First he found a spike-leaved agave among the rocks and pounded it to a fibrous pulp with a flat stone, licking the sticky sap from his fingers as he separated the fibers and stretched them out to dry in the sun. Then he climbed to the site of a recent rockslide and hunted among the jumble of stones, filling his cloak with the other things he needed: heavy pointed stones for digging and small round ones for slingstones; thin, sharp pieces of flint to serve as knives; and all the dry brush and firewood he could find.

It was midday before he had hauled everything back to the sleeping place he had chosen for himself, a flat patch of bare earth that was partially sheltered by an overhanging ledge. Wishing he had his battle-ax instead of a stone to break the hard soil, he scraped and pounded and dug with his fingers until he had hollowed out a shallow pit about two feet deep and as long as he was tall. His stomach was growling but he ignored it, contenting himself with a drink from a stream as he worked his way back down the mountain. He made three separate trips down to the plain and back, each time stuffing his cloak with ichu grass until it resembled a gigantic cloth ball. The climbing exhausted him, but he knew he would be grateful later, after the sun had gone down. Trembling with fatigue, he filled the bottom of the pit with a layer of grass and piled up the rest around the perimeter. Then he made a last effort to dry out the agave fibers, pulling them between his pinched fingers strand by strand.

He took another small drink and urinated twice as the sun was setting, wanting to leave himself no reason to rise in the night. As cold shadows began to creep down the mountainside, he drew his cloak around him and lay down in the pit, pulling armfuls of bunch grass in over him. He packed himself in as tightly as possible and prepared to wait out the night, determined not to move and allow any of his body heat to escape. He did not have much, with his stomach empty and his strength depleted by the day's labors. Darkness fell and the stars came into the sky, and he distracted himself for a while by tracing the outlines of the animals whose dark shapes stood out in the midst of the flowing river of silver light.

But gradually the cold seeped down through the layers of grass and cloth to his skin, and he hugged himself and rocked from side to side to stimulate some warmth. Squirming and shifting his limbs, he would form a comfortable pocket and fall into a doze, only to awaken a short time later with some part of his anatomy exposed and numb. He dozed and woke, dozed and woke, snatching what rest he could between icy awakenings. At some point before dawn, he dreamed that he was being freeze-dried like a potato, and that Sumac Mallqui would come in the morning to press the moisture out of him with his feet, leaving him as flat as a piece of chuño.

He woke at first light and struggled up out of the pit to squat and blow kisses to the sun, making the mocha to Inti and thanking him for the warmth of the day. He felt slightly dizzy but went to work without delay, twisting the agave fibers into threads and braiding the threads together over a frame made of sticks. He tied each knot tightly, not allowing hunger to hasten his fingers. When the sling was finished, he tested it for strength, sending stones caroming off a rock formation some distance away. Satisfied, he filled his cloak with slingstones, said a prayer to Illapa, and went hunting for his food.

Until late in the afternoon he had little luck, missing his only shot at a vizcacha and several at mice and birds. All he had to show for his stalking was a handful of wild potatoes and a small snake he had surprised sunning itself upon a rock. For that he need not have wasted a day fashioning a sling. He could have set traps instead, as Uritu had said he intended to do, or tried to run down rabbits in the way Tomay had described. He wondered briefly how his friends were faring, and if their plans were working better than his own.

Then he caught a glimpse of movement out of the corner of his eye and froze where he stood. Whatever had moved froze, too, for he saw nothing stirring as he swept his eyes over the ground. On his second sweep he saw a small, reddish-brown bird crouching at the edge of a bare patch he had cleared of grass himself only yesterday. It was a yutu, one of the small partridges that lived on the plain. Cusi smiled, for the yutu was not only good to eat but was also notoriously slow-witted, more inclined to freeze or run than to fly. Very slowly, without taking his eyes off the bird, he fitted a stone into the pocket of his sling, keeping another one in his left hand in case he missed. Under no circumstances was this prey going to escape, even if he had to run it down and kill it with his bare hands.

The yutu had flattened itself against the ground and tucked in its head, but it was still large enough to present a reasonable target. Cusi crouched and threw in one motion, sending the stone skimming on a low line. It hit the ground in front of the bird and skipped, striking the bird with a solid and audible impact and knocking it over backward in a flurry of feathers. Cusi was not far behind his stone, snatching the stunned creature by the legs and swiftly wringing its neck. He let out a cry and began to do a victory dance, which was interrupted almost immediately by the sight of a second bird breaking out of hiding a short distance away. This one chose to run, heading for the shelter of the rocks with Cusi in close pursuit. At the last moment, just as Cusi was about to make a grab for it, the bird rose into flight, flying headlong into the side of a large boulder and killing itself instantly. Recognizing that this was clearly a gift, Cusi put aside his desire to dance and said a humble prayer instead, thanking the gods for the food they had sent to him.

Climbing back up to his resting place, he worked feverishly in the dimming light, gutting and cleaning the birds and the snake as best he could with his crude blades. Then he built a fireplace out of stones and filled it with brush and tinder, repeatedly striking two hard stones together until he got a spark. He singed the last of the feathers off the birds in the high flames, finding even that smell mouth-watering, and then laid the carcasses across the flat-topped stones in the midst of the fire. He cooked and ate the thin slivers of snake meat while he waited, then lost patience and ate one of the birds half cooked, ripping at the stringy meat with his teeth. The second bird, though, was perfectly done when he plucked it off the hot stones, and he savored every bite, sucking the bones before tossing them into the fire. He felt so warm and replenished that he ventured down to the stream in the darkness to drink and wash himself.

Clouds had rolled in to obscure the stars, reminding him of the cave he had located earlier as a possible shelter from the rain. For now he had the glowing coals of his fire for company, and he watched them until they faded down to ash. Then he rolled the hot fireplace stones into the pit, sprinkled them with dirt, layered on more ichu grass, and climbed in after them. He drowsed in the luxurious warmth radiating from below, his thoughts inevitably drifting to Tocto. He had been with her on four occasions since their first meeting, each time losing a little more shyness as they talked and touched and explored the remote parts of the Cora Cora, the palace that belonged to the Vicaquirao household. The last time, he had told her about Raurau Illa and his spirit brother, and he had let her put her hand over the stone inside his waistband, which seemed to glow with a heat that threatened to brand his skin. She had kissed him on the lips afterward, leaving them both breathless and aroused to the point where they became shy with one another again.

Cusi felt himself being aroused by the memory and pressed his hands together over his loincloth. Everything and nothing, he thought, wishing he was with her now in some shadowy corner of the garden. But then he remembered where he was and decided to let himself sleep, knowing that the warmth of the stones beneath him would not last the night, while his passion could be rekindled with ease. Tucking his hands up under his arms, he fell into a dream, dancing across the plain while Tocto sat watching from the rocks, calling to him with sweet, whistling sounds.

He woke later to the grating rumble of thunder and the pattering of rain on the ledge overhead. Scooping up the potatoes he had saved from the night before, he bundled them up in his cloak along with his knives, sling, and slingstones and scurried up the mountain to the cave. He ducked in through the narrow entrance just as the rain began to come down in earnest, accompanied by a peal of thunder that made him think the sky was growling at his escape. Cusi laughed at the thought, congratulating himself on his foresight in locating this shelter. It was too large and open to be a suitable den for animals, and no humans had chosen it as a burial site for their dead kin. It was only about ten feet deep, with a small area just beyond the entrance in which he could stand upright before the ceiling abruptly slanted down to meet the floor.

Spreading his cloak under him, he sat and watched the rain pouring down on the plain below. The sky was a solid dark gray in all directions, hiding the surrounding peaks and promising a protracted storm. As time passed and the rain showed no signs of slackening, Cusi began to realize the limits of his foresight. He had not thought to store any extra wood or grass up here, and there was no possibility of digging a sleeping pit in the stone floor. Nor could he risk going out and getting wet if he could not be sure of drying off before darkness fell. He was trapped here until Inti decided to show himself, which seemed no more likely now than it had earlier.

His plan did not accommodate a whole day of rain, which vexed him until he remembered that the point of this ordeal was to teach him how to cope with unexpected reversals. A warrior never knew when he might be cut off from his comrades, and from the pack trains and storehouses that normally supplied the warriors when they were on the march. He had to be tough and resourceful, capable of making new plans when the old ones failed. So, guessing that it was already midday and seeing little hope for a break in the rain, Cusi rolled himself up in his cloak and tried to sleep, saving his strength for the long, cold night that surely lay ahead.

The rain was still falling when he awoke in darkness, no longer able to ignore the cold. He found the place where he could stand up and began to pace in tight circles, stamping his feet and slapping at himself to restore circulation. His hunger had returned, too, made keen again by the feast of the night before, so he gnawed on the hard, bitter potatoes as he paced. They provided more diversion than actual nourishment, but he was still sorry when they were gone. Now he had nothing to sustain him except his thoughts, which seemed to run in circles of their own, closely pursued by the inescapable facts of his hunger and discomfort.

This was the first major test for the initiates as they entered their last year of training, and according to Sumac Mallqui, it often eliminated several boys from the tests ahead. Some became so cold and exhausted that they gave up before the three days were over, and some came back in such poor shape that they clearly would have died if left out for a few more days. The latter would be weeded out by the daylong march that Sumac Mallqui had scheduled to begin immediately upon the boys' return. The threat of failure was real now, and the responsibility for averting it lay solely with the boy himself.

Cusi went on pacing in the darkness, blowing on his hands and squatting occasionally to rest, telling himself that no night could last forever. He knew that he was stronger now, due to a daily diet of meat and maize and the constant burden of his battle-ax. And he no longer suffered from loneliness, with Otoronco, Tocto, and his friends for company. Yet a part of him still worried that his father had been right, and when he was worried, the lie he had told Aranyac seemed like a great, glaring flaw in his sense of well-being. It made him feel that his possession of his spirit brother was still somehow illegitimate, an attachment that might yet be severed with the same cruelty with which he had been separated from his mother. Tocto would be lost to him, too, because without his spirit brother he had no claim to being different, and he doubted that he would have the courage to attempt anything with her.

Wearied by these gloomy speculations, he stopped pacing and felt the cold blackness of the night close in around him. He could see himself reporting in to Sumac Mallqui, shivering from hunger and sleeplessness, obviously too weak for a forced march. The warrior would look at him with disgust and gesture for him to leave the group, and then everyone would see that *this* was the way in which he was different . . .

"No!" Cusi shouted, whirling in place and swinging an imaginary battle-ax at the air around him. He stubbed his toe on a slingstone and stooped to pick it up and hurl it out into the dripping darkness, listening to it land with a defiant clatter. Then he threw the rest of his stones, one after another, until he could find no more on the floor. He stood breathing heavily, waiting for the world to strike back and punish him for his defiance.

The first flash of lightning came without warning, followed closely by a crash of thunder so loud that Cusi jumped and banged his head against the ceiling. Then there was another and another, bright fingers of fire that seemed to reach across the sky without touching the earth.

"*Illapa,*" he exclaimed softly, seeing the vapor of his own breath in the illumination from afar. He groped for the stone in his waistband, prying the stitches apart with his fingers in order to remove it. A piece of Illapa's lightning, Cusi thought, feeling the similarity of shape. He looked at it in the light of the next flash and saw veins within the quartz that seemed to hold the glow after the lightning was gone. He closed his hand around it and stepped closer to the entrance, going to meet the storm that was advancing upon him in a rush of wind.

The stone warmed quickly in his hand and seemed to pull his whole arm upward, as if yearning to fly free into the air. Cusi clung to it tightly, holding it up to the sky as the thunder boomed and simultaneous shafts of lightning split the darkness into jagged pieces. Dazed and deafened, he was certain that he was about to draw the holy fire down upon himself, but he was too awed to lower his arm or move away from the entrance, even as the flashes came closer and closer and the thunder made him flinch. Suddenly the storm was directly over him, so that all he could see were streaks and explosions of light that had no discernible shape, like tiny suns that burst as they were born. With a final crack of thunder, one of the suns plummeted to earth, striking so close to where he stood that he was pelted with mud and sand and stinging bits of shattered rock.

Then the rain came down in a torrent, covering the entrance like a curtain and throwing him once more into darkness. He could not think or move or breathe for a moment, his body vibrating with the impact of lightning against earth. Then sensation returned, and he could feel the mud clinging to his face, the cuts left by the flying pieces of rock, the throbbing lump where he had banged his head. The knowledge that he was still alive filled him with a wild elation, and he threw off his cloak and began to dance in place, bumping his head a second time before he could gain full control of his limbs. He clasped his spirit brother in his fist and beat on his chest as he danced, believing everything Raurau Illa had told him and pounding it into his heart so that he would never doubt it again. From this time onward, he vowed, he would be Illapa's devoted servant, a willing and faithful messenger. And he would be strong in the knowledge that the stone was truly his, and that it made him more than merely different. It made him a brother to lightning.

Huancabamba

F ROM THE WAY Quinti had spoken about it, Micay had expected that Huancabamba would be a city, or at least a large village. But it was something very different, less like an actual settlement than a greatly expanded version of the wayside rest houses that had provided nightly shelter along the Royal Road. It seemed to have sprung up out of nowhere on a windy plain west of the Huancabamba River, with nothing around it except a double row of storehouses and several large corrals for llamas and alpacas. Its buildings were all of one story and were tightly clustered around a huge central square; they looked as if they had all been built by the same hand at the same time. Fully half of the dwellings were empty when the Incas arrived, the clean, barren rooms showing no signs of ever having been permanently occupied.

"Who lives here?" Micay asked Quinti as they arranged their baggage in the half of a room that had been given to them. Quinti referred the question to her father, and Apu Poma came around the long red curtain that divided the room into halves. He addressed Micay with his usual unflagging seriousness, which always made him sound as if he were delivering a report to a superior.

"The governor of the province resides here, of course," he explained, "along with the micho and a handful of assistants, with their families and their servants. Then there are the priests and mamacona in the House of the Sun and the mitmacs we have settled here. I am told that there are communities of Collas and Lupacas from Collasuyo, Rucanas from Contisuyo, and Paltas and Cañaris from north of here. The mitmacs perform the administrative tasks for the governor and provide warriors to help enforce our laws."

The explanation had been so thorough that Micay hesitated to admit that her question had not been answered.

"Are there no people, though," she asked timidly, "who were not brought here from somewhere else?"

"Ah! You mean the Huancas," Apu Poma told her. "They have their villages on the other side of the river, in the valleys that lead to the east. It is warmer there. That is also where we have the fields and terraces that belong to Inti and the Sapa Inca."

"I forgot that you have not stayed in a place like this," Quinti said apologetically. "They are all along the Royal Road, wherever a suitable city does not exist. They were built not for the local people, but for the Incas who govern them, and for the Sapa Inca when he comes to visit."

"Or for his armies, when they come in his place," Apu Poma added. "This time we have both, and we will have even more mouths to feed when the chiefs begin to arrive tomorrow. It is a good thing the royal storehouses are full."

"You are not the micho here, Father," Quinti reminded him teasingly. "You will not have to feed them all."

Apu Poma gave her a brief, tolerant smile before lapsing back into his customary frown of responsibility.

"It will be even worse in Tumibamba," he predicted glumly as he left the girls to their unpacking and went back to his side of the room.

The next day, the procession formed up again and followed the Sapa Inca's litter into the central square, though this time the Incas were not accompanied by their servants and porters and pack llamas, and they had exchanged their dusty traveling cloaks for bright celebratory garments. The column entered from the east, passing through two monumental doorways and then down a narrow street that separated a pair of feasting halls. A great stone dais stood in the center of the square, a massive platform some twenty feet high that supported two carved stone seats. The area immediately around the dais had been left vacant, an island of open space in the midst of a solid mass of warriors, who stood silently with their shields, weapons, and banners in their hands. A wide aisle separated the outer ranks of the warriors from the spectators, who were packed in ten deep around the entire perimeter of the square.

Thousands, Micay thought numbly, having never seen so many people assembled in one place before. Led by the sacred Napa and Huayna Capac's litter, the procession made a slow circuit of the square, moving down the aisle between the warriors and the onlookers, who bowed and blew kisses off their fingertips as the Sapa Inca was carried past. As she followed in the midst of Huayna Capac's retinue, Micay saw the expressions of awe on the spectators' faces and realized that this place *had* been built for them. They were meant to experience the full power and glory of the Sapa Inca, so that they would know why he was their ruler. Awed herself, Micay could scarcely believe she was part of those making the impression, rather than those who were being impressed. She glanced sideways at Quinti and saw that this was nothing new or special to her, simply a duty that had to be performed before the feasting and socializing that would begin later.

After Huayna Capac and the Coya Rahua Ocllo had taken their seats on the dais, the rest of the Incas filled the space around the base of the platform, facing outward. Prayers were offered to Inti and speeches were made in greeting, though Micay could not see any of the men who were speaking and could only guess at their identities. She recognized Huayna Capac's speech because he addressed the crowd as "my children" and said simply that their loyalty and devotion brought pleasure to him and honor to Inti, his father. It was the shortest of the speeches, and the one that was listened to in the most profound silence.

The single most impressive incident, however, occurred at the very end of the ceremony. There was a long silence from above, and then a tapping sound that caused all the people around Micay to turn and look up. Huayna Capac was standing on the edge of the platform above, wearing the multicolored fringe around his forehead and a golden shield on his chest. An attendant handed him a battle-ax with a star-shaped head of solid gold, and the ruler brandished this over the crowd, holding it out in front of him with both hands. The ranks of warriors immediately responded in unison, raising their own weapons and shouting Huayna Capac's name three times. Their voices boomed and echoed off the platform, deafening Micay and sending a chill up her spine. The same shout was then repeated nine more times as Huayna Capac presented himself to the warriors on the other three sides of the dais. Micay left the square with her ears still ringing, telling herself that these men were her protectors and not her enemies.

That night the feasting began in earnest, conducted with a lavishness that had not been possible in the crowded wayside rest houses. The feasting halls were decorated with flowers and colorful rugs, and the servants brought out dish after dish: soups and stews and many kinds of roast meat and fish, along with baskets of fruit and sweet porridges made with honey, cacao, peanuts, and sweet potatoes. The sheer abundance of tastes was as tempting to Micay as it was to the provincial chiefs, though after seeing several of them gorge themselves into a stupor, she found it easier to restrain her own appetite. She tried to follow Quinti's example instead, taking only a small taste of anything that was offered to her.

After the food was cleared away, akha was brought out, and the Inca men began a series of formal toasts to their guests. They did this with a cup in each hand, presenting one to the chief being toasted and drinking from the other themselves. The highest-ranking Incas delivered toasts from Huayna Capac himself, bringing cups carved in the shape of jaguar heads, which had been filled with a special akha brewed in the House of Chosen Women. Only the most important chiefs or those who had performed an exceptional service for the Sapa Inca received this kind of honor, in a ceremony that commanded the attentive silence of everyone in the immediate vicinity.

The Inca women moved among the guests more quietly, seeing that cups were kept filled and that the wives and relatives of the chiefs were drawn into conversation and made to feel welcome. Instead of making toasts, they performed introductions, honoring their guests by bringing other Incas to meet them. The wives had been assigned to the guests they were to entertain by the Coya herself, and Micay quickly perceived that Mama Cori had considerable standing with Rahua Ocllo, the First Wife, because she had been assigned to the family of a Huanca chief who had received one of the first of the royal toasts. Mama Cori brought to the task a retinue that included Quinti, Micay, and six other young women, all of whom were the younger daughters of prominent Incas. They had been entrusted to Mama Cori for their training, a further testament to her prestige in the court.

Displaying an unrelenting graciousness, Mama Cori took her guests and retinue on a circuit of the feasting hall, which was occupied by the members of the five Upper Cuzco households. Mama Cori knew people in each group, and from their titles and lineage, they seemed to be the most important people in each household. They also appeared to be genuinely pleased to see her and to meet her guests, and she reciprocated by bestowing her attention upon *their* guests. Her command of names and relationships, even those learned in passing only moments before, was prodigious, and her interest in the conversations around her never seemed to flag. She is like a chosen woman, Micay thought, impressed by the intensity of Mama Cori's dedication to her role.

"Your mother has many friends," she whispered to Quinti as their group proceeded to the adjacent hall, which served the five Lower Cuzco households.

"She has had years to make them," Quinti said with a kind of grudging admiration. "She has made enemies, as well. Mama Huarcay, for one."

"The Fourth Wife," Micay recalled with a shudder. She gave Quinti a questioning glance.

"You are wondering if that is why she allowed me to choose you for my companion," Quinti surmised. "Actually, that made her reluctant to consider you. My mother is a very careful woman, and she would not antagonize an enemy without meaning to. Secretly, though, I think she approved of the way you spoke to Mama Huarcay as much as I did."

"She did not seem to," Micay said, remembering the skeptical way Mama Cori had regarded her at their first meeting. Quinti laughed.

"She is also careful about what she shows. Surely, you are aware of that by now."

"She has great composure," Micay ventured cautiously, and Quinti laughed again, though without amusement.

"She is not a person who ever lets her heart speak for her," she said flatly, ending the conversation as they entered the hall and confronted another group of new faces and names.

LATER THAT NIGHT, outside the Incahuasi, Micay had her first glimpse of the Royal Rememberer Lloque Yupanqui, Mama Cori's twin brother. Quinti had told her stories about how close the two of them were, so close that they were supposedly aware of each other's feelings even when apart. Yet this man looked nothing at all like Mama Cori. He was not only taller but much, much thinner, so that his flesh looked like ropes wrapped tautly around his bones. His nose was also more prominent, with a slight downward hook to it, and his eyes were sunk deeply in their sockets, with thick folds in his eyelids that gave him a deceptively sleepy appearance. He spoke in an odd, mild voice that also seemed somehow deceptive, since there was no lack of confidence in his gestures.

He had come out of the royal enclosure to inform Mama Cori that the Coya wished to speak with her privately before receiving her guests, a circumstance that caused both of them to apologize profusely to the Huancas. The chief and his wife bowed and waved their hands and assured them that they were quite content to wait for their audience, which would be a great honor whenever it came.

"My daughter will wait with you," Mama Cori told them, glancing only briefly in Quinti's direction before gesturing to the other ñustas in her retinue, taking them off with her and Lloque. Micay stayed behind with Quinti, who took a deep breath and held it for a long time. Then she exhaled harshly, forced a smile onto her face, and signaled to a serving woman to bring them akha.

For a while Quinti struggled diligently to maintain a conversation with the chief and his family. But all the news from Cuzco had already been passed along, and the subjects of crops and herds and the weather had long since been exhausted. Nor were the guests truly at ease speaking Quechua, so that Quinti was constantly repeating her questions or asking them to repeat their answers. Micay often heard things before Quinti did and was tempted to act as an interpreter, but Quinti did not ask for her help and she was afraid that it might be rude to offer, an insult to the guests' effort. The torturous dialogue went on but began to dwindle until they were spending more time drinking than talking, their attention wandering to the other groups waiting around them.

Even Micay's attention wandered and was drawn immediately to the ear-plug man who was working his way through the crowd in their direction. The family resemblance was too striking; it had to be the older brother, Amaru. He was as handsome as Quinti had said, with a strong jaw, thick, sensual lips, and eyes that were bold and searching. He intercepted Micay's gaze and held it, cocking his head to look at all of her and smiling to himself. The frankness of his appraisal made Micay's face grow hot, and she quickly lowered her eyes. When she glanced up again, he was standing next to Quinti, causing her to spill akha from her cup in surprise. He took her by the elbow and turned her away from the guests, whom he had not bothered to greet.

"What are you doing standing here?" he demanded, in a tone loud enough for everyone to hear. "There is someone who wants to see you."

"I cannot leave," Quinti protested, lifting her chin to indicate the people behind her. "We have guests."

"Who is this pretty one?" Amaru asked, baring his teeth and looking straight at Micay, making her lower her eyes again.

"This is Micay, my companion. My brother, Amaru Inca."

"Bring her along," Amaru suggested, as Micay bowed to him.

"I dare not," Quinti demurred. "Mother will return for us very soon."

Amaru clicked his tongue in mock regret. "Ah, and I told Quilaco Yupanqui that I would bring you back with me . . ."

Quinti seemed to rise up on her toes at the name, turning in the same motion to face her guests. "If you will forgive me," she began, but the chief was already bowing and gesturing for her to go.

"Stay with them," Quinti said to Micay, and went off with Amaru, who took her cup from her and drank as they walked away. Too stunned to speak, Micay watched them disappear into the crowd. Then she turned back to the Huancas, feeling utterly abandoned herself yet still responsible for them.

"There is someone she must see," she started to explain, but the chief held up a hand to stop her.

"It is better that she go. Perhaps she will hear something that pleases her, something we could not tell her."

Micay was shamed into a silence she did not know how to break, so she simply stood with the guests, wishing her cup were not empty but too flustered to ask the servants for more. It seemed an agonizingly long time before Mama Cori emerged from the Incahuasi, trailed by her retinue. She took one look and came directly to Micay, shedding the smile she had worn through the gate.

"Where is Quinti Ocllo?" she demanded.

"She went off with her brother, my lady."

"Amaru was here? Was he introduced to our guests?"

"Only to me, my lady," Micay admitted, finding it impossible to make it sound any better. Mama Cori glanced skyward and let out an explosive breath.

"Did you try to stop her?"

"I had no chance—"

"No one should have to stop her. But as her companion, Micay, it is your duty to remind her when she forgets her own."

"Yes, my lady."

"Go and find her, then. Tell her that she is to go to her quarters and remain there until she has spoken to me. I will look after our guests."

Micay bowed in compliance, then made a parting bow to the Huancas. As she turned away, she realized that she had just lost *her* chance for an audience with the Coya, an honor she had yet to have. But she was more disturbed by Quinti's display of willfulness. How was *she* supposed to perform her duty when Quinti might abandon hers on a whim, without any warning? Reminding Quinti would not have made any difference, since she had not forgotten her duty so much as ignored it. Nor was Mama Cori entirely blameless, having thrust the duty upon her daughter in a way that was itself willful.

Micay stopped and tried to drink from her empty cup, scanning the groups of people in front of her. It occurred to her that Quinti and Amaru might have gone to some place she had not even seen yet, in which case she would never find them tonight. The thought left her breathless with dread, so that she had to summon up her composure just to remain calm. There are no chosen women here, she decided, except for me.

Cuzco

CUSI'S FRIENDS had just begun their waiting in the courtyard, so they were surprised to see him emerge from Aranyac's chamber so soon after he had gone in. He had told them that he intended to confess everything, and they knew how much he had to tell. But his lips were shut tight as he walked past them toward the gate, so they fell in around him, exchanging glances to see who should be first to ask. Uritu, who had been the only one of them in favor of a confession, drew subtle nods from Rimachi and Tomay.

"You told him, Cusi? So quickly?"

"He did not want to hear anything. He said that it did not matter why I had lied, only that I had."

"But you had been *drawn* there," Uritu stressed. "Would he not let you tell about that?"

Cusi shook his head glumly.

"I warned you of that," Rimachi pointed out, as they passed through the gate and turned down the narrow street. "What is your punishment this time?"

"I must confess to one of the Grass Men."

Rimachi and Tomay seemed to inhale at the same moment, expressing their common shock with a single sucking sound. Uritu let out a mournful whoop that trailed off like a falling bird. Cusi looked at Tomay, who could not quite conceal his sense of vindication.

"I will not say I warned you," Tomay told him, "because I did not think that an Inca of the blood could be made to do such a thing. Are you certain that it is within Aranyac's power?"

"I could ask for a hearing with all of the teachers," Cusi said with a shrug, "or I could ask Otoronco Achachi to intervene. But I will do neither."

"You will be observed, of course," Rimachi said knowingly. "No one will know what you said to the Grass Man, but everyone will know that you were compelled to go."

"Unless you try to withhold the truth from him," Tomay put in. "Then he is permitted to reveal your crimes to your superiors."

"I will not withhold anything from him," Cusi said in a determined voice. "I must clear myself of this lie, so that I can approach Illapa with an open heart."

Uritu murmured approvingly, but both Tomay and Rimachi remained skeptical. Still, as they stopped at the end of the street, the two boys looked at each other and Rimachi nodded for Tomay to speak.

"We have shared in the concealment of this lie. We will accompany you to the Grass Man, if you wish."

"I am grateful," Cusi told them. "But I can find my own way to Pumapchupan."

"May Illapa give you courage," Uritu said in parting, and the other two boys murmured in assent as Cusi left them and walked down the street alone.

WHEN PACHACUTI had rebuilt the sacred center of Cuzco, some sixty years before, he had conceived of it as a great lion in the mountains. The lion's head was the fortress of Sacsahuaman, with its jagged, fanglike ramparts, and its body was the land between the two rivers, the Saphi and the Tullu, which flowed down from the heights above the fortress. Within this long, tapering triangle were the shrines of the Inca gods, the House of Chosen Women, the House of Learning, and the palatial enclosures of the Sapa Inca and his predecessors. All were grouped around the Haucaypata, the huge, open square that was the heart of Cuzco. The place where the two rivers came together to form the Huatanay was called Pumapchupan, the Lion's Tail.

This was the place where the holy ground of Cuzco ended and the Southern Quarter began, a boundary made visible by the waters rushing together into the deep, stone-lined channel of the Huatanay. As he crossed over to the right bank at a point just above this joining, Cusi had an even more palpable sense of departure, since he was leaving behind the protection of a privilege that was his by birth. Only foreigners and commoners were required to confess their crimes to the Grass Men; the Incas of the blood had always claimed the right to confess privately, in their own hearts. Aranyac had stripped Cusi of this privilege, making him, for this short time at least, no longer an Inca.

There was a cluster of warriors in the center of the bridge, but they were questioning everyone who sought entry to Cuzco from the other direction, and they paid no attention to Cusi as he passed through their ranks from behind. There were other men at the end of the bridge, Cañaris who wore the livery of the Royal Guard, and as he turned onto the path that led down to the river, Cusi was aware that he was being watched. He had changed into his plainest tunic and loincloth, but he could not hide the cut of his hair or the weave of his headband, both of which marked him as an Inca and made his presence here conspicuous. The people he passed on the path were all commoners who bowed hastily but could not conceal their surprise at encountering an Inca in a place meant only for them.

The path sloped down under a small cliff and then leveled off just above the river. The ground was barren and littered with fallen rocks, with only a few ragged weeds as evidence that this was the season of ripening. It suddenly seemed so bleak and cold that Cusi glanced upward to see if the sun had gone behind a cloud. But the sight of two vultures circling in the bright sky overhead made him lower his eyes again quickly, reminding him of how close this place was to the prison called the Sanka Cancha, the Place of the Pit. He turned his gaze toward the row of makeshift huts and lean-tos that lined the riverbank, searching for a black hut with an owl's wing over the doorway. He located it with an unsettling ease, for the black hut was set apart from the others and there were no people squatting outside, waiting for their interview with the Grass Man.

The hut was barely as tall as he was, built of stones and mud that appeared to have been charred in a fire. The owl's wing above the curtained doorway waved like a ragged hand in the breeze that came off the river. Cusi stood for a moment, reflecting nervously on the decision that had brought him here. It had been motivated by his need to *act* on his vow to Illapa, to announce his affinity to those who might help him understand its implications. He had gone to the huaca twice, looking for Raurau Illa, but there was no sign of him. He had thought of going to the elders of the Vicaquirao household, the keepers of the huaca, but they would be certain to consult with his teachers before admitting him to their ceremonies. So he had decided to go to Aranyac himself, hoping that the story of what had happened to him on the mountain might help to justify his previous actions and assuage Aranyac's anger at the lie. He had rehearsed his explanation carefully, trying it out on his friends and on Tocto Oxica, who had been the most encouraging of all. He had felt that he was ready now to establish the authority of his secrets, rather than surrendering them to the authority of others.

But he had not prepared himself for the possibility that his explanation would be bluntly rejected, and he would be sent here instead. He held the black cloth that Aranyac had told him to bring as a gift bundled under one arm, and he stooped to pick up one of the neatly bound bunches of ichu grass that lay in a pile beside the low doorway. Offering a silent prayer to Illapa, he pushed through the heavy curtain and crawled into the darkness on his hands and knees.

He had gone only a short distance before the way was blocked by what felt like a large stone. He came up into a crouch, sensing that the roof was not far above his head, though he could see nothing. The atmosphere was close and stank of sweat and tobacco smoke, a combination that made him want to pinch his nostrils shut. There was a scraping sound, and suddenly a shaft of light struck him full in the face, seeming to burst out at him through an open chink in the back wall. Dazzled, he blinked and started to move aside when a harsh voice stopped him.

"Stay where you are."

A red coal glowed in the darkness just to the left of the chink in the wall, and a moment later a cloud of tobacco smoke washed over him, making him cough and rub at his watering eyes.

"Who are you?"

"I am Cusi Auqui . . . the son of Apu Poma Inca. I was sent here by my teacher, Aranyac."

There was a grunt that, like the voice, seemed to convey a deep, abiding disgust. Then another chink appeared in the wall, lower down, admitting a slender beam of light that illuminated the flat-topped rock Cusi had bumped into earlier.

"Place your hands on the stone," the voice commanded, "and tell me the crimes you have committed."

Cusi put down the cloth and the bunch of grass and laid his palms on the stone, which was so cold it made his fingers curl.

"I lied to the teachers," he confessed. Immediately a stick of some kind came down across the backs of his hands, making him jerk backward in surprise. He caught his breath, which had been driven out of him by the shock of the blow.

"What did you lie about?"

"I—I told them I had lost a memory cord, when I had given it away."

The stick descended again, a light but stinging whip across his knuckles, irritating rather than truly painful.

"What else?"

Cusi understood that he was being asked for admissions, not explanations, and that he had best make them brief.

"I accepted a spirit brother from a stranger without the knowledge or permission of my superiors."

The blow fell, and Cusi paused for only an instant before going on, not waiting to be asked.

"I also failed to report the stranger, though he was a trespasser on holy ground."

When the expected blow did not come, Cusi found himself wincing involuntarily, a spasm that was nearly as bad as being hit. He recovered himself and went on to the last of the crimes that had brought him here.

"I concealed all of this from my superiors, even though I was punished and ordered to tell them the truth."

The stick came down swiftly, breaking the light as it slapped against his wrists. Cusi accepted it with a strange kind of satisfaction, a perverse reward for his honesty.

"What else?" the voice prompted impatiently. When Cusi hesitated, the stick came down again, hard enough to hurt. "To whom else have you shown disrespect? Your father?"

"Yes, but—"

Suddenly blows rained down on him hard and fast, marching halfway up his forearms and raising welts on his skin. Cusi's eyelids fluttered uncontrollably and he had to clench his teeth to keep from crying out.

"Answer for your crimes!" the voice thundered. "They are yours and no one else's! Again, have you betrayed your father with disrespect?"

"Yes," Cusi said forcefully, hunching his shoulders against a blow that did not come.

"What women have you defiled with your hands or your thoughts?"

Cusi immediately thought of Tocto, but had to be struck before he would admit that he had done anything to defile her.

"Only one," he allowed and was struck again, apparently for his reluctance. His arms were trembling and his hands felt flayed, so that it was all he could do to leave them exposed on the stone.

"Is this woman forbidden to you? Is she a sister or a chosen woman or above you in rank? Does she belong to another?"

"Yes. The last," Cusi admitted, and received another welt.

"That is theft! To whom does she belong?"

"She is the sister of Huascar."

"That is a crime against the Sapa Inca himself!" the voice cried, and the stick came down several times in succession. Cusi flinched despite himself and almost pulled his hands away. The pain made him momentarily frantic, and then an enormous anger rose up in him at the way he was being tormented. He felt that he was being turned inside out and emptied of all his self-respect, and it made him want to strike back at his unseen antagonist. But the voice went on.

"Whom have you envied?"

"No one," Cusi blurted, unable to think in his anger, which was inflamed by the blow that followed his denial.

"You forget Huascar."

"Huascar, then!"

"And whom do you wish to murder?"

"*You,*" Cusi said vehemently, meaning it with all his heart. A strange, guttural sound came from the darkness; a laugh, he realized.

"Of course. I am covered with your crimes. I am made hateful by the sickness of your secrets." The stick was suddenly placed on the stone, laid gently between Cusi's hands. "Take that and throw it into the river, so that your sickness will be carried far from Cuzco. Spit out the last of your hatred upon the grass and throw it on the waters, as well. Then wash your face and hands and leave here at once."

Cusi slowly lifted the slender wand from the stone, discovering that it was a hollow stalk with hard, knobbed joints. He put the bundle of black cloth in its place.

"I have brought you this."

An invisible hand drew the cloth into the darkness, out of the beam of light that lay like a vein of pale gold across the top of the stone. There was a rustling and then a soft, popping sound, as if the cloth were being stretched and jerked taut.

"I am satisfied. Do you wish to thank me before you go?"

"No."

There was another of those strange laughs.

"Go, then, and be as truthful in everything else you say."

Holding the stick and the bunch of grass in one hand, Cusi turned and crawled out of the hut, blinking dazedly at the sudden abundance of light. He located the river and walked the few steps to its banks, picking his way between large boulders. The water was a dark, metallic gray, furrowed and flecked with white by the swiftness of its currents. Cusi threw the stick out into the middle of the rushing stream and watched it disappear. He thought at first that his mouth was too dry to spit, but when he saw the pale welts swelling up against the darkness of his skin, marks that crisscrossed the backs of his hands and wrists, bile rose in his throat and he spat viciously on the yellowing bunch of grass. His mouth filled with a bitter taste that he tried to empty onto the grass before he hurled it into the river.

But the taste lingered even after he had washed his face and rinsed his mouth with the cold river water. He numbed his hands and forearms in the water, but they began to burn as soon as he exposed them to the air. At least the skin had not been broken, so there would be no lasting scars. Yet Cusi felt scarred on the inside, as if his heart had been scoured with coarse sand and wrung out by hands that had no gentleness. He understood now why Tomay was so bitter and why his friends' faces always went blank whenever the teachers began to describe the rectitude and honesty the Incas sought to instil in their subjects— as if it were a gift they bestowed upon savages. My brothers know what it is like to have their secrets beaten out of them, Cusi thought; they must conceive of the Inca as an angry man who strikes at them from the darkness, and then asks to be thanked.

He went up the path with his head down, going back to Cuzco, back to the privileges and responsibilities of being an Inca. He would no longer have to feel like a criminal in Aranyac's presence, and he could pledge himself to Illapa without fear that his honesty would be questioned. He had been cleansed of all his crimes, and he supposed that he should have been grateful, or at least relieved. But all he could think about, besides the stinging pain in his hands, was the innocence that had been taken along with his guilt. He had always believed in the stern benevolence of the Incas, who always brought more to their subjects than they took. But he could not believe in it any longer, and never again would he mistake compliance for admiration, or expect to be loved simply because he was an Inca.

Cusipampa

THE THREE WOMEN sat together in the center of the room, facing inward, talking quietly among themselves while they spun alpaca wool into thread in the light from the open doorway. It was late afternoon, and the complex of buildings outside their room was virtually deserted, the rest of the court having gone off with Huayna Capac on a great hunt in the hills. Quinti had wanted to go, too, but she was still winning back her mother's favor, and Mama Cori had found a compelling reason for the two of them (and Micay) to stay behind.

That reason was spread out on the floor around them in the form of the garments that Amaru had worn during his initiation some years earlier. The women were now beginning the task of weaving a similar set of garments for the youngest son in the family, Cusi Auqui, who was training for the rites in Cuzco. Since these clothes would have to be sent back to him from Tumibamba, a two-month journey for even the best bearer, Mama Cori had decided that it was not a task they could put off.

Almost all of the colors and patterns were traditional, and the same tradition demanded that certain items had to be woven by the initiate's mother and elder sister, while the rest could be the communal product of his close relations. Micay had never met Cusi and had been told very little about him, so she would never have put herself forward as a close relation. But Mama Cori had assumed her full participation from the outset and had entrusted her with what seemed like important work, including segments of two tunics and a waistband that she would weave by herself. To Micay it had felt like a reward rather than a responsibility, a visible measure of her place in the family.

During a lull in the conversation, Quinti stopped her spindle and reached behind her to lift up one of Amaru's tunics, frowning thoughtfully.

"The rites are almost six months away," she said. "Cusi might grow considerably by then. Perhaps half size will not be large enough."

"Amaru was large for his age," Mama Cori recalled. "He was one of the biggest boys in his initiation group. Cusi is one of the smallest in his."

"My brother was born early," Quinti explained to Micay. "He was a tiny baby, and very weak."

"The midwives did not expect him to survive," Mama Cori said, her eyes glinting at the memory. "But they had thought the same thing about *my* brother, who was born after me and had trouble breathing at first. So we nursed Cusi and prayed for him until he was strong and healthy."

"*You* nursed him, Mother," Quinti reminded her gently. "Amaru and I were too little to help, and Father was commanding the garrison in Copiapo."

"I only did what my mother had done for Lloque. And Lloque himself was a great help to me. He and the Vicaquirao priests spent many nights praying for Cusi's recovery."

"But you saved him," Quinti insisted. "I remember how you carried him inside your shift, next to your heart, and how diligent you were about making the proper offerings to his huaca. I was young enough to be jealous, but you made it seem like a holy mission."

Mama Cori clicked her tongue and reached down to give her spindle a desultory spin. "The gods and the huaca were kind to me." She pointed with her chin at the tunic in Quinti's hands. "We will make them a little larger than half, just to be safe. He must be able to move his body freely in the rites."

Quinti nodded agreeably and laid the tunic down. But instead of picking up her spindle, she put her hands in her lap and squinted at her mother.

"We were going to join Father in Copiapo," she said slowly. "Why did we never go?"

"Cusi was not strong enough for such a journey. Surely you knew that at the time, Quinti."

"Yes, but I kept expecting that we would go when he was better. He did not stay weak that long. By the time he was three, he was so fast that only Amaru could catch him."

"Do you know how far it is to Copiapo? It is almost as far south of Cuzco as Tumibamba is north, and the great Atacama Desert lies in the way. I had not made Cusi healthy in order to expose him to such a risk."

Quinti seemed to accept that, though she still did not reach for her spindle. Mama Cori had also stopped working, so Micay stilled her spindle out of politeness.

"Do you think it would be . . . different," Quinti said suggestively, "if we had gone to Copiapo?"

Mama Cori gave Micay a swift, hard glance that made her feel, keenly, her true distance from the center of the family. "It" could only refer to Mama Cori and Apu Poma's marriage, which seemed to consist largely of a shared sense of duty that yielded a strained politeness but little open affection. Quinti had dropped hints without ever discussing it openly, but Micay had only to see the way Mama Cori was with Lloque Yupanqui to know how much was being withheld from Apu Poma. Now she lowered her eyes submissively, wondering if Mama Cori was going to ask her to leave. The older woman cleared her throat, then spoke directly to Quinti.

"No, it would not be different. We would have been miserable in Copiapo."

"Different for Cusi, though?"

Mama Cori looked down at her lap, appearing genuinely pained. "Perhaps. We will never know. I did not mean to put him between us."

"I hope that he is well, Mother," Quinti said with sudden fervor, reaching out to touch Mama Cori on the knee. Mama Cori covered her hand, nodding gravely.

"No more than I, certainly. He will know we are thinking of him when he receives his garments."

They went back to work and Micay did likewise, more baffled than enlightened by what she had just heard. They both knew something that had not been spoken, something about this sickly child and his absent father, but Micay could not imagine what it might be. At least she had not been asked to leave the room, which seemed more important than what she had understood. She had the patience of a chosen woman; she could wait for explanations.

They worked in a companionable silence until the light outside was tinged with the hues of sunset. Then Mama Cori suggested that they send Runtu Caya for food and torches, so they could continue their labors. Micay went out to convey the message to the old retainer, who nodded compliantly and walked off toward the awning house on the other side of the enclosure. Micay stood for a moment, stretching her limbs and watching the shadows creep up the sides of the mountains in the distance. Cusipampa, she thought, the joyful plain. They were not far from Tumibamba now, where they would finally have a home of their own: the micho's quarters in the Mollecancha, the palace that was being built for Huayna Capac. The prospect of living in a palace was almost beyond belief, and it made her think ruefully of how Cahua had had to push her to accept the life she was being given.

She was just about to go back inside when she saw a warrior enter the courtyard. At least, she thought he was a warrior because of the spear in his hand and the boldness of his stride, which made his golden earplugs dance above his shoulders. The man paused to give orders to the servant who had come through the gate just behind him, and Micay realized it was Apu Poma. He was holding a cloth bag in addition to his spear, and he was incredibly dirty and disheveled. His face was smudged and his hair stood up around his headband in uneven tufts; his skin and clothing were streaked with dirt and what appeared to be dried blood.

He has come straight from the hunt, Micay thought as Apu Poma sent the servant, who had a bloody bundle in his arms, toward the awning house that served as a kitchen. When he saw Micay, he raised his spear and smiled exuberantly, again looking like a young warrior rather than the Apu Poma she knew. She went to intercept him, uncertain of what she should say but knowing that she should at least slow him down, and not let him burst in on Mama Cori and Quinti without warning.

His smile was still in place when he stopped in front of her, wearing his dirt and bloodstains like battle paint. Micay returned the smile, seeing a resemblance to Amaru she had never noticed before. But then, she had never seen him looking so thoroughly pleased with himself.

"Greetings, my lord. The hunt must have been a great success."

"More than a success! Ah, it was wonderful! We had a thousand drivers going through the forest in a line, shouting and beating on the trees with sticks, driving all the game ahead of them. You would not have believed how much there was, Micay. Deer were bounding everywhere, and there were whole herds of guanacos and vicuñas, and foxes, vizcachas, wildcats, and skunks running past underfoot. There was even a mountain tapir and a puma that Huayna Capac dispatched himself."

He paused and glanced proudly at his spear.

"I killed two deer, so that we would have venison to eat tonight. But then I decided to join the men who were trying to catch the vicuñas, so that they could be shorn of their wool. You have to be swift and agile just to get close enough to cast your net, and all these men were much younger than me. They made jokes about me and called me "grandfather" until I was the first one to catch a vicuña without hurting it. From then on, they were trying to keep up with *me!*"

Micay smiled at him again, finding his enthusiasm infectious and wishing she did not have to quell it. But he was already beginning to move past her, clearly intending to share his success with Mama Cori and Quinti.

"I can see where your son gets his swiftness," Micay said to catch his attention. "I mean Cusi, my lord. We have been talking about him today."

Apu Poma halted abruptly and looked down at her, his triumphant smile vanishing.

"Who has been talking?" he demanded. "My wife? What has she been telling you about him?"

Micay faltered and drew back slightly, surprised by the harshness of his response, and by the implication that Mama Cori would have said something derogatory about Cusi.

"We have been planning the garments we will make for his initiation," she explained. "We talked about his size, and how he had been ill when he was little. Mama Cori and Quinti Ocllo are both very fond of him; they made me feel proud to be able to help make these clothes for him."

Apu Poma licked his lips and looked past her, as if regretting his suspicions.

"So that is what you have been doing today," he said vaguely. "Have you had any visitors? Has my brother-in-law been here?"

"He called, but Mama Cori sent him away. We have been alone."

"Perhaps I should wash," Apu Poma suggested, looking down at himself. He suddenly seemed to remember the bag in his hand and held it out to Micay. "Here. This is the wool of one of the vicuñas I captured today. The Sapa Inca gave it to me as a prize. Perhaps it could be used in the garments you are weaving for Cusi."

The bag was amazingly light, even though it was stuffed full with fine reddish-brown hair. Micay put her hand into the bag and could not believe the softness; it felt like duck down, only smoother and more densely textured.

"I have never felt anything so fine, my lord," she said breathlessly. "It is a gift that honors your son."

"Ask my wife if she will accept it," Apu Poma commanded, looking over her shoulder in the direction of the family's room. Micay turned and saw that Mama Cori and Quinti had come out and were watching from the doorway.

"Ask her," Apu Poma prompted, and Micay began walking toward the women, holding the bag in front of her like an offering. She suddenly felt like a messenger between enemy camps, and it gave her a distinctly queasy sensation. She could not imagine why Mama Cori would want to refuse such a gift, but then why would Apu Poma have to send her to ask?

Mama Cori received her with an expression that was less than motherly, betraying no hint of the intimacy they had shared earlier. Micay opened the bag to display the wool, which had a luster that made it look as if it had been polished.

"It is vicuña wool, my lady," she explained. "A gift from the Sapa Inca to your husband, who captured the vicuña himself. He has asked that we use it in the garments we are weaving for Cusi."

Mama Cori did not even lower her eyes to the bag.

"Tell him he has already made his contribution to his son's manhood. Anything more would be excessive, and hypocritical, as well."

"It is the Sapa Inca's gift, my lady," Micay heard herself pleading. "We could make such fine garments from it . . ."

"Do not take sides in this, Micay," Mama Cori said in a stony voice. "Simply tell him what I said."

Micay cast a desperate glance at Quinti, but her eyes were averted, as if she would not take a side, either. Drawing a breath to steady herself, Micay turned and started back toward Apu Poma with the bag still in her hands. She saw his face stiffen, then turn baleful as he realized that he was being refused. She mustered all her composure as she walked, but there was no moisture in her mouth, and she did not think she would be able to deliver Mama Cori's rebuke. But before she could reach Apu Poma, he spun on his heel and headed for the entrance to the enclosure.

Micay stopped and looked back at Mama Cori, just in time to see her disappear into the room. Quinti lingered in the doorway, staring back over her shoulder at Micay, who stood abandoned in the center of the courtyard, holding a gift that had not been accepted and could not be returned. Then Micay heard a snarl behind her and turned to see Apu Poma rushing at her, his face wild. He dropped his spear and seemed to leap at her, both hands outstretched to grab her. Micay froze in place, holding the bag up in front of her for protection, clinging to it so tightly she was sent sprawling when he snatched it out of her hands. She hit the sand and skidded on her side, feeling a twisting pain in her wrist and a burning friction along her hip, grit in her teeth and eyes. Above her Apu Poma shouted hoarsely, incoherent with rage.

When she was able to raise her head Apu Poma was gone. Blinking furiously against the sand in her eyes, she saw Quinti hurrying toward her from the other direction, her path strewn with wispy clumps of reddish-brown wool. She realized dimly that Apu Poma had thrown the bag at his wife and probably had not meant to throw her down as well. Then Quinti was squatting beside her, helping her to sit up, brushing the sand out of her hair.

"Are you hurt? Oh Micay, I am so sorry . . ."

Micay spat out some sand and flexed her sore wrist, finding that she could move it easily enough, though not without pain.

"I will be all right."

"Are you certain? I will get the healer."

"*No,*" Micay said sharply, holding out her good arm so that Quinti could help her to her feet. As her shift fell away from her hip, the abrasion flamed up with pain, so that she limped when she tried to walk. Quinti hovered over her solicitously, but Micay waved her off and stood on her own. Mama Cori still had not come back out to see what her departure had provoked.

"It is my fault," Quinti apologized. "I should have gone out as soon as I saw you talking to my father."

"I did not want to be his messenger. Or your mother's."

"No, you were caught in between. Like Cusi."

"There is too much I do not know, Quinti. I cannot act like a member of this family if I do not know its secrets."

"That is also my fault," Quinti acknowledged. "I had hoped that you would not need to learn them. Come, let me take you to the bathhouse and tend to your wounds. I will tell you what you need to know."

Micay felt too battered to resist, but the sight of the vicuña wool scattered around the courtyard made her pull back against the grip Quinti had on her elbow.

"We must pick up the wool," she decided. "It is too precious to leave like this."

"I will tell Runtu Caya to come gather it."

"No, we must do it," Micay insisted, so firmly that Quinti released her and stepped back in surprise. Micay bent to pick up a swatch of fine hair, grimacing as her shift caught and rubbed across her hip. Quinti put a hand on her arm to make her stay still, then went ahead to collect the rest of the wool on her own. She came back and put the restuffed bag into Micay's hands.

"That should be yours now. You have suffered for it."

Micay put her swatch into the bag and bundled it shut. She realized, from the way Quinti was regarding her, that she should probably apologize. She had never told Quinti what to do before, and now she had just done it twice. But for some reason, that only made her less capable of the diffidence Quinti had come to expect of her, so that she could not even deny that the wool was hers. She tucked the bag under her arm and started hobbling toward the bathhouse, nodding silently to herself when Quinti finally came up to take her other arm and guide her the rest of the way.

V

INTI RAYMI:
The Solemn Feast
of the Sun

(A.D. 1512)

Cuzco

MIST ROSE off the Rimac Pampa as the sky finally began to lighten, turning from slate to light gray and revealing the shifting shapes of the clouds. A breeze from the east swept down the broad avenue between the two lines of tents that had been erected in the middle of the field, ruffling the plumes and feathers that hung in a woven fringe from the open awnings. There were five tents on either side of the aisle, those of the Upper Cuzco households on the right and those of Lower Cuzco on the left. Cusi stood outside the second tent on the right, in the midst of the story singers of the Iñaca household. They had come here in darkness, accompanying the litter that carried Pachacuti from the Patallacta. The golden-eyed mummy of the dead ruler had been placed on a stone seat inside the tent, and arrayed around him were the mummy of his Coya, Mama Anahuarque; his spirit brothers, including the double-headed serpent of gold that was called Inti Illapa; and the huacas of the many tribes he had conquered during his reign. The tent was crowded with oddly shaped hunks of stone and pieces of carved wood, some nearly formless and some bearing a distinct but grotesque resemblance to condors, llamas, serpents, and great fanged cats.

While mamacona from the House of Chosen Women had tended to Pachacuti's needs, wrapping him in blankets of vicuña cloth and offering him cups of akha and coca leaves, the singers had sung songs to entertain him and the Coya. They had sung until it began to turn light, as had their counterparts in the other tents, for each tent held the mummy of a past Sapa Inca. But now they were all silent, waiting for the procession to arrive and the ceremony to begin. Already a bright orange glow illuminated the ridge line of the eastern mountains, and the horizontal bank of clouds above them began to shred and split in advance of the Sun. Inti had finally reached his northernmost point of rising, the end of his yearly journey in that direction. He was at his weakest and most dim, exhausted by the effort of warming the earth and raising up the crops. But today he would be reborn and would begin to grow once more, and his people had come to welcome him as Churi Inti, the Child Sun, and Huayna Punchao, Young Daylight.

Like those around him, Cusi was barefoot, wearing only his headband and the red, ankle-length robe that was the special garment of the Inti Raymi. He shivered slightly in the cold morning air, feeling light-headed and empty from the three-day fast that all of the Incas had undergone. In the silence that hung over the avenue, he thought he could hear the huacas murmuring behind him, their captive spirits giving off a breathless hum of thwarted power. It had been very strong inside the tent, like a vibration in his bones, and he was not certain how long he could have stayed there, had he not been able to occupy himself with the task of singing. As it was, he had forgotten the words to a whole verse when he had glanced up to see Pachacuti's eyes glowing out of the darkness, mirroring the light from outside.

The procession suddenly appeared at the head of the avenue, a long double column of red-clad Incas led by the sacred Napa, who wore golden tassels in his upright ears and a red cape over his snowy back. While the rest of the column halted where they were, the Napa walked down the avenue with dainty steps, escorted by a group of Sun priests. Cusi and his companions lowered their eyes and made the mocha as the Napa passed, blowing kisses off their fingertips to the living symbol of the First Llama, the emblem of Cuzco. The priests led the Napa to the eastern end of the field, past the last of the tents, to the place where the golden images of Inti, Viracocha, and Illapa stood together on a three-tiered stone dais.

Several moments passed in silence, as the sky turned gray-white and the clouds were lit from below. Then a line of scarlet fire appeared above the distant horizon, turning the beaten grass of the Rimac Pampa a deep pink. At the other end of the avenue, the golden litter that ordinarily carried the Sapa Inca and the Coya was lowered to the ground, and Auqui Topa Inca, the Regent, and Huascar, the Heir, stepped out. They walked out ahead of the column, a tall figure and a short, squat one, both blowing kisses off the tips of their extended fingers. Halfway down the aisle they began to sing, a quiet song of greeting to the emerging Sun. The singers in front of the tents joined the song at the second refrain, keeping their voices low and soft, gently coaxing Churi Inti into the sky. The song would gradually rise in volume until midday, then taper off and fade away with the last glimmer of sunset. It would be sung for nine days, until Inti could be seen to be moving south again, toward his ultimate maturity as Apu Inti, the Lord Sun.

As he blended his voice with those around him, Cusi felt a strong affinity for this Sun who was both old and young, tired and fresh. He felt that he had also completed a long journey, a term of trial that had robbed him of some of his warmth and dimmed the enthusiasm of his boyhood. He had learned many things about his fellow Incas that did not please him, and it was this that made him feel tired and old before his time. He had been subjected to more than his share of scorn and suspicion, even after his visit to the Grass Man, and it had made him wary and slow to trust, protective of his dignity.

Yet his weariness was not physical, and like the Child Sun, he could feel himself swelling and hardening into new shapes, bright with potential. He had grown visibly taller, as tall as Tomay now, and there were days when he thought he could feel the meat he had eaten in the Patallacta being transformed into muscle on the practice field. Some five months remained before the manhood rites would commence, but he no longer worried about being held back on account of his size and strength. He might never be a large man, like Otoronco, but he was a brother to lightning, and he had not lost a footrace to any of his initiation brothers in months.

The Regent and Huascar passed the place where Cusi stood, Huascar wearing a band of yellow fringe around his forehead, the insignia of the Heir. He was a stocky boy but quite short, and he carried himself like a born wrestler, his arms bowed at his sides as if ready to grapple. Cusi watched him pass and felt no trace of envy, though some sympathy for his lack of size. He knew that the expectations placed on Huascar were much greater than those made of any other boy, and he knew at least one person who was already disappointed in him.

Lending their voices to the song, the procession of Incas began to advance down the avenue, following Huascar and the Regent at a respectful distance. At their head were the four lords of the Four Quarters, one of whom was Otoronco Achachi. The old warrior's powerful body seemed ill confined by the long priestly robe, and his scarred face wore an expression of squinting bemusement, a warlord's attempt to display humility and devotion.

Directly behind the lords, in double file, were the members of Huayna Capac's immediate family who had remained behind in Cuzco. Tocto Oxica was three back from the front, on Cusi's side of the column, and the sight of her made him forget the words he was singing, or even that he *was* singing. He had laid eyes on her only once since his visit to the Grass Man, and that glimpse had been at a distance greater than this. Otherwise she had refused all of his requests for a meeting and had stopped sending him invitations to Vicaquirao feasts. Her women always turned him away with the same, curt message: It was not safe.

She seemed even smaller than he remembered, barely larger than some of the children around her. Yet she carried herself like a woman, her head held at an elegant tilt, singing as she walked, her eyes narrowed against the light. Cusi stared at her with a solid ache in his chest, a collision of longing and loss with anger and betrayal. He remembered the way she had pressed her lips to the cut on his cheek, where the stone cast by Illapa's lightning had struck him; he remembered the eagerness with which she had encouraged him to join the Vicaquirao ceremonies and confirm his special relationship with Illapa. He remembered how the Grass Man had beaten him simply for having her in his thoughts.

Then she passed out of his range of vision, which was filled instead by members of the Capac Ayllu household, the household of Topa Inca. Cusi returned his attention to the song, finding that he had begun to sing too loudly and was drawing glances from the men around him. He lowered his voice, realizing that he had not succeeded in his attempt to forget Tocto, to shun her as she had shunned him. It had only made him tired to pretend that he could forget, that he wanted to forget.

A wild yearning made his voice crack, so that he stopped singing altogether, merely moving his lips to the words. He turned his head slightly, into the blinding light of the rising Sun. Even with his eyes closed, he was enveloped by the reddish haze of Churi Inti, and he made his vow to the Child Sun. Before the Inti Raymi was over he would find a way to meet with Tocto, whether it was safe or not. If she had decided to permit him nothing, he would hear it from her own lips and know the reason why. Only then could he begin to grow and move forward again, toward a maturity of his own.

Tumibamba

T HE HOUSE Micay shared with Quinti was the smallest of the dwellings within the micho's enclosure, but they had both been drawn to it at first sight. It had four windows, two flanking the central doorway and one at either end of the long single room, so there was always plenty of light, even on a cloudy day. And it was relatively isolated, wedged in next to the bathhouse on the narrowest of the three terraces upon which the compound had been built. The larger terrace above held Mama Cori's house, an open-sided awning house that doubled as kitchen and eating place, and the house that belonged to Apu Poma. The terrace below had two identical houses set side by side, one for guests and one for Apu Poma's sons when they were present, though both dwellings were now occupied by guests.

From her place just inside the doorway, Micay looked across at the entrance to the enclosure, where two of Apu Poma's assistants, wearing green tunics and headbands, were greeting the people who came to see the micho. She watched them separate the messengers and functionaries from those who could command a personal audience, sending many of the former back out after their messages had been heard and directing the latter up the stairs to the plaza above. There was a small crowd of people waiting outside Apu Poma's house, as there always was when the micho was at home, with more of his green-clad aides working to maintain order among the visitors. Even at night there were messengers coming and going from the upper terrace, disturbing sleep as well as privacy.

When she grew tired of watching the men at the entrance, Micay turned her attention to the interior of the room, contemplating the ways in which she and Quinti might decorate it. They had laid down several mismatched rugs and some llama skins for sitting, but the walls were barren and the niches in the back wall had been used for storage rather than aesthetic effect. There were bundles in the corners that still had not been unpacked from the journey, and bags that had been carelessly hoisted up into the rafters just to get them out of the way.

The clutter offended the exacting sense of neatness Micay had learned in the House of Chosen Women, but she was not allowed to do household cleaning in her present condition, and there had been no time to do so earlier. Upon their arrival in Tumibamba they had gone to work for Mama Cori, decorating the micho's house and then her own, since both would be used for official business and for entertaining. When they had finished with that, it was already time to begin preparing for the Inti Raymi festival, which meant that the houses used for guests had to be put in order. Then the guests had begun to arrive, and once the Inti Raymi had started, two days ago, all work of a personal nature had stopped. The Incas were involved in another grand display of power and generosity, a last round of ceremonies, feasts, and dances before the warriors went north to fight against the Quitos.

Micay had attended the first two days of the celebration before being forced to retire, and what she had seen did not make her regret missing the next four. The Incas were tired and distracted, and it showed in the ceremonies and processions, which were marred by unexplained delays and breaks in the expected rhythm. The feasts were particularly joyless affairs, noisy and over-crowded, due to the fact that large sections of the Mollecancha were still under construction. Micay had overheard so many wistful references to the stately gathering held in Cuzco at this time of year that she had become persuaded of the crudeness of this imitation and could not consider herself deprived. It had even occurred to her, in a tranquil moment, that all of the Incas should have her excuse to rest and recover their composure.

A commotion outside drew her gaze back to the men at the compound entrance, which was only about fifty feet away from where she sat. Amaru had arrived, wearing an orange and red tunic that made him stand out like a flame amid the forest green of Apu Poma's assistants. He was looking in Micay's direction, nodding absently as one of the assistants spoke to him and gestured toward the stairs to the upper terrace, as if inviting him to visit his father. Amaru ended the conversation with what must have been a curt refusal, given the way the assistant backed off and bowed. Then he came toward Micay, following the path of paving stones that ran between the plots of bare earth that would one day be flower beds.

Micay moved back out of the doorway, sitting down on a reed mat against the back wall. The quiver in her stomach that had been coming and going all morning suddenly intensified, though it felt more like excitement than pain. She doubted that the men at the entrance had told him about her condition, or that it would make any difference to him if they had. If he felt like speaking to her, propriety was the last thing that would deter him.

Amaru came right up into the doorway, glancing casually from one end of the room to the other before addressing Micay.

"They say that my sister went off with Quilaco at midday. Where did she take him? Not to the court, I hope."

"I think they went to walk along the river," Micay told him. "Near where you were working on the bridge."

He took a step into the room, regarding her curiously.

"And they left you here alone? What did they expect to be doing in the daylight?"

Micay lowered her eyes in embarrassment.

"I began my bleeding two days ago, my lord. You should not be speaking to me while I am sequestered."

"I am not fasting," he said dismissively, coming closer and sitting down across from her on one of the rugs. He gave her a smile that was both approving and suggestive. "So you are finally a ñusta, Micay. Perhaps now I can think seriously about marriage."

Micay lowered her eyes again, though she was used to this kind of teasing from him. She adopted an arch tone when she looked at him again.

"That will make your mother very happy. She thinks you waste your life in pointless flirtations."

"My mother is never without an opinion. What is yours, Micay? We march north as soon as the Inti Raymi is concluded. Should I be pledging my heart to some ñusta, so that she will worry over me while I am in battle?"

"It is not my place to advise you, Lord Amaru. Nor would I question Mama Cori's judgment. But everyone wonders why you are not serious about any of the ñustas."

"Do they," Amaru said without interest. "Most people only play at being serious. They marry because it is permitted to them and they think they should. Later, perhaps, they will learn what is truly serious in their hearts."

"Is that so wrong?"

Amaru looked at her directly, making her feel naive for even asking.

"You live with my parents. What do you think they have learned from one another?"

Micay remembered Apu Poma's face as he rushed at her, grabbing for the gift his wife had so coldly spurned. She spoke with unconsidered frankness.

"Terrible things. Rage and denial."

"That is a serious answer," Amaru commended her. "Perhaps I *should* marry you, Micay."

"You should leave me," she reminded him halfheartedly, but of course he did not move.

"What do you think of Quilaco as a husband for Quinti?" he asked instead, and Micay hesitated, realizing that Quinti had never asked her this question.

"He is very handsome, and a favorite of the Coya. And Quinti is—"

"Lovesick," Amaru supplied scornfully. Micay gave him a sharp glance, suddenly vigilant on Quinti's behalf.

"Is she wrong to trust him?"

"No," Amaru shrugged, "she is safe enough. He is not like me."

Micay opened her mouth but then closed it again, causing Amaru to bare his teeth in a grimacing half smile. He pointed at her with his chin.

"Why do you swallow the question you most want to ask? It means that Quilaco cares about the opinion that other people have of him. He wants to be admired and respected, so he will do what the Coya, and his commanding officer, and his wife expect of him."

"And you, my lord?"

Amaru smiled at her boldness.

"As for me," he said musingly, "I know that I am brave. I know that I can fight, and build things, and command other men. I know that I am attractive to women. Must I make it my duty to prove what I already know to someone else? All they truly want from me is my obedience or my approval. I obey myself, and I give my approval to those who earn it."

"I see," Micay murmured, amazed that he would speak this way, to her or anyone else. A young warrior was expected to be bold and independent, but Amaru's attitude went well beyond that, approaching disloyalty.

"Do you? Ah, now you will never marry me," he said with mock sadness. "Perhaps you would prefer my brother Cusi. He is about your age, and he is not like me either. But you must be sure not to let my mother suspect you have designs on her son."

"I have no designs on anyone," Micay protested in a flustered voice.

Amaru laughed. "No ñusta remains so innocent for long, especially not one as pretty as you." He reached for her hand, but she would not let him take it, so he laughed again and stood up. "If Quilaco returns, tell him that I will be at the house of Ninan Cuyochi. He can come drink with us there if he can bear to part with my sister."

"I cannot speak to Quilaco," Micay reminded him. "And since he is not like you, he would not speak to me."

"Have Quinti tell him, then."

"Quinti was the one who told me that I was not to speak to men during these days. You would have me tell her I broke the rule on the very first day?"

Amaru crossed his arms on his chest and squinted down at her as if puzzled by her resistance. Micay realized her objection was absurd—they both knew that Quinti would not care about the infraction—but his willingness to compromise her so casually had aroused a stubbornness that was instinctive.

"If it will make you feel more respectable," Amaru suggested scornfully, "you can tell her that I forced myself upon you. You can say that you sat there like a proper stone and did not respond to anything I said. My sister knows me; she will believe what you say."

They stared at one another in silence for a moment. Then he spoke in a voice that was remarkably mild, without scorn.

"But I think you will simply give her my message, Micay. I think you are more like me than you know."

Micay blinked at him, too astonished to speak.

"Perhaps you need to be," Amaru said with a slight shrug. "But you are able to hear me, Micay, in a way that is impossible for the others. You do not deny what you hear or find a way to misunderstand it. I will leave you to think about why that is true."

He turned and went out, showing her his flame-colored back, his golden earplugs dancing just above his shoulders. As he drew near the compound gate, the men in green accosted him again, gesturing toward the upper terrace, but Amaru walked past them without pausing to consider their pleas. Micay let out a breath and looked around her, startled by how large and empty the room suddenly seemed. She wondered if his presence was so vivid for everyone. And did he truly tell other people the things he had told her?

She sat quietly for several moments, trying to empty her mind of questions and confusion. Amaru had a way of slipping past her composure and poking her in places she thought were protected. And he seemed to regard this as a form of flattery. The quiver suddenly reappeared in her stomach, a sharp pang that briefly doubled her over. She welcomed the distraction, but it passed all too quickly. Then she again found herself trying to deny that she was anything at all like Amaru, a proposition that seemed perfectly obvious one moment and perfectly elusive the next. Because to say for certain that she was not like him, she had to know whom she *was* like. And when she thought about all the people in her life, and those she could remember from her recent past, she felt no resemblance to any of them. She leaned back against the wall and folded her hands over her stomach, breathing deeply to stifle a rising fear.

"I am a ñusta," she said aloud. Her words echoed hollowly in the enclosed space, seeming as much a question as an answer.

Cuzco

T HE SAPA INCA'S pavilion had been erected at the western end of the Rimac Pampa, centered over a mound of dark brown stone that rose up out of the earth like the shell of some great subterranean turtle. Two sunken seats had been hollowed out of one face, and the rest of the stone's surface was covered by an intricate array of carved knobs, niches, channels, and ledges. It looked like an architect's clay relief map frozen into stone, though the landscape it depicted bore little resemblance to any earthly locale.

The seats, normally occupied by the Sapa Inca and his Coya, were filled by Auqui Topa Inca and Huascar, who were accepting Inti Raymi gifts on behalf of Huayna Capac. All of the chiefs who had come today were from the Eastern

Quarter, and they were greeted first by Otoronco Achachi, the lord of that quarter. The Chuncho chieftains filed into the huge tent wearing their long cotton tunics, their faces painted and tattooed and their headdresses gaudy with bright feathers, carrying blowguns and tall chontawood bows. They were Campas and Machiguengas and Piros and Mascos, people from the rugged cloud forest that climbed the eastern slopes of the Andes Mountains. There were also some jungle dwellers from the Amaru River region, a few leaders of roving Chiriguano bands, and a delegation of Moxos in jaguar-skin tunics.

Most of them bowed to Otoronco with a reverence that should have been reserved for the Regent and the Heir, addressing him simply as "grandfather." They came before him barefoot and shivering in the dry Cuzco air, each wearing a symbolic burden upon his back, as he would have in the presence of the Sapa Inca. Otoronco greeted them with a few words in their own tongue, offering them coca that had been ground and mixed with ash, Chuncho style, and inquiring about the state of their tribes. Watching from his place to the right of the stone, Cusi thought that Otoronco handled the men splendidly, calming them and bolstering their dignity with his attentions. He was an Inca who had spent many years in their lands, who knew their customs and the names of their fathers and grandfathers. For the occasion Otoronco had put on a jaguar-skin belt and a broad necklace made from the whole skins of tiny green birds, articles that had previously been hanging on the walls of Otoronco's room.

Auqui Topa Inca, on the other hand, seemed stiff and ill at ease, too conscious of the fact that he was occupying the seat of the Sapa Inca. He greeted each group of chiefs with a speech that varied little from group to group, thanking them in Huayna Capac's name for their loyalty and for the gifts they had brought. But he did not try to converse with them, even through the available interpreters, and he was content to let Otoronco supply the personal contact that made these interviews meaningful. Huascar sat beside him in the Coya's seat, his feet just touching the ground, wearing his yellow fringe and a tunic woven in the checkered pattern that was Huayna Capac's own. He would add a short greeting to that of the Regent, and occasionally he would ask to handle one of the chiefs' gifts, bestowing additional prestige upon its bearer.

The major concern of each interview, beyond the display and recognition of the chiefs' loyalty, was the exchange of gifts. The chiefs were required by law to attend the Inti Raymi celebration, but they owed the Sapa Inca no tribute other than the labor and cloth their people had already provided during the preceding year. Still, as a sign of their love for the ruler, they brought gifts of all the rare and desirable things that were grown or made in their lands, demonstrating their prestige among their own people in the process. They could be sure, as well, that the Sapa Inca would reciprocate generously, sending them back to their villages loaded down with goods that each chief could then distribute at will.

Just behind the stone, a cloth partition screened off the rear half of the tent, which was being used as a kind of two-way storehouse. Groups of palace retainers were stationed at both ends of the curtain, one group to carry off the chiefs' gifts and the other to bring forth the gifts specified by Otoronco and the Regent. Squatting all around the stone were the count takers with their counting boxes and piles of colored cords, with which they kept a careful record of every exchange. As Otoronco's assistant, Cusi helped wherever he was needed, conveying goods and messages and making sure that Otoronco's coca bag was kept filled. He was aware that it was an honor for him to be here, so he did his best to remain both unobtrusive and attentive, resisting the urge to get caught up in the spectacle before him.

He was fascinated, though, by the collection of gifts that was gradually accumulating in the back of the tent, and he quickly made himself available whenever there was a chance of being sent behind the partition. He walked the aisles between the neat rows of goods, wondering how the count takers could possibly keep track of such a variety of strange and exotic items. There were large quantities of the things for which the Eastern Quarter was famous: bags of gold dust collected from the mountain streams, bundles of feathers, snake-skins, and jaguar pelts, and bales of fragrant coca leaf. But the chiefs had also brought many live animals, monkeys and birds and creatures of all colors and sizes, some poking their heads through the bars of their cages and others lying trussed on the ground, only their eyes moving. They were surrounded by baskets of fish and frogs and live turtles, stacks of stiff crocodile skins, and a vast array of painted gourds filled with medicines, vegetable dyes, tobacco, and the drugs used for visions and divining. The poorer chiefs had contributed lengths of palm-fiber cloth, baskets of pineapples and sweet manioc, animal-tooth necklaces, and gelatinous clumps of fish eggs and insect larvae.

Huascar appeared to share Cusi's fascination with the gifts, and as the day wore on, he began to surround his seat with the items that most attracted his fancy. A magnificent jaguar skin, with its head attached, was draped over the curving top of the stone, and a green and blue parrot in a bamboo cage occupied the niche at Huascar's elbow; a spotted snakeskin belt hung from a protruding knob on the side of the stone, against which a long black chonta-wood bow was leaning. Huascar was wearing a mantle of reddish-brown monkey fur around his shoulders, one of several garments he had asked to try on. Most had been tailored for a man and had made him look dwarfed and ridiculous, but no one had laughed, and the chiefs involved had seemed immensely flattered by the Heir's desire to wear their gifts.

Cusi had often acted as the go-between, delivering whatever Huascar had requested, and he was intrigued by what he saw of the boy up close. Huascar never noticed *him,* but that was because his enthusiasm for the gifts was so compelling and unabashed that he did not see anything else. Cusi knew that it was a traditional practice of the Sapa Inca to don the garments of his subjects, but Huascar was not merely emulating his father. He was enjoying the gifts as if they had been given to him personally, as if he were a boy on his naming day in a room filled with relatives. Cusi marveled at his lack of self-consciousness before all these men, something Cusi himself could never have emulated. It made Huascar seem younger than his twelve years, and more innocent than Cusi would have expected.

As the next group of chiefs was being summoned into the tent, Otoronco beckoned to Cusi for more coca, and Cusi brought him the bag he had just filled with the ground mixture of coca and ash, which could be chewed without lime. Cusi was about to retreat with the empty bag when Otoronco stayed him and gestured toward the men who had just turned in under the tent's fringed awning.

"I believe you know these people."

Cusi had begun the day hoping he would see Uritu's father and the other Campas from Vitcos, but he had not had time to think of it since. Ozcollo was walking a few steps in front of the rest of the delegation, carrying a painted staff that was topped by a spray of parrot feathers. He was a slender man, smaller than Cusi remembered; Uritu, just behind him, seemed nearly as tall. Looking at the two of them together, Cusi could see how much Uritu had altered his appearance to conform to Inca styles. Unlike his son, Ozcollo wore his hair long beneath his feathered headdress, and his loose, unbelted tunic fell almost to his ankles. Stripes of bright red had been painted across his forehead and over the tattoos on his cheeks, and feathered labrets hung from his lower lip and both of his ears. When he greeted Otoronco in Quechua, Cusi could hear the lilting Campa accent that Uritu, with Cusi's help, had lost long before.

"Greetings, illustrious Lord. It is an honor and a pleasure for me to stand before you."

Ozcollo and all those behind him bowed in unison, and Otoronco accepted their homage with a lordly nod. Then the two men exchanged coca from their bags, dipping with their fingers and making smacking sounds of satisfaction as they chewed.

"You know my grandson, Cusi Auqui?" Otoronco inquired casually. Ozcollo's eyes brightened with a fondness that made Cusi flush with pleasure.

"Of course, my lord. I see him every year when I come for the Inti Raymi. He has been a good friend to my son."

"I have met your son. Greetings, Uritu," Otoronco called, giving Uritu cause to bow a second time. Then Otoronco removed the wad of chewed coca from his cheek and dropped it on the ground. "Come, let me present you to the Regent and the Heir."

Otoronco turned so that Ozcollo could walk with him to the stone, and Cusi fell in beside Uritu, who smiled swiftly in greeting. Auqui Topa Inca made his usual speech in a Quechua that was probably too rapid for Ozcollo to follow, though there was no hesitancy in the chief's reply. Cusi realized that it was Ozcollo's warm, resonant voice that had made him remember a larger man. That, and the enormous respect that Uritu had for his father, a respect that had not been diminished by Uritu's exposure to Inca ways. Yet Ozcollo carried his power lightly, so that a display of modesty did not seem a strain for him and did not reduce his stature.

Huascar said his few words, sounding rather fatigued, and then Ozcollo's companions began to bring forward their gifts. There were the usual bags of gold and sheaves of brilliantly hued feathers—the latter too beautiful to ever seem truly commonplace—as well as a polished turtleshell drum, some painted gourd rattles, and a mantle woven out of shimmering blue hummingbird feathers. Ozcollo earnestly explained where the gifts were from, with Otoronco occasionally translating for the Regent, who had trouble comprehending Ozcollo's Quechua. Huascar showed some interest in the mantle, but not enough to ask for it. He was sitting with his elbow on the stone and his chin cupped in his hand, a posture that made Cusi draw himself up very straight, furious that Huascar would display his indifference so openly. He had no right to act like a tired little boy when he was representing all of the Incas.

"And there is one last gift, my lords," Ozcollo concluded, turning his body so that he was facing Huascar directly. Without looking back, he raised his hand over his plumed head and beckoned. A large dark shape loomed up out of the corner of Cusi's eye, coalescing in front of him as four men, two on either side of a cloth carrying sling suspended from the poles they bore on their shoulders. Water dripped from the sling, which sagged low from the weight of its contents. The bearers put down their poles and spread open the sling, revealing a packed mound of bluish-white snow. Ozcollo had everyone's attention now, and he paused for a moment to let them contemplate the ice, which was shaped like a log and had bits of greenery sticking up out of it. Then he gestured to the porters, who squatted and began to strip away the ice, which was in neat layers separated by palm leaves. When they were done, they stood up and stepped back, leaving two piles of melting snow flanking an enormous, gray-black fish.

Cusi did not know what kind of sound he made, because it was lost in the general outburst of amazement. Everyone in the tent crowded forward for a look, even the normally imperturbable count takers. Huascar jumped down from his seat and squatted in front of the fish's whiskered snout, staring at it intently, as if expecting to see it breathe.

"Is it alive?" he asked tremulously.

Ozcollo could not restrain a joyful whoop of laughter. "His heart was beating until we reached the first high pass in the mountains. Perhaps he knew that he would be eaten by the Incas, and died of happiness."

Ozcollo and his companions whooped as laughter swept the tent; even the Regent laughed, once Otoronco was able to translate for him. Before the retainers came out to carry the fish off, Huascar paced off its length, taking thirteen of his small steps to reach the back fin. After conferring briefly with the Regent, Otoronco sent Cusi after the straining retainers.

"Tell them to have it taken directly to the cooks in the palace."

The retainers had carried their burden only a short distance beyond the partition before setting it down. Huascar was with them, shadowed by two Cañari guards as he leaned over the fish, poking at it with his finger. He seemed totally absorbed, running his eyes up and down its scaly length as if he could not take it all in. Cusi waited politely for a few moments before catching the eye of the head retainer and addressing him in a low voice.

"The lord says it is to be taken to the cooks in the palace."

"The flesh is firm," Huascar said aloud, apparently to himself, since his gaze was still fixed on the fish. He straightened up and put his hands on his hips, bunching the monkey-fur mantle up around his ears. Unnoticed, the head retainer bowed to him and went off to find additional bearers. When Huascar finally raised his head and saw Cusi standing across from him, he appeared startled, as if he had forgotten where he was.

"You—who are you?"

"I am Cusi Auqui, my lord, the grandson of Otoronco Achachi," Cusi said with a bow, finding it odd to address a boy both younger and shorter than himself as "my lord."

"You are the one who went to the Grass Man," Huascar exclaimed, regarding Cusi with a sudden intensity of interest, not unlike the way he had stared at the fish. "Why did you do that?"

"I was sent by my teacher."

"For what?"

"That is a secret, my lord," Cusi said stiffly, "as you know."

"Ah, it must have been bad," Huascar averred, glancing at Cusi's hands with a kind of eagerness. "I heard you were *whipped.*"

"I was cleansed."

Huascar grunted, but he seemed to accept Cusi's reticence. Otoronco's voice came from the other side of the partition, and Huascar's eyes darted once in that direction. He looked back at Cusi and tossed his head petulantly, responding to a question that had not been asked.

"They can finish without me. It takes so little to please these Chunchos. They think any metal is precious if it comes in the shape of a tool. Just give them a few ax heads, some potatoes, and a pot of face paint, and they are happy."

Cusi sucked in his breath, reminding himself that this arrogant, stupid boy was the Heir. Huascar sensed his reaction, though, because his eyes narrowed beneath the yellow fringe and he drew himself up, jerking his chin at Cusi.

"Is that not so?"

"They are happy with any gift that comes from the hands of the Sapa Inca," Cusi said evenly. "But they also know what they need. They do not make metal or grow potatoes or dig cinnabar in their lands. That is why Otoronco Achachi chose the gifts he did. He knows the people of the Eastern Quarter and how to please them."

Huascar blinked in astonishment, as if Cusi had just delivered a speech in a foreign tongue. He glanced over his shoulder at the Cañari guards, whose faces had gone blank.

"I do not like being corrected," he said to Cusi. "Especially not by a boy who has been beaten by the Grass Man."

"I meant no disrespect, my lord. But I must honor what I know to be true.

I know the Campas, and they are people worthy of our respect. They are the same people who carried this great fish over the mountains for you."

"Yes," Huascar agreed tentatively, allowing himself to be distracted by the icy black hulk that lay between them. "Yes, it is a worthy gift."

He crossed his arms on his chest and stared down at the fish, as if reading some message in the arrangement of its fins and scales. Or letting his embarrassment pass, Cusi thought, putting on a blank expression of his own. Huascar raised his head slowly, surveying the area behind Cusi before letting his gaze rest on him.

"I will forgive you, then," he decided, pursing his lips and nodding gravely for emphasis. "It is the Inti Raymi, a time to display our generosity. So you are forgiven. You may go now."

Cusi bowed and departed quickly, before Huascar grew tired of playing the Heir and became himself again. He had not wanted to bring himself to the boy's attention in the first place, and he would surely try not to do so again in the future. He understood now why Tocto had such disdain for this brother. Huascar was ignorant but could not let himself be corrected; he was scornful of things he did not understand because he did not know he needed to understand. He was a child who had been told too often that he owned the world.

The odor of fish was still in Cusi's nostrils, and the memory of Huascar forgiving him made him want to grimace and spit. But he composed his face instead and went back to his place next to the stone. It was the Inti Raymi, a time for rebirth and renewal, and he did not wish to brood about the people who disappointed him. He was already too old for that.

Tumibamba

IN CELEBRATION of Micay's release from confinement, Quinti took her first for a walk along the highest terrace of the Mollecancha, allowing her to savor the freshness of the breeze, the rush of water in the river below, and the wonderful view of the fields and mountains to the east. As they walked, Quinti told her about the people they were likely to meet at the various feasts they would be attending today, dwelling especially on those who would be at the gathering hosted by Chuqui Huipa, the Coya's eldest daughter. Micay listened attentively, memorizing names and titles and household affiliations, and making sure she knew where each person stood in relation to Mama Cori's party in the court. This sort of preliminary exposition had become a habit with them since the altercation in Cusipampa, a way of insuring that Micay would not be caught again in the middle of a conflict she did not comprehend.

When Micay had exhausted all her queries and had had her fill of the open air, they began their descent to the feast that was taking place on the terraces just below. Now all of Quinti's thoughts turned toward Quilaco Yupanqui, an infatuation that Micay found easy to indulge, since Quilaco was only the second male Inca, after Amaru, whom Micay had found truly attractive. He was a year or two younger than Amaru and had an expressive, sharply featured face, with bright brown eyes and a hawk's beak of a nose that almost made him look like a Cañari, though his skin was much darker. He had the self-assured, innately aggressive bearing of an Inca warrior, but there was none of Amaru's teasing ambiguity in his eyes or manner.

When they finally found him, he was standing near a staircase with a cup in his hand, talking to two women. Micay and Quinti had drawn too close to retreat before they saw that the older of the two women was Mama Huarcay, the Fourth Wife.

"Should I leave you?" Micay whispered. Quinti shook her head fiercely. She pointed with her chin at the ñusta standing beside Mama Huarcay. "That is Cori Cuillor, the second daughter of one of Huayna Capac's war chiefs. Mama Huarcay is her sponsor."

Quinti led her right up to the group, receiving a welcoming smile from Quilaco. They bowed in unison to Mama Huarcay.

"My lady," Quinti said respectfully, and gave Cori Cuillor an apparently friendly nod.

"Quinti Ocllo," Mama Huarcay said in a drawling voice, as if tasting the name. "I have not had the pleasure of your company in some time. How are you finding your new quarters in Tumibamba?"

"Very pleasing, my lady."

"And your parents? How are Mama Cori, and your father"—she appeared to falter, blinking rapidly—"Lloque—?"

"Lloque Yupanqui is my mother's brother," Quinti said without a blink of her own. "And I am sure you remember my father, Apu Poma, the micho of Cañar Province."

"Of course, the micho. He must be very busy attending to the needs of our guests and other such matters." Mama Huarcay turned her glance to Quilaco, with a slight nod to her companion. "Cori's father is also busy, as you no doubt know."

"I will be serving under him with the warriors of Upper Cuzco," Quilaco said proudly, bowing to the young woman, who lowered her eyes and returned the bow. Too quickly, Micay thought, having seen the way Quinti and some of the other ñustas could prolong this display of modesty, letting their eyes slowly drop from the man's face, like a bead of water running down a wall. She decided that Cori Cuillor, despite her father's rank, might not be equal to the ambitions Mama Huarcay had for her. She felt Quinti relax slightly beside her, just enough to appear unaffected by Mama Huarcay's ploys.

"And who is this with you?" Mama Huarcay inquired suddenly, looking straight at Micay. Micay saw no recognition in the woman's eyes, but then, Mama Huarcay looked very different to her, too. She seemed sly rather than malicious, and the slyness gave her a strange kind of beauty, one that went well with her veiled eyes and insinuating voice.

"This is my companion, the Chachapoyas ñusta Micay," Quinti explained, turning so that Micay's bows to Mama Huarcay and Cori Cuillor were unobstructed. "She joined our family in Caxamarca."

"Ah," Mama Huarcay said, and Micay saw that she had remembered. What she felt, however, remained thoroughly concealed. She glanced up at the cloth band around Micay's forehead.

"I see you are a recent ñusta. You will be eligible for the next Quicuchicoy, if you have sufficient rank."

"She does, my lady," Quinti assured her, perhaps too briskly, for Mama Huarcay paused to give her a disdainful smile.

"I will be happy to have her in the group, then. I am in charge of preparing the ñustas for the rites."

"The high priestess will also have a hand in their training, will she not?" Quinti suggested, while Micay struggled to absorb this startling piece of information, which had obviously escaped Quinti's notice before this.

"Once Rahua Ocllo is able to choose a new one," Mama Huarcay sniffed. "The woman who has the title now is being stubborn about giving way. I may have to train everyone in the end."

Quinti nodded judiciously at this boast, flicking a sidelong glance at Micay, a signal for her to speak. Micay inclined her head, calling on all her composure to keep her voice steady.

"I will be honored to learn from you, my lady."

"I will expect you to have learned a great deal before you come to me," Mama Huarcay told her bluntly. "The Quicuchicoy confers great status on the girls who undertake it—even the daughters of foreigners. We must be certain they are worthy."

"I am confident that you will be generous and impartial in your judgment," Quinti put in, in a voice that sounded remarkably earnest, as if she truly believed what she was saying. The tone seemed to awaken Quilaco from a state of bemusement.

"The girls could not be in better hands," he agreed, raising his cup to Mama Huarcay with a sincerity that almost brought a smile to Micay's face. He was clearly not at all like Amaru, who would never have mistaken this exchange for an innocent conversation. Quinti raised a hand to her lips and then touched him lightly on the arm, as if she had just remembered something.

"We should probably begin our walk to the Coya's compound. I promised Chuqui Huipa that we would visit with her before the feasting begins."

"Forgive us," Quilaco said to the other women, responding with the same innocence to the power of the Coya's name. After an exchange of bows, the three of them walked off together, threading their way through the crowd. Quinti let Quilaco get a little ahead before turning to look at Micay.

"You will be ready for her," she promised in a low voice.

More ready than I was today, I hope, Micay thought. But she simply nodded to Quinti and hastened her steps to catch up with Quilaco, who had continued on without them.

THE MOON was down and the dark, narrow streets of the Mollecancha were quiet when Micay and Quinti returned to the micho's quarters later. They had stayed with Quilaco until he had to report for his watch; at least, Quinti had stayed with him, while Micay waited at a discreet distance, sipping akha and watching the moon descend in the western sky. She felt incredibly tired and also slightly drunk, a woozy combination that seemed to match Quinti's dreamy euphoria.

"He promised that he would ask for me on his first full leave from battle," Quinti repeated. "He said that he would speak to Father. You must help me remember that while he is gone, Micay."

As they came into the enclosure, a figure suddenly rose up out of the shadows next to the entrance, causing them to jump back in fright. The figure held out his hands, palms up, appealing to them to be calm.

"Forgive me, my ladies. It is I, Acapana, the micho's assistant. He asked me to bring the ñusta Micay to him when she returned."

"Perhaps I should also go," Quinti suggested dimly, trying to muster some sisterly concern. But Micay shook her head and gave her a push in the direction of their house.

"You need to sleep. I will join you shortly."

"I will escort you, my lady," Acapana offered, and Micay went with him toward the stairs to the upper terrace, trying to match her steps to his long, limping stride. He was a tall man around Quinti's age, an Inca of the blood from one of the Lower Cuzco households. The injury to his foot had kept him from being a warrior, but his rank and intelligence had made him the head of Apu Poma's personal staff at a very young age. Micay had watched him from seclusion and had been impressed by his ability to handle the constant flow of visitors without becoming impatient or harried.

As they climbed the stairs together, it suddenly occurred to her that Acapana would not have had to stay here so late unless he wanted to. He could just as easily have entrusted the message to one of his subordinates. Then she remembered the way he always smiled at her, whenever he met her alone; he was too shy even to raise his eyes when Quinti was present. She glanced sideways at his silhouette, which bobbed jerkily as he negotiated the stairs in the darkness. She had a very clear image of how he climbed, swinging his bad foot out to the side and up, so that he put no weight upon it until it was flat on the ground. She remembered his face less well, except for the shyness of his smile, and she could not make out his features now. But she had the distinct and flattering impression that he was looking back at her.

They reached the top and walked across the plaza toward Apu Poma's house, toward the light that shone out around the edges of one of the two curtained doorways. Acapana cleared his throat once, as if to speak, but then apparently changed his mind. Micay felt drunk again and realized she had been holding her breath, waiting to hear what he might say. When they came to the curtained entrance, he stood to one side, out of the light, and spoke in a voice that seemed resigned to its own politeness.

"I will wait to escort you back to your room, my lady."

"I am grateful, Acapana," Micay said, drawing out the name the way Mama Huarcay might have, letting her voice be the equivalent of languidly lowered eyes. Even in the darkness, the effect on Acapana was apparent; she thought she could hear his teeth click as his backbone stiffened. He bowed from the waist as she pushed through the curtain into the room, blinking at the light and realizing that she should have paused to allow Acapana a good look at her. Too quickly, she thought. Then she turned her attention to Apu Poma.

He was sitting cross-legged on a llama-skin rug, his back against the wall. Rushes burned in the niches on either side of him, casting a yellowish light on the knotted memory cords spread out on the floor around him. He looked haggard but quite awake, his jaw bulging around a large lump of coca. He inclined his head to Micay and gestured for her to sit on the rug in front of his own.

"My daughter keeps you out late," he said in a guttural voice. Then he paused to remove the wad of leaves from his mouth and deposit it in a bowl beside him.

"We were in the company of Quilaco Yupanqui, my lord," Micay explained. "At a gathering hosted by Chuqui Huipa, the Coya's daughter."

Apu Poma nodded absently, as if he had not really been concerned about their whereabouts. His eyes went past her and then returned, and she thought for a moment that he was glaring at her. Then she realized that he was simply working up his determination, convincing himself that it was worth the effort.

"I have not spoken to you about what occurred in Cusipampa," he said finally, "though I have known I owed you an apology. It is not easy for me to admit I was so blinded by my anger that I abused you. You would be justified in believing whatever my wife has said about me; I have given you that justification myself. Yet I would ask you to believe that I did not intend to harm you, and that I am sorry for the pain I caused you."

Micay hesitated, knowing a swift answer would not satisfy him.

"I have always believed that, my lord. I knew your anger was not aimed at me."

Apu Poma cocked his head and stared at her for a long moment.

"You are not saying that merely to placate me? Do not be afraid to speak the truth."

"It is the truth, my lord."

He stared at her for another moment before nodding and letting himself relax for the first time, slumping back against the wall behind him.

"I am grateful for your understanding, my daughter. I receive little of it from the rest of my family. You have probably been told that I was cruel to my son Cusi, but I was only trying to make up for the time I did not have with him when he was small. He may hate me for what I did, but he will be stronger for it."

Micay knew better than to respond. Apu Poma toyed with the coca bag and lime container on the floor next to him, nodding to himself in lonely agreement.

"If I had not been made a stranger to my own children," he went on, "they would understand me better today. Perhaps as well as you do, Micay."

Again Micay was silent, though she lowered her eyes at the compliment. She recalled that Amaru also thought she understood him, and he despised his father. When she looked up, she was glad to see that Apu Poma had turned his attention away and would not see her confusion. He was removing a colorful bolt of cloth from a bag next to him.

"This is for you, my daughter. An Inti Raymi gift."

She simply stared as he unfolded the mantle and held it up in front of him, turning it slightly toward the light. It had been tie-dyed in horizontal bands that replicated the colors of the sunrise, a rich vermilion bleeding into a red that brightened to orange and then to a golden yellow. Apu Poma lurched up onto his knees and shuffled forward to wrap it around her shoulders, over the mantle she already had on. Micay looked down at herself, smelling the blend of cotton and alpaca from which it had been woven, feeling warmed by the brilliance of the colors.

Apu Poma reached back for his coca bag and removed a slender piece of gleaming metal, cleaning off the shreds of coca leaf with his fingers and rubbing it against the front of his tunic. It was a long mantle pin of beaten white gold, its blunt end flattened into the shape of a long-billed pelican. Micay held the ends of the mantle together in front of her while Apu Poma gingerly poked the golden pin through the thickly woven cloth.

"There. You have worn a chosen woman's pin long enough. Now you can take your place among the other ñustas."

Micay ran her fingers over the tight weave of the mantle and around the polished edges of the golden pelican, dazzled by their beauty.

"Inti rises all around me," she murmured, looking up at him gratefully. "You are too generous, my lord."

"You are the only one who thinks so, my daughter," Apu Poma said ruefully, managing a weak smile. He sat back down on his rug. "You should go to your rest now. And let no one tell you that you may not keep my gifts."

"Yes, my lord," Micay said obediently, rising to her feet to bow to him. She was almost to the doorway when he spoke again.

"Micay. What became of my other gift? The vicuña wool?"

Micay turned, realizing she had not thought about it since their arrival in Tumibamba.

"I still have it, my lord, in one of our packs. Would you like me to return it to you?"

"No," Apu Poma frowned, "I do not want it back. But since it came from the Sapa Inca, it should not be disposed of carelessly."

"Perhaps I could make an offering to Inti," Micay suggested after a moment. "On behalf of Amaru and Quilaco and the other warriors."

"You have my permission to do whatever you see fit."

Micay bowed compliantly and turned again toward the doorway, blinking at a flash of gold from her new pin. She felt heavy-limbed and light-headed, floating somewhere beyond both fatigue and drunkenness. So many people had claimed her today, as companion, apprentice ñusta, daughter. Perhaps even as a woman to be courted. It was as if she had emerged from seclusion into a new life, one that would not allow her to hang back and watch her steps. She felt dizzied by so much choice.

Yet as she lifted up the curtain to let herself out, some of her self-possession returned and she had the presence of mind to pause for a full moment in the light, so that Acapana would be sure to get a good look at her and would be as dazzled as she felt, wrapped in the radiant colors of her Inti Raymi gift.

Cuzco

CUSI CAME out through the Patallacta's main gate, clutching a flute in his hand and walking with impatient steps, still angry with himself for having forgotten to take the painted wooden flute with him in the first place. He was as much astonished as angry, because his memory almost never failed him in practical matters. And the flute was much more important than that. It was to be his gift to Tocto Oxica, when he finally found her, and half of what he planned to say referred to it. That it could have slipped from his mind was only further proof of how he had been resisting the fulfillment of his vow. After tonight, only one day remained of the Inti Raymi, and he was not even certain that he would see Tocto tonight. He only hoped that she would be at the Vicaquirao dance, toward which he had already started once.

He had gone only a short distance down the street when he was struck by the sudden feeling that he had forgotten something else. But what? He stopped abruptly, slapping the flute against his thigh in frustration. What was wrong with him today? He could not seem to accomplish the simplest things. He glanced up and down the street, which was beginning to grow dark even though he could still see light on the ridge of mountains to the east. The few people passing by did not seem to have noticed his confusion, so he stood a moment longer, trying to resolve his misgivings. Then he saw the boy and the old man standing against the outer wall of the Patallacta, and he realized with a start that the old man was Raurau Illa.

They were not far from the gate, and Cusi had actually gone past them before he stopped. He walked over to them immediately, nodding first to the boy, who stared back at him with wide eyes but did nothing to alert Raurau

Illa to his presence. The boy was perhaps nine or ten, with a broad dark face
and fat cheeks like Tomay's, indicating Colla blood. Cusi cleared his throat,
and Raurau Illa raised his head slightly, his milky eyes staring past Cusi's right
shoulder. Cusi hesitated, uncertain of how to address him. He looked more
respectable in a striped tunic of good cloth, with his face unpainted and his
long, whitening hair bound back by a headband with a jagged lightning design.
Cusi finally let the amazement and relief he was feeling speak for him.

"Grandfather . . . it is I, Cusi Auqui."

The old man's head turned toward the sound, and he nodded.

"Yes. Your voice has changed, Cusi Auqui. It comes from deeper within
you. That is good."

"How did you find me?"

"I remembered the name of your guardian and asked where he lived. How
did you find me?"

"I, ah—" Cusi stammered, remembering the confusion that had made him
stop and the forgetfulness that had brought him back here. He looked down
at the flute in his hand. "I came back to the Patallacta because I had forgotten
something, or so I thought. Perhaps I was summoned—"

"Perhaps," Raurau Illa allowed. "Perhaps your spirit brother wished you
to find me. You have it with you?"

"Yes," Cusi said, unconsciously raising a hand to his waistband. He saw the
boy's eyes follow the movement, then quickly look away.

"What else do you have with you?"

"A flute. That is what I came back for. I intend to give it as a gift to someone
I know."

"To whom?"

"A ñusta."

"Ah," Raurau Illa exclaimed softly, his eyelids briefly covering his silvery
gaze. "Now tell me about how Illapa came to you."

"How do you know about that?"

"I dreamed of it. But many of the herd boys saw the storm," Raurau Illa
added, gesturing to the boy beside him. "Alco saw it. And we knew that the
young Inca warriors were in the hills where it struck. How close did it come
to you, Cusi?"

"It was right over me. I was in a cave, and the lightning hit so close outside
that I was struck by stones and mud."

"But you provoked it," Raurau Illa interjected mildly, as if confirming
something he already knew.

"I—" Cusi suddenly remembered throwing his slingstones into the darkness. "I must have."

Raurau Illa nodded. "Tell me: When the lightning came toward you, how
did it look? Did it come across the sky or down to the earth?"

"It came across," Cusi recalled. "Except for the last burst that struck near
me. That seemed to come straight down to earth."

"Do you understand the significance of that? It is the female lightning that seeks to return to earth, to Pachamama. You must tell me more about this ñusta."

"She is the daughter of the Sapa Inca." Cusi sighed. "Must you question me like this, Grandfather? I have been questioned many times since I last saw you, largely because of the memory cord I gave you. I was finally sent to confess to the Grass Man."

"No doubt you learned a great deal."

"I was punished a great deal. I wanted to talk to you many times, but I could never find you at the huaca."

"In the future, you must walk past it, to the herdsman's hut on the next ridge. If you light a fire there, Alco or someone else will come for you."

"Why did you not tell me this before?" Cusi demanded, irritated by how easily he had dismissed the confession to the Grass Man.

"I had to be certain that I was right about you."

"You mean, that I would not report you."

Raurau Illa gave a dry, scornful laugh.

"Did I not tell you to report me? Do you think I am a trespasser in Cuzco now? I am here for the villcacona, the questioning of the huacas and those who speak for them. I am one of those who speaks for the huaca to which we are both pledged, and I was brought to the Inti Raymi as the guest of the elders of the Vicaquirao household."

Cusi hung his head for a moment, feeling extremely foolish. He remembered his surprise when he had confessed to not reporting a trespasser and the Grass Man had refrained from striking his hands. He must have known that Cusi was not capable of determining who belonged on sacred ground and who did not.

"Are you certain about me now?" Cusi asked in a low voice.

"Yes. You have made the spirit brother a part of yourself, I can feel it. And even if you have not shed your self-importance, you have learned some of its costs. You have even learned to greet me with respect."

Raurau Illa bared his teeth in a crooked smile, rearranging the deep wrinkles around his mouth. There was a tolerance in his voice, as well, that made Cusi feel forgiven, his mistakes accepted as necessary and inevitable.

"I have not asked you, Grandfather," he said with renewed humility, "if you and Alco would like food or drink."

"You must go to your ñusta," Raurau Illa told him brusquely. "She is important to you. Perhaps also dangerous."

Cusi squinted at him anxiously.

"I hope to meet her at a dance hosted by the Vicaquirao household. Will you walk with me to the Cora Cora? Perhaps you have also been invited to the dance?"

"Do not overestimate my respectability, either," the old man said with a mirthless laugh. "It is probably best that we not be seen there together. Have you told the Vicaquirao priests that you know me?"

"I had intended to tell them everything, so that they might guide me. But after I went to the Grass Man, they treated me with suspicion and only reluctantly allowed me to attend the ceremonies to Illapa. If they did not need members so badly," Cusi added bitterly, "they might not have allowed me to participate at all. So I told them nothing."

"That is also for the best. Someone who can draw the lightning to him does not need a guide. He needs only courage and the will to understand. You are learning this, despite yourself."

"But when will I see you again? There are many things I still have to ask you."

"You will see me when you need to. The time will present itself. Go now; take your flute to the one who holds your heart."

Cusi made a reluctant bow.

"Can you tell me if the prophecy of the huaca was a good one?"

"I had only positive answers for the questions the high priest put to me," Raurau Illa said simply, cocking his head in a way that implied innocence. Cusi realized that he was mimicking the face he had put on for the high priest.

"And for the questions he did not ask?"

"Ah, that is very different," the old man admitted, betraying just a trace of a smile. "I still hear sighs and groans, and whispers that mention fatherless sons, and Viracochas, and a Cuzco that is empty at its heart. I do not know what questions these whispers might answer. Perhaps you will help me to know someday."

"They cannot be pleasant ones."

"Then we must know them before all others," Raurau Illa said forcefully. "Farewell, Cusi Auqui. Go in the knowledge that you walk in Illapa's sight. Guide yourself carefully, and do not summon the lightning unless you mean to . . ."

IT WAS fully dark by the time Cusi reached the Cora Cora, the palace enclosure that belonged to the Vicaquirao household. The dance was being held in the plaza and gardens that surrounded a famous fountain, a rectangular stone basin large enough to bathe in. Its water came from a spring that had its source near the fortress of Sacsahuaman, and it was symbolic of the role Inca Roca and his Coya, Mama Micay, had played in bringing fresh water to Cuzco. There were other fountains located throughout the enclosure, including an especially sacred pool within the compound where the mummies of Inca Roca and his Coya were kept.

Cusi used Ayar Inca's name to get past the guards at the gate, but once inside he assiduously avoided all the likely places where his grandfather might be. He knew that Ayar Inca had come into Cuzco for the Inti Raymi, and the fact that he had not sent for Cusi could only mean that he was waiting for Cusi to come to him. No doubt he had heard about Cusi's visit to the Grass Man and regarded it as suspiciously as the other Vicaquirao elders did. No doubt he would want Cusi to apologize for the bad impression he had made, so that his reputation could be cleansed as his heart already had been. He would not understand why Cusi might be unwilling to humble himself a second time, and he would see any attempt at argument or persuasion as defiance, which he would blame on the influence of Otoronco Achachi.

So Cusi had come without an invitation and had to do his best to remain unobtrusive while he searched for Tocto. It was not as easy here as it would have been at an Iñaca dance. In keeping with the Vicaquirao sense of decorum, conversation was more muted, the drinking less conspicuously energetic, and the dancing had not even begun. Cusi had to be careful, as he scanned the crowd, not to catch the ready eyes of one of his hosts, who might feel compelled to provide him with company. He kept moving, staying out of the torchlit areas and away from the largest congregations of people, determined to remain his own guide.

He made a complete circuit of the plaza, finally coming to a halt in the shadows next to the large awning house that faced out onto the fountain. The abundance of torches inside the awning house and the likelihood that his grandfather would be present kept him from trying to enter. He glanced up over the enclosure wall and saw a bright half moon rising above the eastern mountains; in a little while, there would be enough light to search the gardens. He put his fingers over the holes of the flute and lifted the hollow wooden tube to his lips in the darkness, feeling a wild impulse to play, to draw her to him somehow with a single magical note. But prudence made him hold in his breath, so that he sounded the note only in his mind, where it mingled with the lonely melodies he had been playing to himself night after night. He did not play well—not nearly as well as Tomay—but that did not really matter. The flute was an instrument that spoke with the heart's uncertain, quavering voice, a voice that could be eloquent in spite of its imperfections. He had played the songs of love and longing and loss that he had learned as a child, finding that he understood them now, so well that he could devise his own melody when memory failed him.

Cusi was not certain how long he stood there with the flute stopping his lips. The moon seemed to have risen a bit higher and the air to have grown colder. He tucked the flute into his waistband, next to his spirit brother, and pulled his cloak closer around his shoulders. He scanned the plaza one last time before commencing a search of the gardens, and that was when he finally saw her. She was standing next to the fountain, speaking to an elderly woman who was as tiny as she was. Tocto's two women stood nearby, along with several other women who must have been the attendants or companions of the old woman. He could tell nothing about the nature of their conversation, except that it was very intense.

Then Tocto bowed to the old woman, who took her hands and held them for a moment. Cusi used the time to determine the most likely path she would take from the plaza, hoping that she was going to her quarters in the Cora Cora rather than back into the awning house. He began to move in that direction, and when he saw that he had guessed right, he hurried through the shadows and went down the path ahead of Tocto and her women. Torches set on tall poles lit the way through a thicket of dense vegetation into a clearing that was both deserted and unlit except for a slanting shaft of moonlight. Cusi went to stand where the moonlight would fall across his upper body, turning to face the place where the path came into the clearing.

He waited for what seemed like an incredibly long time, until he began to think that he had miscalculated. Or else she had been detained or had turned back for some reason. He was not ready for her when she did arrive, though he kept himself from moving or speaking when she halted and made a startled noise at the sight of him. Then she turned and sent her women back down the path, gesturing so vigorously that she did not have to say a word. As she came toward him, Cusi stepped back out of the moonlight and watched her come through it to stand before him. He could see her face, surrounded by black hair that seemed to have the same liquid sheen as her eyes.

"How did you know to come here tonight?" she whispered.

Cusi spent a moment savoring the throaty sound of her voice before he could reply. "The Inti Raymi is almost over. I had made a vow that I would speak to you before it was completed."

"That is like you," Tocto said, looking at him with a rueful kind of fondness. "Then you did not know that it is safe for us to meet again?"

"I never knew why it was unsafe to begin with. Not that it can *ever* be truly safe."

"I was certain my brother suspected us. He asked me about you shortly after it became known that you had gone to the Grass Man. I do not speak to him often, Cusi, so I had to feel that his interest was not innocent."

"I met him a few days ago. He was still interested in me, but he did not mention you."

"I know. I was wrong," Tocto admitted. "I just learned about your meeting with Huascar from a woman who is a member of his household. He told her he found you very strange and secretive, with an unnatural sympathy for foreigners."

Cusi laughed harshly, remembering Huascar standing over the fish in his monkey-fur mantle, forgiving Cusi for correcting him.

"I do not want to talk about your brother," he decided, and he reached for the flute in his waistband. "I came here to give you this."

Tocto turned the flute over in her hands and looked up at him questioningly.

"It holds everything that was in my heart while I waited to see you again. Everything I hoped and feared."

"What did you fear?"

"That I would never see you again. That you had lost interest in me or decided that my confession to the Grass Man had made me special in a way you could not approve. Others have scorned me because I allowed myself to be cleansed."

"They did not know, as I did, *why* you had gone." She freed a hand and reached out for one of his, holding it up in the spreading glow of the moonlight.

"I was proud of you when I heard, and worried that the experience would make you bitter. Were you beaten because of me?"

"Some," Cusi allowed in a taut voice. "I was beaten for every secret I possessed. Perhaps it made me bitter, but not toward you."

Tocto nodded and held on to his hand, coming closer and looking up into his eyes.

"It has made you even more special to me," she whispered, laying her head on his chest. Cusi put his arm around her back and pressed her against him, rocking back on his heels with his nose in her hair. He did not think he would ever want to move again.

"I saw Raurau Illa today," he murmured into her hair, and immediately regretted speaking when she pulled away from him to see his face. "I forgot your flute, and when I went back for it, I found him in the street outside the Patallacta. Or he found me. He said that the lightning that almost struck me was female lightning. He understood from this that you were very important to me, and perhaps dangerous."

"Another sign of your specialness," Tocto told him solemnly, nodding in agreement. "You must never fear that I will abandon you, Cusi. It is you who will have to abandon me one day."

Cusi swallowed painfully, knowing that she spoke the truth and was not doubting him.

"I will not want to," he managed. "I think I was struck before I ever went to the mountain."

Tocto suddenly tugged on his hand, pulling him toward the path that led deeper into the garden.

"Does your vow permit you to do more than speak to me?" she asked as she led him through a moon-streaked grove of molle trees, toward a narrow passageway between two darkened buildings.

"My vow has been fulfilled," Cusi said in a voice that sounded oddly fierce. He put his hands on her shoulders and followed her eagerly into the enclosing darkness.

Tumibamba

THE DAY chosen for the warriors' departure turned out to be bleak and overcast, with a thin, cold rain that fell like fringe from the gray curtain of the sky. The days before this—five since the end of the Inti Raymi—had all been sunny and dry, but it was unlikely that Inti would show his face today. This would only add to the controversy, Micay reflected as she stood with Quinti on the high terrace of the Mollecancha, watching the warriors assemble on the plain to the east. The delay in leaving was due to a disagreement in the ranks of Huayna Capac's priests and soothsayers, those who helped him discern the shape and portents of the future. Additional inquiries had been sent to the coastal shrines of Pacatnamu, Rimac, and Pachacamac, and though the post runners had returned with the replies very quickly, there had been further contention before the decision was made that this would be the most propitious day to launch the campaign against the Quitos and Carangui.

The ranks of the warriors stretched to the north and south for as far as Micay could see. Beyond them, in the foothills to the east, were enormous herds of pack llamas that would carry the army's provisions and extra weapons. It was a much larger assemblage than any of the ceremonial gatherings Micay had witnessed thus far, and it was different in its demeanor, as well. Sudden waves of movement would periodically erupt in the midst of the diverse regiments, a brandishing of shields, weapons, and banners that would be followed by raucous cries and the chanting of war songs. Sometimes different parts of the same regiment seemed to be contending with each other in displaying their belligerent restlessness, raising howls that made Micay think of hungry beasts. It occurred to her that it was in fact hunger they were expressing, since the fast they had all undertaken to sanctify their departure had been unduly prolonged.

"Your father said fifty thousand men would leave today," Micay said to Quinti, leaning toward her under the umbrella they shared. "With an equal number to follow in ten days. Surely, the Quitos and Carangui cannot resist such an army for long."

Quinti nodded absently but did not reply, her gaze fixed on some point in the distance. Micay made no attempt to arouse her, knowing it was useless. The long Inti Raymi celebration had been a test of everyone's stamina, but it had been particularly draining for Quinti, who had been waging a campaign of her own. The postponement of the warriors' departure had left her totally enervated, unable to rest and recuperate while Quilaco remained in the city, yet also unable to see him while he was fasting. She had fallen into a stupor that could not be penetrated by the cries and shrieks of the warriors, much less by Micay's halfhearted attempt at conversation.

Micay looked back out over the warriors, who filled the fields like a beautiful but deadly crop. Even in the dim, watery light, they were resplendent with color, their shields and tunics bearing warlike designs, their helmets and headdresses tufted with feathers and spangled with medallions of gold and silver. The individual regiments stood in compact squares, divided in two by an aisle that separated the Upper and Lower districts. Space was also maintained between the regiments, which had been called up from every part of the Four Quarters. Micay was able to identify the Cañaris by their wicker headbands, Chimus by their tight conical helmets, Chunchos by their long black bows and gaudy headdresses, and Collas and Lupacas by their knit caps and the slings and bolas they whirled over their heads. There seemed to be many Colla regiments, at least among those within her view. Golden-eared Incas stood at the junctures between the regiments, exercising final command over the foreign chiefs.

Amaru and Quilaco were both down there somewhere, occupying just such positions, Quilaco with pride, Amaru with apparent indifference. Micay wondered which attitude was more dangerous, which most likely to lead to a fatal excess of courage. She thought of the offering she had made on their behalf. The mamacona representing the Women of the Sun had been most pleased to receive the vicuña wool and had pledged their prayers to Inti and Mama Quilla. Despite some lingering misgivings, Micay felt that the offering had not been compromised by the small amount of wool she had kept aside. It was not for herself, after all, and Apu Poma had given her permission to do as she saw fit. During these last idle days, she had had the occasion to dye the wool black and spin it into thread, assisted at times by Quinti, who had been oblivious of what she was doing. Micay preferred having no accomplices; if she were going to take sides, she wanted to have only herself to trust.

"Did you say something?" Quinti inquired dreamily, startling Micay out of her thoughts.

"Too long ago to remember."

Quinti stared down at the warriors.

"Why do they just stand there, getting wet and cold? Why do they not leave?"

"I imagine they are waiting for the Sapa Inca. Your father said that Huayna Capac was going to lead them out of Tumibamba."

"And then he is going to return, and let the army proceed without him," Quinti complained. "The war would go much faster if he were to lead the warriors in person."

Micay had wondered about this herself, but Quinti was the first person she had heard to question it.

"Your father said that the messengers had already begun to arrive from Cuzco with the results of the Inti Raymi accounting. The Sapa Inca must also attend to the rest of the Four Quarters."

"Do not tell me what Father said," Quinti said wearily. "He has no part in this war, and he is content to have the warriors out of the city for a long time. Amaru said that the war chiefs will compete with one another more fiercely with the Sapa Inca absent, and that will slow down the advance."

"But who could stand in the way of so many?" Micay asked, spreading her hand over the plain. Quinti sighed and let her shoulders slump, leaning against the umbrella they held between them.

"No one, I hope."

As they watched, the Sapa Inca's rose-colored litter suddenly appeared at the southern end of the plain, borne above the heads of the warriors who accompanied it, forcing a path through the middle of the assembled regiments. Those closest to the litter were Cañaris, but the rest were all members of the Inca Old Guard, the elite corps of veteran fighters. As the litter passed between them, the regiments on either side raised a ferocious din, beating their spears against their shields and dancing in place. Micay heard Huayna Capac's name being shouted, but it was only one cry among many, and not always the most heartfelt. The litter moved northward until it was out of sight. Then the regiments slowly began to advance, rank upon rank, their war cries subsiding into chants that seemed to blend together into a single, menacing rumble.

"The war has begun," Quinti murmured plaintively.

Micay reached over with her free hand to steady her. "He will return, Quinti. Probably very soon."

"It cannot be soon enough," Quinti said, looking down over the parapet at the river far below. Micay followed her gaze and saw a band of water the color of the sky, rushing swiftly between banks of fitted stone. A rope bridge hung limply in the rain, seeming absurdly frail. She stared at it for a moment, reminded of the House of Chosen Women, of something she had heard or dreamed there. But the memory was too vague; Caxamarca seemed years, not months, in the past.

"I must sleep," Quinti groaned. Micay nodded compliantly, casting a last glance at the plain. The warriors were still streaming northward, chanting their war songs and churning the fields into mud with their feet. She realized belatedly that she had not seen any regiments of Chachapoyas, and she wondered if that were simply a matter of chance or if she had missed them because she had not thought to look for them until now. Those memories were even farther in the past, all but lost to her now.

"I will guide you home," she said to Quinti, taking the umbrella so that Quinti could duck under the branches of the tree first. As she lowered the umbrella to follow, Micay felt the cold touch of raindrops on her head and shivered, wondering if years from now this would still be thought of as a propitious day.

VI

CAPAC RAYMI:
The Royal Feast
of the Sun

(Six months later, A.D. 1512)

Cuzco

STONES CLICKED together down the hill to Cusi's right, fifty feet or so away, probably at the place where all the loose shale had fallen. He guessed that it was Sumac Mallqui, come to harass him and test his alertness for the thousandth time. But Cusi did not move immediately, remaining as long as possible in the shade of the tunic he had stretched over the rocks that sheltered him. The sun was very hot, and he knew the path his intruder would have to take to reach him. Squatting with his left leg stretched out in front of him, he kneaded the sore muscles of his thigh, trying to loosen them for action. Then he unwound the sling from around his forehead and fitted a stone into the braided pocket, twining his fingers through the looped end and clasping the loose end against his palm. Gathering his shield and war club with his other hand, he came up into a crouch with a grimace, molding himself against the rocks as he swiveled to face down the hill. He saw movement among the bunch grass exactly where he had expected it and let fly with his sling, though without the force to injure.

There was a loud grunt as the stone struck its target. Then Sumac Mallqui sprang up out of the grass, swinging a long black chontawood club sharpened to a knife edge on two sides. Cusi waited among the rocks, knowing that the warrior's weapon gave him an advantage on open ground. When Sumac Mallqui was almost upon him, churning up a cloud of red dust as he charged uphill, Cusi feigned a charge of his own, then quickly pulled back. The warrior jerked upright in reaction and launched a wild swing that drove Cusi farther back, the tip of the club splintering harshly on the rocks. Cusi chopped down with his own stone-headed club, almost tearing Sumac Mallqui's weapon from his hands, then leaped out and struck him in the shoulder with his shield, sending him rolling back down the hill. Resisting the urge to pursue him for the kill, Cusi let out a ululating cry, a call that would have brought other sentries to help him, if he were in fact in enemy territory. No one would come today, but Cusi was still required to give the signal.

Sumac Mallqui made one last backward somersault and came up to his feet with his club at the ready, his apparent helplessness a ruse that might have cost Cusi his life. Sumac Mallqui grinned and charged again, hacking chunks out of Cusi's flimsy shield as Cusi dodged among the rocks, striking out defensively with his club. They fought until they were both arm-weary and gasping for breath, without the strength to deal a mortal blow. Sumac Mallqui lowered his battered club and stepped back, as if uncertain that Cusi would respect an unspoken truce. Cusi in fact raised his club to throw it, but then caught himself in time.

"You would have received assistance by now," Sumac Mallqui managed, huffing between words. "You were wise not to pursue me."

"Be grateful I did not throw harder with my sling," Cusi scoffed. "I did not think it would be fair after the noise you made to let me know you were coming."

The warrior laughed and propped his long club against the side of a rock. Like Cusi, he was wearing only a loincloth, and his dust-coated body was striped with running lines of sweat. Cusi picked up his tunic and mopped at his face for a moment, then tossed the black shirt to Sumac Mallqui to do the same.

"Your leg is better," the warrior suggested.

Cusi took an experimental step that he could not finish smoothly. "I forgot about it. I doubt that I could have outrun you, though."

"I am not the one you will have to outrun. Mayca kneed you on purpose, you know. To cripple you for the race."

"I know that," Cusi snapped, snatching his tunic out of the air when Sumac Mallqui tossed it back to him.

"I wanted to be sure you remembered. He and Sutic will no doubt try to hurt you again in the race."

"They will not get close enough to hurt me," Cusi vowed.

Sumac Mallqui smiled sarcastically. "Good. Because I have seen you resist your anger, as if you felt soiled by it. You do not like the way I have made you and your brothers be enemies of one another."

Cusi did not try to deny the charge, since it did not matter what he liked. He stared stonily at Sumac Mallqui, wishing he had thrown harder with his sling.

"Yet you seemed to like it well enough after you beat Mayca in the wrestling," Sumac Mallqui continued tauntingly. "You had never beaten him before, had you? You did not think you *could* beat him. Ah, but your anger transformed you, and made you a fighter!"

"I did not just want to beat him," Cusi said through his teeth. "I wanted to *destroy* him."

"I remember," Sumac Mallqui said with satisfaction. "I had to pull you off of him. His neck must be as sore as your leg. We will see who has recovered best when the race is run eight days from now."

"I can count."

Sumac Mallqui grinned at his disrespectful tone and picked up his long club. Cusi put a hand on his own weapon, having been attacked before when he thought the test was over. The warrior's grin widened in recognition.

"Good. You may leave your post now to wash yourself and drink. But take your anger with you. It is the warrior's only true friend, and his best weapon."

Cusi watched him go down the hill, waiting until he was out of sight before heading toward the stream that lay just to the east of his post. He tossed his tunic over his sweaty shoulders and took his sling and club with him, discarding his shattered shield among the rocks. Now he would have to search for materials to make a new one, since he would be expected to be fully armed when he returned to Cuzco at sunset tomorrow. He cursed Sumac Mallqui roundly as he limped across the side of the hill, keeping his eyes and ears open for signs of other would-be attackers.

It was the seventh day of the Huarachicoy, seven days that had been filled with competition and chastisement, the nights spent out in the cold and rain, sleeping on the hard ground. Tomorrow night he and the other boys would break their fast and sleep indoors for the first time since the rites had begun, though Cusi was past the point where he looked forward to such comforts. Perhaps he did resist his anger, as Sumac Mallqui had said, but it was with him nonetheless, a constant irascibility compounded of hunger, hardship, and unceasing harassment. It had made him scornful of comfort and impatient with anything that stood in his way.

He shrugged the tunic off his shoulders and knelt beside the stream, bending to drink deeply from the icy water. Except for the race down Mount Ana-huarque, the contests between the initiation brothers had been concluded two days ago. With Sumac Mallqui goading them on, pitting the foreign boys against the Incas and then the Incas against one another, the struggle for distinction had been fierce and bitter. Cusi had been first in the jumping and third in the sling (behind Mayca and Tomay), and he had done well, consider-ing his size, in the fighting with shields and war clubs. He had done less well with the weapons that favored size and strength—the bow, spear-thrower, bolas, and spear—and had been eliminated in the early rounds of competition. The wrestling had come last, with the boys divided into groups according to size and weight. Everyone in Cusi's group, including Cusi himself and Tomay, had expected Mayca to be the final winner.

Mayca. Just the name made Cusi's heartbeat accelerate, and he sat up and snarled at his own reflection in the water. For three years they had studied and trained together, competing frequently but without malice. Cusi granted Mayca his superior strength, secure in the respect that Mayca had to pay to Cusi's swiftness. They had been friendly rivals, along with Tomay, who was perhaps the fiercest competitor of the three. They had never been close, but Cusi would not have hesitated to claim Mayca as his initiation brother.

Cusi bent again to wash himself, feeling the tight knot of pain in his left thigh. He had considered himself lucky to have made it to the final round of the wrestling, his path cleared by Mayca's elimination of Tomay. He probably would have been content to finish second, knowing that he was still the favorite in the race, which was the most public of the contests. But then Mayca had spun him by the arm and smashed a knee into his thigh, a blow that had drawn a warning from Sumac Mallqui, though the warrior had pretended at the time that it was not deliberate and had also chosen not to stop the match. Cusi had stared at Mayca's unrepentant face through a film of pain, seeing that he had decided to be first in both the wrestling and the race and that he did not care how he earned the distinction. In that instant Mayca became the symbol of everything Cusi despised, the cause of every injury and injustice he had ever suffered. Cusi had recalled his father's arm shooting out at him, the Grass Man's stick descending out of the darkness, and he had thrown himself at Mayca's head, hating him with a passion that no mere enemy could ever arouse.

Rinsing himself with handfuls of cold water, Cusi stood up and shook off the excess moisture. He was dry almost immediately and soon began to feel the dizzying effects of the sun's heat. He wound his sling back around his forehead and draped his tunic over his head and shoulders like a mantle. In sixteen days Cusi and his brothers would celebrate their manhood in conjunction with Inti's attainment of full maturity as Apu Inti, the Lord Sun. Cusi had half of that time in which to heal and prepare himself for the race, which was a dangerous event for everyone involved. He leaned down and massaged the sore muscles in his thigh, feeling renewed annoyance at Mayca, even though he knew that anger would not help him heal. He needed patience, gentleness, and the humility to pray for wholeness, attributes he had been forced to abandon days ago and could not hope to recover now. Is this the kind of men we are to become? he wondered furiously. Angry men who injure their brothers?

He spat on the ground, remembering Sumac Mallqui's taunts, then picked up his war club and limped off to find wood for a new shield.

Tumibamba

OUT OF THE CORNER of her eye, Micay saw the messenger come through the compound gate and stop short, no doubt arrested by the sight of a courtyard filled with ñustas. Then he glanced in her direction, no doubt wondering why she had been separated from the group and made to stand alone, facing the wall. Behind her Mama Huarcay was still talking about Huayna Capac's pardon of the Quitos, comparing it to past acts of mercy on the part of Topa Inca and Pachacuti. It was a recitation Micay had heard too often lately, whenever Mama Huarcay wanted to goad her into a silence for which she could be punished.

So Micay ignored the drawling voice and bore her punishment, staring up at the colorful frieze that decorated the wall in front of her. It was four feet high and ran all the way around the inside of the enclosure walls, a double horizontal band with pelicans above and leaping fish below, separated by a narrower band filled with geometric designs and bordered by scrollwork that mimicked the waves of the Mother Water. The figures and designs had been carved into the buff-colored plaster that covered the adobe walls and had been painted in vivid shades of red, green, and blue. Many of the Inca wives, including Mama Cori and the Coya Rahua Ocllo, had been appalled when Mama Huarcay had brought in the Chimu artisans and put them to work decorating her modest enclosure in the style of the royal palaces of Chan Chan. They had been especially offended by the band of bright red pumas that had appeared on the *outside* of her compound walls, and it was said the Coya had asked her husband to have it removed. But Mama Huarcay had somehow persuaded Huayna Capac to appreciate its beauty as she did, which made it a success no matter what the other women thought.

The voice behind her stopped, and a rustling, shuffling sound told her that the other ñustas were being dismissed or set to some new task. When Mama Huarcay spoke again from close behind her, Micay had the sudden intuition that the message somehow concerned her.

"You like it, do you not?" Mama Huarcay prompted.

Micay understood that she was referring to the frieze.

"Yes, my lady," she admitted.

"Surely Mama Cori has told you not to like it."

"Mama Cori does not tell me what I should like or dislike, my lady. I have my own judgment, as she has hers."

"Yes, yes, but you have *feelings*, too, Micay. You understand passion, as the Chimus do. That is why you are able to see the beauty of this."

"Yes, my lady."

"Mama Cori will never trust you because of that. You *know* that, Micay. You will never be cold enough for her. Though at least you have not disgraced yourself, as Quinti Ocllo has."

Micay remained silent, as she had earlier when Mama Huarcay had tried to lure her into either defending Quinti or joining in her condemnation. Mama Cori had taught her that she did not have to take a side in personal attacks, and Micay had learned on her own that there was more dignity and less punishment in simply refusing to speak than in trying to reason or argue.

"Look at me," Mama Huarcay snapped.

Micay turned and gazed at her with polite expectation. "My lady?"

"Lloque Yupanqui has sent for you. He gave no reason, but since he is a Royal Rememberer of the first rank, his wishes must be respected. No doubt his sister has told him to rescue you from me, and of course he would do whatever she asked. It is well known how *close* they are—"

This familiar insinuation also required no response, and Mama Huarcay did not seem to expect one. She pointed with her chin toward the courtyard gate.

"So go, Chachapoyas girl, let them give you their protection, though it costs you the friends and favor you might have won here. It is a shame how they use you for their own ends, and an even greater shame that you mistake it for caring. Go, and remember to return here at dusk to serve at the Capac Raymi festivities."

Micay bowed in compliance and turned to go, thinking that she had never had any chance to win friends and favor here, just as there had never been anyone to rescue or protect her. That was simply the nature of her initiation as a ñusta, and she was not a person who yearned for the choices she had never been given . . .

THE ADMINISTRATIVE compounds were on a level well below that of the gardens and enclosures of the court, and as she descended a steep, winding staircase, Micay wondered how Lloque had the time to visit with her in the middle of the afternoon, in the midst of the Capac Raymi. The rank he had attained among the Rememberers meant that he traveled with the Sapa Inca and attended him during important ceremonial occasions. In addition, Huayna Capac had given him the task of establishing the fields, shrines, and huacas that would allow the manhood rites to be held in Tumibamba during next year's Capac Raymi. The last time Micay had come to see him, only a few days before, she had had to wait in a line outside his chamber while he conferred with priests and Cañari officials and a steady stream of messengers. It was both flattering and reassuring to think that he had put such matters aside in order to respond to her concern for Quinti.

She was surprised, then, to find the long, narrow courtyard in front of the Rememberers' rooms empty and Lloque Yupanqui alone in his room without a single servant or apprentice present. He was sitting on a straw mat with his hands open and unoccupied in his lap, an odd sight in itself, since he was usually toying with a memory cord or one of the painted wands he used to help him remember. He smiled slowly from beneath his drooping eyelids and gestured for her to sit on the mat across from him. After the bustle of the crowded streets outside, which had been filled with Capac Raymi celebrants, the silence here seemed distinctly eerie.

"It is different today," Lloque acknowledged in the voice that always seemed too soft on first hearing. "Huayna Capac has had second thoughts about the Huarachicoy. It is possible that he will want to hold it in Quito instead, if his quarters there are completed in time."

The Quitos had negotiated a surrender just before the Capac Raymi had begun, ending a five-month siege of their capital city by the Inca army, which had never been given the order to launch an all-out attack. As part of the terms of their surrender, they were to build a splendid palace for Huayna Capac in Quito, though it seemed most unlikely that they could be driven to finish it as early as next year. Much of the Mollecancha was still under construction, and the campaign against the Carangui would begin in earnest soon.

"I hope your work here will not be wasted," Micay said sympathetically.

Lloque gave a slight shrug. "I believe he will reconsider. Only time will be lost. I chose to watch it pass today rather than joining the others at the ceremonies."

Micay nodded respectfully, understanding the gesture of his being here like this. He was not a man who ever expressed anger or disapproval, or any strong emotion, for that matter. He did not seem to possess strong emotions. So his apparent idleness was, for him, a loud and pointed protest.

"I believe I have found a remedy for Quinti's problems," Lloque went on. "It was suggested to me by the high priestess."

Micay swallowed, resisting the urge to gape at him in disbelief. "The *present* high priestess, my lord? The woman who has defied the Coya?"

"Her name is Chimpu Ocllo, as you undoubtedly know. I had to meet with her over another matter, and I very quickly understood how she has been able to keep her place. She is the mamanchic here, no matter what anyone might think about her beliefs concerning the membership of the cults. She is too holy to be removed simply because Rahua Ocllo wishes to have the same power she had in Cuzco."

Micay had to swallow again. She had heard only complaints and disparaging comments about Chimpu Ocllo from both her teachers, so it was astonishing to hear Lloque attest to her holiness with such calm certainty.

"What has she suggested for Quinti, my lord?"

"She is going to arrange for her to be a teacher of Quechua to the women and children in one of the outlying districts of Tumibamba."

"Quinti has agreed to this?" Micay asked, unable to keep the astonishment out of her voice.

"She said that you would be surprised. But she wants to be as far removed from the court as possible, and she needs a useful task to distract her from her waiting for Quilaco Yupanqui. Perhaps a roomful of Cañari children will make her yearn for the company of well-spoken adults, and she will decide to come back and make her apologies to the court. Or perhaps she will give herself to the task and will learn the patience and discretion that will allow her to return whenever she wishes."

"I cannot think Mama Cori will be pleased to hear of this," Micay ventured. "She is very much on Rahua Ocllo's side in this disagreement."

"I will speak to my sister when the arrangements have been made," Lloque said, seemingly untroubled by the prospect. "Her position in the court makes it impossible for her to admit that Quinti's complaints might be just. Therefore she cannot make Quinti reconsider the wisdom and usefulness of voicing such complaints in public."

"Do *you* believe her complaints are just, my lord?" Micay asked. Lloque raised his eyebrows at the question, forging deep lines in his high forehead and making his sunken, hooded eyes appear owlish. Micay froze, realizing belatedly that she had asked for a candor and trust to which she was not entitled. She could not claim to know him well, having spoken to him alone on only two other occasions. But then Lloque gave her a judicious nod, as if finding the question pertinent and her worthy of the trust.

"There is no question that the warriors have been kept too long in the field without being allowed to fight. Everyone knows that there has been trouble maintaining discipline among the men, just as there has been confusion among the war chiefs because their orders must be brought from Tumibamba. It cannot be said that Huayna Capac has given this campaign his wholehearted attention, and it will not be remembered as a glorious triumph."

Lloque paused and held up a long, bony finger. "But . . . several of Huayna Capac's advisers complained of these things long ago, shortly after the campaign had begun. They are no longer his advisers. And two of the war chiefs came back to Tumibamba to complain that the Quitos were not being treated with the severity that rebels deserve. They were correct, of course, but they are now commanding garrisons in the jungles of the Eastern Quarter. The justice of their complaints had no bearing on how they were received."

His voice seemed dry and very precise, no longer soft. Yet his angular face remained calm and untroubled. He apparently felt none of the anger and disgust and outrage that had finally overwhelmed Quinti's good judgment.

"Perhaps Quinti has been fortunate, then," Micay suggested. "She has at least been able to choose her own place of banishment."

"It could have been worse," Lloque allowed, "given what she said and the nature of her audience. You do not win widespread admiration by questioning the Sapa Inca's courage and generosity at one of his own feasts." He paused and cocked his head at her. "So, my daughter, you are approaching the end of your time with Mama Huarcay, and you seem no worse for it. In fact, you are strong enough within yourself to spare concern for Quinti. Cori was very worried that Mama Huarcay would make it an ordeal you could not bear."

"It was hard at first," Micay admitted, "being singled out and punished for every slip. But Mama Cori had prepared me well, so I was not surprised by much. And now that the end of our training is in sight, Mama Huarcay has become more restrained in her criticisms of all the ñustas. I think she wishes she had been kinder to us, so that we would remember her with more fondness."

"How *will* you remember her?" Lloque inquired curiously, startling her with the question that no one else in the family had thought to ask. They all assumed that her memory of Mama Huarcay would be a wholly unpleasant one, and she had done nothing to contradict their assumptions. Now she felt caught out, unable to deny that it was not that simple.

"I am not certain," she confessed. "I received more of her attention than any of her favorites did, and not all of it was unkind. She has told me many things, stories about her life and the places she has seen, and sometimes . . . when she forgot who I was, who I represent, she treated me almost like a daughter. She is capable of great warmth, my lord . . ."

Micay trailed off guiltily, realizing that she had not spoken this fondly of Mama Cori. It was a contrast of personalities that Mama Huarcay had exploited from the start, half proselytizing, half trying to get Micay to compromise herself. The only time her insistent disdain for Mama Cori's coldness ever slackened was when she was making suggestive remarks about Mama Cori's relationship with her twin brother.

Lloque, this same brother, was gazing at her steadily, and Micay was certain that he perceived her embarrassment. But it seemed not to arouse any suspicion in him. She wondered if he knew the sort of slanders that were passed about him and Mama Cori; she wondered if he cared.

"Mama Huarcay's warmth is well known, especially to the Sapa Inca," Lloque said at last, giving her a thin smile. "That she has shown any to you is a tribute to your character, Micay. I will be proud to stand as your uncle in the final ceremony of the Quicuchicoy."

Micay bowed in gratitude, feeling her cheeks flush and her throat tighten. Both Mama Huarcay and Mama Cori had done their best to influence her, but neither had thought to praise the effort she was making on her own behalf.

"I will not keep you, my daughter," Lloque said when she looked up. "But before you go, tell me something. The waistband we discussed the first time you came to see me—was that sent to Cuzco along with the rest of Cusi's garments?"

"I placed it in the bundle myself. I can only assume that it went off with the rest."

"Good. I think it will please him." He raised a hand in farewell. "May Mama Quilla, Mother Moon, guide your steps in the testing that is yet to come and keep you from going astray. Let her be your teacher, Micay, above all the others you might have."

Cuzco

IN THE STORY SONGS about Huanacauri, he is known first as Ayar Cachi, the eldest of the four brothers who brought the Inca people from their place of origin to their home in Cuzco. Ayar Cachi was also the most violent and warlike, and his younger brothers feared his reckless ferocity, which might be turned upon them. He possessed a golden sling from which his slingstones flew like lightning bolts, shattering rocks and gouging great furrows into the earth, destroying whatever he aimed at. To protect themselves, his brothers lured Ayar Cachi back to the caves of origin, telling him that fine garments and golden vessels had been left behind in one of the caves. When Ayar Cachi entered the cave in search, they walled up the only entrance with huge stones and left him there to perish.

It was later, on a mountain overlooking the Valley of Cuzco, that Ayar Cachi reappeared to his brothers, his voice emanating from the glowing arch of an immense rainbow. He called himself Huanacauri and told his brothers that their home lay in the valley below. He told them that they would be great lords, and that one day their descendents would rule over the lands and people in all directions. But he warned them that they must always venerate the warlike spirit of Huanacauri, and make offerings in his name, and bring their sons to him to be initiated into manhood. When the voice stopped and the rainbow faded away, a stone in the shape of a seated man was found on the summit of the mountain, a huaca that took the name of Huanacauri, as did the mountain itself. From that time onward Mount Huanacauri was revered as a holy place by the Inca warriors, who claimed the huaca as their special patron and prayed to him for success in war.

On the tenth day of the Huarachicoy, as was the custom, the initiation brothers, dressed in white cloaks and tunics, climbed to the shrine at the top of Mount Huanacauri. They were led by the Sun Priests and the sacred Napa and were accompanied by a squadron of golden-eared warriors and their close kinsmen. Cusi walked near the head of the group, flanked by Otoronco Achachi and Ayar Inca. He was still limping, but more out of stiffness than pain, and he was not breathing hard at the top, as both of his grandfathers were.

The entire group spent the night at the shrine, which was illuminated by fires kept alive by the initiates. Llamas were sacrificed and their hearts thrown onto the fires, while the priests drank akha and invoked the spirit of Haunacauri in eerie tones. Prayers were chanted by the elder Incas, and the warriors took turns leading the boys in the war songs Sumac Mallqui had taught them. The spirit of the ceremony was not diminished by the fact that the shrine was empty, for everyone knew that the huaca had been carried north with the warriors, and they all understood why that was necessary.

At dawn the boys were assembled in two lines, facing each other across an open aisle. Sumac Mallqui came down the aisle with aggressive strides, brandishing his black chontawood club and shouting in the boys' faces. He slashed at the air around their heads, screaming threats and watching their eyes for the slightest sign of fear or withdrawal. If they flinched now, when the danger was not real, he told them, they would never be fit to face the dangers of an earplug man. As Sumac Mallqui approached Cusi's place in line, Cusi made himself into a stone, imagining himself as hard and unyielding as his spirit brother, the curve of his spine emulating the bend frozen into the middle of the stone. Saliva sprayed his face along with Sumac Mallqui's hoarse shout, but he did not move or blink as the black club swept past his eyes, so closely that it stirred the hair on his forehead.

The next man to come down the aisle was Otoronco Achachi, a surprising participant due to his age and rank. An honor to me, Cusi thought, letting his pride stiffen him even further. Otoronco had a short thrusting spear with a double-edged bronze tip, and he was challenging the boys with an energy and agility that belied his age. He seemed to be in a rage, his face contorted and his cries barely coherent as he lunged from one line to the next, turning his spear point aside at the last possible moment, so that the flat side of the blade seemed to kiss the flesh it passed.

"Are you ready to die?" he bellowed at Cusi, jabbing his spear past one eye and then the other. "You will have many chances more real than this!"

The spear point cut back and forth under Cusi's chin, and he caught a glimpse of Otoronco's bloodshot eyes, which seemed inflamed with anger, just before the sharp bronze tip ripped through the front of Cusi's tunic with a swift sigh. Otoronco was gone before Cusi felt the sting that told him he had been cut. He ignored it and let the shock of Otoronco's anger travel through him like a vibration through a stone, producing no visible movement. Otoronco's cries seemed to diminish rapidly in intensity as he moved down the line, as if he had exhausted his anger and had begun to remember his age.

Other men came down the aisle, one after the other, harassing and threatening the boys until the sun had fully risen. Then the boys' fathers, grandfathers, and uncles came forward with switches made of grass and whipped the boys on their bare arms and legs, exhorting them to remain brave and unfeeling, so that they might withstand the hardships of war. Otoronco was silent and applied his switch in a subdued manner, though Ayar Inca more than made up for his forebearance by scourging Cusi with a thoroughness that reminded him of the Grass Man. Cusi accepted the punishment without rancor, knowing that he had earned it by avoiding his grandfather and disregarding his counsel. He hoped that he and Ayar Inca would be able to talk later, as men.

From Haunacauri the boys returned to the Hawk Enclosure, their ceremonial quarters perched on a terraced landing halfway up the side of Sacsahuaman Hill. They were to rest here for three days, accepting the visits of their teachers and kinsmen and readying themselves for the race down Mount Anahuarque. Several men from the Iñaca and Vicaquirao households came to tell Cusi how much he had impressed them during the ceremony, standing composed and oblivious as the torn front of his white tunic slowly stained red.

There was a note of sympathy in some of their compliments, a muted suggestion that Otoronco had acted carelessly, without being in full control of his weapon. Cusi would say only that Otoronco had paid him a great honor, speaking with a curtness that was interpreted as modesty and discretion when in truth he simply found it difficult to converse with anyone. He was still part stone, and the fleshly part was drawn tight against intrusion, expecting menace even now. It was not until the second night that he was able to sleep deeply, without being awakened by creatures lunging at him out of his dreams.

He sat alone on the terrace wall the next afternoon, massaging his thigh in the sun and contemplating the fact that neither Otoronco nor Ayar Inca had come to see him. He guessed that they were embarrassed by the enthusiasm with which they had carried out their respective duties toward him. Which made him wonder in turn about himself, about his ability to arouse a violent response in the hearts of his own kin. It was not a talent he cherished, though in his present state it gave him a twinge of vengeful pride.

Tomay came out along the top of the wall and squatted down next to him, nodding briefly in greeting. Cusi went on massaging his leg while Tomay watched him in silence, his broad Colla face expressionless, his eyes slitted against the light. His fat, round cheeks, though, had the darkly burnished color that indicated either uneasiness or high emotion. He and Cusi had exchanged no more than a few words since the rites began.

"Is it better?" Tomay asked, pointing at Cusi's leg with his chin.

"Somewhat. I will be ready."

"Good." Tomay looked away, down into the courtyards of the enclosures at the base of the hill. He adopted a tentative, experimental tone, as if beginning a barter. "We are not allowed to help one another in the race—even if one of us falls."

"That is correct."

"But we could warn each other, could we not, if one of us perceived a danger in the path, or the threat of a collision?"

Cusi opened and closed his mouth on a peremptory reply. The fact that Tomay felt he had to ask was proof in itself of how greatly the trust between them had been eroded. It also showed just how much he wanted to win the race.

"Sumac Mallqui warned me that Mayca and Sutic would probably try to injure me again in the race," Cusi said evenly. "That would be true for you, too, if you were ahead of them."

"Perhaps," Tomay allowed. "Though I am less important to them because I am not an Inca."

"All those who finish will be Incas."

"You understand what I mean. I could beat Mayca and he would still be the first of the blood Incas, the true Incas."

"Not if I beat him, too," Cusi said, flexing the muscles in his thigh without grimacing. "We are brothers, Tomay. You do not need to ask me to watch your back. I would do that even if it were not allowed."

Tomay lowered his eyes, his cheeks darkening even further. "Spoken like an Inca," he said hoarsely, so that Cusi could not tell if he were being sarcastic. "Run well, then. I will whoop like Uritu if there is danger. Do not be too proud to listen."

Tomay rose and walked away without waiting for a reply. Cusi decided to feel heartened by their agreement, despite the awkwardness. He and his friends would come together again when this ordeal was over. Whether they would ever again look upon Mayca and Sutic as brothers remained to be seen, and depended heavily on whether they all survived the race. Cusi went back to work on his leg, as determined as Tomay to do more than survive.

Otoronco came to see him that night, finding his way to the ledge in the hillside above the Hawk Enclosure, where Cusi was standing sentry duty. They stood side by side in the darkness, looking out over a sleeping Cuzco, lit only by the gleam of cooking fires and the torches of guard details. As usual, Otoronco did not waste any breath on amenities.

"You were not cut badly?"

"No, my lord. The healers closed the wound easily."

"I was not thinking about what I was doing," Otoronco admitted, a frown in his voice. "I was thinking about the Quitos. I was thinking about the garrisons they overran when they rebelled, the warriors they slaughtered. Warriors who were commanded by young Incas not much older than yourselves. I looked at all of you and thought that you would soon be going out to face death in the name of Huayna Capac, and that that name should provide you with more protection."

"The Quitos surrendered, did they not?" Cusi ventured, mentally recalling the locations of the other sentries and hoping that none were close enough to overhear this treasonous talk.

"Without punishment!" Otoronco snarled in disgust. "My father or Topa Inca would have struck hard before opening negotiations, out of respect for those who had been killed. Huayna Capac has never faced that kind of death. He does not know what it is like to be surrounded and outnumbered, with no hope of rescue and the enemy closing in, grinning at your fear and telling you what he will do to your body after he has cut your throat. Huayna Capac cannot imagine the humiliation of such a death, so he does not understand the need for vengeance. He does not react like a warlord should."

The pronouncement, tantamount to an accusation of cowardice, aroused an anxiety so deep and instinctual that Cusi found it hard to breathe for a moment. It was treason simply to be present when the Sapa Inca was criticized. Otoronco grunted and went on in a more thoughtful tone.

"Huayna Capac came to the fringe as a child, and it was felt he could never truly be risked in battle. Yet before the succession was settled he was almost killed twice by assassins. Why could he not be risked against the enemy when he had already withstood the assaults of his brothers and cousins? He has been spared the most valuable experience a man can have: to face inevitable death and yet survive. To believe that you have lost everything, and then have it all back. To know you did not save yourself, yet you have been saved. That is when you know that you have huaca, that you are apart from the things of this world."

Cusi started violently, almost dropping his spear. "You have had this experience, Grandfather?"

"It was common in my youth, when we were taking Inca power into places where our name had never been heard. Once, in the land of the Moxos, I stood in a clearing in the jungle, outside a fortress made of logs. My men were behind me, but they were as sick and exhausted as I was, in no shape to attack. I do not know what made me think I could talk my way into the fort, or why I expected them to respect my empty hands. They let me come within shouting distance and then began shooting arrows at me through cracks in the wall. There was no place to run for cover, and not even time enough to throw up my arms. Before I could flinch, there were arrows sticking in the ground all around me and one embedded deep in my leg. I was certain, too, that these were poisoned arrows.

"But somehow," Otoronco explained, shaking his head as if still astonished, "somehow I stood there and called to the Moxo headman until he came out to meet with me. And somehow I made peace with him and let him take me inside to have his healers tend to my wound. I do not remember much of that, because I was delirious from the poison for many days afterward. But I have not forgotten a moment of what came before. I can still hear the bowstrings snapping and feel the wind of the arrows hissing past me as I stood there, calling out in a voice that could not have been my own, a voice that was calm and unafraid, when in my heart I had lost all hope and was utterly consumed by my pain and terror."

Chastened by the memory, Otoronco clasped his hands in front of him and rested his chin on his chest. Cusi remembered to breathe and found that his free hand was clamped over the spirit brother inside his waistband. The anger and disgust were absent from Otoronco's voice when he spoke again.

"It is an awesome experience, and it changes you forever. You cannot hear of an Inca dying in a faraway place without sharing the fear of his last moments and feeling a personal responsibility to avenge his death." Otoronco paused and licked his lips. "Still, it is not an experience that anyone would deliberately seek, and I should not blame Huayna Capac for his lack of it. He has inherited a world we have emptied of enemies. Look how far he must go simply to find an enemy worth fighting! He has the harder task, I think. He must preserve the world his father and grandfather won for him, yet there is little he can add to it on his own account. His accomplishments have been limited by those of Pachacuti and Topa Inca, yet it is only with them that he can be compared."

Otoronco turned to Cusi and held up his hands at different levels, as if balancing two unequal weights, and Cusi nodded to show that he understood. Otoronco dropped his hands after a moment, seeming bemused by how much he had said.

"I came here to inspire you for the race," he said ruefully, "and instead I

tell you things you should not even hear. You will have to do well in spite of
your guardian. The warriors tell me that the current wagering favors a boy
named Mayca."

Cusi grunted and scuffed at the dirt with his foot. "Warriors will wager on
anything. It does not make anyone faster, or the mountain less steep."

"Indeed. Make a name for yourself, then, other than that of the boy who
went to the Grass Man. Give your guardian a reason to be extravagant in his
boasting."

"I will be ready," Cusi said succinctly, feeling there was no larger promise
that he could make.

Tumibamba

WITHOUT PAINT or powder, the face in the mirror seemed much
younger than the one Micay had become used to seeing there. She
held the mirror at arm's length to study the mantle and shift she had
chosen, both light gray edged with a line of dark blue, plain garments to match
the unadorned face. The cloth was mostly cotton, too, which made it a practical choice on a day as warm and humid as this. Micay could not remember
the last time she had worn these clothes; certainly not since she had begun her
training with Mama Huarcay. Mama Cori and Apu Poma had both seen that
she was dressed in a manner befitting a member of their household, contribut-
ing so many new garments between them that old ones like these had been
pushed to the bottom of the pile.

Micay decided that she liked the subdued, austere effect, which seemed to
heighten the contrast between the light bronze of her skin and the glossy black
of her hair. Perhaps she should dress more simply all of the time, and not just
to please Quinti. She hoped that Quinti would be pleased and not think that
she was being mimicked out of disrespect. Micay had only appearances to go
by, since she and Quinti had barely seen one another since Quinti had become
a teacher. Quinti was up before dawn to make the long walk to the north
quarter of Tumibamba and was usually asleep by the time Micay returned
from the feast or ceremony at which she had served. They had not had a
chance to discuss any of the obvious changes that had taken place in the days
since Quinti had assumed her new position. Days, Micay had constantly to
remind herself; days, not months.

Putting down the mirror, she adjusted the wide blue belt around her waist
and left the house by the central doorway, feeling the full warmth of the day
settle on her skin. The sky was overcast but very bright, Apu Inti hovering
closely behind a mask of clouds. The sun's position told Micay that she still
had a little time before she had to leave to meet Quinti—enough perhaps to
see if Acapana found her beautiful in her new, simple guise, or if he would have
trouble recognizing her. She looked ahead to the compound gate but did not

see him in his usual place, which was odd, since Apu Poma was doing business in his house in the upper terrace. There were not as many visitors, due to the Capac Raymi being in session, but there were more than enough to keep the two green-clad assistants at the gate fully occupied.

Then she saw him off to her left, sitting on a bench at the base of the terrace wall, his green tunic blending in with the leaves of the cantut bushes on either side of him and the vines trailing down from the garden above. He sat with his long legs extended in front of him, his head bowed over the hands in his lap. He did not look up until Micay's shadow fell across the bench. Then his eyes showed only a dim recognition, none of the approval or surprise she had hoped for. She lifted her chin and began to turn away, but Acapana was up quickly, hopping slightly on his bad foot and holding out his hands in apology.

"Forgive me, Micay. I was not paying attention."

Micay turned back to face him and saw that he was still not paying attention. He was looking at her without really seeing her, half his gaze turned inward. He did not seem capable of noticing the change in her appearance, much less reacting to it. Another long moment passed before the fact of her presence completely penetrated.

"I was—remembering," he explained. "Tomorrow is the fifteenth day."

It took Micay a moment to comprehend the significance of the date, but then she understood why he seemed so stricken.

"The Huarachicoy," she murmured.

Acapana nodded grimly, his eyes on the ground. "The initiation brothers will be running in Cuzco, racing one another down the side of Mount Ana-huarque."

It was during his own initiation, four years before, that Acapana had injured his foot, falling twenty feet onto a rocky ledge after being forced off the trail. He had managed to finish the race anyhow, proving his manhood at the cost of a foot that would never mend properly. He had won the right to wear the golden earplugs of an Inca, but he could never be the warrior they were meant for.

"I hope that you are also remembering the courage you showed that day," Micay said encouragingly. "Surely you do not regret the memory of that."

Acapana lifted his eyes from the ground, his dark face set in a grimace of doubt. "I wonder now if it was truly courage or just impatience and pride. I could have lain where I was and let the healers come tend to me. Perhaps the bones would have healed correctly, and I could have participated in the rites of the following year. But no, I had to get up and go after my initiation brothers. I was one of the best among them, and the thought of being left behind was worse than the pain in my foot. Now they are all in Quito, waiting to march against the Carangui, and I am here."

"Your duties here are important," Micay reminded him. "The micho depends upon you."

"I would rather my commander depended on me, and the warriors under me."

He was looking at the ground again, clinging to his dejection, Micay thought. He had never shown this kind of self-pity before, not even the first time he had told her the story of how he had been injured. He had spurned any hint of sympathy then. His present attitude, in contrast, seemed self-indulgent and unmanly, and insulting to her, as well. He was here with *her*, after all, which should have been some consolation to him.

"Why do you dwell on the past," she inquired in a voice that rose on its own, "when you can do nothing to change it? You dishonor the life you have been given by yearning for the one you feel you have lost."

Even to her own ears the words sounded unduly harsh, her tone of authority thoroughly presumptuous. She had meant to prod him, not rebuke him. She saw his face go blank and his gaze travel past her, his eyes slitted to close her out. An apology came to her lips but stuck there, seeming wholly inadequate.

"I am grateful for your advice, my lady," he said in a brittle voice. "If you will permit me to leave you, I must return to my duties now."

Numbed by the seriousness of her mistake, Micay let him go without another word. It had taken her months to overcome his shyness, and now it might be that long before he revealed his feelings to her again. She looked down at herself, feeling clumsy and artless in her plain dress. But it was too late to change. She headed for the compound gate, hoping again that Quinti, at least, would approve of her appearance. Certainly she had won no admirers for herself here.

Quinti was waiting for her on the terrace above the river, the place from which they had watched the army depart six months before. Now the fields they had seen the warriors trample into mud were planted with row upon row of crops in full leaf, the foliage so high and dense in places that it obscured the irrigation ditches and low stone walls that divided the fields into hundreds of individual plots. Rectangles of bright green maize alternated with the darker, broad-leafed sprawl of squash and beans, and the quinoa stalks were already taking on their distinctive reddish hue. The sky to the east had darkened considerably, and beneath this somber canopy the young crops seemed to glow with color. The Royal Road looked like a broad, dun-colored stripe across the middle of the checkered landscape, an undeviating path that split the plain in two from north to south.

"We will be going out into the fields soon," Micay said, joining Quinti at the parapet. The river below was deep and turbulent, flecked with foam and scraps of vegetation. Quinti gave her a sidelong glance, scanning her face and clothing with one eyebrow raised.

"To the mountains, as well, I have heard."

"We have heard very little. No one knows what the high priestess has planned for us."

"Only because no one will ask her. She makes no secret of what she believes or how she intends to act. You should find her refreshing after my mother and Mama Huarcay."

Micay examined her curiously. Her face seemed severe beneath the plain tan headcloth, her features sharpened by the weight she had lost during the months of fretful waiting. But she no longer seemed so pinched and haggard, and the glaze of misery was gone from her eyes.

"The teaching she arranged appears to agree with you," Micay ventured. "You seem very fit."

"Even though I am too thin? And dressed like one of the mamacona?" Quinti suggested mockingly. She again ran her eyes over Micay's clothing. "Or is it like a chosen woman? My mother has held you up to me as an example, but perhaps she does not know in what way she is correct."

Micay squinted at her in bewilderment.

"There was a time when you spoke back to someone like Mama Huarcay," Quinti said, "rather than around her. But perhaps you have forgotten that."

"I have tried," Micay began, then stopped in confusion. "I do not understand what you mean. Have I done something wrong?"

Quinti stared at her for a moment before replying.

"No. You have been the perfect ñusta. The whole family is proud of you, especially my mother. She sees a great future for you in the court. And there is a space to be filled in her entourage."

"But I have no desire to take your place! You must believe that, Quinti. Even if such a thing were possible, I would not wish for it."

"It does not matter; I do not want it for myself anymore. That is why it pains me to watch you being drawn into a life that is all clever talk and emptiness."

Micay felt a sudden gloom descend upon her and glanced up at the sky. But the dark clouds still hung over the mountains in the distance, and those overhead seemed unsparingly bright.

"I had hoped you had changed," she said dejectedly. "But you have only gotten worse."

"I *have* changed," Quinti insisted fiercely. "But perhaps you are already too much of an Inca to understand how."

Turning abruptly, Quinti started walking toward the bridge that hung over the river. Micay followed after her numbly, stunned by the accusation, which seemed absolutely bizarre. *Too much* of an Inca? What could that mean? She mounted the steps to the next terrace level and walked out onto the bridge behind Quinti. It was a new structure, strung so tautly that the transition from the hard ground to the woven hemp floor was barely perceptible through the thin soles of her sandals. The middle of the bridge rested on a massive stone column that had been built up out of the river like an island, and the rope guardrails were as thick as a man's arm.

Quinti walked to the middle and went to the left-hand guardrail, facing upriver. Micay joined her cautiously, mystified but uncertain that she desired an explanation. Quinti seemed calm again, however.

"You know that this bridge was built solely for the use of the Cañaris who serve in the palace," she said in a mild tone. Micay could only nod in agreement. "It is so strong that it hardly sways in even the most powerful wind. And look," she added, pointing with her chin at two large boulders that broke the current at the base of the support column, "they have even made the river slip past less forcefully."

"The Incas always build well," Micay murmured, beginning to sense that she was being tested in some way. She drew back slightly from the guardrail, distracted by the view of the rushing waters below.

"Yes," Quinti went on, "they are also building stone houses for many of the chiefs, with enclosures of adobe brick. It impresses the common people, who must walk past these houses when they go to work the Inca's fields or to fetch drinking water for themselves. Though in Cuenca, where I teach, it is sometimes hard to walk anywhere, because the streets flood whenever there is a heavy rain."

There was a definite hint of challenge in the last statement, a reminder of Quinti's past complaints, but Micay did not know what kind of response she was expected to make.

"Have you reported this to your father?" she asked finally.

Quinti let out a sharp, incredulous laugh. "Do you think he does not know? It is the micho's duty to know, and he always performs his duties. But he cannot ask Huayna Capac to wait for his palace while some drainage ditches are dug in the north quarter of Tumibamba. The Mollecancha must be finished so that Huayna Capac can enjoy it before he departs for Quito."

"He is the Sapa Inca—"

"—'Lover of the Poor, as great in his generosity as he is in courage,' " Quinti quoted mockingly. "So generous that he can allow his warriors to stand idle in the field for five months while he decides to forgive the Quitos for their rebellion. So brave that he would not risk an attack on their city, so that he might have it undamaged for himself."

Micay restrained an urge to cover her ears. This was the same way Quinti had spoken at the feast, except that her outrage had hardened into a bitter certainty. Still stinging from the way Quinti had laughed at her, Micay abruptly decided to change the subject.

"What will you do when Quilaco returns?"

Quinti released her grip on the guardrail and made a half turn toward Micay, the hard set of her features relaxing into a defensive blankness.

"I will see him, of course."

"He will expect you to accompany him to the Coya's court."

"I will see him alone first and explain what has happened."

"And what if he does not understand?" Micay pressed her. "What if he wants you to stop teaching and resume your place in the court?"

"You have even begun to *sound* like my mother," Quinti said disdainfully, though she continued to avoid Micay's gaze.

"You will lose him to one of the other ñustas, Quinti. I do not believe that *he* does not matter to you; you cannot have changed that much. It was because of him that you first became angry."

Quinti turned all the way around to face her, her voice low and tight, as if the words were hard lumps in her throat.

"When he left me I grieved for him like a widow. But I was prepared to suffer that, as any Inca wife must be. But then when months passed and he still did not return, I began to realize that when he *does* return, it will only be to leave again. There will be no end to wars that are waged so halfheartedly. And what if he is killed in battle? I realized that you cannot expect those you love to share all of your life, and that what is yours alone should not be wasted in waiting. No doubt you understand this very well."

Micay frowned at this assumption, puzzled by it until she remembered Cahua and the other people who had been taken from her. Then she shook her head impatiently.

"I prefer to dwell on what I have rather than what has been lost."

"Exactly," Quinti said with a grim smile. "That is why my mother and Lloque Yupanqui think so highly of you. You will not dwell on what others may have lost, either, to provide you with what you have. You will learn to be as selfish as I was."

Micay thought suddenly of Acapana, and the way she had scolded him for ignoring her. But she resented Quinti's attempt to shame her too much to give in to her guilt, and so she spoke sharply instead.

"I have worked very hard to make myself a ñusta and earn the respect of those above me. Lloque Yupanqui told me that I should be proud of what I have accomplished. Would you have me believe otherwise?"

"You may believe whatever pleases you," Quinti said shortly. "Even what you are taught about the Incas. I will not trouble you any further with the truth."

For the second time Quinti turned and walked away, back the way they had come, and this time Micay did not follow. She noticed that Quinti even walked differently, with her arms straight down at her sides, her hands curled into loose fists. The purposeful force of her stride made the bridge tremble slightly, a ripple of movement that Micay saw more than felt. She shivered, possessed by a sudden fear of standing out here alone, as if she might somehow lose her sense of balance and stumble too close to the edge. But pride kept her from moving until Quinti was out of sight; she did not want Quinti to think that she was pursuing her, chasing after her to apologize.

As soon as Quinti had disappeared down the terrace steps, Micay gave in to her fear and started walking, staying squarely in the center of the bridge and blinking her eyes to blot out all sense of the drop on both sides. She leaned forward over her clasped hands, walking faster, then dropped her hands and began to run. Her long shift flapped around her ankles and caught on her thrusting knees, and she stumbled once and felt the rope floor recoil beneath her weight, sending a spasm of fear through her midsection. But she righted herself and staggered the last few feet to solid ground, expelling the air from her lungs with an audible sigh.

The fear seemed to depart in the same rush, leaving her sweating and trembling and astonished at her sudden loss of control. She felt ridiculous and glanced around to be sure no one had been watching her. Then she composed herself and walked away from the bridge without bothering to look back.

Cuzco

C USI'S EYES were open and seeing for some time before he realized that he was awake and could make out shapes in the room. He was not certain if he had slept, but he knew there was no more use in trying. Most of his initiation brothers were still sleeping around him, though a few were sitting up and a couple of mats had already been vacated. Cusi quietly stripped off the tunic and loincloth he had on and left them folded on his mat. Then he picked up the bundle of clothes next to the mat and went out to wash.

The mountains to the east were visible in outline against a sky turning silver, but the land below was still in darkness, and mist blurred the features of the immediate landscape. Except for the damp chill of the air, Cusi felt he was walking through a dream as he found his way to the bathing pool. It was still too dark to see his reflection in the water as he washed, keeping his distance from the other two boys who had also risen early. When he was dry he moved even farther away, seeking the privacy of a bench shielded by a low retaining wall. Here he undid the bundle, which was composed of a tawny tunic with white fringe, a boy's loincloth of the same basic color, and a narrow waistband that appeared to be solid black.

The garments had come to him all the way from Tumibamba, and he studied them in the growing light for signs of his success in the race. He remembered when one of the long-distance bearers had come to the Patallacta with the much larger bundle containing all of his initiation clothes. "A gift from your mother and sisters," the man had said, and Cusi had corrected him, explaining that he had only one sister. But the bearer had been adamant that "sisters" was what he had been told, and he had begged Cusi to believe him, since the message was as much a part of his burden and responsibility as the garments themselves.

Cusi lifted the waistband and held it close to his face, so that he could make out its true colors. The black band was thickly woven but only three fingers in width, bordered on both edges by a thin red stripe, the color of the Iñaca household. The central motif was a series of jagged vertical lines in Vicaquirao blue, lightning bolts against a black sky. But when Cusi blinked and refocused his eyes, the black seemed to rise up out of the background, forming a series of thicker shafts outlined in blue, shafts that bore a distinct and startling resemblance to Cusi's huaca.

It was this piece that had finally convinced him to believe the bearer, long after he had accepted the man's story out of kindness. Because there were other items that, by custom, had to have been woven by either his mother or Quinti, and the workmanship on this was very different. And why would they have included the Iñaca red when they knew him only in connection with the Vicaquirao? Tomay had agreed that it was the work of another weaver and had further pointed out that the black threads were too soft and shiny to be anything other than vicuña. None of this had helped Cusi determine the identity of this mysterious weaver, except that she was important enough to have received a royal gift of vicuña wool. Cusi could not conceive who it might be; he did not think that *anyone* knew him well enough to have captured the shapes and colors of his life with such uncanny accuracy.

He briefly put the band down and pulled the loincloth on between his legs, adjusting his genitals inside the supple cloth before binding the ends in place with the band. His spirit brother, hidden inside the thick weave of the waistband, was a reassuring lump against his side, and he patted it once before pulling the tunic on over his head, letting it fall loosely almost to his knees. It pleased him that the tunic fit snugly across the shoulders, evidence that he had grown more than his mother had allowed herself to imagine.

Once dressed, he was too restless to sit still and stood up to stretch his limbs, feeling his stomach clench as the fact of the race repossessed his mind. His leg was ready; he would have all of his swiftness, if he could make use of it. But the trail down was narrow and treacherous, and a slower person could hold back those behind him, and perhaps disable anyone who attempted to pass. And then there was the long run from the bottom of the mountain to the parade ground of Sacsahuaman, which required stamina as much as speed. The boy who won today would have to use his head and heart as well as his legs. *And perhaps the warning of his friends,* Cusi thought, remembering his agreement with Tomay. He decided that he should find his friends and wish them luck before they all began the climb up Mount Anahuarque, and were forbidden to speak to one another.

But Ayar Inca intercepted him on his way back to the sleeping quarters, and Cusi let himself be led off to the edge of the plaza. His grandfather addressed him with heightened formality, acknowledging both the importance of the occasion and the distance that had grown between them. He questioned Cusi closely about the details of his fasting and offerings, and about the nature of the prayers he had made during his nightly vigils. He seemed satisfied in most respects, though he chided Cusi for not offering more prayers to Apu Inti, the Lord Sun for whom the Capac Raymi was being celebrated.

"It is natural for a young man to pray to Haunacauri during this time of trial," Ayar Inca allowed. "But as I have told you before, an Inca man needs more than just courage and ferocity. Apu Inti represents wisdom and the fullness of experience, and as you know, in this aspect he is closely identified with Viracocha, the Creator, the founder of all knowledge and custom. Viracocha," he repeated reverently, "who taught the first people how to live, and what was right."

"I will correct this omission, Grandfather," Cusi promised, "before the race begins."

"Good, though I have already prayed on your behalf." Ayar paused and examined him thoughtfully. "Your attachment to Illapa is also very strong for one so young."

"The god has drawn me to him. You know that I am dedicated to his huaca."

"It is only recently, however, that you asked to be included in the Vicaquirao ceremonies. Your devotion seemed sudden, especially since you have chosen not to explain it."

"I could not explain it to myself," Cusi confessed, "and in my confusion I acted secretively. That is why Aranyac sent me to the Grass Man."

"So you felt no need to explain to anyone else?"

"Not to those who treated me with suspicion even *after* I had been cleansed," Cusi said firmly. "But perhaps I was wrong to have believed you would regard me in the same way as the Vicaquirao priests."

Ayar frowned sharply, the lines in his face deepening. Then he inclined his head in recognition. "Perhaps I would have. I would surely have wanted to know how a boy your age could claim to judge the intentions of one so powerful as Illapa."

Cusi hesitated for a moment, remembering Raurau Illa's ambivalent attitude toward the Vicaquirao elders. But then he decided that if he wanted to regain his grandfather's trust, he would have to display some trust of his own.

"I did not rely on my own judgment," he said abruptly. "I was counseled by a man who speaks for the huaca. A man named Raurau Illa."

Astonishment passed across Ayar's face, and he made an involuntary noise in his throat. "You should have reported this to the Vicaquirao elders."

"I meant to, my lord, but they did not invite my confidence."

"Will you tell them now?"

Cusi slowly shook his head. "No, my lord."

"Why not?"

"There are some things you do not surrender to the judgment of other men," Cusi told him, spreading his hands to show that he meant no disrespect, yet fully meeting Ayar's gaze.

"That sounds like the advice of Otoronco Achachi."

"It is, my lord, but I have taken it into my heart and made it my own. And I must ask you to respect my decision. I do not know how Raurau Illa is regarded by the Vicaquirao elders, but I have a bond with him."

Grasping his chin in one hand, Ayar stared down at him, his lips moving soundlessly, as if he were chewing on his words. He seemed to find none of them to his taste for several moments. Then he grunted and dropped his hand from his chin, allowing a rueful smile to creep onto his face.

"Yes, this is how I would have my grandson speak to me when he is a man. And I would expect him to come to me if he is troubled by doubts in the future."

"I will, Grandfather," Cusi promised.

"Very well." Ayar squinted up at the brightening sky, then looked expectantly at Cusi. "It is the tradition, now that I have questioned you, that you may ask me whatever you wish to know."

The outcome of the race was the first thing that came into Cusi's mind, but there was nothing his grandfather could tell him about that. Then he thought of Raurau Illa and recalled Ayar's earlier mention of Viracocha.

"Is there a legend concerning the return of Viracocha?"

Again Ayar appeared taken aback, but he recovered quickly. "I will not ask where you heard of this. Yes, there is such a legend. It states that when Viracocha and his helpers reached the end of the Northern Quarter and were preparing to depart over the Mother Water, Viracocha looked back and promised that he would one day return to rule over the land he had created."

"Why," Cusi said carefully, "why were we not taught this legend in the House of Learning?"

"There has always been doubt about its authenticity, a doubt I share. Pachacuti, I believe, was the first Sapa Inca to order its exclusion from the teachings of the educators, and his successors have done likewise. This is the kind of knowledge that unsettles the people and gives rise to false prophets. It is best left to the priests and elders."

Cusi nodded respectfully, though he remembered Raurau Illa saying that this was the kind of knowledge they needed to know before all else.

"I am grateful for your frankness, Grandfather. I must go now and say my prayers, and prepare myself."

"I will not keep you longer. You should know, though, that a certain Vicaquirao ñusta will be waiting for you at the end of the race. She asked to take the place of your sister and serve you akha when you have finished."

Cusi had not seen or spoken to a woman since the rites began, and he had tried not to let Tocto into his thoughts too often. He felt his cheeks grow warm under Ayar's knowing gaze and made an additional effort to respond in a forthright manner, as a man should.

"You gave your approval, my lord?"

"My permission," Ayar corrected, though gently. "I asked her to persuade me of the wisdom of this, and though she spoke quite sensibly, she succeeded only in convincing me that it is not wisdom that guides her heart." Ayar paused and gave him a significant glance. "You know I esteem wisdom and proper conduct above all else. Perhaps you think I do not esteem courage highly enough, but that is because you are young and preoccupied with proving your own. You will learn, as I have, that the real courage lies in living with the painful things we must carry in our hearts. I believe that Tocto Oxica can help to teach you such courage, and that is why I will not join those who already stand between you."

Sobered by the implications of his grandfather's apparent leniency, Cusi bowed deeply, touching his hands to his shoulders and holding the pose to show that he honored what he had heard.

"Run well, my son," Ayar said in parting. "Run *wisely,* and let Apu Inti guide you down the mountain."

SUMAC MALLQUI had arranged the boys in a line, the slowest in the middle and the swiftest at either end. The head of the trail was two hundred feet away across a shallow, grassy depression; it was framed by shoulder-high outcroppings of gray rock that formed a kind of gate, with an opening wide enough to accommodate perhaps three men abreast. There was no way to tell which way the trail went beyond the opening, and the boys had not been permitted to scout it beforehand, having been brought to the top by a different path.

Cusi was at the far right end of the line, a compliment to his speed that put him at the greatest possible distance from the entrance to the trail. Tomay was to his immediate left, but he had not looked any farther down the line. A strong, swirling wind was blowing, and the white clouds scudding by overhead seemed close enough to touch. Cusi's excitement was blowing like a wind inside him, alternately gusting into confidence and subsiding into dread, exhausting him with the effort to keep himself still during the priests' final prayers. He simply wanted to run and not think anymore about how much he wanted to win this race, or how much he feared losing it, or how many people he wanted to impress. Just let it begin, and let his legs provide the answer.

But then the priests began a loud chant, invoking the blessing of Apu Inti, and Cusi forced himself to raise his eyes from the ground. He took a deep breath and tried to quiet his heart and regain control of his emotions. Wisdom seemed as elusive as the wind in his present state, but he made himself look down the line of boys, noting their positions in the hope that it might tell him something or at least revive his judgment. Uritu and Rimachi were both close to the center of the line, due to their size and slow-footedness, and stationed between them was the hulking figure of Sutic, Mayca's cousin and confederate. Mayca himself was five places from the other end of the line, which put him that much closer to the entrance to the trail, probably enough to nullify Cusi's edge in swiftness.

As Cusi watched, Sutic lifted his head above the bowed heads on either side of him and looked down the line at Mayca, who was already staring in his cousin's direction. Cusi glanced toward the opening between the rock outcroppings, gauging angles and distance, and suddenly he saw what was about to occur. Sutic was fast for a big man, and powerful enough to bowl over anyone in his way; he would not have to maneuver for position like the smaller boys on the outside. If he were the first one to the opening, with Mayca close behind on his left, he could block off Cusi and Tomay while Mayca passed through on the other side. And if he could hold the others behind him long enough for Mayca to build up a sizable lead, there would be no one who could catch up.

Cusi smiled to himself, seeing that in this instance his wisdom and his excitement were in accord. He had to forget strategy and run as hard as he could for the opening. Even at the risk of not being able to stop himself, he had to beat Sutic to the gap. If the trail turned sharply to the right on the other side, he would be in trouble, perhaps enough to end the race right there. But he was not going to hang back and let those two steal it from him before it had barely begun.

Clearing his throat to attract Tomay's attention, he cast a sidelong glance at his friend and loosely assumed a starting position, bending low at the waist as he did when the race was to be short and furious. Then he straightened up and gazed toward the opening, holding the stance until he saw, out of the corner of his eye, Tomay look in the same direction and nod. Cusi smiled to himself again, realizing that having Tomay close might complicate his own plan but deciding that he should not care. If Tomay could keep up with him, they would find a way to go through together, like brothers.

The priests finally fell silent, and Sumac Mallqui walked out in front of the line and mounted a large rock, turning to face them with his long arms raised over his head. He looked up and down the line, pointing with his chin at the boys who had unconsciously crept forward in their places.

"This is your final test," he shouted above the wind. "Soon we will know who is the swiftest of the new earplug men. When I drop my arms, you are off, and may the gods be with you!"

The warrior paused for another moment, his golden earplugs trapped between his neck and shoulders, then brought his arms sweeping down.

"RUN!!"

Cusi leaped out ahead of the line, hitting full stride after only a few steps, his eyes searching the ground ahead, noting rocks and gullies. As soon as he noticed a space opening to his left, he angled in that direction, cutting across in front of Tomay and the next two boys. Then he had to straighten out again to avoid a collision, lowering his head and digging down for more speed, having to trust the blurring contours of the ground. He jumped a gully without slowing even slightly and saw another chance to cut toward the center, where Sutic was pushing out ahead of the ragged line. Now Cusi had the angle he wanted on the gate and went straight for it, aware that Tomay was close behind him on his right.

He looked up when there were twenty-five feet left and saw the scene just as he had imagined it: Sutic and Mayca running side by side, out ahead of the others, Sutic beginning to veer in Cusi's direction, cutting off the angle between Cusi and the rock ledges that framed the opening. The rocks suddenly seemed very distinct, hard and sharp. Cusi heard Tomay whoop behind him and knew that he should slow down now or give up any chance of dodging the collision that appeared inevitable.

But then Rimachi charged into the narrowing space between Sutic and Cusi, his thick legs churning and his face contorted with effort, pushing himself past his limit. He drew even with Sutic and startled him into moving aside. Cusi saw his chance and shot forward through the gap between the rocks and a lunging Sutic, who threw himself into Rimachi's path in his attempt to stop Cusi. Cusi whooped to warn Tomay as he felt Rimachi and Sutic go down in a tangle just behind him.

Then he was through the opening and was plunging down the trail, which went straight down for about fifteen feet before veering sharply to the right. Cusi skidded through the loose dirt on his buttocks, using every foot to slow his momentum. Mayca had reached the bottom ahead of him and was the first onto the trail that led down to the right. He took the inside half of the path, against the hillside, leaving plenty of room for Cusi to pass if he dared. But Cusi was still recovering from the effort of getting through the gate and was content to follow Mayca at a safe distance, especially when he noticed the prickly pear cactus along the outside of the trail and the steep drop-off just beyond.

The trail narrowed and switched back to the left, demanding another frantic effort to slow down and resist the outward pull of momentum. When he had made the turn and was back on Mayca's heels, Cusi glanced back over his shoulder and saw that it was Tomay whose footsteps he had been hearing behind him. So his friend had also made it through the melee at the gate. Only a couple of others were within sight, and they were some distance back. I owe this race to Rimachi, Cusi thought, if I win it. He was willing to let Mayca set the pace as the path zigzagged down the mountain, continually switching back from left to right. He needed only to be this close at the bottom to know that he would overtake Mayca on flat ground. Then Tomay would be the one he would have to contend with.

They ran one behind another for some time, maintaining a pace that did not make them fight the turns. The distance between switchbacks began to lengthen as they descended, and the drop from one course to the next became less steep and forbidding. Tomay was the first to succumb to the temptation to cut the distance. Cusi heard a crash behind him and glanced back to see Tomay disappear over the side of the trail in a cloud of dust, his arms flailing for balance. When Mayca and Cusi made the turn onto the next course, they saw Tomay up and running a hundred feet ahead, his back covered with a red dust that came off his shoulders in small puffs.

Mayca did not require any pressure from Cusi to respond to the challenge, and after two more switchbacks, they were back in single file with no more than six feet separating one from the other. Then Mayca began putting pressure on Tomay, not allowing him to maintain a comfortable pace and coming up hard behind him on every turn, threatening to bump him over the side or simply make him overrun the turn. Tomay stubbornly held him off, straining hard to keep his balance at the switchbacks, which had begun to widen out into landings as they neared the base of the mountain. Just before one of these landings, a break in the trail forced Tomay to the inside, and Cusi saw Mayca go to the outside and speed up, his shoulder already lowered to crash into Tomay when the path came together again at the landing. Cusi whooped and sprang up behind Mayca, distracting him long enough for Tomay to get through the turn untouched. They all came down onto the next course staggering and out of control. Then Mayca tripped and went sprawling, just missing Tomay's heels as he went down.

There was no time for Cusi to slow down and no room on the path to go around, so he took two hard steps and went up in the air, hurtling Mayca while he was still tumbling forward. Cusi was just coming down when Mayca suddenly threw up an arm and caught Cusi's trailing leg, flipping him over in the air. Cusi crashed down on his side, one arm twisted under him, the other slamming the ground in concert with his head. There was a loud ringing sound and no air in his lungs, and then a sharp pain in his wrist. He was roused by a foot coming down close to his face and he struggled to get up, thinking that Mayca was passing him. But when he was finally able to rise, he saw that it was two other boys who had passed him. Mayca and Tomay were no longer in sight.

Cusi forced himself into a clumsy trot, favoring his bruised hip and pressing his injured wrist against his stomach with his other hand. He felt wide-eyed and witless from the shock of the fall, but he made himself go on, trying to keep the other two boys in sight. It was hard to keep air in his lungs, and every breath seemed to set off swelling pains in his head, hip, and wrist. He wondered vaguely if the wrist were broken or only sprained. Then he wondered if more than two boys had passed him while he was down. The thought brought him back to himself and made him run a little faster, testing his hip, which hurt but did not collapse under him. He also managed to free an arm for balance by tucking up his tunic and grabbing hold of his waistband with one hand, immobilizing his injured wrist against his side. It was awkward and painful to run half hunched over, but it was not impossible. He was no longer thinking about winning the race, simply of not finishing a disgraceful distance back.

So he began to concentrate solely on his running, trying to establish a pace that let him anticipate the dips and rises and breaks in the trail, so that he would not waste any energy or take any risks in getting past them. He could not take another fall and expect to be able to get up again, so he was prudent out of necessity, slowing almost to a walk on some of the switchbacks. The two boys ahead had not lost him, though they were usually turning down onto the next course just as Cusi entered the one above. He had recognized the taller of the two boys as Titu, a boy not noted for his speed but among the best at long distances. He would have to be pleased to be so close to the front with the longest part of the race still ahead. Cusi doubted, though, that any of them would catch sight of Mayca and Tomay again.

As he turned down onto the last course, he saw Titu and the other boy come out onto a wide, well-defined road that wound across a boulder-strewn plain for a short distance before disappearing around the side of another hill. A herd of white alpacas was grazing on one side of the road, and as he came down onto the level ground, Cusi saw that some of the herd boys had come to the roadside to watch the race. Titu and the other boy went past them without stopping, but Cusi approached more slowly and saw that they were standing next to a stone irrigation channel that ran under the road. They were surprised when he stopped in front of them, but they parted quickly enough to let him kneel beside the clear, flowing water. He alternated drinking with washing, so that he would not drink too much at once, and he soaked his swollen wrist in the icy water for several moments to numb the ache. When he rose he could feel the stiffness in his hip and the sting of the abrasions on the side of his head, and he left streaks of blood on his tunic when he used it to pat himself dry. The herd boys stared at him in silence as he limped back up to the road. Their narrow black headbands told him that they were Soras, probably the sons of mitmacs who had been settled here long ago. Cusi remembered the woolen sling around his own head and took it off and began wrapping it tightly around his wrist, grimacing at the pain. He glanced back at Mount Anahuarque and saw figures moving three courses up.

"How many are ahead of me?" he asked the boys, startling them again. The biggest one held up four fingers. Cusi clenched his fist to tighten the wrapping and gingerly swung his arm in circles, testing the movement for pain. He looked again at the boys, remembering the herd boys he had outrun the day he had met Raurau Illa. He felt he should say something, affirm that this was a sign.

"The Soras can carry anything," he said abruptly. "They help carry the Sapa Inca's litter."

The boys nodded warily, too disconcerted to show pride.

"How do they carry their pain?" Cusi asked, and after a moment, the biggest boy risked a slight smile and pointed at Cusi's bound wrist.

"Like that. Like a bundle that belongs to someone else."

Cusi saw the other boys' smiles before he felt the smile that was on his own face, and he was amazed to hear himself laugh.

"I will do that, then," he cried, shaking the arm in a kind of salute as he started off up the road, measuring his pace to let his sore hip loosen up gradually. The water had revived him and allowed him to see that he was not seriously injured. The pain he had to carry seemed much lighter without the additional weight of the fear of not finishing. He would finish, and ahead of all those still behind him, in fifth place at least.

He glanced up and realized that the herd boys were running along beside him, matching his careful pace. Cusi increased his speed but only slightly, only as much as was comfortable. He concentrated on running smoothly and let the boys stay beside him until they fell away of their own accord.

HE RAN alone until he reached the Western Quarter Road, which was lined with the houses of mitmacs and the pleasure compounds of the high Incas. The people came out to watch him pass, and Cusi distracted himself from his pain by recognizing their origins in their clothing and headdresses. There were Soras, Rucanas, Chinchas, Nazcas . . . groups from all the tribes who lived in the Western Quarter.

Only the servants of the Incas watched from the compound doorways, since all the Incas were up on Sacsahuaman awaiting the finish of the race. Occasionally someone would call out to Cusi in encouragement, but most stared at him in silence, bowing respectfully as he passed.

He was near a place called Picchu, still outside of Cuzco proper, when he passed the boy who had been running with Titu. He was sitting by the side of the road, soaking a sore foot in an irrigation ditch, and Cusi would have not seen him at all had the boy not raised a weary hand in acknowledgement. Cusi waved back in surprise, and the boy pointed ahead and shouted.

"Not far!"

Buoyed by this unexpected encouragement, Cusi had to struggle against the urge to pick up his pace. He told himself the boy could only be referring to Titu, because there was no way Cusi could have made up ground on Tomay and Mayca. He had maintained too prudent a speed and had stopped to drink too many times. He decided he was better off without the goad of vain hopes and ran on at the same pace, telling himself only that fourth was better than fifth.

As he passed the guardhouse and approached the Cusipata, the huge square adjacent to the Haucaypata, he finally saw someone in the middle of the road ahead, walking very slowly. But it was Mayca, not Titu. He was still trying to go forward, hobbled by a limp that kept changing from one leg to the other as his muscles alternately relaxed and seized up. As Cusi came up behind him, Mayca cried out and grabbed his thigh, staggering sideways like a wounded man. Cusi saw what he himself must have looked like after Mayca had kneed him in the wrestling, and he was tempted to put Mayca down with a stiff forearm to the back as he passed. Instead he paused beside him, running in place until Mayca looked up at him, his face contorted with pain. The surprise in Mayca's eyes turned quickly to something like hope, surprising Cusi with its sudden intimacy.

"Hurry!" Mayca gasped, waving Cusi on. "Catch them! Do not let the Colla be first!"

Cusi's hatred welled up in a rush that made him want to spit, though his mouth was too dry to permit such a gesture.

"Better him than you," he snapped and ran on, mounting the broadly terraced steps that led up to the Cusipata. The square was half filled with a crowd of warriors, Incas by privilege with their gold and silver earplugs and their stiff battle standards held aloft on the ends of spears. They greeted Cusi's appearance with a roar of encouragement that made him throw back his head and stretch out his legs, forgetting his pain completely. The men on both sides of the pathway through their ranks were shouting at him, gesturing with their spears and war clubs, as if urging him into a battle that lay just ahead.

"Run, Inca!" Cusi heard. "You are almost on their heels!"

Cusi did not know how that was possible, but he could feel the strength that was left in his legs and he began to think again about winning. Then he left the square and started up the long street called Saphi, under which the Saphi River flowed. It was quiet again, with only a few servants watching from the compound entrances, but Cusi paid no attention to them once he spotted the two runners ahead. Tomay and Titu were trotting along side by side at a pace that seemed agonizingly slow, labored rather than prudent. The incline of the street had begun to rise as they approached the base of Sacsahuaman, but Cusi maintained his speed, wanting to overtake them before they began the climb to the fortress above.

Before he could reach them, though, they both stopped to drink from the fountain at the bottom of the steep trail that led up the side of the hill. Cusi had a momentary urge to run right past them and take his drink at the top, but one glance at their weary faces, as they looked up from the fountain, made him slow and come to a halt beside them. They were both as bruised and bloodied from falls as he was, and neither showed the slightest inclination to rush off and protect their lead. Cusi squatted with them and drank, aware again of his own pain and fatigue.

"No one will catch us from behind," he said as they rose in unison and turned toward the trail. Titu was favoring his right foot, and one of Tomay's eyes was swollen shut, so that he had to turn his whole head to glance at Cusi's sling-wrapped wrist.

"Mayca did his best to finish all of us," Tomay muttered as the three of them started up the trail together, working through their various aches and injuries before settling into a patient uphill jog. They climbed steadily, passing the Hawk Enclosure halfway up. Cuzco was below them to their right, and they could see the crowd of warriors in the Cusipata, with the open pathway through their midst. They were nearing the top, reduced to a hard walk by the grade, when Titu began to fade back. Cusi and Tomay faded with him for a while without knowing it, their heads down over the trail. But then they found themselves halfway up the final flight of stairs and realized simultaneously that Titu was no longer with them. They looked back and Titu raised a hand to them, shaking his head as he forced himself up the steps, one at a time.

Cusi and Tomay drank again at the top, staring at each other across the rippling surface of the small pool.

"We owe this race to Rimachi," Cusi said finally, and Tomay nodded emphatically, his puckered eye making him appear to be winking.

"Run well, Inca," Tomay said brusquely, and they took off across the grassy plain in front of the fortress, matching strides in an easy lope. Neither forced the pace, since they both knew a steep climb awaited them once they rounded the wall at its westward end. They would save themselves for the parade ground on the other side of the fortress. Then, in front of the assembled Incas, the race would resume over the four hundred feet of level ground to the finish line, which was even with the stone seat of the Sapa Inca. Cusi was no longer certain how much strength he had in his legs and lungs, and he did not know if he could force his bruised hip into a real sprint. He was grateful to have made it this far, and the opportunity to win still seemed an unbelievable gift. He glanced sideways at Tomay, wondering what the battle with Mayca for the lead had cost him and how much he had left.

Then they rounded the end of the wall and the trail narrowed, bringing them elbow to elbow as the path dipped down and then began a long, twisting ascent to the high ground at the far end of the wall. They ran along the base of the great stone rampart, Tomay on the inside against the wall and Cusi along the outer edge of the trail. To Cusi's left, there was only air and a hundred-foot drop to the gorge below, but he chose to trust Tomay with his safety rather than try to cut in ahead or behind him. This is the last hill you will climb today, he told himself, leaning into the slope and gritting his teeth against the searing pains in his hips and knees.

Shouts from above made him lift his head, and he saw that the crest of the hill was near and that the people on top of the wall beside them were shouting and waving their mantles. He and Tomay came up over the rise and rounded the end of the wall at the same moment, and were engulfed by a great roar of greeting from the thousands of people who lined the ramparts that flanked the parade ground on both sides. The sound seemed to stand the boys upright for a moment, their eyes dazzled by the flashing of gold and silver amid the richly colored garments of the onlookers. Then Tomay let out a whoop and started running, and Cusi went after him, his own whoop lost in the excited cries of the crowd.

Sound blurred and vision shrank, and Cusi was aware only of the boy beside him, arms and legs pumping, teeth bared, one eye glinting sidelong as Cusi drew even. Cusi tried to pull out ahead, but it was as if there were a hand pushing down on the point of his hip, preventing it from rising any higher. He could go no faster than this, and he was not certain he could maintain even this pace all the way to the end. The wind seemed to whip past his face without entering his open mouth, leaving his lungs burning and empty. Tomay began to draw away and Cusi could only watch the distance open between them, thinking, the Colla will be first after all. But then Tomay seemed to falter and came back beside him, and Cusi thought, we will finish together, like brothers. They were running side by side, their strides perfectly matched, and Cusi surrendered to the rhythm with a kind of relief, letting go of his thoughts and devoting the last of his energy to the sole task of making it to the end.

Figures suddenly loomed up ahead and he heard their shouts over the roaring in his ears. Out of the corner of his eye he saw Tomay lift his head and thrust his chest forward, reaching for an extra bit of speed with his whole body, lunging for the chalk line across the grass ahead. Surprised out of his rhythm, Cusi felt a sharp pang of disappointment, and though he tried, he could summon no more from himself. He had even slowed slightly, accepting defeat, when he saw Tomay lose his footing and hit the ground with one knee, arms flailing wildly as he pitched headlong onto the grass, ten feet short of the white line.

Cusi swerved instinctively, and his momentum carried him past Tomay and over the line, his feet kicking up a cloud of white dust as he staggered to a stop. He bent double, gasping for air with his hands on his knees. Immediately people crowded in around him on all sides, putting their hands on his back and shouting incoherently in his ear. He straightened up and tried to turn around, but his way was blocked by the massive figure of Otoronco Achachi, who waved him forward with both hands.

"Do not stop yet!" he bellowed. "Claim your prize before you rest!"

Dazed and breathless, Cusi stumbled forward, seeing the terraced hillside covered with faceless people, rising up like a headdress above the double stone seat that had been carved into the bedrock at the base of the hill. Huascar and the Regent, Cusi thought dimly, though his attention shifted quickly from the occupants of the seat to the group of small white statues laid out on the ground in front of the seat. They were arranged in neat rows, forming a pyramidal pattern, and Cusi stooped to pick up the statue that stood at the apex: a replica of the huaman, the mountain hawk, the swiftest of all creatures. He cradled it in the crook of one arm, feeling the rough grain of its surface against his skin, for it had been carved out of salt. For the first time, he realized he had won the race.

A moment later Tomay stepped past him and lifted up the replica of the guanaco, the fleet wild cousin of the llama. He stepped back beside Cusi without looking at him, facing the occupants of the stone seat. Auqui Topa Inca and Huascar sat in the places of the Sapa Inca and the Coya, the Regent holding a long painted staff that bore the mascapaycha, the royal fringe, at its tip. He tilted the staff at the two boys, who bowed in unison.

"In the name of the Sapa Inca," he proclaimed, "I commend you, my sons. You have shown the courage and fortitude for which the Inca are known, and you have given us a race that we will all remember. A race worthy of the Capac Raymi!" With an unusual display of animation, the Regent struck his chest with the flat of his hand. "Word of this will be sent to Huayna Capac in Tumibamba, and your names will be on the lips of every Inca in the Four Quarters. I salute you, Cusi Huaman, and you, Tomay Guanaco!"

Auqui Topa Inca raised the staff over his head and shook it, at which the hillside behind him erupted in cheers and whistles that were soon answered by a similar clamor from the crowd atop the jagged ramparts on the other side of the parade ground. Cusi felt his skin prickle as the sound swirled around him and he heard his name being shouted aloud. He glanced sideways at Tomay, whose round cheeks were mottled with a high color that could have been pride, disappointment, or simply exhaustion. The eye on Cusi's side was swollen shut, so that he could catch no glimmer of how his friend was feeling. Tomay had not been content to share the victory; he had had more ambition at the end, or a greater need to prove himself. He had risked everything to win, displaying more of the Inca spirit than Cusi had been able to muster.

When the crowd had quieted, the Regent handed his staff to an attendant and gestured for the Heir to speak. Huascar seemed to have grown larger since Cusi had last seen him, though he was still dwarfed by the spacious dimensions of the great stone seat. His eyes were hidden in the shadow of the yellow fringe he wore around his forehead.

"Apu Inti smiled upon you today," he said to Cusi. "The Colla was ahead when his foot slipped."

"He was, my lord," Cusi agreed, with another glance at Tomay. "I thought that I was beaten."

"Yet the god interceded for you," Huascar concluded triumphantly, leaning forward in his seat. Then he sat back and spoke in a sententious tone to Tomay. "You see, Colla, what it means to be one of the sons of Inti. He will never allow his children to be defeated."

Cusi recalled Tomay once saying he would never do anything to provoke the Heir. Now he stood silent, not acknowledging that he saw what Huascar meant or found it of any significance. It had been a pointless boast offered as a piece of royal wisdom, and Cusi was proud that Tomay would not dignify it with a reply. Cusi stood up straight beside him while Huascar let the silence stretch on awkwardly. Finally the Regent interrupted, gesturing with his open palm to the left side of the seat.

"You are weary, my sons. Greet your sisters, then, and refresh yourselves with the akha they have prepared for you."

The crowd next to the seat parted and two ñustas emerged carrying drinking cups and jars of akha. Tomay's sister went to him, and Tocto Oxica stopped in front of Cusi and bowed over her jar. The two young women spoke almost in unison, with Tocto deliberately drawing out her words so that her companion would not fall behind.

"Greetings, Brother Inca. You have run far, and you have run well. Please accept my gift of akha for the honor you have brought to your kin."

Cusi fumbled with his statue for a moment, finally freeing his good hand to take the wooden cup she held out to him. He wanted so much just to look at her that he had trouble remembering the words he was supposed to say.

"I am grateful, my sister," he managed belatedly, and heard Tomay repeat the words after him. The cup felt extremely heavy in his hand, and his arm shook with fatigue as he held it out for her to fill. His embarrassment made him aware of all the people watching, including Huascar, but Tocto merely laughed softly and rose up on her toes, tipping her jar with a generous motion that wet the ground all around them while filling the cup to overflowing with foaming gray akha. Tomay's sister took longer in filling her brother's cup, and Cusi waited until Tomay was ready before turning toward the west and lifting his cup in a salute to Inti.

"To our Father," he said, pouring a small amount onto the ground in a symbolic sharing. Then he raised his cup to the Regent and the Heir before putting it to his lips and letting the cool, nearly flavorless liquid flow down his parched throat. He closed his eyes and lost himself in the wonderful sensation of wetness for a moment, remembering the water he had drunk with the Sora herd boys and their advice on how to carry his pain. He drank to them silently, and to Rimachi, as well. As he lowered the cup, he saw Tocto's quick, dark eyes on him and could not keep himself from smiling. He suddenly felt drunk and incapable of saying anything, but he was rescued by the arrival of Titu, who had just crossed the finish line and was being ushered forward to claim his prize. Cusi remembered to bow in the direction of the stone seat before allowing Tocto to lead him away.

"Did I forget anything?" he asked dazedly, bending to speak into her ear.

"You forgot how a brother is supposed to look at his sister," Tocto told him, not sounding displeased. "But no one will find fault with you today, Cusi Huaman."

" 'Cusi Huaman,' " he repeated. "My mother used to call me that, when I was small and weak."

"Perhaps she foresaw this day," Tocto suggested seriously, "when everyone would recognize your specialness."

Before he could respond, they were confronted by a large crowd of well-wishers that included many of the high-ranking members of both the Iñaca and Vicaquirao households, all subtly jostling one another to be among the first to congratulate him. Tocto quickly stepped in front of him and whispered as she refilled his cup.

"I must not share any more of your fame. I will find you later, at the dance."

Cusi felt a powerful urge to keep her with him, but he did not have a hand free to restrain her, and her eyes warned him off. So he forced himself to let her go without another word, raising his eyes to the people in front of him and pretending that they had all of his attention, that his heart was not following Tocto through the crowd. The sight of Ayar Inca among the Vicaquirao elders only made him feel his abandonment more acutely, as he remembered what his grandfather had said about Tocto earlier. Like a bundle that does not belong to you, Cusi thought, nodding earnestly at the compliments being showered upon him, trying to accept the fame the gods had given to him alone.

Tumibamba

T HE FINAL stage of the ñustas' training took them out of the city on a pilgrimage to the more distant shrines and huacas that were in the keeping of women. Their itinerary had been set by the high priestess, Chimpu Ocllo, who did not appear herself but supplied two mamacona, both Cañaris, to act as guides. These women marched the girls toward the mountains to the east, maintaining a silent, purposeful pace and stopping only occasionally for water. They spent the first night in a rest house on the plain, surrounded by potato fields and grazing flocks of llamas and alpacas. On the second night they reached the Lynx House, an elaborate mountainside complex that belonged to the cult of Mama Quilla. They were fed and allowed to bathe, but none of the resident mamacona came to greet them or show them the shrines in and around the Lynx House itself.

Before they set out the next morning, each girl was given two blankets to carry in addition to the lengths of cloth and bags of coca leaves they had brought as offerings. As Micay slung her consolidated bundle over her shoulder, she saw the other ñustas exchanging glances that ranged from quizzical to anxious. The initiates had never had to be their own bearers when this was done in Cuzco, or so they had been told. The mamacona waited patiently for them to assemble and then started up the trail without a word. They climbed for half a day before stopping at a cave in the side of the mountain. Shedding their sandals and bundles, they entered a long, oblong chamber that narrowed to a crack at its far end. The mamacona led them past the crevice one by one, so that they could feel and hear the warm, murmuring wind that seemed to well up out of the heart of the mountain, the bosom of Pachamama, the Earth Mother. Though the cave was unattended, each of them left an offering along with the prayers they chanted to Pachamama.

Then they again hefted their bundles and climbed still higher, circling around to the other side of the mountain, to another cave that was also the source of a spring. After another ceremony to Pachamama, the girls were permitted to drink from the spring and were given a meal of roast potatoes and wild greens prepared by the two Cañari women who lived in a stone hut next to the cave. The ñustas slept inside the cave itself, wrapped in their blankets on the hard stone floor. Micay was almost too exhausted to shiver when the night cold began to penetrate her blankets, and her head was aching from soroche, the sickness of the heights. She thrust her clasped hands down between her thighs, listening to the moans of the other girls, which mingled eerily with the sound of dripping water. She remembered the warm whisper of wind she had felt in the first cave, a comforting presence that fit her sense of the Earth Mother. Was Pachamama to be found here, as well, in this cold, damp, hollow place where there seemed to be neither warmth nor comfort? Micay was shivering now, despite her fatigue, and she was astonished that Chimpu Ocllo would subject them to this sort of hardship without a word of warning. Then she remembered Quinti saying that no one had asked the high priestess about her intentions. Was this her revenge, her way of showing Rahua Ocllo and the Cuzco wives that she would not be scorned and ignored? It hardly seemed like the action of a holy woman, though Micay was uncertain what to expect from such a person. She did not even know what to expect from their tireless, taciturn guides. Numb with cold and uncertainty, she decided to pray rather than moan, making up her own words to ask Pachamama to warm and protect her, and to give her the strength to rise in the morning.

When the mamacona led them deeper into the mountains on the next day, a number of the girls began to lag behind on the trail. As she moved up in the line, Micay was aware that the laggards were whispering to one another as they climbed, no doubt discussing their predicament. Their weariness had been apparent in their drawn faces and the stiffness of their movements upon rising, and the only food they had been given before departing was a handful of tiny, cold potatoes each. Micay had noticed reluctant expressions on several faces as the ñustas left their offerings of fine cloth outside the hut of the cave's caretakers.

For her own part, Micay was hungry but otherwise did not feel as awful as she had expected. She had somehow managed to get some sleep, and she was becoming accustomed to the aching light-headedness of altitude sickness, which seemed less annoying when she was moving. Since the other girls were not likely to include her in their whispering, she decided to leave them behind and worked her way forward until she was directly following the mamacona. This made her feel even better, since the women were both careful and sure-footed, and their example saved her the work of anticipating the breaks in the trail. It also occurred to her that they were the only ones who knew the way out of this wilderness and where to find what food and water there was, a fact that seemed to leave very little to whisper about.

When they finally stopped next to a mountain stream lined with brilliant green moss, Micay turned to watch the rest of the ñustas straggle in. Those closest behind her were also foreigners, the daughters of high chiefs. Then came the daughters of Incas by privilege and some of the Inca girls from the Lower Cuzco households. The last to arrive were the highest in rank, Upper Cuzco ñustas whose mothers or sponsors were close to the Coya or one of the other royal wives. Four of these girls came up to the mamacona and bowed in unison, presenting themselves as a delegation. A girl named Amancay, a niece of the Coya, spoke for them in a Cuzco Quechua that made the mamacona squint. She demanded to know why they were being marched like recruits for the army, and why they were being starved when they had under-taken no fast. The two Cañari women nodded deferentially, though they did not seem intimidated. The older one spoke succinctly, as if the explanation were too simple to require many words.

"Because we only have eight days, and there are many places we must visit. We will have our share of food wherever we go. Where it is plentiful, we will have plenty."

"Why were no preparations made for our coming?" Amancay persisted.

"We are expected everywhere. That is why we have these places to our-selves."

Amancay glanced around at the deserted landscape, raising her eyebrows in a display of skepticism.

"Who else is there? We have seen no one since we left the high plain."

"That has also been arranged," the mama assured her. "Our solitude will not be disturbed."

"That is what you mean by preparations?" Amancay inquired weakly, looking around at her companions for aid. One of the other girls, a favorite of Mama Huarcay, spoke out in exasperation.

"*Why* must we visit all of these places?"

"Because they are holy," the mama said with a finality none of the girls could contradict. She gestured at the stream with her chin, indicating that they should drink. Then she and the other mama shouldered their bundles and began to cross the stream by means of a stepping-stone bridge. Micay felt the girls' attention shift to her when she picked up her own bundle and started after the mamacona, but she had been alone in their midst all along, so their opinion was not going to deter her now—not when she had been given a reason for going on that made all complaints seem petty and self-pitying, a judgment on the complainer. Because they are holy, she repeated to herself as she stepped out over the rushing water of the stream, watching her feet, knowing that she should not go grudgingly toward whatever lay ahead.

IN THE DAYS that followed, the mamacona led them down into canyons barely touched by the sun and up onto desolate plateaus where the wind shrieked in their ears. They visited hot springs where ferns grew high in the sulfurous steam, and they worshiped at patches of wind-carved rock watched over by solitary women with leathery skin and staring eyes, women who spoke neither Quechua nor Cañar. They saw a waterfall that plunged through the arch of a perpetual rainbow and a mountain that rumbled and smoked, and at night the great white river of stars flowed across the sky, shedding single drops that left silver streaks on the blackness as they fell. As her bundle was emptied of its offerings, so Micay herself felt lighter, emptied of her former concerns. She could see for great distances in the thin air, but in every direction there were only more mountains and forests, extending endlessly, utterly beautiful and utterly wild. The thin air also gave her vivid dreams that were filled with birds and animals, dreams in which she walked on paths rather than streets. In one of these dreams she met her mother, who spoke to her in Chacha and gave her another blanket to keep her warm. Micay did indeed feel warmer, but she awoke in a fright, breathless and unable to recognize her surroundings or the people sleeping next to her. Nor could she recall later what her mother had said to her in the dream.

Soon after this, she saw a condor soaring among the peaks and remembered the dream she had had in the House of Chosen Women. She remembered the bridge bouncing beneath her, the condor recognizing her as he flew past, the way she had moved without willing it, watching the condor fly off over a landscape as vast and compelling as this. When she looked up again, the condor was gone, and she was startled by the vacant blue of the sky. But then the great black bird reappeared out of the shadow of the cliff face, circling lazily over the canyon from which the girls were departing. The trail was steep and narrow, forcing Micay to confine herself to occasional glances upward. I am not the person in the dream, she thought, at least not here. But she understood the terror that had come to her on the bridge in Tumibamba, where Quinti had suggested to her that she had become selfish and forgetful of her past. Now her past was returning to her in dreams and in memories of dreams, making her think that she *had* been walking blindly, her gaze fixed on becoming a ñusta.

They came out of the mountains on the eighth day, returning to the same rest house where they had spent their first night. Waiting to greet them were members of the cult of Axomama, the Potato Mother. Micay was right behind the mamacona, and she watched the expressions on the women's faces— especially those of the Inca wives—change as they got a closer look at the ñustas. Micay suddenly realized how dirty and disheveled she was, her lips dry and chapped, her hair dusty, her whole face wind-burned. She had not looked in a mirror since leaving the city, and none of them had bathed properly since their visit to the hot springs several days earlier. She knew she must look like one of the women who tended the huacas and spoke in voices as wild as the land itself.

The wives seemed to notice, as well, the order in which the ñustas were walking, a reverse ranking that had grown more pronounced during the course of their journey. Amancay and her friends, along with about half of the group, had gone most grudgingly to the holy places, staying just within sight of the mamacona on the trail and delaying as long as possible in catching up. On several occasions they had chosen to go hungry rather than eat food they thought insufficient or too coarse, and they had refused to help gather firewood or fetch water when it was needed. In front of the Inca women, they took on an air of injured dignity, letting their mothers and aunts and sponsors know that they had been made to suffer but had borne it like Incas. It was a somber group that followed the priestesses of Axomama to the potato field that belonged to the cult, which lay close to the rest house.

The ceremony was relatively brief, with chanted prayers to Mama Quilla, who governed the time of planting and harvesting, to Pachamama, who made the earth fertile, and to Axomama, whose spirit lived underground and made the tubers ripen and grow firm and large. Akha was spilled onto the soil, and cups of the drink were ceremoniously passed from the older women to the younger. Then everyone took up short-handled hoes and worked in lines, piling up earth around the base of the young plants. They sang in Quechua as they worked, songs that Micay could understand but which did not touch her as deeply as the indescribable keenings of some of the huaca keepers. She was distracted, too, by the presence of so many people, and she felt tension rather than reverence in the periods of silence between songs.

When they had all retired to the rest house, she heard the explaining and complaining begin in earnest, first in whispers as it had on the trail, then in voices that rose in outrage and disbelief and were meant to be overheard. She had been told that this was the time when the women of the cult would speak to the ñustas about becoming new members, but they were preoccupied instead with eliciting the details of what the ñustas had undergone. They crowded around Amancay and her friends and totally ignored Micay and the few other girls who had no relatives or sponsors present. Micay was content to be ignored, because she was repelled by the complaining and by the eagerness of the listeners, who seemed to take pleasure in their shock. She could not have shared with them what *she* had experienced: the overwhelming power of the mountains and the sky, the raw beauty of a land without people or cities, the peculiar thrill, half fear and half exhilaration, that had possessed her at certain of the huacas. The latter, especially, was unlike anything she had ever felt before, and certainly not something to be spoken of in querulous whispers. So she withdrew from the others and went to sit in the corner with the two mamacona, who appeared oblivious of the controversy and accepted her company with their usual wordless tolerance.

The next day the entire group descended into the valley, down to the maize plots that belonged to the cult of Saramama. These were on terraces above the Tumibamba River, enclosed by low walls of finely fitted stone. A party of priestesses and wives was waiting at the entrance to the field, and Micay again saw expressions of dismay and concern slip through their composure as they perceived the condition of the ñustas. Mama Cori was among the greeters. She, of course, betrayed no reaction, though her eyes traveled all the way to the end of the column before returning to linger on Micay. Micay met her gaze with a firmness meant to convey her lack of injury or complaint, lifting her chin for emphasis. Mama Cori's eyes widened slightly but then went past Micay again, making her wonder if her message had been understood, or if Mama Cori would have preferred to find her at the rear rather than the head of the line.

Shedding their sandals and bundles next to the wall, the ñustas followed the high priestess of Saramama into the field, where the ceremonies of the Maize Mother would be held. They squatted in the aisles between the rows of young plants, at eye level with the leafy tips. Micay's feet sank into the rich, weedless soil beneath her and her nostrils filled with the odors of freshly turned earth and the guano that had been spread as fertilizer. The sun was warm on her head and shoulders, and she found herself feeling drowsy, lulled by the familiarity of the songs and chants. She knew them all by heart, since Mama Cori had taught her with the expectation that she would be asked to join the cult when she was a fully fledged ñusta. She could dimly remember the enthusiasm she had once felt at the prospect, though the effort of remembering only seemed to add to her fatigue. She settled back onto her heels, barely able to keep her eyes open. As exhausted as she had been in the mountains, she had never felt this sleepy. The ceremony seemed to go on forever, and she came close to losing her balance several times. Only the knowledge that her fatigue would be blamed on the mamacona kept her from surrendering to the urge to fall over.

As soon as she could rise and move around, joining the other women in cleaning the irrigation ditch that ran down the center of the plot, her lethargy left her and she felt clearheaded again. She worked hard at the various tasks she was asked to perform, making up in her own heart for the inattention she had suffered during the prayers to Saramama. The rites of the Maize Mother were important to the well-being of the crop, and she did not wish to slight them simply because they did not inspire her as the huacas had.

Afterward, as the women left the enclosure and congregated on the path outside, Micay saw the two mamacona pick up their bundled blankets and start back toward Tumibamba. Their task was finished, since all the shrines still to be visited were within the city and their guidance would not be required. Heads turned to observe their departure, but none of the wives went out of their way to bow to the mamacona or bid them farewell. Micay picked up her own blankets from the base of the wall and slung the empty bundle over her shoulder, intending to go after the women and show them the respect and appreciation they deserved—and at the same time shame all these disdainful women and their whining daughters.

Yet something held her where she was. Perhaps it was the delayed return of prudence, brought on by the thought that she was about to act in a way of which only Quinti would approve. She also realized that the mamacona did not need a public display of her support. They had acted correctly, as directed by the high priestess who was the real target of these recriminations.

"I am pleased you chose not to desert me, my daughter," a voice said behind her. "I would like to introduce you to the women of Saramama."

Micay turned to find Mama Cori standing a few feet away, her arms folded across her chest. Only then did Micay realize how greatly she would have insulted her sponsor by leaving, and she felt her cheeks grow hot with shame.

"Forgive me, my lady," she said hoarsely. "I was not thinking. I only wished to show my gratitude to the mamacona."

"They were so good to you?" Mama Cori inquired skeptically, looking her up and down. "You look no better than the other ñustas, and they do not seem filled with gratitude."

"They resisted what we were shown. If they had gone with open hearts, they would have no regrets."

Mama Cori stared at her intently, giving Micay the feeling that her thoughts were being read.

"You have no regrets of your own?"

"None, my lady."

"Then you did not mean to scowl at me earlier? When I first saw you?"

"Scowl?" Micay repeated helplessly. "I meant to show you that I had not been harmed."

Mama Cori's eyes widened as they had earlier, and she made an exasperated noise.

"You are more tired than you know, Micay. You do not know your own face anymore. Wait here; I will explain to the other women and then we can leave."

She turned back into the crowd before Micay could protest, and after another moment of burning embarrassment, Micay realized that what she felt most strongly was relief. She did not want to meet the women of Saramama in her present state, with the sensations of the mountains still vibrating in her nerves and her face speaking in ways she could not control. She needed to wash and sleep and regain her composure, so she would not be subject to rash impulses. Still, as she waited for Mama Cori to return, she thought of the mamacona departing in silence, alone and unthanked, and she felt an undeniable pang of regret that she had not gone after them and accepted the consequences with an open heart.

THE NEXT morning the ñustas went to the shrine of Mama Huaco, which was on one of the outer terraces of the Mollecancha, surrounded by a high-walled enclosure. Mama Huaco was revered as the First Coya, the wife of Manco Capac and the woman who had taught the Incas how to cultivate maize in the high valley of Cuzco. She was seen as an avatar of Pachamama, and the maize plots around her shrine were always the first to be sown and harvested. Her cult was small and exclusive, dominated by women from the Lower Cuzco households and several of Huayna Capac's secondary wives, including Mama Huarcay. The Coya was a member by right, but the present Coya, Rahua Ocllo, had not chosen to involve herself deeply in the cult's affairs. Her elder sister and predecessor, the Coya Cusi Rimay, had been a devotee of the cult while she lived, and its ranks were still filled with women loyal to Cusi Rimay's memory. Rahua Ocllo had lent her prestige to the cults of Saramama and Mama Quilla instead, leaving Mama Huarcay as the highest-ranking member of her group.

All of this went through Micay's mind as she waited with the other ñustas in the courtyard in front of the shrine. The easy functioning of memory was reassuring, helping to convince her that she was returning to normal. A long night's sleep and a second bath had made her feel more civilized, and Mama Cori had helped her comb out her hair and paint her face, conversing with her about the things that had occurred in her absence. Yet the walk through the Mollecancha had been unsettling, the streets and buildings seeming recognizable but no longer familiar. The palace grounds seemed exceptionally barren, a wilderness of blank walls and empty courtyards, the gardens and groves of trees so neat and circumscribed that they seemed like constructions themselves. Micay remembered once thinking that the whole of the Mollecancha was a garden, but she had not been so aware then of the walls that hid some of the most elaborate plots from public view.

She was also not sure that she was ready to face Mama Huarcay again, and she had been relieved when the Fourth Wife had sent two other cult members to lead the ñustas to the shrine. Mama Huarcay had come out into the courtyard to greet them, but she had spoken in the formal tones of the presiding member of the cult, rather than as the woman who had been training them for three months. Micay had been reminded of the woman she had first seen in the House of Chosen Women: imperious, disdainful, full of her own power. Then Mama Huarcay had gone back into the shrine and had not come out for a long time. The ñustas stood waiting in the middle of the courtyard, watching the sky cloud up overhead and listening to the chants emanating from the curtained doorway of the shrine.

Mama Huarcay finally emerged in the company of the high priestess of the cult and selected a small number of the girls to return with them to the shrine. These included all of Mama Huarcay's favorites and all of the girls who were related to members of the cult. A short time later she came out again and invited several more girls to accompany her; these were all from high-ranking Upper Cuzco families and were unlikely to join the cult even if asked, but respect had to be paid to their blood. A lesser priestess came out next to lead in the rest of the full-blooded Inca girls, leaving Micay standing with the other foreign girls and the Incas by privilege, the same ones who had marched at the head of the column in the mountains.

No one else came out and a light rain began to fall, gradually darkening the flagstones of the courtyard. Micay bowed her head in an attempt to keep her face dry, thinking that it would not be proper to pull her mantle up over her hair. She was resigned to the fact that she and her companions were not going to be invited into the shrine, though she wondered about the times in the past when Mama Huarcay, in one of her affectionate moods, had hinted that she might be willing to sponsor Micay for membership in the cult. Micay had never believed her afterward, but she had not forgotten the precedents Mama Huarcay had cited, or how believable she had made it seem while the mood was upon her.

Micay's hair was plastered down on her scalp and her mantle was almost soaked through before Mama Huarcay again stepped past the curtain. She stood in the shelter of the deep doorway and stared across at the remaining ñustas, appearing not to notice the rain. Finally she called out Micay's name and beckoned to her with a toss of her chin.

As she crossed the intervening space, Micay was so conscious of her face that she could feel the rain cutting channels through the paint and powder on her cheeks. Then she was staring into the face that she had come to know nearly as well as her own, since Mama Huarcay expected to be looked at and admired and always gave her a moment to do so. It was a boldly attractive face, dominated by a classic Inca nose, powerful and straight, the bridge an undeviating line between forehead and blunted tip. Her nostrils flared in regular half moons above her full lips, which curled sensuously around every word she spoke. Her eyes seemed languid, shrouded by drooping eyelids and a thicket of black lashes, yet Micay knew them to be every bit as quick and observant as Mama Cori's. She also knew how proud Mama Huarcay was of her smooth dark skin and unlined cheeks, and how sensitive she was about the lighter spots on her cheekbones, like faint tearstains beneath her eyes.

When Mama Huarcay finally looked at her directly, it was with a distaste that made Micay feel the ravages of the rain.

"You and the others can wait in the compound doorway," she said shortly. "We will not be done for some time."

"Yes, my lady," Micay murmured obediently, then hesitated, wondering if there were more.

The languid eyes flashed with impatience. "What?"

"Nothing, my lady."

"Speak, Chachapoyas girl. Do you have a complaint?"

"No, my lady. I simply wondered why we were brought here today."

"It is an honor for you to be this close to the shrine of our mother," Mama Huarcay scolded her. "Do you think yourself worthy of more?"

"That is not for me to judge," Micay demurred, lowering her eyes because she could not trust them not to contradict her denial.

"No, it is not," Mama Huarcay agreed emphatically. "At this moment you are not worthy of my patience. Take yourself back to the others."

Micay bowed and quickly backed out into the rain before turning to walk away. She relayed Mama Huarcay's message to the other girls and could tell from their expressions that they did not feel any more honored than she did. As she followed them toward the enclosure entrance, her wet clothes hanging heavily on her body, she thought of how close she had come to talking back to Mama Huarcay. She had wanted to challenge her the way the mamacona had been challenged and make her justify having them stand uselessly in the rain. She had wanted to say Yes, if the training I received from you and Mama Cori, and from the mamacona in the House of Chosen Women, is worth anything, then *I* must be worthy of better treatment. If I am not worthy, then neither is what you have taught me.

She crowded into the doorway behind the others, telling herself that she had not *shown* any of this defiance, however much she may have been wishing to. That the wish was so strong told her that she was definitely not back to normal. Maybe she was more tired than she knew, as Mama Cori had suggested, though Micay suspected that it was more serious than that. She wiped water from her eyes, and her fingers came away black with paint. It occurred to her that maybe she did not *wish* to know her own face anymore; that maybe she could no longer look at herself with an open heart and still say she approved of what she saw . . .

ON THE LAST day before the Quicuchicoy would officially begin, the ñustas were taken in small groups to the shrine of Mama Quilla, Lady Moon, the highest of the female gods. Mama Quilla's house was within the Coricancha, the Golden Enclosure of Inti, which stood on a rise overlooking the great square of Tumibamba. Her house stood to the left of Inti's and was the same size and of the same exquisite stonework, though its outer walls were banded with thin strips of silver rather than gold. The interior walls were even more heavily adorned with the shining moon metal, which threw bright reflections across the stone floor and spread the light that came in through the doorway and the two front windows. Mounted in the center of the back wall, facing the doorway, was a large, circular shield of beaten silver, the image of the Moon herself.

Micay's feet were bare and her arms were filled with cloth she herself had woven as an offering. The other four girls, all the daughters of Cañari chiefs, fanned out in front of her, then seemed to disappear as her eyes fell on the silver Moon disc. She was suddenly back in the House of Chosen Women, staring out the window with Cahua, praying to Mama Quilla for wholeness. She could not think of Mama Quilla without also thinking of Cahua, of her devotion and her kind heart. She felt a crushing sadness at the thought of how disappointed Cahua would be to see her now, splintered in spirit and darkened by doubt, hardly a light to those around her. She felt tears coming when she heard the voice and noticed the woman sitting against the wall, directly below the silver image.

"Sit, my daughter," the woman repeated. Micay lowered herself to the floor across from her, startled out of her desire to weep. The woman's hair was entirely gray, but she had a strong, dark face that seemed to resist aging and a wide, mobile mouth that peeled back to reveal pink gums when she spoke.

"I am the high priestess, Chimpu Ocllo. In the name of Mama Quilla, I welcome you to the House of the Moon."

The ñustas all bowed over the offerings folded up in their laps.

"Soon you will begin your fast, and the wives will come to visit you, to test your skills and question your knowledge of the ways of the Incas. Though I did not have a hand in all of your training, I am certain that you will all be found worthy of the title 'ñusta.' "

She paused and looked at them in turn, giving each of them a moment of recognition and consideration, as if she intended to remember their faces. Micay felt her scalp prickle and warmth flow into her cheeks, and she remembered what it was like to feel truly honored.

"Soon after this," the woman continued, "you will be finding husbands and establishing your own households, and taking up your duties in the cults of the gods. You must always be clean and virtuous, my daughters, and kind to the poor and the unfortunate. You must be respectful of those above you in rank and generous with those below. You must give the same attention to your ceremonial duties that you give to your households and children, and you must strive to be the equal of your husbands in courage and strength. You are an example to all of the women in the Four Quarters, and you must always conduct yourselves with humility and good judgement, in the knowledge that you are the daughters of Mama Quilla."

The ñustas bowed again, and when Micay straightened up, she saw that several mamacona had come into the room and were relieving the other girls of their offerings. The high priestess herself held out her hands for Micay's offering, smiling at the astonishment that must have been on Micay's face. She ran her fingers lightly over the cloth before putting it in her lap and accepting the other offerings the mamacona brought her. She examined them one by one, praising the weaving and thanking the girl responsible. After receiving her blessing, the other girls were led out by the mamacona, leaving Micay alone with the high priestess. She had to remind herself to breathe as she watched Chimpu Ocllo take up her offering and study it more closely. The backs of the woman's hands were densely wrinkled and gnarled with veins, showing her age in a way her face did not. She held up the cloth and smacked her wide lips in appreciation, raising an eyebrow at Micay.

"You weave like a chosen woman, Micay, though you were only in the House of Chosen Women for a short time." She paused to smile at Micay's unconcealed surprise. "But then, the Chachapoyas are known to be fine weavers."

"You inquired about me, my lady?"

"That is how one learns, is it not? The sisters told me about the girls who went with them willingly and showed the proper devotion to the huacas. They told me especially about you. Did you have a vision in the mountains, Micay? Have you been called to a life of holiness?"

It had not occurred to Micay that her actions might be interpreted in this way, and for a moment she did not know how to respond. She felt enormously flattered by Chimpu Ocllo's interest in her and was reluctant to disappoint her, but she also knew that she had to tell the truth.

"I had dreams, and memories of dreams, but no visions, my lady. Nor have I ever been drawn to the life of the mamacona. I was happy to leave the House of Chosen Women as soon as I could."

"And now you are unhappy? You appeared stricken when you first entered this house."

Micay glanced up at the image of the Moon, which gave off a mottled glow.

"I prayed to Mama Quilla when I was in the House of Chosen Women. I prayed to her for wholeness and perfection, so that I might be worthy of leaving and having my own life. I felt that she had given me her blessing and her protection. But now . . . somehow I have lost all the certainty I felt."

"That has happened to many of the people who have come here," Chimpu Ocllo said bluntly. "In most cases, it has only made them more arrogant and ambitious. You saw this yourself in the mountains, and you have no doubt seen worse in the court. No doubt you have been told that I am troublesome and provincial; I would expect that Mama Cori and Mama Huarcay would be agreed on that, if nothing else."

Micay had, in fact, heard both women express oddly similar sentiments, so she could only nod in agreement.

"I came here more than twenty years ago, Micay, with my brother, Topa Inca. I was present when Huayna Capac was born, but I did not go back to Cuzco when he and the other Incas did. Mama Quilla had summoned me to her service, and I stayed here to help foster her worship among the Cañari. Naturally, I am troublesome to those who believe, at times, that they are still in Cuzco, and at other times believe that they are free to devise their own customs and traditions. That is why I sent the ñustas into the mountains: to show them what has always been here and will be here after the Incas are gone."

"I saw," Micay murmured. A brief smile creased Chimpu Ocllo's lips, revealing a trace of pink. "Yes, and it has confused you and made you unhappy. That is why you must come to me for instruction once the Quicuchicoy is over."

Micay drew a fluttering breath. "Instruction, my lady?"

"In the cult of Mama Quilla. No doubt you have been told that membership is open only to Incas of the blood. But that is not the tradition here. Our mother accepts all those who truly wish to know and serve her. She accepted me when I, too, was a stranger here. I have always been alert for those who come to her willingly, seeking an answer to their doubts."

"I am honored, my lady," Micay said slowly, her voice suddenly hoarse.

"Yes, and you are wondering what Mama Cori will think, and the others in the Coya's court. But if you did not care in the mountains, why should you care here? Customs and traditions may differ from place to place, but our sense of what is correct must not change. Be true to what you know, Micay. You may leave me now, but expect that I will send for you."

Micay bowed and rose to bow again to the image of Mama Quilla. The high priestess raised her hand in blessing.

"Do not worry that you are troubled by doubts and fears, my child. That does not mean that you have lost Mama Quilla's love and protection." Her broad lips peeled back in a pink smile. "Consider, Micay: Can your life be so wrong if it has brought you to me?"

WHILE MICAY began her three days of fasting, Mama Cori began to weave the belt and head cloth that Micay would wear in the final ceremony of the Quicuchicoy. The two of them were sequestered in the awning house on the upper terrace of the micho's quarters, and the retainers kept all men from entering the area. Apu Poma had even taken himself and his attendants to the governor's compound to lessen the risk of an accidental encounter. While Mama Cori worked at her loom Micay greeted the wives who came to visit her in groups of three or four. She served them food and drink that she had prepared herself and showed them samples of her weaving while they ate. Then she sat with them and answered the questions they put to her. Most of these were straightforward: She was asked to name the past Sapa Incas and their Coyas, the feasts and celebrations of Inti and the other gods, the duties of a woman to her husband and children, the punishments for various crimes, the proper times and conditions for planting maize and other crops. Several women asked her about her namesake, Mama Micay, the Coya of Inca Roca, the sixth Sapa Inca, and Micay patiently repeated the story of how the Coya had brought drinking water to Cuzco.

The most difficult questions came from the two women from the Chima household, who had come as Mama Huarcay's representatives. They questioned her about the penalties for adultery, treason, and theft and for the lesser forms of disloyalty, which had to do with spreading false rumors and speaking against the rule of the Sapa Inca. Then, as if still on the same subject, they began to question her about the recent campaign against the Quitos, asking her to describe the reasons for the conflict and the terms of the surrender. One of the women finally asked her outright if she thought the Quitos had been sufficiently punished for their rebellion, a question so improper that it brought Mama Cori's weaving to an abrupt halt. But Micay did not give her a chance to intervene, telling the woman confidently that the glory of this victory lay not in the punishment that had been inflicted but in Huayna Capac's patience and mercy, and in the calm restraint of his warriors. Now the grateful Quitos would join in the campaign against the Carangui, and their city would be a base for the army. Huayna Capac had shown the wisdom of generosity, Micay concluded; he had won with soft words rather than hard stones.

The women could find no fault with her answer and even felt compelled to commend her before they left. Mama Cori had already resumed her weaving and made no comment to Micay after the women had gone. Micay assumed that she was also satisfied with the answer, which had rolled off Micay's tongue with a shameless ease. The interview with Chimpu Ocllo seemed to have relieved her of her defiant urges and freed her to say what she knew was expected, even if it no longer felt like the truth. The high priestess had recognized her confusion and would help her resolve it later; for now, she had to concentrate on resisting her hunger and completing her examination without incident.

It was not until the second night, when the day's interviews were over and Mama Cori still had not said a word, that Micay began to suspect that she was being deliberately ignored. She supposed that it was what she deserved, since Mama Cori had seen her on the verge of walking away and knew that she had not reckoned the ingratitude of such an act. She probably felt as uncertain of Micay as she did of Quinti, and her suspicions would hardly be alleviated once she heard of the high priestess's offer of "instruction." Micay had been waiting for two days for an opportunity to tell her about the interview, but Mama Cori remained bent over her loom in a posture that actively discouraged interruption.

Micay shifted her gaze away from the circle of firelight, glancing up into the rafters, where strings of peppers and sheaves of dry grass were stored. Twisted around the ropes that held the support beam in place was a limp spray of wilted blue flowers, a remnant from the feasts Apu Poma had given while Micay was in the mountains. The post runners had brought word from Cuzco that Cusi— the boy who had once been so small and sickly, the son who had been scorned as a weakling by his father—had come in first in the Huarachicoy race. The news had been announced in all the squares of Tumibamba, and the retainers were still talking about all the people who had crowded into the micho's compound to congratulate Apu Poma and drink to the success of Cusi Huaman, as he was now being called. Apparently Apu Poma and many others had gotten extremely drunk, and cups and dishes had been broken and several of the flower beds had been trampled. The next day the Sapa Inca had summoned Apu Poma and Mama Cori to congratulate them personally, an honor that had necessitated a second night of celebration.

Mama Cori herself had said nothing about any of this, so Micay could only guess how she had reacted to Cusi's triumph and to Apu Poma's celebration of it. She suspected that it had only made her miss her youngest son even more and respect her husband even less. No wonder she was distant. She was playing mother for Micay, but all her real children were gone: Amaru in Quito, Cusi in Cuzco, Quinti in her estrangement. And for these three days she could not speak to her brother Lloque, a deprivation that probably affected her more strongly than anything else. Everyone in the family was aware of the effect

Lloque's company had upon her and of the fact that she grew restless and irritable if they were separated for too long a time.

The muted shuffling sound of Mama Cori's weaving suddenly ceased, bringing Micay back to full attention. Mama Cori sat for another moment over her work, then sighed audibly and slipped out of the backstrap of her loom. When she turned around, her eyes were narrowed and her brow furrowed, as if she were still studying the close weave of the cloth. But then her face became impassive and her eyes took on a searching intensity, reminding Micay of their first meeting in the House of Chosen Women. She trusts me no more, Micay thought, feeling weak in her limbs and aware of her hunger.

"Tell me," Mama Cori said slowly, "do you plan to stay in this house once you are a ñusta?"

"But of course, my lady," Micay blurted out. "Where else would I go?"

"Mama Huarcay has not offered you a place with her?"

"No, my lady. Why would she?"

"Because she has hinted in the past that she might. I did not hear this from *you,* for all we talked, but there are others who have ears."

"Mama Huarcay hinted at many things," Micay said patiently, "but only to taunt me. Her displays of affection were too infrequent to be trusted."

"The high priestess is known to be more determined in her affections. As perhaps you already know."

Micay sighed helplessly and spread her hands. "I have been waiting for a chance to tell you, my lady—"

"The high priestess singles you out," Mama Cori interrupted, "the only ñusta to be granted a private interview, and you feel you can wait to tell me?"

"I was not certain you would approve," Micay said, immediately sorry she had reached for such a lame excuse.

"And if you thought I disapproved," Mama Cori inquired in a scathing tone, "you would not tell me at all? Come, Micay, you forget how small this city is and how many eyes are watching. These secrets of yours are worth little, but they cost you greatly in trust."

Micay lowered her eyes, blinking back the sudden threat of tears. "I did not think of them as secrets, my lady. And I do not think you have ever trusted me."

The statement caught Mama Cori off guard, and she hesitated just long enough for both of them to see that it was true. She clamped her lips tight and drew a breath through her nose.

"I am slow to trust anyone, even those of my own blood. I have always suspected that your defiance of Mama Huarcay was not as innocent as you pretended. Then you tried to come between me and my husband in Cusipampa. I told you, did I not, not to take sides in the matter?"

"Yes, my lady."

"Yet you used the vicuña in the waistband you wove for Cusi. Did you think I would not notice?"

"Apu Poma gave it to me," Micay murmured defensively. "I gave some of it to the Women of the Sun and made the rest of it my gift to Cusi. It did not seem right to deprive him of its beauty."

"But it seemed right to defy my wishes," Mama Cori huffed. "Do you wonder why I do not trust your judgment? I thought at first that you were shrewd and ambitious, eager to improve your place. That was why you sought to ingratiate yourself with my husband and Mama Huarcay, and with my brother Lloque. But now I see that you are more like Quinti. You obey no one's wishes but your own, and you enjoy being the one who stands against the many, the one who is wiser and more righteous than her elders."

Mama Cori paused for breath, but Micay felt capable only of listening, wondering what she would be accused of next. She could not believe that she was the devious person Mama Cori was describing, even if she had done everything of which she was accused.

"Where is Quinti now?" Mama Cori went on. "Why has she not come to braid your sandals for you, as a sister should? You see how it is when you are loyal only to yourself: Those who are most like you are the last who will come to your aid. You are alone in the world, and you deserve to be!"

For a moment, Micay was almost overcome by the urge to collapse and weep and beg for forgiveness. But she held back against it and felt a growing stubbornness that seemed to rise out of her midsection and push up on her lungs, straightening her back and making her jaw jut out. She blinked the moisture from her eyes before looking up at Mama Cori.

"Quinti has not come because she thinks I am too much like you. You tell me I am too much like her. So how am I to see myself? Do I deserve to be misunderstood?"

"Do not speak to me in anger, Micay," Mama Cori warned, and Micay realized that what she was feeling was indeed anger, an emotion that had been forbidden and forgotten for so long that its presence was both startling and irresistible, like a sudden fever that consumed all other sensations as it rose. She shuddered and spoke quickly, trying to keep her voice steady.

"Must I always talk around you, my lady? Will I never be allowed to make my own judgments and decide for myself what is right? If I am as deficient in judgment as you say, then surely I should not be allowed to complete the Quicuchicoy. Let me break my fast now, so that the disgrace of my failure will be entirely my own . . ."

She reached for one of the food bowls she had put out for the day's guests, but Mama Cori caught her wrist in midair and held it fast.

"That is enough! There will be no failure; you will complete the rites, as you were meant to." Mama Cori squeezed her wrist hard for emphasis. "I have not forgotten my responsibility to guide and support you, even if you reject my advice. I will do what I can to help you, but I cannot watch in silence while you destroy your future, as my daughter has done."

She released Micay's wrist with a thrust that set Micay back on her haunches, well out of reach of the bowls. Then Mama Cori looked up in surprise, and Micay turned her head to see Quinti standing just behind her.

"She is trying to tell you, Mother, that she does not need to be watched by you or anyone else."

"Then why have you been watching from the darkness?" Mama Cori demanded angrily. Quinti simply sat down next to Micay and deposited a small bundle in her lap. "I did not do all the work myself," she explained to Micay. "The women I teach in Cuenca asked to help when they heard I was making sandals for a chosen woman, a sister of the famous Cusi Huaman."

Micay stared back at her speechlessly, turning the soft hempen sandals over in her hands. Her anger had disappeared, leaving her shaken and slightly bewildered. Quinti gave her a brief smile, then looked expectantly at her mother, who appeared to have recovered her composure.

"What has brought you back to us?"

"The high priestess summoned me. She reminded me that my family had need of me and that they had a right to my concern. As you know, she can be most persuasive."

"Not everyone finds her so," Mama Cori said coolly. "She seems to have her greatest success with the young and the very old."

Quinti glanced sideways at Micay, seeming almost amused. "We are old enough to be called 'ñusta.' Perhaps she succeeds because she is kind and truthful and not concerned with rank and prestige."

"Perhaps she is more concerned than you can see. Is it an accident that she has recruited the two of you? She knows how close I am to the Coya."

"She would probably be happy to recruit you and the Coya, as well," Quinti suggested mildly. "I did not come here to argue with you, Mother, I came to sit with Micay during her fast and to take my place in the ceremony."

"And then you will leave us again?"

Quinti met and held her mother's gaze with a seriousness, a purposefulness, that Micay had never seen her display before. She was not asking for approval, but she did seem to want Mama Cori to understand.

"I will still teach, but not every day. The high priestess has convinced me that I must attend to *all* of my responsibilities and obligations."

"I assume that means that you will become active in the cult of Mama Quilla," Mama Cori said tersely.

Quinti nodded. "I am a member. As you are, Mother, and the Coya, too."

Mama Cori ignored her and turned her attention to Micay. "And what has Chimpu Ocllo promised you?"

"She said she would send for me, my lady, to instruct me in the ways of the cult of Mama Quilla."

Mama Cori made a clicking sound with her tongue and then shook her head, glancing from one to the other with a rueful expression on her face. "So . . . I am to take the two of you to the court with me, so that you can listen for Chimpu Ocllo and defend her against criticism. I cannot think of a better way to enhance my popularity."

"You would have your daughters with you," Quinti pointed out, "women who might also speak to Chimpu Ocllo on your behalf."

Mama Cori gave her a pained smile. "You are proposing an alliance, then? Will we have to exchange hostages, or will our words be enough to seal the agreement?"

"Our words," Quinti insisted, deliberately ignoring her mother's sarcasm. "You have mine that I will not embarrass you willfully. But you must trust me to make my own explanations and apologies, as I see fit."

Mama Cori gazed at her thoughtfully for a moment. Then, seemingly making up her mind, she gave an abrupt nod. "I would expect you to." She glanced at Micay. "I will make no excuses for either of you and assume no more loyalty than you show me. You are women in your own right. Choose your own examples and pray that you are not being deceived."

Rising slowly to her feet, Mama Cori gathered her skirt and walked around them and out of the awning house. Micay clasped her sandals against her empty stomach and looked at Quinti, who seemed satisfied with the bargain she had struck.

"Perhaps now we can truly be sisters," Quinti suggested, "if you can forgive me for what I said to you."

"That seems long ago," Micay said helplessly. "So much has happened that I do not understand."

"You will," Quinti said sympathetically, patting her on the knee. "These rites may not teach you, but they will make you a ñusta, and then you can learn from the high priestess."

"I had thought that I would know everything, once I had completed the Quicuchicoy," Micay murmured, so wistfully that Quinti laughed.

"It is just the beginning of what a woman must know. But we will learn together from now on. Come, let us sing your fasting song, the one to Mama Quilla."

"Our mother," Micay began, drawing out the note so that Quinti could join her. The firelight flickered as coals crumbled into ash, and Micay realized how long she had been sitting and how weary she was. It suddenly seemed as if the journey she had begun with the mamacona had only just ended. But it was a relief rather than an effort to sing, and she blended her voice with Quinti's, hearing a sound that seemed mature and womanly, restful to the ear.

VII

LLOQSINA PUÑUY:
Dreams of Departure

(A.D. 1513)

Cuzco

CUSI DREAMED that Tocto was walking backwards in front of him, pulling him along by the hands and urging him to walk faster. She seemed annoyed with him, but it was dark and growing increasingly colder, and he wanted to huddle back against the warmth that remained behind him. Then he lost the image and was aware that he was dreaming, that Tocto was trying to awaken him from a sleep that lay upon him like a stone, so heavy that he could not force his eyes open. He heard his name being called; then a sharp tug on his ear sent pains shooting right up into his head, jolting him awake. He found that the blankets had been pulled off him, exposing his naked body to the cold night air, and that Tocto was kneeling over him, her arms propped against her thighs. He raised a hand to his ear, which was still tender from the weight of the new, larger plug he had recently been given to wear.

"It was the only way I could wake you," Tocto said in apology. "Your friend Rimachi has come for you."

Cusi struggled into a sitting position and began to search for his clothes, shaking his head to clear it. He realized that the curtain over the doorway had been pulled back and someone—probably one of the gate men—was standing outside with a torch. He could hear the hoarse bellow of a conch horn being blown somewhere in the distance.

"It must be a message from Tumibamba," he said, glancing at Tocto, who had not moved. His tunic smelled of her as he pulled it on over his head, and his thighs felt sticky when he tucked his loincloth between his legs. He looked at her again, feeling the tension in her silence.

"It cannot be a victory," he went on, cocking his head toward the doorway, "or there would be shouting, too."

"The gate man is waiting," Tocto reminded him gently. "Do not make him explain his presence to anyone else."

He went over to her on his knees and took the hands she held out to him, pressing them to his lips. Tocto smiled at the gesture, though her eyes were wide and moist. Cusi had to swallow before he could speak.

"I will see you here in two days," he promised. "Send one of your women to Rimachi's cousin if there is a change."

Tocto nodded without conviction and withdrew her hands, pointing with her chin toward the doorway.

"Just let me see you again before you leave," she whispered, shaking her head vehemently to cut off his protest and again urging him toward the door. Cusi caught a brief glimpse of the tears on her cheeks before he turned and rushed out of the room, drawing the startled watchman along after him as he headed for the gate. He knew this part of the Cora Cora well enough to travel without a light, though the man soon caught up and led the way with his torch. Other messengers were coming in through the gate when Cusi came out to find Rimachi waiting in the street, holding a torch of his own. Rimachi was breathing rapidly and seemed very excited, though his voice was grave.

"We have been summoned to the Hawk Enclosure," he reported, and they immediately started up the street together. "Word has come from Tumibamba, and it is not good. The advance column of Huayna Capac's army was ambushed by the Carangui, surprised in the night. Ten thousand were killed and many more wounded, most of them Collas. The Carangui now hold the fortress at Cayambi and have made the Incas fall back around Quito."

Cusi glanced sideways and shook his head in disbelief. "How could this happen? We were told that the Collas had demanded to be in the vanguard; the beginning of the campaign was delayed because of it. Did they post no sentries?"

"Perhaps they grew complacent." Rimachi shrugged. "Or perhaps the Carangui are stronger than anyone thought. It is said they attacked in great numbers."

They walked in silence for a while, passing messengers and hurrying groups of warriors, hearing the sounds of drums and conch horns from many parts of the city. Huayna Capac had no doubt demanded additional warriors to replace those who had been lost, and his wishes would be carried out as soon as was humanly possible. Cusi realized how foolish his promise to Tocto had been and wished he had stayed to hold her instead of rushing out of the room.

"We will be going north, then," he said, more to himself than to Rimachi, who nonetheless responded by giving the torch in his hand a vigorous shake, scattering sparks as he released the excitement he had been holding in.

"Very soon, I expect. To Tumibamba," he said with relish, showing his teeth, "and then to fight!"

"It will be good to see our families again," Cusi murmured, remembering when he had looked forward to leaving Cuzco with the same enthusiasm. When there had been no one he would be leaving behind. Rimachi suddenly poked him with an elbow, and Cusi looked up to see his friend staring down his long nose at him.

"Are you awake? Certainly it will be good. For Cusi Huaman and his friends it should be even better. Everyone will want to meet you and introduce you to their daughters. You will be famous all over again."

"It will take us two months to get there," Cusi reckoned wearily. "At least while we are marching I will not have to race someone every day."

Rimachi stopped for a moment and lowered the torch to peer into Cusi's face. He seemed baffled by what he saw.

"Has it been so hard for you? You have lost only twice, and they were older men, champion runners. Surely you cannot find it trying to accept all the cheers and prizes."

"No," Cusi admitted, gesturing curtly to start them moving again. "But it is hard to sleep when your heart and mind are still racing and your legs are already tensing for the next day's start. The only time I sleep is when I am with Tocto, and then I am like one of the dead and can hardly be roused at all."

"You will not have that problem for much longer," Rimachi told him. "And you knew from the beginning that you would have to leave her someday. As it is, you have been incredibly fortunate that the Vicaquirao has kept your secret so well."

"Huascar has no power over the households," Cusi said scornfully. "Neither did Huayna Capac. That was why he was so eager to go to Tumibamba. It was obviously not the chance to fight that drew *him* north."

"You have been listening to Otoronco Achachi," Rimachi cautioned. "It will be good for you, as well, to get away from his influence. You do not have his reasons to be bitter."

"And you will not allow me my own."

"Once you feared that you would be held back from the Huarachicoy altogether, and then you were sent to the Grass Man for lying. You seemed destined for shame, not fame. So no, Cusi Huaman, I do not think you have any reason to be bitter. I would never have risked being trampled by Sutic if I had thought you would be so ungrateful."

Cusi managed a weak smile, mollified by the teasing tone with which Rimachi had concluded. "You are right," he conceded. "I should not complain, but I am just not as ready to leave as you are."

Rimachi nodded thoughtfully, bending slightly at the waist as they began to climb the long hill toward Sacsahuaman.

"I know what Uritu would tell you," he ventured after a long pause. Cusi gestured for him to go on. "He would say you should go see the blind man."

Cusi stiffened and was not aware he had nodded until Rimachi let out a whoop of laughter.

"I should have let Uritu tell you himself. He should know the influence he has with you."

"What would *you* say?" Cusi challenged him, and Rimachi shrugged.

"I would say we will be lucky if we are given time to pack and polish our weapons. I do not know that I would use what little we have on a blind man."

"That is why I listen to Uritu," Cusi said succinctly. He began walking faster. "Let us find out for sure how much time is left to us. Then I will know what I must do here."

Tumibamba

MICAY HAD BEEN talking to Acapana when Amaru suddenly came through the gate, alone but with a presence that made everyone around him come to attention. Gold glinted from his earplugs and the circular Sun shield on his chest, and the bands of blue feathers around his knees and forearms seemed to make the muscles in his arms and legs stand out more powerfully. He smiled when he saw Micay and walked right past Acapana without giving him a glance, lifting Micay in an embrace that pressed her whole body against his, a hug that was at first fierce and then briefly suggestive before he set her back on her feet. Micay felt her face flush with pleasure and embarrassment, and she cast a quick glance at Acapana, who was nearly as large as Amaru yet seemed to have shrunk into the background. Amaru caught the glance and looked Acapana over himself, his eyes lingering on the green tunic and the small golden plugs in Acapana's ears. Acapana gazed back at him steadily, hardly seeming to breathe.

"The micho's chief of staff," Amaru said finally, nodding in recognition, his arms cocked at his sides. "What is your name?"

"Acapana, my lord."

"I will remember," Amaru promised, and Acapana bowed to him. Amaru turned back to Micay, examining her as frankly as he had Acapana, though with a smile on his lips.

"So, you have grown up while I was away."

"It has been over a year, my lord."

"I know exactly how long it has been," Amaru assured her. He lifted his chin toward the upper terrace. "Is there akha in my mother's house? I want to drink."

"Lloque Yupanqui is with her. And of course there is akha. She has been expecting you for two days."

"That is not long. Come, you can take me to her. You can fill my cup for me and show me what you learned in the Quicuchicoy."

He took Micay by the arm and began to lead her off, then looked back over his shoulder and nodded to Acapana in parting. Micay smiled up at him as they climbed the stairs to the upper terrace.

"I am grateful, my lord," she said.

Amaru pretended to be surprised for a moment, then shrugged his broad shoulders. "It is too easy to be rude in my father's compound. I do not wish to make it worse for those who have to serve him."

There was a large group of men standing silently outside Apu Poma's house, their somber faces reflecting the severity of the defeat the Incas had suffered. As the recognition of who Amaru was came over them, they began to bow and raise their hands to their mouths in gestures of deference and respect, moving aside to open a pathway to the micho's house. But Amaru simply turned Micay to the left and guided her past them without so much as a nod in their direction. He seemed suddenly oblivious of her, as well, his face set in a kind of concentrated squint that made him look older and less handsome. She could not tell if it was pride he was displaying, or rudeness, or a fierce reluctance to claim his own success in the midst of the larger failure. He was one of the few who had not only survived but had won honors for himself, fighting his way out of the ambush and then rallying the remaining warriors into an orderly retreat. At the gate he had seemed unchanged, and he had not given her a chance to think about what he must have experienced on the battlefield. But he could not have lived through so much danger and seen so much killing without being affected. Micay decided he had the right to ignore whomever he chose, including her, and she did not try to intrude on his thoughts as they left the other men behind and crossed the plaza in front of the awning house.

He stopped of his own accord before they got to Mama Cori's house and seemed to come out of his trance, blinking and frowning at his own preoccupation. "Where is Quinti?"

"In Cuenca, the north quarter of Tumibamba. She is teaching Quechua to the Cañaris."

Amaru shook his head impatiently, as if he had not heard her correctly.

"Has the court truly become so tedious?" he demanded.

Micay smiled at his disbelief. "You have been away a long time, my lord. We still attend your mother in the court, but we are also attached to the high priestess, Chimpu Ocllo."

Amaru pondered that for a moment, then shook his head again. "I do not think I wish to understand all this. I will be leaving Tumibamba soon enough. I only want to know that my mother has not been abandoned by the rest of the family."

"We are here for her, my lord, and Lloque Yupanqui visits frequently."

"Of course," Amaru murmured, squinting at the doorway of his mother's house. Then he brought his attention back to Micay. "No doubt Cusi will be coming here soon with his initiation brothers. We were told about him in the field. It was my mother, you know, who taught him how to run."

Micay nodded respectfully, touched by his obvious fondness for his younger brother.

"If you are concerned about your mother's feelings," she said gently, "I should warn you that she knows that you have been in the city for the last two days."

Amaru grimaced and looked toward the doorway again. "It is probably better that she be annoyed with me," he decided. Abruptly he started her moving again, leading her up to the entrance to Mama Cori's house.

As usual, Mama Cori and Lloque Yupanqui were alone and deep in conversation, but they quickly got to their feet to embrace Amaru and welcome him back. Micay went to the corner for drinking cups and a jar of akha, waiting patiently until they were all seated. Then she filled two cups and set them in front of Lloque, so that he could toast his nephew. Lloque ceremoniously raised both cups, extending the one in his right hand to Amaru.

"Greetings, Huaminca, veteran warrior. You showed great courage against the Carangui and saved the lives of your comrades. Even in defeat, you must be saluted. Your name will be kept by those who remember the deeds of Huayna Capac's reign."

Amaru took the offered cup, and both men poured a little onto the floor, for Inti, before drinking themselves. Amaru drained his cup and immediately held it out to Micay to be refilled. She did so, then filled a cup for Mama Cori, who took only the obligatory sip before speaking.

"Tell me, my son, about the seriousness of Quilaco's injuries."

"He has a leg wound and a broken arm, but he will heal. He will probably be ready to fight again in a few months."

"Were you with him during the attack?" Lloque inquired in his gentle, colorless voice.

"Nearby. We retreated together with all the warriors we could rouse and arm. We were fighting for our lives the whole way, so it was not hard to show courage."

"Yet you were not wounded, or even marked!" Mama Cori marveled, looking him over with wide eyes. Amaru took another long drink and gave his mother a mirthless smile.

"I was too drunk to be hurt."

"And I am too old to be teased," Mama Cori retorted, though in a tolerant voice. Amaru's smile hardened, seeming even more false.

"I am not teasing. We had been chasing the Carangui for days, burning their villages as we went. But they would not engage us in the open. Finally we had to stop and wait for the rear guard to catch up, because we were days ahead of them. We had time to brew akha from the maize we carried with us, and then the singing of war songs began, and the boasting and taunting. Most of us were drunk when the Carangui attacked."

In the silence that followed, Amaru held out his cup for more akha. Micay complied, then went back to the corner to refill her jar. Lloque was speaking when she returned.

". . . no mention in the report of the war chiefs. They blamed the ambush on the Collas' being too eager to get to the enemy."

"They were also eager to outdrink their Inca comrades," Amaru told him bluntly. "That is why so many of them died. Do you suppose that this will also be in the story songs of those who remember the deeds of Huayna Capac's reign?"

Lloque straightened his back and cocked his head to one side, as if he were listening to the echoes of Amaru's words and trying to judge their tone, judge whether he was being taunted, his own toast thrown back at him in disrespect. Amaru gazed back at him impassively, appearing to expect an answer.

"It is a disgrace," Lloque said in a deliberate voice, "under *any* circumstance, for so many to die so pointlessly. That is why our songs will be filled with grief and regret and warnings for the future. Would you have me demean their deaths with ridicule?"

"No," Amaru said swiftly. "I simply wished to be sure that this would not be remembered as a victory. You have reassured me, Uncle."

From her place just outside the circle of their conversation, Micay could see only the side of Mama Cori's face. But she could almost feel the force of her frown, which made her recall Amaru's earlier remark about it being better for his mother to be annoyed, a remark that still puzzled her.

"Why do you find it necessary to tell these stories?" Mama Cori broke in sharply. "Do you wish to belittle your own accomplishments?"

"I accomplished nothing. There is nothing gained in a retreat."

"This kind of modesty is perverse," Mama Cori said in exasperation. Lloque quickly interrupted to head off an argument. "How long will you be with us, my son, before you return to Quito?"

"Less than a month. But I am not going back to Quito."

Amaru raised his cup to his lips, watching his mother over the rim and waiting for her to ask him where he was going. But apparently her annoyance or surprise, had rendered her speechless. Lloque finally beckoned to Amaru to explain.

"I am going to the coast with Sinchi Roca, to help him inspect the roads and buildings between here and Pachacamac."

"That is a long journey," Lloque said softly. "You will be gone many months."

"We expect to spend several months in Chan Chan alone."

Lloque glanced sideways at his sister, but Mama Cori still did not speak.

"Sinchi Roca is an estimable man," Lloque said to Amaru, "and you can only profit from an association with him. But I do not have to remind you that there is no war in Chan Chan. You will remain at your present rank while Quilaco and the other young captains earn honors for themselves and rise above you."

Amaru shrugged his shoulders, as if to say that he had enough honors.

"You should also think of your health," Lloque persisted. "You have never been to the Hotlands. It is always warm and the air is hard to breathe, sometimes damp and stinking of fish, other times dry and hot as the desert. When we fought against the Chimus, our warriors had to be rotated back to the mountains every three months or they would have perished from the heat and bad air."

"As you said, we are not going there to fight," Amaru said easily. "Sinchi Roca has already warned me about the discomfort and danger of illness. But they cannot be measured against what I will learn and see. I have already been given my release by my commander."

"Then I can only wish you good health," Lloque concluded, giving Mama Cori a quick glance that seemed to be intended as a warning. But her response was harsh and heedless.

"I can only wonder when you will decide to choose a wife and begin a family, as a man should. Does Sinchi Roca speak to you only of roads and buildings?"

"He is like a father to me. But he knows better than to push his daughters at me."

"An excellent father!" Mama Cori exclaimed mockingly, shaking off the hand Lloque tried to lay on her arm. "Does he not trust you with them? Or does he think you too immature?"

"I must go now," Amaru said in a low voice, bowing to his mother and uncle. Mama Cori turned her face away and did not look up as Amaru rose to his feet; from behind, Micay saw a tear slide down her cheek. Lloque gestured silently for Amaru to leave, then waved Micay out after him. Still carrying the akha jar, Micay caught up with him in front of the awning house. He turned and took the two-handled jar from her and raised the scalloped rim to his lips.

"Why did you have to provoke her?" Micay asked quietly, putting her disapproval into her eyes. "It will not make her miss you any less."

Amaru rested the pointed bottom of the jar against his hip and wiped his mouth with his free hand.

"It might."

"But is that truly how you wish to be remembered?"

"I would prefer not to be remembered at all," he told her flatly. "I would like to be forgotten by all those who feel it is their duty to shape my character and arrange my future."

"Not everyone wishes to mislead you—"

"I can mislead myself," Amaru proclaimed, sounding slightly drunk. He handed her the jar and turned to go, then turned back to face her.

"When my brother Cusi comes, tell him that I am proud of the man he has always been. He will understand my meaning."

Micay stared back at him and shivered, seized by a sudden uneasiness that made her want to detain him.

"You sound as if you do not intend to return, my lord. What do you expect to find in Chan Chan?"

"I do not know. Whatever I have not found here or in Cuzco. Whatever is left for me to find."

"Perhaps you will find what is serious in your heart," Micay suggested boldly. "It is something you said to me before you left the last time."

"I remember," Amaru said. He gave her a smile that alleviated some of her uneasiness. "I told you then that you hear me better than anyone else." He reached out and touched her gently on the cheek. "But you should listen to someone more trustworthy, if you can find such a person."

"The high priestess found *me*," Micay said breathlessly.

Amaru smiled and withdrew his hand. "I am told such things happen." He shrugged and inclined his head in parting. "I will probably see you again before I leave the city. But remember my message to Cusi."

Micay nodded compliantly, repeating the message to herself as she watched him walk away. Its meaning seemed clear to her, far clearer than anything Amaru had said about himself. Yet her cheek burned where he had touched her, her heart was beating hard against her ribs, and her hands felt slippery and weak on the handles of the jar. Why did he always have this effect on her? How did he always get her to care about him, when he seemed to care so little about himself?

She shook herself and turned toward the awning house, looking for a place to put down the jar and collect her thoughts. She would have to discuss what Amaru had said with Quinti and the high priestess, though she was not certain she would be as frank about her feelings. Quinti was already teasing her about being in love with Amaru, and Micay could never deny it with conviction. She tried now to put him out of her mind, to think about Acapana, who had asked to escort her and Quinti to their next visit with Quilaco. But the image of Amaru fighting drunkenly for his life, a disdainful smile on his face, lingered stubbornly, and she knew that this was how *she* would remember him— whether he wished to be remembered or not.

Cuzco

O TORONCO ACHACHI took the matter of how Cusi would spend his last twenty days out of Cusi's hands by summoning him and Uritu to assist him in the palace. Tomay had also been serving as one of Otoronco's attendants since the Huarachicoy, but he had been granted leave to accompany his father back to the Southern Quarter to participate in ceremonies of mourning for the Collas who had been lost in the ambush and to help recruit new troops. It was thought that Tomay's fame as a runner might help attract whatever young men were left in his homeland, but it was also necessary to get Tomay out of the palace. He was obsessed with his grief and bitterness and far too sensitive to be subjected to the rumors and judgments that were being passed so carelessly.

Cusi and Uritu were sorry to lose him, since Tomay was the best of them with memory cords and the retainers on Otoronco's staff saw the world almost solely in terms of their knots and colored cords. Otoronco was an indifferent administrator, and he had inherited his staff from the former lord of the quarter and had never thought to change it, even though he resented his reliance on men who were servants for life, bloodless men without clans or ancestral lands of their own. They sat in closed rooms with their clay relief maps and bundles of cords, tying and untying their knots and telling him about places they had never seen, places where he had lived and fought but that they knew only as strings of numbers. The retainers, for their part, were dedicated, meticulous men who had learned their skills from their fathers and grandfathers and who believed that without the knowledge they collectively held in their heads, the Eastern Quarter would disappear from human memory. They were inclined as a result to be brusque and not overly deferential, anticipating rather than responding to questions.

In the past months, Cusi and his two friends had come to assume the role of intermediaries between Otoronco and the retainers, translating his demands and desires into terms comprehensible to the staff and trying to blunt the effects of his explosive temper. But Cusi came to the present task with a sense of dread, fearing that it might consume all of his remaining time without much visible accomplishment. Otoronco had been in such a rage over the ambush that Cusi was half convinced that he might refuse to comply with Huayna Capac's demand for more warriors or else sabotage the process through angry neglect. The staff were rigid with anxiety and resistance to the ordeal to come, knowing that all of their numbers would have to be changed in order to squeeze out the additional men. Cusi could foresee being caught in the middle of a pointless clash of wills, battling reluctance on both sides until his twenty days were gone.

He was thus surprised and relieved when Otoronco somehow mastered his anger and took command of his duties with the fierce intensity of a war chief planning a counterattack. He sent his swiftest messengers to the governors of the provinces, demanding their most recent tallies of available fighting men and alerting them to the orders that would follow. Then he assembled his entire staff, perhaps a hundred and fifty people, in the eastern corner of the palace and had them squat in a great circle around the wooden stool he occupied as lord. He told them that as the representative of the Sapa Inca, he could simply take the men he needed and leave the discussion of compensation for later. But that would undoubtedly cause ill will, desertions, and possibly rebellion in places where there were too few troops to begin with. So he had decided instead that the terms of recruitment would be worked out beforehand, so that all of the Inca's subjects would know they were being treated fairly. As a first step, he announced that the amount of labor owed to the Inca by each village or district would be reduced in direct proportion to the number of warriors supplied. The Eastern Quarter mostly provided workers for the ruler's mines and coca plantations, and Otoronco instructed that the supervisors of these projects be told that they would have to make do with fewer men in the future. The retainer who kept the cords for the coca plantations, and whose task it would be to communicate some of this unpleasant news, felt compelled to speak up.

"The supervisors will protest, my lord. They will say justly that they cannot be expected to produce as much with fewer men."

"They will not be expected to produce as much," Otoronco told him without hesitation. "That is a cost the Sapa Inca will have to bear. See that they are informed of that, as well."

Cusi and Uritu exchanged a glance, having reached the same conclusion about the target of Otoronco's attack. Obviously he intended to make Huayna Capac pay for his carelessness. Uritu, who seldom spoke up in gatherings, raised a palm to get Otoronco's attention.

"There were some tribes, Lord, who freely gave more warriors than were requested in the last levy. Even with the reduction of the labor tax, they might not be left with enough men to plant and harvest their own crops and hunt for food. They would feel justly that too much has been asked of them."

Otoronco nodded to Uritu but addressed his reply to the whole group.

"We will not ask for men who cannot be spared, and if there is any lack of food, it will be supplied from the Sapa Inca's storehouses. The messengers who carry our terms are to say that these are the terms of Otoronco Achachi, who promises to rectify any unfairness. No one will be made to suffer because of his loyalty to the Sapa Inca."

The staff bowed to him in unison, with a sense of relief that was almost palpable. All of their numbers would still have to be changed, but it made their task much easier to know that requests for compensation would be honored and that Otoronco would bear the responsibility for the cost to the Sapa Inca. They went back to their maps and cords and began to search methodically for the needed recruits. Otoronco summoned Cusi and Uritu to his side.

"Do you understand my intentions?" he demanded. Both of them nodded tentatively. "Let me be plain at least with the two of you: I do not intend to let Huayna Capac bleed the Eastern Quarter dry in order to feed his profligate campaign in the north. I want the two of you to see that nothing is overlooked, nothing asked without something offered of comparable worth. Instruct the messengers yourselves, so that they will speak well for us and inspire confidence rather than resentment. I want acceptance, not mere compliance."

Uritu let out a low whoop of appreciation, and Otoronco bared his teeth in a smile that seemed vaguely angry.

"That is the response I want. Send one of the servants to fetch extra clothing for you. We will sleep here until the final messages have been sent."

None of them left the palace for the next ten days, during which the reports came in from the governors and were tabulated by the retainers, who tied new totals into their cords and began to make comparisons.

On a rare foray into another part of the palace, Cusi ran into Rimachi, who was doing his apprenticeship with one of his uncles, who was a captain of the Royal Guard. Rimachi had been spending most of his time standing guard outside the feasts the Regent was providing for the chiefs who had already arrived in Cuzco. He had seen Tocto on several occasions but had had no chance to speak to her.

"She is acting as Huascar's hostess, and he is meeting with everyone, encouraging them in his father's name. It is clear that he wants to make an impression, so they will speak well of him to Huayna Capac."

"The warriors from the Eastern Quarter will speak well of Otoronco Achachi," Cusi said with certainty, "though I doubt that Huayna Capac will appreciate the cost of their good will."

"I have heard that the other lords are offering prizes of cloth and llamas and coca. And there are rumors that some of the governors are rounding up rebels and troublemakers and emptying the provincial prisons in order to meet their quotas."

Cusi took this information back to Otoronco, who shook his head in disgust, the jagged scar standing out lividly on his cheek.

"That is probably what Huayna Capac deserves," he snarled, though loud enough for only Cusi to hear. "But I want men who have a chance of surviving his ineptitude, men who will return to their homes when the fighting is over."

Finally all the provincial reports had been assimilated, all the old agreements and understandings either altered or adjusted, and the messengers had been given their instructions and tested to be certain they had committed everything to memory. Otoronco dispatched them in person, urging them to be swift but prudent and to invoke his name if anyone should try to deter them.

"That is enough," Otoronco said gruffly when all the retainers had gone back to their rooms and he was alone with Cusi and Uritu in the empty corner of the huge hall. "Let us go clear our throats of orders and our minds of numbers."

"I have been dreaming at night about memory cords," Uritu murmured wearily. "They hang around my head like hair or teeth."

Cusi could barely remember having slept these past nights, much less having dreamed. He dimly wanted to go in search of Tocto. He also thought of asking Otoronco for permission to visit Raurau Illa. But most of all, he simply wanted not to make any more decisions, so he let Otoronco lead him and Uritu to a dance in the Regent's compound. Most of those present were Incas who had been summoned back from the provinces or released from other duties in order to command the troops going north. One of the latter was Sumac Mallqui, who was exultant over the chance to return to the field. Since Cusi and Uritu would be serving under him in the first regiment, he saluted them as comrades, offering them cups of akha with his right hand. He was toasted in turn by Otoronco, who then led him aside and engaged him in a serious conversation, gesturing with the cup in his hand.

Feeling giddy from the akha, Cusi surveyed the crowded enclosure but saw no sign of Huascar or Tocto. When he glanced back, Otoronco was still talking, but Sumac Mallqui appeared uncomfortable, as if he were being asked for a favor he could not grant. Otoronco soon left him and accosted another captain in a similar fashion, seizing the man's attention by means of a flattering toast. Grateful to be abandoned and too tired to tolerate any more drink, Cusi and Uritu slipped out of the compound and went back to their respective rooms to sleep.

A WOMAN with hair knotted like a memory cord was baring her breasts to him and trying to entice him into a dark room, when a pair of powerful hands reached down and yanked Cusi out of his dream. Otoronco was breathing akha into his face and shaking him by the shoulders, having already lifted him to his feet.

"Wake up! What is wrong with you? Are you drunk?"

"I was sleeping," Cusi managed.

Otoronco released him, swaying back on his own heels in a way that indicated that he himself was very drunk. "Where is your battle-ax? Bring it with you."

Otoronco lurched out of the room, and Cusi found the ax with the star-shaped head and went out after him. The moon was nearly full, casting a cold, bluish light over the courtyard. It was the first time in ten nights that Cusi had thought to notice the moon, and he offered a silent prayer to Mama Quilla as he went into the shadows after Otoronco. He found him urinating into the sand pit in the corner of the courtyard and joined him at the edge, relieving himself of a lingering tumescence caused by his dream.

"The Incas have grown small," Otoronco grumbled as he turned away from the pit and headed toward the stairs to the terrace above. "Small and sensible. They flee from anything they think is impossible."

Cusi went up the stairs with him, wondering where they were going. The next terrace held the rooms of the Iñaca elders and priests, and the only thing above that was the Illapa Cancha, where Pachacuti was kept.

"They are afraid to speak the truth," Otoronco continued in a ranting tone, "especially if they think someone of a higher rank does not want to hear it. They would never say something that might be considered bold or startling. Ah! Someone might accuse them of having courage and vision!"

Cusi did not recognize this diatribe or its source, though he was awake enough to recall the conversations Otoronco had been initiating at the dance. They had reached the next terrace, and Otoronco started across a small plaza toward the narrow staircase that led up to the Illapa Cancha. Cusi was suddenly aware of the time of night, Otoronco's drunkenness, and the battle-ax in his own hands.

"My lord—where are we going?"

Otoronco turned at the foot of the stairs. "To see my father. To see a real Inca."

The ax handle became slippery in Cusi's hands, and he felt painfully awake as he followed Otoronco's back up the steps, noticing how smooth and finely cut the stones were. There was a priest standing guard at the top, and though he bowed deeply to Otoronco, he straightened up in indignation when he saw the weapon in Cusi's hands.

"My lord! It is forbidden."

"I know the rules," Otoronco said curtly, glaring at the man in the bright moonlight. He pointed at Cusi with his chin. "This is my grandson, Cusi Huaman. He leaves in ten days for the north, to fight against the Carangui. His weapon will go with him, then and now."

The priest backed out of the way, but two more sought to block the entrance to the compound itself, which was small and narrow and had high walls of the finest stonework. Otoronco seemed to menace them with his whole body without even raising a hand.

"You do not wish to obstruct me tonight," he told them with an earnestness that made them waver and back farther into the doorway. Then a hoarse, quavering voice, a voice that rasped and cracked with weary authority, issued from within.

"Let them enter."

The priests immediately parted and flattened themselves against the sides of the doorway as Otoronco and Cusi walked past them into the tiny, moonlit courtyard. The walls were so high and the space so small that Cusi felt as if he were at the bottom of a brightly painted box. The rest of the enclosure was filled by an open-sided awning house, its interior space hidden in blackness beneath the sharply slanting roof. Otoronco crossed the courtyard in five aggressive strides, ducking his head as he stepped in under the overhanging thatch. Cusi followed him more reluctantly, holding his battle-ax in front of his chest, blinking as he left the light. Gradually, shapes began to emerge from the darkness, the nearest and most visible a cone-shaped bundle set atop a low platform. Cusi had only just recognized this as the mummy of Pachacuti when a pale round face suddenly rose up behind it. A mask, Cusi realized, struggling to maintain his composure. He could feel the unsettling presence of the huacas he could not see, and it made his stomach tense and his jaw clench, his body instinctively drawing in on itself. The hollow, weary voice spoke again, seeming to come from somewhere between the mask and the shrunken outline of Pachacuti's head.

"Otoronco Achachi. Why do you come here in anger?"

"There is a war to be fought!" Otoronco burst out, jarringly loud. "But no one with the will or courage to fight it. Ten thousand lost, killed in their sleep, yet I must stay here and send more to be slaughtered. They say that when Huayna Capac heard of the ambush, he merely laughed and said that men were the food of war."

"The Inca always laughs at defeat."

"And then he seeks his revenge," Otoronco proclaimed. "He does not retire to his palace to wait for reinforcements."

The mask dipped and hovered close to the head of Pachacuti, as if putting an invisible ear to his mouth.

"No," the voice said at last. "He does not."

Otoronco grunted and dropped his hands, which had been grabbing the air in front of him.

"My heart is not old and tired and quiet," he said softly. "Must I stay here, Father, until only the old men are left and I am called up with the last of them?"

The mask rose until it hung over the mummy like a pale moon.

"I cannot intercede for you outside of Cuzco."

"No one will speak for me! They all say that it is impossible, that Huayna Capac would not hear of it, that the other war chiefs would revolt—"

"Who is this other who comes to me bearing a weapon?" the voice interrupted suddenly, sending a tremor up Cusi's spine. He had been listening to the exchange in utter astonishment, wondering who was behind the mask and whose voice he was hearing. He felt Otoronco turn in his direction, as if just remembering that he had a companion.

"He is Cusi Huaman, son of Apu Poma and grandson of my brother, Sinchi Huaman. Like his grandfather, he won his name in the Huarachicoy race."

The voice made a humming sound that seemed to go on for several moments, the mask floating toward Cusi and then drawing back.

"And the weapon?"

"He has carried it for a year to make himself strong. Now he will carry it against the Carangui."

"Let *him* speak for you," the voice decided. "Come closer, Cusi Huaman, and show me the weapon you carry."

It took an act of will for Cusi to make his legs move, and he felt as if he were wading through sand as he edged forward, holding the battle-ax out in front of him. His arms trembled and shook, as they had when he had tried to hold the cup after the race, though now it was fear, not exhaustion, that affected him. The mask bobbed in front of him and suddenly the ax was snatched out of his hands, rocking him back onto his heels. The mask danced before his eyes, streaked with black, and something soft and fibrous whipped across his face. He realized simultaneously that the mask was surrounded by long black hair that was being tossed wildly about and that the person wearing the mask was a woman. Then the ax was dropped back into his hands, so abruptly that he lost it for a moment and caught it again around his knees.

"Win fame with this," the voice told him, sounding like no woman's voice he had ever heard. "Win fame, but do not forget those who came before you. I have spoken."

The mask vanished in the darkness, and Cusi and Otoronco bowed and backed out of the awning house, Cusi finding it much easier to move in that direction. The moonlight blinded both of them, and they stood blinking at one another in the center of the boxlike courtyard. Cusi was filled with a sudden buoyancy, a release of pressure that made him grab the ax by the end of the handle and whirl away from Otoronco, delivering a series of coordinated strokes to the defenseless air. His momentum brought him back around to face

Otoronco from a perfect fighting stance, his body balanced and flexible, the ax poised to strike. Otoronco reached out and lightly touched the studded stone head, but when he tried to take the weapon, Cusi shook his head and backed out of reach. A smile creased Otoronco's rugged face, making the scar climb his cheek.

"That is right. It is yours now," he said and pointed with his chin at the doorway, allowing Cusi to precede him out of the Illapa Cancha.

THEY REMAINED outside in the moonlight, Otoronco sitting in the stone seat in the center of his courtyard, chewing coca and watching Cusi work off a restlessness that sent his muscles into spasms if he stayed still for too long. He demonstrated his skill with the ax, fighting battles with his shadow until his skin was shiny with sweat and his shoulders ached. He put the weapon down at Otoronco's feet but kept pacing, accepting a blanket and a cup of akha from the retainer who had come out to serve them. He wrapped the blanket around his shoulders and drank to ward off the chill of his drying sweat, walking back and forth in front of Otoronco's seat. When his legs were finally as tired as his arms and he had drunk several cups without feeling any effect, he came to a halt before Otoronco, who gazed at him impassively, his cheek bulging with coca.

"Grandfather," Cusi said plaintively, but Otoronco held up a hand to cut him off.

"Do not ask me what you should believe. You must decide that for yourself. Nor will I ask *you* to promise me fame. No man can know what the gods will provide him. But if the favor of Huayna Capac should fall upon you, you must ask him to let me fight again. You must persuade him that I am no threat to his authority, and that I could be useful in the field."

"I am sure that is true, my lord—"

"But?" Otoronco interrupted, his eyes flaring wide. "Would you become small again, Cusi, a man like your father? I thought I had seen you grow large in spirit."

Cusi straightened up and drew the blanket tighter around him.

"You have helped to make me a man, Grandfather. Whatever fame I may win, I owe to you."

"But?" Otoronco demanded again, when Cusi hesitated. "Do not tell me that you are afraid to risk Huayna Capac's displeasure."

"No, my lord," Cusi admitted. Then he took a deep breath. "But there is something I must ask of Huayna Capac before anything else."

Otoronco reared back in his seat, as if to regard him from a greater distance. "What is that?"

"His daughter. In marriage."

Otoronco's mouth fell open, and then he began to laugh, so hard that he had to spit out the wad of coca tucked into his cheek. He slapped the stone on which his arm rested, shaking his head at Cusi.

"Here I was, questioning your willingness to ask the impossible, when already you have more in mind for yourself. Forgive me for doubting you, Cusi Huaman. Can I trust you, then, to ask for me after he has refused you his daughter? It may seem a small thing to him in comparison."

"You have my promise," Cusi agreed. Then he added quietly, "Are you certain he will refuse me?"

Otoronco gave an elaborate shrug, closing one eye and spreading his hands. "I am certain of nothing, especially where you are concerned. Perhaps you are a brother to lightning, a favorite of Illapa. The gods can change anything. So ask for what you want, or take it. Do not grovel for favors."

"Yes, my lord," Cusi bowed, then took him at his word. "I would like your permission, then, to visit the man who gave me my spirit brother."

"Go," Otoronco snorted in amusement. "Anything else? No? You will get to the girl on your own? Good. Then sit for a while, if you can hold yourself still. There is a story I have never told you, a story I have told to only a few people. It is about the vision Pachacuti had on the plain, on the night before he had to fight the Chanca."

"I have sung the song," Cusi murmured, squatting on his heels in front of the seat. Otoronco waited, glancing up at the moon, while one of the retainers refilled Cusi's cup and departed.

"I heard this from Pachacuti's own lips," Otoronco said then, his voice slightly hoarse, "and I have never questioned that it is true. Perhaps when I have told you, you will understand why I consider it the duty of an Inca, *always,* to attempt the impossible . . ."

Tumibamba

ACAPANA ESCORTED her to the entrance of the Coya's enclosure, but then Micay went on alone to the small adobe house Quilaco had been given by the Coya. A servant directed her to the garden that lay on the other side of a grove of molle trees that shaded one side of the house. Micay slowed when she heard voices ahead, then stopped altogether when she caught a glimpse of Quilaco's visitors: Mama Huarcay and her protégé, Cori Cuillor. They were standing next to the bench on which Quilaco was seated, obviously in the process of saying farewell. Mama Huarcay was wearing her warmest smile, and Cori Cuillor appeared both alluring and self-assured as she urged Quilaco to remain where he was, sitting in the circle of sunlight that surrounded his bench. Quilaco was also smiling, though Micay thought she could detect a certain dimness in his response, which she took as a hopeful sign.

She felt even more fortunate a moment later when the two women left the garden by another path, sparing her a confrontation she did not need right now. She had not had an occasion to speak to Mama Huarcay since the Quicuchicoy, but she did not suppose the Fourth Wife had forgotten her, or would not have taken the opportunity to ridicule her attachment to Chimpu Ocllo. Micay took a last peek at Quilaco before going forward, watching him adjust the sling around his arm with a preoccupied frown on his handsome face.

When he saw her come out of the trees, though, he forgot all about his injuries and jumped to his feet, craning his neck to see if anyone was behind her. Disappointment flashed briefly in his dark eyes when he realized that she was alone, and there was an urgency to his greeting that he could not quite mask.

"I am pleased to see you, Micay. Have you brought a message from Quinti?"

"Yes, my lord," Micay said. She paused as if to collect herself. "She has asked me to convey her regrets to you, my lord. She does not feel that she can come to see you anymore. She feels that it will only lead to further misunderstanding."

Quilaco spun on his heel, hiding his face from her for a moment. He turned back more slowly, his expression fixed and hard except for a muscle that twitched in his jaw.

"Very well. You may tell her that I regret her decision."

"Yes, my lord," Micay said with a bow, beginning to back away from him.

"Micay."

"My lord?" she inquired, trying to sound surprised rather than relieved. Quilaco grimaced and gestured for her to sit on the bench beside him.

"You must tell me what has happened to her."

Micay settled herself carefully on the edge of the bench, facing him from a few feet away. She hesitated before she spoke, not wanting to seem too well prepared with her answers.

"She feels that you have already been told by others. And that you have chosen to believe them."

"I did not want to," Quilaco insisted. "I was shocked that I had to learn these things from other people. Why did she not tell me, the first time she visited, *why* she was teaching? Why did she not tell me that she had joined Chimpu Ocllo?"

"You were still weak and in pain, my lord," Micay explained. "She did not wish to trouble you."

Quilaco gave her a fierce sidelong glance, looking past the finely arched beak of his nose.

"She also did not know how she felt about me. I could see that. I could understand it, after more than a year apart. But then she came the second time, and she did not deny the things I had heard about her. She tried instead to *defend* them to me."

"And you would not listen to her," Micay said quietly.

"I could not believe what I was hearing! She showed no remorse for the things she had said about the Sapa Inca. She seemed to feel that it was a foolish but necessary experience. She asked me quite seriously if *I* was satisfied with the way the campaign has been conducted."

"You did not answer her," Micay pointed out more sharply, shedding the guise of an innocent messenger.

Quilaco's eyes narrowed and his face hardened again. "I have no need to make foolish statements. Why are you really here, Micay? Is Chimpu Ocllo behind this?"

"She gave Quinti her advice, certainly. As the Coya and Mama Huarcay have given you theirs."

"The Coya has great affection for me because of my mother. I cannot spurn her advice."

"Has she advised you to spurn Quinti?"

"No," Quilaco said quickly. "She has not lost her affection for Mama Cori, either. But I can tell you that she has no love for Chimpu Ocllo. In Cuzco, the Coya has always been the head of the cult of Mama Quilla."

"Forgive me, my lord, but this is not Cuzco. Nor is it a village the Inca conquered only yesterday."

"You have obviously mastered all of Chimpu Ocllo's arguments," Quilaco said scornfully. "Were you sent here to taunt me with them?"

"No, my lord. I was sent to see if you would risk what you know as bravely as you risked your life. Or if you can believe only what the court chooses to believe."

Quilaco stood up, his eyes flaring with anger.

"What do you think you know about this war that the court does not?" he demanded.

"We know that many of the warriors were drunk when the Caranguis attacked," Micay said, and watched the color leave his face and his anger flag. He glowered at her for a moment, then turned and walked to the edge of a nearby pool, moving awkwardly because of the sling and the bandage around his thigh. He stood looking down at the lily pads that floated on the surface of the water, or perhaps at his own reflection. Micay rose to meet him when he limped back, still glowering.

"Quinti asks much of me," he said in a taut voice.

"She feels she has much to give, my lord. That is why she risked sending me here in her place. She knew she might lose you, but she would lose much more if she lied about her feelings just to appease you. She wants to share what is in her heart, not conceal it."

Quilaco regarded her in silence, and though Micay sensed that he was persuaded, she also felt a certain resentment toward her, as if he were blaming her in some way. She realized that she was the only witness to his capitulation, something she had not considered when she had agreed to act as Quinti's messenger.

"I have heard you," Quilaco said at last. "Tell Quinti that I will visit her in the micho's quarters soon. I will send one of the retainers to arrange a proper time."

Micay bowed in compliance and left him, feeling his eyes on her back as she retreated into the molle trees. She thought she had spoken well on Quinti's behalf, though she had not tried to improve upon what she had been told to say by Quinti and the high priestess. Perhaps in time Quilaco would realize that the words had not been her own and that she had not been trying to trick him into changing his mind. Perhaps he would even come to see his capitulation as an act of courage and independence. Or, Micay thought wearily, perhaps I have again found my way in between a husband and a wife—before a match has even been made.

THOUGH SHE had been offered new quarters in the Mollecancha, Chimpu Ocllo remained in the enclosure that belonged to the high priestess, which was on the same high ground as the Coricancha. The three small houses and one awning house were usually crowded with guests and pilgrims in addition to the staff of mamacona and the women who served in or were being trained for the cult, but Chimpu Ocllo seemed to prefer it that way. She did not mind noise or interruptions or the sound of conversations other than her own, and she encouraged the women to talk while they worked. She had also trained everyone who served her to attend to their tasks and not to her, so that she could come and go as she pleased without an entourage forming every time she moved. She often left the compound and went out into the streets of Tumibamba, accompanied only by those she had invited. She was an energetic walker, and she sometimes took her companions as far as the river before bringing them back at the same pace.

Micay had done this with her once, in a small group that included Quinti, and she had found it an exhilarating experience. Chimpu Ocllo knew every section of the city and the history of the clan that occupied each, and she was known and welcomed everywhere, though the Cañari, too, seemed to know not to detain her when she felt like walking. Micay had returned that day feeling that her knowledge of the world outside the Mollecancha had been expanded enormously, and she had understood for the first time the pride and pleasure Quinti took in being able to find her own way to Cuenca.

On this day, Chimpu Ocllo summoned only Micay as she headed purposefully for the compound entrance, and Micay followed after her quietly, trying not to display her pride in this mark of favor. She was glad that she had worn her most comfortable sandals, because Chimpu Ocllo was setting a typically rapid pace. It was a clear day, with the mountains visible in the east, and Chimpu Ocllo seemed to choose her path so that one or another of the mountains could be seen at the end of the street, framed by the walls on either side. She identified the mountains by name, calling each one "Apu," Great Lord, and she explained that it was no accident that the streets of Tumibamba led directly to the Apus. The paths that had separated the clans in the original village of Tumibamba had been aligned with the mountains, so that the lords of the Earth could look down and bless the people who lived below.

"The paths to the Apus have never been altered," she told Micay, "except for where the Inca took land for the great square and the Mollecancha."

Micay thought of the paths within the Mollecancha, which constantly turned back on themselves, skirting blank walls and guarded gates, restricting both sight and access. This street, which had seemed drab and dusty at first, began to seem spacious and open to the sky, lit by the luminescent glow of the snow-capped peak in the distance. She remembered seeing the same mountain framed by the walls of the canyon where she and the other ñustas had visited the hot springs, and she understood another aspect of why the high priestess had sent them there.

She was disconcerted when Chimpu Ocllo suddenly led her down a narrow side street, and she realized belatedly that they had stopped hurrying. They came out into a small plaza where a group of Cañari women were gathered, and for a moment Micay thought that Chimpu Ocllo had brought her to a Cañari ceremony. But they were sitting and standing in too random a fashion and did not seem to be waiting for the high priestess's arrival. Nor were they working at a common task, and though they were quiet, they did not appear to be in mourning.

"Do you know what this is?" Chimpu asked, drawing her closer to the gathering. About half of the women were sitting in a rough circle on the hard-packed earth of the plaza. In front of them were cloths covered with piles of fruits and vegetables: avocadoes, papayas, and mangos, several sizes and colors of potatoes, big pale green squash, and uchu peppers in brilliant shades of green, orange and red. More than anything else, it was the colors and shapes of the piles that reminded her, and she was surprised when the word came to her.

"It is a market."

Chimpu laughed softly at her surprise and gestured with her chin for her to watch. Micay had nearly forgotten what bartering was like, since there had been none of it in the House of Chosen Women and there was none among the Incas, who received everything they needed from the royal storehouses. These women sat or squatted across from one another, silently adding to their respective piles, potatoes on one side and peppers on the other, until a satisfactory agreement was reached and they simply exchanged piles. Micay looked on in fascination, feeling old memories well up on the edges of her consciousness.

Then she became aware of the conversation going on in Cañar next to her, and she saw that Chimpu Ocllo had been approached by several older women, probably the leading women in the clan. They all had something in their hands that they were trying to get Chimpu to take: a pineapple, some bananas, a string of bright peppers. Chimpu appeared to admire everything but finally accepted only two avocados, one of which she handed to Micay. Micay bowed in gratitude, and Chimpu introduced her in Cañar, of which the only words Micay understood were "Chachapoyas ñusta" and "chosen woman," for which there were no Cañar equivalents. The women seemed most impressed that she had been a chosen woman, raising their hands to their mouths or touching their shoulders as they bowed to her.

Chimpu soon made her farewells and led Micay out of the plaza, carrying her avocado in one hand, near her waist. Micay cupped hers in both hands, feeling both the smooth contours of its shape and the rough corrugations of its greenish-black skin. She suddenly remembered being small, her hands barely large enough to fit around the avocado her mother had given her to hold. She remembered squeezing the ripe fruit with her fingers until it was mushy, then happily biting into the skin, totally unprepared for the bitter taste—

"What are you remembering?" Chimpu inquired, breaking into her thoughts. Micay blinked and looked around at the street before holding up the avocado in response.

"Once, when I was very young, I tried to eat one of these through the skin."

"When you lived in—"

"In Suta," Micay said automatically, then stopped in confusion, blinking harder. The last time Chimpu had asked her where she was born, she had not been able to remember. They were walking very slowly now, Chimpu leaning toward her intently.

"You see, you remember much more than you think."

"I was made to forget in the House of Chosen Women. I see no purpose in remembering now."

"No? What about your dream, Micay? Your body went across the bridge, but your spirit followed the condor, the symbol of your people."

"The Incas are my people."

"Now they are, yes. But you were not a mere child when you were taken. Part of your life has been lost, and you suffer because of it. It is the disease of the Incas, who think they can live anywhere and withstand any kind of loneliness. They build walls like those of Cuzco and make everyone speak Quechua to them and then imagine they have never left home."

"But you are at home here," Micay ventured, still trying to assimilate the startling notion that the Incas were somehow sick, a notion that Chimpu had voiced almost casually.

"I have been here for twenty years," Chimpu said with a pink-gummed smile. "And I understood very early that I was lost. That is how I am able to recognize what has happened to you. But you have no guarantee that you will live in only one place for so long. If you marry an Inca or an Inca by privilege, you might have to follow your husband to many places, perhaps to places where you would be the only Incas. You must be complete within yourself if you hope to bear the strain and confusion of that."

"I have always sought wholeness," Micay averred.

The Coya Pacsa smiled again. "Yes, I know. That is why you must try to remember, even if it is painful. You must watch your dreams, for it is in dreams that the gods and the huacas whisper to us. Listen to what they tell you."

Micay nodded earnestly and was startled when Chimpu tossed her avocado into the air and caught it again. Chimpu laughed and pointed at the avocado in Micay's hand.

"When that is ripe, be sure to peel it carefully. It is only the inside that is nourishing."

Cuzco

I T WAS LATE afternoon before Cusi arrived at the herder's hut. Weighed down by the bundle on his back, he had traveled more slowly than usual and then had spent more time than he planned at the huaca. But he had no regrets about that, and he was still feeling the elation of the gift he had left at the huaca, a gift that had been both a release from the past and an offering to the future.

When he found Raurau Illa's young helper waiting for him in the hut, he told himself not to be surprised. He smiled at the boy, sharing his good spirits.

"Greetings, Alco. I wish to see Raurau Illa."

"You are expected," the boy said curtly, rising from his squat. His broad Colla face had shown no reaction to Cusi's smile, though Cusi saw him glance once at the place on Cusi's hip where his spirit brother was concealed beneath his tunic and the thick weave of his waistband.

"Did he know I was coming today?" Cusi asked, adjusting the bundle on his back as he and Alco started off across the plain at a fast walk.

"He knew you were coming days ago. I have been waiting."

"I had important duties to attend to," Cusi began, then wondered why he was explaining himself. Did the boy mean to sound resentful, or was he merely nervous in the presence of an Inca? "I am sorry if I made you wait," he added, in what he thought was a soothing tone. "Raurau Illa must have better uses for his helper."

"I am not his helper," Alco retorted, giving him a swift, angry glance. "I am his successor."

The resentment was unmistakable yet still startling, and it made Cusi pause to consider what kind of threat he posed to this boy. Who am I to Raurau Illa? he wondered, watching as Alco began to open space between them. He had no answer, but he decided he should not allow Alco to walk away from him so rudely.

"*I* am his *guest,*" he said loudly, and saw the boy's head come up and his pace slacken. Cusi caught up with him, then pulled his bundle off over his head. "I have brought gifts for Raurau Illa and his people. No doubt you are the proper person to carry them for me."

Cusi unceremoniously dropped the heavy bundle into Alco's reluctant hands, nearly pulling him off balance. Still, the boy shouldered it without a word and started off again. Making sure he had his coca bag—a gift from Otoronco that was still new to him—under his arm and his cloak tied loosely around his neck, Cusi went along with him, his hands empty at his sides. He had not brought a weapon with him, expecting to find no enemies this close to Cuzco. Apparently he had already found one, and he hoped, if there were others ahead who resented him, that they were no larger than the boy beside him.

THE VILLAGE was much farther from the huaca than Cusi had anticipated, and the rolling expanse of the plain seemed to angle toward the sky, which had turned a solid gray. Cusi squinted into a chilly northeast wind, feeling slightly breathless, his temples aching from the altitude. He was glad he had thought to bring the cloak; he would need it later. He would have wrapped himself in it already, except that Alco was clad only in his tunic and was barefoot, besides. Cusi had focused on his feet as they walked, noticing that the skin was creased and whitened like old leather, or like the skin of a person much older. He was sorry now that he had made Alco carry the bundle this whole way, but he could think of no way to ask for it back without insulting the boy even further. It will make him strong, he told himself guiltily, like Otoronco's ax did for me.

The ten houses of the village were clustered on high, rocky ground unsuitable for either pasture or the cultivation of potatoes or quinoa. They were built of fieldstone set in mud mortar, and their thickly thatched roofs were bleached and frayed from exposure to the harsh weather of the high plain. Each house was surrounded by a small walled compound that in some cases served as a corral for the family llamas.

Alco led him to the entrance of a compound that seemed no larger or more elaborate than the others, pushing through the wooden gate that kept three white llamas penned inside. The animals shied off into a corner as Cusi entered, distracting him enough that he forgot to put the gate back in place behind him. Alco went back to do it for him, his broad face compressed with a kind of weary vindication. Then he preceded Cusi through the single low doorway of the windowless house, into a darkness that was thick with the odors of smoke, wool, llama grease, and unwashed human bodies. Cusi held his breath, straightening carefully from the stoop he had assumed to get under the stone lintel of the doorway. To his left a woman crouched in the glow of the clay oven she was tending; straight ahead, three men sat on a low platform against the back wall. Alco had deposited Cusi's bundle in front of them and then squatted down to one side of the platform. When he could see well enough to recognize Raurau Illa as the central of the three figures, Cusi went forward and squatted on his heels in front of him, facing him across the shapeless mass of his gift bundle.

"Greetings, Grandfather," he said respectfully, and was surprised when the man to Raurau Illa's right spoke in response, though his words were not directed at Cusi.

"He has come, as you said. We have seen it."

Cusi found Raurau Illa's blank, silvery eyes in the near darkness and saw that they were fixed on him.

"Alco," Raurau Illa said without turning his head. "Tell me how Cusi Auqui has changed since you last saw him."

The boy seemed to freeze in place, facing Raurau Illa, and he spoke from memory, without glancing sideways at Cusi.

"He is bigger and stronger than he was, and he has the earplugs of a warrior. He wears a headband that is red and black and a tunic of fine cloth, and he has a coca bag that he did not have before. He has obviously become wealthy and used to having servants do things for him. He was very pleased with himself when he arrived at the hut."

Cusi was tempted to smile at the mixture of contempt and grudging respect in the boy's voice, but he decided that it might be interpreted as condescension.

"What did he carry with him?" Raurau demanded.

"A heavy bundle of gifts. For you and our people, he said."

"What have you brought us, Cusi?" Raurau asked, abruptly abandoning his examination of the boy. Cusi leaned forward and untied the twisted ends of the large blanket that held his gifts. He spread the bundle open, moving a little to one side so that the light from the doorway could illuminate the contents.

"There are mantles and loincloths and other pieces of clothing," Cusi explained, unfolding a few of the top items and placing them into Raurau's outstretched hands. "Also some sandals and four cups. These are prizes I won for my running. I have also won a new name: Cusi Huaman."

"Show me the cups," Raurau said, passing the items in his hands to the men on either side of him. The men fingered the cloth and made humming sounds that apparently indicated satisfaction. Cusi dug down to the center of the bundle, unwrapping the four wooden cups from the garments he had wound around them for protection. Two were carved in the shape of puma heads, the snarling faces painted vividly in black and red. The third cup had a repeating pattern of lynx heads in low relief around its cylindrical sides, and the fourth had representations of mountains beneath a band of sky symbols associated with Illapa. Cusi handed the latter to Raurau first.

"This made me think of you, Grandfather," he said.

Raurau turned the cup in his hands, tracing the carvings with his fingertips. Then he showed his teeth in a brief smile and put the cup down in front of him, obviously making it his own. "Yes," he said succinctly, holding out his hands for more. Cusi gave him the puma cups, which he distributed to the men beside him, both of whom bowed ceremoniously to Cusi. He lingered so long over the last cup that Cusi wondered if the relief were too shallow for his fingers to decipher.

"They are lynx heads," he supplied helpfully.

Raurau appeared to laugh. "Yes. And you have come to tell me, have you not, that you are going north, to Chinchaysuyo, the Lynx Quarter?"

"I leave in seven days."

"Then whoever possesses this cup will have to think of you in the north every time he drinks. Perhaps you should be the one who decides who will bear the burden of your memory."

He handed the cup back to Cusi, who squinted at him in perplexity. He did not know anyone else in this village; he did not even know the names of the men who had received the other two cups. He briefly considered simply handing the cup back to Raurau, but then realized what the old man wanted him to do. So he swiveled on his heels and held the cup out to Alco.

"You should have this, then, as the successor. We can drink together when I return to Cuzco to celebrate our victory over the Carangui."

Alco accepted the cup with a slight nod, his expression wary.

"There is another favor you can do for us," Raurau said to Cusi, who cocked his head for a moment, feeling that Raurau was prevailing rather freely on his generosity.

"Speak, Grandfather," he suggested, wondering how wealthy Raurau thought him to be.

"A young man from this village has recently been taken by the Inca, as a herder for the pack llamas going north. His name is Urcon; he is Alco's older brother. Will you give him your protection?"

"I am an unproven warrior," Cusi reminded him, "and I will have to go where I am sent. But I will look for this Urcon when we arrive in Tumibamba, and I will do whatever I can to help him."

"I ask no more than that," Raurau agreed. "Tell me: How long can you stay with us now?"

"Only tonight. I must be back by noon tomorrow."

"We must talk, then," Raurau decided. He swiveled his head to the right and then the left, acknowledging his companions. "Return here later, my friends, and I will fill your cups with akha."

The two men murmured their gratitude to Cusi as they departed, and then Alco did the same in a barely audible voice. The woman was still crouched by the stove, boiling potatoes in a pot, and a couple of children were playing in the corner of the room, but Raurau ignored their presence.

"You have coca in your bag?" he asked abruptly, surprising Cusi with yet another request. But Cusi had intended to offer him some, so he dutifully unslung the fringed bag from around his shoulder and passed it over.

"It has already been ground and mixed with ash," he explained, "in the style of the Chunchos."

Raurau grunted and filled one cheek before handing the bag back. Cusi would have liked some for his headache, but he was not certain that he could chew and talk at the same time, so he refrained. He listened to the wet sound of Raurau's chewing, reminding himself that this man had given him his spirit brother and knowledge of his special relationship with Illapa. He had the right to impose on Cusi's generosity.

"You must feel that much has been taken from you and little given," Raurau said then. "But I have assumed that you came here for only one thing. I assumed that you came to hear your future."

"You can tell me that?"

"I can tell you some, if you wish to know. But you must tell me everything that has happened to you, Cusi Huaman. Come, sit closer. I must know the man who owns this future. I must know if he is ready to claim it . . ."

"THAT IS not uncommon," Raurau said when Cusi concluded his recitation by telling him about his deep sleeps. "Your spirit is thinking about dying. It is practicing. This happens to young warriors who are waiting for their first battle."

"But it does not happen when I am with the warriors. Only with Tocto."

"That is when you care most about being alive, which makes death very large and powerful. It will seem even more tempting after you leave her, and you may feel that you do not care about anything. You may feel reckless and brave and ready to throw your life away. You must not indulge such feelings, Cusi," Raurau said sternly, "not even to impress your comrades. You must keep your spirit ready, because you will face death much sooner than you expect."

Cusi drew a slow breath, trying to assimilate the sudden shift from advice to prediction. Obviously Raurau had decided that he was ready to hear his future.

"Will this occur before I reach Tumibamba?"

"I do not know where Tumibamba is. I can only tell you that the danger will come as a surprise."

"Will I face it with courage?"

"You will face it with your whole being, and you will not be the same when you are done. You will survive, but you will be carried away in darkness, and the faces you see will be those of strangers."

"Will I be taken captive, then?" Cusi asked in a tight voice.

"I do not know. I could not see any more. Beyond this, I know only that you will be gone for many years, and that one day you will return to this village. You will come here in need."

Cusi frowned, though now he understood why Raurau had wanted him to make a bond with Alco. But the thought that he would come *here*, so close to Cuzco, in *need*, overwhelmed any sense of gratitude he might have had. It was a dismal conclusion to what seemed a bleak and ominous recital. He had expected to be warned of trials and challenges, but he had also hoped to hear of triumphs and accomplishments, perhaps even a mention of fame. Instead he had been promised only survival, along with vague and frightening hints of blindness or captivity. He felt poorly repaid for his generosity, reduced rather than enlarged in spirit.

"There is more that I can tell you," Raurau added, "but not like this. We must eat and drink first. Especially we must drink. You are under no vow of abstinence?"

"I will be honored to drink with you," Cusi murmured wearily, finding the idea of drunkenness powerfully attractive. He closed his eyes, knowing Raurau could not see him, yet hoping that the old man might somehow sense his

despair. Yet Raurau merely called softly to the woman by the stove, telling
her it was time they fed their guest.

LATER CUSI found himself sitting on the front edge of Raurau's platform, alone
in the middle of the crowded room, and drunk in a way he had never been
drunk before. After they had eaten, Raurau had produced a bag of brown
powder that he said was made from the seeds of the villca tree, along with other
ingredients. He said it would sharpen Cusi's senses better than coca. Using a
hollow piece of cane, he had blown a small amount of the powder up into
Cusi's nostrils, setting off a fire inside his head that had blinded him and made
the tears pour from his eyes. When his vision had cleared, though, there
seemed to be much more light in the room, so that he could actually make out
Raurau's features without straining. His hearing had also become much more
acute and selective, so that the sounds he wished to hear seemed amplified
above the background noise and plain to his ear. He had put this marvelous
capacity to full use as soon as the people of the village began to crowd into
the room, because those bold enough to address him at all did so in shy
murmurs, their faces half averted. Cusi had not always heard everything they
said to him, but he had heard enough to keep from embarrassing himself or
them.

The akha he had drunk had dulled his worry about embarrassment but had
only seemed to heighten his state of alertness, so that he was aware of everything around him even as he lost touch with his own body. The room had
grown quite warm, and he had long since followed the example of the other
men and stripped down to his loincloth and headband. But he was still sweating profusely, radiating an intense heat of his own, and though his muscles felt
taut and swollen with blood, he was no longer certain if they were capable of
movement. Nor did he have any desire to move, or drink, or talk to anyone.
He was simply content to sit and watch the other people in the room, finding
their faces tantalizingly familiar, though still the faces of strangers. He had met
them all, but Raurau was the only one who could talk to him like a man rather
than an Inca.

The space directly in front of him had been left open by the other guests,
out of respect for the map Cusi had laid out on the floor earlier in the evening:
Chinchaysuyo, the Lynx Quarter. The raw wool he had used for mountains
and the stones for cities were still in place, the quinoa stalks representing the
Royal Road still in line, showing the path he would follow to the north, to
places most of these people would never see. They had watched with wide eyes
as he laid down stone after stone, explaining the distance between cities and
the nature of the people who lived in each. In the midst of constructing the
map, he had felt his despair lift, banished by the vastness of the world he was
describing. He realized that it was Raurau's vision that was limited, not his
own future. Raurau had seen as far as he could, but he had seen only a little,
and he had not precluded what he had not mentioned. The dangers he had

foreseen might consume only days of Cusi's life, while he had promised him many years before his return. That assurance had seemed more precious with each cup of akha Cusi drank, a gift both incredible and gratifying.

A gentle poke sent one of his earplugs swinging, and he saw out of the corner of his eye that the little boy was back. He had done this earlier, captivated beyond shyness by the shining golden cylinders that stretched Cusi's earlobes toward his shoulders. There had been a moment when everyone in the room seemed to draw a common breath, waiting to see how Cusi would react. When he had smiled and indulged the child's curiosity, he saw people smile at him who had not been able to meet his eyes before, and he knew that he had won some respect that was not commanded by the earplugs themselves.

He smiled now, and the boy peeked around his shoulder and smiled back. Cusi experimented with the muscles in his neck and found that they did indeed work, enough at least to turn his head and make his earplugs dance. The boy crowed with delight and pointed a stubby finger at Cusi's head, his wide brown eyes filled with golden reflections. He was perhaps two years old and was completely naked, his face and belly still soft and round.

Then some people in the corner of the room started to sing, as they had on several other occasions, and the boy began to dance out in front of Cusi, onto the map. He shuffled through the grass that was supposed to the the Mother Water, kicking up dry yellow waves, then put the port city of Tumbez up into the woolen mountains with a nudge of his toe. He giggled and grinned at Cusi, who grinned back in encouragement. Cusi found himself immensely pleased at the prospect of this child dancing across the world, oblivious of its vastness and its dangers. The boy whirled and sent part of the Royal Road skidding across the floor, drawing the worried attention of several adults, who relaxed when Cusi shook his head at them and laughed.

A moment later Alco came through the low doorway on the other side of the room. Cusi watched him with one eye, then with both when he realized that Alco was carrying the huaman in his arms. He went straight past Cusi, obviously taking the statue to Raurau for his decision. Cusi glanced back at the boy, who had danced over Caxamarca and was doing great damage to the lands of the Chachapoyas, then turned to look over his shoulder, his muscles prodded into action by curiosity. He saw Raurau wet a finger and touch it to the statue, then raise the finger to his lips.

"Cusi," he said, pointing his chin in Cusi's direction, "you left this at the huaca?"

"Yes . . . I wanted to give my fame to Illapa."

"It has flown after you instead," Raurau observed, appearing amused. "What would you have us do? Bury it? Leave it out on the plain to melt in the rain?"

Cusi had turned all the way around to face him, and he saw the boy creep up onto the platform next to Raurau, his eyes on the white hawk in Raurau's hands.

"Use it," Cusi said impulsively. "Share it out among the people who are here."

"Huaman cachi," Raurau proclaimed softly, holding the statue out to Alco. "See that everyone is given some of the hawk salt."

Alco carried the statue into the center of the room, closer to the light from the stove and the single torch over the doorway. The little boy was at his hip the whole way, reaching up for the hawk, but Alco resolutely ignored him. He stood on the edge of the ruined map and held the statue over his head, turning in a circle so that everyone could admire it.

"Huaman cachi," he repeated, and bent to set the statue upright on the floor. The little boy immediately tried to claim it, but Alco held him away with a forearm and pushed him into the hands of one of the women. Then he straightened up and gestured for people to step back, turning to accept a large, oblong hammering stone from someone behind him. Cusi felt his whole body tense as he saw Alco heft the stone and glance once in Cusi's direction, the torchlight giving his eyes a vengeful gleam. Cusi clamped his lips against the urge to cry out in protest, realizing it was too late.

As Alco raised the stone, though, the little boy darted out in front of him, hugged the hawk against his stomach, and toddled toward Cusi as fast as he could. Alco checked his swing with an effort that drew laughter from the people around him, which in turn made the boy look back over his shoulder, chortling with glee at his theft. His feet had already gotten tangled up in a pile of wool that had once been mountains, and the backward glance cost him the last of his balance, so that he stumbled and began to fall forward, his arms still wrapped tightly around the statue.

Cusi sprang before he even knew that he had gathered his legs under him, surprising himself as much as everyone else. He landed in a wide crouch, grunting as he caught the boy in time and broke his fall, easing him gently to the floor. The boy was still laughing when Cusi lifted him to his feet and relieved him of the statue, which he surrendered willingly. Cusi glanced past him at the gaping faces of Alco and the people behind him, realizing that his sudden leap had stunned them into silence. He smiled at the boy and let him touch the hawk, enjoying the feel of it in his own hands. He remembered the solemn way he had offered it to the huaca and realized that he should have been as careful the second time. Fame was too rare to be dispensed with so carelessly.

"Thank you, little one," he said to the boy. "But this belongs to everyone."

He stood up and walked over to Alco, trailed by the boy, who kept Cusi between himself and Alco.

"It flew back to me again," Cusi said, setting the statue down at Alco's feet. "Perhaps I was not quite ready to release it. I gave it once to Illapa; I give it now to you. Dispose of it with care."

Stepping back, Cusi patted the little boy on the head and then walked around Alco toward the doorway, the people parting to make a path for him. The boy followed him but was intercepted and scooped up by a woman presumably his mother, and Cusi ducked through the entrance alone. He heard a muted crack followed by excited cries behind him, but he did not glance back. It was enough to have given his fame away; he did not have to see it shattered into a hundred small and indistinguishable pieces.

MOST OF the guests had gone before Raurau initiated the last round of drinking, though a couple of men had passed out and lay sleeping where they had fallen. The banked coals in the oven provided the room's only light, a dim, reddish glow that barely disturbed the darkness. Raurau was standing in the center of the room, swaying drunkenly from side to side and murmuring unintelligibly to himself. He had the drinking cup Cusi had given him in one hand and a gourd rattle in the other, and occasionally he gave the rattle a limp shake and raised one foot, briefly remembering that he was dancing. Cusi watched in a drunken stupor, his eyes opening and closing of their own accord, all alertness long since drowned in akha. He had been drunk like this before and knew that there was nothing to be learned from it. It was something to be endured rather than enjoyed, and he always regretted it profoundly the next day.

He woke from a doze to find himself toppling slowly sideways, and though he was able to pull himself back into a sitting position, the effort made his head spin and his stomach take a sudden drop. He held back against the nausea that rose in his throat, but he knew that he could not postpone the inevitable for long. Using the wall behind him for support, he rose to his feet in stages, then pointed himself toward the doorway and lurched into motion. The ground tilted under him but he kept himself staggering forward, remembering to duck at the last instant so that the top of his head just grazed the stone lintel as he plunged out into the night. The air felt fresh and delicious after the smoky atmosphere of the house, and he gulped it in for a moment, then made a clumsy run for the corner of the courtyard.

It was a thorough purging, satisfying in its violence, so that he felt no distress even while he was retching on his knees in the cold dirt. He had taken in too much for one day and needed emptying. The heat went out of him along with the akha, and the sweat turned icy on his bare skin. But it felt good to shiver and spit and have the ground stay still beneath him. He let his head bow and his shoulders slump, releasing the tense hold he had kept on himself ever since meeting Alco. It had been his protection against the strangeness of being here, of never knowing what would be asked of him next.

He heard the shuffling of feet behind him but did not turn or try to rise. Perhaps someone else needed to be sick. Then a loud buzzing sound erupted directly behind him, startling him so completely that he ducked and rolled to one side, as if avoiding a blow. He came up onto his knees and turned to see Raurau dancing in front of him, shaking two gourd rattles with such vigor that Cusi felt pinned by the sound. Raurau's eyes were shut tightly, but he shook the rattles right at Cusi's face, hammering on the air between them. Then he stopped and let his arms fall to his sides. When he lifted the rattles again, it was in a slow, measured rhythm, and he began to sing in a hoarse monotone:

> The earth will not hold you, Cusi Huaman,
> The earth will not hold you.
> You will soar like a hawk,
> And plummet like Illapa's lightning.
>
> There are condors in your sky, Cusi Huaman,
> There are condors in your sky.
> One flutters to earth;
> One watches tirelessly,
> With eyes that pierce the darkness.

Raurau repeated both verses, then stopped as abruptly as he had begun. He turned and walked slowly toward the house, pushing out a foot to find his way, the rattles dangling silently in his hands. Cusi struggled to his feet, feeling the earth trying to hold him back. He put a hand to his hip and felt the warmth of his spirit brother before his fingers discerned its shape through the weave of the waistband. It was the only part of him still warm. His skin burned coldly, as if he had been rubbed with ice, and he had the vivid but incredible impression that Raurau had tattooed him with his buzzing rattles. Shivering, he looked up at the night sky, which was lightening as the moon began to rise behind the eastern peaks, and he wondered if he were being watched even now by the condor who saw in darkness.

Alco suddenly appeared in front of him, holding a blanket in his hands. He was followed closely by the three llamas, their white heads bobbing on their long, graceful necks. He glanced pointedly at the hand Cusi had clamped to his hip, and was startled when Cusi abruptly lifted it. To cover his surprise, he held the blanket out to Cusi.

"You are cold."

Cusi was shivering violently, but he crossed his arms on his chest rather than reach for the blanket. He cleared his throat and spoke rapidly, so that his voice would not tremble.

"The stone is mine, Alco. It is pointless to resent me for having it."

Alco frowned and looked down at his feet, pulling the blanket back against his chest. Cusi hugged himself and breathed through his teeth, trying to control his shaking.

"I will be leaving when it is light, and I will not return here for many years. Raurau Illa told me this. He wishes us to be friends."

"He did not tell *me* this."

"Perhaps he wanted you to discover it on your own," Cusi suggested. "He had to teach me not to be rude to strangers."

"You think you have learned?" Alco inquired with such naked contempt that Cusi could only stare at him for a moment. He saw that the boy was shaking nearly as hard as he was himself, though probably not from the cold.

"I have learned many things from Raurau Illa, and I would like to honor his wish. I would like to tell Urcon, when I find him, that his brother is my friend."

"Tell him whatever you like," Alco burst out, his voice rising and breaking. "But do not pretend my friendship is important to you."

"You cannot know what is important to me," Cusi began, but Alco cut him off, stamping his foot so that the llamas behind him shied away and made spitting sounds.

"*You* are important to you! You want us to serve you and be grateful to you and make you feel your own importance. You want us to know that you own the whole world and that you can make us wealthy just with the things you do not need. Why would someone like you ever need my friendship?"

"Perhaps it is our way to ask the impossible," Cusi murmured in resignation. He let out a long, shuddering sigh. "Raurau would not let me persist in my stupidity, but I do not know how to change you. Keep your blanket, then, and your friendship. When I come here again, treat me as you would any stranger. I will expect no more from you."

"I will return the cup," Alco said stiffly as Cusi started past him. Cusi paused just long enough to shake his head in refusal.

"It was a gift. If it troubles you to use it, let it stand empty."

Feeling cold and empty himself, he walked toward Raurau Illa's house, which was now clearly visible in the moonlight. But Cusi was thinking only of darkness, and sleep, and the warm folds of his cloak. For now he was done with looking ahead.

Tumibamba

WHEN THE high priestess appeared at the gate of the micho's quarters at noon, Acapana had just come on duty. She strode past his assistants before they could greet her and ignored their belated bows, surveying the entire enclosure as if she expected to find her own way. There was an urgency in her manner that made Acapana dispense with the amenities.

"How may I help you, Mamanchic?"

"Where is Micay?" Chimpu Ocllo demanded, her voice revealing her distress. "Have you seen her today?"

"I only just arrived—"

"Take me to where she sleeps. Quickly!"

Acapana pointed her along the path between the flower beds that led to Micay and Quinti's house. He nearly had to run to keep up with her, and he was just behind her when she stopped inside the doorway, staring down at the floor. Over her shoulder, he could see what appeared to be a crumpled pile of bedding, until he noticed the bare foot protruding from one end. The high priestess inhaled with a kind of shriek and went down onto her knees next to the bedding. Acapana stood frozen in the doorway, hunched over but unable to move.

"Micay!" Chimpu Ocllo cried, pulling away a blanket to reveal a mass of glossy black hair. "My daughter!"

Then the pile moved, exposing pale, coppery skin among the blankets, and then a face that seemed as creased and rumpled as the bedding. Micay's swollen eyes opened and immediately filled with tears, and she threw her arms around Chimpu Ocllo, letting out a wail of anguish that made Acapana's skin crawl. It sounded like the bleat of a dying llama, and it seemed to hang in the air for a moment before being swallowed up by the sound of Micay's weeping. The high priestess held her and stroked her hair, murmuring to her softly and pulling a blanket around her bare shoulders.

"Is she ill, my lady?" Acapana asked finally, when Micay had become still. He saw Micay's head pull away from Chimpu Ocllo's breast and one eye find him in the doorway—an eye that went wide with fear and instantly hid itself again.

"No," Chimpu Ocllo assured him, glancing back over her shoulder. "She will be fine. Have one of the servants bring us some food and some akha. And see that no one else disturbs us."

Acapana ducked back out of the house, wondering why—if Micay was fine—there had been tears in the old woman's eyes. He went to find one of the retainers, feeling that he had stumbled into something strange and slightly shameful, and that it was no place for him.

THE POOL was a rectangle carved into the bedrock, with a low bench at either end and sculpted headrests in the upper edge. Wisps of sulfurous steam rose from the placid surface of the water, curling upward like vines around the shaft of sunlight that came through the open trapdoor in the bathhouse roof. Micay and Chimpu Ocllo sat facing each other, the blood-warm water lapping at their throats. Micay glanced down at the tiny bubbles clinging to her skin, making her limbs feel languid yet light, not truly her own. When she looked up, Chimpu was regarding her steadily, her long gray hair spread over the headrest behind her.

"Can you tell me now?" she asked.

Micay nodded tentatively, though it was another moment before she could make her voice work.

"I dreamed I was a mitmac."

"You have told me of a similar dream. It was after I took you to see the Yarovilcas who had been settled here."

"It was the same. I was with my mother, inspecting the house we had been given by the Inca. My hair was braided and we were speaking in Chacha. We did not know what to do, because the house was completely empty, and we had nothing with which to fill it. The house was all of stone, and the walls were so smooth that we could not even find a way to hang a cloth. Then I noticed all the people who were looking in the windows at us: They were Cañaris, and their faces were filled with hatred and suspicion, because they knew that we had been brought here to spy on them. I turned to tell my mother, but she was gone, and that frightened me so much that I woke up."

"It *is* the same dream," Chimpu concurred. "Why has it affected you so strongly this time?"

"It made me remember. First I remembered the mitmacs who came to take me from my father. Then I remembered everything else."

Micay felt tears coming again and squeezed her eyes shut against them, shaking her head in denial.

"Tell me, my daughter," Chimpu urged. "What have you remembered that hurts you so?"

Micay lifted both arms out of the water and splashed them down again in frustration, sending a wave across the pool that crested just beneath Chimpu's chin.

"The micho would not listen! He had come to take me, and it did not matter if it was right or justified under the law. My father argued with him and demanded a hearing; he even broke the micho's stick to make him listen. But the micho had his mitmacs with their spears, and he had brought the selector of chosen women with him. He *stole* me from my father and sent me to Caxamarca. That is how I became a chosen woman."

She let her head fall back into the smooth curve of stone behind her, the tears streaming down her face. In her mind she saw the girl who had been Misa climbing up a steep mountain trail, too numbed by shock and exhaustion to feel the fear and grief and loss that flooded through Micay as she watched in memory. Chimpu called her back, talking softly to her while she wept.

"You know that I do not approve of the way the Inca has taken people from their homes, whether they be chosen women or mitmacs or retainers. We disrupt the lives of our subjects more than we ever admit, and then we wonder why they do not love us. After what was done to you, Micay, I would not blame you for hating us."

Micay winced at the suggestion and shook her head.

"I cannot hate anyone. My father hated the Incas. He defied them and refused to serve as their chief. He swore that he would never forget how I was stolen from him. But I forgot him in only a few months. I forgot everything until today."

"You were given no choice," Chimpu reminded her. "You must not think that you betrayed him. That will only prolong the pain."

"It is awful," Micay moaned, "worse than when I came back from the mountains. Worse than anything. I was awake, but I did not want to be. I did not want to breathe or feel or think."

"I was afraid, when I first saw you, that you had done harm to yourself," Chimpu confessed.

Micay looked at her and sighed. "I promised Cahua that I would never do that. She was the one who taught me *not* to dream."

Chimpu stretched out her arms and rose laboriously to her feet, sending water lapping over the sides of the pool. She sloshed the few feet to where Micay sat and helped her up, supporting her until her legs could function well enough to negotiate the slippery steps. The stunning slap of cool air against her wet skin was quickly smothered by the thick towels Chimpu wrapped around her, bundling her like a mummy. Then Chimpu began to dry Micay's hair with another towel, standing naked and dripping beside her.

"You should dry yourself, my lady," Micay murmured, embarrassed at being attended by the high priestess. But Chimpu merely laughed and slapped herself on one bony hip.

"This skin is too old and tough to feel anything," she scoffed. Then she draped the towel over Micay's shoulders and came around to face her. "You are very tender right now, very vulnerable. But your pain will pass, and there will come a time when your memories will no longer make you bleed inside."

Micay regarded her skeptically as Chimpu bent for a towel and began to dab at her breasts and belly.

"When that time comes, how will I be different?"

"You will know the fears and angers you carry with you from the past. Perhaps that will make it easier for you to trust yourself. But you must stop denying what has happened to you, hiding it from yourself," Chimpu warned. "True composure is not a masking of your feelings and beliefs but a calm, respectful embodiment of them. You will understand the difference the day your face truly feels like your own. Like the mirror of your heart."

Micay lowered her eyes, blinking back the tears that mirrored what was in her heart, a pain that seemed far from passing. Chimpu clicked her tongue sympathetically and briefly rested a hand on Micay's shoulder.

"Come, let us dress ourselves. You will stay with me until you are stronger. I am the one who made you dream again, after all. I will not leave you to suffer your memories alone, my daughter. I will not be *that* kind of Inca."

Cuzco

THE LOWER terraces of the Patallacta were already in shadow below him, and the slanting rays of the sun burnished the rooftops of Cuzco, making the thatch look like solid sheets of metal. My last sunset here, Cusi thought wistfully, at least for many years. He was sitting in the back doorway of his room in Otoronco's compound, absorbing impressions to carry north with him, to sustain him through the years he would be away. Such a prolonged absence was truly inconceivable to him, but his trust in Raurau Illa made him feel that he should try to prepare himself. It also helped to keep his mind off of Tocto, and whether she had been permitted to come to the Iñaca feast, and whether the instructions he had given her woman would allow her to find her way to him in the dark. That he would not see her again before he left was also inconceivable, but in a way that made him ache just to consider it.

He heard voices—one that sounded like Otoronco's—behind him and immediately began to devise excuses for why he did not wish to go to the feast. But it was Tocto herself who slipped past the curtain covering the front doorway and came toward him with a smile on her face. Cusi had planned to take her into his arms as soon as he saw her, but the actual sight of her made him too weak to do anything except smile back at her. She stopped before she reached him, in the midst of the belongings he had laid out to take with him. She crouched and ran her fingers over the hard, polished surfaces of his shield and wooden helmet, giving him quick, darting glances that reminded him of the first time they had met. She riffled the quilted folds of his cotton armor and poked at the bundled blankets that held his eating utensils and personal items. The battle-ax was lying on a mat of its own, propped up on two of its six blunt points. Tocto put a hand out over the weapon but then pulled it back, turning her head swiftly to catch Cusi gaping at her in anticipation.

Then she made a kind of hop and was squatting in front of him, holding his head in her hands and kissing him on the face. He reached for her but she backed off to the other side of the doorway, laughing at how she had flustered him.

"How did you get away so soon?" Cusi asked helplessly, happy to be so flustered and to see her laughing.

"Otoronco Achachi brought me. He danced with me at the feast and bragged to me about you. He wondered why you had not come to get me yourself."

"I would not have waited all night," Cusi assured her. "How long can you stay?"

"Until you have to leave. It does not matter anymore if I am missed."

They stared at each other, then looked out over the city as the sunlight winked out and dusk began to settle with its customary rapidity.

"It seems so quiet," Cusi mused aloud. "You would hardly know that all the halls and barracks are filled with warriors. There will be noise and singing later, though."

"Not here," Tocto said knowingly, reaching back to untie her head wrap. "Let us be very quiet for a while, before we talk." She gave her head a backward toss, shaking her long black hair out onto her shoulders. "I want to listen to you breathe . . ."

This time when he reached for her, she came to him willingly, and together they found their way to his sleeping mats and the soft blankets that would not be going with him on the march.

LATER THEY LAY with the blankets bunched up around them like earthworks, warmed by the fire Cusi had kindled in a small three-legged brazier. Even as they talked, they could not stop touching and pressing their bodies together, murmuring with pleasure between words. The sound of singing came clearly from many parts of the city and from the Patallacta itself, but it seemed a celebration of their privacy, rather than an intrusion.

"I was afraid you would be sad," Cusi confessed, "or angry that I had not risked more to see you."

"Rimachi told me that you had gone to see the blind man. He suggested, in that way of his, that perhaps *you* were the blind one."

Cusi drew away from her, prepared to defend himself, but Tocto laughed to let him know she was teasing.

"There was nothing you could have done," she assured him. "Huascar would not let any of us rest. He has begun to realize that he has to make a name for himself, and he saw this as a great opportunity. I used the time I was around him to put another idea in his head, and I think I have succeeded. He talks about it constantly now, as if it were his own."

"You are teasing me again," Cusi warned her.

But Tocto laughed, clearly proud of herself. "First of all, I suggested to him that this could be a long war and that his power here would not grow. I reminded him that Ninan Cuyochi and Atauhuallpa and our other half broth-ers are in the north with Father, proving themselves in the field. It was not difficult to persuade him that he was brave and wished to prove it, and that he should ask to go north when he has completed the Huarachicoy."

"And you would go with him," Cusi concluded, gazing at her with admira-tion. "That was clever. And probably necessary," he added as an afterthought, frowning slightly. "I have been told I will not return here for many years."

Tocto propped herself up on an elbow, her eyes darkening. "You must tell me everything. You must tell me about Pachacuti, too. Otoronco began to boast about how he had finally gotten you to join the Iñaca, but then he seemed to remember himself and tried to swallow his words. He seemed almost sober and said that you were naturally more adept in these matters than he was."

"Adept!" Cusi exclaimed softly, shaking his head at the memory of his fear and bewilderment.

"Otoronco also said that we wanted the same thing from you. What did he mean by that?"

"The impossible," Cusi murmured, and sighed at her quizzical expression. "I must explain about that, as well."

THE SINGING had long since died away outside, and Cusi had added more wood to the fire, pausing in the midst of acting out the sequence of events in Raurau's house. He repeated the old man's final prophecies, shaking his empty fists at Tocto and hissing to duplicate the sound of Raurau's rattles. Then he lay back down beside her, breathing hard, warm and half aroused by his exertions. Tocto put a hand on his chest to hold him down and threw a leg over his hips, straddling him on her knees.

"I will be the condor who watches over you from afar," she told him, her eyes glistening high above him in the darkness. She spread both arms wide, her fingers splayed like pin feathers, then brought her hands down between her legs to grasp and guide him. Cusi felt himself rising to meet her, sinking upward in a warm, wet slide. He groaned with pleasure as she leaned forward over him, brushing his chest with her nipples.

"Stay inside me," she whispered. "Stay until the end this time, in case it is our last."

A tremor of misgiving went through Cusi, a reflex of their past prudence. Tocto rocked backward and then forward again, bending to kiss him on the lips and drive all concern for scandal out of his mind. He threw his arms around her back and they rocked in unison. When the surge began in his loins, he held back against it for as long as he could, then let it take him completely, knowing that further resistance was impossible.

THEY PRAYED together, huddled beneath the blankets, feeling holy despite their nakedness. They wept and held each other and made love again while they were weeping. Tocto urged him to sleep because of the long march he had ahead of him, and Cusi pretended to try for a while. But he could feel her attention upon him, like a hand stroking his forehead, and he finally opened his eyes to gaze back at her. Tocto murmured in protest, but Cusi simply smiled and shook his head. He did not want to sleep now; he did not want to leave her for a dream. He could barely make out her features and the liquid gleam of her eyes, yet she felt closer than his own skin. He wanted *this* to be the dream he took with him out of Cuzco. He wanted it to be the only dream he remembered when next he had to awaken, far away from here.

VIII

CHINCHAYSUYO:
The Lynx Quarter

(A.D. 1513)

Chachapoyas Province

USI AND RIMACHI slipped out of Caxamarquilla just before dark, in the midst of one of the thick, foglike mists that had begun to come daily, watering the lush landscape as thoroughly as any rain. They worked their way through the untended fields surrounding the city, recognizing those that had belonged to Inti and the Sapa Inca by the fact that the young plants had been deliberately trampled and the stone boundary markers overturned. The other plots had been left to grow but were rapidly being taken over by weeds, a testament to how long the fighting had been going on.

They waded across a shallow river where a rope bridge had once hung, soaking the ends of their cloaks and tunics, then scrambled up the muddy bank and plunged into the darkness of the forest. Neither of them had spent much time in forests previous to this, and they were still unsettled by the helplessness the dense vegetation inspired in them, a sense of being both blind and enclosed. They stayed close to each other, walking as swiftly as the failing light would allow, listening for sounds both ahead and behind. They were armed only with short thrusting spears and the slings wrapped around their foreheads, and they were not even certain where in this jungle to find a stone to throw. They could only trust the scouts who had discovered this path and pronounced it safe, and hope that the diversionary attacks their commander had ordered would keep the Chachapoyas occupied elsewhere.

As the scouts had promised, they came out of the forest before night had completely fallen, so they could still find the trail that zigzagged up a steep hillside and then followed the line of a rocky ridge toward the dark, distant shapes of the mountains. Looking back from the top of the ridge, they saw the mist roll over the forest below, enveloping it in a grayish-white cloud that woke the tree frogs and made them sing. Cusi and Rimachi exchanged a rueful smile in the darkness, remembering how the chorus of croaks and peeps had spooked them until Uritu had captured one of the tiny frogs to show them, whooping with laughter at their relief and amazement. Cusi had been reminded many times, since coming here, of Otoronco's stories about the conquest of the Eastern Quarter. The land of the Chachapoyas was cooler and more mountainous, cloud forest rather than true jungle, but there were the same biting insects and draining heat in the lowland valleys, the same brightly colored birds and slow green rivers. And there was an enemy who had greeted them much as Otoronco and his troops had been greeted: with a hail of stones and arrows, followed by a screaming wave of armed, painted men.

The untested warriors who had left Caxamarca and crossed the Marañon River to investigate reports of unrest among the Chachapoyas soon found themselves the veterans of a full-scale rebellion, fighting so fiercely that they had no time to dwell on their new status. Cusi and Rimachi were among the few who had not received a serious wound, though both wore bandages in several places. They had been chosen as messengers because of Cusi's swiftness and Rimachi's ability to hold off an attack by himself, which it was hoped would allow Cusi to escape and carry the message to Tumibamba. Those were, in fact, their orders in case of an attack, and their commander, knowing they were friends, had made them promise that they would not hesitate to part company.

The misty rain overtook them as they picked their way along the ridge, blurring their vision and soaking through their cloaks and the blankets slung over their backs. The rain was warm and made Cusi want to slough off the sodden weight on his back, but he knew he would need all of it later, when they reached the highlands. He hoped it would dry by then but shook off the thought as petty and possibly dangerous. Raurau Illa had warned him that he would face death sooner than he expected, so he had been more prepared than most of his comrades for the threats they had encountered. He could not afford to grow careless now, especially since he had been forced to leave his heavy battle-ax behind. Once they were out of Chachapoya territory and safely on the Royal Road, he could relax and think about being dry and comfortable. Perhaps he could also think about whether the death he had already faced had changed him as Raurau had predicted, or only as it changed any warrior who came out of the killing alive.

But such thoughts were even more dangerous. Their commander had given them twelve days to reach Tumibamba, which left them no time for mistakes or delays. Cusi returned his attention to the slick rocks underfoot and the occasional sounds that penetrated the steady trilling of insects and frogs, going forward one step at a time like any veteran intent on prolonging his career.

IT TOOK them three days to cross the mountains, but they did so without incident, hiding the few times they heard the approach of other people. When they came down over the plain and saw the Royal Road cutting a wide, unerring path across the valley below, they both let out a whoop and began to run, their cloaks billowing out behind them. For a moment they were boys again, enjoying the rush of air past their faces and the clear ground where there were no trees to obscure vision or vines to trip them up. The short grass between the yellowed bunches of ichu grass had just begun to green from the early rains, and the earth felt springy underfoot. Cusi felt his competitive instincts stir for the first time in months, but he resisted the surge to race out ahead and set a pace that Rimachi could easily match. They had hardly spoken to one another in the past three days, but they had lived through every tense moment together, feeling at times that they shared a common set of nerves and senses. Cusi was not about to run away from him now, when the threat of a forced separation was behind them.

Once they were standing on the Royal Road, the seriousness of their mission came back to them, and they glanced around to be certain they had not attracted anyone's attention. It was for the sake of secrecy, after all, that their commander had risked sending them out over the mountains. It would have been safer and faster simply to send the message back to Caxamarca and let the post runners carry it to Tumibamba. But Colla Topa had decided that it was not prudent to have the news of the Chachapoyas' rebellion shouted from one end of Chinchaysuyo to the other, especially since the news of the Carangui victory had so recently traveled along this road in the opposite direction. He would entrust the message to the post runners when the twelve days were up, but he hoped that news of reinforcements would already be on its way to him by then.

So Cusi and Rimachi dusted off their clothing and began to march north, trying not to appear like what they were: men who had just come out of a war. They even avoided speaking about it, though it was what they wanted most to discuss now that there was no longer any danger in raising their voices. Their reticence was enforced by the presence of the post runners themselves, who were stationed at fixed intervals along the road. They usually sat outside their small stone huts, one on either side of the road, their white plumes attached to their shoulders and their conch trumpets on strings around their necks. Cusi had always felt an affinity with the post runners, who had to be both swift and sure of memory, capable of absorbing a shouted message and repeating it back exactly at the end of a hard run. They could carry a message from Cuzco to Tumibamba in less than six days and without losing a word.

The runners along this length of the road were Huancas, provided as part of their tribe's labor obligation but specially trained in Cuzco. As Cusi walked past, nodding in greeting, he at first felt slightly guilty, knowing that he was on this road because his commander did not wish to trust them. Yet he also felt himself being examined by keen and knowing eyes, which could not fail to notice the bandages on his arms and the sorry state of his clothing. For an Inca, as his earplugs proclaimed him, such shabbiness could only mean one thing. And Cusi realized that even though Colla Topa had not sent any messages out, there was no telling how many might have come this way to Caxamarca, inquiring about the "unrest" in Chachapoyas.

"They must know about the rebellion," Cusi decided aloud once the runners were well behind them.

"Probably," Rimachi allowed, hefting his spear. "We have been fighting there for almost two months ourselves. It is hard to hide a war from your neighbors."

"Then we cannot hide it, either. We can only hope to get to Tumibamba before anyone else is tempted to rebel."

Rimachi was silent for a moment, squinting off into the distance. "If what the captives said is true," he suggested, "the Chachapoyas were not tempted. They were provoked."

Cusi gave him a sharp glance. "I heard some things, too. But Colla Topa did not include them in his message."

"He is a war chief, not an administrator. He does not care about how it began, only about how to end it."

"But you care?" Cusi asked curiously. Rimachi gave him a long look that contained none of his usual teasing skepticism. He gestured with his free hand toward the gold and silver plugs in his ears.

"I am an Inca by privilege now. I have killed men and had them try to kill me, and it is not something I wish to do for no reason. Or for a bad reason. That governor deserved to die for his stupidity. It is a pity the Chachapoyas did not go back to their homes after killing him."

"They also killed most of the garrison," Cusi pointed out, "and two hundred of the men who came with us. They also burned the royal storehouses and slaughtered the Inca's herds."

"For which they will have to be punished," Rimachi said brusquely, sounding almost angry. "That should put an end to 'temptation.' "

Cusi looked down at the paving stones beneath his feet, amazed by what he was hearing. Rimachi sounded like Otoronco, whom Rimachi had always regarded as rash and dangerously critical.

"So it has changed you," Cusi said softly. "The fighting, I mean."

"How could it not?" Rimachi demanded. Then he also softened his tone. "You do not know . . . I have not told you . . ."

"I know," Cusi assured him grimly. "I can still see the faces."

"The eyes, anyway . . ."

They fell silent again as they approached another pair of post runners seated outside their huts. As they drew even with the man on the right, Cusi had a sudden impulse and called out to him in a friendly voice.

"Greetings, messenger. What is the news from Chachapoyas?"

"There is fighting," the man said bluntly after only a slight hesitation. "But the troops from Cuzco have gone to end it."

"Good," Cusi declared. He walked on for some distance before exchanging a glance with Rimachi.

"You should have asked if his people had been tempted to rebel," Rimachi suggested, and both of them laughed.

"We risked our lives for nothing," Cusi said ruefully. But Rimachi shook his head in denial, his lips curled in a sardonic smile. "No, not for nothing. For a few extra days in Tumibamba. That was always *my* reason for volunteering."

"Let us walk faster, then," Cusi proposed, picking up the pace. "Let us have *something* to show for our risk."

Tumibamba

UNNOTICED BY MOST of the revelers in the micho's compound, the sky began to darken early, the sunset obscured by a layer of low clouds that smelled of rain. Seeing that both Mama Cori and Apu Poma were preoccupied with their guests, Micay took it upon herself, as a daughter of the house, to see that torches were lit. She threaded her way through the crowd on the upper terrace, exchanging greetings with the people she knew while she searched for Acapana. She was aware of heads turning for a second look at her, especially the heads of young men, but she kept moving and did not allow anyone to hold her eye for long. She knew that if she stopped the young men would find her, and then she would have more helpers than she needed but no freedom to act on her own.

Acapana was standing with one of his assistants near the stairway to the terrace below, and both of them stared at Micay unabashedly for a moment before moderating their gaze. Acapana stammered slightly in greeting and kept his eyes averted the whole time she was making her request, acting as if he were memorizing an important message. He immediately dispatched his assistant to light the torches. Then he looked at Micay but had to clear his throat before he could speak again.

"You are lovely tonight, my lady."

"You are too kind," Micay demurred, lowering her eyes with a modesty she could not truly feel. The fact that she had become beautiful—seemingly overnight—still seemed incredible to her, but it had been impressed upon her too forcefully, by too many people, to be denied. Chimpu Ocllo had been the first to recognize the change that was occurring, and she had brandished mirrors at Micay and tried to prepare her for the reactions of others. She had tried to show her that the only real modesty lay not in gestures but in how she used her beauty.

She looked up at Acapana, who had fallen awkwardly silent, and felt again that her beauty was a punishment to him. He seemed dazed in her presence, as if he had overslept and could not rouse himself. After the day when Chimpu had come to rescue her from her dreaming, he had kept his distance from Micay for a while, apparently regarding the incident as an attack of illness from which she would eventually recover. He had never understood why she had not encouraged a return to their former intimacy, and lately he had begun to take on the defeated aspect of a man who did not expect another chance.

"Will you alert me when the high priestess arrives?" Micay asked when it became clear he had nothing more to say to her.

He gestured toward the crowd with his chin. "If I can find you, my lady."

Several cruel rejoinders sprang into Micay's mind, all having to do with how he had lost her, how he had fled from the sight of her suffering. Chimpu had scolded her for simply withdrawing from him, rather than telling him about her disappointment, but Micay had felt there was justice in her silence.

"I would be grateful," she said now. "I suspect we will all know it if the Coya comes."

She bowed and turned back into the crowd, feeling guilty in spite of herself. This was another symptom of sudden beauty, the sense that she deprived others of pleasure simply by removing herself from their sight. She tried to acknowledge the feeling yet put it aside, as Chimpu had taught her, concentrating instead on the obligations she had chosen for herself. She decided to return to the awning house, where she had last seen Mama Cori, but she had gotten only half way there when she was intercepted by Mama Huarcay, who stepped away from a group of women and drew Micay to the edge of the terrace, under a pole that held one of the newly lit torches.

"So it is true, what I have been hearing," she said, examining Micay with open admiration. "I was not surprised, of course. I have remarked upon your beauty to others many times."

"You often told me," Micay reminded her, "that I was too fat in the face and too thin in the body."

Mama Huarcay smiled and gave a half shrug, making no effort to deny it.

"That is obviously no longer the case," she said smoothly. "Tell me, my daughter: What is your place now that Quinti Ocllo and Quilaco have announced their marriage?"

"I will be helping Quinti prepare for the ceremony—"

"Of course. But after that? It is no secret that Quilaco dislikes you. Do you suppose you could be comfortable in his household?"

"I do not know, my lady," Micay admitted, recalling that it was Quilaco who had insisted that Mama Huarcay be invited to this feast. "Nothing has been decided yet."

"And who will decide for you? Mama Cori? Chimpu Ocllo?" Mama Huarcay made an exasperated noise. "One would arrange a marriage as indifferent as her own, and the other would hide you away among the holy women. Both would try to make you ashamed that you are beautiful and have the feelings of a woman."

Micay could only smile at this assessment of her prospects, which had not altered in all the time she had known Mama Huarcay, except that Chimpu Ocllo had been added as another bad influence.

"What do you think my place should be, my lady?"

Mama Huarcay stared at her thoughtfully, squinting slightly, as if trying to see her anew. "As you may know, it will soon be my turn with Huayna Capac. I will be with him for eight days and nights, along with the women I choose to accompany me. I have told you what that is like, as much as can be described." She paused and widened her eyes at Micay. "Perhaps you also know that he is partial to women with your coloring, especially when they are young."

Micay squinted back at her with unconcealed skepticism. "I have always enjoyed your stories, my lady," she said politely. "But I have never seen a place for myself in any of them."

"Open your eyes, then! Any mirror would tell you that you are beautiful enough to be chosen a second time. And my husband is kind to those for whom he is the first; he opens them gently, like delicate blossoms. Afterwards they are his favorites, and he gives them gifts and lands of their own and arranges marriages with men of high rank. They have great prestige, because they have known the touch of the Sapa Inca."

Micay felt her cheeks grow warm at the thought of being touched and opened, but she looked at Mama Huarcay and silently shook her head.

"Have they already made you ashamed?" Mama Huarcay demanded. "Or are you simply afraid to risk their displeasure? Think of what it could mean to you! Would you rather live out your life with a crippled gatekeeper or with the mamacona?"

The reference to Acapana flustered Micay briefly, then made her angry. She took a deep breath, aware of angers older and more powerful than this one, angers she had carried with her since the first day she and Mama Huarcay had met.

"I would prefer a life I have chosen for myself," she said in a tight voice, her stomach contracting with fear while her heart thudded with a kind of excited yearning.

"I cannot force you to choose the life I offer," Mama Huarcay allowed with just a trace of scorn. "If you lack the courage—"

"I have not heard any offer!" Micay burst out, cutting her off. "I have heard only suggestions, hints of what might be. I have heard such hints before, and I almost believed them. But then I was left standing in the rain outside the shrine of Mama Huaco and was told that I should be honored to have come so close, though I could never enter. I can live without such empty offers."

Mama Huarcay glared at her with a contempt that seemed to make the air between them quiver. "You are a fool, Chachapoyas girl," she growled, spitting out the words one by one. "Chimpu Ocllo will be standing out in the rain herself soon enough. And Mama Cori will be out there with her, now that she has become her defender. What place will you have then? You forget that your blood is worthless and that you are only as worthy as those who sponsor you."

"I know my blood and my worth," Micay said with stubborn pride. "I know who is worthy of my trust."

"You will regret speaking to me this way."

"It is the way I began with you, my lady. Or would you have me believe that you had forgotten?"

"Indulge your arrogance while you can," Mama Huarcay seethed. "Beauty that comes so suddenly often departs with the same speed. You will beg for my favor one day."

She turned away before Micay could reply and went off into the crowd, apparently too angry to return to the group she had been with. Micay turned in the opposite direction, clasping her hands together to keep them from shaking, feeling a kind of exhilaration that was hard to distinguish from fright. She wondered at herself, at the strange but undeniable satisfaction she felt at having deliberately made an enemy. I chose this, she thought, and began again to look for Mama Cori, wearing a smile too personal for others to perceive.

WHEN IT COULD not be put off any longer, Mama Cori gave in and signaled her husband to make the announcement. Apu Poma cleared a space for himself in front of the awning house and prevailed upon the crowd for quiet as Quinti and Quilaco took their places to his right. Micay came forward from the other side with two cups of akha, which she handed to Apu Poma. He smiled at her fondly as he took the cups, letting his eyes linger on her mantle and pin, gifts he had given her himself. He seemed quite pleased with the role he was about to play, as if unaware that anyone was missing from his audience. Quinti and Quilaco were looking at each other and seemed similarly unconcerned. Micay bowed and backed away, returning to her place beside Mama Cori as Apu Poma began his speech of greeting to the assembled guests.

From his place on Mama Cori's other side, Lloque Yupanqui turned his head and looked down at Micay, his thin lips drawn tight in an expression of poorly suppressed regret. He had tried to dissuade Mama Cori from the course she had chosen, arguing that while it was brave and honest, it put too much at risk. He did not appear at all pleased to have been proven correct, though he was struggling to maintain a face in keeping with the occasion.

Chimpu Ocllo was on the other side of the circle of open space, surrounded by the wives of Cañari chiefs. She had kept a discreet distance between herself and Mama Cori all evening, but finally it had not mattered. The Coya had not come. There would be no meeting, no attempt at reconciliation, despite the personal appeal Mama Cori had made. Chimpu's eyes, when they met Micay's, were tinged with sadness, because she also knew what the Coya's refusal meant to Mama Cori.

Apu Poma was toasting his future son-in-law, praising Quilaco's conduct against the Quitos and Carangui and predicting a swift rise through the ranks of the warriors. Micay glanced over the ranks of the guests and wondered how many others were aware of the significance of the Coya's absence. Mama Huarcay had known something, though it was an exaggeration to call Mama Cori a defender of the high priestess. She had gone to speak with Chimpu several times but had strenuously maintained her neutrality, admitting only that some of Chimpu's contentions were reasonable.

It was Quinti who had forced her to act by insisting that both the Coya and the high priestess be invited to this feast. She had left her mother to determine how to issue the invitations and whether to warn each of the other's possible presence. Mama Cori had felt compelled by friendship to tell the Coya that Chimpu had also been invited. Yet her respect for Chimpu, or perhaps simply her own integrity, had prevented her from making an invitation that she knew would be rejected out of hand. So she had prevailed upon that friendship, and all of her credibility with Rahua Ocllo, and tried to act as a go-between. The Coya had listened in silence, but she had not given her answer until tonight.

Now Quilaco was returning Apu Poma's toast, speaking on behalf of his father, who was the governor of the province of Chincha and could not be present. Quilaco's mother had been a close confidante of the Coya, and when she had died some years before, Rahua Ocllo had extended her affection and favor to the son her friend had left behind. Micay did not know if Quilaco had used any of his influence to urge the Coya to come tonight, though he did not seem unduly disappointed by her absence. He was gesturing with the arm that had been broken, unconsciously flexing and unflexing the muscles, as if reminding himself that he was healed. But he has not risked much of what he knows, Micay thought bitterly, and Quinti has not pushed him to do so.

Apu Poma was concluding his announcement, inviting all those present to remain for the drinking and dancing that would follow. A sudden breeze came up while he was speaking, causing all the torches to smoke and flutter, and a few drops of rain pelted down on the guests. Apu Poma laughed with uncharacteristic exuberance and repeated his offer as the crowd began to break up around him, some ducking their heads in anticipation of a more serious downpour.

The rain held off, but in the next moments, while some of the guests, largely Quilaco's warrior friends, came forward to congratulate the couple, many others began to move toward the compound gate. It was a gradual exodus, but unmistakable in its implications. Micay cringed inwardly on Mama Cori's behalf, knowing that she must feel bereft and abandoned. Mama Cori had not moved or responded to any of Lloque's quiet coaxings. He was trying to persuade her to join her husband and daughter and take the place that was hers.

"You mean my place as the micho's wife?" she demanded suddenly, turning on him with an outraged expression. "Or as the mother of children who have all left? I have no place anymore."

"It is not irrevocable," Lloque soothed, trying to calm her. "You simply asked too much at the wrong time."

"Too much?" Mama Cori turned away from him in disbelief and looked at Micay. Her eyes were like pieces of slate: hard, desolate, and dry. "Too much, Micay?"

"She has asked as much of you, my lady. And she is the Coya. She should be generous with her prestige."

Mama Cori's eyes softened slightly, and she nodded to Micay with a rueful kind of gratitude.

"I suggested that to her, though not so plainly. Perhaps that is why she did not hear me." She glanced past Micay and raised her chin. "Here is the high priestess."

Chimpu Ocllo nodded absently in response to Lloque's bow, her attention all on Mama Cori. There was sympathy in her eyes, though she chose not to display it in her gestures or tone of voice.

"I am sorry, my daughter. I know you did not wish to be seen as my advocate."

Mama Cori gave a weary shrug. "I was aware of the risk. I had hoped to be seen as an advocate of understanding and accommodation."

"I share the same hope, as you know," Chimpu asserted emphatically, as if trying to counteract Mama Cori's weariness. "We must not stop trying."

Another gust of wind brought more rain spattering down, and Lloque began to herd them all toward the awning house with sweeping motions of his long arms. Chimpu used this as an excuse to take Mama Cori by the elbow and lead her off, speaking rapidly into her ear, and Micay fell in beside Lloque. He pointed with his chin at the pair ahead.

"She is a powerful woman, the mamanchic. She has won over my sister, even though Cori will not admit it to herself."

He seemed impressed rather than resentful, despite what this had cost his sister. Micay recalled what Mama Huarcay had said about Chimpu and Mama Cori standing outside in the rain.

"Is she powerful enough to keep *her* place?" she asked.

Lloque stopped to look down at her, ignoring the drops of rain that slanted down around them. "It is not luck that has kept her in it this long," he said succinctly. "Rahua Ocllo has asked Huayna Capac to replace her many times."

"He has refused?"

"As you must know, Huayna Capac has a deep belief in omens and signs, and the prophecies of the huacas. He knows that Chimpu Ocllo derives her power from the huacas of this land, and that the Cañari regard her as a holy woman. He will not tamper with such things just to satisfy his wife."

Micay nodded, grateful for the seriousness of his response. It seemed lately that men were serious only in the way they stared at her, unless they were trying to impress her with flattery. Then they became very serious about their own words and interpreted any question as a request for more. She glanced up at Lloque, who seemed in no hurry to seek shelter, even though they were practically alone on the plaza.

"Has there been any word from Chachapoyas?" she asked.

Lloque gazed at her curiously for a moment before appearing to understand why she would inquire. "None since the troops from Cuzco were sent in. They have probably brought peace to the province by now."

Micay imagined golden-eared warriors lining the walls of her father's compound while the micho shook his stick and threatened to take something more from her father. She comforted herself with the thought that her brothers would still be too young to take as warriors, and there were no other daughters left to steal.

"I had almost forgotten that about you," Lloque said, breaking into her thoughts. "I have come to think of you as an Inca ñusta."

Micay met his eyes briefly, knowing that he meant it as a compliment and that he was not given to idle flattery. And it was the compliment she had once sought above all others, before Chimpu had found her and made her remember her past.

"You are kind, my lord," she said carefully. "But I am a Chachapoyas ñusta. It is important that I acknowledge that."

"Important to whom?" Lloque demanded. "Has someone made you feel unworthy?"

"No, my lord. It is important to me."

"Why is that?"

Micay blinked and glanced up at the rain, which had begun to come down more steadily. But Lloque ignored the hint and the rain, too, pulling on his chin as he waited for her answer. She felt she had no choice but to attempt a serious one.

"I was no longer a little girl when I was taken from my family and sent to the House of Chosen Women. I brought feelings and memories with me, and instincts that belonged to another way of life. I was made to forget in the House of Chosen Women, but I was not there for very long. I learned the ways of the Incas, but that did not help me understand all that was inside me."

Lloque's eyes widened in comprehension, and he made a clicking sound with his tongue. He nodded rapidly, then wiped at the moisture on his face as if noticing it for the first time. He started them moving toward the awning house again, putting a hand on the back of Micay's elbow to guide her. Ahead she could see Chimpu talking to Mama Cori and Apu Poma, and Quinti and Quilaco smiling in the midst of a group of ñustas and young warriors. She hoped Lloque would not question her further, because she did not want to tell him that she had come to think of herself as a mitmac within the family, an outsider who had been brought here to live among them yet would always remain apart.

She looked up at him as they came in under the awning house roof and saw that he was studying her intently, his brow furrowed in a frown of concentration. She wondered if he had guessed at the depth of her detachment, which made her feel disloyal and ungrateful at times, despite Chimpu's assurances that it was necessary. Lloque finally sighed and gave her a strained smile.

"I hope, at least, that you will continue to call me 'Uncle.'"

"Oh yes," Micay blurted, surprised and touched by his diffidence. "It is a privilege I cherish, Uncle."

She gave him a smile that drew the attention of several of the young men nearby, but Lloque merely nodded, swiveling to look out over the heads of the remaining guests.

"Let us help salvage what we can of this feast," he suggested, and they parted company easily and resumed their respective duties to the family.

"TUMIBAMBA," Rimachi said distinctly, as they came down onto level ground, and this time Cusi sensed he meant it. He had murmured the word many times during their journey as a kind of incantation against fatigue, but this had been offered as an invocation to the land around them, which was hidden by darkness and rain.

"Are we there?" Cusi asked, unable to see more than a few steps ahead.

"Almost. We should reach the first sentry post soon."

Cusi grunted, knowing better than to ask how much remained after that. There was always more, and thoughts of rest only encouraged the awareness of pain. They had come from the provincial center of Huancabamba—where they had alerted the governor—in six days, trotting where the land was flat and climbing the mountain passes with their heads bent before the wind. They had walked by moonlight and through thunderstorms and once in a falling snow, talking and arguing to keep themselves awake and not caring if the startled post runners overheard. The only secret left between them was how much each of them was hurting, a subject they avoided by mutual consent.

The sentry house, when they came to it, had niches in its outer walls, in two of which torches were burning. Cusi and Rimachi did not see the light until they were almost upon it. The lone sentry standing in the doorway cried out in surprise when he saw them, then stepped out into their path with his shield and spear readied. Three more warriors, all Cañaris, quickly appeared to back him up.

"We have a message for the Sapa Inca," Cusi said sharply, resisting the instinct to raise his own weapon. "Take us to him immediately."

The sentries eyed them warily without giving way, and Cusi realized how suspicious they must appear, with the ill-fitting garments they had borrowed at the last rest house hanging wet and muddy on their bodies and their sandals worn to slips. Rimachi took a step forward so that they could see that he wore a wicker headdress like their own, as well as the earplugs of an Inca by privilege. He spoke in Cañar, though it seemed that the words "Cuzco" and "Chachapoyas" were what the sentries heard most clearly, and what made them apologize as they put up their weapons.

Two of the sentries escorted them past the next three guard posts, and then a young Cañari captain took charge and led them through the outskirts of the city. The captain knew Rimachi's father, and he and Rimachi conversed in Cañar while Cusi silently repeated Colla Topa's message to himself. He wondered if Huayna Capac would hear them in person and if he would question them about what else they knew. He and Rimachi had agreed, during a moment of bravado during the snowstorm, that they would tell the Sapa Inca about how the rebellion had been provoked. Now, feeling more and more at the limit of his strength as their destination drew near, he was not certain that either of them would be so bold.

Rimachi smacked his lips loudly as they walked out onto a bridge that spanned a river Cusi could hear but not see.

"The Tumibamba," Rimachi explained in an eager, proprietary tone. "I used to play here as a child."

He pointed out other landmarks as they passed through a residential district of plain adobe compounds that he said was shared by Cañaris and a clan of Yarovilca mitmacs who had been settled here by Topa Inca. Cusi was impressed by how much his friend could still recognize, even in the rain and darkness, after an absence of some eight years.

They turned onto a wider street that was flanked on one side by a twelve-foot-high adobe wall that extended, unbroken, for as far as they could see. Rimachi put a hand up and ran it along the smooth, even surface. "What is this?" he asked finally. The Cañari captain laughed. "You have been away longer than you think. This is the Mollecancha, the palace of Huayna Capac. Most of it has been built since he came here to live."

Cusi and Rimachi exchanged a glance, remembering Otoronco's diatribes, but they said nothing to the captain, who seemed proud that the Sapa Inca had taken up residence in his city.

The captain bade them farewell at the palace gate, where an old man wearing the light blue tunic of the palace retainers questioned them briefly before turning them over to a boy who might have been his grandson.

"Take them to the war chief Michi."

So it would not be Huayna Capac himself, Cusi thought as they followed the boy into the maze of narrow streets that separated the buildings, gardens, and compounds within the palace enclosure. Cusi decided that he was more relieved than disappointed. It was enough to have brought Colla Topa's message here so quickly; it was not their responsibility to elaborate on the origins of the rebellion. As they began to ascend from one terrace level to the next by means of steep, winding staircases, he felt his legs beginning to rebel, shooting days-old pains up into his hips and back. The boy ahead, perhaps only five years younger, seemed impossibly nimble, but there was no self-respecting way to tell him to slow his pace. Cusi stopped paying attention to what was around him and concentrated on climbing the stairs without huffing or grunting.

Finally, after what seemed an interminable climb, they came to the gate of a large interior compound. The guard here was half veteran Inca warriors and half Cañaris from the Royal Guard, and they were armed and vigilant. Cusi could see that all of the Cañaris recognized Rimachi, though none of them greeted him with more than a nod. The Inca captain listened to Cusi's brief explanation and then hesitated, as if hoping he would go on and reveal what the situation in Chachapoyas was. Cusi sensed the same attentive hope in all of them and realized they would be grateful for the war he had brought them, since it might take them away from guard duty for a while. But he did not say anything more, and the captain beckoned to them and led the two of them to a small house just inside the enclosure. The single room was warm and seemed brilliantly lighted, with rushes burning in all of the wall niches. Several men were sitting on mats on the floor, eating, and the captain pointed them toward a heavyset man with bright black eyes and a golden Sun shield on his chest. Stunned by the light and the smell of the food, Cusi and Rimachi stood silently, dripping water onto the stone floor, until the war chief wiped his lips with a cloth and gestured for them to speak.

"We have a message for the Sapa Inca," Cusi explained, "from Colla Topa, commander of the warriors of Hanan Cuzco."

"The Sapa Inca is with the Third Wife and cannot be disturbed." The war chief raised his chin to indicate the niche behind him, which held a replica of the royal fringe. "You may give your message to me."

"The province of Chachapoyas is in a state of rebellion," Cusi began, and all the men who had continued their eating abruptly stopped. The war chief Michi listened intently as Cusi delivered the full message. Then he glanced at Rimachi, who simply nodded in confirmation. Immediately Michi turned to one of his subordinates.

"Summon the messengers. We must notify the high priest, the governor and the micho, and the commanders of the regiments. Quickly!"

As the man hurried out of the room, Michi turned back to Cusi and Rimachi and asked their names.

"Ah, the famous runner," he said to Cusi, appraising him a second time. "How fast did your legs carry you here from Caxamarquilla?"

"Ten days, my lord," Cusi told him, exchanging a proud sidelong glance with Rimachi.

"You did well," Michi commended them, nodding to each of them in turn. "I will see that you have the honor of leading us back to Chachapoyas once the troops are assembled. And since you are the son of the micho, Cusi Huaman, perhaps you would like the honor of delivering your message to him yourself."

Cusi resisted the urge to glance at Rimachi, who had argued with him about how he should greet his father, trying to convince him to show respect if not forgiveness. Cusi abruptly decided that duty would be even better, and he bowed to the war chief in compliance.

"I will tell him, my lord."

"I will show him the way to the micho's quarters," a familiar voice volunteered from behind them, and Rimachi's father, Choque Chinchay, stepped forward and rested a hand on his son's shoulder. "Welcome home, my son. Welcome, Cusi."

Cusi returned the greeting, even though Choque Chinchay was not really paying attention. The look that passed between him and Rimachi was like a strong embrace that excluded everyone else in the room. Cusi felt a pang of envy that made his legs quiver, and he knew why Rimachi had been able to argue with such conviction.

"Take them, Choque," Michi said expansively. "See that they are well rested. I will send for them when it is time to march."

THE RETAINERS had finished cleaning up and only a few torches were still burning inside the awning house. The immediate family sat around a brazier of live coals, now with Quilaco in their midst. Micay sat just outside their circle, though close enough to feel the warmth of the fire. Lulled by the patter of rain on the thatch overhead, she listened to the self-regarding rhythms of Quilaco's voice and did not have the energy to feel annoyed. He and Apu Poma seemed to be the only ones who had not been utterly drained by the day's festivities. Quilaco was explaining—for the third time within Micay's hearing—why he was sure that he would be given a compound in Quito once the Carangui had been crushed and construction could resume in that city. In the meantime, Micay knew, the Coya had arranged for him and Quinti to have a house in the Mollecancha, with their own garden and bathhouse and a small but adequate staff of servants. Micay had heard that story several times, as well.

She glanced at Quinti, who had been hearing these stories all night and who looked as exhausted as Micay felt. Micay had tried more than once to rescue her and take her off to a quiet corner where she would not have to smile at anyone, but Quilaco had put himself in her way every time. Though she knew he was keenly aware of her presence, he acted publicly as if she did not exist, or existed only to perform trivial tasks. Micay had not needed Mama Huarcay's warning to sense that she would not be a welcome guest in his house, whether here or in Quito.

Acapana suddenly appeared out of the darkness, ducking his head as he came in under the roof. He was followed by a much shorter man who was carrying a spear and had a cloak pulled up over his head.

"A messenger from the war chief Michi," Acapana announced as they stepped forward in the flickering light. Mama Cori started up as if stung, even before the messenger's head had fully emerged from the hood of his cloak.

"Cusi!" Quinti exclaimed softly, apparently the only one able to find her voice. The young man's black hair was plastered down over his headband and sling, and his face seemed pinched and haggard, but the features were unmistakable. He looked at Apu Poma and addressed him in a formal tone, his Cuzco accent very distinct.

"I have a message for the micho. It comes from Colla Topa, commander of the warriors of Hanan Cuzco."

"Speak, warrior," Apu Poma replied with equal formality, pulling the mask of the official over his surprise.

"The province of Chachapoyas is in a state of rebellion. The rebels have killed the governor and trampled the fields of the Inca and Inti. They have looted the royal storehouses and broken irrigation pipes and slaughtered the royal herds. We came to the aid of what was left of the garrison, and we have held the city of Caxamarquilla for the past month. But we have not been able to move beyond it without suffering severe losses. Colla Topa has asked the Sapa Inca to dispatch additional troops to restore complete control and bring the rebel leaders to judgment."

"How many does the enemy number?"

"We cannot tell. We came with five thousand men, and we were always outnumbered in the fighting."

Apu Poma rose to his feet with a show of official distress. "I must leave you," he apologized, making a perfunctory bow to the company. He looked back at Cusi and hesitated briefly, but Cusi simply stood where he was, offering no other greeting as the water gathered in a puddle around his feet. Apu Poma nodded uncertainly, then gestured for Acapana and left the awning house.

There was a long moment of silence. Then Cusi shrugged off the bundle on his back, which landed with a sodden plop. He dropped his cloak on top of it, then his spear and sling. He looked across at his mother and slowly let a smile grow on his weary face, a smile that was shy but heartfelt. Micay was dazed by what she had heard and seemed to see him from a distance. But she remembered Amaru saying that his brother was not like him, and even at a distance, this first smile seemed like proof.

"I prayed I would be allowed to see you again," Cusi said. "The huaca has protected me, and the Chachapoyas have brought me here even sooner."

Mama Cori rose and went to embrace him, followed closely by Lloque and Quinti. Quilaco remained apart, waiting to be introduced, and Micay was aware that he was staring at her, though she did not wish to see what was in his face. She turned away from him and went to fetch some dry clothing and tell the retainers to prepare some food and akha. Runtu Caya, the head retainer, had already stirred up the fire in the back of the awning house, and she waved Micay off with a broad smile.

"I know. Cusi is here. I will bring him what he likes."

Micay nodded wordlessly and walked toward Mama Cori's house, not feeling the rain as she crossed the plaza. The Chachapoyas—her people—had rebelled. This was not mere shouting and the breaking of sticks; blood had been spilled, Inca blood, and there would have to be retribution. She remembered the day, years before, when her father had buried the weapons under the floor of the weaving room. All of the children old enough to understand had been summoned to watch, and her father had told them that the weapons were there in case they ever had to fight the Incas again. In her mind Micay could see the looms pushed aside, piles of earth flanking a raw hole the size and shape of a man.

She found herself going back across the plaza with a tunic and a blanket in her hands but no memory of how she had found them. When she came into the awning house, Cusi was standing close to the brazier with his hands outstretched. He had stripped off his wet tunic, revealing several dark bruises on his chest and dirty bandages around one shoulder and the opposite arm. Standing between Lloque and Quilaco, he seemed a miniature man, well proportioned but scarcely taller than Micay herself. She was about to approach when she recognized the black waistband he was wearing, which made her feel proud in a way that only added to her confusion. So she handed the tunic and blanket to Quinti, who gave her a preoccupied nod and took them to Cusi, who had just finished drying his hair. He pulled the tunic on over his head and sat down on the blanket, carefully folding his legs under him, as if he feared a cramp.

Runtu Caya had brought him maize cakes and stew and part of a roast duck, and everyone sat and watched while he tore into the food with his fingers and teeth, appearing not to have eaten in days. Finally hunger gave way to an awareness of his audience, and he wiped his lips on a cloth and looked expectantly at his mother and uncle. Mama Cori seemed content simply to stare at her son and deferred to Lloque, who said, "Tell me what you know about this rebellion. We had heard only reports of unrest."

"That is what led us there from Caxamarca. But we were fighting almost as soon as we crossed the Marañon, and it has not stopped. Rimachi and I had to leave under the cover of darkness."

"You will return in daylight," Quilaco interjected loudly, raising his drinking cup. "With an army behind you."

Cusi nodded tentatively, appearing disconcerted by Quilaco's enthusiasm or simply too tired to respond to it. He looked back at Lloque and went on with his explanation, seeming to choose his words carefully.

"The Chachapoya captives told us that the trouble began in the eastern villages, where there were protests over the way the governor's agents were recruiting new warriors. The governor took most of the warriors from the garrison and went in person to see that his orders were obeyed. They say he executed several men who had refused to give up their sons, and that that is what set off the uprising. The governor tried to put it down, then tried to return to Caxamarquilla. But word of the executions had traveled, and there had been another uprising behind him. He and his men were caught in the middle and were all cut down."

"Rebels always claim self-defense," Quilaco told him with the weary tolerance of a veteran instructing a novice. "They become especially innocent once they have been captured."

"Rimachi saw one of the captives put to torture," Cusi said in a hard, flat voice. "The man begged to be forgiven, but he would not change his story."

There was a moment of awkward silence before Quinti intervened, tugging gently on Quilaco's arm. "He is tired, Quilaco. Let him finish."

"Yes," Lloque agreed, urging Cusi to go on. "Who are their leaders? Did none of the chiefs try to restrain them?"

"Those who did were either killed or deposed. The leader of the revolt in Caxamarquilla was a chief himself. To taunt us, he has taken the name Uscovilca, after the war huaca of the Chancas. In the east, I am told, the leader is an old warlord named Casca."

Micay froze at the sound of her father's name, which awoke echoes in her memory and made her see her father again, sitting on his stool with his scarred legs stretched out in front of him, his wives and children around him, confronting the Inca without shame or fear.

"They will beg to be forgiven, too," Quilaco said vengefully. "But there is no mercy for traitors. We will stuff their skins with grass and make drums of them, to beat on at our victory feast. We will make drinking cups out of their skulls . . ."

It had become obvious that Quilaco was drunk, though Micay was also certain that his remarks were meant for her. No doubt he wanted her to weep and apologize and retreat even farther into the shadows outside the family circle. But she would not be driven away, she decided, as long as she could still walk.

"The Chachapoyas have always been unruly savages," Quilaco was saying as she rose to her feet and began to walk around the circle, away from him and toward the plaza. Mama Cori's head turned to follow her passage, and she saw Cusi notice her for the first time, his face blanching with a kind of frightened recognition. Micay stopped abruptly and turned to face Quilaco across the circle.

"You must have learned all you know about rebels from the Quitos," she told him, "since you know so little."

"Micay!" Mama Cori admonished. But Quilaco held up a hand to her, baring his teeth in a combative smile. "Let her speak."

"I will speak," Micay averred, "though I know that you will not listen. That is the kind of Inca you are. You would rather judge and punish and remain ignorant of your own crimes. It is Incas like you who have ruled Chachapoyas since before I was born. If we are savages, we have learned it from you."

"You would defend these cowards and traitors?" Quilaco demanded, shaking off Quinti's hand as he struggled to his feet. Lloque was also rising, holding up his hand to attract Micay's attention.

"If you had listened, you would know that they can defend themselves. The only thing left for you to steal is their lives, and those you must take at the risk of your own."

Everyone except Cusi was standing now, and Mama Cori was the first to step in front of Micay and stop the argument.

"That is enough!" she commanded forcefully. "I am disappointed in you, Micay. Go to your room."

Micay bowed swiftly, proudly, and turned to walk out of the awning house, out into the darkness and the falling rain.

CUSI TOOK shallow breaths to calm himself, waiting as the others resettled themselves. He had seen that face—or at least that pale skin and black hair—before, and the eyes had been fierce and icy like hers. He had killed a man, a much larger man, whose pale, unpainted face had seemed as eerie as those decorated for war. He had died believing in the advantage of his size, his face painted with blood.

Quinti was whispering furiously to Quilaco, who had just allowed Runtu Caya to refill his cup. Cusi accepted a cup from her and drank deeply, feeling the effects almost immediately. He set the cup down and caught his mother's eye, reminding her with a glance that once he did not have to ask obvious questions aloud. Mama Cori sighed and nodded in acknowledgement.

"Her name is Micay, as you heard," she explained. "Quinti and I chose her from among the chosen women in Caxamarca to be Quinti's companion."

Cusi looked at his sister, who leaned forward imploringly.

"She has been very sensitive lately, especially about her past. This news must have upset her greatly."

"That is no excuse for disloyalty and disrespect," Quilaco said sternly. "She insulted every Inca."

Quinti closed her eyes for a moment before turning to appeal to him directly. "You must forgive her, Quilaco. She is like a sister to me."

"I would not have her in my house."

"I would have her in mine," Lloque broke in forcefully, causing everyone to sit back in surprise. "She is a Chachapoyas ñusta, and she has no reason to be ashamed of her heritage or her conduct. She spoke to you as you deserved."

"She spoke *treason,*" Quilaco exclaimed, unable to believe that he was being reprimanded.

"She told you the truth about yourself," Lloque insisted. "You have acted rudely tonight, my son. I regret that I did not stop you sooner."

Quilaco stiffened with anger and seemed on the verge of forgetting Lloque's age and rank. He glanced sideways at Quinti, whose head was bowed, then rose to his feet, tipping over his cup in the process.

"Since I cause you such displeasure, my lord, I will remove myself from your company." He bowed curtly to Lloque and pivoted on his heels to address Mama Cori. "The wedding will have to be postponed, my lady, until after I return from Chachapoyas. I will speak to Apu Poma when my duties permit."

"Of course," Mama Cori said in a resigned voice, accepting his bow with a nod. Quilaco gave Quinti a last look, baring his teeth in an angry smile as he turned away.

"I will see you on the march, Cusi Huaman," he said brusquely in passing. "Welcome to Tumibamba."

Cusi gave him a bemused nod as he stalked out of the awning house. Welcome, indeed, he thought incredulously, drinking some more akha. He glanced at the somber faces of his mother and uncle, wondering at his mother's compliance and at Lloque's vigorous defense of the Chachapoya girl. He wondered even more when Quinti looked up and her eyes were dry, displaying none of the anguish he would have expected, given the way her husband-to-be had been humiliated. He drained his cup to the bottom, sensing a depth of complication that he could not fathom. He suddenly began to feel every step he had walked to get here from Cuzco, and when no one else seemed inclined to break the silence, he spoke with the blunt honesty of his fatigue.

"I am drunk and need to sleep. But I think that you have all changed as much as I have."

Tears sprang up in Quinti's eyes and streamed down her cheeks while she nodded in agreement. Lloque gave a kind of shrug, spreading his long hands and glancing at Mama Cori, who spoke for all of them.

"It has been no easier for us to be away from Cuzco," she admitted, "than it could have been for you to stay there alone."

It was the first time Cusi had ever heard his mother express uncertainty about *anything,* and it gave him a moment of panic that made his scalp prickle and his skin break out in a cold sweat. Then he felt a rush of protective feeling that made him want to reach out to his mother and shield her as she had always shielded him. Yet she was regarding him with her customary dignity, letting him know that she was not helpless in the face of difficulty. Cusi straightened his back and tried to speak with equal dignity.

"Your father, Ayar Inca, told me before the Huarachicoy race that true courage lies in living with the painful things we must carry in our hearts. I am still learning the truth of that."

"We all are," Lloque assured him quietly. "It is never learned only once."

There were tears in Mama Cori's eyes now, but she shook her head at Cusi's expression of concern and tried to smile.

"Go to your rest, my son," she told him. "I could not stand to be any prouder than I am at this moment. Quinti, show your brother to his house."

Cusi struggled to his feet and managed to bow without falling over. He took a long look at his mother's face, indulging himself, before turning to follow Quinti, forcing his tired legs into one last march before he slept.

BY HIS THIRD morning in Tumibamba, Cusi was once again able to awaken at first light, without the aching stiffness in his muscles that had made him move like an old man for two days. It had rained during the night, washing the walls of the compound and leaving puddles in the plazas. Steam rose like smoke off of the hot water pipe on the second terrace, and the only creatures moving were two tiny brown birds who were flitting from shrub to shrub in front of the guest house adjacent to his own. Standing in the doorway, Cusi stared up at the pale sky, spotting a vulture already circling high over the city. He thought of the condors in Raurau Illa's vision song and wondered at the fact that he had not seen a single one during the journey from Chachapoyas. He had yet to tell anyone here about Raurau Illa, largely because he had spent most of his time describing the Huarachicoy race and answering questions about the rebellion. This was true even with his own family, and he had decided that it was just as well. His relationship with Raurau, like his visit to the Grass Man and his love for Tocto, was a part of his life too important and complex to be shared quickly, and he would be leaving Tumibamba in another two or three days, as soon as Huayna Capac's soothsayers settled on a propitious day.

Someone was moving on the middle terrace, walking slowly between the cantut bushes that lined the path to the bathhouse. Cusi squinted and made out a long gray and white shift and a dark gray head wrap—a woman. Then the figure stopped in a gap between the bushes and tilted her face toward the sky, and though Cusi could not make out her features, the lightness of her skin told him that it was the Chachapoyas ñusta, Micay. She had been confined to her house since the night of Cusi's arrival, though more for her protection than as a punishment for her outburst. No one within the family seemed angry with her, not even Quinti, but in the rest of the city the attitude toward the rebellious Chachapoyas was decidedly ugly. Cusi had repeated what he knew to a number of people, and their reactions had been much closer to Quilaco's than to Lloque's. That is the kind of Inca you are kept coming back to him as he watched his listeners ignore the details that might have moderated their desire for revenge. There had been enough veiled references to the Quitos, too, to make him think that the Chachapoyas would be made to pay for Huayna Capac's previous display of leniency.

When he looked again, the ñusta had disappeared, probably back into the house she shared with Quinti. Cusi was glad he had not been able to see her more clearly. He had refused Quinti's offer to take him to meet her, knowing that he might soon be confronting another of those pale faces in battle, where he could not afford to hesitate or hold back. If he had to meet death in the way Raurau had predicted, he wanted to do so with his whole being.

Still he made a small bow toward the place where he had last seen her standing, silently saluting her for having escaped her confinement long enough to greet the dawn. He admired her courage and spirit, as Lloque obviously did, and he hoped that he would not be compelled to steal the lives of many more of her people.

ON THE DAY of the warriors' departure, the drums started beating early, and Micay could hear the sounds of singing and shouting even in the confines of her room. She could imagine the regiments stretched out along the Royal Road, waving their banners and weapons and chanting their war songs. They would be facing south this time, led by the Sapa Inca's litter, with its curtained canopy covered with scarlet feathers and medallions of gold. Huayna Capac had decided to attend to this rebellion in person, and unlike the day on which the Incas had left for Quito, this day's sky was clear and the sun shone warmly. Micay wondered if her people would even be given the chance to surrender. She had heard many tales about rebel tribes who existed only in memory, examples of Inca ruthlessness. Their villages and holy places had been destroyed and their lands resettled by mitmacs, and the few survivors had disappeared into the ranks of the retainers.

Micay shivered at the thought and got up to go stand in the sunlight. She had tried to pray, but she had forsaken the gods of her people, and she could not appeal to Mama Quilla to help defeat the sons of Inti—not when Chimpu Ocllo herself would be participating in the ceremonies of departure, praying for an Inca victory. Micay felt even more like a mitmac, cut off from her homeland and isolated where she lived.

The compound was deserted except for two men at the gate, because the rest of the family, including the retainers and most of Apu Poma's staff, had gone to see Cusi Huaman leave. He and his Cañari friend would be marching with the veterans at the head of the column, leading the army back as a reward for having brought word of the rebellion out. Quinti had assured Micay that Cusi had not been angered by her outburst, and that he had continued to speak of the Chachapoyas with respect. But Micay's most vivid impression of him was of the expression on his face when he saw her for the first time. It was as if he had seen the dead come to life, which made her realize later that he had killed Chachapoyas. So it hardly mattered that he did not wish to gloat like Quilaco. He was going back to kill still more. He was an Inca; it was in his blood.   .

She noticed belatedly that one of the men at the compound gate was Acapana, and that he was staring at her. She sat down on the step anyway and turned her face up to the sun. She was not hiding here, since there was nothing left to hide. Let him stare. She did not move when he left his post and limped toward her, though she was startled when he sat down beside her without being asked and addressed her without any of his usual diffidence.

"I heard you exchanged words with Quilaco Yupanqui."

"That is true."

"He was very angry when he left; I saw that myself. And he has not returned."

"He has gone to kill Chachapoyas with the other Incas," Micay said, deliberately trying to shock him. He was leading her somewhere with this recitation of facts, and she did not like being led. Acapana paused to swallow but then went on in the same manner.

"It is rumored that there will be no marriage now."

"There is cause for doubt. Perhaps you should ask Apu Poma."

Acapana ignored the suggestion, sitting hunched forward, his elbows on his thighs and his palms pressed together in front of him.

"I suppose you will be going to stay with the high priestess," he ventured more tentatively, giving her a swift, sidelong glance.

"Why do you suppose that?"

"Quinti Ocllo and Mama Cori must be very angry with you . . . especially now, when Mama Cori has lost the favor of the Coya. I would think that you would look to the high priestess for protection."

"I have her protection," Micay assured him, "but the family has not disowned me. It was Lloque Yupanqui who sent Quilaco away in anger, and Quinti is actually relieved to be freed from her agreement. You understand too little about this family, Acapana, to suppose anything."

He rose to his feet and seemed about to walk away but then caught himself and stood with his hands on his hips. "You will be staying here, then?"

"Do you wish me to leave?"

Acapana whirled on her, his face dark with anger. "You understand too little about me if you can ask that. But then, you do not wish to understand."

"How am I to understand," Micay demanded, rising herself, "when you never speak to me openly? Even today, when you are being bold, you do not tell me what you really mean."

Acapana blinked and looked away, licking his lips. Then the words seemed to erupt from his throat, as if they had been lodged there for a long time.

"I came to tell you that you did not have to be alone. I came to tell you that there is an Inca who would never cast you out if you chose to come into his house."

"So you meant to rescue me from my disgrace," Micay concluded warily. "And that is why you felt free to speak so boldly."

Acapana sighed and hung his head for a moment. But then he met her gaze and held it, speaking in a quiet, rueful voice. "I can never do the right thing with you, Micay. But in my heart I wish to. That has never changed."

Now Micay looked away and had to swallow before she could speak. "I do not know what is in my heart. My life has changed too many times, and each time I know less about where I belong and more about how alone I am. There is no one who can rescue me from that."

"There are many men who will want to try," Acapana assured her in the same rueful tone. "Perhaps it would be better between us if I were not one of them."

"Perhaps," Micay agreed tentatively, not wishing to seem unkind. "I must save myself in any case."

"You will," Acapana said with confidence. "But do not forget my willingness to help, if you have need."

Micay bowed gratefully, feeling at ease with him for the first time in months. The noises in the distance suddenly swelled into one great shout that resounded like a thunderclap, then died away abruptly.

"They are leaving," Acapana murmured, gazing in the direction of the sound. Micay followed his gaze and saw only the cloudless blue of the sky. So she sat back down and refused to look again, holding tight to her memories of Chachapoyas, as if they might evaporate in the hard clarity of the Tumibamba air.

IN ADDITION to the twenty thousand warriors who followed him out of Tumibamba, Huayna Capac had brought a hundred retainers for his personal service, the same number of Soras and Rucanas as litter bearers, and a pack train of llamas to carry his food and clothing and the furnishings of his office. But he had not brought any of his wives along, and most of his advisers and soothsayers had been left behind. He seemed intent on moving swiftly and purposefully, without ceremony or celebration, so that all those who saw him would be made aware of his displeasure. He had had the side curtains removed from his litter and often sat holding a battle-ax with a golden head, his face stern and unforgiving, displaying no recognition of the crowds of people who humbled themselves and blew kisses to him as he passed.

The warriors marched eagerly in his wake, buoyed by the knowledge that there were no delegations of old men preceding them, bearing gifts and soft words that might end the battle before it could begin. They had been held back from the Quitos and then had been surprised and embarrassed by the Carangui. This time, however, they were going not merely to threaten, but to *fight*, to show the world that the sons of Inti were still to be feared.

Cusi and Rimachi traveled somewhat uneasily in the midst of those at the head of the column, feeling more like guests than comrades. They were questioned endlessly about what the fighting had been like, and the more details of the danger and the killing they supplied, the more their listeners wanted to hear. It was clear from the envious responses of the younger warriors that most had never fought a concerted battle, day after day, against an enemy that only grew in numbers and determination. The veteran warriors of the old guard had to cast back many years, some as far as the original wars against the Chachapoyas, to recall examples that matched what Cusi and Rimachi were describing. There were some awkward moments with the warriors of Quilaco's age and rank, who would condescend to Cusi and Rimachi because of their youth and lack of insignia and then realize belatedly that these two "boys," fresh from the initiation rites, had already outstripped them in terms of true battle experience. Cusi and Rimachi were careful not to condescend in return, but it required an effort that made them yearn to be back among their initiation brothers.

When they were two days south of the provincial center of Huancabamba, close to the place where Cusi and Rimachi had come out of the mountains, the two young men were summoned by Michi and Yasca, the war chiefs who shared the command of the column. Michi explained that the Sapa Inca had given permission for two of his sons, Ninan Cuyochi and Atauhuallpa, to lead a small advance party to Caxamarquilla by means of the trail Cusi and Rimachi had taken out. Cusi would guide the hundred warriors led by Ninan Cuyochi, who would travel a half day's march ahead of the hundred commanded by Atauhuallpa and guided by Rimachi.

"It will be dangerous," Michi warned them, but Cusi and Rimachi merely smiled at one another before bowing in compliance.

Yasca, a man with a rough face and a fearsome reputation, spoke up as they were turning to leave the tent. "You have already fought in this war, so you should know to respect your enemy. Do not let ambition lead you into an ambush."

Ninan Cuyochi and Atauhuallpa were waiting outside the tent, and while Ninan merely nodded to Cusi in greeting, Atauhuallpa grinned at Rimachi and clapped him on the shoulder.

"We will see you in Caxamarquilla," he called back to Ninan as he led Rimachi off. Ninan nodded again and gestured curtly for Cusi to follow him in the opposite direction, toward the tents of the Upper Cuzco regiment. Cusi had met Ninan once before and had found him rather cold and distant, his narrow face fixed in a perpetual half frown of what seemed to be suspicion. He was the only child of Huayna Capac's first Coya and was said to be a favorite of the Sapa Inca, even though he had been passed over as Heir. He was only a few years older than Cusi, and his preoccupied manner did not make him seem any more mature or confident in his ability to lead. Cusi would not have minded a grin and a slap on the shoulder to take with him into the mountains.

When they were seated under the open awning of Ninan's tent, however, and Ninan began to speak, Cusi quickly perceived that what he had taken for distance was really shyness, and that Ninan had been thinking about what lay ahead rather than about how to greet his guide. He had obviously memorized everything he had been told about the trail, and he had already devised ways to detect an ambush and to get his men swiftly past the exposed places. He discussed these with Cusi, posing questions to test Cusi's competence before deciding to put him in charge of the forward scouts. He also met Cusi's eyes the whole time, so that the furrow in his brow came to seem a token of earnestness rather than suspicion. When he finished speaking, it was Cusi who smiled.

"I do not know how I was chosen to be your guide," he told Ninan, "but I consider myself fortunate. You have given me confidence that I will see my initiation brothers again."

Though his expression did not change, Ninan dipped his head to acknowledge the compliment. "I chose you myself. Your brother, Amaru, is a friend and a warrior I admire. I wish he were going with us, as well."

"I wish I had been able to see him," Cusi said wistfully. "I still do not understand why he wanted to go to Chan Chan at this time."

"He is a restless man, and he does not care about rank or reputation. He fought recklessly in the retreat from the Carangui, risking himself many times to save others. Those who saw him said he seemed restless to die. Perhaps it is best that he go somewhere peaceful for a while."

Cusi nodded reluctantly, wondering if Amaru had changed so much in the time they had been apart or if he, Cusi, had simply been too young to recognize the restlessness in him. Remembering Raurau Illa's prophecy that he, too, would be changed by a confrontation with death, he looked across at his young commander.

"It will not be peaceful in Caxamarquilla," he said with grim assurance.

Ninan's thin lips parted slightly, in what almost seemed a smile. "That is why we are going there. Draw whatever supplies you need from the supply keeper; tell him to give you the clothing of a scout. Then prepare yourself as a warrior should. We leave at dawn."

TO THE BEATING of drums and the blowing of conch trumpets, Huayna Capac was carried into Caxamarquilla seven days after the arrival of his sons. He barely paused to greet them, though, before ordering a full-scale attack on the Chachapoya forces that still surrounded the city on three sides. The Chachapoyas held their ground through two days of fierce fighting but then began to buckle as regiment after regiment of fresh troops were poured into the battle. In danger of being outflanked, they drew back into the eastern end of the valley, where a rear guard held the pass through the mountains for another day before being overrun.

Losses had been heavy on both sides, but the greater part of the Chachapoya army had managed to escape through the pass, and it was all the war chiefs could do to hold their men back from pursuit until the Sapa Inca could be brought forward to give the command. Huayna Capac descended from his litter to pass out praise and promises of reward to his commanders and captains, and it was during this inspection that he learned of the nearby fortress where a small band of Chachapoyas had taken refuge.

The stronghold was not large but seemed impregnable, set atop a narrow, rocky crag that rose so steeply toward the sky that the fortress could be reached only by ropes or ladders. It was some distance from the place where most of the fighting had occurred and could not menace the pass through which the Incas had to march. Ordinarily it would have been ignored, or a small force would have been left behind to starve the defenders out. But Huayna Capac was determined to leave no enemies alive behind him, so he summoned Atauhuallpa and Ninan Cuyochi and pointed toward the stronghold.

"Take the men who are with you, my sons, and light a fire the whole province of Chachapoyas will see. Make them know that the Inca will tear down mountains to punish those who rebel against me."

Cusi had continued to serve under Ninan Cuyochi after reaching Caxamarquilla, and the last rotation had brought him together with Rimachi, Tomay, and Uritu again. They eagerly joined the column of men streaming toward the crag, led by Atauhuallpa, who whooped and brandished a spear, and by Ninan, whose customary frown was deepened to a scowl by the squint he assumed in an effort to survey the terrain. Both had distinguished themselves during the past days of fighting, constantly leading their men into the thick of the battle and pushing the enemy back. The fortress was their reward, a chance to test the limits of their courage and resourcefulness; to prove, again, that there was no fortress the Incas could not storm.

Despite the eagerness of the warriors, however, the attack was slow to take shape. Only one narrow path wound up the side of the crag, and the men behind the walls above were throwing down rocks in earnest, knowing only too well where the climbers would be exposed to their aim. Atauhuallpa and Ninan Cuyochi sent squads up the mountainside on both sides of the path, to scale the rock face with ropes and climbing axes, their shields lashed to their backs for protection. They also sent bowmen and dart throwers and slingers up onto the surrounding heights to shoot their arrows and stones down into the fortress. The main force continued its harried progress up the path, carrying the ladders and grappling hooks that would be used in the final assault.

It was Uritu, from his place among the Chuncho bowmen on a nearby ridge, who first noticed what appeared to be a path that climbed the sheer face of the cliff that fell off behind the fortress. He sent word down to Ninan, who dispatched a scout to inspect the path at first hand. The scout returned to say that there was indeed a way up, but that it was very narrow and very steep, a track more fit for a vicuña than a man.

Ninan sent his captains among the men to ask for volunteers, specifying that they be small and slender, with good balance and no fear of heights. He wanted six men brave enough to climb the cliff and assault the stronghold from the rear. There were perhaps no more than twenty Chachapoyas inside the fortress, so six would have a chance if they attacked without warning. But Ninan also told the captains not to shame anyone into volunteering, since this was a mission that offered glory but was more likely to provide an early death.

Cusi and Tomay were among the handful of men taken aside by their captain, and when Cusi heard what was being proposed, he knew immediately that this was the challenge Raurau Illa had described. He felt a chill that made his stomach contract, forcing the air out of his lungs. He knew that he was going to volunteer, that he *had* to volunteer, but he was overwhelmed for a moment by an enormous sense of convergence. This was also his chance to win fame, to test his huaca in the way Otoronco had told him about, by attempting the impossible. He was still trying to find his voice when Tomay spoke up beside him.

"I will go. I will climb any cliff to kill a traitor to the Inca."

"So will I," another voice proclaimed. Cusi turned his head to see Mayca standing behind him. Mayca was holding a rigid pose, and his eyes went past Cusi without seeing him.

"I will go, as well," Cusi blurted, so hastily that the captain stared at him for a moment, giving him a chance to reconsider. Cusi nodded emphatically to show he understood what he was agreeing to.

"That is enough," the captain said. "Three others have already been chosen. Your leader will be a man called Condor Tupac."

Cusi felt a second chill, remembering the condors in Raurau's vision song. *One flutters to earth. One watches tirelessly, with eyes that pierce the darkness.* Which would this be, if in fact it were either? Cusi shook himself, trying to shrug off the chill as he walked toward the assembly point with Tomay and Mayca. Whatever was to come, he had to face it with his whole being and not trust to prophecies to save him.

He recognized two of the other volunteers and was pleased to see both of them. One was a scout named Paucar who had been on the trail with Cusi and had taught him some of the secrets of his craft. The other was a young Colla warrior named Huañu whom Tomay had helped to recruit and promote. Both were tough and dependable, exactly the kind of comrades Cusi would have chosen himself, since Rimachi and Uritu were too large to be considered.

Condor Tupac, on the other hand, was a short, dark man who was at least fifteen years older than any of them and a good deal thicker through the shoulders and torso. He wore the earplugs of an Inca of the blood but spoke in an oddly accented Quechua, introducing himself as the micho of this province. Apparently noting their surprise that a man of his age and rank would be a member of this group, he went on in a low, taut voice.

"I have a debt to pay to these savages. They have destroyed everything we built here, everything we tried to give them. They deserve total destruction, and they will have it! I will be the first into the fortress, and the first to put it to the torch!"

He scanned their faces for signs of disagreement, but his eyes were fixed and glaring, like those of a man with a fever. He cannot see us, Cusi thought; he is tireless only in his desire for vengeance, or perhaps for vindication.

"I will be second, then," Mayca announced suddenly, drawing a nod of approval from Condor Tupac. Cusi glanced around at the rest of his companions and saw that none of them found this bidding any more appropriate than he did. Paucar, as the oldest and most experienced, finally broke the silence.

"Let us pray we all reach the top together," he suggested quietly, a sentiment none of them could scorn. Cusi lowered his eyes, filled with an affection for Paucar so strong that it embarrassed him. He would gladly face death with such a man, and with Tomay and Huañu. For a moment he was afraid he was going to weep.

Then Condor Tupac gave the command to move out, leading the way with Mayca falling in behind him. The other four all hesitated, looking at one another, before both Paucar and Tomay gestured for Cusi to take the next place. Not wanting to show reluctance at such a time, Cusi went after Mayca and Condor Tupac without a word, though he did not get too close to them. There could be no turning back now, but he would have to tell Ninan Cuyochi later that he had made a mistake in trusting so much in age and rank. Cusi glanced up at the sky, offering the thought of "later" as the first of his unspoken prayers.

THEY BEGAN their ascent in the middle of the afternoon, when the cliff had already fallen into shadow but there was still enough light by which to see. They had removed their earplugs and rubbed their skin with ashes, and they had put on gray tunics—mourning clothes—to help them blend in with the rocks. As weapons they carried flat bronze knives in sheaths secured to the back of their waistbands and their woolen slings wrapped around their heads.

Condor Tupac went first, then Mayca, Cusi, Tomay, Huañu, and Paucar. They had agreed among themselves, promised one another, that if one began to fall he would not reach out and pull his comrades down with him. They would stay an arm's length apart and regroup at the top, if they made it that far. There would be no talking, for every sound would echo off the rocks.

Cusi did not allow himself to look up at the whole extent of the cliff, keeping his eyes on Mayca's back as they started up the steep trail. It was wide enough here to walk without turning sideways, though it soon became necessary to lean to the left, in toward the cliff. They climbed up out of the brush before making a switchback in the other direction, picking their way over piles of fallen shale and past the thorns of the cacti that clung stubbornly to the side of the mountain. Now Cusi was following Mayca's gray-clad buttocks, both of them bent almost double against the incline. All of them were breathing hard, gulping at the thinning air, so that Condor Tupac finally signaled for a rest, to guard against their being heard by whomever might be above. Cusi leaned back against the rock face and turned sideways to look at Tomay, who was also avoiding looking down. Their fear of heights had been thoroughly tested during the Huarachicoy, but they knew that all their weight, even that of their attention, had to be concentrated on keeping themselves on the path. They had to think only of what lay ahead, not of what was below or behind.

Beyond the next switchback, the trail narrowed precipitously, becoming little more than a declivity traversing the sheer face of the cliff. It had been used by some other human, though, for rudimentary handholds had been chipped into the rock at the most difficult places. They had to move sideways now, facing inward and feeling their way along. Whoever had come this way before had been an exceedingly small human, perhaps a child used as a messenger in times of emergency. Cusi squeezed the excess air out of his lungs in order to press himself more closely against the rock face, never more grateful for his lack of bulk. He could tell, from the number of times he had to wait, that Mayca and Condor Tupac were struggling to keep their weight balanced. At such times, he put all of his thoughts upon his spirit brother, which was a hard lump against his belly. He imagined it as a stake or a pin of stone that held him fast to the mountain, a piece of the living rock that could not be broken away. Once, though, out of the corner of his eye, he saw a hawk fly past below him and the sight broke his concentration and made his whole body waver, so that fear pricked his skin and sweat poured down his sides. But he held on and did not move again until he was calm, edging forward with his whole attention upon the next handhold.

His waiting had opened space between himself and the two men ahead, and he could hear Tomay close behind him. He repressed the urge to hurry, sliding his bare feet sideways bit by bit as he kept himself flattened against the rock. He was aware now of all the air behind him, but his immediate problem was an overhanging shelf of stone that seemed to lower itself toward his head with each step he took forward. He bent his knees as much as he could without threatening his balance but still had to tuck his head back into his shoulder to make it under the overhang. The posture made him look back at Tomay, and he saw that the two fingers of height his friend had over him was forcing Tomay to assume a precarious crouch beneath the shelf of rock. Suddenly the knob of stone beneath Tomay's forward hand snapped off with a muted crack, and Cusi saw the fingers come free and hang in the air, helplessly splayed, grasping at emptiness. Then his own hand clamped down over them and pinned Tomay to the rock, an action so swift and instinctual that Cusi did not feel his own movement and was surprised by the sensation of flesh beneath his fingers.

Tomay grunted softly in gratitude, his eyes still wide with panic. Slowly his fingers found another grip and Cusi withdrew his hand, leaving Tomay to negotiate the rest of the overhang by himself. The terror of nearly falling seemed to have shrunk him, so that he did not slip again and was right behind Cusi when he made the last turn and came up on top of the overhanging shelf. Here the path was wide enough for two men to stand abreast, a small plateau some twenty feet below the top of the cliff. The six men squatted to rest and recover their strength, looking over the edge at the canopy of trees that filled the bottom of the gorge, several hundred feet below. The drop seemed perfectly perpendicular, and the greenery would have provided no cushion from such a height. Except for Cusi, each of the men had carried a small piece of stone somewhere on his person, and they deposited these in a small pile, silently thanking the mountain for allowing them to climb its face. Cusi also thanked the mountain, patting his waistband to show that he carried his own kind of apachita.

They went on in single file, grateful to be walking upright, testing the weary muscles in their legs and adjusting their loincloths and the knives attached to their waistbands. They wound part of the way around the cliff, able now to hear the sounds of fighting from the other side of the fortress. The sun, Blessed Inti, would be shining full into the eyes of the defenders, warming the backs of those who sought to scale the fort's walls. If they could strike now from behind, out of the shadows, the Chachapoyas would never be able to hold the walls, and the stronghold would be taken.

Then the men ahead stopped, and Cusi could see past them to the last obstacle that lay between them and success. The path grew narrow again for a distance of perhaps twenty feet and then ended abruptly some four feet short of a landing that appeared to lead into the fortress itself. They would have to walk sideways for twenty feet and then make a standing leap over the gap, hoping no one was hiding behind the masonry wall that jutted out onto the landing.

Condor Tupac eased himself out onto the narrow ledge, standing with his back to the cliff, so that he would be able to swing a leg out at the end and throw himself over the opening. He moved cautiously, his eyes fixed on the empty landing ahead, his arms out at his sides, hands feeling for a grip on the wall of rock behind him. Mayca followed him in the same fashion, and then Cusi slid out, trying not to let his thoughts rush ahead to the final leap. A great depth of color yawned in front of him, and he could feel the wind plucking at the front of his tunic. Two more steps, toes curled against the slide of bare skin on dusty stone, fingers digging into cracks, searching among the moss and debris for a better purchase. The noise of the fighting was very loud, drowning out the sounds of dislodged pebbles and anxious breathing. Then Cusi's forward hand touched that of Mayca and he stopped, feeling Tomay touch him a moment later.

Another long moment passed, while Condor Tupac gathered his courage and offered a last prayer to Inti. Cusi prayed to Illapa, and to his spirit brother and his huaca and the spirit of Pachacuti, calling on all of the powers he knew to help him survive and conquer. Then he heard a cry and saw Condor Tupac swing his leg up and out and throw himself toward the landing, flailing for balance with his arms. He seemed to hang in the air, as Tomay's hand had earlier, and as he came down, a man in war paint and feathers stepped out from behind the wall and struck him a glancing blow with a spear, knocking him off the landing before his feet were fully on it. Mayca reacted instantly, shuffling forward to throw himself at the landing, hoping to reach the Chachapoya sentry before he could raise his spear to strike again. But he left the ledge too soon, misjudging the length of the gap, and he got only one foot onto the landing before pitching backward to his death. He screamed as he fell, a sound that echoed out over the gorge, keen and helpless.

Reflex had carried Cusi almost to the end of the ledge, but there he froze, just out of range of a spear thrust from the other side. The Chachapoya stared at him for a moment, his eyes wildly alert in a face that had been painted half red and half white. Then he saw the way Cusi was clinging to the rock face behind him, and a white smile split the red paint around his mouth. He backed off a step and began talking in his own language, grinning at Cusi and gesturing for him to jump.

Cusi looked down at the short piece of ledge and then the empty expanse that separated him from the landing. He had jumped greater distances before, many times, but never with so much whirling space beneath him, waiting to claim him if the bronze point of the sentry's spear did not. He imagined himself falling, impaling himself on the trees, shredding his flesh on the rocks, ending as a sack of torn meat for the vultures to pick at. His throat closed as a cold, prickly sweat broke out all over his body.

"Jump, Inca," the Chachapoya taunted him, speaking now in bad Quechua. "Show me how you fall, Son of the Sun."

Cusi could feel Tomay and the other two men behind him and understood that there was no possibility of retreat now that they had been discovered. They would be easy targets for rocks from above, and they could never make it back down in darkness. He was the leader now, and it was his duty to throw himself on the spear and give those behind him a chance. He glanced down at the ledge again and calculated the short hop he would take as he swung his leg out, then the long leap to the other side. But there was no strength in his legs and no desire in his hands to release their desperate grip on the rocks behind him.

"Let yourself fall, then," the sentry jeered. "I would not bloody my spear on a coward."

Feeling a sudden warmth on his leg, Cusi realized he had wet himself. He did not know why he did not simply let himself fall and put an end to his shame, except that he was as numb to his shame as he was to his hatred for the taunting Chachapoya. He felt both, yet neither could move him. He remembered Raurau Illa's prophecy that he would live to return to Raurau's village, but it seemed utterly meaningless, without the power to put courage back into his heart. He thought of Otoronco's story about Pachacuti, whose madness had allowed him to survive certain defeat. But Cusi was not mad and had lost none of his senses. He saw everything too clearly: the vast, featureless space below him, the ledge and the landing, the vigilant stance of the man with the spear. He saw death everywhere, and could not bring himself to face it . . .

Then his right hand suddenly sprang free behind him, still grasping a piece of the cliff, and his muscles came alive with the terror of lost balance. He pivoted on his toes, trying to swing his body back into the cliff but finding there was no room—he would hit the wall and fall. A howl of denial burst from his lips and he hopped forward on one foot, swinging his arm in a frantic circle and pushing off into space, amazed by the spring in his leg, the remembered strength—he could jump *high* as well as far—that launched him toward the startled sentry, who jerked backward in self-defense. Cusi released the stone in his hand in midair, aiming for the painted face but throwing wildly past it. Then he came down and felt a slashing pain rip through his ribs just before his shoulder crashed into the sentry's chest and his knees and elbows struck the hard stone floor. There was no air in his lungs for a moment and red spots swam in front of his eyes; he felt his body still flying through space, leaving the rest of him behind.

Then he was aware of his cheek pressed against the dusty stones of the landing and his mouth sucking desperately for breath. Careful hands turned him over and raised him into a sitting position, which made it a bit easier to breathe. Tomay, Huañu, and Paucar were squatting around him, holding their knives with blades like shining half moons. Tomay's blade was bloody, and there was no sign of the sentry.

"Can you move?" Paucar asked softly. Cusi nodded, letting them help him to his feet. Tomay hastily stripped off his own tunic and pressed it against Cusi's side, trying to keep him from seeing the blood. Cusi could see it and could feel it wetting his fingers through the cloth, but he could not yet connect it with any pain; the effort to breathe was too consuming. Paucar hefted the spear that had belonged to the sentry and gestured for the others to help Cusi along.

"The next weapon belongs to you," he promised in a tone of deep respect, and Tomay and Huañu murmured their assent. Cusi let himself be led along, wondering why they did not simply leave him, since he was in no shape to handle a weapon. And how could they speak to him with respect? Had they not seen how terrified he was? He had been paralyzed by it, frozen in place, and it was only the fear of falling that had finally made him jump—fear and the piece of stone that had come free in his hand, pushing him off the mountain.

The pain came over him as he stood in the shadows, leaning against the mud-plastered wall of a storage hut, waiting while the others searched for weapons. From the other side of the hut the shouting of men and the clattering of stones and arrows were very loud, but the pain would not let him attend to anything else. His knees and elbows felt as if they had been broken by stone hammers, and every breath seemed to tug at his torn ribs. He groaned and sank slowly to the ground, clutching the blood-soaked tunic to what felt like a burning hole in his side. Tomay appeared beside him with a spear in one hand and a battle-ax in the other.

"We have taken our weapons and set fire to the hut," he reported excitedly. "Now we will kill those who come to put it out."

"I cannot fight anyone," Cusi managed, his voice a croak.

"You have done enough. You have great huaca, Cusi Huaman." Tomay put the battle-ax down beside him and grasped Cusi's free hand, bowing his head over it briefly. "I could not have done what you did. You saved us all."

Then Tomay was gone, and smoke was swirling around him where he sat. He coughed and groped for the spirit brother in his waistband, closing his fingers around it. He remembered what he had felt as he jumped, the despairing sense of having no choice and no control and a wild, ferocious anger that he could do no more with his life than throw it away. He had not been trying to save anyone except himself. His last thought had been of Tocto, sitting alone in Cuzco, waiting but never hearing from him again . . .

He was aware later of being moved, of many people around him in a flickering yellow light, of hands touching him, of wet cloth pressing against his face and parched lips. He was lying on his back, lashed to a litter with strong ropes across his chest and legs. When he could make out the faces leaning over him, he was able to recognize only that of Ninan Cuyochi, and he was seized by the guilty notion that he was the only one of his party who had survived.

"Tomay—"

"Tomay has told us what you did," Ninan assured him. "Now you must lie still so we can lower you down to the healers, who wait below. Your wound must be closed before you lose all your blood."

Cusi closed his eyes, relieved that the others were alive and could speak of what he had done. He did not want to have to speak of it himself. He felt the litter being raised and carried, then lowered through the air in a slow, jerky descent that made his ribs throb with pain. He was still conscious when the ropes were untied and the healers began to pry the makeshift bandages off his wound, but then the pain overwhelmed him and he slid downward into darkness.

IX

HAMPI CAMAYOQCONA: Healers

(A.D. 1514)

Tumibamba

C USI WAS carried back into Tumibamba on a litter with a canopied roof and curtained sides, borne on the shoulders of six of the Sapa Inca's own Sora bearers. They took him directly to the micho's quarters, lowering the palanquin as they came through the gate into the compound, where the family and all of the servants were waiting. An honor guard of four warriors in bright tunics of sumptuous cumbi cloth was leading the way, and among them Micay recognized Ninan Cuyochi, the son of the first Coya and a favorite of Mama Huarcay. Behind the litter came another group of eight or ten men whose strange appearance made Apu Poma hesitate in his greeting to Ninan Cuyochi. They were long-haired men who wore animal-skin headdresses and tunics of foreign weave, with necklaces of claws and teeth around their necks and feathered coca bags hanging under their arms. They gave off a collective odor of herbs and wood smoke, and they seemed oblivious of everything except themselves and the litter. Several were shaking gourd rattles and chanting in low voices as they shuffled forward.

"Huayna Capac's healers," Quinti whispered to Micay, and they both cast a glance at Mama Cori, whose face—already taut from days of anxious waiting—seemed to tighten even further at the sight of these disreputable-looking men.

Apu Poma led everyone down to the lower terrace, where the guest house Cusi had last occupied had been converted into a sickroom. The bearers set their burden down on the walkway in front of the house, and at an order from Ninan Cuyochi they lifted the side curtains and folded them over on top of the canopy. The healers pressed in on both sides, but Apu Poma stepped back and spread his arms, opening a space for Mama Cori to kneel beside her son. Quinti and Micay slipped in behind her and peered over her shoulder at Cusi, suppressing the exclamations of distress that rose to their lips.

He was wearing only a loincloth and was bound to the litter by leather straps across his chest, waist, and calves. His face looked ghastly: thin and drawn, his eyes sunk deeply into their sockets, his lips pale and cracked. He had pulled himself over onto his uninjured side, so that his bandaged ribs thrust up into the air, the white cloth tinged with pink. There were dark bruises on his knees and forearms and raw, bloody patches where the twisted straps had cut into his arms and legs. He drew each breath with a groan and expelled it with a shudder, grimacing at the effort, which was exhausting simply to watch.

"Water," Mama Cori commanded urgently. But when Micay turned to obey, she found her way blocked by two of the healers, who made no move to clear a path for her. A man wearing a gray fur headdress was addressing Apu Poma from the other side of the litter, gesturing toward the guest house behind him.

"He cannot stay here, my lord. There is not sufficient room for us. We must take him to the Coya's compound."

"We must remove these bonds," Mama Cori cried, looking around in distress. "Tomay, help me. Use your knife."

The warriors seemed to have disappeared into the tight ranks of the healers, who were all larger men, but now one of them—a fat-cheeked Colla in a knit cap—knelt down on the other side of the litter and produced a crescent-shaped knife from a sheath in his waistband.

"Lord Micho, we cannot stay here," the head healer insisted more stridently. "It is best we take him with us now."

The warrior named Tomay stared up at Apu Poma with slitted eyes, the knife poised above Cusi's bonds. Apu Poma cleared his throat and then spoke with unusual force.

"He is my son. He stays here."

Tomay's knife made a rasping sound as it slashed through the leather strap, which sprang loose in both directions like an uncoiling snake. Cusi moaned and shifted his limbs, settling down onto his back. Another warrior, also a Colla, shouldered his way through the healers with a bowl of water in his hands. He squatted and passed the bowl across to Mama Cori, who wet her fingertips and began to moisten Cusi's lips.

"Where can we stay, then?" the head healer asked in grudging resignation. Mama Cori answered without looking up. "You can go. We do not need you."

"The Sapa Inca has ordered us to attend him," the man persisted, still addressing himself to Apu Poma. "We must—"

"I will heal him," Mama Cori interrupted, rearing back in anger. "Look at how you bring him to me! Did you ever think to feed him or give him water? He should never have been moved. I would have gone to him anywhere."

"The choice was not ours, my lady," the healer explained, spreading out his hands in a show of innocence. "We have done everything we could for him . . ."

Tomay suddenly stood up and turned to confront him, holding the knife loosely in front of his chest.

"You have had enough of him. You have poked at him and said your spells over him and questioned him in his sleep. Leave now, before I drive you away."

"Tomay!" Ninan Cuyochi admonished, stepping in between them. But the face he turned toward the head healer was even less sympathetic. "You are released from your duties, Titu, by my order."

"My lord, the Sapa Inca will be most—"

"Go!" Apu Poma added in a stony voice. "Go before I decide to report your negligence as well as your insolence."

The healers immediately lowered their eyes and backed away, heading for the compound gate. Apu Poma told the bearers to remove the canopy altogether and then had them carry Cusi inside on the litter. Tomay, the second Colla, and a third warrior—another short, wiry man who wore the earplugs of an Inca—gently transferred Cusi to the soft bed of mats and llama skins that had been prepared for him, and then stood back to let the women take over. Micay knelt and held the water bowl for Quinti, who sprinkled Cusi's lips while Mama Cori cut off his bandages with a thin obsidian blade.

"He is still bleeding."

"I will make a poultice," the third warrior offered, moving toward the mat where Mama Cori had laid out her medicines. "I am Paucar, my lady, from the Aucayhaylli household. I was with Cusi on the cliff."

"So was I," the second Colla said in heavily accented Quechua. "I am Huañu, my lady, from Hatuncolla."

"We are grateful to you," Mama Cori murmured, dabbing gingerly at the raw, puckered wound with a wet cloth.

"My father is waiting for all of us in the great square," Ninan Cuyochi reminded them. "He will want the heroes who took the fortress to stand on the dais with him."

Paucar nodded but stayed where he was, watching Mama Cori apply a mass of wet green leaves to the gash in Cusi's side. At the first touch Cusi coughed and moaned and tried to roll away from the pain, but Quinti gently restrained him. Mama Cori patted the poultice into place, and they all watched as Cusi's straining body gradually relaxed.

"The coca leaves are numbing the pain," Paucar observed with satisfaction. Tomay squatted next to Cusi's head and helped Quinti lift his upper body, so that Mama Cori and Micay could wrap a cotton bandage over the poultice and around his back. Then they lowered him down again, Quinti and Tomay keeping their hands on his shoulders for a moment as if to help steady his breathing. When the harsh, labored sound of his respiration seemed to ease and modulate, Paucar and Huañu stood up and began to move toward the doorway, where Ninan Cuyochi was waiting. Tomay simply looked up from his place next to Cusi's bed.

"You two go," he said to his comrades. "I will stay here. I would not be alive to enjoy our fame if not for him. I cannot celebrate without him."

Apu Poma escorted Ninan and the two warriors out of the room, then returned to squat at the foot of the bed. He looked across at Tomay and seemed about to speak, but then thought better of it and joined the others in waiting for Mama Cori to break her silence. She was staring down at Cusi with her hands in her lap, as if she had to reach some decision before she touched him again. Micay noticed for the first time that he was wearing the waistband she had woven for him, though it was so stained with blood as to be almost unrecognizable.

"We must feed him," Mama Cori declared abruptly. "Someone must be here whenever he awakes, to give him whatever food and water he can swallow. His wound is healing, but he is weak from the blood he lost and from the neglect of these healers. We must give him the strength to survive." She looked sideways at Tomay, clenching her hands in frustration. "Why did they not feed him?"

Tomay's cheeks colored again and he lowered his eyes for a moment, as if ashamed.

"He was attended by the healers from our regiment at first; they were the ones who stopped the bleeding and sewed the wound shut inside. These others met us in Huancabamba on the way back; the Sapa Inca had summoned them. I went to check on Cusi the next night and found them all squatting around him, waving feather fans over his body and touching him with stones and roots and their fingers. The one called Titu Atauchi was leaning over Cusi's face, repeating back to him things he must have said in his sleep, because he was not awake.

"I made them stop that time," Tomay said in a hoarse voice. "But after that none of us were allowed near him, by order of the Sapa Inca. We heard rumors that Huayna Capac himself visited him on several occasions."

Mama Cori glanced over at Apu Poma.

"Lloque was right. He said Huayna Capac had claimed Cusi and would want to keep him close while the power of his heroism was still with him. Lloque could tell from the nature of the messages we received, which spoke of something more than courage and daring. Huayna Capac covets anyone he believes possesses huaca."

"What did he *do,* Tomay?" Apu Poma asked, unable to restrain himself any longer. "We know only that he climbed a cliff and led an attack on a fort, during which he received this wound. Surely you are all heroes; what did he do that the rest of you did not?"

Tomay took a deep breath and then shrugged, as if he could find no other way to describe it.

"He *flew,* my lord. He leaped off a ledge no wider than your foot and soared into the air like a hawk, and threw himself onto the warrior who had surprised us. The man had a spear, and he had already sent two of our number to their deaths. I expected to die the same way, and I wanted to get it over with. I could barely stand it when Cusi waited, pretending to be afraid, letting the warrior grow complacent and careless. I thought I was going to fall a hundred times, and I almost did when Cusi screamed and made his leap. He came down on the man like a stone and knocked him senseless, which was a good thing, since my legs were so weak that I barely made it to the landing after him." Tomay paused and shook his head, his awe undiminished. "I still see him in my memory, but I cannot fully believe what I saw."

They all looked down at Cusi in the silence that followed Tomay's testimony, again hearing the ragged sound of his breathing. Mama Cori leaned forward and carefully sprinkled a few drops of water onto his lips. Suddenly Cusi's eyelids fluttered and the tip of his tongue licked out blindly.

"He has not stopped fighting," Mama Cori proclaimed, "and neither must we." She looked across at Quinti and Micay, holding their eyes for a moment. "Will you help me watch over him? One of us must be here at all times, day and night, until he is strong again."

Micay and Quinti nodded without hesitation.

"When I am not with him," Quinti added, "I will pray for him at the House of the Moon."

"I would like to sit with him as well, my lady," Tomay put in. "For as long as I am in Tumibamba."

"I also want to sit with him," Apu Poma said quietly, drawing a sharp glance from Mama Cori.

"You cannot bring your other duties here. He must be allowed to rest when he is not being fed."

"Acapana can handle my duties. They are not as important as this."

Mama Cori appeared flustered by the sincerity of his response, and her features slackened for a moment, showing the weariness and concern her composure was holding at bay. She tipped her head to Apu Poma and then to Tomay.

"You may join our vigil, then." She reached down and touched Cusi's forehead, speaking to him in a fervent whisper. "We are here for you, my son. We will not leave you again, I promise. We will be with you for as long as you need us."

HE HAD lost his breath somehow, perhaps he had given it away, and surely that was why the Grass Man had beaten him so severely, so that the blood ran down his arms onto the yellowing bunch of grass and then flowed into the river, turning the water scarlet and staining everything with his crimes. He gave himself gladly to the river's embrace and was carried away by it, out of Cuzco and into this darkness, where he felt himself falling again, his limbs waving weakly in the winds that buffeted him from side to side and chafed at his skin, falling endlessly and alone . . .

He woke once to find himself bound and immobile, yet still moving through the darkness, which was filled with the sound of shuffling feet. He knew then that he had been taken captive, and when the faces of his captors loomed over him, taunting and threatening him, he hid in the darkness behind his eyes, bearing the tortures they inflicted on him and saying nothing that might reveal the whereabouts of his comrades. Even when he felt a cold presence beside him and saw the leering, skeletal face of Death out of the corner of his eye, he did not yield to their questions or beg for his release. He fell deeper into the darkness, away from them, preferring to die of hunger and thirst rather than ask for comfort from his enemies.

The light when it came was liquid and glaring, and it puzzled him at first, until he understood that he was under water. His captors spoke to him from above in voices that were garbled and echoing, and he regarded them with a contemptuous annoyance, wondering why they did not comprehend the fact that he could not speak under water. The water lay heavily on his body, which felt too weak to resist its weight. He was exhausted from the constant movement, from pursuing the full breath that always eluded him, from the dreams of falling. His failure only made the Grass Man angrier, so that he stabbed at Cusi with his stick and commanded him to answer for his crimes or die.

But Cusi had no answers and no strength left with which to utter them. As he lay waiting for death to claim him, he saw the Grass Man's face emerge from the darkness, a warped and shrunken face with papery skin and golden circles where the eyes should have been. Cusi felt a pang of regret as fleeting as his strength, regret that this secret would die with him, and no one else would ever know, as he did now, that the Grass Man was Pachacuti . . .

IT WAS late at night and raining when Tomay brought Cusi's other two friends to see him. Micay was sitting with Runtu Caya, who had been telling her stories about Cusi's childhood to help keep them both awake. The old woman bowed to the young men and retreated to a corner to stir the broth she had simmering on hot stones, showing proper deference to these Incas by privilege but not about to leave them alone with a ñusta. Micay allowed Tomay to introduce her, though she already knew that the tall, handsome Cañari had to be Rimachi and the Campa with the feathered headdress, Uritu. They both had blanket-wrapped bundles in their arms, and they set them on the floor in front of them when they squatted down on the other side of Cusi. After they had all stared down at Cusi for several moments, their faces impassive but their eyes glittery in the light of the rushes burning in the wall niche, Rimachi was the first to speak.

"How is he?"

"Very weak," Micay said frankly. "It exhausts him simply to swallow a few sips of water. But Mama Cori got him to take some broth this morning for the first time."

Rimachi nodded and they all fell silent again, though now they were studying her rather than Cusi. They seemed uneasy in her presence—Uritu especially—but she could not tell if it was her beauty that bothered them or the fact that she was a Chachapoya. Tomay had already demonstrated how loyal they were to Cusi; perhaps it disturbed them to see one of the enemy tending to their friend. That was the feeling Uritu gave her, though she thought she detected an appreciative glint in Rimachi's eyes. Hoping she was right, she pointed with her chin at the bundle in front of him.

"What have you brought with you?"

Rimachi brightened immediately, as if he himself had been trying to think of a way to open a conversation. He unwrapped his bundle with a flourish.

"We have brought Cusi's possessions." He rifled through a pile of garments whose brilliant colors were apparent even in the dim light, finally selecting a tunic and holding it up to her. It was buff-colored vicuña with a border of tocapu—small, individually woven squares filled with intricate designs and symbols. "These are the gifts of the Sapa Inca, rewards for Cusi's bravery."

"It is beautiful," Micay murmured, glancing sadly at Cusi, whose emaciated body seemed much too small for the garment.

"Uritu has his personal belongings," Rimachi prompted, turning to the Campa, who had made no move to open his bundle. Rimachi gestured with his hands, acting surprised.

"Come, she is a daughter of the house," he said, glancing at Micay for a confirmation he did not seem to need.

"Cusi did not give me his things to display," Uritu said gravely, his gaze focused on the far wall. Rimachi made an exasperated sound and spread his hands in apology to Micay, who did not know where to put her own eyes.

Suddenly Tomay spoke up from Uritu's other side, addressing her in a shrewd tone, as if he had just figured something out. "Did you help to weave Cusi's initiation clothes?"

Micay stared at him blankly, still flustered by Uritu's show of distrust and unable to see what her weaving had to do with it. She nodded in bewilderment, and Tomay smiled, his eyes nearly disappearing behind his cheeks.

"The bearer who brought them to Cuzco insisted to Cusi that they had come from his mother and 'sisters,'" Tomay explained. "Cusi did not know what that meant. He showed me a waistband that was different from the others—that one, I think," he added, pointing with his chin at the stained band around Cusi's bony hips. "It was vicuña."

"I wove that myself," Micay admitted. "I went to see Lloque Yupanqui, who showed me what colors and symbols to use."

"Where did you get the vicuña?" Tomay asked curiously.

Micay sighed at the memory. "From Apu Poma, who had received it from the Sapa Inca. But the decision to use it was my own. Mama Cori had refused to accept it."

There was a moment of silence that seemed filled with disapproval, making Micay wonder why she had told them so much, so truthfully.

"You knew how Cusi felt about his father?" Rimachi inquired delicately, looking down his long nose at her in a searching but not unkindly way. She could not bring herself to see what was on Tomay's and Uritu's faces.

"That was when I learned what Apu Poma had done. But I did not think Cusi should be deprived of such a great gift because of what had happened in the past. I thought I could make it *my* gift, so that no bad feelings would be attached to it."

"It was his favorite," Uritu said emphatically, looking directly at Micay for the first time. She noticed that he had thin black lines painted on his broad cheeks and an empty perforation in one nostril, and she sensed—perhaps because of the importance he attached to Cusi's preference—that he cared for Cusi in a way different from the other two. He suddenly dropped his eyes and reached down to unfold the bundle in front of him. He lifted out a battle-ax with a black stone head and placed it carefully on the edge of Cusi's bedding.

"That was a gift from his grandfather, the Lord Otoronco Achachi. It was blessed by Pachacuti himself."

Micay nodded quizzically, familiar with the names, but not in relation to Cusi.

"I was told that his grandfathers were Sinchi Huaman and Ayar Inca," she said politely. All three nodded in agreement.

"Otoronco Achachi is the brother of Sinchi Huaman," Rimachi explained. "He was Cusi's guardian in Cuzco."

"This is another gift of the lord," Uritu said, laying a fringed coca bag beside the ax and patting it proudly. "He chews his coca as the Campa do, ground with palm-leaf ash."

Rimachi and Tomay both smiled indulgently at this boast and Rimachi raised his eyebrows at her, as if impressed by the compliment Uritu had paid her. Uritu removed a round, red and black shield and propped it against the handle of the ax without comment, then seemed to hesitate for a moment before producing the last item in the bundle. To Micay's surprise, it was a crudely carved, unpainted drinking cup.

"A gift from the blind man," Rimachi murmured in a bemused tone, shrugging slightly and not responding to Micay's questioning glance. Just then Cusi coughed and moved his head, immediately drawing all of their attention.

"Runtu!" Micay called softly. "Some broth."

She nodded to Tomay and Uritu, who had already moved into position to lift Cusi, and reached behind her for her water bowl.

"Slowly," Tomay cautioned, having done this before. "He weighs almost nothing."

They lifted him into a sitting position, buttressing him with their bodies and supporting his head with their hands. Micay waited until his breathing calmed somewhat and his eyelids began to flutter, signs that he might be able to swallow. She gently cupped his chin in one hand and tipped the wooden bowl to his lips, permitting him only the smallest sip before pulling the bowl back. He grimaced but did not cough, which encouraged her to give him a larger drink, then one more, almost emptying the small bowl. She waited again, studying Cusi's gaunt face and listening to the sound of his breathing, fighting a rising excitement that she knew might make her careless. When he seemed able to continue, she turned and exchanged the water bowl for the bowl of broth Runtu Caya had brought to Rimachi, who was squatting beside her. He seemed huge this close up, and Micay instinctively avoided his eyes as they made the exchange, certain somehow that he would break her concentration.

She tested the broth with a finger and found it just warm, smelling richly of the fresh llama meat from which it had been made. Cusi's lips seemed to part willingly for the first sip, and she was close enough to see his nostrils quiver and his tongue curl back as the broth flowed down his throat. She was aware of Tomay and Uritu smiling on either side of him, sharing her elation as he accepted a second sip, and a third. She felt she could see color coming back into his face, and she suddenly understood the rapturous sense of triumph that belonged to a successful healer.

Then Cusi coughed, his head jerking down toward his injured side, and Uritu let out a whoop that so startled Micay that she spilled some of the broth onto Cusi's chest. Tomay and Uritu caught his head as it lolled back, and suddenly his eyes popped open and he seemed to look straight at Micay. He spoke a single, breathless word.

"Tocto."

Then his eyes rolled back, showing white, and he went limp in his friends' arms. Micay hastily signaled Tomay and Uritu to lower him back down, praying she had not given him more than he could stand. It would make him weaker, not stronger, if the feeding made him vomit or set off a coughing fit. Mama Cori had warned her of the dangers of trying to cure him all at once. Micay found herself praying to the healing spirit of Mama Quilla, praying in a way she had not even attempted since the night Cusi had arrived with the news of the rebellion.

She felt rewarded when Cusi did not cough or vomit but subsided into sleep instead. She, Tomay, and Uritu all seemed to relax at the same moment, letting out a common sigh of relief that made them laugh at themselves. Uritu whooped as he had earlier, and Tomay shrugged and smiled, his round cheeks flushed and shiny, as Micay felt her own to be. Uritu took a cloth and wiped the spilled broth off Cusi's chest, grunting with satisfaction and giving Micay a shy smile when he was done. Micay pulled a blanket up over Cusi's legs, and they all moved back and sat on the floor. The rain had begun to come down harder outside, drumming audibly on the thatch overhead.

"Has he spoken before this?" Rimachi asked quietly. Micay turned and met his gaze, which was more admiring than inquisitive, betraying the fact that he had asked the question primarily to get her to look at him. But he maintained a certain restraint, not courting her too openly, which would have embarrassed her in front of Uritu and Tomay.

"He has said things in his sleep," she told him, "but not sitting up, with his eyes open." Having given Rimachi his look, she addressed herself to all of them. "Do you know what 'tocto' means?"

There was a moment of silence. Then Rimachi laughed.

"It means he is healing. He will sleep well if he is dreaming of her."

"Oh, it is a name," Micay murmured, noticing that Tomay was frowning slightly and that Uritu had gone blankly impassive again, as if this were another matter not to be displayed. But finally Tomay felt compelled to explain.

"Her name is Tocto Oxica. She is a daughter of the Sapa Inca by the Coya."

A forbidden woman, Micay realized, though she was not scandalized by the notion, as Tomay seemed to be. The Coya's other daughters had their 'secret' admirers, she knew, and flirtations that were not so secret. But she sensed that Tomay and Uritu would not want to hear this from her and would not respect her for telling them.

"Is there also someone named Ichuri?" she asked instead, hoping it was an innocent question. But they all went blank, even Rimachi, who exchanged a glance with the other two and would not return the look she offered him.

Micay sighed and decided to retreat. "Forgive my curiosity. You are his friends, and it is right that you keep his secrets. But you should prepare yourselves, because Mama Cori will ask you the same questions."

They exchanged another glance, then nodded to her one by one. After a respectful pause they all stood up, Rimachi and Uritu gathering up the blankets in which they had carried Cusi's things. Micay knew Rimachi would be the one to speak, and she looked up at him calmly.

"We will come again, my lady, if we may. Your company has been a great pleasure."

"You have been good for him," Micay said, letting her gaze rest lightly on each of them in turn before she inclined her head and bowed to them in farewell. She let them disappear into the rain before she straightened up, pretending not to see the backward glance Rimachi sent her as he ducked through the doorway.

Runtu Caya came over and bent to take the rest of the broth and the water bowl from Micay. The old woman rested the bowls against her hip and stared down at Cusi, her mouth puckering fondly, seemingly unperturbed by his frailness.

"He will live," she said succinctly. "There is too much in his life for him to leave it."

Micay nodded compliantly, looking over at the stack of richly colored garments, the proof of his fame. And there was the daughter of the Sapa Inca, and someone named Ichuri, and a blind man who was equally mysterious. Plus his family and three friends who loved him. Even *she* had prayed for him, she who could not pray for herself or the safety of her people. You are too important to too many, Cusi Huaman, she thought, and she moved closer to him so she could hear his breathing above the muted beating of the rain.

IT WAS the reddish-gold glow of a sunset that finally began to bring him out of the pain-wracked world of his dreams and back to awareness. The rich light seemed to slip gently beneath his sagging eyelids, filling his head with a soothing redness that did not stab at his sensitive nerves. He suddenly remembered the transition from day to night and then day and night themselves, the regular and trustworthy alternation of light and dark. He realized then that he had left the darkness where he had been bound and tortured, and that he was being cared for. He let himself be handled and fed, no longer trying to hide from his captors, though the effort of breathing and the pain of movement kept sweeping him back into unconsciousness.

Then his eyes blinked open and he saw the roof beam above him, a clean, straight, barkless timber that did not waver out of focus as he continued to stare at it. He could see beyond it, too, to the latticework that held the plaited layers of thatch in place, a gridded pattern just visible in the upper darkness. And the darkness did not descend to blot out his vision or fill with menacing shapes and faces that swelled and shrank in time with his breathing. The roof stayed where it was and the bedding beneath him did not soften and begin to swallow him up, as it had in some of his dreams of falling. In my dreams, he thought. Had he ever truly fallen? How had he hurt himself, then? He could not remember.

He closed his eyes to stop the questioning, which made his head ache. When he opened them again, he saw faces leaning over him, and he heard, very distinctly, his name being spoken. The faces were so clear, so familiar, that he wanted only to stare at them, afraid that if he tried to speak, he would use up all his strength. But then he saw them exchange a concerned glance and realized they were wondering if he was truly awake.

"Mother," he managed, in a voice that sounded hoarse and dry to his own ears. "Uncle," he added, when the first effort did not overwhelm him.

"Yes, Cusi, yes," Mama Cori said, smiling at him with tears running from her eyes.

"You are back with us," Lloque put in, and Cusi slowly shifted his eyes—still testing them—to his uncle's long, angular face.

"How . . . long?" Cusi asked, finding it as difficult to frame a question as it had been to entertain his own.

"Ten days since you were brought to us," Mama Cori told him. "I do not know for sure how many days since you were wounded."

Wounded. Yes, he remembered the spear, the blood. But had he fallen, too? He hurt in many places besides the large, constant ache in his side. He blinked, confused by memories he could no longer trust, even though they had the vivid feel of actual experience.

"Was I a captive?" he wondered aloud, and saw the answer in their surprise.

Lloque laughed softly. "No, my son. Your heroism enabled your comrades to take the fort and light a fire for the Chachapoyas to see. They surrendered to the Sapa Inca soon afterward."

"The fort," Cusi murmured, beginning to remember too many things at once, so that confusion overwhelmed him and made him close his eyes. He felt a cool hand on his forehead and heard his mother's soothing voice.

"Rest now, my son. You are still weak."

Weak with fear, Cusi recalled, unable to shut out one particular memory, a vision of himself frozen against the cliff face, his limbs as useless to him as they were now. The image made him want to squirm with shame, and the desire itself was enough to send sharp twinges of pain arcing outward from his ribs. He gasped but felt the worst of the pain pass quickly, leaving him with sufficient strength to open his eyes and talk some more if he wished. The knowledge that he had such a choice was immensely reassuring, proof that he was healing and would be able to awaken again. So he chose to sleep rather than talk, leaving questions and memories for later and returning to the more familiar confusion of his dreams.

QUINTI WAS sitting with Lloque Yupanqui when Micay arrived to relieve her, carrying a bowl of warm maize gruel. Quinti rose up on her knees, preparing to leave, but then sank back down again and leaned forward over Cusi.

"You are awake, my brother," she said excitedly, signaling to Micay to bring water and food. When Micay returned, they had him sitting up against the wall, with mats and blankets piled up behind him for support. Quinti held the water bowl for him and then fed him gruel with a wooden spoon, waiting after each spoonful until he opened his mouth for more. He ate five spoonfuls before closing his eyes and shaking his head slightly in refusal, grimacing at the pain the movement cost him. Micay took the bowl and spoon from Quinti and set them on the floor beside her, grateful that he had diverted their attention from her. He had awakened twice before while she was attending him, seeming much more alert the second time, when Tomay rather than Apu Poma had been with her. He had not spoken to her either time, though she had felt that he recognized her by sight.

He sat with his eyes closed for several moments, the muscles in his throat working visibly beneath the taut layer of skin. Then he belched and opened his eyes, looking first at Quinti, then past her at Micay, again saying nothing, though his gaze lingered with what seemed like interest. Finally he turned toward Lloque, and Micay was struck by the resemblance between them, now that the flesh had been melted off of the fine bones of Cusi's face. He had the same cleft in his chin and the same triangular ridge of cheekbone above his hollowed cheeks, and the lack of expression caused by fatigue seemed to mimic Lloque's characteristically emotionless mien.

"Tell me, Uncle," Cusi said in a dry, deliberate voice that seemed to belong to someone much older. "How did the war end?"

Lloque raised his eyebrows. Then he nodded and composed himself, and began to recite from memory, speaking in the measured rhythms of the Royal Rememberer.

"It is said that when the Chachapoyas saw the smoke from the burning fortress, they began to break ranks and flee for the hills. Huayna Capac brought his warriors through the pass and was about to send them in pursuit of the fleeing rebels, when he was met by a delegation of Chachapoya women who had come to plead with him for mercy. A white-haired woman who had once been one of Topa Inca's women spoke for them, and it is said that she addressed the Sapa Inca boldly, with fire rather than fear in her voice. And she said to him:

" 'Sole Lord, Son of the Sun, what is it that you are about to do? Will you destroy, in your anger, this province that your father, Topa Inca, conquered so long ago? Will you forget the mercy he showed to us then and the kindness we have come to expect from the Inca in all the years since? If you indulge your wrath today, will you not regret it tomorrow, when your eyes clear and you can see all that might have been saved? Why do you not remember your title, Lover of the Poor, and take pity on my people? Can anyone be poorer than these wretches who have violated your trust and taken up arms against you, who have desecrated your fields and temples and destroyed all the things you built for them? I ask you to remember your reputation for clemency and generosity, a reputation that was your father's before you. Do not allow your anger to stain the glory of your reign with the blood of those who have already surrendered. Remember that the greater their crimes against you, the greater will your mercy seem to those who hear of it. Remember, Child of Inti, the pride the Incas have always taken in their wisdom and restraint. I beg you to heed the wisdom of your own heart, Great Lord, and spare my people. And if you will not grant me this wish, then I ask you to end my life now, so that I will not have to witness the final destruction of the Chachapoyas.' "

Lloque's hands, which had been fingering an imaginary cord while he spoke, stopped along with his voice as he paused to be sure that Cusi was still listening. Cusi's eyelids had begun to slide downward, but they opened again at the sudden silence, signaling Lloque to go on.

"It is said that Huayna Capac was silent for a long time, considering the woman's words. The woman and her companions prostrated themselves before him, weeping pitifully and begging him for mercy. Finally Huayna Capac went to the woman and raised her up with his own hands. And he said to her:

" 'I am grateful to you, Mamanchic, for you have reminded me of my reputation and my honor at a time when anger ruled my heart. Surely you are right that I would regret tomorrow the destruction that tempts me today; surely I would want to call the dead back to life. You are truly my mother, for you have changed my heart. And you are the mother of your people, for you have redeemed their lives and saved their villages and fields from burning. Let it be as you ask, Mamanchic. Go back to your people and tell them that they have my pardon, and ask what else they might need to begin their lives again. It will be given to them by my order. As further proof that I have forgiven them, I will take my warriors back with me to Tumibamba and leave only those officials necessary to restore peace and order. I trust that this will ease their hearts and revive the loyalty that is owed to the Sapa Inca.' "

Lloque paused again, and this time Cusi spoke. "What is said . . . about me?"

Lloque appeared taken aback for a moment, but then smiled proudly. He spoke without his previous formality or hand gestures, as if he had told this story many times in an unofficial capacity.

"It is said that you and five others volunteered to climb a steep cliff and assault the fort from the rear. For this alone, your courage must be saluted. Your comrades were the scout Paucar, Mayca Yupanqui, Tomay Guanaco, the Colla Huañu, and the micho of Chachapoyas, Condor Tupac."

Micay could not help the sound that escaped her throat, a gasp of both surprise and recognition. She had not heard that name in any of the previous recitations of this story, and it seemed to echo in her head, like a voice out of a dream. Lloque had stopped to stare at her, and she saw Cusi's eyes widen and fix on her before she looked down in embarrassment. After a pause that seemed agonizingly long, Lloque went on.

"Condor Tupac led you to the top, where the trail narrowed to a ledge and a leap had to be made over an open chasm. Condor Tupac jumped first, but he was surprised by a Chachapoyas sentry who had been hiding behind a wall. The sentry pushed him to his death and did the same to Mayca Yupanqui, who followed him bravely. We mourn the deaths of two so courageous warriors. You were third, Cusi Huaman, and now the leader, so you did not rush ahead to your death. You waited and gathered your strength, ignoring the taunts of the sentry and lulling him into carelessness. Then it is said that you made a great leap out over the chasm, shouting the name of Illapa and throwing a stone you had worked loose from the cliff, flinging yourself at the sentry like a hungry puma or a diving hawk. You were wounded, but still you over-whelmed him, so that your comrades could come behind you and attack the defenders of the fort. It is your comrades who have told us what you did; they speak of it still with awe and disbelief, honoring the huaca that saved their lives. It will be remembered as the act that brought the war against the Chachapoyas to an end."

"You are a great hero, my brother," Quinti added softly. "The Sapa Inca inquires about your health every day, and messages of praise have come from Cuzco and many other places."

Cusi sighed and his eyelids fluttered down, making him appear to be frown-ing. He spoke haltingly, as if words had begun to elude him.

"I . . . have . . . fame."

Quinti hesitated, uncertain if it was a question or a statement. Cusi's eyes were shut and his head seemed to wobble.

"Yes, great fame," Quinti told him. "The whole of the Four Quarters knows your name. Whatever you want will be yours."

A shudder jerked Cusi's head back, and his eyes flared briefly in their sockets, wild and disbelieving, unable to focus on anyone.

"But I should have died," he whispered harshly, his gaunt face contorted in a kind of weary snarl. Then he seemed to lose his strength all at once, closing his eyes and letting his head droop toward his chest. Lloque and Quinti quickly recovered from their shock and moved to lower him back down onto his bed. Lloque gestured for them to withdraw, and they all rose and went to stand at the foot of the bed.

"Why did he say that?" Quinti murmured in distress.

"Men who have experienced what he has are often confused by it," Lloque explained, staring down at Cusi. "They do not know where their strength and courage came from, and they feel unworthy of their fame, perhaps even of having survived."

"He should not have to suffer that way," Quinti protested. "We must make him understand what he has done."

"He will have to come to that understanding by himself," Lloque said gently.

But Quinti shook her head, her distress hardening into determination. "I will go to the House of the Moon and pray to Mama Quilla to enlighten him and ease his heart." She turned suddenly and gave Micay a challenging look. "Will you join me there later?"

Micay stared back at her stubbornly, unwilling to be shamed into prayer. Quinti finally sighed in resignation, bowed to Lloque, and went out through the doorway. Lloque watched her go, resting his chin on the tips of his long fingers.

"She will reform all of us," he mused, "now that she has no husband to distract her."

Micay returned to her place next to Cusi and pulled a blanket up over his legs. She was aware that Lloque was regarding her with his customary seriousness, and when she glanced up at him she saw that of course he had noticed her slip and remembered it.

"You knew the name of the micho."

"Yes. He took me from my father."

"Ah. Are you glad that he is dead?"

Micay paused, still uncertain of what she felt. "Many others have suffered because of him. I cannot grieve that he is gone."

"Perhaps justice has been done," Lloque suggested in a doubtful tone. "Does that free you in any way, my daughter?"

"I do not know. I still have not heard if my father is alive."

"I will inquire again," Lloque promised. He glanced out the doorway, gauging the light. "I must return to my duties. No doubt someone will join you before long."

"I will be fine," she assured him, bowing in parting. She looked up to see him lingering in the doorway, gazing back at her.

"The rebellion is over, Micay," he reminded her softly. "*You* must learn to live again, too."

CUSI WAS awakened in the night by the need to urinate, and he was mildly surprised to find that his father was the only one sitting with him. But Apu Poma raised him up with an ease and gentleness that was also surprising, and he did not fumble as he loosened Cusi's loincloth and held the gourd for him. He seemed so natural in the role of nurse that Cusi was slow to recall that his father had never done this for him when he was a child.

"Do you wish to sleep again?" Apu Poma asked when Cusi had finished and the gourd had been put aside. Cusi was still so weak that he could fall asleep almost at will, and he had done so on every other occasion when he might have spoken to his father. He could barely see his father's face in the darkened room, but he was aware of how eager Apu Poma was for them to talk. Cusi had put him off when he was last in Tumibamba, promising they would speak when he returned from Chachapoyas.

"No," he said now. "I will sit with you for a while."

"I am grateful," Apu Poma murmured with audible relief. "You know how much I have wanted to speak to you, even before you went back."

"Yes."

"I wanted to tell you then that I had misjudged you grievously, and that I had treated you without the respect you deserve. That is even more true now, and I can only ask you to forgive my poor judgment."

"You lied to me and struck me without reason."

Apu Poma looked down at his hands, unable to face him even in the darkness. "I am ashamed of what I said and did. I told myself that I had done it for your own good, but that was also a lie. I was angry and disappointed, and so I acted cruelly. I was wrong to send you away from your mother on that day."

Cusi remembered arguing with Rimachi as they marched, telling him that Apu Poma would never admit that he had been wrong; that he would try to command Cusi's forgiveness the way he claimed to command respect. Cusi had sworn that no apology would be good enough, and that he would let his father speak only for the chance to reject him. Now he merely pursed his lips in a painless version of a shrug, able to recall his arguments but none of the anger behind them.

"It does not matter. I was meant to go to the huaca that day."

Apu Poma's head came up, but his voice was hoarse and hesitant. "Then you will forgive me?"

It truly did not matter to him anymore, but something kept Cusi from simply agreeing. He remembered the question he had asked himself over and over in those first lonely days when Aranyac was punishing him and Otoronco had forgotten he was alive.

"Why have you always hated me?" he asked his father now, more curious than accusatory. Apu Poma made a sound of denial but then was silent for a long time.

"You were born when I was in Copiapo," he said at last. "It was because of you that Cori would not bring the family to join me. Or so she said. She had other reasons for not wanting to leave Cuzco."

Cusi's strength was flagging, and he was increasingly aware of the strain sitting up put on the lacerated muscles in his side. But he bore the pain and made himself listen, sensing somehow that his father had not told him everything.

"I took another wife in Copiapo," Apu Poma continued abruptly. "A Lupaca woman. She stayed behind to have my child when I was called back to Cuzco. It was also a son. They were both killed in a rockslide on their way to join me. I never told anyone about them until now."

The silence in the room seemed to reverberate, and Cusi felt his thoughts slipping away from him, along with his sense of balance. Then his father was lowering him onto his back, responding to a desire Cusi could not remember having voiced. His father's hands seemed strong and capable, yet his voice quavered and caught, as if he were weeping.

"Sleep," Cusi heard him say. "It is all in the past now. It is all like a bad dream . . ."

WHEN HE WOKE again, it was with the sensation of having been jostled and rearranged, which made him fear that he was back in captivity. He rose warily to consciousness, listening to the murmur of voices above him. Gradually they separated and became more distinct. His mother. Tomay. Uritu. He realized again that he had never been a captive. He had never fallen. No one knew how afraid he had been on the cliff.

"It is too filthy to keep," he heard his mother say, and he opened one eye as Uritu replied with what seemed like unusual force.

"I will clean it myself, my lady. He will want it."

Then Tomay's face appeared directly above him, teeth bared in a smile that seemed ferocious so close up.

"He is awake."

They sat him up and fed him as they always did: water, warm broth, some kind of thin porridge. He had no real hunger and could barely distinguish one taste from another, but he sensed that it pleased them to see him eat. So he ate until it became too tiresome, then closed his eyes and rested for a few moments.

"You must be washed, my son," his mother told him. "We will do it now if you think you are strong enough."

Cusi tilted his head slightly in acquiescence, realizing for the first time that he was naked except for the bandage around his chest. He crossed his arms in front of him and took a weak grip on his own wrists as Tomay and Uritu lifted him off the bedding and onto a nearby mat, straining to make the transition a slow and gentle one. He felt like a limp bundle in their arms, which made his own seem like mere sticks, the muscles shrunk back to the bone. They held him upright while his mother washed him with warm, soapy water and a soft sponge. She was deft but insistent with the sponge, scrubbing him everywhere the bandage did not cover, sometimes with a vigor that made him clench his teeth against the raw ache in his side.

By the time they finished washing his hair and drying him off, he was exhausted, and they laid him down to sleep on the fresh bedding the retainers had put down for him. He dreamed that he was lying next to Tocto on top of a steep hill that overlooked Cuzco. They were together under a blanket with their bodies just touching, yet they felt entangled, breathing with the same pair of lungs and knowing each other's thoughts without speaking. But then Cusi had to get up and leave her, because he had lost something and had to go and look for it. Or perhaps it was some*one* he had lost. An overwhelming sense of urgency made Tocto and the hill vanish, and then he was awake so swiftly that he was left breathless.

His mother and Tomay were having a conversation across him, gesturing to one another with the pieces of cloth they had draped over their wrists. Uritu had his head down and his hands busy with something in his lap, so it was several moments before they noticed that he was awake and helped him to sit up. The sense of misgiving was so strong that he had trouble focusing his eyes on any one of them.

"I have lost something," he blurted, blinking to try to clear his vision.

"You have been asleep, my son," his mother said soothingly. "We have been with you the whole time."

"What is missing?" Cusi cried in frustration, and his mother and Tomay put out their hands to restrain him. Then Uritu spoke sharply and emerged out of the blur holding a thin black rope in front of his face.

"He wants this."

Uritu gave one end of the rope to Mama Cori and the other to Tomay, and only when Cusi felt them wrap it around his waist did he realize what it was. He sighed gratefully and put a hand down, groping until his fingers found the hard lump of his spirit brother and closed around it. He looked at Uritu, who had a brush in his lap and balls of colored fluff sticking to his skin and clothes, and wished that he had the strength to whoop like a Campa.

"I did not realize the importance this had for you," Mama Cori apologized, with a curious glance at the place where Cusi was holding on to it. He hesitated, trying to think of excuses, instinctively guarding his secret. He felt his breath coming faster and realized the effort that concealment cost him and would continue to cost him if he temporized with his mother now. He had had too many secrets for too long, and it suddenly did not seem worth the effort.

"It holds my spirit brother," he said to his mother, who showed her surprise by sitting back and casting a quick glance at Tomay and Uritu.

"Forgive me. I did not know you possessed one. Was it a gift from Otoronco Achachi?"

"No. From a blind man, a sorcerer named Raurau Illa. He met me at the huaca on the day you left Cuzco."

"You were young to be consorting with sorcerers," Mama Cori suggested in a disapproving tone that made Cusi grimace with annoyance. Explanations seemed as tiresome as evasions, and equally pointless.

"My age did not matter to him," he said curtly. "He regarded me as the messenger of Illapa. I have come to believe he was right."

"Indeed," Tomay murmured appreciatively, and Cusi caught a glimpse of an admiring smile out of the corner of his eye. He did not turn his head to see more, because Tomay's devotion—which he had sensed before this—was also tiring to him. He watched his mother and saw her decide to let him have his way.

"Perhaps you will tell me more when you are stronger," she conceded. "Now you must choose a loincloth to wear. The Sapa Inca has sent you many beautiful ones."

"Whatever pleases you," Cusi murmured indifferently. He held still while they arranged the strip of cloth under him and pulled the ends up through the loops in the waistband. Then Mama Cori produced a short red and black band and showed him the small silver badge and the two tiny white feathers that were pinned to it. It took Cusi a moment to realize that this was not his old Iñaca headband, but a new one.

"Lord Otoronco Achachi sent you this from Cuzco, along with a message. He congratulates you on your fame and reminds you of your promise to use it wisely."

Cusi hooded his eyes and smiled to himself as his mother tied the band around his forehead with the badge in front.

"Lloque and I had hoped to see you in Vicaquirao blue," she admitted ruefully. "Otoronco must have been persuasive."

"He was good to me."

"To all of us," Tomay put in, and Uritu grunted softly in agreement. Mama Cori's expression remained rueful.

"Did you tell this to your father? He said you spoke to him last night."

"Yes," Cusi said tentatively, as the memory came back to him. "We spoke of other things."

"He believes you have forgiven him."

"It does not matter anymore. He has pain of his own to carry." Cusi let his eyelids slide shut. "I must sleep now."

"You have matured greatly, my son," his mother whispered as they laid him down. "You are worthy of your fame."

No, Cusi thought dimly, feeling shrewd and deceitful because he knew better than to say so aloud. Not until he had used it. Then he would have no more secrets to protect and could give his fame away. Then he could tell the truth and lose it.

NINAN CUYOCHI'S compound was tucked high up in the southwest corner of the Mollecancha, a long walk from the micho's quarters. Micay made it even longer, taking Rimachi on a roundabout route down her favorite streets and past her favorite buildings, reacquainting herself with the palace. She had not wanted to accompany Rimachi to this dance, but Mama Cori had all but commanded her to go, urging her to get out and see the sky and breathe some moving air again. So she made Rimachi take the air with her, even though the sky was overcast and the air heavy with warmth and humidity. She walked until her shift began to cling damply to her body, shedding her misgivings on the familiar ground of the rain-washed streets and fragrant garden paths. Rimachi knew most of the Cañari guards and was known by the Incas, who inquired about the health of Cusi Huaman before waving them through whatever gate they wished to enter.

"We can go to the dance now," Micay said finally, when they had paused to rest at the top of a flight of stairs. "I am grateful for your patience, Rimachi."

"It requires no patience to walk with you, my lady," he assured her with a gracious smile. "I am content to walk some more, if you wish. I have been to many dances since we returned."

"No," Micay decided. "I have not been to a public gathering since you and Cusi brought word of the rebellion. It is time I faced people again."

"You have nothing to fear; there is no hatred left for your people. They fought valiantly and have been forgiven. And you will see what it means to be associated with Cusi Huaman. Half of the warriors who will be at the dance owe their promotions to him, if not their lives."

"But I am only a member of his father's house."

"That is enough," Rimachi averred. "And even if you were not, you are still my guest, and *I* am associated with him. You saw what the Inca guards were like. I have had to learn not to accept every toast that is offered to me on his behalf, or I would be too drunk to hold a cup."

"But you have a reputation of your own. Surely you would prefer to be known for your own accomplishments."

"Of course, but I have no choice. *We* have no choice," he corrected, putting a hand under her elbow to guide her toward the next staircase. "His fame is too great not to touch everyone who is near him. But if you bear it lightly, like a garment that is not really your own, you will find that it is not too terrible a burden."

THE CROWD inside the compound was young and boisterous, a swirl of bright cloth and glinting metal that seemed to give off noise and laughter in waves. Two different groups of musicians were playing furiously on their flutes and drums in opposite corners of the enclosure, but there was no room for dancing, even if anyone had shown an interest. As Rimachi had predicted, he was recognized by the greeters at the gate, who ushered them toward a group of ñustas and warriors congregated in front of the awning house that occupied one side of the compound. Ninan Cuyochi was at the center of the group, looking sober and preoccupied, allowing his half brother Atauhuallpa to preside over introductions. Atauhuallpa accosted Rimachi like an old comrade, pressing a cup of akha into his hand and making an exuberant if unceremonious toast to the man who had led him through the mountains to Caxamarquilla.

"If only my brother and Cusi Huaman had not turned the trail into mud ahead of us," he complained mockingly, winking at Ninan, who simply raised his cup to Rimachi and gave him a respectful nod. Micay could see Amancay and Cori Cuillor among the ñustas behind Ninan Cuyochi and Atauhuallpa, but they displayed no recognition as Rimachi drew her forward to be introduced.

"This is the Chachapoyas ñusta Micay, a daughter in the house of the micho, Apu Poma."

A broad smile appeared on Atauhuallpa's face, touching off similar smiles on the faces of many of those around him, though not those of Amancay and Cori Cuillor. Micay heard Cusi's name being repeated behind the murmurs of greeting, which seemed genuinely friendly.

"Welcome, my lady," Ninan said earnestly, with what almost seemed like a frown. "Can you tell us how he is?"

Micay realized that she could have been a Carangui in full war paint and no one would have noticed or asked her a different question. She was aware of a sudden silence immediately around her.

"The wound has not closed completely and he is still weak," she told Ninan, whose frown deepened and made her go on. "But he eats regularly, and he is conscious more often."

A small cheer went up from the listeners, startling Micay. Rimachi nodded encouragingly, as if the cheer had been for her.

"I hope he will be strong enough to have visitors before we leave for Quito," Ninan said. "The rains will be diminishing soon, and I would like to see him before we march north."

This brought whoops from the warriors present, and a few of them raised their cups to Inti, who was still hidden behind a bank of grayish clouds.

"Perhaps, if there is no fever," Micay allowed. But then she felt them straining toward her and gave in to the pressure of their eagerness for some positive news. "He has fought bravely to recover as far as he has. I am sure he will be back among you as soon as he is able."

"It cannot be too soon!" Atauhuallpa proclaimed, sloshing akha out of his cup with a vigorous salute. "He has been the example we have needed; he has reminded all of us of what it means to be an Inca. We will need his kind of courage and daring to storm the strongholds of the Carangui!"

This time the cheering was so prolonged and enthusiastic that Ninan could only smile and shake his head, allowing the group around him to dissolve into smaller, celebratory clusters. Rimachi leaned down to speak into Micay's ear as she accepted a cup of akha from a servant.

"You see how little encouragement they need," he said dryly, and Micay laughed, feeling slightly giddy. He had warned her, but it was still astonishing to say so little and elicit such an overwhelming response—and to be heard without scorn or suspicion or the desire to judge. Cusi Huaman had not only ended the war, he had effaced the bitterness of its memory.

The giddiness wore off as Rimachi introduced her to a succession of warriors and ñustas, some of whom she already knew, though even these greeted her with a warmth that had been missing since she attached herself to the high priestess. Neither Amancay nor Cori Cuillor displayed any warmth, acting as if this were their first introduction, but they were careful in their gestures and intonation, employing none of the small signs of disrespect the men would not have noticed. Cori Cuillor was in the company of a young Inca captain named Challcochima, a tall man who kept his arm around her shoulders as if a marriage had already been arranged. So Quilaco did not go back to her, Micay thought, and realized that her social instincts were beginning to return.

"Shall we move from here?" Rimachi suggested once no more people were pressing in for an introduction. "Uritu and Tomay should be here somewhere."

Holding her cup in both hands, Micay let him lead her into the crowd, which no longer seemed so amorphous and overwhelming. She was able to recognize individual faces and the colors of the various households and the shades of rank indicated by the size and workmanship of mantle pins and earplugs. She could tell from the fresh shine of the gold and silver which of the warriors had been recently promoted and which of the ñustas were soon to be wives, and she found herself memorizing details to relate to Quinti and Mama Cori later. Occasionally someone would catch her eye and bow in recognition, but her responses were as keen as her perceptions, so that she never hesitated over whether to show deference or expect it. You were trained for this, she reminded herself, feeling her capacities swell and stretch like muscles that had lain dormant for too long.

Then their way was blocked by a group of warriors who were toasting one another and singing a war song, and they backed away into a corner formed by a staircase that went up to a terrace above. Rimachi stared at her over the rim of his cup as they drank, his eyes bright with admiration.

"If I may say so, my lady," he ventured, "your composure has been splendid. If this has been difficult for you, it has not shown. You do not seem to have been away from the court for a moment."

Micay smiled and gave her head a rueful shake.

"I have not forgotten everything I learned. But you must know how long I have been away. I know that you have been asking."

Rimachi smiled unabashedly, not even pretending to be surprised or embarrassed. "I have heard many things," he conceded. "But only two that are of importance: that you were a chosen woman, and that you are attached to the high priestess. The rest only makes you more fascinating."

"And you think well of Chimpu Ocllo?"

"I am Cañari!" he laughed. "My mother served in the cult of Mama Quilla before we went to Cuzco, and she would join again in an instant if the Coya would allow it. She was very excited when I told her about you, and she would like very much to meet you."

The admiration was back in his eyes, and Micay shivered even as she felt herself grow warmer. All of her misgivings about coming here suddenly seemed remote, the nagging complications of a past she did not have to justify to him. Her arms felt light and buoyant as she lifted her cup in a two-handed toast.

"I am Chachapoya, and I do not know if I will ever serve in the cult of Mama Quilla. But I would be honored to meet your mother."

Rimachi drained his cup with a flourish that made his gold and silver earplugs dance beside his face. Then he simply stared at her and smiled, paying her the compliment of having nothing clever or eloquent to say.

Finally they were interrupted by a young captain who introduced himself as Ucumari and presented Rimachi with a fresh cup of akha. Ucumari was bowlegged and thick-browed, so muscular through the chest and shoulders that his tunic gathered around his neck and made him appear hunched over, bearlike, as his name suggested. He greeted Micay politely and asked the usual questions about Cusi's health, but it quickly became apparent that his real interest lay in recruiting Rimachi into his squadron. So Micay withdrew a few steps and courteously turned her back so that the two men could speak in private.

The group of warriors in front of the stairs had begun to disperse, and through an opening in their ranks she suddenly caught a glimpse of Tomay. Then she could see all of him, and though he stood without swaying, he was obviously quite drunk. His round face was shiny with perspiration, his cheeks were the color of a deep bruise, and his knit cap had been pushed onto the back of his head. He was being toasted by an older, larger man who wore huge golden earplugs and a golden Sun shield on his chest, the insignia of a war chief. The man's skin was weathered and grainy like unrubbed stone, and an expression of forbidding impatience seemed to have been etched permanently onto his features. Micay could not tell from either face if this was a friendly toast, though there was nothing on the faces of the onlookers to indicate otherwise.

Then another couple moved out of her line of vision, and she saw a woman standing a few steps behind the war chief—a Chachapoyas woman. Her hair was braided and wrapped around her head, and she did not wear a mantle over her light, gauzy shift, which was knotted at one shoulder and left the other shoulder bare. She had her arms crossed in front of her breasts, hugging herself, and every few moments she raised her eyes from the ground to take a timid, darting glance around.

When she finally noticed Micay, her eyes went wide and the glance became a yearning stare that revealed how utterly lost she felt. Micay did not recognize the woman's face, but she knew what it felt like to stare like that, and the shock of such uncommon empathy left her too stunned to smile or nod. The woman blinked and seemed to see the rest of her—her mantle and pin and the head cloth that covered the back of her head—and hastily lowered her eyes, dipping her braided head in apology.

"Forgive me," Rimachi said, appearing suddenly at her side. Micay could only point with her chin, but she saw his face tighten as he followed her gaze. "This has been happening too often," he said tersely, "and Yasca is not someone who tolerates disrespect, even from a drunken hero. Let us join them."

Micay realized that he was referring to Tomay and had not even noticed the woman. She let him start forward without her, waiting until he turned back in surprise.

"Who is that woman?" she demanded, and he had to look again before he saw whom she meant. When he turned to her once more, he seemed to understand that he should be careful of what he said.

"I would imagine she is the widow or daughter of someone who was killed in the fighting."

"Lloque Yupanqui told me that no prisoners had been taken in this surrender."

"We took no warriors, certainly. But obviously . . . some women were taken as wives."

"As prizes, you mean," Micay said flatly. Rimachi seemed about to equivocate, but then he swallowed what he was going to say and nodded.

"Yes, as prizes. Lloque Yupanqui is a wise and honorable man, but the Royal Rememberers do not choose what they must remember on the Sapa Inca's behalf. Surely you know that, Micay."

His tone was patiently sympathetic, a reminder rather than a rebuke, but Micay was suddenly so infuriated that she had to turn away before she cursed him or spat in his face. She wanted to spit in all the graciously smiling faces she saw around her; she felt betrayed by everyone, though most of all by herself. She saw the gate and had a powerful urge to dash her cup to the ground and walk out.

"If you wish to leave, my lady," Rimachi offered quietly, "I hope you will allow me to accompany you."

Micay took a deep breath, realizing that her anger was out of proportion and that she was surrendering to it too easily. If she walked out now, she would only carry it with her, and her absence would make no difference to anyone, except perhaps to the Chachapoyas woman, who might feel that much more abandoned.

"No," she said to Rimachi. "I want to talk to her. You can look after Tomay, if you wish."

"Yasca can be intimidating, but he knows me," Rimachi told her as they walked up to the edge of the circle of space that surrounded the two men with cups in their hands.

"I am always second to Cusi," Tomay was saying to the war chief, his tone humble but his lips pushed out with a kind of belligerence. "Even in toasts."

Yasca's arms were crossed in front of him, his chin resting on the rim of his cup as he stared down at Tomay. He glanced sideways at Rimachi and bared his yellowish teeth in what might have been a smile. Then he snorted and gestured at Tomay with his cup.

"No," he said in a voice as harsh as his face. "No, you are the first Colla I have ever toasted. That is one distinction Cusi Huaman cannot claim."

Tomay had stiffened at being contradicted but then appeared taken aback by the war chief's strange compliment.

"Indeed!" Rimachi exclaimed, raising his cup in a salute to the two of them. The circle of onlookers was startled into doing the same, and many prolonged their acclaim when they realized they were helping to avert a possible quarrel. Tomay could only smile weakly and bow to Yasca before lurching off to have his cup refilled. As if fulfilling a promise, Rimachi immediately brought Micay forward to meet the war chief. Yasca nodded absently at the introduction, his eyes straying in the direction Tomay had gone.

"You should look after your friend," he said to Rimachi. "His fame has made him careless and disagreeable."

"I will see to him, my lord. Perhaps you will permit Micay to speak with your new wife."

"What for?" Yasca demanded impatiently, then took a good look at Micay for the first time. "Ah, I see. Of course, talk to her! She is afraid to talk to me."

"That is probably true of your own warriors," Micay said sharply, her anger still with her, though at a more controllable level. Yasca glared at her for a moment, then struck himself on the chest with his cup and laughed.

"It is," he agreed, amusement making his eyes appear surprisingly soft in that granite face. "But I have no reason to want *her* to fear me. Tell her I intend to be kind to her, Micay. Tell her I will treat her with the respect due a wife. Her name is Quespi."

"You will have to make your own promises," Micay told him, but she went over to the woman and took her hands, which were clasped tightly in front of her. Her fingers were cold and trembled in Micay's grasp, and it took her a full moment to raise her eyes to Micay's face. Micay again saw that stare of desolation and yearning disbelief, and the greeting she had prepared died on her tongue. She found herself speaking in Chacha, the words tumbling out almost without thought, feeling oddly shaped as they passed her lips.

"Greetings and welcome, my friend Quespi. I am called Micay."

"Greetings and welcome," the woman whispered, tears welling up in her thickly lashed eyes. Then she was overcome and could only bob her head over Micay's hands in gratitude. Aware of Yasca and Rimachi listening behind her,

Micay coaxed the woman back up and led her a few steps away. She waited while Quespi blinked back her tears, then nodded encouragingly for her to speak.

"I am from the Puma clan of Caxamarquilla," Quespi began slowly, glancing up to guage Micay's attentiveness. Reassured, she began to speak more rapidly, telling Micay about her life in a dialect of Chacha that Micay could barely follow. She was indeed a widow, though she had been married for only a few months before her husband was killed in the uprising against the governor. Her father and brother were killed later, and since her husband had no brothers to claim her, there was no one to protect her from the Inca's officials. She seemed to understand that she had been taken as a wife, not a prisoner, and she even seemed to be aware of Yasca's rank and to be impressed by it. But there was something else that was making her fearful, something she had not told Micay or that Micay had missed.

"Yasca says that he will treat you like a wife," Micay told her in halting Chacha. "He does not want you to be afraid."

Quespi swallowed, again looking at Micay's mantle pin and head cloth with a kind of residual suspicion. Then she sighed, as if she had no choice but to trust Micay and speak.

"What will he do with my child?"

Micay cast a startled glance at Quespi's midsection, but she was a stocky woman and showed no obvious signs of being pregnant. She caught the glance, though, and nodded anxiously.

"Perhaps three moons."

"Ah." Given her own feelings about Inca duplicity, Micay was in no mood to reassure Quespi or predict Yasca's reaction. Her anger began to return, and she gave Quespi's hands a rough shake, startling her.

"Come, we must tell him. He would know soon enough, anyhow."

Quespi pulled her hands free and stared at her with outright suspicion, and Micay realized that she had spoken in Quechua. She held up a hand to calm her while she searched her memory for the appropriate Chacha words.

"Did you know the mamanchic who spoke to Huayna Capac?" she asked finally. Quespi nodded, still wary but heartened somewhat by the memory. "That is how we must speak to Yasca," Micay told her. "I will speak for you, but you must look him in the eye and make him believe his own promises. That is the only way to make an Inca act like an Inca."

Quespi glanced over her shoulder at the war chief, seeming both perplexed and fearful. But when she looked back at Micay her mistrust was gone.

"Speak well, my friend Micay. It is my first child."

Rimachi had disappeared, but Yasca was waiting in the same place. The men he had been talking to fell silent and backed away as Micay and Quespi approached. Micay could tell from the war chief's bemused expression that Quespi was doing her part, and she seized the advantage and addressed him boldly.

"You say that you will treat her with kindness and the respect due a wife."

"I will," Yasca managed, barely able to take his eyes off of Quespi's resolutely upraised face.

"And you will treat her children with the same kindness and respect?"

"Of course. I am a father to all of the children born in my house."

"That is admirable," Micay concluded. "Then you would be a father, as well, to a child that was brought to you from Chachapoyas."

Yasca had already begun to nod impatiently, but comprehension caught him in midnod, jerking his head back so abruptly that his earplugs swung wildly. He raised his eyebrows at Quespi and scratched his chin with his free hand, then turned back to Micay with a shrewd smile on his face.

"If this child is as handsome as its mother and as bold as you are, it would be my favorite. I would treat it like a child of my own blood."

The exchange had been in Quechua, but Quespi had obviously understood enough, because she suddenly bowed and went to Yasca's side. She looked up into his surprised face without fear.

"I will serve you well, my husband. I will give you many children."

Yasca nodded awkwardly and took a drink from his cup. He looked at Micay but could not seem to find anything to say.

"I would like to visit Quespi, if I may," Micay said, "and help her learn the ways of her new home."

"You are welcome in my house, Micay. You have obviously learned those ways yourself, and well."

"I am only beginning to learn," Micay murmured, half to herself. She bowed to him and gave Quespi a parting smile as she withdrew from their presence. She had spotted Rimachi's head coming through the crowd, and now he and Uritu both came into view. They were holding Tomay upright between them, bumping him constantly with their shoulders to keep him going in a straight line. Tomay was alternately laughing and trying to resist his friends, his eyes rolling dreamily as he careened forward in their grip. He began arguing with them again as they brought him to a halt in front of Micay.

"Do not tell me I cannot dance, if I want to dance."

"Not *alone,* Tomay," Rimachi said impatiently. "This is not that kind of celebration. People were laughing at you behind their hands."

"No one laughs at me anymore!" Tomay snarled. "And no one tells me what to do except Cusi."

"I will dance with you," Micay put in. Tomay blinked at her, seeing her for the first time. Then he became flustered and glanced sideways at Rimachi and Uritu, who nodded to one another and simultaneously let go of his arms. Tomay swayed wildly for a moment before catching his balance, and the effort seemed to deflate him.

"I am too drunk to dance, my lady," he muttered.

"Then there is no reason for us to stay here any longer," Micay said briskly, drawing a subtle, approving nod from Uritu and a vaguely incredulous stare from Rimachi, who was no doubt wondering where her anger had gone. Tomay belched and shook his head stubbornly, losing the cap off the back of his head.

"I can leave by myself. Rimachi will never forgive me if I ruin his time with you."

"I will still be with him," Micay pointed out, "and with you and Uritu, as well. I could not ask for a better escort than the three brothers of Cusi Huaman."

Uritu was moved to a solemn bow and Rimachi to a smile of appreciation, but it seemed to Micay that it was the mention of Cusi's name that most persuaded Tomay. She cared only about the result, which was that he meekly surrendered himself to his friends' guidance as Micay led the way to the gate.

"Did you settle Yasca with his wife as easily as you settled us?" Rimachi murmured to her as they walked down a narrow street between enclosure walls, looking for a set of stairs wide and safe enough for Tomay.

"Nearly," Micay allowed. "We persuaded him to accept both her and the child she is carrying."

"Yasca? He is not known for his openness to persuasion, though you seemed to know how to make him hear you. None of his *captains* would have dared to speak to him that way."

"I was angry," Micay said simply, "but I wanted to *do* something with my anger."

"Besides making enemies, you mean," Rimachi suggested, and Micay had to smile; she was feeling too pleased with herself not to.

"Yes, besides that. I think I have finally understood what the high priestess has been trying to teach me: what she means when she says that she only wants the Incas to be true to themselves."

"What?" Tomay demanded, leaning forward to look at her with a surge that made Uritu and Rimachi grapple to keep him from pitching forward onto his face. His eyes were bleary but wide open, and he seemed to understand what he was asking. Micay spread her hands, gathering words out of the humid air to describe what had come to her out of her anger and her desire to make it useful.

"She means that they must be constantly reminded of who they are supposed to be, or else they will forget and treat the rest of us like their property. Or like retainers."

Now they were all looking at her with wide eyes, and Micay realized that what she had said was close to treason. But there was no disapproval on their faces, and no one spoke to contradict her.

"They treat the Collas worse than retainers," Tomay said in a low voice. "They think it is a great experience to toast one of us."

"Then it is an experience you must give them," Micay told him, "over and over, until it becomes natural to them. The mistake is to assume that they will do what is right on their own and then to feel betrayed and angry when they act no better than other men."

"Some of them can be trusted," Uritu said mildly. "The old ones, like Otoronco Achachi, and the young ones who know us, like Cusi."

Rimachi gave Uritu a glance that was distinctly disturbed, as if he had expected stronger disagreement from him.

"I think I would trust more of them than that," he ventured.

Tomay snorted, though he seemed more exasperated than envious. "That is because the Cañaris have been favored since the time of Topa Inca."

"It does not matter who is favored," Micay interjected on Rimachi's behalf. "It is not easy for *anyone* to live among the Incas."

They were silent for a moment, and then Uritu suddenly let out one of his startling whoops, reminding them that they were standing in the middle of the street staring at one another. Tomay whooped in imitation, producing a loud, hiccuping sound that made them all laugh. They started moving down the street again, away from the pounding of the drums and the percussive huffing of the flutes. Rimachi looked down his nose at Micay and smiled proudly.

"I think, my lady, that it is *you* who are escorting *us,*" he said to the loud agreement of his friends, and the four of them continued down the street together, whooping like Campas who had just come into the city for the first time.

WHEN NINAN CUYOCHI and Titu Atauchi entered the room, Cusi was sitting up with his back against the wall and his legs folded under him. Despite the warmth of the day, he was wearing one of his gift tunics, and he had put in his earplugs and had his coca bag hanging beneath his left arm, over his wound. The two men squatted down at Cusi's right, across from Mama Cori, who sat on his other side.

"My lady," Ninan said to Mama Cori, before turning his earnest gaze upon Cusi. "My friend . . . it eases my heart to see you looking so much better. We have all been praying and making offerings for your recovery."

Cusi kept his eyes on Ninan's face, struggling to contain the emotions that the sight of Titu Atauchi had aroused in him. He had recognized the man immediately, even though he had seen him only in what he had thought were dreams. That was the face—surrounded by gray fur and a fringe of sharp teeth—that had leered at him out of the darkness, the face of his captor and chief torturer. A residual shiver of fear gave way to a distaste so sharp and savage that it made Cusi salivate.

Yet he also felt the power of the healer's presence, a force of personality that intruded on Cusi's consciousness even though he tried to shut it out. Cusi restrained the urge to reach for the spirit brother at his side, though he was certain somehow that Titu Atauchi already knew about it. He decided instinctively that he should not be alone with this man and that he should not show any weakness in front of him.

"I am grateful for your concern," he said to Ninan. "My family and friends have given me their constant attention, so that I could not help but heal."

"My father has sent us to see if you are strong enough to receive a visit from the Sapa Inca."

"I would be honored," Cusi averred. "I am surprised, though. It would be more proper for me to go to him when I am able."

"He wants to see you before the army marches north," Ninan explained. "He is going to lead us to Quito himself."

Cusi nodded in acknowledgement, closing his eyes for a moment to collect himself, and to see if Titu's presence remained as strong. It did. Cusi opened his eyes and looked directly at the healer.

"And why are *you* here?"

"I would like to examine you, my lord," Titu said with a polite bow, "to be certain your wound—"

"No," Cusi interrupted rudely. "There is no need for that. I am strong enough."

"My father holds the two of us responsible," Ninan began, but Cusi cut him off, too.

"There is no one who can claim responsibility for my being alive. Not even me. Tell the Sapa Inca he may come whenever he wishes."

"Very well," Ninan conceded. But Titu rose up slightly next to him, his eyes narrowed and his lips drawn tight. The fringe of teeth above his forehead shook as he spoke.

"I must prepare you for your interview, then," he insisted. "There are questions the Sapa Inca will no doubt wish to ask you . . . especially about your past." He glanced discreetly at Ninan and Mama Cori. "Perhaps we should have this discussion in private."

"There is no need for that. What questions?"

"My lord, I beg you to reconsider. When you were in our care, you spoke out in your dreams and told us many things. Some you might wish to keep to yourself."

"I will wait outside," Ninan offered, but Cusi simply shook his head and addressed himself to the healer.

"If I could not keep them from you, why should I keep them from my mother and my commander?"

"My lord," Titu sighed, spreading his hands in a display of pained reluctance, "we have already sent to Cuzco to confirm what you told us. We know, for example, of the visit you made to Pumapchupan—"

"To the Grass Man," Cusi said sharply, startling all three of them. "I am prepared to speak of that if the Sapa Inca chooses to ask. What else?"

Titu hesitated, his gaze turned inward for a moment, and Cusi realized that his instincts had been correct. Titi had obviously counted on getting him alone, no doubt with the intention of using Cusi's own secrets to make him speak well of how he had been treated. No more, Cusi thought, though he was suddenly aware that he was sweating heavily inside the tunic and that there was a slight ringing in his ears. He was relieved when Titu finally shrugged in capitulation.

"I see you do not wish to hear my advice—"

"Not about what you heard me speak in my sleep," Cusi said swiftly, determined to finish this before he gave away the one secret he wanted to keep. "But perhaps the Sapa Inca will wish to know what I imagined while I was being carried here. Should I tell him that I became convinced that I was a captive being subjected to torture? Should I tell him that Death rode beside me in the litter, and I was certain my captors had put him there to make me speak? Perhaps he will wish to know whom I saw as the chief of my torturers."

Cusi's voice had risen involuntarily and the sweat was running freely down his face and arms, but Titu did not appear in any condition to notice. His face had turned the color of his headdress, and his hands were clasped in front of his stomach, as if he had been stabbed.

"Leave us," Cusi told him curtly. "You may find your own excuse for why you do not wish to accompany the Sapa Inca when he comes to visit me. I do not wish to see you again."

Titu rose and turned away in a single motion, and was gone before Cusi could blink. The abruptness of it made him dizzy, and Ninan's face momentarily became a blur.

"You have a fever, Cusi," Ninan said in an anxious voice as both he and Mama Cori moved closer.

"This tunic is too warm for the day," Cusi murmured, raising his arms so that they could remove his coca bag and then the tunic, which was so wet that it clung to his body. As soon as the air touched his damp skin, he began to shiver, setting off tearing pains in his side. A blanket was hastily wrapped around him and they lowered him onto his back.

"When did this start?" Mama Cori asked sternly, and Cusi gave up his secret through trembling lips.

"Last night. But I want to see him."

"Quinti was negligent. I would not have allowed this visit had I known."

"She was praying. I want to see him while I am still important to him."

"You will always be important to him," Ninan assured him.

But Mama Cori waved him back, tucking another blanket around Cusi. "He must rest now, my lord. If you see any of his initiation brothers as you leave, please send them to me."

"Tell him I am strong enough," Cusi urged hoarsely.

Ninan stared down at him for a moment before addressing Mama Cori. "I do not think that my father will come immediately. Alert me if you feel the visit should be postponed."

Cusi watched him go in silence. His chills had passed, but he felt utterly drained. His mother slipped off his headband and mopped at his forehead and hair with a dry cloth.

"You must make me well," he said to her, and she sat back on her haunches to examine his face.

"I must know that you are *not* well first," she admonished. "And I do not think you wish to speak to the Sapa Inca with a fever clouding your mind. Titu Atauchi is a powerful man, and you attacked him recklessly."

"I felt his power," Cusi sighed. "I wanted to be rid of him while I had the strength to do so."

Tomay and Uritu came part of the way into the room, still holding the weapons they had been cleaning.

"How can we help you, my lady?"

"Find your friend Paucar and anyone else you know who might have medicines for a fever. The ones I have employed to prevent it have not worked."

"You suspected," Cusi said after his friends had ducked out again. Mama Cori loosened the blankets and dabbed at his chest with her cloth.

"I could smell the wound after you had been washed. You should not have tried to conceal it from me."

"Forgive me," Cusi muttered, closing his eyes and surrendering to his weariness. "I do not want secrets . . ."

He felt a cool hand on his forehead and heard his mother murmur something he could not understand, though he dimly sensed that she had asked him a question.

"The Grass Man is Pachacuti," he told her. Then he slept.

AS MICAY came out of Cusi's house into the sunlight, she found Apu Poma about to enter. They stepped back away from the doorway, shading their eyes with their hands. Micay spoke without having to be asked.

"Paucar's remedy has made the fever recede, but it has not broken. He is getting weaker and having trouble keeping food and water down."

Apu Poma nodded and dropped his hand, frowning against the light. "Is Cori still with him?"

"She stayed all night with me. Lloque Yupanqui is with her now; he has been trying to convince her to rest."

"It has become a vigil again," Apu Poma said sadly. "It was easy to forget how frail he was, once he was able to sit up and speak to us."

"He was strong enough to drive away the Sapa Inca's healer."

"He was," Apu Poma agreed, attempting a smile. "No, I will not underestimate him again. But I had better join Lloque and see if together we can persuade my wife to rest. She will be sick herself."

Micay bowed, remembering when Apu Poma could not utter Lloque's name without a grimace of distaste and would not have willingly entered a room where his brother-in-law was alone with Mama Cori. This vigil had healed some wounds, even if Cusi himself was still not out of danger. Apu Poma was still regarding her when she straightened up.

"Have you heard about Acapana?" he asked.

"Lloque told me that he was to be named the micho of Chachapoyas, but I could hardly believe it. He is so young!"

"He is trustworthy and capable, and we do not have anyone older to spare, not with the campaign about to begin again. Besides, he has earned the chance.

I am sorry to lose him, of course, but I spoke strongly on his behalf." He squinted at her and shrugged ruefully. "I think, though, that my words did not matter as much as the fact that they were spoken by the father of Cusi Huaman."

"How soon will he be leaving for Caxamarquilla?"

"Probably not until after the warriors have gone north. We are still assembling the mitmacs he will take with him, along with all the officials and cord counters and men to supervise the rebuilding of the city. He was at the gate a moment ago, if you wish to speak to him."

Inclining his head to her, he turned away and went through the doorway without further delay. Micay walked toward the stairs that led up to the middle terrace. Acapana was still at the gate, though he was surrounded by a knot of people who made it impossible for her to get close to him.

The rumor had somehow spread that Cusi Huaman was fit to receive visitors, and the result had been a steady stream of supplicants: young warriors with weapons in hand, hoping for the touch of his huaca; fathers with sons who had been praised for their swiftness; sign readers, sorcerers, and curers of all kinds; even a few older women with ñustas they hoped to present to him. Micay thought of Cusi as she had seen him during the night, shivering and sweating and raving deliriously about Pachacuti and Huascar and others whose names she did not recognize. He had even tried to sing once, a confused song about hawks and condors and mountains falling. When Paucar's potion had finally begun to work, he had looked up at her and called her Tocto and had fallen asleep with a shuddering smile.

We cannot lose him now, she told herself fiercely, and realized that she had closed her eyes in concentration. Praying, she thought. She opened her eyes to see two men, one short and one tall, detach themselves from the group around Acapana and begin to move in her direction, as if to find their own way down the stairs. But one of the Cañari warriors guarding the gate moved to intercept them, and they stopped in front of Micay instead. The short one, with his knit cap and Colla features, looked like a common herdsman; the taller man was much older and had bags and bundles slung over his narrow shoulders and tied around his waist, as if he were about to embark on a long journey or were in the midst of one. He seemed to be following the shorter man's lead, though otherwise he appeared oblivious to his surroundings, reminding Micay of the Sapa Inca's healers.

She was aware that the Cañari guard was coming toward them, so she was not surprised when the small man turned to her and made a brief, bobbing bow. But instead of the desperate appeal she expected to see on his face, he gave her a smile that split his face from cheek to cheek and seemed to light up his eyes from behind. It was perhaps the most guileless, ingratiating smile she had ever seen on a grown person, the smile of a child who had yet to learn cunning.

"My lady, I do not know what to do. I was told by my grandfather to see Cusi Huaman, but every time I come here, I am turned away."

"Many are turned away," Micay said soothingly, disarmed by the smile. "He is really not well enough to receive visitors."

"That is why I have brought Hanp'atu. He is a Callawaya."

The guard suddenly intervened, using the haft of his spear to prod the man back away from her. "You two must leave. You have no business here."

"My grandfather, Raurau Illa, is a friend of Cusi Huaman," the man insisted plaintively, still trying to explain. "He sent me a message that I was to see him."

The guard grunted scornfully and began to herd both of them toward the gate with his spear. Then Micay remembered she had heard that name before, and very recently at that.

"Wait. Let them stay. I will be responsible for them."

The guard stared at her reluctantly for a long moment but then stepped aside and went back to his post. The short man bobbed back in front of her, beaming with gratitude.

"I am called Urcon, my lady. Will you take me to Cusi Huaman?"

"I do not think I can do that, but I will take a message for you. How does your grandfather know Cusi?"

"They are dedicated to the same huaca. Cusi came one day when my grandfather asked for a sign from Illapa."

Micay blinked, uncertain that she had heard correctly. For all the awe in his voice, he might have been speaking of a meeting on the street.

"Does Cusi know *you*?"

"No, my lady. The rest of us went away that day. But he promised my grandfather, after I had left, that he would find me in Tumibamba and be my sponsor."

"I am certain that he will, then, when he is well enough. I will remind him that you are here."

"But Hanp'atu can make him well!" Urcon assured her with that same smile. "The Callawayas are the most famous curers in all of the Four Quarters."

"I still do not think—" Micay began. Then she trailed off when she saw Tomay and Huañu come through the gate. She decided to let Tomay help her settle this, and she beckoned to him as soon as he had seen her. He gave Urcon and Hanp'atu a suspicious once-over as he approached and watched them out of the corner of his eye as Micay tried to explain who they were. But the hard set of his features changed completely when she mentioned that the tall one was a Callawaya, a tribal name that had meant nothing to her. Tomay seemed to regard the man with instant respect.

"I have been searching, and I was told there were no Callawayas in the city. When did you get here?"

"He arrived only days ago, my lord," Urcon explained, and the tall man nodded gravely. "He came from Cuzco with a pack train of long-distance bearers. He brought his medicines and a message for me from my grandfather."

"And who is your grandfather?"

"He is called Raurau Illa, my lord."

"He is a blind man?"

"Yes, my lord. The lightning of Illapa took his sight many years ago."

Tomay drew a deep breath and turned back to Micay. "We must take them to Cusi," he declared, staring at her with his lips pushed out, as if he expected an argument. Micay had been ready to accede, but suddenly she sensed that he did not really want her support or agreement. He needed to do something of his own for Cusi, something to weigh against the life he felt he owed him. His cheeks had darkened, and there was a fierce kind of eagerness in his eyes.

"I did not want to take that responsibility," she told him, putting on a skeptical frown. "Mama Cori is with him, and she is tired and irritable. She turned away the man Uritu brought yesterday because she did not like the way he smelled."

"I know. But I am willing to risk her anger for this."

"Very well. He is *your* initiation brother."

"He is," Tomay said succinctly, making it sound like a vow. He gestured to Huañu and the two men and led them toward the stairs. Micay glanced at Acapana, who was still involved with the crowd at the gate and had not noticed her presence. She realized she might not have many more opportunities to speak with him, though the same would be true of Cusi if his fever did not break. She turned and went after Tomay, deciding he might need her support even if he did not want it and telling herself that Acapana was leaving only the city, not the world of the living.

SLEEP SURROUNDED him thickly, like a dense fog, but then an angry voice rose up beside him and he flinched reflexively, imagining the Grass Man. He saw the stick descending and fled from it, bringing himself awake. He felt rather than saw that there were many people around him, several of whom seemed to be speaking at once. At last he was able to distinguish his uncle's voice, though it, too, seemed sharp and admonitory.

"It will not help to raise your voice, Tomay," he warned. "You must respect my sister's wishes."

"But you asked us to find medicines for a fever, my lady," Tomay protested loudly. "No one knows more about these things than the Callawaya."

"That may be so," Mama Cori said impatiently, "but I did not ask you to bring strangers here. *I* do not know this man or his grandfather."

"Cusi does," Tomay insisted, and Cusi managed to get his eyes open to see his friend standing over him, casting a shadow across his face. "Cusi!" Tomay said urgently, bending to look at him. "I have brought you a Callawaya healer. And the grandson of Raurau Illa."

"That is enough," Apu Poma declared, pushing himself to his feet and forcing Tomay to straighten up and back away. The threat of violence brought Cusi fully awake, and he finally understood what Tomay was trying to tell him.

"Urcon?" he said aloud.

Everyone around him seemed to freeze in their places, his father and Tomay standing nearly chest to chest. Then another man stepped up next to Tomay and leaned forward, wearing an incongruously bright smile.

"I have come to you, Cusi Huaman, since you could not come to me." His smile dimmed perceptibly as he saw how weak Cusi was. "But you must let Hanp'atu tend to your wound. He is very skilled, and he has medicines from everywhere."

"Come closer," Cusi murmured, and turned his head to look at his mother, who was tight-lipped with disapproval. "Please . . . you have done what you could . . ."

Mama Cori finally nodded reluctantly and rose to her knees to back away. Then Tomay and Urcon were lifting him into a sitting position, and a tall man with a flat, expressionless face was opening bags and pouches on the bedding beside him. Cusi looked into Urcon's smiling face and could perceive only a slight resemblance to Alco and Raurau Illa, whom he had never seen smile. He was surprised when Urcon reached for his hands and inspected first one and then the other, as if expecting to find Cusi holding something.

"Where is your spirit brother? It should be with you."

The healer grunted in agreement as he slit Cusi's bandages with an obsidian blade and carefully peeled them away. Cusi held still until he was done, wincing at the stinging touch of air against his wound. Then he looked back at Urcon and patted his waistband.

"It is here," he assured him, and Urcon smiled with such pleasure that Cusi almost had to laugh. He was astonished at how much better this man made him feel, simply by squatting there next to him.

"You are not like Alco at all," he suggested.

Urcon nodded and shrugged. "He has always wanted to be like Grandfather. He grew up trying to be old and wise."

"And you?"

"I can wait to be old," Urcon said with another shrug, "and I do not expect to be wise. I am a herder; I keep count and take good care of my llamas."

"That is enough?"

Urcon seemed to become self-conscious for the first time, glancing bashfully at Tomay.

"Perhaps a wife someday, and land to build a house."

Cusi could only nod, distracted by the pain from which he had been trying to distance himself. His wound was itching and throbbing, and he could feel the invasive presence of fever prickling beneath his skin. Out of the corner of his eye he watched the Callawaya make a thick paste out of llama fat, a grayish powder, and several kinds of aromatic herbs. Then the healer removed another pouch from his waist and looked up, addressing his words to the air.

"I need some akha, weakened by half with water."

The very thought of akha made Cusi queasy, and he could feel sweat break out on his forehead. He felt even worse by the time Micay squatted down next to Urcon and handed a cup across to Hanp'atu. The healer tapped powder into the cup from his pouch and swirled the mixture together with a circular motion. Then he handed the cup back to Micay and beckoned her closer.

"Please if you will help him to drink, my lady, while I apply the ointment." He glanced at Tomay and Urcon. "It will burn at first, so you must hold him still and keep his hands away."

The other two men took a grip on Cusi's arms, and Micay moved into position with the cup. Cusi closed his eyes and opened his mouth to breathe, certain that he was going to vomit soon. But the first taste of akha surprised him with its sourness, which made him salivate and then swallow without thinking. Micay quickly gave him a second sip, and now he could feel fingers dabbing at his wound, hurting him, until suddenly a new sensation overwhelmed all others and all he could feel was the sharp, searing pain of a flame licking across his ribs. Tears forced his eyes open and he gasped, spraying akha at Micay's blurry face. He tried to pull away from the fiery pain, but the hands on his arms held him fast. He groaned helplessly and found the cup hovering near his lips again. He let himself drink, hoping the sour liquid might somehow quell the burning in his side.

"That is enough," he heard the healer say, and the cup was withdrawn from in front of his face. But the burning went on and on, until he could not hope or even think. His last sensation was of a hand pressing down on his own, flattening his palm over the hard zigzag shape of his spirit brother.

HE WAS SURPRISED, when he finally awoke, to find Rimachi sitting next to him, rather than the Callawaya. He had dreamed, over and over again, of the time he and Rimachi had climbed through the mountain pass in a snowstorm. In one of the dreams Rimachi had been carrying him, something Cusi was certain had not happened in real life. The clarity of this last thought made him realize that his fever was gone. He turned his head and saw that Micay was still where he remembered her being, though Uritu rather than Urcon was next to her, and his father and mother were nowhere to be seen.

"Where has everyone gone?" he asked, hearing his voice reverberate through his body. He felt light and hollow, like a dry stalk.

"You have been asleep for almost two days," Micay told him gently. "The fever broke last night, and your mother and father finally went to sleep themselves."

Runtu Caya had come over with several bowls balanced on her outstretched palms, and Cusi allowed Rimachi and Uritu to sit him up against the wall. His whole body trembled with weakness, but there was no pain in his side and the prospect of eating did not make him nauseous. He drank some water from the bowl Micay held up to his lips, then rested while she waited for the broth to cool sufficiently.

"I dreamed we were in the mountains," he said to Rimachi, giving him a sidelong glance. "In the snow."

"I remember it too well," Rimachi laughed, and pointed with his chin in Uritu's direction. "But there is your snow."

As Cusi turned his head, Uritu moved aside to reveal what appeared to be a sodden pile of blankets. But once Uritu had peeled away several thick layers of cloth, Cusi could see the glittering white lump of ice inside. Uritu gave him a sly smile.

"It did not come from my father, though," he said, shaking his feathered head in mock disappointment. "So there was no fish inside."

Cusi blinked, then remembered the gift fish that had so impressed Huascar. He smiled at Uritu, who whooped at his own joke. The smile felt strange and brittle on Cusi's face, the muscles too long unused, so that they could not fully express his relief and pleasure. The worst *had* to be past if Uritu felt he was well enough to joke with.

"Uritu's father brought an enormous fish to Cuzco for the Inti Raymi," Rimachi explained to Micay, who appeared baffled and slightly annoyed by their amusement. "It caused a great sensation."

"I am sure it did. *Your* father sent his men to the mountains for the ice," Micay said to Cusi, "so that we could cool you when the fever rose." She held up the bowl of broth and gave the other two men a scolding look. "You must let him eat now."

The smile had slipped off Cusi's face while Rimachi was speaking, as the memory of Huascar called forth other memories and made him recall why he had wanted to be well again. He nodded to Micay, grateful for her sense of duty.

"Feed me," he told her. "I have been asleep too long, and my dreams cannot sustain me."

ALONE IN HIS room, Cusi heard sounds from outside that told him that the Sapa Inca had arrived at the compound gate. He would be dismounting from his litter to greet Apu Poma and the rest of the family, who would bow and make the mocha to him, displaying their reverence and their gratitude for the honor of this visit. Cusi felt a nervous flutter in his stomach and put a hand over his spirit brother, silently repeating the chant he had devised to fortify himself: *You are the famous Cusi Huaman, brother to lightning, winner of the Huarachicoy race, hero of the Chachapoyas War; you have faced the Grass Man and Otoronco Achachi and Pachacuti himself; you have the huaca of one who has returned from a certain death.*

The chant worked less well now than it had when this audience was still days away rather than moments. He had devised it after concluding that he could not afford to play the role of a fortunate but modest young warrior if he wanted his request to be taken seriously. He had to inhabit his fame and convince Huayna Capac that he possessed the powers that had been attributed to him, that he was a man so rare and valuable as to be worthy of the Sapa Inca's own daughter. Cusi had had to convince himself first, which was not easy, given that he felt small and emaciated and was still too weak to stand. He had used the chant to help build his composure, practicing an aloofness he hoped would disguise his physical frailty.

A stocky man with a square, humorless face and an elaborate cloth head-dress suddenly appeared in the doorway, surveying the room for a moment before entering. Cusi recognized him as Topa Yupanqui, the high priest of Inti. Cusi bowed in a way he had also practiced, crossing his arms on his chest to protect the damaged muscles in his side. The high priest made a circuit of the room, murmuring to himself and blowing kisses off his fingertips. Then he stood at the foot of Cusi's bedding and raised one hand with his thumb and forefinger extended, the royal command to listen.

"The Sapa Inca Huayna Capac, Herder of the Sun, honors you with his company, Cusi Huaman. May Inti Viracocha guide your heart and tongue in his presence."

Cusi bowed in compliance, holding his ribs as he carefully straightened up. The priest was staring at him, his eyes narrowed skeptically, exerting a force of presence not unlike that of Titu Atauchi, though this man seemed much more powerful, beyond the healer's devious sort of arrogance. Cusi stared back at him without blinking, simultaneously trying to show that he had nothing to hide and that he was not intimidated. The high priest finally relaxed his gaze and nodded. Then he went back out, giving Cusi no indication of the impression he had made. Cusi breathed deeply, suddenly aware of the effort he had been expending, which made him feel as if he had been holding back the walls with his eyes.

A few moments later, two men wearing the blue livery of palace retainers came in, one carrying two puma-head drinking cups, the other a three-legged carved wooden stool inlaid with gold and mother-of-pearl. They left the stool on the place where the high priest had just stood, the cups on the floor beside it. Ninan Cuyochi came in after them, carrying a battle-ax with a star-shaped head of solid gold, the sacred champi the Sapa Inca carried with him into battle. He bent to lay the weapon on the bedding in front of Cusi, straightening up with an expression that seemed almost pained in its seriousness.

"Prepare yourself, my friend. He comes."

Cusi nodded, feeling the nervous flutter spread upward like a beating of wings, driving the air out of him for a moment. This was the Sapa Inca, the Sole Lord of all the Four Quarters, a man to whom men like Topa Yupanqui and Titu Atauchi were humble servants. Surely he would see right through Cusi's disguise to the boy who had stood frozen on the cliff, wetting himself in fear, a boy who was a hero only by accident and who deserved nothing.

As soon as the figure appeared in the doorway—gold glinting from his armbands and earplugs, the thick multicolored fringe around his forehead—Cusi bowed his head and began making the mocha, plucking hairs from his eyebrows and blowing them off his fingertips in the direction of the Sapa Inca. His eyes lowered, he saw sturdy brown legs wrapped at the knees with bands of iridescent feathers and sandals trimmed with jaguar fur. There was a moment of silence after the man settled himself on the stool, and Cusi waited, wondering why he had yet to feel the emanations of his presence.

"Lift up your face and look upon me, Cusi Huaman, for you are greatly favored by Inti, and by his son, Huayna Capac."

Cusi bowed from the waist before raising his eyes, his gaze sweeping slowly upward from the feathered kneecaps to the bright, checkered weave of his tunic, then to a strong, handsome face held at a haughty angle, so that the golden spools of his earplugs cast glowing reflections across his cheeks. His hands were propped against his hips, displaying arms that were muscular and unblemished by scars, the biceps banded with gold. He seemed to radiate fitness and vigor, his lips curved in the distant half smile of someone who had never been tired or troubled or uncertain of himself. Solid and austere, he seemed almost too perfect to be true, and Cusi could only stare at him speechlessly.

But then the dark eyes beneath the multicolored fringe moved, and they were Tocto's eyes, swift and darting, meeting Cusi's gaze but holding it only briefly, taking in the rest of him before returning to his face. Cusi emerged from his trance and realized that he could not *feel* this man, at least not in the way he felt the presence of Titu and the high priest. He has no huaca, Cusi thought, and for the first time he began to believe that he himself did.

"We have met before," Huayna Capac told him, "though you were not able to acknowledge me. You spoke to me out of a dream and told me you had nothing more to confess. No doubt you thought I was the Grass Man."

"It is true, my lord," Cusi said simply. "I surrendered all my secrets to him so that I could face death with a clear heart."

Those swift eyes had fastened on him expectantly, testing his reaction to the Grass Man, but now they widened with admiration, abandoning all pretense of suspicion.

"You not only faced it, you defied it! Forgive my curiosity about your past, Cusi. Tell me how I can reward you for what you have done."

When Cusi hesitated, Huayna Capac went on, as if he had anticipated a modest response.

"I will give you lands and a compound of your own, of course, either here or in the mountains or in Quito, along with retainers to work the fields and tend your herds. But that is not nearly enough for one who has served me so well. Speak, Cusi. Do you wish to join the old guard and lead the way into battle? You are young, but you have earned the honor."

"I would like to join the scouts, my lord, when I am strong enough."

"You shall be their commander! What else? Is there a ñusta you desire to marry? I will see that she is kept for you until you are old enough."

"There is a ñusta, my lord . . ."

"What is her name? You will have her, even if she has been promised to another!"

"Her name is Tocto Oxica, my lord," Cusi said softly. "Your daughter."

Huayna Capac's mouth fell open, and he clapped his hands down onto his thighs. Cusi felt the blood rush to his face and struggled to keep his gaze steady and his expression calm. He managed not to flinch as he watched Huayna Capac's amazement dissolve into an anger that contorted his handsome features.

"So that is true, as well," he said at last. "Why do you even dare to ask me, Cusi? You know it is impossible."

"So was my leap from the cliff," Cusi retorted. "But I have learned from Pachacuti himself that an Inca must always attempt the impossible."

Huayna Capac cocked his head, his eyes fixed in a glare of outrage and astonishment that did not so much see Cusi as try to consume him. Cusi held his breath and tried to exert all of the force that was in him, all of the huaca he was said to have. But he only succeeded in causing the ruler to tear his eyes away with an exasperated grunt.

"You have made your attempt, then," he told Cusi in an unrelenting voice. "I would give you your pick from the ñustas in the House of Chosen Women, Cusi Huaman, but you may not have a daughter of the Coya."

Despite himself, Cusi let his shoulders slump and hung his head in defeat, crushed by the denial he had never let himself believe he would hear, even though everyone had told him it was inevitable. After a moment, Huayna Capac spoke in a more kindly tone.

"You have great courage, my son, and I cannot expect you to confine it to the battlefield. So I will forget that you even thought of marrying my daughter. Tell me what I can give you instead."

Cusi shrugged weakly and spread his hands open in his lap, unable to rally his spirits. Agitated by this show of lassitude, Huayna Capac clapped his hands sharply and called over his shoulder for akha.

"Revive yourself, Cusi," he commanded as Micay entered the room carrying a wide-mouthed jar. He held up the two cups for her to fill, gazing at her admiringly as she poured.

"Stay, my daughter," he said when she was done. "You have not just come to Tumibamba, have you?"

"No, my lord," Micay said in a small voice, keeping her eyes lowered. "I have been here for over two years."

"Then you have been to the mountains? Yes? Do you by chance know the estate that is called the Rainbow House?"

Micay seemed to catch her breath, as if the name had startled her.

"Yes, my lord. It is near the Lynx House, which belongs to the cult of Mama Quilla."

"You know it, then," Huayna Capac concluded with an enthusiastic smile. "Do you not agree that it would be an excellent place for Cusi to rest and recover his health?"

Micay cast a sidelong glance at Cusi, her eyes wide with a recognition that startled him, since it seemed to include him in a coincidence unknown to him.

"Most excellent, my lord," she said to Huayna Capac. "There is a beautiful view down the valley and a waterfall where there is always a rainbow."

"It is a huaca that belongs to the cult of Huanacauri," the ruler told her with satisfaction. "Most appropriate for a man who has been blessed with so much courage. It is yours, Cusi. Let us drink to the bravery that won you such a prize." He lifted the cups and spilled a little akha from each onto the floor. "To Inti, our father . . ."

At a nod from Huayna Capac, Micay put down her jar, took the cup from his outstretched right hand, and carried it to Cusi. She remained kneeling beside him, her hands poised to help, but Cusi warned her off with his eyes, wrapping both hands around the head of the puma and holding the cup out in front of him with an effort that made his arms shake.

"To Inti," he replied, and took a sip of akha before lowering the cup down between his crossed legs. He watched as Micay backed away and went to refill Huayna Capac's cup, noticing the curious glance she cast at the golden-headed ax on the bedding before him. He realized then that Huayna Capac had brought it here for his blessing, for the touch of his famous hands. That brought him back to himself and made him remember his promise to Otoronco.

"I am grateful, my lord," he said, looking up at Huayna Capac, who was wiping his lips with the side of his hand. "There *is* a favor I would ask you, if I may."

"That is better. Speak."

"There is a warrior left behind in Cuzco who wishes to join in the fight against the Carangui. He is old, but he has lost none of his fierceness."

"What is this warrior's name?" Huayna Capac asked, his generosity suddenly tinged with wariness. Cusi gave him a wan smile, trying to show that he did not wish to surprise or anger him.

"He is my grandfather, Lord Otoronco Achachi. He does not seek the command he once held, my lord; he would serve wherever his leadership might be useful."

The cool, detached smile had returned to Huayna Capac's face, though it seemed a bit forced, as if he were determined not to let Cusi shake his equanimity a second time.

"Perhaps I should bring him north," he said casually, "before he returns all of the wealth of the Eastern Quarter to the people who live there. But it would not be easy to find a place for him, no matter what *he* is willing to accept. What war chief or commander would want a legend serving under him?"

"I do not know, my lord," Cusi admitted. "I only promised I would speak to you on his behalf, if I were given the chance."

"I will honor your promise, though I will have to consider what is appropriate for a man of his rank and prestige. Does that satisfy you?"

Cusi bowed in acceptance, knowing that he had already asked for far too much. Huayna Capac grunted and set his cup down on the floor beside his stool.

"Then lay your hands upon the sacred champi, so that your spirit might accompany the Incas to Quito."

Moving deliberately, Cusi rested both of his hands on his waistband, over his spirit brother, a gesture Huayna Capac seemed to comprehend and appreciate. Then he reached out and grasped the handle of the ax with both hands, gritting his teeth against the expected pain in his side.

"May you sweep the Carangui before you, my lord," he said in a taut voice, "and make their lands your own."

"Inti has willed it," Huayna Capac declared, rising to his feet as Cusi removed his hands from the ax and sat back. He watched the ruler bend and scoop the weapon up in a single motion, his muscles flexing effortlessly.

"*This* for rebels and traitors," he proclaimed, slashing the air with swift golden strokes. He stared down at Cusi with a reckless smile on his face, seeming splendid and self-assured. "You must come to me when you are recovered, Cusi Huaman. I count you among those who are my support and the strength of my hand."

"I am honored to serve you, Lord Inca," Cusi said, bowing and making the mocha as a sign of his sincerity and his deference. Huayna Capac accepted his allegiance with a nod, gazing at him past the head of the ax. His smile had become fond and indulgent, almost fatherly. Then he darted a last admiring glance at Micay, who was also making the mocha, and turned and strode out of the room with the ax in his hands. Cusi let out a long breath and stared down at his own hands, which seemed fleshless and spindly, without spirit to confer. It was over. He had used his fame and his huaca, and they had not been enough. He would never be allowed near Tocto again.

He did not look up when the retainers came in to remove the stool and the cup the Sapa Inca had used. They left Cusi his cup as a gift, and he strained to lift it for another drink, rolling the akha around in his mouth before swallowing. He finally glanced over at Micay, who was standing in the same place with the jar in her hands, appearing dazed with what he realized had to be relief.

"You performed flawlessly, my lady," he told her.

She started briefly at the sound of his voice. "I did not expect him to speak to me," she confessed. "It was enough of a surprise that he chose me to serve him."

"No doubt," Cusi agreed wearily. "But it is over now."

"He was very generous," she suggested, nodding as if to encourage him. "The Rainbow House is a rare and beautiful place."

"So you said. It was not what I wanted, but he would not give me that. No matter what I had done." He glanced down at the cup between his legs and pointed at it with his chin, making no attempt to lift it. "Take this from me, if you would. I do not want to think about his generosity anymore."

Micay put down her jar and came to kneel beside him, picking up the cup with the care usually reserved for ritual vessels.

"This is a great gift," she murmured. "I will put it aside for you to drink later."

"No, take it away. It only reminds me of what I have lost."

"To whom shall I give it, then?"

"Anyone," Cusi said indifferently. "Whoever you wish."

"It is a great gift," she repeated, turning the puma head in her hands. "Perhaps, my lord, you would like to give it to Tomay. He was the one who brought Urcon and the Callawaya to you. He would prize a gift from you."

Cusi had been on the verge of telling her irritably just to leave him alone, but this suggestion—this pronouncement—made him straighten up so suddenly that he hurt his side. She was regarding him calmly but with a glint of challenge in her dark eyes.

"You know Tomay so well?"

"We have watched over you together. I have seen how he is around you, and away from you, as well. It is hard for him to owe you so much."

"He owes me nothing," Cusi protested. "I acted only to save myself, out of fear. I can tell him that now."

Micay paused, showing respect for the honesty of his statement. But then she slowly shook her head in disagreement.

"He will not believe you. He was also afraid on the cliff, which made him revere you even more for what you did. You will only make it harder for him if you try to deny what he has said on your behalf."

Cusi exhaled sharply, grimacing at the painful tug on his mending rib muscles.

"Then I can tell no one," he concluded.

Micay shrugged and nodded, as if she saw no other choice. "Tomay is not the only one who wishes to believe in your courage. I do not think you could change that, no matter how many denials you made."

Cusi closed his eyes for a moment, though he knew in his heart that she was right. He remembered the huaman cachi, the hawk that had flown after him to Raurau Illa's village, bearing the fame he could not elude.

"I am slow to learn some things," he said to Micay. "Please take the cup to Tomay. Tell him that he saved my life and I am grateful."

"I will tell him," Micay promised, rising gracefully with the cup in her hands. The folds in her shift made a whispering sound as they unfurled around her legs, a sound that reminded him of Tocto and brought a bitter lump to his throat. So he did not speak as Micay bowed and walked out of the room, though he wanted to tell her that he was grateful to her, as well. He wanted to tell her that *she* was the generous one. But he was afraid he might begin to weep if he spoke, and he did not want her to think he had relapsed into self-pity.

When she was gone he stretched out his legs and let himself slide down onto his back. He closed his eyes so that anyone who looked in would think he was sleeping and would leave him alone. But his thoughts would not let him rest, and behind his eyes he saw Tocto's face emerge from that of her father, staring at him sadly, with all the swift eagerness gone from her gaze. I have lost you, he told her silently, and he felt the tears flow out from beneath his eyelids, leaving her image unblurred in his mind and his heart still aching with disbelief.

X

HUANACAURI HUASI:
The Rainbow House

(A.D. 1514)

The Rainbow House

WHEN MAMA CORI had heard everything the messenger could tell her, she sent the man off to be fed. Then she stood silently, impassively, for several moments, and Micay could almost feel her hardening herself against the disappointment this news had surely caused her. When she finally turned to Micay her eyes were like flint, and her voice was no softer.

"I should have expected this. Go tell Cusi, if you can find him. It may not make any difference to him, but tell him anyway."

Micay nodded compliantly and went out, grateful to have an excuse to get away. She had felt the tension building inside Mama Cori during the last few days, as they came to the end of all the cleaning and decorating they could reasonably do here. Supplies had been transferred from the storerooms, the bathhouses and guest rooms had been put in order, and the household servants had all been rehearsed in their duties. The estate was ready to be used again as a place of leisure and renewal and family pride, and Micay knew Mama Cori had looked forward to Amaru's arrival as the occasion for the house's first feast. The whole family would have been together for the first time in years. Now she could only wait for Apu Poma to confirm the misgivings she had obviously had all along.

Checking all the houses and courtyards and questioning the retainers as she went, Micay found her way out of the complex, which was built on several terraced levels against the side of a mountain. The construction incorporated

outcroppings of the gray bedrock as foundations and stairways, and the standing stonework was exceedingly smooth and well fitted, a constant reminder
that this retreat had originally been built for royalty. The final set of stairs had
been carved into a hollow between two banks of solid rock, which cut off the
sunlight and made her feel as if she were climbing up out of a cave. It was also
much colder in the shade at this altitude, this late in the dry season, so she
pulled her mantle tighter around her shoulders until she was out in the light
again.

She followed a zigzag path up the hill, using the tops of the terrace walls
to move horizontally and climbing from one terrace to the next by means of
the stepped walls that divided each terrace into a number of long, narrow plots.
Some of the plots had already been planted with early potatoes, and in others
the reddish earth had been tilled and broken in preparation for the planting
of oca and ullucu. Almost the entire mountainside had been terraced, and as
she moved laterally she could see two of the retainers digging in one of the
maize plots far below, down near the gleaming band of the river. The land rose
more steeply on the other side of the river and was used only for grazing,
though a broken pattern of ancient terracing could still be seen through the
patchy clusters of yellow bunch grass. By squinting, Micay could make out
brown and white shapes that had to be a herd of llamas or alpacas moving
single file across the face of the mountainside.

Despite the somber news she carried, the spaciousness of the view had its
usual exhilarating effect upon her, and she had to remind herself to go slowly.
She no longer suffered much from the altitude, but her head still felt light, and
she knew it would be many more days before her body would be fully accustomed to this height. The path had left the terraces behind, winding its way
upward through bunch grass and then cacti, over ground too steep and rocky
to be cultivated. With little hope of finding Cusi, she had begun to look ahead
to her favorite resting place, a place she knew to be ideal for watching the
sunset. She had visited it often during the times she had stayed at the Lynx
House, which was in the valley behind this one.

She stopped to catch her breath at the top of the ridge, so it was another
moment before she realized that her favorite place was already occupied. It was
Cusi, sitting cross-legged on the long, flat rock that collected the sun's heat and
held it well beyond the fading of the light. Micay knew the properties of the
stone from experience, and she was impressed that Cusi had found it on his
own. Perhaps he was beginning to lay claim to the Sapa Inca's gift, after all.

He had obviously been walking hard, because he did not have his earplugs
in and his gray tunic was dark with sweat and clung limply to his upper body.
The legs folded under him appeared strong and muscular, even at a distance,
but his arms still seemed almost fleshless, the dark skin stretched taut over
every knob and point of bone. He was staring out over the valley to the west,
his eyes narrowed and his face bared to the changing light.

As she approached, Micay realized she had not been alone with Cusi since

Huayna Capac's visit, now almost four months ago. It had not seemed deliberate on his part, not with all the other visitors he had had and the time he spent exercising and walking. And she had not wished to intrude on him, to be part of the unending crowd that wanted to be close to the famous Cusi Huaman. She wondered, though, if he had told anyone else what he had told her, the secret she had persuaded him to keep. She wondered if he regretted having told her.

"My lady," he said in surprise, when he finally noticed her presence. Micay bowed, giving him a moment to collect himself.

"A message has come from Tumibamba," she reported. "Sinchi Roca's party has returned from the coast, as expected. Amaru, however, was not with him. Your father is coming to the Rainbow House to tell us what he knows of this."

"Has something happened to him?" Cusi demanded. "Is he ill?"

"Not that we have been told. Apparently, he has chosen to remain in Chan Chan."

Cusi frowned and looked away for a moment, as if he found the message difficult to assimilate. Then he shook his head, as if he did not wish to try. He looked up at her and pointed with his chin at the other end of the stone.

"Will you sit with me?"

Micay seated herself on the warm stone, arranging her shift over her knees. Following Cusi's silent example, she gazed toward the west, where the sun, now a deep reddish-orange, was framed between the steeply sloping sides of the valley. The top half of the mountain across from them had turned golden brown, and shadows stretched out in dark sheets across its lower half. Gnarled trees and spike-leaved cacti stood out distinctly where the light still touched, and the ragged clumps of bunch grass along an exposed ridge looked as if they had been set afire. Micay felt she could see forever, as she had in her dream, and her exhilaration returned with a rush that left her light-headed and breathless. She was startled when Cusi spoke.

"You are smiling," he said softly.

"It is beautiful," she murmured without turning her head. "I used to come here to watch when I was staying at the Lynx House."

"Ah—so that is how you knew about the Rainbow House when the Sapa Inca asked you. What drew you here?"

The air before her eyes seemed to be washed with gold, and mist was rising from the river like gray smoke, rolling up to conceal the lowest terraces. In the stillness, the high-pitched call of a herd boy carried across the valley. Reluctantly she turned to look at Cusi, wondering why the beauty in front of them was not an answer in itself.

"I wanted to be alone," she recalled. "I was not involved in the activities of the cult, so I was free to wander and explore. Sucso and Cachi were pleased to have a visitor of any kind, and they did not disturb me if I sat here or by the waterfall."

"Did you know that the waterfall was a huaca of Huanacauri?"

"Not until the Sapa Inca said so. I simply felt peaceful there. The water is never quiet, but it is never too loud for your thoughts."

"And you feel peaceful here, as well?" Cusi prompted, leaning forward with his elbows on his thighs.

"I do," Micay said tautly. "At least I do when I am not being interrogated about how I feel."

Cusi blinked and sat back, releasing her from a pressure that was almost physical, as if he had been resting his weight upon her. He was immediately apologetic.

"Forgive me, Micay. I have spent too much time talking to strangers, and I have learned that it is better to question them than to answer the same questions about myself over and over again. If I am rude, they pretend not to notice. I did not mean to be rude to you, my lady, though I envy your peacefulness."

Micay was still slightly stunned by the force of his attention, which made her understand why some of his visitors had gone away feeling intimidated or offended. This was the "coldness" and "arrogance" they had complained of as they left. But the Cusi in front of her seemed sincere in his apology, and he was sitting back, waiting for her reply.

"I am not offended," she told him finally, "and I do not think you have any reason to envy me. After all, the Rainbow House belongs to you now."

"Does it?" Cusi inquired in a doubtful tone. "In Cuzco I would not even have a *house* until I was married, and it would belong to my household, not to me. Only the Sapa Inca is allowed to hold lands of his own."

"This is not Cuzco," Micay pointed out. "And you are not the only warrior with a compound of his own. Paucar has one in Tumibamba, and Tomay has been promised one in Quito."

"I know, and they would probably think me foolish for resisting what has been given to me. You probably think me foolish, too. But it is not right for one man to have so much, and to have it so far away from Cuzco. What will happen when our work here is done and it is time to return?"

Micay was silent, recognizing that he was arguing with himself, not her. And she had no answer to such a question, which made him sound like an Inca who had just come north and was still looking back. She had not heard such sentiments in a long time, except from the white-haired old warriors who would always be looking back.

"Huayna Capac gave me this," Cusi went on, "as consolation for what he denied me. If I accept it, have I been consoled? Have I forgotten what I truly wanted?"

He had been speaking to the air, his gaze focused inward, but then he came out of it and looked at her directly.

"You are smiling again," he said in surprise, and Micay realized that she was indeed. She found it touching and amusing that it had taken him this long to reveal the real source of his resistance.

"*Have* you forgotten her, my lord?" she asked gently, so that he would not feel he was being mocked. "I do not see how accepting this estate would affect your memory. Nor do I see what consolation there is in refusing it."

Cusi stared at her for a long moment, his face set in a stubborn frown but his eyes wavering, considering.

"I have not forgotten," he said in a toneless voice, surrendering to her logic without embracing it. He looked past her, then out over the valley. The sun was a reddish mass that seemed to be dissolving as it sank into the clouds of mist that filled the valley bottom, and the mountains were dark brown silhouettes against the deepening blue of the sky. In the distance a pair of turkey vultures drifted in broken circles above a pink-tinged peak.

"Vultures," Cusi murmured. "Only vultures."

"Not hawks?" Micay ventured.

"Not condors," he said flatly, lowering his gaze and turning to look at her. "What is it?"

"Nothing," Micay said too quickly, flustered by the coincidence. "I was thinking of condors—"

"Just now? Why?"

"I have dreamed of them. The condor was the first god of my people."

"The Chachapoyas," Cusi said thoughtfully. Then his eyes flared eagerly and he leaned toward her again. "Condor Tupac . . . who fell to his death in front of me. Why do I think you knew him? *Did* you know him, Micay? What was your dream?"

He seemed about to leap at her, and Micay shook her head vehemently and slid her legs off the stone.

"I must go back—"

"Wait," Cusi pleaded, trying to untangle his legs and rise in one motion. Halfway up, he winced and groaned loudly, putting a hand down to steady himself. Arrested by his cry, Micay stopped a few feet away and turned to look back. Her concern must have shown in her face, because he grimaced and shook his head, holding his side with both hands.

"It is nothing," he muttered. "Go, please . . . I cannot expect you to forgive me a second time."

Micay was too confused by what had just occurred to argue with him, so she turned and went down the path, searching the ground ahead of her in the failing light and carefully watching where she put her feet.

STEPPING BACK out of the herd, Urcon caught Cusi's attention by holding up a fist. Very deliberately, he opened and closed his fingers four times, then finished by holding three fingers aloft.

"Twenty-three," Cusi said aloud, and found the two large knots and three smaller ones on the cord that counted this part of the herd. "It is exactly as you said, Sucso. I am pleased." He wrapped the master cord around the others and handed it to the old man. "All has now been counted, and all is in its place."

The traditional expression of satisfaction drew a solemn bow from the old man, who tucked the cords under his arm. He looked up at Cusi without meeting his gaze, waiting politely until Cusi gestured for him to speak.

"My lord—at the feast to welcome your father—will your mother and sister be present?"

"Of course," Cusi said, though he understood why Sucso might have his doubts. "I will speak to them myself."

"Very good. You asked that six places be set, my lord. May I ask who is to be the sixth guest?"

"Urcon," Cusi said, pointing with his chin at the herder, who had waded back in among the herd and was talking to the llamas.

"Within the family circle, my lord?"

Cusi stared at him for a moment, understanding the reason for this query, as well. The rules of rank and blood had been strictly observed here in the past, and his mother had given the retainers the impression that they would continue to be. Cusi considered an explanation of who Urcon was to him, but he finally did not have the patience for it.

"That is my wish," he said curtly. "See to it."

The old man bowed and departed without a murmur of complaint, though the arrogance of Cusi's response echoed in his own ears. He was trying to correct that in himself, but the retainers seemed to invite it. And he had certainly given Sucso enough of his time and attention in the past two days to justify some impatience. It did not matter to *him* that every scrap of cloth and kernel of maize was accounted for; the gift of the Rainbow House was beyond such petty reckoning. But he had nonetheless participated fully in the accounting, knowing it was the only meaningful way he could demonstrate his regard for Sucso's worth.

That much was done now, and at least in the eyes of the retainers, he had established himself as the master of the house. His mother, once she learned of it, would be proud that he had taken up his responsibilities, and Quinti could stop praying for him to recover his enthusiasm and his gratitude for all the favor the gods had shown him. Perhaps even Micay would be persuaded to think better of him. He cringed whenever he considered what she must think of him: sulking, selfish, arrogant . . . wanting to be consoled for his good fortune.

He needed to start over with all of them, most of all with himself. He had fulfilled his promises to Tocto and Otoronco Achachi, and he had lived through the dangers Raurau Illa had foreseen for him. He had paid for his fame and good fortune in pain and fear and blood, and it had changed him in ways he still could not comprehend. But he was determined now to learn, and where better to start than with those who had once known him best?

He whistled to Urcon and started back toward the Rainbow House, reminding himself to speak to his mother and Quinti. He wanted everyone there when he finally learned why Amaru, his only blood brother, had chosen to stay away.

THE AWNING house on the middle terrace had a gabled roof and a window at each end; its open side faced west. As Cusi had instructed, the retainers had laid down a circle of reed mats just inside the shelter, though it seemed less and less likely that he would have a sunset to share with his guests. The clouds had thickened as the day wore on, dulling the colors of the landscape and putting a persistent chill into the air. Before they were done, they would probably need the fire that had been built in a pit in front of the awning house. Cusi stooped to examine the topmost logs, which had been stripped of their bark, polished, and carved with symbols of the Moon and the stars and the other gods of the sky. As they were consumed by the flames, their smoke would rise skyward as an offering. The wood had been a gift from one of Cusi's visitors, a chief from Tumbez who had been trying hard to impress him.

Cusi walked around the circle of mats, counting the six places indicated by the arrangement of spoons and bowls and drinking cups, and went to the back of the awning house, which seemed dark and even chillier than outside. His mother had decorated the niches in the back wall with strips of bright cloth and a sampling of the many other gifts he had received during his convalescence. He had admired the beauty of her handiwork yesterday, and it was one of the reasons he had chosen this place for the feast. But now he went right to the gift that had stayed in his mind since that visit: a spray of green parrot feathers fanned out across the back of the niche, behind an array of stones carved in the shapes of llamas, frogs, and ears of maize.

He saw only the feathers, which awoke a memory that made his scalp prickle with a kind of delicious dread. He could remember the giver vividly: a Shuara sorcerer who wore a jaguar-skin cape, a feathered ornament through his upper lip, and two shrunken heads attached to his waistband. His presence—his huaca—had been so strong that Cusi had tried to leave the room, an attempt the sorcerer had prevented simply by squinting at him. His name was Kirupasa and he had turned out to be friendly, though Cusi had felt like a helpless child the whole time he was with him.

"There is no safety in ignorance for those who can feel," Cusi murmured, recalling what Kirupasa had said when Cusi had responded equivocally to an offer to visit the man's village. He decided the man had been right to scold him, though he also decided not to touch the feathers. He only needed to remind himself that the time for avoidance was past. When he had done so, he turned and went back to await the arrival of his guests.

THEY BEGAN the feast without Quinti, who had apparently warned Cusi that she might be late returning from the Lynx House. Her absence left a gap to

Micay's left, separating her from Mama Cori and Apu Poma. Urcon was present on her right, but he was trying his best to be invisible in this company, which left another kind of gap between her and Cusi. She would have felt exposed had she been called upon to speak, but Cusi was directing his remarks to his parents, glancing occasionally in her direction like a proper host. The glances were genuine—he was aware of her presence—but he was clearly not going to interrogate her tonight.

He was trying not to interrogate his parents, either, but they were not making it easy for him. Mama Cori had come out of her self-imposed seclusion at Cusi's request, but she remained withdrawn to the point of sullenness. Apu Poma had arrived in a preoccupied state and then seemed to take offense at his wife's unresponsiveness, which made him lapse into a sulk of his own. Neither had much to say about Cusi's earnest account of his inspection of the Rainbow House, and Apu Poma had to be coaxed to repeat the little he knew about the activities of the court, which had gone north to Quito along with Huayna Capac and the army.

The food was good, but even that occasioned little comment, and as Micay watched Cusi begin to flounder, she wondered what he had expected this feast to be like. He could hardly believe that Amaru's defection was a cause for family celebration, especially after the way his mother had reacted. He had to suspect that something was wrong, unless he was too impressed or loyal to his older brother to question him. Micay suddenly remembered the message Amaru had given her for Cusi, a message she had yet to deliver. Perhaps Cusi was just as proud of the man he thought Amaru to be. Rimachi had once insisted to her that Cusi was naive in many ways and expected too much honesty from too many people. Yet Rimachi had also said, with a different sort of disdain, that Cusi was drawn to prophecies and powers that could not be seen and other matters best left to priests and sorcerers . . .

Micay turned to look at him and found that he was looking back at her, waiting for someone else to realize that the circle had fallen utterly silent. When she nodded in sympathy he gave her a rueful smile that seemed neither naive nor mysterious, as if he had known it might come to this. Without a word of explanation he pushed himself to his feet and walked out to the pit filled with wood in front of the awning house. Sucso's wife, Cachi, quickly brought him a flaming torch.

"We have tolerated the cold long enough," he declared, glancing up at the gray sky for a moment before thrusting the torch down into the kindling at the bottom of the pile. The fire smoked and crackled, and then the flames rose swiftly, forcing him to step back as they shot up over his head. He turned back to his guests, smiling when he saw that he had gotten their attention.

"We have been silent long enough, too," he said, raising his voice above the snapping roar of the fire. "Come, Father, you have spoken to Sinchi Roca. Tell us why Amaru has chosen to remain in Chan Chan."

Apu Poma cleared his throat, nodding in resignation. "The supervisor of building for Chimor Province had to be replaced, and Amaru volunteered for the post. Sinchi Roca tried to dissuade him but then felt compelled to appoint him. He was the only Inca with sufficient rank and competence who wanted to continue living among the Chimu."

"How long will he stay?"

"As long as he wishes," Apu Poma said with an angry shrug. "There are few enough builders available for everything Huayna Capac wants done here and in Quito, and even fewer who will volunteer for duty in the Hotlands. He might be summoned back to fight, but that is unlikely to happen soon."

Cusi nodded thoughtfully, then signaled for the servants to bring out the akha. Standing with his back to the fire, he took two cups and toasted his father in the traditional manner, welcoming him to the Rainbow House for the second time. The cup he kept for himself, Micay noticed, was the crude, unpainted vessel he had been given by the blind man, Urcon's grandfather. He held it against his chest and looked down at his father with polite expectation.

"Must we beg for the rest?" he asked. "Surely, Sinchi Roca had some notion of *why* Amaru chose to stay."

"He did," Apu Poma admitted reluctantly. "But what he told me is not pleasant. I see no reason to make everyone share my shock and disappointment."

"Perhaps we can help you bear it," Cusi suggested, and Micay heard a definite edge in his voice, an unwillingness to let the discussion lapse again. Apu Poma drained his cup and held it out to Cachi to fill.

"Most of what I know is only rumor and speculation. And some of it is disgraceful."

"I understand disgrace," Cusi said, baring his teeth in a relentless smile. "It can be borne."

"Tell us, Apu," Mama Cori said sharply. "If Amaru were here, he would not hesitate to tell us himself. *Especially* if the news were disgraceful or disappointing."

Apu Poma's lips curled in distaste, and he shook himself and grunted fiercely before he could speak. "They say that he has become a captive of the Chimus, a willing captive. He dresses like them and imitates their gestures, and he lets them speak to him in Mochica rather than Quechua. He shuns the other Incas and spends his time off duty with the young nobles from the court of the Grand Chimu, or at the compounds of the women of pleasure. When he does attend one of the governor's feasts, he drinks heavily and does not hide his drunkenness."

Apu Poma trailed off, looking down at the matting in front of him and shaking his head in a way that made his earplugs flash erratically in the firelight.

"Is that all?" Cusi inquired. Apu Poma's head came up, and he glared at Cusi for a long moment. Then he glanced once at Mama Cori and went on in a harsh, angry voice, as if to punish all of them for their curiosity.

"No, there is more . . . there is worse. The sentries found him one night, naked and drunk on something more powerful than akha, talking and singing to himself as he walked out into the waters of Mama Cocha. They pulled him out before he drowned himself, but it took four of them to do it, and he broke one man's jaw in the struggle. That is a fact. What is rumored is even worse. Stories about sorcerers and rebels and secret rites forbidden by the Inca— stories about dances given by boys who paint their faces and dress like women." Apu Poma spat the last words out, gesturing at Cusi with his cup. "Is *that* enough for you?"

Cusi stood very straight and drank from his plain wooden cup, frowning thoughtfully at what he had heard but showing no signs of shock or disappointment. Micay recalled the things Amaru had said about himself in the past and could not be surprised, either, though she doubted that he had ever said them to Cusi. He had claimed that Cusi was not like him.

She was watching him with fascination now, unable to predict what he might say next, and she saw his eyes widen and catch the firelight, giving off an impulsive gleam. He stepped forward and surprised everyone by addressing himself to Urcon.

"What would you do, my friend, if you had heard this about *your* brother?" he asked. Patiently he waited while Urcon deliberated on his answer. Urcon was quick with smiles, but not advice.

"Alco would never want to leave the village," he explained, looking only at Cusi. "But if he had gone instead of me and I believed he had lost his way, I would go to find him and lead him home."

"Of course," Cusi said succinctly, coming back around to assume his former place in the circle. He put down his cup and glanced sideways at his father. "When will you next send a party to Chan Chan?"

"Half of the governor's warriors are due for rotation in two months," Apu Poma reported before he could catch himself. "But what are you thinking? No, I could not allow you to damage your own career for his sake."

"I would not damage my career by leading the warriors there. I will bring Amaru back with me."

"And if he refuses to come?" Apu Poma demanded. "You would have wasted months traveling back and forth, when you could have been with your comrades in the north."

"It will take months before the muscles in my side are fully healed," Cusi told him. "Hanp'atu warned me of that, and I know it every time I try to breathe deeply or lift something heavy. In the meantime all I can do is walk, and it is better if I have a destination and a purpose."

"Cusi, please," Mama Cori broke in. "I know you will have to leave me soon enough. But I beg you, do not make me watch you throw your life away on Amaru. Too many Incas have perished in the Hotlands."

Cusi lifted his cup to his lips but did not drink, only stared at his mother over the rim. From Micay's angle, he appeared suddenly daunted, touched by the note of pleading in Mama Cori's voice. Unless he were more like Amaru than he seemed, he would have to yield to such a plea. But then Micay saw his eyes widen and take on that same bold gleam, and his lips peeled back in a smile that he kept to himself for a moment before lowering the cup to show it to his mother.

"Do not watch from afar, then," he suggested. "Come with me. Quinti and Micay could come, too, and Urcon could lead the pack train. We could look after one another."

The top logs suddenly collapsed into the fire, sending up a shower of sparks and causing everyone except Cusi to jump. Micay's heart seem to hang suspended after the rest of her had settled back down, buoyed up by the stunning audacity of his suggestion, which he seemed to have plucked out of the air. And he had invited *her,* too. The image of Mama Huarcay's frieze flashed through her mind, along with a confused thought about passion and beauty that warmed her cheeks. A smile rose irresistibly toward her lips and she quickly lifted her cup to conceal it from Mama Cori.

"This is a rash proposal," Mama Cori finally said. "It is impossible even to contemplate."

"The impossible must *always* be contemplated," Cusi insisted, but then had to look up as Quinti came into the awning house. She bowed in greeting to her father and mother before offering a breathless apology to Cusi.

"Forgive me, my brother, I was delayed at the Lynx House." She sat down in the place left for her and glanced around the circle. "So it is true, then? Amaru has not returned from Chan Chan?"

"He has apparently decided to stay and make himself into a Chimu," Mama Cori said with unconcealed disgust. "Cusi is suggesting that we all go to Chan Chan to bring him back."

"That is generous of you, my brother," Quinti said, smiling at Cusi. Then she grew serious, resting her chin on her clasped hands, a pose that reminded Micay of Chimpu Ocllo. "I am afraid, though, that I could not think of leaving now, when I am just beginning to find a place for myself within the cult of Mama Quilla." She lifted her head and glanced from Micay to Mama Cori. "But that should not prevent the rest of you from going. What is there to keep you, Mother? You have decorated all the rooms here, and Tumibamba is empty, now that Lloque and the rest of the court have gone to Quito."

"You are kind to remind me of my uselessness," Mama Cori said drily.

"You would be most useful to me," Cusi put in. "Amaru could not refuse both of us."

"Micay should go, too, if she wishes," Quinti said. "She knows Amaru and can talk to him."

Micay could not hide behind her cup again, so she looked across and met Mama Cori's penetrating gaze, which swept over her like a cool, suspicious wind.

"She might be better off *not* knowing him," Mama Cori suggested. "Besides, she had just begun her training with Chimpu Ocllo's healers before we came here. She might not wish to leave her place, either."

"Hanp'atu would probably be happy to travel with us," Cusi said quickly, glancing at Urcon for confirmation. "He could teach her things about healing that only the Callawaya know."

Mama Cori's eyes had not left Micay. "She might also wish to be in Tumibamba when Rimachi and the other warriors return for their leave."

The insinuation froze Micay's responses for a moment, so that she glimpsed the stricken expression that passed across Cusi's face. Then she felt her cheeks flush, first with guilt and then with anger. Mama Cori had never spoken to her about Rimachi or any other potential suitor. She was simply using this to resist Cusi, to punish Amaru rather than try to rescue him. Before Micay could think of what to say, Apu Poma broke in.

"Do not ask her to decide, Cori, when you have not decided yourself. Amaru is a grown man, but he is also our son. He should not be abandoned so easily."

"You are hardly the one to speak of that!" Mama Cori snapped.

Apu Poma rose up slightly, throwing his head back. "I am precisely the one to speak of it. If you will not go with Cusi, I will find a way to go myself. Even if I must resign my post."

Mama Cori stared at him in disbelief, then looked past him at Cusi. "You seem to have infected everyone with your boldness, my son. Are you certain you want your cautious mother for a companion?"

"You are the first I asked," Cusi reminded her.

"Then I must accept. Have you also decided, Micay?"

"I have heard many things about Chan Chan," Micay said, knowing that Mama Cori would understand from whom she had heard them. "If I am welcome, I would like to see them for myself."

"Of course," Mama Cori said, with a lack of conviction that was lost on Cusi, who clapped his hands and signaled for more akha.

"Let us drink to our journey," he proposed, raising his cup and beaming at all of them. Quinti laughed, sharing his elation, which seemed to falter slightly when he caught Micay's eye.

"Just bring him back," Apu Poma said gruffly, holding out his cup to the servant. "And yourselves, as well."

THE SUN was still high when Cusi and Micay made their farewells to Quinti and the mamacona and left the Lynx House, descending to the river by means of the stepped path that led from one terrace level to the next. At the bottom Micay turned to wave back up to Quinti, who was still standing with several of the mamacona in front of the buildings high above. Cusi waved absently, his attention on the rope bridge that hung over the river and the path that zigzagged up the terraced slope on the other side. It was the most direct route back to the Rainbow House and a fairly easy climb; they would not have to rest or otherwise prolong their return. He shook his head impatiently, unwilling to have this end too quickly.

"When you last stayed here," he asked Micay when she turned back to him, "what was your favorite way to walk?"

Micay's dark eyes seemed to consider him for a moment. Then her eyes widened with interest, and she smiled slightly and pointed with her chin toward a narrow path that ran along this side of the river and led deeper into the valley.

"Will it take us to the Rainbow House?"

"Eventually . . . though not without some work. I wanted to be alone then. I did not go where it was easy for anyone to follow."

"I can use the work," Cusi said, and paused briefly to swallow. "That is, if you do not mind being alone with me."

"I do not mind," Micay said in a neutral tone. She bent to tighten the bindings on her sandals and roll up the bottom of her shift, precautions that required no explanation. There had been an unusually heavy rain the night before, and any path this low in the valley was bound to be muddy. The river, which was only about thirty feet wide here, was high in its banks, the water dark, swift, and flecked with debris.

Straightening up and turning without a word, Micay set off down the path at a pace that became more brisk as she learned to trust her footing. Cusi followed closely, noting that she was nearly as tall as he was, though much less thin. She wore a red head cloth doubled over on the back of her head, briefly confining the glossy black hair that then fanned out and hung to the middle of her back, obscuring the brilliant sunset-colored mantle around her shoulders. Her shift was tan with a faint red stripe, and the wide belt around her waist was the same red as her head cloth. The specks of reddish mud on her exposed ankles and calves seemed startlingly dark against her light skin, like spots of paint, or blood. Cusi felt a familiar stirring in his stomach, an uneasy mixture of excitement and misgiving that made him think again of Rimachi.

The terraces of the Lynx House were far behind them now, and the land on both sides of the river had grown increasingly steep and barren, dotted with thorny cacti and clumps of brush and bunch grass. Adroitly Micay picked her way past the places where the runoff had eroded the path or left deep puddles, moving quickly through the cold shadows where sunlight did not reach. Cusi reminded himself to watch his own feet, since admiring her gracefulness was no protection against an embarrassing tumble into the river.

She finally slowed and came to a halt on a flat-topped stone that had been set into the riverbank to form a crude landing. Three similar stones had been placed in a line across the river, their tops just visible above the water, which foamed and eddied around them. They seemed much too widely spaced for Micay to attempt in her shift, and while he once would have crossed in two swift hops, he now had to consider what the jolt of landing might do to his ribs.

"Do you intend to cross here?" he asked doubtfully, and Micay gave a small laugh.

"It is the best place. There are two more stones just under the water. You will see them when you are over them. Just be careful to put your foot down flat. Watch . . ."

Lifting her shift away from her legs, she stepped out onto the first stone and then out onto the rushing surface of the water, which flowed up over her foot but did not carry her away, apparently supporting her weight as she carefully swung her other foot up onto the second dry stone. Then she stepped down into the water again, up to the third stone, and onto the opposite bank. When she turned to look back, Cusi spread his hands and bowed, shaking his head in amazement. He stepped out onto the first dry stone and found that he could indeed see the next one under the water, though it took a certain amount of courage to trust its solidity in the face of the fiercely eddying current. The coldness of the water was a shock, numbing his toes in the instant it took to plant his foot and step up to the next stone. The second descent into the icy flow was less daunting, but he forced himself to be just as careful, having realized while watching her that it would be impossible to save her if she slipped. Micay laughed with a kind of relief when he hopped up onto the bank beside her.

"I did not realize how it looked," she explained. "I kept expecting you to sink, even though I knew the stones were there."

"I would never have tried it if I had not seen you do it first. You would make a good scout, my lady."

"I have had to find my own way many times," she said with a rueful smile. Then she turned to lead him up the path behind her. Small birds flitted through the undergrowth, which was dense near the river but thinned rapidly as they climbed laterally and switched back in the other direction. The path became less muddy but was interrupted more frequently by rock and mud slides. Micay had shortened her stride as the trail rose, but she approached the slides without much hesitation and her instinct for finding the best way around seemed unerring. Cusi found himself walking confidently in her footprints, grabbing onto the same exposed roots she used as handholds and left swaying behind her. It was clear now that she would be an able traveling companion for the journey to the coast, probably more able than he was himself.

The first twinge in his side came about when he expected it: just when his legs were feeling warm and loose and ready to be tested, just when his lungs needed to expand and give him more air. He ignored the pain for a while, trying not to breathe so loudly that Micay would hear him, but he knew he could not push himself for long. He had tried often enough in the past and had learned over and over again that some kinds of pain had to be obeyed.

"My lady . . ." he said finally, causing Micay to stop and look back. "I must rest."

He lowered himself to the ground, sitting with his knees up and his back against the hillside behind him. He made himself breathe slowly and evenly, and almost immediately the ache in his side began to diminish.

"Forgive me," Micay said, sitting down on a rock next to him. "I was not thinking."

"I will be fine in a moment," he assured her, mustering a smile to show her he meant it. "You are a strong walker, Micay. Stronger than some warriors."

"I was looking ahead to a place I wanted to visit."

"I am sorry to delay you," Cusi said, pulling his feet in under him. But Micay put a hand on his shoulder to keep him from rising.

"There is no rush. I assumed, when you suggested a different path, that you did not only want to *walk* with me."

"No," Cusi admitted, feeling his stomach stir. "We have not had a chance to speak since the feast."

"I know, and there is something I must tell you."

Cusi heard the note of apology in her voice and knew what was coming. He stared at her composed features and felt disappointment settle in his stomach like a stone, crushing all stirrings beneath it. He sighed and nodded for her to go on.

"It is a message Amaru gave me for you long ago, before he went to the coast."

Cusi blinked in surprise, still waiting to hear Rimachi's name.

"Amaru?" he repeated foolishly. "What did he tell you?"

"He said to tell you that he was proud of the man you had always been," Micay quoted. "He said you would understand what he meant."

Cusi was so confused that he understood nothing for a moment. But then the meaning of what she was saying penetrated, and he remembered the last time he had seen his brother. He remembered the arm Amaru had put around him, his attempt to intervene, his voice raised in argument after Cusi had been sent away. However he had changed, he had remained loyal to Cusi, as this message proved.

"I do understand," he said to Micay, "and I am grateful to you for telling me. It makes me even more certain that I am doing the right thing."

"I should have told you sooner, but there was never the right time."

"It helps me more to hear it now," he insisted. He smiled and shook his head at the memory of what he had expected to hear from her. "I was afraid, when you said you had something to tell me, that you had changed your mind about going to Chan Chan."

Micay squinted at him quizzically. "Is there a reason why I should?"

"No," Cusi said swiftly, "not at all. I want very much for you to go with us. It is only what my mother said . . . about Rimachi."

"I heard her before I made my choice."

"I knew he was an admirer of yours," Cusi went on, "but I did not know how serious. My father seems convinced you will marry him; he thinks Rimachi is the reason you did not go back to Chachapoyas with Acapana."

"He is wrong," Micay said bluntly. "I never spoke to Acapana about returning to Chachapoyas, and I have not spoken with Rimachi about marriage."

"And Amaru?" Cusi asked.

This time she hesitated, her eyes going past him. "Amaru used to tease all
of the ñustas."

"But he confided in you."

"Sometimes. He told me once that I heard him better than anyone else,
because I was like him. He said I should marry you, because you were not."

"I have made you angry," Cusi suggested, and she confirmed it by rising
abruptly and continuing up the trail. He pushed himself to his feet and went
after her, though a prudent regard for his tender ribs kept him from trying to
catch up with her immediately. He followed her around another switchback
and saw that they had reached the final segment of the path, a straight, steep
stretch that rose all the way to the ridgeline. Micay was climbing at an angry
pace, with her head down, so she did not see the break in the trail as soon as
he did. But she saw it just as he was readying himself to call out a warning,
and she was still standing at the edge, examining the slide, when he finally
caught up with her.

A boulder the size of a man had slid down from above, plowing a path down
through the rocks and scrub until it intersected with the man-made trail. It
was now lodged in the midst of a pile of rubble that covered the trail for a
distance of about ten feet. There was no way to walk around it, and one glance
at the eroded slope below told Cusi that any attempt in that direction would
send them sliding all the way to the river. The only alternative was to climb
over the top of the boulder and hope it did not slide out from under them. Or
they could go back the way they had come. Cusi looked at Micay, who had
been studying the position of the sun, a hand raised to shield her eyes.

"It will be dark on this side of the valley before we could get back to the
river," she said in a flat voice that seemed calculating rather than daunted. She
lowered her hand to look at him, and Cusi nodded.

"I do not think we could walk on the water in the dark. But we could look
for another place to cross, or we could build a shelter and . . ." Cusi trailed
off, realizing what he was suggesting just as the image of a warm, dark hut
stirred him from head to foot. He saw the color rise in her cheeks and did not
know if he should smile or look away, so he simply stared at her helplessly
until she turned and pointed with her chin at the slide.

"Or we could climb over the top of this. Do you think it will hold us?"

Cusi shook himself and stepped up beside her, poking at the dirt and rocks
piled up around the boulder with his toe.

"It should if we are careful. You must let me try first, my lady. If it begins
to slide, I can jump to safety."

"You might reinjure yourself," Micay objected, though it was more a warning than a protest.

He nodded and smiled grimly. "Perhaps, but I have done that just walking.

And I know that I am not meant to die here. Stay back in case I have to jump back this way."

Stripping off his sandals, he tied them into a bundle and tossed them over the pile, hearing them land on the path on the other side. Then he backed off a few steps, took a last look at Micay, and with a running start scrambled up to the top of the boulder, knocking a small avalanche of stones and dirt loose behind him. He paused briefly at the top to scan the way down, but suddenly the stone shifted under him and he went down on one knee. Out of the corner of his eye he saw rocks spray out into space and heard them land with a clatter far below. Then the boulder held, and he did not try to rise but sprang from a crouch, landing feet first in the rubble and springing again before the resulting slide could carry him away, finally skidding down through the loose dirt on his buttocks and coming to rest a few feet from where his sandals had landed.

He sat still for a few moments, his heart pounding too hard to let him feel anything else. Once his breathing returned to normal, he could feel the throb of a bruise on his knee and the dull ache that told him his ribs would be stiff and sore tomorrow, but nothing worse. A sudden elation made him get to his feet too quickly, but even that did not hurt him. He realized that he had not been afraid, he had not frozen even when the rock moved under him and he was aware of how far he could fall. He realized, as well, that he had been wondering about his own courage; waiting, without knowing he was doing so, for a chance to test it.

He walked forward to where a slight curve in the trail allowed him to see Micay on the other side of the pile. She raised a hand to her breast in relief, and he displayed himself to her, shaking his limbs and gesturing to indicate that he was not hurt. He smiled encouragingly, and though she did not smile back, she threw him a bundle that contained her sandals, mantle, and pin. She had already rolled her shift up past her knees.

"Go lightly and quickly," he called, "and do not hesitate at the top."

He saw her nod, though she was staring intently at the jumbled pile of dirt and stone, rocking back and forth on her heels. He was admiring her concentration when suddenly it occurred to him that this was an utterly foolish risk she was taking. She could be crippled or even killed, and for what? Ñustas did not have to prove their courage. He could tell her to wait while he went for men with ropes and torches. The embarrassment of that was nothing compared to the possible consequences of a bad fall.

But something kept him from calling out again, and it was not only the fear of breaking her concentration and actually causing her to fall. It was a sense that she would never forgive him for doubting her courage and judgment, for acting as if she did not understand the risk and had no right to take it. She clearly did not feel that she owed her life to anyone, at least not to any man. She has found her own way many times, Cusi reflected; perhaps that was what she needed to prove.

So instead he put a hand over his spirit brother and began to encourage her in his heart, calling upon Illapa and the power of the huaca to bring her safely to him. When he saw her start forward, he murmured a last prayer and went forward himself, positioning himself at the edge of the slide, where he would have a chance to catch her if she fell.

He heard the rattle of falling stones for what seemed like a long time, and then the top of Micay's head appeared above the stone, her black hair streaked with red dust. Slowly and methodically, she brought the rest of her body up onto the boulder, rising into a crouch that revealed the pale flesh of her thighs as she crab-walked across the top of the stone. The boulder had not moved, but the sound of the rocks and dirt leaking away below was constant, and Cusi wished she would stop hesitating and make her jump. But she continued to scan the rock-strewn slope that separated her from the path, looking up and down it as if she had all day to plan her descent. Then, to Cusi's utter astonishment, she stood up and stepped straight off the stone onto a narrow earthen ledge left when part of the hillside had fallen away in a chunk. Cusi had never taken the time to notice it before he felt compelled to jump, though now he could clearly see the path it made down the slope, above the pile of loose rubble. Micay came down it with the same lack of haste, alternately searching for roots to grasp and watching the placement of her feet, her free arm held out for balance. She came even with the place where Cusi had positioned himself before she had to abandon the ledge and come down through the remnants of the slide. There were no roots to grab onto now, and it would have been safest for both of them had she slid the rest of the way on her buttocks. But she stayed upright, her arms outspread and waving slightly to compensate for the incline, her eyes seeking out the next place to step. She slipped several times and gathered downward momentum as she righted herself, but she never lost her concentration or gave up control.

As she closed the distance between them, Cusi saw that he would have to check her momentum and turn her to the right or she would miss the path. He was tempted to wrap her in a congratulatory embrace and swing them both onto the path, but at the last moment he decided it was better to let her finish on her own. He braced himself and stretched out his right arm, his hand cocked back stiffly, angling his body so that she would either have to collide with him or turn to the right. Micay saw him and instinctively dug in with her back foot, swiveling her hips to avoid a collision. She also sighted in on his upraised hand and swung her arm toward it as she hurtled down on him. Their palms smacked together with a jolt Cusi could feel all the way down to his hips, and he saw her bounce off and whirl sideways, her arms held up over her head as if she were dancing. Still upright, she went several feet up the path before she could stop.

Cusi let out a triumphant shout and churned his way out of the pile of dirt and stones that had drifted up around his legs. She was still standing with her back to him, her shoulders rising and falling rapidly with her breathing. He paused to pick up his sandals and her bundle and then approached her respectfully, waiting until she turned to face him. Her cheeks were flushed and her eyes were wide and bright; she looked as elated as Cusi had felt when he had made it over. He smiled in recognition, and she laughed and clapped her hands, shaking her head in exhilarated disbelief.

"You were magnificent, my lady," he told her. "Now I have seen you walk on water and dance down a rockslide in the same day."

"I held myself steady," she said in a thrilled voice, gazing past him at the boulder. "I saw every step before I took it."

"And each one was right," Cusi agreed, seeing that she *had* proven something to herself. He handed her her bundle, which she simply tucked under her arm, her eyes scanning the slope as if she were memorizing every detail. Finally she looked at Cusi, regarding him rather dreamily.

"Shall we go on?"

"I will follow anywhere you lead, my lady," Cusi said, crossing his arms on his chest to bow. She smiled the same way she had at the sunset, a smile not meant for anyone else, and turned and started up the path at a pace that seemed almost languid. Her feet were bare and her shift was still rolled up around her knees, reminding Cusi of the glimpse he had seen of her thighs and of the warm, dark hut they might have shared. He let the thoughts stir him, but he had no regrets about what they had done instead. He had seen more of what was in her heart this way, and it had only made her more alluring. He walked behind her with his sandals in his hand, no longer worrying about Rimachi or Acapana or Amaru, feeling that he would be content to walk like this for as long as she wished. The journey to Chan Chan suddenly began to seem barely long enough.

XI

YUNCAS:
The Hotlands

The Royal Road

THEY HAD gone south from Tumibamba for two days, then turned west onto the road that crossed the mountains to the coast. The road had quickly become a narrow trail that wound its way around the snow-capped peaks, and for several days they had been climbing in and out of canyons and over cold, airless passes, following the paths of the rivers and streams that had their headwaters here. They had walked in single file most of the time, in a silence enforced by the danger of a misstep, and they had spent their nights crowded together in the mountain rest houses, which were often so small that the warriors had had to sleep outside on the ground.

Finally word was passed back from the head of the column that this was the last pass they would have to climb, and when Micay looked ahead, she could see an expanse of blue sky unsullied by either clouds or further peaks. She relayed the message to the woman behind her, one of two Inca wives whose husbands had recently been posted to Chan Chan. Both women were confeder-ates of Mama Huarcay and had treated Micay coldly from the outset, though the current news actually made the woman smile. She relayed the message over the heads of her children to the second wife, who in turn passed it back to the count takers and their families in the rear. Somewhere behind them were the rest of the warriors, and then Urcon with the pack train. The Callawaya healer, Hanp'atu, was probably back there, as well.

They were proceeding slowly now, one steep step at a time, and Micay could hear the harsh whistle of Mama Cori's breathing as the older woman struggled forward ahead of her. The air seemed very thin, and Micay was half winded herself, the blood pounding in her head. Then she could see the top of the rise, where each of the warriors paused for a moment before disappearing down the other side. Cusi was standing at the crest, saying something to each of the warriors as they passed, drawing smiles from several. He was holding a large stone in one hand and was flanked by Acunta, the Chimu guide.

"Rest, my mother, and look," he said to Mama Cori, drawing her aside with his free hand and pointing her toward the west. Mama Cori hung on his arm, breathing too hard to straighten up, and Cusi used the moment to look over her head and smile at Micay. He beckoned with his chin, rolling his eyes to indicate the view. Then she could see it for herself, and the sight momentarily distracted her from the problem of breathing.

"Mama Cocha," Cusi said solemnly. The land that stretched out from the foot of the mountain was low and rolling and brilliantly green, split by several slow, winding rivers. In the far distance the green seemed to stop abruptly, and beyond there was only blue, as if the sky had descended and swallowed up the land. Micay had to squint to make out the hazy shimmer that distinguished water from air, the air that covered everything and the water that went on forever. She could feel Cusi's excitement, the almost reverential pleasure he took in anything that was strange and wonderful, and she had to restrain herself from looking at him, aware that Mama Cori had recovered and was standing between them.

"It is so green," Mama Cori mused aloud. "But in the highlands the rains have barely begun."

Cusi turned toward Acunta, a man of perhaps fifty years whose thin lips and long, straight nose made him appear habitually reticent. Micay was always surprised by the ease and assurance with which he spoke, once his opinion had been asked.

"Mama Cocha flows in different directions, and sometimes she is warm, sometimes cold. This year she has brought her warm waters as far south as Tumbez, and with them come the rains. When that does not happen, the Valley of Tumbez is as dry as the valleys farther south, and without irrigation, nothing would grow."

Micay noticed the respect with which Cusi attended to the Chimu's words. He had been uncertain at first of their need for a guide, since the Royal Road was clearly marked and hospitality was assured by the fact that Cusi was traveling as the personal representative of the Sapa Inca. But she had seen Acunta grow on him, until Cusi was telling her that he had decided to cultivate the Chimu and exploit the man's knowledge of the coast. Micay thought it was Acunta who had done the cultivating, and expertly. He had not flattered or tried to ingratiate himself, maintaining a dignified reserve that had drawn Cusi to him out of curiosity. It was much the same way Micay herself would have set out to attract Cusi's interest, if she had had to.

"Let us go down," Cusi suggested, pointing out a gap in the line created by one of the count takers, who was waiting for his wife and children to catch up. Cusi went first, curling his stone up against his chest and extending his other arm behind him to help his mother. Acunta stepped back and made a slight bow, cocking his head to indicate that Micay should precede him, a gesture that made his silver eartubes flash in the sunlight.

Micay returned the bow and went down the path after Mama Cori, aware that Acunta had fallen in behind her. There was nothing particularly sinister about him, and she did not see how his explanations could do Cusi any harm, even if they were lies. But she could not read the man's eyes, and again she remembered Rimachi telling her that Cusi was naive in many ways and that he expected too much honesty from too many people. Neither she nor Rimachi had suspected at the time that she might find such a quality attractive, but it made her want to watch Cusi's back for him.

So she would keep a wary eye on this Acunta, who claimed not to know Amaru and had simply been available for this journey, having recently guided another procession to Tumibamba. She heard his footsteps behind her and thought of his hard, wiry legs and leathery feet, which proved at least that he was a strong walker and had probably been to all the places he spoke of. Beyond that, she would have to see for herself. But she was a strong walker, too, and she would keep her eyes open all the way to Chan Chan.

CUSI BLINKED and squinted and shaded his eyes with his free hand. That had to be Urcon in among the llamas, but he should have been able to see him clearly at this distance. Cusi reached into the fringed bag under his arm and added another pinch of powdered coca to the wad in his cheek. He felt drowsy and sluggish, and he was sweating profusely inside his cumbi-cloth tunic. They would be arriving in Tumbez by midday, and he had to look the part of the Inca's representative, no matter how warm and humid it was in this valley. He heard parrots squawking in the trees as he walked toward the corral and felt for a moment that he was back in Chachapoyas, which quickened his nerves more effectively than the coca did.

Urcon was inside the corral, loading the llamas with the help of Hanp'atu, who was unencumbered by his usual bundles and bags of medicines. They were accomplishing their task with quiet efficiency, Urcon calming the llamas and holding them steady while Hanp'atu balanced and secured the cloth packs that hung down on both sides of the beasts, joined by a broad woven strap that went across the llama's back. There was none of the shying and spitting that had occurred often during the first days of the journey, when Urcon was still getting to know the herd. They know him now, Cusi thought admiringly, waiting by the fence for them to finish. One of the loaded llamas wandered over to him, and Cusi took the wad of coca out of his mouth and held it out to the animal, which sniffed at it briefly, then lapped it out of Cusi's hand with one swipe of its tongue. It chewed for a moment, its long jaw swiveling sideways, then saw there was nothing more in Cusi's outstretched hand and trotted away.

Urcon came over with a smile that seemed brighter—or at least more relaxed—than it had in days. Cusi noticed that he had removed his knit cap and changed into a cotton tunic that looked light and cool.

"You have won their trust," Cusi praised him, nodding toward the llamas. Urcon shrugged and shook his head, though his smile remained in place.

"It was not that. They are not mountain llamas, they were raised on the coast. They were not happy in the highlands, but they are at home now. A flat land feels right to them."

"It does not agree with me," Cusi said, nodding in greeting as Hanp'atu joined them. "I do not feel right, and I cannot see as well as I should."

Urcon and Hanp'atu exchanged a knowing glance, and Urcon laughed and gestured for the Callawaya to explain.

"What you feel is normal, and there is nothing wrong with your eyes. The air here is thicker, heavy with dampness and dust. It is harder to see through, and your lungs will have to get used to breathing it. But it will not hurt you."

"You should wear a lighter tunic," Urcon advised.

Cusi shrugged, wiping at the sweat on his forehead. "I have to meet the governor and the chiefs of Tumbez later, and it is enough that they will find me young and inexperienced at making speeches. I must do something to impress them."

"They will be impressed to meet Cusi Huaman," Urcon pointed out, "whatever he is wearing."

Cusi hesitated, but only because the solution seemed too simple for him to have overlooked. He realized again that he was still not comfortable at the head of the column.

"You are right," he said, and he peeled his tunic off over his head. "I let myself get nervous and forgot why Huayna Capac chose to make me his representative. Do you have another cotton tunic?"

Urcon nodded and went back into the herd, searching for the right pack. Cusi looked at Hanp'atu, who had begun to attach his bags and bundles to various parts of his body. He had to remind himself that this man was also his subordinate, dependent on him for permission to travel.

"Are there people you wish to see in Tumbez?" he asked. When Hanp'atu nodded, he went on, "Once we are quartered, you may go wherever you wish. I hope to leave at dawn on the third day."

"I am grateful, Lord Cusi. I will give you no reason to regret your trust."

"I am sure. Perhaps, when there is time, you would be willing to share some of your knowledge with the ñusta Micay. She is training to be a healer."

"I would share with her," Hanp'atu agreed, nodding his head for emphasis. "She was the one who brought us to you the first time."

"I thought it was Tomay," Cusi said in surprise.

"Him, too. But she was the first to see us."

Urcon returned and passed a pale blue tunic over the cane fence. It felt like nothing in Cusi's hands as he slipped it on over his head. He smiled and rolled up his own tunic, displaying it to them.

"I will save this for later, when it is truly needed."

"Where is your stone?" Urcon asked teasingly. "Surely you will want to have it with you when you meet the chiefs."

"I left it with Micay," Cusi said, and saw Urcon's eyes widen with a kind of gleeful recognition. Urcon glanced sideways at Hanp'atu, trying very hard not to smile.

"What?" Cusi demanded. "Have I been so obvious?"

Urcon shrugged innocently. "The warriors are impressed with how often you check on the back of the column. They think you are a very careful commander, like Ninan Cuyochi. Or perhaps simply concerned about your mother."

"But you think otherwise," Cusi prompted, not really displeased that his friend had seen.

"I was with you at the Rainbow House after your mother and Micay went back to Tumibamba. I did not think it was your mother you were missing so much."

"No," Cusi admitted. "Though it is better if my mother thinks it is her I have come to check on."

Urcon shrugged again and nodded in compliance, though his eyes showed some puzzlement at the need for such secrecy. Cusi did not feel compelled to explain, since he doubted he could deceive his mother for much longer—if, in fact, he had deceived her this far. He tucked his rolled-up tunic under his arm and nodded to them in parting.

"I will see you in Tumbez, my friends. Then we can begin to unload some of those gifts your llamas carry."

THE DAY had finally begun to cool, and she had found the coolest spot near the corral, a place that was in the shade of an adjacent building and in the path of a breeze that had a slightly salty smell. She had draped her mantle over the top of the cane fence, and she leaned her elbows on it as she talked to Urcon, who was trimming the excess wool from the coats of his llamas. He could not shear them, he had explained, because the packs would chafe against their skin, but he wanted to make them as comfortable as possible. He worked in a crouch, his hands and arms shiny with grease and his feet buried in a pile of wool.

"Did Cusi keep his stone with him?" he asked, glancing up at her.

Micay laughed. "Mama Cori was furious with him about that, especially after he changed his tunic in full view of the honor guard. But he did not try to hide the stone, and of course it drew the interest of everyone who was there. So instead of giving a speech, he told the story about how his grandfather gave him a battle-ax to carry to make him strong, and how he had to make himself strong again, though his wound would not permit him to carry anything so heavy."

"I have the ax with Cusi's things," Urcon told her. "Did they like his story?"

"I do not think they had ever heard an Inca speak to them like that. Even the governor seemed amazed. But it made them forget their fear about saying the wrong thing, and they liked Cusi for that. It became a great joke among the chiefs to ask him if they could examine his 'weapon.' "

Urcon grunted and laughed, startling the animals around him, so that they put their ears back and shyed away from him. He stood up, holding a bronze knife in one greasy hand and using the other to brush at the swatches of wool that clung to his sweaty body. He looked badly in need of a bath, a condition Micay felt she shared, even though it did not show as plainly. She had had to draw heavily on her composure to get through the ceremonies of greeting without wilting openly. At one point she had gazed out over the painted walls of the compound and had seen the tops of palm trees, which had aroused a wistful memory of Chachapoyas and the light, gauzy garments she used to wear there. She had allowed the memory to linger, using it to distract herself from the suffocating closeness of the air.

But now she needed a cool bath, and it seemed pointless to wait any longer in the hope that Cusi would appear. He was as famous here as he had been in Tumibamba, and he was trying harder to attend to those who wanted to meet him. She sighed, straightened up from the fence, and was reaching for her mantle when Urcon suddenly turned and smiled in welcome. Cusi was crossing the courtyard toward the corral, and when he saw the two of them together, he let out a Campa whoop and trotted the rest of the way, cradling his stone in the crook of one arm. He set the stone down on top of a fence post with an emphatic thump, then unslung his coca bag and looped it over the same post. His richly colored tunic was plastered limply against his body, as if he had been caught in a downpour, and he grunted with effort as he pulled it off over his head, revealing the livid white scar on his side. He slung the tunic over the top of the fence with a wet slap, appearing wild-eyed with relief.

"I promised myself," he said breathlessly, "that when all the greeting was over, I would go to the shore of Mama Cocha and bathe in her waters. Will you go with me?"

"Now? The feast—"

"I am told it is not far; we can be back in time for the feast. Come, we will not need our sandals."

"We cannot go barefoot through the streets of Tumbez," Micay protested weakly, even as she bent to untie her sandals. Cusi took off his headband and hung it around the post; his black hair stuck up in spiky tufts on either side of the flattened ring around his forehead.

"We can go barefoot to Mama Cocha," he declared, sounding both reckless and resolute. He suddenly held out his hands to her. "Come, please. I have obeyed all the protocols today. I have earned the right to satisfy myself, and so have you."

Micay nodded and took his hands, surrendering to his enthusiasm despite her better judgment, which told her that Mama Cori would blame *her* if this led to a scandal. Cusi rewarded her with a big smile, squeezing her fingers and pulling her toward him as if to embrace her. But he held back at the last moment, bracing her on his cocked wrists and looking into her eyes with their faces close, so that she could see how much he wanted to embrace her.

"Urcon!" he said as he released her, and Urcon hopped the fence and fell in on her other side as Cusi led them toward a servants' entrance at the rear of the compound. Once out in the street, they turned right and headed west toward the setting sun, which hung in the sky like a ripe red fruit. Their presence was noticed almost immediately, probably because Cusi had not removed his golden earplugs, which seemed even more conspicuous without the usual accompanying regalia. People stopped in the street to watch them pass, and a group of young boys began to follow them at a discreet distance, with a few of the bravest darting up for brief, closer looks. Micay could barely imagine what they must think of an Inca warrior who seemed so small and frail, his ribs showing as prominently as his scar, walking through their city clad only in a loincloth, accompanied by a herder and a ñusta with bare feet and no mantle. She did not want to imagine what it would sound like when it finally reached Mama Cori's ears.

Cusi had seemed utterly oblivious of the attention they were drawing, but suddenly he turned his head and looked past Micay, catching the eye of a boy who had just come abreast of them.

"We are going to Mama Cocha," he announced with solemn assurance, nodding to the boy as if certain that he would understand and approve. The boy seemed to, nodding vigorously and calling back "Mama Cocha! Mama Cocha!" to his friends, before eagerly running down the street ahead of them. The name of Mama Cocha came back to them in echoes and murmured greetings, and people began to appear in doorways and side streets, some looking puzzled and suspicious but most smiling and bowing to this young Inca lord, this son of Inti, who was going in so humble a fashion to visit Mama Cocha. Micay found that the three of them had adopted an almost stately pace, and she realized that what had begun as a reckless, self-satisfying adventure would likely become, in the retelling, a kind of personal pilgrimage that had brought honor to the people of Tumbez—and added a generous luster to the reputation of Cusi Huaman. She glanced sideways at him, and he gave a slight shrug, as if he knew what she were thinking.

"I did not plan this. I only knew that they have a high regard for Mama Cocha."

"Your mother will still think this is scandalous."

"She will also see how it pleases our hosts. They have been telling me all afternoon how I must see the great foaming waters. Now they will know how well I listened."

"You are not as naive as some people think," Micay said cryptically. Cusi gave a short laugh but did not ask her whom she meant.

Following the boys, they turned left onto a side street that led them out onto the long pontoon bridge that spanned the Tumbez River. To their right, the river broke into several strands that spread out over the floodplain, cutting winding channels through the banks of silt deposited in the past. The water was glazed red by the low, slanting rays of the sun, and hundreds of water birds wheeled and dived through the glaring light. They could hear the rumbling murmur of Mama Cocha, though the shoreline itself was shrouded in mist. The breeze blowing upriver was moist and smelled of fish.

There were only a few buildings on the south side of the river, and then they were skirting an expanse of marshy land where totora reeds grew up over their heads and tall white birds waded delicately through pools of standing water. The boys accompanying them had gradually begun to fall away, either out of respect or because sunset was very near. Cusi spoke to the last two, asking their names and telling them his, making them feel important before sending them back the way they had come.

The three of them went on alone, walking blindly into the light so that they almost stumbled into the first of the sunken gardens they came on. The long rectangular plots had been dug out of the soft soil at the edges of the marsh, and neat rows of crops were already sprouting, watered by seepage from below. The earth that had been excavated when the plots were dug had been piled up to form dikes along both of the long sides, and these provided a solid, level path through the maze of adjoining gardens. The whole area smelled power- fully of the guano and fish heads that had been used as fertilizer, a stench that seemed to hang in the air despite the breeze, forcing them to breathe through their mouths until they climbed down off the last dike.

Now there was sand beneath their feet, still warm despite the waning of the sun's heat, and they could see the expanse of golden water in front of them, stretching north, south, and west for as far as they could see. It rippled and swelled in intricate patterns as it rushed toward the shore, surging up into ridges of foaming white that suddenly collapsed with a breathy roar, spewing forward and then sliding back into the path of the next wave. The three of them had abandoned their stately pace and were loping across the shell-strewn sand, Cusi hugging his elbows in against his sides, holding himself back, Urcon running easily with his head back and his mouth open to the breeze, Micay holding her shift doubled up past her thighs, running as no ñusta was ever supposed to run, for the sheer pleasure of it. The sand became hard, then wet, and they were running down the gentle slope toward the crashing water, going too fast to stop, Cusi whooping and Micay laughing wildly as they splashed through a gauzy sheet of rolling water and saw the ridge form and crest in front of them, throwing out a wave that hit them waist high.

Micay instinctively pulled back at the impact, and she floated up off her feet for a moment, her shift billowing up around her like a tent as the water surged up between her legs, surprisingly warm and soothing after the initial shock. Her feet sank back down into the soft sand and she regained her balance just in time to see Cusi charge headlong into a cresting wave, which picked him up and threw him over backwards like a piece of driftwood, washing him back up onto the shore. Micay sloshed sideways through the knee-deep water, pausing to brace herself against a wave that broke against her thighs and threw water up onto her face and hair. By the time she got to Cusi he was up on his knees, laughing and spitting and wiping water out of his eyes. He turned his head to let the end of another wave wash over him, then struggled up to his feet.

"Now we can say we gave ourselves to Mama Cocha," he said with a grin, almost shouting to be heard above the sound of the surf.

"Yes, and she threw you back," Micay laughed, and Cusi rolled his eyes and shook his head in agreement. They turned to look for Urcon and spotted him farther down the beach, sitting cross-legged at a point where the water rolled right into his lap and slid by him without making a splash. He was staring out over the water with a smile on his face. The sun was half gone and seemed to be pulling in its light as it sank, so that the air was suddenly clear and empty of color. Micay saw that the water was a deep greenish-blue, and for the first time she noticed the tiny gray shore birds that scooted along the edges of the incoming waves and the gulls that hung in the air farther out, their wings arched to hold the breeze. Cusi reached over and gently plucked a strand of seaweed from her hair, letting his hand linger, touching her neck and bare shoulder.

"I was slow to see you, Micay. Now I cannot see anyone else."

"Not even Tocto Oxica?" Micay suggested.

He paused for a moment and drew a slow breath. Then he shook his head decisively. "Only in memory. I have stopped grieving for what was denied me. I stopped the day you came to watch the sunset with me."

"Am I your consolation, then?"

"You are much more than that," Cusi insisted. He gestured toward the narrow band around his waist. "Even when I was in Cuzco, and did not know you existed, you touched my life. Yes, Tomay told me that you wove this for me, and Hanp'atu told me that you were responsible for bringing him to heal me. There have been many signs, once I was able to see them, and they all tell me that you are the one Raurau Illa sang of: the condor who watches tirelessly, with eyes that pierce the darkness."

Micay remembered her dream and shivered, unsettled by the prospect of being the object of a prophecy uttered long ago by a blind man who lived far from both Chachapoyas and Tumibamba. Yet she could still see the condor soaring down the valley, and she knew that watchfulness was one of her deepest traits, learned first in the House of Chosen Women and perfected among the Incas.

"I have felt that distant, that lonely," she murmured plaintively, and she felt Cusi's hands on her shoulders, drawing her toward him. She shuddered slightly as their wet bodies touched, and he held back for a moment, his fingers splayed out across her back, then gave a shudder of his own and pressed himself against her, wrapping his arms tightly around her. They molded together with an ease that astonished her and made her realize that Rimachi had always been too large for her. They had never fit together like this, so perfectly that neither had any desire to move. She was dimly aware of the warm water swirling around their ankles, of darkness falling around them, of the breeze on her wet back. Her cheek was pressed against Cusi's, so she felt him forming words before he spoke.

"Urcon is coming," he said in a resigned voice. "It is dark."

Reluctantly he released her from the embrace, keeping his hands on her shoulders when she wobbled dizzily. His features were indistinct except for the white gleam of his smile.

"I will watch over you, too," he promised. "I will not let you be lonely again."

Urcon had stopped at a discreet distance, and when Cusi turned and nodded to him he started off ahead of them without a word, leading the way up onto the dry sand. As they went to follow, Cusi took Micay's hand and held on to it, a gesture that warmed her and made her realize she was not dreaming this. She glanced back over her shoulder and saw the waves still coming in, their white crests glowing in the darkness before being extinguished on the shore. She squeezed Cusi's fingers, trusting in his promise as much as her watchful heart would allow and offering a silent prayer of gratitude to Mama Cocha for sending him back to make it.

The Royal Road

IMMEDIATELY SOUTH of the valley of Tumbez, the land became flat and arid, a sandy, brush-dotted plain that separated the waters of Mama Cocha from the mountains to the east. Unimpeded by hills or rivers, the Royal Road ran straight across the center of the plain, well inland from the shore and seldom more than a half day's march from the foothills of the mountains. The road was smooth and well maintained, flanked by low walls that kept back the drifting sand, and it was wide enough to permit Cusi's party to travel in a compact group, while leaving room on both sides for the passage of post runners. The messengers were often the only other people they would see, for there were no settlements on the plain, and the rest houses where they spent the nights were up in the foothills. The walking was easy but the landscape was monotonously barren, supporting only stunted shrubs and an occasional cactus. The travelers recognized their progress by the changing colors of the sand and used oddly shaped dunes as landmarks, knowing that the wind would wipe them away after they passed.

It took three days for them to reach Sullana, the first river valley south of Tumbez, and each day was a replica of the one before. They would rise and set out in a drifting fog, with gray clouds hanging low overhead and the air filled with a fine mist that somehow left no trace of moisture on the skin. The clouds would begin to lift around midday, but it would be warm even before that, and if the clouds broke sufficiently to reveal the blue of the sky, the sun's heat could be quite intense, reflecting off the road in shimmering waves. The afternoons were bright and dry, with a gritty wind blowing in their faces and no doubt in their minds as to why this land was called Yuncas, or the hotlands.

They arrived outside Sullana late on the third day, footsore and covered with dust, squinting from the glare and the blowing sand, feeling parched in all their senses. Despite Acunta's assurances, Cusi was not certain they had arrived anywhere until the road began to rise ahead of them and he could see gulls circling in the sky along with the ubiquitous vultures. Then large cacti and gnarled algaroba trees appeared at the side of the road, and Cusi found himself climbing, a form of exertion his legs had almost forgotten. The incline was modest, and he and the warriors with him took it eagerly, opening distance between themselves and those behind. When they topped the rise, though, they all stopped and stared, even though Cusi had given no command to halt.

The road ahead was lined on both sides with fruit trees, and it descended in sections into a valley that seemed impossibly lush and green. Cusi hefted his stone and gazed toward the east, where the river cut its way down from the mountains. Houses with brightly painted walls and peaked roofs of reed thatch lined the high slopes, and all of the land below was planted with maize and cotton and other less familiar crops, the fields threaded together by an elaborate system of canals and irrigation ditches. Cusi thought of his own fields, which he had helped to break and plant before he left the Rainbow House but which would still be waiting for the onset of the rainy season. The crops here seemed well advanced in their growth, their leaves an emerald green that was almost painful to his eyes.

"Have the rains come here, as well?" Cusi asked when he realized that Acunta was standing beside him. The rest of the group had come up around them and spread out across the road, murmuring and shaking their heads as they stared down into the valley.

"It never rains here," Acunta told him. "But there is always water in the river, and none of it is wasted. That is how people have been able to live on the coast. There is no life outside the river valleys."

"So I have seen," Cusi muttered, brushing the dust from the front of his cotton tunic, a gift from the governor of Tumbez. He saw a delegation coming up the road toward him, so he stepped out in front of the group and began to wave them back into their ranks. Micay appeared with Mama Cori just behind her, but instead of returning his smile, she cast a significant glance at his head, reminding him of the headdress Acunta had given him earlier in the day. It was a stiff, flat-topped cylinder of cloth that fit snugly around his forehead, with a loose flap hanging down behind to cover the back of his neck, a typical Chimu headdress. Cusi had immediately appreciated the way it protected his head from the sun, and then he had grown so used to it that he had forgotten he had it on.

He snatched it off his head with his free hand and handed it to Micay, though not swiftly enough to prevent his mother from witnessing the act. Acunta was also watching, his narrow face impassive, and Cusi felt his cheeks warm with embarrassment. He wanted to apologize to Micay for not heeding her warning about Acunta, but he also felt a defiant urge to take the headdress back and show his mother that he would not be bound like a prisoner by custom.

He did neither, simply nodding gratefully to Micay and turning back to await the advancing delegation. He again saw the trees and the green fields separated by ribbons of bright water, but it still did not seem real to him after the barren emptiness of the plain. What a strange land this is, he thought, beginning to reconsider everything Acunta had told him, searching for the path he had been following without knowing he was being led.

Piura

THE SUN TEMPLE built by the Inca was situated on a high ridge on the northern side of the valley, overlooking the larger of the two rivers that watered the valley. Climbing up to it, Micay had been struck by the prominence of its site, which could be seen from everywhere. As she and Mama Cori were leaving, however, she was struck more powerfully by its isolation. It was far from the fields and no houses had been built nearby, and not a single person had come to visit the mamacona during the whole time Micay and Mama Cori had been there. It was further proof of what Micay had begun to learn in Tumbez, that the coastal tribes gave their primary devotion to Mama Cocha and the Moon Mother, whom the Chimu called Si. The people of Piura had accepted Inti's temple into their midst, and they worked the fields that supported his cult, but they showed him no more reverence than was required.

They had gone only a short distance down the path, out of sight of the temple, when Mama Cori stopped next to a rough stone wall and let out a sigh that was almost a groan. Micay was not surprised, since she had felt the older woman holding back her impatience during the latter stages of the audience. She had been gracious enough but not genuinely sympathetic to the loneliness of the mamacona and their desire for more encouragement and support from Tumibamba. She had acted as if her being there, bearing the Coya's gifts and blessing, should have been encouragement enough.

"You must wonder why I asked to be the Coya's representative," Mama Cori suggested, "when I no longer have the patience for this kind of duty."

"I assumed you wished a reconciliation with Rahua Ocllo, my lady, and a chance to resume your place in the court."

"I could have had both without *this*," Mama Cori said scornfully, lifting her chin toward the temple behind them. "This will only give her another reason to restore me to favor."

"You want something more from her, then," Micay ventured.

Mama Cori gave her a cool smile that somehow made the suggestion seem crude, yet exactly what she had expected from Micay. "Perhaps. Primarily I did it to protect myself from Amaru's reputation. I did not want to be regarded simply as a mother come to save her renegade son—a person who might be treated with a disrespect meant for him."

Micay nodded wordlessly, understanding that Mama Cori had finally decided to talk to her after twenty days of sharing quarters but speaking only of practical matters. No doubt she had been provoked by the amount of time Cusi had begun to spend talking to her. Micay told herself to be very careful, knowing that Mama Cori had much more power than Cusi wanted to believe.

"It will also help," Mama Cori went on, "if we have to exert pressure in order to free Amaru from his captivity. The governor will have to listen to me as well as Cusi. Once we get Amaru back to Tumibamba or Quito, then perhaps the Coya's favor will be useful, if we are to have any hope of finding him a suitable wife."

Micay opened and closed her mouth, deciding not to add that being Cusi Huaman's brother would not hurt Amaru's prospects, either. It might seem like a taunt, and she was certain that Mama Cori would get to Cusi soon enough on her own.

"I have not entirely given up on Quinti, either," Mama Cori declared, giving Micay a challenging look. "She is drifting toward the mamacona, but she has changed her course often enough in the past, and always without warning. She could grow tired of prayer and change again. Her reputation would also have to be overcome, but it could be done." Mama Cori paused, the challenge in her eyes becoming stern, almost a threat. "Then there is my youngest, my Joyful Hawk—so famous that the Sapa Inca offered him any woman he wanted, and so impetuous that he asked for the Sapa Inca's own daughter. That has only added to his reputation, of course, and made him more desirable as a husband. I was glad that Huayna Capac went north before Cusi was strong enough to visit the court. He would have been overwhelmed by the attentions of the ñustas and their mothers and sponsors. He is used to being flattered, but not at the hands of the most beautiful women in the Four Quarters. His head might have been turned, and he might have pledged himself to a wife who did not have the blood or breeding to share the high rank that will be his."

Micay nodded again, knowing better than to try to speak for Cusi or defend her own qualifications as a wife. Irritation flashed across Mama Cori's face, and she pointed at Micay with her chin.

"And you, my daughter. Apparently Acapana was not good enough for you, or perhaps you had already lived in the household of a micho and were looking higher. I had thought Rimachi might suit your ambitions perfectly. He is not an Inca, but he will rise as a warrior and you would always be close to the court and to the high priestess. I was surprised, as I am sure he will be, by how easily you discarded his affections."

"A young heart changes," Micay said evenly, quoting a sentiment she had first heard in the House of Chosen Women. "I made no promises to Rimachi."

"He might think otherwise. He might expect at least that you would not throw yourself at his closest friend, his brother. No doubt he will blame Cusi and their friendship will be destroyed. That would be a fine marriage gift!"

Micay stared back at her stubbornly, feeling a kind of relief that she had finally been accused. "I have never thrown myself at anyone."

"As always, you did it slyly. I saw the way you insinuated yourself with him, encouraging him to be willful and careless, just as you did with Amaru. For a short time I thought that it was Amaru you were after, but now I see he is not good enough for you, either. You will not be satisfied until you have ruined Cusi's life."

"You have often been wrong about me, my lady," Micay said coldly, "but never more wrong than you are at this moment."

"This ridiculous courtship is wrong, and it must stop! It must, Micay, you have to see that it is impossible . . ." Mama Cori trailed off, panting for breath, her face livid with urgency. She clasped her hands together under her chin and shook them as she spoke. "Listen to me, Micay. Do not do something you will regret for the rest of your life. I will arrange a good marriage for you, with Rimachi or anyone else you want. You will have land of your own and servants, and you will be the first wife, the one whose place cannot be taken. I promise you I will see to that, even if the man is an Inca of high blood. And you will always have my respect, and my favor . . ."

Micay turned away, looking out over the valley without seeing anything. She felt close to tears, though she was not certain whether it was anger or sorrow that moved her. An iridescent blue dragonfly hovered in front of her, suspended on invisible wings, and she watched it for a moment, feeling weightless herself. Then she looked back at Mama Cori, who was regarding her with a dreadful kind of earnestness.

"To earn your favor, then," Micay said slowly, "I must accept that I am unworthy of your son." She waited until Mama Cori nodded reluctantly in agreement before going on. "Then I would also have to accept that all the women who have trained me and tried to shape my character have failed. That *you* have failed most of all, since you taught me more than anyone else."

"Believe what you must," Mama Cori began, but Micay cut her off abruptly.

"I do *not* believe it. Nor do you, my lady. If you did, you would have gone to Cusi first and tried to convince *him* that I was unworthy."

"He will hear me when the time comes."

"He knows you do not trust me. But he will still expect you to speak the truth."

"I should have known you would defy me," Mama Cori said in disgust. She dropped her hands and brushed past Micay, starting down the path by herself. But then she turned and looked back, her jaw clenched with determination. "He is my son, Micay. You will never have him. Never."

We will have each other, Micay thought defiantly, but she did not say it aloud, she did not shout it at Mama Cori's retreating back as she wished to. It seemed too fragile a thing to trust to the air or to anyone's ears except Cusi's. So she kept it to herself and began to follow Mama Cori at a discreet distance, feeling the same peculiar sort of relief she had felt earlier. Defiance and distrust had characterized their relationship from the beginning, as if they had been drawn together only to collide, time after time. But this had to be the end, the final act of defiance, and she hoped that this time, at last, she would not have to act alone.

SOUTH OF Piura was the Sechura Desert, a vast lake of sand where there was no water at all and no protection from the dust storms that sent waves of sand rippling across the plain. The Royal Road went east, making a long circle around the desert that added several days to the journey. But the terrain was more varied and interesting as they climbed in and out of the foothills, and they saw more people, and wild creatures other than lizards and vultures. The morning fog collected against the hills, condensing like dew and producing a band of vegetation that looked like a green banner stretched across the sides of the yellow-gray hills. They passed herds of llamas and alpacas that had been brought down from the mountains to graze on the short, tender grasses that appeared only in this season.

On their third day out of Piura, early in the afternoon, they came upon a shallow swale that opened out between two low hills. They were below the elevation where the fog condensed, but the swale was thickly carpeted with grass and wildflowers of many colors. It looked like a mountain meadow at the height of the rainy season, yet the hills on both sides were completely barren.

"The rain has come here," Acunta explained as Cusi halted the column. "Probably for the first time in years. But the desert is always ready to bloom."

It was nearly time for the next rest, so Cusi gave the signal and the whole column immediately moved toward the meadow, the children running out ahead and squealing when they felt the grass beneath their feet.

"Be sure to drink," Cusi reminded the warriors nearest him, making sure they passed the word. "The desert is still all around us."

He stayed on the road until it was empty and he could see that no one was coming in either direction, except for a lone messenger far behind. Then he followed his people into the meadow, which was not as thickly covered as it had at first appeared, though still a miracle to the eye. He found a patch of grass that had not been too thoroughly trampled and sat down on it, dropping his stone onto the ground beside him. He wiggled his toes against the slender blades of grass and reached out to pluck a reddish-gold flower, which came out of the earth without resistance. Past a cluster of warriors who were lolling in the grass, toasting each other with their water gourds, he could see Micay stooping next to Hanp'atu, who had deposited his bundles in a pile around his long legs. They straightened up at the same time, each with a handful of flowers, which they held out to each other like offerings. They began to talk without looking into each other's faces, their heads bent over the flowers, occasionally pointing at one or another of them.

It took him another moment to locate his mother, who was sitting by herself on the other side of the swale, part of the way up the hill. Her water gourd was in her lap and she was twisting grass around the fingers of one hand, staring vaguely in Micay's direction but not appearing to be watching her. He wondered when she would decide to talk to him and what she would have to say. Micay had waited two days before telling him about their conversation, and two more days had passed in silence since then. He had wanted to confront her immediately, but Micay would not permit it. She had her own history with Mama Cori, much of which he did not know, so she would not allow him to be outraged on her behalf. He was still waiting for the chance to be outraged on his own.

Acunta cleared his throat and squatted down next to him, holding a rolled piece of leather in his hands. Cusi had been aware of his presence for some time but had been ignoring it.

"Perhaps you would like to examine the map, my lord," Acunta said tentatively, offering the roll. Cusi ignored that, too, twirling the flower between his fingers so that it turned from gold to red to gold again.

"I examined the map last night, and I have not forgotten what I learned. In four days we will be in Motupe, where the ancestral lands of the Chimus begin. After that is Apurle, where we will see some of the huacas built by the Mochicas in ancient times." Cusi put on the obliging face of an especially earnest student. "Would you like me to name the rivers and valleys that come after the Motupe?"

Acunta swallowed and stared down at the grass between his feet, his fingers unconsciously rolling the map tighter.

"I have offended you, my lord," he said in a low voice. Cusi had to take a moment to compose himself, because he was angrier than he had known and he did not want to let his anger speak for him. He had not meant to mock the man, but he had not been able to stop himself once he started. He dropped the flower and picked up his stone, feeling a twinge of strain in his side.

"I am young for my rank," he said to Acunta, "so I must learn from those who serve under me. That is why I let you teach me all that you have. I knew you wanted me to think well of your people, but I did not think you would try to take advantage of my youth. You should not have offered me Chimu clothing, even to escape the heat. It is too soon for me to pay such an honor to your people, and you knew it."

"It was premature," Acunta admitted, "and no doubt presumptuous. But it was not your youth that made me bold. It was the fact that you have been generous with your respect in all of the places we have stopped, more generous than any other Inca I have served. You must forgive me if I was jealous and eager to have you show the same respect to my people."

Cusi gave him a hard look, feeling flattered despite himself, which only made him more suspicious. But the Chimu met his gaze and held it steadily, as if he wanted to be believed even at the risk of insolence. He had never felt to Cusi like a man who needed to flatter or lie, though suddenly it occurred to Cusi that he ought to test his perception.

"Am I more generous than my brother?" he asked abruptly, catching

Acunta by surprise and making him blink. But he did not jerk his eyes away or try to feign innocence. Finally his lips parted in a thin smile and he nodded in resignation.

"Perhaps. I have only met your brother once."

"You claimed not to know him at all."

"I was told to say that. But I was also told to reveal myself if you became suspicious. It was not my task to spy on you in secret."

"What *was* your task, then?"

"To guide you and to teach you about the Chimu if I could. To see if you were a man of reason or a man of force." Acunta paused and again met Cusi's eyes. "I will report that you are both, and clever enough to trap me in my pride, as well."

"Report to whom?" Cusi demanded, shaking his head at the flattery. "Who gave you this task?"

"Men who are close to your brother. I was sent with his consent."

"That does not answer my question. What men? And what do they have to do with my brother?"

"I was asked not to say, my lord, by your brother himself. He asked that you save your questions for him. He awaits your arrival in Chan Chan."

"Why Chan Chan?" Cusi persisted, despite the man's smoothness in evading him. "You told me yourself that the governor and the court of the Grand Chimu are in Chiquitoy. Why is he not there?"

"He is the chief of building," Acunta said simply. "He is supervising projects in the Chimor Valley."

Cusi drew a breath to fuel his next question but then realized that insistence was not going to yield results with this man. So he used his stone as a prop and pushed himself to his feet, performing the movement with a practiced hitch that saved him pain. Acunta rose to face him, inclining his head so that he would not seem to be looking down at Cusi.

"I see that you intend to honor my brother's request," Cusi said brusquely, "so I will not command you to answer, as I could. But you must assure me that in future I will not have to trap you into truthfulness."

Acunta bared his teeth in a sardonic smile.

"I would not wish to be embarrassed a second time. You may trust my word, Lord Cusi; I have no desire to mislead you."

"Let us go on, then," Cusi declared, raising his stone up over his head and letting out a shrill whistle. "I hate secrets, and my brother is waiting to enlighten me."

The Leche Valley

THE FIVE of them had left the rest house near the Royal Road at dawn, walking westward through fields planted with cotton, peanuts, gourds, and broad beans. The trail ran along the top of the earthworks of one of the major canals for a while but then branched off and went through the center of the fields, crossing the numerous irrigation ditches by means of log bridges. Though they walked for half the morning, their destination was always ahead of them: a jagged, buff-colored hill that rose up in the middle of the flat river plain, standing out starkly against the surrounding vegetation and the overcast sky.

The trail finally turned and approached the hill from the south, and they could see it was set on a rocky plateau elevated above the level of the plain. Buildings, some with painted walls, were clustered at the base of the hill, and to the east were several of the flat-topped adobe pyramids that had been built by the Mochicas, the ancestors of the Chimus. These man-made hills were as large as or larger than those the travelers had seen at Apurle and Sican, but they appeared almost modest beside the towering vertical thrust of the natural hill. Acunta had told them the Mochica name for this place, translating it into Quechua as Huaca Urcco, or Sacred Hill.

The trail ended at the foot of a long, narrow earthen ramp that rose at a steep angle to the top of the plateau, some fifty feet above. Silent and immobile, five Chimu priests stood blocking the entrance to the ramp, their impassive faces showing no recognition of Acunta's greetings. Nor did the sight of Cusi's earplugs seem to impress them, perhaps because of his age and size or the fact that he had a water gourd and carrying bundle slung over his back like a common warrior. The priests were all well advanced in years, their hair gray or white beneath the stiff cylindrical headdresses.

Acunta approached them alone, bowing repeatedly and addressing them in Mochica. He began quietly but gradually became more animated as his explanation was met with few words and many gestures of disdain and denial. Finally he bowed again and came back to confer with Cusi, who was standing next to Micay, with Urcon and Hanp'atu behind him. The guide's narrow face was taut with embarrassment.

"They do not want to admit us," he said tersely. "They had no notice of our coming, and they do not recognize the name of Cusi Huaman. They say that the representative of the Sapa Inca would have been brought here in a litter, with a retinue of retainers and warriors. It is my fault, my lord. I should have thought to send a messenger from Apurle to announce us."

Cusi dismissed the apology with a shake of his head, then glanced sideways at Micay and gave her a small smile. "They do not know me here," he murmured, seeming almost pleased. He nodded curtly to Acunta. "Tell them we are common pilgrims, then, with gifts and offerings for their temples."

Acunta turned halfway around to relay the message to the priests. One of them—a large, fleshy man with haughty eyes—responded with a brusque, dismissive statement that hardly required Acunta's translation.

"They say they will take them up for you."

"Tell them," Cusi said, raising his voice and looking straight at the priest who had spoken, "that we have walked here from Tumibamba without their help. Tell them we have the strength to walk away again, carrying our gifts with us, if they do not show us the same respect we have brought to them."

Acunta flinched slightly at the directness of the challenge, but before he could turn back to translate, the priest stepped past him, drawing himself up to his full height and puffing out his chest, his face a mask of indignation. Micay drew back instinctively and only just saw, out of the corner of her eye, a flash of movement as Cusi shifted into a fighting stance that brought the priest up short. She glanced at Cusi and saw that he had barely moved and that his hands were poised but open at his sides. Yet she had the overwhelming sensation that he was about to hurl himself at the priest's throat; the threat was so palpable that she had to blink to be certain she had not already seen him do it. The priest recovered and glared down at Cusi, who altered his stance only slightly, straightening up so that the man had to raise his eyes. Micay could not see what was in Cusi's eyes, but it seemed to make the priest pause and reconsider the wisdom of trying to intimidate him. A chill passed over her and she shivered, a movement that gave the priest an excuse to avert his eyes from Cusi.

"Who are these others?" he demanded in Quechua, looming toward Micay. "This is not a place for women. Why have you come here?"

"Because it is holy," she told him without hesitation, just as she had told Mama Cori the night before. It silenced him, as well, and then Cusi intervened.

"They are with me, and they have come here with open hearts. Will you receive us or not?"

Unable to meet Cusi's gaze for long, the priest glanced back at his silent companions, then made a reluctant, belated bow. "I will take you to the high priest," he conceded, and he turned to lead the way up the ramp.

Micay felt Cusi's hand under her elbow as they started up the incline, but she was afraid for a moment to look at him, afraid she might see the face he had shown to the priest. But when she did look, it was the Cusi she knew, his eyes warm and full of approval.

"Because it is holy," he repeated softly, cocking his head and nodding ruefully, as if wishing that he had thought to say it himself.

THE HIGH PRIEST, whose name was Nofan-Nech, was well past eighty years of age and seemed too frail to support the magnificent sunrise headdress that fanned out above his white head. He seemed relatively indifferent to the visitors' presence, though he was willing to appoint a guide to show them through the buildings and temples that surrounded the great hill. They were leaving his chamber when he suddenly called them back, speaking in a voice that was no longer so dim and weary. Cusi saw that the gift bundles—which the old man had accepted with barely a murmur of gratitude—were open beside him, and he had a string of red shell beads stretched loosely between his bony fingers. He spoke in a heavily accented Quechua that he had not employed in greeting them.

"These are fine gifts," he said bluntly, dropping the beads back into the bundle. "But you did not present them in the name of the Sapa Inca."

"No, my lord," Cusi admitted. "They are my own gifts and those of my companions."

"You must be a man of importance or the son of such a man."

Cusi saw the priest who had confronted him sitting behind the high priest, with his eyes averted, and he realized that no attempt had been made to explain who he was.

"As I told your subordinate, I am leading a party to Chan Chan as the representative of the Sapa Inca. Many of these gifts were given to me in Tumbez and Piura and Motupe, where I made official visits."

"This is not an official visit, then," the high priest concluded.

"No, my lord."

"And the chiefs in Motupe and Apurle did not suggest that you should come here?"

"They told me about this place, but only after Acunta"—Cusi inclined his head toward the guide, who was standing just behind him—"had already informed me of its existence."

"And none of them offered to lead you here?"

"No, my lord."

Nofan-Nech straightened up slightly and looked around at the other priests in the room.

"We cannot expect the Inca to honor us when our own people do not," he admonished them, though his voice was resigned rather than angry. He squinted at Cusi and spread his hands in apology. "You must forgive our lack of courtesy, my son. There is a time within all of our memories when the choice to come here would not have been yours. You would have been sent here by the Sapa Inca, and all the chiefs along the way would have wanted to accompany you. We would have known of your coming for days, as we did the times Topa Inca came here himself. It has been many years since then, but our memories are long and we have not yet learned to be grateful for those who come here unannounced, out of curiosity."

Cusi suddenly felt the impertinence of his decision to come here alone, leaving behind all those who preferred to rest for the next day's journey. He had not made much of an effort to persuade them of the importance of this place, largely because no one except Acunta had made that effort for him. He had felt certain of his welcome simply because he was an Inca.

"You must forgive—" he began, but the high priest refused to hear him out.

"Tell me what you wish to see and know."

"I would like to see whatever you wish to show me," Cusi said humbly, since he did not truly know what was here. "I would like to know more about the Chimus and their gods."

Nofan-Nech gestured to his assistants, who removed the flaring scarlet headdress from his head, then helped him to his feet. He started toward the open doorway, beckoning for them to follow.

"I will show you myself. I will tell you about the Chimus—more, probably, than you are prepared to learn. But I must begin with the first people, the people who built most of what you will see: our ancestors, the Mochicas . . ."

THEY STAYED much longer than they should have, so that the sun was low in the west before they made their farewells and started back along the trail by which they had come. Though they knew they would have to complete the journey in darkness, they could not bring themselves to hurry. They walked along in silence, breathing in the moist green scent that was rising from the fields and trying to assimilate all they had seen and heard at Huaca Urcco. Micay knew she would visit the place again in her dreams, whenever she finally got to sleep that night. She had only to close her eyes for a moment to see stepped patterns and curling waves and geometric swirls, all in vivid colors, repeating themselves endlessly along a cracked plaster wall.

Acunta and Hanp'atu were walking a short distance ahead of her and Cusi, Urcon trailing a few feet behind. Cusi finally looked over at her, his eyes bloodshot and his expression dazed, as if he had drunk much more than the one cup of weak akha the high priest had offered in farewell. He had listened intently to everything the old man had told him about the long history of the Mochica, about the kingdom that had risen in the Lambayeque Valley after the Mochicas had declined, and about the Chimus who had come last and ruled the entire coast until the coming of the Inca. Nofan-Nech's memory was a thousand years long and filled with names that could not be pronounced, much less remembered. He spoke of men who had been dead for hundreds of years as if they were his grandfathers, and he was disinclined to leave any of them out of his recitation. Micay had become lost early on and had thereafter confined her attention to his descriptions of the gods and his retelling of the legends. She felt sorry for Cusi, who had been unable to close his ears or turn away to stare at the ruins around him, even for a moment. She wondered if he had captured any impressions of his own to take away with him.

"What will you remember," she asked him suddenly. "What will be the first thing?"

Cusi cast his eyes skyward in a gesture of helplessness. Then he pursed his lips and closed one eye, keeping the other eye on the trail ahead of him. He seemed surprised himself by how quickly he reached a conclusion.

"The pyramids," he said hoarsely. "I was disappointed by how worn and eroded they were, so that they could not even be climbed. I wanted to imagine them as they were in the time of the Mochicas, but they were too badly damaged. But then he took me to the center of the plaza, with the pyramids rising up around me on three sides and the Sacred Hill towering over everything, blocking out all but a patch of the sky directly overhead. I forgot what was outside: the plain, the mountains, the Great Waters. I felt like I was at the center of the earth. And the stillness when he stopped talking . . . the power that was still there after so many years. Then it did not matter that the pyramids were in ruins. It seemed right."

He nodded to himself, then blinked in surprise, realizing he had been speechifying. Micay nodded in acknowledgement, though the high priest had not taken her or the others out onto the plaza, conferring that honor on Cusi alone. She glanced back at Urcon, who nodded to show that he had been listening yet still took several moments to deliberate over his reply.

"I will remember a dead city," he said finally, "with roofless houses and empty rooms where the swallows build their nests. I will remember the drifts of sand piled up in the side streets and the way our footsteps echoed ahead of us, even though we walked very softly. I will remember feeling the presence of the dead all around us like shadows where there is no sun."

"You did not like it, then," Cusi concluded, sounding both surprised and disappointed.

Urcon simply shrugged. "I did not want to look too closely," he allowed. "Still, I saw enough to tell my children and grandchildren some day. If they will believe me."

He smiled then to reassure Cusi, and they both laughed, agreeing at least that what they had seen challenged belief.

"And you, my lady?" Cusi prompted.

Micay spoke without hesitation. "I cannot forget the wall paintings, especially the ones around the plaza. I could not believe that the colors could still be so bright and the images of the gods so clear. That is when I could understand his stories the best, when I could see the legend before me. There was one, not much faded and broken in only a few places, that showed the Hawk Attendant, a creature with the body of a man and the head of a hawk and earplugs that were serpents' heads. There were waves both above and below, and he was standing on a raft—"

"—fighting the Crab God," Cusi broke in, "with a battle-ax like mine."

"Fighting him over and over," Micay marveled, "for the whole length of the wall. Just as he protects Si, night after night, as she makes her journey through the depths of the Great Waters. There was a time when I looked around the plaza and wanted to weep, because I could see that once all the walls had been painted and how little there was left—how much will never be seen again."

They fell silent, watching their feet as they crossed an irrigation ditch by means of two logs packed together with mud. The sun was disappearing behind them and blue-black swallows were swooping low over the fields, which had begun to take on the color of the night. Cusi glanced ahead, as if to be sure that Acunta and Hanp'atu were still out of earshot.

"Did you not find their beliefs very strange?" he asked, sounding bemused rather than scornful. "They pay little honor to the Sun, though he is so constant that they can plant two crops a year. Instead they are devoted to the Moon, men and women both, even the warriors. And they believe that Si dwells beneath the Great Waters, not in the sky. Most of their gods dwell in the water or the mountains, not the sky."

"The sky is always the same here," Urcon pointed out. "Perhaps the sky is empty of gods, or they are hidden by the clouds."

"They get their water from the rivers, which come from the mountains," Micay added, "and they get food and shells from Mama Cocha. They do not have to pray for rain or worry that frost or hail will destroy their crops."

"They fear the rain," Cusi said, showing the whites of his eyes in the failing light. "Nofan-Nech told me that he had seen it rain only three times during all the years he has been alive, but each time there were floods that did great damage to the canals and fields and buildings. There was a ruler of Lambayeque who was sacrificed by his people because he could not make the rain stop."

Urcon grunted softly, and Micay thought that if Uritu had been here he would have whooped in appreciative amazement. On several occasions today she had felt like doing so herself.

"It may seem strange to us," she suggested, "but they have believed these things for a very long time. Far longer, I think, than there have been Incas and Chachapoyas."

"That is true," Cusi said ruefully. "I often felt, listening to him, that our people are very young, and we have known greatness for only a short time. I tried to imagine Cuzco abandoned like that, tended only by a handful of priests, but I could not make myself see it. Perhaps it is bad luck to imagine such a thing."

The glow winked out behind them and it was suddenly dark, though the trail was easily distinguishable from the crops on either side. Micay felt the weariness in her legs but tried to ignore it.

"You promised the high priest you would return," she said.

Cusi grunted in assent. "On our way back to Tumibamba. I will bring the whole party the next time, and food and akha. I will pay Nofan-Nech the respect he deserves."

"And the priest who tried to threaten you?"

Cusi was silent for a moment, and she could not tell if he was looking at her or past her.

"He apologized to me as we were leaving. I should not have threatened him, but he did not give me time to think."

"How did you threaten him? I *felt* it, but I only saw you look at him."

"Huaca," Urcon murmured from behind, but Cusi did not respond immediately. She was certain now that he was looking at her, though she could not make out his features in the darkness. She was surprised by his reticence now, after all the other secrets he had shared with her.

"I cannot tell you exactly," he confessed. "It is a power I have had since

I . . . returned. I felt it first in other men, like the healer, Titu Atauchi, and the high priest and some of the sorcerers who have come to visit me. It is the power of their presence, and I have used mine mostly to defend myself. I have misused it, too, like a weapon I did not know was in my hands, a weapon too big for me. You have felt it yourself; you told me so, on the ridge above the Rainbow House."

"Yes," Micay recalled, beginning to understand why that conversation had had such an impact upon him.

"After that I did not want to be so careless again. I felt I should have more control over my effect on others, especially those I care about."

"Is that the reason you wish to visit places like Sican and Huaca Urcco?"

"Yes, because they are holy," Cusi agreed. "Because I might learn what I need to know. A Shuara sorcerer told me there is no safety in ignorance for those who can feel."

Micay fell silent and heard Urcon stir behind her. He cleared his throat before interrupting.

"The others are no longer in sight," he pointed out. "I will go ahead and tell them to wait until you catch up. We should not be separated in the dark."

A shadow slipped by on Micay's right and was quickly swallowed up by the darkness.

"He is uneasy with such talk," Cusi said after a moment. "He is willing to accept what he does not understand. Have I made you uneasy as well?"

"A little," Micay admitted, "though I prefer to understand, if I can. I will know to tell you if you ever use your power on me."

Cusi laughed and touched her arm, then linked it with his own.

"You have more power over me than any of the sorcerers do," he assured her. "They could not cast a spell that would capture my heart more thoroughly."

"I want to believe that," Micay told him, squeezing his arm for emphasis. "But there are others who have power with you. Your mother, for one . . ."

"You would not let me speak to her, and she has chosen not to speak herself. But I will not let her come between us, Micay, I promise you that. She will never have that power."

They could hear voices just ahead, and Cusi briefly drew her toward him and pressed his lips against her cheek before releasing her arm.

"Because it is holy," he added in a whisper, then raised his voice to greet the others, who were standing together in the dark, waiting to resume the journey.

THE LAMBAYEQUE VALLEY was the largest river valley on the entire coast, with a broad, flat floodplain that fanned out almost to the shores of Mama Cocha to the west and extended north all the way to the Leche Valley, a two-day march. The river split into three parts to water this vast expanse, and a system of canals that began high in the hills carried the water to every foot of arable land, most of which had been planted in cotton. The river waters were so abundant that canals carried it north to both the Leche and Motupe valleys, snaking across the hills like a giant serpent, while another canal went straight south to the Zaña Valley.

The settlements of Cinto and Collique were in the upper part of the valley, occupying hilly ground that was unfit for cultivation but ideally situated for control of the major canals. Light rains were not uncommon in these hills, so the houses and administrative buildings were surrounded by fruit trees and cantut bushes and climbing orchids where hummingbirds came to drink. The settlements were half Chimu and half Inca, for the Inca had settled families of mitmacs here after the war, many of them from the Cuzco area. Both groups built their houses and compounds out of adobe brick and mud plaster, but the Cuzcoquiti left their walls unpainted or etched them with black lines meant to resemble the close joining of stones. They also wore cotton garments woven in traditional Cuzco styles, the patterns and colors altered only slightly over the course of fifty years. Only the oldest and most important of them had ever seen the Holy City, but all considered it their true home. Here Cusi was a hero not because of his exploits in the Chachapoya War, but because he had won the Huarachicoy race. Their interest in the news from Tumibamba and Quito was merely polite, but they would listen raptly to any story he had to tell about Cuzco, as many times as he could be brought to tell it.

The Chimu chiefs, for their part, were flattered by Cusi's interest in the huacas of their ancestors, and they took him to visit several of the more impressive sites in the valley, all of which were well away from the areas now under cultivation. Some were still in use as Chimu ceremonial sites, while others lay abandoned to the wind and the drifting sand. East of Collique was an enormous huaca that was as tall as the Sacred Hill, though shaped much like the rectangular adobe bricks with which it had been built. The rains of hundreds of years had cut deep gullies through the ramps that climbed its long sides, making it impossible now to reach the summit, where the crumbling walls of ancient shrines could still be seen. Cusi stared at it in awe, thinking of the thousands of hands and the years of labor it must have taken to erect such a colossal edifice, a man-made mountain. His guides disagreed among themselves over who had built it and why, and there were no priests with long memories available to resolve the dispute. There is nothing so great that it cannot be lost from memory, Cusi had thought. It was a thought that disturbed him profoundly yet made him feel less young, less attached to his own fame and importance.

Wearing a cotton tunic of Inca design, a gift from the mitmacs of Cinto, Cusi marched his party from Collique to Zaña in one day, the Royal Road flanked for the entire distance by a wide canal that carried water south to the smaller, drier valley. Three more days of hard walking through desert hills brought them to the Inca administrative center of Farfan in the center of the lush green Jequetepeque Valley. Here the accumulated fatigue of the journey, compounded by all the nights spent talking or drinking or stealing away with

Micay, finally caught up with him. He woke on the second morning with his side aching and his limbs so weak he could barely turn over. He fell back asleep until one of his men came in to check on him, and then he could rouse himself only long enough to tell the man that he would not be leaving his room today and should not be disturbed. Then sleep sucked him under, and he dreamed that he was lying on a raft with Micay and the Hawk Attendant standing over him, descending into the swirling, bottomless depths of the Great Waters . . .

When next he awoke, the room was dark except for the flicker of a fire burning in the sunken hearth in the corner. His first thought was that he had not slept so deeply since the times in Cuzco with Tocto, when it had been almost impossible to awaken him. His second thought was that he had awakened from this by himself, without any lingering grogginess. He saw his stone on the floor next to his sleeping mats and instinctively flexed his right arm, feeling the muscles move beneath the skin, languid but responsive. He rolled over and suffered no more than the normal, restraining twinge in his side, though his stomach told him he was hungry. Then he saw his mother sitting cross-legged on the floor a few feet away.

"I did not expect I would have to do this again so soon," she said. "I had hoped my vigils for you were over."

"They are," Cusi told her, stretching more of his muscles and finding them remarkably functional. "You need not have worried, Mother. I admit I pushed myself too hard, but I am strong enough now that I can recover quickly. I will run again before this journey is over, and I will carry my battle-ax back to Tumibamba in my own hands."

Cusi smiled at his own boast, then felt foolish when his mother simply stared back at him, appearing neither amused nor impressed. But as he pushed himself up into a sitting position, he also felt it was true: the long sleep seemed to have restored him completely. Perhaps he had tested his stamina too recklessly, but it had not failed him.

"I will be more careful in the future," he promised, hoping to mollify her. But her voice had an edge like flint.

"That should not be difficult. I have watched you exhaust yourself needlessly, and I have wondered why your duties as the Sapa Inca's representative were not sufficient to occupy your energies. I wondered why you had to act, as well, like a wide-eyed boy eager for adventure."

Cusi sat up straight, his face burning. He remembered all the angry conversations he had had with her in his mind during these past days, while he waited for her to speak to him. That had worn on him, too.

"Perhaps you should have spoken earlier," he suggested, "if my actions were so repellant to you."

"Perhaps I was waiting for you to speak to me. But you did not seem interested in my advice."

"That did not stop you from inflicting it on Micay."

"My words were meant for her ears alone," Mama Cori said sharply. "She should not have repeated them to you."

"Why not? You claimed to speak on my behalf, did you not? You made offers and threats, and you spoke to her about marriage before I had done so myself. Should I be ignorant of that and let you arrange my life however you wish?"

His mother's eyes flared in outraged disbelief, as if he had slapped her or spat on her. Then she turned her face away, refusing to look at him. Her voice was low and harsh, the rasp of flint upon bone.

"Perhaps it was not *my* words you heard, though obviously you wish to believe them. I cannot be surprised, since I do not know you anymore. I knew the son who first came to me in Tumibamba. He had grown into a man, but I recognized his smile and the kindness in his eyes. Someone else returned to me from Chachapoyas, someone cold and distant, as if he were still lost in the darkness of his dreams. He dwells there still, punishing those who remember and love him as he was . . ."

Tears were streaming down the side of her face, and she began to rock back and forth in mourning. Cusi felt the blood rush from his face and his chest constrict so that he could not breathe or speak. He heard her abandoning him, blaming him for the way he had changed, as if he had done it to spite her. As if he did not yearn for what he had lost on the cliff and fear that his new power was truly an absence of something human, an emptiness at the heart of him. Tears rose in his eyes and he blinked them back, blurring his vision. His voice sounded strangled.

"I woke from the darkness into a world of strangers. You cannot know how alone I have been, even with my friends and family around me. But I am done grieving for myself," he declared, anger opening his throat, "and I will not have you grieve for me. I am not someone you have lost."

Her face still averted, Mama Cori gathered her legs under her and rose to her feet. Cusi held out his hands to her in appeal, his anger turning just as quickly to pain. It cannot end like this, he thought desperately. But she would not look at him.

"I lost everyone long ago," she murmured, and walked out of the room with her head down. Cusi collapsed back onto his sleeping mats with a groan, squeezing his eyes shut in despair. For all of his anger, he had never imagined that they would not finally be reconciled, that he would not persuade her and win her approval. He groaned again and drew his knees up to his chest, stabbed by a remorse that was as sharp as the sentry's spear. Perhaps he had been as cold and heartless as she said; perhaps he had never fully returned to the living and never would. It was unbearable to think he might never know whether he had or not. It was unbearable to think—to know—that his mother had spurned him. He squirmed and dug deeper into the blankets, but there was no escape into sleep. All of his thoughts seemed unbearable. He lay back panting, trying to find the courage to bear the painful commotion in his heart.

THE ROAD from Jequetepeque to the Chicama Valley ran well inland of Mama Cocha for most of its length. The last rest house before they would reach the

Inca capital of Chiquitoy was at the edge of the northerly spread of cultivation, so that its buildings and compounds were flanked on one side by the barren desert plain and on the other by a dark green field of cotton. A breeze blew in off the water, cooling and freshening the air and carrying the steady murmur of the surf.

There had been a magnificent sunset, followed swiftly by a night that seemed unusually clear. Breaks in the clouds revealed glimpses of the great river of stars that flowed overhead, and the air was warm and soft, caressing the skin like vicuña. Micay and Cusi spread their blankets out among the dunes above the beach and lay down in each other's arms, their bodies cushioned by the fine, loose sand. They had spent parts of several previous nights like this, touching and whispering and murmuring with excitement and pleasure, learning to love with their lips and fingers as well as their hearts. Their caresses had become more and more sensitive and intimate, far beyond anything Micay had experienced with Rimachi yet also new to Cusi, who found no lingering memories of Tocto in his flesh. The wonderful fit of their bodies drew them inexorably toward a consummation that neither resisted, and this would have been a perfect night to reach it.

Yet they lay together in silence, subdued rather than eager, their clothing loosened but still between them. Cusi fumbled halfheartedly with the copper pin that held her shift together at the shoulder, then gave up and lay motionless on his back, staring up at the stars. Micay could feel the weight of his depression, like a great slab of stone that flattened his spirit beneath it. She had tried to warn him, but he had been unable to hear her. Now, as she had feared, she could not console him, she could not even penetrate the pain and confusion Mama Cori had stirred up in him. They had talked about it, and he had acknowledged her warnings and his own promise. He had even claimed to recognize the cruelty and unfairness of what his mother had done, though he did not seem to believe it. She had made him uncertain of everything he believed and felt, so that he had only to reach a conclusion to begin doubting it.

Micay pressed her lips tightly together, unwilling to break the silence again. There was nothing she could say now that would not sound like recrimination, and she knew he already felt guilty enough. She had to wait, trusting that his confidence would return and that he would realize his mother *could* be so wrong about him. Yet tomorrow they would be in Chiquitoy, where their official duties would resume in earnest, and Cusi would begin his unofficial task of rescuing Amaru from his captivity. From the little Acunta had revealed, that task seemed more complicated than ever, and possibly dangerous. Cusi was not fit for it in his present state, and she could only see him coming to harm, being taken from her in some way more brutal than anything Mama Cori could effect. She had to speak to him now; she had to make him hear her before he lost himself completely in doubt and misgivings.

Patches of silvery light appeared on the crests of the dunes surrounding them, and she knew without looking that Mama Quilla had risen from behind the eastern mountains, half full but growing in wholeness. Micay thought of Cahua and the House of Chosen Women in Caxamarca, which lay just beyond those same mountains. And she knew all at once how to make Cusi listen.

"When the micho of Chachapoyas, Condor Tupac, took me from my father, my name was Misa. Before I reached the House of Chosen Women, I had lost even my name."

Cusi grunted sharply and rolled over onto his side to face her, raising himself up on one elbow.

"Misa," he repeated, testing the name with his tongue. "Tell me, Micay . . . tell me what happened to her."

She had never told anyone about the House of Chosen Women, and even he had not thought to ask. But now she told him all of it, beginning with the appearance of Condor Tupac and his warriors in her father's compound. She told him how she had been led to Caxamarca like a prize llama and there shorn of everything that belonged to Misa: her clothing and language, the gods and customs of her people, the memories and attachments of her past, even the right to think, feel, and react as her instincts told her. She told him about her loneliness and desolation, her struggle to cease her "dreaming," and the process by which Cahua, Yutu, and the mamanchic had influenced and shaped her, gradually making her accept the life that had been chosen for her.

Cusi did not stir, but she could feel his attentiveness, so she went on without pause. She told him Cahua's story about the girl named Inquil, who had chosen to die when the uta took her beauty, and about Cahua's own choice to live on and be a light of hope and encouragement to those around her. Micay could not tell the story without weeping, and Cusi sighed and put his hand on hers to comfort her, waiting until she recovered. Then she went on to recount her dream of the bridge and the condor in detail, knowing he would want to hear all of it, and concluded with a description of her clash with Mama Huarcay and her subsequent interview with Quinti and Mama Cori, which had led to her departure from the House of Chosen Women.

Her voice had grown hoarse by the time she finished, and Cusi reached out and lightly touched her throat, then her cheek.

"So Misa is gone, and Micay has lived on in her place," he said softly. "I am selfish enough to be thankful for that, though it hurts me to know how you were made to suffer. I want to believe you were chosen so you could be with me, but Condor Tupac was a man who served only himself. That is the kind of Inca he was."

"You saw him die?"

"I saw him fall. He was our leader, but none of us wanted to follow him too closely. The war your father brought had ruined him, and he was wild with the need for vengeance, which drove him to his death. It was too late to help Misa, but he paid at last for his provocations."

They were silent for several moments, staring at one another as a shaft of moonlight pierced the clouds and spread its pale glow over the dunes.

"My father has never surrendered," Micay told him. "They say he has fled into the lands of the Shuaras. I do not know if my mother is with him."

"Can he be persuaded to return?"

"Acapana has promised to try," Micay said with an uncertain shrug. "He asked me what he should say to my father, but I could not tell him. Why should my father accept the Sapa Inca's promises now, when they have always been broken in the past? And who am I to urge him to do so? He would not recognize the person I have become, except perhaps as proof that the Inca's theft had been a success. I would still be lost to him. I told Acapana not to speak of me unless my father asked."

Cusi sat up and took her hands, widening his eyes to see her in the moonlight. His hands were much warmer than hers.

"I know a powerful man among the Shuaras. I will send a message to Acapana and tell him to use my name. At least he will be assured of finding your father." Cusi paused, chafing her fingers to warm them. "I understand now why you did not wish to go back to Chachapoyas. You could not be his daughter again any more than I could be the son my mother remembers." He paused again to swallow. "Perhaps, though, since you have chosen to remain among us, you would also choose to be my wife."

Micay pulled back slightly, though she did not let go of his hands. "Only moments ago," she said warily, "I felt your mother lying here between us, like a wall. Is she truly gone, or have I merely distracted you from your pain?"

"She is not gone," Cusi conceded, "and neither is the pain. But can I be less brave than you have been? I have been motherless before and survived it. I will carry my pain the way the Soras do: as if it belonged to someone else."

He lowered himself down beside her, their hands still clasped between them, their faces close. She could feel he was entirely there, warm and eager and undistracted, drawing strength from his own vow.

"We are still too young to marry," she murmured, feeling heat rise between them.

Cusi's teeth gleamed against his dark skin. "We may have to wait for the ceremony, but a match could be announced. Huayna Capac would do that for me without consulting anyone. I will ask him when we return."

"Will I be the first wife?" Micay asked, freeing her fingers and flattening her palms against his. He smiled again, but his tone was solemn with conviction, as if he were making another vow.

"The only wife, Micay . . . the one whose place could never be taken by another."

Her watchfulness gave way then, with a kind of inward lurch that pushed her forward into his encircling arms. He molded himself against her, kissing her lips and throat while his hands flowed over the arch of her back, smoothing and stroking her long hair. Their clothing slipped away piece by piece until only skin separated them. Cusi rose above her briefly, his body dark and wiry, the muscles in his arms and neck stretched taut as tent lines. He looked into her eyes and lowered himself cautiously, entering then drawing back when she gasped at the sudden tearing pain. Shoulders trembling, he held himself back for another moment, then slipped forward and was engulfed, covering her as she took him in and wrapped her arms around his hard, bony back. He moaned and began to rock gently, creating a friction that burned yet stirred her intensely, obscuring the pain with bursts of a new and indescribable pleasure. Micay opened her eyes and caught a glimpse of silver moonlight on the furled crest of a dune, and she heard the liquid voice of Mama Cocha murmuring in the distance. Then a cry that seemed to come from beneath her drew her back and she was reabsorbed, and they clung together, deeply joined, heeding nothing outside themselves.

Chiquitoy

THE ROYAL ROAD ran straight through the center of Chiquitoy, pausing in the broad, open square at the heart of the settlement. At the foot of the stepped dais that stood just east of the road, Cusi and his party were formally welcomed by the governor of the province of Chimor, Mayta Yupanqui. Cusi returned the greeting, then watched as the people he had led from Tumibamba disappeared from around him. The wives and their children went to their husbands and fathers with eager cries and much joyous weeping, the count takers and their families were quietly led away by the chief of counts, and the warriors were delivered to their new commander. Before marching off, the warriors raised their spears and shields over their heads and shouted Cusi's name, a salute that warmed his heart and told him that he had won their respect, the first duty of a commander.

Then he was alone with his mother, Micay, and Acunta. Urcon and Hanp'atu had taken the pack train to the corrals and would join them later. Ignored for the moment by the governor, who was introducing the wives to the other members of his delegation, and by his mother—who was completely closed to him now—Cusi exchanged a glance with Micay, who appeared watchful and wary. She no doubt felt as isolated and outnumbered as he did, finding little solace in the fact that all of these strangers were Incas. Cusi nodded and smiled at her with his eyes, encouraging her and being encouraged in return by the recognition that passed across her face. Then he was aware of Acunta standing at his elbow, and he stepped aside to talk with him.

"I must leave you in the governor's hands now," Acunta said, inclining his head respectfully. "But no doubt I will see you again, perhaps in Chan Chan."

"I will go there soon, if that is where Amaru is."

The guide cast an amused glance at the stone in Cusi's hand. "Will you go there armed?"

"Perhaps. Will I not be among friends?"

"You will have to decide that for yourself. They will know you are not a man who is easily deceived."

"Farewell, then, Acunta. Tell my brother to expect me."

"I will, Cusi Huaman," Acunta promised, bowing again. "Enjoy your stay," he added. Then he lowered his voice so that only Cusi would hear the scornful tone of his parting words: "Here in the *capital* of Chimor . . ."

WHEN THEY had been shown their quarters and the women had retired to prepare themselves for the feast later in the day, the governor offered to give Cusi a tour of Chiquitoy, alluding to the fact that he had heard about Cusi's excursions to the Mochica ruins. He spoke of it with a kind of conspiratorial amusement, as if it were a piece of cleverness on Cusi's part. Cusi found this offensive but chose not to contradict him, assuming that the tour was an excuse to speak to him privately about Amaru. So he willingly walked back toward the square with the governor and his micho, a man of about thirty named Topa Roca.

It quickly became apparent, however, that Mayta Yupanqui had no intention of discussing Amaru or anything else of a serious nature. He allowed Topa Roca to describe the buildings and compounds they were passing and contented himself with an occasional expostulation about Cusi's age and rank. He was a large, heavyset man who carried his girth with assurance and a certain dignity, as if he had earned the right to eat. His size had also led him to underestimate Cusi and to think that he could flatter him carelessly in an incredulous tone that was itself condescending.

"So young, yet so famous! At your age, I was just learning to command a squad of mitmacs in Huanuco. And here *you* are, still getting your growth, but already traveling in the name of the Sapa Inca—it is truly astonishing. I must introduce you to my daughters later . . ."

They had crossed over to the eastern side of the square, where the buildings clearly belonged to the Chimu. The walls presented a series of continuous friezes etched into the plaster in low relief and painted in vivid shades of red, yellow, blue, green, and black. The patterns were intricate but repetitious, with long rows of pumas, pelicans, dragonflies, and fish bordered by waves and geometric swirls and the symbols of the moon and the stars. None was as striking and impressive as the Huaca Urcco murals, yet the unbroken expanse of brightly painted figures was pleasing to the eye and made the plain adobe compounds of the Incas on the other side of the square seem unduly drab and solemn.

Cusi noted this while struggling to contain his anger. The governor, in his jovial way, was trying to loom over him and make him feel small and insignificant, just as the priest at Huaca Urcco had done. Cusi's first impulse was to turn on him and back him off. I have killed larger men than you, he thought. Then he realized the same thought had been in his mind when he had faced down the priest. That was what he must have shown the man: a glimpse of the death he had witnessed and caused—and might cause again.

"That is the western side of the Grand Chimu's compound," the micho was explaining, gesturing toward the longest section of wall. "The entrance is in the northern end, according to Chimu custom."

Cusi nodded absently, shaken by what he had realized about the source of his power and by how close he had come to misusing it again. However obnoxious, the governor was not his enemy, and it would be a serious mistake to make him one. The people around Amaru might be dangerous, and Cusi had no warriors of his own behind him. So he drew a slow breath, mastering his anger and deciding there were less drastic ways to stop this man from treating him like a precocious boy. He waited until Mayta Yupanqui and Topa Roca were a few feet ahead and had their backs to him. Then he raised his stone to shoulder height and dropped it hard onto the sun-baked earth. It landed with a boom that echoed across the square and made both his companions jump. Mayta Yupanqui probably had not jumped so high in years, and Cusi just managed to stifle a laugh at the sight of that top-heavy, bowlegged body hurtling off the ground in fright.

"Forgive me," he said calmly, bending to retrieve the stone. "My arm must have grown weary."

The governor was gaping at him, one hand flattened against his chest, his breath coming in short bursts. Topa Roca had recovered his composure quickly and was regarding Cusi with a mixture of anger and curiosity. Cusi hefted the stone in his hand and glanced expectantly from one man to the other.

"Before we go any farther, perhaps you will tell me about my brother."

"Amaru?" Mayta Yupanqui blurted. "What is there to tell? He is in Chan Chan, working."

"Working on what?" Cusi demanded. "Did you send him there?"

"He is supervising the reconstruction of one of the major canals in the Chimor Valley," Topa Roca intervened. "It is his own project, though of course he consulted with the governor first."

"Yes, he has my permission," Mayta Yupanqui agreed, "and my blessing. It is good to see him show such energy and ambition."

Cusi glanced at Topa Roca, whose expression seemed pointedly neutral. "We heard other things about him in Tumibamba. Concerning his conduct."

"Ah, yes, Sinchi Roca was not pleased to leave him behind," the governor recalled, "and I must confess that I was concerned about him myself. Enough so that I called him in for a serious talk. But all he truly needed was a task worthy of his talents, and he has found that now. The last time I saw him he was clear-eyed and clearheaded, and I am told he has stayed that way in Chan Chan."

Mayta Yupanqui had fully recovered from his shock and was growing expansive and unctuous again. Cusi decided to let him talk, though he believed none of it.

"Who are the people around him?"

"Young Chimu nobles, mostly," the governor admitted, though he did not seem distressed by the fact. "The foremost is Ancocoyuch, the son of the

Grand Chimu. The others are all of royal blood, younger sons who are exempt from the labor tax but have no lands or holdings of their own. There are fewer places for them since the Grand Chimu's lands were broken up and put under our administration. Amaru has done us all a great favor by putting them to work. I told him that an Inca was true to his blood and training only when he was leading other men, and he appears to have taken my words to heart."

"I am certain you have been a great influence upon him, my lord," Cusi said in a voice as neutral as Topa Roca's expression. "Still, I want to go to Chan Chan as soon as possible."

"But you have just arrived!" Mayta Yupanqui protested. "There are feasts scheduled, and a dance, and meetings with members of the Grand Chimu's court . . . everyone of importance has requested an audience with the Sapa Inca's representative. It is expected you—"

"I know my duties," Cusi interrupted, "and I will discharge them fully. And when I make my report to the Sapa Inca, I doubt he will ask me to describe the feasts I have attended. He is more likely to be interested in the reconstruction of a major canal and the lands that will be reclaimed in his name."

The governor frowned at the curtness of Cusi's reply, but then a shrewd smile spread across his fleshy face as he realized the possibility of accruing some favor with the ruler. Somehow Cusi had known that would appeal to him.

"In that case, I will see you are released from your obligations here as soon as possible," he promised. "Perhaps you would like to have Topa Roca accompany you."

"That will not be necessary," Cusi said, meeting the micho's eyes and giving him a respectful nod. "Though perhaps he could tell me more about this project before I leave."

"He is at your disposal," Mayta Yupanqui said grandly, waving a hand and nodding to himself as if satisfied that everything had been settled. "Now—shall we continue our walk?"

"I think I have seen enough, my lord," Cusi demurred. "I would prefer to rest before the feast."

"Certainly," the governor allowed, turning them back in the direction they had come. "But we must talk some more later. You are a remarkable young man."

"I have had to be," Cusi murmured.

The older man laughed. "Perhaps you will tell me why you carry that stone with you everywhere," he said in an amused tone.

Cusi shrugged, smiling to himself at the memory of how he had made the governor jump. "It makes my arm weary," he said simply, and he was pleased to see—for just an instant—a smile cross Topa Roca's impassive face.

THE FOUR of them assembled at first light and left Chiquitoy while the fog still hung low and thick over the ground, limiting their vision and causing them to come up on the sentries without warning. Micay was reminded of the morning they had left for Huaca Urcco, except that today Acunta was not along to guide them. They were traveling without porters or an honor guard of warriors, though Cusi had been offered both. The warriors, in particular, had been urged on him, but Cusi wanted to go to Chan Chan as a brother, not an official of the Inca, so he had been adamant in his resistance to any kind of retinue. He had succeeded largely because he already had a reputation for unconventional behavior and because he had earnestly espoused a confidence in his own safety—which Micay, for one, knew he did not really feel.

He was clearly excited to be on the march, but he also seemed somewhat nervous and preoccupied as he led them past the last sentry post and out onto the Royal Road. He kept shifting his stone from hand to hand and shrugging at the carrying bundle and water gourd he had slung over his shoulder, and the pace he was setting was rapid but uneven. Micay had seen too little of him, at least privately, during the past several days, so she did not know what he might have learned. The night before, she had thought she heard him singing to himself in the next room, but she had been unable to understand the words and she had finally forced herself to stop listening. The sound of his voice had only made her more lonely for his company and more aware of the obdurate silence in the room she shared with Mama Cori. Mama Cori would not even acknowledge their leaving, much less bid either of them farewell.

They were well away from the Chicama Valley before the fog finally lifted, revealing the six-foot walls that bordered the road on both sides and the familiar barren plain that lay beyond. At a place where there was a break in the wall and some flat-topped stones for benches, Cusi gave them their first rest. Micay removed her cloak and rolled it into her bundle, then drank from her gourd in recognition of the growing warmth of the day. But like Urcon and Hanp'atu, she was really waiting for Cusi to speak. He had his gourd raised to his lips but was lost in thought, staring out over the desert. Then he came out of it and saw them waiting, and he stoppered the gourd and put it down on the bench next to his stone. When he spoke, Micay heard the voice he used with his warriors, the shrewd, somewhat sardonic voice of a leader who relied on strategy rather than exhortation.

"We will be in Chan Chan by late afternoon. You all must know by now that it is not an empty ruin inhabited only by aged priests. My brother is there, but the micho has warned me that some of the men around him are of questionable character and loyalty. The Grand Chimu is also suspicious, even though his own son is one of their leaders. They both fear that something more than a canal is being built in Chan Chan, though they are reluctant to say so openly. The governor refuses to believe that anything could be seriously wrong in his province. He gave his permission for the rebuilding, but since it did not involve any of the Inca's workers, he did not feel it was necessary to inform Cuzco or Tumibamba. If he had, someone might have recognized the significance of the Moro Canal. Someone might have recalled the story songs of the conquest of Chimor, as I did last night."

Micay murmured appreciatively, understanding what he had been singing in his side of the wall.

"The war against the Chimu lasted almost ten years," Cusi explained, his voice taking on a trace of the song's stately rhythm, "and many warriors were killed on both sides. Topa Inca brought three separate armies against them, one from the north, one from the south, and one that came down through the mountain passes to the east. The Chimu fought fiercely, and they surrendered only because the Incas cut their canals and they could no longer feed themselves. The last canal to be cut was the Moro, the one that brought water from the Chicama River to the fields around Chan Chan itself. That is the canal my brother is helping to restore."

"The war has been over for many years," Hanp'atu pointed out.

Cusi nodded in agreement. "Almost fifty years. And the canal was rebuilt once, shortly after the war ended. But about thirty years ago it was broken again to force the Grand Chimu to move his court north to Chiquitoy. The present Grand Chimu, Huaman Chumu, was the Heir then, and he remembers the move with a bitterness he cannot conceal even now. Chan Chan is his Holy City, and all of the Grand Chimus who came before him are buried there."

"The Chimu herders could not believe I was going there," Urcon reported. "They say it has been abandoned for many years and that only those of royal blood are allowed to go there for ceremonies."

"That was true," Cusi allowed, "until Amaru and his friends took up quarters there. I suspect they want to restore not just a canal or some fields, but Chan Chan itself."

"If that *is* what they want," Micay mused aloud, "is it such a bad thing? If you had been moved out of Cuzco, would you not want to return?"

"Yes," Cusi agreed, and gave her a fierce smile. "And then I would want to raise an army and drive out those who had made me move."

"That is because you are an Inca," Micay told him sharply, "and you do not know what it is to be conquered. Perhaps the Chimu only want to grow their crops and live in peace, close to their ancestors."

"Perhaps," Cusi said, still smiling. "That is what I intend to find out. I will need your help," he added, addressing all three of them. "I will need you to question me like this, and to tell me what you think and feel. You must be my comrades and keep watch for me while my back is turned. I am going there to see my brother, but the people around him will care only about what I might report to the Sapa Inca. Innocent or not, they are likely to perceive me as a threat to their interests."

"But you carry the Sapa Inca's name," Urcon protested. "There would be war if you were harmed. That is a worse threat."

"I would not expect an open attack," Cusi told him. "But there might be an 'accident,' or something might be done to discredit me, so that I would be reluctant to speak against them. I do not fear a knife across my throat but a push on a dark flight of stairs or a powder slipped into my drinking cup."

"They have such things in Chan Chan," Hanp'atu affirmed. "They trade heavily with the medicine men in Chiquitoy."

"You must prepare me, then, as we walk," Cusi said, and he reached down for his bundle and his stone. As they resumed their march, Micay and Urcon fell in behind Cusi and the healer, but Cusi gestured for them to come up on either side.

"We must all know everything," he said emphatically, and Micay felt a surge of loyalty and affection that surprised and baffled her, because it seemed so unlike what she ordinarily felt for him. It was the response of a trusted comrade rather than that of a lover, she realized, and she was amazed that it gripped her with nearly equal force. But then she was listening to Hanp'atu explain about mushrooms and cactus buttons and their effects on the senses, and she made herself pay strict attention, wanting to know anything that might protect them from the dangers that lay ahead.

Chan Chan

THEY PASSED several large huacas on the arid plain north of Chan Chan, and then they could see the walls of the city itself, their bright colors visible even at a distance, shimmering through the waves of heat that rose from the Royal Road. Pyramids topped by shrines of wood and cloth stood out above the walls, and in the far distance were the steep hills that formed the southern boundary of the Chimor Valley. They could see nothing of the valley because the city filled the whole plain in front of them. Despite everything they had been told, they had not been prepared for the vastness of the site, which made Chiquitoy seem a mere village in comparison.

As they drew closer, the plain around them was crisscrossed by a network of low walls and shallow ditches that must once have defined and watered a broad expanse of adjoining fields. Now the dun-colored earth between the walls was baked hard and the only things growing were the cacti and scrub brush that lined the ditches. A strong wind whipped ropes of sand across the ground, and vultures circled in a sky unmarred by smoke.

They came at last to a great wooden portal that spanned the road, its façade carved in deep relief with a row of snarling pumas that seemed to glare down at them as they passed underneath. There were no guards at the gate and no one in sight among the buildings immediately in front of them. Nor was there an obvious way to proceed. The Royal Road seemed to end here, and though they could see several narrow corridors opening between the buildings, they could see only more walls and buildings beyond, no hint of a square or major street. The silence was so vast it seemed to swallow even the sandy rustle of the wind. Then a conch horn blew and they heard the nervous bleat of a llama from somewhere nearer at hand, sounds that were distinct yet impossible to locate.

"*Someone* is here," Cusi muttered under his breath, "but how do we find them?"

Then a figure emerged from one of the passageways and came toward them, smiling in greeting. After a moment of confusion, Micay realized it was a young man. He was wearing a white headdress and a long, loose tunic that fell below his knees, and he was as slender as a girl, and as graceful. He held his palms open in front of him and bowed low, speaking in heavily accented Quechua.

"Welcome, Lord Cusi Huaman. I am Fempellec. I will take you to your brother."

"Greetings, Fempellec," Cusi managed, unable to keep himself from staring at the other man's face. It was a face many women would have envied, delicate and sleek, without angles or bumps, as if there were no bones beneath the smooth, dark skin. His eyes were a liquid black that caught the light, and they were surrounded by lashes as thick and luxuriant as Mama Huarcay's. Micay found herself considering how she would paint such a face to make it truly striking, but then Fempellec glanced in her direction, and there was something undeniably masculine in the tilt of his head, and in the way his eyes swept over her appraisingly. She thought she saw a trace of surprise at her presence and a bit more at the sight of Urcon and Hanp'atu, though he covered it quickly. He also seemed unperturbed by Cusi's staring, though he finally made another small bow to break the spell.

"You must be tired and thirsty," he prompted. Cusi blinked and mumbled an apology, gesturing for the other man to lead the way. As Fempellec turned, the wind blew his long white tunic tight against his body, making it obvious that he was not wearing a loincloth underneath it. Micay caught the wide-eyed glance Cusi gave her, but she could only shrug, having seen nothing like this in Chiquitoy, either.

They entered the passageway and had to fall into single file as the walls closed in on both sides and the overhanging roofs shut off the light from above. Their path twisted and turned between freestanding walls and the backs of buildings, moving from sunlight to deep shadow and back again with a frequency that stunned the senses. Given their size and rough construction, the buildings might once have been houses or workshops, but they were crowded together in such a disorderly way that it was impossible to identify their functions or even to tell where one left off and another began. They all seemed to be intact, but the few doorways that opened onto the narrow street were all covered with curtains that hung gray and heavy with dust, and no sounds of life came from within.

Micay had quickly lost all sense of direction, and she began to wonder how Fempellec was able to remember such a dizzying route, suspecting that he was deliberately trying to confuse them. She began to hunger for a square or a public garden, someplace where she could lift her head and not feel closed in on all sides. Apparently the Chimu did not share the Incas' need for places that were open to the sky, unless this crowding had come about by accident, something else utterly unlike the Incas.

Then they passed some empty corrals whose cane fences had fared less well over time than the buildings and came out into a long street that ran along one side of an enormous enclosure. The wall was at least fifteen feet high and seemed to go on forever, carved and painted in bright colors along its entire length. The other side of the street was lined with smaller enclosures and more of the densely clustered houses, all of which seemed to have their backs to the street. The great wall was so high that most of the street was in shadow, and when they were halfway down Micay could look both behind and ahead and see that both ends of the street were eventually blocked by other walls and buildings, leaving no view of any of the hills or mountains in the distance. Who were these people, she wondered, who had no desire to look upward or beyond themselves?

They turned the corner at the end of the wall and encountered the first people they had seen, a crew of workmen who stopped and stared at them in much the same way they had stared at Fempellec earlier. Cusi nodded to them, his golden earplugs glinting in the light, and the workmen all bowed hastily, making belated gestures of deference. Fempellec went past them without a second glance, leading the way toward the entrance of an enclosure that seemed small in comparison with the monumental compound they had just passed. The unguarded doorway was deep and framed by a wooden portal much like the one they had seen outside the city, but once they had stepped through it they were confronted by another blank wall only a few feet within. Fempellec turned left and led them down the narrow corridor between the two walls, a space as cool and dark as a cave. He turned right at the very end, just when it seemed they had reached a cul-de-sac, and they followed him into a paved courtyard large enough to be filled with sunlight despite the height of the surrounding walls and the low angle of the afternoon sun.

Fempellec continued across the courtyard toward an exit on the other side, but Cusi and his companions slowed and trailed after him, blinking and gulping air like creatures who had just come up from underground. They were almost to the exit before they noticed the other people in the courtyard: a pair of elderly women cooking over a sunken hearth in one corner and five men sitting on benches against the far wall, under a sunshade made of poles and matting. The men were wearing boldly patterned tunics and headdresses, and they stared impassively at the visitors, showing no response at all to Cusi's nod of greeting. Micay was still trying to absorb the notion that room to lift your head and look at the sky was a privilege reserved for those who lived behind the double wall, so she naturally interpreted the men's lack of welcome as the arrogance of privileged ones. She was more intrigued than insulted, however, and wondered why they huddled under a makeshift shelter when they could have been out in the light and air.

After waiting for them to catch up, Fempellec led them down another blind corridor and through a series of small, connecting courtyards lined with what appeared to be storerooms. They went up one short ramp and down another. Finally they came around the corner of an interior wall and found themselves in a small but spacious courtyard. There was a row of storerooms along one side and three small houses against the back wall, but the dominant structure was a kind of freestanding awning house, a U-shaped building with a flat earthen roof that stood in the center of the courtyard. Fempellec went ahead of them and disappeared into the building's open side, and a moment later Amaru emerged from the shadowy interior, his arms spread wide in greeting.

"Cusi!" he exclaimed softly, wrapping his brother in an embrace that lifted Cusi up onto his toes and made him flail awkwardly with the hand that held his stone. Cusi laughed and Amaru released him, holding him at arm's length for another moment to look him up and down.

"I do not need to mention how much you have grown; your deeds told me that long ago. But you seem to have recovered from your wound, as well."

"Nearly," Cusi allowed, and turned to introduce his companions. But Amaru's eyes had already found Micay, and they widened along with his smile.

"Ah, I was expecting my mother, and instead I see my favorite ñusta. Have you missed me so much, Micay, or have you come here in Mama Cori's place?"

"Neither," Micay said, feeling the familiar warming effect of his teasing. "I have come here with Cusi."

"We are going to be married," Cusi declared. Amaru raised his eyebrows and looked from one to the other as if to find the truth in their faces. Then he nodded once and smiled at both of them, no longer teasing.

"I suggested this once, did I not?" he asked Micay. "So how can I deny it now? But I understand now why our mother is not with you. She would never approve of something so natural." Amaru waved a hand dismissively and pointed with his chin at Urcon and Hanp'atu. "But who are your other friends?"

Cusi introduced Urcon as the grandson of his "benefactor" in Cuzco, a deliberately vague term that made Amaru raise his eyebrows again, though he did not ask for an explanation. He seemed captivated by Urcon's smile and spoke to him with extraordinary gentleness, coaxing him out of the shyness this strange and overwhelming city had induced in the young herder. Then Cusi told the story of what Hanp'atu had done for him, and Amaru bowed to the healer in a show of respect.

"I am grateful you saved my brother, Hanp'atu; you are most welcome here. There are a number of men who will be equally grateful to trade with you for the things you carry."

"That is why I carry them," Hanp'atu said compliantly, returning the bow. Fempellec and an elderly serving woman had come out of the awning house with mats to sit on and water gourds and bowls of fresh fruit, and Amaru prevailed upon his guests to drop their bundles and sit where they were. Micay did so gratefully, giving in to the fatigue and thirst she had been ignoring for some time. She accepted a damp towel from the serving woman and pressed it against her eyes, which felt raw from squinting into the gritty wind and worn out from too much looking.

"We have no baths here," Amaru was saying, "but there is a well in the next courtyard with a pool for washing."

Micay kept the towel over her eyes, listening to his voice while she tried to recall the image she had kept of him in her memory. *That* Amaru would never have apologized for the lack of baths or anything else; such matters would have been beneath his regard.

"Will there be water for baths when the Moro Canal is restored?" Cusi asked.

There was a brief silence before Amaru laughed. A different laugh, Micay decided; detached and amused, rather than bold and disdainful.

"There was once," he acknowledged, and laughed again. "Acunta told me you were blunt and forthright in your questioning. You will have your answers, Cusi, I promise you. But must we rush to that? Is there not time to refresh yourself and enjoy my hospitality? It is something I have learned from the Chimu."

Micay lowered the towel and looked at him, and the fact of how much he had changed struck her forcefully. It was not the kind of change she had anticipated; there were no signs of dissipation or self-neglect. If anything, he seemed even leaner and more handsome. But there were fine squint lines around his eyes, and his gaze seemed distant and almost placid, as if he no longer expected to be surprised by what he saw. He even sat with a kind of languor, displaying none of the physical flamboyance she remembered so well. His black hair was unbound and had been allowed to grow longer, so that it hung down below his ears, concealing his empty earlobes.

He had persuaded Cusi to accept a slice of pineapple and was urging more on him when he suddenly became aware that Micay was studying him. He gave her a knowing smile and made a subtle gesture that brought the serving woman to remove Micay's towel and leave her a clean one. Shortly afterward Fempellec quietly set a bowl of mixed fruit down in front of her, the different-colored slices arranged in a spiral pattern.

"You must try some of this, as well, Micay," he coaxed. "Though no doubt you were well feasted by the Grand Chimu. He still commands some excellent cooks."

"We were served most elegantly at the court," Micay agreed, carefully removing a piece of mango so as not to disturb the pattern in the bowl. "And the food was delicious."

"If only the governor would learn from him," Amaru said, exchanging a brief smile with Fempellec, who had come to sit beside him.

"Mayta Yupanqui feels you have learned from him," Cusi said. "That is why he is not suspicious of what you are doing here. He is the only person in Chiquitoy who is not."

Amaru grimaced and waved a hand in front of his face, as if swatting at an insect. "He has a talent for banishing concern . . . his only talent. But do not waste any of your breath on him; you have come too far today to tire yourself needlessly."

"I am not tired," Cusi said curtly, "and I have not come this far to talk about feasting. I find frankness refreshing."

Micay stopped chewing, surprised by Cusi's sudden aggression after he had apparently acceded to Amaru's request for a postponement of serious talk. She was even more surprised that Amaru did not rebuke him for his rudeness or at least show some annoyance. His voice was remarkably even, tinged only slightly with disappointment.

"You are impatient, Brother. It is a common flaw among the Incas, one I shared once. What is it that you cannot wait to know?"

"I want to know why you have stayed here."

"Where is it you think I should go?"

"There is a war in the north. My initiation brothers are fighting there, and so are yours."

"Ancocoyuch is here. He was one of my initiation brothers, as you may recall."

"I recognized the name," Cusi allowed, "but I did not recall that you were ever close to him. In Cuzco he was better known as a dancer than as a warrior."

"No doubt you heard that from me," Amaru said ruefully. "In Cuzco I was scornful of many things. That is another flaw of the Incas."

"I can name other flaws if you wish," Cusi told him. "But that does not change my blood or yours. And like Otoronco Achachi, I can never forget how few of us there are."

"No doubt the Carangui think there are too many," Amaru suggested. He gave Micay a sardonic smile. "Was that not true of the Chachapoyas, my lady?"

It was the sort of provocative question he had used to ask her, a "serious" question, but he turned back to Cusi without waiting for her reply. He was simply fending Cusi off, she realized, using her to deflect Cusi's demand for frankness.

"The Chachapoyas were provoked," Cusi said tightly, "and I take pride only in having helped to bring the war to an end. But the Carangui are a true enemy. They slaughtered our garrisons and killed the emissaries who came to them with offers of peace and reconciliation."

"So did the Quitos, and they were forgiven easily enough once they had surrendered what Huayna Capac wanted. Do not try to convince me or yourself of the righteousness of this war. It has only one cause, and that is Huayna Capac's desire to conquer lands in his own name. I assume you have met him, Cusi. Is he a greater man than the rest of us? Is he so like a god that we should heed his every whim? Or is he just a man who has always had so much that he cannot recognize when he has enough?"

Micay had heard him speak like this before, too, though never with so little passion and resentment. He did not truly seem to care what sort of man

Huayna Capac was, as if treason were simply another twist in the argument, another diversion.

"I am pledged to serve the Sapa Inca," Cusi said stubbornly, obviously struggling with his anger. "But my sense of duty does not begin or end with him. I am also pledged to Huanacauri and to Illapa and to the memory of our ancestors. All these things tell me I should be with my comrades, avenging the Incas who have died."

"Then you have no need to think or judge for yourself," Amaru began, but Fempellec suddenly interrupted, stretching out his long, graceful hands in a gesture of appeal.

"Is there not a sense of duty between brothers?" he asked plaintively. "Are they not bound to love and understand each other? Tell me if I am wrong to think this, because I have no brothers of my own."

Cusi and Amaru exchanged a startled glance. Then both dropped their eyes, shamed into silence. Amaru was the first to look up. He gazed thoughtfully at Cusi for a moment, then turned to Fempellec and placed a hand on the young man's shoulder.

"No, you are not wrong, my friend. You know how much I have looked forward to seeing my brother after all these years apart." He reached out and put his other hand on top of Cusi's, which was resting on his stone. "You are the only person I would want to have visit me here, Cusi, and I did not mean to treat you like an ordinary guest. I meant instead to tell you how grateful I am that you have come here, even if you have come to save me from myself."

Cusi raised his head and stared at Amaru, at Fempellec, and, it seemed, at the hand on Fempellec's shoulder. His face was impassive, but his voice was thick.

"I came because I could not accept the rumors I had heard about you. I felt I should learn the truth for myself and help you if you needed help. If I am impatient, it is because I have waited a long time to hear what Acunta said you would tell me."

Amaru smiled and nodded vigorously, as if he were greatly encouraged by Cusi's response. He gave Cusi's hand a shake that made the stone roll out from under his palm.

"We will yet understand one another, I am certain. But the answer to your question is not simple, and there are things that can be shown better than they can be told. You must be patient and let me share my life with you, and then make your judgment."

Cusi gently disengaged his hand from Amaru's grasp and recovered his stone. He hefted it as he glanced sideways, first at Micay, then at Urcon and Hanp'atu on his other side. His expression seemed deliberately bland, an acquiescence that was not to be mistaken for satisfaction. Then he looked back at Amaru and nodded compliantly.

"If my comrades can be that patient, so can I. We have all come here to see Chan Chan."

"And you will," Amaru promised, beaming at his guests as if the matter had been settled. Micay found herself smiling along with everyone else, relieved that the tension had been broken. But she had heard the message in Cusi's reference to his "comrades," and she knew he had not been moved by Amaru's assurances. He put down his stone and accepted some fruit, and at Fempellec's suggestion was gazing up at the sky, admiring the colors of the sunset. Micay saw Amaru put his arm around Fempellec and give him a brief, congratulatory hug, and she wondered if he believed they had won Cusi over. Perhaps he no longer knows what frankness is, she thought, turning her eyes toward the red-streaked sky with a renewed feeling that their task here would be difficult and the truth—if they ever found it—would very likely be dangerous.

AFTER TEN DAYS Cusi felt he had been introduced to most of the aspects of his brother's life in Chan Chan. He had visited the various work sites, which were split between the sunken gardens that provided the workers with their daily sustenance and the canals that might one day return much larger tracts of land to productive use, and he had been shown the plans for each, as well as the actual work in progress. He had also toured two of the great palace enclosures that had belonged to former Grand Chimus, had met and talked with Amaru's friends and fellow workers, and had survived two nights of heavy drinking and conversation with Amaru himself. The only thing he had yet to experience was one of their celebrations, but that would be remedied in a few days, when the Feast of the New Moon would be held. He had already heard many stories about these feasts, which were reportedly examples of Chimu hospitality at its most exuberant.

Over the course of these same days, the reason Amaru and the others were here had also been revealed to him. The project had been the inspiration of Ancocoyuch, who had decided to make a peaceful conquest of unused lands, reclaiming them as a gift to the Sapa Inca and the Grand Chimu, thereby proving himself a worthy heir to his father and a loyal subject of the Inca. Ancocoyuch himself, in an apparently impulsive moment of candor, had confided to Cusi that he had a deeper motive: that he intended, once he was Grand Chimu, to revive the ceremonies venerating the Chimu ancestors, a duty his father had neglected in recent years. For this reason he wanted to see the city surrounded by green again, its streets and buildings maintained by those the fields would support. He had laughed heartily at Cusi's suggestion, offered as a joke, that Chan Chan itself might be restored to such an extent that Ancocoyuch would be tempted to move his whole court here. Cusi had laughed, too, agreeing that such a possibility was beyond imagining, and that of course they would all wish to return to Chiquitoy once their work here was done.

None of this, however, even if it were true, explained Amaru's interest in the project. He claimed to be drawn by the challenge to his skill as a builder and by the chance to help his initiation brother and win the favor of the next Grand Chimu. But he had not displayed an overwhelming affection for Ancocoyuch, whose favor was worth little at present and would never be very great as long as he ruled under the Inca. And the challenge of resurrecting the Moro Canal seemed more like a wild hope, given the number of workers Amaru presently had available. Why would he dedicate himself to years of thankless work with so little immediate reward and such a large chance of failure?

Yet Amaru remained fundamentally evasive despite all the talking they had done. When pressed he referred vaguely to powerful experiences he had had both in Chan Chan and at the shrine in Pachacamac, experiences that had supposedly stripped him of vanity and ambition and changed the way he viewed his life. But he refused to elaborate, claiming an inability to put these things into words and an unwillingness to see them distorted in the attempt. Cusi found this reticence especially frustrating, because he sensed—as he seldom did otherwise—that Amaru was telling him something like the truth.

Feeling the need to be away from his brother and Fempellec and the others who were always around to guide and explain, Cusi asked to visit the great huacas of Mama Cocha and the Moon, which were well south of Chan Chan, on the other side of the Chimor River. Hanp'atu was engaged in trading with those who were planning the feast, and Urcon chose to stay with him, so only Cusi and Micay went south with the guide Amaru had provided, a young Chimu named Pongmassa. They passed through the cotton fields on the flood-plain of the river, then ventured out onto the windswept dunes that surrounded the enormous pyramids, the largest structures ever raised by the Mochica. Gazing at the towering adobe shrines, the size of small mountains, Cusi was seized by the sudden conviction that the descendants of these people would not be content merely to water a few fields and then go back to their homes. No amount of hearty laughter made that seem appropriate.

I have seen everything, he thought, but I still understand nothing. Or had he only seen what Amaru wanted him to see? Where else should he look, and for what? As Pongmassa began to lead them away from the huacas, Cusi looked ahead into the green Chimor Valley and recalled a suggestion the micho Topa Roca had made to him. He did not know how it might help, but suddenly it seemed worth the small effort it would require. So he stopped Pongmassa and told him to take them into the valley so that he could pay a courtesy visit to the official who was responsible for the fields and herds that belonged to the Inca. The guide was visibly reluctant to depart from their original itinerary, but he was too young to contend with someone of Cusi's rank and not clever enough to think of a compelling excuse.

They turned inland and found the official at the small Inca administrative center halfway up the valley. He was an Inca by privilege from Chincha, but he recognized Cusi's name and had known that he was in the area. He was surprised and flattered by the visit, but above all he was anxious to tell the Sapa Inca's representative about his recent difficulties. He wanted to explain in advance about the bad luck that would reduce this year's tallies through no fault of his own. Cusi encouraged him politely, and the man told him about the unusually low birthrate among the herds, the llamas that had been lost to disease and marauding pumas, and the rash of accidents that had carried off a number of young men and women, among them some fine craftsmen and weavers. Then there were the requests from the governor to release workers to Chan Chan for extended periods; surely the governor had been aware that these transfers would make it harder for the remaining families to fulfill their labor obligations. Surely Cusi could see that and would not let the governor forget.

Cusi heard the man out and did his best to reassure him that he would not be punished for matters beyond his control. It was not easy, for the man was extremely worried and Cusi himself was eager to be away and alone with his own thoughts—because he thought he was finally beginning to understand. But he had the presence of mind to ask one question before he left.

"Tell me, did the llamas and alpacas bear fewer twins this year?"

"Why—yes!" the man said in amazement. "How did you know? That is the major reason the herds have not increased."

"It is a phenomenon I have observed elsewhere," Cusi said blandly, concealing his own excitement at the confirmation he had received. Once outside he concealed it from Pongmassa, as well, acting bored and disgruntled as if the visit had been a waste of time. Micay automatically put on a similar face, though he could feel that her curiosity had also been aroused. They walked down out of the valley in silence, Cusi turning things over in his mind, arranging and rearranging what he had seen and heard and dwelling especially on the odd bits of information he and his comrades had collected. When they were once again on the plain and Pongmassa had drawn far enough ahead on the road, he turned eagerly to Micay.

"What do you make of what the official said?" he asked.

She gave a short laugh, as if she had been about to ask the same question. "He has either suffered the most terrible luck," she guessed, "or he is the victim of some very clever thieves. Thieves that steal people as well as animals."

"The Chimu seem to fear thieves, do they not? They build their storerooms inside their enclosures rather than out, and they block the way to them with walls and corridors and guardhouses."

"They believe that Si watches over their possessions during her nightly vigils," Micay told him. "I had thought that was a peculiar role to attribute to the Moon Mother, but perhaps it comes from a knowledge of themselves."

"No doubt. These thieves may be too clever even for Si. Did you not tell me that you had seen one of the post runners stop to talk to Ancocoyuch?"

"Urcon saw it, too. We were both surprised that the messenger would stop for so long. Fempellec was with us, and he said that was how they learned the latest news from Chiquitoy and Tumibamba."

"What if they *send* messages as well as receive them?" Cusi suggested, and saw her eyes widen with comprehension.

"The governor's requests," she whispered.

Cusi nodded with grim satisfaction. "Mayta Yupanqui told me that none of the Inca's workers were involved in this project, and no doubt that is true as far as *he* is concerned. The only better way to steal workers would be to have their chiefs report them as dead or missing, so that they would be removed from the labor tallies altogether. Gone forever—like a llama dragged off to the puma's den."

"What is the significance of the twins?" Micay asked, frowning intently.

Cusi smiled at her for a moment, loving her for her concentration, her desire to understand all of it. "It is something Urcon noticed. Do you remember how he told us about that day he heard a llama bawling and slipped away from Hanp'atu and their guide to investigate? And he found the corral filled with young llamas?"

"He said the crying llama had been weaned too soon," Micay recalled, "and the herder did not seem to know it or what to do about it."

"He was a guard, not a herder, and he would not allow Urcon to stay around to help. But Urcon got a look at the whole herd, and he was struck by the fact that there were no two alike. In a herd of that size he would have expected several identical pairs."

"So one is stolen and one is left to be counted," Micay concluded. "And the Inca's official anguishes over his bad luck but sees no reason to be suspicious."

"Exactly," Cusi said. Then he had to break off the conversation, for Pongmassa was waiting just ahead. They had reached the outskirts of the city, and from this distance Cusi could see smoke rising up above the walls in several places. More places, in fact, than he would have expected. Yet he knew that once he was inside those walls, he would only be able to see what was directly in front of him, and he would have to rely on Pongmassa just to find his way back to Amaru's compound. From there he would certainly see nothing important, nothing that might corroborate his suspicions.

To postpone that eventuality and because he could think of no better excuse, he told Pongmassa that they should stop at the nearest well for water and a rest.

"I cannot go any farther without a drink," Micay complained in a peevish tone she must have learned from some other ñusta, because he had never heard her use it before. He smiled at her behind Pongmassa's back as the guide sighed in resignation and led them into a high-walled compound that appeared to be very old, its buildings and painted walls damaged by more than one of the infrequent rains. The well was at one end of an interior courtyard; at the other end was a colonnade that had collapsed for half its length, so that the buckled roof leaned up against the outer wall like an earthen ramp. Pongmassa pulled back the well's wooden cover and filled a gourd with water for them, then went to squat in the shade beneath the undamaged part of the colonnade.

"There are more people here than we have seen," Cusi said as they drank from the gourd. It was hot in the open, but he had no desire to share their conversation with the man in the shade.

Micay squinted at him doubtfully. "Perhaps they are not here."

"They must be. I should have seen it earlier. The sunken gardens can feed many more people than Amaru has shown us, and why would he want a surplus? And too many of his friends are not fit for the sort of work they pretend to do. You said as much yourself. You said they were creatures of the court and that they did not regard you with the hunger of men who were deprived of women. So where are the women? All we have seen are gray-haired cooks."

"Perhaps they have been moved away while you are here," Micay suggested. "If they are as clever as you say—"

"They are, I know it," Cusi insisted. "But it would be safer to hide the workers here than to move them. You could hide an army in this city."

"Then where do you begin to look?"

Cusi spread his hands and exhaled heavily. "I do not know. I cannot see through these walls, and I could not find my way around them, even if I were free to do so . . ."

He trailed off in frustration, realizing that he had woven a whole fabric out of his suspicions without possessing even a thread of evidence. He and Urcon had returned to that corral the next day only to find it empty, swept clean of both tracks and droppings.

"Perhaps you could see *over* them," Micay said abruptly. Cusi looked up at her in surprise, not understanding until she inclined her head toward the colonnade. The collapsed part of the roof appeared solid enough to hold his weight, at least until he could jump to the part that was still intact. From there he could easily climb to the top of the wall and might be able to see where the smoke was coming from. But then he saw Pongmassa squatting below.

"I do not know how much I will see from up there," he said to Micay, "but Amaru would certainly be alerted to my suspicions."

"Does that matter? If what we suspect is true, he is not going to offer you the proof."

"No," Cusi agreed. he stood up, handing her the gourd. "We will have to see for ourselves. Stand where you can see both me and the sun, and try to remember where I point."

He started toward the colonnade, walking casually, as if he were coming to announce another delay. Pongmassa looked at him but did not rise, and then Cusi was close enough to see the steep angle at which the roof had fallen and the deep gullies the rain had cut through its covering of dirt. He realized that if he hesitated or lost his momentum, he would break through or slide back down and end up looking like an utter fool. So he put his head down and began to run, feeling a wild surge of elation as his legs lifted him up and propelled him forward. Out of the corner of his eye he saw Pongmassa jump up and shout a warning, but then he flew past and sprang up onto the ramp, landing with a sharp cracking sound but never slowing, flailing with his arms as he churned upward through the crusty layer of sand and earth. He heard canes and timbers snapping amid the clatter of debris, and he saw a section of the roof ahead of him buckle and open, but he was already high enough, on a level with the flat roof to his left, and when he jumped he felt another burst of enthusiasm, remembering the joy of soaring through the air.

The whole roof shuddered when he landed, but it held him. Pongmassa was calling to him to come down before he hurt himself, but Cusi ignored him and jumped again, catching hold of the top of the wall and pulling himself up with a grunt of effort. He sat for a moment, breathing hard and feeling a pain in his side for the first time. When it passed he stood up and smiled down at Micay, who was watching him from the middle of the courtyard. Then he stared out over the maze of walls and rooftops, trying to get his bearings. The way he had been led around by his guides had prevented him from formulating a coherent map of the streets, but he had learned to orient himself by means of the major pyramids, which varied in size, shape, and degree of deterioration. Shading his eyes with his hand, he located the low, smoothly finished pyramid that was the burial place of Minchancaman, the last Grand Chimu to rule Chan Chan. Amaru had his quarters in an annex just to the north of Minchancaman's palatial enclosure, and in that direction Cusi spied several plumes of smoke rising up into the still air. Farther north and well to the east, a single dark column was visible against the sky, and Cusi reckoned that it had to be coming from the canal work site, where the workers were probably burning brush. Turning slowly back toward the west, he saw a similar column rising up to the left of Minchancaman's pyramid, in the area he associated with the sunken gardens. More innocent smoke.

Then he turned another step and saw what he had been looking for—due west, almost directly in the descending path of the sun. The smoke was concentrated in a single area but was rising from a number of sources. More than just cooking fires, Cusi thought. To the south was a large, apparently ancient pyramid that he did not recognize, and he realized that none of their tours of the city had taken them near it. He glanced down to get Micay's attention, then raised his arms straight out in front of him and put his fingertips together, forming an arrow that pointed directly at the smoke.

When he got back down to the front edge of the roof, he lowered himself part of the way over and then let himself drop, landing in a crouch. Micay was nodding to him, her eyes bright with shared triumph, but Pongmassa was staring at him as if he had lost his mind.

"I want to go toward the Great Waters," Cusi told him pointing toward the sun with his chin. "Toward Inti. There is a pyramid I have never seen."

"It is not allowed," Pongmassa protested in bewilderment.

Cusi cut him off sharply. "You are my guide, and that is where I wish to go. Do as I say."

Pongmassa was about Cusi's age, but he was considerably larger and had a strong upper body. Anger came into his eyes for an instant, but Cusi never gave him a chance to dwell on it, fixing him with a glare that seemed to well up from deep inside, carrying all his dark memories of injury and death and some of the fierce joy he had felt in running and jumping again. Pongmassa shrank back and turned without a word to lead the way, and Cusi lurched after him in a kind of daze, feeling Micay take his arm to steady him. When he was able to look at her again, there was concern rather than triumph in her eyes,

and she shook her head sternly when he opened his mouth to speak. It is the
only weapon I have, he thought, since he could not say it aloud. And the thrill
of running had somehow made it stronger and more available. That was
something else he would have to remember to tell her later.

Pongmassa displayed no desire to run, but neither did he try to lead them
astray. The lowering sun made it easier for Cusi and Micay to assure themselves of that, though they had to shield their eyes with their hands to keep
from being blinded. Finally Pongmassa brought them to the juncture of two
avenues, at the corner of a huge enclosure that stretched away to the south
and west. The high walls were old and eroded, the paint faded and flaking off
in patches. The guide pointed sullenly toward the top of the pyramid, which
could just be seen rising above the walls at the southern end of the enclosure.

"Good," Cusi said absently. He looked down the avenue to their right,
following Micay's line of vision to the smoke she had already spotted. They
started walking simultaneously, Cusi calling back over his shoulder to Pongmassa. "We will go this way."

The young man caught up with them quickly, running backwards in front
of them and making frantic gestures of denial. "No, my lord, please . . . the
walls have fallen there and the way is blocked. It is a dangerous place!"

"Then why are people living there?" Cusi demanded, seeing no point in
concealing his suspicions any longer. Pongmassa opened his mouth but then
dropped his hands and fell silent, stepping aside to let them go ahead of him.
They continued down the avenue, smelling the smoke now and catching
occasional glimpses of it above the crumbling walls of a smaller compound to
their right. They rounded the corner of the compound and found themselves
in a crowded quarter of small single-room buildings, much like the area they
had passed through on entering the city. Some of the outer buildings had
indeed broken down and lacked roofs, but the narrow gaps between them were
still open and there was a clear path beaten into the dust, leading into the
interior. Remembering caution, Cusi went through first, following not the path
but the sound of voices he could hear ahead and the cooking smells that drifted
to his nostrils. They passed through the middle of two deserted clusters of
buildings and were about to enter a third when Cusi spied a swift movement
in the shadows and froze, throwing out his arms to keep Micay back. Then
he laughed and started forward again, causing a tiny animal to scurry out into
the light.

"Guinea pig," he said over his shoulder as the long-haired little rodent
disappeared under the ragged curtain that covered the doorway of an abandoned building. That was another sign of occupation, because guinea pigs did
not live in the wild. Three llamas were penned up between two buildings in
the next cluster, a superfluous sign as he began to identify sounds that had
baffled him at first but that now told him what these people were doing here:
the steady, clinking tap of stone hammers on metal, the muted screech of a
woodworker's rasp, the clack and shuffle of weavers at their looms. The smell
of wood smoke was very strong as he approached the next gap, and as he came

out of the dark corridor he saw two Chimu women squatting beside a large fire pit in the middle of a courtyard. They were dumping handfuls of dirt onto the fire, smothering it in what seemed a very even and methodical manner. Potters, Cusi thought, having learned from Acunta how the Chimu produced their shiny black pots.

The women finally glanced up from their work, and their heads jerked back in shock at the sight of Cusi and Micay. They seemed too stunned to move or speak, so Cusi nodded to them and began to lead Micay past.

"See to your fire," he said. The women simply stared up at him, their hands still filled with dirt. A child appeared in the opening ahead—the first child they had seen in Chan Chan—but turned immediately and ran back the way he had come. By the time Cusi entered the next courtyard with Micay and then Pongmassa behind him, the small, irregularly shaped space was beginning to fill with people. They stood silently with their tools in their hands, their faces and arms smudged with soot and paint, their clothing tufted with bits of wool or wood shavings. A few of the women still sat on the wooden benches next to the doorways or on the ground near the poles to which their looms were tied. Cusi glanced through an open doorway and saw that benches and bins had been built in against the back wall, no doubt to accommodate some similar but long dead group of craftspeople.

Behind him Pongmassa and another man were speaking in low voices, in Mochica. Cusi simply waited, since he did not know what to say now that he was here, with his proof standing all around him. Finally the guide came up beside him and dipped his head in a bow.

"They want to know if the Inca has come to punish them."

Cusi scanned the faces around him, seeing both fear and deference in the way they hastily lowered their eyes. They obviously knew they did not belong here, yet they had just as obviously established lives for themselves here, lives he could shatter with just a few words of disapproval. He saw several of the children staring at his earplugs with undisguised awe, as if they had never seen an Inca of the blood before.

"Have they been brought here against their will?" he asked. Several others besides Pongmassa shook their heads in denial.

"No, my lord. This is how their grandfathers lived, and their grandfathers before that. They wish to live here."

But who has given them that choice? Cusi thought, though he did not say it aloud. They would not be the ones to answer for that crime. He glanced at Micay and found her regarding him with a kind of wary expectation, not as a lover or a comrade, he realized, but as an Inca. That chilled him slightly, but it also made him consider his responsibility to these people, who had been safe here until he had come looking for evidence.

"Tell them," he said to Pongmassa, "that I am the Sapa Inca's representative, not his spokesman. It is not in my power to punish or forgive. But tell them, as well, that I will speak on behalf of their right to stay here and live in the way of their grandfathers."

Several people bowed in gratitude before Pongmassa had even begun to translate, and when one had the boldness to smile at him, Cusi beckoned to the man and drew him aside, away from the sound of Pongmassa's voice.

"Tell me, my friend, does Ancocoyuch keep his women near here? The women who do not work, I mean . . ."

The man smiled again knowingly, and gestured with his chin. "Behind the palace of Minchancaman," he said in rough Quechua. "Boys, too, pretty ones, very skilled. But the guards let no one come close."

Pongmassa had stopped speaking, and Cusi turned to acknowledge the bows he was receiving. Then he took Micay's arm and looked back at the man with a smile of his own.

"I have no need to go there," he said. The man cast a glance at Micay and laughed appreciatively.

"Go where?" Pongmassa asked with renewed apprehension, but Cusi simply laughed and shook his head.

"Another place I am not expected," he told the guide, and bowed in farewell to the people in the courtyard. "Come, lead us back to our quarters. We have seen enough for one day."

FROM HER place in the doorway of the guest house, Micay saw Cusi come around the corner of the awning house and walk toward her. He carried his stone casually in one hand, but it did not detract from the authority of his appearance. His golden earplugs and the silver household badge on his headband had been polished to a high shine, and he was splendidly attired in a cumbi-cloth tunic of buff-colored vicuña with a border of red chevrons, wristbands woven from scarlet feathers, and his fringed coca bag under his arm. He considered himself to be the only Inca who would attend this feast, and he had made sure that no one would mistake him for a pilgrim or a common warrior.

His expression, though, was grim and troubled, and she guessed that Amaru had managed to evade him again. He squatted in front of her and set his stone on the ground, and Micay hesitated before holding out her hands to him, knowing that the coldness of her fingers would alert him to her own anxiety. But he merely frowned in sympathy and gripped her fingers more firmly, unable to smile or find words of comfort.

"He would not hear you?" she suggested.

Cusi exhaled through his nose and gave an angry shrug, his earplugs casting wavering reflections onto his cheeks. "He was not there. He sent a messenger to say he had been detained and would meet us at the feast. Urcon and Hanp'atu are waiting with the messenger, who will take us there."

"It is not too late to leave," Micay said halfheartedly. "We could make an excuse to the messenger and slip away undetected. They will not leave their feast to come after us."

"If the Inca's name does not protect me at the feast, it will not protect us on the road. And if I am forced to flee, I will have to bring troops back to punish those who made me go. Then all the work here will be destroyed."

"It may well be destroyed anyway, once the Sapa Inca learns of the thefts that have been committed."

"I know," Cusi allowed. "But if I am the one who must bring that about, I cannot run now, before I have even been threatened. If it is possible to resolve this peacefully, I am the only one who can do it. I owe it to those people, and to Amaru, to have the courage to try."

Micay had known she would not sway him, but she also knew it made him stronger to speak his reasons aloud. She freed her hands and reached up to touch him on the cheek.

"Be brave, my love, but come back to me."

Cusi bared his teeth in a failed attempt at a smile. "I would feel safer if you were going with me. Safer for both of us."

"I would, too," she agreed, "but I do not belong at this feast for many reasons. No one will bother me here. If they should," she added, reaching down to withdraw the long bronze needle she had stuck through her belt, "I can protect myself."

"Trust no one," Cusi warned, though he had to smile at the way she brandished the needle. "Do not trust a summons unless it is borne by either Urcon or Hanp'atu."

Micay nodded as she replaced the pin in her belt. Then she reached out with both hands and scooped up his stone and held it out to him, surprised at how heavy it was.

"Take your weapon. And do not hesitate to use your other weapons, or to run. Do not let anyone close enough to hurt you."

Cusi took the stone from her and pressed it against his chest as he leaned forward to kiss her on the lips. He lingered until his balance was threatened and he had to rock back on his heels.

"I am not meant to die here," he said solemnly, "and I have you to live for now. Watch for me, Micay; I will be back."

He rose in one motion—no longer needing to put out an arm to brace himself—and turned to walk away. But he had not gone very far before he looked back over his shoulder, and he continued to stare at her until he turned the corner of the awning house and disappeared from sight.

Micay shivered and pulled her mantle closer around her shoulders. The day had only begun to cool and the sun was not fully set, but there was no heat in her body. Her bleeding had begun two days earlier, during the dark of the moon, and she had chosen not to hide the fact, even though it barred her from the feast. It would not have barred her from a feast of Mama Quilla, but the priests of Si were men, and their distaste for a woman's blood had driven her into seclusion. It was what she wanted, anyway, since she would have been the only ñusta at the feast, the only woman not there to serve or entertain. And Hanp'atu had told her and Cusi about the array of herbs and powders that would be offered to the guests along with the food and akha, medicines that

made healthy men see visions and speak from trances and dance until they
dropped. She would have been no help to Cusi under such circumstances; more
likely, he would have had to protect *her*.

The sky was red but fading, and already she could hear drums beating from
the direction of Minchancaman's enclosure, where the feast was being held—
where Amaru and the Chimu would be waiting to welcome Cusi into their
midst, knowing that he was aware of their crimes. He had hoped at least to
know where Amaru stood beforehand, but Amaru had given him no chance
for a confrontation and had said nothing to Cusi about their day with Pongmassa. It was a guilty silence that had almost persuaded Cusi to abandon his
brother and leave for Chiquitoy.

But he is not that kind of Inca, Micay thought with an affection that was
as rueful as it was admiring. He would not call for the warriors until he had
heard and said everything that might prevent their coming. It was the way an
Inca was supposed to act, the way she wanted him to act so that she would
not hate him for his power. Yet the thought of losing him now filled her with
a despair she could not face; she would want to die, too. So although the moon
was only beginning to rise, somewhere beyond the eastern mountains, Micay
began to pray to Mama Quilla, calling on the Moon Mother to protect her son.
She prayed that the Chimu would not be tempted to add murder to their crimes
and that Amaru would not let himself betray his brother. Above all, she
prayed—with all her heart—that the blind man was right.

THERE WERE perhaps fifty people standing in the forecourt of Minchancaman's pyramid. They were massed in the center of the square plaza, which
could have accommodated several times their number. Yet in their midst a
single figure stood surrounded by open space, with no one else within twenty
feet of him. Cusi had been led to this spot by a priest after being separated from
Urcon and Hanp'atu at the gate. They had been turned back because they were
commoners, an obstacle Cusi should have foreseen but which he could not
dispute with the drums beating and everyone around him maintaining the
solemn decorum of the ceremony. The priest had left him in the plaza, and
none of the other celebrants had come to stand beside or in front of him,
though he could feel their eyes on his back.

While the light lasted, he watched the Chimus of royal blood—the only ones
allowed beyond the forecourt—climb the walled ramp that zigzagged up the
northern side of the pyramid. A fire was burning on the top platform beneath
a cloth canopy stretched over a framework of tall poles. The platform gradually filled with men, priests in long robes and nobles in brightly colored tunics,
standing three to four deep around the canopied area. Cusi wondered if Amaru
had been allowed that high or if he had been held back at one of the lower
levels. The Chimus restricted everything according to rank, even, as Micay had
pointed out to him, access to the sky above.

When night had fallen and the bright crescent of the rising moon could be seen above the eastern walls of the enclosure, the prayers and singing began, accompanied by the beating of drums and the blowing of flutes and conch horns. The ceremony was conducted by a priest who wore a silver crescent on the chest of his black robe and a black Chimu headdress over his long white hair, which flowed onto his shoulders. Backlit by the fire, he was a dramatic figure when he came to the edge of the platform to exhort those standing below and those who listened in adjoining courtyards. Cusi could understand nothing of what he said, except for the name of Si, but the man's voice was distinct and compelling, even at that distance.

That would have to be Naymlap, Cusi decided. Hanp'atu had heard him described as a powerful sorcerer and healer, an exile from the priesthood in Chiquitoy who had been living in the desert and the mountains for many years, seeking visions. Cusi could feel his presence from where he stood, and he wondered if he would have to face Naymlap before the night was through. He had no idea what or whom to expect, because Amaru had given him no clue. The people around him began to sing in Mochica, making him even more aware of his isolation in their midst. He understood how Otoronco Achachi had felt outside the fortress of the Moxos, waiting for the arrows to fly; how Pachacuti had faced the prospect of fighting the Chancas, knowing he was impossibly outnumbered. Too many crimes had already been committed, and he knew too much about them. They might hasten a reckoning by killing him and his comrades, but then again they might postpone it while they found some way to conceal their other crimes. They were clever people; they might even find a way to explain the deaths and escape all punishment.

Perhaps Amaru will explain for them, Cusi thought, and felt the anger that had been building inside him turn hard and cold. If he had fled with the evidence he already possessed, he might still have been able to argue for the innocence of the craftsmen and their families. But he could not have defended Amaru, who had been a passive witness to treason and thus deserved as harsh a punishment as any of the traitors. Cusi had stayed to save him from certain disgrace and death, yet he had no reason to believe Amaru would lift a hand to defend him in return. Amaru had yet to offer a word that was helpful or worthy of trust.

As the ceremony above him began to conclude, Cusi held his stone against his hip and put his other hand over the spirit brother in his waistband. Si was a god foreign to him, and he did not know if Illapa's power reached into this rainless land. But he had faced death before, and he would face it again if he had to, with his whole being. He shut out the memory of the fear that had paralyzed him on the cliff and thought only of the hatred he had felt for the sentry who had taunted him for his helplessness. The earth will not hold you, he chanted silently, you will soar like a hawk and plummet like Illapa's lightning . . .

He had closed his eyes to draw in on himself, and when he opened them again a line of men was coming down the ramp of the pyramid, each man holding a torch overhead. The people around him began to break ranks and

make way for the servants who had come into the courtyard, their arms filled
with reed mats and baskets of flowers. Cusi stood where he was. No one came
near him or blocked his view of the bottom of the ramp, where the first torch
bearers had just appeared. They streamed into the courtyard with celebratory
smiles on their faces, calling to their friends and handing their torches to
servants, who took them to wooden holders set out around the perimeter of
the plaza.

Most of the line had descended before Amaru appeared, a testament to his
standing with the Chimu. Cusi actually recognized Fempellec first, because
Amaru was wearing full Chimu dress and was not immediately distinguishable
from the men around him. Fempellec had reddened his lips and darkened his
eyes and was wearing a long, gauzy tunic that clung to his slender body,
making it impossible *not* to distinguish him from the other men.

Amaru smiled in greeting as he came toward Cusi, followed by Fempellec
and five or six other men. Cusi recognized Pongmassa and Acunta among
them, but he gave no sign of recognition to either of his former guides. Nor
did he return Amaru's smile.

"Welcome, my brother," Amaru began.

Cusi cut him off with a curt shake of his head. "We must talk, Amaru. I
will have the answer I came here for, or I will leave now without it."

"But we have not broken our fast! It is rude even to suggest—"

"I owe no courtesy to those who would deceive me. Do not put me off again,
or it will be the last time we speak."

Before Amaru could reply, Pongmassa took a belligerent step forward from
behind him. Cusi felt his anger billow up inside him, raising him up onto his
toes with his stone curled in one hand. In his mind he could see their bodies
coming together, the arc of his arm as he smashed the stone against Pongmassa's forehead. But Fempellec gasped in fright and Amaru thrust himself
in front of Pongmassa, holding up his palms to Cusi. He nodded, appearing
shaken.

"Come, then, and we will talk. There is a place prepared for later . . ."

Fempellec retrieved a torch from one of the holders and led the way out of
the couryard. Cusi stalked off after him, not looking back to see who followed.
He was still ready to strike someone, and it would not have mattered who;
anyone who gave human shape to his sense of being threatened would do.
Fempellec was trotting to stay ahead of him, and Cusi followed without regard
for where they were going, stamping his feet occasionally in an attempt to
dispel some of the deadly energy surging through his body.

He was led into a courtyard about the size of a large room, with niches in
all four walls and a low bench built along one side. Fempellec fixed the torch
in a holder near the doorway, and Cusi saw that mats and cups and other
feasting implements had been laid out on the floor and along the bench. He
walked past Fempellec into the middle of the courtyard and stood with his
back to the door, breathing deeply until he felt calm and clearheaded again.

When he turned Amaru was standing a few feet away, frowning at him, and Fempellec was a few feet behind him.

"Alone, Amaru," Cusi said. Fempellec lowered his eyes and began to back away. Amaru turned as if to stay him, then thought better of it and let him go without a word. He turned back to Cusi, his face tight with annoyance.

"You have no cause to treat *him* with scorn."

"I do not know who he is or what place he has in your life. Perhaps I do not wish to know."

"Perhaps you are afraid to know," Amaru suggested, and Cusi grunted in disgust. He crouched down and picked up a bronze tube that was lying on the mat at his feet. It was hollow and about a foot long, with a flared lip at one end. He put down his stone and fished in his coca bag, removing the small leather pouch that Raurau Illa had given him long before.

"Tell me, then," he said, offering the pouch and tube to his brother.

A startled curiosity replaced the anger on Amaru's face, and he squatted down across from Cusi and took the implements into his own hands. He examined them for a moment, opening the bag and using a wet fingertip to raise some of the gray powder within it to his lips. He grimaced at the bitterness of the taste and gave Cusi a sardonic smile.

"This is how the Chimus first came to trust me. Unlike the Incas and their spies, I was not afraid to accept a tube of vilca or a bowl of huacacachu. I was not afraid of what I might see—or say—when I was in the place of visions."

"This will not give us visions, but perhaps it will help us hear each other. Before it is too late."

Amaru squinted at him skeptically, then shrugged and busied himself with the pouch, carefully pouring a small amount of the gray powder into the flared end of the tube. Then he held the tube out between them. Cusi fitted his nose into the flared opening, and Amaru blew hard into his end. Once the fire had gone out in Cusi's head and his eyes had stopped watering, he took the pouch and tube and repeated the process for Amaru. They sat back on their haunches and stared at one another for several moments, sniffling and licking their lips as the drug began to take effect. Cusi felt the clarity of vision he had possessed in the highlands return to him, giving him a momentary surge of confidence. But he still could not read Amaru's expression, which seemed incongruously calm, given the way his eyes glittered in the torchlight.

"What do you feel you must report to the governor?" Amaru asked finally.

Cusi paused for a moment to consider the way the question had been phrased. As if there might be some things he would wish to forget.

"Everything," he said flatly. "And it will be reported to the Sapa Inca as well by messengers that can be trusted."

"But what can you say? What have you actually seen? A few craftsmen and their families—"

"—who were stolen from their clans and removed from the census count under false pretenses."

"Yet you promised to defend these people," Amaru pointed out. "Would you betray them first?"

"I will speak for them, but not for those who brought them here. And not for those who have stolen llamas and alpacas from the royal herds and workers from the Chiquitoy Valley. That is not just theft but treason. So is the use of the post runners to carry false messages."

"Indeed, but what proof could you offer for any of this?"

"A royal inspector would find the proof, if the governor's inspectors did not find it first," Cusi assured him. "The theft of the workers would have been discovered soon, in any case. You had to know that, Amaru. It was too bold a crime to conceal for long."

"There are some here who are very impatient, and they do not consult with me before they act. They are the same ones who believe you and your companions should not be allowed to leave here alive."

Cusi drew a slow breath, aware of the dryness in his mouth and the accelerated beating of his heart. Again he envisioned himself smashing his stone against Pongmassa's head.

"They must be impatient fools," he said emphatically. "Do they think they can kill the Sapa Inca's representative with impunity? They would pay with their lives and those of all their descendants."

"They think Huayna Capac is preoccupied in the north," Amaru shrugged. "In the past, he has shown himself to be slow to take revenge. He might even forgive them, as he did the Quitos."

"Not for the death of Cusi Huaman. And if anything happens to prevent my return, our mother would lead the troops here herself. No one in Chiquitoy would believe that an accident claimed all four of us."

Amaru held up a hand to him. "I am not the one you must convince. Though I must tell you, you will convince no one here that you are harmless if you speak to them as you have spoken to me. It would be better to acknowledge the weakness of your position and prepare a more humble response, even if you are Cusi Huaman. Because of what you said to the craftsmen, there is a majority who would trust you to leave. But you would have to swear to them that you will say nothing to jeopardize what they have here."

"Better?" Cusi repeated incredulously. "To ignore treason is to make it your own. Or have you forgotten everything here?"

"You saw no treason," Amaru reminded him. "You could say that truthfully. It is your only hope, Cusi. If you value your life and the lives of Micay and your friends, you must swear to be silent."

Cusi came forward onto his knees and picked up his stone. But he spoke with quiet conviction.

"No."

"No? Then—"

"Then what, my brother? Will you stand by and let them kill us?"

"The choice to live is yours, not mine."

Cusi stood up and stared down at him, grasping the stone with both hands so he would not be tempted to use it.

"You *have* forgotten everything, if you would choose to live with my blood on your hands. But it will not happen, Amaru. I am not meant to die here, and I will not let you make traitors of both of us. We must find another way."

"There is no other way," Amaru said wearily.

"We must devise one, then," Cusi snapped, gazing desperately around the courtyard for a source of inspiration. His eyes fell on the pouch at his feet, and he remembered Raurau Illa telling him he would return there in need. He needed another of Raurau Illa's visions to guide him now. Or one of his own. He looked back at Amaru. "You were not afraid to go to the place of visions with the Chimus. Would you go there with your brother?"

Amaru opened and closed his mouth and then stood up himself. "We would be helpless while we were there."

"You say I am helpless here, anyway. We must see if that is true."

Amaru stared at him for another moment, then nodded once, curtly. His face was no longer calm, but he seemed wary of his own excitement and did not smile.

"Prepare yourself, then," he said, and turned toward the doorway. "I will return with the huacacachu, and we will go together."

MICAY HAD BEEN promised a portion of the feasting food, so she was not startled when Fempellec and two male servants suddenly appeared from around the corner of the awning house. One servant carried reed mats and a torch to light their way; the other had a large basket covered with a cloth. Fempellec carried only a painted drinking gourd and seemed to drift along beside the servants.

"Greetings, my lady," he said in his sibilant Quechua, making a perfunctory bow. Then he gestured to the servants and spoke to them in rapid Mochica, giving them detailed instructions on how to lay out the food and flowers that were inside the basket. There was enough food for several people, though it came in the form of a number of small, separate dishes, in accordance with the Chimu preference for variety and color over sheer abundance. Micay felt feasted simply by the smells that rose from the steaming bowls of soup and stew and the plates of roast meat and baked fish.

When the meal had been arranged to Fempellec's satisfaction—in a perfect semicircle ringed with flowers—the servants fixed the torch into the wall holder behind Micay and disappeared into the darkness with the basket. Fempellec, however, remained where he was, staring down at the food as if he expected to find some flaw in its arrangement. His black hair hung loosely around his soft, sensual face, which he had painted in a manner Micay found rather crudely seductive, though not unlike the way the women in the Grand Chimu's court made themselves up. His tunic was so sheer that she could see the dark circles of his nipples and the tight, sculpted cluster of his genitals, which showed him to be more a boy than a man.

"Would you eat with me, Fempellec?" she prompted. "I would be grateful for your company."

He blinked in surprise, as if he had forgotten her presence, and she saw that his eyes were glassy with drink or something more powerful. He slowly sank to the ground on the other side of the food, holding his gourd in his lap. He gave her a crooked smile and gestured with his chin, inviting her to begin.

"You are kind, my lady. Please try some of the duck. I saw it taken off the spit myself."

Micay complied, finding the meat moist and tender beneath the crisp skin, which tasted of wood smoke and herbs. She also sampled a stew of mussels, tomatoes, and uchu peppers, a succulent filet of white fish in a spicy peanut sauce, and a sweet bean porridge topped with slices of avocado. The food was so delicious that she was almost able to forget her concern for Cusi and her wariness of Fempellec's presence. He had taken only a single piece of fruit for himself but had drunk twice from his gourd. He alternated between watching her like a host and drifting off into his own thoughts, which seemed to sadden him.

"I should not keep you from the feast," she apologized. "Though you can hear it quite clearly from here."

"I hear it," Fempellec said in a dull voice, lifting his head toward the music and shouting in the distance. "I heard everything they said. And so did those who were listening to me. Now there is no hope."

Micay felt a pang of dread that put an end to her appetite, but she had to wait until Fempellec looked at her again.

"I do not understand," she said.

Fempellec nodded in agreement. "It is impossible to understand. I have done nothing to make him hate me. No one here has insulted or mistreated him. Yet he would destroy everything just to take Amaru away from me."

"Cusi," Micay said breathlessly.

Fempellec nodded again, as if she had agreed with him. "He is mad . . . he will not listen to reason, even to save himself. There is such violence in him! He would have killed Pongmassa and then me."

"There was a fight?"

"Amaru stopped him, but there was death in his eyes, I could see it. When I led him away he made me run, stamping his feet like a hungry beast. He is frightening."

"He is a warrior," Micay explained, hoping to soothe him and make him more coherent. "And because he is smaller than most men, he reacts strongly to any threat."

"I have known men who could not separate their passion from their anger," Fempellec said with a shiver, his gaze turned inward. "Amaru was like that when I first knew him . . . when he was still ashamed of what I made him feel. He would use me and then cast me out in disgust, threatening to kill me if I returned. But I always came back, and I was still there when his anger and shame were gone."

"I see how gentle he is with you. That is how Cusi is with me."

"Why has he done this, then?" Fempellec burst out. "If he will not save himself, why must he take Amaru with him? Because I know Amaru. He loves Cusi, and he will be bound to him even more when they return from the place of visions. He will have to leave with Cusi or die alongside him."

"What has happened?" Micay demanded in alarm. "Why have they gone to the place of visions?"

"To find a plan, Cusi said." Fempellec spread his hands and a single black tear slid down his face and stained the front of his tunic. "But it is too late. Pongmassa and the others were with me outside the courtyard. They would not trust any promise Cusi made now, even if he spoke from a vision. And Amaru will try to stop them, and they will have to kill him, too."

Micay dropped her hand cloth onto the food and stood up, shaking with anxiety. She briefly recalled Cusi's warning, but Fempellec had not come to summon her, and she did not think that his drunken despair was feigned. Still weeping, he had begun to lift his gourd to his lips again, but she stepped around the food and snatched it out of his hands before he could drink.

"We must help them," she said sharply, discarding the gourd behind her. "If Amaru has to leave, you can come to Tumibamba with us."

"You only want to help Cusi," Fempellec retorted, looking past her indignantly. "I know what the Incas would think of me. Amaru told me himself. He would never take me to live among them."

Micay leaned down and grasped him by the shoulders, forcing him to meet her eyes. For a moment she wished she possessed Cusi's terrifying presence, so that she could simply make him obey her. But there was enough fear in Fempellec's eyes, which stared out at her from a face disfigured by misery and smeared paint. She spoke to him with a gentle urgency that was nothing like the desperation she felt inside.

"We will make him take you, Fempellec. But we must have the courage to save him first. That will bind him to you as he is bound to Cusi. As I am bound to Cusi."

Fempellec sighed and hung limp in her hands. But then he sighed again and struggled to his feet, leaning against her for support.

"You are only a woman," he muttered. "And I—"

Keeping one arm around his back, Micay reached up with her other hand, using three fingers to draw lines through the tear-streaked paint on his cheek. Then she dabbed at his other cheek in the same manner.

"Now you are painted for war," she told him, walking him in a slow circle. "Now we must go and protect the ones we love."

THE DARKNESS of the corridor was soothing to his eyes after the glare of the desert, but he was still burning hot and his mouth felt parched and shredded.

Dragonflies followed him, glowing blue and yellow in the darkness, hovering around him with a menacing hum like vultures waiting for him to drop. He had wandered, hiding at times from the enemies who hunted him, from the black man with no face, the man with the bloody clawed stick. There was a woman . . . she gave him water and pressed herself against him, she was naked and roused him with oiled fingers, closing her mouth around him and drawing all of him in . . .

Fear blossomed in his chest and the dragonflies hummed louder. She had stolen his spirit brother. No, he had it still. He ran from her, swollen and exposed, and people laughed at his nakedness and the drunken way he ran. He could not outrun the dragonflies, who could smell his fear. They hung in front of his face, showing him their teeth and humming hungrily. They feasted on the flesh of the helpless, he knew that now; he dared not fall again. He stopped to rest and looked into the courtyard that opened beside him. A man stood with his back to the entrance, the stone tip of the spear he was holding visible over his shoulder. He turned sideways and Cusi saw that it was the Chachapoya sentry, his face painted in halves, angry. *I did not kill him, then. He will kill me if he sees me.* The dragonflies buzzed loudly, trying to attract the sentry's attention. Cusi was trembling so hard that he was certain to be seen, but he could not move out of the doorway. He realized he was not meant to live after all.

Then something nudged his hip and he was aware of a presence beside him. He did not turn his head—he knew somehow not to do that—but he understood that it was his spirit brother. He was tall and calm, cool against Cusi's burning skin. He murmured unintelligibly and Cusi saw that the sentry had turned around again. He slid across the opening, his legs wobbling under him, and felt his spirit brother flowing beside him as if they were attached at the hip. He staggered down the corridor, the dragonflies gone now, but then he had to stop again, arrested by a voice. He looked into another courtyard and saw a boy seven or eight years of age. The boy opened his mouth to speak, but it was Amaru's voice that Cusi heard, coming from somewhere behind him.

"You are back. Stay then, and listen. *Listen,* Cusi. This was before you were born. Before anyone knew you *would* be born. Father was away fighting and Mother took us to live with Lloque Yupanqui, whose first wife had just died."

Behind the boy, Cusi saw the stone houses of his uncle's compound, with dim, shadowy figures moving inside the awning house on the upper terrace.

"Then Father returned, wearing the insignia of a commander, and he took us back to our own home. But it was only a short time before he was ordered to Copiapo to command the garrison. He wanted to take all of us with him, but Mother refused. She said the post was beneath him. It was too far from Cuzco, and she did not want to raise her children among savages. She was angry because he would not use his influence to have his duty changed."

"That is the kind of Inca he is," Cusi heard himself say.

The boy gave him an exasperated look. "The kind who does what he is told," Amaru's voice said, "and expects his wife to do the same. He pleaded with her and then shouted at her, and finally he struck her. I did not see that, but I remember the bruise on Mother's cheek."

"He struck me," Cusi said, and tried to shrink back out of the doorway when he saw Apu Poma come out of the awning house and advance toward the boy. But his spirit brother held him in place, and Amaru's next words made the man fade and suddenly disappear.

"Yes, and I am trying to tell you why. Listen. Mother took us back to Lloque's compound, and we stayed there until after Father had left for Copiapo. I did not see him again for six years. Lloque acted as my father and yours, when you came. Early, the midwives said, counting from the time Father was in Cuzco. Father must have counted, too, where he was, and he must have found the time suspiciously short. He was not able to see how small and sickly you were, so why should he believe you were born too soon? He had always been jealous of Lloque."

There was violent movement inside the awning house, but Cusi could not see what it was. Confusion was making him drowsy, and he felt his spirit brother begin to push him away from the doorway. The boy and the voice were both fading.

"Listen . . . *you* are the one who is hiding now. I am telling you why he has always treated you so badly. In his heart, he has always doubted that you were his. Cusi! I am not saying it is true . . . I do not know, but . . . they are twins. Wait, there is more. Cusi . . ."

He felt better to be moving again, down the dark corridor, away from the disquieting voice. His spirit brother was murmuring beside him, below hearing, and at first the sound was soothing. But then it took on a warning tone that brought all his fear back, fresh and potent. He stopped short in fright— someone was standing in front of him. The acrid odor of wood smoke and dirty wool stung his nostrils.

"What is your message?" a familiar voice asked. "Why have you summoned me?"

"Grandfather," Cusi breathed, and then he could see the deeply lined face with a band of black painted across the closed and useless eyes. Cusi wanted to weep with relief, but his eyes were too parched for tears.

"What is your message?" Raurau Illa demanded a second time.

"I need help, Grandfather. I am lost and surrounded by enemies . . ."

"There is only one enemy," the old man said unsparingly, "the one who will bring the pacha puchucay, the end of our world. If brother fights brother, who is left to watch for signs? If fathers abandon their sons, who is left to guard the lands of their birth? Our strength must not be squandered . . . you must make peace here."

"But they want to kill me!" Cusi cried.

"Are you not a brother to lightning? Trust the one who is with you and strike quickly. But when the danger is past you must forgive them, you must show them the mercy of the truly strong. You must help them undo what has been done."

There was a sudden explosion of noise—angry voices contending in a foreign tongue—and the darkness around him deepened so that he could no longer see Raurau Illa's face. He felt danger swirling around him like a wind that clawed at his skin.

"Grandfather! I cannot see!"

"You will, my son, and then you must act with all your swiftness. Use these eyes and see, Cusi; use the eyes Illapa took from me."

Two glowing eyes appeared in the darkness, large and yellow, with black pupils that suddenly began to expand, swelling out from the center until only slivers of golden light shone out around them. They floated toward him, and he let himself be drawn forward . . .

He woke sitting up with his back against a wall, his forehead resting on his crossed arms, which were propped against his upraised knees. He felt a raging heat in his body and an awful thirst in his throat, and for the first time he remembered the bowl of huacacachu he had drunk and knew he had wandered in the place of visions, not in the desert as he had thought. He opened his eyes and saw the paved floor beneath him and his stone, which was resting between his heels. They seemed richly textured, like fine cloth, but they remained solid beneath his gaze, and it did not hurt his eyes to look.

Out of the corner of his eye he saw a body lying beside him, a body that twitched spasmodically and let out low moans. Amaru, he heard, or thought. Then he was aware of the expectant presence crouching close on his other side. I hear you, brother, he thought, remembering the danger and the need to strike. He raised his head and saw that the courtyard was ringed with men, all frozen in place, all staring at him. Directly across from him, two men stood out from the others, holding short thrusting spears in their hands. One of them was Pongmassa, and from the excited expressions on their faces, Cusi understood that they were the ones who meant to kill him.

Taking his stone in one hand, he struggled to his feet, stumbling backward against the wall as a wave of dizziness swept over him. He felt the drug surge through his veins like poison, sickening him so that he clutched at the wall with his free hand and would have fallen if his spirit brother had not held him up. Then the dizziness passed and he could hold himself up, though he was trembling uncontrollably, his muscles twitching under his skin.

He turned back to face his enemies and saw that Pongmassa and the other man had separated and were slowly coming toward him, their spears held at the ready. Cusi stepped away from the wall, shaking so hard he could barely keep both of them in view. Pongmassa sneered at him and lowered his spear as a sign of contempt. Anger stiffened Cusi's spine but only made him shake harder. Then he felt arms come around him from behind and was wrapped in an embrace that stilled him completely. His attackers also stopped and exchanged an uncertain glance. *The stone for Pongmassa*, Cusi heard. *When he moves again, strike.*

Pongmassa grunted and took a bold step forward, and Cusi felt all his muscles jump at once as his spirit brother released him. *Strike!* He whirled and threw his stone underhand as hard as he could, coming up off his feet and aiming for Pongmassa's startled face. Instead it struck him in the ribs with a crack that drew a collective gasp from the onlookers. Pongmassa went down, and Cusi let out a scream only he could hear and leaped at the other man, who jerked back and swung his spear wildly in front of him, blurring the air. Cusi landed out of range and feinted to the right, planting his foot and springing back to the left as the man thrust viciously and missed, lurching past him and almost losing his balance.

Do not let him close, Cusi heard, *but do not let him rest. You do not have to kill him.* Cusi could not rest or stay still. He was driven by the frenzied energy of the drug, which made him run in place as he circled in on the man with the spear. He swooped in, dodged twice, and danced back out of reach, leaving the man thrusting at air. Cusi was back at once, ducking and spinning and faking blows with his fists, goading the man into an impetuous charge, then slipping past him and giving him a hard slap on the side of the head as he went by, sending his headdress flying. The man staggered to a stop and whirled in anger, but Cusi was already behind him, and this time Cusi kicked him in the back of his knees, knocking his legs out from under him. He went down and tried to roll away, but Cusi gave him another kick in the back and a slap across the face before he could regain his feet.

Cusi harried him from one end of the courtyard to the other, making him spin and stumble, abusing him with kicks and blows that were meant to humiliate rather than disable. "Helpless!" Cusi snarled. "Feel how it is to be truly helpless!" The man charged twice more, and both times Cusi tripped him and sent him sprawling on his face. Finally the man was too winded to move and simply stood with one arm thrown up over his bloody face, the spear dangling uselessly in his other hand, its point broken off in the last fall. Cusi was gasping for breath himself, but he could not bring his vengeful, manic dance to an end, not while there was a target for his anger. The man was swaying and about to drop when Amaru suddenly sprang up from his place against the wall and hurled himself forward.

"Cusi!" he bellowed, and lifted the man right off his feet, carrying him for five steps before slamming him headlong into the opposite wall. Then he fell on the man's back and began to curse him and pummel him with his fists, as if the man were conscious and resisting. Several of the onlookers jumped in to restrain him, and Amaru began to fight with them, too, calling them cowards and assassins. Cusi had stopped without knowing it, since his muscles were still pulsating from their exertions, and before he could will himself into motion Acunta appeared in front of him and held up his palms in a gesture of forbearance.

"Stop now, Cusi. It is finished."

Finished. The word seemed to awaken his body to what he had done and what it had cost him. He hurt all over and could not get enough air into his lungs, and as he sank slowly to his knees he felt the last of the violent energy drain out of him. Amaru was still struggling with the men around him, but

Cusi saw they were not armed and were not trying to harm him, even though he had hurt several of them. He wanted to call to his brother to stop, but he was breathing too hard and his throat was too dry and raw to let him speak. Acunta was trying to reason with Amaru over the heads of the men holding him, but Amaru was in the grip of a frenzy that made him oblivious to words. Protecting me, Cusi thought, as Amaru continued to shout his name.

Suddenly there were shouts of alarm and Cusi saw a ball of fire shoot into the courtyard. No, it was someone waving a torch, swinging it wildly like a club. It was Fempellec, painted and screaming like a savage as he rushed toward the men around Amaru. Acunta stepped into his path and Fempellec swung the torch at his head with all his might, painting a swirl of fire across the air. But Acunta ducked and the torch flew out of Fempellec's hands and sailed across the courtyard, smashing against the wall and showering the onlookers with sparks and bits of flaming wood.

The screaming and commotion seemed to end abruptly, and Cusi saw Fempellec held fast in Acunta's arms and Amaru standing still, blinking and staring around him dazedly. Cusi was surprised to feel an arm go around his back, since he had lost all sense of his spirit brother's presence. But it was Micay. Her wide brown eyes swept over him with a kind of tremulous disbelief, and then she burst into tears and pulled him against her. Cusi felt that familiar softness, the sweet smell of her skin, and let himself go limp in her arms, believing at last that he was safe. *Watch over me,* he murmured voicelessly, and then he gave up his hold on consciousness.

"He has a fever," Micay said to Hanp'atu as they lowered Cusi to the floor. He had lost his tunic somewhere, and his bare skin was hot to the touch, though perfectly dry. His cracked lips and contorted features made him look as if he had been lost in the desert for days, and his breathing was extremely labored.

"It is the huacacachu," the healer said succinctly. "We will have to wake him and make him drink."

Hanp'atu's words echoed in the sudden stillness that had fallen over the courtyard, and Micay looked up, realizing she still had her needle in her hand. It was coated with the blood of the guard who had tried to keep her out of the courtyard after she had heard Amaru scream Cusi's name. Fempellec had set the other guard's tunic on fire with a blow of his torch, and everyone else had gotten out of their way.

Coming toward her from the far end of the courtyard, where he must have been the whole time, was a tall, white-haired priest dressed totally in black except for the silver crescent that hung on his chest.

"Naymlap," Hanp'atu whispered to her as the priest stopped to say something to Amaru, who was sitting with his head in his hands and Fempellec's arms around his shoulders. Acunta was beside the priest when he came over to where Cusi lay, and the guide introduced them to Naymlap, high priest of Si. Micay and Hanp'atu bowed respectfully, though the priest appeared not to notice. He stared down at Cusi for a moment, appraising him with a kind of arrogant fascination.

"Revive him," he said to Hanp'atu. "We must hear what he has to tell us."

"My lord—" Hanp'atu began. But Micay held up a hand to him and rose to her feet to confront the priest. Naymlap frowned at her forcefully, and behind him Acunta made a gesture of warning, but Micay was not daunted by either of them. After what she had been through tonight—what she had felt when she heard Amaru scream Cusi's name—she had no more fear left.

"You are said to be a great healer, Lord Naymlap. Surely you can see that he cannot speak to you now. He must be allowed to rest."

"An ordinary man, yes," the priest said dismissively. "But he brought great power back from the place of visions. We must know what he saw there. If he sleeps, he may forget."

"Then he will forget," Micay snapped. "Why should he tell you anything? Did you stand and watch while they tried to kill him?"

Naymlap raised his eyebrows, appearing more surprised than offended by the question. "Of course I watched. He was threatening to report us all as thieves and traitors, and he boasted that he was not meant to die here. It was our duty to test him and to kill him if he was not worthy of his claims."

"So you gave him huacacachu and set an assassin on him," Micay concluded. "Or was it two?"

"It was two," the priest agreed. "You see where they lie. They could not touch him."

"You will not touch him now," Micay said. The priest glanced down, making her aware that she was holding the bloody needle out in front of her, pointed toward his chest.

"Are you a warrior, too, my daughter? Would you pierce my heart with that?"

"If you try to harm him, yes," Micay vowed. She nodded toward Hanp'atu. "We are healers, and we will decide when he is strong enough to speak to you."

Naymlap stared down at Cusi, who was moaning and grimacing in an uneasy half sleep, his eyelids fluttering. The priest sighed and nodded in resignation.

"No one will harm him now. No one would believe they could. Put away your weapon," he said to Micay, "and heal him. Help him remember when he awakens, and send for me when he is ready."

As Naymlap walked away, Micay looked over at the two men who were lying on the ground being tended to. One of them was not moving, the other was writhing in pain. Acunta and the rest of the men in the courtyard were staring at her blankly in a silence that was heavy with misgiving. She stared back at Acunta for a moment, letting him know that she would not forgive him for allowing this to happen. But then she let the needle fall from her hand, producing a ringing sound that broke the spell and made the onlookers blink and stir.

"Bring us water and a litter," she said to Acunta, who bowed and turned to relay the order to those behind him. Micay knelt back down beside Cusi and, laying a cool hand on his forehead, began her watch.

WHEN CUSI FINALLY awoke fully, a day and a half later, Micay saw that no one would have to encourage him to remember. He acknowledged Micay and Urcon with a groggy smile, but then his gaze turned inward and he let them handle him as they would, submitting limply to their continued ministrations. They washed him and massaged the cramps out of his muscles, and they soaked his bruised hands and feet in cold well water to reduce the swelling. Then they gave him warm coca tea to soothe his sore throat and began to feed him a honeyed maize porridge one spoonful at a time, trying to intrude on his reflections as little as possible. He chewed and swallowed indifferently for a while, but then appetite overwhelmed his memories, and he came out of his reverie and beckoned for something more substantial.

As soon as he was full he wanted to speak, but Micay held a finger up to her lips and made him sit for a while longer and drink more coca tea. He did so with surprising patience, gazing thoughtfully at the three of them as if the sight of them were helping to put things in order. Micay was impressed by how calm he seemed after a sleep that had been disturbed many times by agitated dreams. He finally nodded and looked to her for permission, which she gave with a smile.

"I am back," he said hoarsely, "and we are still together. I am grateful, my friends."

"We did nothing," Micay demurred. Urcon hung his head, feeling derelict because he had been at the feast and had taken no part in Cusi's rescue.

"You would, had you been needed. I will need you now, because I have been shown what we must do—by your grandfather, Urcon."

All of their heads came up, but before Cusi could begin to elaborate, someone stepped into the doorway behind them, blocking the morning light. Cusi looked up and beckoned.

"Enter, Acunta."

The guide came in hesitantly, glancing once at Micay before he bowed and squatted down across from Cusi. He placed a bundle on the floor in front of him and unwrapped it for Cusi to see. It was Cusi's tunic, and inside were his headband, wristbands, and coca bag, along with a slender bronze tube Micay did not recognize.

"These are yours, my lord."

Cusi nodded. He picked up the headband and slipped it on over his tousled head, centering the silver badge above his forehead.

"There is also a message," Acunta added. "The micho Topa Roca and the Coya's representative, Mama Cori, have set out from Chiquitoy and will be arriving late this afternoon. They are bringing fifty warriors with them."

Cusi toyed with one of his earplugs for a moment, appearing bemused by this belated rescue attempt. He glanced toward the doorway as if gauging the time of day, then raised his chin and spoke decisively to Acunta.

"When they have been shown to their quarters and allowed to wash and refresh themselves, see that my mother and Topa Roca are brought to Amaru's awning house. Amaru should be there, too, and your high priest . . . Naymlap. Is he still in the city?"

"He has been waiting to speak to you, my lord," Acunta said tightly, casting a sidelong glance at Micay. "But he may wish to leave the city now."

"No one is to leave Chan Chan," Cusi declared. "Tell him he should come here instead, unless he wishes to bring the full punishment of the Inca down on himself and all of his people. Tell him that I intend to resolve this peacefully, without punishment. But I will not spare anyone who does not have the courage to stay and face me."

Acunta cocked his head, as if doubting what he had heard or trying to discern another meaning behind it.

"What about those who attacked you?"

"I doubt that they are in any condition to flee," Cusi said with a grim smile. "Let them be an example to anyone else who dreams of raising his hand against the Inca."

"I will relay your message," Acunta promised. "Would you also like Ancocoyuch to be present?"

Cusi frowned and licked his lips, as if there were a bad taste in his mouth. "Was he there—in the courtyard?"

"No, my lord."

"But he knew? He approved?"

Acunta nodded silently.

"Then I do not want to see him now," Cusi decided. He looked around at his friends. "Is there anyone else who should be included?"

"Fempellec," Micay said. Cusi squinted at her skeptically before acceding with a shrug. "Fempellec, then. And you, Acunta."

The guide nodded in surprise, then bowed compliantly and left the room. Micay let out a long breath, feeling she would burst from the questions she wanted to ask. Cusi looked at her and let out a short, barking laugh.

"Speak—only do not tell me that it is impossible."

"But—with no punishment at all?" Micay asked incredulously. "With the micho and your mother here? You cannot pretend that these people are innocent, yet you do not have the authority to absolve them of their crimes."

"They are guilty," Cusi agreed, "and my absolution would be useless. But it would be wasteful to punish them. There is a war in the north and perhaps a more serious threat elsewhere. We must settle this in a way that will not require a garrison after we are gone. We must undo the wrong that has been done and see there is no chance that it will be repeated."

The calm with which he offered this proposal was breathtaking, and Micay was reminded of the way he had taken command of his feast at the Rainbow House, the occasion that had brought them all here. Now, though, he seemed to be taking command of something much larger; he was speaking for the Inca, but in his own voice.

"The Chimu will heed you," Urcon put in. "I have been asking and listening, and they all know what you did. You *are* the Inca to them."

"No punishment," Hanp'atu said tentatively. "Does that mean you will allow them to stay here?"

"Some of them. We must decide which ones and under what circumstances. What will seem fair to them, yet still be acceptable to the governor and the Sapa Inca?"

He spread his hands, turning the question over to them, and reached for more coca tea. Micay still had many questions of her own, particularly about how he was going to persuade Mama Cori and Topa Roca to heed him, but she realized she would only be making him waste his breath and the voice he would need to persuade them. We must decide, she thought, and let herself assume, as he did, that the responsibility and authority were indeed theirs. Suddenly, with only themselves to answer to, it did not seem so impossible.

"Let *us* talk now," she said to Cusi, drawing nods of agreement from Urcon and Hanp'atu. She thought for a moment, beginning to grow excited. "Perhaps we should think first of the victims of these crimes and where the evidence of them will appear. I am thinking of the official in the Chimor Valley . . . the man who has suffered such bad luck."

"His luck could be reversed," Hanp'atu suggested. "The workers who were borrowed might suddenly return, carrying gifts of gratitude from those who borrowed them."

"The gifts might walk by themselves," Urcon said, smiling at his own joke, "and help fill out the royal herds."

"Gifts might also be sent to the Sapa Inca, the governor, and the Grand Chimu," Micay added. "Fine craftwork done in the traditional style of the Chimu, from the holy city of Chan Chan."

Cusi smiled over the rim of his cup and gestured for them to go on. Together they began to work out a plan, a fair and acceptable one, that would allow them to leave Chan Chan in peace.

WHEN CUSI and his comrades arrived, the others were sitting in front of the awning house in pairs: Topa Roca and Mama Cori across from Acunta and Naymlap, Amaru at the top of the circle with Fempellec just behind him, on the side away from Mama Cori. They were sitting in silence, though the cups of akha in front of them testified to the fact that Amaru had performed the necessary toasts and introductions. The tension between them was palpable as Cusi stepped into their midst, and he felt it coalesce around him as he bowed and spoke to his mother in greeting. He could tell she was genuinely relieved to see he was all right, and he lingered over his greeting so that she would note how carefully he had dressed himself, with the requisite splendor of the Sapa Inca's representative.

Topa Roca, on the other hand, was too uncomfortable and suspicious of this gathering to be impressed by Cusi's dress, and he kept glancing past him at Naymlap, who seemed to be the source of his discomfort. Cusi nodded to both Amaru and Acunta, who were regarding him with a deep but guarded curiosity, then turned to introduce himself to the priest, whose glowering presence he had felt behind him the whole time.

"We have seen each other, my lord Naymlap, but we have not met. I am Cusi Huaman. I believe you know the Chachapoyas ñusta Micay."

"Your protectress—"

"Indeed. And these are my friends Urcon and Hanp'atu. I am pleased that you heeded my message."

"I trusted your word in coming here," Naymlap reminded him balefully, exerting a force as powerful as any Cusi had encountered. But Cusi had nothing similar with which to respond nor any urge to do so. The huacacachu had burned all the anger and violence out of him, at least for a while, and their absence made him feel like his spirit brother, cool and quiet and imperturbable.

"You have tested my word," he said mildly. "Do you not owe me your trust?"

The priest pursed his lips but did not reply, and Cusi bowed politely and turned to take a seat next to Micay, with Urcon and Hanp'atu sitting a little behind on either side. Amaru was sitting directly across from him, and Cusi noticed that he had put on his headband and golden earplugs. Fempellec, behind him, had also bound back his hair and put on a dark tunic that made him seem less slender and girlish. No doubt on Micay's advice, Cusi thought, but then he turned his mind to what he had to say. He did not have to ask to speak; they were all waiting.

"I have been told many things about what is being done here. In Chiquitoy I was told that land was being reclaimed in the name of the Sapa Inca and that some young Chimu nobles were being put to useful work. Upon my arrival I was told by Ancocoyuch of a plan to revive the ceremonies venerating the ancestors of the Chimu. Still later . . . I met some craftsmen who had come here to live and work in the manner of their grandfathers." Cusi paused and slowly looked around at his listeners. "I have found that this project is all of these things, as well as others that cannot be explained in such innocent terms. It is a dangerous situation, one that threatens the peace that has existed between the Chimu and the Inca for fifty years. I have brought you all together because I hope to resolve this situation, and I will need your cooperation to do so."

"What are these—" Topa Roca began, but Cusi held up a hand to forestall his protest.

"Hear me out, Lord Micho. I know my rank and the limits on my authority. But I have risked my life and those of my companions to uncover the truth here. I claim the right to act on what I know and what I think is best. You may dispute that claim with the governor if you wish, but listen first to what I propose."

"I am willing to listen," Topa Roca assured him. "But who is here to represent the Chimu? I see a guide and a man who lost his standing within the Chimu priesthood. Where is Ancocoyuch?"

Cusi sat still for a moment, unaffected by the animosity radiating between the priest and the micho and unwilling to put himself in the middle of it.

"Ancocoyuch is going back to Chiquitoy," he announced. "Along with those who are most closely attached to him. He is not to return to Chan Chan except on ceremonial occasions. Those who remain here will be under the care and instruction of their high priest, my lord Naymlap, and they will be led by their new chief. I will ask the governor to appoint Acunta to that post."

Naymlap drew himself erect, his eyes flashing with outrage.

"You would presume to name me high priest?" he asked indignantly.

Cusi shook his head. "I would merely recognize the standing you already have here. Would you refuse such recognition?"

The priest grunted and lowered his shoulders, glancing at Topa Roca through narrowed eyes. When he looked back at Cusi, a shrewd smile played upon his lips.

"I might accept it," he allowed, "if it were meaningful."

"It cannot be done," Topa Roca declared emphatically. "The Grand Chimu and his priests would be furious. They have asked many times for the right to reopen Chan Chan, and the Sapa Inca has always denied it to them."

"It will be open to them, but only as a place where they can worship their gods and preserve the memories of their ancestors—not as a place where the Grand Chimu or his heir might establish a court and raise an army of rebellion. It will be a holy city, like Pachacamac or Huaca Urcco, and its high priest will be responsible for guarding against anything that might jeopardize its sanctity."

Cusi watched as the implications of his statement sank in and the two men realized the opposition he was setting up between Chiquitoy and Chan Chan and the limitations it would impose on both sides. They stared at each other warily, forgetting Cusi as they calculated the advantages and disadvantages of such a scheme. Amaru used the opportunity to speak for the first time.

"Who else will be allowed to remain in this holy city?" he asked. Cusi glanced around at his comrades, silently acknowledging the words they had given him.

"Only those who are necessary to sustain it properly," he told Amaru. "Enough workers to maintain the sunken gardens and to keep the streets swept and the buildings in repair. They may take wives from among the women who are here, in matches approved by the chief. The craftsmen who are here may also stay, on one condition: that their work be dedicated to their gods and their ancestors, rather than to the enrichment of their leaders. Some of what they produce may be used to obtain new materials, and some will have to go to the Inca and to Inti. The rest should go to support the priests who tend the huacas in other parts of the province, so that they might share in the renewal of the holy city."

"You speak only of the sunken gardens," Amaru pointed out. "What about the rest of our work?"

"The work on the Moro Canal must be abandoned," Cusi said flatly. "Perhaps the small canal to the east could be completed, so that there is water for bathing and purification. But that is all. The workers who were 'borrowed' from the Chimor Valley must be sent back to their homes, with gifts to compensate their clans for their absence. And a substantial gift of llamas and alpacas should be made to the Inca official there to restore his goodwill."

Cusi had addressed his words as much to Acunta and Naymlap as to Amaru, and while they all—even Amaru—seemed resigned to the necessity Topa Roca rose up in protest on his other side.

"Cusi, hold! If I understand you correctly, you are speaking of crimes you have no right to forgive."

"Do not understand me too quickly, Lord Micho," Cusi warned. "I will tell you everything that has been done, so that you can see it is not done again. You may station whatever officials you wish here, and you will come periodically to inspect for yourself. The chief will be responsible for providing you with an accurate accounting, and he will show you proof of his tallies. You should also maintain a close contact with the official in the Chimor Valley."

"I asked about your right to forgive," Topa Roca said stiffly, "not about the duties you think are mine."

Beneath his calm Cusi felt a stirring that told him he would not be without anger forever. He quelled it but heard his voice grow stern.

"If we seek forgiveness for these crimes, it will have to be revealed that they occurred under the watchful eyes of the governor and the micho. Is that what you wish? Or would you rather explain to Mayta Yupanqui how the danger was averted and the peace assured? I will have to explain the same thing to the Sapa Inca, and I expect he will be satisfied to hear such an explanation rather than a request for a royal inspector and judges and warriors to carry out punishment."

Topa Roca grimaced and swallowed with difficulty, as if he were being squeezed around the throat.

"Such leniency might be an invitation to lawlessness," he muttered.

Cusi turned away from him, addressing his words to Naymlap. "Not if it is justified by a greater threat. There is only one enemy, the enemy of all of us, the one who would bring the pacha puchucay, the end of our world. Do you know of this, my lord?"

"I have heard," the priest said, with a deliberately vague gesture, "of those the Incas call Viracochas . . . those who dwell in waiting at the edges of the world . . ."

"Then I would ask you, as I was asked in the place of visions: If brother fights brother, who is left to watch for signs? If fathers abandon their sons, who is left to guard the lands of their birth? Our strength must not be squandered. There must be peace between us."

"I hear you," Naymlap said respectfully. "Though perhaps these are questions meant only for the Inca. We no longer guard the lands of our birth—only our holy places."

"They are part of our strength," Cusi told him, and the priest nodded and fell silent. Cusi let out a long breath and looked around the circle, searching his mind for anything he had forgotten to say. But he had said everything he needed to. The four men were all looking down or away, reckoning what his plan meant for each of them. The only person who had not spoken was his mother, and he knew he had to recognize her. If she challenged his authority—or worse, scolded him in front of these men—Topa Roca would probably decide to balk and the whole arrangement would collapse. Cusi hoped she had noticed that his plan spared Amaru along with everyone else, but he could not read her expression and he was no longer certain how she might act. She had mourned him as one of the dead, and she could bury him now with a scornful word. But he could not pretend she was not there.

"You have not spoken, my mother," he prompted. "What is the opinion of the Coya's representative?"

The men all looked up from their calculations, paying her an extra measure of attention because they had forgotten her presence. Mama Cori inclined her head to them, then spoke directly to Cusi.

"You have assumed responsibilities that are much greater than your rank should allow," she told him bluntly. "But perhaps this is a time that requires such boldness from those who serve the Sapa Inca. He is fighting one war and does not need another to distract him." She paused and looked around at her other listeners, holding their attention. "My father, Ayar Inca, taught me that the laws were strict and binding upon everyone, but that no law should ever be more important than the people and property it was meant to protect. If this settlement is acceptable both to those who must live under it and to those who must enforce it, it will be acceptable to those who must hear of it in Tumibamba and Cuzco. If you wish, I will be an additional witness to the final agreements."

Topa Roca and the two Chimu bowed to her. Cusi stared at her speechlessly for a moment before bowing himself. She had spoken with a voice that seemed to come out of his past, a voice that made him remember how powerfully persuasive she could be. He knew that Topa Roca would not balk now, and indeed, it was the micho who suggested to Naymlap and Acunta that the three of them go off together to discuss the matter further. The priest accepted the offer with an alacrity that seemed almost like respect, and after Cusi promised to join their discussions later, the three men made their farewells and left.

Then it was quiet in the courtyard, and Cusi turned to Micay, who rewarded him with a smile and an embrace. Urcon reached over to pat him on the back, and even the habitually dour Hanp'atu appeared pleased with the success of their plan. The serving woman brought out cups and fresh akha for them, and they drank without formality, in thirsty celebration. Cusi gazed upward over the rim of his cup and saw a white gull hovering in the reddening sky. He saluted it silently as a sign of the life he had helped to preserve here.

"So, my sons," Mama Cori said, breaking the silence, "will you return with me now to Tumibamba?"

Cusi lowered his cup and saw Amaru do the same. Their eyes met for a moment, then Amaru smiled wryly and shrugged.

"My brother has left me little choice. I no longer have any work here."

"You could remain in Chiquitoy," Mama Cori pointed out. "The governor has told me repeatedly how fond he is of you."

Amaru let out a mirthless laugh and looked across at Cusi. "No, I will honor what my brother has done for me. He has given me no choice in that, either. He would not desert me, and he would not let me abandon him. Perhaps he will regret that someday. For now, though, I will be his brother Inca, if that is what he wishes."

"And you, my son?" Mama Cori asked, turning to Cusi. At first he wondered why she had to ask, but then he realized how much he had assumed because of the way she had supported him. She might have been speaking only as the Coya's representative, not as an approving mother.

"I have always assumed we would return together," he said carefully. "Whether you would be speaking to me was another question. You spoke *for* me only moments ago, and I thought I heard the voice of someone I knew."

"Someone who had been away?" Mama Cori suggested. "As you were away in the darkness of your injury?"

Cusi smiled slowly, recognizing the subtlety of this voice, too, and realizing that this was as close as she would come to admitting she had been wrong.

"I am back," he said.

"So am I," she assured him, and glanced at Amaru. "As your mother, not your judge."

Amaru pursed his lips and nodded, appearing impressed by her promise. Cusi felt compelled to test it.

"You should know then, my mother, that I intend to ask the Sapa Inca for permission to marry Micay."

Mama Cori stared at Micay for a long moment, apparently without rancor, though Cusi could not tell what else might have passed between them. They had their own history, he recalled, apart from him.

"I am not surprised," Mama Cori said, "and I will accept the Sapa Inca's decision. You are young to marry, but you have his favor."

Cusi decided not to ask if he had hers, resigning himself to the hard limits of her pride. He saw the same resignation in Micay's eyes, though she seemed pleased with the way he had spoken for her. She cast a significant glance in Fempellec's direction, reminding him of their earlier agreement. It was the only piece of the plan he had forgotten, his memory carrying on the reluctance he had supposedly surrendered to Micay. He nodded to her and looked across at Amaru.

"I assume, my brother, that you will be taking your apprentice with you. He still has much to learn about being a builder."

For a moment, Amaru sat perfectly still; not even his eyes moved. Obviously

Micay and Fempellec had chosen not to warn him but to test him cold, in front of Mama Cori. Amaru raised a hand to one of his earplugs, then slowly turned his head to look at Fempellec.

"Would you wish to do that?" he asked, seeming genuinely bemused. "You have never lived in the highlands, and I will be away fighting, at least for a while. I would not be there to teach you."

"I have no family here, my lord," Fempellec told him, as if they had never discussed such matters before. "I would wait for you and learn from whomever I could."

Amaru opened and closed his mouth, then shrugged. "I owe you that opportunity," he decided. He looked at Cusi. "Is there space for another in your column?"

"There is," Cusi said, and was surprised when Fempellec rose and came toward him, holding something cupped in both hands against his stomach. The weight of his burden, plus the unfamiliarity of the loincloth he was wearing, made him amble slightly, an awkwardness that only seemed to add to the boyish appearance Micay had achieved with the headband and dark tunic. He seemed an unformed youth rather than one formed too prettily. Cusi darted a glance at his mother and saw only mild curiosity on her face.

Fempellec bowed and squatted in front of them, meeting Micay's eyes but slipping quickly past Cusi's. His burden, which drew his thin arms taut as he set it down, was Cusi's stone. Fempellec smiled at Micay and deftly removed a bronze needle from the hem of his tunic. He held it out to her like a prize.

"Your weapon, my lady," he said proudly. "I rubbed it clean for you."

"It shines like a torch," Micay said as she took it from him. "It will remind me of the night we were warriors together."

Fempellec was more tentative as he lifted the stone with both hands and held it out to Cusi, and his eyes widened with alarm when Cusi shook his head and did not reach out to take it.

"That is yours now, Fempellec. Carry it with you to Tumibamba and let it make you strong. You will need strength to live among the Incas."

Fempellec curled the stone back against his chest, appearing no less alarmed and doubtful, and Cusi realized that he did not understand such a stern form of encouragement. He had never had a guardian like Otoronco Achachi. Cusi smiled to reassure him.

"My grandfather gave me a similar gift," he explained, "when there were those who thought I was too small and weak. It is a burden you carry for your own benefit."

Fempellec still seemed puzzled, but Cusi's smile seemed to alleviate his immediate fears, so that he was able to execute a clumsy bow and lug the stone back to his place behind Amaru.

"You must all be hungry," Amaru said abruptly, raising his hand for the serving woman. "You must allow me to feed you."

The sun had fallen below the level of the surrounding walls, and night was descending rapidly. A swallow swooped low over the courtyard as Cusi drained the akha in his cup. He felt half drunk and curiously wistful, as if some part of him were resisting the conclusion he had struggled to bring about.

"You never answered my question," he said to Amaru, in a voice that sounded dreamy to his own ears, "about why you stayed here."

Amaru examined him skeptically. "I tried when we were in the place of visions. It has to do with you. But you fled from me; you had visions of your own to pursue."

Cusi frowned, struck by a sudden uneasiness. "There are gaps in what I can remember . . ."

"That is the nature of huacacachu," Amaru told him. "Often it is the most unpleasant things that cannot be recalled," he added, with a swift glance at Mama Cori. "But they will come back to you later."

There had been a warning in Amaru's glance, as well as in his words, and some nagging shred of memory told Cusi that he did not want to speak of this in front of his mother. Amaru was looking at him expectantly, as if prepared to go on, but Cusi simply nodded.

"We will talk later, then."

"I will not let you forget," Amaru promised. "But now I insist—you must suffer my hospitality while I am still able to provide it."

Cusi impulsively lifted his empty cup. "Let us drink, then. To the holy city of Chan Chan."

"To Chan Chan," Amaru repeated softly, and they sat looking at one another in the near darkness, waiting for their cups to be filled.

◄◄XII►►

AUQA AUQA
PACHA:
A Time of War

(A.D. 1516)

Quito

Outside the cold, crowded courtyard, a bright sun was shining on the city of Quito. Cusi could see it above the unfinished walls, which were just high enough to block out the light and its warmth. He had been told that the climate in the valley was always mild, but the city itself was situated on a plateau on the side of a volcano, and at this altitude the difference between sun and shade was painfully apparent. He wrapped his cloak more tightly around his shoulders and still had to make an effort not to shiver, because the flagstones were icy cold beneath his bare feet and he had had no chance to eat before coming here. He had not expected that he would be made to wait.

The men waiting with him were war chiefs, officials, and messengers of all kinds, and he told himself that their business should probably take precedence over news from the peaceful province of Chimor, even if it was borne by Cusi Huaman. And Cusi had been told that he might be granted a personal audience with the Sapa Inca, an honor few of these other men could hope for. He could bear his cold feet and empty stomach for a chance to ask for Micay.

As the morning wore on, however, he began to suffer a restlessness that was worse than his hunger. He found a place where he could stand in the light and warm himself, but that only made him more aware of time passing and opportunities slipping away. He and Amaru had arrived well after dark the night before, and by the time they had cleared all the sentry points and reported in to the war chief Michi, they had been too tired to do anything but sleep. They had had no chance to look for any of their friends and comrades or even to learn who was here and who still at the front lines. Then the messenger had come for Cusi at first light, so that he had seen only tantalizing glimpses of the green valley below the city and the massive, twin-cratered volcano that rose up behind it.

Just as Cusi was considering approaching the Cañaris guarding the inner door a second time to remind them of his presence, the war chief Yasca strode into the courtyard. He walked up to the guards and spoke to them brusquely, appearing fierce and implacable and clearly impatient. Cusi expected him to be ushered through the doorway without delay, but instead he was made to wait while one of the guards disappeared inside. A few moments later the guard returned with his captain, who happened to be Choque Chinchay, Rimachi's father. Cusi had the impression that Choque Chinchay recognized him in the moment before Yasca claimed his attention. The war chief spoke to him with a kind of glowering urgency, obviously delivering a message he meant to be repeated with some exactitude. Choque Chinchay bowed in compliance and went back inside, and Yasca turned to leave the courtyard.

But he paused to scan the faces around him, and when he saw Cusi he came over to greet him. The men near Cusi discreetly backed away, some of them bowing in Yasca's direction.

"I heard you had returned," the war chief said with his customary abruptness. "Are you fit to fight?"

"I leave tomorrow to join Paucar and Tomay and the other scouts. Unless they are also here?"

"No, they are watching the fortress for us. Harassing the Carangui, too, probably." Yasca rubbed his chin and laughed. "Your friend the Colla always wants to draw some blood after he has done his scouting. He is good at it, too, though he likes to think that with a few more men he could sack the fort by himself. The other scouts call him Guanaco, because he is so swift and wild."

"Guanaco," Cusi repeated with a smile. "Soon he will have at least one more comrade."

Yasca cast a sour glance at the interior doorway. "Tell him that is all he will have." Then he looked more closely at Cusi, noticing his bare feet and the bundle slung over his back. "You expect an audience?"

Cusi hesitated, recalling the way the war chief had been turned back. He did not wish to seem arrogant about his own favor.

"I was told it might be possible. I went to Chimor as the Inca's representative, and I have not made my report."

"You may have a long wait," Yasca advised him, seeming annoyed, but not with him; not out of jealousy. He started to turn away, then stopped. "You have just come from Tumibamba?"

"Yes, my lord," Cusi said simply, knowing what he wanted but waiting for him to ask, as Quespi had requested.

"Well. Did you happen to hear of my Third Wife? She is a Chachapoya, like the ñusta in your father's house."

"I saw the Lady Quespi," Cusi confessed. "I was there when she came to visit Micay. With your son."

"My pale-skinned son!" Yasca snorted. "Does he look like me?"

"He is big, and he grasped my finger as if it were a war club. They are both well, my lord, and asked to be remembered to you."

The war chief nodded curtly, as if embarrassed by the gratitude that showed in his eyes. He glanced around the courtyard again, his expression turning sour.

"Do not wear out your spirit here," he said in parting. "You would not be the only Inca he has refused to see."

Cusi bowed and watched him leave, unsettled by the implications of his warning. Why would Huayna Capac want to turn him or any other Inca away? The news he had heard in Tumibamba had all been good, and the morale of the warriors, from what little he had seen, seemed high. There had been heavy fighting and equally heavy losses, but the forts at Cochisque and Huachala had both been taken. The Carangui had been driven back into their stronghold in the Mira Valley, where they could only wait for the massive assault the Incas were preparing to launch against their fortress. Huayna Capac should have been pleased with how much had been accomplished.

Cusi shifted the bundle on his back, which was meant to be symbolic, a sign of deference to the Sapa Inca. Cusi's bundle was more than that, containing finely wrought pins and metal and shell jewelry made by the craftsmen of Chan Chan. He had hoped that these gifts might make his explanation more palatable, since he intended to be frank about the potential for trouble in Chimor Province. Now he was not certain his report would be heard at all, and it made his frankness seem like a fool's gift, never asked for and never owed.

He went up to the guards at the inner doorway, prepared to exert some force upon them, but he arrived at the same moment that Choque Chinchay appeared on the other side and beckoned to him to enter. He had prepared himself for the guilt that clutched at his insides, so he was able to smile in greeting and meet Choque Chinchay's eyes as the older man gripped his arm. The grip made him remember how big and strong Rimachi was.

"Welcome back, Cusi Huaman. Your trip to the Yuncas seems not to have harmed you."

"I am well again and ready to fight. I need to make my report before I leave tomorrow. I have messages from the governor."

Choque Chinchay turned to indicate an elderly Inca who was sitting on a bench against a side wall.

"The representative of the lord of the Northern Quarter will take your report. He will see that it is relayed to both the Sapa Inca and the lord in Cuzco."

"So I will not have an audience?"

"I cannot say," Choque Chinchay told him. "You were not summoned through me, so I will have to check. It is doubtful, Cusi, but you will still have to wait."

Cusi nodded in resignation, beginning to take Yasca's advice to heart. If he allowed this to humiliate and anger him, he would be wasting more than his time. Better to save his anger for the enemy.

"Rimachi is here in Quito," Choque Chinchay said as he escorted Cusi toward the old man on the bench. "He will be eager for news about you—and your family."

Cusi saw the older man's knowing smile but could only nod in acknowledgement, clutched by the guilt again. He did not think Choque Chinchay had noticed, though, and then he was alone with the lord's representative. The old man was accompanied by two retainers who would help him remember and transmit the proper messages. So, putting aside the more elaborate story he had prepared for the Sapa Inca, Cusi told him in the plainest terms about the situation that had developed at Chan Chan and about the way he and the governor and the micho had decided to resolve it. He emphasized the terms of the settlement, but he did not avoid naming the crimes that had been committed, omitting only the attempt on his own life, the one crime he felt was his to forgive.

"We felt it was best to forgo punishment at this time," he concluded, "because of the reinforcements that would have been required."

"You did well to settle this," the old man said bluntly. "A request for warriors would not be heard now."

Cusi stared back at him, hearing no regret or outrage in the man's voice. He was simply stating a fact.

"What if there were an uprising," Cusi inquired, "and officials of the Inca had been killed?"

"That is not what you have described to me."

"It might have been. We were fortunate to have intervened when we did. And we acted in the belief that we would not be forgotten by those who sent us to Chimor."

"You acted well, as I said," the old man told him, rising from the bench and gesturing for the retainers to gather their cords. "I am sure you will be commended for your efforts."

"Commended," Cusi murmured in disbelief as the three men walked away. Everything he had done in Chan Chan had been a fool's gift. He sat back down on the bench, stunned by the old man's apparent indifference, which he saw as a reflection of the Sapa Inca's own. He knew now, beyond all doubt, that he would not be granted an audience today. The only question was how long he would be made to wait before the spurning was made final. He scanned this second courtyard, which was smaller but less crowded than the first. Most of those waiting were messengers and Cañaris of high rank; there were no other Incas among them. The curtained inner doorway was also guarded by Cañaris of the Royal Guard, making Cusi wonder if all the Incas had been displaced by the men from Tumibamba. Huayna Capac had been born there, he reminded himself, and he had always had a great fondness for the Cañaris. But it still made no sense at this point in the campaign. The Incas were the core of the army, and they could not be displaced from there without inviting disaster.

He had stopped paying attention to the doorway while he pondered the situation, so that he felt Titu Atauchi's presence before he looked up to see him approaching. The healer was wearing his fur headdress with its fringe of teeth, and on his chest was a fan-shaped pectoral of green parrot feathers. Cusi examined him impassively, not bothering to rise from his seat.

"So . . . the hero has returned," Titu drawled, smiling unpleasantly. "It took you long enough to heal."

Cusi returned the smile in kind. "You are hardly the one to judge."

"And you, my lord? Have you been waiting here long? Perhaps you would like me to carry your name to the Sapa Inca . . . no doubt there is another of his daughters you would like to ask for."

It occurred to Cusi that the summons had come from Titu himself—or, more likely, that he had arranged for Huayna Capac to make it and then forget he had done so. It did not matter which. That this man had any authority at all with the Sapa Inca was an affront to all other Incas. But Cusi was representing only himself now, and he was not going to let this humiliation touch him. It was a burden that belonged to someone else.

"Carry yourself away from here," he said curtly. "But know that I will be thinking of you the first time I have to kill. It will be your face I will see beneath my battle-ax."

Titu Atauchi boldly stood his ground for a moment, but Cusi did not even raise his eyes and the man soon went away without another word. Cusi sat quietly with his eyes open, letting himself fall into the numbed alertness of a sentry, awake to his surroundings but not to the hunger in his stomach and the restlessness in his legs. He was a warrior and an Inca, and both knew how to wait. He would use his waiting to clear his heart and mind for battle.

Inevitably, though, he began to think about Micay, missing her keenly as he had all the way here from Tumibamba. He had made Amaru do weapons drills with him to exhaust himself at night, and then they had talked intensely, often until the fire had burned low and everyone else in the rest house had gone to sleep. Yet he had still lain awake most nights, aching to feel her beside him, touching and whispering and sharing their secrets. He had lost Hanp'atu long ago to a caravan going to Caxamarca, and Urcon more recently to the supply herds, but Micay was the one comrade he could not replace. Even his conversations with Amaru, who had been as frank as he had promised, seemed incomplete because he could not discuss them with her afterward.

He found himself frowning, thinking of the possibility that Lloque Yupanqui was his true father, as Amaru claimed their father believed or suspected. Amaru had seen Apu Poma in the place of visions, wearing a mask with no eye slits, the "mask of duty," Amaru had called it—a mask that blinded him to what was in his own heart, to the rage and jealousy that had made him mistreat Cusi on that day of parting in Cuzco. That was the day Amaru had abandoned his belief in the superiority of the Inca and had begun to seek another purpose to his life. Which had brought him finally to Chan Chan . . .

A commotion at the doorway brought Cusi fully alert. The curtain was pulled aside and Choque Chinchay appeared, followed closely by a man nearly as tall but much thinner: Lloque Yupanqui. Cusi stood up as his uncle came forward alone, smiling and shaking his head.

"Cusi, my son . . . I am afraid there has been a mistake. There is little hope—"

"So I understand," Cusi said shortly. "Though I do not think it was a mistake."

Lloque accepted the challenge in Cusi's voice without blinking. Nor did he try to deny his accusation.

"The Sapa Inca is an impatient man. He had expected to move more quickly against the Carangui, and he has mistaken the stubbornness of their resistance for a lack of effort on the part of his commanders."

"But he has been here to see for himself."

"That is part of the problem," Lloque said in a low voice, "as you will learn. But come," he added more briskly, gesturing toward the bench, "will you sit and tell me about your family, and your visit to the coast?"

"That could take a very long time," Cusi warned, resisting the lure of his uncle's company, a familiar pleasure that suddenly seemed strange, perhaps even perverse. If he were not an uncle, but a father . . .

"I have time," Lloque said, then saw the way Cusi was staring at him. "Unless—have *I* done something to offend you, my son?"

"No," Cusi said quickly, lowering his eyes and thrusting Amaru's suggestion out of his mind. "No, Uncle, you could not do that. If you have the patience to listen, I will tell you everything."

Lloque laughed and took a seat on the bench, motioning for Cusi to begin his recitation. They sat together until late in the afternoon as the sky clouded over and darkened with the promise of rain. Cusi gave him the full report of his journey and his experiences in Chan Chan, telling him much more than he would have told the Sapa Inca, since he did not have to conceal Amaru's role or the fact that his own life had been threatened. Lloque, as always, was the perfect listener, calm but thoroughly attentive, drawing Cusi out without seeming either suspicious or judgmental. Cusi did indeed tell him everything: about his feelings for Micay and his argument with Mama Cori; about what he had seen and heard in the place of visions; about how his spirit brother had helped him fight for his life.

When he was done, Cusi sat back against the wall and let his uncle ponder what he had just heard. The uneasiness he had felt at the beginning had totally disappeared, and he realized that *this* was the kind of report he had truly wanted to make. He felt a sense of completion that the lord's representative had not allowed him and that an audience with Huayna Capac would not have provided either. He glanced at Lloque, feeling a great affinity for him, yet seeing little resemblance to himself in the man's gaunt, angular features and mild eyes. Amaru had to be wrong, because Cusi could not believe Lloque would have denied their true relationship for all these years.

"We have not had a chance to talk like this since you came north," Lloque said at last. "When I knew you in Cuzco, you had a boy's concerns. Now you speak to me of visions and spirit brothers and the end of our world. I am moved by how much you have grown and the kind of man you have become."

Cusi lowered his eyes, warmed by the uncharacteristic emotion in his uncle's voice.

"The Sapa Inca must hear of this, as well," Lloque went on. "He should know how well you served him and at what risk. I will tell him at a time when he is feeling more generous toward his fellow Incas. That could be days or even months from now, but you know I will not forget."

Cusi nodded, though he was suddenly struck by the thought of Micay back in Tumibamba, living with his mother, who had promised only to abide by the Sapa Inca's decision. He had not reckoned on there being no decision to report.

"I expect no reward," he said to Lloque, "though I had hoped to ask for permission to marry Micay."

"Ah," Lloque exclaimed softly, giving him one of his rare smiles. Then he had another thought that made him shake his head. "I would be pleased to ask for you, my son, today or at any other time. But Huayna Capac is with his fourth wife, and no doubt you know the enmity that exists between Mama Huarcay and Micay. She would do her best to prevent the marriage if she heard of it."

"I told both Micay and my mother that I would ask. They expect to have word from me."

"I will give them word," Lloque promised. "I will soon have leave to return to Tumibamba, and I will explain to them what has happened. Have they moved into the governor's compound?"

"My mother has already begun to decorate it," Cusi told him with a smile. "When Micay and Quinti are not helping her, they are training to be healers. They may come to Quito in a few months to help tend to the wounded."

"And your father? Is he happier now that he has the title he deserves?"

Cusi cocked his head, thinking he detected a slight edge to the question. He had never seen Lloque return any of the animosity Apu Poma had long shown toward him, even though it would have been a natural response.

"He does not celebrate too openly," Cusi said carefully. "But he is pleased."

"Does he know your hand in it?"

"You mean because I asked for Otoronco Achachi? I did not know Huayna Capac would make him a royal inspector and send the governor to replace him as lord of the Eastern Quarter. And my father *does* deserve the title. Compared to the governor of Chimor—"

"Of course," Lloque interrupted gently. "But I think you are telling me he does not know."

Cusi sighed and spread his hands. "It is better between us now, but I still cannot speak to him as easily as I do to you."

"I have had more time with you," Lloque pointed out, "and we are dedicated to the same huaca. Though it has never reached out for me as it has for you," he added quietly. "I have even met this blind man of whom you speak, but I never thought twice about him. It was a powerful vision that let you see him in Chan Chan and a powerful message he gave to you. You must keep it with you and ponder its significance."

"I will not squander what has been given to me," Cusi promised.

Lloque made an abrupt gesture with his chin. "Do not waste any more time here, then. Go find your brother and your other comrades, and see that you are well fed before you go into the field. I will testify that you answered your summons, should anyone question."

Cusi stood up, feeling his carrying bundle slap lightly against his back. He stripped it off and held it out to his uncle.

"These are gifts from the craftsmen I allowed to stay in Chan Chan. Perhaps you could present them to the Sapa Inca whenever you decide he is ready to receive them."

Lloque took the bundle without comment and rose to his feet. "Farewell, my son. Come to me when you have leave, and I will tell you about Micay and the rest of your family. Until then, may Illapa continue to guide and protect you and keep your arm strong."

"Farewell, Uncle," Cusi said, hearing the word again in his mind and finding it both correct and inadequate. Perhaps what his father suspected was right, even if it was not true. Perhaps Lloque was his spirit father. Cusi gave him a last look and then turned and headed for the outer doorway, satisfied with what he felt, if not with what he knew. He passed between the Cañari guards, barefoot and empty-handed, but with all his duties discharged. He went to find Amaru and to prepare himself for war.

Tumibamba

T HE MAN made a clicking sound deep in his throat, just before he stopped breathing. It was a sound Micay had heard Urcon make to summon his llamas, and she wondered if the man were calling to the spirits of his ancestors, begging them to take him out of his pain. He should have never lived this long, with a deep stab wound in his abdomen and his neck broken from a fall. It would have been kinder to let him die in Quito.

Micay sat back on her haunches and looked across the man's prostrate body at Quinti Ocllo, who had her eyes closed and her hands clasped in front of her.

"He is gone," Micay said quietly. She murmured a brief prayer commending his spirit to the next world, then picked up the coca bag that held her medicines and rose to her feet. Quinti opened one eye for a moment but stayed where she was, and Micay turned away and walked out of the awning house, suppressing a sharp surge of annoyance. This was not the first patient she had lost, and she had known from the first not to linger needlessly or indulge in the mourning that was better left to comrades or relatives. A healer did not want to carry thoughts of death to her next patient, and it seemed more respectful simply to walk away and allow the spirit to depart in peace.

The light in the courtyard was dimmed by the thick cover of clouds overhead, and the warm air smelled of rain. Micay took several deep, slow breaths, expelling the man's death from her own spirit. Only when she felt clear did she allow herself to wonder how long Quinti was going to stay behind, which brought her annoyance back in force. She accepted the Inca belief that some aspect of the spirit remained with the corpse, even though she had never come to share it. But this man had been a Palta, not an Inca, and Micay doubted that Quinti either knew or cared about what the Paltas believed. She was simply resisting the task she had been given, pretending to be a priestess rather than a healer.

In anticipation of the rain, some of the men in the courtyard were being moved inside, and Micay went to help rather than waiting for Quinti. All of the men had lost limbs or suffered crippling injuries, but Micay smiled and joked with them as they hung onto her arm, knowing that her beauty distracted them and gave them some momentary consolation. She did not feel any of the pity or revulsion many of them felt toward themselves, and she did not let them see the fear their injuries inspired in her. She was always reminded of the blind man's prophecy that Cusi would return to his village in need, a prediction Cusi sometimes seemed to regard as a promise of present invulnerability. It seemed not to have occurred to him that he might be incapacitated like this, left in a state of need that would be with him wherever he went, as long as he lived.

Thoughts of Cusi inevitably made her think of Quito, where she would probably be sent once she had helped to train Quinti and Quespi and some of the other novice healers. The fact she herself was no longer considered a novice was a testament to the thoroughness of Hanp'atu's teaching and to how quickly and naturally she had taken on the spirit and manner of a healer. Though many of the mamacona were also healers, Chimpu Ocllo conceived of it as a practical craft requiring competence and composure rather than any special form of reverence. So she had been quite satisfied with the way Micay had been trained and had not hesitated to put her in charge of the others. She had told Micay that it was the form of devotion best suited to her, bringing wholeness to others in the name of Mama Quilla.

When Micay returned to the courtyard, Quinti was standing outside the awning house, wearing the vacant expression that Micay had come to think of as her praying face.

"We have done what we can for today," Micay said shortly. "It would probably be wise to return to the governor's compound before the rain comes."

Quinti's head jerked slightly, and she focused her eyes on Micay with lofty disapproval. "You are quick to abandon the dead."

"I have been taught not to linger. It is our task to tend to the living, not brood over the dead."

"I am not surprised that you cannot distinguish brooding from prayer. You should not expect *me,* however, to share your indifference."

"Chimpu Ocllo expects me to share my knowledge with you," Micay reminded her. "I cannot do that if you will not listen."

"I must listen to my heart," Quinti insisted, glancing across to where the high priestess was supervising the loading of some pack llamas. "Even if she will not."

Micay sighed in exasperation. "I am going, anyway. Your mother expects us."

Quinti gave her a withering look which said plainly that she did not care what Mama Cori expected either. Micay shrugged and started walking toward the gate, leaving Quinti to do what she would: either follow or stand brooding until the rain came to drive her home.

MICAY ARRIVED at the gate to the governor's compound just as the rain began to fall. As she took shelter inside the deep, trapezoidal doorway, she met Mama Cori on her way out, accompanied by three of the young ñustas who had recently been put in her care. All four women were immaculately dressed and made up, wearing long cloaks to keep their hair and clothing dry.

"We are going to the Coya's compound," Mama Cori explained. "You are welcome to join us if you wish."

Micay glanced at the other ñustas, who were probably close to her in age but seemed much younger, even with their faces skillfully painted. They were also much cleaner.

"I am grateful, my lady," Micay said. "But I have kept the company of the wounded all day, and I must cleanse myself."

Mama Cori nodded agreeably. "Perhaps you could also look in on Amaru's apprentice," she suggested. "His latest master sent him home again. For good. This is the third man who has rejected him, and I do not think we could find another. If we cannot find something useful for him to do, perhaps he should be sent back to Chan Chan."

"I will speak to him," Micay said swiftly, as if to head off the prospect of anything so drastic. Mama Cori stared at her, her expression and tone both thoroughly neutral.

"After Amaru, you know him best. I will trust you to decide what should be done."

Briefly inclining her head, she turned and led her charges out into the street. Micay went in the opposite direction, out onto the plaza that occupied the middle section of the compound. The smoothly paved expanse was slick with rain and empty of people, for all those waiting to see the governor had crowded into the enormous awning house at the western end of the enclosure. There were two guest houses next to it, and Fempellec lived in the first of these, having originally shared it with Amaru. As she walked toward it, Micay recalled how terrified Fempellec had been the first few times he had seen it rain. His first master had sent him home in disgust after Fempellec had become incoherent with fright during a thunderstorm, trying to hide himself under a blanket. The second master had been more patient about such eccentricities, but at a certain point, he had wanted Fempellec to stop listening and asking questions and do some work with his hands. He soon learned that any tool that blistered Fempellec's fingers somehow got broken, and that any stone too heavy for him to carry got dropped along the way. The master's patience had come to an abrupt end the day he overheard Fempellec trying to persuade another apprentice to do his work for him.

She stopped just inside the doorway of the guest house, calling Fempellec's name and blinking to adjust her eyes to the interior dimness. She found him sitting against the back wall with his knees up and a blanket wrapped around his shoulders, despite the warmth of the day. As she approached, she noticed he appeared sullen rather than distraught over this dismissal. She also noticed, in the niche above his head, the stone Cusi had given him, which had ridden most of the way back to Tumibamba on the back of one of Urcon's llamas.

"Mama Cori told me," Micay said. "We must find something else for you to do."

"Like what?" Fempellec demanded petulantly, giving her an accusing glance. "You knew I would never fool anybody here."

"The question is how to serve . . ."

"I will not be a common servant."

"No, of course not," Micay agreed. "Though I have not forgotten the meal you served to me in Chan Chan. You made it seem a feast, even though you were drunk and downcast."

"So? I have been serving at feasts since I was a small child. But the Incas attach no importance to it. They simply want to fill their bellies and then get on to the drinking and boasting."

Micay gave him a tolerant smile. "That may have been true in Chiquitoy, but it is not true in the Mollecancha. You have not been observing very carefully. Otherwise, you might know that the former governor had a member of his staff whose only duty was to oversee the feasts and dances the governor was required to hold. He considered the man so valuable that he took him with him to Cuzco."

Fempellec's head came up slowly. "What good would it do me to know that?"

"It might cause you to see that Apu Poma has no one similar on his staff. It would have to be someone who could work with the retainers . . . someone clever enough to please both Mama Cori and Apu Poma."

Fempellec shrugged. "I have no trouble with the retainers. We are not so different. And I have seen enough of Amaru's mother to know what pleases her."

"And Apu Poma?" Micay prompted. Fempellec's smooth face tightened back to the bone, and he dropped his gaze. When he finally looked up, his eyes glinted like hard black stones behind the thick fringe of his lashes.

"He looks at me as if he knows too well what I am. He makes me feel I could never do anything to please him."

"I told you in Chan Chan," Micay reminded him, "that it is not easy for anyone to live among the Incas. You must convince them that you deserve their consideration."

"How do I do that with a man who hates the sight of me?" Fempellec demanded.

Micay smiled, hearing the interest implicit in his anger. "You serve without being seen. The retainers prepare most of the governor's meals without supervision. They could be persuaded to let you make one special. Apu Poma would not even have to be told, unless he were so impressed that he inquired."

Fempellec grunted softly and fell silent for a moment, considering the offer. "What if he is not impressed? He is an Inca, after all, and he has not been to Chan Chan."

"Then you try again. But you will have to keep the cooperation of the retainers. I will speak to Runtu Caya for you only once."

"Now?" he asked. Micay nodded and rose to her feet, and he shrugged off his blanket and stood up with her.

"You are like him," he said.

"Like who?"

"Cusi. Only you are kinder. You do not give me stones to carry."

"You have enough burdens," Micay said lightly, and together they turned toward the doorway.

The Mira Valley

BEFORE SETTING out they removed their tunics and sandals and hid them among the rocks along with their weapons. Then Tomay picked up a small stone which he displayed to Cusi with a grin before tucking it into his loincloth.

"An offering stone," he said, warning Cusi again that this would be a serious climb and reminding him of the cliff they had climbed in Chachapoyas, the last time they had fought together. Cusi did not neglect the custom this time, choosing a stone that bore a vague resemblance to the spirit brother inside his waistband. Tomay nodded in approval and started off across a narrow crevass that was spanned by a single log, with a deep drop below.

Then the path ended and they were climbing upward, moving from ledge to ledge and handhold to handhold, avoiding the thorny cacti that grew even at this altitude. The sun shone down hotly through the thin air, which seemed to mock Cusi's efforts to breathe, making him painfully aware of how short a time he had been back in the highlands. But while he could not conceal his huffing from Tomay, he did not let himself lag far behind. Tomay had been glad of his return, but he had also been testing Cusi in various ways, giving him opportunities to display his fitness and his fighting instincts but also watching to see how much authority he would try to assume. For his part, Cusi had no desire to assert his rank and take command of men who had been in the field for months without him, and he was relieved that Tomay had abandoned his worshipful attitude. It was better to have to compete with him and alleviate his supsicions, even if it meant proving himself all over again.

The last part of the climb took them along the sheer face of a cliff on a ledge only a little wider than the one they had used in Chachapoyas. Cusi felt sweat run down his spine as he pressed himself against the rock wall, sliding sideways foot by foot, nothing but air behind and below him. Fear made his stomach and lungs contract but did not freeze him in place, and he kept himself moving along the ledge, emulating the calm, upright presence of his spirit brother.

The ledge widened at the end, and then they scrambled on their hands and knees up to the top of the promontory. As they flopped down on a flat slab of rock, Tomay removed the offering stone from his loincloth and placed it on top of a small pile of similar stones, murmuring his thanks to the spirit of the mountain. Cusi did likewise, offering his prayer with deep sincerity.

"Most of those are mine," Tomay said proudly, pointing at the pile with his chin. "But I knew you would not be afraid to come with me."

"It must have been hard the first time."

"No harder than it was for you just now." Tomay shrugged, though he was not refusing the compliment. They rolled over onto their bellies and crawled forward to the edge of the cliff. As Tomay had promised, they could see the whole fort from here, and it was an imposing sight. They were at the extreme northern end of the valley, where the bottom land grew narrow and then rose steeply to the only pass through the encroaching mountains. The first wall of the fortress spread itself across the pass halfway up, and the next four walls rose behind it at stepped intervals, forming concentric rings of defense all the way to the top of the pass. Each rampart was lined with warriors, and in the leveled areas between the walls there were more warriors, and piles of stones, and stacks of spare weapons. There were no ramps or stairways connecting one fortified level with the next, so that passage up and down could be accomplished only by means of long rope ladders.

"Were the forts at Cochisque and Huachala like this?" Cusi asked, trying not to sound daunted.

"They were strong," Tomay allowed, "but not so well situated. Each wall here will be a fortress in itself."

"And each one steeper than the one before. Like fighting up a mountain."

"But look below us," Tomay said, pointing with his chin. Cusi peered over the edge and saw, far below, a row of blackened shells that might once have been storerooms. "We did that ourselves," Tomay explained. "Red-hot sling-stones onto dry thatch. It only took a few of us."

Cusi smiled, remembering Sumac Mallqui telling their initiation group about that trick. Tomay had always been an attentive student.

"But we should be making serious attacks from up here," Tomay insisted, "and from the other flank, as well. We could send rockslides down on them and make them divert men from the wall. They would have to fight uphill to keep us off their backs. As it is now, there are so few of us that they can send out patrols to hunt us."

"I told you what Yasca said. He seemed willing to give us more men, if the choice were his."

Tomay turned his gaze out over the valley to where the Inca troops were massed on the plain. He sighed in frustration.

"I asked for Uritu and a few other bowmen; they could do so much damage from here. But their whole regiment is kept stationed near the Sapa Inca's litter, so that he can watch them shoot their arrows."

Cusi grunted in acknowledgement, having heard similar complaints from others, usually expressed with more bitterness. Tomay was not one to openly criticize the Sapa Inca, but it had not taken Cusi very long to understand what Lloque had meant about Huayna Capac's presence being part of the problem. The ruler wanted to participate personally in the conquest of the Carangui, but he had never served as a war chief in the field, and he did not feel that it was either necessary or appropriate for him to descend from his litter and mingle with the common warriors. So the Inca Old Guard, the elite corps of veteran warriors, were compelled to stay with him, performing Royal Guard duty while younger and less experienced commanders led the attack. Huayna Capac had also insisted on a full frontal assault of each stronghold, having little interest in maneuvers that would occur out of his sight. He was the Son of Inti, and he believed his sacred presence should inspire his warriors to surmount any obstacle.

"Otoronco Achachi told me this would be a long war," Cusi murmured, but Tomay had suddenly stopped listening, his attention focussed on the mountainside below them and to their left.

"Carangui. They have seen us."

There were ten or twelve of them, bristling with weapons, working their way up the zigzag trail that would eventually bring them to the spot from which Cusi and Tomay had set out. Their leader was indeed looking in their direction, shielding his eyes from the sun. Cusi realized how exposed they were up here, even lying flat.

"We must get to the log bridge before they do," Tomay said urgently, "or we will be trapped here."

Cusi did not argue, though when he found himself creeping sideways along the ledge and recalled all the other obstacles they had had to overcome going up, he could not see how they could possibly make it back in time. He tried to put such thoughts out of his mind, along with his anger at Tomay for leading him into such a trap. He was only partially successful, and his anxiety made him rigid and clumsy so that he skinned his hands and feet and banged his knees on rocks. All the way down he was tormented by the expectation that they would reach the log bridge and find a grinning Carangui warrior waiting for them on the other side, spear at the ready. Sliding down a gravel slope on his buttocks, his breath coming in ragged bursts, he did not feel ready to face that again, not with his whole being.

But when they finally reached the bridge it was unattended, and they bounded across it and ran for the place where they had hidden their weapons. The feel of his battle-ax in his hands gave Cusi back his confidence, but he had only a moment to savor it before the Carangui came screaming up the path toward them, whipping their spear throwers over their heads and sending wooden darts rattling off the rocks. To Cusi's utter amazement, Tomay grinned at him happily.

"This way!" he shouted, taking off up a path to their left, running hard with a short spear clutched in his hands. Cusi went after him, hunched over his ax to make himself a smaller target, no longer worrying about his wind or what might lay ahead of him. The danger was behind him now, and all he had to do was outrun it. They went over a ridge and plunged down a side trail that descended into a gully and then rose toward a second ridge that was topped by large piles of boulders. Carried by their momentum, they flew down the slope, Cusi hard on Tomay's heels, certain that once they reached the boulders, they would be safe from the Carangui spear throwers. Halfway up the opposite side of the gully, though, Tomay suddenly glanced back over his shoulder and slackened his pace, so that Cusi almost ran up his back.

"Let them come," Tomay huffed. Cusi looked back and saw half the Carangui coming down the slope after them, while their comrades had stopped at the top of the ridge to let fly with their slings and spear throwers. A dart sailed past Cusi's shoulder and embedded itself deeply in the ground beside the path. He put his forearm into the small of Tomay's back and gave him an urgent push, and Tomay laughed and started running again.

As they gained the crest of the ridge, a slingstone ricochetted off the rocks and hit Cusi in the back of the thigh, but it only served to propel him over the top, in among the sheltering boulders. Tomay began to slow again, and Cusi was about to prod him in the back with his ax when he suddenly noticed men crouching among the rocks on both sides of the trail. Their own men, waiting in ambush. I have been used as bait, Cusi realized as he and Tomay kept going at a trot, not stopping until they heard the chorus of screams that told them the trap had been sprung.

They turned then and saw the Carangui being cut down, except for the leader, who lashed out with his club, spun free, and came charging down the path toward them. He was a large man and carried a shield along with his club, but he rushed at them with the recklessness of one who did not expect to survive. Cusi and Tomay split apart and made a charge of their own, using the man's headlong momentum against him. He swung wildly at Tomay with his club and threw up his shield toward Cusi, and though Cusi could easily have taken out the man's legs, he made the shield his target, taking a two-handed grip on his battle-ax and coming up off his feet with the force of his swing. The shield exploded into fragments of painted wood, and the man lurched sideways helplessly, letting out a final shriek as he was impaled on Tomay's thrusting spear.

In the silence that followed Cusi could hear the labored sound of his own breathing, and he could still feel the blow he had struck vibrating in his hands and shoulders. He was aware that Tomay and the others were all looking at him, waiting to see how he would react. He glanced down at the ground, still feeling a trace of anger at the way he had been deceived and the anxiety it had cost him. But most of his anger had exploded against the Carangui's shield, and he had to admit that it had been a satisfying blow. He looked over at Tomay, keeping his face impassive.

"Well, Lord Guanaco," he said slowly, "do you have any more of these restful tasks for me today?"

Tomay grinned and Cusi let himself smile. Then they were all laughing, Huañu and Paucar and the other scouts crowding around to slap Cusi on the back.

"My initiation?" Cusi suggested, raising an eyebrow at Tomay.

"I wanted our flight to seem convincing," Tomay shrugged, laughing. "We were almost *too* fast, though."

"Next time I will know to pretend," Cusi said dryly, and Tomay laughed again. Then the two of them followed the example of the other scouts and went to strip the corpse of the warrior they had killed.

Tumibamba

L ong strokes," Micay emphasized, using both hands to scrape a piece of root across the rough, ribbed surface of a grinding stone. "The larger the fibers, the better the poultice will hold together."

Quespi pursed her lips and studied Micay's hands for a moment, lengthening her own grinding stroke in imitation. Then she put her head down and did not lift it again until she had worn her root down to a stringy sliver. She sifted through the pile of orange fibers with her fingers, nodding to herself before she looked up at Micay.

"I will not waste my approval on you," Micay said with a smile. "I just wish the other women were as diligent."

Quespi shrugged. "They are young, and they do not have my desire to go to Quito." She reached into the basket for another root.

"It has made you a good healer."

"I do not have your gift," Quespi said frankly, glancing at her son, who lay sleeping beside her. "And I would prefer to tend only to my own family. But I do not want Yasca to forget me—or Huallpa."

"That is wise. But you know, of course, that the Incas believe a wife should not lie with her husband while she is still nursing. They think the child will be deprived and will turn out a weakling."

"An ayusca," Quespi said, drawing the word out so that it sounded ridiculous. "The first and second wife have reminded me many times. I bow to them most respectfully, but I do not tell them what I choose to believe. Or what Yasca will believe—and do—when he sees me again."

Micay laughed, delighted by the defiance in Quespi's eyes. She had needed few lessons in how to act toward the Incas, especially the Inca who was her husband. They went back to their grinding for a few moments but looked up in unison when Mama Cori and Chimpu Ocllo emerged together from the high priestess's house. They were not smiling, but they did not seem dissatisfied either. After Mama Cori had disappeared through the compound gate, Chimpu Ocllo turned and beckoned, calling Micay by name. Micay wiped off her hands and followed Chimpu through the open doorway into her sparsely decorated room, which had splints and bandages piled up in all the corners. Chimpu sat down on the bench against the back wall, gesturing for Micay to take the mat on the floor in front of her.

"What do you think is wrong with Quinti?" she asked abruptly.

Micay hesitated for a moment, wanting to be fair. "She seemed fine before we went to the coast, but she believed then that she would be allowed to join the mamacona. She is disappointed and bitter because you have refused her the honor."

"She is not worthy of it. But do you truly believe she was fine before? Or was she simply lost in her own dream of devotion? Speak plainly, Micay. I may not have you with me for too much longer."

"Plainly, then, my mother . . . I think she is lost again. I do not think she knows or cares about what is required of a mama. She is simply following her heart, as she has always done."

"Of course. Only she is older now," Chimpu added, "and she sees fewer places she might claim. As I told Mama Cori, her desire is not enough, since she will not subject it to discipline. Quinti was aware that my asking her to become a healer was a test."

"I warned her about that myself."

"Now she is so miserable she will not leave her room. I have told Mama Cori to tell her that she must dream a purpose for herself. I want you to go to her, my daughter, and help her through this. Be patient with her and see she does not harm herself."

"I will be a sister to her," Micay promised.

Chimpu nodded and then looked at her with bemusement. "Would you believe me if I told you that Mama Cori came here to ask me to grant Quinti's request and admit her to the mamacona?"

"I would question my hearing," Micay admitted.

The older woman gave her a broad, pink-gummed smile. "She did not approve of it any more than I did, of course. But she felt she should support her daughter's wishes, since she could not persuade Quinti to change her mind."

"As I told you, my mother," Micay said, "I cannot explain the change that came over her in Chan Chan. But she has been much kinder to everyone, less quick to judge."

"I think that she has finally abandoned the expectations she brought here from Cuzco," Chimpu declared with satisfaction. "I think she has accepted that she cannot arrange her life, or the lives of her children, with the same certainty."

"Perhaps, my lady. I will be more willing to believe that when Cusi and I are married."

Chimpu cocked her head for a moment, then nodded slowly. "Yes, perhaps it is best to be wary of the depth of such sudden changes. She also brought me overtures from the Coya, and they were not all they should have been. Rahua Ocllo feels she can be generous with her recognition now that she expects to move her court to Quito when the palace there is finished. She does not understand that recognition has value only when it is given freely."

"So we must both wait for the reconciliation we desire," Micay concluded.

Chimpu gave her a rueful smile. "We must, indeed. Go to Quinti, my daughter. The fighting has begun again in the north, so it may not be long before you are needed in Quito."

"Let us pray that the fighting is over quickly," Micay murmured, and the high priestess nodded and raised a hand over her in blessing.

"Let us also be prepared to do our part," she said, and sent Micay from the room.

THE PRIVATE residences of the governor and his family were at the extreme eastern end of the enclosure, set on a natural eminence that rose some fifty feet above the level of the main plaza. The face of this bluff had been buttressed with ascending terraces that were so thickly planted with flowers, vegetables, and decorative shrubs that it seemed as if a wall of greenery supported the three stone houses at the top. A wide central stairway and narrower, steeper staircases at both ends provided access to the upper level, and open channels of cut stone carried water down from one terrace to the next, irrigating the garden plots and filling the reflecting pools at the base of the bluff.

As Micay climbed the steep staircase that led most directly to the house she shared with Quinti, she glanced down to her left and saw Fempellec conferring with Runtu Caya and some of the other retainer women in the open space between two of the pools. They were surrounded by piles of mats, baskets of flowers, and other feasting paraphernalia, and they were all so engrossed in their planning that Micay had no chance to catch their attention. She hoped that meant that Quinti was better, because she had asked both Fempellec and Runtu to check on her periodically and to stay with her if her mood seemed dangerous. They had not failed her in the past, but then Fempellec had not been responsible for a feast quite as important as this one before. It was perhaps his final test, and his earlier successes had given the retainers cause to share in his ambitions.

But the curtain was pulled back from the doorway of their house, and as she approached, Micay could see Quinti sitting just inside, visible in profile. She had a long-handled mirror in her hand and was holding it at various distances from her face, staring at her reflection. She looked up when Micay stepped into her light, and Micay could not contain a gasp of surprise. Quinti's face had been painted in a fashion that could only be described as grotesque, with large vermillion splotches on her cheeks and circles so deep and dark around her eyes that she seemed to be staring up out of holes. Micay swiftly knelt beside her, trying not to show her horror.

"Fempellec did this for me," Quinti explained, examining herself once more in the mirror. She sounded distantly satisfied, or perhaps simply detached.

"He has a heavy hand with a brush," Micay suggested gently.

Quinti's hollowed eyes suddenly flashed with unexpected impatience. "I asked him to paint me like this. This is how I looked in my dream."

Micay murmured an apology and suppressed the urge to ask about the dream. Quinti did not want questions or interpretations; she had made that clear to Micay from the start. She would reach her own conclusions, no matter how slowly they came.

"I saw myself at a feast," Quinti said finally. "My face was painted like this, but I did not seem to know it. I walked through the crowd as if I expected them all to bow to me. I was smiling at them and not seeing the contempt and pity on their faces. My eyes were open but I seemed asleep." Quinti paused for a moment and frowned, which made her look desperate and haggard. "Then I woke up and turned on them in anger, scolding them and ordering them into rows, like disobedient children. They obeyed me, but they shrank away from me in fear, staring at me as if I were deranged."

Micay kept her own face impassive, though she wanted to reach out for Quinti in sympathy. It was a terribly harsh vision of how others perceived her, painful in its honesty yet exaggerated all out of proportion.

"That is how I have been," Quinti went on, "either a pathetic fool or a madwoman. Do not try to deny it, Micay. You have seen enough of both. And both are useless."

She picked up the mirror and made as if to throw it against the wall, but then simply let it drop onto the mat beside her with a thud. Micay forced herself to remain still, finding it a good sign that Quinti was not weeping. Quinti sat looking at her hands, breathing out her frustration in deep exhalations that gradually lost their force. She gave a final sigh and looked back at Micay.

"Why is it that you and Cusi find guidance in your dreams, while my dreams mock me?"

"I did not understand my dream for a long time," Micay reminded her. "I forgot it."

"But it came back to help you, like Cusi's benefactor. I have no vision, no huaca. The high priestess is right to spurn me."

"No one has spurned you," Micay told her firmly. "And no one expects you to have visions or powers. That is not what qualifies a woman for the mamacona. My friend Cahua, who by now must be a Woman of the Sun, had no special gifts."

"What did she have that I do not?" Quinti demanded.

Micay squinted at her, sensing that the time had come to abandon her restraint and answer. "She had the courage to live with her deformity and to make others want to live with whatever they had suffered. She made her life a gift to Mama Quilla, and she asked for nothing in return."

Quinti was silent for a moment, her gaze turned inward as if gauging her own feelings. Finally she shook her head and looked at Micay with pained resignation.

"No, I am not that brave or that selfless. I want to know that my life counts for something. I want to *see* it and *feel* it."

"Then you would not be happy among the mamacona."

"No," Quinti agreed, and fell silent again. Then she got up abruptly and went to stand in the doorway, staring out over the rest of the compound. After a respectful moment, Micay rose and went to her side.

"When does Lloque Yupanqui arrive?" Quinti asked wearily.

"Not until late this afternoon. You can rest awhile, if you wish. There will still be time for us to bathe and repaint your face."

Quinti touched one of the splotches on her cheek and grimaced at the sight of her reddened fingertips.

"I have not thought about such things in a long time," she confessed. "I wanted to be done with being a ñusta."

"It is what I want for myself, as well," Micay told her. "I do not know why it has to be so hard."

"Perhaps we only learn from what hurts us," Quinti suggested with a wan smile, turning back into the room. "If so, I am surely destined to be very wise . . ."

IN RESPONSE to Mama Cori's insistence that the feast of welcome be a small, private affair, Fempellec had created a kind of alcove in the space between the two reflecting pools. He had used the terrace behind, which was planted with dense, dark green shrubs, as the back wall, and had arranged ferns and palm fronds and potted plants into low side walls of greenery that extended out from the terrace's retaining wall and curled around the perimeters of the pools. The ground had been covered with dark green cloth, and orchids, lilies, and mountain flowers had been tied into the walls of leaves, sometimes in bunches and sometimes individually, creating a pattern of dots and bursts of bright color against the field of green. Fempellec had been working on this artificial glade until just before Lloque Yupanqui arrived. Then he had disappeared into the kitchen and had not shown himself again.

In his place five serving women appeared, one for each of the guests, each bearing a wooden tray covered with a light cloth. The women all had white lilies tied into their hair, even gray-haired Runtu Caya, and they seemed to move in unison, setting their trays down in front of the guests and removing the covering cloths in a simultaneous gesture that released a cloud of fragrant steam into the air. The women departed with the same quiet precision, leaving the guests staring speechlessly at the colorful array of bowls and dishes on their trays, an arrangement that was as pleasing to look at as it was to smell.

Lloque Yupanqui seemed stunned by the display and was slow to reach for his food. Once he had sampled several of the dishes, though, and found it difficult not to keep sampling them, he became effusive in his praise, claiming he had not tasted anything so delicious since he had left for the north. He addressed his compliments to Apu Poma and Mama Cori, who were sitting side by side in front of the retaining wall, Mama Cori on a small pile of mats and Apu Poma on the three-legged stool he had inherited from the former governor. Lloque was sitting to their right, his back against the stone embankment of one of the pools, and Micay and Quinti were sitting across from him in front of the other pool.

Mama Cori exchanged a brief glance with Apu Poma before shaking her head at her brother's compliments.

"I cannot claim any credit for this," she explained with a smile. "Amaru brought a young Chimu back with him from Chan Chan, and he has found a place for himself in our kitchens."

"He must be a treasure," Lloque enthused, looking at Apu Poma. "You must be careful not to let the Sapa Inca hear of him, or he will be snatched away in an instant."

"I plan to make him my chief of feasts," Apu Poma announced with a judicious nod, as if he had had it in mind all along. It was, in fact, his first acknowledgement of Fempellec's new role, though he had been aware of it for some time.

"Perhaps if Huayna Capac had someone to serve him feasts like this," Lloque said in a more sober tone, "things in Quito would be better than they are."

There was a moment of silence, in which the tinkling of water draining into the pools seemed unnaturally loud. Apu Poma leaned forward on his stool, looking suddenly like a governor rather than a host, and gestured for Lloque to go on. As Lloque, in his mild, comforting voice, began to describe the rift that had occurred between Huayna Capac and the other Incas, Micay stared down at the bowl of boiled potatoes in front of her, their wrinkled red skins flecked with herbs and shiny particles of salt. What she heard made her lose her appetite, so that the potatoes began to seem hard and opaque, like decorative objects carved out of wood and cleverly painted. She felt a sympathetic hand come to rest on top of her own, and she knew without looking up that Quinti had also realized there would be no marriage to announce.

"But what can he want?" Apu Poma protested in disbelief, once Lloque had completed his bleak summary. "The other forts were taken in good time, and in the face of strong opposition."

Lloque spread his long hands and shrugged. "It is my guess—and it is only a guess—that he wants a victory like the one he achieved in Chachapoyas. He would like the enemy to break and flee before him and then come to him begging for mercy." Lloque paused and shook his head ruefully. "But the Carangui continue to fight even when they are forced to retreat. They will not give him that kind of victory."

"You speak as if you no longer shared his confidence," Mama Cori pointed out. "Has he withdrawn from his Rememberers, as well?"

"From all of us," Lloque admitted. "He spends most of his time with his women and his soothsayers and priests, and a few of the foreign war chiefs. He would not even receive his own representative to the province of Chimor."

"You saw Cusi?" Mama Cori asked eagerly as Micay's head came up.

"I did. He had been summoned to the court under the illusion that he would be given an audience—a cruel trick of Titu Atauchi's, I am afraid. But it allowed me to spend some time with him and to hear about his experiences in Chan Chan. He seemed fit and in good spirits, and he asked to be remembered to each of you." Lloque looked across at Micay and smiled. "Especially to you, my daughter. He told me that he intended to ask for you in marriage, and though that is not possible just now, I promised him I would convey his request to the Sapa Inca at a more propitious time."

Micay bowed in gratitude, feeling a swelling of relief that cushioned and diminished her disappointment. At least she knew that Cusi had tried and that Lloque would try again. That in itself should be a message to Mama Cori.

"I hope that you also approve of this match," Lloque continued, looking now at Apu Poma and Mama Cori. "I honored Cusi's wish because I felt he knows his own heart, and because I respect and cherish the woman he has chosen."

"I have already given Cusi my blessing," Apu Poma said. "And I am happy to keep Micay within our family. She has been a good daughter to us."

Micay lowered her eyes, her cheeks burning, but she could not keep herself from looking to see what was on Mama Cori's face. Nothing, it seemed. No discernible resistance, but no surrender either.

"Let us hope Huayna Capac returns his brother Incas to favor," Mama Cori said quietly, "so that this war might be brought to an end, and we might think again about things like marriage."

Lloque stared at her in silence for a moment, as if waiting for her to say more. When she did not, he sighed audibly and let the matter drop. Instead he looked at Quinti, raising his chin to attract her attention.

"I must not forget, my daughter, that I also have regards for you from another warrior. A man who came to see me in Quito to apologize for his past rudeness."

"Quilaco?" Quinti blurted, giving Micay a startled glance. Quilaco had appeared in several of her recent dreams, though not in any way that had seemed significant to either of them.

"He hoped that you had not forgotten him completely," Lloque told her. "And that you might one day forgive him for the way he acted toward you. He was most anxious to win my pardon before he went into battle, and I was convinced of his sincerity."

"Perhaps I would be, too," Quinti murmured with such uncertainty that Lloque blinked at her quizzically, as if she might be joking with him. Micay glanced over at Mama Cori and saw the same imperturbable expression. She is as slow to hope as she is to concede, Micay thought. Perhaps she no longer allows herself any expectations at all.

"Well," Apu Poma interrupted awkwardly, again assuming his duty as host, "let us eat this food before it grows cold. There is still akha to be drunk."

Micay saw Quinti pick up a spoon and begin to eat, displaying an appetite for the first time in days. Micay felt mildly reassured, but skeptical. Quinti had tried to find her purpose in Quilaco once before, and it had not sustained her. Micay sustained herself with the thought that she would soon be going to Quito, where her own purpose would be clear to her and Mama Cori's stubborn reticence would not matter. With a defiance visible only to herself, she plucked one of the potatoes from the bowl and bit through the skin, tasting salt and herbs before the blander flavor of the inner flesh swallowed them up. She ate all of it and then reached for another, knowing she might not see food like this for some time to come.

The Mira Valley

T O THE EAST a jagged crack of light had appeared between the snow-capped peaks and the slowly lifting clouds. Mist was rising in white sheets from the valley below, which was still covered in darkness. Cusi squatted next to Tomay on their high viewing platform, their flanks unabashedly pressed together for warmth, each wrapped in the single blanket they had dared to carry up here with them. Cusi flexed his bare toes against the icy stone beneath him, reminded of his wait in the Sapa Inca's court. Except that the company here was better; he and Tomay had become comrades again in their month together in the field, finally putting to rest the competition that had always existed between them. With so much real risk to be faced, it had suddenly seemed childish and dangerous to be contending with one another, even in a friendly way. Cusi had been able to speak frankly of the fear that had paralyzed him on the cliff, and Tomay, in turn, had revealed the jealousy and resentment he had felt at living in the shadow of Cusi's heroism.

Yet it had taken Cusi until now to tell Tomay about his love for Micay and to ask him how he thought Rimachi would react. Cusi had managed to avoid seeing Rimachi during the short time they were both in Quito, a bit of cowardice he had told himself was for the best, though he did not try to say so to Tomay.

"I have seen him . . . three times since we came into the field," Tomay recalled. "He is even bigger and stronger than he used to be, and a favorite of Atauhuallpa and Challcochima and the other young commanders." Tomay looked at Cusi in the dim light, his knit cap pulled down over his forehead. "And every time I saw him, he found a way to talk about Micay. He talked about her the same way you just did, only with more longing."

"But he knew her for such a short time. They had never even spoken about marriage."

"That has not stopped him from dreaming about it," Tomay said flatly. "We have been out here for over a year, Cusi. That is many nights of sentry duty and sleeping on the cold ground. What else does a warrior have for company except his dreams and memories?"

Cusi was silent, accepting the fact that there would be no easy way to dispel Rimachi's sense of betrayal.

"What is your company," he asked Tomay, "while you are waiting to fight?"

"I have no woman," Tomay shrugged, "and I have to think hard to remember my home. But I saw the place that will be mine."

"Where?"

"East of Quito, in the foothills on the other side of the valley. There are only a few buildings and some potato fields, but there is plenty of pasture for the herds and a family of retainers to tend them."

"This was your gift from the Sapa Inca?"

"I was offered a compound in Quito, not far from the palace. But the palace is not even built yet, so it might have been years before I would even have a wall around me. So I chose the other instead."

"The Guanaco House," Cusi suggested.

Tomay grinned. "I will call it that once I am allowed to go there for more than a visit." He pointed with his chin toward the fortress below. "Once we have left those walls in ruins and made our northern border safe."

The mist had dissipated, and the dark, sinuous shapes of the Carangui ramparts stood out clearly, looking like a giant rope that had been laid down over the pass in smooth, even coils. Cusi and Tomay had wanted to be up here at first light to see whether the Carangui had made any changes in the deployment of their troops during the night. They had already sent back the cords with their count of the enemy forces stationed at each level, information that would be dutifully correlated with the reports of the scouts on the other flank. They did not expect, though, that their count or a report of any subsequent change would have much effect on the plan of attack. For days the Incas had been launching one assault after another on the first line of defense, attacking the wall itself as much as the men guarding it. They had battered at it with axes and clubs and great logs carried by several men at once, carving out handholds and niches from which to fight the warriors above. There had been little attempt at subterfuge, except in the rates at which fresh troops were sent into battle. The Incas had made it plain that they were going to go over the wall, no matter what the Carangui did to stop them.

After a deliberate two-day lull, during which the attackers had displayed signs of fatigue, an all-out assault had been ordered for today. That was the real reason Cusi and Tomay were here. They expected that the first wall would be breached before the day was through, and they wanted to study the way the Carangui would react: whether they would withdraw or send in reinforcements, and how they would move their warriors from one level to the next. It seemed likely that valuable information could be gained for the future, since the other walls were certain to stand beyond this day.

So they waited in silence, feeling the first rays of the sun strike their backs and knowing they would not have to wait much longer before the first cries of battle reached their ears.

IT WAS not until midday that the first rampart was breached. Using ropes and ladders and the steps they had cut into the face of the wall, the Incas and their allies swarmed over the top, fighting the Carangui at close quarter for the first time. The screams of the warriors and the clash of stone and metal echoed off the rocks in an unceasing din, and dust and smoke billowed up in a hazy cloud that obscured the scene of the battle.

Cusi and Tomay sat with their blankets doubled over their heads to protect them from the intense heat and glare of the sun. From their lofty perch, the warriors on the first level looked like ants, and it was impossible to tell who held the advantage. In the far distance, on the crest of a ridge overlooking the battlefield, they could see the lozenge shape of the Sapa Inca's red and gold litter, held aloft on the shoulders of his bearers. There was a broad ripple of movement around and beneath it, as if the ground itself were shifting, and the lozenge began to move forward, down the slope. Huayna Capac had obviously decided to lend his presence to the fight.

The two scouts turned their attention to the fort below, noting that the groups of warriors that had been gathering on the second and third levels had grown larger. They had been coming down from the levels above for some time, using long rope ladders that could only hold a couple of men at a time. It was unclear what use they could be, since the ramparts at both levels were fully manned and there was no good way down to the fighting. Yet these warriors, with their lacquered shields and helmets and their obsidian-studded clubs, were working themselves up for battle, singing their war songs and dancing around fires that were almost invisible in the bright sunlight. Cusi and Tomay exchanged a quizzical glance, wondering where they expected to go.

Then the shrilling of bone whistles came to their ears, piercing through the noise of the fighting, and they saw the groups on both levels begin to move en masse toward the ends of their respective walls. Cusi considered the possibility that this was some kind of drill, because there was no way *around* the walls, either. But that did not explain the dancing and singing, which should not have been wasted on a drill. As they moved, the groups drew themselves out until they were marching in double file, and suddenly the lead warriors turned and headed for some wooden storage huts that had been built against the base of the rampart. A shrine? Cusi wondered, but then he saw the pairs of men disappear into the huts one behind the other, the line slowing but not stopping. And no one came out on either side.

"Tunnels!" Cusi and Tomay exclaimed simultaneously, recalling the subterranean passages beneath Sacsahuaman, where they had performed some of their initiation rites. Tomay immediately stood up and waved his blanket to attract the attention of Paucar, who was stationed below. Then he dropped the blanket and urgently gave the signal indicating an enemy counterattack, slashing at his forearm with a stiffened palm.

"He was already building the fire," Tomay reported as he squatted back down next to Cusi. "He must have seen it himself."

A solid stream of Carangui warriors was moving across the second level at both ends, disappearing into the huts that disguised the tunnels' entrances and no doubt coming out on the level below, on the flanks of the attacking Incas. More warriors were pouring down from the upper levels of the fortress by means of similar tunnels, the long rope ladders hanging empty like the clever deceit they were.

Large puffs of black smoke suddenly came into view to Cusi's left, rising in rapid succession from Paucar's signal fire. A moment later a similar signal went up from the mountain on the other side of the fort, and then watchers in the hills farther south began to pick up the message and repeat it. Cusi squinted in that direction, looking beyond the rising haze of battle and scanning the slope until he located Huayna Capac's litter, which looked like a long red boat riding low in a lake of indistinguishable men. It had stopped going forward and now started back, only to stop again, spraying a golden glitter in all directions. Cusi thought of sunlight striking the waves of Mama Cocha, then realized he was seeing reflections from the earplugs of the Old Guard as they tried to move in concert with the litter.

"Go back," Tomay muttered fiercely, his keen herder's eyes trained on the same spot. But their warning had come too late. As they watched, two rippling waves of color—one at each flank—came rolling up the slope, converging on the litter. From their viewpoint it happened with agonizing slowness, yet the Caranguis' charge must have been swift. The two waves collided with those massed around the litter and set off a general upheaval that made the red boat rock backward and bob in place for a moment, striking sparks of gold all around it. Then it went under and disappeared completely from view.

Cusi and Tomay were both on their feet, though too stricken to speak. They stared desolately at one another, not wanting to believe what they had seen. The Sapa Inca spilled from his litter, possibly killed or captured . . . it was impossible to conceive.

"We must go," Tomay managed. "We must join the retreat before we are cut off."

Cusi nodded, feeling an anger and helplessness that filled his throat and made his legs quiver. Seeking to calm himself, he bent down and picked up his discarded blanket. With a glance at Tomay he carefully folded the blanket into a neat square and laid it on the place where he had sat, holding a hand over it while he offered a silent prayer to Illapa. Tomay nodded in agreement and followed Cusi's example. Then, without speaking, the two of them turned and began their descent, leaving their blankets behind as a sign that they intended to return.

Tumibamba

I T WAS during one of the first days after the warriors had begun to return—when the wounded were pouring into the high priestess's compound and the demands on the healers were frantic and overwhelming—that Micay saw Rimachi. The feeling of being watched made her glance up from the man she was tending, and there was Rimachi, about ten feet away, leaning against one of the posts that held up the roof of the awning house. He had bandages on both arms and a scar on his right cheek, but he was dressed in clean clothes and seemed strong and fit, in stark contrast to the men who lay at his feet.

He made no sign of greeting, and the expression on his angular face told her immediately that he knew. His features seemed frozen into a mask of grim impassivity, and the glint of admiration that had always been in his eyes when he looked at her was gone. Micay could not recall the last time a man had appraised her so coldly, and she shivered and lowered her eyes. She realized he would never look at her with pleasure again, and she felt a quaver in her throat and a constriction in her chest, as if her heart were shrinking.

When she looked up again Rimachi was gone, and she let out a ragged breath, feeling both disappointed and relieved that he had not asked her to speak. She had spoken to his mother some time ago, to spare her the embarrassment of hearing from someone else, and while it had been difficult and painful, they had parted with mutual respect. Micay had no way of knowing whether Rimachi had heard from his mother or whether he had met up with Cusi in the field. However he had learned, he clearly had not been persuaded to forgive the betrayal. Nor did he look as if he wanted to forget.

A few days later Uritu appeared, unhurt but seeking word of Cusi and Tomay, who had not reported in to their regiment during the general retreat.

Micay had made inquiries of her own among the wounded but had nothing to tell him, except for the frequently expressed comment that scouts had to find their own way back when the battle was lost.

"They will come," Uritu said, softly but adamantly. "The Carangui could never catch them."

Uritu himself had been part of the huge retinue accompanying the Sapa Inca's litter, a force that had included not only warriors but also priests, advisers, servants, and several hundred extra litter bearers. They had been crowded too closely together to begin with, with everyone jostling to get close enough to hear Huayna Capac's words, and it had only gotten worse as they moved downhill toward the battle. When the signals of the counterattack were first seen, Uritu claimed, there was still time for the litter to be withdrawn. But there were too many people giving commands, and some of the bearers became confused and had panicked. The warriors had begun to push and shove, some trying to get to the litter and others trying to clear enough space to defend it. They were off balance before the Carangui struck, Uritu said, and they fell the way a great tree falls in the jungle, taking all the vines and smaller trees down with it.

Unable to make effective use of their long bows in such a melee, the Campas had withdrawn to higher ground to provide cover for the retreat. Uritu had seen Huayna Capac emerge from the cloud of dust hanging over the battle and come up the slope on foot, his face and clothing covered with dirt, his golden battle-ax dangling limply from one hand. He had refused all offers of assistance, cursing anyone who tried to approach him, and when he had reached the top of the ridge, he kept on walking without once looking back at the desperate fight the Old Guard was waging behind him.

"The Old Guard suffered heavy losses holding off the Carangui, but he did not even stay to urge them on." Uritu touched one of his gold and silver earplugs and let out a low whoop that sounded vaguely sorrowful. "I wish I had turned my eyes away in time."

"He has blamed the Incas for the defeat," Micay said, "especially the Old Guard and the scouts. He has ordered that none of the usual honors be paid to them."

Uritu nodded. "He has even cut our monthly rations of food and cloth. As if hunger might restore our pride."

Uritu stayed with her a while longer, chewing coca while she told him what had happened to Cusi in Chan Chan and how the two of them had been drawn together during the course of the journey. She also told him about Cusi's attempt to ask for permission to marry her and about the way Rimachi appeared to be taking the news.

"The condor who watches," Uritu murmured, with what Micay interpreted as approval. "I will try to speak to Rimachi. He must know that Cusi would not do this to hurt him."

Uritu had to return to his regiment, which was camped just outside the city, but he came back the next day and every day that followed, questioning the new arrivals among the wounded and sitting with Micay to help ease her waiting. Amaru, who had survived the assault on the fortress with only minor injuries, also came to visit on several occasions. He took a wholly disrespectful pleasure in the fact that Huayna Capac had been dumped from his litter, scoffing at the defeat in order to disguise his anger and his concern for Cusi. Almost a month had passed since the day of the battle, and the border north of Quito had been secured ten days before. The number of lost and wounded coming back to Tumibamba had diminished to only a few a day. Then, one afternoon when she and Uritu were shaving and smoothing splints, he looked up and dropped his coral rasp into his lap.

"They are here."

There was a small crowd at the compound gate, and Micay focused on the first pair of golden earplugs that caught her eye. For an awful moment she thought it was Cusi lying on the makeshift litter. But then the man lifted the arm he had been holding over his face, and she saw it was Paucar. He and all the men standing around him looked as if they had just come out of battle. She saw Tomay next, and then Cusi as he stepped forward to greet the high priestess. He was incredibly filthy and disheveled, wearing a sling in place of his headband, cotton armor that was shredded and stained with blood, and sandals that had lost half of their soles. Yet he was moving, limping only slightly, his limbs were straight and he had all of his fingers, and he was not holding his side. Micay kept herself from weeping because she wanted to see him clearly every moment she could.

He made a rather perfunctory bow to the high priestess, and his first words to her, to Micay's surprise, appeared to be sharp and contentious, as if he expected resistance. Chimpu Ocllo stared back at him for a long moment, during which Cusi's back stiffened and the annoyance on his face slowly changed to a kind of startled recognition, then to outright apology. He stepped back and executed a proper bow, revealing the shield and battle-ax strapped across his back. The high priestess rewarded him with a smile when he straightened up, then put a hand on his shoulder and turned him toward the place where Micay and Uritu were sitting.

He was there almost before she had a chance to drop her tools and stand up, and she noticed that he forgot to limp. His teeth gleamed against his dirty face and he gave a laugh that was half a sob, wrapping his arms around her waist and pulling her against him. Her hands groped futilely for a hold on the shield on his back before settling on his shoulders. He stank of sweat and blood and wood smoke, and the padded armor was like a tattered cushion between them, but their bodies still managed to fit together. Micay wept on his shoulder, and he whispered her name over and over, stroking the long hair that hung down her back.

"I will soil your clothes," he said finally, releasing her so that they could exchange greetings with Uritu and Tomay and Huañu.

"The mamanchic said my splint was well placed," Tomay boasted. "Paucar will march with us the next time."

"He broke his foot," Cusi explained. "That is why it took us so long to get back. The Carangui chased us deep into the mountains, and we often had to hide rather than run." Cusi paused, his face hardening. "Then we got to Quito and they would not give us any bearers, so we had to carry him here ourselves."

"They treated us like deserters," Tomay said bitterly. "On orders from the Sapa Inca."

"It is the same for all the earplug men," Uritu told them. "Except for his sons and brothers."

"You are back, though," Micay interjected. "That is what matters."

Cusi and Tomay exchanged a bemused glance.

"Yes, we are back," Cusi said quietly. "What about Amaru?"

"He is fine. He was here yesterday, waiting with us."

"And Rimachi?" Tomay deliberately addressed the question to Uritu, who glanced at Cusi and nodded.

"He is also in the city. But I do not think you want to see him, Cusi."

"I had to tell his mother," Micay told him. "Then he came here one afternoon and simply stared at me without speaking. He knows, and he has not chosen to forgive."

Cusi sighed and put an arm around her shoulders to comfort her. He held out his other hand in an apologetic gesture to Uritu and Tomay.

"You must forgive me, too. I did not wish to make you choose between your brothers."

"We will go to see him later," Tomay offered, with a glance at Uritu for confirmation. "Perhaps we can take the edge off his anger."

"I will be grateful." Cusi spread his arms to include Huañu in the group. "Come, let us go to the governor's compound. He will not begrudge us a bath and some food. He will not turn us away simply because we are Incas."

CUSI GROPED his way into the steamy darkness of the bathhouse, whispering Micay's name. He heard an answering murmur, then felt arms come around him from behind and pin his arms to his sides.

"You must promise me," Micay whispered, pressing her breasts against his back, "you will not touch me until I say you can."

"Am I being punished?" Cusi laughed.

"You are being pleasured."

"Ah . . . then you have my promise."

The arms released him, and he felt her hands pull up the bottom of his tunic, lifting it to his shoulders, where he pulled it off over his head and tossed it aside. Now he could feel the shape of the breasts pressed against his back, and her hands came around his waist and slid down into his loincloth, wrapping around him as he began to rise.

"Remember your promise," Micay chided him when he groaned and let his hands flutter at his sides. She massaged him with both hands, loosening his waistband by pushing against it with her wrists, until it came undone and the loincloth fell off. Still holding him from behind, she bumped him gently and forced him into a stiff walk, leading him over to the bed she had made out of piles of soft cotton towels. The dim glow of moonlight filtering in through the ventilation ducts mixed with the steam rising off of the sunken bath, making him feel as though he were walking in a dream. Only the smooth hands that caressed him were real.

She made him lie down on the towels with his arms at his sides, and then he could see her face, blurred but beautiful, as she knelt over him and slid her hands over his thighs and across his belly, brushing his chest with his nipples. His mouth fell open and he smiled helplessly, feeling his muscles tremble and quake beneath her fingers and lips. She kissed and touched him everywhere, her long black hair falling over her shoulders and dragging across his skin like a feathered hand. He moaned and mumbled incoherently, his back arching and his hands twitching with the desire to pull her down on top of him.

Then she was straddling his loins, smiling down at him as she lifted one of his hands and rubbed herself against it, holding his fingers together but letting him feel the wetness between her legs. Cusi let out a long moan, and she dropped his hand and rose up on her knees, fitting him inside her with one swift motion, then sinking slowly down upon him, her head thrown back and her mouth opened in a silent cry.

"Now you may touch me," she whispered, rocking forward and bringing her face down close to his. Cusi's arms lifted on their own and wrapped around her back as she kissed him on the lips and began to rock, sending him into a delirium that made everything blur and then disappear as pleasure roared through him like a wave that broke and broke and finally collapsed back upon itself in a shattering burst.

They lay enmeshed for an unreckoned time, until their breathing quieted and their skin began to cool. Then Micay gingerly lifted herself off of him and they lay side by side, Cusi making avid use of his right to touch her.

"I could not have withstood such teasing a few nights ago," he murmured, still incredulous.

Micay laughed softly. "I waited to be sure your heart could stand it."

"I am not certain it has. Where did you learn such a wonderful trick?"

She hesitated for a moment, staring into his eyes.

"From Fempellec. He got very drunk the night he was named chief of feasts, and he started talking about the other ways he knew to entertain. I listened because I did not want him talking to anyone else."

"You listened and learned," Cusi said emphatically, smiling at her. "Amaru told me, on the way to Quito, about the things he had experienced in the houses of pleasure on the coast. About the many ways there are to take pleasure from your body, or another's, ways that we were taught were wrong, perverse, despicable. He did not convince me completely that the Incas disdain these practices only out of fear and ignorance and because the Sapa Inca does not want them to be distracted from their duties. But he made me see—"

"The attraction?" Micay suggested teasingly when he could not finish. Cusi shook his head stubbornly, though he had to smile.

"You have shown me that, better than he or Fempellec ever could. No, he made me see that it had not hurt him or made him weak and cowardly, as we were told it would. Though . . . it could hurt him greatly in another way if anyone else were to hear the sounds that sometimes come from their house late at night."

"Are they different from the sounds you just made?" Micay asked with a mocking innocence that made him pull her against him in a fierce hug that could not stifle her laughter.

"Are you also intent on corrupting an Inca?" he demanded.

Micay surprised him with a serious answer. "I am intent on having his child, even if I may not marry him. The midwives told me the moon is right for me."

"Let us hope it is," Cusi said after a respectful pause, leaning back to look at her face. "And we *will* marry, once Huayna Capac has been brought to his senses. That may be soon, since the earplug men have suffered his scorn for as long as we can stand. We are meeting tomorrow night, outside the city."

"You did not tell me," Micay said apprehensively.

"I only heard tonight. No one else must know, especially not my father."

"What can you do? You are sworn to serve and obey him."

"He is sworn to respect and lead us, but we are not even allowed to see him. There are those who say we should take Huanacauri and march back to Cuzco."

"Will it come to that?"

"I pray it does not. That would be the end of the Incas . . . brother fighting against brother, fathers abandoning their sons. It would be the disaster Raurau Illa warned me of, a squandering of all our strength. We cannot let it come to that."

"Neither can Huayna Capac," Micay decided, regaining her courage. "He cannot win this war without you."

"Let us hope he remembers in time." He reached out and brushed the hair away from her forehead, letting his hand linger on her cheek. "I do not wish to leave you again until I have to."

"I do not wish you to leave, ever . . ."

Cusi pushed himself up on one arm and bent down to kiss her. She raised her hands to his face, and he pressed his lips against each palm as he came up onto his knees beside her. He smiled as he took her hands and gently pinned them down at her sides.

"The moon is still right," he said suggestively, holding himself poised above her. "Now you must promise *me* . . ."

THE INCA warriors assembled after dark in a recently harvested maize field on the other side of the Tumibamba River. They built bonfires out of the discarded husks and stalks, no longer caring if they were noticed by the foreign troops camped all around them. They had kept the planning for this meeting as secret as possible to prevent its disruption by a sudden order from the Sapa Inca, but once begun a gathering of three thousand men could not be hidden. If his spies had not already alerted him, Huayna Capac would probably receive the news during the feast he was giving for the Cañaris and Quitos, the latest feast from which the Incas had pointedly been omitted.

The atmosphere around the fires, when Cusi arrived with Tomay and Amaru, was unlike anything he had ever experienced at a feast. The Incas seldom came together in one place except for celebrations and ceremonies, and then they were usually separated by rank and household affiliation. But tonight the men mingled freely, war chiefs with raw apprentices, and although they were kinsmen and initiation brothers and comrades in arms, they greeted one another with a heightened sense of recognition and mutual respect, reaffirming their larger common bond. Cusi was moved by the warmth of the greetings, which made him recall Otoronco Achachi's statement that he could never forget how few Incas there were.

Moving from fire to fire, Cusi and Tomay met up with several of their initiation brothers whom they had not seen since Chachapoyas, and they spoke of the battles they had been in and the comrades they had lost. Cusi's old adversary Sutic gripped Cusi's arm in front of the others and spoke solemnly of his cousin Mayca, who had been the first of their number to die. Cusi accepted the offer to bury their past differences and praised Mayca's courage on the cliff, saying that the manner of his death brought honor to them all, a claim that made Sutic tighten his grip and pound Cusi on the back in gratitude.

Sumac Mallqui, their teacher in Cuzco and now a high commander, came up to join them, and it was through him that Cusi at last made the acquaintance of some of the young commanders who had distinguished themselves in the recent fighting: men like Challcochima, Quizquiz, Tomarimay, and Ucumari, who had fought valiantly in spite of the restrictions imposed by the Sapa Inca's presence. They knew Cusi by reputation but had never had a chance to meet him because of his long convalescence, and they regarded him now as a noteworthy defector to their cause, proof that even those most favored by Huayna Capac no longer owed him any loyalty. They plied him with invitations to join their regiments and assured him that none of the field commanders blamed the defeat on the work of the scouts.

Conspicuously absent from this group were Ninan Cuyochi and Atauhuallpa, who, like all the other royal sons and brothers, could not risk being suspected of plotting to usurp the fringe of the ruler. It was said, though, that Atauhuallpa—the more distant son—had given his blessing to the meeting and that Ninan Cuyochi, much as he revered his father, had agreed not to oppose whatever action the warriors decided to take. Knowing Ninan Cuyochi's careful, judicious ways, Cusi considered the latter, if it was true, the most serious defection of all.

Gradually word was passed to assemble, and the warriors formed an immense semicircle around the central bonfire, the closest sitting on the broken earth while those behind sat on the field walls or stood back in the shadows. Cusi found a seat on a wall between Tomay and Amaru and looked toward the place where Michi and Yasca and two other war chiefs stood waiting to address the crowd. As Michi stepped forward to speak, however, the moon suddenly appeared above the eastern mountains, flooding the field with a pale light that glistened on the thousands of gold and silver earplugs. The moon is right for us, too, thought Cusi, feeling a thrill of recognition pass from man to man. Michi looked up and raised his arms over his head in supplication.

"Mama Quilla, Mother of the Incas!" he cried. "Look down upon your sons and show them your guidance and mercy. They have suffered a scorn and a punishment they have not earned!"

A low, rumbling murmur arose from the crowd, half reverential and half defiant. Cusi felt something like a growl escape from his own throat, and he gazed up at the nearly full moon, thinking of his brief meeting with the high priestess and recalling the power of her presence, the force she had exerted upon him when he had spoken to her rudely. She had not made him feel threatened and overpowered, as other men had, but simply wrong and foolish. It was the kind of power that needed to be exerted upon Huayna Capac, who called himself the Herder of the Sun yet had no huaca of his own.

"My brothers," Michi said when they were once again silent, "I must tell you first what you all know: It was not the fault of the Incas that this battle was lost; it was not the fault of the scouts and the Old Guard that Huayna Capac was thrown from his litter and disgraced. We know it was not the warriors who failed in their duties!"

The men roared in agreement, throwing their fists into the air and brandishing imaginary weapons. Their shout echoed out across the valley, breaking against the walls of the city.

"I must also tell you," Michi continued, "that the four of us were summoned by the high priest today. He assured us in Huayna Capac's name that we were still held in his favor and that we would receive the rewards and recognition we deserve. But we were not given an audience nor any assurances that you, our brothers and kinsmen, would also be restored to favor. We are here because we find such an arrangement most unsatisfactory."

A few of the younger warriors cheered this show of loyalty, but their cries were drowned out by the deep humming sound produced by the veterans as a sign of their respect and approval. They expected their war chiefs to be like the warlords of old, whose first loyalty was always to the fighting men.

"This is our plan," Michi told them. "Let us assemble at first light in the plaza in front of the Coricancha, dressed and armed for a march. We will lay claim to Huanacauri, our patron and the strength of our arms. If Huayna Capac refuses to grant us the respect and gratitude we are owed, we will take the huaca and march back to Cuzco. Let him fight alone if he believes we are worthless!"

Rising to their feet as one, the warriors signaled their assent by shouting the name of Huanacauri loud enough for the Sapa Inca himself to hear. Glancing around in the din, Cusi noticed that Tomay appeared doubtful but accepting, while Amaru smiled at him with genuine delight.

"I am grateful now that you brought me back," Amaru said, leaning toward him to be heard. "I would not have missed being a part of this."

As they began to disperse with the other warriors, they were intercepted by a dark, handsome man with a hooked nose who greeted Amaru with the enthusiasm of an old friend. He seemed vaguely familiar to Cusi, too, though Cusi did not know why until the man turned and introduced himself.

"I am Quilaco Yupanqui," he said with surprising humility, as if he did not expect to be remembered. "Yasca sent me to alert you, Cusi Huaman. You are one of eight who have been chosen as the honor guard for Huanacauri."

"But I have been back in the field for only a short time," Cusi protested. "There are others more deserving."

"Perhaps, but few who are as well known to the Sapa Inca. I was also selected because of my closeness to the Coya. The war chiefs want him to feel the affection and loyalty he has lost."

"I am honored, then," Cusi said, glancing at Tomay, who did not appear envious of this distinction. Quilaco drew himself up in front of Cusi as if he had another message to deliver.

"Since we may stand together tomorrow," he said solemnly, "I must ask you now to forgive me for the rudeness I displayed in your presence on the night you arrived from Chachapoyas. I insulted your sister and your uncle and the ñusta Micay, and I am sorry."

Cusi blinked at him in amazement, having all but forgotten the incident. So much had happened since that made it seem almost trivial, though it was clearly not trivial to Quilaco.

"That was long ago, and I have held no grudge against you," Cusi assured him. "And surely on this night we are all brothers and must forgive one another everything."

"I am grateful," Quilaco said, bowing deeply. Then he nodded to Tomay, clapped Amaru on the shoulder, and disappeared into the crowd. Cusi watched him go, scanning the faces for the two brothers he had not seen tonight.

"What was he talking about?" Amaru asked in a puzzled voice. "And why did he never marry Quinti? The match had been made before I left for the coast."

"I will tell you later," Cusi promised, still surveying the crowd. He finally turned to Tomay. "Why have we not seen Uritu and Rimachi?"

"That was our plan," Tomay said succinctly. "There is some forgiveness that will not come so easily."

"Not even tonight?"

"Especially not tonight," Tomay assured him. "We could not risk an argument here. You will have to risk it yourself at another time."

"I can wait, then," Cusi decided, and he started them moving toward the edge of the field. "Let us retrieve our weapons, and begin our argument with the Sapa Inca."

BY THE TIME Inti's first pink light began to spread over Tumibamba, his sons the Incas were already standing in the great square at the heart of the city. They had worn their finest tunics, along with the necklaces and armbands and Sun shields they had been given for past acts of bravery, but otherwise they were dressed for a march, their helmets, shields, and cloaks tied into a single bundle on their backs and their weapons in their hands. They stood grim and unmoving, their backs to the Coricancha, the Enclosure of the Sun, and their eyes on the main gate of the Mollecancha on the other side of the square. The stone dais of the ruler rose up in the center of the plaza, partially obscuring Cusi's view of the gate, from which a steady stream of curious, apprehensive people had been issuing. They drifted to join the crowd that was gathering around the perimeter of the plaza, showing their fear in the tentativeness of their movements and the fact that their eyes never left the warriors. Only the muted shuffling of their feet disturbed the silence, which was heavy and brooding, the silence of power deliberately withheld.

Cusi had barely eaten and he had not slept at all, having spent the night talking with Tomay and Amaru and Micay and Quinti—and, at the last, with his father, as well. But the excitement and dread that seemed to surge through him by turns left him no opportunity to dwell on his fatigue. He had not felt this way since the day of the Huarachicoy race, only this time the future of *all* of the Incas was at stake.

He was standing in the front rank with Quilaco Yupanqui and the rest of the honor guard, which included Sumac Mallqui, Challcochima, Ucumari, and three members of the Old Guard. On the ground in front of them, sitting on low, stiltlike legs, was the litter upon which the huaca of Huanacauri had been carried here from Cuzco. The narrow wooden frame was draped with a red and blue cloth woven entirely of feathers and spangled with medallions of gold, silver, and abalone shell, and there was a round seat with a high lip sunk into its middle. For all the vows Cusi had sworn to Huanacauri during the Huarachicoy, he had yet to see the huaca itself, because it had been here, confined in the Coricancha when not leading the Incas into battle. Today they would free Huanacauri from the confinement of Huayna Capac's arrogance, and perhaps he would lead them away from this battle, back to Cuzco.

A movement to Cusi's left caught his attention, and he saw a small retinue of women cross the corner of the plaza and pass behind the warriors. Their leader was the high priestess, and Cusi assumed that they were going to the Coricancha. Micay and Quinti were with her, and by now they had probably told her about the way Mama Quilla had appeared at the meeting of the warriors. Cusi did not know if Chimpu Ocllo would have any part in this, but she was the only one who might have the power to intercede if neither side would yield. There was no one else who could pretend to neutrality any longer.

A low murmur swept the crowd ringing the square, and Cusi looked past the dais to see the Sapa Inca's litter being carried out of the Mollecancha. He should have walked, Cusi thought, feeling a ripple of displeasure pass through the men around him. The litter was preceded by a group of priests and advisers—among whom Cusi recognized both his father and Lloque Yupanqui—and was accompanied by a large contingent of the Cañari Royal Guard, whose presence caused the Incas to tighten their grips on their weapons. It had never occurred to Cusi that Huayna Capac might try to use force against them, and the possibility shocked him deeply, even as it made him glad of the battle-ax in his hands.

The procession halted on the other side of the dais, and the high priest climbed to the top of the stone platform and stood looking down at the warriors. Finally he hailed them in the name of the Sapa Inca, demanding to know why they were here, since they had not been summoned. The four war chiefs, who stood in a row in front of the troops, stared back at him without speaking. The high priest asked again, and again there was no reply. He asked a third time, and finally, after a prolonged pause, Michi answered him curtly.

"We are here because we must leave this city. We are being driven out by hunger, and by the scorn and disrespect of the one who should love us like his own sons. We cannot allow ourselves to be mistreated in this manner any longer."

While the high priest stared down at them speechlessly, Michi and his companions turned, and a path was opened for them through the ranks of warriors. The war chiefs walked down this path toward the Coricancha, and the honor guard formed up and followed, the four tallest carrying Huanacauri's litter on their shoulders. Michi led them up the long flight of stairs, and priests and mamacona stepped back out of their way as they entered the sacred enclosure and went directly to the gold-banded house that belonged to Inti. A single priest stood in the war chiefs' way, and Michi strode up and glared in the man's face.

"He belongs to us, not you," Michi snapped, and the priest backed away and let the war chiefs enter the shrine. The honor guard waited outside, the bearers lowering the litter to the ground. Cusi found that he was panting, though more from emotion than effort. It had been a relief to move his legs, but as he had climbed the stairs, feeling that every eye in the square was on him, he was struck by the awful seriousness of what they were doing. They were violating every protocol and prohibition, committing treason with every step they took. They might be remembered as the men who brought the reign of the Inca to an end.

Cusi glanced over at the House of Mama Quilla and saw only a few mamacona standing in front, witnessing this unlawful seizure of the huaca with horrified expressions on their faces. But Micay and Quinti and the high priestess were not among them, and he was encouraged by the thought that they were inside praying. *Someone* should be praying, seeking the wisdom to resolve this before it went any further, before everything that bound them together as a people was destroyed.

Michi and one of the other war chiefs emerged from the shrine carrying the huaca between them, grimacing at the strain it put on their arms. Huanacauri was a piece of brown, weathered stone, shaped vaguely like a seated man, its fissured surface carved with ancient symbols and the images of hawks and snarling pumas. Cusi put down his battle-ax to make the mocha, blowing kisses off his fingertips while the two war chiefs carefully lowered the huaca into its seat on the litter. Cusi and the others went to help the bearers lift the burden onto their shoulders, a feat the eight of them accomplished with a loud collective grunt.

They walked slowly back across the courtyard, Cusi and Quilaco reassuming their place behind the war chiefs and ahead of the litter, their weapons once again in their hands. When they came out through the high trapezoidal gateway, they were greeted by a great shout from the assembled warriors, who had turned to face them with their weapons raised in salute. The blast of noise washed over Cusi like a gusting wind, filling him with an exhilaration that made him want to leap and brandish his weapon, displaying the reckless, warlike spirit of Huanacauri. He suddenly felt the rightness, as well as the necessity, of what they were doing. It could not be treason to defend the honor of the Incas; it was their duty to do so here, just as they had on the field of battle. There were some things that should not be left to the judgment of others.

Somehow Cusi managed to resist the urge to make a display of himself, though it seemed that he and his companions floated through the midst of the warriors, wafted along by a tumultuous emotional wind. The litter was set down facing the dais, and the honor guard took up positions on either side of it, the war chiefs lined up to their left. As silence settled back over the square, Cusi became aware of the presence of the huaca beside him, exerting a subtle pressure he felt on the back of his neck, so that he was tempted to turn and look behind him. In his mind he saw not a stone but a seated man, his face fixed in an obdurate scowl, prepared to hear of nothing but war. Cusi cast a brief sidelong glance at Quilaco, wondering if he felt any of this. He did not appear to; his attention seemed completely focused on the dais, where they all expected Huayna Capac would appear.

To their surprise, the ruler came around the platform on foot, trailed by a small entourage of priests and advisers. He wore a magnificent feathered cape over his checkered tunic, and gold glittered from his wrist and leg bands and the pectoral on his chest. He stopped in front of the war chiefs and crossed his arms on his chest, staring at them sternly. Cusi felt an involuntary tremor, a reflex urge to bow his head in deference to the Sapa Inca, the Sole Lord of the Incas. Had the war chiefs bowed, Cusi was certain he and the others would have done the same, The instinct was that strong.

But the war chiefs remained silent and unbending, and Cusi thought he saw

Huayna Capac's eyes narrow behind the fringe of many-colored tassels that hung from his headband. Finally the ruler spoke.

"Come, Michi," he said in a tone of hearty exasperation, "speak to me. Tell me why you have lent yourself to this act of defiance and disrespect."

"You have driven us to this," Michi told him bluntly. "We came here to fight for Inti and Illapa and Huanacauri, as our fathers and grandfathers have done. But you have betrayed our trust and repaid our loyalty with contempt. You have left us without a leader, so we have taken possession of the one whose warlike spirit has always guided the Inca warriors."

Huayna Capac did not respond for several moments, his chest rising with his breathing, his eyes darting from side to side behind the fringe. Like Tocto's, Cusi thought, looking for an escape from her life. Huayna Capac suddenly dropped his arms and stepped forward to take Michi by the elbow.

"Surely you must be mistaken," he said urgently, drawing the four war chiefs into a walk. They began to pace up and down in front of the ranks of warriors, discussing their respective grievances in voices that veered easily from reasoned argument to righteous indignation. The warriors heard their leaders express complaints that went back as far as the campaign against the Quitos, and they heard Huayna Capac speak of the defeats and disappointments he had suffered, and why they justified him in his anger. The desire for a reconciliation was mentioned again and again by both parties, but there was no agreement on who should apologize and who forgive.

Still deadlocked, they finally stopped their pacing, back at the place where they had begun. Huayna Capac left the war chiefs and came over to stand in front of the litter. Instead of making the mocha to Huanacauri, he simply bowed, as one warrior would to another. The Herder of the Sun, Cusi thought incredulously. He believes he is the equal of the gods. Yet it was also clear to Cusi that Huayna Capac did not feel the huaca's emanations, which was undoubtedly why he did not regard it with more awe. It struck Cusi that he was a profoundly irreverent man, despite his belief in signs and prophecies.

Then Huayna Capac raised his eyes to the members of the honor guard, and his face grew wistful at the sight of men who had once basked in his favor, yet who now would not so much as bow their heads to him. His gaze lingered on Cusi, whose age and size made him conspicuous in this group. He seemed about to speak for a moment, and Cusi braced himself, wondering if he was going to be threatened or cajoled and whether he should respond to either. He had no desire to add to his reputation for presumption, or to be the one whose face Huayna Capac remembered whenever he recalled this day. Yet he could not allow himself to be any less blunt and honest than Michi, who had spoken for all of them.

Huayna Capac must have seen this in his eyes, because he suddenly clamped his mouth shut and blew air through his nose in frustration. Then he turned and walked back to the war chiefs with short, rapid strides.

"I must consult with my priests and with those who speak for the gods and the huacas," he announced.

Michi glanced at Yasca and the other war chiefs before replying. "We will wait," he said, and Huayna Capac turned away without waiting to see if anyone would bow at his departure.

WHEN THE war chiefs had come to remove the huaca of Huanacauri, Micay and Quinti had been standing at the two windows that opened onto the courtyard of the Coricancha. They had taken turns describing the incident to the high priestess, who sat beneath the silver moon disc in the back wall with her eyes closed and her hands folded in her lap. She had been particularly interested in the demeanor of the men as they performed their task, and she had grunted with satisfaction when Quinti had reported that Quilaco seemed frightened and Micay that Cusi appeared entranced. That was how they should look, Chimpu Ocllo had told them, and had listened to the rest of their description without comment.

Then there was a long period during which the courtyard was empty except for the mamacona who came to report on what was happening in the square. Micay leaned against the deep sill of the window, imagining the warriors standing silent in their ranks while Huayna Capac and the war chiefs conducted their walking parley in front of them. The fact that he had stayed to talk—after they had refused to bow to him—seemed promising, a sign that he recognized the weakness of his position. When she heard that he had left again, though, she wondered how long the warriors would remain standing so patiently. Her own legs were beginning to ache, and they had no windowsill on which to rest their elbows or their weapons.

"Now he will send for the images of the gods," Chimpu Ocllo said from her place against the wall. "For Churi Inti and Chuqui Illa and Collca and Mama Ocllo."

Micay straightened up at the window, and after another period of waiting the high priest came into the courtyard, accompanied by a large group of priests and mamacona and by men bearing several cloth-covered litters. They dispersed toward the various shrines within the Coricancha, obviously intending, as Chimpu Ocllo had suggested, to remove the effigies of the gods. Micay began to describe the activity she was able to see, but the high priestess gently cut her off, telling her it did not matter.

"All of these effigies are personal to Huayna Capac," she explained. "Those we inherited from our ancestors are in the Coricancha in Cuzco. The warriors know this, and if they will not bow to him, they will not heed his priests. Come sit with me, my daughters. I want to speak with you before the Coya comes."

Her eyes were open when Micay and Quinti sat down across from her, and her gaze was clear and calm, as if she had just awakened from a refreshing sleep. Micay felt far from rested herself, but she complied when Chimpu asked her to repeat Cusi's account of the warriors' meeting one more time. The older woman nodded when Micay was through, then turned to Quinti.

"Quilaco Yupanqui has not made a match with anyone else since yours was broken," Chimpu observed. "And he has made a great point of apologizing to your uncle and your brother. If he has truly changed for the better, could you marry him now?"

Quinti cast a bewildered glance at Micay. "Micay keeps reminding me not to look to Quilaco as the solution to everything, and I know she is right. What are you suggesting now, my lady?"

"The Coya will have to come to me soon," Chimpu said with quiet assurance, "to ask me to speak to the warriors. She knows I will do this, but she also knows she will finally have to pay me the respect I am owed. What I ask will be painful for her to give, but she will give it to me. Once we have made our arrangements an intermediary will be needed, and I want to suggest you, my daughter. I want to propose, as a gesture of mutual trust, that you be married to a man who is close to her, if it is agreeable to both you and Quilaco."

"But—I would live close to the court if I married Quilaco. Who would I obey?"

"You would obey what you know is right, as your mother does. She is another reason why you will be acceptable to Rahua Ocllo. But as I said, the match must be acceptable to you after you have spoken with Quilaco."

"I had planned to speak to him," Quinti confessed.

"See that you are given the respect you are owed," Chimpu advised. "Be sure he understands that you have responsibilities of your own."

Quinti nodded compliantly, and Chimpu was silent for a moment, looking from one to the other. Micay heard no sounds from the courtyard and guessed that the priests had departed, carrying the effigies with them. If they failed, only the high priestess was left, and Micay wondered if she truly had the power to sway the Incas.

"Did you make plans to follow the warriors?" Chimpu asked abruptly. Micay could only nod, feeling vaguely disloyal. "That was prudent," Chimpu allowed, "but you will not have to use them. Go outside now, and greet the Coya when she comes. I must dress and prepare myself to speak to my sons."

THE WARRIORS bowed in unison when the effigies of the gods were carried into the square on their litters, accompanied by the holy ones who spoke for them. When the men straightened up, they saw that the procession was being led not by Inti or Illapa, but by Mama Ocllo, the First Mother of the Incas. Her effigy was a seated woman wrapped in gold cloth with a golden death mask for a face—the mummy of Huayna Capac's own mother, Cusi knew. Her speaker was a tall Cañari woman whose black hair was streaked with white and hung down in front of her face, as if she were in mourning. She stopped not far from where Cusi stood and turned to face the warriors, raising her arms with her palms out, as if to feel the heat they were giving off. She spoke in a voice that was breathless with distress and disbelief, so that her words came out in echoing bursts.

"This cannot be, my sons. Why are you here? You cannot mean to violate the vows that bind you to your lord. You cannot wish to disgrace the memories of your fathers and grandfathers. Where will you go with no one to lead you? Who will protect the women and children when you are gone?"

After the first flush of shame, Cusi felt a rising annoyance, both in himself and in the men around him. He could feel her power but he could not see her face, and her Cañari accent seemed to become more pronounced as she continued to accuse them of betraying everything their ancestors had held sacred. What had made Huayna Capac think that he could send a woman to scold them? And a Cañari, no less! Cusi closed his ears to her, wondering why Huayna Capac could not understand the significance of his own gestures. Even now he had to remind them of how he had separated himself from them and put the Cañaris in their places.

The speakers representing the other gods made similar appeals, some more forgiving in tone, but the warriors listened in a silence that grew progressively more sullen. It was now past midday, and they were tired and hungry and thirsty, no closer to being satisfied. Soon the march to Cuzco would begin to seem less trying than waiting here.

When the effigies had gone and Huayna Capac did not reappear, the war chiefs turned to their regiments and gave the men permission to put down their weapons and stretch their limbs. Cusi ran in place, rotating his shoulders and flexing his aching arms. The battle-ax had begun to feel like the painful burden Otoronco Achachi had originally intended it to be, though Cusi blamed his present discomfort on the Sapa Inca. Otoronco had complained long ago that Huayna Capac was not a warlord, a leader proven in war, which was in fact the reason they were standing here today, their weapons useless and heavy in their hands.

Cusi squatted, bouncing slightly on his heels to exercise his knees and ankles. There was no longer any exhilaration or dread to sustain him, and he had to struggle to keep his hopes of a resolution alive. He glanced across at Quilaco, who was doing knee bends on the other side of the litter. He had once been as blind and arrogant as Huayna Capac, but apparently he had changed. Quilaco intercepted Cusi's glance and grimaced in recognition, appearing worn and impatient. Cusi guessed that it was the fighting that had changed him, the confrontation with death close up and on the ground, rather than from the safety of a litter. He nodded to Quilaco, sharing a moment of comradeship that did little for his hopes, since it only made their distance from the ruler more apparent.

At a signal from Michi, Cusi and the warriors around him retrieved their weapons and reassumed a waiting stance. Clouds had been passing in front of the sun all morning, and now a dark band obscured Inti's face entirely, cooling the air and bringing the sky down low over their heads. Some of the men stirred nervously, but Cusi found the strange twilit atmosphere reassuring, a sign that the gods of the sky were not angry with them. Then he heard movement behind him and glanced over his shoulder to see the warriors parting to open a path

through their ranks, bowing as they backed out of the way. The high priestess
came slowly through their midst, her hands held open in front of her, turning
her head from side to side to gaze into the men's faces as she passed. There
were loops of polished silver around her wrists and neck, and the pattern of
silver threads in her long gray shift shimmered brilliantly in the dim light. She
was followed by four white-haired mamacona, each of whom carried a painted
pottery jug.

A warm, flowery scent came to Cusi's nostrils as Chimpu Ocllo came past
him and stopped in front of Huanacauri. She made a deep, stately bow,
fluttering her fingers in front of her lips so that her silver bracelets jingled,
whispering a greeting that sounded almost loving. Cusi felt her presence sweep
over him and back again with renewed force, as if she were drawing power
from Huanacauri. The air seemed to close in around him, shutting off his
hearing and making his muscles slacken involuntarily, so that he almost let go
of his ax. The other members of the honor guard bowed in awe, but Cusi could
not move; he had to see her face as she straightened up. She met his eyes
without a blink of surprise, as if she had felt him staring, and there was
recognition in her gaze, both of who he was and what she was making him
feel. He was aware of the presence of his spirit brother, swelling up inside him,
tall and utterly calm like the high priestess herself, like Cusi wanted to be.
There was approval in her eyes but still he yearned to please her, to prove he
was worthy of that benevolent regard. Accept me, Mamanchic, he thought
helplessly, letting the weight of his ax pull him over into a bow.

Her departure left him swaying on his feet, the wind pulled out of his lungs,
part of him gone with her, adding to her power. He saw her wield it upon the
war chiefs, searching their faces with a compassion and understanding that
made them blink and lower their eyes. She spoke in a voice that was strong
and direct, without a trace of pleading or disapproval.

"I do not have to ask you, my sons, why you are here. You gathered in the
sight of Mama Quilla, and she has heard the prayers you made for her guidance
and protection. She has heard the grievances you voiced today, and she has
witnessed the dignity and respect you have shown, even in your defiance.
Always she has looked upon you with pride and favor, as her own sons. She
looks on you with the same love today."

The war chiefs and all the men behind them bowed again in a spontaneous,
ragged flurry of movement.

"What has happened here is a grave matter," Chimpu went on, "one for
which we have no precedent and no rites of settlement. It cannot be undone
and it must not be ignored, yet it is beyond apology, beyond forgiveness.
Perhaps it can only be left to heal. That is the hope that has brought me here,
my sons. Let this wound be healed; let the Incas be whole again."

"What do you ask of us, Mamanchic?" Michi inquired hoarsely.

Chimpu spread her arms wide in a gesture that made her silver bracelets
slide down her forearms. "I have been assured that Huayna Capac wishes to
be reconciled with you. That he wishes to provide a feast for you and restore

your honors and privileges. And that he is willing to consult with you about the future conduct of the war. Is that not what you have come for? I ask you to lay down your grievances, my sons, and accept what has been offered. I ask this not on his behalf, but on behalf of all the Incas and all those under Inca rule. I ask in the name of Mama Quilla, to whom you will always be precious, never to be replaced, never to be forgotten."

The warriors all around Cusi had lowered their weapons, and some were weeping openly. Chimpu turned slightly and summoned the mamacona forward.

"I will leave you to consider your decision," she said to the war chiefs. "I know this waiting has been a hardship for you, so I have brought you water from the sacred well in the Coricancha. May it refresh your senses and help you to choose wisely."

The mamacona presented their painted jugs to the war chiefs, who held them carefully against their bodies as they bowed. Michi dipped two fingers into his jug and touched them to his lips before he spoke.

"Surely, Mamanchic, you have shown us the only choice."

The high priestess raised a hand over them in blessing, then led her women back through the ranks of warriors, back to the Coricancha. Cusi saw one of the water jugs coming his way, passing slowly from hand to hand, but before it could reach the honor guard, Michi gave the order to return Huanacauri to his shrine. He sent Yasca and another war chief to lead the way, and Cusi saw that Yasca's rough-hewn face was wet with tears.

"She has great huaca," Cusi murmured to him as they prepared to move out.

Yasca bared his teeth in acknowledgement. "She has won a great victory," he said, softly but distinctly, "and left no one defeated . . ."

THAT NIGHT Huayna Capac came in person to the great feast in the Coya's compound. In a screened-off section of the plaza, he met his warriors face to face, seated on a stool covered with jaguar skin and holding a drinking cup made of gold. He offered no explanations or apologies to the men who came before him, toasting them as if he had never had any reason to question their courage and loyalty, as if the last battle with the Carangui had ended in victory rather than defeat. He also gave them gifts worthy of victors: land and herds and places to live; rights to water, wood, stone, and the labor of skilled workers and retainers; use of servants, messengers, and litter bearers; and the customary rewards of coca leaves, fine cloth, and gold jewelry. He sat surrounded by his stewards and a crowd of count takers, who were responsible for recording and remembering the details of his generosity.

Many of the younger men, like Cusi, wanted wives, and the Sapa Inca granted their requests without exception, giving them women from the House of Chosen Women and his own household and using his influence with the parents of desirable ñustas. He greeted Cusi with the obligatory toast—offered a bit stiffly, as if perhaps he remembered Cusi's place in the honor guard. But he let his gaze linger on Micay while he listened to Cusi's request, and his stern face gradually relaxed into a smile that made him appear youthful and magnanimous.

"I remember this ñusta well," he said. "Almost as if she were one of my own daughters. Do you ask for her as your first or second wife?"

"My first," Cusi said proudly. "The one whose place cannot be taken."

"Let it be done, then," Huayna Capac declared. "Your father and uncle have already assured me that there are no objections to this match, and certainly I can see none. You may hold the ceremony whenever your duties allow you the time; I will have my cooks send food for your wedding feast."

He acknowledged their expressions of gratitude with a curt nod, leaning back on his stool with one hand propped against his hip and the other holding his cup balanced on his thigh. He was smiling again and seemed reluctant to dismiss them.

"Now that my other daughters are safe," he said in a leisurely tone, "what else can I give you, Cusi? I have heard of the duties you performed for me in Chan Chan, and I wish to reward you."

"I have had my reward, my lord," Cusi told him. "The trip to Chimor made me strong again, and you have already given me the Rainbow House and the woman I love. What more could I ask?"

"What about you, my daughter? You are now the mistress of the Rainbow House. Perhaps you would like more servants or some women to keep you company when your husband is away fighting."

"I am grateful, my lord," Micay demurred, "but I have a task of my own. I am a healer in the cult of Mama Quilla."

Huayna Capac grunted and stared at them silently for a moment, his eyes narrowed behind the fringe of colored tassels.

"The high priestess is a great healer," he said, pointing at Cusi with his chin. "They say that you gazed back at her with great boldness today, but she finally made you bow to her."

"It was not boldness, my lord, and she did not need to make me bow. She knew that I bowed to her in my heart."

An expression that seemed both pained and envious passed across Huayna Capac's face, and he turned to address one of his stewards.

"See that Cusi is sent a basket of fresh coca leaves and some leather sandals for the march. And for you, my daughter," he added, turning back and gesturing to another servant, "some fine Chimu beads and a mantle pin to wear on the day you become Mama Micay. They were brought to me by my representative to Chimor."

Micay took the cloth-wrapped bundle from the servant but made no attempt to open it, because Huayna Capac was raising his golden cup to signal an end to the audience. She and Cusi bowed and made the mocha as they backed out of his presence and were swallowed up by the crowd of those still waiting for an interview. They found their way out of the screened-in enclosure and

stopped in the shadows at the edge of the torchlit plaza, where finally they
turned, put their arms around each other and stood swaying together for a long
time.

"It is done, Micay," Cusi whispered into her hair. "No one can come
between us now."

They walked out into the light of the torches, though they hung back from
the crowd of drinkers concentrated in the center of the plaza, around the place
being cleared for dancing. Inside the gift bundle, they found what Huayna
Capac had promised. The beads were tiny, the dark scarlet of mullu shell
alternating with the pink of coral, each bead carved on two sides with the
delicate, wavelike symbol of Mama Cocha. The golden pin was almost a foot
long, its blunt end fashioned into the elongated fan shape of the Chimu sunrise
headdress.

"These were made in Chan Chan," Cusi said, as he placed the beads around
her neck. "By the people we discovered on our walk."

"The generosity you showed them has been returned, then," Micay decided,
gazing down at the beads and the pin in her hands. Lost in their memories for
a moment, they did not see Rimachi until he was looming over them, Uritu
and Tomay poised warily on either side. Rimachi looked down his long nose
at them, his nostrils flaring with the force of his breathing.

"So—brother. Do you have everything you want now?"

"Everything except your friendship—brother."

"Ah, *that*. A small thing, surely. Perhaps you would like me to arrange it
for you. I am good at clearing the way for you, am I not? You move quickly
behind my back."

"If you are referring to the Huarachicoy race," Cusi said quietly, "yes, I owe
you that."

"But you could not stop there, could you? You could barely wait for me to
be gone before you trampled on my trust, and took what you knew I wanted
most."

"We did not mean to hurt you, Rimachi," Micay interjected. But he ignored
her and glared down at Cusi, who slowly drew himself up, his face hardening.

"You are too small for me to strike the first blow," Rimachi said scornfully.
"Let me show you my back again. Perhaps that will give you the courage you
need to show your true feelings. Come, this is the kind of treachery you know
best—"

"Not *here*," Tomay urged, trying to restrain him, but Rimachi shook him
off and displayed his back to Cusi, his tunic bunched up around his massive
shoulders. Cusi started forward, but Uritu stepped in front of him, shaking his
head even when Cusi held up his hands to show his peaceful intentions. Then
they heard Amaru's voice, high and loose with drink, addressing Rimachi in
mock disbelief.

"And what is this, Rimachi? You turn to greet me and then give me this
terrible scowl. Are you so displeased to see me?"

"It was not meant for you," Rimachi said tersely, and Micay saw Amaru crane his neck to see over Rimachi's shoulder.

"For my brother, then? I would gladly help him bear the insult."

"Stay out of this, Amaru. I have no quarrel with you."

"Oh, but you do, when you think you have the rank to order me away. You Cañaris have been spoiled by too much royal favor. You need to be reminded of your place."

"I thought your place was in Chan Chan," Rimachi shot back, "with the Yunca women."

Tomay and Uritu moved first, trying to wedge themselves in between as the two men closed and swung at each other with their fists. Tomay intercepted a blow and went down, grabbing on to Rimachi's leg and making him stumble into Amaru, who elbowed him in the jaw and sent his wicker headdress flying. Uritu fought his way in and bumped Amaru backward, giving Cusi room to jump in and thrust himself in Amaru's path, locking his arms around his brother's waist and straightening him up with a shoulder to the chest. Rimachi freed an arm and cuffed Cusi across the back of his head, but Cusi simply dug in with his heels and used the strength of his legs to push himself and Amaru out of reach.

Then Micay stepped into the space that had opened between the combatants, holding the golden mantle pin in her hand and brandishing it like a weapon. Amaru flailed out over Cusi's head but jerked his arm back with a yelp when Micay stabbed him in the forearm.

"Stop this!" she commanded. She whirled to face Rimachi, thrusting the needle at his stomach so purposefully that he had to back up to avoid being stuck. He looked down at her with wide eyes.

"If you have a quarrel, it is with me, as well. And you will not settle it this way. Look at you," she said, turning sideways to include Amaru in her scorn, "fighting like boys in the street. Were you not among the men in the square today?"

Both Amaru and Rimachi averted their eyes and dropped their hands, so that Cusi and Uritu felt safe in letting them go. They stood breathing heavily, their hair and clothing in disarray, aware for the first time that it was quiet in the plaza and people were watching them. As the spectators finally began to turn away, Uritu knelt beside Tomay, who was still on the ground, holding the side of his head. Rimachi bent to pick up his headdress and held it against his hip, looking not at Amaru but at Micay. His eyes followed her intently as she wiped the point of her pin clean and handed the cloth to Amaru to bind his bleeding forearm.

"You have chosen the proper weapon," Rimachi said, pointing with his chin at the golden needle in Micay's hands. "I have no defense against that. Perhaps I should have thrown myself on it."

Micay's cheeks colored and she held the pin down at her side, shaking her head stubbornly. "Forgive us, Rimachi. Let us be your friends again."

"We did not set out to betray you," Cusi added. "You must believe that. We were drawn together."

"By what?" Rimachi flared, the anger back in his eyes. "By your famous huaca? Your huaca gives you everything, so that you can claim to have done nothing yourself. That is very useful for you, but do not ask *me* to believe in your innocence." He turned from Cusi to Micay. "Nor in yours, my lady. You know what the Incas are like, and you know what you allowed me to believe and hope. Forgive yourself if you can. I cannot forget as easily as you do."

Drawing himself up to his full height, he turned and walked toward the compound entrance, carrying his headdress in his hand. Uritu helped Tomay to his feet, and Micay collected herself sufficiently to examine the lump on his head and advise the application of cloths soaked in cold well water.

"I know where there is some ice," Uritu replied, and he led Tomay off toward the kitchens. Cusi and Micay led Amaru in the opposite direction, to one of the benches that separated the plaza from an adjacent garden. They discovered in the process that he was thoroughly drunk and could barely walk straight.

"What is wrong with you?" Cusi demanded, standing over him while Micay retied the binding on his wound. "Drunk as you are, Rimachi might have broken you in half."

"I fight well when I am drunk," Amaru drawled. "Besides, he was drunk, too."

"This was not your quarrel. You knew that."

"I knew you did not want it, but I *did*. I needed to hit someone, and he made himself available." Amaru pulled his arm away from Micay and gestured with both hands. "You have had your audience with Huayna Capac? Did you listen politely while he toasted your courage and offered you gifts for a battle we lost?"

"Yes," Cusi said firmly. "That is part of the healing that must be done."

"Healing!" Amaru snorted. "It is playing at respect, nothing more. I had to be drunk to stand still for that."

"What did he offer you?"

"A compound in Quito, if this war is ever won. And then, when I pretended to be grateful, he gave me a wife."

Cusi straightened up and glanced at Micay, at a loss for words.

"A ñusta?" Micay asked.

"A chosen woman. A Quito girl given in the surrender. She is only twelve or so, still learning to speak proper Quechua. The mamacona will keep her in the House of Chosen Women until she is old enough to marry."

"Has she been given a name?" Micay inquired sharply.

Amaru acknowledged her with a guilty nod. "She is called Parihuana. I saw her for a moment. She is thin but pretty, and thoroughly terrified of men."

"Of course she is. You must be kind to her."

"I have no desire to hurt her, Micay. But I did not ask for her, either.

Mother must have done this, through the Coya—her way of slowly restoring me to respectability."

"Did you try to refuse?" Cusi asked.

Amaru grimaced and shook his head. "No. I was too drunk to think of a good excuse, and . . . there is no good excuse. I am aware of what is being said about me. Perhaps I was even a bit relieved, because it was *not* a ñusta." He paused and shook his head again. "Though I doubt Fempellec will appreciate the difference."

"He has known something like this was inevitable," Micay said. "But you must be kind to him, too, and tell him before he hears from someone else. Someone like Mama Cori."

Amaru looked at her in alarm and pushed himself to his feet. "You are right. I will go tell him now." He started off, then caught himself and came back, smiling as he rested a hand on Cusi's shoulder. "I almost forgot. He gave you permission to marry?"

Micay displayed the golden mantle pin, and Amaru laughed and put a hand over the bandage on his arm.

"Yes, I have felt that. May it prove less painful to you, my brother. You have chosen a warrior for a wife."

"A comrade," Cusi corrected.

Amaru laughed and clapped him on the back. "*Someone* should want to be married," he said with a shrug, and he lurched off into the darkness, leaving them together to contemplate the life they had been given.

XIII

YAHUARCOCHA:
The Lake of Blood

(A.D. 1520)

The Rainbow House

THOUGH IT WAS the middle of the night and Micay had tried not to cry out, Mama Cori heard the sounds of her labor and came to help. She had just put some sticks onto the brazier for warmth and light when Micay brought the baby forth, cupped in sticky, trembling hands. It was not much longer than her hand, pale and bloodless, with an oblong head and a face still unformed, the eyes and mouth mere indentations, like thumbprints pressed into soft clay. Yet the tiny hands and feet were perfect and complete; in spite of herself Micay counted the fingers and toes. Mama Cori cut the birth cord, and Micay laid the child down in the fine cloths she had kept ready for the last two months, ever since she had felt the child die inside her. She took a last look but could not determine if it would have been a boy or a girl, which relieved rather than disappointed her and made it easier to close the cloths around it.

Mama Cori helped her expel the afterbirth, then left her for a moment and returned with one of the retainers. Together they washed Micay with warm water and wrapped her in a clean shift, then cleaned the place on the floor where her water had broken and spilled. There had been very little blood and only a few moments of real pain; it had been not unlike the cramps she had suffered from drinking bad water on the coast, and she had mistaken it for that for a while. Then she had been glad that it was finally happening. Now she felt flaccid and empty, with strange aches in the muscles of her thighs and abdomen and a vague burning in her vagina.

"I lost two like that," Mama Cori said when they were alone. She was brewing coca tea over the brazier. "One before Amaru and one after Quinti. I thought I was going to lose Cusi the same way."

"I have waited so long," Micay murmured. "Then it was there, and I knew it. Just as I knew when it was gone . . ."

"Yes, I remember. I remember, too, how I blamed myself and thought back to all the things I might have done to injure the child. But I had done nothing, just as you have done nothing, Micay. It is the will of the gods."

"Perhaps I should have stayed in Quito . . ."

"Nonsense. There were no midwives there." Mama Cori turned back from the brazier and handed her a steaming cup. "Heed me in this, Micay. I know the grief you are suffering. Do not make it worse than it has to be."

The coca tea had a musty flavor, but its warmth was soothing and seemed to fill a little of the emptiness. Micay stared at Mama Cori over the rim of the cup, noticing the lines that had appeared in her face in the last several years and the touches of gray in her hair. Quinti had already made her a grandmother once.

"You are kind to me, my lady," Micay said. "Though you must feel that you were right about this marriage. Cusi should have a wife who can bear the children of his blood."

"You are still young," Mama Cori scoffed. But then she looked at Micay seriously. "No, I know now that I was wrong to oppose your marriage. I am reminded every time I see him come back to you. I see the anger and pain begin to go out of him as soon as he is with you, and you make him whole again before he leaves. You are the reason he has lived through these defeats without being harmed."

Micay blinked at her in surprise. "But I have hardly seen him. It is his huaca and the fact that he has Tomay to guard his back."

"You are a part of his huaca," Mama Cori insisted, "if only because he believes that you are. I want my son to live through this war, Micay. I want all of us to return to Cuzco together and live the lives of Incas. I will treasure the grandchildren you will give me, but I am not impatient and I do not consider them a measure of your worth. No child could be what you are to Cusi."

Micay lowered the cup and pressed its warmth against her stomach. For the first time since the child inside her had died, she felt the urge to weep, and she reacted angrily against it.

"You never said this to me, even after we were married. I have never stopped fearing that you would arrange for him to be given another wife."

"I did not think it needed to be said," Mama Cori confessed, appearing surprised at Micay's anger. "I thought I made it clear in Chan Chan that I would no longer question his choices or try to interfere in his life. Have I not treated you like a daughter since that day?"

"Yes," Micay conceded, and she began to weep in spite of herself. "But you never gave us your blessing, until it no longer mattered."

"It never *did* matter. That is what I realized when I was alone in Chiquitoy: that I had no influence over my children, and could only drive them farther away by pretending I did. That was not easy for me to accept, even after I knew I had no choice. I am sorry, Micay," she said in a softer tone. "I thought it would be enough for you to know that you had won."

"Won!" Micay repeated incredulously. She gazed down through her tears at the cloth-wrapped bundle beside her. Mama Cori took the cup from her shaking hands and helped her to lie down on the blanket-covered mats. Then she turned and poked the brazier with a stick to settle the coals and lessen the light in the room.

"Forgive me, my daughter. I meant to console you, and I have only upset you more. You must rest and recover your strength."

"I have no strength," Micay moaned. "I am empty."

"That will pass," Mama Cori assured her, "and you will feel whole again. You must believe that, Micay. You must heal and regain your spirit, because Cusi needs you. And I need you."

Micay forced her eyes open, but Mama Cori shook her head and put a hand on Micay's forehead, making her close them again. The hand lingered, gently stroking her brow.

"Do not ask me now. Just sleep. I will sit with you and see that nothing troubles your dreams. Sleep, my child . . . I will be here with you."

Silvery shapes unfurled and shot through the blackness behind Micay's eyes, but the hand smoothed away her shudder and a soft blanket settled down over her shoulder. A cord snapped and she floated downward, feeling sleep close around her like a thick, dark cloth.

Quito

THE TWO of them came up to the palace gate side by side, their shields strapped across their backs and their weapons held out in front of them, ready to be surrendered to the Cañari guards.

"Cusi Huaman and Tomay Guanaco," Cusi said curtly. "Commanders of the scouts of Upper Cuzco, the regiment of Ninan Cuyochi. We have been summoned by the Sapa Inca."

"You are expected, my lords," the head guard told them. He bowed and waved them through, shaking his head at the proffered weapons.

"This is a show of trust," Tomay observed as they walked toward the inner doorway.

"Certainly a change since the last time I was here."

Tomay spoke to the second set of guards, and they were passed through with the same deference, their weapons still in hand. Cusi grunted softly in appreciation, cradling his battle-ax in the padded crook of his arm. It had never been easy for him to part with it, and his attachment had only grown more intense with each battle he had survived. It was too much a part of his protection to leave in anyone else's hands.

The inner courtyard was filled with golden-eared Incas, and Cusi quickly perceived that they all held the rank of commander or above, though apparently none of the war chiefs was present. There were many familiar faces in the crowd, though Cusi had not seen most of them since the day they had stood together in the square in Tumibamba. He and Tomay exchanged nods of greeting with the men they knew, some of whom added a shrug or raised an eyebrow to indicate their bemusement at being here at the Sapa Inca's summons, with weapons in their hands.

One of those without a weapon was Amaru, whom they found leaning on wooden crutches, talking with Quilaco Yupanqui.

"I will find Uritu and Rimachi," Tomay said.

"I will be here," Cusi assured him, instinctively noting the direction of his departure before turning to greet his brother and brother-in-law. Amaru straightened up under Cusi's inspection, holding his splinted left leg slightly behind the other.

"The arm looks healed, and you are not as thin," Cusi decided. "How is the leg?"

Amaru shrugged. "It will heal in its own time. I have had no one to chide me about it since Micay left."

"Has there been any news from Tumibamba?" Cusi asked, glancing at Quilaco, who shook his head.

"Only that the Inti Raymi was successfully celebrated."

Cusi snorted. Other than the rites of war, the last ceremony he had attended had been his own marriage, three years earlier. And now that he had finally managed to return to Quito, Micay was gone.

"What is this about?" he said impatiently, gesturing with his ax toward the crowd. "When did Huayna Capac come north? The last we heard, he had gone into seclusion while more troops were being mustered."

"They are still being mustered," Quilaco reported. "But when he came out of seclusion, he came here directly. On foot. He is inside now, meeting with the war chiefs."

"On foot," Cusi repeated, cocking his head uncertainly. "Is he angry?"

"Quite the contrary, I think," Quilaco said, looking to Amaru, who stood hunched over his crutches for a moment, shaking his head in disbelief.

"He came to see me a few days ago," he said to Cusi. "By himself. He left his entourage outside my compound and just walked in to see me."

"What did he want?"

"Nothing, apparently. He did not say anything about the war or my wound or the last defeat. He saw the model I had built of my compound, and we talked about that for a while and about the work I had done on the coast. He was *most* interested in my visit to Pachacamac."

"You told him about that?" Cusi asked incredulously.

Amaru gave him a crooked smile. "Since he did not ask me stupidly or command me to tell him, I saw no reason not to tell him. He seemed to understand, or at least not to be surprised. He was like you were when you were asking, only more eager and less earnest, as if it were all new and exciting to him. I had a feeling he had taken vilca, or something like it, before he came to see me."

"And then he just left?"

"Yes. He did not try to recruit me or enlist me in his cause, and he did not offer me any gifts." Amaru looked at Quilaco and laughed. "And I had complained to him about needing workers to finish my compound."

Cusi let out a skeptical grunt and glanced over his shoulder, searching for Tomay. They had formed their opinion of Huayna Capac long ago, and they had not missed his presence in the field, even if they had suffered another defeat without him. Cusi doubted that a taste for vilca had made him a better leader.

There was a commotion at the far end of the courtyard, and the men began to move in that direction, obviously being invited farther into the palace. Amaru nodded for Quilaco to go ahead and hung back to speak privately with Cusi.

"Another thing . . . Fempellec is here."

"How? Has Father come north?"

"No, Fempellec has left the governor's service. He has attached himself to the Fourth Wife, who came here with the Sapa Inca." Amaru smiled wryly. "He is now her chief of feasts."

"Mama Huarcay?" Cusi recalled. "She is an old enemy of our mother, and she hates Micay."

"What do I care about court squabbles?" Amaru scoffed. "This is Quito, and it was his only way to get here. Why are you frowning? Would you begrudge me some pleasure while I am healing?"

Cusi pinched the bridge of his nose with his free hand and blinked several times. He had been frowning, though not with conscious disapproval, more because these matters seemed distracting and intrusive, irrelevant to his safety. He looked at the battle-ax crooked in his arm and realized that he did not have to be concerned with his safety here.

"I have been in the field too long," he said to Amaru. "I have forgotten about pleasure."

"That is your reward for avoiding this kind of pain," Amaru said with a grimace, levering himself forward to display his splinted leg. Cusi gazed at the shrunken limb, recalling Micay's doubts that Amaru would ever be able to fight again.

"Has it begun to mend?"

"It hurts in a different way, and Micay said that was a good sign. The splint comes off soon, and then I will see."

"I brought you back for this," Cusi said ruefully. Amaru simply snorted and lurched forward on his crutches, forcing Cusi to jog to catch up with him.

"I have lost too many comrades to consider myself unlucky," Amaru said. "I am satisfied to be alive and still able to take some pleasure."

They fell silent as they joined the end of the line that was filing through the doorway into another, larger courtyard. Cusi thought of all the comrades *he* had lost in the last assault on the fortress. Paucar had died on the field and Huañu during the retreat; there were only a few scouts left who had been with them from the beginning. And they had come so agonizingly close to victory before the Carangui had thrown them back; only the fifth and final wall had remained to be breached. Then the rock had come down on Auqui Toma, killing him instantly and depriving the Incas of their war leader, giving the Carangui war chief Pinta an opportunity to launch a counterattack. Auqui Toma had been one of Huayna Capac's brothers, but he had been a true warlord, perhaps too much of one.

Tomay was waiting inside the next courtyard, and he gave Cusi a quizzical look that made him realize he was frowning again. He rearranged his face and greeted Uritu and then Rimachi, who actually faced him long enough for a respectful exchange of nods. Cusi felt warmth rise to his cheeks as he followed Rimachi's broad back toward the center of the courtyard, where the other commanders were assembled. He glanced sideways at Uritu, who gave him a brief smile of confirmation, his feathered head held rather stiffly erect, the result of a back injury he had suffered in the retreat.

The men were standing in a loose semicircle in front of a cloth canopy erected in the form of an awning house. Sitting on stools underneath the canopy were the Inca war chiefs: Michi, Yasca, and Colla Topa were there, along with their counterparts from Lower Cuzco, and Sumac Mallqui now had a seat in their midst, as did Ninan Cuyochi and Atauhuallpa. It took Cusi a moment to realize, as he and his companions found places for themselves at one end of the semicircle, that the man sitting in the center of the war chiefs, on a stool no larger than theirs, was Huayna Capac.

The ruler stood up and walked out from under the canopy, forestalling their bows by holding up a hand with his thumb and first finger touching, the royal command to listen. He was dressed rather plainly in a checkered cumbi-cloth tunic that fell to his knees, cloth arm and leg bands, and the royal fringe around his forehead. He stopped and looked from one end of the group to the other, his pursed lips gradually pulling back into a fierce smile.

"Greetings, my sons. You have fought well in my absence, even though victory has eluded you. I salute your bravery. I have come to join you. I have come to take my brother's place and to avenge his death."

Cusi found himself humming with the other men, affected by the conviction with which the statement had been uttered and its blunt appeal to an emotion they all recognized.

Huayna Capac made a broad gesture that seemed to include the entire sky. "The huacas were questioned in Cuzco during the Inti Raymi, and their answers have been brought to me, along with those of the speakers at Pachacamac, Rimac, and Pacatnamu. I have called on Inti and Illapa and the spirits of my ancestors for guidance, and I have gone alone to the place of visions." He paused and drew a long breath, his hands braced on his hips. "Everywhere, from all sides, I have been told that I must come here and claim my honor with my own hands. I have left it in the hands of others for too long."

The silence that greeted this admission was so total that Cusi thought everyone had stopped breathing. Perhaps they had.

"I have seen how this war will be won," Huayna Capac continued. "I have told my plans to the war chiefs, and they have given me their approval. As soon as the regiments are fully assembled, we will begin the drive north again. I will be with you, but there must not be any carelessness or undue haste. Many of the men who are coming to us from Cuzco are so young their earplugs still hurt, so we must exercise restraint until they are ready to prove themselves. When they are, we will lead them against the fortress, and I will bring Pinta's head back to Tumibamba on the end of my spear!"

The warriors hummed and murmured in approval, shifting their hold on their weapons. Huayna Capac turned and went to the far end of the semicircle. He began to walk along in front of the men, speaking to them and greeting some of them by name. Cusi watched him in astonishment. This was not the same arrogant, self-regarding man who had stood before them in the square four years ago. He spoke like a man who meant to fight, and Cusi believed him, despite the fact that he had never risked himself in battle before. He even walked differently, exuding the muscular restlessness of a much younger man.

Huayna Capac stopped in front of Quizquiz, a veteran commander whose wiry body and narrow face bore the scars he had earned along with his reputation as a fearless leader.

"So, my son," Huayna Capac said, "no doubt you have seen this Pinta in battle?"

"I have seen him. He is always there, on top of the wall, when the fighting is heaviest. He dresses all in red, like a flame, and he makes the men around him fight like wild beasts."

"I sent some Carangui captives back to him as my messengers. I sent him weapons and a shield, and I challenged him to come out of his fortress and fight me."

Quizquiz cocked his wedge-shaped head to one side, then shook it slowly, making his golden earplugs swing.

"He will never come out until we pull him out."

"We will," Huayna Capac assured him. Then he stepped back to address the group. "I also told him—and I tell you now—that the captives I sent to him are the last we will take alive. Show no mercy to any Carangui who surrenders. Spare only one and make him witness the death of his comrades before you send him back to Pinta with my message. Tell him that the Inca is coming to destroy him."

He snapped the words out, so that they echoed sharply off the courtyard walls. Quizquiz's eyes widened. Then a smile split his face and he raised his spear in a salute, a gesture swiftly taken up by the other men with weapons. Huayna Capac nodded once in acknowledgement.

"There is food for you, my sons, and akha. I invite you to stay and replenish yourselves. I will be here to speak with you and hear your suggestions."

He turned and walked back toward the canopy, leaving the men with their weapons still raised. Next to Cusi, Uritu let out a soft whoop.

"Perhaps we have a new warlord," Cusi suggested, glancing at Tomay and Amaru.

Amaru smiled tauntingly. "Perhaps you will want to tell him about *your* visions."

Cusi shrugged and hefted his battle-ax, which he had raised in salute along with the other men. But he was not certain how much to trust Huayna Capac's transformation, especially in regard to something as personal as his visions. In the field, he had thought about them often, but he had not spoken to anyone about them in a long time. They were like his spirit brother, a part of his protection that he preferred to keep hidden.

When the summons came, though, it was for both him and Tomay, and they left their food and went in under the canopy with their weapons still in hand. Huayna Capac was sitting with Ninan Cuyochi and Atauhuallpa on either side of him, the royal fringe hanging on a standard behind him. It was the first time Cusi had seen him without it, and it made his face and head seem naked and his eyes extraordinarily prominent. Cusi could feel the probing force of those eyes as Huayna Capac greeted the two of them by name, and it did not diminish after the ruler sat back on his stool and gestured for Ninan Cuyochi to speak.

"You have reported that the Carangui have completed their harvest," Ninan said, "and that it was a good one."

"The warriors were out in the fields," Cusi said, "some guarding while the others helped pick. They have all gone back to the fort now, where the work continues on restoring the walls."

Ninan nodded. "We will be ready in time to prevent another harvest. But my father wonders if a small band of men, or several small bands, could do some damage to the crop that has already been harvested."

Cusi and Tomay exchanged a glance. Cusi nodded for Tomay to speak, feeling distracted by Huayna Capac's presence, which seemed to exert a constant tug on his attention. It was more persistent than powerful, and Cusi felt his own presence begin to rise up in annoyance.

"Several bands in different areas would be the most effective," Tomay said to Ninan. "We know where their storehouses and drying yards are. If we had the right men, we could set it all afire and be gone before they knew we were there."

"You would be totally on your own," Ninan cautioned. "It would be months before we would be close enough to give you any support. They will surely come out to hunt you before then."

"They have hunted us before," Tomay assured him. "With a few bowmen and some swift runners, we could make them pay dearly to keep their crops."

"Not just their crops," Atauhuallpa interjected, "but their herds and houses, too. Destroy whatever you can, and leave fear behind you. Give them a taste of what is to come!"

"No captives anywhere?" Tomay suggested, glancing from Atauhuallpa, who was known for his impulsive ferocity, to Huayna Capac.

The ruler nodded firmly. "Spare no one. Take whichever men you wish. Everyone who returns will be granted a twenty-day leave."

"We will earn it, my lord," Tomay said, and he and Cusi bowed. Huayna Capac suddenly stood up, causing his sons to do likewise. He held out his hands to Cusi.

"May I see your weapon, my son?"

Cusi nodded obediently, but then was stricken by a spasm of reluctance that stopped him with his arms half extended.

"This was given to me by Otoronco Achachi," he explained hastily. "It was blessed by Pachacuti himself."

"I understand why you cling to it, then," Huayna Capac said patiently, his hand still outstretched. "But it will not suffer from my touch."

"Forgive me," Cusi murmured, and surrendered the battle-ax into his hands. He hefted it and examined the shaft and the star-shaped head, which were nicked and battered from much hard use.

"It is light," he decided, "but well balanced. It has obviously served you well." He held it out for Cusi to take back, meeting his eyes during the brief moment of exchange. "You know that I have made Otoronco Achachi the governor of Chachapoyas."

"I was told," Cusi acknowledged.

"I need a strong man there at this time. We have enough strong men here to do what must be done. And when it comes time for the final attack, I want you to be with me, Cusi."

"I would be honored, my lord," Cusi replied. Feeling Tomay stir beside him, he cleared his throat politely. "My lord . . . may Tomay Guanaco also stand with us? We have kept each other alive for a long time."

Huayna Capac laughed. "Of course. We will need all of our swiftness on that day. As I said, I have *seen* this."

There was a note of triumph in his voice, but the eyes that searched Cusi's face did not expect him to be impressed, and they were looking for something more than mere agreement—a shared knowledge, perhaps. There was the eagerness Amaru had mentioned, too, a kind of ardent fascination that gave his presence a particular urgency. Cusi felt old and jaded in comparison, his curiosity much more guarded.

"You have seen things, too," Huayna Capac suggested. "But you hold them closely, like your weapon."

Cusi could only nod in agreement. "I have been told of an enemy greater than the Carangui, one we cannot yet see. But it is impossible to look ahead now, with the Carangui still in our way."

Huayna Capac gave him a rueful smile.

"No doubt that is prudent. We will talk again later, then, when the way is clear." He smiled at Tomay and nodded in dismissal. "Return to the feast, my sons. I will send for you when it is time to end this war."

They bowed over their weapons and backed out from under the canopy before turning to walk away. They stopped at the edge of the feasting crowd, which had put aside food for akha and was beginning to become boisterous.

"Well," Tomay prompted, "do you believe him?"

"I want to," Cusi confessed. "He could be wrong about what he has seen, but he is not simply wishing. Do *you* believe him?"

"He speaks like a warlord . . . but I will believe him more if he is still in the field, fighting, when our turn comes to watch his back." Tomay paused and surveyed the crowd in front of them. "Who should we take?"

"Uritu, of course, if his back is healed. And his two cousins."

"What about Rimachi? He is good with the spear thrower, almost as good as a bowman. And if we had to flee, he could hold the trail by himself."

"Would he go with me?"

"He will go with *us,*" Tomay said emphatically. "The four of us have not fought together since Chachapoyas. We might never get a chance like this again."

"Let us take it, then," Cusi agreed, and they started forward into the crowd. "For once, let us all go together . . ."

The Mountains

T HE TRAIL was narrow and hugged the steep, rocky side of the mountain, high above the ribbon of water that filled the bottom of the canyon below. Micay and Parihuana were halfway along it when the rain began to come down, driven by the wind that had been blowing in their faces all morning. They took off their sandals, pulled their cloaks over their heads, and kept going, hoping to find a cave or a side path that might lead to shelter. They finally had to stop to rest beneath an overhanging ledge, which kept off only some of the rain and none of the wind. Micay's cloak was a sodden weight on her back, and she could feel the dampness seeping through to her hair and clothes. Parihuana was shivering openly, and she looked pale and pinched around her eyes and mouth.

Micay relieved her of the leather pack slung over her shoulder, waving off the girl's feeble protest with a curt shake of her head. She had begun to doubt her own judgment yesterday, when they had been rained on for the first time, but when they had found the woodcutter's hut that was on the map and had dried themselves in front of a fire, Micay had convinced herself not to worry.

Now, though, there were no more huts to be expected, and it seemed unlikely that they could make it to the huaca before dark. She glanced at Parihuana, who was huddled beneath the limp bedroll she still carried on her back, and thought that Mama Cori would never forgive her if she made this girl sick.

"Let us go on," Micay suggested. "Perhaps there is a cave ahead."

Parihuana nodded with weary compliance and took the lead at a gesture from Micay, who had to rearrange her own bundles to accommodate the additional pack. Both of them flinched as they stepped out into the lashing rain, which made it difficult to raise their eyes from the ground. Micay followed Parihuana's back, still struggling to settle her burdens over her cloak-wrapped shoulders and worrying about the danger of mudslides. They had just come around a slippery bend in the trail when Parihuana stopped dead and let out an ear-splitting scream. Micay jumped in fright and bumped into her from behind, nearly knocking them both down.

Then she saw the puma crouched in the center of the trail, its rain-matted fur standing up stiff along its arched back. The puma snarled and Parihuana screamed again. Micay slung the pack that was hanging off her arm, an awkward heave that landed just in front of the cat and skipped off the side of the trail. The puma went straight up into the air, its legs stiff and its tail flailing like a whip, its teeth bared in what seemed to be a grimace of outrage. Then it hit down and immediately bounded sideways, disappearing up the mountainside in a tawny blur.

Parihuana turned and tried to speak, but the only sound that came out of her mouth was a high-pitched squeak that made both of them laugh. They hugged each other, laughing and weeping and shaking with the fear they had barely had time to feel. Micay's limbs felt hollow and buoyant, as if she might float upward if Parihuana let her go, and she was aware of the rain on her face without feeling its cold sting.

"We are safe," she murmured, patting the wet girl's back. Parihuana pulled away from her, gesturing with her hands, her thin face more animated than Micay had ever seen it.

"I almost walked right into it, Micay . . . all I could do was scream."

"That is what frightened it away. I missed with the pack." She looked over the side of the trail but saw no sign of it. Then she realized which pack it was. "That was the rest of our food."

Parihuana encouraged her with a smile. "We do not have that far to go, do we? The Pachamama will feed us when we get there."

Micay forced herself to smile. She meant that Macas, the woman who tended the huaca, would feed them. Micay had only told her a little of what she knew about Macas, and she realized she would have to tell her the rest very soon. But not now, not while she was feeling so grateful to be alive.

"We will get there," she promised, "but not by standing here in the rain. Come, we will be warmer if we move . . ."

The rain stopped shortly afterward, and though the wind dried out their outer garments, it also made them move vigorously in order to avoid taking

a chill. By the time they found the cave, the light was failing and they were
growing clumsy with fatigue, so Micay called a halt. The cave was spacious
but dark past the first few feet, so they crawled into it on their hands and knees,
tossing pebbles ahead of them to frighten off snakes or other animals. To
Micay's delight, they discovered that the cave had been used by herders to
shelter their flocks, who had left the floor littered with dung and remnants of
fodder. She took this as a favorable sign and thanked Pachamama as she and
Parihuana gathered every scrap of precious fuel.

They used what was left of the light to collect stones for a hearth, and all
the brush and firewood they could find. Since most of the wood was wet, they
used it to construct drying racks around the hearth, hoping to dry it out along
with their clothes. With the firesticks she kept in a leather pouch around her
neck, Micay kindled a swift-burning fire of dry grass and powdered llama
dung. Then she and Parihuana held sticks in the flames until they were dry
enough to be added to the blaze. For a long time, they were too busy feeding
the fire and turning garments on the racks to exchange more than a few words,
but their silence was comfortable. The firelight reflected warmly off the ceiling
of the cave, and they could no longer feel the wind that swept past in the
darkness outside.

When their blankets and clothing were sufficiently dry, they sat back and
gave in to their fatigue, which put Parihuana to sleep almost immediately.
Micay had wanted to talk with her, to explain about Macas and their reason
for being here, but she was exhausted herself and thought it was probably
better to let the girl sleep. So she banked the fire, covered Parihuana carefully,
and fell asleep within moments of covering herself.

Hunger woke her later, and she sat up in the darkness, tucking her cloak
and blankets in around her. The circle of black sky she could see through the
cave mouth was spangled with silver stars, and the night air had grown still
and cold. She listened to her stomach growl and thought of the pack still in
her possession, which held offerings of cloth and food for the keeper of the
huaca. They could not touch the food, of course, except to save themselves
from starving. They were not close to that yet, but they would be if they had
to go back without finding any provisions. And the high priestess had warned
her that Macas's sense of hospitality could not be trusted: she would certainly
not receive them without the expected offerings, but she might not feed them
in return. That was why Micay had burdened them with the other pack, the
one that had been sacrificed to the puma.

"We must go back," she said aloud, realizing just how dangerous their
situation was.

"Why, my lady?" a voice asked. Micay jumped and clutched at her heart.
She saw Parihuana's face rise up out of the nest of blankets beside her.

"You are awake."

"Something jumped at me in my dream," the girl explained. "Then I could
not go back to sleep, and I heard you awaken."

Micay poked her hands out through her blankets to revive the fire, which flared up reassuringly. Parihuana sat up next to her and moved closer, her fingers fanned out toward the flames.

"Why must we go back?"

Micay stared at her in the firelight, and though the girl would not meet her gaze for long, she still seemed far less timid than she had when they had set out two days ago.

"That is the first time you have asked me a question of your own," Micay pointed out. "And on the trail, after we saw the puma, you forgot yourself and called me 'Micay.' Perhaps it is working, after all."

Parihuana raised her eyes with an effort, clearly perplexed.

"I do not understand, my lady."

"That is why you must ask questions. You never asked me the purpose of this journey, or why I wanted you along. You did not even seem aware that I was offering you a choice."

"But you asked me to come," Parihuana protested. "You said that the keeper of the huaca spoke the language of the Quitos."

"Her name is Macas, and she knows Quechua, too, though most of the time she will not speak it. Often, she will not speak at all. The high priestess told me that she has not allowed anyone near the huaca in more than a month."

"Then . . . why have we come?"

"I have my own reason for wanting to visit the huaca. I brought you with me because I wanted to shock you and make you less of a chosen woman."

The girl stared at her speechlessly, too astonished to look away.

"Has no one told you that I was also a chosen woman?" Micay asked. "No, I see that is something else Mama Cori has left for me to explain. I was thirteen when I was taken, and I did not stay in the House of Chosen Women for very long. But still, I was like you are, timid and self-effacing and unable to choose for myself. I had been taught to accept the life I had been given, but not how to understand it. The initiation rites did not teach me that, either, but they brought me to these mountains, and that is where I began to understand."

Parihuana's narrow face seemed to bend inward around the frown trapped between her eyes. "Mama Cori has told me that I must be bolder. Is that what you mean?"

"You must be more than that. You must be responsible for yourself, for everything that happens to you. You have been brought to live among the Incas, but you will have to find your own place in their midst."

"But the Incas honor the chosen women. And I will be the wife of Amaru Inca, will I not? What are you saying, Micay? You are frightening me . . ."

"There is no time to be more gentle," Micay apologized. "I will be returning to Quito before too much longer, and there is no one else who will tell you the things you need to know. Listen to me, Parihuana. We could have been killed or badly injured today, but the puma ran from us. And then we found this cave and the makings of a fire. We have shared the kind of danger and good fortune that should make us trust each other."

Parihuana looked down at the hearthstones, her face contorted in the firelight, twisted with fear and confusion. It is too soon for her to hear this, Micay thought, and too much for her to comprehend. She sighed in resignation and Parihuana's head came up, her eyes glittering with desperation.

"These things I need to know . . . what are they?"

Micay sighed again, and nodded. "You need to know what kind of man Amaru is and why you are being married to him. You need to know what that could mean for you. I will tell you what I can, but you must make me explain anything you do not understand. That is the first thing you must learn: that you have the right to question and decide the truth for yourself."

Parihuana stared at her with determined boldness, her lips trembling and her eyes darting as she struggled against the compulsion to look down and away. Micay resisted the urge to encourage her, knowing it would not help.

"Are we going back?" the girl finally managed.

Micay nodded approvingly. "I think we must. If we go on, we will have to give the offerings to Macas. But we cannot trust that she will feed us or provide for our return. She may simply turn us away. No, it is better to go back now and not risk starving on the trail."

Parihuana reached out and put another stick on the fire, glancing at Micay over her shoulder.

"If you were alone . . . would you go on?"

"Perhaps. It is important to me." Micay paused, then decided not to make her ask. "I have been with Cusi for five years, but I am still childless. I remembered this huaca from my first visit to the mountains, and I decided to go there to appeal to the Earth Mother."

"What would you eat," Parihuana asked quickly, "if you were alone?"

Micay squinted at her. "There are roots and plants I could eat . . . we passed them on the trail. They would probably be enough to sustain me, if Macas gave me nothing."

"Then they could sustain me, as well."

"No—" Micay began. But then she caught herself, remembering what she had said about making choices. "Would you want to take such a risk?"

Parihuana bobbed her head tentatively. "I never saw a live puma before. Or slept in a cave. If we go back . . . we will never know what would have happened to us at the huaca."

Micay raised her eyebrows, staring at the girl until she turned her head away in embarrassment. Micay felt trapped by her own words, as if the judgment she had doubted were having its revenge.

"Danger and good fortune," she repeated ruefully. "Mama Cori would never forgive me if I brought you back sick or injured."

"Maybe I will come back bolder instead," Parihuana suggested.

Micay could only smile. "I am sure of it. Let us try to rest, then, since we are going on."

Parihuana gave the fire a last poke and lay down with her head near Micay's.

"I do not think I can sleep, my lady."

"I know," Micay said, turning so that they faced each other in the darkness.

"But close your eyes and just listen. Do not ask me any questions now. Let me tell you about the family into which you have come. Into which *I* came years ago, a chosen woman like you, trying to be whatever I was asked to be, yet lost to myself . . ."

AS THEY CLIMBED toward the huaca, Micay was struck by how well she remembered this place and how little it had changed. She and Parihuana had left their cloaks and bundles at the cave on the lower slope, the cave with the warm floor where Micay and the other ñustas had slept during their visit. The two of them carried their offering bundles in their arms as they followed the path up and around the mountainside, past the clumps of brush and patches of bunch grass that seemed to spring up out of the rocks. They were well above the tree line and near the end of the dry season, yet the vegetation was uncannily lush and green, nourished by the warm, sulfurous water that seeped and bubbled up out of the earth. The pools where the water gathered steamed in the cool air, their basins ringed in vivid shades of red and amber and gold. Parihuana coughed and gagged slightly as the gaseous odor of the water grew stronger, overpowering the thin mountain air despite the breeze that was blowing.

The trail ended at the foot of a broad tongue of stone that jutted out over a deep canyon. To their immediate right was the cave of the huaca, a black hole in the rock face. To their left, standing at the end of the jutting ledge with her back to them, was the tall, angular figure of Macas. This was exactly the way Micay had seen her on her first visit, though the wildly tangled hair that swirled around her head and upper body was now completely white. She wore a beltless brown shift that was threadbare even at a distance, and her elbows and feet were chapped white by exposure.

Then Macas turned and saw them, and Micay caught a glimpse of bared teeth and one glaring eye behind the ropes of hair as the woman lurched toward them, staggering as if her feet could not feel the ground, her arms flailing out at her sides. All of the weariness and discomfort Micay had been feeling disappeared in a rush of fear, and she had to call on her composure to make herself stand still and bow over the offering in her hands. Out of the corner of her eye, she saw Parihuana do the same, and she was glad the girl was still that much of a chosen woman.

She looked up into eyes that reminded her of the puma and seemed to glow with the same luminous ferocity. She froze, and Macas snatched the bundle out of her hands and jumped back, hugging it against her chest as if she expected Micay to try to take it back. When Micay simply stared at her, the woman made a chortling sound and freed a hand to seize Parihuana's offering, as well. Then she turned and staggered off toward the cave with both arms wrapped in a tight embrace around the bundles.

Micay let herself breathe, wondering if this would be the end of it. For the first time, the prospect of surviving on roots and grass for the next three days seemed inviting, and she could guess from Parihuana's rapid breathing that she would also be happy to leave without seeing the huaca. But then Macas emerged from the cave and came to confront them again. She pointed a bony finger at Micay's golden mantle pin, the wedding gift of the Sapa Inca, and surprised her by speaking in Quechua.

"Inca wife . . . give me."

Micay complied without thinking, removing the long golden needle and handing it over, holding the end of her mantle together with her other hand. But Macas wanted the mantle, too, pointing at it wordlessly and making smacking sounds with her lips. It was Micay's favorite, the sunrise mantle Apu Poma had given her, but she had no choice but to surrender it to Macas's clawlike grasp. Macas took her belt and headcloth, too, piling up the garments on the ground behind her. Then she undressed Parihuana in a similar fashion, calling her "girl" and sneering openly at her plain silver pin, her hooked nose piercing the curtain of hair that hung down in front of her face. What Micay could see of her eyes convinced her that the woman was mad, even more deranged than Chimpu Ocllo had feared.

Dumping Parihuana's garments onto the pile, Macas turned back and gave them a smile that seemed absolutely greedy and malicious, her lips peeled back from a mouth that was missing half of its teeth. She pointed at the copper pin that held Micay's shift together at the shoulder and waved her arms in a peremptory gesture, indicating that they should strip completely. Micay took a breath and slowly shook her head, deciding that she would not be sent away from here naked.

"Do not ask that, my lady. We have come here as pilgrims; we do not deserve to be humiliated."

Macas threw up her arms and let out a shriek of outrage that made Parihuana flinch and shrink back slightly. Macas turned in a circle, stamping her bare feet and swinging her head down between her shoulders, like a llama in pain. She came back around to face Micay with her hand raised to strike.

"We come with the regards of the high priestess Chimpu Ocllo," Micay said bravely, and was stunned when the woman shrieked again and slapped her across the side of the face, spinning her halfway around. Through the pain and flashing of light, Micay felt Parihuana catch her under the elbow and hold her upright. But then a second blow caught her across the top of the head and knocked her free of Parihuana's grasp and off her feet.

"Run!" she cried, rolling out of range as Macas awkwardly tried to kick her. Micay scrambled to her knees, trying simultaneously to untangle her legs from the loose folds of her shift and put some distance between herself and the madwoman. Then she heard Parihuana's high, quavering voice, speaking in Quito, shouting the command to stop. She glanced toward the voice and saw the girl poised in a half crouch, brandishing a stone in one hand and threatening to throw it at Macas. Macas lunged toward her and Parihuana threw. As the stone sailed past her head, Macas suddenly stiffened, her head jerking back to reveal an eye that was completely white. Then she collapsed backward onto the ground, her limbs twitching uncontrollably.

Breathing heavily, Micay rose and stood looking down at her for several moments before she realized what she was seeing. Such fits were not uncommon among warriors who had suffered head injuries, and she knew that the violence was not directed at anyone and would soon pass. She knelt and tried to cradle Macas's head, to keep her from banging it against the ground. Parihuana knelt with her, her breath squeaking as she pulled the matted skeins of hair away from Macas's gaunt, tortured face.

"I did not mean to harm her!"

"Your stone missed," Micay assured her, as Macas twisted and thrashed between them. "She has a sickness."

Macas moaned and went limp, her lips circled with a white froth, and Micay gently set her head down, bending over her to be certain she was breathing. She heard Parihuana gasp and looked up to see the girl weeping, her face fearful and stricken.

"You did not harm her," Micay repeated. "And she can no longer harm us."

"I know," Parihuana whispered. "I remember . . ."

"Remember what?"

"My uncle . . . long ago, like this. He never meant to harm anyone, either."

"It is good for you to remember," Micay soothed, reaching across to take one of her cold hands. "It is your old life coming back to you. Let it come . . . accept it."

When Parihuana felt stronger, they half carried, half dragged Macas to the cave, making a bed for her out of the garments they had removed earlier. The cave itself, as far as they dared to enter, was completely empty, though the air was thick with a damp, sulfurous warmth. They sat beside Macas's prostrate body, listening to the steady hiss of steam emitted by the huaca, which was a natural pool where cold spring water mixed continuously with a hot current that boiled up from the heart of Pachamama. Micay and the ñustas had been permitted no closer than this during their visit, allowed only to breathe the rich, life-giving fumes that rose from the huaca.

Micay breathed them in again as she waited, feeling weak and dizzy and wondering if they should leave before Macas awoke. But she was aware, as well, of the gift bundles that lay where Macas had left them. She had seen men awaken after a fit with no memory of what had happened, all their responses gentled by the violence of what they had undergone. Perhaps Macas would be no different; perhaps she would even remember some generosity.

Still, both she and Parihuana assumed a wary crouch when Macas finally began to stir. Micay's cheek felt bruised and there was a lump swelling on the top of her head, beneath her hair. She had prepared Parihuana to flee at the least sign of further violence. But Macas's eyes were dim when she opened them, and she held a hand to her head as if it hurt her. When she was able to focus on Micay and Parihuana, she stared at them without recognition, though without suspicion, either.

"You have come to bathe in the waters of our mother?" she murmured weakly.

Micay allowed herself to relax, though only a little. "If you find us worthy, my lady. We are from Tumibamba. I am Mama Micay, and my companion is Parihuana."

Macas began to try to raise herself, and they helped her to sit up with her back against the wall of the cave. She looked at each of them in turn, squinting in the steamy light. She seemed fully conscious now, a trace of shrewdness in her eyes.

"You are not Incas," she observed, "and you are not sisters."

"I am a Chachapoya, and Parihuana is a Quito. My husband is an Inca, and she has been given in marriage to his brother."

"Why have you come?" Macas asked, addressing herself to Micay. "Are you barren?"

Micay flinched at the bluntness of the question. "I lost a child two months ago. It was the first to come to me in five years."

"And you?" Macas said to Parihuana, who immediately dropped her eyes. Macas spoke again, in Quito, and the girl straightened up and answered her in the same tongue, lapsing into Quechua only for the words "chosen woman." Macas nodded, then winced and closed her eyes, raising a bony hand to her forehead.

"Is there something we can get you, my lady?" Micay asked. "Some water perhaps . . . ?"

"No, we must bathe," Macas said, the hand still covering her eyes. "Pachamama will heal me. She has been angry, terribly angry, but she is quiet now. She will fill us with peace."

Macas lowered her hand to her shoulder and plucked at the knotted ends of her shift, finally allowing Micay to untie it for her. She shrugged off the shift, revealing a body that appeared dessicated, the skin slack and wrinkled, falling away in loose folds from the stringy muscles and protruding bones. There were fresh scratches across her withered breasts that looked to be self-inflicted.

Micay and Parihuana helped her to her feet, then removed their own shifts, Parihuana hesitating even after Micay had signaled her assent. Micay knew the girl was self-conscious about her body, which was lean and supple like a boy's, with hips and thighs that seemed fleshless and breasts that were barely defined. Micay was aware of the fullness of her own body, the extra flesh she had not shed with the birth.

Without a word, Macas led them deeper into the cave, moving slowly as the light disappeared completely. The floor sloped downward and became warm beneath their bare feet, and the air was dense with a moisture that settled slickly on their skin. The splash and drip of water echoed off the unseen walls, producing a low drumming sound behind the constant hiss of steam, which had grown louder and sharper, like the sound of sizzling fat. Micay groped her way forward, breathing shallowly through her mouth, fighting a fear that she was about to fall into emptiness. She kept one hand extended behind her, touching Parihuana's fingers, which were cold despite the warmth of the damp air.

There was a splashing sound just ahead of her, and then she was up to her ankles in water so hot that she cried out in pain, the cry booming off the walls and deafening her. Parihuana grabbed her hand from behind just as another, more powerful hand clamped down on her wrist, pulling both her and Parihuana forward with a jerk. She lost Parihuana's hand and stumbled, up to her thighs in water that stung but no longer burned. Macas let go of her wrist and caught her around the waist, her hands surprisingly sure in the darkness. Micay felt herself being drawn forward into an embrace, her breasts flattening against Macas's bony chest, a knee gently prodding her thighs apart. Macas lifted her hands to Micay's shoulders and spoke directly into her ear, through the loud hissing of the steam.

"Come, little mother . . . open yourself to me. Let me touch you and fill you with life. Let me touch you, little mother . . ."

The pressure of her fingers on Micay's shoulders was light but insistent, steadying her as she sank down into a squat, the water so hot against her loins and belly that her skin itched and tingled. Waves lapped up over her breasts and onto her throat as Macas took her hands away and moved to find Parihuana, who was somewhere to Micay's right. She heard murmuring, and then a sudden swell against her side as Parihuana lowered herself down. Micay swayed back onto her heels, unable to feel her lower body, which seemed to be melting in the great heat that enveloped her. She could barely breathe, she was fainting, the hissing like a rattle inside her head, a stuttering, sibilant voice that suddenly spoke one word: "Twins."

"Yes?" Micay cried out, lurching upward in surprise and yearning, hoping to hear more, to be certain she had heard that word. Her legs buckled at the knees and she pitched forward, but Macas somehow caught her on an out-stretched arm and kept her upright. Then Macas spun her around and gave her a light push in the direction from which she had come, speaking in a voice very different from the one Micay thought she had heard.

"Go," she urged, and Micay splashed forward, hopping instinctively at the first touch of the scalding water in the shallows. Her feet slapped down on dry ground and she could see a glow of light ahead; she walked toward it on rubbery legs, her body still pulsing with heat. The glow coalesced into the distinct shape of the cave mouth, and then she could see through it to a landscape softened by the rich golden light of sunset. The beauty of it brought tears to her eyes, and she braced a hand against the wall and let them flow down her cheeks, feeling grateful simply to be above the earth once more.

Splashing sounds echoed up out of the cave, and she looked back to see Macas and Parihuana emerge from the darkness with their arms looped around each other, water streaming off their bodies. Micay could not tell who was supporting whom until they were beside her and Macas abruptly parted from the girl, who would have fallen had Micay not caught her by the arm. Macas peeled a tangle of wet white hair away from her face, so that Micay could see her disapproving frown.

"Why did you stand? I had not released you."

"I—I thought I heard a voice."

The frown disappeared, and Macas grunted thoughtfully. "What did you hear?"

"Only one word: 'Twins.' "

"So you are the one," Macas said, nodding to herself. "No wonder you came while I was sleeping . . . while Pachamama was peaceful. So it will be; our mother has spoken. If one or both is a girl child, you must dedicate her to Pachamama and this huaca."

"I will bring her here for your blessing, my mother," Micay promised bowing her head. When she looked up, Macas had turned away and gone to squat next to the offering bundles. Parihuana squeezed Micay's arm and smiled at her, appearing giddy with relief, as if she had survived something more frightening than a puma.

"Here," Macas said, turning in her crouch. She tossed them two of the lengths of cloth that had been wrapped around their offerings. "Dry yourself."

Micay and Parihuana each took a cloth and began to dab at their wet hair. Micay could feel the air now, cool and tingling on her skin, drying her without touching the interior warmth. She felt no urgency, no fear of a chill, and the gesture of concern was itself immensely reassuring. She and Parihuana watched as Macas held up a string of uchu peppers, caressing it with the side of her face, her hooked nose buried amid the brilliant green, orange, and red bulbs. She put down the peppers and shook the sacks of maize and quinoa and salt, grunting to herself. Micay and Parihuana exchanged a glance and began to dry themselves more assiduously, looking around on the floor for their shifts.

But then Macas rose and came toward them, a length of cloth draped loosely over her sunken shoulders and her cupped hands filled with potatoes and strips of charqui. She held the food out to them, grunting and gesturing with her chin until they had relieved her of most of it. She took one of the remaining pieces of blackened, freeze-dried meat and tore at it with her widely spaced teeth, smacking her lips and working her jaw from side to side like a llama. Micay and Parihuana forgot about their shifts and squatted down with Macas to eat, Micay giving Parihuana a sharp glance to remind her to go slowly. Following Macas's example, they stared out over the canyon while they ate, letting the air dry them completely.

When Macas had finished the little she had kept for herself, she wiped her fingers on her bare thighs and fixed her gaze on the ground in front of her. Micay and Parihuana also stopped eating and waited with her, keeping the rest of their charqui and potatoes in neat piles beside them, close at hand. Micay again located her shift. When Macas finally spoke, it was in Quito, and Micay had to look to Parihuana for a translation.

"She says we must leave now," the girl whispered. "She is weary."

They quietly got up and helped each other into their shifts, and after a covert glance at Macas, who appeared oblivious, they also put on their belts and picked up their mantles and pins. Micay bundled their food up in her head cloth while Parihuana spread the offering cloths out on the ground to dry. Macas was now sitting on her buttocks with her feet planted in front of her, rocking back and forth between her upraised knees. Micay could feel another attack coming on, the return of the madwoman who had greeted them with shrieks and blows. And she knew now, from the way Macas had handled her in the water, just how powerful the woman was.

She gave Parihuana the food bundle and motioned for her to precede her out of the cave. Macas was rocking harder and murmuring to herself, her hair hanging like a veil in front of her face. Micay resisted the impulse to flee, remembering the woman who had embraced her in the darkness and called her little mother and promised her twins. She decided to take one last risk for *that* Macas. Sticking her pin through the thick weave of her belt, she approached the seated woman and carefully spread her sunrise mantle over her hunched shoulders and back. Macas went completely still, and fear rose up in Micay's throat and almost made her run.

"We are grateful, my mother," she said hoarsely. Macas shuddered and dropped her head to her chest, letting out a deep groan. Even as she edged away, Micay wished she had the courage to stay and try to heal this woman. She wished there were a medicine for the violence that made her a danger to herself and everyone who tried to come near her. Once outside the cave, Micay glanced back and saw that Macas had not moved, except to raise a hand to touch the edge of the mantle.

Micay caught up with Parihuana and the two of them headed swiftly down the trail that led away from the cave. They were halfway around the mountainside when they heard the first scream, a howl of pain and anger that echoed off the rocks and frightened birds out of the undergrowth. Micay and Parihuana exchanged a glance but did not look back, having seen all they were meant to see here.

The Mira Valley

THE HERD BOY abandoned his herd and ran when he saw the three of them come down over the ridge. Rimachi and Sutic kept going toward the herd, Rimachi fitting a dart into his spear thrower and Sutic untangling the strings of a bola. Cusi chased after the herd boy, staying above him and forcing him toward the place where Tomay would be waiting. The boy was stocky and could not run very fast, and as Cusi closed on him, the boy cast a terrified glance over his shoulder, then lost his footing and went sprawling on his face in the grass.

"I have him!" Cusi called out, and Tomay emerged from the gully just ahead. Cusi grabbed the boy by the back of his tunic and turned him over, showing him the blade of the flint knife in his other hand. The boy's eyes darted from the knife to the empty holes in Cusi's earlobes, and he did not struggle; he was perhaps eight years old.

With the boy between them, Cusi and Tomay walked back toward the place where the herd had been. Six dead alpacas lay like bloodied heaps of snow on the fresh green grass; the rest of the herd had scattered in all directions, menaced but not pursued by Rimachi and Sutic.

"Look," Tomay said, pointing with his chin toward the valley below. A column of warriors was moving rapidly in their direction, climbing the trail that led upward through the potato fields. Cusi estimated that there were forty of them, and they were not ones they had seen before. That made three groups that were hunting them.

"This will be the last of this," Cusi said to Tomay as they came in among the dead alpacas.

"Good," Tomay said curtly. Cusi nodded in agreement. He did not have Tomay's background as a herder, but every llama he had killed had made him think guiltily of Urcon, until he could not bring himself to slaughter any more. It was one of many distasteful duties he would be glad to leave behind.

Rimachi and Sutic had also seen the warriors, and they waved their weapons and called down to them tauntingly, encouraging them to run faster.

"We should leave now," Rimachi suggested more soberly. All four men looked at the herd boy, who hung limply in the grip Cusi and Tomay had on his tunic. They had killed boys as young as this to prevent being discovered, and they knew that if the war went on long enough, this boy might one day hold a weapon on them. It was Tomay who decided for them, jerking the boy out of Cusi's grasp and holding him at arm's length, a fan-shaped bronze knife flashing in his other hand.

"The last of this, as well," he said. Reversing the knife, he pressed the wooden handle into the boy's hands and spoke to him in the crude Carangui he had picked up questioning prisoners. "That is for Pinta," he said, pointing with his chin at the knife. "Tell him the Inca is coming to kill him."

Tomay let him go, and the boy rocked back on his heels, staring in amazement at the knife in his hand. When he looked up, Tomay was standing with his arms crossed on his chest and a knowing smile on his face, tempting him to try his courage. For a brief instant, hatred flickered in the boy's eyes and his hand tightened on the handle of the knife. But then he cast a doleful glance at the nearest dead alpaca and turned and ran. The men laughed and shouted encouragement at his retreating back. Then they, too, turned and ran for their lives.

THEY HAD BEEN running for most of the last month, ever since the rains had driven them to higher ground and the Carangui patrols had begun to hunt them in earnest. Before that, they had waged a campaign of terror up and down this side of the valley, appearing out of the darkness to set fire to anything that would burn and to kill anyone who tried to stop them. They had welcomed the patrols at first, finding warriors a more worthy prey than farmers, and they had dropped landslides down on them and lured them into ambushes on the steep mountain trails. But soon there were too many, circling in from too many directions, and they had found themselves hiding more often than they fought. They had suffered their first casualty ten days ago, when an ambush had been laid for them, and one of the three young scouts they had brought along had fallen to a well-thrown dart. The rest had fought their way free, but they had decided shortly afterward that it was time to withdraw.

There were seven left in the band now, because as soon as they had removed themselves from immediate danger, they had sent the other two scouts ahead, carrying plans for a final ambush to Ninan Cuyochi and the advancing Inca troops. They had then gone into a deliberately seductive flight, showing themselves often enough to lure the Carangui on while trying not to let them get too close. The latter had proved more difficult than they had expected, due to the ever-increasing number of their pursuers, which made it seem as if the whole valley were out hunting them. Showing themselves had also become all too easy, so that finally their flight had become desperate rather than deliberate.

Cusi crouched beneath an overhanging rock, peering out through falling rain while he wrung the water from his cloak. Rimachi lay sprawled next to him, and Uritu sat with his sore back pressed against the rock wall, chewing coca with audible determination. Uritu's two cousins were hidden a short distance away, and Sutic was somewhere back down the trail, standing rear guard. They were all waiting for Tomay to return and tell them which was the safest way to proceed—if there was such a way.

"You say this canyon is two days ahead?" Rimachi queried, propping himself up on an elbow.

"If we do not have to double back or go out of our way," Cusi allowed. "That may not be the end for us, though. If the scouts did not get through, or the troops could not be brought up in time—"

"They will be there," Rimachi said easily. "You worry too much, Cusi. You should learn to trust your own huaca, as the rest of us have."

Cusi glanced at him in annoyance. "That would be a good way to grow careless. We have already lost one man."

"One out of ten. Given the damage we have done, that is a small cost. The Carangui have not had a peaceful night in months, and they hate us so much that we could lead them all the way to Quito if we had to."

"Be still, Rimachi," Uritu scolded softly. "It is bad luck to boast too soon."

"It is only the truth," Rimachi said with a shrug, sitting up and looking at Cusi. "Tell me that you have not been thinking ahead to Quito and what you will do with your twenty-day leave."

"I have," Cusi admitted reluctantly, "but I know better than to let myself dwell on it."

"Why not dwell on it? What else do we have to keep our minds off of being tired and wet and hungry? It is the only thing that keeps me from feeling like a hunted animal."

"It is safer to feel that way," Uritu put in.

Rimachi ignored him, his eyes fixed on Cusi. "Tell me you have not been thinking about Micay."

"I have," Cusi said, squinting at him in the watery light. The strange glimmer in Rimachi's eyes seemed to bring forth the question of its own accord. "Have *you*?"

Rimachi suddenly grabbed him by the arm, his teeth bared in a smile that was cruel and predatory.

"Why not? All those times when it did not look like you and the other scouts would make it back . . . I thought about going to tell her you had died. I imagined her welcoming the comfort I could give her in her grief." Rimachi grimaced and let go of Cusi's arm. "But you always came back and brought everyone back with you. And I realized it is true, what Tomay believes about you . . . your huaca is like a spell around you that protects you from harm and brings you good fortune, without your even willing it. After that, whenever I thought of Micay, I saw her with a mantle pin in her hand, holding me at bay."

Cusi stared at him speechlessly, his arm still throbbing from the force of Rimachi's grasp. The glimmer was gone from Rimachi's eyes, which were bleak but dry. He blinked once and went on in a resolute voice.

"The last time I saw my father, he told me Micay had gone back to Tumibamba to bear your child. He also told me again that I could carry my jealousy forever and it would still bear me nothing. So I have decided to discard it. I am going to use my leave to go back to Tumibamba and have my mother arrange a marriage for me."

Uritu let out a low whoop and reached out to put a hand on Rimachi's shoulder, a gesture that managed to be both consoling and congratulatory. Cusi hesitated for a moment, then did likewise, and Rimachi did not shy away from his touch. He exhaled heavily and let his wide shoulders slump beneath their hands.

A small stone suddenly skipped past them, and a moment later Tomay crawled in with them, gesturing accusingly with his spear.

"Be glad I am not a Carangui," he scolded. "Come, there is a way, if we move quickly."

"I will get Sutic and the others," Rimachi said hastily, gathering up his cloak and war club and lurching out into the rain.

Tomay wiped water from his face and cast a quizzical glance at Cusi and Uritu. "What makes you so careless today?"

"We were looking ahead to our leave," Cusi explained as he and Uritu struggled into their wet cloaks and picked up their weapons.

"You were *what*?"

"We were being men, not animals," Uritu said, and he and Cusi whooped in unison as they pushed Tomay out ahead of them and headed up the trail.

Quito

THE WAITING crowd let out a cry of greeting when the triumphant warriors came into the main square, led by Ninan Cuyochi and Atauhuallpa. From her place between Amaru and Lloque Yupanqui, Micay immediately spotted Cusi and his comrades, who stood out like poor pilgrims amid the gaudily attired warriors at the head of the column. None of them was wearing his earplugs or headdress or any other sign of rank, and their cloaks and bedrolls were slung over the backs of their drab, dirty tunics. They had no shields and carried only light weapons, and none of them bore the captured Carangui insignia that the other warriors were displaying like banners.

As always, Cusi was marching next to Tomay, and Micay felt a familiar swelling of love and gratitude that included both of them. Even at a distance, they appeared tired and ill nourished, their faces set in a hard squint that made them seem utterly indifferent to the cheering of the crowd. The war chiefs halted in front of the place where the Regent and governor and other dignitaries were gathered, but Cusi had seen her now and he just kept coming, breaking ranks with a lack of hesitation that took even Tomay by surprise. Micay caught her breath as she saw heads turning to follow his progress, the expressions on the faces of the dignitaries ranging from astonishment to plain disapproval. Heedless, Cusi came on with his spear in his hand, his eyes darkly circled with fatigue but bright with expectation and concern, searching her face and empty arms. Before he reached her, Lloque Yupanqui took a step forward to intercept him.

"You are being rude, my son," Lloque said with gentle urgency.

Cusi seemed to rear up at him, his whole posture radiating a dangerous impatience. "I have been worse than that," he snapped. Lloque took an involuntary step backward, his face aghast. Cusi ignored him and turned toward Micay, his eyes losing their terrible coldness, becoming plaintive as he stretched his free hand out to her. "Micay . . ."

"Our child was stillborn," Micay said softly, aware of the silence that had descended on the square and of the eyes still on them. Cusi stood stunned, blinking in surprise at the tears that flowed down his hollow cheeks. Herself weeping, Micay put her arms around his waist and pressed herself against him, wanting to shield his pain from the curious glances of the onlookers. She was grateful when she heard the Regent finally begin his speech of welcome and felt the attention of the crowd shift away from them. Only then did she rise up slightly on her toes and whisper in Cusi's ear, squeezing him reassuringly.

"I have been to the huaca of Pachamama. She has promised me twins."

Cusi stiffened, then relaxed into her embrace, both arms coming around her back, one hand still grasping his spear. The speeches went on while she held him, feeling his warm breath on her neck and the rough cloth of his tunic against her chin. She thought of the way he had acted—the way he had used his presence on Lloque—and realized that this duty had made him wild in a way she had never seen before. It was not the wonderful victory it was for these others.

The Regent brought the speeches to an end with the announcement of the feast ordered by the Sapa Inca, which would be held in ten days. The crowd cheered this even more lustily than they had the appearance of the warriors, who now broke ranks at a signal from Ninan Cuyochi. In the ensuing commotion, Micay again spoke into Cusi's ear.

"You must apologize to your uncle. You threatened him."

Cusi pulled back from her, regarding her with disbelief that was only gradually replaced by a grimace of pained recognition. He nodded and let her go, turning to face Lloque.

"Forgive me, Uncle," he said hoarsely. "I could not—I did not think—"

Lloque stared back at him, his head cocked to one side and his eyes narrowed, as if examining a stranger whose intentions were unknown to him. He did not seem offended so much as shocked and disturbed, beyond the reach of apology. Amaru leaned in from Cusi's other side, supporting himself on the staff that had taken the place of his crutches.

"You can be forgiven anything, my brother," he put in. "You have given this city a reason to celebrate, the first we have had in a very long time."

Cusi hesitated for another moment, but Lloque remained unbending, so he turned reluctantly to address Amaru.

"Has the war gone so badly, then?"

"It has not gone badly at all," Amaru said in surprise. "But the Carangui fight and flee, as always. They will not give us a real battle. From the reckless way they pursued you, you must have made them hate you enormously."

"That was the task we had been given," Cusi said curtly, looking past Amaru with a kind of relief as his initiation brothers came up to join them. Micay was startled to see that Rimachi was with them, and even more startled when he met her eyes and gave her a shy, rueful smile.

"I think you made the speeches shorter," Tomay said to Cusi. "But I do not think you made a friend of the Regent or the governor."

"That hardly matters," Amaru scoffed. "You have made Ninan Cuyochi his father's favorite son, and he is the only one you truly have to account to. The feast will make the others forget."

"Will the Sapa Inca return for the feast?" Tomay asked.

Amaru smiled and gave his head a vigorous shake. "No, he has not come out of the field for anything, not even the Capac Raymi. It will be a warlord's feast . . . one for which the warlord has no time."

Tomay grunted and exchanged satisfied glances with Uritu and Rimachi. Cusi hefted his spear and put his free arm around Micay's waist.

"Let us go," he suggested. "Have you built your bathhouse yet, Amaru?"

"There are no workers to spare," Amaru said, "but you know where the one nearby is. I have had Fempellec's cooks prepare some food and akha to celebrate your return. I hope you will all do me the honor . . . and you, my uncle."

Lloque took his eyes off Cusi and made a slight, preoccupied bow. "I am grateful, my son, and I will want to hear your stories later," he added, glancing at Cusi's brothers. "But you must excuse me now. I must hear Ninan Cuyo-chi's report on the ambush while the details are still fresh in his mind. My daughter," he said to Micay, giving Cusi a last, cold look, "I will speak with you another time, as well."

Cusi looked down at the ground in the awkward silence that followed Lloque's departure. Micay finally signaled Amaru with her eyes, and he banged down his staff to break the spell.

"Let us go, then," he urged. "Fempellec will never forgive us if we let his food grow cold."

Rimachi and Tomay laughed loudly at that, and even Uritu mustered one of his rare smiles. They began to move across the square, toward the street that led to Amaru's compound. Amaru limped ahead, drawing the others with him, so that Micay and Cusi were soon out of their hearing. Micay kept her silence, though, sensing the depth of his confusion and remorse and knowing she could not speak to it. The misunderstanding with Lloque could only be a small part of it, or he would have managed a more convincing apology.

Just as she was about to speak, to remind him of her presence if nothing else, he suddenly straightened up and shook himself, looking around at the walls and rooftops with a kind of wonder. Then he he looked at her in the same way, tightening his grip on her waist.

"My wife . . ."

"Yes, my husband?" she said lightly. "I still know you, even if you do not know yourself."

His eyes glittered wetly, but he bared his teeth and forced a short, strangled laugh.

"You do," he agreed in a weary voice, pulling her closer so that their hips bumped as they walked. Just before they reached the entrance to Amaru's compound, where the others were waiting, he laughed again, to himself, and leaned over to whisper a single word into her ear: "Twins?"

CUSI AND TOMAY and their comrades came into the crowded courtyard in a group, and they were accorded the kind of reception with which Cusi had become too familiar: the sudden hush and swift turning of heads, followed by an eager rush to be near the heroes, to greet them and praise them as extravagantly as possible, hoping to be recognized in return with a word, a special glance, a touch of the hero's hand. Small nods of recognition were the best that Cusi could manage as they worked their way through the well-wishers, though he found he was not as annoyed as he had expected to be. He had not wanted to attend the feast at all, but now that he was here, he found himself responding to the brilliant swirl of colors around him and the rich smells in the air. It was as if his senses had been starved for these things for too long to pay any heed to the nagging ambivalence in his heart.

They finally reached the places that had been reserved for them, which were not far from the low dais Mama Huarcay had erected for herself at one end of the courtyard. She had asked to be put in charge of this feast because of her fondness for Ninan Cuyochi, who was sitting on the dais with her, along with a number of women and a select group of Inca dignitaries. The governor and micho of Quito, the famous architect Sinchi Roca, the high priest, and Cusi's uncle Lloque Yupanqui were among the ones Cusi recognized, as well as Titu Atauchi. They smiled and nodded in greeting to the warriors, but they were obviously going to wait until later to greet them in person.

As food was brought out, Cusi felt his ambivalence begin to battle with the excitement the feast had stirred up in him, producing a kind of restless impatience. His first taste of the food—which Fempellec, as Mama Huarcay's chief of feasts, had prepared—aroused intense memories of Chan Chan, of hot dusty winds and the feeling of unfriendly eyes on his back. He glanced sideways and saw that Micay was staring up at the people on the dais, her eyes narrowed slightly as if measuring an adversary. Cusi did not have to look in that direction to know that Titu Atauchi was staring down at him in the same way. He had been feeling the man's presence ever since he had sat down. Why are we here, he wondered, allowing such people to honor us?

He glanced around at his brothers, who appeared wholly diverted by the food, talking and laughing while they ate. They had also had bad dreams and lingering misgivings about the things they had done in the hills, but they had obviously found some way to put them out of their minds. Tomay had gone to the Guanaco House and had discovered some unanticipated comfort in the form of one of the retainer women; Rimachi had gone even farther, back to Tumibamba to arrange a marriage with the daughter of the high chief. Perhaps that was all it took—some real reward—to make these empty gestures tolerable. The only person who intercepted his glance was Uritu, who was chewing impassively, his appetite apparent only by the number of empty bowls in front of him. He had refused a gift of land in the north and had accepted the rights to a coca field in Vitcos instead, postponing his reward until the war was over and he was able to return home. He seemed to regard Cusi with a certain expectancy, as if aware of his restlessness.

When Fempellec's servants had spirited the empty bowls and platters away and had brought out cups and jars of akha to set in their place, Cusi's group waited before drinking, wondering if a toast would be sent down from the dais. Instead they heard toasts being offered to Ninan Cuyochi as the commander who had arranged the ambush, so they raised their cups to each other in a silent salute that recognized the risks they had taken to make that ambush possible. Even with food in his stomach, the akha had a powerful effect on

Cusi, making his head lift and his presence expand precipitously, as if he had inhaled a tube of vilca. Suddenly he felt dangerous, capable of anything— except perhaps of what was expected of him. Micay tugged on his free arm, and he looked at her out of eyes that felt large and glowing.

"What is it?" she asked, examining him closely. He thought she had never looked more alluring, and he was suddenly sure she was already carrying the twins she had been promised, though he did not know how he knew this.

"What do you see?" he asked in return.

"It is more what I *feel* . . ."

Cusi could only nod in agreement before Tomay leaned in from his other side, pointing with his chin and the cup in his hand.

"They are finally coming down to greet us."

They rose to their feet as Mama Huarcay descended from the dais, carrying herself like the Coya, her blue-black hair bound back by a pale violet head cloth, her neck and wrists encircled by multiple strands of fine gold beads. Beneath a light mantle, she wore a shift of Chimu weave, the same violet bordered in black and cut with diagonal panels of a gauzy material that let the dark reddish-bronze of her skin show through, revealing the tops of her breasts and a slice of midriff above her wide black belt.

"Your enemy," Cusi murmured, watching her with fascination.

"But not yours," Micay warned. "You do not need to add to your reputation for rudeness, Cusi."

Mama Huarcay had stopped a short distance away, and Ninan was introducing her to Rimachi, Sutic, and Uritu. Cusi watched the seductive way she leaned toward Sutic as she addressed him, bringing a helpless, flustered smile to the warrior's face. Even Rimachi seemed bemused, flattered in spite of himself.

"She has a powerful presence," Cusi observed.

Micay sniffed disdainfully. "You mean she is exciting to men."

"That, too," Cusi allowed with a smile. "But she reminds me of her husband. They both want influence, rather than trust."

Ninan was bringing her toward them now, followed closely by Lloque Yupanqui, Titu Atauchi, and what Cusi first thought was another woman. He realized belatedly that it was Fempellec, who had allowed his hair to grow long again and was wearing a tunic that fit his slender body snugly. He no longer looked like an awkward boy, though he had stopped short of face paint. Tomay again spoke in Cusi's ear.

"Look who is with her. The great healer."

Ninan stepped forward to perform the introductions, raising his puma-head cup to Cusi and Tomay before turning back to include Mama Huarcay.

"My mother, no doubt you have heard of the exploits of Cusi Huaman and Tomay Guanaco, the commanders of my scouts. There are no others I esteem more highly, and none more skillful at clearing the way for the rest of the warriors. They are the ones who have made the Carangui fear the very thought of the Inca. And this is Mama Micay, Cusi's wife and an estimable healer."

They all bowed. Then Cusi and Tomay exchanged a brief toast with Ninan, who could not repress a laudatory smile. Cusi swallowed slowly, feeling the heat of the akha rise from his stomach at the same moment that he met Lloque's cool gaze. Observing my conduct, Cusi realized, judging my courtesy and respect. But not toward him or Ninan; toward these others, a man he knew was Cusi's enemy and a woman he knew was Micay's. Cusi wanted to shake his head in disbelief. This was not why he had risked his life in the hills, staining his hands with innocent blood and letting the Carangui hunt him like an animal.

"I have indeed heard of the famous Cusi Huaman," Mama Huarcay agreed, giving him a smile that totally excluded Micay and Tomay. "My friends in Chimor tell me you are responsible for bringing the holy city of Chan Chan back to life. And of course you brought Fempellec to live among us," she added with a laugh, "to provide us with feasts like these. Or was it your brother who was responsible for that?"

Cusi smiled at the insinuations that seemed to ooze out around her loosely assumed innocence, like sap from an overripe pineapple. He realized that Titu Atauchi's presence was no accident; she *wanted* to put him on his guard.

"In fact," he said, turning so that she would have to include Micay in her gaze, "it was Micay who suggested to Fempellec that he could have a life here. My brother and I merely gave him our support and protection." He paused and caught Fempellec's eye. "He has our protection still, should he ever need it."

"That is *most* unlikely," Mama Huarcay proclaimed, fluttering her hands around Fempellec's shoulders, as if framing him for display. "He is indispensable to me. Who else could have made delicacies out of the poor fare that is available to us? The shortages are terrible, with the Sapa Inca away."

Cusi shrugged and turned toward Tomay, coaxing him with his eyes. "It is a warlord's feast, is it not?"

"A feast for which the warlord has no time," Tomay concurred forcefully, making Mama Huarcay look at him but not paying her any more courtesy than she had shown to him. "We are honored most by his absence."

Mama Huarcay blinked her thick black lashes, as if her eyes had been soiled by looking at a Colla. She again addressed herself to Cusi, raising her chin and leaning toward him from the waist, so that he could smell the scent of orchids and see the deep V between her breasts. "Still, you must help my husband subdue these savages without delay, so that he can return to us."

Cusi found himself smiling in apparent agreement, though it was a smile that made his teeth feel sharp. He realized there was no reason to show disrespect when what he truly felt was no respect at all.

"After what we did to them, my lady," he told her, "they would be justified in thinking that *we* are the savages."

"We took no captives," Tomay added, "and we left the survivors with nothing but scarcity and grief."

"Certainly nothing that might be made into a delicacy," Cusi agreed, still smiling his wicked smile, which appeared to confuse Mama Huarcay. She stared back at him speechlessly, causing Ninan to intervene.

"It has been a hard struggle, my mother, but this time we will drive them out of their fortress and scatter them before us."

"It cannot happen too soon," Mama Huarcay declared, glancing over her shoulder at Titu Atauchi. "The Sapa Inca has higher duties to which he must attend."

"Indeed, my lady," Titu confirmed, stepping up beside her. "He is the Herder of the Sun, the most beloved son of Inti. The people need the protection of his holiness."

"Just as we need the strength of his arm," Cusi agreed, surprising the sorcerer by raising his cup in a salute. Tomay mimicked the gesture, his tone skirting the edge of outright mockery.

"We will also need healers in the field. Will you be going north with us, Lord Healer?"

Titu Atauchi puffed out his cheeks and began to rise up at Tomay, the fringe of teeth on his fur headdress shaking as if caught in a light wind. But he arrested himself in midmotion, his eyes darting sideways at Cusi, who had simply lifted his chin expectantly, a subtle movement that was just disconcerting enough. Cusi managed not to laugh as Titu seemed to deflate in front of them, sinking back down into the feather pectoral he wore on his chest.

"Someone must attend to the rites and omens," Mama Huarcay said on his behalf, though there was annoyance in her voice.

"Then we will carry your regards to the Sapa Inca," Cusi said to Titu. He made a gracious bow to Mama Huarcay. "And yours, my lady."

"May Inti give you strength," Mama Huarcay said curtly, and swept away without acknowledging the bows of Tomay and Micay. Ninan Cuyochi glanced back at Cusi with a kind of puzzled exasperation, but Lloque Yupanqui did not so much as turn his head as he departed.

"That was rash," Micay said, letting out a long breath. "And you both enjoyed it too much."

Cusi and Tomay looked at each other and laughed.

"You did not?" Cusi inquired, lifting an eyebrow until she gave in with a smile of her own.

"I have seldom seen her at such a loss for words. She is used to a different kind of false smile."

"Like those she gave us," Tomay said dryly. Cusi drank from his cup and slowly shook his head, no longer smiling.

"I only wonder," he said, "why Ninan and my uncle continue to give their respect to such useless people . . ."

STANDING WITH Uritu among the onlookers, Micay watched Cusi take his turn in the center of the circle of dancing men. She saw him spring upward and spin completely around in the air, his arms outspread, then land lightly on one foot and dance back to his place on the circle. Some of the onlookers cried out in admiration, and Micay herself was impressed, though not at all surprised. His presence was strong today, and he seemed to have discovered that he could release it in ways that were exuberant rather than aggressive. He had not been rude to anyone since his encounter with Mama Huarcay, and even then he had not used his power to threaten.

A movement beside her caught her attention, and she turned to find Amaru leaning on his staff, staring at the dancers without seeing them. He was wearing an expression that seemed extraordinarily sober and thoughtful, almost chastened.

"Amaru?" she said softly, and he nodded and drew her aside, away from the crowd and the noise of the music. The gravity of his expression alarmed her, so she was surprised when he began with a question.

"Do you know about my visit to Pachacamac?"

"Cusi told me," Micay admitted.

"I fasted and abstained from everything for a month in order to be admitted to the highest shrine. I asked the huaca to tell me how I was meant to serve: as a warrior or as a builder. The sounds I heard were like groans from inside the earth, and the priest who spoke for the huaca told me that the time of conquest was coming to an end, and that death would be the only victor in the wars to come. He also told me, if I would build, to build far from the places that men would fight to keep."

Micay nodded respectfully. "Cusi said you found it pointless to pursue either course. And so you stayed in Chan Chan."

"Yes . . . until Cusi came to get me. Now I have been told I have a month in which to choose one or the other."

"What have you been offered?"

"It was an ultimatum, not an offer. Sinchi Roca wants me to retire as a warrior and become his chief assistant in charge of building the palace here. The war chiefs, for their part, would give me only a month to make myself fit to march and hold a command again." He exhaled angrily. "They are all punishing me for my past, of course."

"Of course," Micay agreed. "And for your present, as well. You have not rushed to complete your healing."

Amaru glared at her for a moment, then looked down at his leg and sighed. "You were not here, but Fempellec was, and it was easy to pretend I would not be forced to choose. But I know I can no longer deceive myself." He looked up and met her eyes. "I have decided I want to march with my brother and the other warriors who stood in the square and made me feel proud to be an Inca. I want to fight while there is still the chance of a victory that means something."

"What do you want me to do?"

"Help make me fit again. Push me and scold me the way you did before you went back to Tumibamba."

Micay was silent for a moment, weighing her reply. She could not doubt the sincerity of his desire, but she wondered how long it would hold him.

"I will help you work on your leg," she said at last, "though a month may not be enough."

"I will make it enough," Amaru vowed.

"Good. You must promise me one thing in return."

Amaru held up his hand, nodding in acquiescence. "I will marry her, Micay, once the war is over. I know I must."

"That is not good enough for Parihuana. She is a fine young woman, Amaru, brave and loyal and thoughtful. She deserves a husband who is her equal."

Amaru let out a mirthless laugh. "It is a pity, then, that she was given to me."

"*No,*" Micay said emphatically, "it is your good fortune. I told her about you and about Fempellec, and she did not weep or ask to return to the House of Chosen Women. She is ready to take the place that is hers, and to give you the respect and support of a wife."

"Fempellec may not be as tolerant. He has a place and power of his own now, or so he believes. He is not so easy to bend anymore."

"If he loves you, as I think he does, he will bend to this. You must make him see that it is for the protection of both of you, of all *three* of you. Otherwise, the disgrace you escaped in Chan Chan will surely find you here, and all your lives will be ruined."

Amaru's face had softened at her contention that Fempellec loved him, and it gradually reassumed the expression with which he had begun the conversation, as if he were grappling with what was truly serious in his heart.

"I cannot control what Fempellec will do," he allowed, "but I will make him hear me. And I will be kind to Parihuana and try to give her what she expects from me. Is that enough to satisfy you?"

"For now," Micay said, and Amaru smiled for the first time. He turned and stretched out an arm, indicating they should return to the feast.

"I am grateful, Micay," he said as they walked back toward the dancing. "Let me persuade you of that now, since I may forget once you begin to whip and scold me."

"I am persuaded," Micay laughed. "For now . . ."

CUSI WAS still cooling off from the couples' dance when he spied his uncle's head bobbing above the crowd, moving toward the gate. He quickly thrust his half-empty cup into Micay's hands, startling her out of the conversation she was having with Rimachi.

"I am sorry . . . Lloque is leaving."

He dashed off without waiting for a reply, dodging through the crowd with what he could feel was diminished nimbleness. Given all the toasts he had received, he should have been too drunk to walk, so he could not complain.

He could not complain about anything that had happened at this feast, and even now he was being given the chance to settle the misunderstanding between himself and Lloque. He had more than luck with him today.

"Uncle!" he called as he broke free of the crowd and saw Lloque on the edge of the deep shadows that hid the gate. Lloque stopped and came back to meet him, out of the path of the other guests who had also begun to quit the feast. He did not seem as pleased as Cusi by this chance to talk, and he did not respond to Cusi's bow of greeting.

"I may not see you again before I return to the field," Cusi said breathlessly. "I did not want to go into battle knowing that you were displeased with me."

"I am," Lloque said in a firm voice. Then he waited in silence for Cusi's apology.

"I am sorry I was rude to you on the day of my return," Cusi began. "I was not—"

"Rude?" Lloque inquired sharply. "You raised your hand to me!"

Cusi blinked at him in surprise and had to consult his memory of what Micay had told him afterward.

"No, my lord, I did not raise my hand. But I know I threatened you, and I am sorry about that."

"So you are able to threaten without raising your hand," Lloque concluded, shaking his head in amazement. "Should I be comforted by that? Is this what you have learned from your visions and your seeking? How to impose your will upon others?"

"I have made mistakes in the past, but I am finally learning—"

"You have learned quite enough," Lloque interrupted. "You seem to have made yourself a master of insolence and intimidation. I saw the way you toyed with Mama Huarcay, smiling while you taunted her and Titu Atauchi and encouraging Tomay to do the same. It did not make me proud of the part I had had in raising you; you did not learn such things from me, or your mother, or the teachers in Cuzco."

Cusi could only stare back at him, seized by a disappointment so profound it made him sway on his feet, feeling his weariness for the first time. He had never received this kind of reprimand from Lloque before, not in all the years they had known one another. And that it should come today, here, over *this.*

"I have had many teachers after you," he said slowly. "They have taught me that it is in the nature of the Incas to impose their will upon others. Those who deny that fact fool only themselves, and they are usually the first to abuse their power."

"Such arrogance," Lloque murmured in disbelief. "What has made you the judge of the Incas? Are you so much better and wiser than the rest of us?"

"I can judge the Incas because I have been one," Cusi told him. "In Chan Chan, I *was* the Inca, and it nearly cost me my life. If I had not been able to impose my will upon the Chimus, I would not be alive today. I would not be here listening to you scold me on behalf of people like Mama Huarcay and Titu Atauchi."

"I scold you on your own behalf. But I do not think you are truly willing to listen."

"Nor you to hear *me*. But you must believe me, Uncle, I have no desire to defy you. I do not know how to make you understand that the lessons of Cuzco are far behind me. We have had to learn other things here; that is true even of Huayna Capac. He has learned that respect is not owed if it has not been earned. So have I."

"Such a belief does not earn my respect," Lloque said flatly. "It is simply an excuse for behavior unworthy of an Inca. Farewell, Cusi Huaman."

Cusi stood up to him stubbornly, shaking his head. "Do not leave me this way, Uncle. It is as wrong as what my father did on the day he left me in Cuzco."

"Do not confuse me with your father," Lloque snapped, and he turned on his heel to go.

"Others have," Cusi murmured under his breath. Lloque jerked to a halt and whirled back around to face him. Crescents of white showed beneath his hooded eyelids and his lips were peeled back in a grimace of indignation. But Cusi was too angry himself now, and he did not shrink away.

"What did you say?" Lloque demanded.

"I said I had been abandoned before by those who should love me like a son. I have always found a way to survive. Farewell, Uncle."

Lloque stared down at him for another moment, clearly not believing him but just as clearly daunted by the force of Cusi's anger. Finally he turned without a word and stalked off into the darkness around the gate.

Cusi's anger departed almost as swiftly, and he was suddenly exhausted and dizzy with drink. He belched, tasting akha, and decided the feast was over. Turning unsteadily, he started back toward Micay and his comrades, those who would stand by him and accept his presence without question. Those who mattered . . .

The Mira Valley

I T WAS LATE in the dry season when the summons finally came from Huayna Capac. Cusi and Tomay and their scouts—who now constituted a sizable force—had completed the task they had been given. They had taken full command of the mountains on this flank of the stronghold, confining the Carangui within their fortress and leaving no one alive outside it—no one who might aid the enemy or spy on the movements of the Incas. They had also prepared the trail that led in from the valley flanking the Mira, making sure it was sturdy enough to withstand the passage of a large force. Cusi and Tomay had not been told *why* they were to do this, but they had felt little need to speculate. They had conducted flanking attacks during the last campaign, with some success, though the steepness of the terrain and the lack of cover had limited the amount of real pressure they could bring to bear on the fort's defenders. How exactly a larger force was going to overcome that limitation remained a mystery, but one they could live with until they reached the front lines.

They came down from the heights well behind the Incas' forward line, which was dug in just below what had once been the first level of the fort. The first wall had been completely destroyed, and those on the second and third levels had been breached many times, though the Carangui came down every day and defended what was left of the ramparts. Only the two highest levels of the fortress remained intact, and the warriors massed behind them were crowded together so tightly they had to sleep in shifts. Cusi and Tomay had seen this from their spy platform, and it made them wonder now if the Sapa Inca had not summoned them prematurely. There were too many Carangui still fighting—and fighting desperately—to assume that they could be overrun very soon.

There was no longer any need to post sentries in the foothills, so the two men came down unannounced into the encampment at the edge of the marshland that filled the low eastern side of the valley. They were used to finding a regiment of Collas here, some of them men Tomay had once helped to recruit. Now, however, they found themselves among the campfires and rude shelters of what appeared to be a regiment of boys. The camp was orderly enough, but many of its inhabitants were smaller than Cusi and looked overmatched by the weapons they carried. They fell silent as Cusi and Tomay passed through their midst, and a few even bowed at the sight of the golden earplugs. Cusi glanced at Tomay and saw him shake his head in disdain, just before there was a sudden flurry of movement and they found themselves arrested in the center of a circle of inward-pointing spears. The spears were held with surprising steadiness, the faces behind them young but deadly serious.

"Who are you two," an officious voice called from behind them, "to walk through our camp as if it belonged to you?"

"We are Incas," Cusi snapped. "Call off these boys before we teach them some respect."

The boys crouched lower behind their shields, raising the tips of their spears and scowling at Cusi's threat. Cusi looked at Tomay out of the corner of his eye and began a slow, silent count to ten. But the voice spoke again in a mocking tone that sounded familiar.

"You were boys once yourselves, were you not? The smallest ones in your initiation group. Some even thought you would not be strong enough to pass the Huarachicoy . . ."

"Amaru?" Cusi asked, and at some unspoken signal the boys lowered their spears and stepped back, grinning proudly at one another. Tomay coughed, and he and Cusi suddenly whirled in unison, flailing out with their weapons while putting themselves back to back. The boys scattered in surprise, dropping their spears and falling over each other, though a few managed to recover quickly enough to hold their ground. Amaru commended those few by name as he came in among them, using a long spear as a staff.

"The one with the battle-ax is the famous Cusi Huaman," he explained to the group, "the brother I have been telling you about. The Colla with the spear is Tomay Guanaco, also a famous warrior. They were already heroes when they were your age, and they were no bigger than you are now."

The boys all inclined their heads respectfully, and Cusi and Tomay laughed, having received few bows since they came back into the field.

"Let me speak to them alone," Amaru continued. "Perhaps I can persuade them to stay and eat with us."

The boys went back to their campfires, and Amaru led the two of them up to a low ridge that overlooked the open water of the marsh. The sun had fallen behind the western mountains, which cast long, jagged shadows across the valley. The plain below and to their left was filled with the camps of the warriors, and they could hear faint shouts from the front lines, where the day's fighting was ending with the usual taunting and sniping.

"So this was your reward for proving yourself fit," Cusi said, giving his brother a rueful smile.

Amaru shrugged good-naturedly. "They are eager to learn, and they believe whatever I tell them about my past."

"This seems an odd training ground," Tomay suggested. "What happened to the Collas who were here before?"

"They were marched back behind the crest of the ridge; we passed them when we were brought in. It seems unlikely we will be used in their place, though. I have been informed of the manner in which we are to march to the rear, but nothing has been said about going forward."

"So you are here for the sake of numbers," Tomay concluded.

"What else?" Amaru agreed. "We were not the only ones brought up from the rear. Veteran troops are being drawn off and kept hidden. And now he has sent for the two of you."

Cusi and Tomay exchanged a glance, their eyes widening with comprehension.

"I am remembering what he said about needing our swiftness," Tomay said slowly. "And a story Sumac Mallqui once told us about the war against the Huancas, who also had to be lured out of their fortress."

"Otoronco used that trick, as well," Cusi added. "It is so old it must be known to everyone."

"*We* have all been taught the same history," Amaru pointed out, "but the Carangui know only what we have shown them. This is the third time we have assaulted the fort, and twice before we have broken and fled. If we did so again, do you not think they would come out after us?"

Cusi thought of the warriors massed behind the walls on the upper levels of the fortress, living with the knowledge that there was no hope of retreat yet forced to wait for the attack to come to them.

"Yes, they would come out. Unless—no, there is no one left to give us away except ourselves. They will come if we make them believe we have lost our courage."

"Convince them, then," Amaru urged. "If we have to climb over the walls to pull them out, we might be here long enough for these boys to become men."

Cusi laughed and reached out to clap his brother on the shoulder. "You look fit, Amaru, and you seem to have good rapport with your warriors. Surely you are not eager to surrender your command?"

"Not until I have led them through the fortress," Amaru admitted, "and back to Tumibamba in triumph. But I tired of warrior's food in the first month, and though they all listen to me as if I spoke for a huaca, none of them can talk to me like a man."

"We will stay and eat with you, then," Cusi offered, drawing a nod from Tomay. "But tell me first how Micay was when you last saw her."

"They should be grateful they do not have *her* to train them," Amaru snorted. Then he smiled at Cusi. "She was still attending to her duties as a healer, but she knew she was carrying your child. Your twins, she is sure . . ."

"She must be close to her time," Cusi said quietly, staring out at the mist that was rising off of the marsh.

"Quespi and the other women will be with her. She is in good hands. But that is another reason to finish this war; or else your children will grow up without you."

"Let us eat, then," Tomay suggested, nudging Cusi with his elbow. "The Sapa Inca wants us there for the finish."

"Fatherless sons," Cusi murmured. Then he shook himself and hefted his battle-ax. He nodded to Tomay and Amaru and started back toward the campfires with them, reminding himself of where he was and where he could not be, even in his thoughts. He briefly freed a hand and touched the place on his waistband where he once had carried his spirit brother, before he had given it to Micay. He was glad now that he had obeyed the impulse to leave it with her. Part of him would be with her at the birth, even as he went, with his whole being, into a different kind of battle.

Quito

SITTING IN Amaru's courtyard beneath a bleak, bright sky, Micay looked up at the vultures circling overhead and let out a sigh that rapidly descended into a groan. She truly wanted to scream, to bellow out her frustration and discomfort, but that might awaken the serving woman Lloque had sent her, an old Quito woman who spoke little Quechua and slept whenever she had no specific task to perform. She would be useful when Micay's time came, but she was no help with the waiting. Her mute, listless presence only made Micay feel more lonely, more idle and useless. There was nothing she could do anymore and no place she could go, not even anyone to whom she could complain.

She lowered her eyes to the great mound of herself swelling up beneath the cloth of her beltless shift. She thought they must both be boys, the way they kicked in the night when she tried to sleep. But she was not sure, and that uncertainty puzzled her and contributed to her loneliness. She was aware of them, alive inside her, at every moment, yet she had had no glimpse of their spirits, not even in dreams. It did not seem right that they should be so much a part of her and still be strangers, like mitmacs who had been settled there by someone else's order. She found herself resenting Cusi at times like this, imagining that *he* was seeing their faces in dreams, even though he had no part in carrying their weight.

Her back hurt, and her legs and feet were painfully swollen so that she could no longer wear sandals. This seat that she had hollowed out in one of the mounds of earth was the only place where she was at all comfortable anymore. She resisted the urge to reach for the small leather pouch that hung between her breasts, suspended from a thong around her neck. She had called on Cusi's spirit brother too many times during the past few months, until the stone and the image it brought to her mind had begun to lose their calming powers. The tall, cool presence that Cusi had described to her always made her feel ashamed of her resentment, reminding her that she was Cusi's comrade as well as his wife. But she did not feel brave and stalwart today, and she had no desire to be reminded of her responsibilities. She wanted to be comforted and cared for, not goaded to further stoicism. It had been a mistake not to risk the journey back to Tumibamba, she thought bitterly. Mama Cori and Quinti and Chimpu Ocllo would never have abandoned her like this, leaving her to sit alone and wait to be delivered from her suffering . . .

She was surprised by the sound of voices, and when she looked up and recognized the two slender figures coming through the compound gate, she let out a cry that made them hasten toward her in concern. She wanted to laugh and reassure them, but she was weeping uncontrollably and could not find a voice to express what she was feeling.

"Micay, what is it?" Parihuana demanded in alarm. "Are you in pain? Is it time?"

Micay managed to hold up a hand and shake her head, smiling through her tears.

"I am only happy to see you. And you, Urcon."

Urcon smiled then, a wide, luminous smile that made her remember the day he had come to cure Cusi and the many days they had spent together on the coast. Parihuana was also smiling with relief while she rubbed Micay's hand between her own.

"The governor sent me north with a herd," Urcon explained, "and told me to visit you."

"And I begged Mama Cori to let me come, too," Parihuana said. "To help you with the twins."

Micay dabbed at her eyes with the edge of her mantle. "I believe it was Pachamama who sent you in answer to my prayers. I am greatly in need of comrades."

"Why are you alone?" Parihuana asked. "Your message said there were good midwives here."

"There are. But they are healers, and they must tend to the wounded until I truly need them."

"You will not be alone anymore," Parihuana promised, unslinging the carrying bundle from around her back. Urcon also removed a bundle and began to unwrap it in front of Micay's seat. She strained to look over her swollen abdomen and saw him remove two wooden cradles from the folds of cloth. He displayed them proudly, showing her the short legs that raised one end up higher than the other and the wicker loops that would support the baby's head.

"These are a gift from Sucso, the head retainer of the Rainbow House," Urcon said. "He hopes you will bring your children back to their father's estate."

"Soon, perhaps," Micay allowed. "The final assault on the fort cannot be far off."

"Have you heard anything from Cusi or Amaru?" Parihuana asked.

Micay shrugged, digging her elbows into the dirt behind her. "One of the wounded told me some time ago that the scouts had driven the Carangui out of the mountains. Amaru was given command of a regiment of recruits, so he is no doubt far from the fighting. We must talk about him later."

"I saw Fempellec in Tumibamba," Urcon reported, rising from his bundle. "He is an important man now, an adviser to one of the Coyas."

"You spoke to him?"

"He saw me in the street and sent for me. He has his own house in the Coya's compound, where the walls are painted like those in Chan Chan. I was very impressed, but I think he misses his home in Chimor. It is all he talked about while we ate."

The thought of Fempellec confiding in Urcon surprised Micay until she remembered the friendship the two of them had developed during the march back to Tumibamba. She had a sudden intuition that it might have been more than that, though Urcon seemed as open and innocent as ever. Perhaps it was the fact that he also seemed older, a man who should have had a wife before this.

"Did Fempellec seem sad or angry?" she asked.

Urcon pondered the question for several moments before replying. "There are many people who serve and obey him, but they are not his friends. When he got drunk he made jokes about them, even about the Coya herself. He says he can tell her anything and she will believe him, and he has only to look at something longingly and she will give it to him. He laughs when he says these things and does not seem grateful." Urcon shook his head in disbelief. "He still has the stone Cusi gave him, but he uses it now to crack peanut shells."

Micay wanted to ask him more, specifically if Fempellec was angry with *her,* but she suddenly realized what a poor host she had been. She dug her hands down into the dirt and pushed herself to her feet, shaking her head at their offers of assistance.

"You must let me offer you food and drink," she insisted. "I am grateful to have a reason to move, hard as it is. Parihuana, there is a woman in the house straight ahead. She speaks Quito better than Quechua."

"Then I will know I am back," Parihuana said, her eyes darkening briefly before she turned and went ahead of them.

"I have become useless," Micay decided as she waddled along beside Urcon. "I forgot completely that this was once her home."

"She did not speak of that to me," Urcon said. "Just that she was coming to be with you, to help you as you had helped her."

"She will be a great help. Can you stay with us for a while?"

Urcon gave her another smile. "There is work for me here as well as in Tumibamba. The governor said I need not return until there was news of a victory or a birth."

"You will not have to wait too long for the second," Micay laughed, swaying so that he gently took her arm to steady her. His fingers were greasy and he smelled of llamas, but she leaned on him gratefully, thanking Pachamama, Apu Poma, and the good fortune that had brought her comrades like these.

The Mira Valley

IN THE TEN days since they had reported to the front, Cusi and Tomay had yet to receive a greeting or summons from Huayna Capac, though they saw him nearly every day. He had simply made them part of the squadron that accompanied him into battle, so that when they did speak, it was in the curt language of warriors at risk. And they were always at risk, because unlike his brother and predecessor, Auqui Toma, who had been everywhere during a battle, Huayna Capac left command and exhortation to his war chiefs and plunged directly into the thick of the fighting. Like a warlord of the most traditional sort, he let his weapons speak for him, and the message he had conveyed to his troops was an unwavering determination to destroy Pinta, the red-clad Carangui war chief who strode the ramparts waving his obsidian-studded war club like a banner. He had made the war a personal contest between himself and Pinta, which kept the sights of his warriors fixed upward even as they fought for every foot of ground on the levels below the remaining walls.

Unaccustomed to fighting in the midst of a mob, where their speed could not compensate for their size, Cusi and Tomay were bruised and battered during their first days with the squadron, each receiving a number of minor wounds. They had quickly learned to place themselves in the second rank, roving back and forth and striking whenever an opening presented itself. Still, the night a summons came from the Sapa Inca, Tomay was nursing a spear wound in his foot, and Cusi hesitated for a moment after the warrior who had brought the message had gone away.

"He did not ask for me," Tomay said impatiently. "Go. Take him my greetings. Find out how much more of this punishment we will have to take."

Cusi left his shield and helmet but took his battle-ax with him. As he threaded his way around the campfires, he again noticed that this was a regiment of the young and the fleet. Most of the Old Guard had been posted elsewhere, perhaps with the troops being hidden in the rear. Ninan Cuyochi and Atauhuallpa were waiting outside the Sapa Inca's tent, which was large and well lit within, so that Cusi could see the silhouette of a man moving about inside.

"Cusi," Ninan said in a warning tone, "be careful with him. This is no time to be too clever or presumptuous. He is in the grips of something—"

"Vilca?" Cusi asked.

Atauhuallpa shook his head and pointed at his own chest. "Something here. You know about signs and visions, Cusi, or so I have heard. See if you can calm him down."

Cusi looked back at him steadily but did not reply, having no desire to encourage the belief that he was a sorcerer. Atauhuallpa's presence was powerful but unconscious of itself, much like his father's once had been. Cusi sensed that he was as concerned as Ninan, but he had no patience for anything he could not see and put his hands on.

"Do what you can," Ninan urged. "He needs to rest sometime."

They opened a way between them, and Cusi lifted the tent flap and went inside. Thick blankets covered the ground, and wicks floating in bowls of tallow filled the room with yellow light. Cusi blinked rapidly, taking in the piles of clothing and cotton armor, the racks of gold-tipped weapons, the painted wooden stool, and the pile of tawny vicuña hides for sleeping. Huayna Capac was pacing back and forth behind the stool, and Cusi waited until he stopped before he bowed over his battle-ax and made the mocha with one hand.

"Sit, Cusi," the ruler said, and he straddled the stool to look down at him. The royal fringe around his forehead concealed his eyes, but not the agitation in his face. He was up off the stool almost as quickly as he had sat down, pacing to the back of the tent to handle some object he kept in a small wooden chest inlaid with gold. A spirit brother, Cusi surmised from the way Huayna Capac hid his manipulations with his body. Then the ruler filled his cheek with coca and lime, removed the fringe and hung it on a standard, and came back to the stool. His eyes were pinched and darting, and Cusi felt a presence that was wild and incoherent, tearing at itself like an animal in a trap. Cusi grew very still in response, feeling the presence of his spirit brother well up inside him, a core of calm readiness.

"Do you know my plan?" Huayna Capac demanded, speaking around the wad of coca in his cheek. "Have you *seen* it?"

"I have only guessed at it," Cusi allowed. "I think you intend to feign a retreat and lure the Carangui into an ambush."

"You simply guessed this? Then Pinta will see it, too."

"No, my lord," Cusi said. "Pinta has not been where I have nor seen what I have seen. And there is no one left to spy for him. He must believe by now that you will tear down the walls to get at him."

"He *must,*" Huayna Capac insisted passionately, swiveling on the stool and rolling his shoulders as if trying to shrug off some painful burden. "But what if I am wrong? Am I mad to believe this? Perhaps it will not happen as I saw it . . . perhaps our flight will be real!"

He jumped to his feet again, but Cusi was ready this time and rose with him, surprising him out of walking away. Cusi extended his battle-ax, held horizontally in both hands, like an offering.

"I told you, my lord, that I received this from Otoronco Achachi. Before I left Cuzco, he took me to the shrine where Pachacuti dwells. Pachacuti's speaker took this from me and swung it as lightly as a grass wand, promising that it would bring me fame."

Huayna Capac took the ax from him and sat back down, balancing the weapon across his thighs. Cusi squatted in front of him, noticing a long scar on the ruler's right leg but not allowing it to distract him. He had to speak while he had the man's attention.

"That same night, my lord, Otoronco told me a story he had heard from Pachacuti himself. It is about the vision that came to Pachacuti when he wandered alone on the plain, waiting for the Chancas to descend on Cuzco and destroy it."

"Tell me," Huayna Capac commanded, his forearms bulging as he unconsciously gripped the handle of the ax. Cusi composed himself, recalling Otoronco's words.

"He wandered through the darkness, blind with despair, seeing no hope for himself and the Incas. He could not flee as his father and brother had done, but he saw no chance for victory or even survival. He was not afraid to die, but to be the man who lost Cuzco was unbearable. There could be no greater failure."

Huayna Capac grunted forcefully, as if he understood this fear too well.

"When the god spoke to him, it was not in a voice that came to his ears, but like a wind that rose up out of his heart and blew all of his fear and doubting away. It told him that if he wished to survive, he must have an ambition equal to his risk. It was not enough simply to defend Cuzco; he had to look beyond, to the time when Cuzco would rule all of the Four Quarters. If he was to accomplish what his mind told him was impossible, he had to lose his mind and all its restraints. He had to be mad enough to believe that he could turn the world upside down and make it his own.

"And so he did, my lord," Cusi continued quietly, "as the story songs tell us. He took the name of the Inca into every quarter, wherever there were men to hear, and always he sought to do more than the minds of ordinary men thought possible. He built roads where there had only been paths; he terraced the steep sides of valleys and brought water to grow maize; he abolished scarcity and hunger and gave the wisdom of Viracocha and the strength of Inti to the people he conquered. He made it the duty of every Inca to do the impossible as a matter of choice, not necessity."

Cusi paused, feeling the full force of Huayna Capac's presence bearing down on him. The ruler was hunched forward on his stool, his eyes fixed on Cusi's face, his jaw so rigid that the lump of coca stood out like a rock. Cusi drew a long breath, aware suddenly of every blow he had taken during the day's fighting. This was more wearying than fighting.

"So if you are mad, my lord," he concluded, "it is because you must be. You must be as true to your vision as Pachacuti was to his."

Huayna Capac nodded abruptly and sat back on his stool, remembering to chew. As he reduced the lump in his cheek, he seemed to return to himself, gazing down at the ax in his lap with a kind of delayed recognition. His agitation had passed, but when he looked back at Cusi, there was no gratitude in his eyes.

"It will not be easy to run from Pinta," he said in a curiously neutral tone, as if testing a strategy out loud.

"It cannot be an orderly retreat," Cusi agreed, "or they will know not to follow. We will truly have to make ourselves vulnerable."

"That is not what I mean. It will not be easy for *me*. I will have to act like a coward in front of the other Incas, when I know how ready they are to question my courage."

"Not anymore," Cusi said without hesitation. Immediately he wished he could take the words back. Huayna Capac's eyes flashed and he stood up with the ax in both hands, gesturing with his chin for Cusi to rise and face him. Cusi got to his feet with a weary reluctance he could not conceal.

" 'Not anymore,' " the ruler mimicked angrily. "I have not forgotten how you stood against me, Cusi. I have not forgotten any of those who did. But you—you who had basked in my favor at so young an age. It was intolerable to me to see you there, defying me with your silence and your unbowed head, looking upon me without sympathy or respect. It was like a blow to me, to think that all my generosity had earned me this ingratitude . . ."

Abruptly, he thrust the ax back into Cusi's hands, rocking him back onto his heels.

"That is why you are here now and why I have allowed you to speak to me so boldly. I wanted to be sure you stood with me again."

Cusi simply bowed over his ax, feeling that anything he said would only feed the ruler's resentment.

"I have not forgotten the part Mama Quilla played in Tumibamba, either," Huayna Capac went on. "In three days, when she is whole, we will attack for the last time. The other commanders are being told as we speak, and the warriors will be told the night before. Then it will be in the hands of the gods. Leave me," he added curtly, nodding in dismissal. "You have made me tired."

Bowing and making the mocha, Cusi slowly backed out of his presence, feeling exhausted himself. He found Ninan Cuyochi waiting outside, standing in the gray light of the rising moon.

"I have made him tired," Cusi reported when Ninan simply stared at him expectantly.

"Forgive me, Cusi," Ninan said in relief, "I should never have doubted you. You have always been special to him."

I made him attend to me, Cusi thought, and understanding why he was so depleted and why Huayna Capac had turned on him in anger. He had had no choice but to use his presence on the ruler, and Huayna Capac could recognize that kind of manipulation now, even if he could not resist it. Cusi had calmed him, but he had also held him against his will, and the Sapa Inca could never be grateful for that.

"It is difficult to convince him he must rest," Ninan said. "You have done us all a great service."

Cusi nodded, though he felt he had done himself no service at all. Huayna Capac had made himself a warlord, but he would rather have remained the ruler he was before, the Sole Lord, a man who had no cause to prove anything to anyone. And he would always remember Cusi as one who had denied him that and made him change. Special, indeed!

"I am weary," Cusi said flatly, and he raised his ax in a parting salute.

"May Inti Illapa bring us victory," Ninan called after him.

"May Mama Quilla keep us whole," Cusi whispered to himself. Then he followed the moonlit path back to his camp.

Quito

IN THE DREAM, Micay was in the mountains, sitting on a ledge overlooking a deep valley. It might have been the landing outside Macas's cave, because there was mist and the smell of sulfur in the air, but she felt completely alone and unthreatened. Then she heard the sound of chewing and turned to see a deer standing next to her, watching her with soft, liquid eyes, its jaw swiveling tirelessly around its cud. Micay admired the light russet coat and the shiny velvet on the antlers, realizing it was a buck. Then the deer stopped chewing and spoke to her in a language she could not understand. When she shook her head, the deer spoke in Quechua, asking her where Cahua and Sinchi were.

They are here, Micay said, and began to turn toward her other side. But the movement set off a twisting, lurching pain that made everything turn red. She

woke and understood immediately what was happening, and she cried out to
Parihuana that her labor had begun.

It was not until later, when the initial alarm and excitement had worn off
and the force of the contractions had finally slackened, that she understood
the message of the dream. She was squatting naked with her back against the
wall, padded all around with blankets and clean cloths. Parihuana and Quespi
were crouched on either side of her, and there were three older women in
attendance, one an experienced midwife named Mama Cisa. Mustering her
breath, Micay told them about her dream, feeling the names take on meaning
as she spoke them aloud.

"A girl and a boy," Quespi said with a congratulatory smile.

"The girl for Pachamama," Parihuana reminded Micay, squeezing her
hand.

"And the boy for Illapa," Mama Cisa concluded, resting her hands on
Micay's upraised knees and peering between her legs. "It was Illapa who spoke
to you. The deer is his spirit animal, and he is greatly attracted to twins."

"His father is a brother to lightning," Micay said.

The midwife nodded gravely, pushing out her lower lip. "He will be a son
of lightning, and you will have to perform the proper rituals for him. But that
is for later. Now you must open yourself wider and let these children into the
world."

Come, little mother, Micay thought, and the contractions resumed as if she
had willed them. She felt strong again, girded around by these women, supported above and below by the gods, by Illapa and Pachamama, and by Mother
Moon, Mama Quilla, who stood watch over women giving birth.

There was both daylight and moonlight; rain, at some point, and possibly
thunder. The only certain things were the pain, which seemed beyond endurance, and the overwhelming fatigue, which became inseparable from the pain
and made her want to flee her own body. The voices, both soothing and sharp,
blended into a single command to push. *Open yourself to me.* She felt Macas
looming over her, the water burning her thighs, the claws of the puma raking
her skin. She screamed and opened out, seeing the passage in her mind even
as the first dark, bloody head appeared between her legs, coaxed and cradled
by the sure hands of the midwife.

The girl, Cahua, came first, though her brother was swift to follow. They
seemed to squall with one voice as they were washed by the women, who
exclaimed loudly over their size and the straightness of their limbs. Then the
women abruptly fell silent, causing Micay to turn in the grip of Quespi and
the other women who were washing her.

"What is it?" she cried, her voice a hoarse croak. Mama Cisa came over to
her with one of the babies bundled in her arms, its cries muffled by the cloths
around it.

"They are healthy, and they have your skin," the midwife said. "Except
where they have been marked by the gods."

She crouched next to Micay and opened the bundle, revealing the tiny, squirming girl, whose wrinkled face was clenched in a frown of displeasure. Micay immediately noticed the smear of red that ran down one side of the child's throat and onto her chest, as if someone had painted her sloppily with their fingers. The mark was vivid and startling against the paleness of her skin, which was light copper in color.

"There is another that will be hidden by her hair," Mama Cisa added, "and a small mark on the back of her shoulder."

She rewrapped the infant and placed the bundle in the crook of Micay's left arm.

"Cahua," Micay murmured, kissing the black hair on the top of her daughter's head and pressing her gently against her breast. The child let out a whimper and then grew quiet, her tiny lips moving soundlessly. Parihuana came over with the other bundle and handed it down to the midwife.

"He has a mark on his back like his sister's," Mama Cisa said, "and one on his foot."

She stared at Micay for a moment, then placed the bundle inside Micay's encircling arm, opening the cloths so that Micay could see the child's face. Despite the warning in Mama Cisa's glance, Micay caught her breath. The blood-red mark completely surrounded the boy's left eye, sprawling onto his cheek and temple in ragged spatters. As if sensing Micay's reaction, he began to wail, and his sister responded with a whimper.

"Sinchi, my son," Micay soothed, her voice breaking and tears running down her cheeks as she hugged both of them against her.

"The god has touched him," Mama Cisa said solemnly. "You must call him Sinchi Illapa when it is time for him to be named."

"Cusi will approve," Quespi put in. "He will be a brave little warrior."

Both of them were quiet again, and Micay looked from one to the other, her breath ruffling the hair on their heads. They were here, her children, her twins. The love that had gripped her like grief began to loosen its hold on her heart, letting her feel the wonder of simply holding them in her arms.

"They are beautiful children, Micay," Parihuana said softly.

Micay looked up at her and tried to smile. "They are," she agreed, and she bent her head over them again as Mama Cisa and the other women began to sing, in light, whispery voices, a song of praise to Mama Quilla.

The Mira Valley

A T DAYBREAK, drums began to beat and the Inca war god Huanacauri was brought down through the ranks of the warriors in a solemn procession. His cloth-draped litter was carried by six war chiefs and was preceded by the Sapa Inca himself, walking and carrying his golden war club in his own hands. Over his tunic, Huayna Capac wore a chest piece of cotton armor the color of the sky, and the multicolored fringe of the ruler was wrapped around a blue and gold helmet surmounted by a crest of short white feathers. Each regiment bowed and made the mocha, then began to sing their war song as the huaca passed through their midst. The warriors all knew about the planned retreat, but they had also been told to attack without restraint until the signal was given, and the sight of Huanacauri, accompanied by their warlord, was meant to ensure there would be no withholding.

The litter was brought forward to where Cusi and the other members of his squadron stood waiting, ranked around a makeshift dais built out of stones taken from the fort's first wall. As they bowed over their weapons and made the mocha, Huayna Capac climbed to the top of the crude platform. The drums stopped beating, and the ruler gazed out over his troops for a long moment, letting the silence grow deep and ominous. Then he turned his back to them and faced the fort, raising the golden-headed war club in one hand and shaking it at the walls.

"Pin-taaa!" he shouted, so that the name echoed up and down the length of the valley. "Pinta, today you will die!"

Whirling the war club over his head, he jumped down from the platform and charged toward the Carangui lines. Cusi and his comrades ran to catch up with him, swept forward by the great roar that burst from the throats of those behind, a sound that was fierce and avid, the eager cry of men closing in for the kill.

FOR SEVERAL days before this, the Inca attack had been deliberately sluggish and hesitant, displaying confusion in the command and some visible reluctance in the ranks. So the Carangui were not prepared for the headlong assault that quickly overran the defenses on the first two levels and stormed the crumbling wall that remained on the third. Huayna Capac led the attack with a recklessness that was a goad to his own men and a distraction to the enemy. He was constantly pushing ahead, offering the Carangui a chance at him that most of them could not resist, even if it meant abandoning their defensive positions. So far, though he had appeared to be surrounded or cut off many times, he had always managed to hold his ground until some part of the regiment came to his aid.

As Cusi followed Tomay through a gap in the wall, his shield raised in front of him to ward off slingstones, he caught a glimpse of blue armor and saw the golden war club flailing wildly in the midst of a crowd of Carangui. Sumac Mallqui and Quilaco Yupanqui were the first to reach the ruler's side, throwing themselves bodily into the melee to clear space for him. Tomay went in behind Sumac, thrusting his spear at those their former teacher had knocked to the ground, while Cusi sprang to the defense of his brother-in-law, who was on his knees, clubbing a man he had pinned down beneath his shield. Another Carangui rushed forward with his spear leveled at Quilaco's chest, but Cusi leaped in from the side and smashed the man in the face with his shield, sending the polished helmet flying from his head. Cusi spun and struck out blindly with his battle-ax, hitting someone who screamed and thrust a spear past Cusi's face, nicking the bottom of his golden earplug.

Then a wall of men seemed to surge up in front of him and throw him back, and as he tripped and went down, he saw Huayna Capac stagger backwards and fall over Quilaco. Cusi rolled and tried to get to his knees, but he was kicked and trampled by men rushing in from both sides, and several large, struggling bodies crashed down on top of him, jarring the wind out of him and pushing his face down into the dust. He felt himself being smothered, and a burst of sheer panic made him thrash and kick until he could pull some air into his lungs. I am not meant to die here, he thought frantically as he lost his shield and helmet and felt something stab him in the calf. Some of the bodies pinning him down were no longer moving, but other hands groped and struck at him, trying to tear off his armor. A sandaled foot came down on his hand and he lost his battle-ax, which almost made him lose his hope, as well. Just when the pressure seemed certain to crush the life out of him, the pile of men above him suddenly toppled sideways and he was free, rolling over and over until he came up onto his knees, spitting blood and trying to clear the dust from his eyes.

A body loomed over him and he ducked instinctively before he recognized Tomay, who grinned at him out of a bloody face and gestured with the spear in his hands.

"We have them now!" he shouted. "Are you hurt?"

Cusi was too dazed to know. Before he could muster a reply, everything seemed to stop, and there was Huayna Capac, standing on the heaped-up bodies of the fallen. His armor was torn and streaked with blood and his broken helmet hung down over one ear, but the golden war club was still in his hands.

"Which of you thinks he can kill me?" he taunted, thrusting out his chest like a target. "I am the Inca, and I will destroy all of you before I am through!"

"Get down," Tomay growled under his breath, but the Carangui facing the ruler were too stunned to react, except for one badly wounded man who tried to rise from the pile of bodies at Huayna Capac's feet. With one swift, savage blow of his war club, Huayna Capac flattened him again, the signal for his men to charge past him and throw the Carangui back.

Tomay found Cusi's battle-ax and scavenged a shield and helmet for him, and the two of them pulled back to the shelter of the wall behind them, which was now in Inca hands. Cusi was amazed to find that he had not sustained a disabling injury, though he would not have wanted to see his face or the bruises on his back. The stab wound in his calf was still bleeding and needed to be bound, so they took a gourd from one of the water carriers and crouched in the shadow of the wall, drinking and waiting for one of the roving healers to appear. While they waited, the bodies of two members of the Old Guard were carried past, and then the limp body of Sumac Mallqui, his long arms trailing in the dust.

"Quilaco," Cusi remembered suddenly, but he had just risen to his feet when he saw his brother-in-law come through the gap in the wall, supported under one arm by an apprentice warrior and attended by an old man with medicine bags slung over both shoulders. There were thick bandages around Quilaco's forehead and one of his legs, and the healer had him sit down against the wall so that he could put a splint on his broken left arm. Cusi squatted down on the other side and held a gourd so Quilaco could drink. His face was so raw and swollen that it was barely recognizable, and one of his eyes was completely swollen shut. Cusi was not certain for a moment that he was recognizable himself, but then Quilaco managed a pained smile.

"I saw you, Cusi," he said through clenched teeth. "Before I was . . . buried."

Cusi repressed a shudder at the memory. "I saw you, too. Then I did not think I would ever see anyone again."

"The Carangui only wanted Huayna Capac. I do not know how he escaped."

Quilaco groaned as the healer knotted the splint in place and stepped back, gesturing to Cusi and Tomay to help him to his feet. They held him upright until the apprentice had positioned himself to bear most of the wounded man's weight.

"Get him to the rear without delay," Cusi told the apprentice. "Do not stop to rest any more than you have to."

"I will be out of your way," Quilaco promised, training his good eye on Cusi. "Just be sure to bring yourselves out after me. It is dangerous to believe you cannot be killed."

Cusi and Tomay exchanged a glance but remained silent because the healer had noticed Cusi's wound and was kneeling beside him, washing the cut with a solution that stung viciously. Cusi watched Quilaco depart through tearing eyes, remembering how they had stood together in the square in Tumibamba. Sumac Mallqui had been with them, too. The whole honor guard had been asked to join this regiment; Huayna Capac had truly not forgotten any of them.

When the healer had bound a dressing in place, he tapped Cusi on the leg and went off to tend someone else. Cusi and Tomay pulled on their helmets and picked up their shields before they looked at one another again.

"A warlord does not stop to count the dead," Tomay said, giving the old saying a bitter edge. "Especially not his own."

"Let us stay together, then," Cusi suggested. "And away from those who bare their chests to the enemy."

"He has *always* been dangerous to us," Tomay muttered, as they began to walk toward the gap in the wall. "No matter where he is."

FOR A TIME it had seemed as if the second wall of the fort might actually be breached, so fierce was the Inca attack. But Pinta had appeared atop the ramparts and had rallied his men to throw off the Incas' ropes and ladders and to rain stones and darts down on them. The Incas continued to attack, sweeping forward in waves from the barricades they had erected for themselves, but the prospect of a swift victory no longer drove them on. Nor did Huayna Capac. Though the order to attack kept coming down the line, the ruler had not shown himself in some time.

Crouched behind the barricade on the left flank of the Inca line, Cusi glanced up through the dust-filled air at the sun. Then he looked around at the men crouched on both sides of him, many of whom returned his gaze. They also knew it was time to flee; perhaps past time. Their arms and legs told them that, without their looking at the sun. If they did not run soon, they would not have the strength to run at all.

Tomay had gone to check the end of the line, and when he returned, Challcochima and Quizquiz came with him, bent over at the waist to keep their heads below the top of the low rampart.

"Has the order come yet?" Tomay asked as the three of them squatted down next to Cusi. The warriors on either side moved away a bit to let them speak in private, though they were all watching the conclave out of the corner of their eyes.

"Not yet. He has not shown himself, either."

"We are wasting men," Challcochima said in disgust. "We will be fleeing in darkness if he waits much longer."

Quizquiz muttered something unintelligible and spat into the dirt. He looked as battered and weary as Cusi felt, his narrow face animated only by the anger in his eyes. When the expected messenger arrived with the order to advance, the four commanders looked at one another and then simply ignored the man. The messenger hesitantly repeated the order, glancing from one to the other but receiving the same impassive stare from each. The man finally retreated in confusion, ducking his head as he ran back toward the center of the line. Cusi saw the warriors along the barricade nod and poke one another as the messenger scuttled past and the commanders stayed where they were. No doubt they thought the ruler's plan was finally being put into action, and perhaps it was, though by refusal rather than acquiescence.

Ninan Cuyochi came back down the line, his face stark with disapproval and reproach. His expression changed, however, when he saw the four of them sitting together. Challcochima was his initiation brother and Quizquiz a close comrade; he could not speak to them as he might have to Cusi and Tomay alone.

"Was the order not clear?" he asked quietly, addressing himself to Challcochima.

The tall warrior shrugged. "Clear enough. But so are the pleas of our captains. They know their men cannot keep fighting like this and then be expected to run."

"The Sapa Inca says he will know when it is time."

"If he were still fighting with us," Quizquiz interjected, "he would feel in his legs that it is time."

"Perhaps you would like to tell him that," Ninan suggested.

"Have you?"

"Yes, and so has Atauhuallpa. Someone else must try—someone he will hear."

Ninan was staring at Cusi, who stubbornly shook his head.

"Do not ask me again, Ninan. I do not have the favor you think. This would make him hate me, I know it."

"That will not matter if we do not act soon," Challcochima pointed out. "We will die here or they will catch us from behind when we run."

"*We* will always know what you did, and why," Quizquiz said bluntly.

Ninan nodded vigorously in agreement. "I will give you what protection I can, Cusi."

They were all staring at him now, and only in Tomay's eyes was there any understanding and sympathy. The others simply trained their urgency on him, making him feel the keenness of his own. They had to end this now or risk never ending it at all. A despairing laugh rose in Cusi's throat and he jumped to his feet, ducking down again when a stone whizzed past his head.

"Remember me, then!" he shouted, pulling his shield and battle-ax in close to his body as he turned and started down the line, Ninan not far behind. The noise of the fighting filled his ears again and he noticed stones and darts flying by just overhead. He recalled their last attack on the wall, the huge rocks descending toward him, the shock of landing when the ladder was dislodged and he had to jump clear. He decided that Challcochima was right. Favor was the least of what he might lose today.

Accompanied by Ninan, he passed through the thick cordon of golden-eared warriors that surrounded the place where the jumbled stones of the barricade had been raised to a height of almost ten feet. Huayna Capac was standing with his arms held out in front of him, drying his hands on a towel while two servants tied a fresh blue chest protector around his upper body. His tunic and helmet were also new and unblemished, and his face and hair had been washed. Even with the bandages on his arms and legs, he seemed as physically magnificent as he had the day Cusi had first seen him. But his eyes, when Cusi looked up from his bow, were those of a man past exhaustion or with a fever. They were bloodshot and reflected too much light, and Cusi was not sure they recognized him.

Atauhuallpa was standing just behind his father, but it was the war chief Rumiñaui, an older man with a cruel face and one eye that did not move, who spoke for the ruler.

"Why have you not attacked as you were ordered? Why do you come here instead?"

"We have to know if we are going to fight on here or pretend to run. We can no longer ask the men to do both."

"Then *tell* them!" Rumiñaui snapped. "It is the command of the Sapa Inca."

Cusi felt his anger rising but decided there was no point in arguing with this man, whom he knew by reputation only. He turned slightly and appealed directly to Huayna Capac, who had dropped the towel and had taken a golden-headed battle-ax from an attendant.

"My lord, I beg you . . . the men have only so much strength. If we are going to flee, let us do so while we are still strong enough to defend ourselves. Another attack would be pointless. Let us fulfill your vision, my lord, and bring the Carangui out."

"Stop your whining," Rumiñaui growled, stepping forward with his spear held loosely in front of him, the point tilted upward at Cusi's chest. Cusi barely heard the words, but he felt the threat with his whole body and reacted without thinking, swinging his ax in a swift loop that came down on the shaft of the spear and snapped it right out of the war chief's hands. Before Rumiñaui could recover, Atauhuallpa grabbed him from behind, and Ninan seized Cusi in a similar fashion. A golden blur suddenly cut the air in front of Cusi's face, and he saw Huayna Capac appear behind it, the battle-ax rising against the blue of his armor. Ninan tightened his grip on Cusi's arms, holding him fast.

"Let him go," Huayna Capac commanded. There was recognition in his eyes now, and the hatred Cusi had predicted.

"He speaks for the other commanders, my lord," Ninan said. "He does not mean to defy you."

"He *always* means to defy me. Let him go!"

Ninan reluctantly complied, and Cusi flexed his arms to restore circulation and spread his feet in case he had to jump. He kept a wary eye on Huayna Capac, who held his battle-ax across his chest, his wrists cocked beneath the handle.

"I should kill you," the ruler threatened, "and be sure of your loyalty once and for all."

"I am not your enemy, my lord," Cusi told him, waiting for him to strike. The threat was far more palpable than anything Rumiñaui had offered, and Cusi struggled to quell his instincts, reminding himself not to strike back.

"No?" Huayna Capac queried loudly. He glanced back over his shoulder for a moment, and Cusi braced himself, watching the man's wrists. But when Huayna Capac looked at him again, there was a smile on the ruler's face. A triumphant smile, perhaps, though his feverish eyes made it seem maliciously self-satisfied. "I have a better use for you, then," he announced. "You will be my coward . . . my betrayer. You will be the first to desert me."

Cusi exhaled slowly, seeing that he would have to surrender his pride along with his favor. He told himself that it was worth it, that it would accomplish what he wanted, what they all wanted. But he hated Huayna Capac for inflicting it on him, and he could not bring himself to voice his compliance.

The ruler, however, did not wait for him to agree. He snapped out orders to Ninan and Atauhuallpa, who were to create a commotion in the crowd around them, as if contention had broken out between the warriors.

"When I finish with the coward and let him run, send half of them after him. Then give the signal to the rest of the line."

As the war chiefs moved to obey him, Huayna Capac lowered his ax to his side and reached out with his free hand, grasping the edge of Cusi's shield and tossing it aside when Cusi let him take it. He made a similar gesture toward

Cusi's ax, but Cusi shook his head and held the weapon down behind his hip.

"Not for you or any other man," he vowed, but the ruler merely laughed and smiled the same, malicious smile. He reached out again and curled his fingers through the rips in the front of Cusi's cotton armor, lifting him up onto his toes.

"*Now* refuse me," he commanded. "Let everyone see your defiance and your disloyalty. Coward!"

He thrust Cusi roughly away, sending him staggering backwards. Cusi caught his balance and held up his hand imploringly, keeping his ax hand tight against his hip.

"We cannot fight any longer!" he cried. "Please, Lord, let us flee now!"

Advancing on him, Huayna Capac slapped him across the face and gave him another hard push. This time Cusi tripped over a rock and went down on his buttocks in the dust. He was aware of the crowd swelling out around them, shouting and waving their arms.

"You will obey me, traitor! You will fight!"

"No more!" Cusi pleaded as he scrambled to his feet. The ruler cuffed him on the shoulder and feinted with his battle-ax, and Cusi jumped back, instinctively raising his own weapon. Huayna Capac straightened up, his eyes wild with indignation.

"You raise your weapon to me? You *are* the enemy, and I will have to kill you!"

If you can, Cusi thought fiercely, feeling his presence expand with the desire to fight. They were outside the shelter of the barricade now, and slingstones had begun to fall around them, kicking up puffs of dust as they thudded down. One of them bounced and hit Cusi in the stomach, causing no pain but bringing him back to his senses.

"Let me run, Lord," he urged the ruler. "Let us put an end to this."

"I will put an end to *you,*" Huayna Capac vowed, and he lashed out at Cusi with his golden ax, swinging from the side with every intention of killing him. But he was more tired than he knew, and Cusi dodged the blow easily, backing away so he would not be tempted to strike at the ruler's exposed legs. Huayna Capac swung and missed again, grunting in exasperation, and it suddenly occurred to Cusi that he should simply turn and run.

"Sorcerer!" the ruler cried, raising his weapon over his head.

But Cusi danced back out of range before he could bring it down. "We are finished, my lord," he said bluntly, releasing his anger in a parting taunt. "You will have to catch me if you wish to kill me."

Huayna Capac shook his ax in vehement denial, but before he could charge a stone hit him in the back of the head with a crack that made Cusi flinch just to hear it, and the ruler fell forward onto his face. There was a sudden, motionless silence all around and then a great tumult overhead, as the Carangui let out a shout from atop their ramparts.

Cusi went down onto his knees next to the prostrate figure as the crowd closed in around them. The back of Huayna Capac's helmet was splintered but not broken, and the blue chest protector rose and fell with his breathing. Suddenly he lifted his head and looked at Cusi, blinking furiously. His head swiveled from side to side, scanning the other faces around him with growing apprehension.

"No! You will not have me!" he screamed, and he seemed to come to his feet in a single motion, flailing with his arms to drive everyone back. He staggered in a dizzy circle that left him facing the fort, and he stared at it, wide-eyed, as if he had never seen anything like it. Then he turned and pushed Atauhuallpa out of the way and began to run, and the crowd parted for him and then began to follow, their shields raised over their heads.

Cusi had risen quickly to avoid being trampled, and he let himself be carried along by the fleeing crowd, holding onto his battle-ax with both hands. Finished, he thought, but he kept his legs moving at a measured pace and did not let himself believe it just yet.

THE DESPERATION of the Inca retreat required no pretense, for they were exhausted and the Carangui who came pouring out of the fortress after them were fresh and vengeful and full of pent-up fury. They drove the Incas down from one level to the next, sensing victory so strongly that they did not even pause to finish off the wounded. Pinta was leading them in person, waving his war club and shouting Huayna Capac's name.

Cusi had no notion of the ruler's whereabouts and no time to look around for him. He had been fortunate enough to have found his way back to the group of warriors Tomay, Quizquiz, and Challcochima had gathered around themselves. They retreated in as orderly a fashion as conditions allowed, taking turns fighting in the rear guard while those behind threw slingstones over their heads and helped carry the wounded away. The Carangui pursued them relentlessly, giving them no chance to rest or regroup and threatening constantly to turn their flank. By the time they made it down to the plain below the fort, they had lost half their original number and could no longer tell the wounded from the able.

They stopped halfway up the long slope of the plain, among the remains of their own camps. The plain behind them was empty of reinforcements, and the Carangui were flowing down over the wall-less lower levels of the fort in a living stream, gathering at the bottom to make a final overwhelming charge. Cusi and Quizquiz arranged their remaining men in a staggered double rank, doing their best to fill their place in the ragged Inca line. Tomay came back from the rear, where he had left Challcochima with the other wounded. He had found a mesh bag of slingstones, and he had just lifted it up to show Cusi—an ironic display, under the circumstances—when he dropped it and pointed urgently with his chin. Cusi whirled back and saw columns of black smoke rising up from behind the walls on the upper levels of the fortress. A cheer went up from the weary men along the line, though only a few had the strength to raise their weapons. A conch horn bellowed behind them, and Cusi glanced over his shoulder to see a wave of warriors come over the crest of the ridge, led by Yasca, Colla Topa, and the litter bearing the huaca of Huanacauri. The trap had been sprung.

The men on the line moved together, opening wider gaps in their ranks to let the reinforcements pass through. The warriors came down the slope on the run, shouting and waving their weapons as they rushed toward the stricken Carangui. A contingent of Cañaris came toward the gap where Cusi and Tomay stood, and Rimachi suddenly sprinted out ahead of his men and came skidding to a halt beside them.

"Brothers!" he cried, waving his men past him. "You have brought them out for us to kill!"

"Do it," Tomay said curtly, and Cusi could only nod wearily in agreement. Rimachi grinned and raised his notched spear thrower in a hasty salute before dashing off to catch his men. The warriors continued to stream past, disappearing into the cloud of dust that obscured the battle at the base of the fort's first level. Lifting his eyes, Cusi could see flashes of gold as the Incas who had sacked the fort descended on ropes and ladders to close the trap from behind. It would be finished very soon.

When the last of the reserve warriors had gone by, some of the men on the line followed after them, but Cusi and Tomay simply sank to the ground and sat leaning against each other shoulder to shoulder. They dropped their shields and weapons and took gourds from a water bearer; the healers ignored them in favor of those unable to sit up. They watched as the battle slowly moved toward the eastern side of the valley, where the expanse of marshland had prevented the Incas from surrounding their enemy completely. Before an Inca column could come around the other side of the water, several hundred Carangui, including the red-clad Pinta, escaped into the foothills. Cusi felt Tomay move against him and realized his friend was laughing.

"Go on," Tomay said breathlessly, "it is your turn to run."

Cusi also laughed, a strange sound that gurgled in his chest and died quickly after passing his lips. But it gave him pleasure—at least as much as his aching body would permit—to realize he did not begrudge Pinta his life. He had been a worthy enemy, and Huayna Capac was the only one who would feel cheated by his escape.

The Carangui who had not escaped with him were gradually cut down or driven out into the marsh, where they floundered around in the water, begging for their lives. There were more than a thousand of them, and their pleas for mercy rose in a chorus as the Incas closed in solidly around the shallow lake. Cusi and Tomay found the strength to rise and watch as the Sapa Inca's litter was brought down to the water's edge. Huayna Capac had removed his helmet and armor and wore a fine cumbi-cloth tunic, with a golden Sun shield on his chest and the ruler's fringe around his forehead. The Carangui crouched among the reeds fell silent as he rose from his seat on the litter and looked down at them. Then he lifted his gaze in the direction of the burning fort and slowly turned until he was facing the sun, which was sinking below the rim of the western mountains. Raising both arms over his head, he called out Inti's name, an echoing invocation that was soon picked up and prolonged as a chant by the warriors, who bowed over their weapons in gratitude.

"Inti Illapa," Cusi murmured, plucking hairs from his eyebrows and blowing them off his fingertips toward the sun and the sky, paying honor to the forces that had brought him through this war alive.

When it was quiet again, Huayna Capac turned back to survey the men in the lake. He let the silence gather around him, then abruptly raised a hand and brought it down in a swift, unmistakable cutting motion. The Carangui screamed in unison, a terrible sound that was cut short by the dense cloud of darts, stones, and arrows that fell upon the marsh. The Carangui jerked and crumpled over, staining the water with their blood as they sank. When the slingers and bowmen finally stopped, apprentice warriors waded in to dispatch the survivors. Huayna Capac remained standing until there was no one left to beg him for mercy. Then he gestured to his war chiefs and sat back down, and his litter was turned and borne slowly back up the slope. Cusi and Tomay stared down at the lake filled with floating corpses, its water a lurid red in the dimming light.

"No captives," Tomay said softly. "Anywhere."

Cusi turned away and took off his helmet, still seeing the lake of blood in his mind. He picked up a water gourd and poured what was left in it over his head, letting the water run down over his face and hair, cutting channels through the dirt and dried blood that was caked on his skin. He wondered briefly if so much death could ever be washed away. Then he sat with Tomay beside him and waited for a healer to tend to their wounds.

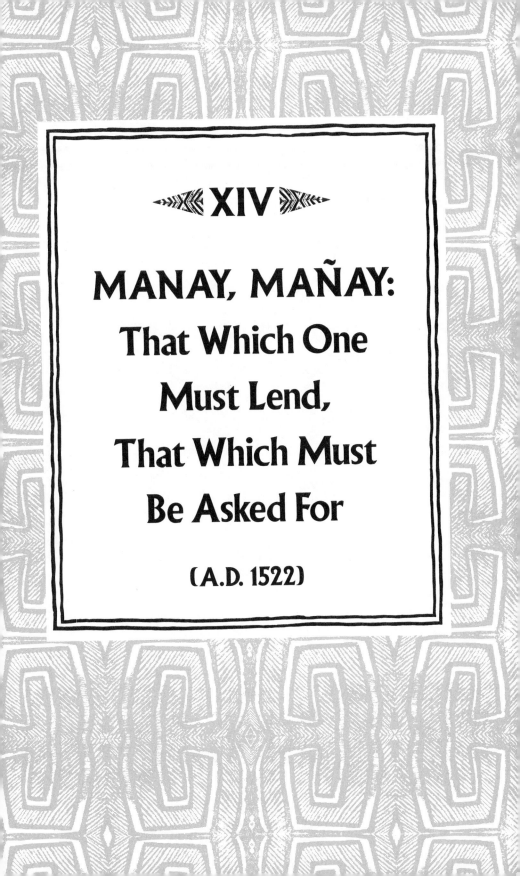

XIV

MANAY, MAÑAY: That Which One Must Lend, That Which Must Be Asked For

(A.D. 1522)

Tumibamba

CAREFUL, SINCHI," Micay cautioned, glancing up from the clump of soft wool she was separating with her fingers. The boy grinned and gave her a wobbly sidelong glance that almost cost him his balance. He was keeping himself upright by holding onto the high end of his cradle, yet he had also just discovered that he could make the cradle tip by leaning his weight on it. New as he was to standing, Micay doubted he understood the consequences of trying to do both at once, though he seemed determined to learn.

Cahua had already tired of pushing her cradle around and was standing next to the embankment of finely cut stone that surrounded the pool across from where Micay sat. The low wall came up to her shoulders, so that she could rest her arms on top of it while standing flat-footed. But she did not have the strength to pull the rest of herself up, and her arms were not long enough to let her reach the water. She looked over her shoulder at Micay and made a yearning sound.

"Yes, the water is pretty," Micay agreed, "but you have already had your bath. I will be pulling the two of you out of there soon enough."

Cahua went back to trying to boost herself up, and Micay gave her spindle a spin and let it drop down in front of her, twisting a long thread out of the clump in her hands. She was sitting on the edge of the pool with her back to the compound gate, ignoring the noise of the messengers and officials who flowed in a constant stream between the gate and the awning house at the far end of the plaza to her left. From the plaza above, she heard the women singing and talking as they plaited mats and wove cloth and drew up plans for the feasts and dances for which they were responsible. The planning for the victory celebration had begun almost ten months ago, within days of the fall of the Carangui fortress, and the preparations were now entering their final stages. It was expected that Huayna Capac would march his triumphant army back into the city before another month had passed.

The twins had been Micay's excuse for not involving herself more deeply in this task, which had come to consume the energies of most of the inhabitants of Tumibamba. Even today, they were the reason for her withdrawal, because Mama Cori had felt their presence would be too distracting to the other women. Mama Cori was totally involved in the celebration, which she and some of the other wives conceived as an opportunity to persuade Huayna Capac that it was time for the Incas to return to Cuzco. The fact that the celebration itself should by tradition have been held in Cuzco had only made them more determined in their efforts.

For her part, Micay did not share their yearning for Holy Cuzco, and if she could have found someone to accompany her, she would have taken the children to the Rainbow House long ago. She was waiting only for Cusi to return, hoping he would be given sufficient leave to allow him to go there with them. He had seen the twins twice since they were born, for a total of twenty days, and the last visit had been six months before. She had heard his regiment had returned to Quito, still without Pinta, and would wait there to join the Sapa Inca's grand procession, which was slowly coming south from the newly established border.

The twins were both resting, Cahua sitting with her back against the bank of the pool and Sinchi standing draped over his cradle with his head thrust down inside it. Micay smiled to herself, finding them beautiful in repose, their round, light-skinned faces framed by feathery black curls. Then their heads came up, almost simultaneously, and they stared past her in the direction of the gate.

"Who is it?" Micay asked without turning. "Your grandfather?"

One of the governor's green-clad assistants suddenly came around in front of her and executed a hasty bow.

"My lady, your husband is here."

Micay dropped her spindle and turned as she rose. Tomay and Uritu were coming toward her, weapons in hand but smiling in greeting. They parted so that she could see Cusi sitting up on the litter being borne in behind them, a heavily bandaged foot sticking up in front of him. He smiled at her and shrugged ruefully, pointing at the foot with his chin.

"He tried to outrun a rockslide," Tomay explained as they came up between the pools. Cusi saw Sinchi standing by his cradle and had the litter bearers lower him down a few feet away. He slid himself off the litter without assistance, extending the injured foot stiffly in front of him. Sinchi gaped at him from the other side of the cradle.

"Look at you, Sinchi," Cusi marveled. "You stand to greet me!"

Sinchi glanced at the bandaged foot, then back at Cusi's face, his mouth still open.

"Do you remember me, my son?" Cusi prompted. Sinchi cocked his head to one side and nodded so solemnly that Micay was almost persuaded he had understood the question and could indeed remember his father. Cusi laughed in delighted disbelief.

"But you were only a baby when I saw you last! You hardly left your cradle!"

Sinchi nodded more emphatically, rocking the cradle back and forth until he lost his grip and went down on his backside. Uritu let out a whoop and Tomay and Cusi both laughed. Micay came out of her shock to go to her son's aid, afraid that he might feel humiliated by the laughter. But Sinchi was grinning, as if he had made a joke, and the men rewarded him with more laughter. Micay picked him up and carried him over to Cusi, who had spotted Cahua crouching next to the pool.

"What about you, my prudent one? You are as watchful as your mother."

"She is the first one into everything," Micay assured him as she lowered Sinchi into his arms. Suddenly shy, the boy squirmed away from Cusi's kiss and looked back over his shoulder at his sister. Cahua glanced at Tomay and Uritu, who had taken seats on either side of Cusi, piling up their shields, helmets, and weapons on the ground next to them. Then she put down her head and crawled up into Cusi's lap with her brother, kneeing Cusi in the groin in the process. He winced but hugged them both to his chest, laughing with pleasure. Micay knelt down to examine the splint on his foot.

"It was a clean break," Tomay said, "and we took him to the healers of your order in Quito. The old woman who tended him said that she had taught *you* how to splint."

"Mama Ticlla," Micay guessed, finding the wrapping more than satisfactory. "It should heal well," she added. Then she caught Cusi's eye and smiled. "Though it could take a very long time."

"Ninan Cuyochi knows how much leave I am owed," Cusi said, clicking his tongue at Sinchi, who was pulling on an earplug. "He supplied the litter and sent me ahead."

"And you, my friends?" Micay asked Tomay and Uritu, who both had a hand out to keep Cusi from going over backward. Tomay snorted.

"We will take whatever leave we can get. Since we have our feet, we will probably be sent back out after Pinta once the celebration is over."

"He has fled into the land of the Shuaras," Uritu explained. "Into the low jungle."

"Let the headhunters have him," Tomay said wearily. "I am tired of chasing him."

They were interrupted by the sudden appearance of Mama Cori, who had come down the stairway behind them. Micay was impressed that she had abandoned her duties to greet her son, but then she saw she had not left them fully. If she even noticed Cusi's injury, she did not react with any distress.

"Welcome, my son. Welcome, Tomay Guanaco and Uritu. I can only take a moment to greet you, because much remains to be done before the day we celebrate your victory."

"So I see," Cusi said, glancing around at all the activity in the enclosure. "We heard that it was to be as grand a celebration as any that were ever held in Cuzco."

"As large, perhaps," Mama Cori allowed, "but not as grand. The more we plan, the more we realize that it cannot be the same as it would be in Cuzco. No other square can take the place of the Haucaypata, and nothing can substitute for the presence of the Sapa Incas and their households."

Cusi squinted at her curiously. "Surely Huayna Capac knew that to begin with. Are you saying he will be disappointed?"

"We intend to please him, but we also expect he will see what is missing. There will be reminders of Cuzco everywhere, reminders of how much richer and more complete his triumph would be if it were being celebrated there."

Growing restless with their father's inattention, the twins wriggled out of Cusi's lap and crawled around behind him. Micay moved to make sure they did not get into the weapons.

"Here, though, his triumph is his alone," Cusi said to his mother. "He does not have to share it with the households or anyone else."

Mama Cori lifted an eyebrow. "Are you speaking of yourself, my son? I have heard you have fallen in his regard."

The cool, unsparing tone of Mama Cori's voice made Micay turn to look at her, and she noticed Cusi was sitting up as straight as his outstretched leg would allow.

"I have certainly received little mention in the official reports of the battle," Cusi said stiffly, "though I was close to him through all of it."

"Closer than anyone," Tomay added.

"Still, you seem not to have won his gratitude," Mama Cori went on in the same tone. "Are you certain you wish to advise me on how to influence him?"

Cusi let out a short, incredulous laugh. "Forgive my presumption, Mother. But if I wanted to make him think about returning to Cuzco, I would not appeal to tradition. You would do better to whisper to him of dreams and portents, of visions that saw him standing in the Haucaypata again."

"What do we know of such things?" Mama Cori demanded. "We are wives, not sorcerers. Nor are you a sorcerer, my son, even though you say things that give people that impression."

"You have spoken to Lloque Yupanqui," Cusi concluded.

"I have. I will not take a side in your disagreement; that is for the two of you to settle between yourselves. But I also cannot accept your advice, when what you suggest is neither honorable nor proper. It is our aim to persuade the Sapa Inca, not to trick him. We will try to awaken the memories that are in his heart, and then we will appeal to him openly and directly. That is all we can do."

"Then do not let me keep you from your task," Cusi said, inclining his head with forced graciousness. Appearing unperturbed, Mama Cori nodded to the rest of them and went back up the stairs. In the silence that followed her departure, Micay first located Cahua, who had stopped her explorations to observe the exchange between her father and her grandmother. Sinchi, Micay saw, had gotten himself eye to eye with Uritu, standing on the man's thighs and holding onto the front of his tunic with one hand. She could see only her son's left eye, and she was struck, as she was only in the presence of people from outside the family, by the vivid red mark that surrounded it. She had not thought he was aware of it himself, despite the way strangers sometimes reacted to his appearance. But he had discovered the thin black lines tattooed on Uritu's cheeks and was staring at them with great fascination. Uritu gazed back at him impassively as the boy raised his stubby fingers toward Uritu's mouth.

"The marks of courage, Little One," Uritu told him, the words slightly muffled by Sinchi's fingers. "Like yours."

Sinchi suddenly sat down in Uritu's lap, leaning his head against the man's chest and hugging him around the middle as if he had found a friend. Uritu appeared dumfounded for a moment—the first time Micay had ever seen him show surprise—then surprised Micay by wrapping his arms around the boy and singing to him softly in Campa.

Cahua crawled over to them to listen, and Micay rose up on her knees and embraced Cusi from behind, putting her lips close to his ear.

"You deserved a better greeting than that."

Cusi sighed and leaned back against her. "I did not expect to have to defend myself so soon."

"You know how much she wants to return to Cuzco," Micay reminded him. "She has put all of herself into this effort, so she has to believe that Huayna Capac is fair and open to persuasion."

"She will be as disappointed with him as she is with me," Cusi predicted. Then he fell silent and pointed with his chin at Uritu and the twins. Uritu was still singing, looking down at the boy cradled in his lap, who was moving his mouth in a soundless imitation. Cahua had a hand on Uritu's knee and was humming her own version of the melody.

"*This* is my greeting," Cusi said softly.

Micay laid her head on his shoulder and gave him a fierce hug. "Welcome home, Cusi Huaman," she whispered. "Your presence will always be celebrated here."

TAKING A MOMENT from the task Mama Cori had given her, Micay stepped to the edge of the plaza and gazed down over the terraced side of the bluff.

The area around the pool was crowded with guests, many wrapped in cloaks against the cool, swirling wind. Cusi and the twins had moved toward the compound gate and up onto the first terrace, where they had found an empty garden plot that was sheltered on both sides by cantut bushes. The plot had been plowed up in preparation for planting, but they were putting it to a different use, building a dirt-walled enclosure big enough for all three of them to sit in. They had completed two of the walls and were working on the third, with Sinchi and Cahua fetching clods of earth that Cusi then packed into place.

Micay laughed to herself, recalling her reluctance to leave them alone with him. She had been afraid that one or the other would crawl away when Cusi was not looking and would get hurt before he could get there on his crutches. But he had abandoned his crutches somewhere and was sitting down in the dirt with them, and the twins were obviously too involved in the project to stray. Cusi was talking to them, though he did not seem to be instructing them, and neither child appeared to be paying attention. She realized that he was really talking to himself, no doubt brooding out loud.

That would not hurt them, she decided. Let them hear what it was like to be an Inca before they were old enough to have to understand for themselves. Perhaps they would be better prepared when the time came. Certainly it would not hurt Cusi to share his doubts and yearnings with these little ones, who could only heighten his hopes and give him more reason to master his anger and disappointment.

She turned back to the plaza, to the frenzy of preparation in which even she had finally had to take a part. Only two days remained until the Sapa Inca's triumphal entry into the city, and everyone who could walk had been pressed into service. Micay saw Parihuana in the awning house and went to speak to her, secure in the knowledge that Cusi and the children would be perfectly fine without her, safe within their private compound.

"WE SHOULD have gone to the Rainbow House," Cusi said, sifting a handful of dirt through his fingers. "That would truly be the way to celebrate what the end of this war means to me."

Sinchi, at that moment, was pissing vigorously on a corner of the wall, taking great interest in the damage he was doing. Cahua might have been listening, though, as she rearranged the row of stones she had set up in the center of the enclosure.

"Perhaps you have inherited my memory," he suggested aloud. "Perhaps you will remember what I am telling you now and keep it with you until you are old enough to understand the words."

Cahua grunted eagerly and crawled off after another stone; Sinchi had begun to plaster the wall with wet mud. Cusi snorted softly, a sound they also ignored.

"Or perhaps you will learn to forget instead. To carry your memories like a burden that does not belong to you."

"Cusi," a voice called from close behind him, "what are you teaching those children? Those walls are uneven."

This time Cusi had no trouble identifying the voice, and he saw recognition on the twins' faces, as well, before he turned to greet his brother—and found him standing at the retaining wall with Otoronco Achachi beside him.

"I met the lord governor at the Mollecancha gate and offered to lead him here," Amaru explained, grinning at Cusi's surprise. Otoronco lifted one bushy eyebrow, the one split by a scar.

"So, is this where your fame has brought you, Cusi Huaman? Commanding the nursery garrison?"

Amaru laughed and hoisted himself up onto the terrace, sitting down outside the compound walls. The twins stared at Otoronco with unconcealed wariness, then went to Amaru, who had already begun to reshape the wall. Cusi lifted his bandaged foot, then the rest of his body, up over the low ridge of dirt.

"Grandfather . . . welcome. These are my children."

"They seem healthy enough," Otoronco observed, showing no inclination to join them on the terrace. The ten years since Cusi had seen him had grayed his hair and added wrinkles to the scars on his face and body, and some of his bulk seemed to have descended toward his waist. But his eyes were sharp and his presence was as formidable as ever. He jerked his chin at Cusi's foot.

"Is that why I heard so little about you in the reports of the victory?"

"This came afterward, chasing Pinta," Cusi said. "I was there, in the final battle. There are those who can attest to that, even if others will not."

"Quilaco would," Amaru said, glancing up from his work. "He told me how you came to his rescue."

"There are others, as well, though Huayna Capac is not among them. It seems I have had my share of fame and favor."

"You used what you had," Otoronco told him, with an embarrassed grimace that Cusi remembered was his way of displaying gratitude. "You fulfilled your promise."

"It was only what I owed you."

"Others owed me more. You did what they would not even attempt, and I will not forget it, Cusi. You cannot know what Cuzco was like after all of you left. A city of old men and count takers, and women no one could touch! Worse than a prison . . ."

"Holy Cuzco," Amaru murmured mockingly. Otoronco grunted but did not correct him.

"How have you found Chachapoyas?" Cusi asked.

"Much too quiet and orderly, and I have only made it more so. It helped to know what you had the Callaway healer tell me, and I have an excellent micho, your father's man. But still, the people are alive there; they do more than count on cords and prepare for the next ceremony. But you know that," Otoronco laughed. "You married one, did you not?"

"What are you doing?" Amaru cried suddenly, and Cahua and Sinchi burst

into a chorus of conspiratorial giggles. They were systematically destroying the
section of wall Amaru had just finished, and his show of distress only goaded
them to a greater effort. A clod of dirt flew backward out of Sinchi's hand and
sailed past Otoronco's head.

"That is why the Incas always build in stone," the old man said dryly. When
Cahua laughed and dumped a pile of dirt in Amaru's lap, he gave up and joined
in the destruction, muttering to himself.

"I was told to build far away . . ."

"Has someone seen to your people?" Cusi asked Otoronco, remembering his
manners. Otoronco nodded.

"I only brought a few with me. I did not have to be told to come here
quietly."

"My father will come to greet you as soon as he is free."

"You are the one I wanted to see," Otoronco said. "Even in Chachapoyas,
I heard about you. They showed me the trail behind the fort, the place where
you jumped. You must tell me about it later, when I can drink to your
courage—your huaca."

"I will take him to the guest house," Amaru offered, dusting himself off and
giving each of the children a parting poke. "We should have set you on the
Carangui fort," he told them. "You would have demolished it by yourselves."

The twins squawked halfheartedly at his desertion, then crawled toward
Cusi, plowing right through the wall behind him. Cusi opened his arms and
welcomed them into his lap.

"Your great-grandchildren, my lord," Cusi said. Otoronco cupped his chin
with one hand and shook his head in bemusement.

"I have lived too long," he murmured gruffly, and he turned to let Amaru
lead him away.

TWO HIGH-BACKED chairs, richly decorated in red and gold, stood on the great
stone dais in the center of the square. The Coya Rahua Ocllo sat alone in one
of them, facing the place where the road from the north came into the square.
Surrounding the dais, in ranks six deep, were the other members of the royal
family, the high priests and mamacona, the provincial governors and their
wives, and the most important of the foreign guests. They were surrounded in
turn by a large open space meant for the warriors, then by a solid ring of
spectators, packed ten deep around the perimeter of the square. Those without
the rank to merit a place in the square filled the nearby streets or sat atop the
walls of the palace or the peaks of the house roofs. Every high place in the city
held its crowd of onlookers.

The arrival of the Sapa Inca was heralded by the sound of drums and
singing. A group of retainers in blue livery came into the square first, ritually
sweeping the ground and scattering flower petals in the ruler's path. Behind
them came the Inca war god Huanacauri, his litter piled high with the banners
and insignia of the defeated Carangui, and the huaca itself wrapped in a feather

cape. A conch horn blew, and everyone in the square and all those watching, from whatever distance, bowed and raised their fingers to their lips, making the mocha as Huayna Capac was carried in, seated on his litter and flanked on both sides by a double file of the Inca Old Guard. The column of warriors behind him was singing a victory song, a deep, repetitive chant punctuated by shouts and a rhythmic stamping of feet.

Huanacauri was brought directly to the Coricancha, his litter carried up the broad steps by six high-ranking warriors, all brothers or cousins of the ruler. They passed close to where Micay and the other healers of her order stood, a place of honor earned by their service in the war. Huayna Capac dismounted from his litter and climbed the stairs alone, appearing oblivious of the people bowing to him on both sides. His eyes were shrouded by the royal fringe, and his golden earplugs and arm bands and Sun shield cast arcs of brilliant light in all directions. The high priest and high priestess stood waiting at the Coricancha gate, and the three of them paused for a moment on the threshold, then turned and entered together.

Keeping her head bowed, Micay gazed back down the stairs to the square. The warriors were still streaming in, rapidly filling the space that had been left vacant for them. She could no longer see Cusi, who had been waiting for his regiment with Amaru and Quilaco and some of the other wounded. They had been swallowed up by the thickening mass of warriors, who carried weapons and banners and wore garlands of flowers around their necks. The singing and drumming continued until Huayna Capac reappeared. He came through the gate with the high priest and Chimpu Ocllo behind him, and all those lining the steps knelt as they had been told to do beforehand. Huayna Capac raised both arms over his head as the square fell silent.

"Inti, our father!" he cried, looking skyward. "Inti Illapa! Inti Viracocha! Victory is ours!"

As soon as he lowered his arms, the warriors took up the chant, adding Huayna Capac's name and shouting louder and louder. Then the standing spectators joined in, and those on the walls and roofs, producing a booming, echoing din that seemed to make the sky quiver overhead. As the Sapa Inca went past her down the steps, Micay rose to her feet and called out the names of Mama Quilla and Illapa, feeling the sounds in her throat but unable to hear herself at all. There was a kind of delirium around her, people swaying and tossing their heads and appearing to howl, some laughing and some weeping. Micay found herself bellowing incoherently, releasing all the pain and frustration of the last ten years, of month after month of waiting and worrying and watching the men being brought in maimed and dying, of seeing them die beneath her hands, and seeing Cusi twitch and moan in his sleep, reliving the killing and the fear. An end to that was surely what victory meant.

Huayna Capac had reascended his litter and was being carried in a circle around the dais, receiving a salute from each of the regiments he passed. Micay wondered what Cusi was feeling at this moment; whether he was standing silent on his crutches or shouting with the rest. Tomay and his other comrades—those who knew what he had done—would be around him, and perhaps they would make him share their pride in having lived to see this day. Huayna Capac could not deny him that.

The litter had disappeared behind the dais, and Micay knew the Sapa Inca would soon climb to the top of the platform, where he would be greeted and embraced by the Coya, his sister and consort. Then there would be prayers and offerings and speeches, and the singing of the story songs of the victory. It would be a long day, and then there would be the first of the feasts and dances, which would go on for another nine days. Gifts and honors would be distributed, and there would be ceremonial gatherings of the cults and the households, and less solemn reunions of families and friends. And marriages: Rimachi with Llampu, and Amaru with Parihuana, if Amaru's stated intention could be trusted.

The shouting continued all around her, but she no longer felt overwhelmed by it or compelled to add her voice to the din. The war was finally over, and now they could begin to heal their wounds and make themselves whole again. Now they could attend to the affairs of life, not death. Perhaps even Cusi will be able to take satisfaction in that, she thought, once the name of Huayna Capac stops echoing in his ears.

AT THE Sapa Inca's feast, the commanders and captains who had distinguished themselves in the fighting were rewarded with purapura—strings of small gold discs to be worn around the neck as proof of their valor. Supported by his crutches, Cusi stood in the line and received his from Ninan Cuyochi, who whispered, as he placed the jingling strand around Cusi's neck, that no warrior deserved the honor more. Afterward, though, he was not summoned out of the crowd in the Coya's courtyard for a royal toast, as were Quilaco, Quizquiz, and Challcochima. Nor did any of the war chiefs seek him out to deliver one on the ruler's behalf. Yasca came twice, to salute Rimachi and then Uritu, and Michi brought a cup to Tomay, along with the ruler's promised gift of forty alpacas from the Carangui herds.

"At least my disfavor has not spread to them," Cusi murmured to Micay as they watched Tomay and Michi drink to each other.

"Yasca had a word for you, as well," Micay pointed out, and he nodded agreeably.

"He stood with me in the square the last time, when we let our silence speak for us. I am content to be silent now."

"I see that, and I am proud. It is the only response to his pettiness."

Cusi leaned sideways to press his lips against her cheek, wishing his arms were free. She had been more than a comrade to him during these past days, listening to his arguments and complaints with sympathy and attention, yet leaving their resolution to him. She had made it possible for him to accept what he had lost, and to understand that it had no value.

He looked up to find himself confronted by a delegation that included Ninan

Cuyochi, Challcochima, and Quizquiz, with Tomay lending encouragement from the side. Each of the three men had a pair of drinking cups in his hands, and Micay stepped aside with a parting smile and let them surround Cusi. Ninan's toast was solemn and heartfelt, an elaboration on the words he had whispered earlier. Cusi hung on his crutches and took the cup with his right hand from Ninan's right hand, the hand of equals. The akha was cool and foamy and slid down his throat before he tasted the slight tang of molle berries. Micay unobtrusively reached in and removed the cup from his hand, so that Challcochima could present him with another. The tall warrior thought for a moment, then shrugged and made no attempt to emulate Ninan's formal manner.

"We cannot change what is in the story songs," he said as he held out a cup. "But we will not leave you out of *our* stories."

Cusi drank again, though he did not try to drain the cup as Challcochima did. Quizquiz barely waited for Micay to relieve him of the cup before extending a third. He spoke with characteristic brevity, nodding his head for emphasis.

"You made him run. I will not forget."

After drinking a third time, Cusi thanked them in a voice that sounded surprisingly calm to his own ears. He was moved by their reassurances, yet he was past needing them. Some part of him had decided he could live without praise or recognition.

Ninan lingered after the other two had departed. He cast a significant glance at the half-empty cup in Cusi's hand.

"You drink with restraint."

"These crutches were not made for a drunk," Cusi said lightly. "I do not wish to fall on my face."

"A warrior who is bitter and angry is prone to accidents," Ninan persisted.

"Do you mean here, or in the field?"

"Both."

"I will not forget to watch my back, or my tongue."

"But you will keep your bitterness inside," Ninan said sadly. "It will poison your spirit, Cusi, and make you cold to everyone."

"Not everyone," Cusi disagreed. "Not to those who matter. Like yourself, my lord. *You* I would always serve without hesitation, and with my whole heart."

Ninan took a drink and studied him over the rim of his cup, no doubt considering who it was that did not matter. He seemed thoughtful rather than troubled, though.

"If my father—if the court returns to Cuzco, would you be willing to remain here?"

"I have thought about it," Cusi admitted. "Have you decided that for yourself?"

Ninan spread his hands in a kind of shrug. "There is already an Heir in Cuzco. But my father would need someone here whom he could trust."

Cusi tried not to seem surprised, though this was the first time Ninan had ever revealed anything like personal ambition. He had always thought him too loyal and obedient for this kind of calculation.

"What if he does not go back?" Cusi asked.

"You think he will not?"

"Not soon. Not unless the wives go stand in the square."

Ninan gave him a rare, sardonic smile. "Perhaps they will. There are too many of us to stay here forever. But consider the possibility that you might be one who does. That is all I would ask of you now,"

"I will," Cusi promised, and they briefly raised their cups to each other. Ninan stepped back and gestured for Micay to join them.

"I will leave you to enjoy the feast. I should tell you, though, that Otoronco Achachi spoke to me earlier. He wants to help me capture Pinta."

Cusi laughed at his grandfather's boldness; *there* was someone who could teach Ninan about ambition. "He has dealt with the Shuaras, at least those on the borders of Chachapoyas."

"But how can I ask such a man to serve beneath me?" Ninan asked. "Even if he claims to be willing?"

"Believe him," Cusi advised. "He does not want the glory, only the chance to fight again. You will not be sorry."

"I will ask for him, then. My lady," he said, inclining his head to Micay as he left them. Micay leaned forward and emptied one of her cups into the cup Cusi held, laughing when some of the foamy liquid spilled over the top.

"I did not think you would be left to go thirsty," she said. He could only nod and lift his cup for an unrestrained drink.

CAHUA HAD one hand coiled among the shell beads around Micay's neck, the other on her mother's shoulder. She was watching the ceremony intently, her head cocked to one side to hear Micay's whispered description of what they were seeing. Talking to her was the only way to keep her still for long, Micay had discovered. Even if she could not understand all the words, she seemed to know that they applied to what was happening in front of her, and that making the match was a kind of participation in the event.

"Now your Uncle Amaru is giving Parihuana a pair of sandals. Look, he is kneeling to put them onto her feet . . ."

Micay glanced sideways at her son, who had a similar perch in the arms of Urcon. Sinchi was simply rapt. He would sit and stare all day if the scene were sufficiently interesting and his sister did not distract him. He especially liked to watch people, so he had been no trouble at all during all the recent ceremonies and gatherings.

"Now it is her turn to give him sandals . . . oh look, Cahua, he will not let her kneel. He is tying them on himself."

Micay heard murmurs of approval from the guests standing behind her, a recognition of the tenderness of Amaru's gesture. Cusi glanced at her over

Cahua's head, and she saw that he was impressed, too. Given the nature of this marriage and the apparent abruptness of Amaru's decision to go through with it, they had both been afraid the ceremony would be a perfunctory affair. Instead, Amaru seemed intent on making it a thing of beauty.

"The mantles are the last of the gifts," Micay whispered to her daughter. "See how they drape them over each other's shoulders, promising each other warmth and protection. Ah, it is a Chimu mantle he has given her. Chimu," she repeated, when Cahua grunted quizzically at the strange word. Amaru himself was wearing a tunic of Chimu design, a blue cotton garment with a pattern of stepped waves in red. He was relaxed and smiling, looking much younger than his thirty years, so that Micay recalled the effect his smile had had upon her when she was Parihuana's age.

"Look, now your grandfather is tying the ends of their mantles together and joining their hands. It is almost over . . . listen to what your grandfather is saying . . ."

Speaking as the governor, Apu Poma admonished the couple to support and care for each other, to raise their children properly, and to be equals in courage, wisdom, and generosity. With their hands around the knot that bound them together, Amaru and Parihuana bowed to him in gratitude and then embraced as husband and wife.

"Now they are married," Micay said, and Uritu let out a whoop that broke the silence and made everyone laugh. As the guests began to crowd in around the wedding pair, offering gifts and congratulations, Micay turned to Cusi, who was leaning on a single crutch.

"Go ahead," he suggested, indicating his unwillingness to risk his foot in the crowd. "Give this to them for me."

He held out a small stone figurine, a conopa meant to bring prosperity and good fortune to the household of its owner. It was a brown frog with white water symbols painted on its back, one of the frogs that croaked to welcome Illapa's rain. Micay let Cahua take it from him, but she made sure her daughter knew it was not hers.

"It is a gift, Cahua. A gift you must give to your uncle and aunt."

Micay glanced at Urcon, who gave her a brilliant smile and went forward with her, knowing Sinchi would want to go wherever his sister did. Behind her she could hear Cusi speaking aloud to himself, his voice lightened by a wonder he could not seem to assimilate.

"Now they are married . . ."

THE CONVERSATION began innocently enough, with Apu Poma asking Rimachi about his decision to accept a captaincy in the Royal Guard. Rimachi was sitting next to his bride of two days, Llampu, a tall, graceful young woman with olive skin and bright, expressive eyes, and he gave her a fond glance before he replied.

"I have sacrificed some rank, I know," he told Apu Poma, "but like my friend Amaru, I want to live a while in my own compound. I have been away from Tumibamba long enough, and it is time to give my parents some grand-children."

Llampu darkened and lowered her eyes with an embarrassed smile, and Cusi saw Amaru acknowledge Rimachi's reference to him with an equally friendly nod. But Mama Cori interrupted before her husband could respond.

"But you would return to Cuzco with the Sapa Inca, would you not?"

Rimachi hesitated, no doubt feeling how the whole circle had come to attention, pulled out of their private conversations by the pointed nature of the question. Only the children remained oblivious, playing with the food in front of them.

"I could be sent back at any time, my lady," Rimachi said, "to relieve those who guard Huascar. But my father has assured me that that is not likely very soon."

"Your father expects to remain here?" Mama Cori persisted.

Rimachi spread his hands in a conciliatory gesture, aware of her reason for asking. "He has not spoken of leaving, my lady. No one in the Royal Guard has, at least not in my presence."

"Do they not repeat to you what the Sapa Inca says? I have heard that he has complained about the crowding of the guests."

"I have not heard that," Rimachi said. "I have only heard that he was not pleased with the quality of some of the delegations sent to honor him. Puna sent no one, and the Huancavelicas seemed to think the usual ambassadors would be sufficient. I suspect they will both receive a delegation of warriors in return."

Mama Cori did not reveal her disappointment, but she also chose not to press him any further. Cusi stared at her from the other side of the circle, feeling no sympathy for her but no desire to gloat, either. Then the implications of what Rimachi had said sank in, and he realized how Huayna Capac was going to resolve the problem of staying here peacefully. It was so simple that Cusi chastised himself for not seeing it sooner. If it was troublesome to keep the warriors here with him, he could send them somewhere else. All he needed was an excuse, a reason to punish someone.

Cusi glanced around the circle and saw a similar apprehension on a number of faces, especially those of the warriors. He felt an urge to say it aloud, to share the sudden fear it awakened in him, a fear he had not reckoned with before this. He wanted to tell them that *he* also wished to live in his own compound for a while. But then he saw his mother's face and that of Lloque beside her, equally impassive, and he could not bring himself to speak. He kept his silence, feeling that they deserved no more warnings from him; that they deserved, finally, whatever rewards their respect for Huayna Capac brought them.

"AS YOU KNOW, your friend Acapana arrived there well ahead of me," Oto-ronco said, leaning his shoulder against the support pole and gazing out at the rain falling on the deserted plaza. "He sent messages repeating the amnesty, specifically calling on your father to surrender."

Micay cast a last glance back into the awning house and saw the twins were playing with Quinti's two daughters, the four of them surrounded by a loose circle of adults. So she gave Otoronco her full attention.

"Was there any reply?"

"A number of those who had been with Casca came down out of the hills and were allowed to return to their villages. When more time passed and it could be seen that no revenge had been taken against those who had surrendered, even more came out of hiding. But not Casca."

Otoronco paused to drink from his cup before going on.

"When I arrived in Caxamarca, I was met by the Callawaya, Cusi's friend. He repeated the things Cusi had told him to say, about how the rebellion had been provoked and how the Chachapoyas deserved to be treated with kindness. He made a special plea that I find your father and restore him to good standing.

"At that point, given what Cusi had done for me," Otoronco added with a smile, "I was quite ready to trust his judgment and do what I could for him. So I was a stern but forgiving inspector, and I sent both messages and gifts to the few rebels still in the mountains. Then I made my tour of the province, and I went to Suta and inquired for myself. Two of his wives were there, but they would not speak to me about him, out of loyalty. The other people spoke of Casca with both affection and regret, because they admired him but did not expect him to return. He had vowed that he would never bow to the Inca again, and they said he had taken refuge among the Shuaras. When I mentioned your name, they told me your mother was with him."

"Did they remember me?" Micay asked wistfully.

"Oh, yes. They called you Misa. One old woman even dared to tell me that you had been wrongfully taken as a chosen woman. They seemed impressed when I told them that you were to be the wife of Cusi Huaman, the man who had captured their fort. I did not actually know that then, but I assumed it from what the Callawaya had told me."

"I doubt my father would be impressed," Micay murmured. "Is that the last of what you heard?"

"I told you, I felt I owed Cusi for my escape from Cuzco. So I sent delegations to the Shuaras, with gifts for their chiefs and assurances that I meant them no harm. But they are a fierce and independent people and very suspicious of outsiders, especially Incas. My men heard rumors of a small band of Chachapoyas, but it was always the next village that might know, and every inquiry seemed to push them farther out of reach. Either your father is determined not to be found or the Shuaras do not wish him to be found. Certainly they do not want anyone entering their territory to look for him. That is all I can tell you."

"I am grateful, Grandfather," Micay told him. "You have done more than anyone could ask of you."

"I intend to do more, at least for Cusi," Otoronco began. But then he raised his head and fell silent as Lloque Yupanqui came up to join them.

"My lord," he said, bowing his head to Otoronco. "Forgive my interruption, but I have been summoned back to the palace, and I did not wish to leave without conveying a message to Micay."

Otoronco leaned back against the pole and gestured for Lloque to speak, not offering him any of the privacy he might have expected. Lloque hesitated for only a moment, though, before proceeding with his message.

"The Vicaquirao priests have spoken to me about the rituals you have requested for your son. Some of them have reservations about Cusi's reputation, but they are all agreed that the signs of this child's affinity for Illapa are unmistakable. So . . . with my recommendation, they will do what you ask."

Micay bowed in gratitude, but before she could frame a reply, Otoronco spoke up in a tone that was mild yet carried a hint of challenge.

"What is wrong with Cusi's reputation? He is known as a hero in Chachapoyas, and surely he has proven his courage and loyalty many times since."

Otoronco was still propped against the pole, his arms crossed, the painted cup curled in one hand against his chest. Lloque acknowledged his contention with a polite nod.

"His courage is not in question, my lord. But there are serious doubts about his character."

"Envy," Otoronco suggested.

"No, my lord. I am afraid I share these doubts myself. I have seen him display an arrogance and disrespect that borders on treason. Worse, he has admitted his willingness to intimidate and influence other men against their will, by means more suitable to a sorcerer than a warrior."

Otoronco slowly straightened up, pushing himself away from the pole without using his hands. Micay felt suddenly small beside him, and she saw Lloque blink in bemusement, as if he had been stricken by the same sensation. He was half a hand taller than Otoronco, yet the old man seemed to talk down to him.

"When I was as young as Cusi, in the time of Pachacuti, no one bowed to us simply because we wore the earplugs. We had to display an unwavering arrogance, because anyone we could not influence or intimidate, we had to fight. We have fewer enemies now, but still, in the places that do not accept our rule, it is no different today."

"Perhaps not," Lloque allowed. "But Cusi has shown that arrogance here and in Quito, not in the lands of our enemies."

"Has he no enemies here?" Otoronco inquired, gesturing broadly with the cup in his hand. "What about those who attack his reputation and spread rumors about him? What about those who envy his huaca and deny him the praise he has earned?"

"He has acted arrogantly toward *me,* my lord," Lloque pointed out. "Surely you do not count me among these enemies?"

Otoronco simply stared at him in silence, an insult that made Lloque stiffen in surprise.

"You do me an injustice, Lord Governor . . ."

"I think not, Lord Rememberer. Were you not one of those who composed the story songs of the final battle?"

"I was."

"Then you know that Cusi was among those who fought beside Huayna Capac at the head of the attack. That much was sung. But did you not find it strange that he earned no recognition for himself, when all around him his comrades and initiation brothers were fighting with distinction? He was not wounded. Was he hiding? What did you think when he disappeared from the telling?"

"I cannot discuss how the songs are composed," Lloque said sternly, "as you know."

"I have participated in such things in the past," Otoronco told him. "I know how it is done. I know that many brave men must go unrecognized, and that only the most worthy will have their names sung aloud. But did no one ask the name of the warrior who pretended to fight with Huayna Capac? Surely he played an important part in luring the Carangui out of their fortress."

"He was a common warrior," Lloque said reluctantly, frowning at the need for such revelation. "Several names were suggested, but no one was sure. It is believed he was lost during the retreat."

Otoronco gave him a hard, prolonged stare, as if again counting him among Cusi's enemies.

"He was cast off, not lost. And he is a most uncommon warrior, as Huayna Capac knows. As his own *uncle* should surely know . . ."

Lloque blinked several times and then went still, his hand raised in a gesture he could not complete. One by one, the implications of Otoronco's statement flared up in his eyes, each leaving him dimmer as it faded. He glanced once at Micay, who could only nod in confirmation. Then he seemed to droop, hanging his head as the sound of rain on the slanted roof overhead filled the silence.

"I have heard you, my lord," he said hoarsely, making no attempt to meet Otoronco's unsparing gaze. Then he turned and walked out across the rain-swept plaza. Otoronco watched him go, then seemed to relent physically, releasing the powerful outward pressure of his presence. Micay swayed on her feet, as if she had been leaning into a wind that had suddenly died.

"I must have more to drink," he announced. He glanced sideways at Micay, betraying a trace of misgiving. "Someone must say these things, since Cusi will not speak for himself."

"He cannot," Micay said. Impulsively she took his arm. "But no one could have spoken more forcefully on his behalf. He will be grateful, Grandfather."

Otoronco snorted derisively, but he smiled and kept her on his arm as he turned back into the awning house.

"I only say what is true," he scoffed, "and there are few enough I can make hear me . . ."

AT THE CONCLUSION of the feast, Amaru and Parihuana again tied the ends of their mantles together, and the family and guests escorted them to Apu Poma's house, singing a marriage song and carrying torches to light their way. Cusi limped along on his crutch next to Micay, feeling a lingering amazement at the fact that he was singing this song for his brother. Perhaps it was the Chimu garments they were wearing, which reminded him of an Amaru who had believed in nothing and been responsible to no one. And Parihuana, from the rear, appeared as slender and hipless as Fempellec, a resemblance Cusi thought might be fortunate, even though it made him uneasy.

He wanted to ask Micay what she thought, but the group had come to a halt in front of Apu Poma's house and Amaru had turned in the doorway to address them. He thanked his father for the loan of his house, his mother for the fine feast, and his family and friends for their gifts, including the gift of their company. Cusi listened with growing skepticism, finding the speech a bit too traditional and his brother's manner a bit too polished. But then Amaru stopped and looked into their faces, his lips curling upward in a familiar, taunting smile.

"Many of you thought you would never see this day," he said with good-humored bluntness. "You thought you could always count on me to evade what was good for me. I cannot blame you for that, but from now on you can direct your concern toward other things. Look to what is serious in your own hearts."

Cusi was the first to laugh at this astonishing pronouncement. Then his initiation brothers and Quilaco joined in, shaking their torches in a salute. Some of the older family members simply shook their heads. Amaru smiled down at Parihuana, as if sharing the joke with her, and then the two of them disappeared through the doorway, letting the cloth curtain fall back in place behind them. Those outside quietly said their farewells and began to disperse, leaving the retainers to clean up in the awning house. Cusi saw his brothers off and was about to start after them when Micay restrained him with a light tug on his free arm. He realized they were alone in the plaza, hidden by darkness now that the torches were gone.

"Runtu Caya is with the children," she reminded him, coming up close. "And I would guess the bathhouse is empty . . ."

Cusi immediately turned about on his crutch, then laughed and pulled her to him with one arm, smelling the sweet scent of her hair.

"Do you think that they . . . that Amaru . . . ?"

"We must not stay here to listen," Micay scolded, and started them moving toward the bathhouse, which lay in the deep shadows beyond the governor's house. "Besides, Parihuana knows what to do if Amaru is hesitant."

"You have made her so bold?" Cusi teased.

"I have done my best," Micay said proudly. "Actually, Amaru himself has—oh!"

She grabbed Cusi's arm so forcefully that he was almost pulled off balance, and he came down hard on his tender foot in the attempt to right himself. But he did not feel any pain until the alarm had passed through him like a cold, prickly fire. Then he was able to recognize the person facing them in the darkness.

"Fempellec," he managed. "You are welcome here; you do not have to hide in the shadows."

Fempellec laughed harshly and came closer, his teeth bared in a mirthless smile.

"Should I sit outside his house like a boy once did in Chan Chan?"

"You could have come to the ceremony," Micay said softly. "You knew that this had to happen, Fempellec."

"That is what *he* said. But I have seen him with her, and I heard him just now. He says he knows what is good for him. He has decided that I am not."

The pain in Cusi's foot made him want to agree, but he felt more than saw Micay's warning glance and kept silent. She had never lost her sense of responsibility for Fempellec, even after he had attached himself to Mama Huarcay.

"Has he been unkind to you?" she asked.

Fempellec gave the same harsh laugh. "He does not think so. He invited me to visit him—to visit *them*—when I am in Quito. As if I could share his respectability . . ."

"You are respected for your own accomplishments. Why not believe that Amaru offers you his friendship? Why not accept what he can give you?"

"Even if it is nothing?" Fempellec said sarcastically. "That is usually what the Incas offer—generous words and an empty hand. A hand that knows only how to take."

"You know better," Micay admonished him. "You know that Amaru is not that kind of Inca. He learned not to be in Chan Chan. That is why he wore a Chimu garment on his wedding day and gave one to his bride. He remembers what he learned when he was with you; why will you not learn from him?"

Fempellec blew air through his nose and shifted his feet, but he did not reply immediately. Cusi received another warning glance from Micay, who had obviously sensed his growing impatience. He held himself still, though he had a strong urge to give Fempellec a shake and remind him that he had been chief of nothing in Chan Chan.

"You always know what to say to me, Micay," Fempellec muttered, "to make it sound like there is reason to hope. Then I go back and I am alone again, and I wonder what made me believe you."

"You are not the first or only one to be left alone," Micay reminded him. "I was alone in Quito, but you never came to visit me. You do not have to tell Mama Huarcay that I am the one you are going to see."

"I do not have to tell her anything," Fempellec declared, the sullen whine gone from his voice. Micay nodded in approval.

"Then I will expect you to visit."

Fempellec cast a swift glance at Cusi, as if expecting some objection. Then he threw up his hands in a helpless gesture, nodded to Micay, and disappeared into the darkness, heading for the steep back stairs.

"You are kind to him," Cusi said. "Perhaps kinder than he deserves."

"I understand his loneliness," she said quietly.

Cusi put his arm around her shoulders, feeling an ache well up in his chest. "I have left you alone too much. And I am afraid I will be sent away again once I am healed."

Micay gave a small shudder and hugged him around the waist, speaking with her mouth close to his ear.

"I heard what Rimachi said. But there is time for us to think and plan . . . I will not release you until you are fully healed."

Despite the ache, Cusi managed to smile.

"Perhaps a bath would be beneficial . . ."

"A long, slow bath," Micay agreed, and she led him limping into the shadows.

The Rainbow House

CUSI CHOSE the path that passed the shrine almost without thinking, because it was firm and level and easier on his foot. He walked along it with his head down and his ears closed to what few sounds there were, the loudest being the steady tap of his staff. His eyes were on the ground and the placement of his staff, but he did not really see them. In his mind he saw a garrison outpost in some remote territory, a cold, mountainous place near a copper mine, a village of crude huts without streets or compound walls, where the only stone house belonged to the Inca commander. Where no one spoke Quechua except to him, and then badly. He saw himself with Micay and the twins, huddled in blankets around a sputtering fire, while outside the wind shrieked across the barren ground and mitmac warriors stood guard at the gate. They would be together but homeless, which might in fact be worse than being fatherless.

Gray suddenly flashed in front of him, a glimpse of an angry face and hands raised against him, a threat that put him into a fighting stance with the staff thrust out in front of him like a spear. His attackers stopped short and he saw that they were old women, two of them, both wearing the light gray shifts of the mamacona. His swift reaction had frightened them, but already outrage was back in their faces, and a glance beyond them showed him the reason why. A third woman stood with her back to him in front of a shrine, a deep niche hollowed out of the rock face that flanked the trail. She was tall and her shift shimmered with threads of real silver, and he did not have to see her face to know he had stumbled upon the high priestess herself.

He immediately lowered his staff and bowed in apology to the mamacona, who did not seem at all mollified. Cusi could not blame them, since he knew how close he had come to striking out at them, and they must have felt his intention. They advanced on him and he began to back away, finding the movement awkward and hoping his foot would not cause him to stumble. Then the high priestess spoke without turning to look.

"Cusi Huaman . . . come forward."

The angry faces of the mamacona suddenly went blank, and they parted to let him approach the shrine. He stopped beside Chimpu Ocllo, who was taller than he was even with her head bowed. But she did not radiate the magnificent calm he remembered from her appearance in the square. To his surprise, her presence vibrated with an urgency that seemed to seize his attention and hold it tightly, avidly, as if to know everything that was in his heart. He resisted instinctively, putting his free hand over the spirit brother in his waistband and hardening himself against her. Chimpu Ocllo gave a small sigh and nodded in recognition.

"You must make an offering," she commanded. "You must ask Mama Quilla to forgive your intrusion."

Cusi remembered the coca bag under his arm and removed a handful of the fresh-ground coca Uritu had recently given him. For you, my mother, he prayed, silently begging the Moon Mother's forgiveness as he stepped forward and deposited the powder inside the niche, where there were already offerings of maize and cloth and feathers. He stepped back and made the mocha with one hand, fluttering his fingers in front of his lips. The prayer had softened him, but he no longer felt the pressure of Chimpu Ocllo's presence. She completed her own prayer and gestured to him with her chin, and the two of them backed away from the shrine with their heads bowed. Then she turned and led him a short distance up the path before stopping to face him. The mamacona waited farther up the path, out of hearing.

"I have wanted to speak to you for some time, my son—since you stood with Huanacauri in the square and stared at me so boldly. What has brought you to me today?"

The expectation in her voice made Cusi hesitate, remembering another ceremony he had interrupted, and his first meeting with Raurau Illa. He swallowed and spoke truthfully, though he knew she would find his answer inadequate.

"I was not watching where I walked, Mamanchic. I allowed my injury to choose the path."

Chimpu Ocllo did not conceal her skepticism, which bordered on scorn. "A commander of scouts who does not watch where he walks? What could possibly occupy your attention to such an extent?"

"I was thinking of the future, Mamanchic, of where I might be sent once I am fully healed."

"So you wandered here by accident, thinking only of yourself?" the priestess demanded incredulously, and threw back her head to look at the sky. "Surely I am being mocked!"

Cusi realized that she was not accusing *him* of mockery, but still he felt belittled by her tone. And when she looked back at him, down at him, her urgency seemed to shake him roughly by the shoulders. He drew himself up deliberately, emulating his spirit brother and resisting her with calmness rather than force.

"You are seeking a sign, my mother?" he asked quietly. "A message?"

Chimpu Ocllo drew back slightly, studying his face with renewed respect. "Yes, of course you would know about such things. I have heard, Cusi, that you have been to the place of visions. That you saw danger ahead for us."

"I was warned of it," he acknowledged. "I was told of an enemy greater than all others, one who would bring the pacha puchucay, the end of our world. My brother was given a similar warning at Pachacamac."

"Who could this enemy be?"

"I do not know, my mother. I was not shown that."

"So you have simply put your knowledge aside? How could you know such a thing and not be obsessed with it? How could you think instead of what your place will be?"

"I have carried this knowledge for many years," Cusi retorted. "Am I to blame because it has only just come to you?"

They faced each other in anger for a moment, Cusi struggling to regain the calm he had lost yet unwilling to bow to her. Then Chimpu Ocllo blinked and seemed to remember herself, looking around at the place where they stood with a kind of wonder. She shook her head as if to clear it.

"Forgive me, Cusi. I have no right to scold you. I have felt the danger in my dreams, but I have not seen its cause. I see our people dying, but not the enemy who strikes them down."

"I did not mean to defy you, Mamanchic," Cusi assured her. "I feel the weight of my knowledge, but I can only carry it in silence. I have no voice in the court, as you must know, and I do not expect to be consulted about our future."

"When I saw you in the square," Chimpu Ocllo said wistfully, "I felt you would do anything for your people."

"That was your doing, my mother. You had great huaca that day."

"And today? No, you do not have to tell me; I know how impatient I have been. Perhaps your coming here was a message, a sign of how desperate I have become. You are one of the few who can resist me."

"I would rather serve you, Mamanchic," Cusi said, and she smiled for the first time, a smile that seemed to peel away and discard the tension that had existed between them.

"Perhaps you can, my son. You must tell me more about what you know, because *I* certainly have a voice in the court. Micay has already said she wishes to see me. Come with her to the Lynx House and bring your children."

"She wishes your advice on how to approach Macas," Cusi said, bowing in compliance.

"I will tell her what I can," Chimpu Ocllo promised. She raised a hand over him in blessing. "I must go on alone now. Try to watch where you walk, commander of scouts."

"I will be more attentive in the future," Cusi told her, bowing again as she left him.

MICAY TOOK Sinchi with her and left Cahua and Cusi sitting together next to the waterfall, Cahua entranced by the arching rainbows, Cusi by his own thoughts. Sinchi could not have been left in such self-absorbed company, since most of the things he wanted to do around the waterfall put him in constant risk of falling in. Micay also thought it was healthy to separate the two of them, now that they would permit it to happen. As long as each had a sense of where the other was, they did not mind being apart for short periods, at least during the daytime.

Holding on to Sinchi's hand, she let him walk up the long slope by himself, a task that still presented a challenge to his balance, if not his stamina. His stubby legs wobbled frequently and sometimes went out from under him, but he always picked himself up and kept going. Matching his slow but earnest pace, Micay glanced to her right, down into the valley. The terraces descending to the river were planted solidly with a variety of crops, gold and red and green, so that the hillside appeared covered by a mantle of richly striped cloth. It was a sight that never failed to please Micay's eye, even on days when the sky was dark. They had arrived here in time to participate in the planting of the late crops and then the ceremonies of thinning and weeding and shoring up the new shoots. Now they could see what their diligence and their prayers to Pachamama and Saramama had accomplished, the bounty of the Earth Mother surrounding them like the walls of a fortress.

Micay knew Cusi shared her pleasure in this place, and she was fairly certain of what his decision would be. It had seemed clear during their interview with Chimpu Ocllo, who also loved these mountains and had forgone her own chance to return to Cuzco long before. She had made Cusi look hard at everything that had a claim upon him, forcing him to distinguish loyalty from love and duty from dedication. He was still deliberating, but only, Micay felt, because he feared the decision would be taken out of his hands.

Sinchi let out a triumphant cry when they finally reached the middle terrace of the complex, and Micay released his hand and gave him a pat on the head, following closely as he toddled into the awning house. Sucso, the head retainer, was standing over the small pile of packs, blankets, and carrying bundles they had assembled for their journey. He bowed his white head to Micay and pointed with his chin at a compact bundle of firewood tied with rope, which Sinchi was already trying to lift off the ground.

"The lord said no more than that," he reported in a doubtful voice. "But he is a warrior; he is used to the cold of a mountain night. The little ones, though . . ."

"There are places to shelter," Micay assured him, "and we can carry no more. We could not carry this much if Urcon were not going with us."

"My son could carry for you . . ."

"Your son must attend to the herds. He will not have Urcon to help him with the birthing."

"I could see to that, with my grandsons."

"What is it, Sucso?" Micay asked, staring at him curiously. It was unlike the old man to force his suggestions on her. He acknowledged this with an apologetic shrug and spoke without raising his eyes.

"The smoking mountain to the north of here has begun to throw fire into the sky, and the sorcerers of the mountain people have heard the thunder from inside the earth. They say that Pachamama is very angry."

"Yet she has blessed our crops and made them flourish."

"They say . . . the Pachamama of the huaca is filled with anger, very dangerous to anyone who comes near. There have been pilgrims who never returned from there."

"That is not true," Micay said firmly. "She has driven many people away, but she has not hurt anyone. The high priestess told me this herself."

"Forgive my presumption, Lady . . ."

"No, I am grateful for your concern, Sucso. But we will all return safely, I promise you. This is our home, and we want to live many years here."

A glint of satisfaction appeared in the old man's eyes, and he put a fist over his heart and bowed as deeply as his stiffening muscles would allow. He went away without another word, apparently reassured. It was a reassurance he could not seem to hear often enough, Micay had found, having gradually come to understand the peculiar devotion of the retainers. She knew that if she and Cusi were to perish, Sucso would mourn their absence more than their actual deaths. An empty compound would make him a mere caretaker again, rather than a family retainer who could claim a relationship to the rank and blood of his lord.

Micay squatted down next to Sinchi, who was tugging happily on the ropes around the firewood, rolling the bundle from side to side. He grinned at her, having discovered for himself that this was not something he could break.

"You will be glad we have this," she told him, "if the rains find us on the trail."

He gurgled and tested the rope with his new front teeth, ignoring her hand when she reached out to smooth his touseled black hair. She thought of Sucso's warning and felt a sharp pang of protectiveness, a fierce reluctance to expose her children to any sort of danger. She had tried, unsuccessfully, to imagine herself placing Cahua in Macas's outstretched arms, trusting the woman not to grasp her too roughly or dash her to the ground. It seemed an impossible act, despite the vow she had made to Pachamama. She had not been a mother herself then; she had not known what it was like to feel utterly responsible for another being.

Sinchi had begun to push the bundle toward the back wall, lifting up on it with his legs bowed and squealing with pleasure when it spun out of his hands and rolled away from him. Micay rose and walked along behind him, ready to catch him if he went over backward. He rolled the wood against the wall beneath one of the niches, cast a quick glance over his shoulder at her, and then clambered up on top of the bundle, grabbing onto the front edge of the niche to hold himself upright.

"Where did you learn that?" Micay asked in surprise, and he turned his head to grin at her, showing by his own lack of surprise that he had had it in mind all along. She realized that the objects in the niches would no longer be safe, since Cahua undoubtedly knew this trick, too, and was even more curious about the niches than he was. Sinchi's nose was level with the edge of the niche, so that he could see inside, but he made no attempt to reach for anything. The last time she had held him close enough to reach, he had grabbed a figurine, then had dropped it and seen it break on the ground. She could tell he remembered; he had been so upset that neither she nor Cusi had thought to scold him.

She put a hand on his back to brace him and leaned down into the niche. She had recently rearranged the contents of most of the household niches, replacing some of the objects Mama Cori had chosen with mementoes from the journey to Chimor. The bottom of this one was lined with bright cotton cloth from Lambayeque, and there was a glossy black Chimu water jar with a ringed spout in one corner and a Chimu headdress in the other. Scattered among the figurines were polished shells and smooth stones from the shores of Mama Cocha, and gleaming in their midst was the bronze needle she had used as a weapon in Chan Chan. Knowing that Sinchi could not listen for long without wanting to touch, she reached in and picked up the spray of green parrot feathers that stood propped against the base of the black jar.

"This was a gift to your father from a powerful Shuara sorcerer," she explained, putting the feathers down near his hands. "Your great-grandfather, Grandfather Jaguar, has gone into the lands of the Shuaras, leading the warriors."

"Mu-mu-mu-muu!" Sinchi vocalized, mimicking the sound Cahua made whenever she spied one of the air serpents, the amarus. He let Micay hold him up and seized the feathers with both hands, waving them in front of his face.

"Gently," Micay cautioned, though she had adopted Cusi's trusting attitude toward letting them handle precious objects. He had allowed Sinchi to hold his spirit brother during the ritual to Illapa, and Sinchi had tried to chew on it in a most unreverent fashion. After a few moments, she pried the feathers from his fingers and put them back in their place by the jar. She heard a throat cleared behind her, and Urcon squatted down on the other side of Sinchi, so as not to block his light.

"My lady—"

"Comrade," Micay corrected, and reached for the stiff cylindrical headdress in the back corner of the niche. She set it on Sinchi's head and then lifted him off the firewood and set him on his feet. "That is the headdress your father was given by Acunta, the chief of Chan Chan."

Sinchi reached up with both hands to hold the headdress on his head, peeping out from under the rim at her and Urcon. They both burst out in laughter, which pleased Sinchi so much that he danced in a circle, jumping flat-footed and alternately hiding and uncovering his eyes. Then he sat down, pulled it off, and began to examine it more closely, tugging on the cloth flaps and tracing the patterns with his finger.

"You are finished with the herds?" Micay asked Urcon, who had washed and put on a clean tunic and smelled only slightly of greasy wool.

"Twin llamas today," Urcon said with a big smile. "Black ones, male and female."

"Ya-ya-ya," Sinchi chattered excitedly, the same sound he made whenever Illapa's name was mentioned. But he knew what llamas were; Cusi and Urcon had taken him and Cahua to see the newborns only two days before.

"Can we see them as we leave tomorrow?" Micay inquired.

Urcon nodded judiciously. "The trail goes near the pasture. They are too small to move far."

"Tomorrow, Sinchi," Micay said, but the boy had the headdress on backwards and could not hear her. She looked at Urcon. "You are ready for the journey?"

"I have prayed," he said simply. "We must not let Cusi carry too much, so he does not hurt his foot again."

"I will take things from him and give them to you. What does the sky tell you?"

"There is little sign of rain," Urcon reckoned, "though we will have some in this season. There is ash on the wind, from the smoking mountain, the retainers say. They think it is an evil omen."

"Sucso told me. What do you think?"

Urcon pondered the question for a moment and then shrugged. "I know little about smoking mountains, except for those I have seen between Tumibamba and Quito. You must also know the place, near the mountain called Sangay, where the ash sometimes lies ankle deep on the Royal Road. It dirties the llamas' coats and makes it hard to breathe, but I do not think it has ever hurt me."

Micay smiled, comforted as always by his plain good sense, the trust he had in his own experience.

"Sucso also warned me about Macas, and I must confess, she worries me more than any omen. The high priestess sent two women to her with supplies, and she surprised them on the trail and drove them off with stones."

"There are three of us, and one is Cusi Huaman," Urcon reminded her. "He would never let her harm the children."

"No, of course not," Micay agreed, though she was not certain she should rely on Cusi to intervene. It was not *his* vow, and it was possible Macas would welcome her but turn him away. But she did not want to burden Urcon with her worries. She bent and deftly plucked the headdress off of Sinchi's head, drawing a loud squawk of protest.

"You can play Chimu again another time," she told him, putting the headdress back into the niche. "Let us go call your father and Cahua. It is almost time to eat."

"Mu-mu-mu-mu," Sinchi pouted, gazing longingly at the niche. But he took Micay's hand and walked back to the front of the awning house, and Urcon picked up the bundle of firewood and returned it to its place among the packs.

"Cusi has thought of everything."

"Everything he can foresee," Micay allowed, and she scooped Sinchi up into her arms, giving him a hug that made him cry out in surprise. She kissed him on top of the head and loosened her grip slightly but kept him in her arms as she stepped out to call her husband and daughter.

BY THEIR third day on the trail, they had refined the rhythm of their march, knowing just how long they could carry the twins before putting them down to walk. Then the adults could rest, sharing out the packs and stretching their muscles while the children toddled and explored. The first day they had gone too far and carried too much, exhausting themselves but not the twins, who had fussed and cried well into the night. Micay's neck and back had been painfully stiff the next morning, and Cusi's foot was so sore he had been forced to use his spear as a staff. So they had taken a slow second day to recover their strength and adjust the pace, stopping frequently to rest and survey their surroundings. The sun shone warmly, and they could see for great distances in the clear, thin air, spying deer moving through the undergrowth on the lower slopes and guanacos picking their way single file along a high ridge.

It was toward the end of the second day that Cusi began to emerge from his preoccupation with the future and take notice of what was around him. He suddenly realized that he had made as much of a decision as he could and that nothing was to be gained by dwelling on it further. The Sapa Inca would do what he pleased in any case, but he could not touch Cusi here. That thought alone made Cusi's foot feel better and seemed to lighten the burden on his back. He began to talk to whichever child he was carrying, the way Micay did, though he told them the things a scout saw along the trail, rather than the herbs and edible plants visible to a healer. As always, Cahua was the more attentive listener, though Sinchi was quicker to spot anything that moved, and his excitement at seeing a wild animal made Cusi laugh with pleasure.

As he walked at the rear of the column on the third afternoon, with Cahua dozing in the sling on his back, he noticed that a change had taken place in Micay, as well. There was no longer any sign of the stiffness that had made it hard for her to straighten up the day before, and the face she turned to Sinchi appeared animated and without fatigue. The partial fast they had been observing seemed to have sharpened her features and made her even more beautiful, and Cusi felt a swelling of desire as he gazed at her. He knew that it was not merely the result of the abstinence they had maintained along with their fast, sleeping back to back every night. Micay had told him about the power she drew from these mountains, but this was the first time he had seen it for himself. It made him feel proud and guilty at the same time, aware of how selfish he had been in his considerations.

"Your mother has huaca of her own," he murmured to Cahua, feeling her stir behind him. "She must have a future that does not squander *her* gifts, either."

Cahua murmured back, and he turned his head to look at her just as a great shadow swept over them, blotting out the sun with a suddenness that made him raise his spear in alarm. Then he saw it was a condor, passing directly overhead, so low he could see the reddish talons curled in against the black body and the white patches on the underside of the broad wings. He brought his gaze down in time to see Micay staring upward, wide-eyed, a smile of awe spreading slowly across her face. Sinchi saw the bird once it was past and tried to climb the back of Micay's head to get a better look.

"It is the Great Condor of the Chachapoyas," Cusi said to his daughter, who had pulled herself up on his shoulders. "He watches over your mother, just as she watches over us."

Urcon had also stopped, and they all stared as the huge black bird beat its way out over the canyon ahead, appearing clumsy and ill proportioned until it caught an updraft beneath the canopy of its wings and rose effortlessly, sailing off in the direction they were headed. Only when it had dropped out of sight behind a distant ridge did Micay turn and look back at Cusi.

"You are not dreaming," he told her. "He blesses your presence here."

Micay exhaled and nodded solemnly, reaching a hand back to loosen the tangled grip Sinchi had on her hair. Then she signaled Urcon, and they started walking again.

"Yes, we must stay," Cusi said, half to himself, though Cahua heard and made a noise in his ear that he chose to interpret as assent.

THEY ARRIVED at their destination at midday and rested in the lower cave, allowing the children to finish the nap they had begun. The clouds had finally come in, though there was as yet no threat of rain. Cusi could feel the tension in Micay as she removed the gift bundles from their protective packs and smoothed their cloth wrappings. He crouched next to her and surprised her by taking her hands, which were cold and trembling.

"We have come here reverently, in fulfillment of a sacred vow," he reminded her. "We have fasted and abstained from lovemaking, as is proper, and we have brought fine offerings. If Macas turns us away, we will leave the offerings and go quietly. But you have nothing to fear in approaching her, Micay. You were meant to come here, and you have the power to turn back any threat she might make."

"You have not seen her," Micay said, breathless at the memory. "You do not know the strength of her violence."

"No, but I have seen the condor, and I know the power you have to calm and heal. You must believe in your own huaca and trust it to protect you."

Micay squinted at him skeptically, as if doubting that his words applied to her.

"I do not fear for myself," she said, and they both looked over at the children. Cahua had awakened and was gazing at them drowsily, her thumb in her mouth. Cusi pressed Micay's hands between his own.

"Trust your instincts, as well. You have your mantle pin; use it if you must. Urcon and I will be near."

They set off up the trail as soon as the twins were fully awake. Micay went first, with Cahua on her back; then Cusi with the gift bundles in his arms; then Urcon with Sinchi. The children wrinkled their noses and coughed at the sulfurous odor of the hot springs, but they seemed to understand that this was not a time to complain. They were quickly distracted by the brilliant colors of the wildflowers that grew in clumps along the trail, and by the birds and butterflies that flitted and hovered around the green thickets that surrounded the steaming pools.

They were more than halfway up, past the point where the vegetation began to thin out, when Cusi spoke a soft warning.

"Look up, to your left. There . . . among the red rocks."

Micay had had her head down, her attention focused on what might await them at the top, so at first she saw nothing unusual in the direction he had indicated. But as she slowed and scanned the rocky slope a second time, she spotted Macas crouching near some broken boulders that were streaked with red and orange stains. Her long white hair was plainly visible, though the mantle she was wearing seemed to blend in with the rocks. *My mantle,* Micay thought.

Macas suddenly stood up, evoking a small cry from Cahua, who apparently had not seen her until she moved. Macas pointed at them with her finger, shaking her head and making a keening sound. Then she made a wild gesture with her other arm, which Micay did not recognize as a throw until a stone crashed into the brush about ten feet away from her. Macas had another stone in her hand and was making threatening gestures with it, though she had also begun to back away up the slope. Micay realized that if she fled now, they most likely would not see her again. They could leave their offerings and depart without having to face her. Micay felt a relief that surprised her by not being as strong as she had anticipated. She also felt Cahua touch the back of her neck, and she remembered the spirit in which the vow had been offered, the joy of having her prayer answered.

"Should we go to her?" she whispered to Cahua and was not surprised, when she turned her head, to see the girl nod. Perhaps she remembered the ceremony for Sinchi in which she had had no part, even though she had cried to be included. Or perhaps it was the effect of huaca, what Cusi had implied when he said that she was "meant" to be here.

"Wait here," she said, turning back to Cusi and Urcon. Cusi stared at her for a long moment, a rueful expression on his face, then nodded in compliance. Urcon bobbed his head in a gesture of encouragement, and Sinchi simply gaped at her with his mouth open. Micay stepped off the trail and began to pick her way through the brush, climbing the slope toward Macas. It was hard going with the child on her back and the rocky soil crumbling beneath her feet, one eye always on their destination. Macas watched them come for a while, then threw a stone that came much closer to its mark, snapping branches as it ricocheted past the spot where Micay had been only a moment before.

Micay touched the end of her pin but kept going, trying to keep her head up to protect Cahua. Thorns caught at her shift and she panted for breath in the thin air, but she did not pause to give Macas a stationary target. When she was thirty feet away, she saw Macas stoop for another stone, and a jolt of fear went through her. There was no place to hide here, and she did not have the energy to dodge. In desperation, she found her voice.

"Mother! Surely you remember me? Surely you would not hurt the child I have brought for your blessing?"

Macas held the stone out at her side, glaring down the slope at Micay. Her dirty white hair was bound back from her face with a piece of frayed rope, and the sunrise mantle, now faded and torn, was held together at the breast by a sharp sliver of bone. The improvement in her dress gave Micay some hope, though it was belied by the wild, animal suspicion in the woman's eyes.

"Mother," she said again, less sharply. "I came to you two years ago, with a Quito ñusta. You took us to the huaca and let us bathe in the holy water. I was told that I would have twins, and indeed, they have come to me. This is the girl child I promised I would bring to you."

Macas gave no sign of comprehension, though she did not raise her arm to throw. On impulse, Micay reached back and pulled the sling around her shoulder so that she could lift Cahua out. She set the child on her feet, holding on to her hand. Macas's head jerked as she looked from Micay to Cahua, and her glare seemed to lose its forbidding intensity. Cahua stamped her feet and squirmed in Micay's grasp, eager to move her legs, so Micay began to lead her slowly up the slope, watching Macas closely. She realized her impulse had been a sound one: she could protect Cahua better this way, now that she was free to intervene with her whole body. And the sight of the child seemed to have allayed Macas's suspicions, or at least given her reason to pause.

They came up among the red-streaked rocks and stopped a few feet away from where the woman stood, separated from her by a barrier of knee-high stones. An unpleasant smell came to Micay's nostrils, and she could hear the breath whistling in and out of Macas's beak of a nose.

"This is Cahua, my mother," she said softly. "I have come to dedicate her to Pachamama."

Macas looked down at the child, the first indication that she understood what was being said to her. Micay hesitated for a moment, reluctant to take her eyes off of the woman, but then Cahua pulled on her hand and made her glance down. The child was twisting her body and looking up at Macas from behind her shoulder, giving her a coy, sidelong glance, as if she and the woman were playing some kind of game. She was holding her other hand behind her back, and as Micay watched in amazement, she extended the hand in front of her, her fingers closed in a fist. Then she let out a triumphant squeal and her fingers fell open, revealing a tiny white stone she must have picked up while climbing the slope.

Micay's vigilance returned and she looked up to see Macas's reaction. The woman blinked several times, then slowly opened her own hand, staring down at the stone in her upturned palm as if she could not remember how it had gotten there. Cahua squealed again and toddled forward, pulling Micay with her. She went right up to the rock Macas was standing behind and plunked the white stone down on top of it with a decisive click, as if concluding a barter.

Macas backed off a step, appearing slightly dazed. Then she squatted down and thrust out an arm, putting her own stone next to Cahua's. Cahua held back for a moment, glancing up at Micay with wide eyes. Micay nodded and released her, and Cahua reached out with both hands and gathered up the woman's stone, hugging it against her chest and abruptly sitting down in the dirt. Micay squatted down next to her and gazed across at Macas, who stared at the tiny white pebble without reaching for it.

"We have brought you other gifts, my mother. Offerings to the huaca and Pachamama."

Macas's head came up and she shook it in vigorous denial.

"No! Angry, angry . . . she burns. Burns!" she repeated, and stood up so abruptly that Micay sat back on her heels and raised her hands protectively, trying to put herself in front of Cahua. But Macas simply put a long, bony foot up on the rock in front of her. The skin on top of the foot looked as if it had melted and run like wax, then cracked and bled from the fissures. Her toes were swollen and had lost all of their nails, and the open blisters gave off the odor of rotting flesh.

"You must let me treat you, Mother," Micay pleaded. "I have medicines in the pack I left below."

Macas grunted dismissively and pulled the foot back, turning away from Micay to stare down the slope in the direction of Cusi and Urcon and Sinchi. She muttered something unintelligible, then clearly spoke the Quito word for the Incas, an honorific form of the words "golden ears."

"It is my husband," Micay explained, rising warily to her feet. "He is with our son and our friend. They mean you no harm, my mother."

Macas ignored her for another moment, then turned back and spoke in a remarkably calm voice, in Quechua.

"The spell will fall on the golden ears, too. No one will escape, not the great ones or the small . . . nothing will save them. Nothing will wake them from the spell of death."

Micay felt Cahua lean against her leg, and she saw that the child was gazing up at Macas, listening intently. Micay's voice sounded hoarse and reluctant to her own ears.

"Who could cast such a terrible spell?"

"It will fall from the sky and rise up out of the earth . . . it will attack from every direction and never be seen." She paused and met Micay's eyes, making her feel the force of her conviction. "Go, tell the golden ears that death will soon be upon them."

Micay cradled Cahua's head against her thigh without looking down, afraid the girl would see the fear in her face. Macas lifted her chin and regarded her imperiously, indicating that she expected her command to be obeyed. Micay bowed her head in compliance, wishing that she could call this madness, though she could no longer see much trace of it in the woman's eyes. She seemed as certain of this as she had of the birth of the twins.

"I am going, Mother," Micay said. "Will you give my daughter your blessing before we leave?"

Macas frowned and pulled on a tendril of hair, then squinted down at Cahua, who grew shy under the scrutiny and pressed herself against Micay's leg. Macas suddenly grunted in surprise and straightened up, jerking her chin at Cahua.

"She is already marked. Death will not take her."

It was hardly a blessing, yet it had been offered with the same certainty as the prophecy. Micay bowed in gratitude and relief, and when she looked up again, Macas was gone. So was the white pebble. Then Macas reappeared farther up the slope, climbing through the brush without looking back. Micay exhaled heavily and bent down to lift Cahua into her arms.

"You will live, my daughter," she whispered, pressing her lips against Cahua's soft cheek. Cahua squirmed away from her and held up the stone Macas had given her, displaying it like a prize. Micay laughed and kissed her again, feeling tears spring up in her eyes. She could hear Sinchi making fretful noises from below, so she pulled the sling around in front of her and began to fit Cahua into it.

"Let us go back to your father and brother," she said, "and tell them what we have learned."

Once Cahua was in place on her back, the child dropped the stone, and Micay stooped with a grunt to retrieve it. As she straightened up, something black floated down in front of her face and she pulled back, thinking it was an insect. But it was a drifting piece of ash, and when she brushed it away from her, it crumbled and vanished in the air. Clutching the stone tightly in her hand, she blinked back her tears and started down the slope.

WHEN THE NEWS of Pinta's capture was brought to the Rainbow House, Cusi went out alone to one of the far pastures where the ground was fairly level and there were no herds grazing. In the month since they had returned from their journey to the huaca, he had worked hard to build up his strength and stamina and regain full use of his injured foot. He knew now what he planned to do, so he had been able to concentrate on making himself ready. Only the final test remained.

Taking a deep breath, he offered a brief, silent prayer to Illapa, then started forward in a trot, building slowly to a run. He felt a certain tenderness at first, coupled with a habitual inclination to favor the foot, and he let it hold him back for a while. But then he was distracted by the wind in his face and the whip of bunch grass against his shins, and the ground blurred beneath him as he let the deep, familiar thrill of running take him over. He felt as if he were discovering his swiftness all over again, breaking a fast that had gone on for so long he had forgotten the pleasure he had given up. He leaped over a field marker and reversed direction without slowing down, skimming over the grass like his namesake, the joyful hawk, as he headed back to tell Micay it was time to leave.

Three days later they came down out of the mountains into the valley of Tumibamba, he and Micay walking on either side of the llama that carried the twins in his woven carrying bags. Urcon followed a little behind, clicking his tongue and singing softly to the other three llamas, which carried their belongings. The leafy tops of the crops stood well above the rough walls that divided the plots, and squadrons of warriors had set up their encampments in the fields that were being allowed to lie fallow. As they passed the camps, Cusi noted the apparent readiness of the warriors and wondered what it meant. He had made little attempt to obtain news from the city, so he knew only that Huayna Capac had instituted an accounting from the whole of the Four Quarters, and that he had sent out his personal inspectors to assist the provincial governors in this task. Perhaps the inspectors had encountered resistance or discrepancies in the count that would require correction and punishment.

The streets of the city were crowded with warriors and messengers and pack trains of llamas loaded down with supplies, and Cusi saw Micay recoil from the noise and dust. During one of the many delays, he reached across the back of the llama to take her hand, though he had to speak loudly to be heard above the din.

"You would not know the war was over," he suggested.

Micay nodded wearily. "Perhaps another has already begun."

When they finally reached the Mollecancha gate, their way was again blocked, this time by a mixed contingent of palace retainers and Cañari warriors. There were an unusually large number of them guarding the gate, and they were questioning everyone seeking entrance. Their manner was aggressively suspicious, especially toward anyone not an Inca or a Cañari, and they appeared to be detaining some of those they questioned. Cusi spotted an opening through the crowd and prodded the llama forward, using his own body to protect Sinchi, who hung suspended in the carrying bag on his side. Micay did the same for Cahua, and they pushed their way forward until they were within the shadow of the deep gateway. Then a Cañari warrior in a wicker headdress stepped into their path from Micay's side and shook his spear in the llama's face, causing the beast to spit and rear back. Cusi hooked an arm around the llama's arched neck and came around in front of it, calming it the way Urcon did, though it took him longer to bring the animal under control. Cahua began to cry and Sinchi quickly joined in. Cusi turned on the warrior, who saw his earplugs for the first time and executed a hasty bow.

"I am Cusi Huaman, commander of scouts. Why are you in my way?"

"Forgive me, Lord. I must know where these others are from."

"These others are my wife and children and my friend," Cusi snapped, feeling his anger expand outward with a swiftness that surprised him. "Let us pass."

"I must know where—"

"I have told you all you need to know," Cusi said tightly, getting a hold on his anger before it added another incident to his reputation. As it was, the warrior looked as if he had been slapped. Then someone much larger gripped the man's shoulders from behind and moved him aside.

"Listen to him," Rimachi advised the warrior. "He is not a man you should question." Rimachi turned and spread his arms, smiling at Cusi and Micay. "Come, my friends . . . welcome to Tumibamba."

"Some welcome," Cusi muttered as Rimachi ushered them through and led them a short distance away from the gate. Micay signaled to Cusi, and they lifted the children out of the carrying bags at the same time. Urcon came up to quiet the llama, speaking to it as if it were a frightened child. Cahua was still crying in Micay's arms, but Sinchi forgot his tears as soon as he saw Rimachi looming over him.

"What is this for?" Cusi asked, cocking a hip to support the boy. "I expected preparations for a celebration."

"You *have* been away a long time," Rimachi said dryly. "Pinta has been all but forgotten. The Sapa Inca simply wants the warriors back so that he can use them elsewhere."

"Where?"

"Wherever corrective measures are required. Several expeditions have already been announced: a small one to Piura and a larger one against the Huancavelicas. Perhaps a serious campaign against Puna. There is even trouble in the Southern Quarter."

"Has Ninan Cuyochi been assigned? I have heard a rumor that he might be named Regent of the northern lands."

Rimachi raised his eyebrows in surprise, then gave Micay a shrewd smile.

"I forgot the high priestess. I heard the same rumor, even before she began spreading it. In any event, Ninan has not been assigned and probably will not be until he returns in a few days."

"I must see him as soon as he does. Should I conceal myself until then?"

"Your return has already been noticed," Rimachi told him, jerking his head toward the gate. "Our task is to find anyone who might be a spy, either for or against us. But the retainers report everything to the palace. You would have done better had you limped and not shown yourself so ready to fight."

"I am more ready than I knew," Cusi admitted. "I want to attach myself to Ninan before I can be sent elsewhere. Tomay and I talked about it before he left."

"If anyone inquires, I will tell them it has already been decided," Rimachi promised. "And I will see what I can learn. The circle of men around Huayna Capac includes few Incas of the blood, except for the high priest, and fewer still who will confide in me. You probably do not know that your uncle was dismissed from his post."

Cusi exchanged an amazed glance with Micay.

"Over me?"

"I do not know. No one will say how he earned the Sapa Inca's displeasure. Your father has made him one of his advisers."

Cusi again looked at Micay, though he could not think of anything to say. She hefted Cahua higher on her hip and glanced around her briefly before addressing Rimachi.

"Have there been any reports of mysterious deaths anywhere?" she asked quietly.

Rimachi stared down his nose at her for a moment, his brow furrowed with concern. "Not that I have heard. Should there be?"

"You must come and eat with us," Cusi suggested. "Even though we have been out of the city, we have learned things."

"I will try," Rimachi said, shrugging his broad shoulders and gesturing vaguely at the gate. "The first thing you will learn here is that everyone is too busy for talk. So if I do not see you, be alert for Ninan's return. I will surely find a way to greet Tomay and Uritu."

They watched him walk back to the gate, where he joined the interrogation of a man wearing a Chimu-style headdress. The man appeared to be protesting his own innocence, his gestures becoming increasingly frantic as the questioning continued. Cusi realized there was no hope for him if his people were under suspicion. He would either have to spy for the Incas or be considered a spy against them.

"You were right," Cusi said to Micay as they began to move up the street. "The war has begun again."

"Perhaps we are already under the spell," Micay said bleakly, and they fell silent as they walked toward the governor's compound, carrying their children in their arms.

IT WAS WELL past the middle of the night when Micay awoke, thinking she had heard one of the children cry out. The moon, a waning crescent, had risen high enough to provide a gray light that streamed in through the windows and open doorway. Micay heard nothing from the twins and was about to lie back down when she heard the slap of a hand against stone and a sharp whisper: "Cusi!"

Cusi was curled up beside her, sunken in the seemingly depthless sleep that had claimed him every night since they had returned to the city. He did not even stir when she took the light blanket that had been over both of them and wrapped it around herself, then rose and went to the doorway. Apu Poma was squatting just outside the entrance, and he put a hand against the wall to help himself rise as she stepped through the doorway. There was fog drifting across the plaza in front of her, and the warm night air left a coat of moisture on her skin.

"What is it, Father?" she asked when he was standing.

"They have arrived. Ninan and Atauhuallpa and the troops."

"They came at night, in the fog?"

"Why not?" Apu Poma shrugged, sounding vaguely angry. "They were told not to expect a ceremony of welcome."

"Where shall I tell Cusi to find them?"

"I had food and akha taken to Ninan's compound. I expect that most of the commanders and captains will be there, toasting themselves."

"Cusi will be grateful," Micay told him with a bow. "I will tell him you brought the message yourself."

"I was awake. And I know what this means to him. If he wishes to stay here as a warrior, Ninan is the best protector he could have. Otherwise he might be sent to the Hotlands to frighten farmers and fishermen and die in the heat."

"You do not approve of these expeditions, either, my lord," Micay suggested softly, struck by the contempt in his voice.

"Most of them are unnecessary. The governors could put matters right with a few extra troops. Instead we have to supply the army all over again from stores that are still depleted from the last campaign. We are sending all the way to Caxamarca for supplies. And we still have not sent everything that is owed to the mitmacs who have settled on the Carangui lands . . ."

Apu Poma trailed off abruptly, shaking his head and letting out a long, exasperated sigh. He glanced around at the fog-shrouded plaza and lowered his voice.

"Forgive me, my daughter . . . I should not complain. But he asks us to do the impossible, then asks for even more the next day, and more the day after that. It might be better to be sent away than to try to serve him here." He stopped and seemed to realize what he had just said. "I do not mean that for Cusi. Go and awaken him, Micay, if I have not already done so. Tell him to be alert for sentries and courteous to them."

Micay made a perfunctory bow and went back into the house. As she expected, Cusi had not been roused by their conversation; he had not even altered his position, and she had to bend close to hear his breathing. She knelt beside him and began to shake him gently by the shoulders, feeling the urgency that Cusi himself had instilled in her, though he had tried to remain outwardly calm. The strain of that—of waiting and praying he would not be summoned for assignment before Ninan returned—had put him into this sleep. She knew that talking would not work and would only awaken the twins, so she tried rubbing his cheeks and forehead. Finally, she tickled his nose with the edge of the blanket, and the resultant sneeze brought him awake with a jerk. It also woke Sinchi, who began to whimper.

"Ninan has arrived," she whispered, and had to repeat it twice before comprehension showed in his eyes and he reached for his clothes. While he dressed, Micay managed to quiet Sinchi and put him back to sleep. Then she went to Cusi's side and told him what Apu Poma had said, emphasizing his warning about the sentries. Cusi had already put in his earplugs and tied the Iñaca headband around his forehead, but he dug into his belongings and pulled out the string of golden discs he had been given at the victory celebration.

"So they will hear me coming and know my rank," he said as he tied the string around his neck, and Micay knew then that he was fully awake. She leaned forward and pressed her lips to his cheek, putting a hand on the spirit brother in his waistband.

"Find him quickly," she urged. "I want to keep you with me, along with your spirit brother."

"I will find him," Cusi promised, giving her a brief, fervent hug before he rose and went out the door, his golden medals jingling around his neck.

AS HE CAME through the gate into Ninan Cuyochi's compound, Cusi thought for a moment that his father had sent him to the wrong place. He had expected torchlight and loud voices, but the courtyard was dark and silent, inhabited only by the fog, which had settled on the ground in vaporous mounds that continually spilled over and spread. He detected a murmur of voices and followed them up a steep flight of stairs to the second level of the compound. Memory told him that an awning house was straight ahead, but he had to wade through the fog before he could see the structure and then the warriors inside. There were at least twenty, perhaps more, sitting silently in the darkness, surrounded by shields and weapons and bowls of food. Most had cups in their hands, and they regarded Cusi with the weary indifference of men who had just come out of the field.

He did not see Ninan or Atauhuallpa among them, but he found Tomay and Uritu sitting with Otoronco near one of the support poles. He squatted down in front of them, squinting at their faces in the uncertain light. Tomay appeared thin and haggard, his eyes half closed, and Otoronco seemed lost in some gloomy contemplation; only Uritu gave him a nod of recognition. All of them had bandages wrapped around various parts of their bodies, and they smelled of sweat and wood smoke and something distinctively sharp and foul—the ointment used to keep off insects.

"Grandfather . . . brothers," Cusi said quietly. "I salute your success and your safe return. What has been done with Pinta?"

"The war chiefs took him to the Sapa Inca," Uritu replied when neither of the other two chose to speak.

"So that is where Ninan is?" Cusi asked, glancing up as a serving woman brought him a cup and filled it with akha.

"He and Atauhuallpa promised that they would wake their father and make him accept his captive," Tomay said hoarsely. Then he winced and doubled over, clutching at his stomach with his free hand.

"You are ill, Tomay . . ."

"The insects eat you from the outside," Tomay growled, "and the worms eat you from within."

"Micay has medicines to purge such things. You must let her tend to you."

"Later. Let them fatten on akha for a while. It is the first thing they have allowed me to keep down."

"They are Shuara worms," Uritu observed, his teeth flashing in the darkness, "and the Shuaras are great drinkers."

"You met with them, then?" Cusi asked, glancing at Otoronco, who was sitting with his back against the pole, his cup balanced on a splayed thigh. He stared back at Cusi but did not speak, even though Uritu waited for him out of deference.

"They met with us," Uritu explained, "once they saw we would not go away without Pinta."

"They gave him to you?"

"To Grandfather," Uritu said, inclining his feathered head toward Otoronco. "The sorcerer would not barter with Ninan or Atauhuallpa, because they were too young. But he knew the name of Otoronco Achachi."

"No," Otoronco said suddenly. "He knew my name, but it was more important to him that he knew my grandson. He would not trust his people to my word, but he would accept the word of Cusi Huaman."

Cusi drew a sharp breath. "It was Kirupasa? What did you promise him in my name?"

Otoronco shifted his position, looking past Cusi and then back to him. "He did not believe that we had only come after Pinta. He was sure that we had come to scout his lands so that we could attack him later. One of his men had seen the maps we were making."

"What did you promise him?" Cusi repeated when Otoronco paused and took a drink from his cup. He had to force himself to meet Cusi's insistent gaze, which seemed to make him angry.

"I gave him the only thing he would take," Otoronco snapped. "My promise that the Incas would not invade his lands or harm his people. Your promise, too. I had no choice. It did not matter to him that I did not have the authority to speak for the Sapa Inca. He wanted the word of someone whose spirit he knew and could touch, or so he said."

Cusi shivered, remembering the unsettling power of the man's presence. "And if this promise is broken?"

"Then he will take his vengeance on you and me," Otoronco said bluntly. "Wherever we are. He said he would find us in a dream and kill us with his magic darts."

Cusi sat back on his heels and looked around to be sure none of the other warriors were close enough to have heard. Otoronco held up a hand and went on before Cusi could speak.

"Ninan Cuyochi is the only other one who knows this. He agreed that it would not be wise to tell his father, since *none* of us had the authority to speak for the Sapa Inca. But he has no desire to fight with the Shuaras again, and he will see that our promise is kept, if it is in his power to do so."

Cusi felt his lips curl back in a snarl that he could not voice. He bowed his head and breathed deeply, knowing he should not blame Otoronco. Had he been there himself, he no doubt would have made the promise on his own. And he had already decided to put his life in Ninan's hands. It was the thought that his spirit had been offered as a hostage to Huayna Capac's goodwill that made him want to spit.

"We met someone else there," Otoronco said, and he put down his cup to dig among the weapons and bedrolls piled up next to him. He slid what appeared to be a spear wrapped in cloth across the ground to Cusi. Cusi took it and backed out of the shadow of the roof into a patch of moonlight, feeling the fog settle wetly on his skin. The cloth, he saw, was a tunic of Inca design and weave, once a fine garment but now ragged and extremely dirty. The spear was a single piece of black chonta palm, one end of which had been shaved down to a sharp point. He experienced a moment of confusion as he studied the rings and barbed lines painted on the shaft, finding the markings familiar even though the weapon itself was not. He had fought against *someone* who marked their weapons in this manner, though it could not have been the Shuaras.

"Those are for your wife," Otoronco said, and then Cusi recognized the markings as Chachapoya. "They belonged to her father."

"Belonged? He is dead?"

"I killed him."

Otoronco drew a breath to go on but was interrupted by the sound of voices in the courtyard below. Cusi glanced over his shoulder and saw torches glowing in the fog, then the shapes of several men coming up the stairs. The men inside the awning house straightened up when they saw that the group was led by the war chiefs Yasca and Michi. Cusi scanned the others and saw Rimachi but not Ninan Cuyochi.

"Greetings, my sons," Michi said with a formal bow. "I come to commend you in the Sapa Inca's name. He is greatly pleased with the captive you brought him."

The men under the roof received this praise in silence, without so much as a murmur of acceptance. So pleased he did not even bother to meet them in the square in daylight, Cusi thought. Michi cleared his throat and went on.

"The Sapa Inca offered Pinta his life if he would pledge his loyalty to Inti and the Inca. The Carangui answered him with silence. He will be killed tomorrow at dawn, sacrificed by the priests of Inti and Huanacauri."

Cusi felt an urge to hum in approval, out of respect for the courage of their enemy, but the other men did not break their obdurate silence. He realized that the fate of the captive did not matter to them, since his capture had gone virtually unrecognized. Nothing would persuade them now that their effort had been appreciated.

"For his part in this," Michi said, "Ninan Cuyochi has been named Regent of the Northern Provinces. Atauhuallpa will share the command, with me, of the warriors who will be sent against Puna."

This brought a concerted hum of approval from the seated men, and Cusi hummed with them, feeling a sudden welling of hope in his chest. Chimpu Ocllo had been right; perhaps the plan would work, after all, and he would be protected by the power of the Regent. Michi had no more to say and turned to go, taking most of the torch bearers with him. Cusi stood up with the spear and tunic in his hands, looking for Rimachi, who would probably know where Ninan could be found. But Yasca came toward him first, gesturing at Cusi with his chin.

"Good, you are here, too," the war chief said, drawing him back toward Otoronco and the others. He gave Otoronco a deferential nod, then turned so he could address both Cusi and Tomay.

"You two are going with me to Cuzco and then to the Province of Charcas. The Chiriguanos are threatening Cochabamba and must be subdued. We will collect our forces in Cuzco."

Cusi exchanged a glance with Tomay, too stunned to speak. He could not have heard correctly. Cuzco? Cochabamba? Amaru had fought there long ago as a young warrior, against these same Chiriguanos. They were nomads and raiders from the other side of the Andes, little more than bandits.

"We march in ten days," Yasca concluded. "Make yourselves ready."

"Do you have a place for me, as well?" Otoronco asked.

Yasca shrugged and shook his head. "I have not been given that honor, my lord. I was told to take these two and Quizquiz, no others. Those were the Sapa Inca's orders."

Yasca gave Cusi and Tomay a curt nod and disappeared into the fog. Rimachi came up beside Cusi and rested a hand on his shoulder.

"Cuzco," Cusi murmured in disbelief.

"I heard," Rimachi said. "I was there when the order was given. He was most emphatic that you be taken."

"Ten days," Tomay groaned. He struggled to his feet. "I cannot wait to purge myself. Can we rouse Micay?"

"She will be awake . . . waiting for different news." Cusi realized that he still had the spear and tunic in his hands, and he looked down at Otoronco. The old man reached out and took the weapon and the garment back.

"Go to your wife," he commanded. "I will tell her myself later. She should not lose her husband and her father in the same night."

Rimachi helped Tomay gather up his belongings, handing Cusi a helmet and a shield to carry. Cusi went out into the fog with them, flanking Tomay on one side but unable to think about what he was doing. He told himself he was leaving, going back to Cuzco. Part of him refused to believe it; part of him had expected it all along . . .

THE TWINS squatted down on either side of her and watched intently as she removed the cloth that was draped over the top of the basket. Tomay craned forward, as well, his tongue darting out to lick at his cracked lips, his eyes large with anticipation. First Micay took out a water gourd and set it down in front of him.

"You must drink water," she told him. "Large quantities of it every day. It will take the poison out of your body."

Tomay nodded impatiently, his eyes back on the basket after a cursory glance at the gourd. Micay removed one small covered bowl and then another, putting them down next to the gourd. Tomay gingerly stretched his hands out, circling one of the bowls as if it were a ritual vessel.

"There is turkey broth and a maize porridge with herbs and greens. Eat only a little at a time," she warned, producing a wooden spoon of the size the children were just beginning to use. Cahua and Sinchi laughed in recognition, and Tomay grinned at them and waved the spoon like a wand. Then he took the covers off the bowls and instantly became serious. Micay unslung her medicine bag and had him stretch out his left leg so that she could examine the most serious of the wounds she had cleaned and bandaged for him. A dart from a Shuara blowgun had struck him in the fleshy part of the calf, causing comparatively little damage until he had tried to pull it out and had discovered that the point was barbed.

"Cusi has gone to see Ninan again?" Tomay asked, making himself wait after each sip of broth, each spoonful of porridge. Micay applied some arrow medicine to the wound with her finger and began to wrap it with a fresh bandage.

"He has gone," she replied. "But he has little hope that Ninan's request will be honored, if he has even been able to make it. Huayna Capac's intentions are too clear."

Tomay took a careful sip of broth and held it in his mouth as long as he could before swallowing. He smacked his lips and groaned with pleasure, his eyes half closed.

"You cannot know how good that tastes," he said. Then he opened his eyes and grimaced apologetically. "I am sorry, Micay, but I think you are correct about Huayna Capac's intentions. He is separating the warriors who stood against him in the square and is sending them to different places. Cusi, of course, must be sent to the farthest place."

"Of course," Micay agreed. She looked up at him and forced a smile. "And there is no need for you to apologize. I know this is a chance for you to return to Hatuncolla, and I do not blame you for welcoming it."

"It has been many years since I have seen Hatuncolla," Tomay said, unable to restrain a smile of his own. "We must pass through it on our way to

Cochabamba, and my family will surely block the road if Yasca tries to avoid being feasted. Perhaps I will take some leave there afterward, as well. But I will not let them keep me," he added hastily. "Cusi and I will return here together as soon as we have completed our duty."

"The journey itself takes months," Micay pointed out, "and then you will have to fight."

"The Chiriguanos have always fled in the past, once they were met with sufficient force. I do not know why the troops sent out from Cuzco could not have done that by themselves," he said with a shrug. "Perhaps Huascar led them."

"Perhaps," Micay allowed, and then fell silent so he could eat. She clicked her tongue at Cahua, who had begun to crawl through the doorway of the guest house, and beckoned for her to come back to where they were sitting. Sinchi had been wrestling with the wicker basket, but suddenly he thrust an arm in the direction of the awning house and let out a loud cry: "Cha-chee! Cha-chee!"

"Do not point with your finger," Micay corrected gently. "It is not polite." She turned to see Otoronco Achachi separating himself from the stream of messengers and count takers who passed constantly between the awning house and the gate. His eyes were on her as he approached, and after a moment of dread and reluctance Micay decided there was no point in putting off what he had to tell her.

"Cha-chee," Cahua and Sinchi said in unison, though their voices trailed off timidly as Otoronco sat down cross-legged next to Tomay. He ignored them and gestured with his chin toward the guest house.

"I have something for you, inside."

"I know," Micay said softly. "Cusi told me that you found my father. And that he is dead."

Cahua had come up close beside her, her head against the side of Micay's breast, her eyes on Otoronco. Sinchi sat listening where he was, the basket overturned between his splayed legs. Tomay had his head down over the porridge bowl, which he was scraping clean with his finger.

"He was alive when we found him," Otoronco told her. "It was after days in which we had seen only glimpses of the Shuaras. They set traps on the trail and shot at us with their blowguns, then disappeared into the forest. It seemed they would do that forever, until we were worn down and had to give up. But then . . . one day . . . a man was waiting for us on the trail. He was not a Shuara; his skin was pale beneath the war paint. When we got closer, I saw that he was old and sick and had to lean on his spear to stand. His nose and mouth had been eaten away by the uta, so that he breathed through a hole in his face."

Otoronco paused to swallow, glancing longingly at Tomay's water gourd. Then he licked his lips and went on. "Somehow I knew who he was even before I recognized his tunic, which was like the ones Acapana and I had sent out as gifts long ago. He prepared himself to fight with us, but he stopped and looked at me when I called him Casca. I told him who I was. I told him that his daughter Misa had married Cusi Huaman, the man who had brought the last war to an end. I told him that you were a healer and that you had two fine children.

"He did not answer me . . . I do not know that he could. But he nodded his head to show that he had heard. Then he lifted his spear and came to fight me. He was so weak we could have captured him easily, but I could see he wanted to die. He wanted to die fighting the Inca. So I honored his wish with my own hand."

Micay had not wept when Cusi had come to tell her he was being sent away, but she wept now, hot, helpless tears that rolled down her cheeks and dripped onto the front of her shift, onto her red shell beads, her long golden pin, even onto her daughter's head. Cahua looked up at her with surprise and then fear, and Micay pulled the child into her lap to reassure her. Otoronco grunted and swept a hand across his face.

"It was because of the way I treated your father that the Shuara sorcerer— the one called Kirupasa—came out to speak with me. He had great respect for Casca, who had fought for him against the other Shuaras before he became too sick. He told me Casca's wife had died of an illness two years before."

All gone, Micay thought, and she remembered weeping in the arms of another Cahua, the friend for whom the child in her lap had been named. The friend who had made her whole and had sent her out to live the life the Inca had given her. Micay hugged her daughter with one arm and reached out a hand to Sinchi, who looked as if he were about to weep, too.

"He was a brave man, my daughter," Otoronco said, "to the very end of his life."

Tomay hummed softly in agreement, and Micay could only nod, breathing slowly as her composure returned. She felt suddenly empty and knew she would not mourn her father and mother after this. The last of her old life was gone, and the life to be was in her arms. She freed a hand and dried her eyes on the edge of her mantle, then gently lifted Cahua off her lap and directed her toward the empty bowls in front of Tomay. She gave Sinchi a brief hug and got him to help her right the basket, a task that got his mind off weeping. Micay looked past him at Otoronco.

"I am grateful, Grandfather. I am honored that it was you."

Otoronco sighed and nodded, looking down at his hands. "I will bring you his spear and tunic."

Micay slung her medicine bag over one shoulder and stood up with the basket the children had loaded for her. They each grabbed a handful of her shift and stood up beside her.

"You must both come and eat with us later," she said to the seated men. "Cusi will want the company of his family and friends."

"He will have it," Otoronco promised. Tomay suddenly remembered the wooden spoon in his lap and handed it to Sinchi, who brandished it like a weapon.

"Cha-chee!" the boy said boldly. Then he turned with his mother and sister and walked away from the guest house, waving the spoon at a messenger who strayed into their path.

THE SUN had begun to sink below the rim of the western mountains, casting the lower level of the governor's compound into shadow and illuminating the upper plaza with a rich golden light. From inside the awning house, Cusi could see only the silhouette of the man who had just come up the central staircase, but he immediately recognized the tall, narrow figure of Lloque Yupanqui. His uncle walked with a kind of stoop now, as if he had suffered a wound that had made him bend inward on himself. He seemed to hesitate at the top of the stairs, then turned and went toward Apu Poma's house, where he had slept since being turned out of the quarters of the Royal Rememberers.

Micay leaned over to whisper in Cusi's ears. "Go to him," she urged.

"He should come to me," Cusi insisted halfheartedly, as the same thought had occurred to him.

"This is not a time to be stubborn about what you are owed. He is your uncle."

Nodding in agreement, Cusi rose and went out into the plaza, stepping around the pile of weapons and traveling gear that he, Tomay, and Uritu would be taking with them. His mother, who was holding Cahua on her lap, seemed to give him an approving glance as he left, which probably meant that she had also seen Lloque. He wondered why she had been able to put aside their differences and bid him a proper farewell, while her brother had not.

Squinting in the powerful wash of light, he made his way to his father's house. Lloque was sitting against the back wall, his head bowed in thought or prayer, his long fingers playing over the memory cord spread across his lap. He looked up slowly when Cusi stepped into the doorway, blocking the light.

"I have made my farewells, Uncle," Cusi said, after waiting for a greeting that did not come. "Except with you."

Lloque stared up at him for a moment. "I did not think it would matter to you." His voice was mild, apparently without rancor or self-pity, though he still had not invited Cusi into the room.

"I would not be here if it did not matter to me. I leave tomorrow, as you know."

"I know."

Cusi exhaled through his teeth. "I intend to come back here to live, but I have seen nothing that makes this certain. Indeed, I have seen and heard of omens that warn of danger and death for our people. There is always the chance we will not meet again."

"That is true," Lloque concurred in the same mild tone.

Cusi bristled angrily, feeling that he was being taunted. "Would you deny me again, then?" he demanded. "You only have to tell me, and I will leave you to your counting."

Lloque lifted the cord and studied it, the colored, knotted strings dangling down from his hands. Then he looked back up at Cusi.

"This is not for counting. It holds a memory that has been buried . . . a song that will never be sung again. You should have it."

He held the cord out like an offering, but Cusi did not move from the doorway to take it.

"What does it have to do with me?"

"It holds your name. The name that was left out of the story song of the final battle against the Carangui." When Cusi simply continued to stare at him, Lloque shrugged and dropped the cord onto his lap. "It has served its purpose. I sang it for the other Rememberers and for the story singers who are taking the songs of victory back to Cuzco. As I had expected, they found reasons why it could not be substituted for the original song we had composed. But I knew none of them would ever forget what they had heard."

Cusi blinked and put a hand against the doorframe to steady himself. "You did that for me?"

"I did it for myself," Lloque said forcefully. "Out of my duty to the truth."

"So that is how you lost your place among the Rememberers," Cusi concluded.

His uncle gave him a sardonic smile. "Perhaps I should have expected that, as well, though I did not. The reaction was exceedingly swift, a testament to the power of your name and reputation."

Confused by the smile, which seemed to mock him, Cusi came into the room and squatted down in front of his uncle. Lloque appeared to have aged since the last time Cusi had seen him this close up, his gaunt features shrunken back against the hard, bony mask of his skull. His eyes were hard, too, and his presence seemed grudging and wary, as if he were poised to fend Cusi off.

"If I had not come to you," Cusi asked, "would you have kept this from me? Would you have let me leave without knowing what you had done?"

"Why not? It changes nothing for you. I did not expect it would."

"You kept my name from being buried completely. Surely you knew what that would mean to me, especially now, when he is sending me away. Why would you refuse me the chance to show my gratitude?"

"I did not want you to mistake my intentions," Lloque said. "Understand me, Cusi: I did not do this to impress you, or to defy the Sapa Inca on your behalf. I am not part of your struggle with him. I have done nothing that would earn your respect."

Cusi grunted and sat back on his heels, feeling his face grow warm. He had to clear his throat before he could speak.

"It was just a gesture, then," he suggested. "You lost your place for nothing."

"The truth is nothing? Perhaps to you . . ."

"To me, the truth would be worthy of more than a gesture." Cusi put his hands to the floor and pushed himself to his feet. The sting of being rebuffed was still with him, but his anger had faded quickly, taking on an exasperated distance. For the second time, Lloque had shown himself to be utterly, willfully irrelevant. Cusi looked down at him and shook his head. "I should have known I could not be reconciled with everyone—especially not with those who are content to stand back and let Huayna Capac do whatever he wishes. That is not just *my* struggle. You had power, Uncle; you were close enough to influence him. Now that power will fall to Titu Atauchi and his kind, men who serve only themselves."

"I have never sought power," Lloque said, "so I cannot regret its loss. There are other places I can serve."

"Harmlessly, no doubt," Cusi said, unable to conceal his disdain. "Far from the decisions that truly matter. I would rather have a reputation as a sorcerer and a rebel than to be so blameless, and so useless. Keep your farewell, Uncle, and your cord. I want nothing more from you."

Resisting his instinctive urge to bow, Cusi turned toward the doorway but stopped when Lloque spoke.

"I never believed you did. I suspected you had come to taunt me with vicious rumors about me and Cori. That is an insult to which *I* can never be reconciled."

Cusi turned halfway back, remembering the apology he had been prepared to offer. There was no point to it now. "It is what Apu Poma once believed, is it not?" he said instead. "It is the reason he hated the sight of me when I was a child."

Lloque suddenly snatched the cord into a ball and threw it at him. Cusi caught it against his chest, though one of the trailing cords whipped him across the face. He blinked rapidly, tasting blood.

"I hate the sight of you now," Lloque snapped. "Remove yourself from my presence. You are unforgivable!"

"Yes," Cusi agreed, baring his teeth in what he hoped was a bloody smile. "And I am certainly no son of yours."

He gathered the cord in his hands, briefly contemplating throwing it back at his uncle. Then he snorted contemptuously and simply let it fall to the floor, and walked out of the room without looking back.

MICAY HAD no memory of when the whispering and touching had stopped and she had drifted off to sleep. But she was immediately aware of Cusi's absence when she awoke, and a sharp pang of loss made her sit up out of her blankets. The darkness had begun to gray with the coming light, giving vague shapes to the objects in the room. She found Cusi sitting a few feet away, his chin resting on his upraised knees, staring down at the twins. Micay took a blanket with her and crawled to his side, draping the warm cloth over both their shoulders.

"He even *sleeps* like Sinchi," Cusi whispered, showing her the whites of his eyes. Micay looked down at the motionless lump that was her son. Next to him

Cahua stirred, throwing off the only blanket that still partially covered her. Cusi reached out and drew it back over her. "*She* is never so lost to the world. She is aware of us even in her sleep."

"You have come to know them well," Micay murmured, putting a hand on Cusi's knee and pressing herself against his side.

"They will be so different when I return. And they will no longer have any memory of me."

"Do not be so sure. Anyway, they will come to know you again."

Cusi nodded absently. His arm rubbed against her breast and his hand found the thong around her neck, then the leather pouch that held his spirit brother.

"If danger comes, take them to the mountains. Your huaca is strongest there."

"I will keep them safe," Micay assured him, wondering why he was telling her this again. They had been over all the contingencies days ago. "Did you have a dream?"

"I could not sleep. I kept thinking about how much I will miss them, and you."

Micay smiled sadly. "I should not be glad of that, but I am. I know you will keep us in your heart."

"Always," Cusi vowed, rising to his knees to embrace her. The blanket fell away, but the chill of the air seemed to evaporate swiftly as his arms came around her back. She led him back over to their bed, aware that he was weeping even as he returned her caresses and grew hard beneath her hands. She pushed him down onto his back and came on top of him, as she so often had during the time when his foot was healing. She was weeping herself, but she did not need her eyes to find how they fit together.

"I will keep you inside me, as well," she whispered, stretching out to cover him and press her lips to his face. She tasted salt and felt his hands cup her buttocks, pushing him in deeper. There was light in the room, enough to see the tears clinging to his lashes as his eyes widened and he murmured her name. Micay put her lips over his and shut her eyes, and they began to move together for the last time.

XV

HUAMAN RUNACONA: The Hawk Men

(A.D. 1523)

Cuzco

T HE STONE huacas in the meadow below, the shapes of the dun-colored hills that shouldered in on the road, even the particular gray of the sky: all had a familiarity that was deep yet eerie, like something recalled from a dream. It had been working on Cusi ever since they had crossed the great bridge over the Apurimac, lulling and exciting him at the same time, making him withdraw into himself. When he saw the messenger coming down the road toward him, he realized that he and Quizquiz had been marching in step at a steadily increasing pace, despite the rising inclination of the road. They and the small vanguard of warriors with them had outdistanced the rest of the column, unconsciously striving to be the first to see Holy Cuzco.

They halted reluctantly and listened to the messenger, accepting the message on behalf of Yasca, who was farther back in the line. Cusi felt the sweat begin to cool on his body and wondered why they had been hurrying. Cuzco would look the same no matter when they saw it; a few moments would not change whatever shock or gratification lay in store for them. He glanced at Quizquiz and saw no similar realization on the warrior's hard-bitten face, which did not surprise him. Quizquiz was a man who moved by instinct rather than reflection, and his most natural impulse was to go forward.

"I will wait and tell Yasca," Cusi offered, and he stepped to the side of the road as Quizquiz raised his spear and resumed the march. The warriors were quickly past, only thirty left out of the thousand who had departed from

Tumibamba three months before. The rest had been released along the way, sent back to their cities and home villages along with another thousand craftsmen, weavers, and workers who had also served their turns. The column now numbered only a few hundred, and of those only four—Cusi, Tomay, Quizquiz, and Yasca—would be going on beyond Cuzco.

Cusi hefted his battle-ax and looked around at the hills, allowing himself to see them and to remember the times he had come here with his family or his initiation brothers. The meadow below, Quiachilli, was venerated by the Iñaca household, for it was there that Pachacuti had finally broken and scattered the Chancas who had menaced Cuzco. Offering a silent prayer to the memory of his ancestor, Cusi gazed down over the rock-strewn plain, noting that the bunch grass had already begun to yellow. He wondered what Pachacuti would think of the Incas if he had walked the length of the Northern Quarter as Cusi had, and had seen what had become of the kingdom he had created.

The next members of the column to reach the place where he stood were the count takers, some twenty of them, who had been sent to assist with the great census Huayna Capac had ordered. They had been cheerful travelers, curious about the places they passed on the Royal Road. But with Cuzco so close, most of them had donned the mask of duty, their eyes fixed on the road and their faces set in expressions of diligent attention. After them came the story singers, each carrying a painted wand as a symbol of their task. Cusi felt their glances but ignored them, refusing to acknowledge that he shared any secret with them. They were followed by several whole families—though none with small children—all wearing the blue livery of the palace retainers. *They are the ones who truly carry my reputation,* Cusi thought, as the servants went past him with their heads bowed. It occurred to him that he might still be considered a hero in Cuzco, though his stature was certain to diminish as soon as the retainers began to relate the news they had carried from the court in Tumibamba. Cusi snorted softly and shrugged the thought aside. His concern for his own reputation had diminished with each step he had taken away from Tumibamba, and he had no illusions about returning to Cuzco in triumph. He would enter the city as he was: tired, hungry, dirty, and itching from the lice that had been with him for half the journey.

Yasca finally appeared in the midst of a group of Cañari goldsmiths, and Cusi raised his battle-ax in a brief salute as the war chief came over to the side of the road to greet him.

"A message came for you, my lord," Cusi reported. "The Heir and the Regent have prepared a feast of welcome for us in the Amarucancha."

Yasca grunted thoughtfully, no doubt impressed that Huascar had lent his name to the invitation. The Heir could not have been pleased by the announcement of Ninan Cuyochi's regency, and he probably knew that Yasca was carrying the official confirmation of the act.

"Well, he has had three months to recover his equanimity," mused Yasca. Then he swept Cusi with a warning glance. "Keep watch over your friend the Colla tonight. He was asking me if he would be made to visit the Grass Men before he could enter Cuzco. Though what he asked was whether anyone would *try* to make him visit the Grass Men."

"What did you tell him?"

Yasca snorted scornfully. "My commanders share their secrets only with me. But if anyone should challenge him, see that he has the good sense to send them to me."

"Does Uritu have your protection, as well?" Cusi asked.

The war chief nodded brusquely.

"I expect *you* to protect yourself. I know the governors and michos told you things they were afraid to say to me. Think carefully, Cusi, before you choose to repeat them."

Cusi squinted at him skeptically. "Are we not far enough from Tumibamba? I had gotten used to speaking frankly again."

"That is the only way an Inca should speak," Yasca growled. "How *freely* you speak is another matter. I want to return to Tumibamba when our task is completed; I do not wish to be given a post in Chuquiabo or someplace worse. So I will let the governors and the census takers make their own reports. I do not want my name associated with bad tidings, and neither should you."

"I hear you, Lord," Cusi said in a chastened voice. "I will watch what I say. What if we are asked directly?"

"Then we will answer directly. But not as if we were the inspector, sent out to make a judgment. You understand me now? Good, let us go, then . . ."

"I will wait here for Tomay and Uritu," Cusi told him. "We left Cuzco together; we should return the same way."

"After ten years," Yasca said, as he stepped back out to join the column, "it is probably the only thing that *will* be the same."

THE PATALLACTA, however, seemed exactly the same, except that its many terraced levels were nearly deserted. All of the Iñaca members were either gone or working in the palace, the head retainer explained as he led Cusi and his friends up to the compound Otoronco Achachi had once occupied. It did not appear to have been occupied since, though its houses and the courtyard with the stone seat were spotlessly clean. The retainers were grateful to have someone to serve, and more of them than were needed appeared to help the warriors make themselves fit for the feast. The men soaked in a steaming hot bath and scrubbed themselves with yucca roots while the servants took their lice-ridden garments away to be brushed or burned and inspected their clean clothes to be certain they were not similarly infested. Then a retainer with a large collection of flint and obsidian blades cut and trimmed the men's hair, and his helpers combed it straight with fine-toothed, oiled combs that removed any eggs the lice might have left behind.

Cusi felt civilized again when they were done, and the feeling seemed to release all the memories he had of this place. He stood in the back doorway of the house he had occupied when he lived here, looking down over the gray and yellow rooftops of Cuzco and beyond to the mountains that ringed the city. He remembered feasts and ceremonies he had attended here, and conversations with Otoronco, and his visit to Pachacuti in the enclosure above. But inevitably all his thoughts came back to Tocto Oxica, with whom he had spent his last night in Cuzco, in this very room. He could barely conjure up the image of her face, but the memories of that last night sent waves of heat through his body and paralyzed his limbs with a kind of confused yearning.

He was still standing in the doorway when Urcon came in to find him. Even though he would not be attending the feast, Urcon had also submitted to the ministrations of the retainers, so Cusi received no warning scent of llama before the herder was beside him.

"I did not mean to startle you," Urcon apologized. "Your friends are waiting outside."

Cusi shook himself and turned away from the view, which was disappearing into shadow as the sun set behind the mountains.

"I was not as ready to be back as I had thought," he said softly. "I had thought about the place, but not the people I knew here."

"There *are* no people here. The last time I was in Cuzco, you could barely move through the streets. Now you are surprised when someone appears in your way."

Cusi experienced a moment's confusion, then remembered that Urcon had left Cuzco before him, with the Sapa Inca. "I had two years to get used to the empty streets. They are even emptier now, and poorly swept in places." He paused and gave Urcon a long look. "No doubt you will be going back to your village tomorrow. I am sorry we cannot spend this last night together."

Urcon shrugged and shook his head slightly. "I had no chance to tell you before. I have been asked to tend one of the pack trains for the warriors going to Cochabamba."

"But you have been released!" Cusi protested. "And you have served your family's turn many times over. No one can make you do this against your will, Urcon. I will speak for you—"

"There is no need," Urcon assured him. "I agreed to go. I was offered four alpacas—two breeding pairs—as a prize. For that, I can wait a few more months to go back."

"No one offered me such a prize," Cusi said wryly. Then he smiled at his friend. "But I am glad that we will be comrades for a while longer."

"I have seen Mama Cocha," Urcon said gravely, "but not Lake Titicaca." Then he gave Cusi a smile that was boastful in its brilliance. "I want to tell my grandchildren that I have seen both."

Cusi laughed and clapped him lightly on the shoulder. "The lake does not roar like Mama Cocha, but you will not forget the sight, I promise you. And perhaps there will be time to visit your village before we head south again. I will find out tonight."

"Are you more ready now?" Urcon asked, as they turned and walked toward the front doorway.

"As always, you have lightened my spirit," Cusi said gratefully. Then he cocked his head and gave it a rueful shake. "But no, I had three months to prepare myself, and somehow I never could." He shook his head again and stepped out into the courtyard. "Perhaps there are some memories we can never be ready to meet . . ."

ONCE THE THREE warriors had been passed through the palace gate, Uritu was sent on ahead to the courtyard where the feast was being held. A member of the Royal Guard, a Cañari who knew Rimachi and asked as many questions about Tumibamba as he could get in, led Cusi and Tomay to a different courtyard, where five men stood in a small circle in front of an awning house, surrounded at a distance by an equal number of torch bearers. Cusi and Tomay exchanged a swift glance as they came up next to Yasca and Quizquiz and saw that the fifth man was their former teacher, Aranyac. The two men beside him, predictably, were Huascar and the Regent, Auqui Topa Inca. Cusi and Tomay concealed their surprise and made a proper mocha to the Heir. Then they bowed in turn to the Regent and Aranyac.

"Cusi Huaman and Tomay Guanaco," Yasca said in introduction. Then he turned to them to recapitulate what had already been said. "Our forces have not yet assembled, but we cannot wait for the rest of them before we march. The Chiriguanos are threatening Cotapachi and Incallacta, where many of the storehouses are located, so the people have no place to store the crops they have just harvested. We will have to take the warriors we have and provide a garrison for them."

Cusi nodded impassively, though he was astounded to hear that an attack force had not been mustered in the time it had taken them to march here from Tumibamba. Perhaps it had become necessary to offer prizes to the warriors, too.

"All we have so far from the Western Quarter is a contingent of Soras and Rucanas," Yasca continued. "Quizquiz will be their commander. There is another contingent composed of mitmacs from the immediate area; they are yours, Cusi. Tomay will have the Collas and Lupacas who should be waiting for us in Hatuncolla and Chucuito. I will command what is left of the Charcas' own defenses, as well as whatever warriors come from the Eastern Quarter."

"How many are we facing?" Cusi asked carefully, struck by the vagueness of Yasca's accounting. The war chief gave the Regent a hard glance before responding.

"At present . . . two or three times our own number. Though more may come over the mountains before we arrive. I expect each of you to have your men ready to fight, and fight hard, by the time we reach Cochabamba. We depart in two days."

The three commanders bowed in compliance, and Yasca looked back at the men across from him.

"Is there anything else, my lords?"

"We have been promised a full regiment from Chincha and Ica," the Regent said in a defensive voice. "We will send them after you without delay."

"Good," Yasca said curtly. He lifted his chin toward Aranyac. "Lord?"

"I have sent my own men ahead to prepare the way for you," Aranyac told him. "You will have all the supplies you need, and the warriors of the Southern Quarter will be waiting for you as expected."

Yasca nodded more politely, as if impressed by the conviction in Aranyac's voice. Then everyone looked to the Heir, granting him the final word and the power to dismiss the meeting. Huascar stepped up to the commanders and began to inspect them, his eyes half hidden by the yellow fringe around his forehead. He had grown considerably since Cusi had seen him last, adding layers of hard muscle to his stocky wrestler's frame. He had the arms and shoulders of a stonemason, and though he bore no battle scars, his presence was not that of a man grown soft from sitting. Cusi had heard that Huascar had won his Huarachicoy race some years ago, but until now he had never believed it might have been an honest victory.

"Your deeds have been sung here, my brothers," Huascar said, his voice deep with admiration. "Everyone has heard of the courage and daring of Quizquiz and Cusi Huaman and Tomay Guanaco. Cuzco is honored by your presence, and I am confident that with leaders such as yourselves and the valiant Yasca, our warriors will drive the Chiriguanos back over the Andes. I only wish I could march with you."

"We can use every man, my lord," Yasca said suggestively. But the Regent intervened forcefully, shaking his head in denial.

"It is inconceivable. Do not tempt yourself, Huascar. There is too much that requires your presence here."

"As always," Huascar snarled, and he spat on the ground with a violence that shocked Cusi and made the men around him stiffen. Aranyac was the first to recover, and he spoke with the authority granted him by virtue of the white in his hair.

"You forget yourself, my son," he said sternly, but Huascar did not even turn to look at him.

"I am forgotten," he muttered. Then he threw up his hands in a gesture of dismissal. "Let us eat, then. That much I can share with you, at least."

Cusi bent with the others to make the mocha, but Huascar simply walked past them toward the exit, followed closely by the Regent and the majority of the torch bearers. Blinking in the sudden darkness, Cusi found Yasca looking over at him. The war chief grimaced knowingly, reminding him of their earlier conversation and Yasca's prediction that nothing would be the same. Cusi nodded in acknowledgement, though in his own heart he wondered if things were not, in fact, too much the same.

AT FIRST, in the flickering light of the torches, Cusi did not recognize the frail, stooped old man who was standing with Uritu just inside the courtyard where the feast was being held. So he looked past both of them, scanning the small but sumptuously dressed crowd, expecting at any moment to meet Tocto's dark eyes looking back at him. He still did not know what he would say or do when he saw her again; he simply hoped he would have a moment to gauge his feelings and collect himself before they were face to face. But while there were several young women in sight who bore a family resemblance to Tocto— no doubt her sisters or half sisters—there were none who required more than a second look. Gradually Cusi's gaze returned to Uritu and his elderly companion, and he realized with a start that the old man was his grandfather, Ayar Inca. He hurried over and bowed low before him.

"Forgive me, Grandfather . . ."

"I have aged, I know," Ayar said tolerantly, putting a hand on Cusi's shoulder as he straightened up. They appraised each other for a moment, and Cusi saw a kind of shrewd sympathy in the old man's watery eyes. "So have you, my son. Let me say it plainly, then: she is no longer here. She has become the high priestess. She lives now on the Island of the Moon in Lake Titicaca."

"The high priestess," Cusi repeated blankly. The knot of tension inside him began to loosen and uncoil, as if some threat had been removed.

"The position came open two years ago," Ayar continued, his hand still gripping Cusi's shoulder, "and it can be filled only by a woman of royal blood. Tocto Oxica proved herself the most willing and worthy."

So she had taken herself out of Huascar's reach, as she had vowed. Her own huaca had rescued her when Cusi's had failed. He wondered if she knew he had tried and felt a sharp pang of disappointment that he would not be able to tell her himself. But the regret had come belatedly, well after his initial relief, and he realized that although he had wanted to see her again, he had also wanted to be safe. He had not wanted to be tempted to love her again.

"I needed to know that," he confessed, meeting his grandfather's eyes and nodding in gratitude. "The memories were too powerful to be denied. Even though I have a wife whose place could never be taken by anyone."

"It would not be like you to forget," Ayar said. "Certainly I had not. But come, the food is being brought out." He lowered his hand to Cusi's elbow and steered him and Uritu toward the mats that had been laid out in the center of the courtyard. "Uritu has been telling me about your life in Tumibamba, but you must tell me more as we eat. I could not recall a ñusta named Micay, though perhaps she is younger than you. Whose daughter is she?"

"You could not have known her, my lord, or her parents. She was a chosen woman from Chachapoyas."

Ayar stopped at the edge of the mats and squinted at him curiously. "A gift from the Sapa Inca?"

"From the gods, perhaps," Cusi allowed. "She was taken into our family as a companion for Quinti Ocllo long before I ever arrived in Tumibamba. It was more years before I knew I had to marry her."

"You say she is the first wife?"

"The first and only," Cusi insisted. Ayar rubbed his chin and glanced briefly at Uritu.

"Uritu also told me that you already have an estate of your own."

"It is called the Rainbow House," Cusi said proudly. "It is in the mountains east of Tumibamba. It *was* a gift from the Sapa Inca."

"To the Iñaca household?"

"To me. The households possess little in the north beyond their prestige."

Ayar looked from Cusi to Uritu and back again, shaking his white head in disbelief. Finally he pointed at the mats with his chin. "Sit, my sons, and fortify yourselves. You will need your strength—and all your patience—to help an old man understand the kind of life you have led away from here. I fear I may know nothing about it . . ."

AT A CERTAIN point late in the meal, as he filled his mouth with a spoonful of thick turkey stew, Cusi thought to himself that this was real Inca food. Potatoes, quinoa, maize, and meat—all thoroughly cooked and heavily seasoned with salt and uchu peppers. Good food that had been made to seem plain and humble, even to a warrior's taste. He realized that what he truly meant was real *Cuzco* food, since the Incas in Quito and Tumibamba did not eat like this at a feast, not with people like Fempellec overseeing the kitchens. Not with the wide variety of foods that came daily from the Hotlands and the coast.

The thought of Fempellec made him realize, in turn, how much he and his brothers had been leaving out of the stories they had been telling his grandfather. It had proven easier to heed Yasca's advice than Cusi had expected, partly because of how much there was to recount but also because of how easily Ayar was shocked. In telling him about Quinti, Cusi had spoken proudly of her role as a mediator between the Coya and the high priestess, never thinking that Ayar might find the need for such a mediator controversial in itself. That slip had cost Cusi a long, difficult explanation that had nearly led him into matters that were truly controversial. He had been more careful thereafter, so careful that they had concluded their shared account of the Carangui War without mentioning the day they had stood in the square with Huanacauri in their midst, threatening to leave. That was a subject that definitely required a direct question, and so far Ayar had not asked it.

Tomay had been talking about the Guanaco House, slyly testing Ayar's response to a *Colla* having land of his own, a test Ayar passed by remaining consistently amazed and doubtful about the practice of ownership itself, without regard for the blood of the owner. There was a lull in the conversation, and Cusi glanced across at Aranyac, who had joined them some time ago but had yet to speak. The teacher—now the lord of the Southern Quarter—intercepted the glance, and Cusi saw an impatience in the man's eyes that made him feel like a student again—a student who had not been thinking carefully about his answers.

"So, my sons," Aranyac began, "we have heard about your successes and your rewards. Tell us what you saw coming here."

Cusi hesitated, exchanging a glance with Tomay, to whom he had conveyed Yasca's warning earlier. Then they both looked at Uritu, who was of course waiting for one of them to speak.

"Come," Aranyac demanded. "Are we such children that you must watch your tongues around us? I can tell you some of what you saw. No doubt you walked on roads and bridges in need of repair, past many fields that had been left to lie fallow. In those that had been planted, you saw women and old men and children working, though probably not as many children as you would have expected. You saw extra guards around the Inca's storehouses, and the officials you spoke to sounded frightened and harassed, perhaps even angry. If you listened to them with sympathy, they would try to tell you what it was like, to be always asking for more when you had less and less to give."

The three friends exchanged another glance, stunned rather than hesitant, and this time Tomay spoke up.

"You have eyes that travel, my lord," he said with a grim smile. "We have seen all of these things. And every place we stopped, the people were summoned to see *us*. They were told that we were the army the Sapa Inca had sent to punish the rebel Chiriguanos, even though in each place some of our number would be released to their families as soon as the ceremony was over. We did that until we had released so many warriors that we no longer had enough to impress anyone. Then, finally, we could march on as if we meant to get here."

Aranyac grunted in acknowledgement and looked expectantly at Cusi and Uritu. Cusi deferred to his friend, who spoke with unusual bluntness.

"Little joy was shown at our coming, except in the places where warriors and workers were released or where our purpose had been misunderstood. Near Xauxa some of us were sent out to gather firewood, and when the people in the fields we were passing saw our bows and spear throwers, they greeted us like heroes. They thought we had come to hunt. They said the governor had not organized a hunt in three years, and they showed us what the deer had done to their crops." Uritu paused and licked his lips. "When we told them that we did not have permission to hunt, they begged us to send someone back to request it. We finally did, but we were refused. Yasca said he could not afford the delay. When we came back the same way with our bundles of wood, no one even looked up from their work."

Cusi was aware of Ayar sitting up straight beside him, no doubt struck by the different tone of these stories. But it was Cusi's turn to be frank, and he could not evade the challenge in Aranyac's insistent gaze.

"I spoke to many of the officials," he said flatly. "I listened to the complaints they would not express to Yasca. More than one told me that the labor tax had been stretched beyond the limits of fairness, and that to ask for any more was to risk rebellion. I heard stories of men who had abandoned their homes and fields and become outlaws, and of others who committed crimes and then presented themselves to be punished, hoping to be made into retainers. One chief said he could no longer punish the women of his clan for adultery, since it was the only way they could get children to help them with their work. He did not know if the husbands would be angry or grateful when they returned, but it had been so long since *anyone* had returned that he could not blame either the women or himself."

There was a long silence when Cusi had finished, and when he finally brought himself to look at his grandfather, he found Ayar staring back at him accusingly.

"You have been humoring me," Ayar scolded. "Do I appear so old and foolish that I should be told only pleasant things?"

"Do not blame Cusi, my lord," Tomay intervened. "Yasca warned us to be careful of what we said here."

"Careful with those of your own blood?" Ayar demanded, still glaring at Cusi. "With those who are above you in experience and rank? And the two of you are scouts—what kind of scout tells his leader only what he wishes to hear?"

"A bad scout," Cusi conceded. "But there are such men in Tumibamba and probably here, as well. They have a way of blaming the scout for what he has seen, as if he had caused it."

"You do not seem to have suffered," Ayar began, but Aranyac held up a hand to forestall him.

"This has happened to you?" he asked quietly.

Cusi nodded. "You will probably hear soon that the Sapa Inca is displeased with me. I do not know what will be said: that I am disloyal or disrespectful or untrustworthy. Perhaps that I am a sorcerer or a caster of spells. I do not claim to be innocent or helpless, my lord; I have not always been careful about what I have said and done. But I have served the Inca well, and I do not think I deserve the accusations that are made against me."

"I *know* he does not deserve them," Tomay declared, and Uritu grunted forcefully in assent.

Aranyac studied each of them in turn. "You have made a serious accusation of your own," he said at last. "If I am to believe you and not what is said about you, I must hear more of what you have left unspoken."

"Would you allow the Sapa Inca to be criticized in your presence?" Cusi asked, turning slightly to include his grandfather in the query. Ayar bared his teeth in a grimacing half smile and gestured with his chin for Aranyac to speak.

"It is no secret that all is not well in the Four Quarters," the lord said. "Yet Huayna Capac refuses to heed our pleas that he return and assume his rightful place. That in itself leaves him liable to complaint. Say what you must, my sons, only let it be honest and worthy of our consideration."

Ayar nodded emphatically in agreement, and Cusi looked at his brothers to see if either of them wished to begin. Tomay raised his head and pursed his lips thoughtfully.

"We must go back to the second campaign," he suggested, "when Huayna Capac came into the field for the first time."

"On his litter," Uritu added, and the five of them drew closer together, ignoring their food as Tomay began a new account of the Carangui War, a harsh, unsparing account that nonetheless raised Cusi's spirits and made him feel—in a way that simply being in Cuzco had not—that he had come a great distance from Tumibamba.

WITH THE first rays of Inti's light shining in their faces, the three friends walked up the street called Hatun Rumiyoc, heading for the training field just outside the city, where Cusi's mitmacs were being gathered for his inspection. As they passed the palace of Inca Roca at the summit of the hill, Cusi felt a fresh pang of yearning for Micay, who bore the name of the former ruler's famous Coya, Mama Micay. Uritu must have been struck by the same thought, because he turned to remind Cusi of the conversation he had had with Micay on their last day in Tumibamba.

"She was willing to have him come to me, as you heard," Uritu said. "You will have to arrange to send him when he is old enough. Better still, bring him yourself."

Cusi wondered briefly if Micay had been serious about her offer to send Sinchi to Uritu, or if she had merely been caught up in the emotion of a farewell she could not voice. But no, she knew Uritu too well to make such a mistake; she had to have known he would take the offer seriously.

"I will see that he visits his uncle in Vitcos," Cusi promised, and Uritu gave him one of his rare smiles.

"I will teach him how to hunt with the bow and the blowgun, and how to chew coca and drink sweet manioc akha."

"And how to melt in the heat and be devoured by insects," Tomay grumbled, recalling his experience in the land of the Shuaras.

"He will not mind that," Uritu said confidently. "He has the spirit of a Campa."

"He was drawn to you, certainly," Cusi allowed. "I will send him, but I will see that he is initiated as an Inca first, to be sure he comes back."

They continued down the street, laughing a bit too loudly at their own jokes. They were all carrying their weapons, but Uritu also had his bedroll and a bundle of personal belongings slung over his shoulder. He was not going all the way to the field with them today, nor would he be marching south with the new column when it left on the day after tomorrow. He was going home, perhaps never to march with them again.

Halfway up the next hill, they came to the compound that had belonged to Cusi's family. Cusi peeked through the curtained doorway to find it uninhabited, with dust gathering in the corners of the courtyard and swallows nesting in the brittle thatch atop the houses. He let the curtain fall back abruptly, reminded of the abandoned Mochica cities he had visited on the coast and of his own unwillingness to imagine Cuzco in such a desolate state. There is nothing so great that it cannot be lost to memory, he recalled, feeling that some of his own memories had already been abandoned here.

He did not share these thoughts with his friends, however, not wishing to arouse the sadness that was already so close to the surface in all of them. Instead he brought up something Aranyac had told them, a plan that Huascar had suggested some time ago, in which the adopted kin who ran the administrative affairs of the city would be brought in from their crowded villages on the outskirts of Cuzco and lodged in the compounds left empty by the Incas of the blood. Aranyac and the other lords had supported the plan, but the Regent had wavered, and the households, to whom most of the compounds belonged, had refused to consider it. So the plan had died, and the officials continued to spend part of each day walking between their homes and their tasks in the palace.

"I would rather have seen someone living there," Cusi said, "no matter who they were. Better commoners than birds and mice."

"Perhaps if someone other than Huascar had suggested it," Tomay reasoned, "it might simply have been seen as sensible. But the households remember how his father resented their wealth and power, and it can only be worse for Huascar. Where will he go to establish himself, now that the northern provinces have been given to Ninan?"

"He will go to the Eastern Quarter," Uritu predicted. "The Shuaras have never been conquered."

Cusi glanced at him in alarm, but Tomay grunted scornfully.

"Nor will they be, not by us. Besides, they have nothing worth taking. Though . . . if anyone is foolish enough to attempt it, it would have to be Huascar."

"We might march together again after all," Uritu suggested.

But Cusi shook his head and banged his battle-ax against his shield. "Forgive me, my friend, but I hope not. Anywhere else, but not against the Shuaras. Have you forgotten Otoronco's promise?"

"I heard him make it," Uritu said, sounding surprised. "But it was never his to keep. I think he knows he will suffer for it."

"And me?" Cusi demanded.

"Perhaps you will suffer, too, but you are Cusi Huaman. You have survived greater threats. You are meant to."

Uritu stopped, and Cusi saw that they had reached the place where the path to the training field diverged from the street that would soon become the Eastern Quarter Road: the road that would take Uritu over the mountains into the Yucay Valley and then northward to Vitcos. Cusi abruptly forgot the Shuaras and looked at his friend, reminding himself not to let a farewell slip out.

"It is not too late to come with us," Tomay urged, though without much conviction. "Yasca would be pleased to have you."

"He is pleased to have anyone," Uritu said, baring his teeth to show them he was teasing. "Fight well against the Chiriguanos, my friends. I will be in Cuzco for the Inti Raymi each year, should you also be here."

"If any of your people are sent north, have them come to us," Cusi offered, rushing out the words to keep them from catching in his throat. "We will look after them for you."

Uritu freed a hand to touch each of them, gripping Cusi by the shoulder, Tomay by the forearm. His dark eyes glittered and his nostrils flared, and the thin black lines tattooed on his broad cheeks seemed to rise to the surface of his skin.

"You are my brothers," he said hoarsely. Then he turned and walked away rapidly, his long black bow in his hand, his feathered head held high.

"You are mine," Cusi whispered, and heard Tomay murmur something similar. Then Tomay nudged him with an elbow, and the two of them turned and went down the path toward the field, keeping their heads down, looking only ahead.

Tumibamba

THE MAN LAY on his right side while Micay removed the bandages and the dressing that covered the back of his head. He had received a heavy blow, probably from a battle-ax, just above and behind his left ear, and the healers who had treated him in Piura had been forced to remove an oblong piece of his skull in order to relieve the pressure on his brain. The skin of his scalp had then been sewn back over the wound, leaving a shallow, oblong indentation in the middle of the shaved area. Micay inspected the sutures that held the flap of skin in place, noting that they were still tight and that the puckering of the flesh around them had receded. The healers in Piura had been extremely skillful, she thought with renewed admiration as she applied a fresh dressing and gently bound it in place.

"Very good," she said, helping him to sit up with his back against the wall and a rolled-up blanket cushioning the back of his neck. "It is healing well."

The man sat with his head cocked to the left and his eyes focused on a point just above and to the right of her head. Micay did not alter her own position to meet his gaze, knowing he would only raise it higher. This was the way he saw now. She had learned from one of the men who had come back with him that his name was Paucar Rimay, and that he was an Inca by privilege from the Sañu clan of Cuzco. He had been a captain in the force sent to punish Piura. He responded to his name and could even say it, but otherwise Paucar Rimay—Gaudy Speaker—could not speak for himself. He could repeat words and utter brief, bewildered exclamations, but he seemed to have lost the names of even the most common objects, and he promptly forgot whatever she tried to teach him.

The other eight men in the room, all of whom had suffered equally grievous wounds, had already lost patience with him and considered him hopelessly deranged. Yet Micay could see the struggle going on behind his eyes, and she could feel the terror his confusion caused him, so that he would sometimes thrash his limbs in frantic helplessness, twisting his body as if to meet an enemy who was always behind him. She could not abandon him in his struggle, even if she did not know how to help him beyond treating his wound and calming him with her presence.

"I am Mama Micay, Paucar," she told him, as she always did. She had no doubt that he recognized her, but he had yet to say her name. She took his hand and lifted it up between them. "This is your hand, Paucar. Your hand. *Hand.*"

"What is . . . no . . . what is . . ."

His head wobbled on his neck, his mouth gaping as if waiting for words to fill it. Micay rubbed his hand between her own to warm it, feeling the looseness of the skin. He was a much larger man than Cusi but probably weighed less. She did not know how he had survived the journey back from Piura, unconscious and in the hands of warriors who would not have had the patience to feed him. He still did not know how to eat by himself and forgot what he was supposed to be doing if someone was not there to put the spoon in his mouth.

"Your hand, Paucar," she repeated stubbornly, and heard her words echo loudly, though she had not raised her voice. She realized that the conversations going on around her had suddenly ceased, and she looked up to see Quinti standing in the doorway, Sinchi holding one of her hands and Cahua the other. They seemed frozen in place, Quinti tall and elegant in a buff-colored shift and mantle, gold gleaming from her mantle pin and the bands around her wrists. Micay could not believe that her sister-in-law, who had once trained as a healer, had forgotten what kind of men were kept in this house—that she did not realize this was no place for a friendly visit and no place to bring children.

But then Quinti bowed to the prostrate men, who all seemed to have curled into themselves, hiding their bandages and the stubs where an arm or a foot had been. She spoke in a clear, unembarrassed voice.

"Greetings, my friends. I am Quinti Ocllo, the wife of your commander, Quilaco Yupanqui. As you know, he is still in Piura, holding the city against the rebels. So I have come in his place to pay my respects to his brave warriors."

Micay glanced around the room and saw expressions much like Paucar Rimay's, men lost for words. She squeezed Paucar's limp hand and thought she felt a tremor of response.

"I am also the sister-in-law of your esteemed healer, Mama Micay," Quinti went on, and lifted the hands of the children at her sides. "These are her children: my niece, Cahua, and my nephew, Sinchi."

"Sin-chee!" the boy repeated emphatically, and then let out a whoop that would have made Uritu proud, though it momentarily deafened everyone in the room. Micay was about to admonish him when she heard another sound start up around her, a sound she could not recall having heard in this room before. The men were laughing. Sinchi grinned and broke free from Quinti's grasp, and then came right over to Micay and gave her a hug, ignoring the fact that she was still holding Paucar's hand. She saw that Cahua had stayed with Quinti and that the two of them had knelt down in the midst of the men, who were rearranging their blankets and trying to raise themselves up on their elbows.

Sinchi let go of Micay and stooped to disengage her hands from Paucar's. She thought he was displaying more of the possessiveness that had arisen with Cusi's departure, but instead he kept hold of Paucar's hand and glanced at her for approval. He was trying to help.

"This is Paucar Rimay," she explained, smiling at her son. Sinchi cocked his head in imitation and closed his right eye, staring at the injured man with his marked eye.

"Poker Rimi," he mimicked clumsily, giving the man's hand a shake. Paucar blinked rapidly, as if dazzled by the light.

"Why is the . . . I—I can . . . say how . . ."

Micay put an arm around Sinchi and got him to lower Paucar's hand back into the man's lap.

"Paucar was hurt while fighting for your Uncle Quilaco," she told the boy, who had tired of looking at Paucar sideways and had straightened up. He seemed perplexed by the fact that Paucar continued to look over his head.

"Head hurt," Sinchi said, pointing at the bandages with his chin. "Head hurt fighting."

"Yes," Micay agreed, deliberately lowering her tone. "That is why you must speak to him softly, with respect."

"Speak softly," Sinchi echoed, casting a doubtful glance at Paucar, who mumbled something utterly unintelligible. Losing interest, the boy turned, shrugging off Micay's arm, and went to see what his sister was doing. Cahua and Quinti had moved to the other side of the room to visit the men there, and Micay watched as they talked to a man whose arm had been amputated at the elbow. Cahua was staring unabashedly at the bandaged stub, but the man seemed too awed by Quinti's presence to mind. He even smiled at the child and tossed his head dismissively, as if his loss were nothing that should distress her. Quinti kept her hands clasped in front of her, touching the men only with her voice and the flawlessness of her appearance. When Sinchi squatted down next to her, one of the men greeted him by name, and there was more laughter and teasing comments that Sinchi accepted as praise. Watching, Micay was suddenly ashamed that she had underestimated Quinti and deeply grateful that she had come. These men needed her recognition as much as they needed medicine and rest.

Finally Quinti rose and got the twins to stand up with her, and they began to make their farewells. Micay turned back to Paucar Rimay, whom she had all but forgotten. She saw that his face was horribly contorted, his lips twisting and flapping as if he had been poisoned. She came up into a crouch beside him, afraid that he was having an attack of some kind. His hands were clenched into fists, and suddenly he spoke, spitting the words out with such force that everyone in the room turned to hear.

"Head! My . . . *head.*"

Then he slumped back against the wall, exhausted and panting. Micay quickly lowered him onto his side, arranging the blankets so he could sleep. His emaciated face had gone slack but his eyes were still open, staring past her. But *seeing* her, she knew, however imperfectly. She laid a soothing hand on his forehead and smiled down at him.

"Rest now," she told him gently before she rose to follow Quinti and the twins out of the room. "Rest now, Paucar Rimay, and believe that the healing has begun, *inside . . .*"

"IT WAS KIND of you, Quinti," Micay said, as they watched the twins run off to join Quespi's children in the far corner of the enclosure. "You help them heal in a way that we cannot."

"It was little enough," Quinti scoffed. "I do not stain my hands with their blood, as you do. The children were wonderful; you should take them with you more often."

"I will now," Micay promised. She squinted at Quinti in the bright sunlight, seeing lines of fatigue that her face paint could not conceal. "Had you been to see Chimpu Ocllo?"

"Of course," Quinti said. She sighed, shaking her head in bemusement. "Do you know, when I came to find you, I was going to ask if you would come back to the court with me."

Despite herself Micay laughed out loud. "Quinti! Have you forgotten whose wife I am? Or how much Mama Huarcay hates me? You cannot be serious."

"Oh, I see now how foolish it was," Quinti allowed, though she did not smile. "Your work here is much more important, much more useful. It is just that I have missed you, my sister."

Micay was sorry now that she had laughed, though she was as surprised as she was moved by Quinti's plaintive tone. She took Quinti by the elbow and led her toward the awning house where Quespi and the other women were working.

"I thought you were happy in your role as go-between. Finally you did not have to scheme or dissemble or make friends for a reason. And you have been so successful . . . you have won the respect of nearly everyone."

"I *was* happy," Quinti admitted, "though it is lonely when you cannot join any of the factions except as a guest. And it has only gotten lonelier, as you probably know."

They stopped just under the awning house roof, out of hearing of the other women. Micay did have an idea of what Quinti meant, but she decided to draw her out anyway. So she simply shrugged and spread her hands. "I am afraid I know little of what happens in the court anymore."

Quinti let out a long breath, but then she spoke without her usual circumspection. "It is more divided than ever. There is my mother and her allies among the older wives, who want to return to the life they led in Cuzco. Then there are the younger women who have forgotten Cuzco and who like living here, or who do not want to risk the prestige they and their husbands have established here. The royal wives fall into both groups, mostly depending on their closeness to Huayna Capac or the Coya. Some will encourage him in whatever he seems to desire, simply to gain favor for themselves. Some do it to undermine Rahua Ocllo's prestige with him. There is even a group that wants to restore the primacy of the first Coya, Cusi Rimay, and have Ninan Cuyochi made the rightful Heir."

"And the Coya herself?" Micay asked when Quinti paused for breath.

Quinti made a waving motion with her hand. "Implicitly, she is with those who want to return. She sees her daughters growing old here, while the only man they could marry remains in Cuzco. But she cannot openly join my mother's party for fear that the other wives might use it against her."

A sharp comment hovered on Micay's tongue, but she held it in, letting Quinti go on without interruption.

"Then there is the high priestess," Quinti said. She sighed again. "You must know yourself how she has changed. She used to be a force for reason and cooperation, but now she is impatient with everything I tell her. She barely listens, then talks to me instead about omens and earthquakes and reports of unexplained deaths. I come here from the court and feel as if I have somehow entered a foreign land."

"Has she told you about her dreams?"

"Many times. She tells me about other prophecies and visions, as well, and she wants me to spread her fears throughout the court." Quinti held her palms up in front of her, appealing to Micay with an exasperated grimace. "I am willing to carry her message, but she will not tell me the source of these other warnings. She says she must protect the people who have confided in her. But who will heed the warnings of nameless people? If they are to be trusted, they must have the courage to come forward and be recognized."

"Can Huayna Capac be trusted not to punish them?" Micay asked.

Quinti drew back slightly, regarding her with a sudden coolness. "That is the kind of question she asks, as if the answer were obvious to everyone."

"It is to me," Micay told her bluntly. "That is why I serve her. I believe in what she is trying to do."

"Then you must have little patience with my concerns."

"I have little patience with the court, I must admit. But I respect you for trying to make it better. You have made a place for yourself that is valuable to us all." She held Quinti's eyes to show that she was serious, then softened and laid a hand on her arm. "And I care about you like a sister, Quinti. Nothing has changed that. If I do not show it more openly, it is because I do not wish any harm to come to your reputation."

Quinti covered Micay's hand with her own and looked down for a moment.

Then she gave Micay a pained smile. "I have never hidden the fact that Cusi is my brother, and I would not distance myself from you, either."

"Still, if we are to be seen together, let it be here or in the governor's compound. Let no one think I am trying to influence you."

"Am I to believe that, as well?" Quinti asked skeptically.

Micay shook her head. "You must be aware at all times that I am trying to influence you. How else can I be certain that you are listening?"

Quinti laughed and released Micay's hand, gazing at her with a kind of wistful respect. "You always did have to take a side."

"As I told you, I have taken this side because I believe in it. I am one of those who brought a prophecy to Chimpu Ocllo. Cusi is another."

Quinti stared at her for another moment, then nodded briskly and glanced up at the sun. "I will let you tell me another time, my sister. As long as you will listen to my complaints about the court."

"We can complain about our husbands being gone, too," Micay assured her. "That is something we have in common with all sides."

"I must go, but you have reminded me that Cori Cuillor asked about you the last time I saw her. I was never certain what she wanted, though she seemed to think highly of your reputation as a healer."

"I cannot imagine why she would be interested in me," Micay said, stepping out into the sunlight to see Quinti off. "Is she still attached to Mama Huarcay?"

"I am not certain of that, either. She has become a close friend of the Coya's eldest daughter, Chuqui Huipa. I tell you so that you will know that you have not been totally forgotten in the court. You will have to decide if that pleases you."

Leaving her with a wry smile, Quinti turned and walked toward the enclosure gate, her long, glossy black hair swaying behind her. Micay was again aware—as she had been in the sickroom—of the drabness of her own appearance: the loose, dark-colored shift and belt that let her move freely while hiding stains; her plain, unpainted face and the lack of a mantle or jewelry. She did not miss such things often, especially now that Cusi was gone, but occasionally their absence made her feel neglected and insignificant. Why should Cori Cuillor or anyone else in the court be interested in her?

Then she conquered the feeling and turned back into the awning house, telling herself that no one would be healed by her vanity. Telling herself that recognition should not matter to her. And wishing Cusi were here to prove her wrong.

WHENEVER FEMPELLEC came to the governor's compound, he usually went first to visit his friends among the retainers. He would send one of them ahead to tell Micay that he was coming, though he would not appear at her house until well after dark. He was convinced that Mama Huarcay had spies everywhere, and he had given Micay sufficient examples to make her believe that his fears, if somewhat exaggerated, were not unfounded.

This night, however, he came unannounced, slipping in through the curtained doorway while Micay was still putting the twins to sleep. She saw him immediately, in the light from the fire she had burning in a brazier, but he gestured silently for her to go on and then squatted near the doorway to wait. As she smoothed the blankets around Cahua and Sinchi and lulled them with a song, Micay reflected on the fact that it had been more than a month since Fempellec's last visit. At that time he still had not been to Quito to see Amaru, but he had found some consolation in the form of another young Chimu whom he had recruited for his staff. She wondered if that had led him into trouble or if it was something else that had brought him here like this.

When the children were at last asleep, she gestured to him and moved to the other side of the brazier. He rose with his heavy cloak still wrapped around him and came to join her, though he paused on the way to look down at the twins, his lips pursed in a thoughtful frown. Micay followed his gaze and saw that the dark blot surrounding Sinchi's eye was clearly visible in the reddish glow from the fire, a sight that roused a vague, anxious stirring in the pit of her stomach.

Fempellec squatted down across from her and held his hands out toward the fire, shivering despite the cloak. She studied his face for a moment and could not tell if it was cold or agitation that was making him shiver, because he was clearly quite agitated.

"Do you have coca?" he asked abruptly, though not without a note of pleading. Micay gave him a searching glance, then reached behind her and brought forth her coca bag, a lime container, and a silver spatula.

"She has forbidden me the privilege," Fempellec explained as Micay passed the items over. "She says coca makes me rash and irresponsible."

Micay waited while he filled his cheek with a wad of coca leaves, added the powdered lime, and began to chew. She did not have to ask who "she" was. Nor was she surprised that he had finally lost Mama Huarcay's favor, though he had kept it much longer than she had ever expected.

"How did it happen?" she asked once he had reduced the size of the lump in his cheek and seemed calmer. The combination of the coca and his Chimu accent gave his voice a hissing wetness, but she could understand him well enough.

"I made a mistake. No, two mistakes. Do you remember the boy from Farfan I told you about? Yes? Well . . . he has earned himself a promotion to her personal staff."

"He betrayed you to her," Micay concluded, and Fempellec nodded and swallowed with a grimace, as if his throat hurt.

"I overheard him talking to another of my assistants, repeating something he had heard Mama Huarcay say. I could have ignored it, but I was annoyed with him for things he had said to me, so I scolded him and told him not to spread false rumors." He grimaced again. "That was the first mistake: accusing her of speaking falsely. The second was in believing that whatever I said would be kept between the two of us. I went to him later to apologize, but he had already gone to tell her. Now it seems likely to me that he had been waiting for the opportunity all along."

"What was the rumor?" Micay asked.

He evaded her eyes for a moment, plucking the chewed coca from his mouth and dropping it onto the coals of the fire, where it sizzled and then briefly blossomed into flame.

"It was about you," he said, and swiftly held up a hand. "I am not claiming I did this on your behalf, Micay. I know you do not need me to defend you from rumors."

Micay nodded impatiently. "You have told me why you did it. Tell me what she said."

"It was about your children. She is telling people that the marks they bear are the signs of adultery. She claims that their real father is the Cañari captain Rimachi, and she reminds everyone of the fight Cusi and Rimachi once had at a royal feast. That is apparently all the proof she offers, but it is something many people remember."

Despite herself, Micay thought of all the times recently that she had allowed herself to be seen with Rimachi. But then fury rose up and wiped out such considerations, leaving her blind and shaking with hatred. It was several moments before she could speak, her voice crackling with rage. "She is a vicious, hateful woman. Not even children are safe from her lies. I told you she was dangerous!"

"You did," Fempellec agreed. "Now I believe you, and I want to be free of her."

The resolution in his voice made Micay pause, and some of her composure returned. His smooth-featured face seemed hard and his eyes glinted in the firelight, reflecting a kind of desperate cunning.

"How do you mean to be free of her?" she asked. He leaned toward her, lowering his voice even further. "If there were a poison . . . something the other healers would not recognize . . ."

"No," Micay said without hesitation. "I cannot use what I know to take a life. Not even hers."

"Just tell me the name," Fempellec urged. "I will find it for myself. Your hands will be clean."

"Say no more, Fempellec," she commanded. "My vows to Mama Quilla forbid it."

"I knew you would not do it," he said with a scowl, sitting back on his heels. "Cusi would never be so kind to an enemy. The Incas kill anyone who stands in their way."

"The Incas kill poisoners by crushing them beneath large stones," Micay reminded him. "My refusal is a kindness to you. You are no murderer, Fempellec; you could not withstand the suspicion that would be cast upon you."

"Then help me go back to Chimor. Persuade Otoronco Achachi to take me with him."

Micay stared at him for a moment, feeling both manipulated and mystified by the sudden request. Had the talk of poisoning simply been a prelude to this? But her curiosity finally won out.

"What makes you think Otoronco is going to Chimor? He has said for the last month that it was time for him to return to Chachapoyas."

"I only know what is said *about* him," Fempellec replied. "He has been mentioned as one of the leaders of the force that is going to march on Chimor. I know it has not been announced, but it will be soon. The rebels in Piura were not alone."

There had been rumors of such an expedition for months, but Otoronco had shown no interest the one time Micay had asked him about it. He had claimed to have his heart set on going to Puna, and when all hope of that had vanished, he had bitterly declared his desire to return to Chachapoyas—bitterly *and* loudly, to anyone who would listen. Micay suddenly saw that it had all been a pretense, a masterful ruse that had used Huayna Capac's perverse sense of reward to Otoronco's advantage. He had known he would never be given what he appeared to want. Micay also realized Otoronco would probably come to her again, this time with his interest unconcealed.

"If this is true," she said to Fempellec, "what I know of Chimor would be useful to Otoronco. He might also appreciate a Chimu guide he could trust."

"I had the same thought," Fempellec said dryly. "Will you speak to him for me?"

"I would—if you are certain this is what you want. There will be punishment this time, and killing. Some of your people will see you as a traitor."

"I have been called worse things. I have to leave, Micay. *She* was waiting for this opportunity, too, and I have seen what she has done to others. She will make me pay for every bit of favor I received in the past."

"You will have to bear it until the warriors are ready to leave," Micay pointed out. "That could be several months."

"That is why I came now; she has only begun to threaten and humiliate me. But this must be kept a secret. If she knows Otoronco wants me, she will never let me go. She would denounce me first."

"Otoronco can keep a secret," Micay assured him with a smile. He looked down for a moment as if shamed by the smile, then nodded in gratitude and rose to his feet, gathering his cloak around him.

"If there were another way," Micay asked, "would you prefer to stay here?"

"Here or in Quito," he allowed. "I do not *want* to help the Incas kill my people."

"Then make no more mistakes. Something we cannot foresee may yet occur."

"Spare me your hopes," Fempellec snorted, and turned to go. At the doorway he turned back and gave her a wistfully sardonic smile. "I would rather have a good, swift poison . . ."

"WHAT MORE can you possibly do for this man?" Mama Cori asked. "You have healed his wound and restored him to health. But only the gods could heal what has happened to his mind and spirit."

Micay attached another thread to her spindle and gave the conical piece of wood a spin as she let it drop, pulling the thread out of the clump of alpaca wool in her lap. The Inti Raymi was less than a month away, and she was helping Mama Cori make cloth for offerings.

"We have found places for all of the men who were with him," Micay told her. "But he has no immediate relatives here, and the members of his clan say they have no one who could care for him. He is truly helpless, more dependent than these two," she added, gesturing with her chin at Cahua and Sinchi, who were playing between the pools. "But he is much better than he was, and he *tries* so hard. It may take him half a day, even two days, to remember the word he wants, but he still recognizes it when it finally comes. And he can eat by himself now, as long as someone puts the spoon and bowl in his hands."

Mama Cori watched Sinchi lug a large rock over to the retaining wall of the pool, so that he and Cahua could climb up onto the top. She gave Micay a skeptical glance. "He will never catch these two, however hard he tries. I admire your dedication, Micay, but this man needs a caretaker, not a healer. You will not have time for him once the wounded begin to return from Puna and the land of the Huancavelicas."

"I know," Micay admitted sadly. "Quespi has been working with him, too. If only we could somehow give him enough memory to make himself useful again . . ."

Something at the compound gate had captured Mama Cori's attention, and Micay followed her gaze and saw Lloque Yupanqui standing with the micho. Lloque had a pair of bundled memory cords in his hands, and he gestured with one of them as he spoke to the younger man.

"There is someone whose memory is being wasted," Mama Cori said wistfully. "He carries the cords because the count takers need and expect them, but he keeps every count in his head."

Micay watched as Lloque gave the cords to the micho, and she wondered, with an exasperated yearning, why she could not have just a little of his enormous capacity to give to Paucar Rimay. If only memory could be exchanged as easily as those cords . . .

"What is it?" Mama Cori asked in alarm when Micay suddenly stood up and jerked her spindle back up into her hand.

"I think I know what he needs."

"My brother?" Mama Cori began, but then dropped the query when she saw Lloque coming toward them. He seemed old and preoccupied, shuffling his feet slightly as he walked.

"Greetings, my sister . . . Micay." He cast a curious glance at the thread tangled around the spindle in Micay's hand. "Please, do not let me interrupt your work."

"I need your help, my lord," Micay said. Lloque raised an eyebrow at the blunt urgency of the request. The two of them had not spoken in a serious way since Cusi's departure, and they both knew that the avoidance was not accidental.

"My help with what?" he asked finally.

"I need you to make a memory cord. A cord to help a man remember how to live."

He settled himself on the edge of the pool across from them, next to the children. He smiled back when Cahua looked up and smiled at him, and he gazed for a moment at Sinchi, who was staring fixedly at his own reflection in the water, occasionally stirring the image with his hand. When Lloque looked back at Micay, he seemed less reluctant to meet her eyes.

"Who is this man?"

"His name is Paucar Rimay," Micay explained. "He is an Inca by privilege from Cuzco. He was badly wounded in Piura . . . the back of his head was crushed in. He has recovered from the wound, but it has robbed him of the ability to remember anything. Even the names of simple things elude him, so that he cannot hold a thought or a task in his mind."

"How do you propose to help him?"

"When I saw you with the memory cords, it suddenly occurred to me that what he needs is something he can touch. Something he can *feel,* like the spoon he eats with, to remind him of what he should be doing."

Lloque leaned forward with his elbows on his thighs. "Can he see colors?"

"I think so. I came one day in a light-colored shift, and he seemed very startled. He is used to seeing me in dark clothes."

"He was a captain of the warriors," Mama Cori interjected, "so he must have learned the use of memory cords."

"Anyone can learn the cord," Lloque said with a certainty that was dismissive. "It is in our blood and on our fingertips. I have taught it to men who did not know a word of Quechua."

Mama Cori was about to say more but restrained herself, drawing a swift glance from her brother. Micay saw something unspoken pass between them, and she realized that Mama Cori did indeed see this as something Lloque needed as much as Paucar Rimay. Lloque put his hands down and pushed himself to his feet.

"I will come and see this man if you wish," he said to Micay, who put both hands around her spindle and bowed over it.

"I would be most grateful, my lord. So will Paucar Rimay, though he will not be able to show it."

Lloque gave her a pained smile. "I am accustomed to that kind of gratitude. I will come tomorrow with my cords."

With a last oblique glance at his sister, he turned and walked out onto the plaza, heading toward the crowd in front of the governor's awning house.

"He has been so withdrawn," Mama Cori remarked as Micay sat back down beside her. "Ever since he lost his place with the Rememberers. Or perhaps it was something Cusi said to him. He has been wounded so deeply that he will not speak of it."

Micay tensed slightly, having heard all of it from Cusi. But Mama Cori simply resumed her spinning, apparently willing to wait until Lloque told her himself—or did not tell her. Micay began to untangle her own spindle, though she was tempted to break with politeness and tell Mama Cori what she would not ask to hear. This kind of reticence was like a bandage without a dressing beneath it; it merely hid the wound, allowing it to bleed and fester.

But Mama Cori's impassive face seemed to warn against such an attempt, so Micay kept her silence, thinking about the cord Lloque had tried to give Cusi, the cord that held a forgotten name and a song that would never be sung again. She prayed he would provide something more useful for Paucar Rimay.

Chuquiabo

C USI AWOKE with a dull, throbbing pain in his temples, panting for breath in the thin, icy air. He thought immediately of coca, the best remedy for altitude sickness, but he would have had to extricate himself from the cloak and blankets he had wrapped so tightly around his body, and the air he could feel against his face was too cold to risk the loss of warmth. He lay back in the darkness, aware of his men sleeping around him, and thought instead of Tiahuanaco. The memory of the place filled him with an immediate sense of well-being, an inner strength that defied physical discomfort, even if it could not banish it entirely. His foot was still sore from the march and his throat had not recovered from the speech he had made there, but it was at Tiahuanaco that he had discovered he was meant to make this journey.

He could no longer recall the exact impulse that had led him to ask Yasca for permission to take his warriors there. Partly it was a selfish desire to visit the holy place he had been told about in Hatuncolla and Chucuito, though he had not mentioned that to the war chief. Instead he had tried to justify his desperate notion that his troops needed to undergo a trial, a common ordeal that might bring them together as a fighting force. Because what he had led out of Cuzco was not a unified regiment of two hundred men but ten separate squadrons of twenty or so, each wearing its distinctive native dress and following its own battle standard. They were all Cuzco mitmacs, their families having been settled near the city generations ago, so they had an innate respect for an Inca of Cusi's rank, and they had all heard the stories of his exploits. They accepted his orders without question and were eager to learn from a warrior who had faced a real enemy, as most of them had not. But whenever he had tried to get them to recognize each other as comrades, he had seen them close their faces and hearts with a singular stubborness. Some harbored ancient hatreds that went back to their original homelands, though most of the animosity seemed to arise from more recent disputes over privilege and property around Cuzco. One group had spied on another, or had stolen water rights, or had deliberately insulted the other's customs and beliefs. Cusi had quickly stopped listening to their complaints about each other, to keep from being made a judge.

Yasca had not been wholly persuaded of the wisdom of this excursion, so he had allowed Cusi only three days to rejoin the rest of the column. To meet this requirement, Cusi had led his ten squadrons on a forced march across the plain, pushing them so relentlessly that by midday they no longer had the strength to compete with one another and had focused all their hatred on him. Yet he would not let them rest, leading them past the grazing herds of llamas and alpacas while a cold rain fell from the dark, empty sky. There was thunder and lightning for a time, as well, but he rejected their pleas to seek shelter, telling them that he was a brother to lightning, a favorite of Illapa. The boast seemed wild and presumptuous even to him, but he was too exhausted and desperate to temper his words. He did not know what he would find at Tiahuanaco, and he could only pray that it would somehow make up for the pain of the march. He prayed constantly to Illapa, having been told that the founders of the site, the ancestors of the Collas and Lupacas, had been worshipers of the ancient Aymara sky god, Thunupa.

As they came over the last set of hills, the wind suddenly came up and the sky began to clear. Shafts of sunlight broke through to warm their backs as they marched in among the broken walls and fallen pillars, the priests and pilgrims who had come before them standing back out of the way. At the end of a long paved plaza, Cusi found what he had come for: an open doorway, set in the middle of what appeared to be a single, massive piece of stone. The walls flanking the rectangular doorway were blank and polished to a fine smoothness, but the lintel above, which rose like the crest of a great headdress, was carved with rows of winged figures, centered on a much larger figure that seemed to emerge from the stone directly above the doorway. Tarapaca, the Lupaca captain who had led them here, made the mocha and whispered in Cusi's ear.

"Thunupa," he said reverently, and Cusi bowed and made the mocha himself, blowing kisses to the figure, whose square head was surrounded by a halo of rays or lightning bolts, some of them ending in puma heads. He held a hawk-headed spear thrower in his right hand and a double-headed serpent staff in his left, and round tears descended from the blank orbs of his eyes. These were all symbols of Illapa, as well, though carved in a geometric style that reminded Cusi of the Chimu and Mochica friezes he had seen on the coast. Such a coincidence seemed incredible to him, but as he gazed up at the figure,

he was struck by an even more powerful recognition: this was the god described in the story song of Pachacuti's vision, the god who had urged him to
lose his mind and undertake the impossible.

Interrupting politely, Tarapaca pointed with his chin at the rows of winged
creatures, who seemed to run to serve Thunupa, carrying serpent staves of
their own.

"Huaman runacona," he murmured, his eyes wide. "Hawk Men, like you."

"Like all of us," Cusi decided, and stepped up into the doorway, discovering
that it had been cut for a man exactly his size. There was only a finger's breadth
of space above his head when he turned and gestured for the men to sit and
listen. The sun was now shining down on them fully, drying their wet clothes,
and the lingering clouds cast black shadows on the terraced hillsides. Cusi felt
the beauty and power of the place, and when he was finally able to speak he
addressed the men with a passion and eloquence that seemed to flow into him
from the outside. Afterward, he could not remember everything he said to
them, though he recalled pointing to the ruins that lay all around them and
asking if they would let this be the fate of Holy Cuzco. He recalled telling them
that the Chiriguanos would fight as one man against them and that they would
perish if they did not band together with the same trust and loyalty. He told
them they must form a clan of warriors; that they must be Hawk Men, not
Huancas or Lupacas or Paltas. Then he turned, stepped through the doorway,
and beckoned for them to follow, greeting each man on the other side and
making him stand with his comrades, not his countrymen.

Cusi came out of his reverie and saw that it had begun to grow light, so that
he could make out the individual blanket-wrapped bodies filling the courtyard
around him. Propped against a nearby wall was a shield that bore a crudely
painted image of one of the Hawk Men, black against a red background. Cusi
thought of the battle standards that were being woven for him from a much
more precise rendering, and he was suddenly eager to resume the march to
Cochabamba. He freed himself from his blankets and stood up, feeling the cold
like a slap against his bare arms and legs. The great snow-capped mountain
Illimani glowed against the sky to the east. Cusi picked up his battle-ax and
crept toward the compound gate, stepping carefully around the prostrate
bodies in his path. His breath hung in a cloud in front of his face, and he could
smell his own sweat and the stink of the llama fat he had rubbed into the seams
of his clothes to prevent lice.

To be fair to the sentry, who had no reason to suspect danger from this
direction, he dragged one sandal slightly as he approached the gate. But then
he sprang through the opening in one bound, landing in a crouch with his ax
at the ready—and found the sentry crouched behind his shield, the point of
his spear leveled at Cusi's chest. The man, a Cana whom Cusi had caught
sleeping at his post in Chucuito, grinned proudly from beneath his knit cap.

"Good," Cusi said curtly. "Perhaps you will stay alive, after all."

"I am a Hawk Man," the sentry boasted, tapping his spear against the
winged creature painted on the front of his shield.

"You may carry one of the battle standards, then," Cusi told him, stepping past him into the street. "I am going to get them now. Rouse your comrades and tell them we march at first light."

"I hear you, Lord Huaman," the man declared, and turned back into the compound. Cusi went on toward the weavers, hearing the sentry shouting behind him in Quechua rather than Cana, so that all the men would understand and rise together.

Nasakara, Charcas Province

AT THE PLACE where the road finally leveled off and there was no more mountain to climb, the pile of small stones left by previous travelers stood shoulder high. Cusi added his offering to the pile, murmuring a breathless prayer of thanks to the mountain for allowing him to reach the summit safely. Then he went over to where Yasca was standing alone, his long cloak flapping around him in the cold wind. A short distance beyond the war chief, Tomay and some of his captains were conferring with a delegation of Charca warriors, who must have come from Cochabamba to meet them. Beyond them Cusi had his first glimpse of the Cochabamba Valley, a startling green against the dull browns and yellows of the surrounding mountains.

Yasca said nothing at first, and Cusi stood beside him in silence as his men marched past, pausing only to leave their offering stones on the pile. Despite the fact that they were all breathing hard from the climb, their ranks were tight and orderly, and it was impossible to tell one squadron from the next. They had done well, too, in the drills and mock combats Yasca had arranged during the course of the march from Chuquiabo. Cusi was proud of the progress they had made, though he had yet to hear a word of praise from Yasca.

Finally, as one of the stiff red and black battle standards was being carried past in front of them, the war chief thrust out his chin and spoke.

"What is that? Some more of your sorcery, or something you learned from Otoronco Achachi?"

Cusi could not tell from Yasca's tone whether he was amused or impressed or offended, or possibly even suspicious. But it surely did not sound like praise.

"It is our battle standard, my lord," he said carefully. "It is one of the Hawk Men from the doorway of the Sky God in Tiahuanaco."

"Ah. I have heard about your performance at Tiahuanaco. Are you a priest now, too, or do you simply devise a ceremony whenever it suits you?"

"I told you why I went there," Cusi reminded him. "Surely you can see how they stand together now."

"You did not tell me you planned to give them your own name and a battle standard in the colors of the Iñaca household."

"I did not tell you because I had not made a plan. And those are the colors of Pachacuti, whom I believe was also inspired by the god of Tiahuanaco.

What is your complaint with me, Lord? Should I not use everything I know to inspire them and make them better warriors?"

"That is what *I* want to know," Yasca replied, turning to loom over him. "Have you made them better, or simply yours? Will they fight on if something happens to you? Or do they require the inspiration of their warlord?"

"I am no warlord," Cusi snapped. "They will fight for whoever leads them. They have always been loyal to the Inca; I have simply tried to make them loyal to one another. If that displeases you, my lord, you have the power to remove me from their command."

Frowning ferociously, Yasca gave him a hard, prolonged stare, then looked away toward the distant green of the valley. Cusi was aware of his men going past behind him, and his pride in them almost made him regret his angry words. It would be painful to lose them now, though he tried not to let this show when Yasca turned back to him.

"I am not displeased," the war chief admitted, "though I must know one more thing. You have not promised them more than they were offered in Cuzco, have you? You know we will not be allowed to keep whatever we take back from the Chiriguanos."

"I do not know what they were offered in Cuzco," Cusi said truthfully. "All I have offered them is a chance to return there alive."

Yasca grunted, appearing satisfied, or at least reassured. "We are two days from Cochabamba. I will stay there to rally the Charcas and wait for the rest of our troops. I am sending Quizquiz and his men to Cotapachi to guard the royal storehouses. You and Tomay will go to Incallacta and hold it against the Chiriguanos when they return."

"They have gone?"

"They were not driven out," Yasca warned. "The Charcas think they went back over the mountains to harvest their crops. So there is no immediate danger. You should have time to scout the area and establish your defenses."

Cusi nodded. "Will we have enough men to hold them?"

"Perhaps. The Quillacas who live there should provide some help, since they have suffered the most from the Chiriguano raids. You may be called upon to relieve the garrison at Chuquisaca, but otherwise you are to stay where you are and let the enemy come to you. Is that clear? Your Hawk Men might be eager to try their wings, but you will keep them on the ground and ready. I will not tolerate any unauthorized attacks."

"I have heard you," Cusi said, at last understanding the reason for the war chief's suspicious questions. He risked a smile. "Did you think I had decided to win this war by myself?"

"You are young," Yasca said with a shrug, "and not accustomed to being out of favor. It might have occurred to you, perhaps at Tiahuanaco."

"I have not forgotten that we are outnumbered and untested. I want to return alive, as well."

"Go join Tomay, then. The Charcas have been telling him what kind of enemies these Chiriguanos are. Apparently they have a leader who is a foreigner, though they think he is a god."

"Do the Charcas also believe this?"

"They believe it is what has made the Chiriguanos so dangerous. They have always sent raiding parties over the mountains to steal metals and women, but now they seem to want more. Go ask the Charcas. Have them tell you what the Chiriguanos do to those they kill or capture."

Cusi bowed and began to turn away, but Yasca's taunting smile made him cast an inquiring glance back. "What is that?"

"They eat them," Yasca said bluntly, waving him toward Tomay. "Let your Hawk Men ponder *that . . .*"

Tumibamba

MICAY and Quespi had brought their feasting clothes with them to the high priestess's compound, and when they had completed their work for the day, they went to the women's house to wash and dress. As Quespi combed out her hair for her, Micay watched her in a hand mirror and was suddenly reminded of her dream.

"I had a dream last night," she said. "We had all cut our hair as short as a boy's."

"How awful," Quespi said, pausing and then pulling the comb downward with a shudder. "Had we been punished for something?"

"I do not know," Micay confessed. "We had also painted our bodies with some kind of shiny paint, like a grease, and we wore masks that covered our faces, though we could see through them. I think we were tending the wounded, but our movements were slow and very solemn, like those of a ritual . . ."

Quespi stopped combing altogether. "Have you told this to the high priestess?"

"I did not remember it until just now. It was so strange, Quespi. Later the men were all naked, and so were we, and we were carrying their clothes on long poles held out in front of us."

"You must tell the mamanchic," Quespi advised.

Micay nodded. "I will, though not until tomorrow. Tonight I want to eat and dance and enjoy myself, and not think at all about injuries or omens."

"Or children," Quespi agreed with a laugh.

"Come, Rimachi will be here soon," Micay said, and they got down to the task of fixing their hair and painting their faces. They barely knew Rimachi's youngest sister, whose marriage feast they would be attending, but the opportunity to wear their best clothes and make themselves beautiful had been more than welcome, and they had both been looking forward to it for days. They laughed at their initial clumsiness with the slender paintbrush, though their skill came back to them rapidly and they were soon admiring one another without reservation, lapsing into Chacha in their excitement.

They had just finished when they heard Rimachi's voice outside asking about them, so they quickly gave each other a last inspection, plucking loose threads from garments and patting errant wisps of hair into place. Micay debated leaving her medicine bag behind but then slung it over her shoulder, deciding that she would find someone trustworthy with whom to leave it at the feast. It would probably be safe here, but she had gone to too much trouble gathering medicines in the mountains and on the coast, and there were some— given to her by Hanp'atu—that simply could not be replaced.

Rimachi rewarded their efforts with a smile of admiration that made the scar on his cheek climb toward his eye. Then he spread his hands in a helpless gesture and bowed, offering his speechlessness as the ultimate compliment. When he spoke, though, it was with his usual eloquence, and he addressed most of his flattery to Quespi. There was a trace of self-mockery in the compliments he paid Micay, a subtle acknowledgement of the nature of the friendship they had established since Cusi's departure. Micay smiled and teased him back, grateful that there were no ambiguous glances or concealed longings between them.

"Always the healer," Rimachi sighed, looking down his long nose at the bag under her arm. "My sister is clearly lovesick, but I do not think she wishes to be cured."

"Some conditions are better left to heal themselves," Micay told him. "I will recommend seclusion and bed rest, with her husband to attend her."

"I am sure they will find that a tolerable remedy," Rimachi agreed. Then he looked past her, his smile fading into an expression of bemusement. Micay turned to find Paucar Rimay standing a few feet away, blinking at them in confusion. He seemed dazzled by the bright colors of their clothes and jewelry, his mouth hanging open in the foolish grin he always wore in company. Micay doubted that he had any more control over the expression than he did over his cockeyed gaze.

"I can . . . help?" he asked in a timid, jerky voice. Micay went to him and took his right hand, which was holding one of the cords tied to the waistband he wore over his tunic. She removed the cord, which had a single large knot at the end, and held his hand between both of hers, in the grip that belonged to her alone.

"Mmmm," she murmured to remind him, and after a moment he stopped blinking and his fingers tightened on her wrist.

"Micay," he blurted out, and she rewarded him with a smile. She cast a swift glance around the courtyard and saw no one in need of the kind of help he could provide.

"You must rest now, Paucar. Rest," she repeated, and finally he nodded and lifted his hands away from his sides, dropping the colored cord he held clenched in his left hand. There were two different sets of cords tied to the waistband. Those on his right hip were all brown and had various kinds of knots tied into them: a fringed one for sweeping, knots on top of knots for carrying, the single large knot simply to ask to help. Those on his left hip were unknotted but of several different colors, each corresponding to a cloth streamer that hung above the doorway of one of the buildings in the cancha. Micay undid the two cords that had brought him here, each of which had been wrapped several times around the waistband, so they would be the first to come to his hand. Then she took the red cord—for the storeroom where he slept— and wrapped it around the band in a similar fashion. On his right hip she wrapped the cord that ended in a series of identical tiny knots, wondering as always how Lloque Yupanqui had chosen them to represent sleep.

When she stepped back, Paucar's hands came down and fumbled to find the short cords, and he arched his neck to see the color of the one on the left. His mouth, still grinning loosely, formed the shapes of unspoken words, and then he captured the command and turned away while he had it, shuffling off in the general direction of the house marked in red. Micay restrained the urge to call out a farewell, knowing it might only distract him and cause him to lose his way.

"So that is the man," Rimachi exclaimed softly. "Llampu has told me about him, and only yesterday Apu Poma was complaining to me about how his brother-in-law had become a nurse."

"He has been tireless," Quespi said in Lloque's defense. "None of us could have taught him so much."

"What will he do now?" Rimachi asked. "Just sleep?"

"Perhaps," Micay allowed. "Sometimes he talks to himself or practices the names of the cords. He likes to draw on the floor with charcoal."

"What does he draw?"

"Shapes and patterns," Micay said. "Some of them are quite beautiful, though they are always incomplete."

Rimachi rolled his head on his neck and shrugged his powerful shoulders as if to reassure himself that the muscles still worked. "Forgive me," he said, obviously embarrassed that he could not conceal his discomfort. "It is injuries like his that warriors fear most. Perhaps more than death."

"Their wives, too," Quespi added, and Micay took each of them by an arm and started them moving toward the compound gate.

"Let us be grateful, then," she suggested, "that we have not had to be as brave as Paucar Rimay."

RIMACHI'S GRANDMOTHER, to whom Micay had entrusted her medicine bag, came to find Micay while she was resting between dances. The old woman drew her away from the circle of light, holding the bag by its strap in front of her.

"Another wife asks for you. I think you will want this."

Micay accepted the bag reluctantly. The heat of dancing was still flowing along her skin, and she had only just begun to feel smooth and supple in her movements. She had no desire to leave now, before she had even had a second cup of akha. But then it occurred to her that something might be wrong with one of the twins, and she thanked Rimachi's grandmother and hurried toward the compound gate. A cloaked figure stood waiting, her back turned to the torch affixed to the wall next to the entrance. Micay had to draw close before she could recognize Cori Cuillor's face beneath the hood of the cloak.

"You must come with me, Micay," the young woman said immediately. "Chuqui Huipa needs your help."

"Is she ill?"

"She is bleeding terribly. We cannot stop it."

"Surely the royal healers . . ."

"We cannot call them. The bleeding . . . she is losing a child."

"I will come," Micay decided, and they went out through the gate together, into the dark streets of the city. "When did the bleeding start?" she asked as they walked rapidly toward the Mollecancha. "Did she fall or receive a shock?"

Cori Cuillor was silent for a long moment. "It was nothing like that. She intended to lose the child. She took a potion of herbs someone had gotten for her."

"Who? The father?"

"No! I do not know who gave it to her. That is the truth."

"And who *is* the father?"

"I cannot tell you that," she insisted, and Micay deliberately slowed her pace, forcing the other woman to turn and look back for her.

"You are involving me in a crime," Micay said in a hard voice. "Two crimes."

"Nothing will fall on you, Micay, I promise! But you must save her!"

"I may not be able to, and you may not be able to keep your promise. I must know with whom I share this crime."

Cori Cuillor made a choking sound and twisted away from Micay for a moment. Then she whirled back and spoke in a hiss.

"Ninan Cuyochi."

Micay grunted and came to a complete stop, moving again only when Cori Cuillor gestured frantically for them to go on. Micay gradually resumed her former pace, but she was nagged by the implications of Ninan's involvement.

"There is something else I must know," she said finally as they walked across a corner of the plaza toward the palace gate. "Does Mama Huarcay have a hand in this?"

"No!" Cori Cuillor said vehemently. "Why would she?"

"She is one of those who wish to make Ninan the Heir, and you used to be attached to her. I know the hold she can have, and the evil she can do. If you think you can serve Chuqui Huipa and her, too, you are—"

"I serve only Chuqui," Cori Cuillor interrupted. "This was no scheme. She loves him!"

Her voice had risen uncontrollably, so that the sentries at the gate all came to attention. Micay put a hand on her arm to calm and guide her.

"Then I have no more questions," Micay said. "Let us go and save her."

THE DOORWAY and the windows at both ends of the small room had been covered with blankets, and the air was thick with acrid smoke from the brazier in the corner. In the lurid red glow of the coals, Chuqui Huipa lay curled up on her side, moaning and weeping with her hands over her face. The fear in the room was nearly as palpable as the smoke, and Micay made an instinctive brushing motion, as if to keep it away from herself.

"Open the windows and doorway and fan some of the smoke out of here," she told the other women. "And kindle a torch."

Cori Cuillor hesitated, no doubt fearing detection. One of the other three women was Amancay, who had trained for the Quichuchicoy with Micay. They were all young wives, and Cori had said that none of them had had any experience as a healer or a midwife. Micay snapped her fingers sharply.

"I must have light and air," she commanded. "Go stand guard if you are afraid of someone coming. But first bring me whatever is left of what she drank."

This time they all moved, one of them going out to guard the gate of this deserted compound. Micay squatted next to the woman on the floor and examined the sodden cloths heaped up near her feet. In the light from the coals, they appeared blood-soaked, but they felt too wet and not sticky enough. When the torch flared up in Amancay's hand, Micay saw that it was not all blood, perhaps not even half. Encouraged, she looked up and took the cup that Cori Cuillor held out to her. It was nearly empty, but the aroma of the herbs was still powerful and distinctive, and Micay recognized it instantly. She breathed out in relief, silently thanking Hanp'atu, who had insisted that she be able to identify the drug, even if its use was forbidden by the Incas. She touched a drop to her tongue, remembering him saying that women would always use it if they had to, no matter what the Inca said. It was oily and bitter, exactly as she remembered. She spat onto one of the cloths and handed the cup back to Cori Cuillor.

"She was given what she asked for," Micay said, "and she seems to have taken the proper amount. She should not be lying down; that only makes the pain worse."

Cori Cuillor and the other woman knelt on either side of Chuqui Huipa, who cried out in pain and clutched a blanket to her as they began to raise her up. At Micay's direction, they brought her up into a squatting position, and Amancay padded the wall behind her with blankets so she could lean back against it. Micay put down her medicine bag and knelt in front of Chuqui Huipa, whose eyes were squeezed shut against the light. Micay had met the Coya's eldest daughter many times, but the person before her was barely recognizable. Her dark face was streaked with tears and face paint and twisted into a shape of pure misery, as if trying to disappear into itself. Every breath she took was a moan, and her whole body jerked as pains shot upward from her womb. Micay took a clean cloth, wet it in a basin of warm water, and gently began to wash the woman's face. She recoiled at first, then submitted with a shudder, her face going slack. Micay washed and dried her face and neck, then drew the blanket out of Chuqui's hands and began to clean her belly and thighs. She felt Chuqui's eyes on her before she was through, but she did not look up or hasten her movements, gradually working inward to clean and spread the lips of the vagina. When Chuqui did not recoil from this, Micay knew that the power of her presence was having an effect. She rinsed out the cloth and folded it neatly over the rim of the basin before looking up.

"Micay . . . help me," Chuqui whispered, and her brown eyes filled with tears. Micay briefly inclined her head.

"That is why I am here. You must finish what you have begun, my lady. You must bear the pain and let the drug take its course."

Chuqui started to look down at herself, then quickly jerked her eyes back up. "It hurts so much . . . it is like claws inside me."

"It is not a gentle medicine," Micay agreed. "But fear only makes it worse. You must relax and open yourself. The only danger now is in anything remaining behind. Tell me, how long did you wait? More than one moon?"

"Only one. I did not dare to wait once I knew. The smallest suspicion could get him killed!"

She jerked and grimaced in pain, twisting in the hands of the women who held her. Micay nodded and dipped her head to examine the gelid substance that was slowly seeping out of her.

"It is better for you, as well, that you did not wait."

"I wanted to ask you to help me," Chuqui said breathlessly. "But I was told you would not do this for me."

"Not for you or anyone else," Micay declared, speaking as much to the other three women as to Chuqui. "It is a violation of my vows to Mama Quilla. You are fortunate I was even able to recognize the drug you had taken."

Chuqui frowned and then burst into tears again, as if she had been scolded. Micay had to remind herself that this woman was some four years older than she was; her helplessness made her seem much younger. But Micay merely waited, tempering her words with the calmness of her presence. She had spoken the truth, and Chuqui would have to accept it in the place of the reassurance she wanted.

"Do you despise me, then?" Chuqui asked, in a voice that quavered and died. Micay slowly but firmly shook her head.

"I have come here to heal you, my lady, not to judge you. I cannot say I would not have done the same in your place. You have been denied much that should be yours as a woman."

Amancay drew a sharp breath, and the torch overhead wavered. Even Chuqui appeared shocked for a moment, as well, and Micay realized that she had probably never criticized her father for what he had done to her, not even

to herself. Micay gazed back at her calmly, sensing that she desired understanding rather than sympathy. Chuqui dabbed at her glistening eyes with the
back of her hand but shook her head when Micay offered her a cloth. Instead
she bared her teeth in a semblance of a smile and extended a hand to Micay.

"Will you stay with me?" she asked softly, and Micay saw her instinct
confirmed in the gratitude that shone in the young woman's eyes. She took the
hand, which felt light and smooth between her own, a hand that had never held
a grinding stone or tied on a splint.

"Of course, my lady," she promised. "For as long as it takes. Until you are
whole again . . ."

BY DAYBREAK, both the pain and the bleeding had stopped, and Micay was
as satisfied as she could be that the womb had been emptied. She gave Chuqui
one of Hanp'atu's preparations to prevent fever and made her lie back with
her upper body elevated and her knees raised and spread. She was asleep even
before a blanket was pulled over her. Micay and the other women stood up,
their joints cracking as they stretched their cramped limbs. Cori Cuillor
reached down and carefully brought up Micay's medicine bag, which Micay
slung over her shoulder with a weary nod. They walked out together into the
chilly morning air, their eyes smarting from smoke and fatigue.

"Send someone for me tonight," Micay said, "when I can come to her
unseen. It would be best if she were not moved for a day or two."

"We will always be grateful to you, Micay," Cori Cuillor told her. "If you
had not come . . ."

I was meant to come, Micay thought, but she did not say it aloud. She looked
down at herself and saw that the hem of her fine shift was stained with blood,
but she was too tired to be disturbed by it. She was a healer, but perhaps more
than a healer, as well. She did not know why she had been drawn back toward
the power of the court, but she could not turn away from it at a time like this.
It occurred to her that Chimpu Ocllo would be pleased, though all she could
do was sigh and put the thought away until later.

"Take care of her until I return," she said to Cori Cuillor, and bowed
vaguely in parting. "I must go and see my children."

Incallacta, the Cochabamba Valley

THE SUN was hot on Cusi's back as he labored alongside his men, fixing
sharpened stakes into the bottom of the trench and lifting stones to shore
up the earthen wall they had heaped up behind it. The trench and
rampart ran across the middle of the plaza and then curved back toward the
great hall, forming a defensive enclosure in front of it. Cusi made sure the work
was done right, even though they had nowhere near the number of men it

would take to defend the wall against a serious attack. It still had a purpose to serve, and the men who were guarding it when the time came would be grateful for the chance it would give them to pull back safely. Cusi could hear the Chiriguano drums beating off to the east, where the forest began, and he knew that that time was not far off.

A commotion at the other end of the wall brought the men's heads up, and all of them instinctively reached for the weapons they kept close at hand. Then those who could see best let out a triumphant shout.

"It is Tarapaca's squadron!" one of them yelled back to Cusi. "They have taken a captive!"

Cusi climbed up out of the trench and squatted on top of the wall. Even at a distance it was easy to pick out the captive, whose naked body was painted black and adorned with numerous metal ornaments that glittered in the sunlight. A chief, Cusi deduced from the regalia, feeling a fresh hope swelling in his chest. They had been waiting for a captive, and the rank of this one showed that Tomay's plan had huaca. Cusi watched as Tomay confronted the man, who was being held upright with his hands tied behind him. Tomay appeared to ask him a question, and the Chiriguano responded by rearing his head back and spitting in Tomay's face. Tomay slapped him hard across the mouth and then gestured for the Hawk Men to take the struggling captive to the great hall.

This also conformed with their plan, and Cusi found the place where he had left his things and began to wipe the sweat from his face with a towel. Tarapaca trotted up to him, proudly displaying the feathered staff that had belonged to the captive chief.

"They did not flee for a change," he reported breathlessly, his eyes bright with excitement. "They came after us and tried to take their chief back. But we held our ranks and bore him away."

"You have done well," Cusi commended him. "Tell Tomay I will join him shortly. Remind him to march the captive around inside, so that he has a good look at what the hall is like."

Tarapaca had helped formulate the plan, so he simply nodded in agreement and held out the feathered staff. Cusi began to reach for it but then took his hand back. He wanted nothing that might interfere with the power of his own presence.

"You keep it for now. Stay near the captive."

Tarapaca smiled broadly and waved the staff over his head, drawing a cheer from the other warriors before he trotted off.

"Finish this," Cusi told them sharply, waving them back to work. "You will understand very soon why it is necessary."

He turned away from them and finished wiping himself clean, letting his body cool down before donning the fine tunic he had brought with him. It was the best one he had, red and yellow checked cumbi cloth with a woven fringe of red feathers, a garment fit for a warlord. He took out his earplugs and polished them, then did the same to the silver badge on his headband, which he centered above his forehead. As he paused to drink from a water gourd, he stared across the enclosed portion of the plaza at the enormous gabled building around which this settlement had been built. The side facing the plaza was two hundred and fifty feet long and had twelve doorways, with narrow windows in between. It was as large as the Cassana, the royal meeting hall in Cuzco, and it could easily accommodate several thousand people under its thickly thatched roof. The Chiriguanos called it the Great Lodge of the Inca, and their leader, the foreigner with the pale skin and the dark hair on his face, had told them that they must burn it.

Cusi picked up the shield with the black Hawk Man painted on a red background and lifted his battle-ax with his other hand. He thought of Pachacuti and of Pachacuti's son, Topa Inca, who had ordered the great hall to be built here. It was a symbol of the confidence of Topa Inca's reign, a place that was never meant to be defended. No doubt Topa Inca had been unable to envision a time when the Chiriguanos would pose such a serious threat and the Incas would respond with such an inadequate force. Cusi and Tomay had four hundred men, barely enough to fill a corner of the hall, and their scouts told them the Chiriguanos had four or five times that number. They had informed Yasca that an attack was imminent, and he had sent back the message that they should dig in and defend themselves. He had not told them to defend the hall, knowing such a thing was impossible. It was Tomay who had made the impossible into a plan.

As he began to walk toward the hall, Cusi realized that in his heart he had been resisting the plan, simply because it was Tomay's and not his own. He resolved now to do his part to make it work, which meant convincing the Chiriguano captive that the Incas were in fact so brave and arrogant that they would try to defend the huge meeting hall with only a handful of men. So mad, Cusi thought, and felt his presence expand around him. He thought again of the ancestor who had conquered the Cochabamba Valley and turned it into one vast garden. Topa Inca would not have stepped aside and allowed savages like the Chiriguanos to destroy everything he had established, and Cusi Huaman would not do so in his place. Not if he could draw the savages down into this plaza, to this building that seemed a hopeless trap for those who held it . . .

His spirit brother was with him like a second backbone bracing the growing force of his presence, which he nourished with all the anger and desperation he had stored up during the past months. The doorway suddenly seemed small to him, so that he ducked needlessly as he went through it. The interior of the building was dim and cool, the cavernous space broken by the three rows of heavy wooden beams that held up the roof. Cusi paused, breathing deeply and trying to temper the violence of his feelings. He wanted to impress the captive, not kill him, though he hated the Chiriguanos more than any of the other enemies he had faced. They *were* savages, raiders and thieves who destroyed but built nothing of their own, the kind of warriors who stopped in the middle of a battle to strip the bodies of the fallen. Only their superior numbers and this leader, the Bearded One, made them worthy of respect.

Calmed by his contempt, Cusi started forward again, toward the small group of men out in the center of the hall. The Chiriguano was standing with his back against one of the support beams, bound to it by a rope wrapped several times around his chest. Tomay had the point of his spear at the man's throat and was forcing his head back, threatening him in Aymara. Cusi stopped a few feet away and thrust his shield and battle-ax into the hands of one of his Hawk Men, who cast a glance at Cusi's face and hastily backed away.

"That is enough," Cusi commanded, and Tomay whirled on him in unfeigned anger, apparently not recognizing his voice. They glared at each other for a moment before Tomay blinked and remembered himself. Then he bowed as if a sudden weight had come down on him, touching the tip of his spear to the floor. He moved aside, and Cusi trained the same glare on the captive, who narrowed his eyes protectively. The Chiriguano was naked except for a loincloth and the gold and silver ornaments around his arms and neck; up close, the black paint on his body appeared thin and granular, a mixture of grease and soot smeared on in streaks. There was a bloody lump on his shaved forehead, and his mouth was bleeding where the feathered ornament in his lower lip had been torn loose. He could feel the force of Cusi's presence—Cusi could see that in the way his whole body pressed back against the beam—but he summoned hatred into his eyes and spat a reddish stream onto the floor at Cusi's feet.

Cusi had already located Tarapaca out of the corner of his eye, and he moved with neither haste nor hesitation, snatching the feathered staff out of the startled captain's hands and striding forward, swinging the staff from the side in a long arc that sent all the onlookers ducking out of the way. He came up onto his toes with a final lunge, snapping the staff in two against the side of the thick post, right next to the captive's head. The crack of the blow seemed to echo back and forth down the length of the hall, and the Chiriguano shuddered inside his bonds, his face averted. Cusi dropped the splintered piece of staff still in his hands at the captive's feet and looked around for the Quillaca scout who acted as their interpreter.

"Tell him I have a message for his leader, the one who is not a Chiriguano," he said to the scout, who gaped at him for a moment before addressing the captive. The Chiriguano's head slowly came up as he listened, and he gave Cusi a disbelieving glance.

"Tell the Bearded One," Cusi went on, speaking directly to the captive even though the man could not understand his words, "that the Great Lodge is sacred to the Incas and their gods. Tell him we will never surrender it and it will not be taken from us. We will dance to our god, and he will destroy anyone who comes near this place in anger."

The scout went on at some length, making sweeping gestures that seemed to expand from the vastness of the hall to that of the sky above it. The Chiriguano grunted and licked at his torn lip.

"Has he heard me clearly?" Cusi demanded. A few more words from the scout brought a grudging nod from the captive. "Ask him, then, if it is true that the Chiriguanos eat the flesh of their enemies."

This time the captive actually smiled, showing blackened teeth. Then he spoke a few words in a hoarse, guttural voice. The scout hesitated, swallowing before he looked at Cusi and translated.

"He says, 'Only the brave ones.' "

Cusi caught the captive's eye with a glance that froze the smile on his face.

"Tell him he is being spared to carry my message. But if he dares to return here, I will kill him myself. And then I will flay the skin from his body and make a drum out of him for my children to play on at feasts."

The scout relayed the message, making beating motions with his hands. The Chiriguano grimaced defiantly but said nothing, his eyes roving past Cusi. Cusi stepped back and gestured brusquely with his chin, and Tarapaca and the others removed the rope and led the captive out of the hall, prodding him with the butts of their spears. Someone handed Cusi his shield and battle-ax and he took them absently, surprised by their weight. Tomay waited until the two of them were alone, then bent and picked up the jagged piece of staff that Cusi had dropped.

"You came very close to his head," Tomay said softly. "You convinced everyone that you meant to kill him."

"I—was not thinking of the risk," Cusi admitted. "I wanted to make sure he heard me."

Tomay gave a short laugh. "He did. And I think they will come to us now. *I* would certainly test you in their place."

"We must make ourselves ready," Cusi said, though he was unable to summon any urgency.

"We have been doing so," Tomay reminded him. "Rest awhile and let the men talk among themselves. My plan will seem safe and sensible now that they have heard what you said."

There was a slight edge to Tomay's voice, and his round cheeks were still dark with color. Cusi could see that he had not appreciated being cowed along with the captive, even if it had made the performance more convincing.

"Your plan is a good one, Tomay," he said in propitiation. "It has huaca. I am sorry if I have seemed reluctant to acknowledge that."

"You have," Tomay said bluntly, but then he tapped the broken staff against Cusi's shield and smiled. "It did not come to me in a dream or a vision. But I saw no reason not to take inspiration from my memories of the Carangui."

"Indeed. If we had *their* fort, even one wall of it, we could hold off the Chiriguanos forever."

"It may take that long for reinforcements to arrive," Tomay said. He gazed up into the rafters with a kind of rueful satisfaction. "This will do. For what we have in mind, this will do *quite* well . . ."

TO KEEP them alert, the warriors manning the ramparts in the plaza were rotated frequently, though at least fifty were kept in place at all times to make the defense appear credible. Several sharp-eared scouts were also stationed out beyond the wall, ready to sound the alarm should the Chiriguanos leave off their drumming and dancing and come on the attack.

The second line of defense was inside the great hall and consisted of fifty more men crouched in pairs beside the doorways and windows that opened onto the plaza. They were all armed with bows or spear throwers and had stacks of arrows and darts piled up next to them. It would be their duty to cover the retreat of the men at the ramparts, allowing the Chiriguanos into the plaza but then holding them at a distance until the next phase of the plan could be set in motion.

Campfires burned in the rear of the hall, warming the men who slept around them and casting a wavering yellow light on the back wall, which was lined along its entire length with shallow rectangular niches. Otherwise, the four-story wall was completely blank, without doorways or windows to permit escape. The two gabled end walls each had four windows, but they were set so high that only the birds that nested in the rafters could use them. The hall was a great box with its only openings in the front, a fact that Cusi and Tomay hoped the Chiriguano chief had noticed.

Yet it was also this blank, imposing back wall that had given Tomay his inspiration, leading him to devise his own version of the hidden tunnels the Carangui had used to ambush the attacking Incas. The wall was built into the side of the hill that rose behind it, and the roof slanted down to rest on it, even with the ground behind. Instead of tunnels, Tomay had suggested cutting trap doors in the thatch of the roof and lowering rope ladders to the floor of the hall. If the enemy could be delayed long enough, they could empty the hall before the Chiriguanos had a chance to enter, and pull up the ladders after them. Then, while the Chiriguanos were still discovering how they had been tricked, they could come around the ends of the hall and attack from the low ridges that flanked the plaza to the east and west.

The traps were open to the night sky, and lines of men were practicing climbing the rope ladders, their shields and weapons fastened to their bodies with straps fashioned just for this purpose. When Cusi approached one of the lines, the men began to move aside for him, but he brusquely waved them back and took his place at the end. He disliked the kind of deference his confrontation with the captive had inspired in some of the men, the involuntary half bows and the glances that were at once worshipful and uneasy. He had played the mad warlord too well to have them believe now that he had only been pretending, and Tomay had discouraged him from making a disclaimer, saying that it gave the men courage to believe their leader was favored by the gods.

I have become what Yasca feared, he thought as he looped his shield around one wrist and secured the strap that bound his battle-ax over his shoulder.

Feeling curious eyes upon him, he concentrated on going up the swaying ladder in an exemplary manner, swiftly and steadily, without wasted motion. He came out into the pale light of a last-quarter moon, which allowed him to see the men spread out over the face of the hill, digging trenches and building walls that connected the existing structures into a complex of makeshift fortifications. It was hardly a fortress, but the hill was a natural defensive position, and higher up there were several storehouses, a corral for llamas, and a spring-fed well. This was the only part of the settlement they had ever intended to defend, and it was the place to which they would retreat if the ambush failed and the hall was taken. Tomay was up there now, supervising his Collas and Lupacas, who were natural builders.

Cusi turned in the other direction and saw more men scuttling over the broad plane of the roof, hauling themselves up toward the peak by means of ropes tied to stakes that had been driven down through the thatch. Tarapaca had asked to be put in charge of defending the roof, and he had recruited a squadron of thirty light, nimble men, most of them—like Urcon—not warriors. Their major duty was to keep the thatch from being set ablaze by a flaming arrow or a hot slingstone, and they had spent the darkest part of each night wetting down a different section of the roof. But Tarapaca had also had them practicing with slings and bolas inside the hall, and he had recently requested a number of rather strange items from the storehouses: wax, pitch, and gourds of paint and cooking oil. Cusi had consented to the request but felt he should see what his captain was up to, since none of this had been included in the original plan.

A fire was burning a short distance up the hill, and he found Tarapaca and Urcon among the men sitting around it. They were surrounded in turn by piles of stones and ichu grass, coils of rope and stacks of llama hides, and a loose assortment of bags, baskets, gourds, and pots. One large, forbidding pile was composed of various kinds of cacti, some of which had been fitted with wooden handles as if to be carried or thrown. Cusi stepped around it carefully and came into the group, his nostrils flaring at the sharp, resinous odors emanating from the pots that were sitting on stones in the fire. The men glanced up at him and then averted their eyes with what appeared to be sly smiles, their hands busy wrapping stones with rope and tying the dry, shredded grass into tufted bundles. Tarapaca had one such bundle in front of him and was pouring an oily substance onto it from a wooden bowl. He pretended to be absorbed in the task, and Cusi stood with his hands on his hips, outwardly skeptical but inwardly enjoying the fact that they would tease him and make him ask for an explanation.

"So," he said finally, "I suppose this is all for the purpose of putting out fires."

Tarapaca straightened up and cast an innocent glance at the supplies around them.

"The llama hides, when they have been soaked, should be the best thing for that."

"And the rest of this?" Cusi demanded. "What is the cactus—your battle standard?"

Grins appeared on the faces of everyone around the fire, though Tarapaca tried mightily to suppress his.

"No, my lord. It is something that will fall on the Chiriguanos from the sky and make them know that the gods are angry with them."

Cusi grunted appreciatively, imagining the thorny plants raining down out of the darkness. He pointed with his chin at the oily bundle in front of the captain. "How else will the gods show their anger?"

"With fire," Tarapaca explained. He stood up, lifting the bundle by means of the six-foot length of rope attached to it. He moved to the open side of the circle, and Urcon got up and went to him, carrying a flaming brand from the fire. They exchanged a few words, and Urcon sprinkled a handful of some kind of powder onto the bundle, which was resting on the ground. Then Tarapaca stood back from it, stretching the rope taut, and Urcon touched his torch to the bundle and jumped back out of the way. The grass went up instantly in a brilliant burst of blue and green and yellow flame, and Tarapaca whirled and swung it over his head, going around twice before he let go of the rope and sent the fireball flying toward an uninhabited area of the hillside. The men around Cusi all stood up to watch, exchanging excited comments about the color of the flames and the fact that they kept burning even after the bundle landed and bounced down the slope. Cusi also rose and met Tarapaca as he returned, laying a hand on the captain's shoulder.

"I wondered why you asked for the roof, my friend. Now I see that you have also been inspired."

"The dyes were Urcon's idea," Tarapaca allowed. Then he gave Cusi a bold smile. "But it is natural for the Hawk Men to strike from the sky, is it not?"

"Let us hope the Chiriguanos find it most *un*natural, and unsettling. Anything you can do to frighten and confuse them is to our advantage. Take any supplies you need, and more men if you need them."

Tarapaca nodded perfunctorily, as if he had known all along that Cusi would approve. He smiled and looked around at his men, sharing the praise with them. "First we will show the Chiriguanos that the roof cannot be burned," he vowed. "Then we will make them wonder who it is they are fighting."

"I leave you to prepare yourself," Cusi said, giving him a final clap on the shoulder. He went out to meet Urcon, who had gone after the flaming bundle and had managed to retrieve both the rope and the stone that had given the bundle its weight. The two of them sat down on the hillside and looked up at the stars and the shining slice of moon, which was barely more than a crescent. Off in the distance, the Chiriguano drums beat on, sounding closer than they had the night before.

"They say the Bearded One is here," Urcon ventured, seeming more curious than fearful.

"One of the scouts got a look at him," Cusi acknowledged. "He wears a silver helmet and chest protector and carries a long war club of the same metal."

"And his face is covered with hair? Like a monkey's?"

Cusi laughed at the image, recalling the stories Uritu had told him about the legendary Monkey Men who lived deep in the jungles of the Eastern Quarter. "No, it is only on his chin," he told Urcon. "But it is black and thick, not like the few hairs some of our grandfathers have. Still, he is a man, even if we do not know what *kind* of man. The Chiriguanos follow him because they think he is blessed in war, but they do not worship him. When they are dying, they pray to the spirits of the forest and to their dead ancestors."

Urcon nodded tentatively. "Why does he wait to attack? Even if he cannot see what we are doing, he must know we are making ourselves ready."

"I do not know what he knows about the Incas," Cusi admitted. "He fought against Quizquiz at Chuquisaca and Tarabuco, but the numbers were more equal and he withdrew both times. What he knows about me is what I had the captive tell him, and what he thinks he sees. I think he sees a chance to do more than just burn the great hall. I think he wants a great victory over the Incas and their gods, perhaps to make the Chiriguanos believe in themselves and in him. So he will wait until the dark of the moon, when it is our custom to dance, and then try to overrun us."

"I have never been in a battle before," Urcon said softly. "Tarapaca has warned us that it is very exciting and confusing, and that it is easy to lose your head. He reminds us constantly that our first duty is not to fall off the roof."

"Obey him; he is a good leader. And if the battle turns against us, do not linger on the roof. Go up to where your llamas are and let the warriors man the barricades. I did not bring you here to fight, and I intend to return you safely to your grandfather."

Urcon snapped the scorched rope against the ground in front of him and gave Cusi a sidelong glance, a hint of a smile on his lips.

"Tarapaca says that if we help defeat the Chiriguanos, you will make us all Hawk Men."

"Tarapaca has great trust in my indulgence," Cusi said dryly. "You would like to go back to your village a warrior, then?"

"If I do not fall off the roof," Urcon allowed. "But you would have to tell them for me. They would not believe it from me."

"I will tell them," Cusi promised. Then he stood up and shook himself, feeling uncomfortable with all the promises he had been making. "Come," he said gruffly, "it is dangerous to look too far ahead—and bad luck."

"I will stay low to the roof," Urcon murmured in agreement, and the two of them turned and walked back toward the fire.

AT SUNSET, with the warriors assembled in their ranks in front of the great hall, Cusi and Tomay made offerings to the gods, burning cloth and coca leaves in the ceremonial fires that had been lit on the plaza. As he made his prayers to Illapa and Huanacauri and Thunupa, asking for strength and courage, Cusi heard the Chiriguano drums go silent in the distance. Still, he and Tomay maintained the solemn pace of the ritual, out of both reverence and an awareness of the Chiriguano scouts who were watching. Then their own drums began to beat, the warriors formed themselves into a long double file behind the two of them, and they began to dance. They circled out toward the ramparts, stamping and shuffling in time, shaking their weapons and battle standards in a salute to the men who guarded the wall. Darkness was falling with its customary swiftness, and the shrill whistle of a hawk sounded from several places, the first warning that the enemy was coming. The dancers circled back to the hall, hearing more signals, and war cries in the distance. Cusi and Tomay separated at the stone dais in front of the hall, Tomay leading his line ahead to the six far doorways while Cusi and his men turned and slowly danced through the six near ones.

Once inside, Cusi called out "Hold them!" to the bowmen and spear throwers crouched next to the doorways. Then he took off on a run for the rear of the hall. He held himself back to let his men keep up, checking out of the corner of his eye to be sure they divided themselves equally among the available ladders. The climb to the top seemed much longer and slower than Cusi remembered from his practice, and his hands were slippery on the thick, braided rungs. This was the point at which they were most vulnerable, when they could actually be trapped inside the hall. They had to free the ladders so that the men behind them could make their escape.

Then he came up through the opening in the roof and saw other men emerging at the same time, silhouettes in the failing light. He unslung his battle-ax and turned to the right, moving along the well-beaten path toward the eastern end of the hall. The Inca drums were still beating inside the hall, but he could also hear screams and the sounds of fighting from the plaza. Hold them, he prayed silently, picking up his men as he trotted along the path. A scout met them at the end of the building and led the line slowly down a path that skirted the jumbled wall of stone they had erected to keep the Chiriguanos from going around the hall. The path turned east and went down through a narrow ravine before climbing again to the ridge overlooking the plaza. Another scout met them at the end of the ravine, and Cusi halted the line and went on ahead with the scout, toward the screaming and the noise of battle. They got down on their bellies and crawled the last several feet to where a third scout lay sprawled behind a barrier of broken rock. The scout leaned close to speak in Cusi's ear.

"The men at the wall held off two charges before retreating. They lost only a few. There are Chiriguanos on the ridge to our left, so raise only your eyes above the rocks."

Cusi crept forward on his elbows and raised himself slowly. The brightness of the fires burning in the plaza blinded him for a moment and made him realize that it was completely dark. Then he saw the enormous crowd of Chiriguanos that had filled the outer plaza and was lapping over the ramparts in waves that advanced and then retreated in the face of the arrows and darts emanating from the doorways of the great hall. The ground in front of the building was littered with the black-painted bodies of those who had attacked too recklessly, and a kind of standoff had been reached, with the main body of the Chiriguanos hanging back around the ramparts. They were dancing and singing and screaming threats at the men inside the hall, waving clubs and torches and shooting barbed arrows that rattled harmlessly against the stone façade of the building. The sight of them made Cusi's stomach tighten in fear, even though his mind told him that the plan was working. As he watched, several of the black-painted warriors danced forward, displaying their courage by exposing themselves to the bowmen and spear throwers in the hall. One of them went down immediately with a dart in the leg, but the others ducked and whirled and kept going forward, appearing to taunt the building itself to strike them down. When they were not hit, other dancers started to advance, and Cusi suddenly saw the individual acts of recklessness coalescing into an undisciplined but effective charge. Stop them now, Cusi thought urgently, wondering if the marksmen had begun to panic and leave their posts.

But then a hail of darts and arrows came flying out of the hall and cut down all but one of those who had come within range, and as the last man turned to flee, a single arrow struck him full in the back and brought the attack to a complete halt. Cusi let himself breathe, and as the din raised by the Chiriguanos subsided for a moment, he heard the drummers inside the building change their rhythm, the signal that all the warriors, except for those at the doorways, had gotten out of the hall. The Chiriguanos continued to hold back, their ranks thickening into a perimeter, just out of arrow range. Cusi realized that they were waiting for their leader, and he hoped the Bearded One would come slowly and give the men inside time to slip away and use the rope ladders.

One of the scouts tapped Cusi on the shoulder and told him that the Chiriguanos had abandoned the ridge, and Cusi gave the order for the men to come up and take their positions. He went forward along the ridge himself, finally crouching down behind a hump of earth at a place where he had a clear view of the whole plaza. His men filtered in behind him, carrying bags of slingstones and quivers of darts for their spear throwers. Cusi put down his shield and ax and untied the sling from around his forehead, gazing down at the massed Chiriguanos with stark anticipation. It would be hard to miss with any throw, and the Chiriguanos did not protect themselves with helmets and armor.

There was movement in the middle of the black, feathered crowd, and a path was cleared for the Bearded One, who came forward surrounded by four gaudily attired chiefs. He was not an especially large man, and his silver helmet and chest protector were badly tarnished, giving off only a dull gleam in the light of the torches. His long, double-edged club seemed of a shinier metal, and he raised it over his head as he climbed up on top of the ramparts.

Just then the drumming inside the hall stopped, and the Chiriguanos turned to their leader and let out a great cry, as if his presence had silenced the Inca drums. Cusi smiled to himself, recognizing the silence as the final signal. The hall was now empty; at this moment, the drummers were probably climbing the ladders to safety. The Bearded One snapped out a command and pointed at the roof with his thin silver club, and a moment later, an arrow with a flaming tip arched through the sky and imbedded itself in the thatch. The Chiriguanos gave another cry as the flame flared up, then seemed to swallow the sound as the fire was abruptly blotted out. Llama skins, Cusi thought, as a second command was given and several fiery arrows went up simultaneously. But none burned for more than a moment or two before being extinguished. The Chiriguanos began to mill around in frustration, and suddenly one of the chiefs standing near the Bearded One waved his feathered staff and charged toward the hall, drawing a wave of men with him. They crouched and zig-zagged as they ran, expecting arrows that did not come. They ran right through the doorways without stopping, and the rest of the Chiriguanos surged across the plaza behind them.

Then there was fire in the sky overhead, an uncanny golden-blue ball that seemed to hang and wobble at the apex of its flight, then plunged straight downward in a shower of sparks. The men beneath it, arrested in midcharge, belatedly threw up their arms and tried to scatter, knocking each other down. More of the flaming bundles came arching over the roof, along with stones and pieces of cactus and gourds fitted with burning wicks. Most of the wicks went out in the air, but the explosive splattering of oil and paint when the gourds landed seemed as unnerving to the Chiriguanos as the fire. They screamed and waved their weapons and shot arrows straight up into the air, unable to find anyone to fight. Cusi fit a stone into the pocket of his sling and vowed that he would make every one of Tarapaca's men a Hawk Man. He heard a familiar whoop echo across the plaza, and he stood up and whooped back and slung the stone down into the crowd of Chiriguanos below. Immediately the whole ridge erupted with war cries as the Hawk Men rose up and rained stones and darts down on the plaza. Tomay's men struck with equal ferocity from the opposite side, and the bowmen and spear throwers who had been inside the hall added arrows and darts to the deadly barrage coming down from the roof. The Chiriguanos began to fall everywhere, and those who did not fall began to run.

Cusi threw stone after stone, avenging himself for all the fear and despera-tion the Chiriguanos had made him feel. When he finally found himself aiming at individual running targets, he wound the sling back around his forehead and picked up his shield and battle-ax. Most of the Chiriguanos were in headlong retreat, but their silver-clad leader still stood atop the ramparts, waving his shiny club and trying to muster a force around him. Some of those who had entered the hall were still coming back out, running from the missiles of Tarapaca's men, who had come far down the front of the roof to snipe at them. A shout went up on the other side of the plaza, and Cusi saw Tomay lead his Collas and Lupacas over the ridge and down onto the enemy. Cusi jumped up on the mound of earth but then paused, making sure the Hawk Men were all armed and ready before he gave the signal to attack.

"Together!" he shouted, knowing how dangerous a fleeing enemy could be. They charged down the slope in a line that quickly drew in on itself, forming a compact wedge that sliced through the shattered ranks of the Chiriguanos. They met little resistance until they neared the ramparts, and then the Chiriguanos fought only because there was no room to run. Cusi stayed close to the men beside him, lashing out with his ax and ducking back behind his shield. He caught a glimpse of blackened teeth and bloody green feathers as a body crashed against his shield, but the men behind held him up, and he threw the man off and finished him with a blow to the skull.

The resistance wavered and broke, and Cusi saw Tomay up on top of the ramparts, his shoulder lowered behind his shield, knocking a Chiriguano backward into the trench. Cusi used a fallen body as a bridge and scrambled to the top of the wall, looking around for the Bearded One. He and Tomay spotted him at the same time: outside the wall, drawing away in the middle of a dense crowd of warriors who were facing backward, fighting as they retreated. Pursuit was tempting but much too risky at this point, and Cusi urgently signaled Tomay to hold. But Tomay was staring at the armored man and paid no attention to the signal. Instead he dropped his shield and hefted his spear in a curled hand, raising it up to his shoulder. Then he ran forward and threw the spear with all his might, falling to his knees upon release and nearly tumbling into the trench. The spear flew toward the silver chest protector as if drawn to it, and Cusi watched in awe, possessed by the sudden certainty that Tomay was *meant* to vanquish this stranger.

The spear struck with a ringing crash that Cusi felt in his teeth, and the flint tip shattered against the metal. The Bearded One went over backward but was quickly lifted to his feet, and Cusi saw the man's eyes, dazed but open, and a flash of teeth amid the blackness of his beard. There was a large dent in his chest protector, but no blood had been drawn, and the man stayed on his feet, only his helmet visible as he turned and was carried off by the crowd.

Cusi shouted to his own captains to hold, then strode down the wall, stepping over bodies and discarded weapons, shouting the same command to Tomay's troops. Tomay was still on his knees in the dirt, and he looked up at Cusi with an expression of stunned disbelief.

"You have great huaca, my friend," Cusi said, bending to help him to his feet. Tomay shook his head, tilting his helmet to one side.

"It cannot be silver," he murmured. "Silver is too soft to withstand such a blow. Even bronze . . ."

"I was certain you had killed him. That you were meant to."

"I was—I did," Tomay insisted dazedly. "I felt it as the spear left my hand, but . . ."

They were interrupted by two of their captains, both of whom addressed themselves to Cusi, asking what should be done with the Chiriguanos who were still alive. Cusi looked around at the bodies littering the plaza, hearing the moans and pleas of the wounded for the first time. He suddenly realized how tired and thirsty he was, yet he mustered the strength to straighten up and make Tomay meet his gaze.

"This is your victory, Tomay Guanaco," he said firmly. "You decide how we should end it."

Tomay put his hands on his hips and nodded, glancing around at the wreckage in the plaza, the crumpled figures that lay writhing in the flickering light of the fires.

"Not with a Lake of Blood," Tomay decided, and he addressed himself to the captains. "Spare the ones who will heal, but see that they are bound securely, one to another. Drag the dead and the dying out to the edge of the plaza and leave them. Perhaps the Chiriguanos will get hungry and come back for them."

The two men laughed and raised their weapons in a salute as they went off to convey the command. Cusi looked back toward the hall and was surprised to see a patch of red flame rising up from the roof, high up near the peak. He pointed with his chin and Tomay followed his gaze, smiling ruefully. As the thatch began to burn more vigorously, they could see the men who were already up there fighting the blaze, beating at it with what looked like black blankets.

"Llama skins," Cusi murmured.

Tomay snorted softly. "Rope ladders and balls of burning grass. Yasca will be certain now that we are mad."

"We were," Cusi said succinctly. "Let him be thankful. I will see about the fire," he added, and he climbed down from the wall and started walking toward the great hall, picking his way between the bodies and the debris of battle, expecting to find Urcon and Tarapaca still up on the roof.

Tumibamba

MICAY HAD just finished dressing for the feast when Otoronco Achachi announced himself outside her house. He briefly filled the doorway, a golden Sun shield gleaming on his chest and bands of jaguar skin around his knees and forearms.

"You look splendid, Grandfather," Micay told him, and he nodded in agreement.

"I want to honor Apu Poma. I owe him for his hospitality." He glanced around the interior of the room. "Where are the little ones?"

"I left them with the women in the awning house so that I could dress in peace. They are excited about your feast."

Otoronco rubbed his chin, seeming bemused. "When I came here, they were crawling and babbling. Now they run up and down the stairs and call me by name. Cahua calls me 'Old Jaguar.' "

Micay laughed, though this display of fondness surprised her. She had thought that he liked the children, but he had never been easily affectionate, and there were times when he seemed totally unaware of their existence. She invited him to sit, and he settled himself cross-legged on a llama skin, grunting as he lowered himself down. Micay wondered if he had more questions about Chan Chan, though she could not think of anything they had not already discussed. Then she saw the way he was looking at her, his head cocked in a wistful squint, and she realized that he had not come for information.

"What is it, Grandfather?" she prompted.

Otoronco nodded gratefully, acknowledging that he had come to talk. "It is this leaving, Micay. It is something I have been doing all my life, often against my will but seldom with much remorse. I never expected to be able to stay with any of my wives for long, and I was always being sent to places where they could not follow. So I went and gave them what I could, when I could. The same is true of my children. Perhaps you will think me unfeeling, but I cannot say that I ever missed any of them."

"Do you miss them now?" Micay asked. He grimaced and shook his head, making his earplugs glitter. "Them, no. But I have missed Cusi since he left, and now I will be leaving the rest of you, and this compound. It is a peculiar feeling. I do not leave until tomorrow, yet I am already looking back with longing. My heart must be getting old along with my legs."

"It is a *young* heart that feels longing," Micay pointed out. "And we will miss you, too. But surely you will come back once order has been restored in Chimor."

Otoronco stared at her for a long moment, and there was no trace of wistfulness in his eyes. "No, my daughter, I do not think I will see Tumibamba again. If I do not perish in the Hotlands, I will probably be ordered back to Chachapoyas or sent to put down another rebellion somewhere else." His eyes grew even harder and his lip curled upward in disgust. "I saw Huayna Capac yesterday. He looks like a bad omen himself: soft and bloated and nervous. He greeted us with all the usual flattery and then let Ninan Cuyochi speak for him while he conferred with his sorcerers and sign readers. I had a foolish moment when I wanted to speak to him as his father's brother and tell him to go back to Cuzco before he forgot everything about being an Inca."

"Foolish only if you expected to be heard or heeded. We all know how he repays good advice."

"We do," Otoronco agreed, "so I gave him none. But there was an edge to his flattery that told me I have done as much for him as he will allow. Any more and he would have to recognize my importance, and that would make me a threat to him." He sighed heavily. "I am tired of this pettiness, Micay. It makes us weak. It makes me believe that the omens of our downfall speak the truth."

Micay remained silent, unable to argue or to urge hope on a man of his age and experience, a man who clearly felt the nearness of his own death. *That* was what he had truly come to tell her, and she felt moved and honored that he had chosen her. After a moment Otoronco shook himself and cleared his throat.

"Enough of such gloomy talk. Now that I have said it, I can go to my farewell feast and be courteous and dignified, and pretend that none of us has any cause for worry." He glanced at Micay with his customary directness. "The Chimu you told me about, the cook, has never come to me. I could use another guide if he is still available."

"I found another place for him, my lord. In Quito."

Otoronco raised his split eyebrow. "I am impressed, my daughter. The situation you described to me did not sound easy to resolve. Did you have help? From Chuqui Huipa, perhaps?"

"Our friendship is no secret," Micay said easily. "Certainly not from someone as wise in the ways of the court as yourself."

Otoronco gave her a sardonic smile. "I will not ask you to explain how the wife of Cusi Huaman—a man in great disfavor with the Sapa Inca—becomes a friend of the ruler's own daughter. I know you are capable of extraordinary things. Nor would I ask you to respond to the rumors about the nature of Chuqui Huipa's illness. I am only interested in the rumors that concern Ninan Cuyochi."

For a moment Micay's instinct was to feign ignorance and fend him off. The danger to everyone involved was too great. But then she caught herself and met Otoronco's knowing gaze, seeing the man who had killed her father and then come to tell her, a man she would probably never see again, though he would be there always in Cusi.

"Say what you mean, Grandfather. You understand how careful I must be."

"I do. But a promise was made to the Shuaras, and Ninan is the one who will have to keep it. I reminded him when I saw him yesterday. He is an honorable man, but I have no other hold on him, nothing that would compare with the power of his father's favor. Perhaps you do, Micay. Perhaps there will come a time when you will want to remind him, as well."

"Perhaps," Micay allowed, though she frowned at the possibility. "I am aware of the power of what I know, but to—"

"*Use* it, Micay," Otoronco said. "If he wavers, use it. For Cusi's sake, and for the sake of all the men who would die uselessly in the jungle. Be as ruthless as the Shuara will be in revenge."

"I have heard you, Grandfather," Micay said with a finality that made him sit back and spread his hands in apology.

"Forgive me, my daughter, if I speak to you as I would to Cusi. It is because I know you have a heart like his. That is why he will come back to you, wherever they send him."

"I will go to him, if I have to."

"I know," Otoronco said, and paused to lick his lips. "And when you see him next, Micay, tell him . . . tell him that his old guardian misses him."

"I will," Micay whispered, her voice catching in her throat. Otoronco's eyes glittered, and he looked at the floor for a moment, then abruptly put down a hand and pushed himself to his feet.

"Come, then, let us go celebrate my leaving. You can help me say my farewells."

"I can," Micay agreed, and she rose to let him escort her from the room. "It is something I have been doing all of my life."

⟫⟪ XVI ⟫⟪

PAHUAC ONCOY:
The Swift-Running
Sickness

(A.D. 1525)

Chuquiabo

THOUGH THE SUN was still setting in the west, its rays merely glanced across the rooftops of the city, which was set in a deep, craterlike hollow between the surrounding mountains. The air had already turned cold, drawing the men in around the fires they had lit for cooking. Having grown accustomed to the mild climate of the Cochabamba Valley, Cusi was grateful for his warm alpaca cloak, which had seen little wear in the last two years, and for the knit cap that covered his head, a gift from Tomay's father on the journey out. As he warmed his hands by the fire, he watched Tarapaca conclude his conversation with Yasca and come back across the courtyard, weaving his way between the fires and the seated men. The captain's face was glum as he squatted down and poked at the potatoes roasting in the fire with a stick, grumbling to himself about how slowly things cooked at this height.

"He said no," Cusi suggested, and Tarapaca dropped the stick and nodded. He mimicked the war chief's gruff, dismissive tone.

" 'The Hawk Men will soon fly off to their homes. There is no need for them to visit the nest where they were hatched.' "

"You asked to go to Tipycala?" Tomay inquired, using the Aymara name for Tiahuanaco. Tarapaca nodded again and looked at Cusi.

"I told him this was our idea, not yours, but he said that made no difference. 'Tell your warlord not to ask me, either,' he said."

"I knew he would accuse me of that," Cusi said with a laugh. "I am sorry,

Tarapaca. It would have been appropriate to return and thank Thunupa for his protection."

"I would have asked with you if you had told me," Tomay said. "Tipycala may be in Lupaca territory, but it is also sacred to the Collas."

For a moment Tomay and Tarapaca stared at each other through narrowed eyes, reenacting the long history of animosity and distrust that existed between the Collas and Lupacas. From the other side of the fire Quizquiz broke in irritably.

"Why would *any* of you want to add to the march?" he demanded. "We are still many days from Cuzco, and who knows where we will be sent from there?"

"True," Cusi agreed, glancing from Tarapaca to Tomay to break the face-off between them. He held Tomay's eyes. "Though . . . the Royal Road passes close by the lake. It would not be a great excursion to go to Copacabana."

"Ah," Tomay exclaimed softly. "I should have known you were saving your favor for a reason."

"Copacabana?" Quizquiz repeated, disbelief and disgust competing for space on his narrow blade of a face. "I was made to go there once. It was crowded and noisy, and the streets and squares were filled with priests and mamacona and sellers of charms and remedies. Pilgrims were everywhere, weeping and praying and crawling on their knees to the shrines. I would sooner spend my time at a Chiriguano feast."

Tomay laughed but kept his eyes on Cusi's face. "It is from Copacabana that the boats go out to the islands of Titicaca and Coati, places even more sacred than Tipycala. Places of great huaca."

"Yasca cannot give you permission to go there," Quizquiz scoffed.

"No, but the high priestess could," Tomay said. "If she remembered an old friend."

"I think she would," Cusi said and smiled. "She might even remember you, my friend."

"Then tell me when you want to go to Yasca," Tomay declared. "He could not deny the request of *two* warlords."

"Warlords," Quizquiz muttered, lifting and dropping his hands in disgust. "If you go off chasing after mamacona, do not expect the rest of us to wait for you. I only want to get back to Cuzco, where the women are fit to touch and we are allowed to touch them."

"We all know what makes you march, Quizquiz," Tomay told him with rough good humor, and Quizquiz smiled crookedly, taking the remark as a compliment. Cusi and Tomay exchanged a nod of agreement, and Cusi sat back to find Tarapaca crouched close on his other side, regarding him with a yearning that was nearly palpable.

"You want to go, too," Cusi concluded.

"My lord, to go to Coati Island, for a Lupaca . . ."

"I will take you if I can," Cusi assured him. He was about to add a cautionary statement when he saw Tarapaca's eyes go past him, widening in wonder. Quizquiz and the others around the fire were staring in the same direction, and Cusi turned to see that a column of warriors had come part of the way into the courtyard and then stopped, finding little room for themselves among the seated men. They were not Charcas and they were carrying too much gear to be local mitmacs on a law enforcement mission. The gear was all new, the shields shiny and unscarred, the cloaks and bedrolls dusty from travel but still unmended. A number of them were wearing stiff, cylindrical headdresses similar to those worn by the Chimus, and from this and the symbols of Mama Cocha on their shields and battle standards, Cusi deduced that they were from the coast, though not a part of it he had seen.

Their commander, who wore the gold and silver earplugs of an Inca by privilege along with one of the headdresses, went up to Yasca and presented himself with a deep bow. The courtyard was completely silent, the veteran warriors on the ground surrounded by their battle-worn gear and the chonta-wood bows and feathered headdresses they had taken from the Chiriguanos staring up at the young, untested troops with their gleaming shields and Cuzco-issue cloaks. Cusi could see the effort the young men were making to remain impassive, though some of them seemed to be suffering from the altitude and could not disguise their nervousness and discomfort.

Yasca listened to the commander's explanation without expression, but then his rocklike face seemed to crack in the middle, and he threw back his head and laughed. It was a loud, raucous sound, more exasperated than amused, and none of the men joined in. Then Yasca put a hand on the commander's shoulder and appeared to apologize, drawing a reluctant nod from the man before stepping past him to address the whole group.

"Make room at your fires for the warriors from Nazca and Ica," he commanded. "They have come from the Western Quarter to help us fight the Chiriguanos."

A wave of astonished laughter swept across the courtyard, but the men around the fires immediately began to move aside and make room for the new arrivals. Yasca said a few more words to the commander, pointing with his chin and sending the man in the direction of Cusi's group. Cusi and his companions rose to meet him, opening a place for him in their circle. The commander stepped into it, his face and body rigid with anger. Only his lips moved when he spoke.

"I am Acari, commander of the warriors of Nazca. The war chief said you would tell me what I should know about the Chiriguanos."

He was facing Quizquiz, so it was Quizquiz who replied, looking the man up and down as if gauging his ability to fight.

"The first thing you should know . . . is that the Chiriguanos are gone. We chased them out of the valley and across the Chaco Plain almost a year ago. I doubt they will want to return very soon."

"We have been in the valley for more than two years," Tomay added. "The other reinforcements from the coast came long ago. Some of them are manning the forts we built to guard against future raids."

"They came late," Quizquiz said unsparingly, "but soon enough to be useful."

"We came when we were sent," the commander said through his teeth, shifting his stance to confront Quizquiz more directly. He looked like a man who knew how to fight and was ready to, yet Cusi had been aware of the man's presence from the moment he arrived, and it told him something very different from what his eyes perceived. There was a pleading quality to his presence, a kind of bewilderment or helplessness, as if the ground were shifting beneath his feet. Cusi had never felt anything like it before, a presence that was a projection of vulnerability rather than power. No one else seemed aware of it, not even the man himself, so Cusi was slow to realize that he should intervene. When he finally did, he stepped forward and bowed to attract the commander's attention.

"Forgive us our rudeness, Acari," he said quietly. "We have been in the field too long. I am Cusi Huaman, and these are my fellow commanders, Tomay Guanaco and Quizquiz."

The commander stiffened in recognition, then very deliberately bowed to each of them.

"I know your names and deeds, my lords," he said in a chastened voice. "I must apologize for approaching you in anger."

"That is how Yasca sent you to us," Cusi told him, shaking his head at the apology. "Come, sit with us, and share our food and the warmth of our fire."

Acari seated himself between Cusi and Tomay and accepted the potato Tomay speared for him with a stick. He nodded in gratitude, then glanced around the courtyard to see how his men were being treated before biting through the blackened skin of the potato. He immediately tilted his head back and made fanning motions in front of his mouth.

"Hot," he managed, and the other men laughed and reached for sticks to pluck their own dinner from the coals.

"You will not have to eat potatoes in Cochabamba," Tomay said as he chewed. "They grow every kind of food in the valley, and the harvest will be in by the time you get there."

Acari stared at him for a moment, as if to be sure that this was not another taunt.

"It was over quickly?" he asked. "The fighting?"

Quizquiz grunted scornfully. "Once we had enough men."

"We were badly outnumbered for many months," Cusi explained. "The Chiriguanos came close to overrunning us at Incallacta. That is why the war chief laughed when you reported. Your arrival now seemed to mock the desperation we felt then."

"I see," Acari said in a low voice, neglecting the half-eaten potato impaled on the stick in his hand. "None of us laughed when we left our homes and families to come here. We did not think it was a mockery."

"Of course not," Cusi agreed. "But we left Tumibamba two and a half years ago, and when we reached Cuzco, we were told that the warriors from the Western Quarter would join us shortly."

"We came when we were sent," Acari repeated stubbornly. Then he relented under Cusi's expectant gaze and gave in to the desire to defend himself. "I remember when the Regent first asked us for troops. The men who had returned from the north had been back only a short time, and we owed the Inca no more for at least another year. There was no way for the governor and the chiefs to comply, and they told that to the Regent. Then, after the year had passed and we had begun to muster our warriors, we received a command from Tumibamba ordering us to march to Chimor. So we waited while the runners carried messages back and forth, until Cuzco and Tumibamba finally agreed that we should come here. That took several months. By then, of course, the Viracochas had been seen in the north, and the priests would not let us depart until the omens were more favorable." Acari stopped and looked at Cusi with sudden suspicion, as if his word were being doubted. "You are surprised by that? You think we should have defied our priests?"

"No," Cusi said hastily, holding up a hand to him. "Do not misunderstand. We heard nothing in Cochabamba about these 'Viracochas.' Who are they?"

"They . . . no one knows who they are," Acari shrugged. "That is only what some people call them, because of the legend. They came in a boat made of logs, and the fishermen who saw it say it looked like a house that floated on the water. It went away again and no one has seen it since."

"What did the Viracochas look like?" Cusi asked, aware that everyone around the fire was listening intently. Acari shrugged again, as if he did not wish to be regarded as an expert.

"No one got very close to them. One fisherman said the house thundered and threw a bolt of lightning at him when he sailed too close. Others said they saw men on top of the house who were very tall and had pale skin, like the Viracochas in the legend."

"Did they have hair on their faces?" Tomay asked impulsively.

"That was also reported," Acari concurred. Then he frowned and cast a quick glance at Cusi. "I thought you said you had not heard of them."

Cusi exchanged glances with Tomay and Quizquiz, seeing that they were as stunned as he was. Quizquiz shook his head in denial.

"It is not possible. Where did you say these Viracochas were seen?"

"First near Manta, then twice more farther south," Acari said, still frowning.

"That is the other end of the Four Quarters!" Quizquiz exclaimed. "It cannot be the same people."

"The Chiriguanos were led by a pale-skinned foreigner," Cusi explained to Acari. "We called him the Bearded One because he had hair on his face. He sounds very similar to these Viracochas."

"We did not hear about him in Cuzco," Acari maintained, though he seemed more puzzled than suspicious.

"We have not told Cuzco. Yasca felt it would be better to carry such information back in person. I see his wisdom now."

Acari nodded slowly. "There was great fear on the coast. All of the huacas spoke of evil things. That is why the priests made us wait."

They fell silent, and Cusi heard the other men talking all around them, no doubt exchanging the same information. *Viracochas*. It had never occurred to him to connect the Bearded One with the legend of Viracocha's helpers, who were said to be tall and pale-skinned and bearded. *This* bearded one had not been that tall, and Tomay had proven that he was a man beneath his hard metal armor. Still, if they were the same people, they were dangerous, perhaps the threat that Raurau Illa and Macas and Chimpu Ocllo had all foreseen.

"One of you can tell Yasca," Quizquiz said when Cusi looked up from his thoughts. "You know how to speak about such things."

"I will tell him," Cusi offered, drawing a nod from Tomay before he rose to his feet. He looked down at Acari and again felt the pleading, as if the man were pulling on him to stay. Yet Acari was gnawing on his potato again and looked up only briefly to give Cusi a respectful nod in parting. Cusi turned and searched for a path across the crowded courtyard, wondering why this man made him imagine weakness when none was being shown.

WHEN CUSI returned, the moon was up and the fires in the courtyard had burned low. He was carrying an extra cap, which he had intended to give to Acari. But shortly after removing it from his pack, he had found Urcon and had learned why his friend had moved his llamas to another corral, away from the llamas that belonged to the Nazca column. Cusi was angry now, so he sent one of the sentries into the courtyard to bring Acari out. He waited in the middle of the steep, narrow street, his breath hanging around his head in a white cloud.

"You wanted me," Acari said as he approached, his shoulders hunched beneath the blanket he wore over his cloak.

"You look cold," Cusi said without sympathy. "Are you well?"

"It is just the altitude . . ."

"Is it? Or have you brought something more with you?" When Acari did not reply, Cusi went on. "Our herders heard that there was sickness among your men. Possibly verruga."

"It was not verruga," Acari said swiftly. "The healers called it spotted fever. And we left all the sick men behind in Cuzco. Most of them were part of the second column, which marches five days behind mine."

"*Most* of them?"

"There were a few with us . . . and a few more fell sick in Hatuncolla, so we left them with the healers there. What was I to do?" he demanded. "Go back?"

"You should have told us."

Acari blew twin plumes of steam out his nostrils. "When? After the war chief laughed in my face? Or when you were sharing your food with me?" His hands appeared from beneath his cloak and grabbed at the air between them. "And what was I supposed to tell you? This sickness has a name only because the healers had to call it something. They had never seen it before, and they knew nothing about how to cure it. They did not even know if it kills."

Cusi stared at him in the moonlight, finally seeing a face that matched the plaintive presence he had been feeling all along. This sickness, or the fear of it, was obviously the source of the strange sense of helplessness that surrounded the man.

"Are any more of your men sick?" he asked.

Acari looked down at the ground and nodded. "I thought it was behind us . . . but then two more were stricken yesterday. The fever comes without warning, along with terrible pains in the head and back. I had our healers take them to a place apart from the others."

"So it has followed you," Cusi concluded, and he shivered as his anger dissipated and dread took him over. *It will come from everywhere and never be seen.* Chimpu Ocllo's dream was coming to life all around him, and he suddenly felt very far from all the people he loved.

"This is my first command," Acari murmured, still looking at the ground. "None of the veterans who had been north would take it. They said they had had enough fighting. I wanted my chance to fight, badly enough that I would have defied any omen."

Cusi felt the two of them sinking into a kind of panicked numbness, a despair as seductive as sleep, and he reacted wildly against it, throwing out his arms with a grunt that made Acari jump back in surprise. Cusi held up a hand and shook his head stubbornly.

"You must fight this sickness instead. We do not know that anyone has died from it yet."

"I do not know if they died or recovered," Acari admitted. "We did not stay with them long enough."

"Get your men to Cochabamba," Cusi told him, "as quickly as you can. There are healers there, and it is much warmer than the high plain. But take your sick with you; do not leave any more along the way."

"What will you tell the war chief?"

"I will tell him what you told me, but not until after you are gone. It is too late to separate the men, and you do not deserve any more insults."

Acari gave him a rueful smile. "You are a generous man, Cusi Huaman."

"This is no time to cast blame," Cusi shrugged. Then he remembered the cap in his hand and held it out to him. "I meant to give you this. Your headdress will be suitable in Cochabamba, but it will not serve you on the plain or in the mountains."

Acari hesitated, then accepted the knit hat and put a hand inside to feel its warmth. "I have nothing to give you in return. Nothing you would want to take."

"Perhaps we will fight together some other time," Cusi suggested, "and I will need something of yours."

"You will have it."

"Let us sleep, then," Cusi said, gesturing toward the compound with his chin. Acari turned with him but held back for a moment.

"There is no need for you to risk yourself any further. I could take a message to the others for you, if you wish."

"No," Cusi decided after a moment's hesitation. He started them moving toward the gate. "No, if I cannot warn them, I cannot desert them, either."

YASCA, CUSI FOUND when he was finally able to speak to him, had already learned of the sick men from the rest house keeper, who had provided separate lodgings for them. Yasca had also received a report, while they were still in Cochabamba, of an outbreak of a similar illness among the Chinchas he had left to guard the newly built fort at Savapata. He had chosen then not to share the report with his commanders or anyone else, considering it even more troublesome than the presence of the Bearded One. At Savapata two men had died of the disease.

"So it is behind us and ahead of us," Cusi said.

Yasca gave him a grim smile. "We have no more choice than the Nazcas do. Unless you have some knowledge of this that will help us."

"I have none that is reassuring, my lord."

"Then we will push on to Cuzco and hope it does not overtake us on the road. That means a hard march and no excursions for anyone."

Cusi nodded compliantly and went back to his men, having already relinquished any thought of visiting Tocto Oxica. He would not go anywhere near the Island of the Moon when he might be carrying the spotted fever as an unintended offering.

They marched across the plain and skirted the lower part of the lake, passing the marshlands where the Urus lived and crossing the Desaguadero River by means of a long, low bridge that floated on bundles of totora reeds. They reached the town of Pomata early in the afternoon of their fifth day out of Chuquiabo. So far no one had fallen sick, but they were all tired and footsore, and Yasca decided to call a halt for the day.

The Inca official in charge of the town met them on the road, however, and told them—warned them—that all of the royal lodgings were occupied. The second column from the Western Quarter had arrived two days before, and they were all sick with the spotted fever, which the official called pahuac oncoy, the swift-running sickness. He confided to Yasca that many people were sick in Cuzco, as well.

"We will camp outside the town," Yasca declared. "Is there a place near the shore of the lake?"

The official told him the best place and also agreed to open the royal storehouses to provide him with food and the means to barter for firewood and fresh meat and fish. He balked slightly at Yasca's request for akha for all five hundred men but promised he would send out as much as he could. Yasca gave the signal and led the column north again, through the town and out onto a flat, soggy plain that ran down to the edge of the shimmering blue water of the lake. Cusi and the others trudged through the soft soil behind him, weaving their way around patches of standing water and scattered clumps of yellowing bunch grass. Yasca assembled them at the shore and climbed up onto a rock to address them.

"No doubt you have all heard about the sickness that threatens us. It is in Pomata and in Cuzco, too, and I must tell you that its danger is very real." Yasca paused and let them murmur and complain among themselves for several moments. Then he raised his hand for quiet. "That is why I have brought you here, to the holy waters of Titicaca. It is said that Inti rose out of a rock on the Island of the Sun to bring light and warmth to the earth. Now, while Inti is high above us, let us cleanse ourselves in the holy waters and wash away any taint of the sickness. Afterward there will be food and akha, and fires for dancing. I ask you to feast and dance in the name of all the gods and huacas you know. Call on them to protect us and guide us safely back to our homes."

With that, the war chief began to strip off his clothes, throwing them down onto the shore. The men dropped their packs and weapons and bedrolls wherever it was dry and piled their clothes on top of them, following Yasca as he hopped down from the rock and waded into the water. A naked warlord, Cusi thought, gasping as the frigid water lapped over his feet, numbing them instantly. The shallows were filled with brown and yellow algae that furred their legs and bellies as they splashed deeper, whooping and shouting from the shock of the cold. Orange-billed coots paddled frantically out ahead of them, rising half out of the water with their wings beating, and Cusi flailed his arms in a similar manner as he lost his balance and plunged headfirst into the clear green water.

He came up breathless and incoherent, chilled nearly senseless, and he immediately turned and charged back toward the shore, too afraid his heart might stop to worry about washing. Yasca was already there, sitting on his rock with a hand clamped to his heaving chest, laughing as Cusi came stumbling up onto dry ground.

"We are swiftly cleansed," Yasca snorted. There was laughter all along the shore as the men dragged themselves out of the water and realized they could breathe and feel again. The sun-warmed air seemed to rub itself against Cusi's skin like a live thing, and he sat down on the sand and let it dry him while his heart gradually slowed its furious beating.

When he was ready to dress, Cusi decided to discard the tunic and loincloth he had been wearing, which had picked up lice despite all his precautions. He put on the fine cumbi-cloth tunic he had worn to impress the Chiriguano chief, the only tunic he had left but one suitable for the sort of feast Yasca had commanded—a feast of desperation, yet necessary if they were to have the spirit to march on.

He received a summons from Yasca but had to wait while the war chief conferred with the regimental healers. A pack train of llamas and porters had come out from the town, followed closely by a group of women carrying baskets of fish and meat. The warriors were already lighting cooking fires and erecting bonfires out of dried totora reeds. Yasca left the healers and drew Cusi aside.

"I am going to take some of the healers back to Pomata," the war chief said. "We need to learn more about this sickness. Are you willing to come with me?"

Cusi took a moment to reply, understanding that this was not a command. But he had known in Chuquiabo, when he had walked back into the courtyard with Acari, that there was no way to flee from this threat. Macas had said long ago that no one would escape, not the great ones or the small. The only thing left was to fight it.

"I will go," Cusi told him. "There is no sickness that could withstand the water of the lake."

Yasca laughed harshly. "We can bathe again when we return. Go tell your captains to save some akha for you. You will no doubt have earned it . . ."

THE ROYAL lodgings in Pomata consisted of four back-to-back compounds that shared walls and connecting doorways. When Yasca, Cusi, and the eight healers with them arrived at the main gate, they found it covered over with a curtain but unattended, with pots and baskets of food and bundles of fire-wood piled up against the wall next to it. Though Yasca had not bothered to alert him, the Inca official came hurrying up the street to greet them. In addition to being out of breath, the man could not conceal his astonishment at their return, and it rendered him incoherent. Yasca brushed aside the man's apologies and gestured with his chin at the supplies against the wall.

"Why are those out here?" he demanded, and the official ducked his head and waved his hands helplessly.

"I cannot make my people go inside. I am sorry, my lord . . . they are more afraid of the sickness than of any punishment I can bring."

"Who is tending the sick?"

"I summoned every healer in the area, though only a small number re-sponded. A group of healers and mamacona arrived this morning from Copacabana, and I have sent to Chucuito for help."

"We will take this inside," Yasca told him. "Bring more, and make sure it is the kind of food a sick man can eat. These are warriors of the Inca."

The official bowed earnestly and hurried off down the street, only too happy to have a reason to get away from the gate. Cusi and one of the healers each took an end of a stout pole from which a huge, blackened pot of beans hung suspended, lifting the pole to their shoulders while their companions took up the other supplies. Clamping a large bundle of dried reeds under one arm, Yasca pushed aside the curtain and led them through the gate.

For a moment Cusi thought he was back in the plaza at Incallacta, after they had ambushed the Chiriguanos. A narrow path had been left clear across the middle of the courtyard, which was otherwise littered thickly with gear, weapons, and prostrate men. Other men sat up against the outer walls with blankets wrapped around them and arms thrown up to shield their eyes against the light. The dense, sour odor of sweat and urine filled Cusi's nostrils, wiping out the appetite the smell of the beans had briefly aroused. Then he felt it, all around him, the helpless presence he had sensed in Acari, which he now realized was the presence of the sickness itself. He felt it as a collective shivering and heard it as a high, keening whine that resonated in his chest. The man at the other end of the pole wobbled on his feet, and for an instant Cusi came close to dropping the pot and running out of the courtyard.

They had all stopped, looking for someone who might take charge of the supplies. But they could only see five or six other people who were even on their feet, and they were all stooping or crouching over the men on the ground. A few of the sick were crying out and thrashing in their blankets, but most sat or lay without moving, holding their heads and letting out low moans and coughs that sounded dry and futile. Yasca had to clear his own throat before he could speak.

"They obviously cannot come to get it, so we will have to distribute these things ourselves. Try not to get anything from them in return."

Yasca waved Cusi and the healer forward, toward the doorway that opened into the next compound, where they could see more men lying on the ground. Cusi was glad to move and strain his muscles against the weight on his shoulder. It made him feel purposeful and awake, and it gave him time to summon the calm strength of his spirit brother and every bit of his own presence, as well. He was facing death as surely as if he were on a battlefield, and he had to face it with his whole being.

Some of the men sitting against the wall on either side of the doorway had produced cups and bowls, and they held them out with shaking hands as Cusi and his partner approached with the pot, which swayed heavily in its nest of ropes. The men were shading their eyes with a hand or the edge of a blanket, even though the sun was low and the light had grown soft and diffuse.

"The others will feed you," Cusi told them, and kept going through the doorway into the second compound. They bore the pot through the litter of bodies and gear, out to the center of the courtyard, where there was some open space around a cooking fire that was still smoldering. They set their burden down with a mutual grunt and stood for a moment, rubbing their shoulders and staring around them. There were two older women in the gray shifts of mamacona who were tending to those in the courtyard, but most of the healers were inside the awning house that occupied one whole side of the enclosure. No one came to help them with the food, and most of the men sprawled out around them did not appear capable of eating. Cusi again had an impulse to leave the pot and walk back out, but while he was struggling with it, the healer who had come with him simply picked up a bowl and a ladle from among the utensils near the fire and began to fill the bowl with beans. Shame made Cusi follow the man's example and reach for a bowl of his own.

They went in opposite directions, picking their way past the fallen to those who were still able to sit up against the walls. As he stepped over a discarded shield and squatted down in front of three such men, Cusi was relieved to see that none of them had his eyes open, though all of them were holding food bowls on their blanket-covered laps. He did not want them to look into his eyes, and he kept his gaze lowered as he carefully ladled beans into their bowls. When one of the men coughed, Cusi averted his face, and in doing so happened to see the bare leg of one of the others, exposed fully in the light. The skin was a mottled reddish-brown and was covered with tiny raised bumps, as if the man had been stung by a swarm of insects. *Spotted* fever, Cusi thought, experiencing a revulsion that made him appreciate Micay's courage as he never had before. He could feel the need emanating from the men, the pleading whine of the sickness, and it made him want to draw back and cover his face. He was sure that if he responded they would drain his strength and drag him down to death with them.

"Inca," a voice said, hoarse but clearly incredulous. "An Inca serves us."

Cusi looked up before he could stop himself and saw the man in the middle squinting at him, holding a flattened palm against his forehead to shield his watery, pink-rimmed eyes. There was pain in his eyes, but also astonishment, recognition, and something like gratitude. The man was still there beneath the spotted skin, alive and feeling. The man to the right also pried open his swollen eyelids and grimaced in greeting, and Cusi's cheeks warmed with shame. How could he withhold his recognition, when there was little else that he could give them?

"I am Cusi Huaman, my friends," he announced. "I have brought you some food. What else do you need?"

"Water," the man on the right groaned, and both of his companions murmured in agreement.

"I will bring it," Cusi promised. "Are you warm enough?"

"Hot . . ."

"Burning," the middle man said, though he appeared to be shivering inside his blankets. Cusi noticed that he had patches of the bumps on his arms and neck, but none on his face.

"Eat what you can," Cusi told them. "I will be back."

As he gathered up his bowl and rose to his feet, Cusi felt someone behind him and almost turned to see who it was. But then he recognized the presence of his spirit brother and knew that he did not have to fear for his strength. He walked resolutely toward the next group of men sitting up against the wall, greeting them respectfully as he approached.

"The Sapa Inca," one of them blurted. Then he rolled his eyes and collapsed sideways, apparently delirious.

"Impossible," the man next to him muttered, peering out from under the cloak hooded over his head. Cusi smiled at him.

"Most impossible," he agreed, and he reached out to steady the bowl that trembled in the man's hands.

THE LAST MAN Cusi tended was one of the sickest, probably past his tenth day with the disease. The fever had moved into his head, leaving him unconscious and totally limp, even though at times his heart beat so hard its movement could be seen through the covering of blankets. Cusi crouched over him warily, knowing from experience that he might suddenly erupt into violent motion, screaming and flailing his limbs. Cusi had a painful bruise on his cheek from another man who had unexpectedly sat up out of a deep stupor, cracking heads with Cusi before falling back. This man barely moved with his breathing, and his face looked pale and contorted in the moonlight. Cusi held a wet cloth over the man's mouth and carefully squeezed out a single drop of water, then two more before pausing. He had seen Micay do this with wounded men, and she had made it seem like an easy, natural act. But it took a concerted effort to exert such a gentle pressure with muscles as tight and tired as his, and Cusi was relieved when he saw a tongue lick out between the cracked lips, searching. He gave the man more, drop by drop, talking to him as if he could hear and telling him that he had to rouse his spirit and fight the fever.

"There are men still alive in their fifteenth and sixteenth day," Cusi told him hoarsely. "The healers think they will recover."

The man gave not a flicker of response, though he swallowed a fair amount of water before passing out completely. Cusi gently washed the man's face, keeping the damp cloth between his hand and the man's skin. He had shed his fear and revulsion long ago, but seeing the sickness close up had made him decidedly prudent. He left the cloth next to the man's head, though his hand came away warmed by the penetrating heat of the fever.

He stood up and stretched, aching with fatigue, his empty coca bag flapping against his ribs. He had given away all of his coca to the men who could chew without choking, in the hope that it might relieve the pain of their headaches. The moon was now low in the sky, though there had been a time when its light was so bright it hurt the men's sensitive eyes.

"Cusi," a voice called, and he turned to see Yasca standing near the compound doorway, along with several of the healers. The war chief had apparently been watching him, waiting for him to finish. Cusi walked toward him slowly, realizing that he was still in a kind of trance, a state of awareness he attributed to his spirit brother. He had told himself over and over that as long as he was calm and strong and not afraid, the spell of death would not fall on him. He had made himself believe it by pushing himself past the point of exhaustion, serving these men with his whole heart.

"More healers have arrived from Chucuito," Yasca told him. "Let us go now, if you have learned enough."

"I have learned more than I wished to," Cusi said wearily, "though I have yet to learn if anyone recovers."

"They do," a tall, gray-haired healer next to Yasca interjected. "The fever breaks after twenty days or so, and recovery is rapid."

"This Callawaya says he knows you," Yasca prompted, and Cusi came out of his daze and recognized the flat, impassive face and the lanky body hung with feathered bundles and medicine bags.

"Comrade," he said in amazement and started toward Hanp'atu, his arms outstretched to embrace him. Then he stopped and drew his arms back.

"I must not. I have been tending the sick."

"So have I, in Hatuncolla and Chucuito," Hanp'atu reported. "I saw men recover in both places, though perhaps an equal number died."

"Is there a medicine for it?" Cusi asked eagerly, but the healer looked down and shook his head.

"It is stronger than any medicine I know. It can only be endured, and all a healer can do is feed and encourage, as you were doing. You have learned from Micay."

"I do not have her healing presence," Cusi shrugged, "but sometimes I could feel them respond to my voice, even those who seem lost to the world."

"Let us go," Yasca interrupted curtly. "We have stayed here too long already."

Hanp'atu accompanied them to the main gate, falling in beside Cusi as they followed the narrow path between the haphazard ranks of the sick.

"The war chief said you intend to bathe in the lake. That is good, but you should sweat yourself thoroughly first and go in while your body is still hot. And you should smoke your clothes over coals sprinkled with dried uchu peppers."

Cusi nodded absently, resisting the notion that these few moments were all he would have with Hanp'atu. It felt good to have the healer beside him, like another spirit brother.

"Urcon is with us, too. Perhaps you would like to join us," Cusi suggested hopefully, "and march with us back to Raurau Illa's village. I can arrange it easily, and your return, as well."

They had reached the main gate, and Yasca and the other healers went through the curtain without pausing to look back. Cusi and Hanp'atu turned and surveyed the bodies strewn across the courtyard, the newly arrived healers moving tentatively among them.

"I am tempted by your company, Cusi," the healer told him, "but I am needed here. Take my greetings to Urcon, but do not let him come here. Leave as soon as you can. Do not stay in any of the rest houses or cities along the Royal Road, and do not go into Cuzco. Go to Raurau Illa; *he* may have the power to protect you."

The finality of the response left Cusi unable to argue, so he nodded and mustered a rueful smile.

"At least I have seen you again, my friend. I did not expect to see anything here that gave me pleasure."

"Nor did I," Hanp'atu agreed. "Farewell, Cusi. May the gods and your huaca protect you. We will meet again if we are meant to."

The healer bowed, then put a hand on Cusi's shoulder and turned him toward the gate, giving him a light push that sent him out of the compound and into the dark, deserted streets of Pomata.

Quito

AMARU HAD come first, to confer with Chuqui Huipa about some workers he wished to borrow from her. Then Fempellec had arrived, and the discussion had turned to the preparations for the feast celebrating the surrender of Quito, which was to be held in ten days. It was the last feast they would hold here before returning to Tumibamba for the Inti Raymi, and there was a common desire to make it a particularly memorable occasion, one that would sustain them until they returned. No one was looking forward to going south, and any suggestion that seemed too drab or traditional was rebuffed with the words "leave that for Tumibamba."

Micay listened to the arguments and banter with the detachment of a mitmac, feeling heavy as a stone in the midst of all these light spirits. She could share none of their earnest enthusiasm, since she was contemplating an even earlier departure and the jibes about Tumibamba only made the decision more painful. Certain that her silence would soon be noticed, she slipped away from the group in front of Chuqui's house and walked toward the open end of the enclosure. Sinchi and Cahua were playing with the other children in the open space between Cori Cuillor's house and the bathhouse, though Cahua stopped to watch as Micay went past on the other side of the courtyard. Micay smiled and nodded, though she could tell from her daughter's pensive expression that Cahua had already perceived her true mood. She will not want to leave, either, Micay thought, lowering her eyes to the pavement in shame at her own vacillation. The dream had come to her two nights ago, and she had known then what she had to do. Yet she still had not told anyone or begun the arrangements to leave.

She walked around a bank of flowering shrubs—fuchsias, cantuts, and chinchircumas still dripping with bright blossoms despite the onset of the dry season—and went up to the waist-high wall that left one end of the compound open to the sky. The sun was warm on her face and arms, and she put her misgivings aside for a moment and gave herself to the view. The palace was built on terraced landings that climbed the side of Pinincha mountain, and there were two levels below this one. Then the thatched roofs of Quito spread out to the edge of the plateau on which the city stood, jutting out over the river valley below. Micay stared down into the cleft of the valley, where the green blackened into shadow, then let her gaze float upward over the colorful patch-work of the recently harvested fields to the solid yellow-brown of the high pasture, where Tomay had his Guanaco House, and finally to the snow-capped peaks of the great mountains in the far distance. She sighed and shook her head. In Tumibamba, especially inside the Mollecancha, you had to go in search of such views, yet here they were provided at every turn.

While she was pondering how she could leave this before she had to, she heard her name being called, and she turned to see Amaru limping toward her with the twins running out ahead of him. Amaru smiled in greeting, appearing tall and handsome, the confidence of his gait unaffected by the limp.

"Come, Micay," he chided, "if you have nothing better to do than stare at the mountains, you must come visit Parihuana with us. I am taking these children in any case."

Sinchi and Cahua came skidding to a stop beside her, grabbing on to her shift to halt their momentum.

"Mama!" Sinchi exclaimed breathlessly. "Uncle Maru says we can feed the fish. And the ducks!"

"We can see the Little Palace," Cahua added, cocking her head so that Micay saw the birthmark on her throat. "He promised."

"Your uncle is a generous man," Micay said, noting a certain wariness in the way Cahua was regarding her. "That is why everyone gives him what he asks. I cannot refuse him, either."

"Let us go then," Amaru concluded. "Scouts!" he said to the children. "Lead the way to my compound and see that we are not ambushed."

"Stay in sight," Micay called after Cahua and Sinchi as they ran off giggling toward the entrance to the ramp that led down to the next level of the palace. Micay and Amaru followed at a more sedate pace, Amaru running a proprie-tary hand along the top of the half wall.

"So you have no interest in the feast today," he said suggestively. "Or yesterday, Chuqui tells me. She said I should cheer you up and make you stop missing Cusi."

"That was kind of her, though I never stop missing Cusi."

"So what is different about today and yesterday? What makes you turn your back on your companions and stare at the sky?"

They turned down onto the ramp, which had a low wall along its outer edge and a line of cantut bushes along the inside, against the retaining wall of the landing above. The twins were halfway down the incline, looking back, and when they saw the adults coming they waved their arms over their heads and ran the rest of the way down.

"Was I not meant to admire the view?" Micay inquired, resisting the gentle pressure Amaru was exerting on her. "Was it not the intention of the man who built this palace to open it to the mountains and the sky?"

"It was," Amaru acknowledged, lifting his chin with pride. Then he gave Micay a sidelong glance. "Is it your intention to flatter me rather than answering my question? Coyness is a bad sign in you, Micay."

She leaned back to compensate for the incline, her hempen sandals chafing against the roughened surface of the ramp. Then she nodded and let out a long breath, finally accepting her duty.

"I must go back to Tumibamba. As soon as it can be arranged."

"You have been summoned? But why would the high priestess need you back before the Inti Raymi?"

"The high priestess has not sent for me. I received a different kind of summons. A dream."

"Telling you to return to Tumibamba?"

"Telling me something I must share with Chimpu Ocllo. It was the second time this dream has come to me, so I cannot doubt its importance."

"There are messengers who can be trusted," Amaru suggested.

"Not with this. She must hear it from me."

They found the twins waiting for them at the bottom of the ramp, having been turned back from the next courtyard by a gatekeeper. The courtyard was part of the complex that belonged to Ninan Cuyochi, and the children could not be allowed to run free and possibly disturb the deliberations of the Regent. Amaru took them by the hand and led them through the gate, questioning his scouts about the enemies they had encountered. Micay followed along behind, no longer surprised but still impressed by Amaru's patience and good humor. Quito was his city as much as it was Ninan Cuyochi's, and he was capable of anything here, even kindness to children.

They left the palace and crossed the corner of the square in front of the Coricancha before they could again send the twins ahead and resume their conversation.

"So you must tell her," Amaru conceded, nodding absently to the people who greeted him in passing. "But how soon must she hear it? What difference will another month make?"

"I never told her about the first dream," Micay confessed, "and it came to me years ago. That is why I cannot hesitate now."

Amaru squinted at her skeptically. "How long ago did Chimpu Ocllo have her own dreams, or Cusi his vision of warning? For years there have been bad omens and prophecies of sickness and death, yet we are still alive and healthy, are we not? Here, anyway, if not in Tumibamba."

"The dream is about a sickness . . . the spotted fever, I think, though I could not see it clearly."

"I heard the reports of that," Amaru allowed, "but they were all from the Hotlands and there have been no more in over a year. Perhaps it went away with the Viracochas."

"Perhaps my dream is a sign that it will return," Micay said tautly. "We never learned what it was. Or who the Viracochas were."

Amaru held up a hand, heeding the warning in her voice. "Forgive me,

Micay. I forget that you are not truly one of us, though you seem to belong here. I see that you have made your decision, and I know you are as stubborn about these things as Cusi. But you cannot convince me that you *wish* to hurry back to Tumibamba."

They had arrived at the entrance to Amaru's compound, into which the twins had already disappeared. Micay gave him a pained smile.

"This is our fourth visit to Quito, and each time it has gotten more difficult to leave. Each time Tumibamba has seemed more gloomy and troubled, more futile. When I am there, Quito seems like a wonderful dream, so that I cannot trust my own memories."

"Quito is quite real," Amaru assured her proudly, "and it is ours. Even if Huayna Capac were to come here to sit and brood in his palace, we would not be dispossessed. We have lands and people of our own here, and a leader who knows how to keep both our trust and his father's favor."

Micay stared at him for a moment, reluctant to cast doubt on his accomplishment. She remembered the Amaru who could find no purpose for himself and no task worthy of his commitment.

"Still, you must not think you are immune here," she told him. "You are not as isolated from the rest of the Four Quarters as you want to believe. Were you not told once to build far from the places for which men would fight?"

A frown briefly clouded Amaru's features, but then he nodded, squinting at her thoughtfully.

"I have not forgotten. But even when I survived the war, I did not expect to be granted a second life, a chance to live the way the Incas were meant to. That was the gift of Sinchi Roca, who showed me what could be done here and put me in charge of doing it. Then you gave me Parihuana, and Ninan was made Regent, and Fempellec came here with Chuqui Huipa. How could I question my good fortune? Why would you have me question it now?"

"I would have you be vigilant," Micay said forcefully. "The sky may be clear over Quito, but the threat that hangs over all of us has not gone away. And Cusi is out there somewhere, trying to come back to me."

"He is probably in Cuzco by now," Amaru reckoned, turning to escort her through the doorway. "You know that Ninan's request for his services was granted?"

"Ninan told me. He promised his father he would cure Cusi of his defiance and disrespect."

Amaru laughed. "And you will cure me of my complacency. We will all heal together."

As they came into the compound they were met by a group of stonemasons and supervisors of work gangs, who were awaiting Amaru's instructions. After receiving his promise to let her announce her own departure, Micay left him to confer with the other men and went up the steps to the second and broadest level of the compound. As expected, she found Sinchi at the long, open tank that drained into a reflecting pool at each end. He was helping Amaru's gardener feed meal to the fish, carefully imitating the slow casting motion of the old man's wrist. The gardener gave Micay a deferential bow, but Sinchi simply smiled down at her reflection when it appeared in the water in front of him. The fish were rising for the bits of meal scattered on the surface, their suckerlike mouths creating circular ripples that expanded outward in perfect rings. Sinchi watched with a raptness that had never varied in all the times he had done this.

"Where is Cahua?" Micay asked softly.

Sinchi spoke to her reflection. "She went to see the Little Palace."

"You both know you are not to go there alone."

"Maybe she told me wrong," Sinchi suggested, glancing up at her out of the corner of his marked eye. His voice was hopeful, but she could see he was speaking out of loyalty rather than conviction. He knew if Cahua was in a mood for breaking rules, though he would not want to see her punished. Micay reached down and ruffled the black hair that covered his head like crow's feathers.

"I will find her. Obey this man and do not give the fish more than they can eat."

"I know that," Sinchi said with mild annoyance, leaning back over the pool. "They would get too fat and sink."

Amused by his assurance, Micay turned away, thinking that perhaps he *was* a Campa. Surely in temperament he resembled Uritu more than he did anyone of his own blood. Micay knew that she could wait to tell him they were leaving. He might state his preference by saying something like "Why not stay?", but then he would adapt himself to whatever she planned for him. He did not have Cahua's memory for pleasure and pain, or at least not her urge to repeat the former and avoid the latter.

As Micay walked toward the stairway next to the bathhouse, she was hailed from the terrace above. Parihuana had just come out of her house, attended by several Quito women including Mama Pura, Ninan Cuyochi's wife. Micay smiled and put her palm out at the level of her knee, pantomiming her search for her child. She pointed with her chin toward the small awning house that filled the corner of the enclosure on the terrace below, a structure that was open on three sides but sheltered by stands of slender feather palms. Breathing sulfurous fumes from the bathhouse, she went down the stairs and into the awning house.

At first, as her eyes adjusted to the leaf-shadowed light, she saw no sign of her daughter among the stools and benches and piles of stone and clay. Fully half the space under the high-pitched roof was taken up by a great mound of earth that rose against the back wall in the shape of Pinincha, the mountain that rose above Quito. Carved into the side of the mound were the terraces and landings on which the palace stood, modeled in clay and, according to Amaru, exact in every detail. The modeling had been rough the first time Micay had seen it, but now all the walls were smooth and straight and the buildings had roofs of woven grass propped up on sticks. There were even tufts of green cloth fixed on thorns to indicate groves and gardens. None of this detail was necessary to the plan that Sinchi Roca had laid out years ago, but it was Amaru's record of how he had executed and modified that plan in the actual construction.

Then she spotted Cahua, crouching at the very top of the mound, watching her mother with her chin resting on her knees, an expression of plaintive resistance on her face. Micay removed a bronze snuffing tube from the nearest stool and sat down, beckoning to her daughter with her free hand.

"Come down, Cahua. Very carefully."

"I do not want to go," the girl blurted. "Do not make me go, Mama!"

"Do not disobey me twice. Come down and I will explain."

Cahua pushed out her lips but then turned and disappeared down the other side of the mound. Micay examined the snuffing tube, noting the grayish film that covered the flared end. Despite his newfound respectability, Amaru obviously had not lost his taste for vilca.

Cahua appeared in front of her, reluctantly penitent, her hands wrapped around a wad of reddish-brown clay, her legs and tunic smeared with dirt. She looked so forlorn that Micay had to force herself to be stern.

"You know that you are not to come here alone. This is not a place where you are free to play."

"I waited outside," Cahua insisted, "but you and Uncle Amaru did not come."

"You should have come back to find us," Micay said. Then she relented and patted the stool next to hers. "Come sit, now. Let me tell you why we have to leave."

"Why?" Cahua echoed, drawing the word out into a moan as she climbed up onto the stool. "There are no other children there, and no place where it is free to play. I like Quito more, Mama."

Micay reflected that Chuqui Huipa, who adored Cahua, would have found this conversation uncanny, since Cahua had known without being told that they were going back to Tumibamba. Micay had tried to explain to Chuqui that Cahua simply had her mother's watchfulness and her father's memory, so that she noted all of Micay's moods and remembered their consequences. Chuqui had insisted that *that* was uncanny in a child not yet four, and perhaps it was. Micay only knew that there was no point in trying to conceal her true feelings from her daughter.

"I like Quito more, too," she admitted, "though I miss the Rainbow House. Perhaps we can go there after I have spoken to the high priestess. That is why we must go back, Cahua. I must tell her about the dream that came to me."

Cahua frowned, wrinkling her nose. "Was it a bad dream? Were you afraid?"

"No. It was a good dream, a dream about the healers who serve Mama Quilla. The Moon Mother must have sent it to me, to help us heal the sick."

"Who is sick?"

"Perhaps no one, but we must heed the signs that tell us to prepare ourselves. That is part of our task, our duty to Mama Quilla. So even though I would like to stay in Quito, I must do what my sense of duty tells me."

Cahua looked down at the lump of clay she was kneading with her fingers, swinging her muddy legs under the stool. Micay knew that she understood the importance of promises and vows; it was another thing she seemed to have inherited from her father. When the girl finally looked up, Micay could see she had reached some kind of reconciliation with the idea of leaving, though there was a question in her dark eyes.

"Do I have to tell a dream, too?"

Micay laughed and shook her head. "No, my child. And we can come back to Quito again, perhaps after the Inti Raymi."

"Chuqui Huipa will miss me," Cahua decided with more pride than regret, then abruptly jumped off the stool. "Here come Sinchi and Aunt Parihuana . . ."

She dashed out to greet them, running along the curving path that wound through the garden and made it seem larger than it was. Amaru had left the planning of the garden to Parihuana, but he had built in such a way that the walls surrounding this first level trapped the sun's light and warmth, and he had devised an irrigation system that could draw hot, steamy water from the bathhouse if there were a threat of frost. As a result Parihuana had guava and papaya and cherimoya trees that were already bearing fruit, and in the spaces between she had planted flowering shrubs and peppers and banks of ferns and flowers that had never been seen this high above the valley. It was a garden worthy of her husband's ambition, which Parihuana had made her own.

Micay stood up with the snuffing tube still in her hand, deciding that it was better there than in Sinchi's curious grasp. Parihuana had stopped on the path and was letting Cahua place her hands on her swollen abdomen, letting her feel the child that was growing inside. Parihuana was only in her sixth month, but she was still so slender that the protruding bulge made her appear particularly unwieldy. Micay understood why she had come down the long way, where the stairs were less steep, though she was somewhat surprised she had come alone. Micay had not indicated that she wanted a private conversation, and she had grown accustomed to Parihuana's entourage of women, who were a sign of her status with both the Inca court and the nobility of Quito.

Parihuana came in under the awning house roof and accepted Micay's embrace with a puzzled smile. She inclined her head toward Cahua, who was hanging onto the side of her shift.

"What has she been telling me? You are leaving?"

"We are going to tell a dream," Cahua added, then followed her brother, who had already deserted them for the Little Palace.

"I must, Parihuana," Micay said. "There are things I must discuss with the high priestess."

"They cannot wait until the Inti Raymi?"

"I have delayed too long already, wavering because it is hard for me to leave this city. So please, my sister, accept that I have decided and let me save my explanations for Chuqui Huipa."

Parihuana seemed to stiffen slightly at the name, but then she ducked her head in compliance.

"As long as you will try to return in time to help deliver my firstborn."

"I will try," Micay promised. "I owe you that."

"Mama, look at the painted house!" Sinchi cried. He and Cahua were standing as close as they dared to the mound, peering through the tiny doorways of the clay buildings. One of the houses had indeed been painted, its walls adorned with a stepped pattern that Micay recognized immediately.

"That must be Fempellec's work," she said.

Parihuana nodded. "He is often out here with Amaru, adding to the model and dreaming about what to build next. Fempellec insists Amaru has stolen all of his best ideas from the Chimu."

"The ramps, certainly," Micay allowed, glancing at the model. The memory of Chan Chan suddenly made the bronze tube in her hand seem appropriate, and she presented it to Parihuana. "This must help them with their dreaming."

Micay smiled as she passed the tube over, and she was surprised to see Parihuana stiffen as she accepted it, her face going rigid for a moment as if at some grim recollection.

"Do you disapprove?" asked Parihuana.

"Of Amaru or of vilca? He is a grown man, and he knows its properties and its dangers." Micay stopped and squinted at her curiously. "What is wrong, Parihuana? You have no need to ask my approval."

"Not yours, perhaps," Parihuana murmured, her eyes on the ground. Micay suddenly understood why she had come down here without her entourage.

"Mama Pura?" she inquired softly, and Parihuana's head came up, nodding.

"She says she cannot be polite to you. She believes you help Ninan and Chuqui Huipa to meet in secret."

Micay might have scoffed at the accusation, but she saw how seriously Parihuana was taking it and how torn she was. Her prestige with her own people was important to her, and it had helped Amaru establish his power in this city.

"Even if the two of them needed my help," Micay said, "it would be pointless for Mama Pura to direct her anger at me. I am not to blame for her husband's affections."

"I have told her that. But then she always turns it back on me, bringing up my husband and the rumors about him and Fempellec. Then I have to pretend to be outraged, and worried as she is worried, that discovery could make me a widow. I hate the pretending, Micay. I hate the silence I keep while she says terrible things about Fempellec."

Micay put a hand on Parihuana's arm to calm her, shaking her head in sympathy. "Perhaps Quito is not such a special place. Perhaps it is simply young."

"I refuse to believe that," Parihuana said stubbornly.

"Then you should not pretend with her. Be an example of the kind of tolerance you want to exist here. If Fempellec is your friend, you must say so and risk her scorn. She has more rank than you do, but she is far less secure and she cannot afford to make you her enemy. Teach her that her pettiness is unacceptable to you."

Parihuana let out a long breath. "You make it sound so simple."

"I do not mean to," Micay assured her. "It requires great resolve to be both polite and honest, and in most courts it is simply not possible. Here you have at least the opportunity—the luxury—to try. You should make use of it while you can."

"You think it will not last?"

"I do not know what will last. That is a concern better left to Tumibamba."

Parihuana gave her a smile that was strained but grateful. "I will miss you while you are there. You must give my regards to Apu Poma and Mama Cori and Quinti Ocllo."

"I will," Micay promised. Then she remembered the children, who had been inordinately quiet while the two women were talking. Micay hoped Cahua had not been listening too closely, and when she turned to look that seemed to be the case. The twins were standing shoulder to shoulder in front of the mound, whispering conspiratorially and doing something to the model with their hands.

"Do not touch," Micay said sharply, and the two of them jumped and whirled around in surprise. They both had lumps of clay in their hands, and as Micay drew closer, she saw that they had placed a number of clay figures on the ramps and landings of the miniature palace.

"Did not touch, Mama," Sinchi claimed with wide-eyed innocence.

"They live here," Cahua explained, pointing at the figures with her chin. Parihuana laughed as she came to Micay's side.

"And who are they?" she asked.

Cahua pointed first at two vaguely human-shaped lumps on one of the lower landings. "Those are Grandfather and Grandmother. They are far away, of course."

"Of course," Parihuana agreed easily, smiling at Micay. "Who are these others?"

"Otoronco Chachee, Uncle Maru, Uncle Uritu, Paucar Rimay," Sinchi said, bobbing his head at the figures he had lined up along a ramp. He lingered over the last, glancing back at Parihuana with an earnest expression on his round face. "He looks up all the time, but he can still see."

"Of course," Parihuana said again, and she turned back to Cahua, who was pulling on her shift. Cahua straightened up so that her chin was at the same level as the three headless lumps she had put at the top.

"The Moon Mother and Pachamama and Huaca Woman all live up here," she said proudly. "It is cooler for them."

" 'Huaca Woman'?" Parihuana said to Micay.

"Macas," Micay explained.

"We forgot Illapa," Sinchi cried, and he put a last potato-shaped lump into place before Micay could stop him.

"That is enough now," she said firmly, taking each of them by an arm and pulling them away from the mound. "Your Uncle Amaru will be angry if you make his palace too crowded. Go and wash yourselves now; we must go back to the real palace."

"I will miss *them*, too," Parihuana said wistfully, watching them run off through the garden. "I pray that Pachamama is as kind to me."

"You were at the huaca with me," Micay reminded her. "You received the same blessing. And I will be your midwife if I am free to come back here in time."

They had stepped out into the moist, fragrant atmosphere of the garden, and Micay stopped and looked up through a fringe of leaves at the blue of the sky. It seemed as if it were always clear and sunny in Quito, even though the rains were as frequent here as in Tumibamba. A dream, she thought, a wonderful waking dream . . .

"So you will leave before Chuqui's feast," Parihuana concluded as they started down the sun-streaked path. "She will be reluctant to let you go."

"I know," Micay agreed. She shrugged. "But she knows that others have a hold on me, as well. She will have to understand that there are some dreams more urgent than this one . . ."

The Southern Quarter Road

THE LUPACA TROOPS were given their release in Chucuito, and the Collas left the column a day later, in Hatuncolla. It was here that the sickness first appeared in their ranks, and among those to be stricken was Tomay. He had previously arranged to stay on with his family for a month's leave, so Cusi had been prepared for a parting. But he hated to leave his friend in such a state, his cheeks aflame with fever and his eyes slitted against the pain in his head. Cusi stayed with him, instructing the family on how to treat him and promising him that they would meet again in Cuzco, until Yasca finally sent Quizquiz to pull him away.

The column went on, slowing their pace to accommodate the sick men in their midst. The healthy men carried their gear and gave them the support of their arms, keeping them upright and moving forward, guiding them when the headaches made them blind. They reached Ayaviri before it became necessary to carry anyone, though now the sickest had spots on their chests and were too weak from fever to walk. Yasca assembled them outside the rest house in Ayaviri and reorganized them into groups of forty or fifty with the sick evenly distributed among the groups. Then he had the pack train brought up and their packs emptied of the baggage of war, saving only the blankets, spears, and rope that could be used to fashion litters and carrying slings. He assigned a herder and some of the llamas to each of the groups, telling the men to discard all but the most essential gear and to load that on the llamas, freeing their hands and backs to carry the sick. Each group was to move at its own pace and to be responsible for its own sick; they were to stay together and try to make it to Cuzco, though they were free to seek refuge elsewhere if they had to.

Cusi watched his regiment of Hawk Men dissolve back into a collection of mitmac bands, though he noticed that no one discarded the red and black shields and battle standards. He allowed it to happen, even facilitating some adjustments in the groups Yasca had formed, trading comrades for kinsmen. He knew that if there was to be discipline in the hard days ahead, it would have to be enforced by something stronger than rank or right of command. The Inca could not command this sickness, and only the obligations of blood would make one man carry another for long.

His own group consisted of Tarapaca and his Lupaca mitmacs, along with some Caras and Huancas who were also among his most devoted troops. He made sure Urcon was their herder, then supervised the loading of the llamas, being strict about the winnowing of gear. When litters had been made for those who could not walk and the healthy had been organized into teams of bearers, Cusi marched them out of Ayaviri, leaving the street outside the rest house littered with packs and weapons and the feather headdresses of the defeated Chiriguanos.

The march soon became a walk that covered less ground with each succeeding day, as more men had to be excused from the carrying and still more had to be carried. The burden on the healthy grew in direct proportion to their dwindling numbers, leaving them little chance to rest between tasks and their turns with the litters. They lost their first two men going over the high mountain pass south of Sicuani. One of the sick came awake with a violent lurch, tipping his litter over the edge of a cliff and taking one of the exhausted bearers down with him. The next night, three young Huancas deserted the group, and Cusi could not bring himself to curse them as cowards or to chastise their elders. He knew the temptation too well and was secretly amazed that more of the healthy did not follow the deserters' example.

With fatigue came the despair of knowing, as he tried to snatch some sleep, that he would wake to a nightmare of moaning, coughing men, more of them incapacitated than the day before. He would have to rise and see that they were fed, then get them up and moving, taking his turn beneath the pole of a litter. And he would wonder, through the pain of his labors, if this was the day the fever would come to him. The sickness was a constant hum in the air around him, a vibration against his skin. The rest houses and villages along the road were either filled with their own sick or were empty, abandoned with the maize and quinoa still drying in the yards. There was no one to help and no place to hide, no place where the sickness might not follow or be lying in wait.

In the face of such hopelessness, the calm hold his spirit brother had had upon him began to slip, and Cusi deliberately pulled away, freeing his presence from the restraint of reason. Alone in the darkness, he sang the story song of

Pachacuti's desperate stand against the Chancas, and he let himself go mad as Pachacuti had, believing he could fight this sickness and win. He did not have Pachacuti's grand vision to guide him, only the promise that he would return to Raurau Illa's village in need. He vowed that he and Urcon would make it there, and to accomplish that he would drag these others with him for as long as he had to.

The next day, as they struggled along the road, the healthy bent beneath their burdens and the sick staggering drunkenly, Cusi began to sing Pachacuti's story song. His companions did not know that this was a sacred song meant only for the ears of blood Incas, but they could not mistake it for a mere marching song, something to distract them from their misery. Cusi sang it a second time and made them sing it with him, teaching them the words as if they were apprentice singers. He went from litter to litter, rallying the bearers and speaking to the senseless, lashed-down men as if they, too, could hear him and be inspired. Once more, he became the warlord who had led them to Tiahuanaco, the mad Inca who had defied the Chiriguanos at Incallacta. When he finally went to take his turn at carrying, Tarapaca stepped in front of him and assumed his place among the bearers.

"Lead us, Lord Huaman," he murmured. "We will carry."

The groups of Soras and Rucanas left the disintegrating column at Combapata, following a westward trail that would take them to their homes without going near Cuzco. The remaining groups gradually came together again at Quiquijana, having lost half their number along the way, either dead, deserted, or left where there was some hope of their being tended. Yasca did not ask any of his commanders for a count, and he said nothing to contradict Cusi's vocal assumption of leadership. He and Quizquiz were content to take their turns with the litters and let Cusi coax and push and rave at the men, making them believe, despite the evidence, that they were not meant to die on the road.

When they were still more than a day south of Urcos, Yasca announced his intention to go no farther than Quispi Cancha, which was perhaps four days away. His household had holdings there, and many of the surrounding estates were inhabited only by the retainers who maintained them. They would have food and the attentions of people who were bound by blood to serve them, which was better than they could expect in Cuzco. Cusi added his assent to that of the other commanders and then went to tell the men, able at last to promise them a destination. He spread the word quickly, saying nothing about his own intentions, which he would confide only to Urcon. He found his friend halfway up a grassy slope, sitting in the midst of a circle of scattered packs. His llamas grazed peacefully a short distance away, though a couple of them straightened up suspiciously at Cusi's approach.

Cusi expected Urcon to be tired, since he had inherited another herder's llamas along with his own and had had to do all the loading and unloading himself. But his friend barely raised his head when Cusi sat down beside him, and he could not manage his customary smile. Cusi felt the presence of the sickness emanating from him, even though Urcon showed none of the outward signs of the fever.

"How do you feel?" Cusi asked bluntly.

Urcon gave a languid shrug. "Tired, but that is all. No fever."

Cusi grunted but decided there was no point in challenging him. Instead he explained Yasca's decision to stay at Quispi Cancha and his own desire for the two of them to go on to Urcon's village. The latter proposal finally made Urcon smile.

"Let us go, comrade. It is only a few days further on from Quispi Cancha, by the trail that goes around the narrows."

"You must tell me about this trail and describe the place where it joins the Royal Road."

"I will be with you," Urcon said lazily. "I will point it out to you."

"Tell me anyway," Cusi insisted. "I am a scout; I need to see the path in my mind."

Urcon's head wobbled on his neck, and he suddenly seemed to realize how slowly he was responding. His eyes filled with a familiar pleading. "Am I sick? Has it fallen on me?"

"I think the fever is close," Cusi told him. "You must be brave, my friend, and believe with all your heart that you will survive. I will be with you."

Urcon gripped Cusi's wrist with surprising force. "Take me to my village, Cusi. Do not stop to nurse me, even if I am so sick you must drag me. Take me to Grandfather."

"I am meant to go there, and you will go with me," Cusi promised, putting his hand over Urcon's. "Now, while you still can, tell me all you know about the trail . . ."

URCON MARCHED for another whole day before the fever struck with its customary abruptness. Cusi found him still standing but slumped over the back of one of his llamas, his face clenched against the pain in his head. His skin was hot and dry to the touch.

"It has begun," Cusi said, and he unrolled a bedroll and helped Urcon lie down, tearing up handfuls of the leathery bunch grass to provide a cushion for his head and back. "Rest now, I will take care of your llamas. You must save your strength, because you will have to walk tomorrow. There is no room on the litters."

He went back to Urcon's pack for another blanket, noticing that his friend still had the Hawk Man shield and the chontawood bow he had been given as prizes in Incallacta. Cusi squatted down next to Urcon and examined him for a moment. Then he blinked, doubting his own eyes. What he had taken for sweat stains on the front of Urcon's tunic seemed to be moving; they *were* moving. He flicked at one of the irregular, grayish lines with his finger, and it broke and scattered like salt. Lice, Cusi realized, as the scattered particles began to move. He put his arms under Urcon's back and gently lifted him into a sitting position.

"What are you doing?" Urcon groaned as Cusi pulled the tunic off over his head and threw it as far away from them as he could.

"The lice are leaving your body. You are too hot for them to live on."

Urcon's eyes were still shut, but he bared his teeth and gave a laugh that ended in a cough. "They can go. I have fed them long enough."

Cusi stripped him completely and brought him new clothes and a new bedroll. The lice hardly mattered now, but he wanted to make Urcon as comfortable as he could for as long as he was able. It was all that he could do, and it was nothing. Urcon was curled up on his side, shivering, and Cusi tucked the blankets in around him before rising to his feet. He felt a helplessness that made him want to shake his fists at the sky, and only the fact that the other men were watching restrained him. Even a warlord could not curse the gods. He turned instead to unload the llamas, but his glowering presence preceded him, and the animals put up their ears and shied away from him, huffing and spitting. Cusi stopped and tried to summon some calm, but his fury only seemed to mount. He wanted to be marching on, not unloading. With Urcon sick, the village was many more days away, and each one would be an agony. He wanted to keep moving while he still had his anger to sustain him.

Tarapaca and a couple of his men went past Cusi without a word, gliding in among the llamas and doing his work for him. Cusi was panting, though the force of his impatience seemed to have spent itself. Perhaps he truly was losing his mind. His spirit brother seemed lost already. With a shrug of annoyance he turned away from the llamas and walked back through the camp the men were making for themselves, saying little to any of them but letting them all see that their warlord was still on his feet.

THE COUNTRY estates of the Incas were situated on the terraced hillside north of the Huatanay River, and many of them were indeed empty of their owners. As Yasca had predicted, the retainers did not flee at the sight of a regiment of sick warriors dragging themselves up the slope from the road. When they saw the golden earplugs of the leaders, they came out with food and water, and they summoned their men from the fields to help with the litters. The few Incas who were in residence in the valley also sent their servants with supplies, though they did not come themselves.

Conceiving of it as his final duty, Cusi made sure that all of his men were quartered where none would be forgotten, and he gave instructions to the retainers on how the sick were to be treated. He was impressed enough by the accommodations and wary enough of the ordeal ahead to suggest to Urcon that they stay in Quispi Cancha until he was better and then go on. Urcon had made it this far under his own power, clinging blindly to the thick fleece of one of his llamas, but Cusi knew he would weaken rapidly once the spots appeared on his chest.

"I can go on now," Urcon insisted hoarsely. "We are too close to stop here."

"But you should not be walking when you could rest."

"The sickness gives you no rest," Urcon said, shielding his eyes with the edge of his blanket. "If I must die, I would rather die on the trail to my home."

Cusi found Yasca sitting on the edge of one of the terraces, gazing down at the valley and the river below. His rough-hewn face appeared as old and gray as the stones on which he sat, though Cusi did not detect the presence of the sickness. Cusi told him that he and Urcon were going on to Raurau Illa's village, and he asked for permission to take four of the llamas, along with supplies and the makings for a litter. The war chief nodded his consent.

"You have earned the right to do whatever you wish. If we ever see another messenger from Cuzco, I will send word of where you are. For Tumibamba."

Cusi bowed in gratitude. "Farewell, Lord Yasca. It has been my honor to serve you."

"Expect to have the honor again," Yasca told him, "if we live through this. I will not forget the kind of leader you have been, and I will speak for your promotion to war chief, since we no longer have the rank of warlord."

"Rank saves no one," Cusi said as he rose. "Tell Micay and my children if I do not return. I will do the same for you."

Cusi assembled their packs and the necessary supplies near the corral, then went back for Urcon. Tarapaca was sitting with him, helping him eat, and Cusi stood over them for a moment, not wanting to spend time and breath on farewells. Tarapaca saved him the trouble by glancing up with a knowing smile.

"You must let me go with you, my lord. One man cannot carry a litter by himself."

Cusi glanced at Urcon, who was slumped against the wall and appeared incapable of speech. But he was the only one who could have told Tarapaca that they were going on.

"You have proven your courage and loyalty, Tarapaca," Cusi said. "There is no need for you to risk yourself further."

"The risk is the same wherever I am," Tarapaca retorted. "Let me use my strength while I still have it. Let me be a Hawk Man awhile longer."

Cusi again looked at Urcon, who was peering up at him from beneath the blanket hooded over his head.

"You agree, my friend?"

"He is a comrade," Urcon managed, "and I am useless."

The truth of the statement was so plain that Cusi suddenly felt stupid, the victim of his own single-mindedness. He had not known how he would carry Urcon by himself, but he had not thought to ask anyone else to help. A warlord did not ask for help. Cusi shook himself and spread his hands in apology, realizing how grateful he would be for Tarapaca's assistance.

"Go tell Yasca that I have asked for you," he said to the captain, "and then bring your gear to the corral. There is still enough light to travel." He let Tarapaca go and squatted down in his place in front of Urcon. "So, comrade, you are strong enough to save me from my own stupidity. You must be strong enough to go home."

Urcon gave a weak cough. "I did not want us both to die on the trail."

"We will all live," Cusi vowed, putting an arm around him to help him to his feet. "Do not think again about dying."

BY THE TIME they reached the place where the trail diverged from the Royal Road, Urcon no longer had the strength to walk, even with Cusi and Tarapaca holding him up on both sides. So they made a litter for him out of the materials they had brought, padding the frame with bunch grass and blankets and tying Urcon to it with strips of cloth that would hold him in place without cutting into his skin. Then they each took an end and started up into the hills, with the llamas following along behind.

Even with two men, they could only carry for a short distance before the strain on their arms and backs forced them to rest. It was as much of an effort to go downhill as up, and the hills seemed to roll out endlessly ahead of them. The second day it rained, muddying the trail and driving them to find a sheltered camp while it was still light. Patches of spots had appeared on Urcon's chest, and he was conscious for shorter and shorter periods. He gave up any attempt to advise Cusi on the handling of the llamas, and then he seemed to forget them entirely, not even clicking his tongue or calling to them from his litter. The beasts trailed along uncertainly, confused by the slow, erratic pace and the freedom they were given to graze.

During their rest stops, Cusi and Tarapaca sat on either side of the litter and talked over Urcon, speaking softly but keeping him aware of their presence. Their conversations were awkward at first, because Tarapaca was still too much in awe of Cusi and deferred to him too readily. But Cusi persevered, speaking with utter frankness and asking Tarapaca questions about himself, trying to show him the difference between a comrade and a follower. For a while Tarapaca seemed as uncertain as the llamas, but then, in the course of describing how he had met Raurau Illa, Cusi mentioned that he had been sent to confess his sins to the Grass Man. Tarapaca gaped at him in astonished recognition, then forgot about deference and demanded to know more, not surrendering his disbelief until Cusi had described the hut and the beating he had received. Tarapaca looked down at his own wrists with a grimace of recollection.

"So you know about that. No wonder you do not take our trust for granted."

"I have never forgotten how few the Incas are," Cusi told him, "or how much we depend upon the loyalty of our friends. Come, while the Grass Man is still in our minds, let us carry some more. There is strength in anger . . ."

They went on for two more days, reaching the place that Urcon had described as the halfway point of their journey. The hills rose up remorselessly ahead of them, and Cusi and Tarapaca debated taking a parallel trail that seemed more level. While they were talking across him, Urcon suddenly emerged from his stupor, wide-eyed and urgent, and began to shout at them.

"Why are you driving them so hard? They are llamas, not men! Let them rest now, or they will sit and refuse to go any farther. We should *all* refuse . . . you have no right to drive us to our deaths!"

He began to writhe against his bindings, pulling them loose from the frame and nearly throwing Cusi and Tarapaca off when they tried to hold him still.

"Urcon, stop!" Cusi cried. "The llamas are fine."

"Stop the fever!" Urcon said vehemently, looking Cusi straight in the eye and glaring at him with hatred. "You lie! You cannot stop anything, you cannot save us! The Chimus will murder all of us and bury our bodies in the sand!"

Then his eyes rolled back and he shuddered violently and went limp in their hands. Cusi could not move for a moment, stunned by what he had seen in Urcon's eyes.

"The fever is in his head," Tarapaca said sadly, and he began to repair Urcon's bindings. Cusi finally recovered from his shock and moved to help, telling himself that the hatred had not been meant for him.

"Let us stay on the path we know," he said to Tarapaca as they went to opposite ends of the litter. "Let us try to talk less and carry more."

The next night they camped near a spring and found a lightning-struck tree that provided plenty of dry wood for a fire. They heated water and washed themselves and Urcon, noting that the spots now covered his torso and were spreading onto his limbs. He was barely able to swallow, but Cusi and Tarapaca were diligent in their feeding and helped him get down a little soup and some honey dissolved in warm water. He became agitated again after they laid him down, but his thrashings were feeble and subsided quickly, and they could not understand anything he said.

They thickened the soup with quinoa flour and shreds of charqui and took turns dipping into the pot with wooden spoons. As Cusi ate, he calculated the distance they had left to travel, taking some comfort in the fact that the hills had begun to flatten out and they would soon be up into the high, rolling pastureland where carrying would be easier. They had also begun to see herds and herders, and though none of those they called to would approach them, they might yet find someone willing to help. Even without help, they could conceivably reach the village in two or three days, if neither of them pulled a muscle and they were not slowed by rain. Tantalized by such hopeful thoughts, Cusi only gradually noticed that Tarapaca had stopped dipping into the pot and was sitting with his head pulled in between his shoulders, staring dazedly at the fire.

"Comrade," Cusi said softly and saw how slowly Tarapaca reacted, even though Cusi's voice had startled him. Cusi could feel the pleading, too, as he had with Urcon.

"I feel strange, Cusi . . . like I am not inside my own skin."

"That is how it begins. Lie down now and rest while you can. Save your strength for tomorrow."

"I will help you carry," Tarapaca promised, though there was more desire than conviction in his voice. Cusi put more wood onto the fire and knelt down next to Tarapaca, who was rolled up tightly in his cloak and blankets.

"We are close enough," Cusi said, resting a hand on Tarapaca's shoulder. "We will get there somehow. We did not come back from Incallacta to die here."

"Thunupa will save us," Tarapaca murmured, closing his eyes. "I will pray to him."

"Pray for all the Hawk Men," Cusi told him. He stood up and gingerly tested his muscles, finding them stiff and sore but sufficiently responsive. "Pray that some of us are still standing when this is through . . ."

BY MIDMORNING Tarapaca was feverish, and though he tried to hold up his end of the litter, the pains in his back buckled his knees and made him stumble dangerously. Cusi had already modified the litter, lashing their Hawk Man shields to the bottom of one end, so he told Tarapaca to walk alongside while he stepped between the poles and began to drag the litter behind him. Now he knew the agony Tarapaca had saved him these past days, taking half of Urcon's weight off his tired muscles and supplying half the impetus to get them moving again after they had stopped. Proceeding at a pace that had the llamas walking around and ahead of them, Cusi pulled the litter for the rest of the day, exhausting himself so thoroughly that he never felt the signs of the sickness coming on. The fever hit him as he was pulling the packs off one of the llamas, pain shooting simultaneously through his head and hips so that his whole body jerked and he went over backward with the packs on top of him.

He lay where he was, hearing a ringing in his ears and feeling heat radiating out of him, a dry heat that parched his throat and made his eyes expand in their sockets. The pain in his head seemed to have settled into place, pulsing jaggedly, while the pains in his back and legs came and vanished in sudden stabs. Yet even as the pain made him dizzy and nauseous, he felt somehow apart from it, an onlooker at the battle being waged inside his skin. He knew he should struggle, push back against it, but he could find nothing firm in himself, no place to push *from*. The sickness seemed to have absorbed his presence into itself, baring him to the pain while leaving him no power to resist it.

Grunting at the effort it cost him, Tarapaca pulled the packs off Cusi and helped him get to his knees. Then he collapsed beside him.

"You, too," he panted, and Cusi started to nod but stopped when the pain flared up in his head.

"Me," Cusi agreed, though it felt like a lie, and he wished that it were.

They went on for two days, three, losing count of time and distance as they dragged the litter across the plain. Urcon had developed sores on his back and buttocks from rubbing and bumping against the litter, but they had nothing with which to make a poultice and barely the strength to force food and water upon him. The light hurt their eyes and every movement reverberated in their heads, so that they moved like blind men and attended only to the tasks they could not avoid. When Cusi could bring himself to look upon Urcon's pale, haggard face, the tongue protruding limply through his cracked lips, he knew that his friend was dying. But there was no urgency left in him, no residue of strength that could be shamed or frightened into action, no huaca to make him leap from the cliff. The tips of Urcon's fingers and toes had turned black and begun to swell, but Cusi could only splash water onto his face with shaking hands, hoping some would find its way into Urcon's mouth.

They almost went past the hut, their eyesight shielded by the cloths they had wound around their heads. But a voice called to them, louder than the ringing in their ears, and they stopped and let the litter down and looked at each other in disbelief. The voice had called the name of Cusi Huaman.

"Thunupa," Tarapaca whispered, but the voice spoke again. They turned slowly and saw the hut, the stacks of wood in front of it, and a short, stocky man pointing a spear at them.

"I am Cusi Huaman. Who are you?"

"I am Alco," the man said, coming a few steps toward them with the spear extended in front of him. Cusi thought he was smiling. "Do you not remember?"

"I remember. You must help us. Urcon—your brother is very sick. You must take him to Raurau Illa."

"He sent me to meet you," Alco replied, walking around them without getting too close, the spear still held at the ready, as if they might attack him at any moment. He peered down at the litter, then seemed to smile again, though there was no pleasure in his voice. "My brother is dead."

"No!" Cusi exclaimed loudly, surprising them all and sending waves of pain crashing through his head.

"Look for yourself," Alco suggested tauntingly, backing off while Cusi gathered the strength to turn and kneel beside the litter. He had checked on Urcon only a short time before, it seemed, and they had heard no sound of complaint. Yet it was undeniable: the stiff, contorted limbs caught in their bindings; the waxy, mottled skin; the face fixed in an unchanging grimace. Cusi did not have to touch him to know that he was dead. Comrade, he thought, and he began to weep, coughing and choking helplessly as tears burned his swollen, sensitive eyes. He had never even thought to say farewell.

Alco came back into view, pushing the fire-blackened point of his spear under Cusi's blurred eyes.

"Take off everything you are wearing," he commanded. "Leave it there, by the litter."

"What do you want from us?" Tarapaca asked, coming to stand next to Cusi. "We are sick."

"Take off your clothes!" Alco shouted. "Where is the stone? Give it to me!"

"You would steal from us?" Tarapaca asked incredulously.

"It belongs to me! Give it to me, Cusi, and I will heal you."

Cusi coughed and cleared his throat. "I do not have it. I left it with my wife in Tumibamba."

"You *fool,*" Alco snarled, and he reared back to thrust with the spear. Tarapaca tried to step into the way but lost his balance and fell across Urcon. Instinct made Cusi jerk backward, and pain blossomed in his head like a poisonous red flower, blinding him to everything else. Kill me, he thought, put an end to the pain. But the blow did not come, and instead he felt someone rise up behind him, a presence he had given up for lost. Long, cool fingers seemed to wrap themselves around his head, quieting the pain. He opened his eyes just a slit and saw Alco glaring at him from behind the spear. He was sweating and breathing hard, his eyes glittering with something more than anger. Cusi coughed and spoke in a harsh, croaking voice.

"Take us to Raurau Illa. Or we will crawl there ourselves."

"And give my people the fever? We have kept outsiders away, and we are healthy. That is why he sent me to heal you here."

"With a spear?" Cusi asked.

"I knew you would try to get past me. But your life is in my hands now, so do as I say, take off your clothes. The sickness is on them and on you. You must be purified."

The fever throbbed in Cusi's temples, and he knew the respite his spirit brother had provided would not last. Then his life and Tarapaca's would truly be in Alco's hands. He had to barter now, while he had the strength.

"If we obey you—you must heal both of us."

Alco glanced sideways at Tarapaca, who was somewhere to Cusi's right. Cusi knew better than to risk the pain of a look.

"I do not know this man," Alco told him. "Grandfather sent me to wait for *you.*"

"*Both.* Promise me, on your life. Or go tell Raurau Illa that we chose to die rather than let you near us."

"I have seen how to purify you," Alco declared. "I know what must be done."

"Then do it for both. On your life."

Cusi had to close his eyes against the light, which had become unbearable. But he made no move to comply, waiting until Alco finally spoke.

"On my life, then. Now do exactly as I say: take off everything, even your earplugs and sandals. The sickness that taints them must be devoured by fire."

"He is mad," Tarapaca murmured, but Cusi simply gritted his teeth against the pain and pulled his tunic off over his head. He spread it over Urcon's stiffening body, then removed his earplugs and headband and laid them carefully on the cloth, as if they were burial gifts. He left his sandals and loincloth on the side of the litter and slowly pushed himself to his feet, feeling the motion of the wind against his naked body but not its coolness.

"Now bring the packs from the llamas," Alco commanded unsparingly, and Cusi and Tarapaca went to do his bidding, staggering with their heads down. The llamas were skittish but eager to have their burdens removed, and the two men dragged the packs along the ground back to the litter. Alco had covered Urcon with a blanket and then piled up dry grass, brush, and wood all around and over him, to a height of several feet. The pack in Cusi's hands had his battle-ax lashed to the outside, but he was too sick and weary to try to rescue it. He heaved the pack onto the pile and stumbled backwards to sit down in the grass next to Tarapaca.

Alco paused to murmur a prayer over his brother, then stooped and thrust a burning brand into the base of the pile. The flames rose up swiftly and so brightly that Cusi and Tarapaca had to cover their eyes with their arms. Alco came over and pounded on the ground with the butt of his spear.

"Come, you cannot rest yet. I have built a sweathouse for you."

"I am burning already," Tarapaca muttered as they struggled to rise. Cusi stood swaying, his eyes shut tight against the light and smoke, smelling the odor of burning flesh.

"Farewell, comrade," he said softly. Then he let Alco lead him away from the fire.

Tumibamba

THE STOREROOM was dim and cool, musty with the odors of wood, dried llama dung, and yucca roots. Micay had to turn sideways to move down the narrow aisles that separated the stacks of goods, which in places were piled higher than her head. She checked them over casually, making sure that everything was as she remembered it. Chimpu Ocllo had given her the master memory cord, but Micay had not even bothered to unwrap it, doubting that anything had been removed from here in the two days since Chimpu had last made her check. All the other women knew the purpose for which these supplies were intended, and even though that purpose had so far manifested itself only in dreams, none of them would have borrowed carelessly from this room.

So Micay displayed her trust in the other women by defying Chimpu's command that she make a thorough count. She realized it was a childish gesture, but she resented being given pointless tasks, and more than that she resented being given them in a way that allowed her no chance to protest their pointlessness. Chimpu was treating all of them, even the mamacona, like indolent novices, but she had been particularly hard on Micay. She had formulated her vision in Micay's absence, out of her own dreams and those of many others, so she had shown little appreciation for the dreams Micay had brought to her so belatedly. She had in fact rebuked Micay for her lack of urgency, shaming her in front of the other women with a harshness that had left Micay shaking and unable to defend herself. Quespi and the others had tried to comfort her with tales of the scoldings they had received, but Micay had not been soothed by the knowledge of their common oppression. The high priestess she had chosen to serve so long ago was not a woman she had ever had to fear.

The light in the room was momentarily extinguished as a large person filled the doorway and then came through it. She looked back at the open space in the center of the room and saw Rimachi smiling at her over the large bundle of light-colored cloth he held in his arms.

"Welcome back, Mama Micay. I did not expect you until the Inti Raymi."

"Welcome back yourself, Lord Rimachi. Llampu told me you were in the mountains with the Sapa Inca."

Rimachi gave an exaggerated sigh. "For fifteen days. And he never went out to hunt or inspect his herds, not once. I got back last night, and my mother and Llampu told me I should bring these here as soon as I could. Where shall I put them?"

"You cannot tell?" Micay said lightly, gesturing with her chin toward several tall stacks of garments of the same neutral color. "But let me count them first."

There were four shifts with matching belts in the bundle, all woven from the undyed white cotton Chimpu Ocllo had specified. Micay unwrapped the memory cord and began to add knots to the count of the white string.

"Ah, I am sorry," Rimachi apologized. "You had finished your count."

"Actually, I had not bothered to begin it," Micay confessed. "I knew everything was here."

She looked up from the cord to find him surveying the contents of the room, a bemused expression on his face.

"What is this all for, Micay? Are you preparing for some war I have not heard about? The Chimu have already surrendered, and the Huancavelicas cannot hold out much longer. Before I left, we had not received any more wounded for a month."

"That is true," Micay acknowledged. Then she hesitated, recalling Chimpu's admonition that they not discuss their plans with outsiders. Rimachi crossed his arms on his chest and looked down his nose at her expectantly, reminding her that he was hardly an outsider. He had told Micay about the first reports of the spotted fever over a year before, at a time when Huayna Capac was trying to keep the information to himself.

"It is not a war we expect," she told him, nodding in apology, "but the great sickness we were warned about long ago. Many of us have had dreams that say it is coming, and the high priestess believes it will be the spotted fever. She began her preparations while I was still in Quito."

Rimachi grunted skeptically, rubbing at the scar on his cheek. "In all the time I was with him, I saw Huayna Capac only twice: when he got on and off his litter. And I was never close enough to hear him speak. But the air around him is filled with rumors and prophecies, and the messengers never stop coming and going, dropping shreds of information along the way. Even the dullest sentry learns things he wishes he had not. You know that I listen for anything that might help you, but most of the talk this time was about the Viracochas. Their return is being predicted everywhere, and there is a fierce competition among the soothsayers to be the first to say when and where they will appear." Rimachi shrugged his massive shoulders. "I heard only one mention of sickness, and that was from Chincha, far south of here in the Hotlands."

"Was it spotted fever?"

"Yes, but I was not certain that the rumor did not refer to the outbreak of a year ago. There was no urgency to it."

"Chimpu Ocllo is most urgent," Micay assured him. "As you can see."

"I saw that the bathhouse has been enlarged, as well, and some firepits dug. Does she know so well how to fight this sickness? I thought it was unknown to even the oldest healers."

"It is," Micay admitted, "and no one has told us of a remedy or dreamed one. The dreams we had were about tending the sick, and we all saw ourselves wearing different kinds of costumes, clothing that seemed intended to keep the sickness from getting on our skin or into our eyes or mouths. That is what most of these supplies are for: to protect us while we nurse others back to health. We know that some people can recover if they are tended vigilantly."

Rimachi frowned. "How do those of us who are not healers protect ourselves?"

"Stay away from those who are sick," Micay said. "Send them to us."

"And if there are too many for you? Everyone should know how to protect themselves if you do."

"For years the high priestess has been telling everyone to prepare for this. 'Show us the sick,' they tell her in return, and she cannot. She can only show them our dreams. Would that move *you* any more than it has Huayna Capac?"

Rimachi gave an ambiguous shrug. "Are you saying you are not certain your costumes will protect you?"

"You see? You want to be shown, as well. Chimpu Ocllo believes that dreams are the eyes the gods lend us. She barely sees with her own anymore."

Rimachi blinked in surprise. "Micay! Do I hear you criticizing the mamanchic?"

"Someone must, and soon," Micay said curtly. "But come, I have stayed here long enough to have taken an actual count."

She wrapped up the cord and led Rimachi out of the storeroom, gesturing for him to drop the curtain back into place over the doorway. Paucar Rimay was waiting for her outside, but her attention was immediately drawn to a commotion on the other side of the courtyard, where a crowd was forming in front of the high priestess's house. Chimpu Ocllo was talking to a man wearing the plumes of a royal messenger, and women were streaming toward them from other parts of the compound.

"Micay . . ." Rimachi persisted, looming up on Micay's left. She realized he had not seen the messenger and was still concerned about her criticism.

From across the courtyard Chimpu Ocllo spotted her and beckoned peremptorily. Resisting both of them, she turned toward Paucar Rimay, who was clearly startled by Rimachi's presence but was clinging stubbornly to the memory cord attached to the center of his waistband. There were only three thick strings to the cord, and Micay saw that his fingers were wrapped around the golden string, the one that spoke of joy and pleasure.

"Wait," she said, holding up a hand to Rimachi. She stepped up to Paucar, who gazed cockeyed over her head, his face wearing its customary foolish grin. "Paucar Rimay, my friend," she said softly. "What do you wish to tell me?"

He arched his neck to look down at the golden string, squeezing it so tightly that the veins in his arm stood out. Lloque Yupanqui had made this third cord for him when he had finally understood that Paucar had a need to express his feelings. The black string spoke of sorrow and regret; the red of anger or disappointment.

"See you," Paucar said at last, his head coming up. "See *you.*"

Micay smiled and put her hands over the hand that held the golden cord. She had known he was glad to see her again, but it touched her deeply that he had made this effort to tell her. That he was even able to make such an effort was a miracle he and Lloque had accomplished together.

"It gives me joy to see you, too," she told him.

"Micay," Rimachi said behind her, "the high priestess wants you. Something has happened . . ."

"Something good has happened here," Micay said. But she took Paucar's free hand and found the cord on his hip that told him to remain where he was. "Wait here, Paucar. You may be needed to help carry."

She turned back to Rimachi, and they both started walking toward the crowd around Chimpu Ocllo and the messenger. The women were leaning toward one another and speaking in urgent whispers, spreading the news outward from the center. Even before Quespi stepped out to meet her, Micay knew what the news would be, and she was glad she had taken a moment to share Paucar's pleasure. It might be the last any of them would have.

"It is the sickness," Quespi said in a flat voice. "The swift-flying sickness . . ."

"Where?"

"All along the coast, though it is worst in Chimor and the valleys farther south. Otoronco Achachi and the governor and the Grand Chimu have all died of it." Fear flared up behind the determination in Quespi's eyes, and she gripped Micay's arm with both hands. "And in Cuzco, Micay. Hundreds have died there, including the Regent and all four of the lords."

"Is there any word of our husbands?" Micay demanded.

Quespi let out a long breath and shook her head. "Not that this man has spoken. But the mamanchic has not asked him."

"I must return to the Mollecancha," Rimachi said abruptly. "I will ask about them."

The women behind Quespi suddenly fell silent and began to move aside, and Chimpu Ocllo came through their midst, a silver Moon shield gleaming on her chest, adding to the glow of vindication that seemed to surround her. She fixed her eyes on Rimachi, her lips peeled back from her gums in a grimacing smile.

"Why are you dawdling here, Captain, when there is desperate work to be done? I have already told the Sapa Inca to expect me. Go tell the Coya that I will come to see her afterward. Have her assemble all of the wives and the heads of the cults."

Rimachi blinked once at the reprimand but made no attempt to defend himself, simply bowing in compliance.

"I will tell her, my mother," he promised, and gave Micay an oblique glance as he turned and headed for the gate. Chimpu looked down at Micay for a moment, shaking her head in obvious disgust. Then she held out her hand for the cord, taking it back as if Micay had stolen it.

"I know you saw me. Yet you found it more important to chat with your pet patient than to answer my summons."

"I did, my lady," Micay admitted. "He was the one I could help most at that moment."

She had tried to sound humble and matter-of-fact, yet even to her own ears her tone seemed defiant. She was aware of the other women frozen in place around her, averting their eyes out of sympathy. Chimpu leaned forward, bearing down on her with the weight of her presence.

"So you would determine your own duty from moment to moment," Chimpu concluded, "guided by whatever whim possesses you. I wonder why you bothered to come back from Quito."

Micay's heart was thudding against the base of her throat, and she felt her composure disintegrating beneath Chimpu's relentless stare. Yet she was angry, too, and determined not to accept her humiliation in silence.

"I came back because I am a healer. I did not come back to be scolded and treated like a wayward child. You are squandering our strength, my lady. You say that there is desperate work to be done, yet you stand here chastising me . . ."

The expression on Chimpu's face was so wild and frightening that Micay lost her voice and ducked her head instinctively, reminded of Macas. Chimpu's words struck her like the expected blow.

"Leave this compound, Micay, and do not return until you have learned the meaning of loyalty and obedience."

Micay shuddered and began to turn away, unable to bear any more of Chimpu's scorn. She jumped in surprise when Quespi suddenly spoke up behind her.

"Mamanchic, please, this is not right. Micay is as loyal as any of us, and she is a true healer. We need her with us."

"Do not interfere," Chimpu warned. Then she grunted in surprise as Quespi went past Micay and walked up to her. Quespi reached out and lifted the silver shield that hung from a chain around Chimpu's neck, tipping it up in front of the older woman's face.

"We would not presume to be a mirror for you, Mother," Quespi said quietly. "You must look for yourself."

Chimpu glowered at her and seemed about to strike Quespi's hands away. But then her eyes were drawn down to the polished surface of the Moon shield, and she stiffened in shock, swaying on her feet. Slowly the rigid set of her features crumbled, and her face seemed to collapse in upon itself. She took the shield into her own hands and continued to stare at her reflection as Quespi backed away and came to Micay's side. Finally Chimpu lowered the disc and looked around at the other women, appearing so dazed and stricken that no one would meet her gaze directly.

"Yes . . . I see how hideous I have been," she mused. "I do not blame you for turning your faces away. You must think I am mad."

The women murmured their denials in unison, and Quespi again surprised Micay by speaking up.

"You have made us ready, Mamanchic, but you have taken too much on yourself. You must let us share the burden."

Chimpu passed a hand over her face, nodding wearily as the other women murmured in agreement. Then she looked at Micay, wincing with remorse.

"And you, my daughter . . . you have borne the worst of it. I saw you holding back, doubting me as all the others have done, and I could not stand for it. There was no place for doubt or hesitation. I had waited too long for something I never wished to see."

Micay stared back at her, feeling bruised and shaken from the encounter and slow to forgive. She had to clear her throat before she could speak.

"I did not think we had to be desperate ourselves to do this desperate work. But I have not been here to share the waiting. I was able to forget for a while, in Quito."

"I saw that, as well," Chimpu told her, "and I could not forgive you for it." She shook her head in rueful amazement. "I cannot expect you to forgive me, Micay. That you should believe, even for a moment, that I would ever cast you out . . ."

There were tears in her eyes, a reflection of the pain she had caused, and Micay stepped forward and bowed before her, and felt a hand come to rest on the top of her head, over her head cloth. Then she herself began to weep, and Chimpu lifted her up and embraced her lovingly, pressing her against the smooth silver shield on her chest. When Chimpu finally released her, Quespi and the other women reached out to take her back into their midst. Chimpu dried her eyes on the edge of her mantle and gave them a strained smile.

"While I have the strength, let me tell you what I will propose to the Sapa Inca. I will ask him for two wayside rest houses, one on the road from Chimor and the other at the pass over the mountains to the lands of the Huancavelicas. Everyone coming to Tumibamba will be stopped and examined, and anyone bearing signs of the sickness will be put in our care. If we are vigilant, perhaps we can keep it out of the city." Chimpu paused and seemed to be counting with her eyes. "For now I want only the mamacona and the women without small children to serve in the rest houses. The rest of you will stay here and work on replenishing our supplies, though we will also send you anyone who is suffering from a wound or an illness we know. Micay, you and Quespi will be in charge here in my absence. I know you will remember to respect the judgment of your sisters.

"I must rest now and prepare myself for the Sapa Inca," Chimpu went on, raising a limp hand over them in blessing. "Go to your families and children, my daughters, and forget your duties for one night. We begin our task tomorrow."

After Chimpu disappeared into her house, the other women crowded around Micay and Quespi, patting their shoulders and murmuring words of gratitude and encouragement. Someone handed Micay her medicine bag, and one of the mamacona volunteered to look after Paucar Rimay, who was still waiting in front of the storeroom. Micay was too tired to refuse, and as soon as she and Quespi could extricate themselves, they headed for the compound gate.

"I am grateful—" Micay began, but Quespi laughed and would not let her finish.

"I have not forgotten how you stood up to Yasca for me. Though I almost waited too long to return the favor."

"I could not recognize her anymore. But you brought her back, Quespi."

"She had to return," Quespi said with a shrug. "Now she will be kinder to us."

They came out through the gate, and Micay looked down the long, narrow street, which at its far end framed one of the great snow-capped mountains in the distance. She thought of the lords in Cuzco and then of Otoronco Achachi, realizing for the first time that he was truly gone. Sorrow welled up in her chest, and she told herself that he had died like a warlord, in the field with his warriors. Now he had no more to fear from Shuara sorcerers or jealous rulers. Farewell, Old Jaguar, she prayed silently, hoping the gods would be kinder to those he had left behind.

XVII

YURAQ
HUARMICONA:
The White Women

(A.D. 1525)

The Village

THE HOUSE that Cusi shared with Tarapaca was small and windowless, and it lacked the fenced-in yard that surrounded the other houses in the village. It had belonged to Urcon's uncle, who had died while Urcon was still away in the north. Urcon's relatives had maintained it for him, but since wood was a scarce commodity on the plain, they had dismantled the fence and used it to repair their own. They would have built a new fence for Urcon, had he returned with all the llamas and alpacas he was owed.

With no fence to block the view, Cusi could sit in the doorway and look down the hillside at the other houses, which were clustered or spread according to the availability of level ground. By now he knew which people lived in which houses, and which of the children and animals belonged to them. He knew none of their names, however, and unlike Tarapaca, he had not gone down to visit them in their homes. He simply watched them come and go, and he did not mind when they stared back, watching him sit.

Tarapaca and some of the other village men were just now returning from the fields, walking up the path that wound between the houses. They had hoes and digging sticks slung over their shoulders and were talking and laughing among themselves. Tarapaca appeared taller and thinner than the rest of them, his back as yet unbent by fieldwork. But the others included him in their bantering, at least until Alco came out of his house to intercept him. Then they silently disappeared into their houses, leaving the two men alone on the path.

Cusi saw Alco hand Tarapaca a small black bundle, and then they parted and Tarapaca came the rest of the way alone, carrying the bundle in one hand and a digging stick in the other. He flopped down next to Cusi and leaned back against the doorframe, breathing hard from the climb.

"You still like the work?" Cusi asked dryly.

Tarapaca waved the digging stick like a wand. "It sounds worse than it feels. Each day I find some strength I did not know was there. It does not make my head hurt."

"Neither does sitting."

Tarapaca grunted and set the bundle down between them. "Alco says this belongs to you."

Cusi spread open the black cloth and saw his earplugs and the silver badge from his headband, all three badly misshapen but polished to a high shine. The stone head of his battle-ax was there, too, chipped and scarred but essentially unharmed by the fire. Cusi reached up through the tangle of hair that hung to his shoulder and fingered the leathery loop of his earlobe.

"They would not fit now. And it would wear me out just to hold my head up."

"I could make a handle for the ax, if you wish," Tarapaca offered.

Cusi grimaced and closed the bundle up. "Then I might have to carry it."

"That is Alco's hope, of course. That you will want to make yourself strong enough to carry it, and then you will want to leave."

"I care nothing for what Alco wants or hopes."

"I do not like him, either," Tarapaca conceded. "But he kept us both alive, as he promised. And he is the one who will decide when you are well enough to see Raurau Illa."

"Perhaps I do not wish to be displayed in that way—as his proof that he deserves to be the next sorcerer."

"But—I thought you came here to see Raurau Illa. What does it matter if Alco profits from the meeting? You are not going to stay here forever."

"It does not matter," Cusi said wearily. "None of it matters."

"Do not say that, my lord," Tarapaca protested. Then he caught himself. "Cusi . . ."

"I am just Cusi here."

"But when we go back you will be Cusi Huaman again, one of the conquerors of the Chiriguanos. Yasca will give you new earplugs and clothes that do not itch and a litter to ride in if you are still weak."

"I never want to see another litter," Cusi snapped. "Besides, Yasca may be dead. Everyone in Cuzco may be dead. And if we go to find out, how do we know we will not be stricken again? This was the second time I have come so close to death, and I do not have the strength to risk it again. I have nothing left."

"Perhaps Raurau Illa could—"

"It *began* with him! All of the anger and the violence . . . I do not want any more. Leave me alone, Tarapaca. I need to sleep."

"Sleep, then," Tarapaca said curtly, using the digging stick to help push himself to his feet. "I have been invited to eat." He paused and cast a frustrated glance over his shoulder. "I am welcome because I helped with the work."

Cusi watched him stagger back down the hillside, his legs obviously unsteady but strong enough to keep him upright. Cusi felt no envy, no goading sense of shame; no desire to be helpful or welcome, either. He turned and crawled back into the darkness behind him, collapsing face first onto his blankets and falling asleep almost immediately, without remorse, pain, or effort.

IT WAS RAINING again, yet the boy who was always watching him was back, squatting among the rocks that had once been part of the yard wall. Cusi knew Alco had encouraged the villagers to spy on him rudely and openly, to make him feel the ingratitude of his laziness. A few had tried, but they had been quickly daunted by the way Cusi stared back. Though he did not smile to show it, it gave him pleasure to have people to look at, and he did not care if they frowned or put on contemptuous faces. He could wait to see their faces change as his stare finally made them self-conscious and then uneasy, so that they would leave in a hurry.

The boy, though, was different. He had withstood Cusi's examination many times and seemed unperturbed by it. He was dark-skinned and stocky, close to the age of initiation, perhaps thirteen or fourteen. Cusi thought of himself at that age and knew he would not have spent so much of his time watching a man who seldom moved out of the doorway of his house. He would never have looked twice at such a man, and he wondered why the boy found him worthy of attention.

The return of curiosity was another sign to Cusi that he was getting better, despite his lack of effort. He could no longer fall asleep anytime he wished, and a crawling restlessness had begun to make him uncomfortably aware of his unused muscles. He had even felt a fleeting impulse to talk, and to explain himself to Tarapaca.

It was the same sort of impulse, only stronger, that made him raise his hand and beckon to the boy, summoning him in out of the rain. The boy rose and came to him as if he had been expecting such a summons for a long time, and Cusi gestured for him to sit down in the doorway beside him. He was taller than the boy but felt distinctly frail next to him.

"Why do you watch me?" he asked.

The boy looked down at the ground and shrugged. "I want to see you run."

"Run?" Cusi snorted. "I can barely walk. Who told you I would run?"

"You are the Running Boy, are you not? Everyone says you are the same man."

Cusi snorted again, but decided not to confuse the boy by denying it. "What do you know about the Running Boy?"

"I know what my grandmother told me. She said he was born small and sickly, so that his mother brought him to the huaca and prayed to Illapa to save the boy's life. And Illapa looked favorably on the boy and touched him with his lightning, putting courage in his heart and swiftness into his legs, so that he never stopped running. He became the swiftest of the Incas, and when he won the great race, he gave his prize to the huaca. To *us.*"

The boy jerked a thumb at his own chest, lifting his chin with such pride that Cusi could only nod respectfully, hiding his astonishment. It had never occurred to him that his only visit here might have made him a legend.

"It has been many years," Cusi said slowly, "but I remember the hawk salt."

"That is my name," the boy told him. "I am Huaman Cachi."

Cusi blinked, then straightened up against the doorframe. "You? You are the boy who stole the statue away from Alco? But you were just an infant; you cannot possibly remember."

The boy shrugged. "I have been told about it so many times that it *seems* like a memory. I have been shown how far you jumped to save me from falling. It is much farther than I can jump."

"I was very drunk," Cusi recalled, "and I jumped without thinking." He looked down at his crossed legs, then out at the falling rain. "Now I think, and I do not want to move at all."

Huaman Cachi squinted at him curiously. "Your friend . . . the Lupaca. He is better."

"Yes, he wants to return. He is not afraid of what he might have lost."

"Are *you* afraid?" the boy blurted. Then he realized what he had asked and dropped his eyes in embarrassment. Cusi considered the question for a moment, finding too many answers for it.

"I am empty," he decided finally. "Illapa gave me great gifts, but I have used them up. I have squandered them. I used them in anger, to threaten and kill, and now they are gone. Now I have only the memories of all the enemies I made, all those who suffered and died by my hand. I saw them all again in the fever . . . I saw my children come to me, walking out of the Lake of Blood. I washed them over and over, but still they were marked, stained with their father's crimes. I could not save them . . . I could not save anyone."

Huaman Cachi's mouth had fallen open in astonishment, and it took him a moment to realize Cusi had finished. Then he started and hastily looked away, shifting uneasily on his haunches. Cusi shook himself, amazed that he had said so much, so openly. He glanced at the boy, who appeared most anxious to leave.

"I must rest now," he said curtly, and the boy jumped up without hesitation and went out into the rain. He had gone only a short distance, though, before he turned and came back.

"Can I come tomorrow?" he asked.

Cusi was so surprised that he reacted with suspicion. "Why? I will only tell you things you should not know."

"I am not afraid to listen," Huaman Cachi declared solemnly, trying to mask the eagerness of his interest. Cusi felt his nostrils draw down and his lips twitch in a brief, reflexive attempt at a smile.

"Come, then, if you wish," he shrugged. Then he yawned. "I will not have run away . . ."

Tumibamba

MICAY WAS supervising the loading of the pack llamas when Quinti arrived, and at first she was reluctant to allow herself to be interrupted. But then she saw the cloak Quinti was wearing and the carrying bundle over her shoulder, and the fear and excitement in her eyes. So she hastily completed her instructions to the herders and the men who were helping them fill the packs and left the memory cord to be kept by one of the other women. Then she led Quinti out into the middle of the crowded courtyard, indicating with a shrug that this was all the privacy she could offer.

"Who are all these men?" Quinti asked nervously. "They do not look sick."

"Most of them are healthy now," Micay affirmed. "But they have no quarters, and we could not heal them and then send them out to sleep in the rain."

"I see some of them know how to weave."

"I make them work for their shelter. But come, Quinti, I do not have time for this. Where are you going?"

Quinti's eyes snapped into sharp focus. "I just received word of Quilaco. He has reached the rest house from Chimor, but he can come no farther." She gave Micay a tight-lipped nod. "He has the spotted fever."

"The high priestess will not want you there."

"Would that stop you if it were Cusi? You must allow me to accompany the pack train. The Royal Road is closed to all other travelers, as you know."

"I would be exceeding my authority," Micay protested halfheartedly. "Your father could grant you passage."

"Come, Micay," Quinti said impatiently, "I do not have time for equivocation. I cannot get through the crowd to see my father, and I do not want my mother to know until I am gone. I must go to him. *Help* me."

Micay sighed in resignation, knowing that both Mama Cori and Chimpu Ocllo would be angry with her for this. But she could not deny Quinti the freedom she would want herself if it were *her* husband. So she took Quinti by the elbow and led her back to the storeroom, past the idle men sitting against the front of the building. The room was now more than half empty, and Micay reminded herself, for later, to make better use of the men outside. They could *all* learn to weave, warriors or not.

But first she went to the back corner of the room and retrieved a compact white bundle, which she untied and opened on top of a pile of blankets.

"I prepared this for myself," she explained, "in the event I should suddenly be called to treat the sickness. You may have it, Quinti, but listen carefully. This is what you must do before you enter the place of the sick. First you must make an offering and pray to Mama Quilla, asking her to protect you and assist you in the healing. Then you must bathe and wash yourself thoroughly, including your hair." Micay briefly held up the white cotton towel and the piece of soap root that were inside the bundle. She replaced them and picked up a semicircular bronze knife, gazing steadily at Quinti. "Then you must cut off your hair, to just below the bottom of your ears, so that the headcloth in here covers all of it."

Quinti swallowed audibly, reaching up to touch the shiny black hair that hung down to the middle of her back. "I heard that the women had done that. Even Chimpu Ocllo."

"They have *all* done it, yet two of them were stricken with the sickness, anyhow. One was careless: she found her son among the sick and stayed too close to him, and neglected to change her clothes often enough. The other woman was apparently diligent in her precautions, so we do not know why she was infected. They both died, though," Micay added unsparingly. "I tell you this as a warning. Do not go there if you are not willing to do all you must to protect yourself. Promise me, Quinti. It is a terrible way to die."

"I have heard you, Micay," Quinti insisted staunchly. "What else must I do?"

Micay nodded and lifted up a painted gourd with a cane stopper. "Before you dress, you must oil your body with this. *Everywhere,* except your palms and the soles of your feet. Then you can put on the white shift and belt and head cloth. Last," she concluded, holding up a filmy piece of cloth, "there is a gauze mask to cover your eyes and nose and mouth. It ties loosely around your forehead and neck."

"You have not done this yourself, have you?" Quinti asked as Micay stood back to let her examine the contents of the bundle.

"No, though I have talked to some of the women who have. They say you get used to the oil and the mask and the constant washings, but not to having your hair short as a man's. You must listen to the other women and do what they say."

"What do they say it is like there?" Quinti asked, stepping aside so that Micay could remake the bundle. Micay hesitated for a moment, then spoke bluntly.

"They said it was impossible at first, when the warriors were still coming back in large numbers. The healthy did not want to have to wait with the sick, and some of the Inca commanders refused to let anyone examine them. There were fights and arguments and wounds to be treated along with the fever, and the crowding was terrible. It is somewhat better now, I hear. They have taken over a second rest house and part of a nearby village, and the Sapa Inca has sent out all of the royal healers. But it is still no place for the fainthearted."

Quinti took the white bundle from her and rolled it up in her carrying blanket. She gave Micay a taut smile and slung the burden over her shoulder.

"I will be brave—and careful, too. I promised my daughters I would bring their father home to them, and I will."

"Where are they now?"

"I took them to the governor's compound and left them with Runtu Caya. I told them to obey their grandmother, but to go to you if anything troubled them. I do not trust my mother's judgment; she grieves too deeply for those who were lost in Cuzco."

"They can stay with me and the twins," Micay assured her. "And I will tell Mama Cori myself, once you are out of the city. Are you ready? I will introduce you to the head herder and give you the cord to carry."

"I am ready," Quinti said breathlessly. She wrapped her arms around Micay and gave her a fierce hug. Micay hugged her back, praying this would not be the last embrace they would share.

"May Mama Quilla watch over you, my sister," she murmured when Quinti released her.

"May she keep the sickness away from this city," Quinti said. Then she dabbed at her eyes with the edge of her cloak and turned toward the doorway and the pack train that waited outside.

LLOQUE YUPANQUI came to lift the curtain back from the doorway and invite Micay into Mama Cori's house. The windows had also been covered to keep out the noise of the crowds in the plaza below, and the air in the narrow room was stale and smoky. A single rush burned in a holder in a niche in the back wall, and Mama Cori was sitting just outside the tenuous circle of its light. Her gray-streaked hair hung loose and uncombed on her shoulders, and even in shadow her face appeared to have aged ten years in the last five months. She had lost both of her parents and most of the relatives and friends she had left behind in Cuzco. But worse, Micay thought, she had lost the Cuzco she had carried in her heart for all these years, the Cuzco that remained inviolate and unchanged by time, awaiting the return of the Incas.

Micay squatted in front of her and briefly clasped the cold hands the older woman held out in a weary gesture of welcome.

"Micay . . . it is good of you to come. How are the children?"

"They are fine, my lady. They wanted to come visit you. Coca and Cisa are with them now, and they would also like to see their grandmother."

"Tomorrow, perhaps. You have not allowed them to mingle with the strangers who live below?"

"No, my lady," Micay assured her. "I have explained the dangers to them, and Coca will not let the younger ones disobey."

"And where is Quinti? With the Coya?"

Micay drew a breath and glanced at Lloque, who had squatted down next to his sister. "No, my lady. That is what I have come to tell you: Quilaco is at the rest house on the road from Chimor with the fever. Quinti has gone to be with him."

"Wait," Lloque interrupted hastily as Mama Cori closed her eyes and let her head loll back against the wall. "I was with the governor all day and we heard nothing about Quilaco. Nor did Quinti come to ask for permission to travel."

"The court hears many things before the governor. She did not want to wait any longer than she had to."

"Then the sentries on the road will turn her back," Lloque declared, laying a reassuring hand on Mama Cori's arm. Micay swallowed and spoke in a low voice.

"No, my lord, they will let her through. She is traveling with the pack train carrying supplies to the high priestess."

In the silence that followed her admission, Micay thought she heard Mama Cori's eyelids snap open. But she did not try to evade the other woman's accusatory glare.

"*You* gave her permission."

"I could not have dissuaded her, my lady. She was determined to go to him, as I would be in her place."

"You are a healer," Mama Cori pointed out. "Quinti is merely an anxious wife."

"She has had some training. And I told her everything I could about how to protect herself."

"Everything except to stay here, where it is safe," Mama Cori said through her teeth. "You have sent my daughter to her death. It does not matter what you told her!"

"You have certainly exceeded your authority, Micay," Lloque said sternly. "You should have sent her to Apu Poma."

"You should have sent her to *me,*" Mama Cori seethed. "You owed me that much."

Micay glanced from one to the other. Mama Cori was livid with an anger that seemed to have erased the weary languor of her grief; Lloque was stolidly taking her side, hoping thereby to mollify and calm her. Meanwhile, Micay thought, Quinti was gone and none of this would bring her back.

"I am sorry, my lady," she said, with more stubbornness than apology in her voice. "Quinti did not have the time to argue with you or anyone else. I had to honor her right to decide this for herself."

Before Mama Cori could respond, there was a voice outside and Apu Poma thrust his head through the curtain, then came all the way into the room.

"Forgive my intrusion. But I have news of Quilaco, and I cannot find Quinti to tell her. I sent messengers to her and to the court, but she seems to have disappeared." He paused and frowned. "Quilaco has finally returned, but he has the sickness. He is at the Chimor rest house."

"What do you plan to tell her?" Mama Cori asked.

Apu Poma cocked his head and shrugged, as if he found it a curious question. "I will tell her what I have just told you; that is all the information

I have. I expect that she will want to go to him, and that she will ask me to help her."

"Will you?" Mama Cori asked, so pointedly that this time Apu Poma hesitated and glanced at Lloque and Micay, gauging the prevailing mood. When he again addressed his wife, his tone was decidedly wary.

"I will make sure that she is aware of the dangers, and I would have her consult with Micay before she leaves. But yes, I would help her. The rest houses are crowded and understaffed, and even someone of Quilaco's rank could be neglected. If she wants to go, I will see that she gets to him without delay."

"Micay has done your work for you," Mama Cori told him. "She did not see fit to consult me, either."

Apu Poma spread his hands in a bewildered gesture of appeal. "Cori . . . you have been in mourning. I would have spared you the trouble. We both know what Quinti is like when she has made up her mind. It would be pointless to try to stop her."

"Only because there are so many who are willing to send her off to die. Is it not enough that Cusi is lost somewhere? Must you make orphans of all of our grandchildren?"

Apu Poma drew himself up, showing remarkable patience in the face of his wife's anger. "Should Quilaco die from lack of care," he asked quietly, "while Quinti sits at home with the children? Do you think that will keep her safe? There is no wall around this city to keep the sickness out. We will all have to face it eventually."

"I do not see you leaving for the rest house," Mama Cori pointed out, "or Micay. Only Quinti. But naturally, you would admire a wife who abandons her responsibilities and rushes off to share her husband's danger."

Apu Poma sighed and let his shoulders slump, looking down at her sadly. "This is an old argument, Cori, one I thought we had settled long ago. Is there not enough to trouble us, without looking back? I will leave you to your mourning now. Perhaps Micay will come and tell me about Quinti."

"Of course," Mama Cori sneered. "Micay will be happy to take your side. So go, and do not come here again, either of you. You remind me too much of how the Incas have betrayed themselves."

Micay rose and backed away, stopping next to Apu Poma, who put a protective arm around her shoulders. He looked down at his brother-in-law, waiting until Lloque met his eyes.

"And you, my lord? What would you have told Quinti if she had come to you?"

"I am not her father," Lloque said. "Or the governor."

"An uncle could claim the right to speak," Apu Poma prompted, but Lloque simply stared at him and would not reply. Apu Poma grunted and turned to push the curtain aside, ushering Micay out ahead of him. The sky was overcast and dark, and the night air felt damp and cool against her skin. She and Apu

Poma walked out into the center of the plaza, from which they could see people still moving about on the level below. Torches were still lit in the governor's awning house. Apu Poma braced his hands against his back and stretched, jerking his chin in the direction of his wife's house.

"I had almost come to respect him. But all he can do is humor her, even when she is being unreasonable." He spat into the darkness. "Forgive me, Micay. Tell me what you have done for Quinti."

Micay told him briefly, apologizing at the end for having exceeded her authority as the high priestess's representative.

"No, you have done well," he said, waving off the apology, "and I will say so to Chimpu Ocllo. I have extended this same privilege to several other wives, and she has not complained to me yet. I do not doubt that she can use every pair of hands." He paused and cleared his throat. "How much longer do you think we can keep it out of the city?"

"I do not know," Micay confessed, startled by his apparent fatalism, though she shared it. "I know that many warriors got past the rest houses without being properly examined. And there are reports of clothing being stolen from piles that were supposed to be burned."

"It is inevitable," Apu Poma said grimly, "and look how we wait to meet it, crowded together like an army under siege. All the barracks and guest houses are filled, and everyone has taken in their relatives and the friends of their relatives. The common warriors are camping in the streets and squares and anywhere else they can lay down a blanket. We can barely feed them all. How can we possibly tend to them when the sickness strikes?"

"I do not know," Micay repeated. "We will have no time for anger then, or for grief."

"I have no time for them now," Apu Poma said. As he started them walking toward Micay's house, she felt him turn toward her in the darkness. "I have sent another message to Cuzco, asking what is known of Yasca and his commanders. Perhaps I will receive an answer this time."

"I know that Cusi is alive," Micay told him, touching the stone, which hung in its pouch around her neck. "He was told long ago that he would return to the village of the blind sorcerer."

"I cannot send a message there. Though, as I learned many years after the fact, *I* was the one who sent him to the blind man in the first place." He stopped as they arrived in front of Micay's house. Through the open doorway they could see the children playing in the flickering light of a torch, while Runtu Caya sat like a watchful stone against the back wall.

"Do you have the time, my lord," Micay asked him, "to come in and see your grandchildren?"

Apu Poma hesitated, then smiled and nodded vigorously. "Yes, of course . . . Cori is the one who makes them orphans with her fear and her anger. I will not abandon them. Or you, my daughter."

"That is the only promise that matters," Micay said as she took his arm and led him toward the doorway. "It may soon be the only promise any of us can make."

The Village

THERE WERE five burned-out spots in the grass, spaced out almost evenly on the gentle slope in front of the hut. There was one for each of the llamas they had brought with them from Quispicancha, and one for the litter on which Urcon had died. Cusi walked around each of them carefully, remembering the fires from the time of the fever—and the vultures that had come before the fires were ready. One of his last memories, before the fever took him under, was of Alco standing over the carcass of a llama, throwing sticks to keep the squawking birds at bay. Cusi had wondered at the time why he did not simply allow the death eaters to have their feast, though now he understood the power that Alco's vision of a cleansing fire had had for him.

He squatted down at the edge of the last blackened area, the place where he had last seen Urcon, where he and Tarapaca had given everything they had to the fire. All of the ashes had either soaked down into the scorched ground or blown away on the wind, and bright green shoots of new grass were already poking up through the cinders. He glanced over his shoulder at Huaman Cachi, who stood a few feet behind him, reluctant to come any closer.

"Here is all that remains of Urcon," Cusi said hoarsely, "and of all the memories he had collected."

"But you have kept his memories," the boy said after a respectful pause. "And you have given them to me."

"Those I knew," Cusi allowed. He had told the boy many things while they sat and then walked, though he had dwelled particularly on the places to which he and Urcon had gone together.

"And I have given them to Grandfather," Huaman Cachi went on, "and to the elders of the clans."

Cusi whirled and came to his feet with a swiftness that surprised both of them. But his annoyance faded as quickly as it had been roused, and he realized it was foolish to have assumed that his stories would not be shared. There were few secrets in the village, and a great thirst for stories.

"You told him about the vision I had of him in Chan Chan?" he asked.

The boy nodded. "He made me repeat everything you told me and was disappointed there was no more. He also said you could not be fully healed or you would have ignored Alco and come to him yourself. I told him that Alco kept watch with his spear, but he just laughed. He does not think Alco could frighten you."

"What do you think? Should I be frightened of Alco and his spear?"

"He hates you," Huaman Cachi said bluntly, "and he does not need his spear to harm you. *I* would not try to go past him. He stalked and killed the puma whose skin he wears."

"Yes, I believe he is brave," Cusi murmured, thinking of the way Alco had taunted him to his face, daring him to strike back. Cusi was probably strong enough now to take his spear from him and beat him with it, if the fight were only physical. But he had no desire to fight and no anger to sustain him if he did. He was easily annoyed, but even his annoyance had no force; nothing deeper was ever stirred.

When he looked back at Huaman Cachi, the boy was staring off into the distance, in the direction of the huaca. He had recently suggested that Cusi might like to go there, and Cusi wondered now if that had been Raurau Illa's idea. But then he saw a tiny figure moving over the grass, coming toward them on a run.

"Who is it?"

"One of the herd boys," Huaman Cachi said. "Someone must be coming."

They waited until the boy reached them, then a few moments longer while he recaptured his breath. He kept a wary eye on the burned spots and spoke to Huaman Cachi as if Cusi were not there.

"An Inca comes, with a spear. He stopped at the huaca but made no offering. I must tell Alco."

The boy ran off again, and they looked back in time to see a second figure come over the next ridge. There were flashes of gold around his head, and they could see he carried both a spear and a shield. They waited, straining their eyes. It was an Inca shield, Cusi thought, but then Huaman Cachi spoke.

"He cannot be an Inca of the blood. He wears a knit cap."

"Tomay," Cusi said softly. "My brother lives."

"Your brother who was in Chan Chan?" Huaman Cachi asked, and Cusi smiled, easily and naturally, his first true smile in months.

"My initiation brother, Tomay Guanaco. The brother who went to Co-chabamba with me."

"Ah, the Colla," Huaman Cachi said, and Cusi realized that Tarapaca had been telling his stories, too. As he waited, Cusi ran his hand over the coarse weave of his tunic, feeling the sharp edges of his ribs and breastbone. He had not looked at himself, even in water, in a long time, though he knew he was still thin. He could not imagine how he looked with his hair long and his earlobes empty.

Tomay appeared thin himself, and there were creases next to his eyes and at the corners of his mouth. He advanced on them without seeming to see them, his customary approach to commoners. Then his eyes went wide in recognition, and he faltered and forced a smile.

"Cusi, it is you. Yes, it *is.* Are you well?"

"Well enough. Better for seeing you," Cusi decided, and he went to take the hand Tomay held out to him. He gripped it only briefly, but long enough for Tomay to feel the difference in the force they could each exert.

"Were you sick long after me?" he asked.

Cusi shrugged and shook his head. "Not too long . . . the fever broke months ago. But not the weariness," Cusi added, tapping his chest. "Not the emptiness here."

"Yasca told me about the march to Quispi Cancha," Tomay said with a sympathetic grimace. "He feels you saved many lives, including his own. What about Urcon and the Lupaca?"

"Tarapaca is here, and well. I could not save Urcon." Cusi pointed to the blackened spot with his chin. "That is where his body was burned."

Tomay bowed his head for a moment. "I am sorry. I lost my mother and nearly everyone older than she was, and too many of the young ones." Tomay trailed off, then sighed and forced another smile. "But I have a *wife,* Cusi. Her name is Ñupchu. She is in Cuzco, waiting to meet you."

"Cuzco is safe?"

"The worst has passed there, and she has already had the sickness. She was my nurse, and then I was hers."

"You are certain it cannot strike you again?"

"I recovered in a room filled with sick people," Tomay testified. "And I know of no one who has been taken a second time."

"Who is left in Cuzco?" Cusi asked, knowing he was stalling but unable to voice the question he truly wanted to ask.

"Huascar and his brothers somehow kept themselves above it, but the Regent is dead, and so are Aranyac and your grandfather. Otoronco Achachi, too, in Chimor." Tomay paused and gave Cusi a significant glance. "But at last report, there had been no sickness in Tumibamba or Quito. Huayna Capac has closed the Royal Road to keep it out."

"Then—"

"Then we can begin to march as soon as you and Yasca are ready," Tomay concluded for him. "He is also still recovering, but he vowed no one would stop him from going back."

Cusi could only stare at him, dizzy with relief. Something stirred uneasily inside him, making him suck in his stomach to keep from squirming. Now he had reason to move, to make himself fit. But where would he find the will? Tomay was watching him closely, but then he suddenly turned, shifting his spear back into his free hand. Alco had just come over the rise, carrying his spear and accompanied by three men who were similarly armed. Alco was wearing his puma-skin mantle and had a string of claws and teeth around his neck, and he pointed his spear at Tomay from a distance of about ten feet and spoke before Cusi could intervene.

"You must leave here, my lord," he said to Tomay, though there was no politeness to the command. "We have kept strangers out of the village, and the sickness, as well."

"He is no stranger, Alco," Cusi said. "And he has already had the sickness."

"Nor do I carry it with me," Tomay added calmly. "I am no threat to you or your village, my friend, unless you would make me one with your disrespect. Lower your weapon or prepare yourself to use it."

Alco crouched lower behind his spear but kept the point up, and the other men fanned out behind him, their expressions as tentative and uncertain as their movements.

"Hold, Tomay," Cusi said. "This is foolish, Alco. He is a commander of warriors . . ."

"You do not rule here!" Alco snarled, his eyes flashing at Cusi. In that instant Tomay charged, flying at him so abruptly that Alco tried to jump back and thrust with his spear at the same time. Tomay swerved and deflected the blow with his shield, and as he came past Alco he swung his own spear like a club, delivering a numbing blow to the side of Alco's thigh.

"Die now!" Tomay shouted, feinting ferociously at the nearest of Alco's companions, who immediately dropped his spear and fled. The other two men ran with him, leaving Alco rolling on the grass, clutching his leg with both hands. Cusi realized that he was panting, his heart beating hard from the shock of the attack. Tomay let out a mocking snarl, then laughed and rapped his spear against his shield.

"Forgive me, Cusi. I have wanted an excuse to test my muscles for some time. Is there a reason why you allow him to address you so rudely?"

"He is the one who tended me when I was sick. He would like me to attack him, to prove that I am fully healed."

"I did not mean to rob you of the pleasure," Tomay said. He motioned to Huaman Cachi with his spear. "Boy! Get him to his feet. The lesson is not over."

Huaman Cachi moved to obey, but Cusi simply looked at the spear Tomay was holding out to him and shook his head.

"No, it is over. I have had enough of threats and violence, of imposing my will upon others. Over and over again during the fever, my enemies came to attack me, or I attacked them first. There was no rest from it, as there has been none in my life."

"That is the life of a warrior," Tomay said softly. "You are not alone in having such dreams; it is part of the sickness. When you are stronger . . ."

"You do not understand. My strength will return, but my huaca is gone. My spirit brother is gone. The Cusi Huaman I remember seems like an angry madman to me. I cannot find him in myself."

Tomay squinted at him in disbelief. "The Cusi Huaman I remember was no madman except when he needed to be. His madness saved my life more than once. I can understand why you might need a rest from that. What does the blind man say to you?"

Cusi looked past him at Alco, who was sitting on the grass holding his leg, his face contorted with pain.

"I have not spoken with him yet. Alco is the only one who can say when I am well enough to see him."

Tomay curled his lip disdainfully. "Him? Come, Cusi, this is not something you surrender to the authority of another. Are you ready to see him?"

Cusi considered it for a moment and shrugged. "I do not know. I do not know what I fear more: what he might tell me, or what he might *not* tell me."

"Yasca will not wait forever," Tomay said, gazing at him steadily. "And I know a fine healer in Tumibamba. I promised her I would return with her husband."

"Perhaps *she* has kept the spirit brother," Alco said from his place on the ground. Cusi put a hand on Tomay's shield to restrain him, then went to stand over Alco, who stared up at him with an unrepentant scowl. Cusi searched himself for anger but found only a muted urge to kick him in the leg. The enmity between them had always been so pointless that he still could not take it seriously. He shook his head in resignation and turned back to Tomay.

"I can decide nothing this way. Let us go to Raurau Illa."

"Hold this," Tomay said with a grin, handing Cusi his spear. Then he reached down with his free hand and jerked Alco to his feet, holding him upright until he could stand on his sore leg. Tomay stood very close to him, speaking with deliberate mildness.

"Now that we are done with threats, I assume that we have your permission to visit him, and that you would be honored to take us there yourself."

"I will take you," Alco muttered with his eyes on the ground, and turned, limping badly, to lead the way to the village.

RAURAU ILLA kept Cusi and Alco waiting outside his compound for most of the afternoon, while he spoke first with Tomay and Tarapaca. Huaman Cachi came out once and returned a short time later carrying the black bundle Cusi had left in his house, which he took inside without so much as a glance at Cusi. Cooking smells drifted out to them from the house, along with the murmur of voices, but no one emerged to speak to them or offer them any food. Cusi became aware of hunger gnawing at the edges of his emptiness, a sensation more curious than painful. He could not remember the last time he had been truly hungry.

Finally, as the sun was beginning to set, Huaman Cachi came out and led them back into the house, gesturing silently for Alco to enter ahead of Cusi. Wicks were burning in bowls of oil on the low platform where Raurau Illa sat with a llama skin draped over his legs, surrounded by several other old men. Tomay and Tarapaca were sitting on the floor in front of the platform, to Raurau Illa's right, and there were the usual women and children moving around at the edges of Cusi's vision. He saw that his black bundle and the bag of dried meat and coca leaves that Tomay had brought were both lying open on the llama skin over Raurau Illa's lap.

Alco stopped a few feet ahead of Cusi and bowed to Raurau Illa, the teeth and claws around his neck making a tinkling sound as he straightened up. The old man's voice rumbled wetly in his chest but did not falter.

"Describe Cusi Huaman to me, Alco. Tell me how he has changed since you saw him last."

"He is no longer a young man," Alco said in a surprisingly neutral tone, "and his body bears the scars of war in many places. He is still thin and weak from the sickness, though more because he will not work to recover his strength. He does not look or carry himself like an Inca anymore. His hair is long and tangled, and his ears are empty."

"What else?" Raurau Illa rumbled.

"He has lost the spirit brother you gave him. He has lost the powers Illapa bestowed upon him. He is helpless and pitiful, yet he feels no shame. He does not know why he is alive."

An edge of malice had crept into Alco's voice, and Cusi knew that once he would have made him pay dearly for such a harsh assessment. Now, though, it seemed merely accurate, and Tomay and Tarapaca seemed to recognize its truthfulness in the way they kept their eyes fixed on the ground.

"Cusi," Raurau Illa said, "come closer. I cannot feel you."

Cusi came up beside Alco and bowed. "I am here, Grandfather."

"What have you brought me?"

"Everything I had was burned. Except for the things you have before you."

The old man's gnarled hand settled upon the bundle, spreading the folds of black cloth, so that the shining metal inside caught the light.

"Will you give them to me?"

"Yes."

Tomay coughed sharply, a clear protest, but Cusi did not glance in his direction, and neither did Raurau Illa. The old man brought out his other hand and lifted the stone ax head from the bundle, the stringy muscles in his arms tightening at the effort.

"You must take this back," he said, holding it out in front of him. "I have no use for it."

"Neither have I," Cusi said, but he stepped forward and took the star-shaped ring of stone out of Raurau Illa's hands, slipping his fingers through the hole in its center. Its weight brought back a vivid memory of Otoronco Achachi looming over him, glaring down at him with the full force of He Who Sees All, then laughing and taking the ax from a wall niche, rewarding Cusi for his defiance.

"What is it, Cusi?" Raurau Illa prompted, breaking into his thoughts. "What has the stone told you?"

The old man's face was lifted to him expectantly, the sightless eyes giving back a dull gleam.

"I was remembering my grandfather, Otoronco Achachi. He gave me the ax and made me carry it to make myself stronger. He took me to have it blessed by Pachacuti himself."

"You must keep it," Raurau Illa told him. "It has survived the fire to come back to you. What has happened to your grandfather?"

"I learned today that he died of the sickness in Chimor."

"Do you blame yourself for his death?"

"No," Cusi said, puzzled by the question. "Why would I?"

"I know you blame yourself for Urcon's death," Raurau Illa said flatly. "Yet

Urcon was never meant to return here, not even to die. You carried him beyond his destiny, far beyond what I had asked of you."

"I thought I could do anything," Cusi recalled. "I was prepared to carry him here myself, because I knew that *I* was meant to come here. I should have stayed in Quispi Cancha and tended him there. He would be alive today if I had."

"He would have died there," Raurau Illa said, shaking his head, "and you as well, perhaps. Your regrets are delusions, Cusi, the result of the fever. You will know that once you allow yourself to grieve."

Cusi turned the ax head between his fingers. "I cannot feel enough to grieve. Like this stone, I have a hole worn through my heart."

"Yes," the old man agreed with surprising sympathy. "Not all of you has come back to life. And you are resisting your return, Cusi, you are afraid to claim another life. You have allowed yourself to believe that Illapa has abandoned you."

"How can I believe otherwise?" Cusi demanded. "I have no more powers, only the memory of boasting that I was his favorite."

"Do you think he is done with you, then?" Raurau Illa demanded in return. "He has made you famous, Cusi. He has made you a man whom other men will trust and follow. Why do you doubt that he will give you the powers you need?"

"I see no sign of a change in myself . . ."

"You will see nothing as long as you sit looking inward," the old man scoffed. "You must stop thinking and learn to run again. That is how you will find yourself."

"That will cure only my legs," Cusi objected, but Raurau Illa went on as if he had not heard.

"Huaman Cachi is the swiftest of the boys, and he says he could easily beat you in a race. He will be your trainer until you can outrun him."

"What if I do not wish to be trained?"

"If you do not work, you will not be given any food. You can starve or go back to Cuzco as you are. No one here will interfere or help you in any way, if that is your choice."

Cusi curled the ax head in one hand and rested it on his hip. "So I must become the Running Boy all over again," he suggested without enthusiasm. "What if I beat Huaman Cachi and still do not wish to leave?"

"Then you may stay," Raurau Illa assured him. "Then I will know you were sent to take my place here."

Out of the corner of his eye, Cusi saw Alco stiffen and then frown, so fiercely that Cusi instinctively lowered the hand with the stone to his side, where he could swing it. The response made him realize that a part of him could still choose, if only in the face of a clear threat.

"I will run, then," he said to the old man, who closed his eyes and nodded. Tomay spoke up from where he was sitting.

"We are going back to Cuzco, Cusi. We will make Yasca wait as long as

possible, but you must come as soon as you are fit. You have a month or two
at the most. Come even if you are not fit; we will carry you if we have to."

"Huaman Cachi," Raurau Illa called, and the boy immediately appeared at
Cusi's side. "Begin the training. See that Cusi earns his food and his sleep. Go
now . . ."

Cusi bowed and turned to follow the boy out of the room. Alco turned with
him, glaring balefully, while behind him, Tomay and Tarapaca were nodding
and smiling in encouragement. Cusi ignored Alco and nodded a farewell to his
friends, but as he walked toward the doorway he tightened his grip on the
knobbed piece of stone in his hand, deciding he might have a use for it, after
all.

Tumibamba

T HE MESSENGER was one of Apu Poma's men, and he had obviously run
all the way from the palace. He gave Micay and Quespi a breathless
smile, knowing what this news would mean to them.

"Your husbands are alive, my ladies. The war chief Yasca and the commanders Cusi Huaman, Tomay Guanaco, and Quizquiz have all survived the
sickness. This was learned from Tomay Guanaco himself, in Cuzco."

Micay and Quespi stared at one another for a moment. Then Quespi grabbed
Micay by the arms and began to dance up and down.

"They're safe, Micay, they're safe!"

"I heard," Micay said numbly, and a thought flashed through her mind:
Now it is our turn. Then a shudder of relief passed through her and she had
an image of Cusi, healthy and standing, walking with his battle-ax in his hands.
All her most recent imaginings had seen him lying sick and helpless, his eyes
closed against the light. Now she could see him smile, which made her laugh
and join Quespi's dance while the messenger looked awkwardly on.

Shortly after they had sent the man back to the governor with their thanks,
Chuqui Huipa came through the compound gate, preceded by two Cañari
warriors from the Royal Guard. It was the first time she had come to the high
priestess's compound, and she had come without her usual entourage. The
warriors cleared a path through the crowd for her, and many of those who
were made to step aside then bowed when they recognized the Coya's eldest
daughter. Some probably bowed simply to the intricate weave of her vicuña
shift and the golden jewelry around her neck and wrists, the insignia of royal
rank.

Chuqui took one look at their faces and threw up her hands in mock
exasperation.

"I came to tell you myself, but you have already heard! Micay, I have never
seen such a smile in all the time I have known you."

"Cusi has been gone all that time. Now at least I know he is out of danger."

"Perhaps you will smile more often now," Chuqui suggested, "and come more often to see your friends."

"I am sorry . . . you see what it is like here." Micay gestured toward the groups of men clustered around the courtyard, some working or carrying supplies, some just sitting.

"Here and everywhere else in this city. And I hear it is no different in Quito. I have been thinking of going to the mountains. If I must be lonely, I might just as well be alone."

Ninan Cuyochi had gone back to Quito some time ago, but the Coya had kept Chuqui here. The women who attended her had also stayed, but most of them, like Cori Cuillor and Amancay, were preoccupied with having their husbands back from the field. Nor were there any of the usual feasts and dances, not with the Sapa Inca in seclusion and the city under siege.

"I would go to the mountains in a moment," Micay said wistfully, "if I were free to do so."

"Is it truly impossible?" Chuqui asked. "My father has an estate much closer than the Rainbow House. You could come for a few days and leave the twins to stay longer. Quinti's children, too. It is not healthy for them to live like this."

"I know," Micay agreed, "but Quespi would be worked to death if I were to leave her alone with all this."

"But I am told that the number of sick at the rest houses has begun to diminish and that some of those who have recovered are going to be allowed into the city."

"Apu Poma has been trying to bring Quilaco and Quinti back for some time," Micay acknowledged. Then she shook her head firmly. "People are still dying at the rest houses, Chuqui; our work is far from finished."

"I have no work here," Chuqui muttered, nodding in surrender, "except to share my mother's misery . . ."

"It would cheer the men greatly to receive a visit from the Coya's daughter," Micay suggested. Then she excused herself and went to intervene on behalf of Rimachi's grandmother, who was being kept back by one of the Cañari warriors. The old woman was scolding the guard in Cañar when Micay came up, berating him with surprising vigor. But when Micay took her aside, the old woman's anger vanished abruptly and her eyes showed the desperation that was behind it.

"Grandmother . . . is it Llampu? She is not due for another three months."

"No, my lady, it is Cumpi Illya, Rimachi's cousin. Her husband has just returned from the Huancavelicas and they have been staying with Rimachi." The old woman paused and glanced in both directions, stepping closer to Micay. "She has a fever and great pain in her head."

"Wait here," Micay commanded. She went directly to the high priestess's house, ignoring the startled glances of Chuqui and Quespi. She found her medicine bag and slung it over her shoulder, then picked up the white bundle from its place near the doorway. A prudent impulse made her wrap it up in a blanket before carrying it out. Chuqui and Quespi were waiting expectantly when she emerged.

"A woman is sick at Rimachi's compound. It sounds like the fever."

"You will need firewood," Quespi said. "I will send some after you."

"Do not let the porters suspect what it is for. Pretend it is a gift."

"I will accompany you," Chuqui said. "You will get there much faster with my men to clear the way for you."

Micay nodded brusquely, motioning to Rimachi's grandmother to join them. Now it is our turn, she thought as the three of them followed the warriors toward the compound gate.

THE WOMAN'S fever was so intense Micay could feel its heat without having to touch her; she was holding her head with both hands and moaning softly. Micay looked across at the husband, who was crouched on the other side of his wife.

"It came suddenly?" Micay asked. "She was not sick before this?"

"No," the man blurted nervously. "Except for her eyes, from the dust—"

"What dust?"

He gestured vaguely toward one of the wall niches. "From the tunic I brought back . . . a prize from the war. Cumpi shook it out and the dust got into her eyes; Llampu had to wash them for her. But that was days ago."

"It must be burned," Micay told him. "It should have been burned when you were examined at the rest house."

"I was not inspected too closely," the man admitted. He was Cañari but wore the gold and silver earplugs of an Inca by privilege, and he appeared frightened as well as concerned for his wife. Much too frightened for a seasoned warrior, Micay thought.

"How do *you* feel?" she asked him abruptly, but he simply stared back at her in silence, showing white all around his eyes.

"Stay here," Micay told him as she rose. "Take off all of your clothes and undress your wife. I will return to help you."

Rimachi had joined the anxious group waiting outside his house, and Micay addressed herself to him.

"It is the sickness," she said bluntly. "Everything in that room, especially the blankets and bedding, must be burned. Everyone who has shared the room with Cumpi Illya must burn the clothes they are wearing and then sweat themselves thoroughly before they dress again."

"Take wood from the storeroom and fill the firepit," Rimachi told one of Chuqui's guards, pointing the way with his chin. "I will empty the room myself."

"Do not touch anything with your bare hands," Micay warned. "Use a spear or a long pole and do not let any dust get into your eyes or mouth. Cover your face with a thin cloth."

"I have heard you," Rimachi promised, relieving Chuqui's other guard of his spear. Llampu gathered her three-year-old son and several of the other people who had been sleeping in the house and began to lead them toward the firepit. Micay found Chuqui standing by herself, holding the blanket-wrapped bundle Micay had left with her.

"I am grateful, my lady," Micay said, taking the bundle out of her arms. "Forgive me for not introducing you properly."

"I do not think anyone recognized me," Chuqui said, seeming bemused rather than insulted. "Not even Rimachi."

"They are too frightened," Micay told her. "And with good reason. You should leave now, my lady. It is a risk simply to be here."

"I am not afraid," Chuqui said with a small shrug, as if surprised at herself. "How may I help you?"

"This should be reported to the Sapa Inca—as calmly as possible."

Chuqui shook her head with a weary disappointment that made her seem older. "My father would not hear it calmly. He might try to banish these people from the city."

"No!" Micay blurted out in disbelief. "He could not do such a thing. This is their city."

"I only know that some of his advisers have recommended it," Chuqui said. "They would send people out to the rest houses. No, it would be better to wait to report this until we can say we have contained it."

Micay was silent for a moment, considering the note of command in Chuqui's voice. "Have you decided to make healing your work, then? I cannot refuse your help, if you insist, but—"

"I do insist. What could I do that would be more important than this?"

"You could do much that would be less dangerous," Micay assured her. "The Coya will be angry at you and furious with me. She will believe I lured you into the high priestess's service."

"Why else has Chimpu Ocllo allowed you to visit Quito so often?" Chuqui suggested. "I am not as naive as I appear, Micay, and I have long endured my mother's suspicions about you and Chimpu Ocllo. But I would not let her deprive me of your friendship. Do not deprive me of the chance to be useful now. I can no longer pretend I am saving myself for something greater."

Micay studied the stubborn set of her features, seeing the resemblance to Huayna Capac and imagining the impact upon the court if Chuqui were to appear in their midst with her hair shorn, wearing white. This was indeed what Chimpu Ocllo had had in mind all along, and Micay wondered why her success made her feel devious. She shook her head and undid the bundle in her arms, digging down through the layers of cloth with a kind of anger and finally drawing out a crescent-shaped bronze knife.

"I must go to the bathhouse and prepare myself," she said curtly, brandishing the knife in front of Chuqui. "When I have washed my hair, will you cut it for me? Short, like a man's?"

Chuqui's eyes darted like her father's for an instant, revealing her distaste for the task, but then she composed her face and held out a steady hand.

"I will do whatever needs to be done," she declared, and Micay surrendered the knife with a rueful smile.

"Watch me for now," she advised, "and learn how to protect yourself from the sickness. We must stay well so that we can help the sick recover."

"We will, then," Chuqui vowed, and she led the way to the bathhouse, holding the shining blade out in front of her like a ceremonial implement.

WHEN ALL of the women had gathered in the high priestess's house, Micay and Quespi each took a count, though they knew beforehand that the number would be inadequate. Including the two of them, there were twelve women in white, their skin shiny with oil and their hair completely hidden beneath the white head cloths. Five other women attended them as apprentices, still wearing their own clothes and with their hair uncut. One of these was Chuqui Huipa, whose quick eyes intercepted the despairing glance that passed between Micay and Quespi.

"There are more today?" she asked.

Micay nodded in resignation. "Two more, in places where it has not been before. It means each of us will have to make at least two visits today; some will have to make more."

"But I have ten sick in one compound alone," one of the women pointed out, "and only a single servant left to help nurse them."

"You will have an apprentice," Quespi assured her. "Though wherever we can, we must begin to train those who are still healthy to take our places."

"That is often more work than treating the sick ourselves," another woman said. "They are either afraid to get too close or not afraid enough."

"We have little choice," Micay said. "It was never the mamanchic's intention to have us go out to the sick. That was forced on us by the way the sickness came and the need to be discreet in our response."

"But everyone knows the sickness is here," a third woman insisted. "They know what we are doing. That is why some of them bow to us in the street and others turn their faces away. They call us the White Women . . . or the Women of Death."

"The Sapa Inca, however, has not recognized our presence," Quespi explained, "and the mamanchic has not responded to our pleas for guidance. We know we cannot continue like this for much longer. It has been only a month, and already we are overwhelmed."

In the silence that followed Quespi's blunt appraisal, Micay could hear water dripping off the thatch and the sounds of children playing in the courtyard outside. The rain had stopped but the sun had yet to appear, and she could feel the chill of the air through the thin weave of her much-washed shift. It had been unusually cold for this far into the growing season, and their stock of blankets and—more important firewood, charcoal, and llama dung had been depleted. They had recently had to begin burying the garments of the sick rather than burning them.

"Perhaps it is time for me to cut my hair and go to the court," Chuqui suggested quietly. All the other women looked at Micay, who thus far had persuaded Chuqui to remain an apprentice and was the only one who dared to address her as such. Chuqui was no longer wearing her golden jewelry or her finest clothes, but no one could pretend that she was simply another member of the group. Micay looked across the circle at her and nodded.

"There are too many to banish now," she conceded. "And we need more supplies and more women to follow our example. We would be grateful for your help and honored to have you join us."

The other women murmured their assent, but Chuqui's reply was interrupted by a loud shout from outside, followed by the sound of running feet splashing through the puddles in the courtyard. Micay swiveled on her seat to see a man run past the doorway, his arms filled with blankets, weapons, and various bundles, some of which he dropped as he ran toward the compound gate. The shouting had grown to a chorus, and more men were fleeing across the courtyard, emptying out of the houses and the makeshift shelters they had erected against the enclosure walls. Micay went out the doorway and called to one of the men by name, but he ran past her heedlessly, charging into the jostling crowd trying to squeeze through the gate. The men pushed and fought and finally propelled themselves out into the street, leaving the courtyard strewn with the things they had dropped. The last man to go through was on crutches, carrying a bedroll in his teeth.

Like survivors of a storm, the women crept out into the courtyard, poking at the debris with their feet and gazing around at the sudden spaciousness of the compound. The children had escaped the stampede by crouching against the front of one of the buildings, and Quespi's son Huallpa, at nine the oldest, led them out in a wary group.

"The first man came from there," Huallpa told his mother, pointing with his chin at the converted storehouse Paucar Rimay had been sharing with several of the guests. "He was shouting something about the sickness, but I could not understand him. Then they all came running out!"

"Stay here," Quespi told him. "Do not let the little ones touch anything."

Micay gave the same instruction to Coca and told Sinchi and Cahua to obey their cousin. Then she and Quespi headed for the storehouse, trailed closely by Chuqui and some of the other women. The floor of the small room was a jumble of blankets and bedding, and a bag of chuño flour had been spilled in the doorway. Paucar Rimay was huddled against the wall in the corner, not far from where a man lay facedown on blankets, moaning and shivering. Micay turned back to warn Chuqui and another apprentice not to enter.

"Go to the bathhouse and prepare yourselves," she told them. "We will need you here."

Chuqui lingered in the doorway for a moment, a hand raised to the glossy black hair that flowed out from underneath her head cloth. Then she snorted softly and let the hand drop.

"They will not recognize me in the court," she said. Then she smiled to herself and went off after the other apprentice. Quespi had gotten the man on the floor to roll over onto his back, and she glanced up at Micay and quickly pulled her gauze mask up over her face, confirming that it was the sickness. Micay covered her own face and went to squat next to Paucar Rimay, who was trembling violently, his face hidden in his arms. Micay found one of his hands, which was colder than her own, and held it in the two-handed grip by which he knew her, repeating his name and her own. She doubted he recognized her in the mask, but she was gradually able to draw him away from the wall and saw that his face was bruised and bloodied and his tunic torn at the shoulder. The waistband with his cords was also missing. Micay spotted it coiled among the shards of a broken pot and started to reach for it, then realized that it would have to be burned along with everything else in this room. Paucar would have no memory, no way to express his feelings, until she found the time to get him new cords.

"The idiot gave it to me," the other man said, and Micay turned to see that Quespi had him sitting up with his tunic off. He and his friends were newcomers, let in off the streets only days before, so Micay had never even learned where they were from. The man grimaced at the pain in his head and pointed an accusing finger at Paucar. "I warned him not to look at me like that. I knew he was casting a spell on me!"

It took Micay a moment to understand. Then she lashed out and slapped the man's finger back at him. "So you beat him and tore his clothes? You fool, he does not have the sickness—*you* do. You brought it here, and now your cowardly friends have taken it out into the city!"

The man collapsed onto his back with a groan, clutching his finger, and Quespi simply gaped at her in astonishment, the gauze mask sucking in around her open mouth. Micay realized that she was angry not only at him but at all the men to whom they had given shelter. Their kindness had been repaid with panic and abandonment.

Making no attempt to explain herself, she helped Paucar to his feet and led him out of the room. He shuffled through the spilled flour, kicking up a white cloud that stuck to Micay's oily legs. He clung to her slippery arm with one hand while the other groped futilely at his hip.

"Where—" he muttered, licking at his cut lip, "it . . . where?"

"Everywhere," Micay said grimly. "Everywhere . . ."

The Village

A FIERCE wind was blowing, and storm clouds were already stacking up over the mountains to the east, but Cusi would not allow Huaman Cachi to hurry him. Planting his feet wide apart, he bent one knee and stretched out the opposite leg, pressing down on his thigh with the heel of his hand. *He is no longer a young man,* he thought, smiling to himself as he recalled Alco's description of him. This training had taught him the truth of that: of muscles that warmed slowly and stiffened as they cooled; of old wounds and mended bones that ached without apparent cause; of legs that felt livelier on some days than on others. The Running Boy cast a shadow now that at times looked like that of a straining man.

The wind whipped Cusi's long hair across his face as he repeatedly squatted and stood, working the joints in his knees. Huaman Cachi squatted a few feet away, near Cusi's ax head. He watched silently until Cusi finally signaled that he was ready.

"Leave the stone here today," the boy suggested as Cusi came over to pick it up. "Race me without it."

"Alco might steal it while I was gone. Besides, I am used to running with it."

"Alco gave it to you," Huaman Cachi reminded him. "I want you to race me fairly. You only play at it."

"You should beat me easily, then," Cusi said lightly.

The boy stood up and glowered at him. "I run as hard as I can. You run no harder than you have to."

"Are you sure of that? Perhaps you become swifter with each day, so that I will never overtake you."

"You did that days ago," Huaman Cachi snapped. "You have finished telling your stories, too, but you will not say what you will do next. You simply like to taunt us!"

"Perhaps . . . come, before I get cold," Cusi urged, and he started out of the fenceless yard at a trot, with the ax head tucked in the crook of one arm. Huaman Cachi quickly came up next to him, and they left the houses and their surrounding fields of potatoes and quinoa and went up onto the plain to run. They had done this every day, in all weather, for the last month and a half, a progress through pain and exhaustion to a stamina that Cusi had finally come to trust. And at night, sitting with a crowd in Raurau Illa's house, he had told the story of the life he had led since he first left Cuzco, sharing his memories piece by piece, from the cliff in Chachapoyas to the great hall in the Co-chabamba Valley. He had wept at times during the telling, and though he was never quite certain whether the murmurs of his listeners indicated envy or simple disbelief, he had gradually come to feel he had no cause for lasting regret.

As if nourished by the remembering, his dreams had changed, as well, becoming more colorful and less threatening. He had vivid encounters with Amaru and Quinti and his mother and father, and he dreamed of Micay nearly every night, dreams that left him swollen with desire even when the dream itself was not sexual. Lloque Yupanqui and Otoronco Achachi came to drink with him once, laughing and wearing memory cords on their heads. Uritu met him on a jungle path, and Sinchi was with him, a solemn Campa boy with a tattooed face and a blowpipe in his hand; Urcon and Fempellec stripped off their clothes and plunged into the foaming waters of Mama Cocha, a dream that also aroused him and made him reckon with the shame he expected to feel.

The wind was blowing hard at their backs, bringing in more clouds to darken the sky overhead. The bunch grass beneath their running feet was a brilliant yellow-green, as if all the light had soaked down into it. There was a distant rumble of thunder, and Huaman Cachi shouted something that was lost in the rush of the wind. Cusi leaned toward him inquiringly, shifting the ax head to his inside hand.

"To the huaca?" the boy repeated challengingly. Cusi looked ahead to the long, undulating stretch of plain that rose gradually to the ridge overlooking the huaca. The storm was coming fast, and there was no shelter along the way. Cusi consulted his legs, which felt warm and responsive, their labors eased by the push of the wind. Perhaps it was time to stop what Huaman Cachi saw as "playing."

"To the huaca!" he agreed, and the boy briefly shot out ahead of him until Cusi lengthened his stride and caught up. Huaman Cachi was running intently, clearly making a race of it, and Cusi decided not to disappoint him. A crack of thunder close behind made them both jump, and when they came down, Cusi tucked the stone in close to his body and stretched out into a full run, taking Huaman Cachi by surprise and making him break his stride. Cusi did not wait for him and was halfway to the ridge before the boy caught up, his face contorted and his breath coming hard. Off to their left lightning flashed, followed by a sizzling clap of thunder, but Cusi ran on heedlessly, denying the pain in his legs and lungs, knowing that Huaman Cachi was at his limit while he himself had more. When he could see the barren patch of earth ahead of him, the watching place at the top of the ridge, he suddenly flung the ax head out ahead of him and put on a final burst of speed that made Huaman Cachi stagger and then fall completely behind.

A hard, cold rain, almost like hail, came pelting down just as Cusi reached the watching place, and he collapsed onto the ground and covered his head with his arms, the roar of his breathing mingling with the crash of thunder. The rain ended as abruptly as it had begun, and Cusi rolled over and sat up, still breathing hard. He saw Huaman Cachi rise up out of the grass and walk toward him, stooping along the way to pick up the ax head and bring it with him. He dropped the stone into Cusi's hands and sat down beside him.

"Now I know how swift you are," he muttered breathlessly, "when you want to be."

"You are a good runner. You did not deserve to be taunted any more."

They both ducked their heads as more rain whipped down on them. Huaman Cachi rested his chin on his raised knees and stared at Cusi with a kind of wistful resignation.

"So now you will leave."

"It is past time. I have been dreaming of the people who wait for my return."

"You will wear the earplugs again and be a war chief?"

Cusi nodded slowly. "I expect to be offered that rank, though I doubt we will be called upon to fight very soon."

"You do not want to fight," Huaman Cachi suggested, squinting at him knowingly.

"Not as I once did," Cusi admitted. "Not out of anger or the need to prove myself. But I will fight to defend what I care about."

"I knew you would not stay here," the boy said. He stood up abruptly and jerked his chin over one shoulder. "There is something for you at the huaca."

Cusi rose into the swirling wind and followed him to the edge of the watching place, where they could look down on the huaca. The jagged shaft of stone appeared black against the reddish-brown earth, and from this angle it seemed to have emerged from the soil rather than to have plunged down into it. Huaman Cachi bowed and made the mocha, but Cusi simply stared, remembering Huaca Urcco and Tiahuanaco and the other holy places he had visited, places that had held him and made him stare like this. He understood for the first time that when he had gone to those places, in his heart he had been coming here.

Huaman Cachi finished his prayer and led Cusi down a narrow, muddy path that took them out of the wind and down into the hollow that surrounded the huaca. Cusi walked out onto the hard-beaten ground, feeling the stillness settle over him, shielding him from the billowing energy of the storm overhead. He smiled, astonished by the sense of comfort he felt in the presence of the huaca. He had always been slightly unnerved by the aura of otherness that emanated from the stone, but now he felt completely calm, certain he belonged here.

The boy had gone around behind the huaca, and he returned carrying a rolled-up piece of leather that was tied with thongs at both ends. He presented it to Cusi with a ceremonious bow, and Cusi put his ax head down to take it from him. Then they both squatted down, and Cusi loosened the thongs and unrolled the bundle on the ground in front of him. Inside was a piece of hard, dark wood about as long as Cusi's arm, slightly tapered at one end and wrapped with a rope grip at the other. It was the handle of a battle-ax, and enclosed with it was a loose bundle of leather lashings. Cusi held his hands out over it, then stopped and looked at Huaman Cachi.

"Grandfather had me bring it here days ago," the boy explained. "He said you would take it and make a weapon from it. Or . . . you would leave everything here in pieces, as an offering, a sign that you had truly put aside the life of an Inca warrior."

Cusi moved the ax head onto the leather sheet and picked up the handle by its gripped end, waving it once to test its weight and springiness. He raised his eyes to the huaca, which jutted out over him, solid and impenetrable against the shifting pattern of the clouds. For a moment he felt he shared its ancient aloofness, its disdain for the passing storms of life. Then he heard a growl of thunder in the distance and it seemed a warning, a reminder that he was a man, not a stone. He was not meant to stay here forever.

"No, I cannot leave that life in pieces," he decided. He upended the handle and carefully thrust the tapered end down into the hole at the center of the star-shaped stone. The fit was perfect, and perfectly tight once Cusi banged the ax head against the ground to drive the handle all the way through.

"My mother's brother made weapons for the Inca's armies," Huaman Cachi said proudly. "Your friends, the Colla and the Lupaca, gave him instructions."

Cusi tucked the lashings into his waistband for later and lifted up the ax with both hands, feeling a familiar expansion of the muscles in his forearms.

"*This* to traitors," he murmured reflexively, though he did not adopt a fighting stance, and he brandished the ax in front of him without swinging it. The instincts were still there, but they no longer possessed him as they once had, immediately and without a second thought, imagining a threat even where none actually existed. For the first time Cusi began to see his detachment as a virtue rather than a failing. This was a different kind of huaca, truer to the spirit of the stone, the spirit that had saved the Running Boy and had given him strength and health. He had brought the anger here with him.

He remembered Huaman Cachi and caught him casting an uneasy glance at the sky, then a similar glance at Cusi. Raindrops began to spatter on the ground around them. Cusi looked at the blackened circle in front of the stone and realized he had no offering to leave, so he raised his battle ax in a salute instead, pledging himself again and promising to live a life that would honor Illapa.

"Let us go to Grandfather," Cusi said to the boy, who scooped up the leather sheet and thongs and made a last hasty bow to the huaca. Then the rain began to come down in earnest, and they ducked their heads and ran blindly for the path.

CUSI SAT cross-legged, facing the platform with Huaman Cachi beside him and his battle-ax—the head now securely lashed to the handle—on the floor in front of him. He had just finished promising Raurau Illa that he would send back all the llamas and alpacas owed to Urcon when Alco entered the house and came to stand beside him. He bowed over the drinking cup in his hands.

"Grandfather . . ."

"Alco, my son. Tell me what you know of Cusi Huaman."

"He has cut his hair and put wooden plugs into his ears, and he wears a headband again. He has fashioned a weapon for himself, and it makes him feel strong and very satisfied with himself. He visited the huaca today but left no offering; he acted as if he owed nothing to the gods."

"Where is his spirit brother?" Raurau Illa asked, and Cusi straightened up attentively.

"Inside him, where it has always been. Perhaps he knows that now."

"Have you tested his spirit against sorcery, as I told you?"

Alco exhaled sharply and nodded. "I left things for him to find, things that would make him hurt himself, but he never found them. I sent him threatening dreams, dreams he had told me during his fever, but he would not dream them again. I cannot touch him with my hatred, though it is strong enough to make any other man sicken and die. His spirit brother protects him."

"Is he healed, then?"

"Yes. He should have left long ago."

"He will leave soon enough," Raurau Illa assured him. "Now I wish to know what it has done to you, my son, to have indulged your hatred in this manner."

Alco looked down into the cup in his hands, his jaw working around a reply that he finally decided to withhold. Raurau Illa turned his silvery eyes in Cusi's direction.

"Cusi, tell me what you see in Alco. How has he changed since the last time you were here together?"

Cusi rose to examine Alco, who remained facing forward, his features rigid and blank.

"He is not wearing his lion skin or his necklace of teeth," Cusi reported, looking him up and down from the side. "His shoulders are hunched, as if he were wearing a pack, and his face is thin and tired, as if he has not eaten or slept well." Cusi stepped around in front of him. "Ah, but the threat is still there in his eyes. No doubt his presence is very strong and hostile, though I cannot feel such things any longer."

"Were you aware of his sorcery?" Raurau Illa asked as Cusi stepped back beside Alco.

"I knew that he was watching me and that he came around my house when I was not there," Cusi allowed. "Someone also came prowling in the night several times and I assumed it was him."

"You heard him?"

"I still have the senses of a scout," Cusi said simply, and the old man turned his head toward Alco.

"So," he concluded, his voice rich with scorn, "you see how effective your hatred has made you. If you had stalked the puma in the same spirit, you would not be with us today. Tell me you have learned this at last."

Alco hesitated for a moment, then let his shoulders slump, bringing his head down in a nod of resignation. "I have learned it, Grandfather. I know better than anyone how this has impaired my judgment . . . and made me do foolish and clumsy things. I will not make myself so vulnerable again, not for any other man."

"I believe you," Raurau Illa said, though he cocked his head as if listening for an echo. "Yet you do not seem ready to acknowledge the service Cusi has done you—or to make peace with him."

"It was my vision that healed him," Alco insisted, his posture stiffening. "I owe him nothing more."

"And you want nothing from him?" Raurau Illa prompted. "Consider, my son, what the huacas tell us. The time of the warlords is ahead of us, and we have no other friends among the war chiefs of the Inca."

Alco crossed his arms on his chest and remained stubbornly silent. Raurau
Illa waited patiently for several moments. Then he held out his hands.

"Let nothing remain between you, then. Give me the cup. If you meet again,
it will be as strangers."

Alco complied without hesitation, carefully placing the drinking cup in the
old man's hands. Cusi saw the pattern of lynx heads that decorated the vessel
and realized it was the gift cup he had left with Alco on his last visit. Raurau
Illa lowered it to his lap and gestured with his chin toward the doorway.

"Go to your place in the mountains, my son, and ponder the choice you have
made. Return in two days, after Cusi has gone."

"I have heard you, Grandfather," Alco replied, and he left the room without
so much as a glance in Cusi's direction. Raurau Illa motioned for Cusi to sit.

"Do you still have the cup I gave you?" he asked.

Cusi shook his head. "It came this far with me only to be burned in the fire."

"You will have this one, then, once it has been cleansed of Alco's bitterness
and envy. All these years, he has never been able to possess it. He kept his
hatred instead."

"I never felt I had earned it," Cusi said. "Even now I would have made
peace with him."

"You may have done more for him as an enemy," Raurau Illa suggested.
"He will choose his adversaries more carefully in the future, and he will never
trust his hatred again. That is a lesson that has cost many men their lives,
especially when they learned it at the hands of an Inca."

"Will he still be your successor?"

"Of course. He healed you, did he not? He is a good and righteous man,
Cusi; you are the only one who has ever made him act badly. I am grateful
to you for giving him that opportunity."

"It is a talent I have," Cusi said sardonically. "I want to be sure, though,
that he will not take revenge on Huaman Cachi after I am gone."

"Speak for yourself, my son," Raurau Illa said to the boy. "Do you have
anything to fear from Alco?"

Huaman Cachi shrugged and shook his head. "He would not hurt me if I
stayed here."

"You plan to leave us?" Raurau Illa inquired, seeming only mildly surprised. Cusi found that the boy was staring at him intently, showing as much
pleading as his pride allowed.

"The sickness is still out there," Cusi told him, "and you have not had it.
You do not want to have it."

"It may come to us here," Huaman Cachi said dismissively. "I am not
afraid."

"Courage does not make you immune. It is a long way to Tumibamba, and
if you got sick, I would have to leave you somewhere to recover. Yasca would
not wait for me to tend you."

"So I would recover and come after you. Urcon found his way to you by
himself."

"You would have to live among strangers," Cusi persisted, "and you might never see this village again. Urcon did not."

"Urcon saw many wonderful things before he died," the boy said almost reverently, and Cusi appealed to Raurau Illa.

"Grandfather, surely you do not wish to lose another of your young men?"

"The Inca would take him sooner or later. I cannot think that he is lost if he is with you, and I expect you will remember this village because of him. Perhaps, like Urcon, he will help to bring you back here again."

Cusi gave the boy a hard look, but Huaman Cachi stared right back at him, undaunted as ever. "I should have known this would happen," Cusi said, "as soon as you told me your name. You may come with me, then. I will notify the count takers and see that your turn is counted as that of a warrior."

Huaman Cachi forgot his pride then and smiled, not as brilliantly as Urcon once had, but surely as heartfelt. Raurau Illa told him to go and inform his parents and to bring them here to drink with the man who would be his guardian. After the boy had run off, Raurau Illa sat in silence for a moment, running his fingers over the lynx heads incised into the side of the cup.

"This is the last time we will speak, Cusi," he said at last. "I will not live long enough to greet your return. So tell me what you wish to know from me. The last time it was your future. Is that what you wish to know now?"

"I wanted assurances of fame and glory," Cusi recalled. "No, I do not think I want to look ahead like that, for myself. Though I want to know what the huacas have said about a time of the warlords."

"It is no secret. The huacas everywhere whisper of war and rebellion . . . of great turmoil when this Sapa Inca dies. They say his power will fall to pieces, so that no one man can hold it. Then the warlords will rule."

"Will the Viracochas cause this?"

"No one knows about them," Raurau Illa admitted. "You will have to join those who watch and listen. Look to your vision for guidance . . . it can tell you more than the messenger who brought it to you."

Cusi thought for a moment and realized he had no more questions; he truly did not wish to know more. "I think I am more concerned with what has already happened to me than with what *will* happen. Alco said my spirit brother was inside me, yet I cannot feel his presence. And then today, at the huaca, I felt an affinity so strong, so reassuring . . . I saw no need for an offering other than the life I have dedicated to Illapa."

Raurau Illa's eyelids came down and his mouth opened in a smile that showed the gaps in his worn teeth. "That is what Alco cannot forgive: he labors and yearns for the things that come to you unbidden. But yes, these are things I can explain to you—some of them. Some you will only understand in time, but that is as it should be."

"I must know if I am fit to be a war chief."

"I am not one to judge that," the old man demurred. "But your friends, the Colla and the Lupaca, have no doubt. They say all the warriors respect your leadership and courage."

"They speak of my reputation, not of me."

"Ah, but it is not a reputation that confines you. No one doubts your ability, but no one expects Cusi Huaman to act like other men."

"But I no longer have the anger, the fierceness . . ."

"Those should not be confused," Raurau Illa admonished him. "They are not the same thing. You will have your anger back, but you will be slow to let it move you. You will look on the world from a distance."

"From a distance," Cusi repeated, feeling for a moment that he understood completely and then feeling that he did not understand at all. Raurau Illa held up a hand before he could find words for his confusion.

"First we must eat, and then we will drink and talk. You will sit here beside me, and we will say all the things that must be said between us. And then, before you are too drunk, you will sing the song that is in the cord you gave me. The story song of Viracocha's journey."

"I remember," Cusi said softly. "It is the journey I will be taking myself, north to the Lynx Quarter."

Raurau Illa held up the lynx-head cup and smiled his blind, gap-toothed smile. "Then you must sing it for both of us, for all of those who have heard your stories. So they will know, when their children ask them, where the Running Boy has gone . . ."

Tumibamba

A LIGHT RAIN was falling but the night was warm, and a full moon behind the clouds cast a grayish light over the compound. The soft patter of rain drowned out the coughing of the sick men in the awning house, and the only sounds from the city outside were the slow, sorrowful beating of a drum and the ragged chanting of those who were mourning their dead. Micay sat in the doorway of the high priestess's house with Cahua sprawled across her lap, finally asleep. She stroked her daughter's short black hair, which Cahua had insisted be cut in the manner of her mother and Chuqui Huipa. Micay and Quespi had cut the hair of all of the children and had made cotton clothing for them so that they could wash and change it as frequently as the healers did. So far none of them had contracted the sickness, though it was much milder in children than in adults. Llampu and Rimachi's son, Topa, had caught it and had recovered quickly, while the husband of Cumpi Illya and Rimachi's grandmother had both died.

The thought of Llampu aroused a pang of guilt that made Micay squirm slightly where she sat. Llampu was the most recent to be stricken, and Micay was worried about both her and the child she carried. The spots had begun to appear and she was already delirious, thrashing about dangerously if Rimachi or someone equally strong were not there to hold her still. Micay had meant to check on her today, but other, more pressing tasks had intervened, and she was too tired now for anyone but her own child. The demand for comfort by the sick was so unrelenting that she was frequently drained of all real caring, able to heal with her hands but not her heart. She allowed herself to go numb at such times, even to withdraw into a self-pitying yearning for someone to comfort *her*. She had seen healers who had been in the field too long, and those who did not permit themselves some detachment often became resentful and cruel. So she let herself forget about Llampu and Paucar Rimay and the others who were sick and sat listening to the rain, not thinking about anything at all.

A flash of white drew her attention to the compound gate, through which had just passed a lone figure, shielded from the rain by a palm-leaf umbrella. At this time of night, it could only be Chuqui Huipa, reveling in her freedom to walk the streets of the city unattended whenever she chose. She was wearing her white shift and mantle but not the matching head cloth, flaunting her short hair at anyone who might see her. It was the haircut, more than Chuqui's earnest pleas, that had persuaded the Coya to let Chuqui stay behind when the Sapa Inca had taken the rest of the royal family north to Quito. "My desire to aid the sick was foolish but commendable," Chuqui had told Micay afterward, "but my willingness to make myself ugly was considered a spiteful act. So my wish was granted as a punishment."

Chuqui smiled twice, once at Micay and then again when she saw Cahua sleeping in Micay's lap. She set her umbrella down quietly and came in under the overhanging thatch, sitting down in the doorway next to Micay. Even so Cahua awoke, though only long enough to crawl across into Chuqui's lap and curl up there.

"Sleep, my precious one," Chuqui soothed, clearly as pleased by this half-conscious show of affection as Micay was to have her daughter's weight off her thighs.

"She had a bad dream," Micay explained. "She stepped on a sick man's blanket and her feet were burning. I probably should not have them sleep in different places from night to night, but it is the only way I get to spend time with them."

"I could not sleep myself," Chuqui admitted. "The rumor we heard is true . . . the sickness is in Quito."

"In the palace?"

"Not yet. Among the warriors Atauhuallpa brought back from the lands of the Huancavelicas."

"We have told the healers there what we know," Micay said, "and I sent a personal message to Parihuana, asking her to urge the Quito women to overcome their resistance to cutting their hair."

"Still, many will die," Chuqui said in the flat, grim voice of experience.

"Many will recover," Micay told her. "Ninan is no less strong than Cusi or Tomay."

"We have both seen strong men die. If I hear he is sick I will go to him," Chuqui declared with a vehemence that made Cahua moan and stir in her lap.

"There is no one to stop you," Micay said. Then she heard a creaking sound and turned to see a large, covered litter being carried into the compound, borne on the shoulders of eight bearers. "For you?" she asked, but Chuqui shrugged and shook her head.

"Those are the governor's bearers," she pointed out. "And three women in white. It must be Quinti and Quilaco!"

Micay had already risen and picked up the umbrella. She peered through the rain, recognizing two of the women as mamacona who were close to Chimpu Ocllo and had accompanied her to the Chimor rest house. The third woman had to be Quinti, yet Micay did not actually recognize her until she was quite close. The face beneath the dripping hood of her cloak was gaunt and haggard, the eyes sunk deep in shadow. But she smiled as Micay came to meet her, and there was a wiry strength in her embrace. All at once Micay understood that Quinti had become a healer at the rest house, and that she had done it with her usual single-minded intensity. No doubt she had allowed herself neither rest nor detachment.

The bearers carefully lowered the litter to the ground and then backed away from it, appearing both relieved and nervous. Micay had seen such expressions before and was puzzled for a moment, since Quilaco had already had the sickness and should not have posed a threat to anyone. Then the size of the litter and the presence of the mamacona penetrated, and she understood why the litter had been brought here rather than to Quilaco's compound.

"The mamanchic," she said, glancing at Quinti for confirmation. "She is sick?"

"It is her seventh day," Quinti said softly. "When the litter came for Quilaco, we decided to bring her, too. She is stronger than most are at this point."

Micay handed her the umbrella and pulled her gauze mask up over her mouth and nose, leaving her eyes uncovered so that she could see in the dim light. Taking hold of one of the side curtains, she peeled it back and tossed it up on top of the litter. A pair of hands from the inside did the same with the second curtain before she could even reach for it, and Quilaco leaned his head out, blinking at the rain. He also appeared thin and drawn, but his eyes were bright.

"Is that you, Micay?" he asked, then pulled his head back in and spoke to the other occupant of the litter, who was slumped down in a pile of llama skins. "She is here, my mother. She has not gone to Quito as you feared."

Seven days, Micay thought anxiously as she ducked her head and leaned in over Chimpu Ocllo. The familiar face appeared old and worn, and her long neck and head seemed exposed and vulnerable with only a ragged shock of gray hair to cover them. Chimpu coughed and shielded her eyes with a limp hand when one of the mamacona opened the curtains on the other side of the litter.

"Greetings, Mamanchic," Micay said, keeping her voice steady through an act of will. "We have been waiting and praying for your return."

"You stayed," Chimpu murmured incredulously, "even though I was cruel to you."

"You were never cruel, my lady," Micay assured her. "Rest now, and save your strength so we can heal you."

She straightened up and lowered her mask, exchanging a concerned glance with the mama who was waiting to take her place.

"She does not want to rest," the woman said sadly, though with a kind of pride, as well. "She spoke to us through the curtain all the way here."

"We must try to make her rest, anyhow," Micay insisted. "Can you move her? I must rouse my children and take our things from her house."

She turned to find that Chuqui Huipa had already done this for her. She had the umbrella in one hand, Micay's medicine bag and several blankets slung over her shoulder and other arm, and Cahua and Sinchi clinging sleepily to her skirts. Quinti was kneeling on the wet ground next to her, locked in a double embrace with Coca and Cisa. Micay smiled gratefully at Chuqui and turned back to help Quilaco, who was struggling to rise from the litter on his own. His body felt light and brittle, and there was none of Quinti's strength in the arm he threw around her shoulders. But he was able to stand, and he smiled when he saw Quinti and his daughters.

"It is so good to be back, Micay," he said hoarsely. "So good to be alive."

"You must bathe and change your clothes before you can touch the children," Micay warned him. "Can you walk to the bathhouse?"

"Probably. I am surely tired of being carried."

Quinti rose and made her daughters stay where they were while she went to Quilaco's side. He removed his arm from Micay's shoulders and dabbed at his eyes, then waved to the girls in greeting.

"Coca . . . Cisa . . . I am back, my daughters. I will be with you very soon." Then he recognized Chuqui and straightened up in surprise, bobbing his head in an abbreviated bow. "My lady . . . forgive me. We were told the court had gone to Quito."

"It has," Chuqui agreed. "But someone had to stay behind to greet our returning warriors. Welcome home, Quilaco Yupanqui."

"I am honored by your presence, my lady," Quilaco murmured.

"I will bathe him," Quinti said to Micay, who nodded enviously. Quilaco's arm on her shoulders had brought back all of her memories of nursing Cusi, and she had been imagining a homecoming of her own. She had felt bereft when he had suddenly taken the arm away.

"Bathe yourself, too," she said to Quinti. "There are clean clothes for both of you in the bathhouse."

Quinti led Quilaco off, and the two mamacona, their masks raised, had Chimpu Ocllo up and moving toward her house, her arms draped loosely over their backs. Micay wiped water from her forehead and glanced at the watchful knot of bearers, then back at Chuqui Huipa.

"I will also have to wash. Will you take the children to the women's room and put them to sleep? I must see to the litter and check on the high priestess."

"I doubt these two will sleep," Chuqui said wryly, cocking her head toward Coca and Cisa. "But I will keep them out of the rain until their parents return."

Pulling her mask back up to cover her entire face, Micay went to the litter and began to remove the llama skins that had cushioned the interior, tossing them several feet behind her. She did this slowly and methodically, so as not to stir up any dust. When the interior was empty she pulled off the side and end curtains and the oiled cloth that had covered the top and added them to the pile. Then she stepped away herself, gesturing with her chin toward the bare wooden frame of the litter.

"It is safe for you to take away now," she said to the bearers, who had watched without offering to help. "We are grateful for your courage and the strength of your arms and backs. You have the blessing of Mama Quilla for your service."

The men bowed to her silently, then came and took up the litter and carried it away. Micay found herself standing alone in the courtyard with the rain soaking through the thin cotton of her shift and head cloth. She looked down at the sodden pile of curtains and bedding and quickly decided she could dispose of it later. Then she turned and walked toward Chimpu Ocllo's house, shedding all detachment as she went, determined to heal the woman who had made a healer of her.

WHEN MICAY finally got a chance to check on Paucar Rimay, she found Lloque Yupanqui sitting cross-legged on the floor next to where the sick man lay. He had tied a piece of cloth over his nose and mouth and was sitting at a safe distance from the bedding. Through the film of gauze in front of her face, Micay noticed that his hands were filled with colored cords. He caught her glance and held them up to her.

"I made them shortly after you told me," he sighed. "Then half of our staff was taken by the sickness, and I had no time to bring them. Then I simply forgot. I did not even know he was sick until your daughter told me today."

"It does not matter now," Micay said bluntly, kneeling down next to Paucar. "He does not have much time left. He has forgotten how to speak or swallow."

Lloque looked down at Paucar, whose bare torso was shrunken back to the bone and thickly covered with spots. He was lying on his side, motionless except for involuntary twitches, a bandage on the back of his head where he had reinjured himself during a violent fit of convulsions. Lloque extended one of his long arms toward Micay, holding out a memory cord that had only three strings of red, gold, and black. Micay took it from him and tied it onto Paucar's waistband, at the rise of his hip. She could feel the heat of his fever around his waist, but when she lifted his hand to place it over the cord she found that his fingers were cool and swollen and darkened at the tips. The hand twitched once where she had left it, then slid limply off his hip, leaving the strings in a tangled heap.

Micay looked across at Lloque and saw that he was leaning forward at the waist with his hands clasped in his lap, rocking slightly, so that his tears fell straight from his eyes onto the floor in front of him. She realized, before she forced herself to look away from his anguish, that this was the first time she had ever seen him weep.

"You were kind to him, my lord," she said when he seemed to have recovered his composure. "You let him have what was left of his life."

"Only so he could die like this," Lloque said bitterly. "Voiceless and abandoned, far from home."

"*We* have not abandoned him," Micay pointed out.

"We did not bring him here from Cuzco or send him to fight a senseless battle in Piura. But we are guilty . . . *I* am guilty. I have been blind and mute, with no sickness to excuse me."

"I do not understand, my lord," Micay said. "You cannot blame yourself for the sickness."

"No, it goes back much farther than that. We let him forget the kind of ruler he should be. We let him believe he owed us nothing, so that is what he gave us. Why should he stay to face the sickness with us?"

Micay hesitated, baffled by this sudden diatribe against the Sapa Inca. She did not know how Paucar's condition had inspired it, and though Lloque was staring back at her steadily, he did not seem prepared to explain. He shook himself and gave her a curt nod.

"Attend to your other duties, Micay," he told her. "I will watch over him . . . until he is gone." He glanced up as Micay rose to her feet. "Then I will go to Quito."

"The sickness is there, now."

"So is *he.* Perhaps it will open a place among his advisers."

Micay found this ambition as baffling as his anger, so she merely nodded and left him with Paucar, pulling down her mask and blinking as she stepped out into the sunlight. She reflected for a moment on the powerful effect the sickness had upon the healthy. It had aroused unexpected emotions in Lloque while deadening her own. She had not wept for Paucar yet, and she doubted that she would. Perhaps none of us are truly healthy anymore, she thought wearily. Then she went to tend to those who were sicker than herself.

PAUCAR RIMAY died the next morning while Micay was saying her prayers and getting dressed in the bathhouse. She helped wrap him up in one of his blankets, then summoned the masked litter bearers to take his body away for burial. Lloque Yupanqui followed the litter out of the compound at a distance, still wearing his own mask and still carrying one of the cords he had made for Paucar.

A small crowd of priestesses and mamacona was standing in front of the high priestess's house, all of them women who had been sitting with Chimpu Ocllo since her return, singing and praying for her recovery. From the shocked expressions they wore now, it seemed they had finally understood there would not be a recovery. For thirteen days Chimpu had defied the sickness as no other patient had, refusing to surrender to delirium or unconsciousness. She had participated in the prayers and songs, forgetting words occasionally but never losing track of the sense. The other women had been inspired by this display of willed coherence and had mistaken it for a genuine resistance to the ravages of the disease. The healers had been misled for a time, as well, because Chimpu continued to take nourishment and to sleep fairly peacefully. But when she was awake, she ignored their pleas that she lie still and conserve her strength, even though she could not conceal the increasing effort it cost her to sit up and speak. They had finally realized she had no intention of recovering; she was deliberately using herself up, spending the strength that might have saved her.

Micay found Quespi and Chuqui Huipa at the edge of the crowd and learned from them that the mamanchic had asked that her room be emptied and then had begun to summon the women—some individually and some in small groups—to say farewell. The first to be summoned was a younger cousin, Mama Ticlla, a round, heavyset woman who had served the cult as a priestess rather than as a healer. Chimpu had asked her to be her successor as the high priestess, revealing that she had already sent this recommendation to the high priest and the Sapa Inca.

Several mamacona had just emerged from the house, all of them weeping as they pulled down their masks. One of them composed herself and made her way to where Micay and her companions stood, though it was another moment before she was able to speak.

"The mamanchic asks for the three of you," she said with a special bow to Chuqui, "and the lady Quinti Ocllo."

Micay briefly took the woman's hands, both to comfort her and to make herself feel something. Mostly what she felt was frustration, a sense of being cheated of the chance to heal her benefactress.

"Quinti went to tend to Llampu," Quespi reported, glancing at Micay in apology. "You were with Paucar Rimay. I sent one of the midwives with her."

"I should go," Micay began. But the mama gave her fingers an urgent squeeze.

"You cannot postpone this, my daughter. Go to her now, while you may."

Chuqui and Quespi each took her by an arm and led her toward the high priestess's house, the other women stepping aside to open a path for them. Micay nodded in belated compliance, pulling up her mask as she followed Chuqui through the doorway and into the darkened room. Chimpu was sitting up against the far wall, cushioned all around with llama skins and attended by two mamacona. The three of them knelt down in front of her, Chuqui on her right and Micay and Quespi on her left. Chimpu's eyes were closed, so Chuqui introduced herself in a soft voice.

"It is Chuqui Huipa, my mother. Mama Micay and Quespi are with me. Quinti Ocllo is away tending the sick."

Chimpu coughed and pressed her hands against the silver Moon shield on her chest, taking several moments to gather her breath. One of the mamacona leaned forward and wet her lips with a cloth.

"You must hear me for her, then," she said finally, in a quavering voice. "Our mother has summoned me to her side, my daughters. Soon she will take me from my pain. So listen . . . you are the ones who will have to begin again, once the old ones are gone." She paused to gulp air, and when she spoke again, her voice seemed to have hardened. "With my death, your vows to this order are completed. I would ask you to make new vows to Mama Ticlla, but I cannot be certain she will succeed me. So I tell you only to choose wisely whom you will serve next. You owe everything to those who return your love, but nothing to those who do not recognize its value."

The three younger women exchanged a masked glance, startled by this heretical advice, which made no mention of duty or loyalty or respect for tradition. Chuqui especially seemed taken aback, her throat working but no words coming out of her mouth. Micay felt a surge of love that was both fierce and gratifying, and her smile stretched the gauze taut across her cheeks.

"Even now, my mother," she said, "you ask us to question and choose for ourselves."

"*Yes,*" Chimpu agreed, so emphatically that she began to cough and clutch at her throat. The mamacona held on to her until the fit subsided, dabbing at her face and lips with wet cloths. "Yes . . . you understand, Micay," she went on, appearing visibly weaker. "When this is over . . . when there is nothing more to be done here. Go to the mountains, all of you, and stay there until your hair has grown back. Let the healers in Quito look after the people there. You have earned the right to rest and restore yourselves. Then you begin again . . ."

She slumped back against the cushions, exhausted, and the mamacona signaled sternly that they should ask no more of her. They bowed and made the mocha, murmuring their farewells into their masks.

"Send in the younger priestesses," one of the mamacona said as the three women rose and backed out of the high priestess's presence. The sunlight was blinding, so it took Micay a moment to convey the mama's message to the women waiting anxiously outside. Most of them were weeping, and their curious glances made Micay aware that her own eyes were still dry. But this was no longer due to a lack of emotion, and she was not going to feign a grief she did not feel. Neither, apparently, was Quespi. Only Chuqui was weeping, quietly and helplessly, so they flanked her on both sides and walked her out away from the crowd.

"I did not know her," Chuqui moaned. "I was never allowed to know her."

Micay and Quespi exchanged a glance, and Quespi began to speak in Chacha, then caught herself and began again in Quechua.

"I knew her first through Micay. She made me take hold of my life and speak up for myself. Just as the mamanchic told us today."

"That has always been her message," Micay agreed. "She wanted to say it again clearly before she died."

"I have heard her," Chuqui declared in a thick voice. "And I will not forget."

"It is better to remember than to grieve," Micay said. She glanced around the courtyard but saw no one in need of immediate attention. "Come, let us go and tell Quinti. This was meant for her, as well . . ."

THEY HEARD the dismal rise and fall of a mourning song as they approached Rimachi's compound, and when they realized it was coming from within, they first hastened, then slowed their pace. The sudden appearance of the three White Women caused the singers to falter, and Micay and her companions faltered themselves when they saw the grieving people in front of Rimachi's house. Rimachi's mother had pulled her loosened hair over her face and was biting on the edge of her mantle, held upright by two younger women. Choque Chinchay was holding his grandson Topa in his arms, absently patting the boy's back, his eyes fixed on nothing. The midwife who had been sent with Quinti was waiting outside the doorway, wearing an expression of deep defeat.

"She brought forth the child," the woman reported, "but the strain was too much for her heart. The child had died some time ago."

"Where is Quinti?" Micay asked.

"Inside with the husband. He refuses to leave."

Micay led the way into the darkened room, which was bare except for the mats and blankets against one wall. Quinti was sitting with her back against the wall, her mask down and her hands on either side of a face that appeared as pale as Micay's. Llampu lay motionless on the stained blankets, her knees drawn up toward her chest and her bare feet sticking out of the blanket that covered her. Rimachi lay next to her, his face close to hers and one large arm thrown over her shoulders. A small oblong bundle lay on a blanket of its own a short distance away.

The three women pulled up their masks as they approached, though Micay left her eyes uncovered as she knelt beside Rimachi. Quespi squatted in front of Quinti and pulled her mask up for her, murmuring soothingly.

"Rimachi, my friend," Micay whispered. "Forgive me . . . I was with the mamanchic. I am so sorry . . ."

Slowly Rimachi rose up on one elbow and turned to look at her. His eyes were wet and clouded with pain, so that he seemed unable to focus on her, and his angular face could not stay still. In the dim light, the scar on his cheek looked like a fresh wound.

"What have I done, Micay?" he asked plaintively. "Why are the women I love always taken from me?"

Tears sprang up in Micay's eyes and her throat filled, so that she could not have given him an answer even if she had had one. She had imagined losing Cusi many times, and just the thought of it had been unbearable, beyond the reach of any consolation.

"I can still hear her voice, inside my head," Rimachi said. "How can she be gone?"

Turning away, he threw an arm and a leg over Llampu's body and covered her with his own. After a moment Micay rose and stooped to pry him off, tugging gently but firmly on his shoulder.

"You are exposing yourself to the sickness," she told him. "You must keep yourself healthy. You have a son to raise."

Rimachi's head came up. "Topa," he murmured, and by stages he rose to his feet, swaying over Micay like a great tree. "Topa," he repeated, starting past her toward the doorway. Micay hastily backed up and stepped into his path, putting a palm flat against his chest.

"You must cleanse yourself before you touch him. He cannot get the sickness again, but he could give it to the other children."

Rimachi stared down at her, slow to comprehend, but then nodded in weary compliance. He curled his fingers around her wrist, pressing her hand against his chest before releasing her.

"I will walk with you to the bathhouse," she offered, and he nodded again, grimacing repeatedly as he struggled to regain control of his face. Behind him, Quespi had gotten Quinti up and had begun to lead her toward the doorway. Chuqui was kneeling on the other side of Llampu, waiting for Rimachi to leave before wrapping the body for burial.

"It is good I have not lost you completely," Rimachi said gratefully as she took him by the arm and guided him toward the doorway. His attempt at a smile made her tears begin to flow again.

"We have all lost too much," Micay told him, weeping into her mask as they stepped out to meet the other mourners.

THE CEREMONIES of mourning for Chimpu Ocllo lasted for ten days, and then her mummified body, hidden inside a covered litter, was carried by the mamacona up to the Lynx House. A procession of some thirty White Women accompanied the litter to the edge of the city, walking toward the great peak that rose above the other mountains in the distance. Micay wished that she had the twins with her, and that she could just keep walking behind the litter until they reached the trail that led to the Rainbow House. But it was too soon to heed that aspect of Chimpu's parting advice. The worst was past in Tumibamba, yet while there were fewer new victims with each day, there were still some, and the convalescence of those who recovered was long. Their work here was far from completed.

They stopped where the street became a trail, allowing the litter bearers to go on without them, down through the terraced fields toward the river. The fields had been planted only haphazardly, according to the health of those who tended them, but where they had been the crops were high and rich green. Enough for the number of mouths left to feed, Micay reflected, though everyone strong enough to work would have to be turned out for the harvest. There would be no one to spare for Quito, where the sickness was spreading through the clans of the city, closing in around the palace perched on terraces above it. Huayna Capac was besieged and could flee no farther, and he no doubt wished that Amaru had made his palace less open to the sky and the city below.

When the litter was finally out of sight, Mama Ticlla turned the procession around and started back toward the high priestess's compound. She wore the silver Moon shield of the high priestess, though no word of confirmation had come from Quito and none was expected soon. It seemed unlikely any interest would be taken in their affairs until after the crisis in Quito was past, so the women of the cult had chosen to go on as they had, giving Mama Ticlla their loyalty and support without the sanction of official vows.

As they went up the street their ranks began to disintegrate, some of the women taking side streets off to their homes or the places where they were tending the sick. Micay was saying farewell to Chuqui Huipa, who was returning to the palace, when she heard a sharp cry and turned to see Quinti clap a hand to her forehead and stagger sideways. Another woman caught her before she could fall, and Micay and Chuqui moved quickly to hold her up. Her skin was already hot.

"I was so tired," Quinti groaned. "I see Llampu in all my dreams . . ."

Micay and Chuqui pulled up their masks before putting Quinti between them and draping her arms over their shoulders. Lifting her up onto her toes, they half carried her up the street, Quespi walking ahead to clear the way for them. Quinti closed her eyes and grimaced at the pain in her head, muttering apologies as they bore her along. Micay and Chuqui were completely winded by the time they arrived at the high priestess's compound, but their sense of urgency kept them going until they were able to lay Quinti down on a bed in the awning house. Then they ripped off their masks and collapsed on the ground, gasping for breath, while Quespi and the other women stripped off Quinti's clothes and began to wash her.

Micay was still recovering when the messenger called to her. He was standing next to one of the support poles, keeping it between himself and the women in white.

"Lloque Yupanqui sent me for you, my lady. The governor has the sickness."

"My father?" Quinti cried, rearing up in distress. The other women coaxed her back down, and Micay came over and knelt beside her, gazing at her thin, haggard face with concern.

"You must think only about your own recovery, my sister. I will go to Apu Poma."

"It strikes the older ones hardest," Quinti fretted. "You must not tell him I am sick."

"I will send word to Quilaco, and I will come back to see you later," Micay promised. "Rest until then."

"Rest," Quinti repeated helplessly, allowing her eyelids to slide shut. "Who can rest . . ."

THE GOVERNOR'S COMPOUND seemed deserted without the usual crowds of messengers and count takers, and the people living in the guest houses on the lower plaza had all gone inside. Micay sent the messenger to notify Quilaco and then climbed the stairs to the upper plaza. The twins saw her as she drew abreast of the awning house and came running out to meet her, stopping a few feet away when she held up a hand to indicate that she was not clean. She was aching to hold them, but she was also urgently aware that this was no time to be careless. So she knelt down to talk to them.

"Grandfather is sick," Cahua told her. "Runtu Caya said we cannot play near his house."

"Will he be dead, too?" Sinchi asked, squinting at her with his marked eye. She had told him about the deaths of Otoronco Achachi and Paucar Rimay, but she was not certain he could distinguish between being dead and simply being away, like Cusi and Uritu.

"I must go and tend to him and try to make him well," Micay said. "We must all pray for him later."

"Grandmother is tending him," Cahua reported. "Uncle Lloque did not want her to and they shouted at each other."

"How did you see this?" Micay demanded. "You did not go near your grandfather, did you?"

"No," Cahua said, putting on her most innocent expression. "I went to Grandmother and told her, and she let me walk with her over to Grandfather's house. Only we could not go inside. That was when Uncle Lloque shouted at her."

"He was *loud*," Sinchi agreed, his eyes wide.

"People forget their manners when they are upset," Micay told them, and rose to her feet. She saw Lloque come out of Apu Poma's house, wearing a piece of cloth around the lower part of his face. He pulled the mask down and braced his hands against his back, stretching and staring in Micay's direction. She looked down at the children, again wishing she could gather them up and carry them off to the Rainbow House.

"You may walk with me to your grandfather's house," she offered instead. "But then you must go back and wait for me in the awning house."

Sinchi immediately ran off toward Lloque, but Cahua walked along next to her mother with self-conscious restraint, just as she must have walked with Mama Cori earlier, accepting the reward for her watchfulness. Somehow she had known that Lloque had not told Mama Cori and that Mama Cori would want to know. Micay suspected she also knew, or at least sensed, that her telling might cause some trouble. She seemed to like seeing people forget their manners.

Lloque had squatted down next to the doorway and was talking to Sinchi, who was standing about five feet away.

"No, none of us will ever see him again," Lloque was explaining as Micay and Cahua came up. "It is not just you, my son. He has gone to Inti, Father of the Incas."

At Micay's quizzical glance, Lloque smiled tolerantly. "We were discussing Otoronco Achachi."

"He is dead," Cahua said flatly, with the disdain of one who is simply not interested. "Sinchi thinks he is hiding somewhere."

"It is good that Sinchi remembers him," Micay said, rewarding him with a nod of approval. "Now both of you go and wait for me in the awning house. I will be there in a little while."

The children complained halfheartedly but finally left them, and Micay squatted down close to Lloque so that they could speak without being overheard from within.

"I wanted you to see him first," Lloque said, "but your daughter was swifter than my messenger. And Cori would not be kept away."

"She might be the best nurse," Micay suggested.

Lloque grunted in exasperation. "I saw that he was washed and given clean clothes and bedding, but she will not take any precautions. Not even a mask! I think she welcomes the chance to die while performing her duty."

Micay paused for a moment, trying to think if there were anyone else who might be able to influence her. But the only person who came to mind was Cusi, and that thought only made her sigh.

"She has not spoken to me since I let Quinti go to the rest house. But I will try to make her hear me."

"Do not let her hurt you, Micay," Lloque warned. "She does not care what she says to anyone."

She has never cared what she said to me, Micay thought, but she went silently into the darkened room, pulling her mask up over her nose. Apu Poma was propped up against the back wall, holding a cloth to his forehead with one hand. His head appeared shrunken and naked without his earplugs and headband, and he opened his eyes only briefly when Micay knelt down beside him. Mama Cori was sitting on his other side with a coca bag and a lime container open in front of her and a silver spatula in one hand. She chewed vigorously, then spat a thin stream of coca juice into the cup in her other hand, but her eyes were on Micay the whole time. She chewed and spat again before she spoke around the lump in her cheek.

"I did not send for you, and I do not want your help."

"Cusi would want me to be here," Micay said stubbornly, calling on the only authority she thought might be respected. Mama Cori started to make a dismissive gesture with the spatula, but stopped when Apu Poma suddenly opened his eyes, letting the hand holding the cloth fall into his lap.

"I want her here," he said, his head wobbling slightly as he fixed his gaze on Mama Cori. "Why are *you* here?"

"I am your wife. It is my—"

"You have never wanted to be my wife," Apu Poma interrupted. "I knew that when I asked for you, but I did not think it would matter. I was an Inca and I had earned my reward. Well . . . we have both suffered enough because of that. You do not have to suffer with me now."

"I want to help you recover," Mama Cori said in a low voice.

"By driving Micay away?" he demanded. "How much have you learned about the sickness by sitting in your room?"

"Would you send me away, then?" Mama Cori asked, holding herself so still she barely seemed to breathe. Apu Poma coughed and winced at the pain, closing his eyes for a moment, and Micay was tempted to intervene, to stop him from spurning Mama Cori altogether. But he spoke before she had a chance, and his voice was surprisingly gentle.

"No, I want you to stay. But not because it is your right or your duty. Only . . . because I ask you to. Because I will be helpless soon, and I want to live through it. I want to see the grandson Amaru has given us, and I want to greet Cusi when he returns."

Mama Cori let out a long breath and glanced across at Micay, trying unsuccessfully to conceal her relief. His eyes still closed, Apu Poma suddenly went on.

"And no more arguing, Cori. Not with Lloque or Micay or anyone. Let the past be settled . . . let there be peace between us before I die."

"I have heard you, Apu Poma," Mama Cori said after a long pause. "Let it be settled, then. But we will not let you die."

Apu Poma grunted in apparent approval, then let himself slide down until he was lying on his back. He shivered, and Micay pulled a blanket up over him. Mama Cori had gone back to chewing and spitting into her cup.

"My lady, will you let me give you a mask and clothes that can be washed?" Micay proposed quietly. "We do not think the hair is so important, if it is properly bound back. The sickness seems to cling to soiled clothing and unprotected skin."

Mama Cori nodded reluctantly and spat into the cup. "I will wear whatever you bring me."

"I will get them for you now," Micay said, unslinging her medicine bag and leaving it on the floor as she rose. "The coca juice will be good for him when he next needs to drink."

She left the room without waiting for a reply and found Lloque standing just outside the doorway, nodding with satisfaction at what he had heard. He followed her out onto the plaza for a short distance.

"It is an uneasy peace," she told him bluntly. "That is why I did not tell her that Quinti is also sick."

The satisfaction disappeared from Lloque's face, but he nodded again. "I will tell her. Apu Poma has shown me how to make her listen." He spread his long hands in a rueful gesture. "Why does it take the threat of death to make us see?"

Pulling his mask up over his nose, he turned back toward the house. Micay turned in the other direction, toward her own house and the extra clothing she kept there. The answer to Lloque's question seemed obvious to her, and she wondered instead about twins who had forgotten how to speak and listen to each other, and about an Inca whose only wish, at the end, was to settle the past and have peace. She wondered if those who survived this would see any better, and if it would help them to begin again.

Cuzco

W HEN CUSI came out through the Patallacta gate, he immediately spotted the man Huaman Cachi had described to him. He was squatting near the stairs that led up to the street, pretending to be filling water gourds at the public fountain. Yesterday he had been part of a street-sweeping crew. Cusi went up the stairs and turned north on the street that ran alongside the Cassana, walking at a pace that would allow the man with the gourds to catch up. The real street cleaners were working again today, preparing the city for the great ceremony of mourning that would be held in four days. Cusi had been to only one such ceremony in his life—during a severe drought when he was a child—and he remembered being frightened by it. Now he simply saw it as the last duty he would have to perform here before he could begin the long journey back to Tumibamba.

He turned right at the end of the Cassana's enclosing wall but went only a few steps before he stopped and waited in the middle of the narrow street. It was not long before the man came around the corner with a mesh bag of gourds over his shoulder. He displayed what seemed to be the natural surprise of a commoner confronted by an Inca in the street, bowing quickly in deference and swinging wide to pass. But Cusi reached out and caught him lightly by the arm, bringing him up short.

"You are wasting your time, my friend," Cusi told him. "You do not need to follow me today."

"My lord?" the man said in bewilderment. "Do you want water?"

Cusi smiled at him. "Yesterday you had a broom. And the person who followed you as you followed me said that you later returned to the palace. I assume you made your report to Huascar?"

"I do not know what you mean, my lord," the man insisted. Cusi suddenly tightened his grip and pulled him close, speaking right into his face.

"I mean that it is Huascar himself who has summoned me today, and if you tell me one more lie I will take you there with me and demand that you be punished for your clumsiness."

The man did not reply, but he dropped the pretense of innocent bewilderment and stared sullenly at the ground. Cusi plucked an empty gourd out of the mesh bag and then let the man go.

"No doubt you are better at sweeping than filling water gourds. You were surely not meant to be a spy." He waved the gourd in dismissal. "Go . . ."

Cusi turned away without waiting to be obeyed and continued up the street, recalling how furious Yasca had been when *he* had discovered he was being spied upon. Only his strong desire to leave Cuzco without delay had kept him from killing the spy and dumping him at Huascar's feet. Cusi did not share Yasca's sense of outrage, though he wondered at Huascar's carelessness in making enemies of men who would soon be going back to report to the Sapa Inca. In other ways Huascar had tried to ingratiate himself with the heroes of the Chiriguano War. As the acting Regent, he had feasted them and given them fine gifts from the royal stores, including new earplugs for Cusi. Cusi had felt that his attempts at graciousness were at least partially sincere, though Tomay had insisted that Huascar could not distinguish a gift from a bribe, and Quizquiz despised him for offering warrior's toasts when he had not proven himself in battle.

Turning north again, Cusi started up the steep street that led to the great hill on which the fortress of Sacsahuaman stood. The Collcampata, where he was to meet Huascar, was a broad landing about halfway up the hill, an ancient gathering place that was used by young warriors during their initiation. Cusi had not been back to it since his own initiation, though he had heard that Huascar was planning some construction on the site. As he climbed the broad path that zigzagged up the face of the hill, he pondered the strange sympathy that he—alone among his comrades—felt for the Heir. Certainly most of what Huascar had done since becoming the Regent was detestable. He had filled the Council of Lords and the other high posts left vacant by the sickness with his uncles and cousins and supporters in the Capac Ayllu household, and he had begun a campaign of bribery and intimidation aimed at the other Upper Cuzco households, particularly the Iñaca and Vicaquirao. His spies were everywhere, seeking out hints of treason or scandal, anything that might discredit the households and give him cause to confiscate their property. He had chosen the most direct and vicious way to consolidate his power, and it had won him allies but no admirers.

Yet behind the arrogance Cusi sensed a man who was trapped and desperate, a man who craved respect but had never been allowed to earn it. He had languished here for fifteen years, heeding his father's wishes, only to see his father assign the rich northern provinces to another son. Perhaps he had also heard the prophecies that the Sapa Inca's power would fall into pieces and saw the Quito Regency as the first sign. Perhaps he had begun to wonder if the vision that had made him the Heir so long ago would have the power to survive his father's death.

On reaching the level ground of the Collcampata, Cusi was immediately accosted by several Cañari warriors from the Royal Guard, all of whom seemed to glance at the Iñaca badge on his headband with a certain scorn. But he was expected, so two of them led him forward along a chalk-lined path, past piles of stone and sand and stacks of log rollers. From the extent of the builder's markers, Cusi perceived that Huascar had something much more elaborate than a shrine in mind, though this was hardly a place to be building anything else. There were already a number of shrines on the Collcampata, one of which belonged to the Iñaca.

Huascar was sitting on a wooden stool in front of an offertory niche in the retaining wall. He was wearing the yellow fringe around his forehead, a cumbi-cloth tunic that was richly embroidered with his personal designs, and sandals trimmed with jaguar fur. Standing around him were four of his half brothers: Challco Yupanqui, Titu Atauchi, Atoc, and Huanca Auqui. They were his advisers and the commanders of the warriors under his control. Cusi held the gourd in one hand and made the mocha with the other, bowing his head and blowing kisses to the Heir.

"Be at ease, Cusi Huaman," Huascar said, waving the guards away. He gestured toward the men around him. "You know my brothers . . ."

"My lords," Cusi said in acknowledgement, bowing over the gourd. He had met them all at feasts, but he would not have claimed to know any one of them well. None of them had fought in the north, and in the presence of Cusi and his comrades they masked their envy with a false heartiness that often verged on disrespect.

"Did you require water for the climb?" the one called Huanca Auqui asked facetiously, pointing at the gourd with his chin. Cusi displayed it and listened to them laugh, recalling a time when he would have been insulted by such a jest and would have been compelled to make the man feel his displeasure. Instead he smiled and tossed him the gourd.

"As you see, it is empty. It was supposedly being filled by a man who was waiting outside the Patallacta. But his true duty was to follow me through the streets, so he did not complete his task."

Their smiles disappeared, and Huascar seemed to sit up straighter, regarding Cusi with interest.

"Who is this man?" he demanded.

"I did not bother to ask him his name. After following me yesterday, he went to report to the palace."

"Are you accusing someone in the palace, Cusi?" Huascar inquired, pushing the fringe of yellow cords higher on his forehead. Cusi saw that he enjoyed this game of badly feigned innocence.

Cusi shrugged. "I am merely expressing my surprise, my lord. There is no reason for anyone to have me followed. My purpose here is plain: I am waiting to participate in the ceremony of mourning, and then I will go back to Tumi-bamba."

"Yet you are staying in the Patallacta," Huascar pointed out. Cusi shrugged again, ignoring the implication that there was anything suspect in that.

"It is where I stayed after my parents left Cuzco for the north. I was brought into the Iñaca by my grandfather, Otoronco Achachi."

Huascar rubbed his chin and frowned, as if he heard Cusi's frankness as a challenge or a boast.

"Ninan Cuyochi has requested your services. Why is that?"

"I have served under him for many years. I was his scout in Chachapoyas and then commander of his scouts during the Carangui War."

"So you are loyal to him."

"Of course, my lord. As I am loyal to Yasca, my present commander."

Huascar cocked his head for a moment, then spat out the next question as if springing a trap.

"And why has your wife become a close companion of my sister, Chuqui Huipa?"

Cusi did not have to feign his surprise, though he kept himself from laughing out loud. "My lord . . . I have not seen my wife in almost five years. I have no idea who her friends might be now. I only know that the sickness is in Tumibamba and I must go back to help her fight it."

A common uneasiness passed across the faces of the brothers, who were not veterans of *that* battle, either. Huascar suddenly stood up and came to take Cusi by the arm, turning him around so that they could walk together toward the low wall at the outer edge of the landing. Cusi stepped carefully over the builder's lines and markers, pretending not to notice the way Huascar heedlessly trampled them under his fur-trimmed sandals. They came to the rampart and stood side by side, looking out over the gold and gray rooftops of Holy Cuzco. Huascar finally grunted with apparent satisfaction and turned toward Cusi.

"I find I like you, Cusi Huaman, though I did not expect to. I have not forgotten how you corrected me when we were boys, and I have heard other complaints about your loyalty and character since then. But you do not seem to match your reputation."

Cusi inclined his head and smiled. "If that is a compliment, my lord, I am grateful."

"I mean it as a compliment," Huascar insisted, and he thumped a hand against his own chest. "I am also misunderstood, Cusi. I am reputed to be many things I am not, simply because I have stayed here and performed the duties my father gave me. For this, I am thought to be lazy and lacking in courage and judgment. And because I demand the respect that is due the Heir, I am said to be arrogant and hungry for power."

Huascar stopped and looked at Cusi, who stared back at him expectantly, having heard nothing that seemed to require his agreement or denial.

"No doubt you have heard such things yourself," Huascar prompted.

"I have only been in Cuzco a short time, my lord, and I have not lent my ear to rumors."

"Perhaps you have heard them in Tumibamba or Quito," Huascar suggested, searching Cusi's face for an unspoken reaction. What Cusi felt was annoyance at this constant interrogation, but not enough for it to show.

"Your name is seldom spoken in those cities, my lord," he said bluntly. "They do not know you well enough to complain about you."

"I am the rightful Heir!" Huascar burst out. "And I am here in Cuzco!"

"Yes, my lord, that is well known."

"Does it mean nothing anymore? Have the Incas forgotten where they came from? *This* is the center, the heart of the Four Quarters!"

Cusi simply nodded, allowing him a chance to recover his composure. He did after a moment, lifting his chin for Cusi to respond.

"Some of us will never forget," Cusi told him. "But we have been away for fifteen years. There are boys and girls of initiation age who have never seen Cuzco and who do not think of it as their home."

"I will change that when I am Sapa Inca," Huascar vowed. "I will bring the Incas back here to live."

"There are many in Tumibamba who have yearned for that," Cusi acknowledged. "My mother is one of them."

"But you are not," Huascar said flatly. "You would leave Cuzco in a moment if you could."

"I would," Cusi admitted. "My wife and children and all of my family are in Tumibamba."

"And the estate my father gave you," Huascar added. "The Rainbow House. He must have favored you greatly."

"He did, my lord."

"Though not enough to give you one of his daughters."

"An impossible wish," Cusi said blandly, noting a dangerous glint in Huascar's eyes, though also a certain disbelief. Huascar did not know if the story were true, and Cusi's response was not meant to enlighten him.

"But that was long ago," Huascar said abruptly. "To what favor will you return now, Cusi? My father is in Quito with Ninan Cuyochi, and *he* no longer has any love for you. Though perhaps you are a friend of Atauhuallpa, as well."

"I know him," Cusi allowed. "He is a great leader in battle."

"He is second only to Colla Topa, now that Michi is dead and Yasca is here. And he is Iñaca, like yourself."

"I am aware of that, my lord. But the households do not have the same importance in the north that they have here. They do not bring men together or keep them apart."

Huascar narrowed his eyes beneath the yellow fringe, staring at Cusi as if he had spoken in a foreign tongue. Then he grunted scornfully.

"They have too much importance here. Their storehouses are overflowing and their herds are as large as the Inca's, yet they have barely enough members to conduct their rites. The retainers do everything for them. Perhaps, though . . . if what you say is true . . . they may not have the respect and protection they believe."

"I did not mean to suggest they have been forgotten," Cusi said. "Surely when the Incas come back to Cuzco, they will expect the holdings of their ancestors to be intact."

Huascar clenched one of his meaty hands into a fist and pounded the top of the wall next to him. "Of course! And they will also expect the next Sapa Inca to go out and claim new holdings for himself. But what is there left to claim? Tell me, Cusi; you have seen more of the Four Quarters than most men. What is left besides jungles and wastelands where only ignorant savages can live?"

Cusi had thought about this before coming here, but he took a moment to consider, not wanting his speech to seem rehearsed.

"There is very little that would be worth the efforts of an army," he said finally. "But is it not also the duty of the Sapa Inca to defend the lands we already hold and to make them prosper? There is much *within* the Four Quarters that will require attention once the sickness has passed. We will need a leader who can plan and build and make us whole again. Such a man would be revered, and all that he brought into the royal storehouses would be his."

Cusi ended out of breath, a bit surprised by his own passion. But Huascar merely crossed his arms on his chest and frowned in disgust.

"So you would have me send the warriors home and busy myself with building roads and terraces. And while I am waiting for the storehouses to fill, I suppose I should dress in rags and carry bags of seeds to the poor people."

"The Sapa Inca could bring dignity to any task," Cusi suggested, struck, despite Huascar's sarcastic tone, by the image of an Inca bearing seeds rather than a spear. "In the past the Sapa Inca has been proud to claim the title of Huachaycoyac, Lover of the Poor."

"You must be mad!" Huascar said incredulously. "Do you think I have no pride? What is wrong with you? You speak like an old woman, not an Inca warrior!"

For a brief moment Cusi was tempted to ask him what *he* knew about how an Inca warrior spoke. But insults no longer affected him as they once had, so he could simply entertain the rebuke without feeling compelled to voice it. He stared at Huascar impassively and then made a respectful bow.

"I am sorry if I have disappointed you, my lord. I know no better answer to the question you asked. With your permission, I will leave you now."

Huascar seemed to deflate slowly, opening and closing his mouth and lowering his arms to his sides. His disdainful expression grew slack with misgiving, as if he had only just remembered his intended purpose, now that it was too late to act upon it.

"You may go, Cusi Huaman," he said wearily. "There are no good answers. But you must remind those you see in Tumibamba that I am here and that I will not be denied what is rightfully mine."

"I have heard you, my lord," Cusi said, making the mocha as he slowly backed out of Huascar's presence. He retraced his steps along the chalk-lined path, nodding to the four brothers who were still standing around Huascar's empty stool, watching Cusi leave with expressions that seemed both curious and resentful. Cusi wondered what Huascar had originally had in mind for him. The talk of favor had been leading somewhere, most likely to a proposal that Cusi become Huascar's advocate or spy. But on whom was he to spy? Ninan was an understandable target, but Chuqui Huipa and Atauhuallpa made little sense as threats to Huascar's future.

As he passed through the Cañari guards and started down the steep path, Cusi decided such speculation was pointless. The important thing was that he had come through the interview without making another enemy for himself and without being made into an unwilling ally. He had even managed to make his speech about the ideal ruler, earning only a few insults for the attempt. There was clearly power in this distance of his, just as Raurau Illa had promised.

Yet his satisfaction with his own performance was more than offset by what he had seen of Huascar. Raurau Illa had also told him that his distance allowed him the choice of seeing warmly or coldly; of seeing into people or looking through them. He had tried to view Huascar through sympathetic eyes, but the man's jealousy and rancor were too deep and transparent. He would always feel aggrieved and thwarted, and it would allow him to follow his worst instincts. Though Huayna Capac had abandoned him here, he was still his father's son, and he would rule just as capriciously once the fringe was his.

Cusi slowed, thinking treasonous thoughts and understanding how the power of the Incas might be splintered and broken into pieces—understanding, too, how such a break might be necessary, as it had once been necessary for the warriors to stand in the plaza. The inevitability of it filled him with sadness, and he found himself looking forward to the ceremony, to the chance to grieve openly for all that the Incas had suffered and lost.

AS THE DAY of the Ceremony of Mourning and Penance dawned, the streets and enclosures of Holy Cuzco were empty and silent. All animals, and people who were not Inca by blood or privilege, had been banished to the outskirts of the city two days before, when the Incas had begun their fast. The Incas by privilege came into the great square of Haucaypata from its four corners, entering by means of the roads that went out from here to the four quarters of the empire. The blood Incas, in their household groups, emerged from the palace enclosures surrounding the square, carrying the mummies of their founding rulers on litters inlaid with gold and precious stones and draped with bright feather blankets. The only sounds were the shuffling of bare feet and the mournful lowing of a conch horn, for no one was to speak for the entire day.

The Incas by privilege assumed their places around the perimeter of the square, sitting motionless with their mantles pulled up to cover their heads and hide their faces in shadow. The households and their litters formed an inner circle, leaving a broad open space around the stone dais at the center. The golden images of Inti, Illapa, and the other Inca gods stood in a tight group upon the stepped stone platform, occupying the place that was otherwise reserved for the Sapa Inca and his priests.

At a signal from Huascar, several men from each of the households came out into the open area around the dais. Each was followed by a woman who carried ceremonial replicas of his weapons. The men wore fringed red tunics, feather headdresses, and shell necklaces, garments worn only on this occasion. Their faces and those of the women had been blackened with soot and stained with the juice of bitter red berries. They formed a deliberately irregular ring around the dais and began to move in silence, lurching and staggering like drunken dancers, obeying no rhythm except that of the grief they expressed with grimaces and gestures of supplication. The men punctuated their uncertain progress with random slaps on the small white drums they carried.

At first Cusi had to concentrate to make himself move awkwardly, but as he recalled all those who had been taken by the sickness, he found himself reliving the death march from Pomata. Soon he was staggering under the imaginary weight of Urcon's litter, blinking and twisting his face as the sickness overtook him. He fell once and crawled through the clean sand on his hands and knees, as he had seen men do when there was no one to carry them. He wept unabashedly for Urcon and Otoronco Achachi and Ayar Inca, maintaining only enough self-awareness to keep himself from speaking or crying out.

There were times when the circling stopped and a single man made a lone circuit of the dais, strewing coca leaves and humbling himself before the images of the gods. Huascar took the first turn at this, and he made his squat wrestler's body seem hunched and deformed as he crept around the circle, saluting the gods with the halting gestures of one who has failed and can only beg for mercy. Cusi whacked his drum and curled down into himself as Huascar passed, feeling at one with him, with all the Incas who grieved and asked to be forgiven. There could be no holding back now, no distance. The heart of every Inca had to be bared for absolution.

The dais was circled eight times while daylight lasted, then eight more times in darkness. Some dropped from fatigue and hunger, and those who continued seemed ever more abject and graceless. Cusi was still on his feet when the first light of dawn struck the thatched roof of the Suntur Huasi, the tower that stood in front of the Amarucancha. He looked around at the people scattered in clumps over the broad expanse of the square, who filled less than a third of the available space. As he often had during the night, Cusi thought of Otoronco, who had never forgotten how few the Incas truly were. At this moment they appeared few and forlorn, as they should. Light was spreading over the square, and soon they would be allowed to break both their silence and their fast. The ceremony was over, and perhaps the Incas would be spared and be allowed to renew their greatness. Perhaps they would fall to pieces as the huacas had warned. Cusi was too exhausted to hope for one or fear for the other. It was done; let the gods judge their worthiness and sincerity. Now he wanted only to find Yasca, so that the first words he would hear, when the Incas could again use their voices, were the war chief's promise: "Tomorrow we march for Tumibamba."

XVIII

KHUYAQ MASICONA:
Comrades

(A.D. 1526)

The Rainbow House

MICAY SAT with her legs dangling over the edge of the terrace, gazing down into the valley below. Sinchi leaned drowsily against her side, taking his afternoon rest with her, a habit that lingered from the time of his convalescence. He was almost back to full strength and seemed to be growing right along with Cahua, but he still tired more easily than he had before, and he did not hesitate to come to his mother for comfort. Nor did Micay do anything to discourage his attachment, savoring these moments of intimacy in the knowledge that they would likely disappear once he was fully recovered.

She felt his head come up and glanced upward herself, spotting the circling hawk that had drawn his attention. He had always been fascinated by birds and animals, and his dreams during the fever had been filled with wild creatures who spoke to him or chased him or performed fantastic tricks. Campa dreams, Micay had thought when he had told her about them afterward. He seemed to regard them as revealed truths, so that he looked on hawks and eagles and foxes as his friends and protectors and kept a fearful watch for bears and jaguars, even though he had never seen either of the latter.

"Huaman," he said solemnly, raising a hand in greeting. "He says my father is coming."

"Let us hope he is right," Micay said, wishing she could share his certainty. She had expected Cusi months ago and could not account for the delay, except that the sickness had spread southward through the highlands, carried by those who had fled Tumibamba at the first outbreak. Many of the post runners had been stricken, and the only information coming north from the cities along the Royal Road was the count of the dead.

"He is right," Sinchi insisted, separating himself from her so abruptly that she nearly fell over sideways. "Look, Mama!"

She followed his gaze down past the rope bridge to the place on the trail where visitors first became visible, a place she had looked to so often that her eyes found it unerringly. Her heart jumped, and she put a hand over the spirit brother beneath her shift as she counted the people moving along the trail, followed by three pack llamas. There were five: one woman and four men, two of whom wore earplugs that glittered in the sunlight. Micay blinked; in her imaginings, Cusi and Tomay had always come alone. She held back, afraid of being disappointed yet again. Then she was aware of the spirit brother under her hand, feeling its distinctive shape through both the pouch and the cloth of her shift. It seemed unusually warm, though perhaps it was the heat of her own blood, surging with excitement. When Sinchi scrambled to his feet, she did not hesitate to do likewise.

She found Sucso, the head retainer, standing a few feet behind her, squinting down into the valley with a frustrated expression on his lined face.

"Is it Lord Cusi?" he asked helplessly.

"I believe it is . . . at last," Micay said, and she went after Sinchi, who was running down the path to the waterfall, shouting to attract his sister's attention. Cahua had been watching the rainbows under the supervision of one of Sucso's daughters, and she came running to join them with her chaperone trailing closely behind. Micay sent the young woman back to her father with instructions to begin preparing a feast. Then she smoothed back her hair, which just brushed her shoulders, and caught up with the twins as they climbed the path to the greeting place.

"Maybe it is somebody else," Cahua was saying, clearly jealous that her brother had been the first to spot the visitors.

"Nooo . . . the hawk told me."

"Who are the others, then?"

"Tomay Guanaco," Sinchi said. Then he swallowed and went on swiftly, his tone rising hopefully, "And Uncle Uritu and Otoronco Achachi. And a woman."

"Uritu has gone home and Grandfather Jaguar is dead," Cahua told him. "And Mama already told us Tomay would be with him. You do not know any more than me."

"Maybe she is Grandmother or Aunt Quinti," Sinchi suggested, cocking his head and contemplating the possibility with pleasure.

Cahua smacked her lips in exasperation. "They are dead, too."

"They are *somewhere*," Sinchi said stubbornly. "Maybe Father found them."

"Enough," Micay scolded, as they reached the top of the broad outcropping of rock. "This is no time to be arguing. Let us greet your father with the proper respect."

The children obediently took up positions on either side of her. They waited in silence, hearing distant scuffling sounds that indicated the visitors' slow progress up the steep, winding trail from the rope bridge. Micay had to remind herself to breathe in and out and to keep her expectations in check. She remembered all the times Cusi had returned from the field in the past, often with death on his hands and a dangerous glint in his eyes, a man who needed to be soothed and slowly brought back to himself. This time he had fought not only a war but the sickness, as well, and he had been gone longer than ever before. He would just have learned of the deaths of his mother and Quinti and Runtu Caya—almost all the women in his family—and he would have seen the way his father had aged. Micay smoothed her hair back again and told herself not to expect a joyful smile in greeting.

Then he was there, bent forward at the waist as he came up over the rock, his golden earplugs swinging next to his dark face. Though his arms were concealed by the shield and battle-ax he carried in front of him, her first swift appraisal told her he was whole: no crutches or bandages, no limp or new scars. He even seemed taller somehow, though that illusion vanished as Tomay came up next to him and then as a warrior she did not recognize looked over both their heads from behind.

Cusi's eyes lit up when he saw her, and an expression of wonder crept onto his face as his gaze swept down to the twins.

"Look at you, my children!" he exclaimed softly, lowering his shield and weapon and shaking his head in disbelief.

"Greetings, Micay," Tomay said, grinning at her. "I have brought your husband back to you, as I promised."

"You are late!" Cahua said sharply, startling Micay and drawing a tolerant laugh from Tomay.

"Very late, little one. It is a long way from Cuzco to Tumibamba, and we stopped many times to help the sick people."

"I was sick," Sinchi announced as he trotted toward Cusi, who crouched down to meet him, setting his shield upright on its rounded edge. Sinchi stopped in front of him and put his hand flat against the feathered figure outlined in black on the glossy blood-red surface of the shield.

"A Hawk Man," the boy said, and Micay saw Cusi smile for the first time, a slow, appreciative smile that made him appear, for a moment, to be thinking of something else.

"The Hawk Man of Thunupa," he explained to Sinchi. "You must ask my friend Tarapaca to tell you about Tiahuanaco, where the Hawk Men were born."

The mention of a friend made Micay remember her manners, and she forced herself to raise her eyes from Cusi and to put aside her astonishment at that smile, which seemed extraordinarily calm and untroubled.

"Welcome to the Rainbow House, Tomay Guanaco," she said, smiling in belated gratitude. "Who else have you brought back with you?"

Tomay seemed to swell up with pride, his round cheeks dark with emotion and stretched taut by his smile. He turned and brought forward a short, heavyset woman who wore her black hair in a double braid, without a head-cloth. She appeared younger than Tomay, though she was bobbing her head in deference too rapidly for Micay to get a good look at her face.

"I have brought back my wife . . . the lady Ñupchu, from Hatuncolla."

Once she had completed her bows, Ñupchu looked up without a bit of shyness, her black eyes bright and inquisitive. Her face was as broad and round as a bowl, which made her smile seem enormous. As Micay returned the smile, her healer's eye noticed that the young woman was not in fact heavyset, but quite clearly pregnant.

"Welcome, Ñupchu. I see you have come here with a companion. Welcome to both of you."

Ñupchu laughed and patted her belly, supplementing her uncertain Quechua with energetic hand motions. "A good marcher, like the father. You are midwife, my lady?"

"I have helped," Micay allowed. "There are several good midwives at the Lynx House, not far from here."

Cusi left his shield and battle-ax with Sinchi and stood up, taking over the introductions from Tomay by motioning with his chin for the other two men to come forward. One was the tall warrior, who had a broad Colla face, a hooked beak of a nose, and friendly eyes. He wore his hair long beneath a knit cap and carried a Hawk Man shield identical to Cusi's. The other was still a boy, though almost full grown, wearing a mask of self-conscious dignity that made his dark, handsome face seem vaguely sullen.

"This is my comrade Tarapaca, who went with us to Cochabamba," Cusi said of the warrior. "He is a Lupaca from Cuzco, a captain of the Inca's warriors."

"My lady," the man said graciously, bowing over his shield, "it is an honor to meet you at last."

"And this is Huaman Cachi," Cusi went on, "who has come here as my apprentice. He is from Raurau Illa's village."

The boy met her gaze for the first time and seemed dazzled by what he saw, so that his solemn manner dropped away and he spoke in impulsive bursts. "My lady . . . you are . . . *beautiful.* Like in the stories."

"It is true," Tomay agreed with a laugh. "You look no older than when we left, Micay."

Obviously embarrassed by his outburst, Huaman Cachi had shrunk back next to Ñupchu, who laughed and patted his arm. Micay's cheeks grew warm, and she found Cusi staring at her, as if he were also seeing her for the first time. He came to embrace her, wearing that same calm smile.

"What stories?" she whispered, ducking out of the way of a swinging earplug as their bodies came together and fit.

"The stories the Running Boy told to earn his food," he murmured cryptically, pressing himself against her. "I will tell you later."

"Tell *me,*" Cahua demanded, tugging on his tunic so hard that both of them were pulled sideways. Cusi laughed but did not let Micay go, leaning back so that she could look into his eyes. She saw at once that he had changed, deeply, though not in a way that required taming. Indeed, it was his *lack* of violent emotion that seemed most striking and most uncharacteristic.

"I am back," he said simply, "but I am not the same."

"I see that. For once you have done nothing to frighten me."

"You see well!" Cusi laughed, and he embraced her again before stooping to lift Cahua up into his arms.

"Come, my daughter, let us lead our guests to their quarters. Sinchi," he called, glancing back over his other shoulder, "do you have my shield and weapon?"

Sinchi ran around in front of him, proudly displaying the shield, which he carried in both hands. "Hawk Boy has the war club."

"He means Huaman Cachi," Micay explained, having seen the older boy pick up the weapon. Cusi nodded absently and lifted his chin to Sinchi.

"Lead the way, then. We must wash off the dust of our journey."

"Tell me stories!" Cahua commanded, riding Cusi's hip as he started down the path after Sinchi. Micay hung back to walk with Tomay and Ñupchu, but she heard Cusi's laughing reply.

"Be patient, my daughter, and you will not be disappointed. We will be a *long* time telling all our stories . . ."

IT WAS NOT until late that night, when they were finally able to leave the children and slip off to the bathhouse, that Micay saw Cusi falter and shed his newfound detachment. She felt it, actually, since she could barely make out his features in the warm darkness and he chose not to open the ceiling trap to let in the moonlight. She was eager and aglow from the akha she had drunk, so she laughed at first when he fumbled awkwardly with her clothing, assuming that a similar eagerness had made him clumsy. When he still could not undo her belt, she helped him, discovering in the process that his whole body was rigid with tension, his breath whistling out his nose. She almost stopped then to ask him what was wrong, but sensed that he did not want to explain; that he needed to go through this struggle.

So she simply took over, as she often had in the past when he had been injured, stripping them both and coaxing him down onto their bed of soft towels. He was already aroused but seemed surprised by it, reacting to her caresses with shudders and sharp sighs. For a moment Micay felt a sense of power that seemed slightly perverse and cruel, and she realized that she had resented the calmness of his greeting after five years of absence. His apprentice had seen her beauty before he had; perhaps he did not deserve to end his struggle so easily.

Then her sympathy returned and shamed her, and she raised herself over him and helped him to enter, moving with ginger care as if he were indeed injured. She saw his mouth open in a silent cry as she began to rock gently back and forth, supporting her weight on the heels of her hands as she leaned forward to rub her breasts across his chest. His arms came suddenly around her back and he bucked upward, burying himself so deeply that the wind was driven out of her, and then he clung to her helplessly as spasms took him over and he jerked and moaned to a shuddering finish. It was all Micay could do to hang on until he was through, and then try to get her breath back as he lay gasping beneath her. He seemed to be sobbing or laughing, and when she raised herself off him, he opened his eyes and gave her a crooked smile, his face slack with relief.

"Are you back now?" she asked, lowering herself down beside him. It was several more moments before he had recovered sufficiently to speak.

"Forgive me, Micay. I—I am not always certain what I will feel. Sometimes I think I have no desires at all."

"You cannot think that now," she told him, and he smiled a true smile and propped himself up on an elbow to look at her. He ran his other hand down the curve of her body, his fingers light and searching.

"No, not about you," he agreed. "I should never have doubted what you would make me feel."

Micay shook her head dismissively. "I am not hurt. But you have not told me what happened to you in Raurau Illa's village. You were there a long time."

"It was not a story to be shared with everyone, though the men know parts of it."

"Tell me," Micay commanded, and he nodded and let himself down, turning to her so that both of his hands were free.

"I will," he promised. "But let me touch you, as well . . ."

THE TELLING proceeded slowly, interrupted twice by lovemaking that was both spontaneous and prolonged, so that they rested and dozed in each other's arms before awakening to talk some more. Cusi concluded his account as they sat soaking in the blood-warm water of the bath, the open trap overhead showing a lightening sky.

"You do not sound distant to me now," Micay told him, hearing the weariness in her own voice. "But earlier, when you spoke of how your father had become an old man, and how Rimachi and Quilaco seemed lost without their wives, you sounded cold and uncaring, as if you did not share any of their grief."

Cusi shrugged, sending a ripple across the surface of the pool. "I left my grief in Cuzco, at the Ceremony of Mourning. I grieved for all the deaths I had already seen and for all those I knew I would have to face here."

"But you did not know it would be your mother and your sister," Micay pointed out.

He nodded in agreement. "No. But I had seen enough of the sickness to know that it would claim someone I loved."

"But your *mother,* Cusi! I cannot believe you could grieve for her in advance and then feel nothing more."

"When my father told me, I remembered what I had felt at the ceremony, but I did not feel it again. I was simply grateful you and the children had been spared."

Micay stared at him, feeling the sharp, stabbing ache that accompanied her own memories. "I was with Mama Cori until the end," she said hoarsely. "When the fever was in her head, she kept calling out for you, like a frantic mother who had lost a child too small to fend for himself."

"My father told me how hard you worked to save her—and Quinti. Just as I tried to save Urcon."

"I miss them," Micay blurted, and she began to weep, feeling the ache even more keenly because he seemed not to feel it at all. "I cannot tell you how much I miss Chimpu Ocllo . . ."

Cusi rose and sloshed over to her and helped her to her feet, holding her against him. "Forgive me, Micay," he murmured. "You must tell me all of *your* stories."

"So many end sadly," Micay sobbed, clinging to him and weeping on his wet shoulder, weeping for the loneliness she had denied until now. Cusi held her tightly, stroking her back and whispering in her ear.

"Even if I listen from a distance, I will hear with my heart," he promised. Then Micay slumped against him and began to tell her stories of the White Women . . .

TOWARD THE end of his second month at the Rainbow House, Cusi rose at first light and went out with Sucso and two of his sons to complete the last of their repairs to the irrigation system. He was somewhat surprised that none of his comrades had joined them, but he could not begrudge them their rest after all the labor they had given him. An earthquake had shaken the mountains not long before their arrival, and while there had been little damage to the buildings, the terrace walls and irrigation ditches had cracked and settled in a number of places. Cusi and his friends had devoted a good part of each dry day to repair work, gradually restoring the foundation of stone and earth that made cultivation possible on the side of a mountain. This last piece of work had been delayed for two days by rain, but he and the retainers finished it off fairly quickly, even without the help of the other men.

The sun was well up by the time he returned to the compound, and the promise of a fine day made him contemplate a hunt or perhaps an excursion into the mountains with the women and children. He went through the courtyards without meeting anyone, finally coming out onto the open terrace overlooking the valley. All three of his comrades were there, squatting together on a sunlit patch of earth. They had etched some kind of plan or map into the dirt in front of them and were discussing it intently, Tomay doing most of the talking.

Huaman Cachi was the first to notice Cusi's presence, and he immediately jumped up and came over to where Cusi was standing. Cusi gave him a bemused look, pointing with his chin at the other men.

"Let me guess," he suggested. "A map through the mountains to the Guanaco House, bypassing the Royal Road and Quito."

Huaman Cachi nodded and shrugged. "It seems possible, the way he tells it. Is it?"

"Not for Ñupchu in her present condition. But you two cannot tell him anything about the trails here."

Huaman shrugged again. "I need to learn about maps, and Tarapaca knows them well."

Cusi glanced over at the warrior, who still had his head down with Tomay. He knows how to follow them, too, Cusi thought, when he wants to travel.

"My lord," Huaman said, breaking in on his thoughts, "may I have your permission to join Mama Micay and Ñupchu? They are sitting near the waterfall."

"And you want to sit with them?" Cusi asked in surprise.

"Mama Micay invited me to listen. She is teaching Ñupchu how to act among the Incas, in the palace and the court."

"Which palace? The one in Tumibamba is empty, and the one in Quito is closed to outsiders."

"That will not always be true," Huaman pointed out. "And as your apprentice, I should be prepared to go anywhere with you."

Cusi squinted at him curiously. "Who has been telling you these things? Has Micay taken over your training?"

"No, my lord," Huaman said hastily, ducking his head in embarrassment. "But she knows how new I am to everything . . . to cities and palaces and people of rank. She remembers how much *she* had to learn, all the things the Incas take for granted . . ."

"Even an Inca like me," Cusi snorted. "But go on, learn everything you can from her. She is a good teacher."

Huaman nodded vigorously, too relieved and grateful to be embarrassed, and trotted off in the direction of the waterfall. Cusi cast a glance at Tomay and Tarapaca, who were still absorbed in their map making, and then followed Huaman Cachi at a more thoughtful pace. Micay had obviously made him feel he had important things to learn, things Cusi would not think to teach him. That was no doubt true, but what had made her feel he needed to know them now?

He reached the edge of the terrace and looked down at the landing next to the waterfall, which hung behind it like a thick, ragged white curtain. Huaman Cachi had already seated himself with the two women, and Cahua was a part of their circle, too. Sinchi was standing near the low wall at the edge of the landing, watching the tumbling water and catching the mist on his face. When he saw Cusi on the terrace, though, he called something to his mother and started up the path toward him. Micay looked up briefly, nodding when she saw Cusi, then went back to her conversation.

Cusi suddenly realized that he and his son were the only ones who had not started thinking about leaving the Rainbow House and going back to cities and palaces. He wondered how long he had been missing the signs of restlessness. Tomay had mentioned the idea of an alternate route to the Guanaco House some days ago, but Cusi had thought his arguments against it had been persuasive. Perhaps he had not taken Tomay's arguments seriously enough.

Sinchi was toiling up the long stairs that compensated for the slope, but whenever he raised his head he was grinning. *He* was ready for a hunt or an excursion, any time it could be arranged. But Cahua never stopped asking when they were going back to Quito, insisting on some promise Micay had made to her long ago. And Micay . . . she was the most restless of all, though he had not wanted to see it. All those trips to the Lynx House, to pray at the shrine where Chimpu Ocllo was buried. And the times he had found her alone, sitting by the waterfall or at their sunset stone. He knew she was struggling with what she had lost, groping for a way to go on. But he had let himself believe she could find her answers here, just by thinking and praying. As if this were the proper place to begin—again . . .

"I am here!" Sinchi announced breathlessly, and Cusi laughed and went down on one knee to hug him. He had found he could not see his son coldly, even when he thought he should. Cahua already had a taste for power and prestige, and she could be astoundingly manipulative. But Sinchi seemed to have no instinct for deviousness; even the tricks he sometimes played were meant to be discovered.

"Are you done fixing?" the boy asked.

"Yes . . . finally. I came looking for someone to hunt with me, but everyone is too busy talking."

"I will go!" Sinchi assured him. Then he glanced back at the women and Huaman Cachi. "They are talking about Quito. Is Uncle Amaru there, or is he dead?"

"No, he is there," Cusi said gently. "He recovered from the sickness, and so did Parihuana. They have a son named Roca, a cousin you have never seen."

"Cahua wants to go because Chuqui Huipa is there."

"So is Huayna Capac and the sickness," Cusi said, half to himself. "But their restlessness makes them ignore that."

"What is—?"

"Restlessness? It is like having someone standing at your shoulder every time you turn around, pulling at your tunic and whispering in your ear. Telling you that you will never find what you want here; that you must go somewhere else to find it."

"Find what?"

"Whatever you think is missing from the life you have."

Sinchi clasped his hands over the top of his head and swayed from side to side, frowning thoughtfully. "Am I missing something?"

"Not that I can see," Cusi said with a smile, pleased he could answer so easily and honestly. He put his hands on the boy's hips and gave him an affectionate shake before rising to his feet. "Come . . . before we hunt, let us go talk to Sucso and Cachi. We will need to make a journey into the mountains soon, and they should begin gathering the supplies."

"Where are we going?" Sinchi asked, though he had already started out ahead, leading the way down the terrace.

"To a place sacred to your mother and sister. You have been there once before, though you probably cannot remember."

"To see Huaca Woman!" Sinchi exclaimed, grinning at Cusi's surprise.

"You remember her?"

"Cahua does. She tells me all the time and shows me the stone the Huaca Woman gave her. So I remember, too."

"Of course," Cusi murmured, shaking his head as Sinchi saw Sucso and ran to accost him. "Let us hope she remembers us."

THEY MADE their journey under a cover of gray clouds that dropped rain on them several times and never broke to show the sun. At times Cusi could barely recognize the landscape through which they were passing, so greatly had it been disfigured by the earthquake. The buckling of the ground had uprooted cacti, toppled trees, and dislodged large boulders, touching off rockslides that had blocked the trail in some places and torn it away completely in others. They were forced to proceed at a cautious pace and to make numerous detours, adding a full day to their march and testing their stamina and perseverance.

When they finally reached the cave at the base of the trail that led up to the huaca, they found it had collapsed inward on itself and was now filled with rubble. Rain was still falling intermittantly, blown in gusts by a swirling wind, so they stretched a blanket over some boulders as a shelter for their packs. Tarapaca and Huaman Cachi pulled their cloaks around them and squatted down to wait out of the wind.

"If I whistle, it is all right for you to come up," Cusi told them. "If I scream like a hawk, come running."

Cusi hefted his offering bundle, which was heavy with food, and turned back to Micay and the children. They each had a bundle of their own, and he saw that Micay had tied them into slings they could carry on their backs, freeing their hands for the climb. As he bent to tie the ends of his own bundle together, Cahua came over and opened her hand in a proud, secretive gesture, showing him the stone Macas had given her. Cusi nodded encouragingly and slung his bundle over his shoulder.

"You must keep that with you," he said, briefly resting a hand on his own spirit brother, which was again sequestered inside his waistband. He had not felt any need to take it back from Micay, but he had understood why, at this particular time, she needed to rely solely on her own powers.

She glanced at him now without really seeing him, then gestured for Cahua and Sinchi to fall in behind her and began to lead the way up the steep, winding path. The children obeyed immediately, solemn in their excitement, and Cusi took up the rear, behind his son. As he lifted his face into the wind, it struck him that the stink of sulfur was not nearly as strong as it had been, and as they climbed higher he began to see why. Many of the water holes where the hot springs had steamed and bubbled were now dry, their basins cracked and ringed with orange and red and brown sediment so that they looked like empty bowls set into the hillside. The foliage around them had begun to thin, as well, despite the recent abundance of rain.

Cusi took this as an unpromising sign and wondered if Micay felt any similar sense of foreboding. She was climbing steadily, looking back only to be sure the twins got safely around the many obstacles in their path. She appeared oblivious of the possibility that Macas might be lying in ambush, which made him scan the hillside with added vigilance. She had had some kind of premonition that Macas would not be here, but he did not know how much to trust it. She herself did not know whether to trust it, she had confessed, but that had not made her grateful to him for deciding, on her behalf, that this trip was necessary. She had accused him of looking through her and making choices that properly belonged to her, and though she had finally agreed to go, she had punished him by withdrawing into herself.

She was beginning to come out again, Cusi decided, watching the way she forged a new path around a rockslide. Even in their current state of devastation, the mountains were having their effect upon her, and the shared hardships of the past few days had brought all of them closer together. She seemed to have forgotten her initial reluctance to have Tarapaca and Huaman Cachi along, treating them at times like old comrades. Only Cusi himself had yet to benefit from her reemergence, but patience came easily to him now, especially in light of all the waiting he owed her.

On reaching a fairly level patch of ground near the top, Micay finally called a halt. The last part of the path, which wound up and around to the landing in front of Macas's cave, was clear ahead of them. Micay untied her bundle and remade it for carrying, then did the same for Cahua, leaving Cusi to look after himself and Sinchi. Cusi squatted in front of the boy and ceremoniously placed the refolded bundle in his outstretched arms.

"Now we go to Pachamama?" Sinchi whispered, and Cusi put his hands on the boy's shoulders and squeezed reassuringly.

"With open hearts and reverent faces," Cusi said. Sinchi nodded and put on a frown meant to show his seriousness, hugging the bundle against his chest. Cusi rose with his own bundle, and they lined up behind Micay and Cahua. For the first time Micay met and held his gaze, and there was a kind of rueful

recognition in her eyes, as if she understood the pointlessness of their separation but could not make up for it now. Cusi simply nodded and pointed with
his chin, showing that he was willing to follow wherever she led.

Bowing her head over her offering and moving at a stately pace, Micay led
them up the path. Cusi silently asked Pachamama to forgive him and kept his
eyes raised, straining all his senses for signs of danger. The wind blew damply
in his face, but he heard no sounds beneath it and saw no movements beyond
those of birds and insects. Micay was the first to step up onto the landing, and
she stopped so abruptly that Cahua bumped into her before finding a way
around. Sinchi went right behind his sister, and Cusi bounded up on Micay's
left, seeing nobody in front of him but much too much sky. It took him a
moment to grasp what he was seeing: fully half the landing had broken off and
fallen away, drawing the edge of the cliff that much nearer to the mouth of
the cave. A jagged fissure split the ground and ran back into the cave, its
branches snaking out over the cracked surface of what remained of the landing.

Micay stared out at the drop to the canyon below, then turned to Cusi.

"Wait for me here," she said.

"Walk lightly," Cusi advised, and she went slowly toward the cave, stepping
carefully over the cracks and testing the ground in front of her. Sinchi cocked
his head and looked up at Cusi with his marked eye.

"What is wrong? Is Pachamama gone?"

"Pachamama is everywhere," Cahua reminded him scornfully. "But the
Huaca Woman is gone."

"Part of the mountain is gone," Cusi told them. "You see where the cliff
broke off when the earthquake struck . . ."

They all turned to look at the open semicircle where the cliff had sheared
off cleanly, as if bitten away by a pair of huge jaws. Before Cusi even saw her
move, Cahua was out beyond his reach, walking toward the place where the
fissure split the edge of the cliff.

"Cahua!" he called, but she ignored him, proceeding to the very edge of the
remaining ground. He heard stones and dirt falling below and dropped his
bundle, but he knew he dared not go after her. Sinchi started to, but Cusi
caught him by the arm and held him back.

"No, my son. She must return by herself."

Somehow Cusi's voice remained calm, but his heart was pounding and his
palms were wet as he watched his daughter stand teetering on the edge, peering
down intently at whatever lay below, as if searching for a place to land. Cusi
felt the force of the wind again and tried to call to her, but he found he had
no voice at all.

Then Cahua's head came up and she stepped back slightly, still holding the
offering bundle in her arms. She said something Cusi could not hear and
released the bundle with a shooing motion that sent it plummeting off the cliff.
Then she cocked her arm as if to throw something else, and Cusi remembered
the stone in her hand and sucked in a breath. Young as she was, she knew
better than to show such disrespect for a sacred object; he could not believe

she had discarded her offering so casually. But she changed her mind and kept the stone, and as she turned to walk back toward him Cusi got down on one knee to greet her, feeling too relieved to feign anger.

"Why did you do that, Cahua?" he asked. She cast a puzzled glance over her shoulder, as if there were nothing extraordinary about what she had done.

"She is down there," she said simply. "The Huaca Woman."

"How do you know?"

Cahua shrugged. "I just knew. Then I saw the cloth like Mama talked about, and some bones."

Cusi grunted and rested his hands on his upraised knee, staring at her with bemusement. She had no idea that she had endangered herself and terrified him more thoroughly than any enemy ever had. He looked up to see Micay come out of the cave, blinking at the light and still carrying her bundle. She shook her head several times as she approached, as if trying unsuccessfully to clear it.

"There is no sign of Macas," she said in a dazed voice. "And the huaca is dry. The water has disappeared completely."

"Macas is dead," Cahua reported. "She is down there."

"Down where?" Micay said, glancing at Cusi in bewilderment. Cusi pointed with his chin toward the cliff.

"She went to the edge and saw bones, and the sunrise mantle. She dropped her offering down."

"But I kept my stone," Cahua said, displaying it in her open palm. "She still has the one I gave her."

"Of course," Micay agreed, commending her with a nod. She appeared calmed rather than bemused by Cahua's uncanny assurance, and Cusi saw the expression of stunned disbelief fade from her features.

"Should we go down for the remains?" he asked.

Micay hesitated only briefly before shaking her head. "No. Pachamama has already taken her back. Let us leave our offerings and go. There is nothing more to be done here."

"It is all gone now," Cahua added, nodding solemnly. Cusi glanced around at them, then scooped up his bundle and rose to his feet.

"Is the huaca dead?" Sinchi asked suddenly, and Micay responded with the same blunt decisiveness.

"It has gone back into the earth, into the womb of Pachamama. She is telling us we must find our own way and our own power. The Old Ones are gone, and we cannot look to them for help."

Cusi stared at her, hearing resignation but no despair in her voice. He swallowed the apology he had been preparing, realizing it would not be appropriate. He had expected to find *something* here, but perhaps it was this absence she needed to confront. He extended his bundle, and she let him place it on top of her own.

"Give yours to Cahua, Sinchi," she said. "She will take it into the cave for you."

Sinchi obediently handed his bundle over, and Micay and Cahua walked together toward the cave. Cusi rested a hand on Sinchi's shoulder, and the boy leaned affectionately against his leg.

"Your mother and sister are brave women," Cusi told him.

Sinchi made an incredulous noise. "As brave as a warrior?"

"Perhaps even braver," Cusi said, watching them disappear into the cave. "Few warriors have the courage to face an enemy they cannot see. But *they* do not turn and flee."

"They must be brave, then," Sinchi agreed, and he let out a low Campa whoop that took Cusi by surprise but seemed, finally, to be the most appropriate response to what they had found here.

Tumibamba

THE MESSAGE from Apu Poma had been waiting for them when they arrived back at the Rainbow House. It said only that the sickness had entered the palace in Quito, and that Amaru was being blamed for having let it in. Without pausing to discuss it, they had gathered their belongings, bid farewell to Sucso and his family, and marched back to the city as swiftly as Ñupchu and the children would allow them to travel.

Apu Poma came out of the awning house in the lower plaza to greet them, summoning servants to take care of their packs and llamas and bring them food and water. He led them over to the pools at the base of the terrace gardens, where they could sit and talk in private.

"We are most hungry for knowledge," Cusi said, propping his shield and battle-ax against the retaining wall before taking a seat on top of it. Apu Poma sat down on the edge of one of the pools and let Sinchi and Cahua climb up next to him, and the others arranged themselves in a loose circle around him.

"There is little more I can tell you," Apu Poma admitted. "Only that Fempellec and another man whose name I did not recognize have been accused along with Amaru. It is difficult to get any information from Quito."

"Can we go there?" Cusi asked, and Apu Poma cocked his head and raised one shoulder in a doubtful gesture.

"I can give you passage to the last guard post on the Royal Road, but only a pass from the Sapa Inca will allow you to enter the city itself."

"Is there a way to send a message to the palace once we reach the guard post?"

"To whom?" Apu Poma inquired. "Even now, I doubt Huayna Capac would welcome your presence."

"Ninan Cuyochi might. Or Chuqui Huipa. Either one could get us passage into the city."

"I do not know what power anyone has there. Perhaps your friend Rimachi knows something. He sent a message this morning asking to be notified of your arrival. The guards at the gate should have seen to it by now." Apu Poma paused and looked around at the group, his gaze finally coming to rest on Micay. "But you are not all thinking of going?"

Micay glanced at Cusi, who lifted his chin, encouraging her to speak. "That is what we have decided, my lord," she told him. "No one wished to be left behind to wait."

"But you have not all had the sickness! This little one here, for example," he added, putting his arm around Cahua, "and you yourself, Micay."

"And Huaman Cachi," Micay allowed. "We will have to protect ourselves, as we did when the sickness was here."

"We will be White Women," Cahua declared, poking her grandfather in the ribs with her elbow. "We will heal everyone."

"No doubt you will," Apu Poma said, surrendering with a weary shrug that made him seem more a grandfather than a governor. He appeared to have aged another few years in the months since Micay had seen him last, and he had a habit now of dropping his gaze to the ground and falling silent for prolonged periods. They were all sitting silently when Rimachi arrived, giving Tomay a hard slap on the shoulder as he walked by him into their midst. He was carrying a slender baton that had been painted with stripes of royal blue.

"I assume you have come down from the mountains in order to go to Quito," he said to Cusi after bowing perfunctorily in Apu Poma's direction. Micay saw Cusi's eyes fasten on the baton, which looked like a mere stick in Rimachi's huge hand.

"You have a way to get there?" Cusi asked, and Rimachi gave him a sardonic smile that made the scar on his cheek curl inward. He still had not regained all the weight he had lost during his bout with the sickness, and there was a reckless glint in his eyes that reminded Micay of tending him when he was delirious.

"My father is sick," he said bluntly, "and I am going to take his place with the Guard and see what I can do for him. Since I owe this privilege to your uncle, I thought I should share it with you."

"Lloque?" Apu Poma interrupted, all his alertness back. "Has Huayna Capac made him a Rememberer again?"

"Apparently." Rimachi shrugged. "I was told that he had spoken on my father's behalf and mine, and that he had persuaded the Sapa Inca that outsiders who had already had the sickness were safe." He displayed the striped baton. "This pass is proof that he spoke well."

"When do we leave?" Tomay asked.

Rimachi grinned. "Tomorrow. Good, we will have all the brothers. What about you, Micay? Will you come and help tend to my father?"

"Of course," Micay said. "We are all going to Quito."

"The children, too? I had planned to leave Topa with my mother."

"Bring him with you. He will be company for Sinchi if Cahua comes with me."

"The guards will never believe that that pass was meant for such a mob,"

Apu Poma warned, but Rimachi straightened up and expanded his chest, wearing the same sardonic smile.

"I would like to see them express their disbelief to me. Or to Cusi Huaman and Tomay Guanaco. I think they will prefer to honor the pass."

"We leave tomorrow, then," Cusi concluded, jumping down off the wall. "It will be good to march with you again, my brother, even if it is not to war."

Rimachi hooded his eyes and looked down his long nose at Cusi. "Is it not a war? There will be as much pain and dying."

"We will fight it together," Micay declared, coming up to join them. Rimachi gave her the same veiled look.

"Everyone fights this alone, no matter who is there. Be ready to march at dawn."

With a parting bow to Apu Poma, he turned and walked toward the compound gate, tapping the baton against the side of his thigh. Cusi glanced at Micay, appearing bemused.

"He must still be grieving," he suggested. Apu Poma stood up abruptly, surprising the twins into standing up with him.

"It is possible to survive the sickness, yet never recover from it," he said in a taut voice. Then he bobbed his head in a gesture that included all of them. "I will eat with you later."

He, too, walked away, leaving Cusi standing awkwardly behind. Micay laid a sympathetic hand on his arm.

"We will fight it together," she repeated, and she gave his arm a squeeze that made him look at her. "And we will do much more than survive . . ."

Quito

T HERE WERE four warriors stationed outside the entrance to Amaru's compound, but they were Cañaris who knew Rimachi, and they readily acceded to his request that they allow Cusi's party to enter. Their captain said that their orders were to confine Amaru Inca and permit him no visitors, but he doubted anyone from the palace was going to come out to check.

"You are the first Incas we have seen in months," the man said dryly, bowing to Cusi and Tomay to show that his disdain was not directed at them. Rimachi nodded and waved the party through, drawing Cusi and Tomay aside.

"I must report to the palace and see if they will allow me to enter."

"You know whom to see inside," Cusi said.

"Of course. Send the Lupaca to the main gate to ask for messages. I will refer to you two as Yasca's representatives and to Micay as the White Woman."

Cusi nodded, then glanced at Tomay and hesitated. Rimachi snorted and poked him in the chest with the striped baton.

"What is it? Are you going to tell me to be careful?"

"You used to tell *me* that."

"Did you ever heed me?"

"Probably not," Cusi admitted. "But I needed to hear it."

"Just as you need to hear it now," Tomay said earnestly. "We escaped our youth without throwing our lives away. Let us not grow careless now."

Rimachi snorted again, but then gave them a grudging smile. "I have heard you." He stepped back and waved them toward the gate. "Go see to Amaru. He has been careless all his life."

"I am afraid he is right," Cusi said as he and Tomay turned and went through the gate. They found Micay holding little Roca, the nephew Cusi had never seen, and Cahua had hold of Parihuana's hand and was introducing her to Ñupchu, Tarapaca, and Huaman Cachi. Sinchi had already taken Topa off to see the fish.

Parihuana was weeping when Cusi finally got the chance to embrace her, and she felt thin and very taut in his arms, like a bowstring pulled to its limit. She wiped her eyes on the edge of her mantle and pointed with her chin toward a thatched hut in the lower corner of the compound, beyond the garden that filled the first level.

"Amaru is there, alone. We did not know you were coming."

"He should have expected it," Cusi said, and he excused himself to go to his brother. The garden was flourishing because of the rain, the untended foliage sprawling out to block the narrow, winding path. Cusi noticed the weeds and unpruned limbs and decided this would be their work while they waited to hear from the palace. He pushed past a last overgrown bush and came into the open-sided hut with the great mound of dirt against the back wall. Amaru was sitting on the ground with his back against the base of the miniature mountain, his head resting just below the first level of the model palace.

"So this is Little Quito," Cusi said quietly, admiring the clay walls and houses. "My children have told me about it."

"Cusi," Amaru managed, lifting his chin and staring. Cusi sat down on a stool across from him and stared back.

"The guards outside said they had not seen another Inca in months. But surely *you* are not surprised to see me."

Amaru's jaw tightened, and he closed his eyes for a moment, as if struggling to control his emotions. His voice was flat when he spoke, and his eyes were bloodshot and weary.

"No, I knew you would come if you could. This is disgusting, Cusi; I should not require your rescue. But now that you are here, perhaps you will help me kill them."

"Who? Who has accused you?"

"There are several, but the ones who deserve to die are Titu Atauchi, Mama Huarcay, and Mama Pura."

"Who is accused besides you and Fempellec? I heard there was another."

Amaru nodded. "One of the court retainers, a man named Machacuay. He was the first to be stricken by the fever, and Titu Atauchi had him beaten and interrogated until he put the blame on Fempellec. Now they want him to live to prove the truth of his accusation, so he has not been thrust out of the palace like the others who took sick."

"But . . . how does any of this involve you? You have already had the sickness, and I assume you have been kept out of the palace like everyone else."

"I have. But Machacuay knew that Fempellec had sneaked out of the palace on several occasions to visit me. It is not so hard; many others have done it, including Machacuay himself. When that was beaten out of him, Mama Huarcay and Mama Pura came forward claiming knowledge of the evil nature of those visits."

Amaru turned his head aside and spat into the dirt.

"You still could not have given him the sickness," Cusi pointed out.

Amaru spat again. "That does not matter to them. Machacuay had many other friends besides Fempellec, and some of them are sick now, too. But no one else has been accused."

"They are not even your enemies," Cusi said ruefully, "but mine and Fempellec's and Micay's."

"You will help me kill them, then?"

"No," Cusi said without hesitation. "As much as they deserve it, no. Murder would not free you, Amaru."

"It would relieve my disgust. These people have made me a prisoner in my own city, while they hide behind walls I built myself! I wish I could bring the sickness to all of them!"

"It may already have been done," Cusi told him. "But we are not without friends inside. Ninan Cuyochi owes me more than friendship, and Micay has great influence with Chuqui Huipa, as you know. And Lloque Yupanqui is there, as well. We will see that the charges against you and Fempellec are dropped."

Amaru examined him for a moment, frowning skeptically. "You say that so calmly, Cusi, as if you expected the Sapa Inca to greet your return with joy. Did you leave your memory in Cuzco?"

"Only my anger and impatience," Cusi said, "and I expect I will have those back before long. Where is Fempellec being kept?"

"Somewhere in the palace."

"Has he had the sickness?"

"No. He helped nurse us, but he was careful, the way Micay had said to be." He looked at Cusi in sudden alarm. "He was healthy the last time I saw him."

"Micay should be able to get to him through Chuqui Huipa."

"But if he is sick, there is no telling what the fever might make him say."

"No, there is not," Cusi agreed. "But we will do what we can to protect him. What about Sinchi Roca? Would he still speak for you?"

"He would, but the sickness took him two months ago. Ninan and Atauhuallpa are friends, though."

Cusi slapped his hands onto his knees and stood up. "For now all we can do is wait for Rimachi to arrange entrance for us. Come, you must meet Tomay's wife and my other comrades."

"One thing you should understand," Amaru said, staying seated. "Before you arrange anything for me. I will not confess my crimes to the high priest or any other man. Not if it means my life! They have no right to judge how an Inca takes his pleasure or who he chooses to love. And Cusi . . . I will not disown Fempellec or allow him to be punished in my place."

"Good," Cusi said simply. "I did not bring either of you back from Chimor so that you could be judged here. Now will you come? I have not properly greeted my nephew, Roca."

Despite himself, Amaru smiled, then pushed himself to his feet. "Micay warned me long ago that we were not immune here. She told me there was no place Huayna Capac could not spoil."

Cusi grunted and turned to lead the way out of the hut. "He has not spoiled your garden. Neglect has done that."

"The old retainer died of the sickness," Amaru explained. "We have only two women left to serve us."

"Now you have a brother," Cusi told him. "Tomorrow we will go to work on the garden. It will take your mind off of murder."

"Perhaps," Amaru allowed, limping up to walk next to him. "Perhaps . . . but the thought will never be far."

THE ENCLOSURE was on a narrow side landing that was attached to the rest of the palace by a single walled staircase. Its rough stone-and-mortar buildings had previously been used for storage and as temporary sleeping quarters for some of the palace retainers. Now, apparently, those functions had been combined, and the compound was being used to store the sick and dying away from the man they had served.

Micay stopped at the top of the ramp and squatted down in front of Cahua, who was a replica of herself in white, even to the small medicine bag hanging under one arm. Micay raised the girl's gauze mask up over her nose, testing her with a last question.

"When must you cover your eyes, as well?"

"When someone sick is being moved around," Cahua said through the cloth, "and there might be dust in the air."

Her eyes above the mask had a gleam that reminded Micay of Cusi, of the Cusi who could not pass a huaca or holy place without going to see it himself. Micay had been unable to dull that gleam, not even with long periods of serious instruction and a detailed account of the horrible things a healer had to face. Cahua had decided in Macas's cave that she did not want to play anymore, a decision that had somehow grown into an urgent desire to become a healer. Micay was not certain she was doing the right thing in indulging her daughter's precocious desire to be a part of the larger world, but Cahua had given her little choice. She had simply stopped acting like a child who could be left behind.

Micay pulled up her own mask and led the way toward the unguarded gate, bracing herself for what lay ahead. She could hear coughing and moaning as they crossed the threshold, though the central courtyard of the compound was empty in the bright sunlight. The sick sat or lay in the shade of the open storage shelters, amid bales of wool and stacks of firewood. Micay noticed that the doorway in the far wall—the exit to the staircase—had been sealed off with a slatted wooden barricade.

A woman wearing the light blue of the palace retainers came out of one of the shelters to greet them. She wore a mask over her nose and mouth but had braided her hair and wrapped it around her head rather than cutting it, and there was no oil on her exposed skin. She cast a startled glance at Cahua before bowing to Micay.

"Have you come to help us, my lady?"

"We have both come. May we see Choque Chinchay, the commander of the Royal Guard?"

"Ah, the Cañari," the woman said, leading them toward a shelter just to the right of the barricaded doorway. "He is in his eighth or ninth day. His son has been coming to tend him."

"From inside the palace?"

"No one was allowed before," the woman shrugged. "People were pushed out to us and no one could go back inside. But that has changed somehow; I do not know why."

"Why are you here?" Micay asked, and she shrugged again.

"My husband caught the fever a month ago, and I came with him when he was sent here. When he died, I had nowhere else to go. There are five others like me, and we do what we can for the sick ones. The Sapa Inca's daughter sent us these masks and instructions on how to protect ourselves."

"You have obviously done well," Micay commended her as they entered the cool dimness of the shelter. There were two men sitting propped up against some bundles and coils of rope, and two more lying flat on the ground. Choque Chinchay was easy to spot because of his size and the relative neatness of his blankets and the materials arranged around him. He was unconscious and breathing fitfully, and his bare arms and chest appeared pebbled with the spots. Micay unslung her medicine bag and knelt beside him, and Cahua did the same on the other side, though she did not get as close.

"Has he had food or water today?" Micay asked the woman, who shook her head.

"I have been waiting for the son. He can lift him by himself."

"I will tend to him," Micay assured her, "and to the others in here."

The woman bowed in gratitude and left them, and Micay looked across and found Cahua staring at her reproachfully.

"*We* will tend to him," she corrected herself, and Cahua nodded primly, her lips pushed out against the mask. Micay poured clean water into a bowl and wet a sponge, then began to wash Choque's face and neck, speaking to him in a soothing tone. Cahua crept closer and patted him dry with a towel, giving Micay a wide-eyed glance when she felt the heat of his fever through the cloth. Micay carefully dripped water onto his lips, which made him cough and mumble, his shoulders twitching in a sudden spasm. Cahua pulled back but then returned, watching intently as Micay gave him a few more drops, let him cough and subside, then gave him a few more, persisting until she could see him swallow. She directed Cahua's attention to the movements of his throat, and the girl let out a cry of recognition and nodded vigorously to show that she understood.

Then Cahua sat back on her haunches and began to sing, not one of the healer's songs Micay had taught her, but a planting song about raindrops streaming down to soak the earth and quench the thirst of Pachamama. Muffled by the gauze, her high, thin voice seemed solemn and plaintive, and Micay saw the men sitting against the bundles lift their heads, shielding their eyes with raised hands. It was the perfect song to sing to them, and Micay smiled into her mask, feeling awed by her own daughter. It was a strange and awkward sensation, a thrill that was half a shiver.

When Cahua finished her song, one of the seated men called something to her, and Micay suggested that she take them some water.

"Use the gourd in your medicine bag," Micay said, and Cahua retrieved the long-necked vessel and went to perform the task. As she finished washing Choque, Micay listened to her talking to the men, telling them who she was and why she was here. She seemed to be referring to Choque as her uncle's father, and Micay heard her mention Chuqui Huipa's name more than once.

Then a large shape blocked out her light for a moment, and Rimachi squatted down in the place where Cahua had been. He peered down at his father's face and then looked up at her with an inquisitive frown.

"He took some water," Micay told him, "and he seems to be resting peacefully."

"You mean the pain has left him senseless. There is no rest until the fever breaks."

"You would know that better than I," Micay allowed. "He is strong and fit for a man his age, and I can see that you have tended him well."

"Once I got to him!" Rimachi said bitterly. "Almost nothing was done for him before that. These women are not healers; they are only here by chance. This is the care he gets for all the years of service he has given . . ."

"We all know the man he serves," Micay said, ignoring his anger. "How is it that you can come here and then go back inside?"

"Someone, probably Lloque Yupanqui, persuaded Huayna Capac that it was safe to let certain people pass in and out, if they purified themselves. We will have to discard our clothes and bathe before we can enter. Chuqui Huipa gave me clean clothes for you, white ones."

"My daughter is with me," Micay said, pointing with her chin. He swiveled on his heels, and they both watched as Cahua tipped the long-necked gourd up to one of the men's lips, giving him just a little before lifting the gourd away. Rimachi turned back and looked at Micay with disbelief.

"Why am *I* the one who is accused of being reckless?"

"Because you take risks out of anger and impatience," Micay told him bluntly. He gave a derisive laugh.

"And you? You cannot wait until she is grown to make a healer out of her?"

"*She* cannot wait. And I cannot deny her the chance to be useful."

"Little comrades," Rimachi said mockingly, though his face changed instantly when Choque let out a groan and opened his eyes. "Father," Rimachi breathed, sliding an arm under Choque's shoulders and lifting him up into a sitting position. The older man's head lolled from side to side, his eyes opening and closing.

"Sang . . . who?" he mumbled. Then he gave a violent start, his eyes popping wide open. "Who has the gate? The litter comes!"

His eyelids sagged back down and he coughed and subsided into unintelligible muttering.

"I am here, Father," Rimachi said, but Micay simply reached for the covered bowl of maize gruel that lay nearby.

"Let us feed him while we can," she urged, and Rimachi moved around behind him to provide better support for his head and neck. He tipped Choque's chin up so that Micay could push a spoonful of gruel between his lips, and they both waited anxiously until his tongue gave a sluggish lick and took the food in. Rimachi let out a long breath and nodded for her to continue.

"I got nothing down him yesterday," he admitted, "and he has not spoken in two days."

"He heard Cahua sing," Micay said, getting Choque to swallow another small spoonful. "She still has hope and trust in her voice, and that is a medicine in itself."

Choque started to cough, and Rimachi concentrated on holding him still until he recovered. When he again looked at Micay, he appeared rueful and chastened.

"There is none of that in me anymore. I am looking for someone to punish."

Micay gave Choque a spoonful of water, and when most of it dribbled down his chin, she signaled Rimachi to lay him back down. She dried his chin with a towel and looked across at Rimachi.

"You have been around the Incas for too long. That is how they squandered their strength. Why not join with us instead, and see that no more is wasted?"

"You do not have to recruit me, Micay," he said quietly. "I have always been at your service."

"Yet you scoff at becoming a comrade."

Rimachi shrugged. "I scoff at everything. I do not see what you hope to accomplish with your little band of comrades."

"I hope to make it larger, for one thing. And influential. Someone must begin again when this is all over. Why leave it to those who have brought us here?"

"Because it is theirs," Rimachi said. "Unless you are planning to seize the fringe of the ruler."

"No," Micay allowed with a smile. "But we could be close to those to whom the fringe is passed. There is more than one royal son."

Rimachi grunted and rubbed his chin, regarding her appreciatively. "This sounds like Cusi, but he does not seem to have that kind of ambition any longer."

"Everyone provides whatever they can, whenever it is needed. That is what it means to be comrades."

"Then I will try to be one," Rimachi decided. "Perhaps you will find a use for my anger and impatience." He glanced down at his father, who was sleeping with one arm thrown across his face. "Come, let us go find Chuqui Huipa. I assume you will want to recruit her next."

"Perhaps. But we must tend to these other men first. Unless Cahua has done it for us . . ."

"Ask her to sing again," Rimachi suggested as they rose. "I could stand to hear her myself."

THE RITUAL of purification was brief and seemed improvised, and the young priest who conducted it would not look at Cusi and Tomay directly. He made them bathe and exchange their tunics and loincloths for clothes he provided, but he kept his back turned while they dressed, and he did not notice that Cusi kept his headband and Tomay his cap. As soon as he could, he pronounced them clean and turned them over to an even younger apprentice warrior, who guided them into the palace.

They had both studied Amaru's model before coming here, so that they would know their way around, but Amaru had had no conception of the changes that had been made in his absence. Gates and staircases had been permanently blocked off, and makeshift guard posts had been erected at every juncture, though often there were no guards in evidence. The barricades made their path from one terrace level to the next seem like a maze of narrow corridors and blank walls, reminding Cusi of Chan Chan. They saw few people, but turkeys and guinea pigs roamed freely, scavenging through the trash that was piled up in the spaces between buildings and leaving their tracks in the dust that covered the courtyards. Tomay sniffed audibly, calling Cusi's attention to the rank odor in the air, a mixture of wood smoke, urine, and rotting food.

"It even smells like a city under siege," Tomay said with a grimace. "Do you think we were clean enough to enter?"

Cusi laughed softly. "The priest did not want to get too close, and neither does this boy." He gestured toward their guide, who had stayed ten feet in front of them without ever looking back. They followed him through a guarded gate into a long, narrow compound that Cusi recognized as Ninan Cuyochi's quarters. Three small houses stood side by side on a raised platform, their backs against the retaining wall of the terrace above, their doorways and windows looking out onto the city and the valley below. Cusi remembered Amaru's proud description of this compound, of how he had elevated the buildings and lowered the outer wall in order to enhance the view. Now all the doorways and windows were covered with cloth curtains, and the apprentice led them to a small awning house at the far end of the enclosure, where the only view was of the guards at the gate.

Inside, Ninan Cuyochi was sitting on a cloth-covered stool, and he waited until the young warrior had departed before he rose to greet them. Then he would not let them bow to him, but gestured with upraised palms and, shaking his head, came up to grip their hands.

"No, my friends, you cannot know how good it is to see you again. You have not been shut up behind these walls for the last six months, hearing nothing but rumors from the outside and gossip from within."

Cusi noticed that Ninan's narrow face seemed slightly bloated, the furrow between his brows deeper and more permanent.

"The sickness in the rest of the city is almost gone," Cusi told him. "You would be safer out there."

"So would you," Ninan said dryly, settling back on his stool and gesturing for them to sit on the mats laid out in front of him. "My father will soon know you are here, if he does not already. I cannot say how he will react, except that he is not in a forgiving mood these days."

"I am not seeking forgiveness, for myself *or* Amaru. I simply want to see him freed."

"That is my wish, as well," Ninan assured him. "And he will be, Cusi, in time. The fear and suspicion will pass when the sickness does, and in any case it is not strong enough to bring punishment upon a veteran Inca warrior. I am not in a position to work openly on his behalf, but I will see that no harm comes to him or his family."

"What about Fempellec?" Cusi asked.

"The Chimu? He is hardly blameless, and he will no doubt be made to suffer."

"He must be freed, too," Cusi insisted. "He is being punished as much for his relationship to me and Micay as for his own deeds."

Ninan spread his hands in a gesture of helplessness, then caught himself and grabbed at the air. Cusi watched the anger and frustration boil up inside him, forcing him to struggle for control. He took several deep breaths before he spoke, but his voice was still tight, as if there were a hand around his throat.

"I know what I would choose to do if I had the power. But I have been in disfavor myself. I disagreed with the decision to shut ourselves up in the palace, and I could not keep silent about my opposition. I felt it was my duty as the Regent to speak for the well-being of all the people. My father felt it was my duty as his son to carry out his command without question. He has not sent for me since then."

Cusi and Tomay exchanged a glance, and Cusi nodded for his friend to speak. Amaru and Fempellec were Cusi's concern, but they had both come to speak to Ninan.

"You were right, my lord," Tomay said. "The sickness spreads most quickly where people are crowded and unclean. And the Quitos are not going to rush to your aid now, after they were abandoned."

"Those were my arguments," Ninan said wearily. "But I do not expect to be forgiven for being right."

Cusi gave him a rueful smile. "If I had known this in Cuzco, I could have allayed Huascar's suspicions. He imagines that you are very close to the Sapa Inca, and he envies you for it."

Ninan responded to the statement as Cusi had hoped he would, becoming instantly, almost combatively, alert.

"You spoke with him, then," he prompted, leaning forward with his hands braced on his knees. "I am told that he rules in Cuzco as if he already wore the fringe."

Cusi and Tomay exchanged another glance, and Tomay could not restrain a scornful laugh.

"That is no doubt how *he* would describe it. Someone else might say that he has installed his friends and relatives in posts beyond their rank and competence and that he rules with bribes and threats. He has more spies than warriors, and he has demoralized the warriors he has by making rank a reward for loyalty, rather than a measure of performance."

"He has also made enemies of most of the Upper Cuzco households," Cusi added, "by threatening to confiscate their holdings."

Ninan sat back on his stool. He glanced swiftly from one to the other, then past them at the gate. His eyes seemed bright and shrewd.

"I am grateful for your frankness, but you must be careful what you say about Huascar to my father. He thinks too often about his own death and who will rule after him."

"We want him to think of *you*, my lord," Cusi said succinctly, and Tomay nodded emphatically in agreement.

"What do you mean?"

"We mean that Huascar is clearly not fit to rule. We need a ruler who can hold the Four Quarters together and restore peace and order."

"We need a ruler the warriors can respect," Tomay said ominously. "Or we will find ourselves standing in the square again."

"The warriors do not choose the Heir," Ninan reminded them, though he was not really arguing. He had clearly thought about all of this before.

"We know who chooses the Heir," Cusi told him. "And if he summons us, we will tell him what we told you about Huascar. It is what Yasca told us to say in our report."

"Huascar made an enemy of Yasca, as well," Tomay explained. "War chiefs do not like to be followed through the streets of Cuzco."

"Remember, though, that Yasca is in Tumibamba," Ninan warned. "His name will not protect you from my father's anger."

"It did not protect us from the Chiriguanos," Tomay said with a shrug, "or from the sickness."

"We can defend ourselves," Cusi assured him. "We will make clear that you did not summon us and that you are not responsible for our presence here. You might even wish to display some anger toward us . . ."

"It is too late for that," Ninan said, looking over their heads. "His men have come for you." He nodded abruptly and stood up. "I will go with you. It is my duty as Regent to welcome Yasca's representatives and to see that they are properly treated."

"We are honored by your concern," Cusi began, but Ninan cut him off.

"It is important to do what is right. For the Heir or any other man." He nodded to himself and led them out of the awning house. "Besides, I will not have it said of me, as it is of Huascar, that I let myself be ignored."

UNLIKE THE rest of the palace, Chuqui Huipa's compound was immaculately clean, and the guards at the gate were strict about whom they would admit. One of them went to ask about Cahua and came back with Chuqui herself. Chuqui embraced Micay with a fervor that left her breathless, then knelt down in front of Cahua when the girl would not let herself be picked up.

"You have become a White Woman, Cahua," Chuqui said in wonder. "The youngest one ever!"

"This is too big for me," Cahua said, pulling at the loose front of the tunic she had been given to wear. "They made us change but let us keep our medicine bags."

"There are clothes to fit you here," Chuqui assured her as she rose to her feet. "We have been ready for this for a long time."

The smile faded from her face, and there was a note of resignation in her voice. The lines around her eyes and mouth all pulled downward, and Micay realized she was exhausted.

"How many women do you have?"

"Ten or twelve, counting the apprentices. I have had little success with the court, Micay. Nothing changes them; not even the sickness can make them listen."

"What about the Coya?"

"My mother has withdrawn into fasting and prayer, without forgiving me for my 'peculiar' behavior in Tumibamba. So some will not join me for fear of offending her, while others would only join me if they could be sure it *did* offend her. When I try to tell them what we learned in Tumibamba, they remind me that Chimpu Ocllo herself died of the sickness, as if that proved our failure."

"They will stop worrying about their standing in the court once their children and husbands fall sick," Micay predicted. "Then they will come to you for help."

"We have supplies to share. My father gave me everything I asked for, at least until he learned that I was sending things out of the palace." Chuqui put her hands on her hips and cocked her head defiantly. "We have decided we will go out to help the sick, but we will not allow them to be brought here. We will keep this place safe for ourselves and our children."

"That is wise," Micay agreed. "Tell me, where is Fempellec?"

"I have not been able to reach him. He is being held somewhere outside the palace. They say he was apprehended trying to escape from the city."

Micay gave Rimachi a doubtful glance. "Amaru thought he was here."

"He is," Rimachi concurred. "A special detail of the Royal Guard is guarding him. They take their orders from Titu Atauchi."

Chuqui stared up at him for a moment, her face hardening. "He lied to me, then. About my own chief of feasts." Her eyes flashed at Rimachi. "Will these guards answer to you?"

"They would have to, my lady, if I were acting in the service of the Coya's daughter."

"You are. Take us to him." Chuqui held out her hand to Cahua. "Do you wish to come with us, my daughter? There may be anger and shouting."

"I will sing until they are quiet," Cahua declared, and she reached up to take Chuqui's hand. They started toward the gate, and Micay and Rimachi fell in behind. Rimachi leaned toward her with a smile.

" 'Anger and shouting' ?" he inquired softly.

"Do not sound so pleased. No harm must come to Fempellec."

"No," Rimachi agreed, still smiling. "Not when Titu Atauchi is so much more deserving . . ."

RAURAU ILLA had warned Cusi that he no longer had the power to contend with sorcerers and that he would be vulnerable to the fears and illusions they could arouse in other men's hearts. *Be still, and do not yield to fleeting impulses,* the old man had told him; *look upon them with coldness, and you will see that their powers are trivial and cannot do you lasting harm.*

They had passed through several guard posts before they were ushered out of the sunlight and into a narrow room that was dark and dense with tobacco smoke. Cusi was immediately reminded of the Grass Man's hut, and when he saw Titu Atauchi appear out of the shadows, he realized that it was meant to remind him. The man loomed up over all three of them, huge and menacing, and a rush of fear made Cusi clench his hands and break out in a sweat. Titu wore a dark tunic and a feather cape, and there were glittering amulets and sprays of feathers pinned to his clothing and the fur of his headdress.

"Who are you, that you wish to enter the presence of the Sapa Inca?" he demanded loudly, and Cusi felt Ninan shake himself, as if shrugging off a heavy burden. His voice sounded strained.

"These are the representatives of the war chief Yasca, who has sent them to report on the successful campaign against the Chiriguanos. Me you know."

"You were not sent for," Titu told him rudely. "You must all be purified.

There must be no anger or defiance or disrespect in your hearts when you come before him."

He had produced a gourd rattle from under his cape, and suddenly the men around him threw up their hands in a tossing motion, making the air glisten briefly. Then Cusi felt a fine powder raining down upon his head, and in the next instant his eyes, nose, and throat were on fire, and he doubled over coughing and retching, tears streaming down his face. The rattle buzzed close to his ear and Titu's voice was a cruel hiss.

"Weep for your crimes, traitor . . . soon you will fall."

Cusi swayed blindly, pawing helplessly at his face. The burning made him frantic, and there was something in the powder that amplified every sensation to an unbearable pitch. Tomay let out a growl that was frighteningly loud, and Cusi realized he was about to attack. "Be still," he said, though he may only have said it to himself. He tore his hands away from his face and reached out to either side, grabbing first Tomay's arm and then Ninan's. He meant to restrain them, but what he achieved was a linking that helped them keep their balance, along with a semblance of self-control. Cusi felt calmer immediately, and as he slowly straightened up he felt his spirit brother unfolding inside him, tall and unshakable like a support beam.

His tears had washed the fiery powder from his eyes, and he blinked until he could see Titu Atauchi clearly. His old hatred welled up in his chest and he let it make him cold and lucid, too distant to feel the force of the man's glare. He saw a tattoo of a serpent on Titu's cheek, flecks of foam on his lips, a mad, drunken light in his eyes. Cusi looked into that light and saw a man who did not feel he had to answer to anyone for his actions; a man who had no leader. Tomay and Ninan were sniffling and muttering in outrage, but they did not try to shake loose from Cusi's grasp. Cusi felt no outrage, just a vast amazement that this man had been permitted to forget his place so completely.

"So you have humbled us with your tricks," Cusi said hoarsely, his voice echoing slightly in his ears. "What has it gained you?"

"It was a test of your hidden powers," Titu sneered. "You have proven yourselves harmless."

"You mean we did not disgrace ourselves as you had hoped," Cusi said. "But you have gained more than you think, Titu Atauchi. Because now there are three Incas who will never forget how you abused them."

Ninan suddenly reared up on Cusi's right, freeing himself from Cusi's grip with an angry jerk. "*Never,*" he agreed. "Now take us to my father."

"He is not ready to see you yet," Titu said hastily. "He is with the Fourth Wife."

"You have not told him, have you?" Ninan decided aloud. "You intended to bring them here and provoke an incident for which they would be blamed. Then you would tell him. He will hear of it from me instead. Out of my way."

Titu hesitated for a moment, reaching toward the coca bag under his arm, but then thought better of it and backed out of the way as Ninan swept past. Tomay spat at Titu's feet as he and Cusi went by, but Cusi had his eyes on

Ninan's back, thinking he had never seen Ninan so angry before, or so forceful. Perhaps this *had* been a test of hidden powers, after all . . .

THE YOUNGEST of the four Cañari guards had been appointed their captain. He was the only one who did not know Rimachi personally and the only one who seemed serious about standing in his way.

"You must wait, my lord, until I can confirm this with Titu Atauchi."

"No, my friend," Rimachi said with a thin smile, "we do not wait for Titu Atauchi's permission. You know who I am and who this lady is. What rank does Titu Atauchi hold?"

"You are new to the palace, my lord. He—"

"He sends loyal Cañaris off to die in abandoned storehouses," Rimachi snapped. He stepped past the young man and tore away the curtain that covered the low doorway. "Since when do we keep prisoners in the dark? This man has been accused, not condemned."

"I will have to report this, my lord."

"Report it, then," Chuqui Huipa told him, waving him out of her way. "This man owes his service to me. Tell Titu Atauchi for me that he has committed a crime in hiding him from me."

The captain swallowed hard and left them, and Rimachi led them through the doorway, crouching to get under the lintel. A steep flight of stairs led down into a small, damp chamber, and Micay held tight to Cahua's hand as they followed Rimachi and Chuqui down. There was rubbish on the stone floor and a powerful odor of urine and excrement in the air, causing Cahua and the two women to pull up their masks. The only light came from the doorway, and it barely seemed to penetrate the gloom at the bottom.

"Here he is," Rimachi said softly. Fempellec was huddled in the corner, completely naked and shivering. Even in the near darkness, Micay could see that his face was bruised and swollen, and he made a whimpering sound when Chuqui squatted down and touched his arm.

"He is *cold,*" she announced with relief.

"Of course I am cold!" Fempellec burst out. "They took my clothes and tried to give me ones that had belonged to a sick man."

"I will get him a blanket," Rimachi said, and he turned and went back up the stairs.

"They beat me when I would not talk," Fempellec went on, his voice flat and without affect. "Then they made me stand in one place all night and asked me again in the morning, and beat me some more."

Micay crouched down next to Chuqui. "We will not let them beat you again," she promised. "Cusi is here, too, and he has promised Amaru that he will free both of you."

"She was there, Micay, when they beat me. She watched. How I wished I had Cusi's stone!"

"Mama Huarcay?" Chuqui asked, and Micay nodded. Rimachi reappeared and wrapped a blanket around Fempellec and lifted him to his feet. Fempellec swayed in his grasp for a moment, then nodded that he could stand on his own. He gave a start when he looked down and saw Cahua for the first time.

"I did not see you, little one," he told her. "Have you also come to rescue me?"

Cahua nodded gravely. "They should not punish you if you have not been bad."

Fempellec looked around at the others and let out a weak laugh. "I have been no worse than usual."

Cahua glanced up at Micay, her brow furrowed quizzically.

"Let us rescue him, anyway," Micay said, "because he is our friend."

"Come, friend," Cahua urged, tugging on the edge of Fempellec's blanket. "It smells very *bad* down here."

"It does," Fempellec agreed, following her toward the stairs. "It smells of that woman's revenge . . ."

IT WAS after dark before Cusi and his companions were ushered into the Sapa Inca's presence, their feet bare and their backs laden with symbolic burdens. They were on a high, unwalled terrace that was fringed with palm trees and illuminated by torches fixed on tall poles. Huayna Capac was reclining on a broad bench covered with skins and cushions, attended by several richly attired women. Cusi could not make out any of their faces, which were blurred by the screen of fine gauze that stood between them and the visitors. There were other people sitting or standing on Cusi's side of the screen, including Titu Atauchi and the high priest, Topa Yupanqui, and servants and messengers moved constantly around the periphery.

When they straightened up from making the mocha, Ninan was confronted by the war chief Rumiñaui, who held a staff topped by the royal fringe, the symbol that he spoke for the Sapa Inca. Huayna Capac himself could be seen in profile through the screen, eating and talking to the women. His voice was quite loud, as if he felt the screen were in fact a wall.

Cusi had watched Ninan's anger cool during their wait, hardening into a kind of grim determination. He flared slightly at the sight of Titu Atauchi, here ahead of him, but his father's visible disregard seemed to deflate and sadden him. He was slow to respond to Rumiñaui's curt command that he state his purpose, and he floundered at first, glancing at Cusi and Tomay as if he could not remember what had brought them here. But then he regained his composure and delivered a short speech on the worthiness of Yasca's representatives, praising them for their part in the campaign against the Chiriguanos. He spoke past Rumiñaui, to the indifferent man behind the screen, recounting how he and these brave warriors had been insulted and mistreated by Titu Atauchi, who had pretended to be acting in the Sapa Inca's name.

"These men, and I, have served the Inca well. We deserve to be treated with respect."

Rumiñaui, who had been glaring at Cusi out of his one good eye, leaned on his staff and shrugged rudely.

"No one asked Yasca to send his report now."

Ninan ignored him for a moment, staring through the screen. Huayna Capac grunted, then laughed, a sound that made Ninan's back go up as he slowly brought his hands down to his sides, clenched into fists. He turned and spoke into Rumiñaui's face, his voice sharp and threatening.

"Yasca needs no one to tell him what to do or when to do it. Nor do I. I am a war chief, the Regent of the Northern Provinces, and the son of the Sapa Inca. So I tell you, Rumiñaui, and you, Titu Atauchi, that the next man who disregards my rank and treats me with disrespect will pay in blood. Do you understand me?"

Rumiñaui gripped his staff, his face fixed in a snarl that did not escape his lips. Everyone on the terrace seemed frozen in place, except for the high priest, who interposed himself between Ninan and Rumiñaui.

"You must not threaten violence here," he scolded Ninan, who responded without taking his eyes off of Rumiñaui.

"I am simply reminding these people of their place, Grandfather. *Someone* must."

The silence deepened, and heads turned toward the screen, which was suddenly lifted up and borne away by the retainers. Huayna Capac had left his bench and was beckoning impatiently to Rumiñaui, who knelt and extended the staff that held the royal fringe. The ruler took the fringe in both hands and placed it around his forehead, absorbing himself in the task for a moment. He was wearing a tunic woven with gold and silver threads that glittered in the torchlight, and there were gleaming bands of gold around his wrists and upper arms. When the fringe was in place he drew himself up in front of Ninan, who bowed stiffly.

"Why are you so determined to provoke me?" Huayna Capac demanded in a voice that sounded permanently hoarse. "You are forever boasting that you are the Regent, as if that gave you the right to complain and make threats. You could be removed as the Regent and sent far from here."

"I know that, my lord," Ninan replied. "But if it is my duty as Regent to accept insults from those below me and indifference from the one above, then I would rather you sent me someplace where my authority had real meaning."

Huayna Capa's eyes went wide beneath the fringe of multicolored tassels, and for a moment Cusi thought he was going to erupt into anger. But Ninan had spoken with a conviction that could not be mistaken for boasting or complaining; it was clear he meant what he said and did not fear the consequences of having said it. He had also given his father a clear choice: either treat him with respect, like a son, or banish him. The ruler frowned but hesitated, his eyes darting sideways to Cusi and Tomay.

"*You,*" he exclaimed softly, appearing genuinely surprised. "Why are you here?"

Cusi bowed politely. "Tomay Guanaco and I are the representatives of the war chief Yasca, my lord. We have come to report on our expedition against the Chiriguanos."

"They were vanquished long ago," Huayna Capac said dismissively. "The Cochabamba Valley is peaceful and productive again. What more do I need to know?"

"Lord Yasca wishes you to know the battles that were fought, my lord, and the names of the warriors . . ."

"I do not care what Yasca wants me to know," the ruler interrupted. "What do you know, Cusi Huaman? What have you seen that is worth my attention? Speak, and quickly, because I have no other reason to tolerate your presence here."

Cusi was not daunted by the threat and knew exactly what to tell him. But he paused for a stubborn moment, out of respect for everything else he and Tomay had seen and done in the last five years.

"There is one thing Yasca did not entrust to any messenger, my lord," he said, slowly but distinctly. "It is that the Chiriguanos were led by a foreigner who had pale skin and a beard of black hair on his face. He wore a helmet and chest protector and carried a weapon made of a shining metal, duller but much harder than silver."

Huayna Capac drew a sharp breath and took an involuntary step backward, abandoning his bullying posture completely.

"How can this be?" he demanded in disbelief. "You saw this foreigner yourself? In Cochabamba?"

"At the place called Incallacta, my lord," Cusi explained, "where he and his Chiriguanos had us besieged. We drew them into an ambush and drove them off in defeat, and that is when we saw him."

"You saw him, as well?" the ruler asked Tomay, who bowed and nodded at the same time.

"We all saw him, my lord. He could not be mistaken for a Chiriguano."

"Had you heard about the bearded strangers who were seen along the coast?"

"Not then, my lord. We learned of them later, when we returned to Chuquiabo. They sounded very similar to this man."

"You are certain he was a man?" Huayna Capac inquired, and Cusi felt the onlookers crowd in closer to hear Tomay's response. Tomay glanced briefly at Cusi and smiled thinly.

"He had no magical powers, my lord, if that is what you mean. He could not stop the Chiriguanos from fleeing, and only his metal armor stopped the spear I threw at him."

"You hit him?"

"Here," Tomay said proudly, giving his chest an emphatic thump. "I was certain I had killed him, but he went off with the Chiriguanos."

Huayna Capac crossed his arms over his chest and turned to glare at his advisers, most of whom lowered their eyes and shrank back from his gaze. One of the few who did not flinch was Lloque Yupanqui, though Cusi almost did not recognize him. He had allowed his graying hair to grow long enough to hide his earplugs, and he was wearing a braided headband that bore a tuft of bright red feathers instead of a household badge. He looked as wild and strange as Titu Atauchi and the other sorcerers, though he inclined his head politely when Huayna Capac pointed at him with his chin.

"Is this why you persuaded me to open the palace? So that your nephew could bring me this alarming news?"

"I have not seen Cusi in five years, my lord," Lloque said mildly. "I had no knowledge of his coming or of what he would say."

"But you are not disappointed with what you have heard," the ruler prompted. Then he turned back to Cusi before Lloque could reply. "Your uncle is one of those who have urged me to regard the Bearded Ones as our enemy. No doubt you are in agreement with him."

"I have seen only this one, my lord," Cusi said, "and he had brought the Chiriguanos to kill us and burn the Great Lodge of the Inca. He was definitely an enemy, because he had made the Chiriguanos more dangerous than they were by themselves. But I know little of those who came to the coast. Have they been seen again?"

Huayna Capac squinted at him for a moment, then grunted with apparent satisfaction. "Good. They were not supposed to know in Tumibamba; I wanted no more panic. But yes, the Bearded Ones came again, only a short time ago. They came in their great rafts that are like floating houses, and everywhere they stopped they asked about *me*. 'Who is the ruler of this land? Where does he live? What does he possess?' They did not understand when the people told them that everything belonged to me. They wanted a count!"

"Where are they now?" Cusi asked uneasily, not at all reassured by the fact that this had been kept secret.

"They went away again, out over the Great Waters," Huayna Capac told him. "They took some of our people with them and left two of their own in Tumbez. I sent for them, but they had already caught the sickness, and they died before they could be brought here. It is said that they were very loud and rude, especially toward women, and that they were always asking for things made of gold. They ignored the other gifts they were given, but when they were finally given some arm bands and a string of gold beads, they did not even wear them. They hid them away in a sack!"

The ruler threw up his hands and turned in a circle, causing the men behind him to murmur and shake their heads, sharing his bewilderment and exasperation. He came back around to face Cusi, dropping his hands in a sudden display of weariness. He glanced at Tomay and then at Ninan, letting his gaze linger on his son.

"So . . . you have forced me to attend to you, and you have seen the burdens the Sapa Inca must carry. Do you still wish to be sent away from here?"

"I have never wished for that, my lord," Ninan said earnestly. "I only want to serve you and help you bear those burdens. But I must have the place and the respect I have earned, so that I can serve you with my whole heart."

Huayna Capac began to frown, but then he sighed and let his shoulders slump in a shrug of acquiescence. "You may have a place at my side . . . for whatever time is left." He began to turn away, then stopped and looked back at Cusi. "I did not expect to see you again, ever. But you will stay now. Until the end."

He turned and started back toward his bench, trailed by his entourage. Cusi, Ninan, and Tomay made the mocha and backed away in the other direction, out of the light cast by the torches. They retrieved their sandals and gave the ceremonial bundles they had been wearing on their backs to the retainers. They did not speak until they were crossing a deserted courtyard, with no one else within earshot.

"You were both so calm," Ninan said admiringly. "Especially you, Cusi. I cannot stay calm when he insults and belittles the people who serve him best."

"It was your anger that made him hear us," Cusi told him. "It is a weapon you will have to use again."

"He will hear me now," Ninan said confidently. "And you will be there with me."

"So it seems, though I did not know if I was being threatened or forgiven."

"Forgiven," Ninan said.

"Threatened," Tomay said. Cusi looked from one to the other and laughed. "Maybe they are not so different, after all . . ."

SINCE NINAN CUYOCHI had reasserted his power as Regent, many of the barricades and makeshift guard posts that obstructed passage through the palace had been removed, and there had been an effort to sweep the ramps and walkways and to burn the trash that was piling up around the buildings. Ninan had also given his open support to Chuqui Huipa's band of White Women, going in person to encourage the members of the court to cooperate with the healers.

But the sickness inexorably moved ahead of him, striking guards and gate-keepers and so decimating the work crews that soon there were barely enough to serve as corpse bearers. Many people came to the White Women for help, which they gave willingly, along with instruction and supplies. Cusi, Tarapaca, and a few others who had already survived the sickness acted as bearers for the supplies, and they also made it their duty to carry away everything that needed to be burned. Yet there were whole sections of the palace that remained sealed to the healers, perhaps closing the sickness out, or perhaps closing the people there in with it.

It was not far from Chuqui Huipa's compound to the enclosure that belonged to Mama Huarcay, but the path between them was new to Micay. She followed it alone, having refused offers of accompaniment from Chuqui, Cusi, Cahua, and Rimachi. Mama Huarcay had been her enemy long before she had had any comrades, and Micay had always faced her alone. It seemed important to her to do so now, despite her dedication to building new alliances.

Mama Huarcay did not come out to greet her, of course, and Micay allowed herself to be led to a storeroom in one corner of the narrow, two-tiered compound. A small, dark man wearing only a light blue loincloth lay sleeping on a soiled mat on the floor, surrounded by discarded clothing, crumpled towels, and the rotting remnants of uneaten meals. Micay raised her mask against the stench as she knelt down beside the man on the mat.

"This must be Machacuay," she said to the servant who had guided her here. The woman nodded without coming any farther into the room. "His fever is gone," Micay continued, touching him briefly on the forehead, "and so are the spots. Why is he so thin, and so still?"

"I do not know, my lady. I do not tend him."

Micay was about to ask who did, but the answer was plain in the man's sorry condition. The delirium and stupor usually lifted when the fever broke, leaving the survivor alert but physically depleted for a long time. That had been the case with Choque Chinchay, who had probably fallen ill about the same time as Machacuay. Micay shook him by the shoulder, lightly but firmly, and the man grunted once but did not awaken.

"Bring me water and clean towels," she commanded. "And some broth and maize gruel."

After the woman had left, Micay pulled the gauze up over her eyes and used a rolled-up blanket to sweep the space around Machacuay's mat clear of debris. The woman returned with the water and towels, and while Micay was washing the man's shrunken, unresponsive body she brought food and left it. Micay did not bother to ask her to help or to explain the lumps and lacerations she found on Machacuay's head and upper body as she cleaned him. The thought that this was the man who was going to be used against Amaru and Fempellec made her feel sick with pity and disgust.

When she touched a wet cloth to his lips, though, he responded avidly, and she patiently dripped water into his mouth until he tired of licking and swallowing. She felt encouraged by the amount of water he had taken, though he appeared to have a brief convulsion before lapsing back into his stupor. As Micay got out her medicines and began to tend to the man's cuts and bruises, she thought of Paucar Rimay. She continued to work even after she heard someone come in behind her, and only looked up when she was done.

"What admirable dedication," Mama Huarcay said in a languidly dismissive tone. "Surely the retainer himself would not think he was worthy of such care."

Micay sat back on her haunches and pulled down her mask. "Is that why you have given him none, my lady?"

Mama Huarcay looked down at the prostrate man and shrugged. "We saw him through the fever, but then his mind did not come back. He could not even talk. He has lost all usefulness, now that Cusi is back in favor and you have hidden Fempellec away. You can have him if you wish. Or you can leave him here to die in his dreams."

Micay stared at her, wondering why her cruelty had not deformed or at least aged her. She seemed as beautiful and seductive as ever, smiling with a studied lack of innocence.

"I will take him," Micay said curtly. "Was this just an amusement to you, my lady?"

"That is a rude and foolish question," Mama Huarcay sniffed. "The Chimus are amused by men who are not men; the Incas regard them with disgust, as perverts and criminals. I do not know what a Chachapoya might think."

"That has always been true," Micay agreed, slinging her medicine bag over her shoulder as she rose to her feet. "I will return with a litter to take him away."

"My servants will take him wherever you want," Mama Huarcay offered, moving into her path. "You do not have to flee my presence so quickly. It will not harm you to speak with me."

"No?"

"No," the older woman insisted, suddenly earnest. "Come, Micay, the world has changed for both of us. Mama Cori and Chimpu Ocllo are dead. You were my enemy only because *they* were. I have always hoped to be reconciled with you."

"I do not think the world has changed that much, my lady," Micay said dryly.

"Soon it may change even more. It is no secret that my husband feels that his time upon the earth is short and that he may soon be summoned back to the side of Inti, his father." Mama Huarcay bowed her head for a moment before going on. "You know that I was very close to his first Coya, Cusi Rimay, while she was alive. I was one of those who helped raise her only child, and because I had no children of my own then, I doted on Ninan Cuyochi the way Chuqui Huipa dotes on your daughter. And of course, at that time, we all thought of him as the Heir." She gave Micay a significant glance. "It is also no secret that the Sapa Inca has recently begun to reconsider his choice of a successor. Your husband has contributed greatly to his misgivings, though he is not the only one to come with complaints about Huascar."

"Cusi and Tomay merely delivered Yasca's report," Micay said in a neutral tone, fascinated by this overture while distrusting it completely. Mama Huarcay snorted disdainfully.

"Cusi Huaman is known to speak with his own voice, no matter who he serves or what it might cost him. So he was believed, despite his closeness to Ninan. He improved Ninan's standing enormously, without anyone suspecting that that might be his intention."

Micay almost smiled, recalling Cusi's own much more doubtful assessment of how his report had been received. Huayna Capac had asked him only a few questions and had not spoken to him since. Micay simply stared expectantly at Mama Huarcay, waiting to hear the reason for this flattery.

"What I am saying, Micay, is that perhaps . . . for once . . . we want the same thing. Is that impossible for you to conceive? Or will you just not admit it to yourself? You have always had the courage to oppose and defy me. Do you have the courage now to put aside your grievances and join with me on Ninan's behalf? Think of what it could mean to Chuqui Huipa and to Cusi . . . think of the place you would have in the court, Micay."

Micay had thought of all these things without once perceiving the need for an alliance with Mama Huarcay. Yet she was tantalized by the offer, drawn as always by the woman's passion, her sheer audacity. She never stopped scheming for influence, and there was no one, friend or enemy, whom she would not try to use. She was another of the Old Ones, as indomitable in her way as Otoronco Achachi had been in his. Micay tried to imagine being her ally, conspiring with her and sharing secrets, entering into her schemes. Between them they would have great power, since no one would ever suspect them of working together. But while the possibility of what they might accomplish was enticing, Micay was not certain she was shrewd enough to contend with Mama Huarcay and to sense the inevitable betrayal before it came.

The man on the floor let out a moan that brought Micay back from her thoughts with a start. She glanced down at his battered face, then up at Mama Huarcay's handsome features, which were, as always, flawlessly painted.

"You were there, my lady," she said softly.

Mama Huarcay reared back in surprise. "I was where?"

"When Fempellec was being beaten and humiliated . . . you were there watching. Did you watch them beat this man, too?"

"What if I did? Would you spurn me for that?" Mama Huarcay asked incredulously. "Surely you have seen worse injuries to better men. What is the life of a retainer compared to the fate of the Four Quarters?"

"What is the Four Quarters," Micay retorted, "if a man can be beaten half to death for nothing?"

Mama Huarcay squinted at her, seeming more perplexed than angry. "Come, Micay, you are using this to avoid what is truly important. You were not so squeamish when Chuqui Huipa summoned you to tend her 'fever.' Obviously you did what was necessary, and you did it swiftly and discreetly. Is that so different from what I have done?"

Micay shook her head in amazement. "I *healed* her, my lady. I did not supervise her torture!"

"A midwife would not have called it healing," Mama Huarcay pointed out testily. But then she held up her palms in a mollifying gesture. "I do not wish to argue with you, Micay. You do not have to love and respect me. I only want to know if you will work with me."

Micay shook her head again, this time in frank denial. "I could never be your ally, my lady, not after what you did to Fempellec. The fact that you do not understand that only proves how different we are."

Mama Huarcay slowly lowered her hands, her face hardening beneath its coat of paint. Her voice was brittle with disappointment. "I thought you had learned by now that righteousness is no protection. There are people more ruthless than I, Micay, and some of them hate you and your husband. As an ally, I might have been able to warn you . . ."

Something in her voice—perhaps simply the lack of anger—gave Micay pause. She realized how much Mama Huarcay had wanted this and how much that said about her own lack of allies. Surprised by a surge of compassion, Micay could only gesture awkwardly toward the heaps of clothing and garbage that surrounded Machacuay's mat.

"There is danger here, my lady, for those who are not protected from the sickness. All this should have been burned long ago."

"Go, Micay," Mama Huarcay said wearily, ignoring the advice. "I will have him brought to you at Chuqui Huipa's compound. See if he is as much help to you as I would have been."

Micay bowed in compliance, then went past her and out the doorway into the light and the fresh, untainted air. She breathed deeply, feeling both relieved and certain that she had made the right decision. But along with the dubious gift of Machacuay she carried away with her a muted but palpable pang of regret, the result of knowing she had put another of the Old Ones behind her.

IN THE BACK of the awning house, Fempellec was scolding the new cook for the second time, waving a handful of herbs in the young woman's face and haranguing her in a loud voice.

"Do not even *stir* my soup!" he was saying when Cusi came up behind him. The cook was trembling and appeared close to tears, and she was making no attempt to defend herself. Even though he knew how easily Fempellec could be startled, Cusi came up close behind him and spoke without warning.

"It is like someone always there behind you, tugging at your tunic and demanding your attention."

Fempellec jumped and whirled at the same time, and Cusi caught him by the arm to keep him from losing his balance.

"I am speaking of your restlessness," Cusi explained when Fempellec could only gape at him speechlessly. Keeping hold of his arm, Cusi propelled him toward the open side of the awning house. "Come, you need to walk . . ."

"It is raining," Fempellec protested, his eyes still wild with shock. "Why are you doing this to me?"

"Cahua and Chuqui Huipa are trying to sleep, and your shouting is only making the cook nervous."

"She should not be allowed near food! She could probably manage to ruin potatoes."

"She will not ruin your soup by stirring it. All of the other cooks are helping with the sick." A few drops of rain were still falling from the gray, breaking clouds, but Cusi ignored them along with the puddles underfoot, leading Fempellec toward the end of the compound opposite the main gate.

"Where are you taking me?"

"Nowhere. You need exercise, and I want to show you how much room there is in this compound—so you will remember what true confinement was like."

Fempellec jerked his arm free and stopped short in the middle of the courtyard. "I have not forgotten."

"No? Then why would you risk an escape from here?" Cusi inquired. "I was awake last night when I should have been sleeping. I saw you sneak out of your house, and I followed you to where you had hidden the ladder. I watched you climb to the top of the wall and then come down again. What stopped you?"

Fempellec made a face and started walking again. "There was someone out there, lying in wait. It was only by chance that I saw him, and then he fled when one of the Regent's patrols came along."

"He is not the first," Cusi told him. "Rimachi surprised one of them and almost caught him, but the man threw a knife at him and got away."

"Why did you not stop me at the ladder?"

Cusi shrugged. "I wanted to see how serious you were. You could have waited until the patrol had passed and then gone."

"Seeing that man made me uneasy," Fempellec admitted, stamping into a puddle with one sandaled foot. "And I was not certain that the ways I know to leave are still open. But I have to get out of the palace, Cusi. I dream every night that they are coming to get me again."

"You are safest here, both from the sickness *and* from assassins."

"That is not how it feels to me. Take me with you the next time you go to Amaru's to see your son. There are guards there, too."

"You know that is impossible. You and Amaru are being ignored, but you have not been cleared. You must stay apart until then."

"That could take forever! You have not even spoken to the Sapa Inca about us."

"Huayna Capac does not have forever," Cusi assured him, "and he gives very little of his time to me. He is more concerned with dreams and omens than with anything that would affect you. So you simply must be patient and keep yourself out of trouble for a while. Is that so hard for you?"

Fempellec raised his eyes from the wet ground and smiled ruefully. "I miss Parihuana, too, and little Roca. They are my family now."

"Then keep yourself safe for them," Cusi suggested. He glanced around and saw where their walking had brought them. "You could make yourself useful, as well. You have not been to see Machacuay yet."

"What is there to see?" Fempellec asked. "He is never going to recover."

"Micay thinks he will. He is awake enough to eat and drink, even if he never opens his eyes. She thinks the voice of a friend might help to rouse him."

"What friend? They beat me, too, but I did not tell them anything."

"If you had had the sickness when they beat you, you would have told them whatever they wanted to hear. He is not your enemy and you know it, Fempellec. So come, show your courage a second time."

Cusi turned toward the house where Machacuay was being kept but waited for Fempellec to lead the way.

"You will be giving me another stone to carry soon," Fempellec grumbled, looking down at the herbs he still carried in his hand. "Tell me one thing first: Would you have come after me if I had gone over the wall?"

Cusi laughed but nodded without any hesitation. "Micay has made you a comrade, has she not? So it is my duty to watch your back, especially if you are foolish enough to expose it to our enemies."

"That is another stone," Fempellec said dryly, but then he smiled and started toward the house. "You do not frighten me like you used to," he said over his shoulder, "but you are still not warm."

Taken aback by this assessment, Cusi pondered it for a moment before going after him. He heard voices ahead and found Fempellec arrested halfway through the doorway. As he gave Fempellec a gentle push forward, he recognized Lloque Yupanqui's voice.

"Come in . . . ah, Cusi, too. Come in, my son, and greet Machacuay."

"Machacuay," Fempellec murmured in disbelief, squatting down in front of the man, who was sitting up against the wall. "It is I, Fempellec. Do you know me?"

Machacuay's mouth fell open and he blinked rapidly, appearing too weak even to compose himself. Finally he squeezed his eyes shut and spoke in a faltering voice.

"Fempellec. Your name . . . was called . . . when I was hiding. Or before. Many times."

"He is still confused," Lloque said softly as Cusi squatted down next to him. "He awoke only a short time ago."

"How did you do it?" Cusi asked.

Lloque spread his long, thin hands in a diffident shrug. "He woke by himself. I did nothing we have not been doing for a month."

"How long?" Machacuay blurted, his eyes popping open.

"A month, my son."

"So long," Machacuay murmured, frowning in recollection. "They hunted me, and I hid. I made them think I was dead."

"You did," Lloque agreed, "and they were willing to let you die. But Micay was not."

"I will serve her forever," Machacuay said breathlessly, his eyes closing of their own accord.

"We must let him rest," Lloque said. "Will you stay with him, Fempellec?"

Fempellec nodded as he leaned toward Machacuay, rolling the herbs between his palms and holding them up to Machacuay's nose.

"Before you sleep, my friend . . . something to give flavor to your dreams."

Machacuay's strained face seemed to slacken, and he murmured in agreement, his head lolling forward. Lloque helped Fempellec lower him down onto his back, then came to join Cusi outside. He moved stiffly, groaning as he stretched his back and legs.

"You have been with him a long time," Cusi said sympathetically. "I should have relieved you."

"It is the only useful thing I have done in days," Lloque scoffed. "I only wish Micay could have been there when he awakened."

"She has gone to tend to Atauhuallpa. He has the fever."

Lloque frowned thoughtfully. "Let us pray he recovers; we cannot afford to lose him. I worry about Ninan, too. He is going out with the patrols too often."

"It is his way of feeling useful," Cusi said, "since most of our time in the court is wasted."

"It is his way of seeing Chuqui Huipa alone. Micay had to chase him out of a sickroom yesterday."

"That *is* foolish," Cusi agreed. "I will talk to him."

"We must stop wasting our time in the court, too. We cannot let him close us out again."

"How can we stop him? He sequesters himself with the sorcerers and the omen readers and the messengers from Pachacamac and Rimac, and when he appears before us he is usually preoccupied or drunk, or both."

"You persuaded him once that you were a sorcerer," Lloque pointed out. "He would not punish you for it now."

Cusi smiled ruefully. "I have told you, Uncle: I no longer have the powers that made you question my character. That was not the form my huaca was meant to take."

"Does that mean you cannot even pretend? How do you think I persuaded him to open the palace to outsiders? I told him I had a dream in which I saw the ceremony of purification being performed. Then I simply described some of the precautions the White Women took, along with some prayers I made up beforehand."

"I have already told him about my vision," Cusi said, "and that was when I could make him listen to me."

"So you will not try again?" Lloque demanded. "There is not much time left, Cusi. You have seen the way he neglects and abuses himself. We must get to him before the sickness does."

Cusi drew a deliberate breath and gestured for Lloque to walk with him back to the awning house. "You must forgive me if I cannot share your urgency, Uncle. I want very much to see Ninan wear the fringe of the ruler. But I have no trust in anyone's ability to influence Huayna Capac in that direction. It might be better not to get to him."

"Micay told me how much you had changed," Lloque said bluntly. "But it is hard to believe I am hearing this from you."

Cusi reached up and put a hand on his uncle's bony shoulder, linking them as they walked. "Should we stop listening to each other, then? You have not explained how you have changed, either. Or why you wear a headband woven from a memory cord."

"I wear it in memory of Paucar Rimay. Micay must have told you about him."

"The man who had lost his memory . . ."

"He had lost *everything!*" Lloque said fiercely. "He could not even say who he was or what he wanted. But he was still alive, and he could still feel. His life had been ruined by a ruler who had never been made to care whether anyone lived or died."

"I am only saying that this is the same ruler," Cusi said, squeezing his shoulder before letting him go, "and it is late to expect him to begin caring."

They had reached the awning house, and Cahua suddenly darted out of the adjacent house and ran up to them. Her eyes were bright with excitement, and she jerked her chin peremptorily, directing their attention to the cook, who could be seen moving about in the rear of the awning house.

"She put some medicine in the soup! I woke up and saw her from the doorway."

Lloque glanced at Cusi and laughed. "She is the cook, my child. It is her task to season the soup."

"She knows the difference, my lord," Cusi told him, stooping to address Cahua directly. "What sort of medicine?"

"It was dark and powdery, like chuño flour," Cahua reported, shooting a scornful glance up at Lloque. "It was wrapped in some leaves that she threw into the fire when she was done. She looked all around first, but she did not see me watching from the doorway."

"Perhaps it *was* chuño," Lloque murmured, his skeptical expression reminding Cusi of Cahua's propensity for spreading rumors and stirring up trouble. Cusi saw a trace of that in the eagerness of her approach, but he was also remembering what she said she had learned at Macas's cave: that she could know things by herself, without anyone telling her first. She had been right to trust her senses then, and he saw no reason to make her doubt them now.

"Let us find out," he suggested, reaching down to take Cahua's hand as the three of them walked into the awning house. He realized that they probably should have awakened Chuqui Huipa, since the cook was the niece of her most trusted retainer. But if Cahua was correct, it was best they find out swiftly.

The young woman looked up from the pot she was cleaning and bowed in deference to the two men. She wiped her hands on the cloth tied around her waist and gazed at them expectantly, a servant ready to serve.

"How is the soup?" Cusi asked casually, and the young woman ducked her head, appearing chastened but not especially nervous.

"I cannot tell you, my lord. The chief of feasts told me that I should not even stir it."

"I heard him," Cusi acknowledged, feeling Cahua give his hand a quick tug in protest. "But it looks rather thin. I would not blame you if you thought to thicken it with chuño flour."

"Oh no, my lord, I would never disobey him," the woman insisted. "I have not touched it."

"Then taste it for us," Lloque said abruptly, bending over and coming up with a wooden spoon, which he held out to her.

"I am not worthy, my lord," she demurred, though she took the spoon and ladled some of the soup into a small bowl. She offered the bowl to Lloque with her arms outstretched and her eyes lowered.

"You must have that first bowl," Lloque insisted, pushing it back toward her. "I am overruling the chief of feasts."

"You do me too much honor," the woman said, but she raised the bowl to her lips and appeared to take a small sip. She glanced timidly at Lloque, who gestured for her to continue.

"Finish it. You must tell us if it is flavorful and nourishing."

The woman cast a pleading glance at Cusi in the hope that he might rescue her again, but when he simply nodded in agreement, she tipped the bowl to her lips and slowly drained it. Cusi looked down at Cahua, who pointed to her throat with an affirmative nod.

"I am not used to such fine food, my lord," the woman murmured, staring down into the empty bowl. "I do not know how it is supposed to taste."

"We are not used to poison," Cusi told her, meeting her eyes when her head came up. "My daughter saw you add it to the soup and then burn the wrappings. I assume it will act slowly, but we can wait to see . . ."

There was anguish in her eyes, but Cusi still could not tell if it was guilt or the shame of being falsely accused. She bowed and took a step back, then suddenly dashed the bowl down at their feet and sprang to the right, where she kicked over the whole pot of soup before running for the gate. Cusi had instinctively snatched Cahua out of the way, but just as quickly he set her down and jumped through the fragrant cloud of steam that was billowing up from the doused fire. The woman ran awkwardly in her long shift, and he could have caught her in a few strides or simply shouted to the guards at the gate to detain her. Instead he stopped where he was and let her escape.

The spilled soup was still sizzling on the hearthstones when he returned; it smelled of scorched tomatoes. Lloque was sitting with his knees raised, grimacing as Cahua picked slivers of pottery out of his shins.

"You let her go," Lloque observed, sounding annoyed.

"I saw no point in catching her."

"She tried to kill all of us."

"She will not be back. If she vomits it out soon enough, she will probably live. But she will live in terror until she is sure."

"That is enough? We might at least have learned who she was and who made her into an assassin."

"Was she trying to make us sick?" Cahua interrupted, holding a towel against Lloque's leg as she looked up. Lloque blinked at her, disconcerted by the innocence of the question.

"Yes, my daughter," he told her. "She was sent here to harm us, and if you had not been so vigilant, she might have made us very sick."

"I thought she was playing a trick on us," Cahua said disapprovingly, "like the time Sinchi put a bug in my food bowl."

"That is how your father seems to regard it," Lloque said with a pointed glance at Cusi. "At least he had the wisdom to trust you, my daughter. I am sorry I doubted you."

"You thought I was playing, too," Cahua said. "But I could see she was doing something wrong."

"Yes, and I am going to find out who sent her here to do it," Lloque declared, handing her towel back to her and pushing himself to his feet. "Then I will complain and accuse and demand punishment for the guilty. You probably see no point in that, either."

"I know who my enemies are," Cusi shrugged, "and I do not expect to see them punished. But you might win some sympathy for us, or at least the Sapa Inca's notice."

"At least you understand my purpose," Lloque said dryly, "even if you do not see any value in it. Wait for your chance, then. I must do what I can to create one for us." He gave Cusi a sardonic smile and pointed with his chin at the broken soup pot. "They spoiled Fempellec's soup, after all."

Stooping to pat Cahua on the head, Lloque turned and left them alone in the awning house. Cusi looked down at his daughter and then at the smoldering mess the cook had left behind.

"I will have to bury this," he decided. He looked again at Cahua, who seemed unperturbed by what she had just seen and heard. "Chuqui Huipa must be told about the cook. Can you do that?"

Cahua nodded vigorously. "Should I wake her up?"

"Gently," Cusi advised. "She will not be happy to hear this."

"Yes . . . now we have no one to make the fire," Cahua agreed, and she marched off toward the next house. Cusi watched her go, grateful she still had that much innocence; that she could not truly comprehend the difference between poison and a bug in the food bowl. He turned back to the spilled soup, letting himself dwell on that difference until his distance dissolved and he shuddered violently at the thought of what might have been.

OF THE TEN people who had occupied the compound, six were already dead when they were discovered. A seventh, an elderly retainer, had clawed his way through the thick curtains covering the gate and crawled out into the street, where the Regent's patrol had found him. Micay was summoned along with the corpse bearers, and she found the three remaining survivors living together in a tiny, trash-filled room. Two were retainer women, both quite old and both quite clearly dying. The third, their mistress, was a white-haired Inca wife who had apparently just been stricken by the fever. Sitting up against the wall with her eyes closed against the light, the old woman told Micay that she was Mama Chiclla, one of the wives of Topa Inca and a member of his household, the Capac Ayllu. The retainers had been her servants since she was a child, and she had nursed them as best she could until the sickness came to her, too.

Micay greeted her respectfully, then pulled her mask up over her eyes and summoned Cusi and Tarapaca to help clean out the room. They carried out basket after basket of trash, flushing out a family of guinea pigs that was nesting in the back corner. They also helped Micay strip and change the retainer women, neither of whom could be roused from her stupor. Micay waited until the men were gone before turning to Mama Chiclla, pulling the mask down to her nose. The old woman was regarding her through eyes that were open only a slit, yet when Micay reached for the golden pin that secured her mantle, she held up a hand to stop her.

"You have not told me who you are."

Micay took her hand back. "I am the First Wife Mama Micay, my lady. I am a healer from the cult of Mama Quilla. I must wash you and give you clean clothes."

Mama Chiclla nodded and let her hand drop. But while she submitted to Micay's handling, she continued to question her about her relatives and her rank. She had heard of Cusi Huaman, she said; he was very famous for one so young. She knew his parents and grandparents and Lloque Yupanqui and Otoronco Achachi, as well. She seemed to know everyone Micay named, though she gave no hint as to whether she approved or disapproved of any of them. Somehow they were not enough to establish Micay in her mind, and Micay finally realized that she must have noticed—probably from Micay's light skin—that Micay was not an Inca of the blood. She wanted to know how a foreigner was entitled to the rank of First Wife.

As she bundled up the woman's soiled clothing and set it carefully aside, Micay struggled with a surging impatience. The sickness was at its height, and she had not had any proper rest in days. Her body ached with fatigue, and she was utterly weary of watching people suffer and die. To have to answer to this woman's suspicions at such a time was almost more than she could tolerate.

Mama Chiclla's eyes were open again when Micay turned back, and her tone had become querulous.

"Must you wear that mask? It is rude to hide your beauty."

"I wear it to protect myself from the sickness, my lady," Micay told her. Then she could not keep herself from going on. "If I showed you my face, you would see that I am a Chachapoya. I was taken as a chosen woman when I was thirteen."

To Micay's surprise the old woman smiled, apparently not hearing the anger in her voice.

"A chosen woman," she said fondly. "Forgive me, my daughter, I could not understand how you were eligible to become a ñusta."

"Now you know," Micay said shortly. "You must rest, my lady, and save your strength to fight this sickness."

"I have no more strength," the woman said. "I am old and tired, and I will die soon. Do you have coca, my daughter? I do not remember where I left mine."

Micay took several of the brittle green leaves from her medicine bag and rolled them into a small pellet, which Mama Chiclla took from her and placed inside her cheek. She was too weak to handle the lime container, though, so Micay fed her a small amount of the gray powder with a silver spatula.

"That may help a little with the pains in your head," Micay told her. "But you must stop chewing when your cough begins, or you could choke."

Mama Chiclla was chewing contentedly with her eyes closed and did not bother to acknowledge the advice. Micay wanted to ask her why she cared about the rank of her healer when she did not expect to be healed. But Micay thought she knew. Chimpu Ocllo had once said of the Inca that the men wasted their lives in wars of conquest and the women wasted theirs in wars of prestige. That was the kind of Inca this woman was: one who could never even imagine the need to begin again; one who would rather die than admit the world had changed.

Someone blocked the light from the doorway, and Micay turned away with a feeling of relief, expecting Cusi or Tarapaca. When she saw Ninan Cuyochi instead, she lost her patience completely.

"Do not come in here! Out!"

"I must speak with you, Micay . . ."

"Outside!" she snapped, and Ninan reluctantly backed out of the room.

"Who was that?" Mama Chiclla asked, blinking painfully at the light. "He wore the earplugs."

"It was the Regent, my lady, Ninan Cuyochi."

"And you spoke to him so rudely? You could not have learned that in the House of Chosen Women."

"He is careless with his health," Micay said, ignoring the reprimand. "I have warned him more than once not to come into a sickroom."

"He is the Regent and the son of the Sapa Inca," Mama Chiclla cried. "He can go wherever he wishes. You must not make him wait another moment."

"He is not sick," Micay began, but the old woman would not let her finish, making frantic shooing motions with her hands.

"Go and apologize! I will not have you insult him on my account. There is nothing you can do for me . . ."

"That is true," Micay agreed, and she picked up her medicine bag and left before she could say something truly insulting. Ninan was waiting outside, standing hunched over with his hands clasped behind his back, his narrow face fixed in a frown that seemed directed at himself.

"Forgive me, Micay," he said immediately. "I came to apologize and only succeeded in offending you further."

"Mama Chiclla thinks I should apologize to you. You are the Regent and can go wherever you wish."

Ninan stiffened but remained penitent. "I am sorry. Should I cleanse myself again? I have done what you told me to do this morning."

Micay stared at him blankly for a moment, unable to recall telling him anything this morning. Then the memory of surprising him and and Chuqui came back with a vividness that made her wonder how she had put it out of her mind.

"I had forgotten about that," she confessed. She pointed with her chin at the compound gate. "You do not need to cleanse yourself, but you should not stay here. The sickness is everywhere."

She started walking, and he fell in beside her.

"You were finished here?" he asked, and Micay blew air out her nose.

"I do not know why I came. Mama Chiclla wanted to be sure I was entitled to my rank before she would let me attend her. Then she told me that she expected to die, like all the others had, because they could not bring themselves to fight this and they would not ask for help. I was acceptable to her only because I had once been a chosen woman."

They came out through the gate and walked a short distance up a narrow ramp to a place where they could see out over the palace and the city below. Micay was startled by the softness of the light and the length of the shadows; she did not know where the day had gone.

"I see that you are not angry at me," Ninan said quietly. "But you *are* angry, and probably exhausted, too."

Micay sighed and nodded in agreement. "I have been through this once before, and I learned then that the sickness is bad for everyone, even the healthy. It is the constant demand for a relief you cannot provide."

"Perhaps that is why I have grown so careless," Ninan mused aloud. "I knew I should not be in that room with her . . . I knew that her clothes might be covered with the sickness. But I could not restrain myself, not when she lowered her mask . . ."

Micay could not recall having lowered her own, but she had. She gave into her weariness then, and all her anger seemed to evaporate.

"Chuqui knew, as well," she told him with a tolerant smile. "And she was hardly resisting your embrace."

Ninan struggled against a smile of his own and managed to quell it. "That is no excuse for my conduct or for the way I spoke to you. I was blaming you for my own mistake, and that is not how the Inca—any Inca—should act."

The Inca. Micay heard the slip and smiled with real pleasure, touched and impressed by this gesture, the more so because he had no need to try to impress her. She bowed with a graciousness she had not felt in days.

"It is a shame, is it not, that the Sapa Inca is never allowed to admit a mistake," she suggested. "It robs him of the chance to display the depth of his character and the largeness of his spirit."

"I would think the Sapa Inca could allow himself anything, even humility," Ninan said, and then he did smile. "I will go and sequester myself until I am truly needed." He began to turn away, then turned back, his expression grave. "You heard that Mama Huarcay has the fever?"

"No," Micay blurted. But then she had to check her memory to be sure. "No, I had not heard. She is another who will not send for the White Women."

"She was with my father only four days ago," Ninan said in a flat voice. Then he shook himself, as if to clear his head of unwelcome thoughts. "I am going. Tell Chuqui I am practicing restraint, not indifference."

You are practicing to be the ruler, Micay thought as she watched him go. A thrill that was half hope and half anticipation welled up inside her, momentarily displacing her fatigue. How different it might be with someone like Ninan wearing the fringe! She remembered the passionate embrace she had interrupted, the way he had held Chuqui against him, his lips and hands moving over her face and body with a kind of loving hunger. Cusi had spoken admiringly of Ninan's anger, but they would need his passion even more if they were truly to begin again.

When he was out of sight she followed in the same direction, thinking she had been too tired for Cusi lately, too distracted to lure him back from his distance and remind him of an old hunger. She sighed and decided abruptly that she had done her duty to the sick for today. Someone else could listen helplessly to their moans; she wanted to hear her own and those of her husband . . .

RIMACHI CAME into the compound just after they had finished their evening meal and were sitting around the fire, talking and drinking akha. Chuqui Huipa invited him to sit and Cusi offered him a cup, but Rimachi shook his head and remained standing, indicating that he had come in an official capacity.

"The Sapa Inca sent me to summon you, my lady," he said to Chuqui. "He asked that you bring your chief of feasts with you."

Chuqui looked across at Fempellec, who had frozen in place, half turned toward Machacuay, who was propped up against the wall next to him. Rimachi went on, addressing himself to Cusi and Micay.

"He also sent for the two of you. In fact, he chose me as his messenger because he had remembered that you and I came out of Chachapoyas together to report the rebellion. He wants you to bring your battle-ax—'the weapon blessed by Pachacuti'—with you."

Chuqui and Micay rose and began to comb out their hair and brush each other off, and Cusi went to get his battle-ax.

"Can I go, too?" Cahua asked plaintively.

Rimachi looked down at her with a sympathetic smile. "Not this time, I am afraid. He did not send for your mother as a healer."

"Why, then?"

Rimachi glanced at Micay. "He remembered her, as well. As the ñusta who knew about the Rainbow House."

"He remembered that?" Micay said in disbelief.

"Lloque Yupanqui is with him, and he appeared exhausted."

"How did the Sapa Inca appear?" Cusi asked as he returned, and Rimachi glanced once at Chuqui before speaking bluntly.

"Obsessed. Excited by things no one else could see, and by vilca. He is like a man with the fever, except he will not lie down."

Cusi asked Tarapaca to stand a careful watch while they were gone, and Micay left Cahua in the care of Chuqui's most trusted retainer. Fempellec finally got up and joined them as Rimachi led the way out of the awning house.

"Why does he want me?" Fempellec wondered aloud. "I am not in his memory."

"Perhaps not," Rimachi allowed, glancing back over his shoulder. "But he has sent for Amaru, too."

Fempellec swallowed audibly and hung back for a moment, but then started moving again just as Cusi reached back for him. He marched past Cusi, his soft face set in a grimace of determination.

"Now," he said to himself. "Now . . . we pay."

A FIRE WAS burning in the center of a much larger blackened area in the middle of the courtyard, and Huayna Capac was sitting behind it on a three-legged stool. He was bare-chested except for the strings of beads and precious stones around his neck, though he was wearing a short jaguar-skin mantle over his shoulders and wristbands of the same spotted fur. His unbound hair was disheveled and hung down over his forehead in place of the ruler's fringe, and a long silver snuffing tube rested across his splayed thighs. With his chin propped on one fist, he stared down into the flames in front of him and did not acknowledge the four people who made the mocha to him from the other side of the fire.

Lloque Yupanqui was standing just behind the ruler, Cusi noted, and he did indeed appear exhausted, his shoulders slumped and his head bowed. Behind him, crouched in the shadows where the garden foliage began, were a few others, all apparently wearing the earplugs. Cusi recognized Ninan Cuyochi and Rumiñaui, and he thought the man lying on his side was Atauhuallpa, who was still recovering from the sickness.

There was a small commotion to Cusi's left, and Amaru was led in, flanked on either side by a Cañari warrior armed with a wooden club. Cusi got only a brief glimpse of his brother's face before Amaru and his guards bowed in the mocha, but it did not look like the face of a man who had come here to plead. His appearance jarred Huayna Capac out of his trance, and the ruler suddenly stood up, letting the silver snuffing tube fall to the ground unheeded. He scanned the line of people in front of him for several moments, finally allowing his gaze to settle on Chuqui Huipa.

"Are these your friends, my daughter?" he asked. "Are these the people who will attend you when I am gone and you are the Coya?"

Chuqui made an imploring gesture, and he nodded for her to come forward, extending a hand as she circled the fire. Chuqui bowed over the hand and kissed it, and when she straightened up, her face was wet with tears.

"I cannot believe you will ever be gone, my father," she murmured.

Huayna Capac smiled, though only briefly. "I am summoned in my dreams every night," he said bluntly, taking his hand back. "So I must think about what I will leave behind me. Do you speak for these people?"

Chuqui turned halfway back, dabbing at her eyes with the edge of her mantle. Her voice was surprisingly firm. "Yes, my lord; I would gladly speak for each of them. They are among my most trusted friends."

"Even the Chimu?" Huayna Capac demanded, jerking his chin at Fempellec. "You! Go stand with Amaru. Guards, leave us!"

Fempellec obeyed without raising his eyes from the ground, walking in front of Cusi to take the place of the guard beside Amaru. The ruler followed his progress through narrowed eyes, his teeth bared in a derisive grimace.

"Go ahead, Amaru," he urged, "greet your pretty friend. It is said that he is closer to you than a brother . . . or even a sister."

Amaru looked down at Fempellec, who was shaking, then raised his eyes to meet the ruler's gaze. With great deliberation, he lifted his arm and placed it gently around Fempellec's shoulders, a gesture that denied all shame. Cusi caught his breath as a memory welled up inside him, and he found himself gripping the handle of his battle-ax tightly, ready once again to risk his life for his brother.

"He is my comrade and friend," Amaru said with the same deliberation. "He put his trust in my protection when I brought him here from Chan Chan, and I will not let anyone harm him."

"You harm yourself by defending him," Huayna Capac warned.

"I would harm myself much more if I abandoned him now," Amaru told him. "So put an end to this, my lord, and judge me if you must. I will bear my punishment like an Inca."

Huayna Capac grunted sharply and came around the fire, moving forcefully but with a lurch to his step, as if his muscles were slightly beyond his control. Amaru stood motionless with his arm still around Fempellec, displaying none of the expected signs of deference as the ruler advanced on him. Out of the corner of his eye, Cusi saw the Cañari guards edging back into range, and he turned toward them, instinctively adopting a battle stance. The guards saw him and hesitated, but Huayna Capac marched right up to Amaru, his golden earplugs swinging, the beads around his neck clicking like teeth.

"You could be condemned to death!" he threatened. "You could be crushed slowly beneath heavy stones!"

"I have never been afraid to die," Amaru said calmly.

Huayna Capac turned and spat on the ground. "You deserve to die for your corruption," he proclaimed, and suddenly he strode toward Cusi with his hands outstretched. "Your weapon!"

Cusi felt as if he were watching himself from afar, seeing himself begin to extend the battle-ax and then stop, holding back just as the ruler laid his hands on the handle. Huayna Capac tugged but Cusi would not let go, and they stood locked together for a moment. The man's smell—a rank mixture of sweat and smoke and fur—brought Cusi back to his senses, and he saw the ruler's wild eyes and distended nostrils and heard the deep, uneven rasp of his breathing. Huayna Capac pulled harder, but Cusi could feel that there was no strength behind his fury, and he held him fast.

"I cannot let you have it, my lord," Cusi said, his voice pulled taut by the strain on his arms. "Not to kill my own brother. You would have to kill me first."

Huayna Capac opened his mouth, but he was too out of breath to speak. As he realized his incapacity, the anger seemed to drain out of him, and Cusi suddenly felt he was not so much keeping the ax from him as holding him up with it.

"No, no one must be killed," he murmured, as if remembering a previous agreement. "I have a better use . . ."

Letting go of the ax, he staggered backward, then righted himself and walked toward Amaru, gesturing loosely with his hands.

"You went to Pachacamac," he said, gulping for air between words. "You told me. The huaca said to build far from the places of men."

" 'Far from the places men would fight for,' " Amaru corrected. Huayna Capac shook his head and held up a hand with his thumb and forefinger touching, the royal command to listen.

"I remember what you told me," he insisted. "And now, for once, you will obey the wishes of the gods. I am sending you to Machu Picchu, a place few men ever see and none would fight for. There you will build a shrine to Mama Ocllo and Pachamama, to stand forever in my memory. It was the dying wish of Mama Huarcay, my Fourth Wife."

Over the ruler's head, Amaru sent a sardonic glance to Cusi, or perhaps to Micay behind him. But then he simply bowed to the ruler in compliance.

"You will leave this city tomorrow," Huayna Capac told him. "Take this one with you, and anyone else who is willing to accompany you. Perhaps your disgrace will have been forgotten by the time you are ready to return."

"Farewell, my lord," Amaru said, with a lack of expression that bordered on indifference. Then he bowed again and backed out of the ruler's presence, taking Fempellec with him. Huayna Capac staggered back to his stool and sat down heavily, calling to his servants for coca. He filled his cheek and chewed, nodding gratefully when Chuqui fanned him with a feather fan she had taken from one of the retainers. Finally he looked up and gestured for Cusi and Micay to come closer to the fire. Cusi felt cinders crunch beneath his bare feet as they entered the blackened circle, and he realized they were walking over the remains of offerings, or perhaps of fires that had been used to foretell the future. Huayna Capac had great faith in the sorcerers who claimed to hear prophecies in the rustle of the flames.

The ruler studied them for a long moment, appearing subdued and thoughtful, as if his outburst had purged him of his anger and impatience. In the bright firelight, his dissipation showed plainly in his face, which seemed puffy and bruised around his eyes and mouth and heavy along the jaw. Cusi understood why it had been so easy to withhold the ax from him.

"I remember when you were brought to me half dead," he said at last, sounding almost wistful. "I bent over you, and you thought I was the Grass Man and tried to hide in your blankets. I did not think you would live to speak to me coherently. Then, when you did speak to me, you asked for my daughter in marriage!" He threw back his head in a laugh that became a wet cough and forced him to remove the depleted wad of coca from his mouth. He dropped it into the fire with a flourish, seeming pleased by the way it sizzled. "I gave you the Rainbow House instead, and later I gave you this woman in marriage," he went on, pointing at Micay with his chin. "Has she been a good wife to you?"

Bemused by the question, Cusi glanced at Micay and smiled. "She has been more than that, my lord."

"And you, my daughter," Huayna Capac said to Micay, "you are the one who lured my daughter into the ranks of the White Women."

"I welcomed her into our midst, my lord," Micay allowed. "She made herself into an able healer."

He looked up at Chuqui, who had stopped her fanning. "She will have to make herself into the Coya soon. How can you help her with that?"

"By being a loyal and honest friend," Micay said smoothly. "She knows that I do not come to her owing favors or seeking them, and that I will tell her what I believe is true. And when the time comes, I can be her midwife."

Huayna Capac leaned back and touched a finger to his lips, appearing impressed by the crisp certainty of her reply. "What do you know of Cuzco, though? That is where the new Coya will have to establish her court."

"I have never seen Cuzco," Micay admitted. "But surely after all these years—and after the sickness—it will seem like a new life to everyone."

Chuqui delicately cleared her throat. "Much will also depend on the new Sapa Inca, will it not? Whoever he may be . . ."

The ruler gave her a cool smile. "I do not have to guess whom you would recommend." He glanced across at Cusi. "You obviously do not think it should be Huascar, either."

"No, my lord," Cusi agreed, and he saw Lloque Yupanqui edge in a little closer behind the ruler. "Not when there is another son more worthy of the fringe."

Cusi's words sounded presumptuous to his own ears, and he braced himself for the inevitable reprimand. He could not believe that this was the same man who had tried to wrest his weapon from him only moments before. He appeared to have forgotten that entirely.

"You told me once about a vision you had had," the ruler said, eying Cusi thoughtfully, "of brother fighting against brother and father against son, bringing on the pacha puchucay, the end of our world."

"Yes, my lord," Cusi replied, deciding not to correct the ruler's memory of what he had been told.

"I have had the same vision," Huayna Capac declared, staring down into the fire. "It will begin soon, with my death. Have you seen this, too?"

Cusi was aware that Lloque had raised his chin in a subtle signal of encouragement, but he needed no prompting to recognize that his chance had come. "I was told in Cuzco, my lord, that the huacas everywhere speak of great turmoil when the Sapa Inca is gone. They say your power will fall into pieces, so that no one man will ever hold all of it again."

"Yes," Huayna Capac said, nodding in recognition. "I know this, even though the speakers of the great huacas are afraid to tell me the whole truth. It is inevitable." He paused for a moment, lost in the flickering warmth of the flames. Then he looked up and spread his hands wide, so that the jaguar-skin mantle came untied and slid backward off his shoulders. "So . . . can you deny what your own vision tells you? No one can thwart the will of the gods. If I withheld the fringe from Huascar now, he would surely try to claim it after I was gone. It would be brother against brother, just as you were shown."

"But you are still with us, my lord," Cusi pointed out. "And if you were to proclaim a new Heir and then summon Huascar to acknowledge your choice, he would have to obey your command. He could not prepare for war while he was marching here from Cuzco."

Huayna Capac toyed with the beads and stones hanging across his chest, his eyes on Cusi's face. There was suspicion in his gaze, but also a kind of shrewd appreciation. "So you *would* try to thwart the gods, and you would tell me how to do it. Your uncle told me you had lost your arrogance, but that is clearly not true."

Cusi bowed over the battle-ax in his hands. "My vision was given to me as a warning, my lord. I was told to be vigilant and see that our strength is not squandered. Surely I must heed what the gods have told me, even if it is their will that I fail in my actions."

The ruler gave him a bleak smile. "Yes, just as I must. You understand, then," he concluded, including Chuqui in his glance, "why the matter of my successor cannot be decided by means of consultation and argument. The choice must come to me in a way that cannot be questioned or denied."

Cusi bowed again in acquiescence, and Huayna Capac rose and came around the fire. This time Cusi offered him the battle-ax willingly, and he took it and examined it carefully, turning it over in his hands.

"It is the same one? The shaft is unmarked."

"It was burned when I had the sickness," Cusi explained. "The ax head was returned to me when I had recovered."

"So you returned from the dead a second time," Huayna Capac mused. His arms began to quiver from the weight of the ax, and abruptly he handed it back. "You will carry that when you escort my body back to Cuzco. You will be a member of the honor guard that walks with me in death." He stopped and put his hands on his hips, his eyes glittering with sudden emotion. "I was your warlord, was I not?"

"You were, my lord," Cusi agreed. "You were the warlord who led us to victory over the Carangui."

"Yes . . . you will bear me back to Cuzco in triumph," the ruler said, nodding to himself. Then he let out a long breath and looked at Cusi, his expression becoming rueful. "You should always have been my favorite, Cusi Huaman. Why that could not be . . . is a mystery I will not live to resolve."

With a parting glance at Micay and a nod to Chuqui, he turned and walked past the fire and out of the courtyard, trailed by the retainers, who silently scooped up his stool and mantle and carried them after him. When the ruler was gone and Cusi and Micay had straightened up from their bows, Lloque Yupanqui came around the fire to join them. He was carrying his braided headband, his long fingers moving absently over the knots.

"Now, I think, there is nothing more we can do," he suggested. "Let us go and say our farewells to Amaru."

"No!" Chuqui said emphatically, startling the other three, even though she was speaking to herself. She realized she was still holding the feather fan and discarded it with an impatient gesture. "I must talk to my mother. I will see you when you return," she said to Micay, and she went off in the same direction her father had gone. They watched as Ninan Cuyochi stepped out of the shadows to meet her.

"Do you think it will be . . . as we hope?" Micay asked.

"It depends upon who is the Sapa Inca at the end," Cusi said, "the man who tried to take my weapon in anger or the man who gave it back with regret."

"The man he was or the man he could have been," Lloque concluded, sounding more resigned than bitter. "Come, let us get away from here. I am tired of smelling smoke and guessing at the future. That is no way for an Inca to live . . ."

THE PRIESTS were blowing their conch horns, signaling the middle of the night, when Micay and her party finally left the palace and walked toward Amaru's compound. They had waited so Rimachi could join them and then had stopped to pick up Tarapaca, Machacuay, and Cahua. Cahua was still half asleep, and Cusi and Rimachi took turns carrying her on their backs. The streets were dark and deserted, and the few sentries still at their posts let them pass without question.

Amaru's compound, however, had been lit with torches raised on poles, so that the light was visible above the enclosure walls, and the lively huffing of flutes drifted out through the open gate along with the sounds of voices and laughter. Micay glanced at Cusi and saw that the noise had awakened Cahua, who was draped over his back with her head on his shoulder.

"I had not expected a celebration," she murmured, and Cusi shook his head in bewilderment and gestured for her to lead the way through the gate. The noise intensified as they entered and found themselves in a crowd that must have numbered close to a hundred, spread out over both levels of the compound. Some were eating and some already drinking, and those clustered around the musicians on the upper terrace had begun to sing and dance. They were mostly Quitos, and they politely cleared a path for Micay when they saw the earplugs Cusi, Lloque, and Rimachi wore. Amaru and Parihuana were standing at the top of the steps to the second level, surrounded by people with cups in their hands, and as Micay approached Sinchi and Topa came bounding down the stairs. Sinchi stuck his head into her stomach and hugged her around the waist, surprising her with his strength. Before she could hug him back he pulled away and looked up at Cusi, who was just setting Cahua on her feet.

"Are we going to Machu Picchu, too?" Sinchi asked eagerly, and Topa, who had jumped up into Rimachi's arms, repeated the question to his father.

"To Cuzco, anyway," Cusi allowed. Then he looked up as Amaru greeted them from the top of the stairs. He was wearing a brilliant red and yellow tunic and was holding a puma-head cup in each hand.

"I know I owe you as well, my uncle, and you, Micay. But let me give the first toast to my brother, who would not give the Sapa Inca a weapon with which to kill me."

"He was crazed with vilca," Cusi said with a shrug. "He did not know what he was doing."

"You were ready to fight, though," Amaru insisted, smiling down at him. "I saw you, and so did the guards. You looked like the Cusi I remembered from Chan Chan."

"You looked like the brother I remembered from Cuzco," Cusi told him, seeming mildly embarrassed. "I am sorry that we failed to free you completely."

"But you have!" Amaru said with an incredulous laugh, and he came down the steps, thrusting the cup in his right hand toward Cusi. "Enough of your modesty. To Inti, our father . . ."

Following Amaru's example, Cusi poured a small amount of the foamy liquid onto the ground. Before he could drink, though, Amaru raised his cup again and spilled out a little more.

"And to Pachamama, our mother . . ."

"To Pachamama," Cusi agreed in a baffled tone, which seemed to please Amaru enormously. As the two men drank, Parihuana, Choque Chinchay, and some of the other guests descended the stairs with extra cups of akha in their hands. Parihuana appeared to share Amaru's exuberance and to take the same pleasure in Micay's bewilderment. She seemed to be repressing laughter as she pressed a cup into Micay's hands.

"What is it I do not understand?" Micay asked helplessly. "I did not expect that you would celebrate being banished."

"We had expected far worse," Parihuana told her. "Just to have them back alive seemed like a gift . . ."

"And Machu Picchu cannot be considered banishment," Amaru said, "not when it is so close to Cuzco. It is remote because of its holiness, not its distance from the places where people live."

"It is very far from Quito, however," Cusi pointed out. "I did not think you were eager to leave what you have built here."

"It has come to seem like a prison to us," Amaru said, frowning briefly. "We will come back when we can live here as we were meant to. Besides, I have never been offered the chance to build a shrine."

"A shrine to Pachamama," Parihuana added, giving Micay a knowing glance. "Perhaps her anger with us will be assuaged. You would certainly have ample reason to bring Cahua on a pilgrimage."

"It is a holy place?" Cahua inquired, and Parihuana smiled down at her.

"One of the most holy, my daughter. It is called Old Mountain because it stands on top of a great mountain."

"It is not far from the coca fields and the trail to Vitcos," Cusi mused aloud, reaching down to rest a hand on Sinchi's shoulder. "We could visit your Uncle Uritu, as well."

Sinchi cocked his head for a moment, then let out a resounding whoop that startled the onlookers and made them all laugh. The crowd around Amaru began to disperse, many going back up the stairs to join the dancers. Micay looked in that direction and saw Fempellec inside the awning house, directing the cooks with a cup in one hand and a long wooden spoon in the other. He was dancing in place and making lewd faces that had the women doubled over with laughter.

"He wants to go, too," Parihuana said, coming close to take her arm. "He is glad to be as far from the court as he can get."

"This was to be Mama Huarcay's last bit of revenge," Micay said in disbelief. "And the Sapa Inca's last punishment."

There was a smile in Parihuana's voice. "Then it is our duty to show that they cannot touch us. How long has it been since we danced together?"

"How long has it been since I danced at all?" Micay asked the air, shaking her head ruefully. Parihuana reached down with her other hand for Cahua.

"Come, let us go ask for a women's dance . . ."

"May healers dance?" Cahua asked as they started toward the stairs.

"Everyone can dance," Parihuana assured her. "Everyone who has not forgotten how good it is to be alive and moving . . ."

AMARU'S FRIENDS and neighbors had departed some time before, carrying off, as gifts, all the food, clothing, and other belongings that Amaru and Parihuana could not fit into their packs. A herder had brought the pack llamas and bedded them down in the far corner of the compound, well away from the garden, and the children had also been persuaded to sleep, lulled by their parents' singing and the promise that they would be awakened in time to witness the departure.

Those who remained sat in the cool green of the garden, talking quietly and letting the akha wear off as the sky slowly grew less dark. No one had anything more to say about the Sapa Inca, or the Heir, or the prospect of returning to Cuzco. At Rimachi's urging, Parihuana was retelling the story of the birth of Ñupchu's firstborn, a daughter named Suchi.

"Huaman Cachi came down from the Guanaco House two days ago to tell us," she explained. "You should have seen how proud he was! He had helped with the birth, and he made it sound like a major battle. He was most proud of the fact that afterward Tomay made him an 'uncle by privilege.' Then Tomay attacked him with a broom and almost broke his arm."

"Attacked him!" Rimachi exclaimed. "What for?"

"He said Tomay was training him to be alert and ready to defend himself at any moment. This was the first time he had been caught off guard, so he bore his sore arm like the insignia of a proud uncle. He said Ñupchu threw a cup at Tomay when she heard about it later."

Rimachi grinned at Cusi. "Sumac Mallqui would have been proud of that trick." Then he swiveled toward the compound gate and rose to his feet. "Someone has come. One of my men."

They all watched in silence as Rimachi went to greet the warrior, who was breathing hard where he stood. Amaru also got to his feet, and one by one the others joined him, except for Fempellec, who remained sprawled across a bench. But he was watching, too, as Rimachi dismissed the warrior and walked back into the garden. Rimachi addressed Lloque Yupanqui: "You and I have been summoned to the palace, my lord. The Sapa Inca has fallen ill."

"With the fever?"

Rimachi shrugged. "The man was not told why we should come. But the rumor of his illness was all over the palace."

Amaru came forward, limping slightly, and took each of them by the hand. "Stay close to him if you can," he urged. "Make him do what is right before he dies."

"We will try," Lloque promised, and he went to embrace Parihuana and take the hand Fempellec shyly offered to him. He and Rimachi were still engaged in their farewells when a second messenger came through the compound gate. They all waited while the woman picked them out of the shadows and came their way. She was one of Chuqui Huipa's retainers, and she came directly to Micay.

"She asks that you come to her, my lady. She asks that you come in white."

"Is she tending the Sapa Inca?" Micay asked, but the woman shook her head.

"No, my lady. She is with Ninan Cuyochi."

Micay froze in disbelief and did not move even when Cusi came to her side. "Go to her, Micay," he urged. "I will look after the children."

Parihuana came up on her other side. "Come, my sister. We will say our farewells on the way to the gate."

Still too stricken to speak, Micay allowed herself to be led off, following Lloque and Rimachi out of the garden. The four men who remained stood in silence until Tarapaca glanced up at the sky and politely cleared his throat.

"It is growing light. I will go wake the herder and begin the loading," he offered, nodding to Cusi and Amaru as he left.

"I was afraid for a moment that the messenger was for us," Amaru said to Fempellec, who grimaced and nodded in agreement.

"Come to tell us that our sentence had been changed."

"I think we will be grateful to be away from the places men would fight for," Amaru said dryly. "Perhaps you would like to come with us, Cusi. He said I could take anyone who wished to accompany me."

Cusi shook his head distractedly, still staring in the direction Micay had gone. "No . . . we are too much a part of this, whatever happens. But if we lose Ninan . . ."

"There would be no one who could challenge Huascar's right to the fringe," Amaru finished for him. "The Four Quarters would belong to him, to rule as he pleases."

"To *ruin* as he pleases," Fempellec muttered. They fell silent again, and Parihuana came back to join them. Her face seemed to mirror Cusi's concern.

"She recovered her composure," Parihuana reported, "and she left here determined to save him. But I have never seen her like that, Cusi. She was shaken to her heart."

"So much of what she hopes for depends on Ninan becoming the Sapa Inca," Cusi explained, "and she has no power over the sickness. She was determined to save Quinti and our mother, too."

"Do not remind her of that," Fempellec said sharply. "She has a gift for keeping hope alive, and you must encourage her. You must display some hope of your own."

Cusi squinted at him. "I have not discouraged her or reminded her of anything she does not remember too well by herself. A display of hope will not keep Ninan alive or make him the Heir."

"How do you know?" Fempellec demanded, but Amaru intervened before Cusi could reply.

"This is not a time to be arguing," Amaru scolded, taking Fempellec by the arm and turning him toward the hut at the back of the garden. "Come, let us all have a last look at Little Quito. Let us remember the life we had here, if only for a short time."

"It is a memory we should take with us to Machu Picchu," Parihuana said as she and Cusi fell in behind them. "And to Cuzco."

There is nothing so great it cannot be lost to memory, Cusi thought, but he did not say it aloud. Instead he nodded agreeably to Parihuana, telling himself that if he could not display hope, he should not deny it, either. Perhaps it mattered in a way he could no longer see from his distance. Or perhaps not. But he did not want to be known, now or in the future, as a man who offered his friends only a stone to carry.

XIX

TOPA CUSI HUALLPA:

Huascar

(A.D. 1528)

Vilcashuaman

WHEN THE thunder broke overhead, it momentarily drowned out the many voices in the hall and made faces turn toward the roof. It was a heavy, authoritative sound, as if the sky had cracked like a stone and was slowly falling apart.

The women gathered at one end of the great hall seemed frozen in place. Dressed in their finest clothing and jewelry but barefoot, their heads uncovered, they were arrested in the act of loosening their hair and daubing their unpainted faces with ashes from an offering fire, preparing themselves for another ceremony of mourning. The only clean faces in the group belonged to the Coya Rahua Ocllo and Chuqui Huipa, and Chuqui was made even more conspicuous by the fact that she was still wearing her head cloth. The Coya had been remonstrating with her because of this when the thunder sounded, causing her to break off and glance upward with an exasperated expression, as if the storm were one more thing sent to thwart her. Chuqui chose that moment to turn her back on her mother and walk away, toward the doorway where Micay, Quespi, and the children were standing.

"Can we go, too?" Sinchi asked in a whisper, apparently unaware of the significance of Chuqui's departure but always eager to witness a storm. Micay exchanged a glance with Quespi, then caught the eye of the Coya, who lifted her chin slightly in a gesture of appeal. Chuqui was walking with her head held high and her eyes veiled in a way that made her appear arrogant, making it clear she had no intention of heeding anyone's command to stop. It was that heedless expression, more than the Coya's appeal, that suddenly aroused a great impatience in Micay. It seemed a pointless waste of will, a squandering of strength.

She let Chuqui pass through the doorway before following, taking the twins with her and nodding her assent when Machacuay moved to join them. They came out into a wind that tossed Micay's hair about and made it impossible for her to see until she turned to face it directly. It was blowing from the east, where the green flanks of the mountains were shrouded in mist, the peaks hidden completely behind a huge mass of clouds, some as white as washed cotton, others black as pitch. Micay drank in the dusty, resinous smell of the mountains along with the refreshing damp of the coming rain, and her impatience became a desire for cleansing, for purging.

Sinchi was grinning happily as Machacuay discreetly led him and Cahua farther out onto the open plaza, away from the stream of messengers and retainers who were going in and out of the middle doorways of the hall. Micay went after Chuqui, who had wandered out onto the plaza and seemed to be heading toward the enclosure wall on the other side. To Micay's left was the great dais of the Inca, a massive stone seat that stood atop a stepped pyramid that vaguely resembled the burial temples of Chan Chan. Its front stairway was on the other side, facing the enormous central plaza of Vilcashuaman, where the thousands of people who had been summoned to witness the ceremony were no doubt already beginning to gather. Thunder rumbled again and Micay imagined them standing silently in the rain, taking their last look at Huayna Capac and wondering what was to come next.

Chuqui had stopped at the wall, which formed a compound around the dais and the hall and plaza behind it. She was looking up at the wall and running her hand over the rough surface of the stones, and for a moment Micay was reminded of herself in the House of Chosen Women, searching in vain for a way out. The memory tempered her impatience, but only until Chuqui turned and spoke in a petulant voice.

"Do not tell me I am being foolish, Micay."

Micay let out a breath that was almost an exclamation. "That is hardly necessary. It is the way you always choose when you wish to defy your mother."

Chuqui's eyes narrowed. "Are you taking her side now?"

"She has never shown any interest in having me on her side," Micay said, though she recalled the Coya's gesture of appeal. "And I have no stake in this ceremony. I have mourned for him only as a matter of duty, and I am grateful that this is the last time we will have to blacken our faces and tear our hair for him."

"Then why did you come after me?"

"I suddenly had no more patience for what you are doing. It is senseless to punish your mother with these childish acts of defiance. All you want is a chance to show her you will not listen, as she would not listen in Quito."

"Perhaps she needs to be shown," Chuqui said stubbornly.

"Still?" Micay demanded. "It has been a year, Chuqui—a year today—since your father died. In five more days it will be a year since Ninan died. Does it matter now that your mother would not support him over Huascar? Huayna Capac made him the Heir anyway, but that did not save him from the sickness. You and I could not save him either, and we have punished ourselves for that." Micay glanced up as lightning flashed out of the advancing clouds. "But it is time to stop this. Cuzco is too close. We have to put this behind us and prepare for what is ahead."

"You know what is ahead," Chuqui retorted. "You know *who*."

"Yes—and you will not be able to walk away from him," Micay said unsparingly. "You will need all your strength to stand up to him."

"Stand up to him?" Chuqui said with a mirthless laugh. "For what? I am not meant to have anything good in this life. It does not matter what happens to me, so why should it matter what I do?"

Micay stared at her without sympathy. "Whatever happens to you, my lady, also happens to those who serve you and to their children. I will not throw away what is good in my life for no reason."

Chuqui straightened up, putting a hand against the wall to steady herself. "You would abandon me?"

"You heard Chimpu Ocllo's last words to us: 'You owe everything to those who return your love, but nothing to those who do not recognize its value.' "

Tears welled up in Chuqui's eyes, forcing her to drop her gaze. She began to sob, softly and helplessly, her shoulders shaking. Micay started to reach out to her, then realized her hands were still black with soot. Chuqui looked up at her, her face tear-streaked and forlorn, showing Micay her grief and loss. Her eyes widened but she did not flinch as Micay raised her blackened fingertips and gently stroked her cheeks, soothing her and painting her face with the ash of mourning. Then Micay reached around behind her neck and untied her head cloth, loosing her hair to the turbulent wind.

"We will not stop in five days to mourn for Ninan," Micay explained, "so let us grieve for him today. No one can see into our hearts and know for whom we grieve."

"You will stay with me?" Chuqui asked, still weeping, and Micay took her by the arm and turned her back toward the great hall.

"I will be with you," she promised. "Come, let us go empty ourselves and bid farewell to our grief."

THE OTHER members of the honor guard were squatting near the doorways, their shields and weapons propped up against the wall. They were talking quietly and looking out at the rain that was falling on the plaza. As the inside of the hall had grown darker, Cusi had moved apart from them so that he could watch the high priest and his priests dress Huayna Capac for the ceremony. Under ordinary circumstances only the members of Huayna Capac's household, Tumibamba, would be allowed to witness such an intimate act. But after months on the road and dozens of similar ceremonies, no one bothered to observe such niceties.

So Cusi watched the priests hover around the dead ruler, bowing to him and displaying garments for his choosing. The mummy was an egg-shaped bundle about three feet high, bound tightly in dark cloth that was never removed. The fleshless face was sunk in around bared white teeth and the golden discs that filled his eye sockets, topped by a startling shock of black hair. The bundle weighed almost nothing, Cusi knew from ceremonial duty, and it had an odor that was both musty and vaguely ripe, like a poorly tanned hide. In no way did it remind him of the Huayna Capac he had known, and he felt none of the awe he remembered so vividly from his one visit to Pachacuti.

The high priest bent over in front of the mummy, putting his ear close to the bared teeth, then straightened up and selected a tunic that glimmered with red, yellow, and blue feathers. Two of the priests carefully pulled it down over Huayna Capac's unmoving head, tucking the extra folds of cloth in around the bottom of the bundle. A mirror was brought so that the ruler could admire himself, and the priests bowed some more and murmured compliments. Cusi wondered if he would feel the same lack of emotion and reverence if he went to see Pachacuti now.

He was still wondering when he realized that the high priest had stepped aside and was staring at him. He thought for a moment that Topa Yupanqui was going to upbraid him for his curiosity, since the high priest knew him too well to mistake it for devotion. But then there was a burst of laughter from the men near the doorways, and the priest frowned ferociously and looked past him. Cusi turned and saw that Huaman Cachi had just come in out of the rain, his dark skin glistening and his long black hair plastered down onto his neck and shoulders. He had obviously dressed in a hurry, inadvertently tucking one side of his tunic into the waistband of his loincloth, and it was this as much as his bedraggled appearance that had drawn the men's laughter. Challco-chima reached up and pulled the tunic loose for him, and after a brief attempt at innocent surprise Huaman Cachi shrugged and grinned. He turned and looked around for Cusi, and he must have seen the high priest watching because he sobered instantly and walked toward Cusi with his gaze lowered.

Cusi turned back and found the high priest glaring at him, visiting his displeasure with the apprentice on the master, and Cusi nodded instinctively, acknowledging his responsibility. Huaman Cachi sat down next to him, but Cusi continued to stare at Topa Yupanqui, who was waiting to see what he would do. You have not been so responsible yourself, priest, Cusi thought, resenting the scrutiny even more because it ignored the men who had laughed. The high priest finally understood and turned away with an audible huff of disapproval.

"It is raining hard," Huaman reported after a moment, peeking at Cusi out of the corner of his eye, "and the plaza is filled with people. I saw Chancas, Soras, Rucanas, and many different kinds of mitmacs."

"I know who is here," Cusi said curtly. "Were you with the same woman?"

Huaman looked down at his hands, repressing a smile. "No, my lord. Her older sister."

"I should make you stand in the rain until you have cooled off enough to have some sense. But we will probably have to do that anyway. So instead I will have your promise that this will not happen again. You will not lie with a woman from one day before any major ceremony until one day after."

"But my lord," Huaman protested incredulously, "no one except the priests is keeping the fast and abstaining as they should. Not even the warriors of the honor guard . . ."

The insinuation made Cusi smile wryly. "I thought Micay and I were quiet last night; we did not awaken the children, anyway." He looked directly at Huaman and let the smile fade. "I am not punishing you for your lust. But I cannot allow you to be so careless."

"We did not do it in the plaza," Huaman muttered. "And she is a retainer, not some Inca's wife. Who would bother to report me?"

"The other sister," Cusi told him. "Do not tell me no one would listen, either. You saw the way the priest looked at you. If an example must be made of someone, who do you think is most likely to be chosen? The Incas in the honor guard? Or an apprentice warrior without rank or blood?"

"Why must an example be made of anyone? If no one else is complying . . ."

"That is when examples are most needed. Especially by those who cannot admit that the laws are being flouted and ignored. Cuzco is filled with such people. So you will promise me."

"You have my promise," Huaman said reluctantly, meeting Cusi's eyes before glancing away. "Your uncle is coming . . ."

Lloque Yupanqui was heading toward the men near the doorways, and Cusi immediately got up and went to join the group. There were four older men in the honor guard, cousins and half brothers of Huayna Capac and members of the Inca Old Guard. They sincerely considered it an honor to be escorting the body back to Cuzco. The other four—Cusi, Quilaco Yupanqui, Challcochima, and Ucumari—were the last remaining members of the group that had defied Huayna Capac and carried Huanacauri out of the Coricancha in Tumibamba. They considered this duty as the ruler's last attempt to command their respect, a most dubious privilege. Because of the demands of their ceremonial role, they could not participate in the deliberations of the funeral column's leaders, except at a distance. Lloque waited for Cusi to squat down with them before he spoke.

"We have received another message from Huascar," he said in a tone of weary exasperation. "It is much like all the others. He demands to know why so many armed warriors march with us and why Atauhuallpa stayed behind in Quito. He tells us again that the high priest of Cuzco, his brother Challco Yupanqui, has made him the Sapa Inca in a solemn ceremony. He also orders us not to empty the royal storehouses to provide gifts for those who have been summoned here."

The group emitted a muted chorus of grunts and snorts and other expressions of disapproval and disgust.

"How have Colla Topa and Yasca replied?" Quilaco asked.

"They have reminded him of his father's dying wishes," Lloque said, "and of the fact that the high priest Topa Yupanqui is still alive and still in possession of the fringe. They did not bother to explain again that Atauhuallpa was left behind as the Regent of the Northern Provinces or that Quizquiz took a thousand warriors back with him."

"What about the gifts?" one of the older men asked with concern.

Lloque shrugged with a kind of stubborn satisfaction. "We simply told him our guests will be accorded the generosity they have learned to expect from the Inca."

As the men murmured their approval, Cusi found himself recalling Quizquiz's parting words, spoken after he had volunteered to lead some troops back and alleviate Huascar's suspicions: *An old priest, a corpse, and a woman well past marrying age. That is not much protection. Watch your backs, my friends.*

There was a flash of lightning outside, so bright that it lit up all their faces, and then the rain came down even harder, accompanied by a crack of thunder.

"Illapa, at least, does not seem to welcome this ceremony," Challcochima said dryly. "Will it be postponed?"

"For as long as possible," Lloque allowed. Then he smiled sardonically. "But surely, if the common people can stand in the rain to watch us, the Incas can go out in the rain to perform. Leave your sandals behind and be careful on the steps of the platform."

The men laughed appreciatively as Lloque rose to his feet. Cusi stood up with him, gesturing for Huaman Cachi to stay where he was. He walked with his uncle toward the middle of the hall, where the leaders of the column were hidden behind a crowd of advisers and messengers. Lloque shook himself and spat with a vehemence that startled Cusi.

"This has begun to feel bad to me, Cusi. It is like shouting at a deaf man. Why will Huascar not wait? He knows the fringe is his now."

"He has been waiting all his life," Cusi reminded him. "And he knows Ninan would have been the Heir in his place, had he lived. He cannot abide the thought that he might yet be cheated."

"We have sent him every assurance, and his spies have been with us since Caxamarca. What will convince him that we come in peace?"

"Perhaps when we lay down our weapons and bow to him in the Haucaypata," Cusi suggested, and Lloque stopped to look at him.

"You do not feel it, too?" He pointed with his chin at the nearest doorway. "You do not see this storm as a sign?"

"It is the rainy season," Cusi shrugged, "and I have never expected anything good from Huascar. I only see that we have no choice but to go to Cuzco and face him."

"Of course," Lloque agreed, though Cusi could tell he was not satisfied with the answer. He had never stopped wanting more urgency from Cusi.

"I am sorry, Uncle. I do not mean to dismiss what you are feeling. But what is it you fear from Huascar?"

Lloque grunted in frustration. "It is only a feeling," he admitted. "My mind tells me to ignore it. My mind tells me there are too many of us for him to harm and that he has too much need of the prestige and legitimacy we are bringing him. The feeling, though, makes me wonder if *his* mind tells him the same things."

"In his mind, he has always owned everything," Cusi said. "He will want to possess our prestige, as well."

"Possess it or consume it?" Lloque demanded. Suddenly he reached out and gripped Cusi by the arms, as if to brace both of them. "I have had dreams, Cusi, dreams in which great jaws close over my head and I am devoured. I have never been afraid of death before, but I am terrified in these dreams, and the fear is still with me when I awaken. I think I am seeing something greater than my own death. Something worse."

Jolted out of his detachment, Cusi looked at him with alarm. "Have you told any of this to Yasca and Colla Topa?"

"It is difficult enough to tell you," Lloque said with a grimace, "and you were once thought to be adept at such things. How long do you think Yasca would listen if I began to tell him about my terrible dreams?"

"He would listen to me," Cusi declared. "But I must have something to tell him that he will understand."

Lloque nodded and let his hands drop to his sides. "We must look harder, both inside and outside ourselves. Talk to Micay and the other comrades; perhaps they have heard something or had dreams of their own."

"I will," Cusi promised, and Lloque forced a smile.

"Farewell then, my son, until we again have the time to discuss our true duty."

"Until then," Cusi agreed, and was surprised when his uncle raised a hand over him in blessing before walking away. As if this farewell might be our last, Cusi thought. He shuddered, moved by the gesture but shamed, too. He turned back toward the honor guard, hearing thunder and hoping the storm would not pass before the ceremony began. He had an urgent need to remember what it meant to be a brother to lightning.

The Royal Road

AT THE ROADSIDE vantage point from which the gorge of the Apurimac River could first be seen, the column stopped to make offerings and to cleanse themselves. The Apurimac was an important huaca, and there were many shrines perched on the cliffs above it, including a famous shrine dedicated to Pachamama. Cusi had told Micay that she would be able to see it after they had passed through the tunnel leading to the long suspension bridge that hung over the river at a great height. The bridge itself was a huaca, since it carried the traveler into the ancestral lands of the Incas.

Micay and Quespi had just finished seeing that all the children—their own, Quinti's two daughters, and Rimachi's son, Topa—were washed and dusted off when a messenger came from the Coya, summoning Micay.

"We can look after the children," Quespi assured her with a nod to Machacuay.

"I can look after myself," Cahua asserted, tugging on Micay's shift. "Can I go with you, Mama?"

"You have seen the Coya many times," Micay reminded her, "and she summoned only me this time. But I will tell her how you sang to Chuqui to make her feel better."

As she walked forward past the resting column, Micay realized that she had not dusted herself off, and she beat at her shift and mantle with her hands. She was thoroughly tired of washing in irrigation ditches and living out of packs, and the faces of those she passed reflected the same weariness. The thrill of seeing Holy Cuzco again had begun to pale beside the prospect of a hot bath and a properly cooked meal. Micay wished she could look ahead to something so trivial, that the suspense over how Huascar would receive them was over and they were safe. But Lloque Yupanqui's dream continued to nag at her, even though they had found nothing to corroborate its dire warning.

The Coya's litter stood in the middle of the road, surrounded by a contingent of the Royal Guard. The teams of Rucana bearers sat on the grass at the side of the road, their bare torsos gleaming with sweat in the sunlight. Rimachi, the commander of the guard, stepped out to meet Micay.

"Cusi was just here," he reported. "He has gone forward to speak to Yasca."

"Finally."

Rimachi raised an eyebrow. "You sound impatient with him."

"Look how close we are to Cuzco."

"Has Huascar devoured us yet?" Rimachi asked dryly. "Nor have we thought of anything to persuade Yasca that he intends to devour us. Cusi is trying to do that empty-handed."

"Yasca must be made more vigilant. Quespi says he scoffs at any suggestion that there is real danger."

"Then he will scoff at Cusi, who cannot tell him anything he does not know. You know that Cusi is doing this to please you and Lloque Yupanqui. He would not let me dissuade him, but his conviction is borrowed."

"He never used to lack conviction," Micay heard herself say. But immediately she wished she could take the words back, along with the contempt and resentment that had been in her voice. Rimachi looked down at her silently, and she felt her cheeks flush under his unsparing gaze.

"We all used to rely on his conviction, his huaca," Rimachi reminded her.

"Even though it made him reckless and dangerous to himself. Is it fair to scorn him now that he no longer has such powers?"

Micay's throat was too thick to allow her to speak, though she could not have found words to describe what she was feeling. She was simply stunned by the realization of how much she had resented Cusi's detachment, and for how long. She had never truly forgiven him for coming back a different man, a man who did not care—or who did not show he cared—with the same fierce, impulsive passion. She missed that and blamed him for its absence, but she had never told him. Instead she had complained to his friend.

"The Coya is waiting," she murmured, unable to look at Rimachi, who simply bowed and led her through the ranks of the guards to the Coya's litter. The curtain on the near side had been thrown up over the canopied roof, and Rahua Ocllo was reclining within on a bed of gorgeously colored cushions. Micay made the mocha and prolonged her bow in an attempt to recover her composure. She could not think of what she should say to the Coya when there was so much she needed to say to Cusi.

When she straightened up and was summoned into the litter, she forced herself to take note of the other women present, seeing that they all wore the light blue of palace retainers. This was to be a private conversation, then. The Coya gestured graciously for her to kneel among the fine cumbi-cloth cushions at the foot of her bed. The rich colors of the soft, thickly woven cloth seemed to blossom around her, and she could smell the sweet grass with which the cushions had been stuffed.

"Tell me about my daughter's condition, Micay," the Coya said, and Micay nodded, grateful for a subject she knew how to address.

"She is much better, my lady. The fever is gone completely and her cough is much diminished. As I suspected, it was only the chill she took at the ceremony at Vilcashuaman."

"We are only a few days from Cuzco. Will she be able to sit up in her litter as we enter the city?"

"If she wishes to," Micay allowed. "My daughter, Cahua, sang to her and got her to eat some solid food."

Rahua Ocllo nodded in approval, and Micay noticed the loose skin on her neck and the thinness of her features. Her long nose and narrow forehead seemed more prominent, and though she was still a handsome woman, she was not aging gracefully.

"Speaking of Vilcashuaman," she said, "I expected you would come to me afterward so that I could express my gratitude."

"For what, my lady?" Micay asked, remembering only the cold and wet, standing beneath a canopy that leaked in a wind that blew the rain sideways. The Coya smiled slowly and tolerantly, as if Micay were teasing her.

"For bringing Chuqui back that day, of course. For convincing her to take her part in the ceremony. You seem to be the only one who can persuade her to act sensibly."

Micay remembered trying to get Chuqui down the slippery steps of the dais while she was still blind and nearly insensible with grief. She looked blankly at the Coya, who was waiting for her reply.

"Sometimes she . . . must find her own reason to participate," Micay blurted out, grasping at the first thing that came into her mind. "I am afraid, my lady, that she feels . . . she feels . . . you have not always supported her in the past."

Micay lowered her eyes, feeling confused and out of control, unable to gauge the possible effect of what she had just revealed.

"Do you think she is justified in this feeling?" Rahua Ocllo asked sharply, and Micay made herself look up. There was displeasure but no outrage in the Coya's eyes; she knew how she had abandoned Chuqui. Yet the manner in which she had posed the question invited a denial, and that was clearly what she wanted to hear from Micay: a lie that would alleviate her guilt but, more than that, would show her that Micay's loyalty could be swayed. Then she would want to enlist Micay as an accomplice, an ally, in the task of making Chuqui act sensibly. Another comrade, Micay thought, and she shook herself fiercely, filled with the guilt of her disloyalty to Cusi.

"I was with her in Tumibamba and Quito, my lady," she said to the Coya. "I heard the messages she sent to you, asking you to speak for the White Women. She never received an answer, my lady."

Rahua Ocllo rose up slightly, as if to defend herself. But then she sank back down on the cushions, her painted lips curling disdainfully.

"It is a pity, Micay, that of all the women who had a hand in training you, Chimpu Ocllo should have had the most lasting influence."

"I can only be proud of that, my lady," Micay said, and then was startled into silence by the sudden approach of Rimachi. He bowed rapidly and did not bother to make the mocha.

"Forgive me, my lady. Huascar has sent his personal representative to Colla Topa and the other leaders. He asks that you and your daughter come ahead to Cuzco immediately. He has also summoned the leaders themselves."

"And they have agreed to go?" the Coya asked.

"They are still deciding, my lady. The rest of the column is to remain here until the city is ready to receive them."

"Go tell Chuqui and the other women that we are leaving," Rahua Ocllo said to Micay, "whether she can sit up or not. Rouse the bearers," she told Rimachi, "and tell Colla Topa we are coming."

Micay and Rimachi backed out of the litter together. They had time for only a few words, because the guards and the bearers were already up and awaiting his command.

"Will you keep Topa with you until we are assigned quarters?" Rimachi asked.

Micay bobbed her head in consent. "I must see Cusi," she said urgently. "If you see him, tell him to find me as we pass."

"I will tell him if I can," Rimachi promised. Then he turned away and began snapping out orders to his men. Messengers and servants were running back and forth along the line, and strings of pack llamas were being led forward.

Micay headed back toward Quespi and the children, suppressing the urge to run herself, though she could not shake the feeling that she was being driven to a destination she would not like for reasons she could only dimly perceive . . .

BECAUSE HE WISHED to speak privately with Yasca, Cusi was still waiting for his turn with the war chief when the official arrived. He was carried up the road in a mesh hammock strung between poles, preceded by a priest who held the multicolored fringe of the ruler aloft on the end of a long staff banded with gold. The leaders of the column ceased their deliberations and assembled in the center of the road, and Cusi joined the crowd that pressed in around them. He could get no closer than the second rank, but he was within hailing distance of Lloque Yupanqui, who was standing just behind Yasca and Colla Topa.

Cusi recognized the official as a brother of Huascar named Inca Roca, a short, undistinguished man who had neither the age nor the prestige for such a lofty post. The official spoke with the voice of the ruler, and he had the power to make arrests and levy punishments, including that of death. Inca Roca spoke in a high, nasal voice that made the refinements of his Cuzco accent seem particularly effete. In the name of the twelfth Sapa Inca, Topa Cusi Huallpa, he commanded that the Coya Rahua Ocllo and her daughter Chuqui Huipa, along with all the other royal daughters, come ahead to Cuzco immediately. They were to be accompanied by the leaders of the column, those who bore the final memories of Huayna Capac. The rest of the column was to wait here until the command came to proceed.

There was a jostling in the crowd behind Cusi, and he turned to see a path being opened for the high priest, who carried Huayna Capac's fringe on the end of *his* staff. Cusi watched him come and suddenly understood the import of Lloque's dream. The jaws had come down over his head to devour him, just as the head of the column was now being drawn forward, where it might be severed from its body and most especially from its long tail of warriors.

When the high priest swept past with the three priests who accompanied him, Cusi stepped out behind him and went forward to join the leaders, who had turned in on themselves to confer. Titu Atauchi was the first to notice his presence, and the sorcerer's eyes flashed with hatred.

"What is he doing here?" he demanded, pointing rudely with his finger. Both Colla Topa and the high priest frowned at the intrusion, but Yasca held up a hand to them, lifting his chin in Cusi's direction.

"He holds the rank of war chief, and he can convey our decision to the others. Cusi, you and Quilaco Yupanqui will share the command in our absence."

"That is not possible," the high priest interrupted indignantly. "They are both members of the Sapa Inca's honor guard. They will be with us."

"Huascar has not asked for his father to be brought forward," Colla Topa explained. "Only the Coya, Chuqui Huipa, and us."

"That is impossible!" the high priest proclaimed, shaking his staff for emphasis. He went forward to question the official himself, and Lloque Yupanqui seized the moment to appeal to the men around him. His gaunt face was pale and rigid with emotion, and he held his hands clasped tightly in front of him. Cusi had exchanged only a glance with him, but he had seen that Lloque had also understood the dream and was struggling with the fear it aroused in him.

"We cannot allow this, my lords," he said flatly. "It was Huayna Capac's wish, as we all heard, to be carried into Cuzco in triumph. We cannot just leave him sitting here in the road without his Coya or the men who speak for him."

"We can meet the rest of the column outside the city and march in together," Colla Topa said. "It is probably best that we arrange this with Huascar so that our war cries are not mistaken for a genuine threat."

"He has made no secret of his suspicions," Lloque persisted. "Should we not have some of our own? Huascar is not yet the Sapa Inca, despite his claims. We have the right to insist that he honor his father's wishes."

"Huascar will be the Sapa Inca," Titu Atauchi put in, "even if you and some others cannot forget Ninan Cuyochi. *I* will not defy his command just to prove our rights."

"I am afraid he is right, my friend," Colla Topa said to Lloque. "Huascar will have the power soon enough, and we will have to live with him."

"If he lets us live," Lloque said, though Colla Topa's apparent sympathy seemed to have defeated him. As if he had said something embarrassing, no one responded to his statement, and after a moment Lloque lowered his eyes, as if to concede that he had. Cusi stepped forward in his place.

"My lords, if you will not take all of us, at least take Huayna Capac and his honor guard. Even a small band of warriors can make a difference."

"What need is there for warriors?" Titu Atauchi demanded. "We should have sent you back with Quizquiz and the other troublemakers. You are simply looking for a reason to rebel."

With an effort Cusi ignored him, directing his urgency at Yasca. "My lord . . . this smells of an ambush, and I have never known you to walk into an ambush empty-handed. Do not do so now."

Yasca studied him for a moment, a glimmer of a smile playing across his rugged face. "You still have the nose of a scout, Cusi. But you are wrong about the difference a few warriors might make. They might incite trouble where none was waiting, and they could not do much if Huascar truly intends to harm us. I cannot believe he does, at least not in the way you suggest. But I will leave the decision about Huayna Capac to the high priest."

Topa Yupanqui came back into the group muttering to himself, one hand cupping his mouth and the other gripping his staff. Colla Topa asked him if he was willing to go forward without the Sapa Inca, and the priest answered with an angry jerk of his head, indicating Inca Roca and his companion.

"He sends a brother without distinction and a priest of minor rank to greet us, as if we were a delegation of chiefs from the provinces! They barely knew to bow to me, and they could only say that they had no instructions concerning Huayna Capac."

"Perhaps we should refuse to go forward without him," Colla Topa suggested, and the high priest seemed to draw in his anger, becoming suddenly shrewd and thoughtful. He glanced around at the group, reading their faces and reconsidering the extent to which he had been insulted—or so it appeared to Cusi, who saw the man's indignation founder on the hard consequences of the word "refuse."

"No," he decided finally. "I would rather take my complaint to Huascar himself. Has the Coya been notified?"

"She is coming," Colla Topa said, pointing with his chin. Cusi turned to see the Coya's litter approaching, led by Rimachi and the Royal Guard and flanked on both sides by a double file of women and children. Chuqui Huipa's litter came close behind, though Cusi could not see Micay among the women on the near side. When he turned back the conclave had broken up, and the leaders were going to join the Coya's retinue. Yasca stopped next to Cusi and Lloque.

"I hope for all our sakes that your fears are unfounded," he said bluntly. "But if we are not safe in Cuzco among our own kin, we are not safe anywhere."

"I have been wrong about many things," Lloque confessed. "I pray that I am wrong about this, too."

"My wife and children will be with you," Cusi reminded Yasca, who simply nodded and laid a hand on Cusi's shoulder in parting.

"Mine, too. We will all be waiting for you. See that you bring the column in good order."

Cusi bowed and watched him walk toward the abbreviated column that was forming up at the side of the road. Then he turned to Lloque.

"Uncle . . ."

Lloque gave his head an abrupt shake, making his golden earplugs swing and tangle in his long hair. "You did the best you could, Cusi. Certainly better than I. I felt their disbelief, and it daunted me. I could not let them see my desperation."

"We could not have convinced them anyway," Cusi told him. "They are not prepared to make Huascar act properly, any more than they were with his father."

"Then we have learned nothing," Lloque said darkly, "and we deserve to be devoured." He reached into the neck of his tunic and pulled a string of shiny black beads up over his head. Attached to the string was a polished disc of obsidian edged in gold. "I always meant for you to have this. Since you have a spirit brother, perhaps it should go to Sinchi. It is meant for a son of Illapa."

"You should keep it with you," Cusi said, though he did not stop Lloque from putting it around his neck. The older man's eyes were moist.

"Now go—find Micay and your children. Tell them to stay very close to Chuqui Huipa. She is the only one Huascar truly needs."

"Farewell, Uncle," Cusi said in a thick voice. "May the gods allow us to meet again."

Lloque touched him on the arm, then turned away without another word, walking slowly toward the head of the forming column. Cusi tucked the disc inside his tunic, next to his heart, and went off toward the rear as fast as he could.

THE LINE AHEAD of them was just beginning to move when Cusi finally appeared. Cahua saw him first from her elevated perch in Chuqui's litter, which the bearers had just lifted to their shoulders. He was on the other side of the litter, and his face suddenly appeared at Cahua's height, and he said something that made the girl laugh. Micay caught her breath in astonishment, having forgotten how high he could jump, and by the time she recovered, he was already coming around the end of the litter. He greeted Quespi and the children and gave his hand to Sinchi, but the whole time he was looking for her, and when their eyes finally met, she received another jolt. It was the Cusi she thought she had been missing, his gaze intense and passionate and searching only for her.

"See, he *is* going to Cuzco with us!" Sinchi called up to his sister, tugging possessively on Cusi's arm. Cusi held Micay's eyes for another moment before bending down to speak seriously to Sinchi.

"Not right away, my son. Quilaco Yupanqui and I have been left in command here." Suddenly he knelt down and took a necklace of some kind off over his head and put it around Sinchi's neck. Micay saw a flash of gold as she approached, and Sinchi's eyes were large and round, making his birthmark look like face paint. He nodded earnestly to whatever Cusi was saying to him, and then Cusi embraced him, holding him for a long moment before letting him go and standing up. Micay could see the string of black beads around Sinchi's neck, but whatever had given off the golden flash was hidden inside his tunic, held fast beneath the hand Sinchi clamped to his chest.

Cusi held out his arms and Micay came into them, pressing herself against him even as Chuqui interrupted by calling down a question from above.

"Why did the leaders agree to this separation?"

Cusi exhaled sharply, though it did not ease the tension in his body, which was making his muscles quiver and his breath come in short bursts. His agitation reminded Micay of the first time they had made love after his return, and she chided herself for wishing he could change back so easily.

"They are afraid of Huascar, my lady," he said to Chuqui, "and they think they can placate him."

"You obviously do not agree," Chuqui observed, and Cusi shrugged without dislodging the fit Micay had achieved between their bodies.

"Lloque Yupanqui and I argued against it, and we tried to get them to take

your father and his honor guard, as well. Yasca and Colla Topa left that choice
to the high priest, but he would not challenge Huascar either."

Suddenly the bearers grunted in unison and lurched into motion, and Chuqui, with a weary gesture, sank back inside the litter. Cusi gave Micay a fierce
squeeze and then reluctantly released her so that they could walk alongside
the litter.

"What did you give Sinchi?" Cahua demanded from above, and Micay
looked up, curious herself.

"It was a gift to him from Lloque Yupanqui," Cusi explained. "It is something that cannot be shared with anyone else."

Cahua made a quizzical noise but Cusi refused to elaborate, turning his head
in the other direction to exchange a glance with Sinchi. The coyness of his
response puzzled Micay at first, too, and then made her gasp in amazement.

"A spirit brother?" she whispered, and Cusi spoke in a low, swift tone that
seemed slightly defensive, as if he had not examined his impulse too closely
before acting upon it.

"I know he is too young . . . but so was I, and I think, at this time, he should
have whatever protection we can give him."

Micay put her head close to his, feeling weak as the implications of the gift
sank in. "Lloque expects to die."

Cusi licked his lips and nodded. "He is too much an Inca to tell them that,
but he tried to make them feel the danger. They would not hear him. They
are prepared to be insulted and mistreated, but they cannot believe Huascar
would actually harm them. I do not know if I can believe it myself . . . I keep
hoping we have somehow misinterpreted his dream."

"The signs have not been clear to any of us," Micay reminded him.

"I have not wanted to attend to them," Cusi said, shaking his head in
self-reproach. "Now I cannot tell anything for certain, except that I do not
want to let you go ahead to Cuzco without me."

Tears sprang up in Micay's eyes, and she hugged him so hard she almost
threw him off balance. "You must not blame yourself! You *must* not."

Cusi tightened his arm around her waist to right himself, blinking at her in
bewilderment. Cahua chose that moment to call down from the litter.

"Yasca and Uncle Quilaco are ahead! They see me!"

Micay raised her face to Cusi, struggling to hold back her tears, because he
was there and she could not tell when they would be this close again.

"Whatever happens," she told him, "you are blameless in my eyes. And you
are always with me, closer than a spirit brother."

Cusi pressed his lips to her forehead and then to her eyes and cheeks, their
hips bumping as they tried to embrace and continue walking at the same time.
Then Yasca and Quilaco were with them, Quilaco lifting up his daughters for
a farewell hug, assuring them he would see them soon in Cuzco.

"I will stay with them now," Yasca said pointedly, and Cusi let go of Micay
and reached down to give Sinchi another hug. Then he took a running jump
and reached out over the heads of the litter bearers to touch Cahua's out-

stretched hand, telling her to take good care of Chuqui. He was coming back toward Micay when Quilaco hooked him by the arm and pulled him out of the line of marchers. Micay could only blow him a kiss as she and Sinchi walked past. He had a hand on his hip, over the stone hidden in his waistband, and while he attempted a farewell smile, he could not conceal the anguished yearning in his eyes.

"I will see you all in Cuzco," he promised, leaning away from Quilaco to try to keep Micay in sight. Micay looked back at him over her shoulder until the road curved and Yasca blocked her view. He was walking with an arm around Quespi and his daughter, Yutu, hanging onto his tunic on the other side. Their son, Huallpa, was just behind them, the top of his head almost even with his father's shoulder.

"He will, Micay," Yasca assured her, and Micay nodded and faced forward again, reaching down for Sinchi's free hand. His other hand was thrust rather awkwardly down the front of his tunic, and he was peering downward with his chin tucked in. He let her take his hand but otherwise paid no attention to her or any of the other people around them. Micay tried to keep him walking straight without disturbing his concentration, deciding that he, at least, should approach Holy Cuzco without fear in his heart.

CUSI HAD GONE out to the sentry post in the middle of the night, and Quilaco Yupanqui found him still there at first light, crouched behind a pile of rocks with his shield and battle-ax in hand. Quilaco was unarmed, with a blanket draped over his shoulders and a water gourd in his hand.

"The man you relieved told me you were out here," Quilaco said tentatively as Cusi rose to meet him. "He could not comprehend why a war chief would choose to stand sentry duty."

"I wanted to be alone," Cusi told him curtly. Quilaco came around the rocks, pausing to examine the trampled ground and the undisturbed bedroll. He gave Cusi a searching glance.

"You have not slept."

Cusi shrugged. "I did not wish to. I am not tired."

Quilaco studied him with undiminished skepticism. "You look as if you are ready to kill someone. Why, Cusi?"

"I may need to. If any harm comes to them . . ."

"Who? Surely, you do not think . . . they are with the Coya and the high priest and men like Yasca and Colla Topa. Huascar would have to be mad to harm any of them."

"He would," Cusi agreed, nodding and hefting his battle-ax to show that he did not dismiss the possibility.

Quilaco glanced away, appearing uncomfortable. "Has your apprentice reported?"

"Not yet. They will be taking the herds to water soon, and perhaps he will have a chance to get close to the warriors at the tunnel and hear something from them."

"Perhaps that is him now," Quilaco suggested, pointing with his chin down the hill. The Royal Road was a broad, pale stripe through the center of the plain that led down to the river, and a lone figure, still at a considerable distance, could be seen coming their way. Cusi put a foot up on the rocks and craned out over them to see.

"Huaman Cachi would not use the road if he had learned anything important. And this person is too slender . . ."

They waited, watching the landscape take on color with the coming dawn. The figure on the road, they finally saw, was wearing light blue.

"It is one of the palace retainers," Quilaco concluded, stepping back from the rocks. "No doubt the Coya left something behind."

"Would she make him run all the way back?" Cusi asked without looking back. "This is a boy, and he is exhausted. Let us go meet him."

"The sentries on the road will stop him. They know I am up here."

Cusi climbed up over the rocks, jumped down, and started down the slope. Quilaco caught up to him with surprising swiftness, thrusting a blanket-draped arm in front of him to make him stop.

"Listen to me, brother-in-law. We were told to share this command. Do not walk away from me like that again."

Cusi gathered himself behind his shield, something in him swelling to the challenge, the threat, of Quilaco's anger. He was ready to knock him down and walk over him, and Quilaco saw it in his eyes and backed off, holding the blanket and gourd in front of his chest. Cusi suddenly understood what was happening to him, and he felt his spirit brother bend in acknowledgement, giving way inside him. He lowered his shield and weapon and gave Quilaco a rueful smile.

"Would you fight me with a blanket and a water gourd?"

Quilaco cocked his head and took several deep breaths. "It seemed for a moment that I might have to. What is wrong with you, Cusi?"

Cusi let out a breath of his own and gestured for them to continue down the hill. "I spent the night considering the possibility that I might have sent my whole family to their deaths. What could be more wrong than that? And for what?"

Quilaco gave him a sidelong glance. "I thought I had come to understand you better on this journey. I am surprised to see you so possessed by anger when there is yet no cause."

The other sentries had stopped the person on the road, as Quilaco had said they would, but now Cusi was close enough to see the boy's light skin and to make out his features.

"It is Huallpa," he said abruptly. "Yasca's adopted son."

One of the sentries had a hand under the boy's arm to support him, and another turned to address Cusi as he and Quilaco jogged up to them.

"He will speak only to you, my lord. He says he is not a retainer."

Cusi hastily put down his shield and battle-ax and took the warrior's place at Huallpa's side. There were bloodstains on the boy's tunic and he had lost his sandals, and he was trembling and gasping for breath at the same time. He looked so pathetic that Cusi put an arm around his shoulders, expecting him to weep. But the boy maintained a dazed courage that did not break as his breathing gradually quieted.

"You must tell us, Huallpa," Cusi coaxed. "How did you get the clothing of a retainer?"

"My father . . . he made me change so I would not be noticed. He made me stay with him after the women and children were sent on ahead. At Limatambo."

"Where is your father now?"

Huallpa stared at Cusi without seeing him, his eyes large and achingly dry. "Dead. They are all dead. We came into a courtyard and suddenly there were men all around us with spears and clubs and knives. My father fought with them, and they killed him. The others were tortured until they begged to be killed."

There was a moment of absolute silence before Quilaco reeled back and shook one of the sentries by the arm.

"Go find Challcochima and Ucumari and bring them here. Hurry!"

"You saw this, my son?" Cusi asked gently, and the boy shuddered and focused on him again.

"I was not to go to him if there was trouble. I was supposed to escape and tell you." Huallpa looked down at the ground. "So I did not help him fight."

"You honored him with your obedience. How did you get away?"

"They made the retainers carry the bodies out and throw them off a cliff." He raised his hands, which were bloodstained up to the wrists. "I helped carry the high priest. They laughed and urinated off the cliff after him and did not see me run away."

Quilaco gave his blanket to Cusi, who wrapped it around the boy's shoulders. Quilaco peered at Huallpa sympathetically, then looked up and waited silently until Challcochima and Ucumari had joined them.

"Tell us again, my son," he prompted. "As far as you know, the women and children were not hurt?"

"They did not stop at Limatambo," Huallpa replied. He looked at Cusi with sudden hope, as if he had not realized until just then that his mother and sister might still be alive.

"But all of the leaders were tortured and killed," Quilaco suggested.

The boy blinked and then frowned. "They did not kill the sorcerer," he said. "The one with the fur headdress. He accused my father and the others, so they let him live."

"Titu Atauchi," Cusi growled, and he stooped to retrieve his shield and battle-ax, resisting the urge to whirl and swing the weapon. He looked toward the west just as Huaman Cachi came over the rise and started down toward the road, running swiftly and easily. When he was close he saw Cusi and opened his mouth to call out, but then he recognized Huallpa, as well, and he slowed to a walk and came quietly to Cusi.

"No doubt you have already heard," Huaman said, bowing slightly to Quilaco and the others. "It is all over the camp down there. They say Huascar had Colla Topa and the others put to death for plotting against him."

"Someone is coming to tell us officially," Ucumari observed, pointing with his chin. A small detachment of golden-eared warriors was coming up the road toward them. Cusi counted eleven, noting that the man in front wore the golden Sun shield of a war chief.

"Alert the commanders in the rear to this," Quilaco said to Huaman Cachi. "Tell them to have their troops ready to march."

"Also tell Tarapaca and some of the captains to join us," Cusi added, "with their weapons."

"Ready to march forward?" Challcochima asked Quilaco as Huaman Cachi ran off. "Or back?"

"We cannot attack Cuzco," Quilaco said flatly, as a kind of reflex.

Challcochima snorted. "Cuzco attacked us."

"We do not have the men," Ucumari pointed out. "Most of those we could count on went back with Quizquiz. The rest will be split."

"Then we must go back," Quilaco concluded.

"My wife and children are with Chuqui Huipa," Challcochima objected, and Cusi grunted forcefully.

"Mine, too."

"So are my daughters," Quilaco told them. "But we cannot rescue them now, and we would not help them by throwing our lives away in a useless attempt. We must go back to Quito and wait."

"Quizquiz was right," Challcochima grumbled, but no one argued any further with Quilaco. Tarapaca and several of the captains came up to join them, and one of them handed a spear to Quilaco, who discarded his water gourd and turned to face the approaching delegation. Challcochima and Ucumari lined up on his left and Cusi on his right, with the captains spreading out behind them. Cusi gestured for Huallpa to stay close to him, and the boy complied with a weary nod.

The leader of the detachment, Atoc, was another of Huascar's half brothers, and he had the same squat, powerful build. He carried a short baton painted in Huascar's personal colors of blue, yellow, and red, and he did not pause to introduce himself or state his authority.

"I have come to inform you that a plot to overthrow the rule of the Sapa Inca was uncovered among your leaders. They confessed their treason before they died. I have come to relieve you of your command. New commanders will be here shortly to take charge of your men."

Quilaco stared back at him impassively for a moment, then exchanged a glance with Cusi, who nodded for him to speak.

"You are speaking of the highest of the blood Incas, those who were closest to Huayna Capac and most honored by him. They had come here to convey the fringe to his son Huascar. Now he will never have it."

"They were traitors," Atoc said bluntly. "We heard their confessions, and we have one who will testify to the plot."

Cusi rose up on his toes and banged his battle-ax against the front of his shield, causing everyone to jump and display their weapons. "There was no plot," he snarled at the war chief. "You tortured them and then you murdered them. They had nothing to confess."

Atoc scowled at him but would not meet his eyes for long. He held up his baton and addressed himself to Quilaco.

"You have received a command from your ruler. What is your answer?"

Cusi felt hands restraining him from behind before he realized he had begun to move forward, ready to answer with his weapon. Challcochima let out a scornful laugh.

"Our answer is that you should leave here right now if you do not wish to be murdered in return."

"This is treason," Atoc warned.

Quilaco stepped forward and slammed the butt of his spear against the ground. "We owe our loyalty to Huayna Capac, and you have slain all of those who spoke for him and carried the memories of his deeds. You have committed a crime far greater than treason, so do not pretend to accuse us!"

"You will be punished . . ."

"I hope they send *you,*" Challcochima sneered, and Atoc turned abruptly on his heel, cutting the air with his baton as he led his troops back down the road.

"We should have killed them," Cusi muttered as the hands that had been holding him back let him go. "What chance did they give Lloque and the others?"

"This is no time for revenge," Quilaco said, turning to speak to the captains. "Gather all those who are able and willing to march back with us. Tell them what Huascar has done, and tell them Atauhuallpa will reward them for their loyalty. Take as many supplies and spare weapons as you can."

Tarapaca hung back and walked up the road with Cusi and Huallpa, studying Cusi over the boy's head until Cusi intercepted his gaze.

"Yes," Cusi said curtly, responding to the question in his eyes. "I have my anger back."

Tarapaca smiled and tapped the point of his spear against his shield. "Perhaps the Hawk Men will fly again."

"Perhaps," Cusi allowed. He glanced back over his shoulder. "We will have to do it far from here, though." He let out a sigh that became a groan. "How long will it be this time?"

"Can I go with you?" Huallpa asked in a low voice, and Cusi turned back and nodded emphatically.

"You must go with us. You are our only witness to this crime."

"I want to come back and kill them!" the boy blurted out, and for the first time he began to weep. "For my father . . ."

Cusi looked across at Tarapaca, then at the road ahead, thinking of the months it would take just to return to Quito. It would take more than patience to withstand the waiting and uncertainty and danger that lay ahead.

"We will come back, Huallpa," he promised, "and we will avenge your father and my uncle. No matter how long it takes, we will not forget what we owe them."

"Never!" Huallpa vowed, staring straight ahead. "Never!"

Cuzco

OUTSIDE THE Coya's compound, the festivities were in their third day. Those in the compound could hear the sounds of singing and dancing coming from other parts of the palace, sometimes from quite close at hand, as if processions were being led past on the other side of the enclosure wall. So far, all they had seen of Cuzco was this compound, for they had come into the city under cover of darkness, and before they could venture out the next day they had received the news that Lloque, Yasca, and the others had been killed. The Coya had been speechless with shock and disbelief, and then she had gone into a rage that had yet to subside. She had expelled all the retainers Huascar had assigned to her, keeping only the guards and servants who had accompanied her from the north, and she had ordered Rimachi to bar the main gate and turn all messengers away. The latter had included a Sun priest sent to invite Rahua Ocllo to take part in the ceremonies of welcome that Huascar had prepared for her and Huayna Capac.

From the sounds they heard, the Coya's withdrawal had apparently had no effect on Huascar or his plans. To Micay this was nearly as disturbing as the murders themselves. What kind of man could bloody his hands so flagrantly, then extend them in welcome? And to whom was he extending this welcome? Micay could not believe Cusi and the other warriors had meekly followed their leaders' example, yet they obviously had not threatened Huascar in return. With the gate closed to all news from the outside, it was impossible to know what had happened, and after what Huascar had already done it was unnerving to wonder about what he might do next.

The interior compound that Chuqui Huipa and her women had been given was small and cramped by the standards of Tumibamba and Quito, but everyone was still too stunned and anxious to complain about the crowding. They sat listlessly around the courtyard, holding their children on their laps and listening, with their heads bowed, to the sounds of mourning from those, like Quespi, who knew their loved ones had perished. To keep her own fears at bay,

Micay steeped coca leaves in a pot of hot water and began to dole the tea out to her companions.

"For the altitude," she said as she handed them a gourd, awakening some of them to a discomfort they had not yet noticed. She had put Quilaco's daughter, Coca, in charge of the younger children and had kept Machacuay with her as her pot bearer, sensing that he needed to be near her more than the twins did. This confinement had to have aroused memories of what he had suffered in Quito, and he was subject to fainting spells whenever anything frightened or upset him too greatly.

They had gone halfway around the courtyard when Micay began to see the signs of such a spell coming on. His handling of the pot had become jerky and uncertain, and though he tried to keep his face averted, she could see he was blinking rapidly and uncontrollably. A glance ahead showed her the possible cause of his distress: they were drawing close to the place where Quespi was sitting with her daughter Yutu. Consumed with grief, Quespi was holding on to her knees and rocking back and forth, her hair hanging down over her ash-streaked face. There was no way to look at her without feeling the danger that threatened them all.

So she drew Machacuay aside, took the pot from him, and made him sit down. Squatting in front of him, she filled the gourd dipper and carefully put it into his hands.

"For courage," she told him, and though he did not raise his eyes, he drained the gourd in two gulps and held it out to her for more. She filled it again and watched him grow calmer as he drank, so that the blinking stopped and he was able to give her a guarded glance.

"Forgive me, my lady," he murmured. "I do not wish to fail you."

"You have never failed me," Micay said firmly. "I have come to depend on you like a comrade. Especially now, when I have so few."

"I do little, my lady, compared to what you have done for me."

Micay shook her head. "That is not true. I trust you with my children, and they mean more to me than anything. But you must do one more thing for me."

"Whatever you wish, my lady," Machacuay said swiftly, his head cocked so that he seemed to be looking up at her. His face was round and plump, yet his features were surprisingly delicate and distinct, almost pretty.

"You must believe that it was your own courage that kept you alive in Quito," Micay told him. "You must believe that and let it calm you whenever you feel frightened and ready to faint. You have my permission to neglect your other duties and sit until the fear subsides."

Machacuay began to blink, but then comprehension filled his eyes and held them still for a moment before he bowed in compliance. "I have never been given a duty like this, my lady, but I will try hard to fulfill it."

Before Micay could say anything more there was a commotion at the gate, and Rimachi strode into the courtyard. He was out of uniform, wearing a tan tunic striped with dark brown, several strings of red beads around his neck.

He was carrying a puma-head drinking cup, and his sauntering gait and the loose smile on his face showed that he had been using it.

The women closest to the gate surrounded him immediately, seeing at a glance that he had been out in the city. Rimachi held up his free hand to quiet their questions and began to address them one by one, and whatever he told them made them cry out and turn to their children in obvious displays of relief and gratitude. No one else has died, Micay thought; they got away.

Rimachi worked his way across the courtyard, preceded by Sinchi and Topa, the latter now proudly bearing the puma-head cup. Chuqui had come out of her house with Cahua, and the two of them came over to stand with Micay. Rimachi bowed to Chuqui with an exaggerated flourish that seemed almost mocking, and Micay could tell from the glittering brightness of his eyes that he was fiercely drunk.

"My ladies," he said, spreading his hands and stooping to include the children in his greeting. "I have news about your husbands and fathers. I was summoned to Huascar's feast, where I spoke to other members of the funeral party, those who came into the city after we did. They told me about the ones who had defied Huascar's command and started back to Quito. Naturally, Cusi Huaman and Quilaco Yupanqui were among their leaders. It is said they took most of the warriors with them."

"Father is safe, Cisa!" Coca whispered to her sister, who let out a joyful squeak and repeated the message in a louder whisper to Cahua.

"So is mine," Cahua said in a normal tone, and Rimachi laughed and nodded to her.

"He is away from here, anyway."

Quespi suddenly pushed past Micay and fell to her knees in front of Rimachi, her hands extended in appeal, her daughter clinging desperately to the side of her shift.

"What about my son?" she pleaded. "What about Huallpa?"

Rimachi flinched in surprise and seemed not to recognize her or the name of her son. Then he clapped a hand to his forehead and went down on one knee, bobbing his head in apology.

"Forgive me, Quespi, I should have said this first. Cusi had another member of the honor guard bring me a message. He said that Huallpa was with him and his comrades and they would all be back. Your son is safe."

Quespi let out a cry and sank backward onto her haunches, weeping into her hands. Micay squatted down beside her and looked across her back at Yutu, who seemed too dazed to weep.

"Your brother is alive," Micay told her, and the girl nodded and patted her mother on the shoulder. Micay looked over at Rimachi, who was still kneeling and had an arm around Topa.

"I am taking Topa with me," he announced.

"You have your own quarters?"

"I have a whole compound. I have retainers to serve me and a chosen woman for a wife."

"You have a vicuña tunic and red shell beads, too," Chuqui added. "And a cup from Huascar's own hand."

Rimachi glanced up at her, seeming drunk again. "Yes . . . those, too. Everything a man could want."

"You must be very proud. Huascar is not known for his generosity."

"He must have *some* friends, now that all the Incas fear and mistrust him. He has been generous with the Chachapoyas, too."

"Does that mean you are his friend?" Chuqui asked.

Rimachi pushed himself to his feet, swaying slightly as he reached up to straighten his wicker headdress. He took a deep breath and clamped his mouth shut, as if biting back words, then slowly let the breath out.

"In this city, my lady, you are either the friend of Huascar or his enemy, and we have seen what he does to his enemies. So yes, I am proud to accept the rewards of his favor."

He executed a sarcastic bow that made Chuqui stiffen, and Micay left Quespi in Yutu's hands and stood up between them.

"You are drunk, Rimachi," she told him sharply. "No doubt you have a right to be, but this is not the time or the place to boast about what you have been given. Let that wait until we are allowed to leave here and can come visit you and your wife."

Rimachi could not meet her eyes for long, and he mumbled an apology and let his shoulders drop in a parting bow. He was about to turn away when a sudden memory made him raise a finger to Micay.

"I heard one other thing at the feast: Amaru is here. Huascar kept him here to work on the palace he is building on the Collcampata."

He turned and headed for the compound gate, Topa and Sinchi again clearing the way for him. Cahua looked up at Chuqui and Micay.

"When can we go to a feast?"

"When we can avoid it no longer," Chuqui said tonelessly, looking at Micay with resignation. "When it is our turn to accept the rewards of his favor . . ."

THE CELEBRATION outside finally stopped, and a day later the first emissaries came from Huascar, bearing gifts for the Coya along with a formal request for the hand of her daughter, Chuqui Huipa, in marriage. Rahua Ocllo would not receive them, though she heard their message through Rimachi before sending them away with their gifts still in their hands. Huascar sent different emissaries the next day and a third group the day after that, but his mother would not relent. On the morning of the fourth day he sent a message saying he would be coming in person as soon as he had finished his prayers to Inti.

The Coya immediately summoned Chuqui to her quarters, and shortly afterward she sent for Micay, as well, asking her to bring her medicine bag. The windows in the Coya's house were covered, darkening the still nearly barren room, but Micay found the two women sitting up and showing no signs of illness. Chuqui was even sitting up straight, and she was facing her mother without any of her customary defiance or inattention. Micay made the mocha to Rahua Ocllo and obeyed her gesture to sit next to Chuqui.

"I want you to make a poison for us, Micay," the Coya said bluntly. "Something that would be quick and irrevocable if taken. Chuqui says you can provide this."

"You told me once that you have oleander flowers," Chuqui reminded her, "though you keep them well hidden."

"I do," Micay admitted. "It is a deadly plant, and only the seeds may be used safely. I would not want it to fall into the hands of a child or someone who is angry or distraught."

"I am both," the Coya told her, "but I have no wish to do away with myself or anyone else. I want it as a weapon, Micay. Huascar is nothing without us, and I want him to know that if he tries to take Chuqui by force, that is what he will have: nothing."

Micay stared at her thoughtfully, disturbed by the request but heartened by the fact that Rahua Ocllo had decided to fight. Micay did not like to be associated with poison in any form, but she did not see how she could deny the Coya the means to defend herself. She glanced sideways at Chuqui before looking across at the Coya.

"I will do it, my lady. But I must be assured that it will not be used against another . . . or as a remedy for despair."

"We are agreed on this, Micay," Chuqui said. "We must do what we can to make him treat us with respect. You told me this yourself in Vilcashuaman."

"I remember. How did you plan to carry the poison with you?"

"In these," the Coya said, and reached into her lap. She produced two small silver lime containers, each no bigger than her thumb, each strung on a fine silver chain. "We will wear them around our necks, where Huascar can see them and we can reach them quickly."

She passed them across to Micay, who checked only to see that each had a snug straw stopper. Then Micay began to dig down through the packets, pouches, and gourds that filled her medicine bag, searching for the pocket that tucked in on itself. Even as she dug, she wondered at the ease with which she had agreed. Had desperation destroyed her scruples so quickly? Yet the thought of what Huascar had done to Lloque made such a concern seem utterly trivial. She removed the tightly bound pouch from its hidden pocket, telling herself that this was the world she lived in now, a world in which a mother, the mother of all the Incas, would arm herself with poison before going to greet her son.

RIMACHI AND the other guards at the compound gate went down on one knee and made the mocha when Huascar's litter came to a halt in the street, surrounded by a large retinue of priests, officials, and Cañari warriors. Huascar stepped down from his seat, gold gleaming at his ears, wrists, and neck, the multicolored fringe of the Sapa Inca around his forehead. His pale blue tunic

had the iridescent sheen of feathers, and there was a triple band of tocapu—
each individual square thickly embroidered with intricate symbols—around
the middle. He ignored the people bowing to him and came toward the gate,
walking out of the bright sunlight and into the shadow of the deep threshold.
When he saw the women waiting for him on the other side, he stopped abruptly
and his mouth fell open.

"Mother," he said breathlessly, as if he had not realized until that moment
who the Coya was. Rahua Ocllo had dressed herself fairly simply in warm
shades of red and purple, and she had painted her face to hide the lines and
make herself look young again. She was standing with Chuqui beside her and
a small group of their women arrayed behind them.

"Come no further, Huascar," the Coya commanded. "Your hands are
stained with the blood of your kinsmen. You have dishonored your father and
disgraced yourself."

Huascar looked down at his hands with an innocence that was almost
beguiling. Micay was startled by how young he seemed, since he was only a
few years younger than Cusi and she no longer thought of Cusi as young. But
then he drew himself up defensively and spoke with an assurance that was
neither innocent nor youthful.

"They plotted against me, and they brought an army with them instead of
an honor guard. I only did what was necessary to defend myself and Cuzco.
The punishment for treason—as you know—is death."

"That is nonsense," the Coya said flatly. "You killed the high priest and
your father's Rememberers. Who will sing his story songs now that they are
gone?"

"We know his songs," Huascar insisted. "They were sent here, and we saved
them."

"Not those of his last days."

Huascar suddenly bristled with anger. "He renounced me in his last days,
no doubt after the sickness had stolen his mind. And who was it who persuaded
him to make Ninan Cuyochi the Heir in my place? It was these same men! Now
they serve Atauhuallpa . . . or they would have, had I turned my back on them.
That is what I know about his last days, and it is all I want to know!"

From her place just behind and to the right of Chuqui, Micay saw Chuqui
raise a hand to the silver container hanging between her breasts. Huascar,
however, seemed to shrug off his own anger and go on as if he had not raised
his voice.

"But I am not here to talk about this, my mother. I have come to ask for
my sister in marriage, as tradition demands of the Sapa Inca."

"You have murdered tradition," Rahua Ocllo told him. "You have shown
no respect for that which should have been sacred to you. I do not claim you
as a son, and I will not give you my daughter."

"But you must!" Huascar cried, sounding more incredulous than angry.
"You know that I am meant to be the Sapa Inca. It was prophesied before I

was born, and the gods spoke again when they took the usurper in Quito. They will not allow anyone to steal what rightfully belongs to me."

"I am the only one who can give Chuqui Huipa in marriage," the Coya maintained, "and if you or anyone else tries to take her against my will, you will be responsible for our deaths."

Huascar threw up his hands in disbelief. "You cannot mean this! I have done all that could be asked of the Heir . . . I have earned it! Mother . . . you must see that it is inevitable . . ."

"I see only that you have no shame. Leave me now, and do not come again until you have repented of your crimes. My forgiveness and trust cannot be won with excuses."

Huascar swung halfway around and then back, grabbing at the air in frustration. He stared at his mother for a long moment, his nostrils flaring and his breath coming in loud huffs.

"Do not think you can give her to anyone else," he growled, and he turned without another word and walked directly to his litter, clapping his hands to set his retinue in motion. The street emptied swiftly, and the women inside the compound released their tension in a collective sigh. The Coya said nothing, and they waited while she stared out through the open gate as if still seeing him there. Finally she turned to Chuqui, and the hard set of her features cut new lines through her face paint, destroying any illusion of youth.

"He has aged, but he is the same child I left here seventeen years ago," she said bitterly. "He does not have the humility to repent or the cleverness to know he should."

"Then . . . what have you gained by refusing him?" Chuqui asked.

"Perhaps nothing," the Coya admitted. "He hates being thwarted, but it is the only way to make him think. Now he has to reckon with me, and even if I cannot impress him, perhaps I can make him impress himself."

Chuqui spread her hands in a quizzical gesture.

"One way or another, he will know how important this marriage is to him before I am through," the Coya explained. "He will remember the effort it took to win you."

"Then it *is* inevitable," Chuqui concluded.

Rahua Ocllo shook her head. "You still have your weapon; you can use it any time you wish. Otherwise . . . yes, I will let Huascar persuade me at some point, when it seems most favorable for you. I will even weep and pretend to forgive him." The Coya paused and bared her teeth in a snarl of determination. "But I will never forgive him, Chuqui, and you should never trust him."

The Coya spat in the direction of the gate, shocking everyone, then whirled and strode toward her house, her women belatedly falling in behind her. Chuqui looked at Micay, Cori Cuillor, and the other women with wide eyes.

"Will this help us or hurt us?"

"He obeyed her," Cori Cuillor pointed out. "He made no attempt to take you by force."

"Perhaps he should have," Chuqui murmured. "Micay?"

"The Coya has decided to fight," Micay said with a shrug. "I do not think either you or Huascar could stop her now. But it might be a chance for you to learn something about him before you become his wife."

Chuqui grunted scornfully and fingered the silver container around her neck. Then she shrugged and let it drop. "It is a poor weapon. Let us see if my mother has others she has kept to herself, ones that do not kill the person who wields them. Let us see if we can learn anything at all from her about fighting . . ."

HUASCAR MADE two more unsuccessful visits to the Coya's compound, each time arriving with renewed determination to have his way and leaving in a daze of confusion and self-doubt without having gained permission to marry Chuqui. After the last visit he announced he was retiring to the Coricancha to fast and pray and seek the guidance of his father, Inti. He made the announcement rather defiantly, as if he had found a way around his mother's arguments, when in fact she had planted the idea in his mind herself.

Chuqui and Micay sat through both visits in silence, Chuqui playing her assigned role, which was to remain aloof and alluring, the prize of this contest of wills. It was not difficult to watch in silence, because the Coya needed no assistance in overwhelming her son and the intensity of her performance was riveting. She fought as Cusi had always said a warrior should, with her whole being, and Huascar himself supplied the weapons she used against him: his weakness for flattery and his need for approval; his fearful belief in signs and omens; his easily aroused suspicions of others. Without ever raising her voice, she seemed to make him spin in place, distracting him, leading him, confronting with the difference between what he said and what he had done. Whenever he grew restive and threatened to break out of the verbal hold she had on him, she would launch into a story of a childhood he could not remember, tantalizing him with accounts of the kind of boy he had been.

As she listened to the motherly tone in which Rahua Ocllo told these stories and observed the powerful effect they had on Huascar, Micay felt a chill creep over her. He was no longer a child and he had been away from his mother for all of his adult life, yet his reactions were those of a son, and the Coya was ruthless in evoking and manipulating them. Micay thought of how easy it would be to do the same thing to Sinchi, and it made her feel cruel just to be watching.

Chuqui appeared enthralled by her mother's performance and gave no indication that she shared Micay's misgivings or had any of her own. Toward the end of Huascar's final visit, however, the Coya told a story that made Chuqui stiffen slightly and sit up straighter. It was a story in which Huascar, in a fit of childish anger, had thrown a bowl of hot squash at the retainer woman who was serving him. According to the Coya, he had then been stricken with remorse and had himself gone to apologize, taking one of his mother's finest shifts to replace the garment he had soiled. There were tears of tenderness in Rahua Ocllo's eyes as she related this, and Huascar was completely unable to respond. Soon afterward he gave up trying to reason with her and went to seclude himself in the Coricancha.

Chuqui then went into a kind of seclusion of her own, taking her meals alone and seldom leaving her house, so that two days passed before Micay had a chance to speak with her. When she finally did, Chuqui went right to the story that had made her sit up.

"It was not Huascar who threw the squash," she revealed. "It was me. And when I refused to apologize to the retainer, my mother gave the woman one of her shifts to shame me. I still feel the shame every time I see cooked squash."

Micay drew a sharp breath. "I suspected her tears were not real, but the story itself . . . it sounded like a story she had told many times in the past."

"I thought for a moment that she had simply confused the two of us, but then she began to change it, turning it into a story that both flattered and shamed him. When I saw her tears, I realized how much she hates him and how little any of this has to do with me. It is her consent she has made important, not the marriage."

Micay nodded. "It may still help you, though . . ."

"Possibly," Chuqui allowed. Then she shook her head vigorously. "I thought for a while that she was teaching me what I needed to know: how to influence him and make him act decently. I was telling myself that I could do the same thing, that as his wife I would have even more power over him." She grimaced and shook her head again. "Then I saw where her power came from, and I realized I could never lie to him with the same passionate conviction. If I hated him that much, there would be no point in trying to live with him."

"She has taught you something, then," Micay suggested. "Do you see another way you could live with him?"

Chuqui regarded her warily, her fingers curling around the silver container at her breast. "She has exposed all of his faults, and he has displayed few virtues in defending himself. But when he spoke of all the waiting he had done and how he felt abandoned and unappreciated . . . I knew what he was saying, and I saw very clearly how my mother was avoiding hearing him. She has done it to me for years."

"There is power in sympathy and understanding, too," Micay said quietly. "Perhaps even for Huascar."

"You do not sound confident."

"I hated him when he tried to defend what he had done to Lloque and Yasca," Micay admitted. "He will never be trustworthy because of that. But I felt sorry for him in your mother's hands. He wanted so much to believe that her kindness and affection were real."

"I know that feeling, too," Chuqui declared, and she covered one of Micay's hands with her own. "So . . . do you agree that I cannot use my mother's weapons? Will you help me find another way with him?"

"I agree—and I will," Micay promised, and Chuqui let out a long, shudder-ing sigh.

"Then let us prepare ourselves. When he returns I will go to him, whether my mother approves or not. It is time for her to step aside; I have waited long enough to be the Coya."

AT SUNSET on the fourth day, Huascar returned to the Coya's compound, bringing the gods of the Incas with him. The Coya had been forewarned by a sentinel stationed on a rooftop, so all the women and children were assembled in the entry courtyard when the procession arrived. To the lowing of conch horns, the first litter, bearing the golden image of Apu Inti, was carried through the gate, borne on the shoulders of four apprentice priests. The guards had already prostrated themselves, and at a signal from the Coya, everyone in the courtyard did likewise, plucking hairs from scalp and eyebrows and blowing them at the gods.

When the conch horns fell silent the Coya rose to her knees. The women around her cautiously lifted their heads, keeping their gaze lowered out of respect. Even with her eyes half averted, Micay was dazzled by the gleam of gold and silver, the glitter of precious stones, the shimmering glow of feathered cloth. Standing in a row in front of her were the litters of Apu Inti, Mama Quilla, and Illapa; to one side and a little behind were those of the Morning Star and the Rainbow, the latter a vaguely serpentine figure completely cov-ered with iridescent mother-of-pearl. The litters were so richly decorated that the images stood out more because of their mass than their brilliance: Apu Inti was a great rayed head of solid gold; Mama Quilla, a polished silver disc; Illapa, a golden winged figure brandishing a spear and a sling.

Micay glanced down and saw that Sinchi and Cahua were staring unabash-edly at this awesome spectacle, and since she could barely restrain herself from doing the same she did not try to discourage them. They might never have another chance to see the images of the gods so close, since few people, even among the Incas of the blood, were ever allowed into the Coricancha. The priests and mamacona who were attending the images were tolerant, as well, appearing to find no disrespect in the children's curiosity. Those who came forward to address Rahua Ocllo were all white-haired elders, yet their expres-sions were surprisingly buoyant and eager, celebratory rather than solemn. They had come to plead with the Coya on Huascar's behalf, but there was more gratitude than entreaty in their voices, and the deference they paid to her was both elaborate and personal.

Smiling, Rahua Ocllo rose and lifted her palms to bring her companions to their feet. She addressed the priests and priestesses by their titles, but it was clear she knew several of them and had met with them like this in the past. Since Huascar was not present, they barely referred to him, speaking instead of how much Cuzco had missed the Coya and her court, who were the true heart of the social and ceremonial life of the Incas. Micay understood from some of their comments that Huascar had been neglecting them, which explained their gratitude. No doubt he had been forced to promise them more of his attention in return for this extraordinary favor.

The Coya basked in their regard, smiling and weeping without apparent calculation, the fierce manipulativeness of the past days melting away in the warmth of nostalgia. She had forgotten to bring Chuqui into the conversation, though everyone seemed to be assuming the marriage would now go forward. Micay caught Chuqui's eye and saw her friend's lips curl into a sardonic smile.

"It has been too long since the House of Mama Quilla was graced with the presence of the Coya," the leader of the mamacona was saying. "And we have not had a high priestess since the sickness carried off Mama Coca and both of her successors."

Before Rahua Ocllo could reply, Chuqui stepped forward and bowed to the woman. "When I am the Coya, my lady, I will come to visit you. And I will prevail on my husband and the high priest to appoint a new high priestess."

The priestess glanced once at Rahua Ocllo, then bowed to Chuqui. All the other priests and mamacona bowed, too, murmuring her name in greeting.

"I must speak to Huascar one more time before we agree," Rahua Ocllo said, and Chuqui turned very slowly to face her, her eyes hooded and the same mocking smile on her lips.

"I have already agreed," she said simply. "If Huascar is waiting outside, these people should bring me to him, and we will return together for your blessing."

"He is waiting," the priestess of Mama Quilla acknowledged with another glance at Rahua Ocllo.

"You are so ready to leave my care, my daughter?" Rahua Ocllo asked in a wooden voice.

"I left it long ago," Chuqui said. "I am ready now to be the Coya."

"Go, then, and bring your brother for my blessing. I will say no more on your behalf."

Chuqui nodded abruptly and went forward into the ranks of the priests and mamacona, who closed in around her as they started for the gate, walking between the litters that held the images of Apu Inti and Mama Quilla. Micay let her hands hang down, touching the heads of her children, and thought to herself, so this is how we begin again . . .

Caxamarca

T HE HILL on which Cusi and Quilaco were camped with their men was barren and rocky, with few spots level enough to permit the erection of a decent shelter. But it was easily defensible in case the governor was foolish enough to send his mitmacs against them, and it was far enough from the nearest fields to remove the temptation of an illegal harvest. Cusi was showing Huallpa how to tie a new flint tip onto his spear when Huaman Cachi pointed out the Inca official who was struggling up the hill toward them. The man wore the small golden earplugs of a nonwarrior and walked with a pronounced limp, leaning on a staff banded with silver.

"That is a governor's staff," Huaman observed. "But he is not the same one who drove us away from the city."

"That one would not dare to come here alone," Cusi said, gazing down the hill. The man had stopped to talk to some of the warriors, and Cusi saw Tarapaca rise and lead the man in his direction. There was something familiar about both the man's face and his limp, but Cusi could not place him, and he was not too inclined to try. The sight of anyone from the city, anyone clean, well dressed, and well fed, made him want to spit.

He heard the man's labored breathing as Tarapaca brought him to the place where they were sitting, but he finished Huallpa's spear and gave it back to the boy before looking up. The man was tall and had both hands around his staff, leaning on it heavily while he caught his breath. It was his eyes—attentive but slightly diffident—that made Cusi recognize him.

"Acapana!" he blurted out.

The man smiled shyly. "It has been many years, Cusi Huaman. May I sit with you and rest my foot?"

Cusi pointed with his chin at an open bedroll. "It is all the hospitality I can offer you. You are still the governor of Chachapoyas?"

Acapana settled himself awkwardly, stretching out his twisted foot with a grimace of relief. "Yes, I am still governor," he said to Cusi. "Apparently Huascar could find no one who wanted to take my place."

"That might change if he hears you are friendly with rebels."

"He has not declared you rebels, though he has sent out an order to deny you food and shelter."

"Yes," Cusi said bitterly. "He would rather goad us into taking what we need by force so that he can declare us outlaws and thieves."

"No one here has accused you of that," Acapana assured him. "We have been told that you barter fairly and that you help the people in the fields in return for a share of the crop."

"Who has been told?"

"All the governors and chiefs from this region were summoned to Cax-amarca to reaffirm their loyalty to Huascar. Some were simply replaced, which of course made all the rest nervous. Even so, there were many who did not think that warriors of your stature should be turned away from the city."

"Where were they when the governor of Caxamarca met us with his mit-macs behind him?" Cusi demanded.

Acapana looked down at his hands. "We tried to persuade him not to," he said in a low voice, "but the pressure from Cuzco was too great. No one dared to take your side publicly."

"Then what can you do for us now?" Cusi asked bluntly. "We need food, not sympathy. Can you open the ruler's storehouses?"

"No," Acapana admitted, raising his eyes when Cusi grunted derisively. "No, we cannot do that. But we have all received gifts from Huascar, most of them from stores that rightfully belong to his father's household. There is nothing to prevent us from giving them to you and your men."

Cusi squinted at him in disbelief. "Why would any of you take such a risk?"

"There is little risk if we are careful. Certainly it is no risk compared to what you have experienced on the battlefield. Some of us have not forgotten what we owe our brave warriors." Acapana paused and shifted his outstretched leg, though the discomfort in his eyes did not seem physical. "For me, of course, the debt is personal."

"How is that?" Cusi asked. "We barely knew each other in Tumibamba."

Acapana spoke through his teeth, as if wishing he could bite the words in half. "I was very young, and your father was only a micho himself when he recommended me for the post in Chachapoyas. But he was also the father of the famous Cusi Huaman, and that was enough to get him whatever he wanted. You were still recovering from your wound then, so you never knew how you helped me. It was also because of you, as you do know, that Otoronco Achachi came to Chachapoyas and I had the privilege of serving under him. So . . . even if I were the only one who wished to help you, I would still have to come and offer what I could."

It was the mention of his grandfather's name that awoke Cusi's shame and made him aware of how rudely he had treated this man, who was his equal in rank and who had come here out of friendship. Cusi glanced at Tarapaca and Huaman Cachi, but both avoided his eyes.

"Forgive me, Acapana," he said abruptly. "You do not deserve my anger and suspicion. I am grateful for your offer. I am grateful that there are Incas as brave and honorable as yourself."

Acapana stared at him for a moment, then nodded slowly, accepting the apology. Cusi turned and motioned to Huallpa for the water gourd, which he handed across to Acapana.

"I should at least have offered you water. It is the one thing Huascar cannot deny us."

Acapana took the gourd, but his eyes lingered on Huallpa. "Is this your son?"

Cusi blinked in surprise, then realized that he must have heard he had married Micay. "This is Huallpa, the son of the war chief Yasca. His mother is also a Chachapoya, and she is in Cuzco with Micay and my children. I am his guardian."

"I was sorry to hear of your father's death, my son," Acapana told him. "He was the greatest of our warriors."

"He was murdered, my lord," Huallpa said, gripping the spear that was balanced across his knees. "I will avenge him one day."

Acapana nodded and drank from the gourd, seeming disconcerted by the contrast between the boy's high-pitched voice and the seriousness of his vow.

Cusi waited a moment before introducing Tarapaca and Huaman Cachi, who bowed to their guest with an extra measure of deference.

"What will you do when you reach Quito?" Acapana asked. Cusi briefly considered a polite demurral before deciding to speak truthfully.

"We will prepare ourselves for the war that is to come."

Acapana froze, his eyes the only part of him moving, searching Cusi's face and then those of the others.

"Is there no way to prevent it? We are still recovering from the devastation of the sickness. A war between the Incas might destroy everything."

Cusi lifted his shoulders in a shrug that was not meant to be casual or indifferent. "The huacas have warned of such a conflict for many years. I was given a warning myself in a vision. Now I see it coming true, and I intend to be ready. I will not die a helpless death, denying the signs of danger."

"But if you openly prepare for war, you will only give Huascar an excuse to come against you. And he will have most of the Four Quarters behind him."

"Let him come. He will outnumber us in everything except veteran warriors, and he will finally learn just who it is that fights wars. If he summons the Chachapoyas to fight against us, you should advise them to rebel instead. They would have a better chance against Huascar's men than they would against ours."

Tarapaca grunted fiercely in agreement, and Acapana glanced at Huaman Cachi and Huallpa but found no support there either. He sighed in resignation and nodded to Cusi.

"No one in Chachapoyas wants to fight with you again. Perhaps Huascar will come to feel the same way and will try to make his peace with you. I only ask that you listen, Cusi, and do what you think is right, as your father and grandfather have done before you."

Cusi glanced over his shoulder at Huallpa and saw *never* in the boy's eyes, an answer that appealed to Cusi, as well. But then he looked back at Acapana and saw a man who deserved a more responsible reply, one that respected the validity of his concern. Huallpa would have to learn some time that a man could not live for vengeance alone.

"I have heard you, Acapana," Cusi told him, "and I have taken your words into my heart. Let us hope we can both do what is right, and not have to face each other as enemies."

Acapana lifted his chin, acknowledging the respect in Cusi's voice, then picked up his staff and levered himself to his feet.

"The gifts I mentioned have been taken to the herder's hut on the other side of this hill. Send your men for them once it is dark. The llamas grazing there are also yours."

"Tell your friends we will not forget this favor," Cusi said, rising to grip Acapana's free hand. "They may call on us to return it."

"Give my greetings to your father . . . and to Micay, when you see her again."

"I will tell them," Cusi promised, and bowed in parting. Acapana turned and began to limp back down the hill. Cusi watched him go, then turned to Huaman Cachi.

"Go scout the hut, and do not let yourself be seen. If anyone is watching, we must make sure they do not return to betray our friends. Take Huallpa with you."

"I will never listen to words of peace!" the boy blurted out. Then he ran off after Huaman Cachi before Cusi could reply. Cusi exchanged a glance with Tarapaca, who shrugged and shook his head ruefully.

"May we live long enough to hear them spoken," the warrior said, and Cusi nodded and bent down to gather up his weapons.

Tumibamba

BY THE TIME they reached Tumibamba, the force that Cusi and his fellow war chiefs had led away from Cuzco had been reduced by half, to those who had holdings in the north or strong ties of personal loyalty to their commanders. They were dusty, footsore, and inexpressibly weary, but they marched with the stolid, relentless gait of veterans, as if they never expected to stop.

At the sentry post on the river bridge, they were met by an honor guard of Cañari warriors, who led them into a city that seemed deserted, only a few elderly people standing in doorways to watch them pass. Then they heard drums beating ahead, a sound that made them lift their heads and hold their weapons less casually. Cusi glanced sideways at Quilaco, who seemed equally unprepared for an official ceremony of welcome. They had been climbing a long incline, and as they came up over the rise, Cusi could see that the street ahead was lined with people, and that the square at the end of the street was completely filled with them. The drumming suddenly intensified, but it could not drown out the cries of greeting from the people in the street, who pressed in to touch the warriors' shields and call to them by name. Cusi recognized several smiling faces, Quitos as well as Cañaris, and he realized that Atauhuallpa had brought everyone out to greet them.

A wide path had been left open through the crowd, out to the dais in the center of the square, which was surrounded by the tight, even ranks of the assembled warriors. As Cusi's column came abreast of them, the waiting warriors began to chant in unison, singing the traditional Inca song of welcome to returning warriors, a song of triumph and victory.

We have won no victory, Cusi thought, but the resonant voices of the warriors denied such misgivings, proclaiming a triumph by the sheer force of their enthusiasm. Cusi again glanced at Quilaco and saw that his brother-in-law's angular face was fixed in a grimace of pride and gratification and tears were running down his cheeks. Something moved inside Cusi then, responding to a need he had forgotten he had ever had. He felt a distinct slackening in

the tension between himself and his spirit brother, a bending inward as if his
anger and his distance were melding together. The sensation buoyed him up
and made him forget his fatigue, the ground suddenly soft and pliant beneath
his tired feet.

The column made a half circuit of the dais, finally coming around to the
stairs that ascended to the top of the great stone platform. The honor guard
stepped aside and the war chiefs went up the steps together, four abreast. A
group of Sun priests met them at the top and led them around the high-backed
stone seats that only the Sapa Inca and the Coya could occupy. Waiting on
the other side was a group of perhaps ten men, centered around Atauhuallpa,
who was wearing a brilliant red and black tunic. With the exception of Cusi's
father, who was standing just to Atauhuallpa's left, all the men wore the war
chief's golden Sun shield. One of them was Tomay, his eyes bright with
recognition, his round cheeks as dark and shiny as the bronze head of the
ceremonial lance he held. My brother, Cusi thought with a surge of emotion
that nearly brought the words to his lips.

Atauhuallpa stepped forward and looked out over the crowd below, raising
his arms until it was quiet. Then he turned to address the war chiefs.

"Greetings, brother Incas! As the Regent of the Northern Province, I salute
you and welcome you back to your home. We are proud to embrace those
whom Cuzco has so blindly spurned. We know your courage well, and we
cherish it; we know it is our protection and our strength. I give you now the
insignia of rank bestowed on you by my father, the Sapa Inca Huayna Capac,
the golden shield that each of you has earned many times over . . ."

Atauhuallpa turned slightly, and Apu Poma came forward, opening the
cloth bundle he held in his hands. The first shield glittered in the sunlight as
Atauhuallpa lifted it out of the bundle, stretching open its golden chain so he
could lower it over Challcochima's bowed head.

"To you, the war chief Challcochima," he intoned, and the warriors in the
square raised their weapons and shouted Challcochima's name three times, the
sound booming off the walls of the surrounding buildings. Atauhuallpa repeated the process with Ucumari and Quilaco, each time to a deafening response. When he came to Cusi, he took the last golden shield from the bundle
and raised it high for the crowd to see. But then he turned and handed it back
to Apu Poma, who opened the chain above Cusi's head.

"To you, the war chief Cusi Huaman," Atauhuallpa proclaimed, and the
warriors shouted, and beyond them the people of Tumibamba shouted Apu
Poma's name, saluting the familiar figure of the governor. Cusi looked into his
father's wet eyes as the Sun shield fell against his chest with a solid thump,
and suddenly he was overcome by the realization of how amazingly good it
was to share this moment of honor with his father after all the years of anger
and uneasiness, years when he never would have believed this to be was
possible. Tears came to his eyes and he let them flow, resisting none of the
feelings that filled his heart as his father embraced him there on the dais in
front of the war chiefs, the warriors, and the people of Tumibamba and Quito.

CUSI LEFT his shield and battle-ax with Huaman Cachi before entering the enclosure to which he and the other new war chiefs had been led, just inside the main gate of the Mollecancha. Atauhuallpa was sitting on a three-legged stool with his tunic off, being washed by a pair of servants, and the only other people present were Tomay and Quizquiz. Cusi went to his friend and gripped him by the shoulders, staring at him until Tomay broke into a smile.

"I knew you would be back," Tomay said simply. "I just did not expect you so soon."

"You were wise to stay behind. The only good part of the journey was the return."

The servants were departing, having helped Atauhuallpa into a fresh tunic that was as resplendent as the last and far cleaner than anything Cusi and his companions were wearing. He had also exchanged his Sun shield for the jeweled emblem of the Regent, and his black and red headband bore the silver badge of the Iñaca household, an affiliation he had seldom stressed in the past. He waited until all the servants were gone and then looked at them with a smile of recognition.

"It is good to see you again, my friends. Before you go off to the feasts that await you, let me assure you that the debts you acquired during your return will be repaid, and I will send additional gifts to those you say have helped you. As for your men, you can tell them they will also receive the ranks they have earned, and they will be rewarded for their loyalty with lands and houses and herds. Much has been left vacant and unattended by the sickness, and I am free to distribute anything that does not belong to the households or the clans. There are women for them, too: widows with lands of their own, ñustas of good blood, and orphaned daughters who need husbands." He paused and gave them another smile. "Is it not time that you took another wife, Quilaco? Ucumari?"

The two men exchanged a bemused glance, clearly unprepared for the offer but just as clearly tempted by it. Atauhuallpa nodded encouragingly and raised his open palms to Cusi and Challcochima.

"What about the two of you? I know your wives are in Cuzco, but should you not have a woman to see to your needs here? I am owed a number of women from the House of Chosen Women . . . you could have your pick."

Challcochima looked sideways and down at Cusi, his face impassive but his eyes narrowed and searching. Of the four of them, he had been the only consistent advocate of open rebellion, scornfully rejecting the prudent approach favored by Quilaco and Ucumari. Cusi had vacillated between the two positions, siding with Challcochima whenever he thought of Lloque and Yasca, with Quilaco whenever he thought of Micay and the twins. Now Challcochima gestured for him to speak, watching to see what choice he would make. No doubt he saw Atauhuallpa's offer as a kind of bribe, a diversion from the consideration of their purpose.

"I am grateful for the offer," Cusi said to Atauhuallpa, "and for the fine welcome you have given us. It is something I have wanted for a long time, and it is reward enough for me. I want nothing that might help me forget where my wife is and why I am not with her."

Challcochima grunted appreciatively. "Those are my feelings exactly. I only want to know when we are going to march back to Cuzco."

Atauhuallpa looked from one to the other, rubbing his chin in a thoughtful manner. It was a pose that seemed new to him and not altogether genuine.

"Quizquiz has been asking me the same thing," he acknowledged ruefully, nodding to the war chief, "so I will tell you what I told him. I understand your anger and impatience, but you must understand how it is here. Our stores are greatly depleted, and we cannot expect any support from Cuzco. We must work to make ourselves self-sufficient, so that we can supply the warriors we have and enlist new ones. And we have to secure our flanks. The Huancavelicas have rebelled again, and I had to send Rumiñaui to deal with them."

"So," Challcochima asked, squinting at him, "are the rest of us supposed to work in the fields until he returns? Huascar is also making himself stronger. Given enough time, he will enlist everyone outside of the Northern Quarter."

"He has the means," Atauhuallpa allowed, "since he is looting my father's household. But let him raise a great army, let him try to feed it and make it fight for him. He has shown by the way he treated you that he does not know the value of proven warriors. What will he do with thousands of untested recruits?"

"We should strike before he has time to arm them," Challcochima insisted. "We could scatter them before us. You were always the first to recommend an attack, Atauhuallpa. I never heard you ask if the storehouses were full."

"I did not have the responsibilities of the Regent then," Atauhuallpa said sharply, showing anger. "I was fighting for my father, not against my brother. Huascar has the fringe now, and the Coya. I cannot challenge him without severe provocation. You forget, Challcochima, I am not Ninan Cuyochi. My mother was a royal wife, but she was not a full sister."

Challcochima threw up his hands in disbelief, looking around at the others for support. Quizquiz let out a grunt that drew a swift glance from Atauhuallpa, which seemed to silence him. Quilaco spoke up for the first time.

"He is right, Challcochima. We would be seen as traitors and usurpers if we moved first, and no one would wish to side with us. We must wait until Huascar discredits himself."

"And until we are stronger," Ucumari added. "Look how many men we had to release because we could not feed them. You cannot ask warriors to fight and scavenge at the same time."

"Tomay Guanaco," Atauhuallpa prompted. "You have been supervising some of the repair and reclamation projects for me. How close are we to a full use of our fields?"

"Perhaps two or three growing seasons," Tomay estimated. "Perhaps less, if we have the use of some of the men who just returned."

Atauhuallpa crossed his arms on his chest and stared expectantly at Challcochima, challenging him to go on. Challcochima again looked down at Cusi.

"Well? Are you also eager to trade your weapon for a foot plow?"

As their heads swiveled toward him, Cusi remembered Raurau Illa telling him that his reputation freed him from the expected response and allowed him to say things other men would not. He looked up at Challcochima and smiled, feeling he was finally ready to use that freedom.

"I am willing to do anything that will make us stronger and more self-sufficient . . . as long as we never lose sight of the fact that we are preparing for war. Because if Huascar does not bring it to us, the Bearded Ones or someone else surely will, and I do not think we will have long to wait."

Cusi felt them all recoil slightly at his mention of the Bearded Ones, and Atauhuallpa sat back on his stool, regarding him with a wariness that went back many years, to the time when Cusi's reputation was being formed. The others were blinking in perplexity, as if they did not know how to regard him.

"Then you basically agree with Quilaco and Ucumari," Challcochima concluded, though his tone was doubtful.

"I agree that we must have the means to supply our men. But I do not think we should concern ourselves with how we are seen. Huascar was already suspicious of you the last time I was in Cuzco, my lord," Cusi said to Atauhuallpa, "when your father and Ninan were still alive. He will see you as a traitor and a usurper no matter what you do, so there is no point in trying to disguise our intentions. Indeed, all of the warriors should be told, when you are rewarding them with lands and herds, that they should expect to have to fight for what they have been given."

"Why not simply announce to Huascar that we are rebels?" Quilaco inquired sarcastically. "Or do you expect to swear the whole army to secrecy?"

Cusi gave him a hard look. "You are not listening, my brother. I want our men to be fully aware of our purpose, so they will not grow forgetful and complacent. It does not matter what Huascar knows. Make no announcements, but make no concessions either."

"You are speaking of the Sapa Inca!" Atauhuallpa burst out. "I cannot simply ignore his commands."

"I am speaking of Huascar," Cusi said quietly, "who murdered the only men who could bestow the fringe on him. We should give his commands the same respect."

"I hear you, Cusi," Challcochima said approvingly, and Quizquiz added his voice in assent. Atauhuallpa stood up and thrust out his hands to silence them. He was visibly angry, but he made an effort to calm himself before he spoke.

"As always, Cusi Huaman, you speak your thoughts boldly."

"I speak as one war chief to another, Lord Atauhuallpa. You have taken on the responsibilities of the Regent, and you would like to take on those of the Sapa Inca. Perhaps you will have your chance, though you will not have it by being careful. The time ahead will belong to the warlords, and that is what you must be. Surely there is no one more fit for the task."

The compliment surprised Atauhuallpa and made him swallow his reply and glance around at the other war chiefs. Quizquiz nodded vigorously.

"We did not come back here just to stand in the square and be rewarded. We want to show our Sun shields to our enemies."

"Lead us, Atauhuallpa," Challcochima urged. "We will give you all the legitimacy you need."

Atauhuallpa pursed his lips. "Quilaco?"

Quilaco glanced at Cusi, then nodded reluctantly. "A man who has no leader is lost to himself, a barbarian. The men would claim you as their warlord without hesitation, and perhaps, as Cusi says, they would be stronger because of it. They would know they had a place here, independent of Cuzco."

"Many of us know that already," Tomay put in, "and we have always looked on you as more than the Regent."

"I agree," Ucumari said before Atauhuallpa could ask him.

"We could all die a traitor's death," Atauhuallpa warned. But then he smacked his fist into his palm and smiled menacingly. "But that is a small risk to a warlord. Will you fight for me, then?"

"We will," the war chiefs said in unison, each placing a hand flat against his chest, over his heart.

"Then I will lead you," Atauhuallpa promised. He gave Cusi a curiously satisfied glance. "Against whoever is first to bring us war . . ."

Cuzco

ALMOST immediately upon Chuqui's arrival at the Collcampata, Huascar began to complain. He was tired of the crowd of women she always brought with her, he said irritably, and he had no patience for children today. So half of Chuqui's retinue and all of the children were sent out of the enclosure, which was broad and spacious, with an open side that looked out over the city and a floor that was half grass. It was the children's favorite place to play, the one place in this steeply terraced palace complex where they were both safe and out of the way of the ongoing construction. Micay had to give Sinchi an extra nudge to get him moving, and still he went reluctantly, gazing longingly at the pair of white alpacas grazing in the corner.

Huascar then began to complain about the things Chuqui had been doing, demonstrating that his spies kept him well informed about her movements. He usually did this in private, where Chuqui had ways to distract and mollify him, and the fact that he now chose to do it in front of his coterie of advisers struck Micay as an ominous sign. Despite all of Chuqui's efforts to make him trust her, he seemed determined to catch her out and embarrass her. He was surely looking hard for a reason today.

"Are your quarters in the Amarucancha so poor that you cannot bear to remain there?" he demanded. "The people call you the Coya Who Walks the Streets . . ."

"My quarters are fine," Chuqui said patiently, "and I know what the people call me because I hear it from their own lips. They are usually smiling, so I accept it as a compliment."

"They are laughing at you behind their hands."

"Then they are fools and beneath the attention of the Coya. There are many other people who are pleased to see me and who want to show me their homes and their children and the things they make."

"The households have been glad to see you, too," Huascar pointed out. "Suddenly the Iñaca and Vicaquirao are telling me they will host the second day's feast for the guests from the Southern Quarter. What did you promise them?"

Chuqui spread her hands and looked around at the listeners with an expression of puzzled disbelief, as if wondering if she had heard correctly. It was actually a gesture she had practiced in front of Micay and the other women as a means of deflecting his accusations and keeping herself from responding too sharply.

"I did not have to promise them anything," she said, "except that I would visit the feast and greet their guests. I thought you would be pleased, my husband, since you had made it clear that you did not wish to provide for the occasion out of your own stores."

"Why did they refuse when *I* asked them?"

"I never had the chance to inquire," Chuqui confessed. "They were too eager to welcome me and offer their services. You know that the women of our family have always been affiliated with the households of Upper Cuzco."

Huascar scowled and looked past her, as he often did when she answered him too well. Looking without seeing, Chuqui had put it in an angry moment, just as he listens without hearing. This time he saw something that made him rise up off his stool and point with his chin.

"I said no children. Bring that boy here."

It was Sinchi, trying to hide behind the alpacas in the corner. But the animals shied and fled at the approach of the two Cañari warriors who had sprung into action at Huascar's command, and who now gathered up Sinchi between them and bore him back to the ruler. Micay was too astonished to move. It was not like Sinchi to disobey her so flagrantly and so stealthily. How had he gotten back in without being seen—or had he never gone out? He had not struggled against the warriors who carried him, and he kept his head bowed after he made the mocha to the ruler.

"What is your name, boy?" Huascar demanded, and Sinchi replied in a surprisingly clear voice, though he did not raise his head.

"Sinchi, Lord Inca."

"Let me see your face. Uh . . . I see you are marked for trouble. Who is your father?"

Sinchi did not flinch at Huascar's grunt of disapproval, but Micay saw his mouth draw downward in disappointment. This was not the first time his birthmark had elicited such a response in Cuzco, but she knew it always hurt him.

"Cusi Huaman, Lord Inca," he said more softly.

Huascar grunted again. "No wonder. Where is your father now?"

"At the Rainbow House," Sinchi said, startling Micay with his certainty, since it was not the reply she had taught him. He was supposed to say that his father was in Quito, serving the Regent.

"Why is he not here with you?"

"He is with the Hawk Men," Sinchi replied, then added impulsively: "And the Hawk Boys."

"What do you have around your neck?" a rough voice demanded, and Huascar straightened up and nodded permission for Titu Atauchi to join the interrogation. Panic swept over Micay, though she was distracted from it by the appearance of Amaru, who had stepped forward to take Titu's place in the first rank of onlookers.

"Answer me," the sorcerer insisted, bending over Sinchi and nodding his head so that the teeth and amulets attached to his fur headdress rattled dryly. Sinchi backed away and muttered something inaudible, a hand clamped to his chest.

"Speak up!"

"Hawk," the boy managed, and Micay realized it was the name he had given his spirit brother. It had accidentally come into her hands one night when she was undressing him after he had fallen asleep, and her fingers had traced the faint, feathery outline of some creature incised into the obsidian.

"Show me," Titu Atauchi commanded. But Sinchi looked up at him and slowly shook his head. He had stopped backing away and his hands had dropped to his sides, and for a moment he appeared oblivious of the man looming over him, as if he were listening to some inner voice. Micay saw his fingers flex and then curl rigidly into claws, and his eyes went wide as he gathered himself and leaped at Titu Atauchi, his hands lashing out like talons. The sorcerer jerked backward so abruptly that his headdress went flying behind him and he went backward onto his buttocks. Sinchi's flailing hands just missed the man's face, scratching his neck and tearing feathers from the woven pectoral on his chest.

Micay moved then, leaving Chuqui's side just as Titu Atauchi came back up into a crouch, his hand raised to slap Sinchi down. Micay cried out and there was a swirl of movement that ended with Titu Atauchi dangling oddly, his upraised arm caught at the wrist and a forearm braced across his throat. Amaru tightened the forearm and lifted him off the ground, bending him backward as if to slowly break him in two.

"Would you strike a child, you coward?" he hissed into Titu's ear. Huascar recovered from his shock and waved his guards forward, but before they could close in Amaru tossed Titu aside and displayed his empty hands to forestall them.

"Forgive me, my lord," he said quickly. "This boy is my brother's son. I will see that he is punished for his disobedience, but I will not allow anyone to abuse him."

"He attacked my counselor!"

Amaru cast a sardonic glance at Titu Atauchi, who was lying on his side with his hands around his throat. "Yes, my lord. That is why I came to your counselor's rescue."

Several of the men behind Huascar laughed, and he whirled and silenced them with a gesture. Micay used the distraction to come to Sinchi's side and help him to his feet. He clung to her arm with both hands and looked up at her in bewilderment, as if he were not sure what had happened.

"You are the mother of this wild boy?" Huascar asked when he turned back and noticed her.

"Yes, my lord. I am Mama Micay, the wife of Cusi Huaman."

"She is my friend," Chuqui put in, stepping up beside her, "and a fine healer."

Huascar studied her with an interest that seemed to have little to do with her healing abilities. "So . . . he ran away and left you, too. He has always been a man of uncertain loyalties."

"He has fought for the Inca against the Chachapoyas, the Carangui, and the Chiriguanos, my lord," Micay said steadily. "And he always stayed until the war was won. Wherever he is, I have no doubts about his loyalty."

"Neither do I," Huascar snapped. "He plotted with Ninan Cuyochi, and now he plots with Atauhuallpa. Do not expect to be together with him very soon. Now take this little red-eyed beast out of here and see that he does not trouble me again."

Micay bowed compliantly and began to back away, drawing Sinchi along with her. She heard Huascar address Amaru:

"You have come close to being cast out yourself. Remember that there are other builders and many empty cells in the Sanka Cancha. You could still be rotting there when they have completed what you have begun here.

"Make yourself ready for me," Huascar went on, apparently to Chuqui. "I will send for you when I want you."

Micay had backed far enough away to turn and lead Sinchi toward the compound gate.

"Did I hurt that man, Mama?" he asked.

"No," Micay admitted, "though you came very close to scratching his eyes. He would have hurt you if Uncle Amaru had not stopped him."

"I know," Sinchi agreed earnestly. "Hawk told me."

"Your spirit brother has a voice?"

Sinchi frowned and rolled his shoulders, as if it were too hard to explain. "He tells me, so I know. Are we going away from Cuzco now?"

"Of course not," Micay said in surprise. Then she realized how Huascar might have given him that idea. "We only have to keep you away from the Sapa Inca for a while, until he forgets the trouble you caused today."

"But soon . . ."

"Soon what?"

"Soon we will go away from here, and I will have friends again."

"Did Hawk tell you that," Micay inquired gently, "or are you just wishing?"

They were passing between the guards at the compound gate, and Sinchi glanced up at them warily and did not answer until they were outside.

"Yes," he said then, and he seemed to consider it a sufficient reply, because he let go of her hand and ran off to join the other children without another word.

"TELL ME what he said to you," Micay urged Cahua. They were sitting with Parihuana in the awning house of Amaru's compound, close to the fire because the sun had almost set and the enclosure was in full, cold shadow. Little Roca was playing by himself in the corner, building something, and Amaru was in the next house having a serious talk with his nephew.

"He said," Cahua began, looking from one to the other to be sure she had all their attention, "that he just wanted to see the alpacas. But the Sapa Inca caught him and then a man with teeth on his head tried to take away his spirit brother. But Hawk flew down from the sky to protect him and then Uncle Amaru picked the man up and threw him away." Cahua cocked her head and frowned. "Did all that really happen, Mama?"

"Except for the part about Hawk. Sinchi protected himself; he went for Titu Atauchi's eyes and knocked him over backward. But how did your brother get away from Machacuay?"

"He ran ahead of us and hid somewhere. He is good at hiding."

"Since when?" Micay asked in surprise.

Cahua shrugged. "Since Topa stopped coming to the palace and then Yutu went to live with Rimachi, too. He thinks if he hides somewhere, maybe his friends will come looking for him. He gets away from Machacuay all the time, but Machacuay will not tell on him."

"No, Machacuay would not," Micay agreed, exchanging a glance with Parihuana, who was regarding her sympathetically. They both looked up as Amaru emerged from the next house and limped toward them. He seemed to be favoring his bad leg more than usual, but he scoffed at Parihuana's expression of concern as he came into the awning house to join them.

"It stiffened up from sitting. And because I let myself forget for a few moments that I am no longer a young warrior."

"How is Sinchi?" Parihuana asked.

"Well enough. He fell asleep."

"Is he sick?" Cahua asked.

"No, my daughter. Only lonely and confused."

"Did you punish him for his disobedience?" Micay asked.

Amaru was still standing, and he spread his hands and looked down at Micay. "How could I punish him? He was right to defend himself, and he gave me an excuse to throttle Titu Atauchi, which I have wanted to do for years. I wanted to thank him for that, but he is already confused enough."

"About what?" Micay prompted.

Amaru spread his hands a little wider. "He is not a child who knows how to complain, so it is not easy to tell. But he does not like Cuzco—chiefly, I think, because he has lost all of his friends since coming here." He squinted curiously at Micay. "What is it Rimachi has done? I have not seen much of him lately."

"He was given a compound in the Cañari quarter," Micay explained, "along with a chosen woman for a wife. So Topa lives there now and seldom comes to the palace. Rimachi also married Quespi so that she could quietly leave Chuqui's service. That meant that Yutu left, as well, and Sinchi was alone."

"I am still his friend," Cahua insisted, "and so are Coca and Cisa. But he does not like to go to the court with us. He says there is too much talking and nothing to do."

Amaru smiled wryly. "He is right about that. But he would be happier if he were outside the city altogether. He talks a lot about the Rainbow House but hardly ever mentions Tumibamba or Quito."

"What can we do for him?" Micay asked. "He told me he expects to leave here soon, but there is no place I could take him. I felt Huascar look on me as a hostage when I told him that I was Cusi's wife."

"I told Sinchi he could stay with us for a while," Amaru said, glancing at Parihuana for confirmation. "Roca is a little young for him, but they played together well enough when Sinchi stayed with us in Quito. I do not think he will cause trouble if he is not confined too closely."

"I hope not," Micay said fervently. "And I am grateful for what you did today, Amaru. You took a great risk."

"It was my duty as an uncle," Amaru insisted solemnly. Then he broke into a wide smile. "And it was worth the risk—and a sore leg—to have Titu Atauchi hanging helpless in my hands. I think Cusi would have been proud of both of us."

"Cusi has never sought trouble the way you have," Parihuana reminded him, but Amaru merely laughed.

"He never avoided it, either. Do not worry, Micay. He will be back, whether Huascar likes it or not."

"I know," Micay heard herself say, and suddenly she understood how little difference there was between believing and wishing. She put her arm around Cahua and spoke to no one in particular: "Yes . . ."

THE BEGINNING of the Inti Raymi was only days away—the guests were already streaming into the city—when Micay noticed that Chuqui was again wearing the tiny silver lime container amid her other jewelry. Micay had not seen it since the day Chuqui had decided to become the Coya, some three months before, and the sight of it made her stop and stare in the middle of the crowded, busy courtyard.

Chuqui saw her staring, but she completed her instructions to the retainers she was addressing and dispatched them to their tasks, cords in hand, before drawing Micay aside. They stepped back into the narrow space left between an enormous stack of firewood and the enclosure wall.

"You feel the need for a weapon, my lady," Micay observed, and Chuqui tilted her head in acknowledgement.

"You do not seem entirely surprised."

"How could I be, with the way Huascar has been acting? Has he threatened you in some new way?"

Chuqui put a hand against the smooth stones of the wall and shook her head. "I saw him this morning, and he made no threats at all. He even congratulated me on how well everything has been arranged. That was when I stopped worrying about little things and began to fear he is planning to ruin it all for me."

"He can try," Micay allowed. "But what else could he withhold that we could not replace? Unless his spies have penetrated all of the Upper Cuzco households, he cannot know how many people we can call on or how much we have in reserve."

"He could refuse to participate."

"He has to participate in the ceremonies. He owes too much to the priests and mamacona."

"More likely, he could invent some reason to have me confined," Chuqui suggested in a grim voice. "The priests could not free me if he put guards at the gate, and the households would not even try. They are generous with their supplies because their storehouses are overflowing, and because it is the only safe way they can strike back at Huascar. They would not challenge him on my behalf."

"No, not yet," Micay had to agree.

"Not until they have seen that I can accomplish my aim in spite of Huascar. That is why this Inti Raymi must be an unforgettable occasion and why I must be there to accept the credit." Chuqui touched the silver container on her chest. "Which is why I have armed myself. If I let him ruin this and keep me from establishing myself as the Coya, there is no point in pretending I have a reason to go on."

Micay was silent for a moment, unable to argue with her reasoning, even though it had led to such an alarming conclusion.

"Just be certain, if you have to threaten him with that weapon, that you speak with the same conviction. He would surely believe you."

Chuqui bared her teeth. "He had better."

"He will not ruin anything," Micay predicted out of the boldness of the moment. "For once he will have to stand back and let something be done properly, in a manner worthy of the Incas . . ."

IT WAS only after Huascar had made an appearance at the dance in the Cora Cora that Micay decided she could rest. He had not been overly gracious to anyone—not to Chuqui, not to the members of the Vicaquirao and Iñaca households, not to the guests from the Southern Quarter—but he had come, and he had been gracious enough. The mere fact that he had willingly and peacefully entered the Vicaquirao compound was considered an astonishing achievement, and after he had departed the household leaders flocked around Chuqui to thank her and pay her homage.

Micay used the moment to slip away and find an empty bench at the edge of the garden, one that was still in the sunlight but away from the musicians and dancers. She slumped down on it, trembling with fatigue and what she realized was hunger, her mouth and throat numb from all the coca she had chewed to keep going. When she closed her eyes, bright colors and then images flickered behind her eyelids, vivid pieces of the past days' events welling up with a swiftness that soon became a dizzying whirl. Her eyes popped open of their own accord, and she had to grip the edge of the bench to keep from falling over backward.

A young man wearing a cook's apron and carrying a drinking cup in each hand was coming toward her, and it took her a moment to realize that it was Fempellec. In Cuzco he found it prudent to conceal his beauty, so he kept his hair cut short and wore tunics and mantles that made him appear thicker and more manly. He had also kept his resolve to stay away from the court, turning down Chuqui's offer to again be one of her chiefs of feasts. He had allowed himself to be pressed into service for the Inti Raymi, but only as the supervisor of the cooks and servants he knew from Quito.

He stopped in front of Micay and extended one of the cups with a laconic flourish that mocked his own toast.

"Chuqui is accepting all the praise, but some of us are aware of your part in her success. You are, after all, the only one who could have gotten me to cook the sort of food the Cuzcos favor!"

Micay laughed and accepted the cup, spilling a little onto the ground in imitation of Fempellec.

"To Churi Inti, the Child Sun," he intoned, and took a large swallow of the frothy gray akha. Micay sipped hers uncertainly.

"I broke my fast after the ceremony on the Rimac Pampa," she explained, "but I do not remember if I have eaten since. If I get drunk, someone will have to carry me out of here."

"I am sure the Coya would provide you with a litter," Fempellec said dryly, and sat down next to her. He took another drink and nudged her with his elbow until she did the same. "There . . . at least they know how to make akha in this city."

"You could teach them more," Micay suggested, "if you would join Chuqui's staff."

Fempellec snorted. "Today I could almost be tempted. Even Amaru is impressed by what you have done. He said it is like the Inti Raymis he remembers from his childhood."

"That is what Chuqui wanted; she has the same memories."

"So should Huascar, but he has a well-earned reputation as an ungenerous host. You saw the sensation he caused simply by being polite to these people. He has acted well for days, in fact. I did not think Chuqui or anyone else had that kind of influence on him."

Micay took another sip, feeling the akha loosening her tongue. "I think he is in a kind of trance from the ceremonies. The Sun priests insisted that everything be done according to tradition, and they had the power, because of what he owed them, to make him play his part. The ceremonies had their own power, and I think he began to believe he is the son of Inti and the father of the Incas. I was there on the Rimac Pampa, Fempellec, when the Incas sang to welcome the Young Sun, and for the first time since I came to Cuzco I felt that I was in a holy place."

"Huascar will recover," Fempellec predicted, "and he will go back to being the enemy of everybody. I wish Amaru would finish with the Collcampata and take us to Machu Picchu. Huascar speaks too often, and too fondly, of the Place of the Pit."

"You would truly prefer the loneliness of Machu Picchu?"

He puckered his lips in exasperation. "I would prefer its safety. Come, Micay, Huascar makes Mama Huarcay seem innocent and kindly. And Titu Atauchi is with him now, too. Maybe you and Chuqui can make yourselves safe, but I would rather go somewhere and wait until Cusi and the others return to cast him out."

Micay sat back and studied him over the rim of her cup, struck by how fresh and powerful his sense of jeopardy still was. She realized that her own had diminished considerably over the past several days, lulled by the apparent success of their plans. Perhaps she was the one who was entranced.

Fempellec suddenly slid off the bench and executed a hasty bow, and Micay looked up to see Rimachi smiling down at her, flanked by a man who regarded her impassively from beneath an elaborate feathered headdress.

"Uritu!" she exclaimed softly, and he slowly let his broad face open into a smile. He was wearing his golden earplugs, but his hair now hung to his shoulders and he was dressed in a long red tunic that fell almost to his ankles, like a priest's robe. In one hand he was holding a puma-head drinking cup and in the other a painted staff that seemed to spout feathers from its knobbed end.

"I should have told you the high chief of Vitcos would be attending the Inti Raymi," Rimachi said, holding out a hand as Micay rose unsteadily to her feet.

"Greetings, my lady," Uritu said with a bow. "Rimachi has told me how you came to be here without Cusi. I am sorry not to see you together."

"I am pleased to see you, my friend," Micay told him. "You remember Fempellec?"

The two men exchanged nods of greeting, and Rimachi smiled knowingly.

"I thought the food here was less bland than usual . . ."

"I did my best to disguise the flavor," Fempellec said with a shrug and Micay and Rimachi laughed. Uritu drank from his cup, his eyes fastened on Micay in unspoken expectation.

"Has the Coya received you yet?" she asked, remembering her manners. "I will take you to her myself."

"I would be honored," Uritu said without discernible enthusiasm, his expectant gaze unchanged.

"Tomay's father is here, too . . ."

"I have already greeted Ancoayllu," Uritu told her, and rapped the ground with his plumed staff, as if to wake her up. "I have come for my nephew, Micay."

"Sinchi," Micay breathed as comprehension settled over her like a cold wrap. "Forgive me, Uritu. Everything that happened in the north seems so far away now." She glanced around uncertainly. "Sinchi should be here by now; Parihuana and Amaru are bringing him."

"I must return to the cooks," Fempellec announced, bowing to the men. "I will find him for you and send him here."

Micay took another drink, but it seemed only to speed the beating of her heart. Uritu's eyes were still on her, studying her reluctance.

"Then you will let him go back to Vitcos with me when the Inti Raymi is over?" he asked quietly.

"He is so young, Uritu. I did not expect this so soon . . ."

"A visit could not harm him, Micay," Rimachi put in unctuously. "As long as he is back in time to enter the House of Learning with his initiation brothers."

"I am not speaking of a mere visit," Uritu said without looking at Rimachi. "As Micay knows."

"I will miss him," Micay said in a belated attempt to explain her hesitation, "but if he wishes to go, you may take him."

"Wait!" Rimachi interrupted, startling them both. "Do I understand you correctly? You cannot mean to keep Sinchi away from his appointed group!"

"Cusi and I promised Uritu that he could teach our son the ways of the Campas," Micay replied, and Rimachi waved his cup impatiently.

"But think how long that could take! You remember, Uritu, how Cusi felt when his father threatened to keep him back. Would you do that to his son?"

"Sinchi has the spirit of a Campa," Uritu said mildly. "If he chooses to have the earplugs, too, he can return at any time."

"He has the blood of an Inca," Rimachi pointed out, "so of course he will want the earplugs. And he and Topa were meant to be initiation brothers, as surely as the four of us were brought together."

"If that is true, then it will be so," Uritu said. "It does not affect the promise that was made to me."

"Micay," Rimachi began, but he was interrupted by the sound of a loud whoop and the simultaneous appearance of Sinchi and Cahua. Sinchi wound himself around Uritu's staff, gazing up at the man with an adoration so strong it made both of them shy. Cahua, however, addressed Uritu with her customary boldness.

"Why are you here, Uncle Uritu? You are not from the Southern Quarter."

"No, my daughter," Uritu agreed. "I came to this feast to see you and your mother." He paused and looked down at Sinchi. "And to invite your brother to come back to Vitcos with me."

"He said he was going to leave," Cahua reported as if she had believed it all along. "Hawk told him."

Sinchi gave Micay a triumphant smile, and Micay sat back down on the bench and beckoned for him to come to her. Cahua came with him, standing to one side as he stopped in front of Micay and lightly rested a hand on her knee.

"Are you ready to go with your uncle, my son? You were very young when your father and I agreed to this. I am surprised you remember him."

"I remember," said Sinchi earnestly. "He wears feathers and has marks on his face, like me."

"He is a great warrior and a leader of his people, and you must obey him as you would your father. He is a kind man, and he will take good care of you."

Sinchi nodded. "When will you come?"

"I must stay here and wait for your father. Perhaps when he returns we will come visit you in Vitcos. Or we will send for you. You know you can return to Cuzco any time you wish."

Sinchi frowned uncertainly and glanced over his shoulder at Uritu. "Will I have friends in Vitcos?"

"Everyone will be your friend," Uritu assured him, "and the forest will be your home. You are never alone there."

Encouraged, Sinchi turned back but faltered at the sight of Cahua's sad expression. Micay saw them lock eyes the way they had used to when they were little, when she used to think they were reading each other's thoughts. They had grown apart as they grew older, but they seemed to understand that this was different, and it had made them twins again.

"You could come, too," Sinchi suggested, but Cahua simply pursed her lips and gave her head a shake.

"I belong to the Coya's court, and the Coya cannot live in the forest."

"No," Sinchi admitted. He put an arm around her shoulders and whispered something in her ear that made her sadness vanish.

"Now?" she asked eagerly. Sinchi nodded tentatively, tilting his head toward Micay to indicate that the choice was not his. Cahua put a knee up on the bench and whispered in Micay's ear.

"He is going to let me see Hawk."

Micay nodded in agreement. "Find a place where you can be alone. Then you must find your Uncle Amaru and Aunt Parihuana and tell them you are leaving and thank them for their kindness."

"I already told them," Sinchi said, "but I will tell them again."

Cahua tugged on his arm, and Micay motioned for them to go, forcing a smile. Sinchi looked back at Uritu and whooped before following his sister into the garden.

"He is going to show her his spirit brother," Micay explained. "I must tell you what I know about that before you leave with him."

"I am eager to listen," Uritu said. He looked at Rimachi, his eyes hooded and a hint of a smile on his lips. "There is a Campa sorcerer, a man very old and very wise, who says that many of the Incas will be coming to live among us. He has seen this, and he thinks it is not far off."

Rimachi grunted scornfully. "Does he say that the Huarachicoy will be held in Vitcos?"

The rudeness of his tone brought Micay to her feet to face him. "Why are you interfering, Rimachi? If you knew my son, you would know he is unhappy here. And who is to say how long any of us can be happy here? We have not made a new man out of Huascar with one festival."

"We cannot all send our children into the forest," Rimachi snapped. He drained his cup with an abrupt motion. "Forgive me, both of you. There was a part of Cusi you always understood better than I: the part that did not want to be an Inca. I want my son to have the place I have earned for him, and I would want my nephew to have the same. Right now, I want more akha . . ."

He turned on his heel and walked away, and Micay and Uritu stared after him for a moment.

"Huascar shows a different face to the Cañaris," Uritu observed.

"Yes . . . but I thought Rimachi knew better than to trust him."

"He does. That is what makes it so hard for him. He could be happy here if he could only forget."

" 'There is no safety in ignorance for those who can feel,' " Micay said, quoting something Cusi had said to her long ago. Uritu nodded and bared his teeth briefly in recognition.

"I will give your son knowledge," he promised, "so he can keep himself safe."

Blinking back tears, Micay gathered up her cup and went to his side.

"I believe you will, my friend," she said in a thick voice. She pointed with her chin at the crowd around Chuqui. "Come, let me take you to the Coya while the spell of the Inti Raymi is still upon us, and we can let ourselves feel . . ."

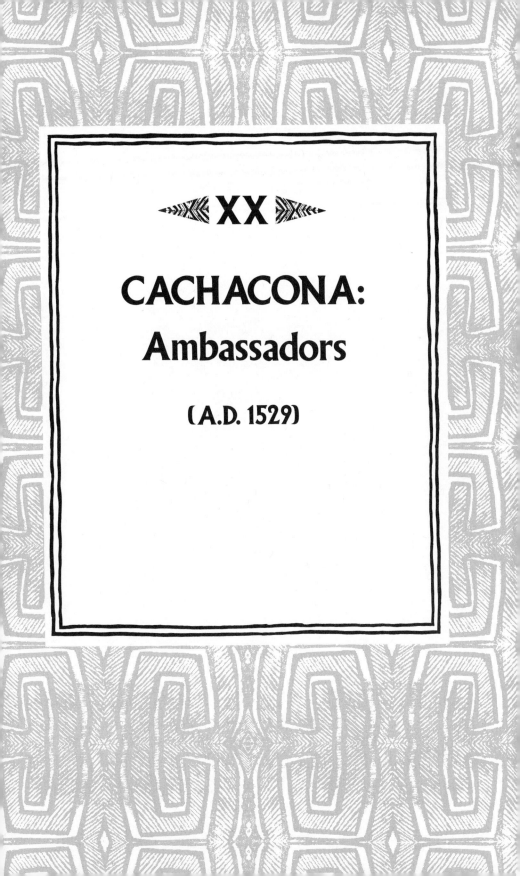

XX

CACHACONA:
Ambassadors

(A.D. 1529)

Quito

THE STEEP, winding trail that led down from the pass finally leveled off and brought them out onto the plain. They stopped and stared out over the rolling expanse of grassland, where nothing grew higher than a man's knee and there was no canopy of trees to obscure the sky and the sun. The three of them looked at one another and smiled, sharing a common sense of return.

Huaman Cachi was the first to break the silence, cracking his spear against his shield and letting out an exultant cry that startled a herd of llamas in the distance. Then he broke into a run that left Cusi and Tarapaca behind for a moment, until they gathered their shields and weapons in close to their bodies and took off after him. Cusi lifted his face to the sun, feeling the thin, dry air whistle past him. Even encumbered by his shield, battle-ax, and the carrying bundle on his back, it felt wonderful to stretch out his legs on firm, open ground, without the fear of slipping in the mud or tripping over a vine. Huaman Cachi had to slow down to secure his own bundle, and Cusi and Tarapaca ran by him on either side, shouting in mock triumph as they passed him.

They all slowed to a walk at the top of the next rise, breathing hard and laughing at their own exuberance. Cusi still felt light and slightly weak from the thorough purging he had undergone, but the exertion of the run had not made him dizzy or overly tired. Gone, too, was the blurriness at the edge of his vision and the occasional flashes of vivid color. Physically, the effects of the ayahuasca—the Vine of the Dead—seemed to have worn off, though the experience of having taken it was still with him in every other way. He decided he had needed such an ordeal, even if he had not been given any glimpses of the future. Whatever dangers he would face in this world—the world he knew—could never be as strange and frightening as those he had encountered in the ayahuasca dreamworld.

"And we survived," he said aloud. Huaman Cachi and Tarapaca both nodded, without having to ask what he meant. Cusi rapped his battle-ax against his shield, deciding that even if he could not see the future he was ready to take his part in what was to come.

HUALLPA WAS sitting on a wall outside the main gate of the city, tying feathers onto darts while he waited. He had apparently been waiting for some time, because it took him several moments to scoop all of his materials into a bag and run to meet them. He greeted them tentatively, staring at their insect-bitten faces and the bands of golden feathers around their wrists.

"Welcome back, my lord," he said to Cusi. "Tomay Guanaco is waiting for you at your brother's compound. Quilaco Yupanqui is probably still with him. They have been waiting to speak to you for two days."

Cusi nodded and led them through the gate. "What news is there?"

"The Huancavelicas surrendered to Quizquiz," Huallpa reported, "and the Coya is trying to arrange a peace between Huascar and Atauhuallpa."

"Chuqui Huipa or her mother?"

"Chuqui Huipa," the boy said. "Though the Coya Rahua Ocllo is supporting her. So are most of the priests in Cuzco and the high priestess of Titicaca."

"Tocto?" Cusi murmured in surprise. Then he gave Huallpa a sharp glance. "You do not seem troubled by the possibility of peace. Why is that?"

Huallpa shrugged, his cheeks darkening. "Quilaco is being sent to Cuzco as Atauhuallpa's ambassador. He wants you to go with him."

Cusi stopped in the street outside Amaru's compound and exchanged a glance with his companions. "Do you remember? How Kirupasa insisted that I had seen what lay ahead in one of my dreams? Even though he would not tell me which one . . ."

"The man who wants to kill you," Tarapaca supplied.

"Yes, the man with the blowpipe," Huaman Cachi agreed, and Cusi nodded, beginning to understand some of the things Kirupasa had told him while he was in his dreams. He looked back at Huallpa, who was staring at the three of them in utter bewilderment.

"There was much to be learned from the Shuaras besides their intentions," Cusi told him. "Perhaps I should not have sent you back with Tomay."

"I was glad to go," Huallpa said without regret. "I hated the jungle."

"So did we," Huaman Cachi assured him, and the three of them laughed and started into the compound. Cusi glanced first at the gardens on the first level, which had been expanded to include food crops as well as fruits and flowers. He had had a hand in the planting before he left for the land of the Shuaras, and he was pleased to see that the retainers had kept up the work. The fields outside the city had been well tended, too, a sign that their effort to supply themselves had not slackened.

Tomay and Quilaco were waiting on the second level near the fish tanks that always made Cusi think of Sinchi. Tomay rose to greet them, looking Cusi over carefully before nodding with apparent satisfaction. Quilaco remained seated, unsmiling, like a man who was struggling to control his impatience.

"I am glad the Shuaras sent you back with your heads," Tomay said as they put down their shields and weapons and shrugged off their bundles. "I should tell you, though, that Atauhuallpa thought you had already lost yours when I told him why you had stayed behind."

"There was much to learn from Kirupasa," Cusi said. "And even though he had agreed to the treaty, he would not have trusted it without the chance to look into my heart and test my honesty."

"You let him do that?" Quilaco inquired sharply.

"I could hardly have stopped him once I drank the ayahuasca. But I had nothing to hide." Cusi looked directly at Quilaco and spoke more sharply himself. "Do not expect me to apologize for my late return. There was no peace proposal when I left, and you were not so impatient to get back to Cuzco."

"So the boy told you," Quilaco concluded, rising to his feet. "Yes, I am impatient, because this is an opportunity we cannot afford to squander. Chuqui Huipa proposed a reconciliation at the Capac Raymi festival, and she has won the support of the households and most of the priesthood. It appears they have finally gotten Huascar to agree to listen."

"Listen to what?"

"A solemn pledge of loyalty from Atauhuallpa. In return he would recognize Atauhuallpa as the Regent of the Northern Provinces, subject to the Sapa Inca's command but exempt from the Cuzco labor tax."

"And you are going to make this pledge?" Cusi asked skeptically. "Huascar will accept you in Atauhuallpa's place?"

"We have no promise of that," Quilaco admitted. "Atauhuallpa is sending Inca Pasac and two of his other brothers along with me."

"The boy said you wanted me to go, too. Whose idea was that?"

"Mine," Quilaco said without hesitation. "Though Atauhuallpa agreed you would be useful. He knows that Micay is close to Chuqui and that you have spoken to Huascar in the past."

"Why do you think I would be useful?"

"For the same reasons," Quilaco began. But then stopped and shook himself angrily. "No . . . I could say I want you because you are brave and trustworthy, and it would be true but not the real reason. I want you because you are more than that, because you have knowledge and powers that might save us when nothing else can."

"The kind of knowledge that might be gained from a Shuara sorcerer, perhaps," Cusi suggested, yielding to the temptation to goad him.

"Whatever has kept you alive in spite of all the powerful enemies you have made," Quilaco shot back. "Your reputation alone makes some people fear you."

"I doubt Huascar is one of them," Cusi said, remembering the man who had stalked him in his dream. "You are telling me, then, that you expect this embassy to be a dangerous one."

"If it were truly safe Atauhuallpa would be going himself," Quilaco admitted. "We both know that. But surely Chuqui has taken a risk in making this proposal, and if there is a chance it could lead to peace, I am willing to risk myself, too. Are you, Cusi Huaman?"

The formality of the challenge made Cusi smile. "I do not think a promise from Huascar is worth anyone's risk, Quilaco Yupanqui. But I would go with you simply for the chance to see my wife and children again. When do we leave?"

Quilaco grunted, appearing relieved in spite of himself. "As soon as the gifts have been assembled. We are allowed a few men to accompany us, and Tomay has volunteered to lead them. I will let the two of you decide whom to take."

He offered his hand to Cusi in parting, and Cusi gripped it firmly, trying to show that he was committed, even if he did not share the other man's hopes. Quilaco nodded impassively and left, and Cusi turned back to Tomay.

"So, my brother, you have made yourself a part of this . . ."

Tomay shrugged dismissively. "We have survived too much together for me to let you go back without me a second time. Ñupchu knew before I told her. She said we should go and bring Micay and Rimachi and all the children back with us."

"We should," Cusi agreed. "It might be our last chance."

Tarapaca politely cleared his throat. "We have also survived some things together. May I be one of your few men?"

"You may," Tomay said for both of them. Then he gave Tarapaca a sly smile. "You may be a Lupaca, but I think of you as a Hawk Man."

"My lord?" Huaman Cachi inquired, and Cusi gave his consent with a nod. That left Huallpa, and Tomay conceded the decision to Cusi with a doubtful shrug that made Huallpa start up in desperation.

"You would not leave me behind?"

"I would if I thought you could not be trusted," Cusi told him. "You may have to face your father's murderers in Cuzco, and if you show them any sign of who you are or what you have witnessed . . ."

"I will show them nothing!" Huallpa promised. "I only want to take my mother and Yutu away from there."

"We may not be able to do that," Cusi said. "We may be threatened and mistreated and forced to humble ourselves. There will be no place for anger or foolish thoughts of revenge."

"I will not betray your trust," the boy vowed, and Cusi studied him for a moment, believing he meant it. He was ready to take his part, too, whatever it might be.

"You are one of us, then. And you will begin your training with weapons on the march. Huaman Cachi will be your teacher."

Huallpa looked from one to the other, appearing pleased but puzzled. Huaman Cachi gave Cusi a searching glance.

"You may tell him about your dream," Cusi allowed. "You must make him ready but not reckless."

"Ready for what?" Huallpa demanded, and Huaman Cachi gave him a cool, hard stare as if to make him feel his age and inexperience.

"Ready to kill Titu Atauchi," Huaman Cachi said, and laughed at the younger boy's shocked expression. "See, he is less reckless already."

Cusi stooped for his carrying bundle and gestured toward the bathhouse. They all began to move in that direction, Huallpa trailing slightly behind.

"What else have you dreamed?" Tomay asked.

Cusi raised his shoulders in a weary shrug. "Many things. I will tell you as we march, and you can help me understand them." He glanced sideways at Tomay but barely saw him, his gaze turning inward. "I must make myself ready, as well. There is a man who wants to kill me, and I believe I will find him in Cuzco . . ."

Cuzco

IN THE UPROAR caused by the Coya's untimely return, Cahua had been kept away from the litter by the crowd of excited women who immediately surrounded it and who began to wail in distress as Chuqui was lifted out by the bearers and carried into her chamber. Cahua tried to fight her way through, but her struggles yielded only a brief, awful glimpse of Chuqui's face: one eye swollen shut and the other leaking tears that made the blood on her lips and chin glisten and run.

Cahua stopped short, feeling suddenly cold, and when she finally got to the doorway the head retainer gently turned her away, saying that only her mother and a few others were allowed inside. Too upset to argue, Cahua looked around for Machacuay, who had been sitting with her when the litter was brought in. She found him standing by himself in the midst of the distraught women, who were tearing at their hair and biting the edges of their mantles. He was blinking rapidly, and he looked down at her as if he did not know who she was, which made her feel cold again.

"Huascar beat her," he said in a strange voice that fluttered and died. Then his body jerked and he collapsed onto the women behind him, who shrieked wildly before moving aside to let him fall.

Though she understood nothing about what had happened to Chuqui, Cahua was at least familiar with Machacuay's fainting spells, so she took charge of him and took refuge in being a healer again. She enlisted two of the bearers to carry the limp, twitching body over to the wall near the doorway, and one of the retainer women brought her blankets and a gourd of water. She wrapped him in the blankets and tended him as her mother had shown her, cradling his head in her lap and murmuring soothingly until the bump in his throat stopped moving and his limbs relaxed with a shudder. When his eyes opened a crack, she gave him a little water, and when he asked where he was, she lied and told him he was safe in his own room.

He believed her and went to sleep, and Cahua was instantly sorry that she had not tried to rouse him, as she again became aware of the other people in the courtyard. The women were huddled together in small groups, whispering and moaning and weeping in one another's arms. Their sounds were so like those of mourners that Cahua had the sudden fear that Chuqui was going to die, and she slid Machacuay's head off her lap and rose into a crouch, eying the curtained doorway. She could sing to Chuqui and make her better. She had done it before, though Chuqui had never looked so bad as now.

Before Cahua could move, the Old Coya entered the courtyard, followed by a group of her women. The wailing women fell silent and bowed as Rahua Ocllo passed through their midst, heading directly for the curtained doorway. She disappeared into the chamber without pausing to acknowledge anyone, leaving her retinue to wait outside. Cahua was briefly tempted to sneak in after her, but there were too many people watching. Besides, the Old Coya had seemed angry instead of worried, so it probably was not true that Chuqui was going to die.

The Old Coya's women had turned to the women already present, and after much whispering they, too, began to moan and wail. But Cahua could tell now that it was not true mourning, not like what she had seen in Quito during the sickness. Probably no one was dying, but something shameful had happened. *Huascar beat her.* Cahua knew Machacuay and Fempellec had been beaten in Quito, but that had been done by some bad men. Huascar was Chuqui's husband, and her brother, too. Brothers did not beat their sisters; they were supposed to protect them. That was what their mother had always told Sinchi, though actually Cahua had hit Sinchi many more times—and harder—than he had ever hit her. She decided something very shameful had happened. Maybe Huascar had let some bad men do things to her, like he had with Uncle Lloque and Yasca. The mourning had sounded a lot like this then, too.

Cahua looked down at Machacuay, wishing he were awake to comfort her, wishing someone would make the women be quiet. Their noises only seemed to make it worse. She thought instead about her father, who was coming to Cuzco and this time was going to come all the way into the city. He had turned away the last time because of what the bad men had done to Uncle Lloque, but now he was coming to make peace with Huascar. Then they would all be together again, except for Sinchi, and maybe they would go to see him in Vitcos.

A sudden silence made her raise her head, and she saw another entourage entering the courtyard, this one led by a short woman who seemed to glow as the light hit the silver she was wearing around her wrists, neck, and forehead. The other women were bowing and making the mocha, but Cahua simply stared in wonder as the Silver Woman came toward her, her hands clasped beneath the large silver disc on her breast. She walked calmly, but her eyes took in the whole courtyard in swift, darting glances, the last of which settled on Cahua and seemed to draw the woman right to her.

"Mamanchic," Cahua murmured, finally recognizing the significance of the silver disc and remembering to bow. The woman smiled and gestured for Cahua to rise, reaching out to touch her under the chin.

"Do you know who I am, my daughter?" the woman asked in a deep voice that seemed to hum in Cahua's ears.

"The high priestess of Titicaca," Cahua ventured, knowing she was right even before the woman nodded.

"I am Tocto Oxica, and I am also the sister of the Coya Chuqui Huipa. I was told these were her quarters. Can you tell me where to find her?"

"She is inside, my lady," Cahua said. She frowned as she pointed to the doorway with her chin. "Huascar beat her."

The woman's smile vanished so abruptly that Cahua quickly lowered her eyes, certain she had said the wrong thing.

"Beaten!" the woman repeated in disbelief. "Do you know what you are saying, child? Who told you this?"

"Machacuay," Cahua said timidly, indicating the blanket-wrapped form on the ground beside her. "He is my mother's retainer."

"Why is he sleeping here?"

"He fainted. He has spells when something makes him feel bad," Cahua explained. "He was beaten, too, when he had the sickness in Quito."

The woman cast a glance at the mamacona behind her, seeming no less doubtful. "You are young to know such things, my daughter. Who are you?"

"I am Cahua, my lady. I am one of the Coya's women and a healer like my mother. She is inside with Chuqui."

"I must go in myself," the woman decided. After a brief hesitation she held out her hand to Cahua. "Perhaps you will take me to her . . ."

Her hand was soft and warm and not much larger than Cahua's. Cahua took a last look at Machacuay, then proudly led the way to the doorway. They pushed through the curtain into the dark room, which was illuminated by three windows high up in the back wall. Chuqui was reclining on a pallet beneath the windows with several women kneeling around her and the Old Coya standing over them all.

"It has been many years, my mother," Tocto Oxica said, releasing Cahua's hand so that she could offer both her hands to the Old Coya.

"I am pleased and honored, Mamanchic," Rahua Ocllo said, taking her daughter's hands and bowing over them. Then she led Tocto up to the pallet, and Tocto knelt down at Chuqui's elbow. Cahua also knelt and looked across the pallet at her mother, who did not smile but did not seem angry, either.

Mostly she seemed fascinated by the Silver Woman, who leaned over Chuqui.

"Sister," Chuqui said in a weak, muffled voice, looking at Tocto with the one eye she could open. There was no longer any blood on her face, but there were bruises and swelling lumps everywhere, and her lower lip had been split open on one side.

"I came to give you my support, Chuqui, as I promised," Tocto told her. "When I arrived I was told that Huascar had left the city and gone to his estate at Calca. Why did he do this to you?"

Chuqui closed her eye and swallowed with a grimace, gesturing with a limp hand for Micay to tell the story.

"He summoned her to the Collcampata alone," Micay said. "He asked her to go to Calca with him and she refused, saying she had to stay to greet you, my lady, and the ambassadors from Atauhuallpa. He threatened her and insisted that the ambassadors could come to him in Calca, and when she still refused, he . . . did this."

"Tell all of it, Micay," Chuqui commanded harshly, glaring out of her one eye. "He forced himself on me!"

"There is a child present, my sister," Tocto cautioned, and Chuqui raised her head until she could see Cahua for the first time.

"Cahua, my child," she said, tears spilling out of her eye. "That you should see me like this . . . come sing for me, my daughter. Sing to make me feel like living again . . ."

The Silver Woman moved back so that Cahua could approach the head of the pallet, and Cahua paused and gave her an expectant glance, just to be certain she was aware that everything Cahua had said was true. The woman seemed startled, but then she nodded and smiled, and Cahua settled herself next to Chuqui and began to sing, choosing a song to Mama Quilla, knowing that would impress the mamanchic even more.

The other women rose quietly and backed away from the pair on the pallet. Most of them left the chamber, but Rahua Ocllo beckoned for Micay and Cori Cuillor to stay behind and speak with Tocto Oxica.

"These are the wives Mama Micay and Cori Cuillor, Chuqui's closest companions," Rahua Ocllo explained, and Tocto accepted their bows, giving a hand to each of them. Her eyes lingered on Micay for a moment, squinting in a kind of puzzled recognition, as if wondering whether they had met before.

"We must decide what to do," Rahua Ocllo said abruptly. "Quilaco Yupanqui and the other ambassadors will be here soon if we do not warn them. Perhaps it would be best simply to tell them to go back."

"But then it would seem that we and Atauhuallpa—not Huascar—have abandoned the effort at reconciliation," Tocto pointed out. "We must keep the idea, at least, alive in everyone's minds. And we must keep the ambassadors alive." She paused, resting a delicate, silver-banded wrist on her hip. "I will go out to meet them myself. Do you have any warriors you can trust?"

"You are closest to Rimachi, Micay," Rahua Ocllo said. "Can we still depend on his loyalty?"

Out of the corner of her eye, Micay was aware of a blossoming of comprehension on Tocto's face, but she answered Rahua Ocllo without hesitation. "We can trust him, my lady."

"He is the captain of Chuqui's personal guard," Rahua Ocllo explained to Tocto, "a Cañari but also an Inca by privilege."

"Yes, I know him," Tocto said, and she smiled at Micay. "I believe I know you, as well, my daughter, though I did not recognize your name at first. Hanp'atu told it to me many years ago."

"I will leave you to become better acquainted," Rahua Ocllo said impatiently. "I must talk to Rimachi and see how close the ambassadors are and if we can get a message to them at all."

With a perfunctory bow she left them, and Tocto again looked at Micay.

"Perhaps you would show me to my quarters now," she suggested, and Cori Cuillor nodded to Micay, indicating that she would stay behind with Chuqui. She smiled wryly and pointed with her chin at Cahua, who was sitting cross-legged with her elbows propped on the pallet, moving her head back and forth in time with her song.

"I will not interrupt the healing," she promised. "And I will see that she is fed if you are not back."

"She is an extraordinary child," Tocto said as the two of them pushed through the curtain into the light. "I did not know why I was so drawn to her until my mother asked you to speak for Rimachi, and I realized you were her mother."

Machacuay was sitting up against the wall outside, drinking hot coca water that one of Tocto's mamacona had gotten for him. Micay gestured for him to remain seated, stooping down to look into his eyes.

"I am fine, my lady," he assured her hastily. "They tell me Cahua took care of me."

"She is inside," Micay told him. "Rest while you wait for her, and bring her to me if she comes out. I am taking the high priestess to the guest quarters."

The mamacona fell in behind as Micay led Tocto out of the courtyard, preceded by a servant who hurried ahead to alert the retainers to their approach.

"Where is Cusi now?" Tocto asked, and Micay realized that it was the first time either of them had said his name, though he was clearly present in both their thoughts.

"He is one of the ambassadors, my lady. I have been awaiting his arrival for two months."

"Ah, I did not know," Tocto said in apology. "I had heard only the names of Quilaco and Inca Pasac. Should we have told them to go back?"

Micay shook her head as they turned into the narrow passageway that led to the gate of the guest quarters. "No, my lady. I agreed with what you said to your mother. And if we can bring him safely into Cuzco, I am certain he can find his way out."

Tocto clicked her tongue appreciatively. "Then he is the same Cusi I knew."

They came through the gate into a small interior compound that did not receive enough light for a garden and so was decorated instead with big pots filled with ferns and moss and freshly cut flowers. Bobbing their heads in deference, the servants showed the mamacona to their rooms, and Micay stepped aside at the entrance to the largest of the houses.

"You will want to rest and refresh yourself after your journey, my lady. The bathhouse is around to the right."

Tocto nodded absently, turning in the doorway to face her. "Before you go, Micay, you must tell me the rest of it. Why did Huascar beat her?"

Micay let out a long breath. "I do not know if he truly expected her to go to Calca with him, since his withdrawal at this point is as much an insult to her as to Atauhuallpa. It was another chance to demonstrate that she has no power with him, to make her plead for her proposal and then laugh at her in front of his advisers. Chuqui survived that well enough, but then when he got her alone, he suddenly grabbed her and started tearing at her clothes. When she fought with him, he knocked her down and tied her hands with her belt, and then he took her like a beast, thrusting as hard as he could to try to hurt her."

Tocto's eyes darted away for a moment, and Micay waited for them to return, reminding herself that she was speaking to the high priestess, who lived away from the world of men and women. But when Tocto brought her attention back and nodded to go on, Micay saw she was reckoning with some inner pain, not flinching at the facts.

"Chuqui survived that, as well," Micay continued. "But when he was done and she held out her hands to be untied, he grinned at her. He released her, but he grinned like a boy proud of his strength, as if he expected her to be impressed with him, too. And in that moment Chuqui hated him so much that she said the one thing she knew would make him wither." Micay sighed at the irrevocability of it. "She looked up at him and said, 'You call yourself a man, Little Brother. Ninan Cuyochi never had to force me.' *That* was when he beat her, my lady."

Tocto's face was stark and unguarded, not the face of a high priestess. "I knew I could never stand to be married to him. That was why I chose the island and the company of pilgrims and mamacona. I knew the memories I took with me would be better than anything I would ever have with Huascar."

"Your memories of Cusi," Micay suggested, and Tocto nodded gratefully, her face softening.

"I never knew whether to believe the rumors about Chuqui and Ninan, but I have always believed Cusi asked for me. It was terrible of me, Micay, I know. I made him risk his life when I knew it was impossible. But still . . . it has warmed me all these years to know he loved me that much."

"He did ask for you," Micay assured her. "It was the only thing he wanted, and he grieved when your father turned him down."

Tocto gave her a pained smile. Then she shook herself, sending out silver flashes. "You are kind, Micay, and you must forgive my self-indulgence. It is one of many ways in which I am unworthy of my title. Will you go with me to meet the ambassadors?"

"I would consider it a great favor, my lady."

"We must salvage what we can of Chuqui's effort," Tocto declared, her wistfulness gone. "I owe her that much."

Micay bowed in compliance, and Tocto sighed as she raised a hand over her in blessing.

"So much has been broken, Micay. I will pray to Mama Quilla to make us whole again," she said as she turned into the house. "Before the pieces are scattered and lost . . ."

Apurimac

THE FIRST contingent of warriors, perhaps twenty in all, appeared behind them as they left Vilcashuaman and stayed there, saying nothing and making no attempt to pass. A second twenty silently took the vanguard in Abancay, and a third detachment stepped out of the rest house at Sahuite to flank them on both sides. The warriors were mostly Cañaris and Chachapoyas, mitmacs from Cuzco led by Inca captains too young to have fought anywhere. Even as their numbers swelled, the warriors kept their distance from the men they were escorting, making them feel isolated as well as outnumbered.

Not counting the two porters, the herder, and his llamas, there were nine in the ambassadors' party. Four of them—Quilaco, Inca Pasac, Topa Poma, and Yahuar Huacac—carried only a ceremonial weapon or no weapon at all, and they regarded the warriors massing around them with a deliberate, disdainful indifference. Cusi and his four comrades were all fully armed, even Huallpa, who had fashioned weapons and a shield his own size. Instead of ignoring the intimidating presence of the warriors, Cusi chose to regard their threat as real and imminent, and during rest stops he and his men quietly worked out their battle signals and a plan to fight their way free if they were attacked. That they would have no chance in such a fight was obvious to all of them and so was left unspoken.

As they came up over a rise and approached the place from which they could see down to the river gorge, the double file of warriors ahead slowed and parted, and they could see another group of armed men waiting in the middle of the road. When Cusi recognized the war chief Atoc as their leader, he glanced over his shoulder at Tomay and Tarapaca and issued a terse warning.

"Keep your weapons ready."

As he brought his eyes forward again Quilaco gave him a sidelong glance and whispered incredulously: "Are you mad?"

"If I have to be," Cusi said brusquely, concentrating his attention on the squat figure of Atoc, who was holding a war club with a notched head of black stone. Even at a distance Cusi could feel the threat emanating from the man, and he drew it into himself like fuel, feeding his presence. He had realized long ago that the man who wanted to kill him would not appear as a Shuara with a blowpipe, as he had in the dream. It could be Atoc instead of Huascar himself, and if it was Cusi would be ready to face him.

Before they reached the waiting group, however, Atoc turned to listen to a messenger, and the men around him all turned to look back down the road. Tarapaca, who was tall enough to see over Cusi's head, leaned forward to speak into his ear.

"Someone else is coming. A procession . . . with a litter."

The line of ambassadors came to a halt in front of Atoc, who whirled on them, angry but distracted, his war club gripped loosely.

"The Sapa Inca has retired to his pleasure compound at Calca and will receive you there," he snapped out. "I will take you after you have made your offerings in Cuzco."

"We had expected to make our pledge of loyalty in the Haucaypata," Inca Pasac objected politely, "in front of all the Incas."

"He will hear your pledge himself," Atoc insisted, but then he had to turn as the men behind him gave way and opened a path for the litter being borne into their midst. It was an open litter draped in sky blue cloth that shimmered with threads of silver, and the woman sitting impassively in the high-backed wooden seat, wearing the silver Moon shield of the high priestess, was Tocto Oxica. The warriors began to drop to their knees as the litter was set down, and when Cusi saw Atoc place his war club on the ground and make the mocha with both hands, he felt free to do the same. The kisses he blew in Tocto's direction came out in forceful blasts as he released all the dangerous tension he had been storing up inside, offering it to her in gratitude.

Her long blue cloak trailing behind her, Tocto descended from the litter and walked past Atoc without a glance, smiling warmly as she approached the ambassadors. The throatiness of her voice was a familiar shock to Cusi's ears.

"Greetings, my sons. I have come to welcome you to Cuzco and to lead you to the feast that has been prepared in your honor."

Cusi bowed along with the other men, struck by the calm authority of her presence and by the way her face had changed with age, so that he could barely see the girl he had known. Nor had she paid him any special recognition, seeming to gaze upon all of them at once.

"Quilaco Yupanqui," she said when they had straightened up, "my mother remembers you with fondness and eagerly awaits your arrival, as do your daughters. But first you must introduce me to your companions . . ."

She turned away from Cusi as she said this, so Quilaco began with Inca Pasac, introducing him as Atauhuallpa's brother and the commander of a regiment in Quito. Topa Poma was also a commander and Yahuar Huacac had been the micho in Tumbez, and both were the sons of Huayna Capac by lesser wives, half brothers who had grown up with Atauhuallpa. Atoc had crept up behind Tocto while Quilaco was speaking, and he waited until she had responded before he tried to interrupt.

"Forgive me, Mamanchic," he said imploringly, and Tocto turned slowly to face him, her smile disappearing. She seemed tiny, barely half the size of the war chief, but the sharpness of her tone made him flinch.

"What do you want?" she demanded. "And why are you here with all these warriors? These men have come in peace, and they do not need your protection."

"My lady, the Sapa Inca sent me. . . ."

"Since I am here, you are not needed," Tocto told him. When he opened his mouth to protest she went on, "And I am certain you do not wish to offend me by arguing any further."

"No, my lady," Atoc agreed hastily, ducking his head and backing away. She watched him retrieve his war club and signal to his captains before she turned back to the ambassadors, who bowed to her a second time. When Cusi looked up and found her eyes on him, he could not hold back a smile, which quickly expanded beyond decorous limits.

Tocto raised her eyebrows in mock amazement. "Are you so pleased to see me, Cusi Huaman?"

"I am, my lady," Cusi admitted boldly. "I greatly prefer your protection to that provided by the war chief."

"Ambassadors need no protection," she said, glancing down at the shield and battle-ax at his feet. "You seem to be the only one who does not believe that."

"I have learned not to trust custom too much, my lady. It did not protect the men who led me here the last time."

"No, it did not," Tocto agreed, and she gave the other ambassadors a solemn look. "We will have to discuss the prospects for your embassy later. For now I would ask you to accept our welcome with an open heart and give us the pleasure of your company."

The men bowed and murmured in gratitude, and this time when Cusi straightened up he saw Micay among the mamacona who had arrived behind Tocto. A whoop escaped his lips before he could think to stop it, and while the men beside him stiffened in surprise, the men behind him simply laughed.

"Does that mean you accept?" Tocto asked, taking Micay by the arm and bringing her forward. Micay's eyes were wet but wide open, and her smile was dizzying.

"I accept," Cusi said wholeheartedly, and he stepped over his shield and battle-ax, reaching out to draw her to him and hold her tight, knowing—for that moment, at least—exactly why he had come back to Cuzco.

Quillarumi

EVEN THOUGH Tocto Oxica was still with them and Rimachi's men were stationed all around the rest house, Cusi had insisted that he and his comrades man one of the sentry posts behind the buildings in which their party was lodged. He had even insisted, over the protests of Tomay and Tarapaca, that he take the last watch himself. Micay had not bothered to protest, because he had been so certain of his need to do this and because she knew she would have him for most of the night. Nor did he seem to tire, even though they had talked and made love and talked some more until well past the middle of the night. Micay was only dimly aware of his departure, and then had gone back to sleep, dreaming about jungles and headhunters.

She awoke before dawn and immediately felt his absence, which was startling, since they had been apart for so many months. Leaving her hair loose, she donned her shift and wrapped a cloak around her and crept out into the courtyard. Rimachi's men were at their posts inside the enclosure, and one of them pointed the way to the back gate, gesturing to indicate that the sentry post was up the hill behind the rest house. The predawn sky was a gauzy shade of gray, so she had no trouble following the path that led upward past terraced fields of quinoa and potatoes, most of the plots dense with vegetation that let an earthy green smell into the chilly air.

The path seemed to end at a large rock formation that jutted up out of the hillside, and Micay slowed as she came up beside it, guessing that Cusi was somewhere above her and wondering why he had not seen her yet. As she continued upward she began to hear grunts and muted exhalations, as of someone hard at work, and she imagined Cusi piling up stones around his position. But there were no accompanying sounds of the labor itself, which made the grunts seem eerily disconnected, as if someone were struggling with the air. Then she heard a low, ticking growl that made her freeze where she stood, her stomach contracting in fear. It was a human sound, but the threat it carried was so palpable it seemed to hang in the air around her, holding her in place. She was only a few feet away from the end of the rock wall, but she could not force herself to take another step.

The growl ended abruptly, followed by a cough and the sound of rapid breathing, sounds that seemed distinctly unthreatening in comparison. Micay's fear dissipated just as swiftly, releasing her limbs, and she understood then that it was not just the growl that had made her freeze. She walked around the end of the rock shelf and found Cusi bent over with his hands on his knees, his chest heaving as if he had just run a long race. His face was shiny with sweat when he straightened up, and he gazed at her without recognition for a moment. Then his eyes seemed to snap into focus.

"Micay . . . did you see?"

Micay shook her head. "I was too afraid to come any farther. It was your presence . . ."

"Yes—good," he said, nodding and smiling to himself.

"Did you mean to frighten me? Did you know I was coming?"

"No, no . . . I was practicing. The face in the dream."

Micay came up to him and dabbed at the sweat on his forehead with the edge of her cloak. "The face you showed to the man who wanted to kill you," she concluded. "You did not tell me your powers were back, though I should have known it."

He took several deep breaths and swallowed, still calming himself. "They are not back, at least not with the same force. I have to summon them, and they do not possess me as they used to. My spirit brother holds me back."

"They felt as strong as I remember," Micay told him. "Strong enough to make me stay where I was."

"Real danger will make it stronger, I think. Enough to keep anyone away."

"Enough to possess you?"

"I do not know," he confessed. "Perhaps. Kirupasa spoke to me and made me notice the face I was wearing in the dream, when I stepped out and confronted the man with the blowpipe. It was a wild and angry face, the face of a rebel or an outlaw, a man who had no respect for authority and no fear of punishment or death. It was a face that said 'You can kill me, but I will never be humbled.' "

He stared at her for a moment, then shivered and turned away to find his own cloak and wrap it over his sweat-soaked tunic. Micay frowned, remembering what else he had told her about this dream last night.

"Yet you *were* humbled by the man in the dream," she pointed out when he returned, his shield and battle-ax in hand. "You said that after you showed him the face and made him lower his weapon, you knelt down before him and let him paint you with the colors of the dead."

"I was weeping, too," Cusi recalled, frowning. He motioned with his shield and led her over to the natural rampart that overlooked the fields and the buildings below. "I did not know what the paint signified until later, when Kirupasa told me. That was about all he would tell me, though he claimed one of the dreams referred to the future. I did not believe him until I got back to Quito and learned that Quilaco wanted me to go to Cuzco with him. All three of us knew immediately which dream Kirupasa had meant."

"I still do not understand how you interpret it," Micay said. "First you disarm the man with your face, and then you let him humble you?"

"Yes," Cusi said succinctly. He gave her a sardonic smile. "Tomay also found that hard to accept. But if this man is Huascar or someone close to him, like Titu Atauchi, I could not attack him even if he were disarmed. Nor would he simply let me walk away. It has become clear to me that what I must do to keep this man from killing me is to convince him that humiliation is a greater punishment than death."

Micay drew a tremulous breath. "How will you know when to submit? How do you know you will not attack instead, as you did in Chan Chan?"

"I do not know what I might have to do," Cusi admitted. "But my spirit brother is keeping his distance and my comrades will be waiting outside to help me escape. We have had two months to prepare ourselves for this, and we have not squandered our time."

"And what if nothing happens?" Micay asked. "What if Huascar treats you with respect and accepts Atauhuallpa's pledge?"

"Then I will be pleased and astonished," Cusi said dryly, "and we will be able to leave Cuzco in peace."

Micay rested her palms on the lichen-spotted rocks and looked down over the thick, orderly rows of crops. "*I* have had no time to prepare myself—or Chuqui—for that. And if Huascar destroys the peace instead, it will be like a second beating to her. How could I desert her then? She would be at her lowest."

"I know," Cusi said ruefully, holding her eyes to show he was not speaking from a distance. "That may be more painful than what I will have to do. But we cannot take her with us, and I will not leave you behind again, not for any reason. I thought about that, too, while I was marching, and I decided we could not risk being separated in the midst of a war. We might never be together again, my wife, and that would be the worst pain of all."

His eyes glittered with emotion, and when she came to him, he let his shield and weapon drop and fitted himself against her.

"I could not bear that," he murmured, and Micay pressed her lips against his neck, tasting salt.

"You will not have to," she promised with a conviction that came to her as she spoke and reconciled her to the lesser pains that lay ahead.

Cuzco

THE FEAST was held in the Coya's compound, but Chuqui Huipa made only a brief appearance, coming out with her mother to greet the ambassadors. The marks on her face had been hidden by skillful application of face paint, but the effect of the beating still showed in her eyes, which were hollow and listless. She offered a few words of encouragement in a near whisper, flinched when Inca Pasac inadvertently raised his voice in reply, and then retired to her quarters.

"She is worse than when I left to meet you," Micay said to Cusi, her face grim. "We will be back."

"We will make her better," Cahua promised, and the two of them went off in the direction Chuqui had gone. Sobered by Chuqui's obvious despair, the guests stood in silence for several moments until Rahua Ocllo gave a signal and the musicians started to play and the servants began to bring out the food.

Quilaco and the other ambassadors joined Rahua Ocllo and Tocto Oxica, who were surrounded by a group of priests and household members waiting to be introduced to the visitors. Cusi hesitated until the crowd came between him and this obligation, then slipped away and found Amaru and Parihuana where he had left them. Servants were laying out ground cloths for them, but no food had yet appeared.

"You must stay here and eat with us," Amaru told him. "Fempellec is preparing some special dishes to celebrate your return."

"And your departure?" Cusi inquired. "I was surprised to find you still here, but you have not told me yet how you got Huascar to let you go to Machu Picchu. Or is he punishing you for something?"

Amaru and Parihuana exchanged a glance and laughed, gesturing for Cusi to sit with them. "It was not really his doing," Amaru explained. "The high priestess of Pachamama finally prevailed on him to honor Huayna Capac's pledge. Perhaps she has also sensed that trouble is coming and workmen might soon be scarce."

"You are content to leave, then?" Cusi asked curiously, looking at Parihuana.

"Quite content," she assured him. "You saw what he has done to Chuqui. She was the one who has made this city bearable these past months. What about you and Micay? Will you stay if there is a peace?"

"No. One way or another we are all going back. We hope to take Rimachi with us, too."

"Tomay and the others are with him now," Amaru said. "But I would not count on any Cañari turning away from Huascar now. He just appointed a new high chief in Tumibamba, a man loyal to him, and there are rumors that our father will be replaced as governor next."

"That is all the more reason why Rimachi should go back with us," Cusi decided. "Tumibamba is too close to Quito and too far from Cuzco to risk making an enemy of Atauhuallpa."

"See for yourself," Amaru said with a shrug. "They are coming to join us."

Rimachi was smiling broadly as he led the group over, but Cusi saw immediately that Tomay's enthusiasm was more restrained, and there was a definite wariness on the faces of Tarapaca and Huaman Cachi. Huallpa was walking next to Rimachi but had his eyes fixed sullenly on the ground, and when Rimachi stopped he kept coming and sat down next to Cusi.

"I came to invite you to eat with us," Rimachi said as he and the other men squatted down with them. "You have not met Tusoc, my youngest wife."

"I will join you when Micay and Cahua return," Cusi promised. "Stay with us awhile and share what Fempellec has prepared for us. Tomay and I need to talk with you."

Rimachi nodded graciously to Amaru and Parihuana and seated himself cross-legged on the cloth. He looked down his long nose at Cusi as a servant unobtrusively set bowl and a wooden spoon down in front of each of them.

"Tomay has already mentioned your plan to take everyone back to Quito," he said lightly. "I would have thought you would be tired of that journey by now."

"I am," Cusi said. "As you know, I have had little choice in the matter, and I suspect I will have little choice again once we are through here. But I would like to see the three of us march north together."

"As we did when we were young warriors?" Rimachi suggested, managing to sound both wistful and skeptical. "When we had no wives and children to think about . . ."

"I intend to take Micay and Cahua with me, of course," Cusi told him. "I do not think any of us should be separated in the days ahead."

"Yet you would have me separate my wives and children from their home, and myself from the rank and place I have here."

"Is Tumibamba not your home, as well?" Tomay interjected. "Atauhuallpa will give you a place. He will make you a war chief, like us, and give you lands and herds and retainers to tend them."

Rimachi spread his hands. "I have that here. Besides, I have not told you yet, but Tusoc and Quespi are both pregnant."

Cusi had almost forgotten about Huallpa, who started up next to him with a grunt of disbelief.

"My mother?"

"She is not an old woman, my son," Rimachi said with a tolerant smile.

Huallpa glowered at him. "I am not your son."

"Huallpa," Cusi warned, but Rimachi held up a hand to him and spoke directly to the boy.

"I would like to call you my son," he proposed, "just as I have come to regard Yutu as my daughter. She will tell you I am not a cruel father."

"Yutu is too young to understand who killed our real father: the man you serve."

"I serve the Coya . . ."

"You say that now," Huallpa sneered, "but where were you when she was being beaten?"

Cusi whirled on him then, but the boy was up and moving toward the compound gate before anyone could restrain him. Huaman Cachi rose without a word and went after him. Rimachi simply shook his head.

"He will have a difficult time in the House of Learning if he talks to the teachers like that."

Cusi and Tomay exchanged a glance, blinking in disbelief.

"I do not condone his rudeness," Cusi said, "but he could never go to the House of Learning here."

"Why not?" Rimachi demanded. "He has a family here now. It may take him awhile to get used to me, but he will want to stay with his mother and his sister."

"Have you forgotten what happened at Limatambo? What he saw there? How would he tell *that* to the teachers?"

Rimachi stroked the scar on his cheek, staring at Cusi with a kind of stubborn exasperation. "He would have to keep it to himself. They would know him as my son."

"And how would he know himself," Tomay asked, "with a secret like that to keep? The Incas have killed *two* of his fathers."

"You are not his father," Rimachi said furiously, "and neither are you, Cusi. This decision belongs to his mother and me."

They were all silent for a moment, realizing they had raised their voices and caused heads to turn. The servants who had been waiting set down their bowls of food hastily and withdrew, leaving the cloth covers still over them. Cusi glanced at Tomay and Tarapaca and saw the same resistance on both their faces.

"No," he said to Rimachi. "Yasca sent him to me, and I did not bring him back here to betray his trust. He is one of us now, and he will stay with us if he wishes."

" 'One of us' ?" Rimachi mimicked. "Are you something more than an ambassador and his helpers? Oh, of course . . . you must all be comrades."

Cusi gave him a hard look. "Let us not pretend this is simply an argument about a boy. We are talking about which side we will fight for in the coming war, and we are asking you not to be our enemy. Join us, Rimachi; I ask you as your brother."

"Join you in what? Atauhuallpa is not Ninan Cuyochi; he has no lawful claim to the fringe. So what kind of war could he wage against the rest of the Four Quarters? It would be like the time we went raiding against the Carangui, killing farmers and llamas and then running for our lives. You would end your days being hunted like animals in the mountains."

"You forget," Tomay pointed out, "how many of the veterans of the Carangui War are still with us. They do not have to be summoned from everywhere and taught how to march in a line."

"It is too late now," Rimachi insisted. "Huascar has put his men in everywhere. Quito is alone."

"Those who serve Huascar would be better off alone," Tomay said in disgust. "He has no loyalty to anyone but himself. If he beats the Coya, what might he do to the commander of her guard?"

Rimachi grunted angrily and pushed himself to his feet. "No wonder the boy speaks to me the way he does. Forgive me, Amaru, but I cannot stay to eat with you. My brothers are dreaming, and my continued presence threatens to awaken them."

"Stay, Rimachi," Amaru urged. "You know they are right about Huascar. Those he favors today will die for him tomorrow."

"Those who rebel against him will die even sooner," Rimachi shot back. "It is too late," he repeated, and he turned away into the crowd.

"You were right," Cusi said to Amaru. "But we will ask him again before we leave."

Tomay shook his head sadly. "He is blinded by his possessions and his privileges. You should have heard him talk about what he has here. You would think he had never had anything in Tumibamba."

"Perhaps he can only remember what he lost there," Cusi ventured, thinking of both Micay and Llamtu.

"He will lose this, too," Amaru predicted, and reached to lift the cloth cover off the nearest bowl.

"I do not wish to be the one who takes it from him," Cusi declared.

Tomay nodded in agreement. "We will ask him again before we leave."

ON THE MORNING Cusi was to leave for Calca, Micay seduced him awake. He had been sleeping so deeply that she had him fully erect before his eyes opened, and she put a finger to his lips to keep him from crying out as she spread her body over him and took him inside. His startled expression relaxed into a smile, his teeth gleaming in the half light. He moved his hips under her and she writhed languidly in response, letting him know she was in no hurry. He pulled a blanket up over her back, holding her inside it and rocking slowly beneath her. With one part of her mind she wondered if he should not be abstaining now, conserving his powers for what lay ahead. But the rest of her attention was distracted by the delicious slide and catch of their joined flesh, which made her think there should be something that was the opposite of abstinence yet was equally purifying and holy. Surely the gods savored pleasure as well as sacrifice . . .

Cusi made a shushing sound and she realized she had begun to murmur aloud. She raised herself up on her elbows, allowing cool air to flow between their bodies, and looked down at his face. His eyes were hooded and he smiled crookedly, appearing on the edge of delirium. Micay stifled a laugh and lowered herself back down, kissing him on the lips as sensations began to build and spiral inside her. She felt reckless and wicked, allowing herself such pleasure when there was so much danger to be faced. She should be afraid for him, afraid of losing him, yet somehow desperation could not reach her. He was too powerfully with her not to return, and surely—surely—the gods would not permit her this joy if they meant to snatch him away.

"*Yes,*" she whispered, gasped, as he began to shudder beneath her and they rushed recklessly, together, toward full delirium.

THE NINE of them left Cuzco without an escort, heading north and east on the Eastern Quarter Road. They had no weapons, not even ceremonial ones, and they carried Atauhuallpa's gifts in bundles on their backs. Tomay had removed his earplugs and tucked the empty loops of his earlobes up under his knit cap, and he and the other three comrades had put on the drab garments and blank, dutiful expressions of porters. Cusi had polished his earplugs and was wearing a tunic with a lightning design along with his Iñaca headband and the wristbands of golden feathers that Kirupasa had given him. *To help you remember your dreams,* the sorcerer had said.

They had climbed up out of the city before they were detained at the sentry post at Illacamarca, where the guards subjected them and their bundles to a thorough search, as if they were assassins rather than ambassadors. In addition to inflicting the intended indignity, the search allowed the guards to send a messenger ahead to Huascar, warning him of the ambassadors' approach. Even though it was a two-day journey to Calca, Cusi doubted they would remain unescorted for too much longer.

So once they were out onto the plain and out of the sight of the guards, Cusi dropped back to walk with the porters. Huaman Cachi and Huallpa had already given their gift bundles to Tomay and Tarapaca and were carrying only water gourds and bags of food. Cusi also noticed with approval that Huaman Cachi had given Huallpa one of the wristbands he had received from Kirupasa.

"Are you ready?" he asked them. Both of them nodded. "You have your map, and you know what to say if you are accosted. Travel by night and wait for us near the bridge with three columns. If we are not back in three days, return to Cuzco and tell Tocto Oxica."

They nodded again, and Huaman Cachi gave Cusi a sardonic smile. "I will bear your fond regards to Alco, my lord."

"Do that," Cusi snorted. He looked at Huallpa, whose pale face was flushed, the boyish features fixed in a grimace of determination. "Watch your comrade's back and heed his warnings."

"I will," the boy promised, his voice sticking in his throat.

"We will see you both again," Tomay said, and the five of them exchanged brief handclasps in parting. The two younger men had gone only a short distance out onto the plain when an angry voice called to them to halt. Cusi saw that the ambassadors had stopped ahead and that Inca Pasac and Quilaco were walking back toward them.

"Go," Cusi commanded, and he went to intercept Inca Pasac, who was still gesturing furiously at Huaman Cachi and Huallpa.

"What are you doing?" he demanded. "Call them back! Huascar knows how many we are. Do you want to give him a reason to accuse us of treachery?"

"If we are asked," Cusi said evenly, "we will say they were boys who lost their courage and had to be sent back."

"No! I will not allow this!" Inca Pasac cried, jabbing a finger at Cusi's chest. "Your fear of Huascar is going to put us all in jeopardy. It is time you acted like the brave warrior you are supposed to be."

Cusi felt his presence swell up without being summoned, and he stuck his chest out so that Inca Pasac's finger thudded against his breastbone, producing a startlingly loud sound. The man drew his hand back with a jerk, blinking in surprise.

"Brave warriors do not walk empty-handed into an ambush," Cusi snapped. "You were the one who would not accept the protection of the Coya and the high priestess."

"You were given your chance to speak," Inca Pasac retorted, "and you were the only one who thought we needed women to protect us. You were the only one who was not shamed by the very idea. If you do not have the courage for this, you should go back yourself."

The insult had an almost buoyant effect on Cusi, feeding his urge to fight, but he restrained himself and glanced past the man, seeing Huaman Cachi and Huallpa disappear over the ridge. Then he looked at Quilaco, who was regarding him with a wary frown, much as he had when Cusi had told him about his ayahuasca dream.

"You were the one who asked me to come," Cusi said. "If you doubt my courage, perhaps you should go on without me."

"Without *us,*" Tomay added from behind.

"We can get other porters," Inca Pasac said disdainfully, though he was also waiting for Quilaco's reply. Cusi challenged Quilaco with his eyes, letting him feel his presence until Quilaco finally had to avert his gaze. He glanced at Inca Pasac, then out over the empty pastureland.

"The other two are gone," he said quietly, "and we are few enough in number. Let us go on together."

"Together!" Inca Pasac snorted in disgust. "You will both have to explain this to Atauhuallpa."

Quilaco watched him walk away, then turned back to Cusi. "Explain it to me first. Where have they gone?"

"To Huaman Cachi's village to get weapons," Cusi told him. "They will wait at the bridge with three columns for our return."

"What if they are captured?"

"Then they are the sons of mitmacs new to the area, and they got lost hunting birds. They may not save us from danger, but they will not bring any more upon us."

Quilaco grunted. "Will you?"

"Do not be surprised by anything I do," Cusi said succinctly, and he started them moving up the road. "Just be ready . . ."

THE DAY had been warm but overcast, and now an unseen sunset was tinting the clouds pink. Micay was sitting with Tocto in the flower-filled guest compound, the two of them exchanging stories in a vain attempt to keep their minds off the ambassadors, who were expected to arrive in Calca by nightfall. For the same reason, the two women had spent most of the day walking around Cuzco, showing it to Tocto's mamacona, many of whom had last seen Cuzco as young women and had grown old without ever leaving Coati Island. The tour had proved a welcome distraction, especially for Tocto, who had fortified her memories by visiting all of her favorite places. Micay had at last tired herself out, though her fatigue seemed to have little effect on the obsessive alertness of her mind. Tocto's attention was beginning to stray, too, her eyes darting around at the slightest sound. She was the one who first saw Chuqui come into the enclosure and called out a startled greeting.

Chuqui did not respond, though she came right toward them, trailed at a distance by Cori Cuillor and several of her other women, who appeared distressed. Chuqui herself appeared decidedly disheveled, her face unpainted and her hair sloppily bound, her pin thrust crookedly through the folds of her mantle. She had a coca bag under her arm, and she was chewing as she squatted down in front of them.

"Greetings, my sister," Tocto said calmly. "It is good to see you outside your room."

"Is it?" Chuqui asked in a thick voice, shifting the lump of coca from one cheek to the other. She looked at Micay with eyes that were tired but angry. "Is it good for you, Micay? I went to your room before coming here, and I saw that your traveling bundles were already filled and tied. No doubt you expected to be gone before I even knew you were leaving."

"No, my lady," Micay said softly. "I have tried several times to speak with you alone, but you have not permitted me the chance."

Chuqui grunted. "You did not try today. Quespi came to see me instead, and she did not care that I was not alone. She pleaded with me to make Cusi give her back her son. She said that Cusi planned to take the boy away with him, and that he had tried to get Rimachi to quit his post with me and go with him."

Suddenly Micay's cheeks were warm, and she lowered her eyes. "That is true, my lady. Cusi and Huallpa cannot stay in the city where their uncle and father were murdered even if there is peace. Cusi and Tomay asked Rimachi because he is their initiation brother."

"So you have planned all along to leave, no matter what became of my proposal," Chuqui said accusingly. "You let me think you believed in it, but it was only a way to get Cusi here so you could desert me."

"That is not true!" Micay protested. "I did not know Cusi would be sent here, or that he would insist on taking me away with him. I do not want to leave you, Chuqui, but he is right: We cannot risk being separated if there is going to be a war."

"You have been apart many times before," Chuqui said, tossing her hand in a dismissive gesture, "and he has always returned to you. You told me in Vilcashuaman that you would not abandon me, and once more, when I decided to marry Huascar. Now that he has ruined everything we have tried to do, you leave me to find my own way."

There were tears in Chuqui's eyes, and she leaned sideways and spat her coca out into a flowerpot, then dabbed at her lips and eyes with the edge of her mantle. When Micay had no reply, Tocto spoke up in her place.

"You are being selfish, Chuqui," she said bluntly. "Micay has served you well for many years, and she deserves the right to be with her husband. You have other able women."

"None who have shared so much," Chuqui insisted, slowly turning her gaze to Tocto. "Who are you to advise me? You will be leaving soon yourself. Whatever happens to me will not touch you on Coati Island."

"You could come back with me," Tocto suggested. "Huascar could not touch you on Coati Island, either."

Chuqui's eyes flared and she reached under her mantle and pulled out the tiny silver lime container. "He will never touch me again, no matter where I am. *Never.*" She gave Micay a smile that seemed almost demented in its spitefulness. "At least you have left me a weapon, Micay. For that you have my gratitude."

"What is that?" Tocto demanded, standing up when Chuqui did. Micay also rose, seeing Chuqui through a film of tears.

"A poison," Micay said, letting the tears flow down her cheeks.

"A final medicine," Chuqui corrected, "for when there is no other cure for this life." She dropped the lime container back inside her mantle and straightened up, tucking a loose tendril of hair back under her head cloth. Her smile was gone and her eyes were dry and haughty when she looked at Micay. "Farewell, Micay. It is true: You have shared enough of my suffering. So go with your husband and do not worry about me again."

Micay bowed and held out her hands, still weeping, but Chuqui simply shook her head and turned to walk away. Tocto put a restraining hand on Micay's arm to keep her from following.

"Let her go," Tocto said gently. "She cannot be more forgiving or more generous. We have our consolations; she has none."

"We were White Women together," Micay murmured numbly, hurt as much by the things Chuqui had not said as by those she had. They had shared much more than suffering.

"It will soon be dark," Tocto prompted. "Let us go wash ourselves before we pray for your husband's return. He should not have to rely solely on his own huaca."

"He has his dream, and his comrades are with him," Micay said, allowing Tocto to lead her toward the bathhouse. She glanced at the sky and saw that the clouds were a solid dark gray; the face of Mama Quilla would be hidden tonight.

"She will hear our prayers," Tocto assured her, as if Micay had spoken the thought aloud. "Even in the darkness she will watch over him, and help him find his way back . . ."

THE YUCAY VALLEY was lower and warmer than Cuzco, lush with crops that would soon be ready for harvest. Insects flashed and hovered in the thick, clinging air, which made Cusi feel as if he were walking underwater, against the current. He had slept so deeply the night before that Tomay and Tarapaca had had to shake him awake this morning, and he still had not emerged fully from his dreams. He had awakened with his spirit brother clutched in one hand

and no memory of having removed it from his waistband, though in his dreams he had stood again upon the cliff in Chachapoyas and had felt a piece of the mountain come loose in his hand as he leaped into space. There had been no paralyzing fear this time; the leap had been exhilarating.

He was still carrying the stone in his hand as they moved along the road to Calca, and it felt good to have *something* in his hand, with Huascar's warriors surrounding him on all sides. He squeezed the slender stone between his palm and fingers, trying to rouse himself. He should be watching the road and memorizing details of the landscape in case they had to flee back this way. He should be gathering his power to face Huascar. Yet his gaze kept drifting impulsively, drawn off by a vivid patch of purple wildflowers or a silver glimpse of the Urubamba River rushing past on their left. He felt lazy and sluggish, far from ready to face a threat.

They stopped to rest at midday, and the warriors opened their ranks so Quilaco could lead his party down to the edge of the river. A short distance downstream was a bridge, and Cusi stared at it for several moments before realizing that it was the bridge of three columns, the landmark he himself had chosen as a meeting place. Wake up, he told himself fiercely as he knelt to drink and wash his face in the icy water. Tomay knelt down beside him.

"Are you all right?" Tomay asked out of the side of his mouth.

Cusi shrugged. "I am still not awake. I cannot make myself pay attention."

"We will do that," Tomay assured him. "Just make yourself ready for Huascar."

Cusi nodded, turning away slightly to dry his stone on the edge of his tunic. He tucked it inside one of his feathered wristbands, so that both of his hands were free to resling his gift bundles and climb the bank back to the road. Displaying their usual disrespect, the warriors along the bank were slow to move out of his way, and as Cusi brushed past, he heard one of them mutter a familiar Cañari epithet. It was one of Rimachi's favorite expressions of contempt, which he had translated for Cusi as "meat for vultures." Cusi took one more step and whirled on the man, feinting right, then left, with a swiftness that took both of them by surprise and sent the man stumbling backward, hitting himself in the chin with his shield. Cusi crossed his arms on his chest and laughed.

"Find some meat you can kill," Cusi taunted, lifting his chin in a gesture that dared the man to attack. He seemed about to, then hesitated and allowed his captain to intervene. Cusi turned his back on both of them and walked toward the road, slipping his spirit brother back out from beneath his wristband. The shimmering golden feathers reminded him of his dream, which he had dreamed again the night before. Once again the man with the blowpipe had not been able to kill him; the poison darts had glowed against the darkness of the jungle, and Cusi had dodged every one. He had not seen what happened next, but he had heard Kirupasa's words: *That is the face you must wear when Death comes too close.*

Cusi was not certain how his face looked at the moment. He might have been smiling, rejoicing in the fact that he was awake and moving easily, in full control of his limbs. He wanted to run but repressed the urge, closing his hand in a fist around his stone and swinging it at his side like a hammer. He marched toward Calca, impatient now to meet his enemy and see the end of his dream.

IT WAS well past dark before the ambassadors were led out onto the terrace landing where Huascar and his companions had been drinking. They had been forced to listen to their laughter and boasting while they waited, until even Inca Pasac's resolute optimism had begun to fade. It was possible Huascar was celebrating the peace in advance, but it surely did not sound like it; nor did the gathering appear peaceful as they were led into the midst of it. Most of the men present held a cup in one hand and a weapon in the other, and their faces seemed drunken and menacing in the lurid, dancing light cast by a pair of bonfires. Cusi had been put into the lead with Quilaco close behind him, and before he had even located where Huascar was sitting he felt the presence of Titu Atauchi, reaching out for him like something with claws. He saw the sorcerer out of the corner of his eye—standing behind Huascar in the gap between the fires—but he did not turn his head in that direction.

The ambassadors had removed their sandals but still carried gift bundles on their backs in addition to the gifts they held in their outstretched hands. They laid the latter on the ground in front of them and made the mocha over them, blowing kisses off their fingertips. At Huascar's hoarse command they slowly straightened up and looked at him. He was seated on a stool covered with jaguar skin, his thick, muscular legs splayed wide and his arms akimbo, staring at them aggressively from behind the royal fringe. The stone in Cusi's hand felt hot and wet as he looked past the ruler and met Titu Atauchi's venomous gaze. The bronze vilca pipe in the sorcerer's hands only confirmed what every instinct already told him: He had found his enemy.

Huascar gestured and Inca Pasac addressed him in a tone of earnest entreaty, using all of Huascar's titles and praising his supposed accomplishments. Cusi barely heard him, preoccupied by the emotions that were billowing up inside him and making it hard to hold himself still. He squeezed the stone in his hand and forced his attention away from the hateful face beneath the fur headdress, scanning the terrace with sidelong glances. Huascar's men were at least four deep all around him, the first rank no more than five feet away. When the attack came, he would have to jump forward, toward the fire. The open side of the terrace—the way out—was in the other direction, behind the warriors.

Quilaco was speaking now, pledging the loyalty of Atauhuallpa and all the warriors under his command. Cusi looked back at Titu Atauchi and saw him smirking with deliberate inattention, as if he knew the words were pointless. A surge of hatred brought a metallic taste to Cusi's mouth, and he realized he could never let this man humble him. He would have to kill him and die himself. That was why he had not seen the end of the dream; Kirupasa had been wrong to think he could thwart death yet again. He would die like an Inca, his hands around the throat of his enemy.

Quilaco stopped talking, and Titu Atauchi suddenly jerked his eyes toward Cusi, betraying a trace of alarm. Huascar pushed out his lower lip and waved his hand at the line of ambassadors.

"Where is Atauhuallpa?"

"In Quito, Lord Inca," Inca Pasac replied, "serving as your Regent. He sent us with his gifts and his pledge of loyalty, which we have already conveyed. We beg you to accept us in his place, Lord Inca."

"You are worthless!" Huascar declared, sounding drunk. He gestured for one of the warriors to bring him Inca Pasac's gift, which was a dark blue mantle brocaded with designs of winged creatures with pearls for eyes and feathers made from gold thread and tiny turquoise beads. Huascar crumpled the cloth between his hands and belched. "This is worthless!" he said loudly, and he threw the garment onto the fire to his right, where it settled, then flared up in a cloud of black smoke. The smell of burning wool stung Cusi's nostrils, but he used the momentary commotion to partially unsling the gift bundle on his back, holding it over one shoulder with his free hand. Quilaco noticed the movement and nodded, though he had no chance to do likewise before Huascar spoke again, grunting out a command.

"Kill him. Kill them all . . ."

"No!" Inca Pasac screamed as men stepped forward out of the surrounding crowd with their weapons raised. But Cusi had already moved, taking a short, skipping hop and kicking the gift bundle on the ground into the fire in front of him, sending sparks and embers flying onto the men on the other side. He landed and whirled in the same motion, swinging out blindly with the bundle from his back, which was heavy with jewelry. It struck a Chachapoya holding a spear full in the face and knocked him sideways into another would-be assassin, who went down with him. A third man—the Cañari Cusi had humiliated at the river—swung a looping blow with a war club, but Cusi saw it as clearly as he had the darts in his dream, and he easily ducked under it. He came up at the man's face with the only weapon he had, striking him three times with the point of his spirit brother, the last blow shattering the man's wicker headband and jarring the stone out of Cusi's hand. The Cañari dropped like one of the dead, and Cusi snatched up his war club in both hands and cut the air around him with vicious strokes, driving two more attackers back into the crowd. Quilaco was down on one knee, bloodied but still fighting with his bare hands, and Cusi let out a war whoop and went to his aid, cutting one man's legs out from under him and hitting another in the back as he tried to flee. Feeling clear space around them, he spun back toward Quilaco, urging him to grab a weapon and get to his feet while he could. When Quilaco simply stared at him, Cusi realized the attack had ceased. Huascar spoke over the heads of the warriors crouched protectively in front of him.

"I said to stop," the ruler repeated in annoyance. "Put up your weapon, Cusi Huaman. You two will carry my message back to Atauhuallpa. You will tell him—"

"I will tell him nothing," Cusi interrupted, brandishing the war club in Titu Atauchi's direction. "He plans to kill me no matter what you say, so I say, let him try now!"

"Stop, Cusi!" Quilaco hissed, but the club felt too good in Cusi's hands, and he had too much power to surrender for a mere promise, not while Titu Atauchi was alive. He spun around once to make sure no one had crept forward from behind, and the force of his presence made several men jerk back. He beckoned to the sorcerer with his weapon.

"Come, Titu," he taunted. "I know you would rather wait until my hands are empty and my back is turned, but I will not give you that advantage."

"Are you mad?" Huascar demanded. "I have spared you, so put down—"

Cusi had not really been looking at Huascar, but now he did, and the sight of the man's arrogant, self-satisfied face made him snarl with anger and defiance. "Spare someone who is in your power," he spat. "I do not fear you and I do not obey your orders . . . I am ready to die, if there is anyone able to kill me. Ah! Titu, you come . . ."

The sorcerer had stepped out from behind Huascar, his face contorted with rage, the vilca pipe clenched in his hand like a weapon. Huascar turned on him indignantly, an arm outstretched to bar his progress.

"Let him come!" Cusi shouted, and he hurled his war club into the fire in an effort to distract the ruler. "I need only my hands for him!"

Everyone ducked as bits of burning wood exploded out of the fire, but Huascar held his ground and Titu Atauchi was soon being borne off in the other direction by a cluster of guards. Huascar turned back and pointed a finger at Cusi, who stood with his hands open at his sides.

"Subdue him," Huascar commanded, *"alive."*

The crowd closed in on Cusi with a rush that he tried to repel with a charge of his own, kicking and flailing with his fists and taking several men down with him in a heap. He fought fiercely, but after only a brief struggle he was pinned down and helpless, being kicked and beaten from all sides. As he writhed at the bottom of an angry pile, trying only to protect his eyes and testicles, he rolled over onto something small but hard, and his hand instinctively dug it out from under his stomach. As soon as his fingers closed around it, he knew what it was and for the first time remembered losing it. Save me, my brother, he thought desperately, curling his whole body around the stone in his fist.

"Enough," he heard Huascar say, and the men lifted their weight off of him, though one could not resist a parting kick to the ribs. Cusi lay gasping and spitting blood, feeling bruised everywhere.

"Strip them both—completely," Huascar said, and as rough hands began to yank at Cusi's clothing he went on, "Now you will see why I spared you. You will serve me now, Cusi Huaman, you will be a perfect messenger . . ."

Cusi did not resist, even when his clothing was gone and they pried out his earplugs with stiff fingers. Then they stood him up next to Quilaco, who was similarly naked. Smiling, Huascar came close and lifted Cusi's chin with two fingers, causing his head to loll back on his neck.

"Tell Atauhuallpa he is a coward and a traitor for not coming here in person. Tell him I have fed his brothers to the vultures, and I will do the same to him. Tell him I think his famous warriors are women." Huascar stood back and beckoned to his servants, who came forward carrying bundles of clothing and pots of face paint. "Dress these women appropriately."

The servants had wrapped a long shift around him and were tying a wide belt around his waist before Cusi fully understood what was happening. Then he began to weep with relief, realizing he was seeing the end of his dream. Huascar snorted in derision.

"No wonder you asked for death. But you will wear your shame back to Quito instead."

The servants had pinned a mantle over the shift, using a long thorn as a pin, and they draped a head cloth over the back of his head, holding it in place with a comb thrust down into his gathered hair. Then they reddened his lips and painted black circles around his eyes and red splotches on his cheeks, wielding their brushes with deliberate clumsiness. Finally they put a mirror into his hands and stepped out of the way, and the men around them began to laugh and jeer and shout out lewd suggestions. Huascar encouraged them by walking around Cusi and Quilaco in a slow circle, patting and poking them and calling them Mama Atauhuallpa. Cusi continued to weep because he could not stop himself, though what he was feeling was not shame but a kind of awed gratitude. His fingers were wrapped tight around the miracle of his spirit brother, which he had forsaken in his madness but which had found its way back to him.

"Escort them down to the road," Huascar announced at last, "and point them toward Cuzco." He grinned at Cusi and Quilaco and blew them a kiss off his extended palm. "Go, messengers. Carry my words to Mama Atauhuallpa . . ."

THE CROWD of jeering, taunting warriors finally tired of their sport and let them go, and Cusi and Quilaco shuffled along the road in silence, their ears still ringing, their gait hobbled by fatigue and the confining folds of their shifts. Cusi had caught a glimpse of Tomay and Tarapaca earlier, fleeing ahead like properly frightened porters, so he was not startled when Tarapaca stepped out of the shadows at the side of the road, carrying his sling and several stones in his hands.

"Keep walking," he advised. "Tomay stayed behind to see who is following. Are you hurt?"

"Everywhere," Cusi groaned, finding it painful just to speak.

"Cusi had the worst of it," Quilaco agreed. Suddenly he spat and hurled the mirror he was carrying into the darkness. Then he tore the makeshift head cloth off his head. "Help me out of these clothes."

Tarapaca untied their belts as they stumbled along in the near darkness, and they made loincloths out of their mantles and wrapped the shifts around their shoulders like cloaks. They were both shivering, even though the night was mild beneath a thick cover of clouds.

Tomay finally caught up with them, breathing hard from a long run. He gestured urgently for them to keep walking.

"Titu Atauchi is behind us," he explained, "with another man, a warrior the size of Rimachi. They each have a spear and a club, and the big man has a shield. They are not hurrying, but they are moving faster than you."

"I can walk faster," Cusi said through his teeth, ignoring the pain in his ribs to prove it.

"Can you walk faster all the way to the bridge?" Tomay asked doubtfully. "We are a little more than halfway there."

Rather than squander any more of his strength on words, Cusi simply grunted in assent.

"Quilaco?" Tomay asked. "If the boys are there with some weapons, we can arrange a proper ambush."

"My legs are fine," Quilaco said curtly. "Lead on . . . I am eager to see some of *them* die . . ."

CUSI WAITED with Quilaco in the middle of the road, resting on one knee in unfeigned exhaustion. In the dim light seeping through the clouds, Quilaco's gaudily painted face, with a gash across his forehead and the loops of his earlobes hanging empty, appeared both clownish and pathetic. Cusi knew he looked even worse himself, but he hurt too much to care and he had no anger to sustain him, as Quilaco did. Quilaco stared back down the road and spoke to him out of the side of his mouth.

"You saved my life twice. If I had not seen you slip off your bundle, I would not have been ready to defend myself. And then you came to help me. I am grateful, Cusi."

"That was why you asked me to come," Cusi said simply.

"I should have stood up with you. If I had known why he wanted to spare us . . ."

"I was out of control by then," Cusi told him. "I was ready to fight all of them to get to Titu Atauchi."

"He saved you. If he had not stepped out to fight you, I think Huascar would have had you killed for the way you spoke to him. For the way you *looked* at him."

"The face," Cusi murmured, remembering his defiant snarl with belated satisfaction. He had been mistaken about his enemy, but he had shown the face to the right man, anyway. A sudden uneasiness made him look up too quickly, awakening fresh pains in the back of his neck.

"He is coming," he warned, and he reached for the flint knife he had placed on the ground behind his knee. Quilaco had a club tucked up under his armpit, concealed by the shift around his shoulders. Two figures materialized out of the gloom, one much larger than the other, advancing on them warily. They stopped about twenty feet away, the big warrior turning to scan the darkness around and behind him. Titu Atauchi came closer, a spear in one hand and a short battle-ax in the other.

"Look at you," he sneered. "It is barely worth the trouble to kill you. You were so eager to fight with me. Where is your eagerness now?"

"You served my purpose," Cusi told him. "I do not care which of us kills you now."

"That will be your last boast. You can go if you want, Quilaco. I have no need to kill both of you."

"You will have to," Quilaco insisted, shrugging off the shift and rising with the club in his hands. A stone suddenly ricocheted off the big warrior's shield, driving him into a crouch. Tomay and Tarapaca came out of the reeds on the left side of the road, armed with spears.

"It is only the porters," Titu Atauchi called to his companion. "Dispose of them."

The warrior feinted at Tomay with his shield and then sprang toward Tarapaca. Titu Atauchi turned and raised his spear to throw it, feinting to make Cusi and Quilaco react. Cusi was gathering himself to dive out of the way when there was a clattering sound and the sorcerer stumbled forward, launching the spear well over their heads. Huaman Cachi came running out of the darkness, following the bola he had thrown, and chopped at Titu Atauchi with a club, hitting him on the shoulder and spinning him around. But the man recovered and drove Huaman Cachi back with his club, then seemed to gesture at him with his free hand. Huaman Cachi cried out in pain and fell down, clawing at his eyes. Titu Atauchi raised his club to strike, but Huallpa suddenly thrust himself into the way, jabbing wildly with a spear to hold the sorcerer off.

"Watch your eyes!" Cusi shouted, and Huallpa ducked away when Titu Atauchi flung out his free hand again. Whatever he was throwing missed, and when he came in behind it Huallpa stabbed him in the knee. Howling in pain, the sorcerer lashed out with his club, knocking the spear out of Huallpa's hands with such force that the boy was thrown to the ground. But Huallpa immediately rolled away, and before Titu Atauchi could go after him Quilaco stepped forward to engage him. Cusi had also risen, the knife in one hand and his spirit brother in the other, though he was in no shape to fight or flee. From what he could see, Tomay and Tarapaca were in the final stages of wearing the big man down, making him lurch back and forth between them.

Quilaco's fatigue also showed in the stiffness of his movements, but Titu

Atauchi was limping from the wound Huallpa had given him, and he did not have Quilaco's experience as a warrior. Quilaco attacked him methodically, making him parry blow after blow and never giving him a chance to use the pouch that was attached to the wrist of his free hand. Unable to turn or look back, Titu Atauchi shouted to his companion.

"Finish them and come!"

He was answered by a hoarse scream, the death cry of the big warrior, who fell with a thud. Titu Atauchi faltered and cast a frantic glance over his shoulder, which gave Quilaco an opening to step in and club him on the side of the neck. Titu Atauchi's club squirted out of his hands and he staggered sideways, reeling toward Huallpa, who was crouched behind his spear, the whites of his eyes visible in the darkness. The boy let out a ferocious yell and surged forward, driving the point of his spear completely through Titu Atauchi's body. The sorcerer grunted once as he doubled over, snapping off the spear and pitching forward onto his face. Huallpa stared down at him for a moment, then drew a flint knife out of his waistband and dropped to his knees beside the corpse. Tearing off the sorcerer's fur headdress, he held it up in one hand and hacked at it with the knife, shredding the fur and scattering teeth and amulets. When there was nothing left of it, he began to hack at the body itself, letting out explosive breaths.

Cusi made himself move then, though Tomay and Tarapaca got there ahead of him and lifted Huallpa off the corpse, holding him between them while he shook and sobbed, the bloody knife still in his hand.

"It is over, my son," Cusi said gently. "You have had your revenge."

"It is not enough!" Huallpa hissed. "He should die many times!"

"There will be more to kill," Quilaco assured him in a grim voice. "Now that the war has begun . . ."

Huaman Cachi came up to join them, mopping at his eyes with a cloth he had wet in the ditch.

"Can you see to carry?" Tomay asked him. "We must hide the bodies before we go on."

Huaman nodded compliantly and began to gather up Titu Atauchi's weapons. Tomay and Tarapaca released Huallpa and dragged the body off by the legs. Cusi tucked his knife into his belt and put a hand on Huallpa's shoulder, motioning to Quilaco with his chin.

"Let us go to the river and wash. We have all been too close to death tonight."

"But we are alive," Huallpa murmured dazedly, allowing himself to be led toward the side of the road.

"We are alive," Cusi agreed. "That much is no dream."

Cuzco

WORD OF WHAT had happened at Calca reached Cuzco a whole day before the surviving ambassadors did, and at Huascar's command, it was carried on to Quito by the post runners. Huascar claimed he had been insulted and provoked, but the bulk of his message concerned the indignities he had heaped upon Atauhuallpa's representatives in return, a response so monstrously disproportionate it could only be seen as a declaration of war. There was open rejoicing among the warriors who patrolled the streets in the Sapa Inca's absence, but the resident Incas recoiled in shock and disgust from the crimes that had been committed in their name, and they found nothing inspiring in the prospect of another war.

A crowd of Huascar's loyalists met Cusi and his companions at the outskirts of the city and escorted them through the streets to the palace, alternately cursing them as traitors and jeering at them as symbols of shame. They were spat upon and had mirrors flashed in their faces and flowery scents splashed on their clothes, to the constant chant of "Mama Atauhuallpa, Mama Atauhuallpa." Rimachi and his Royal Guards turned the crowd back at the palace's main gate, though not without some pushing and shoving that was more boisterous than angry.

Then a path was opened, and from her place just inside the gate Micay saw the six of them march forward in unison, first Huallpa and Huaman Cachi, then Cusi and Tomay, then Quilaco and Tarapaca. They were dressed in rough clothing and had knit caps pulled down over their heads in lieu of headbands and earplugs, and they were moving at a measured pace that defied the pressure of the crowd. Micay realized they were moving slowly to accommodate Cusi, who was limping and holding a hand over his ribs on the side where he had been wounded so long ago. His face was so swollen and mottled beneath the unfamiliar knit cap that he seemed to become less recognizable as he drew closer, and there were welts and abrasions visible on his arms and legs. Micay had never seen him looking more thoroughly battered, yet she also noticed that his head was up and he was not carrying himself like a man who had been beaten. In fact, none of them was. Their hands were empty and their drab clothes were stained with spittle and face paint, yet they marched like warriors who had done their duty and knew it, even if the annoying fools around them did not.

As they came in through the gate, Cahua let go of Micay's hand and ran to Cusi, who held her against his side with one arm rather than attempting to pick her up. Coca and Cisa went to Quilaco, who also kept them at arm's length, gesturing to indicate the filthiness of his tunic. But both men were smiling, and when the gate was closed behind them the six of them released their tension in a burst of harsh laughter, turning to spit and make obscene gestures toward the crowd beyond the wall. Micay came up on Cusi's other side, and he removed the hand from his ribs and gingerly draped his arm around her shoulders, leaning against her for support.

"How badly are you hurt?" she whispered, afraid to put her hands on him. "Have they reopened the wound in your side?"

"No, it is just my ribs . . . and every other place they could kick."

"Did Huascar beat you, too?" Cahua asked, arching her neck back to look up at him.

"He had his men subdue me," Cusi said, his voice both muffled and slightly sibilant, a testament to the blows he had taken in the mouth.

Quilaco spoke up for him: "But only after he had surrendered his weapon. He fought off a whole crowd of assassins before that and saved my life."

"You must tell us all of it," Micay said. "But Tocto Oxica and Rahua Ocllo are waiting to greet you. They thought you might wish to wash yourselves first."

The men laughed at that, even as they agreed it was wise. As they started down the street toward the Coya's compound, Micay freed herself from Cusi in order to greet Tomay and the others, thanking them for their part in the escape. She stopped short when she saw Huaman Cachi's raw, bloodshot eyes, but Tomay kept her going with a gentle nudge.

"What happened, Huaman?" she asked. "Were you with them when they were subdued?"

"After," Tomay said discreetly. "We were followed away from Calca. We will tell you about that, too."

Micay glanced at Huaman again, then past him at Huallpa, who was still carrying himself with the erectness of a returning warrior. Her eyes were drawn to the band of golden feathers around his right wrist, and for a moment she mistook the discoloration for a spattering of face paint. But then she saw how deep and ineradicable the stain was, and she knew what had caused it. Huallpa followed her gaze with a mixture of pride and shyness, his pale cheeks darkening.

"So that dream was true, as well," she breathed, and all of them nodded at once.

"He is still learning to be a warrior," Tomay allowed, "but he has run his Huarachicoy race."

"We should march soon, then," Micay decided, and Tomay shrugged, then nodded in agreement.

"We covered our tracks, but we probably should not linger here."

"Our belongings are packed, and Rahua Ocllo has provided llamas for us," Micay told him, and he nodded again.

"Then we will go. Our task here is completed for now."

MICAY AWOKE at first light and was briefly unsettled by the height and softness of the bedding, which she had piled up for Cusi's benefit. He was still fast asleep, and she had to bend close to examine his face in the dim light. The cold compresses she had applied the night before seemed to have brought the swelling down somewhat, but the socket of his right eye had turned pitch black, and the opposite brow was purple and jutted out like a ledge. He had shown her what had happened to his spirit brother in the fight, and she had decided that their conditions were identical: blunted and splintered but still in one piece.

She rose and dressed as quietly as possible, but Cahua woke anyway and was immediately seized by the excitement of departure.

"Is Tocto Oxica here yet?" she whispered, pulling away from the comb Micay was trying to draw through her hair.

"Not yet," Micay told her. "Probably not until we are almost ready to leave."

"She is going back to Lake Titicaca soon," Cahua reported. "She said I could visit her on Coati Island the next time we come back."

"She is kind, and she likes you," Micay agreed. Cahua had been terribly upset the night before, when she had finally realized that not only were they leaving Cuzco, but neither Chuqui nor Tocto was leaving with them. Tocto had taken her aside and had somehow calmed her down and gotten her to accept the necessity of their departure, a task that to Micay had seemed hopeless.

"We will not be the Coya's women anymore, will we?" Cahua said now, barely making a question of it yet watching Micay for signs of hesitation.

"No," Micay said firmly, "and I doubt there will even be a court for us to attend. But we will be needed as healers before long."

"That is what Tocto said," Cahua concluded with apparent satisfaction. Then she frowned and spoke in a low voice. "I did not tell her about the Huaca Woman, though. Can I still be a healer for Mama Quilla if I am pledged to Pachamama?"

Micay smiled, understanding what Tocto had offered her in exchange for her place in the court. "Tocto knows about Macas. If she said you could join the cult of Mama Quilla, you need no one else's permission."

"Can I go and wait for her at the gate?"

"As long as you get something to eat from the cooks first and promise to stay out of the guards' way," Micay allowed. "Send Machacuay to me if he is out there."

Machacuay was waiting outside, and with his help Micay managed to rouse Cusi and lift him up into a sitting position. He groaned and mumbled incoherently for a few moments, then gradually lifted his head and smiled at her, revealing the sorry state of his lips.

"Is it dawn already?"

"I am afraid it is. Let Machacuay take you to the bathhouse; the hot water will loosen you up. I will come to bind your ribs when you are dry."

Cusi nodded in agreement and let them help him up, grimacing but making no sound of complaint. He had told her he had no right to complain about anything, not after he had willingly given himself up for dead and yet had come back alive. So he bore his pain with a kind of serenity, as if it were a necessary form of penance, an offering after the fact.

She watched him limp off with Machacuay, then gathered up her medicine bag and went out into the courtyard, feeling that her future as a healer was already on her. Huaman Cachi was helping Tomay and Tarapaca load the llamas, but she drew him aside and made him sit against the wall while she bathed his eyes with a solution of tara powder and warm water. Huallpa came and squatted down across from her while she patiently dripped the tara water into Huaman Cachi's eyes, admonishing him for blinking.

"That is worse than what he threw at me," Huaman Cachi complained, though he tried to keep his eyelids still.

"It has already begun to heal the scratches," Micay told him. "I think what he threw was finely powdered salt."

"It felt like a thousand tiny knives . . ."

"He had reminded *me* to watch out for that," Huallpa put in. "Then he forgot to watch out himself."

"I got excited," Huaman Cachi admitted. "I wanted to fight him."

Micay finished rinsing his eyes and put a clean, wet cloth over them, instructing Huaman to hold it in place and sit for a while. As she emptied out the gourd bowls she had been using and replaced them in her medicine bag, she was aware that Huallpa was watching her, and she realized he had come to speak to her, not Huaman. When she looked up at him he quickly lowered his gaze, but not before she had seen the mixture of curiosity and confusion in his eyes.

"Will you leave without seeing your mother?" she prompted, and his head came up abruptly.

"I already saw her. Last night."

"Where?" Micay blurted out in surprise. "Was she here?"

"Rimachi brought her, but she would not come all the way inside. I spoke to her in the garden near the palace gate. She understands now why I am leaving, and that no one is stealing me away from her."

Micay felt a pang of disappointment so sharp she could not speak, not even to acknowledge how responsibly he had acted. So close, she thought, yet she would not come to say farewell. Huallpa went on, his voice rising in frustration.

"She talked to me for a long time, but I still do not understand how she can stay here. She *hates* Huascar, and she knows he should be overthrown. But she says that is not enough to make her change her life again. She thinks she can live quietly among the Cañaris and let the Incas fight among themselves. Even though she knows Huascar will make the Cañaris fight for him . . ."

Micay found her own voice, though its hoarseness betrayed her disappointment. "You cannot blame her for wanting some peace in her life, my son. She has had little enough of it."

Huallpa nodded, though with more impatience than agreement. "She said you would understand. She told me how you saved her when she was brought to Tumibamba and given to Yasca . . . how you spoke up to him and made him claim me as his son. She wept when she spoke of you, my lady . . . she said there is no one she respects more. That is why she would not come to see you in person. She knew you would persuade her to do what was right and come with us."

Tears welled up in Micay's eyes, and she could not muster the composure to hold them back. First Chuqui, now Quespi. The war had not even begun, and already it was tearing them apart. She was aware that Huallpa was also weeping and that Huaman Cachi had lowered the cloth from his eyes and was regarding them with muted dismay. She dabbed at her eyes with the edge of her mantle and cleared her throat, forcing her sorrow back into its place.

"Now all our eyes are red," she announced, and Huaman Cachi smiled in relief. She gathered up her medicine bag, and they stood up with her. "Perhaps that is appropriate. The prospect of a war between the Incas should not bring joy to anyone," she said, and she gave Huaman Cachi a pointed glance. "Not even to young warriors so eager to prove themselves that they forget what they know about their enemy."

"Ready but not reckless," Huaman Cachi murmured, ducking his head in embarrassment. Huallpa spread his hands in a plaintive gesture.

"Do you think my mother and Yutu will be safe here until we return?"

"Safer than we will be, most likely," Micay told him frankly, and the thought made her sorrow recede even further. She turned and pointed with her chin at the pack llamas. "I must see to Cusi. Go and finish the loading of our belongings, before the llamas grow tired of waiting and refuse to carry them away for us . . ."

SWIVELING HIS upper body slightly to loosen the bindings around his ribs, Cusi watched as Tomay slid his red Hawk Man shield down into the pocket of the woven pack that hung down on the near side of the llama.

"What about your battle-ax?" Tomay asked.

"Huaman Cachi is going to carry it," Cusi explained, and Tomay bent to secure the flap on the pack, murmuring soothingly to the llama. The beast had its head turned back to watch Cusi, its liquid brown eyes both curious and wary. But then a large figure came through the courtyard gate, disturbing the air with his purposeful stride, and the llama's tufted ears went back and it shied, making a wet, snickering sound.

"Rimachi has come to us," Cusi said, and Tomay straightened up and led the llama out of the way. Rimachi was carrying a spear, and his angular face was set in a hard, dutiful scowl, as if he intended to make swift work of this visit. When he was close enough to see the welts and bruises on Cusi's face, though, he hesitated and drew a deep breath, planting the spear in front of him and leaning on it.

"I am glad you are back," he said gruffly. "I knew you would not die from being mocked."

"It is good to see you, as well, my brother," Cusi told him. "We had agreed we would speak to you again before we left."

"You had better go while you can," Rimachi said. "I came to tell you that a peculiar message has come from Calca. Titu Atauchi and another man have disappeared, and we were told to detain them if they return to Cuzco without the Sapa Inca's permission."

"Why tell us?" Tomay said with a shrug. "As everyone knows, we were chased out of Calca like women."

"Sorcerers have been known to vanish mysteriously," Cusi added, "especially when they have angered the ruler."

Rimachi rested his chin on the hands he had wrapped around the haft of his spear and looked down his nose at them. "So far I am the only one who knows the two of you well enough to suspect you. But it will occur to Huascar before long."

"We will leave as soon as Tocto Oxica comes to see us off," Cusi assured him. Then he quickly went on, "I know you will not come with us now, Rimachi, but perhaps there will be another chance for you to return to Tumibamba before war is openly declared. Perhaps by then Cuzco will no longer seem so attractive to you. If that happens, do not be too proud to come join us."

"Even after war is declared," Tomay added, "we would welcome your defection at any time."

Rimachi laughed harshly. "You are generous, my brothers. You invite my disloyalty and offer me a share in your rebellion."

"We offer you comrades you can trust," Tomay told him, "and a leader who is a warlord."

"A chance to die in good company," Rimachi concluded dryly, and Tomay blew air through his nose and shook his head in frustration.

Cusi spoke up in a flat, impersonal tone. "There is another reason you should come. Our warriors are ready to fight, and they know they will be fighting for their lives. They know there will be no mercy for them if they surrender or retreat. So they will show no mercy toward those who oppose them. The first of those are likely to be the Cañaris."

Rimachi straightened up behind his spear. "Which side would you expect me to take then?"

"You would be known to both sides," Cusi said. "You would be a valuable man if a truce or a treaty became necessary."

"I have seen what happens to ambassadors," Rimachi said curtly. "No, you must go to your war without me. And soon. I want you out of the city before I am told to detain you."

"We will be back," Tomay promised, and Rimachi raised his spear in a parting salute, hesitating in the middle of the gesture as he had when he first had seen Cusi's face. Then he gave the spear a vigorous shake and spoke in a voice that seemed to catch in his throat.

"I will remember you," he said. He turned toward the gate, startling the llamas with the force of his passage and leaving his brothers staring after him in silence.

THEY WERE loaded and ready to march when Tocto Oxica arrived from her morning prayers, accompanied by only a pair of her mamacona. The impatience everyone had been feeling vanished when they saw she had made herself beautiful for this occasion. Her face was painted flawlessly, and her long hair shone blue-black beneath a head cloth that was itself black. Her shift and mantle were blue with a bold diagonal pattern of black chevrons, and her silver jewelry gleamed like mirrors in the sunlight. After they had made the mocha she smiled and gestured for them to rise. In her hands, she was holding what appeared to be a memory cord, and each of the mamacona carried a gift bundle. At a nod from Tocto the women took the bundles to Cusi and Quilaco.

"Those are gifts from your households," Tocto explained, "from Pachacuti and Inca Roca himself. They want brave men to have them, and they fear Huascar will seize their possessions once he has the war as an excuse."

Each bundle contained a pair of golden earplugs and a headband woven in the household's colors. With Micay's help, Cusi inserted the heavy golden discs into his distended earlobes and tied the band around his forehead, centering the silver badge above his eyes.

"Now I feel whole again, my lady," Quilaco said gratefully. Tocto accepted their bows, then displayed the cord in her hands. It was bound into a tight bundle with silver thread and bore a silver badge that was a replica of the Moon shield on Tocto's breast.

"This makes you my representatives and entitles you to the courtesy and service due the high priestess herself. Simply deliver it to the high priestess in Tumibamba and tell her that I approve of her count."

With a nod of consent from Cusi, Quilaco accepted the cord from her, bowing over it as he stepped back. Then Tocto beckoned to Cahua, who had come ahead to announce her and had stayed with Micay and Cusi. The girl stepped forward eagerly, and Tocto slipped one of her silver bracelets off her wrist and held it out to her.

"Cahua, my daughter . . . this is so you will remember you are special to Mama Quilla—and to me."

Cahua remembered to bow in gratitude, but then she had the bracelet on her own wrist, holding it up to admire the brilliant reflections it cast.

"My brother has a spirit brother, but it is not as beautiful as this. Do I have to hide this from other people?"

Tocto smiled and shook her head as she straightened up. She took a second bracelet off her other wrist and stepped past Cahua to offer it to Micay. She let Micay take it but held on to her hands.

"This is because you are special to Mama Quilla, too. And because you shared the waiting with me and told me your stories of Chumpu Ocllo, Macas, and the White Women. I am grateful I had this chance to know you."

"It has been an honor for me, Mamanchic," Micay said, her tone properly respectful but her eyes warm with the intimacy they had established in so short a time. Tocto held her gaze and smiled, squeezing her hands lightly before letting go. Cahua came back to stand beside Micay, holding up her wrist to compare her gift with her mother's.

Flashing silver, Tocto moved on past Cusi and gave her blessing to Coca and Cisa, then to the four warriors at the end of the line. She lingered in front of Huaman Cachi and Huallpa, touching the head of the battle-ax in Huaman's hands to make him raise his eyes to her.

"Be brave, my sons," she told them with a kind of benevolent sternness, "but do not take too much joy in killing. Spare those who can do you no harm, and do not leave everything behind you in ruins."

Appearing thoroughly dazzled, the two young men bowed over their weapons. Then Tocto came back to stand in front of Tomay. She tilted her head toward Cusi without looking at him.

"So, Tomay Guanaco," she said in her throaty voice, "are you still faster than your brother?"

Tomay glanced at Cusi and laughed. "Right now I am, my lady."

"Better-looking, too," she added, turning to face Cusi, who was holding his sides and trying not to laugh. "Your huaca still protects you, Cusi Huaman, though perhaps not as well as it once did."

"Perhaps it has had to save me too often, my lady," Cusi suggested, giving her a crooked smile. "That is why I surround myself with such good comrades."

"Yes . . . you have always been fortunate in that regard," Tocto agreed, smiling at Micay and Cahua and nodding to the others. Then her eyes returned and fastened on him, and her smile and teasing manner dropped away. "You once told me it is the duty of an Inca to attempt the impossible. Do you still believe that?"

"Otoronco Achachi told me that," Cusi said slowly. "He had heard it from Pachacuti himself." He pursed his lips and raised a hand to the golden disc in his right ear. "Now Pachacuti gives me his earplugs because he is afraid his great-grandson will steal them from him."

"Does that mean the duty of an Inca has changed?"

"Perhaps," Cusi allowed. "Before, we always knew to whom an Inca owed his duty. We have lost that certainty, and we may never have it again."

"But do you believe it is *your* duty?" Tocto persisted. Cusi stared back at her for a long moment, then glanced to the left and the right, seeing how intently everyone was listening. He looked back at Tocto and smiled ruefully.

"No, my lady, not anymore. I am pledged to a warlord, and a warlord's only duty is to lead his men in war. That is what I will do, as well, for as long as I must."

"Only that? Do you serve your people in no larger way?"

"I serve the people who return my love and trust," Cusi said flatly. "I do not owe more to anyone, not even you, my lady. Do not ask me to bear the burden of your hopes."

Tocto looked down at her clasped hands and let out a long sigh. "No, I have no right to ask that of you," she decided. "Not again. Forgive me, Cusi. I ask only that you count me among those who return your love and trust."

"I do, my lady, without question," Cusi said, and he crossed his arms over his ribs to bow. Tocto drew herself up and addressed the whole group, raising a hand over them in benediction.

"Accept my blessing, then, and let me lead you out of the palace. Let me see you safely on the Northern Quarter Road before we say our farewells."

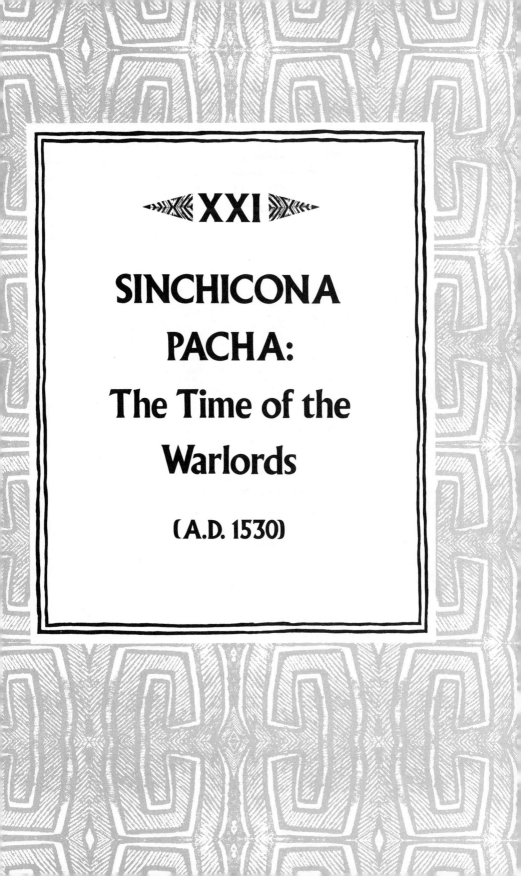

XXI

SINCHICONA PACHA:
The Time of the Warlords

(A.D. 1530)

Tumibamba

TWO PIECES of news had come to Quito before Cusi departed. The first was that Huascar had dispatched a Royal Inspector to conduct an investigation of the affairs of Tumibamba, especially regarding the Sapa Inca's holdings and those of his late father. The inspector was accompanied by a thousand warriors, most of them Incas, and they were said to be marching north at a rapid pace.

The second was that Atauhuallpa had finally called off the campaign he had been waging against the island city of Puna. He had ordered Quizquiz and Challcochima to withdraw their warriors—the bulk of his veteran troops—and march them back to Quito from the coast. Since the campaign had been stalled for months, such a command was long overdue, but it was still being widely interpreted as an anxious response to the threat of a reckoning.

Atauhuallpa, however, remained in Tumibamba, so when Cusi went to report on his recruiting he took two hundred men south with him. They were the youngest and rawest of his recruits, and he and Tarapaca and their handful of veterans used the journey to teach them how to carry their weapons and march like warriors. By the time they reached the checkpoints on the outskirts of the city, they were able to display enough order and discipline to appear imposing, and Cusi noticed the disquieting effect they had on the Cañari guards. Atauhuallpa already had a regiment with him in the city, and given the current situation, the Cañaris would have to see these as reinforcements.

Cusi left them camped in a fallow field near the Royal Road with Tarapaca in command and went on with only Huallpa and Huaman Cachi and two count takers for company. As they crossed the river and entered the streets of the city, Cusi was aware of the wary glances they drew from the Cañaris they passed. No doubt they wondered what message *he* carried. For his part, Cusi wondered why Atauhuallpa had not ordered some of the warriors from the coast to return here if he was determined to stay himself. Tumibamba belonged to the Four Quarters, not the Northern Regency, and though Atauhuallpa had maintained a strong presence in the city, he had done so in spite of the hostility of the Cañari high chief, Urco Colla. An inspector with a thousand warriors could easily bring the unspoken truce to an end, leaving a long and dangerous retreat through Cañari territory to Quito.

Once inside the Mollecancha, Cusi led his companions up several steep flights of stairs, toward the corner of the enclosure where Ninan Cuyochi and Atauhuallpa had once had small compounds. Atauhuallpa was in the process of combining these into one multitiered enclosure, not a major feat of construction but enough reason for Huascar to send out an inspector. Cusi reminded himself to visit his father later, knowing that Apu Poma's days as governor were numbered since he had accommodated Atauhuallpa's desires in an effort to keep the peace between the Incas and the Cañaris.

Inside the entry courtyard of the unfinished enclosure, a crude lean-to provided shade for Quilaco Yupanqui, Ucumari, and Rumiñaui, the trio of war chiefs who along with Quizquiz and Challcochima were Atauhuallpa's closest advisers in the field. Rumiñaui was Atauhuallpa's chief administrative officer, a post that gave him great influence, and Quilaco and Ucumari shared the command of Atauhuallpa's personal regiment. The hierarchy had solidified during the time the ambassadors were in Cuzco, and while Quilaco had been brought back in near the top, Cusi and Tomay had been sent out to recruit what would obviously be a reserve regiment. Since Cusi knew Atauhuallpa did not trust him except as a war chief, he had accepted the task without complaint, content to have men he could train to his own standard.

After an exchange of greetings, Cusi took the master cord from the count takers and presented it to Rumiñaui, who frowned as he began to unravel the cords, tilting his head back to look at Cusi out of his one good eye. The other eye had a grayish cast that had given him the name "Stone Eye."

"It took you long enough," he grumbled, "for just this many."

"Two thousand apiece," Cusi said succinctly, "with only a hundred veterans to start with. We took the time to speak to them in person and draw out the ones who were truly willing to be warriors. We wanted to make sure we did not take men we would have to send home later."

Rumiñaui suddenly grunted and looked up from his examination of the cord. He separated a single black cord from all the others, pulling it taut to display the discreet cluster of knots at the very end.

"What do these represent?" he demanded. "You were not authorized to recruit retainers."

Cusi shrugged. "They volunteered after hearing us speak, and the families they serve agreed to release them. They were all good, strong men who are eager to fight, so we accepted them on our own authority. Do we have so many good men that you would have us send them back?"

Rumiñaui reluctantly shook his head and let the cord fall back among the others. "Where are these recruits now?"

"I have two hundred young ones with me, and Tomay has about three times that number with him in Quito. Those are the ones in immediate need of training. The rest will come to us after the second weeding of the fields."

"We may need them before that," Quilaco said in a low voice.

"They can be summoned," Cusi assured him. "But why? What has Atauhuallpa decided to do about the Royal Inspector?"

Quilaco exchanged a glance with Ucumari before replying. "He has decided to stay and face him like a warlord. Some of us have advised him to withdraw to Quito, but he is stubborn about defending his right to be here. The inspector, you should know, is our friend Atoc."

Cusi stiffened, then bent down and picked up his shield and battle-ax. "He should be intercepted before he gets here, then. Give him time with Urco Colla and this city will be a dangerous place for all of us."

"A warlord does not turn away from danger," Quilaco said in exasperation, obviously mimicking Atauhuallpa's own argument. "You, Cusi, were the one who told him he would not succeed by being careful."

"That is still true, but I was recommending bold action, not carelessness. If Atoc truly has only a thousand men, we should attack him on the road and take him captive. That would freeze the Cañaris in place until our main force returns from the coast. Then they would have no choice but to join with us."

"Atauhuallpa does not fear the Cañaris, either," Rumiñaui broke in, scolding both of them. "Many have already joined him secretly, and the rest are afraid of him. Even Urco Colla respects our power."

"Then we should show him we know how to use it," Cusi said bluntly. "Give me a thousand men and I will go to meet Atoc myself. I will bring him back tied to his own litter."

"You will do nothing of the kind," Rumiñaui told him. "Atauhuallpa will decide when and where we attack. If you cannot control your hatred of this man, you should withdraw to Quito."

"Take your recruits to the Rainbow House, Cusi," Quilaco suggested. "You can train them and spend some time with Micay and the children, too. We will alert you if you are needed."

Cusi had had this in mind himself, so he decided not to argue. "I would ask you to defend my father if he is singled out for punishment. He has earned our protection."

"He has," Quilaco agreed. "I will watch out for him."

"Watch out for your warlord," Cusi advised in parting. "Do not let him embrace danger too closely."

The Rainbow House

THE PATH up above the waterfall was lined on both sides by a variety of herbs and wildflowers, some growing wild and some sown there by Micay herself. She had Cahua and Cisa gathering mint and other easily identifiable leaves along the bank of the stream, and she was trying to teach her eldest niece, Coca, how to recognize some of the rarer medicinal plants. Coca was usually a good pupil, but at the moment she was distracted by the group of young recruits gathered on the landing below. Cusi had led them past a short time ago, huffing and sweating and struggling to keep their shields and weapons up in front of them. Still, Huallpa managed to exchange a glance with Coca as he passed, and it had visibly buoyed him up. For her part, Coca had seemed deaf for several moments afterward, until Micay had spoken sharply to get her attention.

The girl's attention had again wandered down to where Cusi was sitting with his battle-ax in front of his crossed legs and his Hawk Man shield propped up beside him, the young men sprawled out around him in a loose circle. The warlord and his brood, Micay thought. She knew she should scold Coca and remind her of how much she had to learn and how little time there might be before they were called to follow the warriors into the field. But in profile Coca's growing resemblance to Quinti was even more apparent, and Micay could not bring herself to be sharp with her.

"Are they listening to Cusi," she asked instead, coming up beside her, "or are they starting to grow tired of his stories?"

Coca bobbed her head in embarrassed recognition. "Oh, they listen, my lady. Huallpa tells them all again to me."

"Do you find them interesting?"

"Some of them," Coca allowed, "when they are not just about fighting. Huallpa likes the ones about the Hawk Men. That is what he wants to be, more than anything else. Then it will not matter whether he is Inca or Chachapoya."

"He is both, as I am," Micay said succinctly. "Why should that matter to him now? The apprentices are all treated the same."

Coca dropped her eyes for a moment. "He worries about how my father might regard him."

"But your father is not his commander," Micay said before she realized what the girl meant. "Oh . . . you mean as a suitor. But you are too young to even think about such things. You are both years from marriage age."

"We are not so young," Coca said with surprising stubbornness. "I have begun my bleeding. And Huallpa has already drawn the blood of an enemy."

"You will age even more quickly in a war," Micay told her. "But you are still growing, Coca, and you must let yourself become a woman before you think of becoming a wife. You are much too young to be a mother. I say that as a midwife, not a disapproving aunt. Promise me that you will not take that risk."

Coca's lips trembled, but she did not turn her eyes away. "Do not tell me I am too young to love him. We may not get any older."

"I would never tell you such a thing, my daughter," Micay assured her. "If you love him wisely, you will help him come back to you. That is why I ask for your promise. We will have to follow the warriors wherever they go, and you could not do that if you were pregnant. You would be separated from him by more than the war."

Coca seemed flustered by Micay's frankness, and finally she lowered her eyes, murmuring that they had done nothing to worry her.

"Promise me, Coca," Micay persisted, "or I will have to talk to Huallpa and make *him* promise."

"You must not!" Coca pleaded. "He will think I accused him! We have barely touched each other . . ."

Micay put a hand on her arm to calm her. "Then it will be an easy promise, and you will not have to fear touching anymore. You must keep each other safe until this war is over."

Tears welled up in Coca's dark eyes. "Can we?"

"You must believe you can, no matter how far apart you are. I will help you; I have been a warrior's wife for many years."

Coca came into Micay's arms then, weeping on her shoulder. "I have been a warrior's daughter all my life . . ."

"Your apprenticeship," Micay said gently, stroking the hair that hung down her back. "Considering the life you have been given, you have been well trained."

AFTER FIVE DAYS of mock battles that had terrified the retainers and disturbed the peace of the entire valley, Cusi had given his young warriors two days off to rest and prepare a feast for themselves. They had organized their own hunting and wood-gathering parties and had drawn lots to see who would act as cooks and who would spend their time brewing akha from the maize Cusi had provided them. At midafternoon of the second day they came in from their camps, singing war songs and waving the standards they had captured during the battles, bearing haunches of venison and strings of game birds like spoils of victory. They spread their blankets over two terraces and filled the firepits with wood and llama dung, erecting spits on which to roast the meat.

The battles had produced no major injuries but numerous minor ones, so that Micay and her healers were kept busy right up to the moment when a group of healthy warriors came to escort the injured ones to the feast. She and the girls followed them out onto the terrace, where she discovered Cusi had not set aside any space for himself and the family. At first she thought she had to be mistaken, because Cusi had always kept the family slightly apart during the many meals they had shared with small groups of the recruits. But when she asked Sucso, who had been fully involved in all the preparations, the old man spread his hands in a gesture of helpless apology.

"I asked him, my lady, but he just said you would sit wherever you were welcome. He said this was not his feast."

Tarapaca had come up while the retainer was speaking, and he smiled and nodded in agreement. "A war chief cannot be bothered with such things."

"A warlord, you mean," Micay corrected, and he nodded again.

"All of the squadrons would welcome your presence, my lady. But Huallpa and Huaman Cachi would not forgive me if I did not persuade you to sit with us first."

Micay gave Coca a glance that made the girl's cheeks darken, then tilted her head in compliance. "I do not think I would be forgiven, either. Lead the way, then. Cusi will simply have to find his own place . . ."

WHEN CUSI finally returned for her, Micay decided it was best to leave Coca where she was rather than subject her to the stares of all the other young men. Huallpa was at least controlling his own glances in the presence of his comrades, and Cahua and Cisa were more than willing to play chaperone. So Micay joined the tour Cusi had previously been making by himself, going from group to group and tasting whatever they were offered. Cusi seemed to know them all by name, an impressive feat after only a month's acquaintance, though Micay realized she herself was familiar with all their faces. At the beginning of their stay Cusi had arranged for each squadron to spend a night quartered in the compound, allowing them the luxury of a hot bath, a well-cooked meal, and a comfortable place to sleep. Once each squadron had had a turn, a night at the Rainbow House became a reward for exceptional performance, a privilege for which the squadrons competed fiercely. So Micay had met most of them more than once, and the battles had resulted in many of them coming for additional visits to have their injuries treated.

Today they seemed both bold and shy with her, so that they greeted her with admiring smiles but then lowered their eyes and paid her an extra measure of deference, as if fearing that their admiration might be misunderstood. Micay was reminded of the way men responded to Tocto Oxica, recognizing the beauty of the woman for just an instant before the trappings of the priestess made them avert their gaze. She realized Cusi had made her into a similar object of veneration: the warlord's wife and the mother of his cult. Like the Rainbow House itself, she was meant to be enticing but beyond reach, a tantalizing glimpse of the rewards that might be theirs if they were loyal and courageous enough.

Cusi would not permit them to show *him* any deference at all, addressing them without formality and chiding any man who would not look into his face. He bantered with them and teased them about their mistakes, sounding gruff but forgiving, a man they might actually please some day. Micay found herself smiling along with the men, enjoying his good humor, yet also seeing it as a kind of performance. Because there was a certain distance he never surrendered, a part of himself he was holding back until it was needed. She wondered if the men also felt it, if it was another way he tantalized them and led them on.

As if sensing her thoughts, Cusi drew her aside when they had reached the end of the upper terrace, turning to look out over the valley.

"I feel you watching me," he said with a sidelong smile. "Am I acting curiously?"

"Not so anyone else could see," she assured him. "But it would be easier, would it not, if you could simply lead them through the doorway at Tiahuanaco?"

"It would," Cusi agreed with a laugh. "It is not the same to use this compound instead. It sometimes feels like bribery. But we do not have much time." He suddenly looked up and pointed with his chin. "Perhaps no time at all. A messenger . . ."

He left her and went to the top of the stairs to meet the man. The other men were pouring akha for themselves and seemed not to have noticed the messenger's approach. While she waited Sucso brought her a cup for herself and Cusi's lynx-head cup, and she drank without thinking, watching Cusi confer with the messenger. Sucso followed her eyes.

"Is it from Tumibamba, my lady? Has the Royal Inspector arrived?"

"He should have arrived several days ago," Micay told him. "Perhaps he has already begun to render judgment . . ."

Cusi came back and took his cup from her, his face impassive but his eyes roaming out over the valley. When he finally looked at her, he did not seem to see her.

"Collect the girls and be ready to leave. I have news that will end this feast."

Despite the bluntness of the command, Micay knew not to hesitate and started back toward Tarapaca's squadron. Cusi walked out to the edge of the terrace and then along it to the center, a hand raised for quiet. As word of the messenger passed through the crowd, the men on both terraces sat down and fell silent, turning to face the spot where Cusi stood. He spoke to them as bluntly as he had to Micay.

"I have received a message from the war chief Quilaco Yupanqui. He reports that Atauhuallpa has been taken captive by Huascar's inspector with the help of Urco Colla and the Cañaris. The other war chiefs could not rescue him and were forced to withdraw their warriors and retreat to the north. We have been ordered to use the mountain trail and join them in Quito."

Cusi paused to let them consider his message, and they sat staring at him in stunned disbelief. Micay suddenly remembered Rimachi's prediction that they would end their days being hunted like animals through the mountains, and she was seized by a spasm of dread that made everything dance in front of her eyes. Without Atauhuallpa they were leaderless, rebel bands that Huascar could hunt down at his leisure. Then Cusi spoke in a voice that seemed to glower.

"Now we will see if Atauhuallpa has the huaca of a warlord, or if he is meant to be forgotten. Because the time ahead belongs to the warlords, and if Atauhuallpa cannot lead us in war we have no use for him. We will gather the warriors and choose another warlord, as was the custom in the days before there was a Sole Lord."

He walked back and forth along the edge of the terrace, making them follow him with their eyes. They seemed doubly shocked by his ruthless dismissal of Atauhuallpa's importance, but he made no effort to reassure them. He gestured impatiently with the cup in his hand, sloshing akha over the rim.

"You must understand that there is no turning back from this war. Huascar has murdered or humiliated everyone who has spoken of peace to him, and he would murder all of you just as easily. He is an unholy man, a man without vision or huaca, a man whose hands are stained with the blood of those who trusted him. There can be no accommodation with him."

Cusi paused to drink, and they all watched him do it, as if the act had ritual significance. Even at a distance Micay could feel his presence, like a coiled force that gave his every movement an arresting weight. He lowered the cup and looked from side to side.

"You all know my stories. You know how many times I have looked upon death and walked away. That is my huaca, and I have not been spared so often in order to surrender meekly now. The day after tomorrow I will leave for Quito. You have until then to pray to your gods and consider if you wish to accompany me. If you decide to return to your homes or to Tumibamba, I will not try to stop you. If you decide to come with me, I will expect you to stay and fight until we have won. In return you will have my solemn promise that I will never betray or abandon you."

With that Cusi drained the cup and wiped his lips with the back of his hand, a gesture that reminded Micay of Otoronco Achachi. Then he turned on his heel and strode toward the entrance to the courtyard above, leaving them to ponder their choice. Micay waited a moment before leading Cahua and her two nieces in the same direction. They seemed as dazed as the men and came without resistance, though Coca cast a last searching glance at Huallpa as they left. A murmuring started up behind them before they had reached the stairs, but Micay kept them going and did not look back. She knew how she would choose in their place, and she was not startled when a voice behind her called out Cusi's name in a salute that was answered by a chorus of fierce shouts and war whoops. A warlord's feast, she thought, from which the warlord himself is absent. Taking Cahua by the hand, she went to find Cusi, to share the last of their time at the Rainbow House.

LATE THE NEXT day, while Cusi was emptying the last of his storehouses, the sentries at the far end of the valley sent up a smoke signal. Two men were coming; important men. My father, Cusi thought with relief. He, Tarapaca, and the men with them went down to meet the runner who appeared soon afterward. Unable to contain himself, the man shouted his message as he approached.

"Atauhuallpa has escaped! He is coming!"

Cusi and Tarapaca exchanged a wide-eyed glance as the men around them broke out in cheers, though Cusi was not surprised to learn from the messenger that the other man was indeed his father. Apu Poma was the only one in Tumibamba who could have helped once the other Incas had fled.

Cusi sent Sucso to tell Micay and dispatched runners to the various camps. Then he got his shield and battle-ax and went to the greeting place to wait. There were fifty men waiting with him and more streaming in when Atauhuallpa and Apu Poma finally made their way up onto the rock. Apu Poma had a spear, but Atauhuallpa was carrying a bronze prying bar in one hand and a wicker headdress in the other. Dispensing with greetings, Atauhuallpa brandished the bar like a weapon and launched into a speech.

"In the cell where Atoc and Urco Colla put me," he proclaimed, "there was one window with bars that let in air and light but would not allow a man to escape. I fell asleep and had a dream, and in my dream Inti came through the bars as a shaft of blinding light, too bright to look upon. He spoke to me and called me his son. He said I was meant to rule, not perish at the hands of cowards. He told me that my power would come from Ticci Capac, the spirit brother left to me by my father, and that with it I would conquer Huascar and found a new line of Inca rulers. Then, before the light disappeared, he turned me into a serpent, a great amaru, and I slid between the bars and escaped."

Atauhuallpa paused and looked around at the men who ringed him on the flat rock surface of the greeting place. Then he bared his teeth in a triumphant smile and held up the bronze bar, which was scratched and discolored at its curved end.

"When I awoke," he went on, "I was still in the cell. But there on the floor was this serpent maker. No bars could hold me then, and I escaped and made my way to my friend Apu Poma." He turned to acknowledge Apu Poma with a nod, then lowered the bar and displayed the wicker headdress in its place. "He gave me this, so the Cañaris would take me for one of their own and not betray me a second time. That is how I got out of Tumibamba alive." He suddenly threw the headdress down and stamped on it with a sandaled foot, breaking it into pieces. "When I next return there, they will not be so fortunate."

The young warriors hummed fiercely in approbation, and Atauhuallpa nodded, tapping the bar against his open palm. He gave Cusi a challenging glance.

"You know about such things, Cusi Huaman," he suggested. "Was this not a powerful sign?"

"Most powerful, my lord," Cusi agreed.

"Would you say it gave me a claim to the fringe of the ruler?"

"Its meaning seems clear. You have only to take the fringe from Huascar's head."

Atauhuallpa grinned and brandished the bar again. "I will pry him out of Cuzco with this, and when I am done with him I will use his skull for a drinking cup. Now show me where I can rest. Tomorrow we go to war!"

The men raised their weapons and shouted Atauhuallpa's name, and Cusi turned aside to open a path to the compound for him. Apu Poma came up beside Cusi and rested a hand on his shoulder in greeting.

"I have offered your father a place among my advisers," Atauhuallpa said over his shoulder as he strode out ahead. "He has not given me his answer."

Then he was out of earshot and young men were streaming past on both sides, trotting to catch up with him.

"Well?" Cusi asked. "We have never gone to war together."

Apu Poma's smile was slow and rueful, deepening the creases in his cheeks. "Certainly not as rebels," he said. He waited until the last of the recruits were past and the two of them were alone. "I am ready to fight Huascar, but I do not wish to see the Cañaris crushed. It was a Cañari who left the bar in his cell."

"You are the only one who can remind him of that," Cusi pointed out, but Apu Poma grimaced and shook his head.

"He does not listen any better than his father did. I heard four versions of his dream before the one he told you. Each time he remembered a little more. He is grateful to me, but he does not need my advice."

"No," Cusi conceded, as they walked toward the buildings of the Rainbow House. "He is truly the warlord now. He does not have to listen to anyone."

Ambato

SQUINTING DOWN through the dust that rose from the fighting below, Cusi saw Tomay wave the red banner attached to the end of his spear. Cusi counted slowly to twenty, then lifted his shield over his head and signaled to the men stationed on the other side of the pass and then to the men above him and to his right, who were poised behind tree limbs and prying bars that had been driven in under large rocks. The rocks sprang loose in a spray of gravel and began to roll and then careen down the mountainside. Ridges of earth they had undermined earlier gave way beneath the pounding weight of the rocks, and a landslide poured down in a cloud of choking dust to fill the pass below.

Cusi and his men were already retreating before the roaring echoes had died down and the dust had settled. After three months of this kind of warfare, they had learned not to stand gloating over the results of their depredations. The sooner they got away, the more time they would have to rest and plan the next ambush.

They joined up with Tomay's half of the regiment on the Royal Road and continued their march north even as they counted heads. The vanguard of Atoc's army had raced them to the pass, and Tomay had lost a few men in the process of holding them off. That had become more common since Atauhuallpa had pulled his own regiment back to Latacunga and left the holding action to them, but it still had a powerful effect on the young men, who were losing comrades for the first time. Tomay spent some time rallying them before joining Cusi and Tarapaca at the head of the column.

"How long will that delay them?" Tomay wondered aloud, plucking the red cloth from the end of his spear and using it to wipe the sweat-caked dust from his face.

"Perhaps a day," Cusi reckoned. "Cutting the bridge at the river will give us another half day, though there is no cover there for an ambush."

Tarapaca lifted his chin into the breeze. "A grass fire might do just as well if the wind is like this."

"The river would be the place to fight a real battle, if we had the men," Tomay said in exasperation. "How much longer can Quizquiz and Challcochima take to reassemble their men and march them south from Quito? We are almost there."

Startled by this outburst, Cusi realized that Tomay must have lost a captain or a warrior who had impressed him. Usually they kept such complaints between themselves.

"We will send a messenger from the river," Cusi suggested, "and tell Atauhuallpa we are tired of being outnumbered."

Tomay shot him a baleful glance, then seemed to realize he was being chided, not mocked. He nodded and turned his eyes ahead, leaning into the incline as the road began to rise toward a saddle between the hills. On the other side were the Ambato River and the broad, grassy plain where the enemy might be met. So far there had been many skirmishes but only one real battle, a surprise attack by Atauhuallpa that had splintered the Cuzco vanguard but had then been thrown back, with heavy losses on the Quito side. Cusi's regiment had been called in to support the retreat, which was basically what they had been doing ever since, though at a somewhat safer distance.

Before that they had been harassing Atoc from his flanks, distracting him with raids on his supply trains and then ambushing the warriors he sent up into the mountains after them. It was the kind of warfare Cusi and Tomay knew best, and they had used the opportunity to toughen their young recruits and teach them to be clever and stealthy as well as fierce. They had been such an annoyance to Atoc that he had mounted two side expeditions to try to drive them out of the mountains, but it had only cost him more men and more time.

This was the Quitos' own territory, and they were deadly when the sides were even and they could choose the terms of engagement.

Atauhuallpa had yet to find himself in that position, due to the swiftness with which Atoc had gathered his army and marched it north and to the unexpectedly slow return of the troops who had been fighting on the coast. He would have to take a stand soon, though, or they would be fighting at the gates of Quito itself. If they lost there, the war would be over and they would go back into the mountains with no hope of ever returning. Cusi shifted the weight of the bedroll and supplies on his back, feeling the same exasperation Tomay had voiced earlier. Atauhuallpa had led them bravely but not wisely, and no warlord could survive if he squandered his strength.

"Look at that!" Tarapaca said suddenly, and Cusi lifted his eyes to see a man in the road ahead, at the top of the incline, waving a blanket in the direction of the river.

"He is one of ours," Tomay reported, and they all picked up the pace of their march. The man ahead continued to wave his signal blanket, then turned and grinned at them as they came up over the crest of the slope.

"Look at that," Cusi murmured in amazement, for the plain that stretched away on the other side of the river was filled with warriors, who were standing and waving their weapons and banners over their heads in salute. A shout of greeting rolled toward them like a clap of thunder, and the plain sparkled with the reflections of many pairs of earplugs.

"Now we have the numbers!" Tomay cried exultantly. "Now we will make them run from us!"

Cusi shook his battle-ax at the sky, returning the salute, and then they started down the hill at a steady but exuberant pace, going at last to join Atauhuallpa's army.

AFTER BEING personally congratulated by Atauhuallpa, they had been assigned to Challcochima as a reserve regiment, and the war chief had stationed them on a hill to the east of the Ambato plain, out of sight of the enemy. The battle began two days later at dawn as Atoc's army of Cañaris, Paltas, and mitmacs came pouring over the saddle between the hills, led by a thousand Cuzco Incas who wore white helmets and armbands to distinguish themselves from the Quitos. Atauhuallpa had left the pontoon bridge over the river intact and had drawn his warriors back to the middle of the plain, inviting Atoc to come across and fight. The Cuzco forces did so without hesitation, using two other bridges that they brought down in pieces and assembled on the riverbank. A light rain began to fall as the two armies closed the space between them and collided with a great crunching sound that briefly drowned out the screams and war cries of individual men.

Cusi watched it begin from behind some rocks at the top of the hill, Tarapaca beside him. His men covered the side of the hill behind him, able to hear but not see the fighting, so after a while he began to summon them forward for a look, squadron by squadron. These were the groups in which they had fought in the mountains, which had taught them to rely on their comrades and to make their own decisions independent of higher command. But their experience of fighting as part of a larger unit was limited, and many of them had never taken part in the kind of battle being waged below.

For the first few moments Cusi let them watch in silence, the scowls on their faces reflecting their difficulty in making sense of the bloody melee on the plain. Then he began to guide their eyes.

"See the way the yellows have come back to the left, filling in behind the Mocha squadron . . . that is how the squadrons must overlap and fit together, like teeth. If one gets too far ahead or behind, the whole line is threatened. You must think of the squadrons on either side of you as comrades and keep them in sight at all times."

He and Tarapaca took turns repeating the message to the different groups, just as Tomay and his top commander were doing with their men at another vantage point on the hill. They ended each time with Atauhuallpa's final command: "No retreat, no prisoners. Today we conquer or die."

It was midday when the last squadron crept up among the wet rocks for a look at the battle. This was Tarapaca's own group, which included both Huallpa and Huaman Cachi. Their captain, Cusi noticed, was one of the retainers they had recruited, a large, expressionless man named Piqui. He was dressed all in black as if to remind himself of his former status, or perhaps to mock it.

By this time some progress could be discerned in the fighting below. The Quitos had clearly pushed their enemy back toward the river, leaving the field behind them trampled to mud and littered with the bodies of the fallen. The advance was most pronounced on the far side of the plain, where Quizquiz's men had almost succeeded in turning the Cuzco line in on itself.

"The Paltas are at that end," Tarapaca explained. "Look . . . there by the third bridge . . . Atoc is moving in some Cañaris in support. They are his best fighters, and you should take no chances with them."

"You knew that already from the mountains," Cusi acknowledged, "but they are even more dangerous now. They know if they lose here Tumibamba will fall." He looked around at them, then addressed himself to Piqui, indicating the warriors massed directly below their lookout. "You see Challcochima's situation: he is facing mostly Cañaris, and he is closest to the bridges, so more keep coming over. In his place, where would you have us attack?"

Piqui bobbed his head in a deferential nod, thereby avoiding Cusi's challenging gaze. He stared down at the battle for several moments, then spoke to the air in a low monotone.

"The first bridge has no guard on it, and it would not be far if we came around the other side of the hill. The men along the river are mitmacs, not Cañaris. It might cause panic among the others if they thought the bridges were threatened."

Cusi again looked around at the others and saw the respect they had for their comrade. "You have sharp eyes," he commended the man, "and I am told you are a fearless fighter. So why do you speak to me like a servant instead of a captain?"

He had spoken gently, so most of them were slow to register their shock at the criticism. Piqui, though, heard it immediately and met Cusi's eyes for the first time, appearing bewildered.

"Cusi—" Tarapaca intervened, but Cusi held up a hand to him without taking his eyes off Piqui.

"He is a man; he can speak for himself. Come, Piqui, soon we will go down there to fight, and death will be all around us. You must face that with your whole being if you hope to survive. You cannot look away if you meet an Inca on the battlefield."

"I will fight whoever is in front of me," Piqui said tersely.

"You must lead these men, as well, and you cannot do that in silence, not in this kind of battle."

"We hear him," one of the other men put in, and Cusi nodded agreeably.

"The other captains must hear him, too, and so should his commander and the war chiefs. That is what is different about the Hawk Men: Rank does not silence anyone. The blood we shed is all the same."

Piqui squinted at him doubtfully. "But only a few have won the shield."

"Only a few have earned it. Today the rest of you will have your chance. If we win here, we will be different men tomorrow. We will be conquerors, not rebels. Those who survive will know they have a right to paint their shields. You may tell the others as you return to your places."

"I will, then," Piqui decided. "I am still the captain?"

"If these men will follow you."

"Come," Piqui said as he turned away, and the others moved as one man, departing without a backward glance. Tarapaca watched them go and laughed softly.

"Forgive me, Cusi. I was afraid you might humiliate him in front of the men. He does not use his tongue as well as he does a weapon."

"We need every weapon, even our tongues," Cusi told him. "Go tell Tomay about the bridge. I suspect he will have seen it himself. Have him send a messenger to Challcochima if he agrees."

Then Cusi was alone with the noises of the battle and the soft patter of rain on his helmet. He put one hand on his battle-ax and the other over the stone in his waistband, feeling an excitement tinged with dread building in his chest. He began to pray to Illapa and Huanacauri, his guardians in war, and then to the ancient sky god Thunupa, patron of the Hawk Men. In your name, he prayed, we were created out of nothing. Do not let us return to the dust from which we were raised . . .

WITH THE canny patience of a true war chief, Challcochima waited until the middle of the afternoon before he signaled Cusi and Tomay to attack. First he had his own men give ground slightly, drawing the Cañaris out away from the bridge, and then he redoubled the attack in order to hold them there.

The wait had built up so much tension and impatience in Cusi's men that when he and Tomay waved them forward they burst from their places and charged over the hill on a dead run. Cusi and Tomay ran side by side in the center of the pack with Tarapaca and the other commander out on the wings, and between them they kept the group compact without slowing their forward momentum. The Cuzco forces along the river were largely composed of warriors who had been sent back from the front to rest, and their reaction to this unexpected attack was sluggish and disorganized, so that the Hawk Men were already on them before many had even heard the alarm.

The first ranks broke and went down before the charge of the vanguard, but those behind collected themselves and stood to fight, forming a wall of men. Soon Cusi was in the midst of it, lashing out with his battle-ax while struggling to keep his shield up and his legs under him. Together he and Tomay cut a hole in the wall, and the men on both sides of them thrust forward to widen it, turning hip to hip to keep the enemy from pouring back in. Even as he fought for his life, Cusi was aware of how well his men were fighting around him, surging and backing off to protect their flanks, hammering methodically at the wall.

Then the wall broke and fell apart before their eyes, and they saw the men in the rear ranks turn and run toward the bridge.

"Run, cowards!" Tomay shouted derisively, throwing a man backward with his shield. The men still fighting seemed to realize all at once that they were being abandoned, but the realization merely immobilized them and they were cut down before they could turn to flee.

"Stay together!" Cusi yelled as they chased the fleeing warriors toward the bridge. He saw no one who could intercept them in time, but he did not want them to be caught strung out along the riverbank after they had cut the bridge. A shrill whistle from Tarapaca made him glance to his right, where he saw that a group of Cañaris had detached themselves from the front line and were coming in their direction.

"Ahead, too!" Tomay shouted in his ear, pointing across the river, where another column of warriors was moving rapidly toward the bridge. They began to run even faster, hugging their shields and weapons in close to their bodies and calling to the Hawk Men to show their swiftness. They overtook the vanguard and were on the heels of the fleeing mitmacs when they reached the bridge. The mitmacs kept going, fighting each other for room on the swaying balsawood deck, but Tomay stopped on the bank and began deploying his men as they arrived, assigning some to cut the thick cables that held the bridge in place and others to hold off an attack from the other side. At the moment the bridge was hopelessly clogged with fleeing mitmacs, who were trampling each other and falling through the rope guardrails in their effort to get away.

Cusi turned back and ordered his men into a battle line to face the Cañaris, who were charging toward them with the desperate fury of those who saw their escape being cut off. Cusi put the largest men in front and made the others put down their shields and clubs and fill their slings and spear throwers. He did the same, feeling naked with the enemy looming so large and close.

"Throw low!" he bellowed, and, whipping his sling over his head, shouted, "Now!"

The volley of stones and darts hit the onrushing Cañaris like a stiff gust of wind, dropping many in the vanguard and making the rest waver. Cusi was stooping for his shield and battle-ax when he heard a chorus of loud whoops behind him, and he looked over his shoulder to see Tomay leap to shore as the bridge pulled away and drifted sideways with the current, already beginning to break into sections. When he looked back at the Cañaris, he could tell they had seen it, too, because they seemed frozen in place, their commanders shouting and gesturing frantically but no one moving forward.

The space around Cusi suddenly filled with warriors and Tomay appeared beside him, grinning. He took one look at the indecisive posture of the Cañaris and his grin widened.

"Challcochima did not say we had to stop with the bridge."

"Before they recover, then," Cusi agreed, and they raised their weapons and brought them down just as quickly, and the Hawk Men charged forward with a roar. Some of the Cañaris came to meet them, but others hung back, and out of the corner of his eye Cusi saw a squadron at the far western end of the Cañari line break away and run for the second bridge. With them went his fear of being exposed and surrounded in the middle of the plain, and he plunged in among the enemy with an abandon that swept his men forward with him. They overran the first ranks completely and never gave the rest a chance to regroup, so there was no wall of men to be battered down this time, only clusters of stubborn comrades and a wider scattering of wildly determined individuals.

After the initial charge Cusi remembered himself and reassumed his role as war chief, dropping back and moving laterally to direct the squadrons and urge the younger men on. He saw Huaman Cachi slip in the mud and lose his shield deflecting a spear thrust, but even as Cusi went to help him, the young warrior, still on his knees, took a two-handed grip on his war club and cut his opponent's legs out from under him. Huallpa was there to finish the man with his spear before Cusi arrived, and the two of them grinned at him in triumph before turning to rejoin their squadron.

The Cañaris had been fighting their way west, and now the bulk of them broke and ran for the second bridge. As space opened up around them, Cusi and Tomay both saw how far they had come from the river and how close they were to the front lines, and they shouted to their captains to hold and regroup.

"Let them go!" Cusi yelled, halting the men who had begun to pursue the fleeing Cañaris. One man, however, kept going, and Cusi recognized the black tunic with a flash of surprise and anger.

"Piqui! Let them go!" he shouted, but the man ran on, dropping his shield and club and throwing himself headlong onto the back of one of the Cañaris.

By the time Cusi got to him Piqui had one knee planted on the Cañari's spine and was pushing the man's face down into the mud, then pulling him up again by the hair.

"Did you hear me?" Cusi demanded angrily. "I said to let them go. We do not need any prisoners."

Piqui looked up at him wide-eyed, still gasping for breath after his run. "This . . . is . . . high chief," he managed, pointing with his chin at a feathered spear on the ground next to him. "His staff . . ."

As Cusi stooped to pick up the staff Piqui jerked the captive's head sideways, and despite the coat of red mud Cusi recognized the face of Urco Colla. The Cañari's voice came out in a croak.

"Kill me . . ."

"Not before we have displayed you to your followers," Cusi told him without remorse. "Then we will give you to Atauhuallpa to answer for your treachery."

Cusi straightened up and handed the staff to Huaman Cachi. "Bind his hands," he said to some of the other men. "Then wipe him off and find his headdress. We want him to be recognized."

Piqui stood up and let the others take charge of Urco Colla. Huallpa handed him his shield and war club, and he stood looking at the ground for a moment, swinging his head from side to side until he finally brought it up and met Cusi's gaze.

"Only a retainer would recognize insignia in the middle of a battle," Cusi said quietly. "But it was a Hawk Man who wisely disobeyed his commander in order to end the battle. Come, let us show him to the Cañaris and break their spirit. When this is over he will be your gift to Atauhuallpa."

Yipping and whooping, the men tightened their ranks and bore their captive back toward the Cañaris who were still engaged with Challcochima's men, knowing that victory was inevitable and that they would soon be painting their shields.

Riobamba

MICAY CAME south as part of a long caravan composed of women and children, servants, porters and herders, and more than a thousand pack llamas. The porters and llamas were carrying all the supplies and extra weapons Atauhuallpa had stockpiled in Quito against the possibility that he would have to take refuge there. His wives and court functionaries had been left in Quito, as well, and they marched at the head of the column, escorting the litter that carried Atauhuallpa's principal wife, Mama Amancay, a young daughter of Huayna Capac by his second wife. Micay had friends among the members of Amancay's court, which was still evolving, but she had politely refused their invitations to join them. It seemed a hopeless enterprise to try to maintain the elegance of a court while on the march, and she had no desire to dress in fine clothes and paint her face every day, only to be rained on or coated with the mud and dust of the road.

Instead she marched with Ñupchu and their children, along with about forty other wives and daughters of the veterans in Cusi and Tomay's regiment. During their months of waiting in Quito, Micay and a few others with experience had trained the rest as healers, practicing their skills on the wounded who had been brought back from the coast. They had also used the time to amass a large supply of bandages, medicines, and splints, which was being carried by a small pack train of their own.

They received more practice when the caravan stopped for the night in Latacunga, where the most serious of Atauhuallpa's wounded had been brought after the battle of Ambato. It was a brief but sobering experience for the new healers, who were confronted by many men so badly maimed that there was little anyone could do for them except to sit with them while they died.

They went on from Latacunga to Ambato, and their passage through the battlefield made them wish they had turned back earlier. Seen through a cowl of scented gauze, which still could not keep out the stench of rotting flesh, the plain was a landscape from the underworld. The Royal Road had been cleared of debris, but bodies lay everywhere, sometimes in piles, sometimes half buried in the mud. The air was filled with buzzing flies, and clouds of carrion birds rose and settled with rapacious cries, screeching and fighting and tearing at the dead with their hooked beaks. It was said that twenty thousand men had died here, and it seemed to take forever to walk past their remains, so that while no one doubted the number, no one felt the glory of the victory either.

They came within sight of Riobamba in late afternoon, when the city already lay in the shadow of Chimborazo, the great mountain that had once smoked and spat fire but now collected snow on its cone-shaped peak. A short time later, while they were still in the sunshine and still at a considerable distance from the city, they came on the first outposts of Atauhuallpa's encampment. About half of the cultivated plots had recently been harvested, and these and every other open piece of ground had since sprouted a thick crop of warriors. The men came out of their tents and makeshift shelters and lined the road as the caravan passed, staring at the women in silence until Amancay called out a greeting from her litter. Then their faces lit up with smiles and they shouted their welcome with a heartiness that would have shown disrespect for a Coya but was probably appropriate for the wife of a warlord.

From that point onward there was no break in the camp, which spread out on both sides of the road and extended well up into the foothills. Micay remembered the huge army Huayna Capac had led out of Tumibamba so many years ago, and a rough reckoning told her this one was equally as large. Going back where they came from, Micay thought, only this time to lay waste to Tumibamba and perhaps Cuzco, as well. She shook herself as she walked, realizing that the memory of Ambato was still darkening her thoughts.

Huaman Cachi and Huallpa met them at a side road, clearing a path through the crowd so Micay's group could leave the main column. Both young men were carrying red and black Hawk Man shields, and as they led the way down the narrow road they gave the women an ebullient account of their attack on the bridge and their subsequent capture of Urco Colla, which had caused the Cañaris to break and run. Micay was pleased to hear of their success and of the small number of casualties they had incurred, but she was also struck by their apparent indifference to the casualties they had inflicted. She realized they had left the bodies behind them and had not looked back, so that all they could feel was the glory.

The road had become a trail as it wound its way up a hill, passing other camps and plots of unharvested crops. Soon they came on more men bearing the Hawk Man shield and were greeted with bows of recognition rather than hungry stares. Men who had wives and daughters in the group came forward to join them, while the younger men remained at a respectful distance. In many places the tents and shelters were so thick there was barely room to move between them, and they passed one terrace plot where three groups of men were working one behind the other: one cutting and bundling scarlet stalks of quinoa, another turning over the stubble with foot plows, the last erecting tents on the cleared ground.

"How quickly it has turned," Micay marveled. "In Quito these last months, all we heard about were desertions and defections and troops that had been promised but never sent. It was not encouraging."

"We had begun to wonder ourselves," Huaman Cachi admitted. "But once we were all together Atoc was no match for us. He was captured, too, and all of the Incas he brought with him were killed."

Micay could not repress a shudder. "It does not sound right to hear Inca deaths reported with pride rather than sorrow."

"I am sorry, my lady," Huaman said hastily. "I should call them Cuzcos, because the true Incas are with us."

Cusi and Tomay were waiting on the terrace landing in front of the compound they had commandeered, holding out their arms in a greeting that also displayed the soundness of their limbs. Cahua got to Cusi first, and he lifted her off the ground in a hug. Then he did the same with his niece, Cisa, speaking to both her and Coca.

"Your father told me to convey his regards. He is in the city with Atauhuallpa."

"And you are out here with the Hawk Men," Micay said dryly, coming into his embrace after he set Cisa down. "Did you not turn the battle for your side?"

"We did," he allowed, pulling her close, "and we were honored by Atauhuallpa. But we persuaded him and Challcochima that we were most effective as a reserve regiment."

"And as mountain raiders," Tomay added, holding his drowsy daughter in the crook of one arm and Ñupchu in the other. Cusi gestured toward the compound behind him, into which most of the other women and their husbands had already disappeared.

"The courtyards are all filled with drying maize, but we reserved the houses for you. There is even a bathhouse," he added suggestively, and he seemed surprised when Micay did not return his smile.

"I feel a great need for cleansing," she told him, "after seeing Ambato."

Cusi grunted and put an arm around her waist, letting the others precede them into the compound. "I would not have wanted to come after us, either," he admitted. "We gave them no chance to muster a retreat. They ran and we cut them down from behind."

"Did you kill any Incas?" Micay asked, and he flinched slightly before shaking his head.

"No, but too many Cañaris. If Rimachi . . . no, nothing could have stopped it. Just as nothing will save Tumibamba now. Atauhuallpa must make an example of the people who betrayed him."

"Even if they surrender?"

"Huascar has already dispatched another brother, and another twelve thousand men, to see that they do not." He stopped in the gateway and looked at her. "Ambato was just the beginning, Micay. Huascar will send many more against us, and we will have to scatter them in the same way."

"I know," Micay said. She sighed heavily. "I know. I only hope we will not have to march three days behind you ever again."

"I will try to keep you closer," Cusi promised. He put his arm around her again and squeezed her reassuringly. "We did not say so to Challcochima, but that is another reason for staying in the rear. Indeed, that may be the best reason we have . . ."

The Lynx House

WITH FOUR warriors marching ahead and four behind, Micay and Cahua crossed the river and followed the trail that zigzagged up the rocky hillside to the east of the Lynx House. They came out through a stand of stunted willows and forded a narrow stream by means of stepping-stones that were barely visible in the moonlight. From here the path went directly to the shrine, so when the captain glanced back at her inquiringly, Micay held up her hand to signal a halt.

"It is not much farther. Wait for us here."

"Let me send a man ahead first, my lady," the captain suggested. "Just to be certain no one else is about."

"No," Micay said flatly. "We do not need protection here."

"There are Cañaris quartered at the compound . . ."

"Those are the governor's friends."

"Still, my lady, Cusi told me—"

"*No,*" Micay repeated, and she started forward with Cahua beside her. "And do not send anyone after us. It would be a violation of sacred ground."

The captain let them pass, and they walked up the path together with their offering bundles in their hands. Micay was aware of Cahua's sidelong glances, and she knew she had spoken more sharply than was necessary. She had not wanted warriors with her at all, but Cusi had insisted, pointing out that the mountain people still owed their loyalty to Tumibamba and could not be trusted too far, despite the leniency he and Tomay had shown them. His argument had been given added force by the fact that the head mama at the Lynx House had refused to extend the customary welcome, saying simply that she could not open her shrine to rebels.

Rebels. The word echoed in Micay's mind as she and Cahua entered the shrine, which was a natural hollow in a tall shelf of stone that jutted out of the hillside. This had been Chimpu Ocllo's favorite place of prayer, and her mummified body was hidden somewhere in the caves and crevices above and behind it. Bowing and murmuring the requisite greetings, they placed their offerings in one of the niches in the back wall and squatted down in the moonlight to pray.

As she sought to open herself to the spirit of Chimpu Ocllo, Micay found herself distracted by her feelings of illegitimacy, of having been compromised by the actions of the side she had taken. She had never walked across a battlefield before and seen the carnage so close, the damage no healer could mend. And then she had heard how Atoc and Urco Colla had been killed, and how their bodies had been made into drums and their skulls into drinking cups, and though she had not actually seen these awful trophies, they had lodged vividly in her imagination. They made her shrink back in guilt from her part in the victory, from the fact that she was as much a part of Atauhuallpa's army as any warrior, perhaps even more so since her skills could allow many men to return to the fighting.

I still serve you, Mama Quilla, she thought desperately, fingering the silver bracelet around her wrist and searching her heart for conviction. She heard drums beating in the distance, at the Rainbow House, where Cusi and Tomay were preparing the Hawk Men for battle. Tomorrow they would begin their advance on Tumibamba, and she would be with them, healing their wounds and praying for their success. How could she expect Chimpu Ocllo to forgive her then, if the Cañaris and their city were destroyed?

"How has it come to this, my mother?" she moaned aloud. "Inca against Inca . . . Inca against Cañari. And no one who can stand between them as you once did."

Cahua stirred uneasily. "That is not a prayer, Mama," she scolded.

"No . . . but sometimes you must let your heart speak in its own way. Sometimes you must let it cry out for help."

"Why do we need help?" Cahua asked. "We are winning the war."

"We may be losing much more," Micay said softly. "If Chimpu Ocllo were alive, there would still be hope of mercy and reconciliation. She had the power to move the hearts of the warriors and make them relinquish their anger. Now that power has been lost, and it is only anger that moves us."

Cahua gave her a doubtful glance. "Are you still angry at the captain?"

Micay shook her head. "No, my daughter. I am only sad and in need of absolution."

"Do not be sad," Cahua urged, and the concern in her voice brought tears to Micay's eyes. Then Cahua began to sing the song of the apprentice healers, the song that asked Mama Quilla to guide their hands and put wisdom in their hearts, and Micay bowed her head and let her tears fall onto the sacred ground. Behind the hopeful quaver of her daughter's voice she could hear the warriors' drums still beating, and she prayed to Mama Quilla to put mercy as well as courage into the hearts of her sons, and she asked Chimpu Ocllo to forgive her for taking the side she had in a world where the sides could meet only in violence.

Tumibamba

THE WANING moon hung skewered on the peaks to the west, shedding a lurid yellow light, and when Micay looked behind her, the mountains of the east were outlined against a sky graying with dawn. Then some unspoken signal was given, and the warriors around and ahead of her began to move, sweeping forward in a great silent wave. The women went with them down a slope into shadows that still held the cold of the night air. Micay glanced down at Cahua beside her and saw that her eyes were wide and bright and that one arm was clamped over the medicine bag under her arm. Next to Cahua, Apu Poma moved through the brittle bunch grass with measured strides, walking erect with only a war club in his hand, the one man not caught up in the excitement of their stealthy advance.

They went up the side of the next hill, into the growing light, and Micay could see the warriors spread out on both sides of her, some of them carrying ladders to throw across the Cañari defenses when the time came. The forward sentries, who had made sure no Cañari scouts had come into the hills, stood up out of their hiding places and joined the wave of men as it reached them. They went over the crest of the hill, down into a gully, and halfway up the next hill before the men ahead began to slow and then came to a halt, lowering themselves down onto the grass. Cusi came back through their ranks and showed the women to a somewhat level patch of ground near a spring that was almost hidden by the reeds and shrubs that had grown up around it. He gestured for them to sit and lay down their bags and bundles.

"Now we must wait until we are summoned," he whispered to several of the women, who passed the word to the rest. He made sure they were all settled before he drew Micay and his father aside. Cahua had already let go of Micay's hand and was hanging onto the fringe of Cusi's tunic.

"Come, I will show you the battlefield," Cusi offered, and he led the way up the hill, threading a path through the crouching warriors. Micay caught glimpses of eyes and teeth shining up out of painted faces, but it was still too dark to recognize anyone. Tomay and Tarapaca were at the top, crouching in the yellowing bunch grass with their weapons and Hawk Man shields propped up beside them. Tomay grinned at Micay when she squatted down next to him. He pointed with his chin at the plain below.

"You see the wall and ditch they have built," he whispered, and Micay nodded. The defenses looked like a thick black ribbon that snaked out from the river and then curved back to form a lopsided semicircle with the river as its base. Within this enclosure were many smaller dark shapes—men, Micay realized—most of them massed at the northern end.

"They are defending the bridges to the city," Tomay explained. "You see how strong they are in the north and how weak on this flank?"

"But surely they know you are here," Micay said, and Tomay lifted his shoulders in a shrug.

"We are an open secret. They know we are here because we killed all the scouts they sent into the hills. For the same reason, they do not know how many we are. So we will stay out of sight until they are not thinking about us at all. Then we will swoop down and drive them off the wall."

"So that is why Atauhuallpa sent Quilaco with the other men."

"He liked our plan," Tomay agreed, "and we have the numbers this time."

They fell silent, and Micay heard Cusi whispering behind her, obviously giving Apu Poma a similar explanation. He had just concluded when Quilaco came up and squatted down with them. He had arrived the day before with another two thousand men, a testament, he had said, to how thoroughly the Hawk Men had captured Atauhuallpa's imagination.

"It is just as you said," he told Cusi and Tomay. "We could overrun them even now."

"We will wait, anyway," Cusi said, "until they respond to the pressure from the north."

"Are your orders to cut the bridges or cross them?" Apu Poma asked, peering at them intently. Cusi and Tomay deferred to Quilaco, who had just come from the head war chiefs.

"That is for us to decide—if we reach them," Quilaco said. "We will have to protect ourselves if they turn on us."

"Cut them," Apu Poma urged. "Let them flee southward past you, away from the city."

Quilaco shot Cusi a glance. "We will do what we must, Father," he said to Apu Poma. "Atauhuallpa will have his revenge, but I do not think he will destroy the city. He plans to assume the fringe and the title 'Apu Inca,' and he would probably do so in the Mollecancha."

"No doubt this came to him in a dream," Apu Poma said dryly, and Quilaco responded in the same tone.

"He brought his spirit brother into battle with him, on a litter. He still walks himself, but I think before long . . ."

"As long as he stays out of our way," Tomay growled.

"You are his favorites, as I told you," Quilaco said. "He calls you the Mountain Warlords. Besides, Quizquiz and Challcochima are conducting the war, and they would not tolerate interference."

"It is almost light," Cusi interrupted, and Micay suddenly realized she had been seeing their faces clearly for some time. On the plain below, the shapes behind the rampart had taken on a human form, and they were moving. Cusi kissed Cahua on the top of the head and nudged her toward Micay.

"Stay in the hills until we come for you," he advised.

"Can we go to Tumibamba then?" Cahua asked over her shoulder, and Cusi glanced at his father.

"Perhaps. I hope so."

"Cut the bridge," Apu Poma urged again. Then he picked up his club and led the way back down the hill to begin the waiting.

AT DAYBREAK, with a chorus of screams and war cries that echoed down the valley, the warriors commanded by Quizquiz and Challcochima attacked the rampart along its northern front. The Cuzco and Cañari forces, led by the Inca war chief Huanca Auqui, fought back with desperate ferocity, filling the double ditch in front of their wall with the bodies of the dead. By midmorning, though, the wall was in danger of being breached in several places, and some of the reserves stationed near the river were sent forward on the run. A short time later the regiment that was standing in reserve behind the eastern rampart was called up in a similar manner, leaving an open space behind the double rank of warriors guarding the wall itself.

The Hawk Men came down out of the hills first, attacking in a compact mass that forced the wall's defenders to pull in their flanks in order to hold the center. Then Quilaco brought his men down just to the south and stormed over the barricade almost without opposition. They were soon cutting down the Cañaris from behind as the Hawk Men pushed them back off the wall.

From the top of the hill Micay and Apu Poma watched the three war chiefs regroup their men on the other side of the rampart and then charge toward the river. The enemy camp lay in the middle of the plain, and they destroyed it as they ran through, setting fire to the tents and shelters as a signal to everyone that they had broken through the defenses. They were met on the far side of the camp by a sizable force of Cañaris who had come out from the river to intercept them, and these were not so easily overrun. The headlong charge was blunted and absorbed into a flailing confusion of bodies, the sides impossible to distinguish amid the swirling clouds of smoke and dust.

"What is happening?" Micay cried, but Apu Poma did not reply immediately, swiveling to look north and then craning his neck as if to see past the place where Cusi was fighting. When the wind blew some of the smoke away,

Micay could see large movements taking place within the enclosure. The reserves near the river were advancing out into the field, while the men at the northern rampart were pulling back, covering their retreat with a hail of stones and darts.

"A planned retreat," Apu Poma said at last. "The Cañaris are taking over from Huanca Auqui's men. Unless it is a trap . . ."

"Cusi will be caught in the middle!"

"He is already," Apu Poma said grimly, his eyes fixed on the battlefield. "If they counterattack, he is done for. If they do not counterattack, the Cañaris are done for. Unless they are all planning to pull back into the city . . ."

For an agonizing length of time Micay could not see the Hawk Men at all. Men seemed to be running in all directions at once, colliding haphazardly in explosions of dust that concealed their struggles. Apu Poma directed her attention to a group of white-helmeted Incas, their golden earplugs glinting through the veil of dust.

"That must be Huanca Auqui . . . he is south of where the Hawk Men are. There! Where all the red shields are. They have made a circle to defend themselves." He glanced northward again. "The Cañaris seem to be holding the Quitos back. If it is a trap, he should turn soon . . ."

Micay concentrated on the circle of red shields, which stood out like a rock in the midst of a rushing stream, surrounded on all sides by the surge of men. Hold your ground, she prayed, do not let them sweep you away. She imagined Cusi and Tomay standing shoulder to shoulder with their comrades, fighting off every attack. Then Apu Poma let out a loud sigh and settled back on his haunches.

"He is retreating south. He is abandoning the Cañaris."

Micay moved her gaze slightly and saw space opening up around the red circle, the stream of men flowing past them in a concerted manner. Then they were clearly visible in their isolation, a clot of color in the midst of the burned-out camp. As the dust of the retreating warriors settled around them and the Cañaris perceived their abandonment, a second retreat began. Fighting every step of the way, the Cañaris backed toward the river, finally massing in front of the bridges for their last stand. The Quito forces closed in around them with triumphant yells, but the Hawk Men did not move to join in the slaughter. Some of the Cañaris managed to flee across the bridges, but most were cut down on the bank or forced into the river to drown.

Then the Quitos halted to rest, and it was quiet for the first time that day. There was a ripple of movement as a litter was carried forward through the ranks, and the warriors began to cheer and wave their weapons.

"Atauhuallpa," Apu Poma said. Then he glanced at the Hawk Men, who seemed to have collapsed where they had fought. "Come, let us go down to them," he suggested. "If they do not have strength to celebrate the victory, they do not have it to come back for us."

"They held their ground," Micay said, slinging her medicine bag over her shoulder as she rose. "That is all that matters."

WHEN THE furious siege they had been under suddenly lifted, none of the Hawk Men could believe it. They stayed frozen in place, crushed together inside the low stone wall of the maize field where they had taken refuge. They were all wounded and ready to drop from thirst and exhaustion, but no one lowered his weapon as the crowd of warriors surrounding them backed off and began to disperse, the Cañaris going one way and the Cuzco Incas the other. The enemy continued to flow and eddy around them for some time, and they kept bracing for a renewal of the attack. But no further threat was made, and finally they were left alone with the dead, the battle moving westward toward the river without touching them again.

No command was given, but one by one the men inside the field wall dropped their weapons and sank to the ground, too stunned and exhausted to speak. The dead were piled three deep along the wall, and the wounded comrades they had managed to rescue lay moaning in the center of the field. Still standing, Cusi turned to survey the field of reclining men, trying to remember where he had left Tomay. The two of them had fought everywhere along the perimeter, it seemed, rushing in to fill the gaps that kept bursting open as Hawk Men fell. He vividly remembered seeing Tomay fall, but the memory was only one of a welter of ferocious images that spun past behind his eyes, swift and disturbing and utterly without sequence.

He saw Quilaco coming toward him across the field and went to meet him, limping and dragging his battle-ax behind him through the dirt and maize stubble. He no longer had a shield or a helmet, and he noticed dimly that blood was seeping through the cloth he had wrapped around the gash on his forearm. He could not remember being cut, and he still did not feel any pain from it or from the blow to his hip that was making him limp. More striking to him was the expression on the faces of the men who looked up at him as he passed, a kind of numbed disbelief that matched what he was feeling so well that he could only nod in recognition and reach out to touch the hands they held up to him. Now they all knew what it was like to face certain death and come out alive.

Before he reached Quilaco, he saw where Tomay was and altered his path, gesturing to Quilaco to join him there. Tomay was lying unconscious on a blanket, held in place by Tarapaca and another man while one of the regimental healers poked at the bloody wound that covered one side of his head. Not far away, Huallpa was sitting up in the midst of his comrades, his face fixed in a grimace of pain and his skin too pale even for a Chachapoya. One bloody leg was thrust out stiffly in front of him, the feathered end of a dart sticking up out of his thigh. Cusi stood swaying over them, certain his legs would give out if he tried to squat. The healer was young and seemed exhausted as well as daunted by the seriousness of the wounds; his hands shook as he gingerly removed a splinter of wood from Tomay's mangled scalp.

Quilaco came up beside Cusi and rested a hand on his shoulder, and the two of them leaned on each other for a moment. The shredded remains of Quilaco's cotton armor hung across his chest like a fleecy scarlet necklace, and with his other hand he was holding a bandage against his side. He spoke in a croaking whisper, pointing at Tomay with his chin.

"How did it happen?"

Cusi tried vainly to wet his lips, seeing it again in his mind. "It was an Inca, an earplug man. He jumped to the top of the wall and cut down Tomay from the side; Tomay never saw him. Piqui and Tarapaca killed him."

"I killed two of the white helmets myself," Quilaco rasped. He shook his head wearily, his chin almost touching his chest. "Where did they all come from, Cusi? It was like an ambush. And they were all so . . . *wild* to kill us."

"Like Chiriguanos," Cusi murmured, and he shuddered. Then the men behind them let out a hoarse, ragged cheer, and he and Quilaco turned to see Apu Poma coming over the field wall, pushing the bodies out of the way with his war club. He was followed closely by Micay and Ñupchu and then by the other women, who began to spread out across the field, carrying medicine bags and strings of water gourds over their shoulders. For a moment, as his father and Micay approached with the children just behind them, Cusi thought he must be dreaming, that he could not truly be seeing his wife and daughter picking their way across the battlefield.

But then Ñupchu must have realized that Tomay was not standing with them, because she rushed past Apu Poma and past Cusi, too, letting out a piercing cry when she saw Tomay on the ground. The anguish in her voice made Cusi flinch, jarring him out of his numbness, which had let him stand here feeling nothing for his friend. He flinched again when Micay put a cool, clean hand on his arm and peered into his eyes. Her face, so close up, seemed immaculate and severe, harrowed by what she had seen and feared, and her eyes were sharp and searching. I am not back yet, Cusi wanted to say, but she seemed to understand that, nodding and patting him on the arm in a way he found immensely reassuring.

She had just begun to turn away when Coca suddenly let out a cry similar to Ñupchu's and bolted past Micay, ignoring Quilaco's startled attempt to greet her. The girl went right to Huallpa, and Micay sighed and gave Quilaco an apologetic glance as she went after her, unslinging her medicine bag with a practiced motion. Cusi found his father standing in front of him, holding his unbloodied war club with awkward diffidence.

"I must go on," Apu Poma said. "It appears Atauhuallpa has stopped outside the city. Perhaps I can reach him before he decides to destroy it."

Cusi glanced over his shoulder at the river, aware for the first time that the fighting had stopped completely. The shouts he had been hearing were those of warriors celebrating their victory.

"What happened to us?" Quilaco asked. "How did we suddenly become the vanguard?"

"It looked like a planned maneuver," Apu Poma explained. "Huanca Auqui pulled his men back from the wall as the Cañaris came up fresh. I suspect the

Incas were supposed to counterattack or withdraw to the other side of the
river. Instead they fled south."

"Go, then," Quilaco urged, "and speak for mercy in my name, too. We have
killed enough Cañaris."

"You speak for me, as well," Cusi added, and Apu Poma raised his war club
in a parting salute.

"I will have him send more healers to you, and litter bearers," he promised,
and he set off for the river with long strides. Cahua suddenly tugged on Cusi's
tunic.

"Father! Mama said I should tend to you."

Cusi looked down at her and felt again that he was dreaming. Quilaco's
youngest daughter, Cisa, was with her, and she handed a water gourd to each
of them, staring up with timid eyes. Surrendering, Cusi put down his battle-ax
and sat next to it in the dirt, feeling his legs go limp as soon as he took his
weight off them. He gave his injured arm over to Cahua's care and raised the
gourd with his other hand, losing himself completely for several moments in
the soothing delirium of slaking an awful thirst.

"Drink slower," Cahua cautioned, as she unwrapped the blood-soaked bandage. Cusi winced as the air awakened the wound and made it burn and throb.
He looked away from his daughter's bowed head and saw that Micay had
spread open her medicine bag in the space between Tomay and Huallpa. She
was kneeling next to Huallpa, holding a poultice and some bandages in her
hands. She looked around at Huaman Cachi and Piqui and the others who
were holding Huallpa up; Coca was holding one of his hands to her lips,
weeping silently with her gaze fixed on his pinched and anguished face.

"Could the dart be barbed?" Micay asked the warriors. They glanced at one
another and shook their heads. "Then it must come out . . . preferably with
one pull. Who has the strength?"

The young healer was one of several who averted his eyes, and Huaman
Cachi ruefully displayed the broken fingers on his left hand. Who has the
courage? Cusi thought, feeling weak and slightly nauseous himself at the
prospect. He was aware of a movement above him as Quilaco took a step
forward, but Piqui spoke up first.

"I will do it, my lady," he said, coming out from behind Huallpa and
kneeling across from Micay. Bracing his elbows against his hips, he reached
out and carefully wrapped his large hands around the slender shaft. Huallpa
groaned and tried to pull back, his eyelids fluttering, and the men holding him
tightened their grip. Quilaco came all the way forward this time and squatted
down, straddling the wounded leg and pinning it to the earth.

"Be as brave as you were on the road from Calca, my son," he said quietly,
and though Huallpa only groaned again, Coca looked at her father with wide,
wet eyes. Piqui had not altered his position, his face utterly impassive as he
waited for Huallpa to be still. Then he let out a harsh grunt and jerked his
hands upward, and Huallpa seemed to come up with him, screaming once
before going limp in the hands of his comrades.

"The point is still attached," Piqui reported as Micay moved swiftly to stanch the bleeding and pack the wound with the poultice. When she had done that, she handed the bandages to the young healer and told him to bind the wound securely but not tightly. Then she immediately turned toward Tomay, only to turn back for another glance at Piqui, who was looking up from the bloodstained dart in his hands.

"You are a brave man, Captain," she told him, recognizing his rank from the markings on his helmet. "Huallpa is fortunate to have you for a comrade."

Then she did turn to Tomay, and Cusi had to pay attention to what Cahua was doing, because the pain in his arm was suddenly a searing flame that licked at all his nerves and made sweat pop out on his forehead. He looked down and saw her dabbing a yellowish paste onto the raw, jagged wound with her fingers, poking down into the cut where it was deep. Cusi's gorge rose and he had to tear his eyes away.

"Hold still," Cahua scolded without looking up. "This is arrow medicine. It will stop the hurting once I cover it up."

"How do you know?" Cusi asked through his teeth, trembling from the effort of holding himself still. Cahua looked up at him in surprise.

"Because Mama told me so," she said simply, rolling her eyes in exasperation as she returned to her task. Cusi looked over at Micay as she straightened up and sat back on her haunches, holding a bloody cloth and a pair of bronze tweezers in her hands. Ñupchu was cradling Tomay's head in her lap, her broad cheeks tear-streaked but her eyes dry and anxious. Micay gave her an encouraging nod.

"I can find no breaks in the skull," she reported, "just splinters from his helmet. And only the lobe of his ear was damaged when the earplug was torn out." She glanced at Tarapaca. "Has he come to at all?"

"Twice," Tarapaca said. "Once he asked for water, and once he told me to stop shouting in his ear."

"Could he drink?"

"While he was awake he could," Tarapaca allowed, and Micay gave Ñupchu another nod.

"Come, let us clean and dress the wound and sew his scalp back in place. Keep talking to him . . . let him know we are here and waiting for his return."

The two women went back to work, and Cusi let himself relax, discovering that the pain in his arm had subsided to a dull, aching throb. Cahua finished tying the bandage in place and looked up at him expectantly.

"You are a fine healer, my daughter," Cusi told her, finding he was able to smile. "You have brought me back."

Cahua squinted at him. "Where were you?"

"In a kind of dream . . . a terrible, frightening dream."

Just then a shadow passed over them, and they both looked up and saw vultures and condors circling overhead. Cusi realized they could not stay here, and so even though he was feeling every blow he had taken, he pushed himself to his feet. He picked up his battle-ax with one hand and offered the other to Cahua.

"Come, little healer, let us go see who is still alive and make them fit to travel."

Cahua gathered up her medicine bag before taking his hand. "Are we going to Tumibamba?"

"If it is still there," Cusi said. Then he went to count his losses.

APU POMA returned before dark, leading a large group of healers and warriors who had volunteered as litter bearers. The latter had been sent to salute the Hawk Men as well as transport them, and their congratulatory greetings had an invigorating effect on those who had thought themselves too weak to stand and walk. Leaving Micay and the women to supervise the loading of the wounded, Cusi and Quilaco went to speak to Apu Poma, who was standing outside the field wall, staring at the mountains to the east. He no longer had his war club, and Cusi and Quilaco approached him cautiously, sensing his dejection even at a distance.

Earlier they had heard a brief outburst of screaming and shouting, as if the battle had resumed or was being reenacted. Then there was a general but orderly movement among the warriors massed on the other side of the river, who began to chant war songs as they marched into the city. A short time later individual columns of smoke began to rise from different parts of the city, darkening the sky but then dying out before they could join and spread.

They halted next to Apu Poma, who was not so much staring at the mountains as looking away from the city. He spoke in a voice that was brittle with despair.

"I bring you the greetings of the Apu Inca, Atauhuallpa, and the high war chief, Challcochima. They are aware of your part in the victory, and they are waiting to honor you in the Mollecancha."

Cusi exchanged a glance with Quilaco. "What happened, Father?" he asked gently. "Has the city been spared?"

"Most of it. Only the houses of the chiefs were ordered destroyed."

"What about the Cañaris?" Cusi prompted.

"The ones left in the city were spared," Apu Poma said. He turned to look at them for the first time. "The ones who came out to plead for mercy . . ." He had to stop and draw air before he could go on, and his gaze went past them again. "They were the last remnants of the noble families of Tumibamba, priests and mamacona and the leaders of the clans and their wives and children. Choque Chinchay and his wife were there, along with many others I have known for years. They came bearing branches of green leaves, and they humbled themselves in front of Atauhuallpa, making the mocha and begging to be spared.

"And Atauhuallpa . . . he sat on a stool covered with jaguar skin, with his spirit brother on a cloth beside him. He heard their pleas in silence, like a proper ruler, and he allowed me to plead for them, as well, in your names and my own. Then he sat with his head cocked toward his spirit brother, as if listening to *its* pleas. Finally he stood up and told the mamacona to rise and gather the children in the crowd and lead them back into the city. As this was being done, he proclaimed that no one in the city was to be harmed and that only the homes of the chiefs were to be destroyed."

Apu Poma paused for breath, his face haggard and shiny with sweat. "Then he turned and smiled at me and said: '*There* is your mercy. Now I must have my revenge, so that all will know the penalty for betraying the trust of the Apu Inca.' Then he turned away and nodded to Quizquiz, whose men were in place all around the Cañaris. They killed all of them, quickly and almost quietly, because no one fought back. No one even rose from the ground . . ."

He trailed off, and the two younger men were silent with him. Tarapaca came up to join them, waiting for a nod from Cusi before he spoke.

"We are ready to move, my lords," he reported, and Apu Poma's head came up.

"Do not take the main road," he said bluntly. "The bodies were left to be seen. Take the second bridge."

Cusi nodded again to Tarapaca and told him to lead the column out. Then he put a hand on his father's shoulder.

"You are not coming with us," he said, unable to make a question of it. Apu Poma simply nodded.

"I am going back to the Rainbow House. I am through trying to understand why we do these things to ourselves. The Four Quarters are yours, my sons; save what you can of them. I will wait and pray for your safe return."

He started to turn away, but Cusi restrained him and they embraced awkwardly, Cusi bumping his forehead against his father's chin but still giving him a strong hug. Quilaco stepped in to grip Apu Poma's hand and murmur a farewell, and then Apu Poma walked away across the battlefield, toward the hills from which they had come. He had the stooping gait of a tired old man, and Cusi wondered if they would live to see each other again.

"Farewell, my father," he said softly, and he limped off with Quilaco in the other direction, joining the column that was slowly making its way toward Tumibamba.

Huancabamba

THE RAINY season was well advanced before Atauhuallpa's warriors, forty thousand strong, marched southward out of Tumibamba. They had been delayed twice: first by another unsuccessful attempt to secure their coastal flank against the depredations of the Puna islanders; then by a Cuzco counterattack that had taken the Quitos by surprise and had very nearly overwhelmed them. Had the Cuzco war chief Huanca Auqui pressed the attack when the advantage was his, he might have inflicted a major defeat upon the Quitos, perhaps even driving them out of Tumibamba. But he had hesitated and then abandoned the fight and retreated down the Royal Road, withdrawing all the way to the Inca administrative center at Cusipampa.

Two days after the warriors' departure, a second group left Tumibamba, led by an honor guard of earplug men and followed by a huge herd of pack llamas. Atauhuallpa was now being carried alongside Mama Amancay in a litter studded with shells and mother-of-pearl that had belonged to his father, and the size of their entourage had grown considerably, now that it was the court of the Apu Inca. Micay and her healers again traveled on the fringes of this group, accompanied by a handful of warriors who were still recovering from their wounds. The rest of the Hawk Men had been sent out ahead of the main force as raiders and advance scouts, so there had been no possibility of the women and children staying with them.

Their group was four days behind the warriors when the first battle took place on the plain outside Cusipampa. The post runners, who had not left their posts even as one army retreated past them and another swept in, brought news of the victory to Atauhuallpa. The Cuzco forces had not been greatly outnumbered, but they had again fought tentatively after a fierce initial rush, and they had retreated before the day was out. Quizquiz had gone in pursuit and had cut down one whole regiment, but the rest had escaped in a heavy rainstorm.

By the time the court reached Cusipampa, the dead had been cleared from the plain, probably by the same people who were still picking through the debris of battle for whatever might be salvageable. A great crowd was waiting in the square to greet Atauhuallpa, who got down from his litter and climbed to the top of the dais to address them, assuming the place where only the Sapa Inca had stood before. Atauhuallpa stood there alone, without a single priest or noble to attend him, and he told the assembled people that they were under his protection now and that they owed their loyalty and their labor to him. He was the Apu Inca, the true son of Inti, and his father had told him he would found a new line of Inca rulers even greater than those who had gone before. Let them look upon him now and believe—and obey.

There were wounded from the battle who needed treatment, so Micay did not take much part in the great feast Atauhuallpa gave to celebrate the victory. She had been amazed to learn that the storehouses that lined the hills above Cusipampa had not been looted or torched by the fleeing Cuzcos, as if Huascar had not given his brother permission to destroy his property even to keep it out of the enemy's hands. His more distant brother, Atauhuallpa, had no such scruples, and he gifted his new subjects lavishly, rewarding them for the loyalty they had already pledged out of fear. The gifting was conducted with an exuberant disregard for protocol and proportion, so that one bemused chief went away with only a bag of potatoes while commoners were carrying off feather capes, silver spatulas, and other items for which they had no use. Micay watched from the side and remembered when she had done this with Quinti and Mama Cori, when every gift was a matter of careful discrimination and the greatest gift was the attention the Incas gave their guests. This display, despite the lofty title Atauhuallpa had given himself, was simply that of a warlord distributing the spoils of war.

They marched on to Huancabamba, seeing signs of the warriors' passage but none of battle. Huanca Auqui had reportedly withdrawn his forces to Caxamarca, where reinforcements from Cuzco were waiting for him. The Quitos were said to be closing in on him cautiously, securing the countryside as they advanced. Atauhuallpa stopped in Huancabamba to gather the local Huancas and impress them with his power and generosity, emptying more of Huascar's storehouses in the process. On the second day of the festivities, however, he received an urgent message—carried by a priest—that made him leave his guests and confer with his commanders. Then he withdrew altogether and was not seen in public for several days. It was said that he was alone with his spirit brother for most of that time and that he had seen Mama Amancay once but would not let her stay to sleep with him.

He was finally lured out of seclusion by the arrival of a column of two thousand Chachapoyas warriors, defectors who had been brought over by the former governor of the province, Acapana Inca. They had been led back through the Quito lines by Huaman Cachi, who was invited up onto the dais along with Acapana. Atauhuallpa gave a speech quite unlike those he had given before, veering between an excited sense of vindication and a glowering repudiation of false prophecies, and lapsing frequently into incoherence. He referred to Acapana throughout as "the Inca governor," and at one point he took Huaman Cachi's Hawk Man shield and held it in front of his own chest, beating on it with a clenched fist and proclaiming that he had been given signs of his own.

The speech was followed by a feast and dance at which the defectors were honored guests and Acapana and Huaman Cachi were seated on either side of Atauhuallpa. Huaman Cachi was the first to get away and come looking for Micay, carrying his shield and war club along with the drinking cup Atauhuallpa had given him. Huallpa went to intercept him, and Huaman Cachi made a show of assessing his fitness, frowning skeptically and poking him with the end of his club. Then he grinned and nodded and offered his shield and weapon to Huallpa, who accepted them with a proud smile. As she was watching this, Micay heard a cry behind her and turned to see Coca cover her face with her hands and run off through the crowd. Cahua and Cisa stared after her in bewilderment.

"She has just realized Huallpa will be leaving her soon," Micay explained, and she sent the two of them off under Machacuay's protection to find and comfort her. When she turned back, Huaman Cachi had given his drinking cup to Ñupchu and was holding Suchi, his niece by privilege. He jiggled the girl up and down while answering Ñupchu's question about Tomay.

"He still does not talk much, and he does not like anyone to stand on the side where he cannot wear an earplug. But his hearing is fine, and he can march all day now without tiring. Cusi is fine, too, my lady," he added for Micay's benefit.

"How did Acapana find his way to you?" she asked.

"We found him. He was about to march into an ambush when Tarapaca recognized him. Anyone else would have attacked without hesitation, because the rest of the Chachapoyas have been forced to join the Cuzcos."

Micay squinted at him curiously. "So why should this defection mean so much to Atauhuallpa?"

Huaman gave Suchi a last hug and handed her back to Ñupchu, trading for his cup. "I cannot tell you, my lady. We certainly did not expect to be received like heroes. Or like some kind of sign from the gods. I did not understand half of what he said in his speech."

"I do not think anyone did," Micay said. "Has anything happened on the battlefield that would upset him?"

"Nothing that I know about. We are closing in on Caxamarca, and they are not making much of an effort to stop us."

"The messenger was a priest," Ñupchu reminded her, and Micay could only nod in resignation. They would know when Atauhuallpa wished to tell them, and not before. Huallpa finally broke the silence with a question of his own.

"Where has Coca gone, my lady?"

Micay pointed with her chin at the shield in his hand. "She saw you take that, and she understood what it meant. You obviously have not prepared her as well as you prepared yourself."

"But she could see I was better," Huallpa protested. "She has been watching me train with the other warriors."

"So you assumed she was looking ahead in the same way you were," Micay said, gazing at him until he dropped his eyes.

"I will find her," he murmured, and he returned the shield and war club to Huaman Cachi before going off into the crowd. Huaman Cachi tucked his cup under his arm and gave the women a rueful glance.

"I did not think. I wanted to make him feel like a Hawk Man again."

"You are not responsible for Coca's feelings," Micay assured him. "Huallpa must learn that he is. But come, you can help me find my old friend Acapana. Perhaps we can rescue him from Atauhuallpa's embrace."

"I think he would be grateful," Huaman decided as he turned to lead the way. "He does not know why he is a hero either . . ."

"HE WAS IN the middle of telling me—again—that he would make me governor of Caxamarca, when he suddenly fell silent and looked up, as if someone had called his name aloud." Acapana mimicked the action, appearing fiercely reflective. "No one had, of course, but everyone with him fell silent. Then he simply got up and left, and no one went with him. He seems to have no advisers."

"Only Ticci Capac," Micay said. "So you do not know what sort of message he received?"

"It was a prophecy, I believe, but he did not want me to know what it said. Only that it was false and he would defeat it."

"Without anyone's help," Micay sighed. She looked up as Huallpa and Coca came out of the crowd around the dancers and presented themselves to her. They appeared reconciled but still tentative with each other, so that Huallpa was a moment behind her in his bow. Micay introduced them both to Acapana, who smiled at Coca.

"You have your mother's beauty, my daughter. It is a pleasure to meet you. Huallpa and I have met once before," he said to the boy, "when he and his comrades had been turned away from Caxamarca."

"We will not be turned away this time," Huallpa vowed.

"Let us hope not," Acapana agreed, gazing at him steadily. "But you should know before you go into the field that among those defending Caxamarca will be several thousand Chachapoyas. Many of them are no older than you, and most were conscripted against their will."

"Why did they not defect with you?"

"Huascar's recruiters came in force without warning. I was lucky to get away with as many as I did. My men are brave and ready to fight against Huascar. But not against their own people, their uncles and cousins and nephews. Cusi understood that and sent us back here instead."

"I have been back here long enough," Huallpa protested, his cheeks mottled with spots of high color. "Besides, I am a Hawk Man before I am a Chachapoya or anything else. I will fight anyone who stands against us."

"A shield does not change your blood or the color of your skin. Think of how it would feel to meet another Chachapoya in battle."

"I am an Inca, too," Huallpa said harshly, "but I have killed Incas. Huascar did not hesitate to kill my father."

Acapana blinked and drew back slightly in shock, resting a hand on the staff propped up beside him. His voice was a disappointed murmur. "Are we no better than Huascar, then?"

Huallpa glanced sideways at Coca, who looked back at him with a cool expectancy that seemed beyond her years.

"Are you?" she asked, softly but distinctly. Huallpa turned to face her, his cheeks glowing and his chest rising and falling with his breathing. The stubborn set of his features slowly relaxed into a kind of thoughtfulness, and he drew himself up straight.

"Yes. At least I know when to yield to those who are giving me good advice." He turned back to Micay and Acapana and bowed.

"Forgive me, my lord. You are right, and I will try to stay out of any battle with the Chachapoyas. I will ask to be a messenger instead."

Acapana made a humming sound deep in his throat, nodding in approval. Coca took Huallpa's arm and addressed herself to Micay.

"We came to ask your permission to dance in the couples' dance, my lady. May we have it?"

"You may," Micay said without hesitation. "Let it be a memory that will sustain you until you are together again."

Murmuring in gratitude, they bowed and turned away, holding hands as they walked toward the dancing area.

"One moment we are talking about killing Incas," Acapana mused aloud, "and the next we are talking about dancing. Yet you do not seem to find it strange at all."

Micay smiled tolerantly, struck by the innocence of his observation. "The war has just come to you, my friend, but we have been living with it for months. Very little can seem strange to us anymore. We must live as the war permits."

Acapana clicked his tongue in sympathy, but then returned the smile. "I am glad to see you are still strong. But since we have been permitted this time together, can we talk about the lives we led before this war took them over? I would like to hear about your children and about Apu Poma and his family."

"I would like to hear about your life in Chachapoyas," Micay agreed. "I assume you have a wife and children of your own."

"*Two* wives, both Chachapoyas. And six children."

Micay tucked her legs up under her on the bench, smoothing her shift down over her knees. "Let us talk, then. Let us hold onto the past for a while longer . . ."

Cochahuaylas

WHEN HUANCA AUQUI suddenly marched his warriors north out of Caxamarca, some parts of the Quito vanguard were slow to give ground, displaying their disdain for an enemy they had chased from the field three times. They quickly learned that this was not the same enemy, at least not in spirit, and the lesson cost most of them their lives. Cusi and Tomay had been made cautious by Tumibamba, so the Hawk Men were the first to withdraw, retreating into the mountains when they found themselves being pursued. Even so, they were harried constantly by a mixed band of Caxamarcans and Huamachucos who would not be deterred by landslides or ambushes and who seemed to welcome every chance to fight. Instead of backing off from an ambush, they would try to fight their way through it with a reckless disregard for their own losses.

During the days of skirmishing and sniping that preceded the battle, Cusi and Tomay gradually learned what had inspired this new, aggressive spirit. They heard it first in the taunts and threats that flew back and forth between the two sides, especially at night. A new taunt referred to them as "godless rebels," and they were told over and over, with a kind of gloating righteousness, that they were doomed to die a horrible death. Catiquilla had decreed it, they were told, and so had Pachacamac; they would die on their knees, the same way they had slaughtered the Cañaris.

They learned the rest from a Huamachuco scout who was captured after killing one of the sentries. The man had left himself no way to escape and had been badly wounded in the capture. He was slowly bleeding to death, but he spat defiantly when Cusi offered the services of a healer in exchange for information. He was similarly oblivious to the threat of being kept alive in order to suffer more refined tortures.

"Tell me about Catiquilla," Cusi suggested on an impulse, and for a few moments light came back into the man's eyes. He spoke proudly of the huaca, which had its shrine in his home city of Huamachuco, a few days south of Caxamarca. Huascar had performed a great ceremony of penance and propitiation in Cuzco, and then he had sent emissaries with rich offerings to Catiquilla and Pachacamac and all the other important huacas, pleading for forgiveness and a sign of victory. Both Catiquilla and Pachacamac had spoken forcefully, declaring that the gods were angry at Atauhuallpa for his crimes and would punish him by stealing the will from his warriors and leaving them to be destroyed.

"The usurpers will die," the scout concluded, coughing and spitting blood. Cusi glanced at Tomay, who was frowning and tugging unconsciously on the earflap of his cap, unaware that Cusi was looking at him. So Cusi met Tarapaca's eyes instead, and saw a concern bordering on alarm. Catiquilla was a powerful huaca, and it had offered this bold prophecy while standing directly in Atauhuallpa's path. And Pachacamac, the most venerable huaca in all of the Four Quarters, had confirmed it. Cusi leaned forward over the scout, whose eyes fluttered open but could not focus.

"Huascar can never be absolved of his crimes," Cusi began, but the man's eyes rolled back and he died with a soft shudder, leaving Cusi poised foolishly with his mouth open. He found Tomay regarding him with a curiously flat expression.

"Who knows if Huascar matters?" Tomay said. "Either Catiquilla is correct or it has uttered its last prophecy." Hefting his spear and shield, he stood up and nudged the body of the scout with his toe. "This one believed, but he still died," he said, and he went off to check on his men, leaving Cusi staring after him.

The battle began a few days later, and the first day of fighting ended indecisively, with losses on both sides but no ground lost or gained. The Hawk Men had come down from the hills to act as a reserve force on the eastern flank, and they had been called into action early and kept there by an enemy who for the first time matched them in both numbers and zeal. There had been no swift, sudden breakthroughs; just a stubborn back-and-forth struggle that tested will and endurance as much as courage. That night the Cuzco forces could be heard celebrating around their campfires, as if they had achieved a great victory simply by staying on the field.

Cusi squatted on a rocky knoll with some of the other Hawk Men, listening to the raucous sounds that drifted to them from the other camp. Tarapaca had confirmed Cusi's sense that the Hawk Men were still in good spirits; the fighting they had done today, while fierce, could not harrow them after what they had experienced in Tumibamba. But Huallpa and the other messengers were reporting an almost palpable uneasiness among the other regiments, who for the most part had grown accustomed to easy victories. Everyone, apparently, had heard about the prophecies, which made the sudden Cuzco resistance appear ominous rather than simply challenging.

"How are your men?" Cusi asked when Tomay came up to join them.

"They are ready," Tomay allowed. "The men around us, though, are awfully quiet, and they jump at sudden sounds."

"A messenger came from Challcochima," Cusi told him. "He asked for our observations and suggestions."

"I expect he already knows the men are nervous," Tomay said dryly. "No doubt he would like you to tell him how to silence the voices of Catiquilla and Pachacamac."

"We do that by winning the battle. I think we must tell him about the Chachapoyas."

"Tell him what? They were not even deployed today, from what I could see."

"Huanca Auqui will have to use them sooner or later," Cusi said, "given the losses he took today. We must tell Challcochima to aim the attack at them wherever they are deployed."

"He would probably do that on his own," Tomay shrugged. "But it would give him something to tell his men."

Cusi grunted in annoyance and turned to find a messenger. "Huallpa, take this message to Challcochima: Tell him Huanca Auqui has several thousand Chachapoyas, most of whom were brought here against their will. Tell him they are young and inexperienced and unlikely to take much inspiration from the words of Catiquilla. They should be attacked as soon as they are deployed."

To Cusi's surprise, the boy simply stared back at him, and Huaman Cachi spoke up in his place.

"I will take the message, my lord."

"What is wrong with you, Huallpa?" Cusi demanded. "You asked to be a messenger."

"I have heard you," Huallpa announced abruptly, and he jumped up and ran off into the darkness. Cusi looked at Huaman Cachi for an explanation.

"He asked to be a messenger, my lord," Huaman Cachi said, pausing to swallow, "so he would not have to fight against the Chachapoyas. The governor spoke to him about that in Huancabamba."

"Acapana had some notion we could save them," Tomay put in when Cusi did not respond. "He assumed we shared it."

"I *did,*" Cusi snapped, whirling on him. "I had hoped to lure more of them into defecting. But we must save ourselves now, or Acapana and all the others will die with us."

Suddenly furious, Cusi stood up and rapped his battle-ax against his shield, then stalked off up the knoll, picking his way among the rocks and startling the sentry who was posted at the highest point. He told the man he was taking his place and sent him back down. He was staring out at the enemy camp, taking deep breaths to calm his anger, when Tomay came up to stand beside him.

"I apologize for saying that about Acapana," Tomay said, "and for making you justify yourself in front of the men."

Cusi fought back a torrent of angry words, recognizing most of them as self-justification. "I cannot justify what I did to Huallpa. I was thinking only of the message, not the messenger."

"You said it better than I would have," Tomay allowed. "Challcochima will be reassured."

Cusi peered at him in the near darkness. "Why do you scoff at that? You have seen how low the morale is in the rest of the camp; the men need reassurance more than anything else."

"I am not scoffing . . ."

"Yes, you are," Cusi insisted. "You have been scoffing at everything, as if nothing we did mattered. As if we should just wait and see if the prophecies come true."

"You are the one who knows about these things," Tomay accused him, "but what do you have to counter the voice of Catiquilla? What do any of us have? Huanacauri is in Cuzco, under Huascar's control, and Inti . . . who can say what side Inti will take? Atauhuallpa's dream is an inspiration only to him, and where is he? Where is the warlord to whom we pledged ourselves? He sits in Huancabamba, consulting with his spirit brother and inventing titles for himself . . ."

Cusi was silent for a moment out of respect for the passion with which Tomay had spoken. "So . . . you are not scoffing," he conceded. "You are feeling like a godless rebel."

Tomay emptied his lungs with a sound that was almost a groan. "I am not a brother to lightning or anything like that. I do not have dreams and visions that tell me what I should believe. So when I see the enemy fighting like new men, drawing great courage from their huacas, I wonder where *we* are supposed to find the strength to match them."

"But this was the first time they have matched us," Cusi pointed out, "and they did it because they are fresh and full of spirit, and we were tired and overconfident. They will not be as fresh and eager tomorrow or the next day, but we will still be veteran warriors."

"Will that be enough?" Tomay asked. "That is what the men are asking themselves, because they feel they are fighting more than just another army."

"We are fighting Huascar's army," Cusi said forcefully. "You know what kind of man he is. Can you believe *he* has won the favor of the gods? I cannot, no matter what Catiquilla and Pachacamac have said."

"They spoke only of the punishment Atauhuallpa has earned."

"They were answering Huascar's pleas," Cusi insisted. "He is not known for his mercy either."

Tomay turned to look at him, baring his teeth in a half smile. "I never doubted you would find a way to defy these prophecies. I have been trying to find my own ever since I woke in Tumibamba and found half my ear gone and my head held together with thread. It did not help to learn that an Inca had done it to me. Nor did it help to learn what Atauhuallpa had done to the Cañaris. I am grateful to be alive, but I lost more than an earplug and a piece of my scalp."

Cusi was again silent, recalling the time he had surrendered his own earplugs to the sickness and had not wanted them back. He realized that the Cuzco camp had grown quiet, as well, the spirit of celebration finally exhausted.

"We should rest and prepare ourselves for tomorrow," he suggested. "The battle will be won on the field, not in a shrine far away. If we are alone, as you fear, we must be ready to fight with our whole being."

"I will fight with what I have left," Tomay said wearily, and he tapped the point of his spear against Cusi's shield in parting. Then he was gone, and Cusi squatted down in the darkness and listened for sounds like a sentry. When he had identified the few he could hear, he began to prepare himself as a warrior. Before he could pray, though, he thought again of what Tomay had said, and he had to ponder the implications of his own reply: *If we are alone . . .*

THE THICK gray clouds that had filled the sky during the night delayed the appearance of dawn, so that mist was still rising from the field when the Cuzcos attacked. They came headlong and screaming, and the Quitos met them with a desperate ferocity, the response of veterans to their own doubts and fears. For a while the battle raged at an unsustainable pitch, each side trying to break the other early. Then there was a mutual backing off as the dead and wounded were cleared out of the way and reserves poured in on both sides to replace the exhausted warriors in the front line. The fighting then resumed as another tense, step-by-step struggle.

Gradually, though, the Cuzcos began to push the Quitos back, so that by midday the Hawk Men were defending the knoll on which Cusi and Tomay had stood the night before, a position that had been well behind the Quito line when the day began. The warriors they had relieved earlier should have returned by now to relieve them, but the messenger Cusi had sent to Challco-chima had not made his way back, and the fighting around the knoll was too heavy now to try to send another. The Huamachucos kept charging up the slope at them, shouting "Catiquilla!" as they fell beneath the rocks and darts the Hawk Men hurled down at them. The air was hot and close beneath the blanket of clouds, and sweat poured off Cusi's body as he moved from squadron to squadron, shouting encouragement and instructions.

When his thirst became overwhelming, he pulled back and found a water gourd and took it with him up to the highest part of the knoll, where he crouched behind his shield and drank. He had been hit by a stone on the ridge of his right cheekbone, and the lump was swelling up into his line of vision. As he made his way in among the sheltering rocks, he found Piqui stretched out on the ground, grimacing while Huallpa wrapped his ankle with a strip of cloth. Cusi knelt down and handed Piqui the water gourd.

"Broken?" he asked.

Piqui shook his head. "I stepped in a hole," he said tightly, prying the stopper out of the gourd to drink. Raising his shield before him, Cusi stood up and scanned the field below and on both sides of the knoll. Despite their fatigue, the Hawk Men were holding their attackers off, but Cusi did not have the same confidence in the regiments on their flanks, and he had no intention of allowing the enemy to cut them off and surround them again. He made sure the flanks were holding before he glanced out toward the center of the battle-field, where the Quito line was definitely sagging. Where are the reserves? Cusi wondered desperately, unable to believe Challcochima and Quizquiz had used them up already. The Cuzcos were moving even more troops forward, rushing them toward the sagging middle of the Quito line.

Cusi heard a rumble of thunder overhead at the same time as he recognized the troops. His cheek flared with pain when he squinted to see, but even through tears the condor banners and gaudily painted helmets of the Cha-chapoyas were unmistakable. Huanca Auqui had obviously saved them until he had a clear advantage, and he was deploying them in a way that gave them no chance to flee or defect. They could only go straight ahead, into the heart of the battle.

Piqui came to stand beside him, leaning heavily on Huallpa for support. They watched in silence as the Chachapoyas, commanded by golden-eared Incas, spread out and filtered through to the front ranks, taking the place of a weary regiment of Caxamarcans. The Quito line seemed to sag back even further, drawing the enemy with them, and then Cusi saw the trap being sprung. Two columns of warriors suddenly coalesced behind the Quito line and came forward at a run, converging into a wedge-shaped mass that carried the whole line with them as they plowed into the middle of the Chachapoyas.

"In the yellow," Huallpa blurted. "Quizquiz is leading them himself."

"That is where our relief went," Cusi said as the Quitos surged and then surged again, driving the Chachapoyas back and cutting them down as they fell into each other. There was panicked movement throughout the Cuzco line, which drew back in sections and then broke completely. Cusi realized that stones were no longer clattering around him, and he looked down and saw the Huamachucos retreating down the slope, stumbling to keep from turning their backs. His own men had risen along the knoll and were looking expectantly in his direction. Piqui detached himself from Huallpa and urged the boy to take up his shield and weapon.

"I can follow on my own . . . take your place in the victory."

Huallpa nodded and looked at Cusi, his mouth set in a grim line.

"You were only the messenger," Cusi told him. "The responsibility—the blame—is mine."

Very deliberately Huallpa shook his head, then turned to face down the slope, awaiting Cusi's command. Cusi raised his battle-ax over his head and shook it, bringing the men on the knoll up onto their toes.

"This to Catiquilla!" he shouted, and he plunged down the slope behind Huallpa, hearing more thunder and thinking dimly that it sounded like approval.

Caxamarca

CUSI HAD LEFT the city at dawn, accompanying Atauhuallpa south to Huamachuco on what he assumed was a mission of revenge. Micay and Cahua rose to see him off, then bathed and dressed in their finest clothes. Micay painted her face with care, using the familiar motions to steady her trembling hands. Cahua was too excited to notice her nervousness and pulled her along by the hand as they went to join the women who were assembling outside the high stone walls of the House of Chosen Women. On a previous stay in Caxamarca, Micay had briefly contemplated a visit to her friend Cahua, but the prospect of being confined by those walls again had aroused too much dread for her to pursue it.

Think of it as a rescue, she told herself now, repeating Cusi's advice. Surely this was preferable to accepting the presence of another wife, which had been Atauhuallpa's intended gift. Still, her heart seemed to have lodged at the base of her throat, and her lungs were laboring erratically as she and Cahua lined up with the other wives and their daughters. There was a long delay while Mama Amancay spoke to the guards at the gate, who kept bowing and making gestures of helplessness. Apparently no one was going to open the gate from the inside, and the guards were reluctant to risk intruding on a domain forbidden to men. Finally Mama Amancay overcame her timidity and ordered two of her women to push the gate open. It swung back easily, and after more hesitation Mama Amancay led them in.

"Mama!" Cahua whispered urgently, and Micay realized that she had taken her daughter's hand in a fierce grip, as if to keep her from being torn away. The women ahead had spread out as they entered, and Micay saw a flurry of gray as the chosen women formed themselves into lines on the other side of the courtyard. Obviously they had not been warned about this visit, and there was another delay while the mamanchic was summoned. Micay lifted her gaze to the sky, trying to shut out the looming walls, trying not to feel the terror of a girl named Misa. She was aware that Cahua was watching her closely, which made her struggle to compose herself. *Think of it as a rescue . . .*

When the mamanchic finally arrived, it was a different woman from the one

Micay had known, a younger but more haggard woman who greeted Mama Amancay with great trepidation, stumbling over her words and bowing too deeply. Mama Amancay seemed equally uneasy with her role and spoke rapidly, waving her hands in a way that seemed only to confuse and unsettle the poor woman even more. The mamanchic shook her head helplessly and turned to the mamacona behind her, waiting until one came forward from the rear and whispered into her ear. The speaker kept a hand raised in front of her face and quickly stepped back behind the mamanchic, but not before Micay caught a glimpse of scarred and furrowed flesh.

"What?" Cahua asked in surprise, and Micay realized she had murmured her friend's name aloud. She felt the dread lift like a weight from her shoulders, so that she could breathe normally, and she was immediately aware of the uncertainty and embarrassment in the women around her. Most of them had no idea of how a transaction like this should be handled, but they could tell this one was being handled badly.

"Come," Micay said to Cahua, reaching down again for her hand, "let us go greet your namesake."

Heads turned as she led her daughter to the front, where they stopped and bowed to Mama Amancay. The young woman was so flustered that she seemed grateful for the interruption.

"I have been here before, my lady," Micay explained. "Perhaps I can be of some help."

"She does not understand who I am," Mama Amancay said in frustration. "She keeps asking for a memory cord. I have no cord."

"My mother," Micay said to the mamanchic, inclining her head in deference. Over the woman's shoulder she could see Cahua's eyes, squinting as if to make her image sharper. "I am Mama Micay, my lady, and this is Mama Amancay, the wife of the Apu Inca Atauhuallpa."

The mamanchic stared back her her blankly. "Who . . . what is the Apu Inca?"

"He is the leader of the Incas from Quito, those who have rebelled against Huascar. They have driven Huascar's warriors out of Caxamarca."

"We heard the noise," the mamanchic admitted in a dazed voice. "But the huacas had promised a victory . . ."

"They were mistaken," Micay told her, quietly but firmly. "Atauhuallpa rules here now. He has sent his wife to claim some of your chosen women."

"How many?" the woman asked, and Micay deferred to Mama Amancay.

"Twelve of the oldest to be given as wives, and another thirty as companions and servants."

The mamanchic swallowed and drew herself up. "What if I refuse?"

Mama Amancay made a sputtering sound, but Micay spoke first. "We are all wives, my mother, and we will treat the girls with respect and kindness. The others will be married to Atauhuallpa's commanders and captains, men of high blood. You would do them more harm to keep them here, hoping that Huascar will regain his power."

"Not to mention the harm you will do yourself," Mama Amancay put in, "if my husband has to come here himself."

"Please, my lady," Micay said, turning to give her a pained look. "There is no need for threats. I am sure the mamanchic can see what is best for the girls."

Cahua was again whispering in the mamanchic's ear, and the woman was nodding slowly, sighing with each nod. She turned back and bowed to Mama Amancay in surrender.

"Let me introduce you," she suggested, "and tell you something about the girls you choose . . ."

Mama Amancay nodded with satisfaction and started across the courtyard with her, the other women following behind. Micay let them go, holding Cahua back and pointing with her chin at the gray-robed mama who stood waiting with her back turned and her head lowered. Micay went up and put a hand on the woman's shoulder.

"Cahua, my friend," she said softly, noticing that there were streaks of white in the black hair that hung down from beneath her head cloth. The warbling voice seemed to dance around Micay's ears before she could capture the meaning of the words.

"I am Mama Cahua now, Mama Micay. Who is the young one you have with you?"

She turned then, her smile appearing crooked and tentative beneath the desolate cavity of her nose. Micay glanced down and saw Cahua staring up at the woman with her usual curiosity but no fear or disgust; she had seen face wounds more devastating than this.

"This is my daughter, who is also named Cahua. We have come to choose a companion for her."

For a moment Mama Cahua's eyes grew large and shimmered wetly, and she murmured something Micay could not understand. Then she composed herself and looked down at the girl, speaking slowly and as distinctly as possible. "How old are you, Cahua?"

"I am eight, my lady."

"Do you want a companion your same age or older?"

"The same."

"And what will your companion do for you?"

"She will be my friend and go everywhere with me. I will teach her to be a healer, as my mother taught me."

Mama Cahua turned slightly and pointed across the courtyard with her chin. "The girls your age are at the far end of the line, do you see? Would you like me to introduce you to them?"

"Can I talk to them myself?" Cahua asked, giving Micay an uncertain glance that made her realize how poorly she had prepared her daughter for this.

"Of course," Mama Cahua said. "Go and introduce yourself, and we will come after you."

Cahua smiled at that and walked off toward the gray-clad girls without a backward glance, as if she had done this many times before. Mama Cahua clicked her tongue in appreciation.

"She may be too old for any girl her own age. Is she your only child?"

"She has a twin brother who is in Vitcos with his uncle. They were my gift from Pachamama."

"And who is the Inca who made you his first wife?" Mama Cahua asked with a knowing smile, reaching out to touch the long golden pin that held Micay's mantle together.

"He is the war chief Cusi Huaman. He is the youngest son of the woman who took me out of here."

"I have heard his name sung in praise," Mama Cahua acknowledged, and her smile faded. "He is now among the rebels?"

"Huascar murdered his uncle and then tried to murder him when he came to Cuzco as Atauhuallpa's ambassador. The Incas in the north had no choice but to rebel."

"And you said that they were victorious here, even though the huacas had spoken against them. Obviously Huascar is being punished for his crimes." Mama Cahua shook her head sadly. "I can say this to no one else, but I have felt it, Micay. We have been asked to provide so many special prayers that the words have become stale and our voices no longer produce an echo. I have wondered if Inti had grown tired of our pleas."

"I have no love for Huascar," Micay said after a respectful pause, "but it gives me no pleasure to hear you say that. We have just heard that the bearded strangers have returned in the north."

"Ah . . . who will speak to them for the Incas?"

"My husband thinks they should be captured or killed," Micay said bluntly, and Mama Cahua stared at her in shock.

"What if they are the Viracochas, as some of the priests believe?"

"My husband fought against one of them, and he believes they are men— very dangerous men. The sickness came when they did, and there are those who suspect they cast it on us like an evil spell."

Mama Cahua clasped her hands in front of her and appeared to study them for several moments. When she finally looked up her eyes were glazed with pain and her voice cracked and whistled. "This is not a life for which we have prepared anyone."

Micay could only nod in agreement. "No one outside is prepared either. We all go on without knowing what the world will be like when we finish."

Mama Cahua held out her arms then and they embraced, just as they had twenty years earlier, only now it was Cahua who seemed the more lost. Micay had been uncertain about the propriety of an embrace, and over Cahua's shoulder she could see some of the other wives turning to stare. But their opinion of her was the last thing she cared about now. She hugged Cahua fiercely before letting her go, and they looked at each other and tried to smile.

"At least I will always know you remembered our friendship," Mama Cahua said. "That is *my* gift from Mama Quilla. Come, let us find the daughter you named for me . . ."

The mamanchic and the wives were still inspecting the older girls, and the younger ones quickly reassumed their ranks when they saw Micay and Mama Cahua coming. But they could not fully take their eyes off of Cahua, who was showing them the silver bracelet she had been given by Tocto Oxica. Micay could only guess at what she might have told them about herself, though their expressions seemed to range from awe to utter disbelief. When they all bowed in unison, Cahua looked over her shoulder in surprise, then smiled proudly.

"I have found the one, Mama!" she announced. "Her name is Ococo, and she is a Campa."

"A Campa here?" Micay murmured to Mama Cahua, who seemed pleasantly surprised by the choice.

"Her parents had gone to Chachapoyas as mitmacs," she explained. "That was where the selector of chosen women found her."

Cahua had coaxed forward a girl slightly thinner and taller than herself, with a smooth, seemingly boneless face and liquid black eyes that had not been dulled by the discipline of the house. Her manner was gentle and self-effacing, so different from Cahua's that Micay wanted to let out a Campa whoop of astonished acceptance.

"She has heard of Vitcos, but she has never seen it," Cahua reported. "She does not believe my uncle is the high chief there."

Ococo gave a small shrug, appearing neither embarrassed by the accusation nor defensive about her disbelief. "Are you not Incas, my lady?" she asked quizzically, and Micay smiled at the aptness of the question.

"We are, and the uncle to whom she refers is a Campa. You should have explained, Cahua, that Uritu is not your uncle by blood but your father's initiation brother."

Cahua nodded impatiently at the correction. "Anyway, we will visit Vitcos when we go to get Sinchi," she added. But Ococo just nodded and glanced expectantly at Mama Cahua, who in turn looked at Micay.

"She speaks Campa and Chacha in addition to Quechua, and she has been adept at everything we teach here. She is perhaps as ready as anyone for the life that awaits her."

"Mama?" Cahua prompted, but Micay continued to stare at the girl. Not because she had any reservations about the choice—there could hardly be a more appropriate chosen woman to rescue than one who had come here from Chachapoyas and was a Campa, as well. Her appropriateness was so striking, in fact, that it had caused Micay to recall Uritu's prediction that many Incas would be going to live among the Campas. It made her wonder if there were not still some signs to be heeded, apart from the loud, deceptive proclamations of the huacas.

"*Mama,*" Cahua said more insistently, bringing Micay out of her reverie. She spread her hands in apology and smiled at Ococo in an attempt to make up for her staring.

"Welcome to our family, Ococo," she said warmly. "Wherever we may live, my daughter, I promise you that you will always have a place among us."

There was a startled gratitude in the girl's eyes, as if Micay had answered a question she could not have asked. She bowed deeply, and then Mama Cahua sent her and Cahua off to collect Ococo's belongings. Micay saw Mama Amancay looking their way, but when the younger woman got a good look at Mama Cahua, she grimaced and quickly turned away.

"I am sorry," Micay began, but Mama Cahua sniffed and cut her off with a curt shake of her head.

"It is unimportant, except that it means I can be of no help in introducing the girls." She took Micay by the arm and led her in the direction the two girls had gone, steering wide of the other wives. "How much longer will you be in Caxamarca?"

"I do not know," Micay confessed. "It depends on whether we travel with the warriors or with the Apu Inca's court. You have already had an example of why I would prefer to travel with the warriors."

Mama Cahua halted at the mouth of the dark passageway into which the girls had disappeared. Micay caught a glimpse of shadowed doorways and imagined the barren rooms within, an image that made her shudder.

"You can come to see me here," Mama Cahua suggested softly, "if you can bear to return again. Do not bring Ococo, though; it would only confuse her."

"I will try," Micay promised, "and I will not let my fear of these walls keep me away. It was hard, though, Cahua, until I saw you."

Mama Cahua smiled crookedly. "For many people, that is harder. I must go now and help the girls who are leaving. Come again if you can. You have always been in my prayers, Micay, but now I will see you there in front of me when I ask Mama Quilla for her blessing. You are the proof that she has listened."

They embraced again, releasing each other only when they heard Cahua's voice echoing down the passageway. Mama Cahua waited for the girls, then escorted the three of them to the gate before saying her farewells.

"Be as good a friend to Ococo as your mother has been to me," she told Cahua in parting. "Hold each other in your hearts."

"We will be like sisters," Cahua declared as Mama Cahua backed away and Micay pulled open the gate, the two of them taking a long last look at each other as the girls went through. Then Micay turned and pulled the gate closed behind her, leaving the House of Chosen Women with her heart too full to distinguish relief from regret.

Ticci Capac, Cusi thought, pondering the name for the thousandth time: Foundation Prince. For three days he had been marching alongside the litter on which the spirit brother rode, studying the hunk of dark gray stone with its bands and inlaid pockets of gold. It was about the size of a cornerstone and appeared at first glance to be an architect's model for a fort or an elaborate dais. A closer inspection, however, revealed an irregular surface covered with an incredible array of knobs, niches, and ledges, which together formed a construction too intricate for any architect to have contrived. In some places the stone had been rubbed to the smoothness of obsidian, while in others it had been left rough and crystalline, preserving the mysterious shapes of animals and symbols that seemed to rise naturally from the rock. If it was a model of anything, it was not of a place meant to be occupied by humans.

Glancing at the road ahead, Cusi hooded his eyes as far as possible, screening out the bright sunlight and the presence of the bearers and the other members of the honor guard. He had to quiet himself completely before he could feel the emanations of Ticci Capac, which were as ambiguous and convoluted as its physical appearance, nothing at all like the spare, upright presence of his own spirit brother. He longed to lay his hands on it, as Atauhuallpa undoubtedly did in private, though Cusi could not imagine what it might convey to him. It had taken him years to become familiar with his own spirit brother, and this one was so much more subtle and elusive, like a voice whispering in a maze of tunnels. Atauhuallpa spent long periods sequestered with it, but he had only had it for a matter of months, and as far as Cusi knew no one had ever instructed him in its secrets. It was hard to believe this warlord was equipped to discover them by himself, though Atauhuallpa was certainly displaying his effort.

Gradually, as his thoughts drifted to Atauhuallpa, Cusi became aware of another, more demanding presence, and a quick glance across the litter caught Quilaco staring at him in annoyance. Annoyance and resentment had become Quilaco's most common expressions ever since it had become apparent that Atauhuallpa had brought them along solely to serve in the honor guard and had no intention of conferring with them about anything: not about the war or the return of the Bearded Ones; not even about what they were going to do in Huamachuco.

The captain of the bearers blew a single bellowing note on his conch horn, and the column slowly drew to a halt to allow the teams to change. Atauhuallpa's litter was lowered to the ground, and he rose from his canopied seat and stepped to the side of the road, where his servants were hastily erecting a tent and digging a hole in the event he might wish to relieve himself. Quilaco had gone to the other side of the road, and Cusi went over to him, noticing for the first time that they had come within sight of Huamachuco. Instead of the usual herds of llamas and alpacas, the grazing land around the settlement was occupied by the tents of the warriors Atauhuallpa had sent ahead.

"So . . . we are almost there," Cusi said, and Quilaco's sour expression took on a sarcastic edge.

"I wondered if you planned to arrive with your eyes closed. Or was Ticci Capac guiding your steps?"

"Since he is Atauhuallpa's only adviser, he may well be guiding all our steps," Cusi pointed out.

Quilaco snorted. "Has he told you where? Or why?"

"I think you know that yourself."

"So he must have his revenge on Catiquilla," Quilaco allowed. "Why does he need me for that? I know nothing about such things."

"Perhaps he wishes to show you what he knows," Cusi suggested. "So you will know the difference between a warlord and the Apu Inca."

Quilaco paused, his eyes narrowing thoughtfully. "You mean beyond the fact that he no longer consults with anyone and will not let us see him pissing?"

"Well beyond that," Cusi said with a rueful smile. "We chose him as our warlord and gave him the power to lead us in war. I think he wants to show us that he possesses even greater powers and owes them to no one."

The conch horn sounded again, and they turned to go back to their posts. Quilaco cleared his throat, as if embarrassed by his own question.

"Has Ticci Capac told you what kind of revenge he will take?"

"Ticci Capac tells me nothing I can understand," Cusi said with a shrug. "But as we both know, Atauhuallpa has never needed anyone's guidance in the matter of revenge . . ."

THE COLUMN stopped for another change of bearers outside the main square and then proceeded without so much as a ceremonial pause past the lines of cheering warriors and up the well-beaten path to the shrine of Catiquilla, which stood upon an eminence overlooking Huamachuco. Before this Cusi had seen the shrine only from a distance, because of the crowds of priests and pilgrims who were always in the way and the prolonged fast that was required to approach any closer. Now the path was lined with warriors, who were holding back a crowd of Huamachucos with their spears. Cusi heard the warriors shouting that no one was going to be hurt, but the Huamachucos were weeping and pleading in a manner that demonstrated their disbelief in such reassurance.

Quizquiz was waiting at the base of the broad steps that led up to the shrine, and he greeted Cusi and Quilaco with a gloating smile, tapping his notched war club against their shields. Everyone present bowed in silence as Atauhuallpa descended from his litter, clutching a bronze prying bar—his "serpent maker" from Tumibamba—in one hand. He gestured brusquely at the shields and weapons Cusi and Quilaco were holding.

"Put those down," he commanded, and when their hands were empty he gave Cusi a flaming torch and Quilaco a long chontawood club with sharp serrated edges. He motioned for them to follow and led the way up the steps, taking them two at a time despite their steepness. They climbed into an even deeper silence than that behind them, and Cusi realized he was feeling the presence of the huaca. He felt it even more powerfully when they reached the top and stood before the curtained doorway of the shrine, which was a narrow enclosure built of rough reddish-brown stone so ancient that thick bands of gray-green moss had filled the sunken joinings. The carvings that flanked the doorway were badly eroded but still showed the fangs and claws of some great cat, which appeared again in the faded weave of the curtain.

With his free hand Atauhuallpa tore the curtain from its hangings and threw it to the ground, trampling it beneath his sandaled feet before gesturing to Cusi.

"Burn it," he commanded, and Cusi had to force his muscles into action, feeling the almost syrupy resistance of the air and a warmth that did not come from the sun or the torch in his hand. The curtain ignited instantly, jerking and twisting like a live thing as it flamed and then shriveled into a blackened coil of ash that was picked up by the wind and borne out over the crowd below. The Huamachucos moaned and covered their heads with their arms, but Atauhuallpa simply turned and went through the doorway.

Because it is holy, Cusi thought as he followed, caught in the ambience of the huaca, which had none of the menace or fierceness he had expected. It reminded him too much of his own huaca, of things abiding and ancient, untouched by the fleeting anger of men. He wanted to squat and humble himself, but instead he walked with the others, holding the torch above his head.

There were naked beams overhead, cutting the sunlight into blocks and striping the floor with shadows. Only the rear portion of the enclosure was roofed, and out of that shape-filled darkness stepped a man who looked as old as the shrine itself. His white hair streamed out around a face that was a mass of compacted wrinkles, and he shaded his watery eyes with a gnarled, spotted hand. He was wearing a long robe decorated with red mullu shells and pieces of iridescent abalone that clinked together as he tottered forward.

"What do you want, Atauhuallpa?" the old man asked in a voice that was thin and hoarse but not at all feeble. "Why do you violate the sanctity of this shrine with your anger?"

Atauhuallpa was momentarily taken aback by the man's directness, but then he responded with vehement force. "You know why, priest. You betrayed me to Huascar. Your lying prophecy gave his army strength."

"I did nothing on Huascar's behalf," the priest insisted. "I only repeated the message of Catiquilla: that you would be punished one day for what you did to the Cañaris. And you *will* be punished unless you perform great acts of penance."

Atauhuallpa snarled as he gave his prying bar to Quizquiz. Then he startled Quilaco by plucking the chontawood club out of his hands.

"I gave the Cañaris what they deserved," he told the priest. "Now you will have yours."

The priest dropped his hands but did not try to flee. "You cannot murder the truth," he said, as Atauhuallpa advanced on him with the club in a two-handed grip, his wrists cocked loosely. The old man had time only to murmur a last prayer before Atauhuallpa swung the club in a hissing arc and struck his head off with one blow. Blood spurted into the air and the headless priest actually took a step forward, his arms flapping like broken wings, before crashing to the floor. Screams erupted from the rear of the enclosure and burst in shrieking echoes around Cusi, who had reeled backward when the priest's head flew past the place where he was standing.

Atauhuallpa tossed the bloody club back to Quilaco, who let it fall with a clatter and then doubled over to vomit on the floor. Atauhuallpa grunted scornfully and grabbed the bronze bar Quizquiz held out to him.

"Come, bring the torch," he said to Cusi, but Cusi heard himself say no. Atauhuallpa stopped and glared at him, but Cusi only spoke more forcefully.

"No, my lord, do not do this. It is unholy."

"No enemy of mine is holy!" Atauhuallpa roared, and he whirled toward the rear of the enclosure, brandishing the bar. Another priest rushed out to plead with him, but Atauhuallpa clubbed him to the ground and kept going. Quizquiz came over and calmly took the torch out of Cusi's hand.

"Warlords do not care about holiness," he said with a smirk, and he went off with his club in one hand and the torch in the other. Cusi heard the clang of metal against stone amid renewed screaming, then the concussive sound of rock shattering and ricocheting off the walls. He could see Atauhuallpa in the gloom, tearing down wall hangings and flailing wildly with the bronze bar, hitting flesh, stone, and wood indiscriminately. Cusi's head was pounding and he felt sick to his stomach, and he knew if he stayed he would faint. So he staggered over to Quilaco, who was standing like a statue, and got him moving toward the doorway. Quilaco's face was ashen and his skin was as cold as Cusi's, but he managed to pull himself erect as they came out of the shrine. As soon as they were outside, Cusi's headache and nausea disappeared, and he realized he had been sharing the death agony of the huaca. His next thought was that he had defied Atauhuallpa to his face. That cleared his head completely, and he marched down the stairs ahead of Quilaco and picked up his shield and battle-ax. Anger at what he had been forced to witness—helplessly—began to well up inside him, and he decided that while Atauhuallpa might be justified in ordering his death, he would not have it easily.

When he looked back up, black smoke was billowing up out of the shrine, and a moment later Quizquiz appeared in the doorway and tossed out the limp, headless corpse of the priest. A few of the warriors yowled in approbation, but Cusi saw Quilaco and some of the others around him shudder or wince. Atauhuallpa came out after Quizquiz and strode to the top of the stairs, holding the bronze bar in one hand and a melon-sized chunk of black rock in the other. The multicolored fringe around his forehead was crooked and sweat ran down his face, but his expression was exultant as he held up the piece of rock.

"Catiquilla stood against me," he bellowed to the prostrate Huamachucos and the gaping warriors. "This is what is left of Catiquilla!"

With that he smashed the rock down onto the platform beside him, shattering it into a thousand fragments. Then he waved the bronze bar in the direction of the shrine.

"Destroy it . . . level it to the ground," he commanded, and a line of warriors carrying picks and bars and stone hammers went past Cusi and climbed the stairs. As Atauhuallpa started down, he gestured broadly toward the Huamachucos with his free hand.

"Go back to your homes. Forget there ever was a Catiquilla."

Cusi heard a great surge of noise and movement behind him, but he did not turn to look. With sidelong glances he checked the positions of all the nearby warriors, noting with satisfaction that Quilaco had armed himself and appeared vigilant. Then he fastened his gaze on Atauhuallpa, watching for the slightest signal and determined not to be taken by surprise. He felt his presence expanding around him, swollen with an anger that was bitter and righteous, but Atauhuallpa came all the way down to stand in front of him, obviously feeling no more than he had in the shrine. Quizquiz, however, was staying close and eyeing Cusi with undisguised wariness.

"You both failed me," Atauhuallpa said, looking first at Quilaco and then jerking his chin at Cusi. "And you defied me!"

Cusi did not respond, keeping his face impassive while he decided whom to strike first, Atauhuallpa or Quizquiz. But Quilaco spoke up indignantly.

"You never told us what to expect here," he pointed out. "We vowed to fight for you, my lord, not help you murder priests."

"You showed how much stomach you have," Atauhuallpa said scornfully. "And you, Cusi Huaman . . . where were your famous powers today? Your *huaca*. You spoke to me like a woman, like someone who deserves the mirror and face paint Huascar gave you."

Quilaco thrust himself forward so abruptly that everyone reacted defensively, Cusi and Quizquiz going down into a fighting stance and Atauhuallpa holding the bronze bar out in front of him. Quilaco had not lowered the point of his spear, but he was quivering with anger and looked as if he wanted to leap at Atauhuallpa.

"Would you dare to scorn us as Huascar did?" he demanded. "We risked our lives for you in Calca, and it was because of you that we were beaten and humiliated. It was because of Cusi's powers that we survived. If you spit on him now, you spit on all of us, and you deserve no one's loyalty!"

Atauhuallpa tried for a moment to glare him down, but Quilaco would not yield. Atauhuallpa lowered the bar and turned it in his large hands, glancing once at Cusi, who was still poised to strike. "I commended you for the courage you showed in Calca," he said finally, and seemed to regret the concession immediately. "But you disappointed me today. I had thought, Cusi, that you were the one I should send to meet the Bearded Ones and bring them to me. But you might lose your courage again and try to tell me *they* are holy."

"I tried to kill the only one I have seen," Cusi growled. "I would do the same to the rest of them."

"Then you are obviously unfit for the task," Atauhuallpa said flatly. "I will see what manner of men they are before I kill them. If you fear them so much, it is better that you go to Cuzco."

Cusi heard the insult but ignored it, hearing a pardon in the statement, as well. He slowly relaxed and straightened up, and Quizquiz did the same a moment later, baring his teeth in recognition of how seriously he had taken the threat.

"Do we have your permission to summon our men from Caxamarca?" Quilaco asked stiffly.

"You do," Atauhuallpa agreed. Then he walked away from them without a word of dismissal or farewell. Quizquiz came up to them and gingerly tapped his war club against their shields.

"He told me above that he intended to have your heads, too," Quizquiz informed them with a smile. "I suspected you might be reluctant to give them up."

"Who would he find to do it for him?" Quilaco asked. "You?"

Quizquiz shrugged. "Cusi was ready to attack me the whole time. Were you not?"

"I would have gone for *him* first," Cusi said succinctly, and Quizquiz laughed.

"Challcochima will be pleased we did not lose you, one way or the other. We march south tomorrow, but you will have time to catch us before we reach Xauxa, where the Cuzcos are."

Quizquiz went off after Atauhuallpa's litter, which was already proceeding down the hill. The hillside was almost completely clear, except for a few Huamachucos who had fainted or been injured in the rush to get away. Above them the warriors were hacking away at the shrine with their tools, even as its furnishings continued to burn. Cusi lowered his shield and weapon and looked at Quilaco.

"This time, you saved us. I could not have argued with him."

"He is as mad as Huascar! That is the difference between a warlord and the Apu Inca: One takes his strength from his war chiefs, and the other thinks they are his to kill."

"He thinks the Bearded Ones are his to kill, too," Cusi said quietly. "They might also be reluctant to comply."

"Let him be his own envoy, then," Quilaco said, and he spat on the ground as they started down the hill, away from what had once been the shrine of Catiquilla.

XXII

PACHACUTI: The World Turned Upside Down

(A.D. 1532)

Abancay

MICAY HAD just been thinking about Cusi when he suddenly walked into the central courtyard of the rest house, followed by a squadron of Hawk Men. She had not expected to see him again until after the battle, so she simply stared for a moment until she noticed the bundle of memory cords in his free hand and understood why he had returned. Then her surprise turned to delight tinged with lust, because she had been thinking about the last time they had made love, in a crowded room in Vilcashuaman. She rose and summoned Machacuay.

"Do you remember the empty storeroom we discovered this morning?" she asked. Machacuay gave her a puzzled nod. "Would you prepare it for later, for my husband and myself?"

Comprehension brought an appreciative smile to his delicate face, and he went off without delay. Cusi had led his men into the awning house, where a pair of white-plumed post runners were stationed. Cusi had taken the messengers aside to explain the cords and whatever messages went with them, and the warriors had put down their weapons and were drinking gratefully from the water gourds the servants had brought out. When Micay arrived, Ñupchu was sitting with Piqui and Huaman Cachi, plying them with questions about Tomay. Micay caught a fleeting glance from Huaman Cachi that made her think that he was being diplomatic in his answers; Piqui, as always, was without expression.

The only one still standing was Huallpa, who was carrying Cusi's battle-ax and obviously did not feel he could put it down without permission. Coca was standing very close to him, whispering in his ear, while Cahua and Ococo hovered at her elbow. As Micay approached, Coca stopped whispering and drew away from him slightly, showing Micay a face that seemed brazen in its innocence. She will break her promise tonight, Micay thought, and realized she had no desire to try to stop her. She only wondered if her niece had found a storeroom of her own.

"So you were sent back with the final count," she said to Huallpa. "Is it a good one?"

He hesitated, and for a moment Micay thought he was going to say he did not know. She would not have believed that from a Hawk Man, and he finally decided not to pretend.

"Not as good as we would have liked, my lady," he admitted. "But numbers often do not mean strength."

"How many do Quizquiz and Challcochima have?" Micay persisted.

"Less than twenty-five thousand. We have not made up the losses we took at Yanamarca and Ancayaco."

"And Huascar?"

"Perhaps twice as many," Huallpa said, and hurried on when Coca caught her breath in shock. "But they are from everywhere, my lady, and not many from any one place. Some of the regiments are so mixed that we do not know what to call them . . ."

Though she tried not to show it, Micay was as dismayed as her niece by the numbers. The Quitos had won five victories since Caxamarca, and they had killed many more than they had lost in each of the battles. Micay had seen the battlefield at Yanamarca, where Quilaco had been wounded, and the carnage had been even more appalling than that at Ambato. It seemed impossible they should be outnumbered again.

"I have heard that Huascar—" she began, but the young people suddenly glanced past her and bowed, displaying a deference that struck Micay as peculiar since she knew it had to be Cusi who was coming. Even Cahua hesitated slightly before going to him, and Micay let herself feel his presence before turning to look. He had given his hand to Cahua, and he bared his teeth to the rest of them in what he must have thought was a smile, though there was no warmth or pleasure in it.

"We came back with the final count," he explained needlessly, and the smile transformed itself into a scowl. "And because we hoped Atauhuallpa might have sent us some of his warriors. But there have been no messages," he added, looking at Micay as if he wished to be contradicted. She could only shake her head in agreement.

"How long can you stay, Father?" Cahua asked, and Micay was astonished when he actually glanced out at the sun, which was sinking behind a bank of threatening clouds.

"At least for the night," Micay said sharply, hoping to jar him out of his preoccupation. But he seemed to take the suggestion seriously.

"It looks like rain, so we might as well. Is there food for the men?"

"It is coming," Micay told him. "The retainers know how to feed warriors."

"Of course," he agreed absently. Then he squinted at her, as if finally perceiving her annoyance. "I must talk with you, Micay . . ."

"Yes. But take back your weapon first so Huallpa can sit and eat with the others."

Cusi had to let go of Cahua to take the battle-ax, but since he had not been paying any attention to her anyway, she willingly went back to Ococo.

"Tell your captain he is in command," Micay said to Huallpa. Then she took Cusi by the arm holding his shield and led him out of the awning house, into the first scattered drops of rain.

"Where are you taking me?" he complained, pulling back against her lead. "I need to make a map for you."

Micay shook her head impatiently, propelling him down a passageway between two of the buildings. "A map of what?"

"Of the trails to Machu Picchu and Vitcos. In case we are pushed back from the river."

"Why would that happen?" Micay inquired sarcastically. "Because you are outnumbered two to one? Or because Huanacauri has promised Huascar a victory if he leads his warriors in person?"

"So you heard that lie," Cusi concluded, but Micay did not respond. Machacuay was squatting outside the storeroom, and he jumped up and moved away from the doorway so Micay could inspect his handiwork. He had swept the tiny room clean and laid out a bed of llama skins and blankets on the floor; he had also supplied them with dishes of food and a jar of akha and a bowl of blue and yellow flowers. Micay smiled at him in gratitude, feeling the rightness of her original impulse.

"Shall I see no one disturbs you?" Machacuay offered, and at her nod he went off to guard the end of the passageway. She went into the room without waiting for Cusi, who stood blinking up at the rain for a few moments before following her in. She took his shield and battle-ax from him and propped them up in a corner, then unpinned her mantle and began to untie her headcloth.

"You could not have known I was coming," Cusi ventured, sounding bewildered. "It was Tomay's turn, actually, but he is still favoring his foot and did not want the extra march."

"I did not know you were coming," Micay admitted, dropping the head cloth on top of her mantle and smoothing back her hair with both hands. "But I knew how to respond to the sudden gift of my husband's company."

Cusi spread his hands in a helpless gesture, appearing pained. "Micay, I did not expect to be back here so soon. I had begun to prepare myself for battle . . ."

"No," Micay told him flatly. "No, I saw you gathering power to face

Huascar, and it was very different from what you are doing now. Now you are simply removing yourself, and you have been doing it ever since you saw Catiquilla destroyed."

Cusi's face seemed to close at the mention of Catiquilla, and his voice was icy. "Perhaps I have needed to. There has been no time to gather power and too many reasons to expend it. I cannot squander what little I have left."

"Perhaps you already have," Micay suggested unsparingly. "Your presence has grown thin and cold, and the children bow to you out of fear, not love. You do not even see them do it."

"I cannot think about children in the middle of a war!"

Micay turned and reached behind her to unlace her belt. She looked back at him over her shoulder. "Is that also true of your wife?"

The challenge seemed to bring him up short, and he blew air through his nose and sat down on the bed.

"Why are you telling me this now?" he asked plaintively, and Micay slipped off her sandals and sat down beside him, her shift tenting loosely around her. She put her hands on his arm, feeling the jagged outline of the scar he had received in Tumibamba.

"Because I was given the chance," she said more gently. "When I saw you today, I simply wanted you. The war had released you to me for one night, and I knew how we should use it. But then you started talking to me about a map to Vitcos without first telling me about the fears that made you think a map was necessary, and I realized just how distant you had become. I decided I had to bring you back."

"For one night?" Cusi murmured incredulously. "And then you would send me back to battle?"

"I would send you back stronger," Micay insisted, giving his arm a slight shake. "Do you remember how we made love before you went to Calca? Did that weaken you? Or did your passion make you fight to stay alive? You have forgotten the many ways there are to gather power."

Letting go of his arm, she lifted up his tunic and began to untie his waistband while he looked on in bemusement. She pulled the woven band free and fished the slender piece of reddish-amber stone out of its hidden pocket. She briefly held it against her cheek and then put it into his hand.

"Here is one, and it is warm. Blunted from being used as a weapon, but still warm."

She let him look at it for a few moments, then reached up and carefully removed his golden earplugs and the Iñaca headband and placed them in his cupped hands along with the spirit brother. "Those once belonged to Pachacuti, the greatest of the Incas. They came to you from him, but also from Tocto Oxica, who has never stopped loving you. And your battle-ax," she added, pointing toward the corner with her chin, "the gift of Otoronco Achachi, who loved you more than he loved any other Inca. How long has it been, Cusi, since you let yourself feel their power?"

He stared down at the collection in his hands, then at his shield and weapon, then at her. Tears welled up in his eyes and his voice shook, spilling them down his cheeks.

"Micay . . . if you make me feel again, I will have to feel all the pain and suffering, the loss of those who will die."

"But if you do not feel any of that," Micay asked him quietly, "how can you believe you are facing death with your whole being? What will keep you fighting when your anger and determination are exhausted?"

"They *are* exhausted," Cusi groaned, tilting his head back and closing his eyes in a vain attempt to stop the flow of tears. Micay put her arms around him and lowered them both down onto the blankets.

"Then you must rely on your comrades," she whispered. "You must draw your power from the caring that binds all of us together. That is the only thing that can still sustain us."

He briefly turned away from her and emptied his hands onto the blankets behind him, then came back into her embrace. Micay fit herself to him, then slipped the knot at her shoulder and wriggled out of her shift, and helped him remove his tunic and loincloth. She touched his wet cheeks with her fingertips, then moved down his body, pressing her lips against the scars that stood out like trails through the taut landscape of muscle and bone. He was only half erect when she took him into her mouth, but he swelled quickly as she teased back the foreskin with her tongue, employing a technique Fempellec had revealed to her long ago. Cusi murmured her name and stroked her hair with trembling, feathery hands, and when she finally raised her head, he drew her back to him and kissed her face and neck and breasts.

"Do not think again about maps," she told him. "We will all go to Vitcos together when you are through. Think about how much we want you with us. Let that give you the power to return."

"I will return," he vowed in a thick voice, and he tried to pull her over on top of him. But Micay slid away and rose to her knees, turning to look back at him over her shoulder.

"I want you behind me, comrade," she said, reaching a hand back between her legs as he brought himself up against her. "But very close, and very deep . . ."

Cotapampa

SINCE THERE HAD never been much hope that Atauhuallpa would part with any of the warriors he had kept with him in Caxamarca, Quizquiz and Challcochima had already formulated their strategy before Cusi returned to confirm their expectations. In truth, Huascar had left them little choice. He had emptied the storehouses and removed the herds from the area the Quitos now occupied, so their supplies were running low, limiting their ability to wait. He had also stationed his warriors on the high ground along the western bank of the Apurimac River, concentrating them around the only two crossings, and he had refused to be lured down into a battle in the open. Whether he was being shrewd or cowardly did not truly matter; either way he was forcing the Quitos to attack his much larger force head on.

The first crossing was the sacred bridge that spanned the deep gorge of the Apurimac at Corahuasi. Since the bridge could be approached only by means of a long tunnel through the rock, it was easily defended and easily destroyed if in danger of being taken. The second crossing, at Cotapampa, was more open to attack, and here Huascar had deployed the bulk of his recently recruited troops, maintaining a sizable force on both sides of the river. The Quito plan was for Ucumari to put pressure on the Corahuasi crossing with a token force of a few thousand men while Quizquiz and Rumiñaui led the main body of warriors in a direct attack on the defenders of the Cotapampa bridge. In their only attempt at a surprise, Challcochima was to lead five thousand men south to Huanacopampa and then circle back to attack Huascar's left flank.

The Hawk Men had been made the vanguard of Challcochima's column, and they marched out at first light, concealed by hills that were well behind the Quito lines. The bunch grass was high and green, as were the smaller grasses that grew in between and were usually cropped by the herds of llamas and alpacas. Many of the fields they passed had been planted, but the crops were dying from a lack of water or were being choked out by weeds. There were no people to be seen anywhere.

Their route soon took them into territory that had not been adequately scouted and where there were many high places from which they could be seen. Cusi felt watched on more than one occasion, but there was nothing to be done about it. They were relying on speed more than stealth, gambling that they could outmanuever or fight their way past any force that was sent out in haste to intercept them. So they marched at a fear-driven pace and prayed that no one had already been sent out to lie in wait behind the next hill.

Cusi frequently fell back and then caught up again, urging his men to maintain their vigilance and keep the squadrons tight and in close touch with one another. He did the same with Tomay's men, who were marching in double file alongside his own, the two regiments separated by a narrow aisle of open space. A few of the captains seemed to resent his interference, but the rest understood what he was doing and why Tomay could not do it himself.

Cusi worked his way up the central aisle, rapping shields with his weapon and bantering with the men he knew, deliberately meting out recognition as well as commands. Judging from the effect he was having, Tomay's men were even more starved for attention than his own.

Tomay was limping along manfully at the head of the column, his shield strapped to his back and his spear held upright like a staff. His right foot had been heavily wrapped and padded, but he still could not put his full weight upon it. His single earplug dangled on Cusi's side, casting golden reflections across the broad planes of his face.

"You have the rank to be carried in a hammock," Cusi suggested half seriously. "We could make one for you easily enough."

"I can march," Tomay assured him gruffly. "I can even run if I have to. It is more tender than painful."

Cusi doubted he could run far, but he knew better than to force the issue. And he was struck by how well the description fit the way he was feeling himself: more tender than painful. He was keenly aware of what the men were feeling—the daily battle each of them had to wage against fear, fatigue, injury, and utter war weariness—and it disturbed him to have to ask even more of them when all he could offer in return were gestures of appreciation and encouragement. Yet he made the gestures anyway and saw their effect on the men's spirits, and he had to accept that it was better than the cold, impersonal exercise of command.

He had tried to explain to Tomay the conversion that Micay had wrought in him in Abancay, but his friend was preoccupied with his foot in addition to being generally resistant to inspiration. His men had begun to display a similarly dour attitude, and Cusi was trying to think of a way to warn him about that when Tomay suddenly spoke up, leaning toward Cusi so they would not be overheard by the men ahead and behind.

"I dreamed last night that we met Rimachi in battle."

Cusi drew a long breath. "I have been wondering about him, though not in my dreams. What happened?"

"We fought furiously, but we were the same size and we could not hurt each other. I hated him, though; I wanted to kill him," Tomay said, and he swallowed hard. "Then something frightened him and he ran away, and other things happened. When I saw him again we were sitting on top of Punishment Hill, and we were boys again. We were waiting for you, and we were laughing because you were in trouble again and Sumac Mallqui was making you run the hill. We were going to run back down with you, but the dream ended before you arrived."

Cusi shook his head in astonishment, stirred by the memory of the boyhood they had shared. "It seems like a good omen," he ventured, and Tomay shrugged with a force that threw him off stride and made him hop and use his spear as a crutch.

"Neither of us died," Tomay allowed, "but we were enemies. I do not expect we will be boys when we meet again."

"Perhaps it is a sign that you must remind him if you do meet in battle. I do not think I could fight him even if he attacked me first. I would have no heart left if I killed him."

"You would be lucky to kill him," Tomay said harshly, "given the size he really is. But you would try if you had to. Who else has a chance of matching him?"

"No," Cusi said, and he stepped out into the aisle between the regiments without breaking gait. "I will not let myself be the one. Neither must you."

"We will all do what we have to," Tomay told him as they parted. "Just make sure that you are the brother who lives . . ."

BY LATE AFTERNOON they were almost to the place where they would emerge from the hills and circle north to join the attack. Cusi could see it ahead at the end of this ever-narrowing valley, which was now no wider than a ravine. The rocky creek bed at the bottom had forced the regiments to split, each moving up the slope in search of some semilevel ground on which to march. The recent rains had softened the earth and made the footing treacherous, and in places the slopes were so steep that the men had to dig in with their weapons to keep from sliding downward. They had already strapped their shields to their backs, because they intended to come out of this valley on the run and ready to break through an ambush.

When the ground leveled out slightly Cusi was able to glance across the ravine at Tomay, who was traversing his slope by sliding himself along on one knee. His method actually appeared easier than trying to walk upright, and Cusi smiled to himself, reassured that his friend would find some way to run if he had to. He glanced ahead just as Tarapaca slipped and his outside leg shot out sideways, kicking loose a shower of mud and stones. Cusi grabbed the back of his tunic with his free hand and held him just long enough for Tarapaca to sink his spear into the hillside and pull himself back. Tarapaca started moving again before glancing over his shoulder at Cusi.

"I think I am awake now," he muttered, and Cusi laughed softly as he gestured to the men behind him to watch their step. He froze in midgesture as the stillness was shattered by a chorus of wild screams and a wave of warriors swept over the crest of the opposite ridge and literally flung themselves down onto Tomay's men, tumbling like rocks all the way to the bottom. Cusi saw Tomay spear one man from his knees and then go down under three more, their war clubs rising and falling.

In an instant the opposite slope had been swept clean of Hawk Men, and more of the enemy were pouring down over the ridge. Cusi tore his eyes away from the place where Tomay had been and gestured with his battle-ax.

"Up to the top!" he shouted, and he started scrambling up the slope, feeling the wind as a dart flew past his shoulder and embedded itself in the ground. The enemy was not far behind when he and his men reached the ridge and turned to fight, and Cusi saw that most of them were Collas. Tears of anger flashed briefly at the edges of his vision, and then he took a two-handed grip on his battle-ax and swung with all his might at the first man who came into range, sending him rolling back down the hill.

"Tomay!" he screamed, and he fought on with a ferocity that stiffened the will of the warriors along the ridge, though it was a long time before he was able to notice.

Abancay

THE MAN had come from the north at the head of a pack train loaded with spare weapons, Atauhuallpa's belated contribution to the war. Micay noticed that he was not carrying the cords for the pack train and that while he wore the large earplugs of an Inca warrior, he had only one arm. A messenger, she guessed, watching as he spoke to the captain of the warriors stationed in the rest house and then started toward the awning house where she and the other women were packing splints and bandages and filling their medicine bags. They looked up at him curiously as he came in under the roof, blinking at the sudden dimness.

"I was told that the wife of the war chief Cusi Huaman was here," he said awkwardly, and Micay inclined her head in greeting.

"I am Mama Micay, the wife of Cusi Huaman. This is Ñupchu, the wife of the war chief Tomay Guanaco."

"I fought with them both against the Carangui," the man said, bowing to each of them. "My name is Poma Mallqui. I have come from Caxamarca with a message for the war chiefs, but I am told it is too late to go to them in the field."

"The battle has begun," Micay confirmed. "We have been waiting for messengers from the other direction."

Poma Mallqui rubbed his chin and grimaced. "I will have to wait with you, then, though I had hoped not to linger. My own wife and family are in Tumbez, and I have not seen them in many months."

"Perhaps I could convey the message for you," Micay suggested. "The war chiefs know me and would trust my word."

"It is not pleasant news," the man warned, though he was clearly tempted by her offer. "It concerns the Bearded Ones. The Viracochas."

Micay motioned for him to sit, and her lack of hesitation seemed to decide him. He sat and drank from the water gourd Ñupchu handed him.

"The last we heard," Micay reported, "they had landed their floating houses at a place on the coast called Coaque, somewhere north of Manta."

"They are in Tumbez," Poma Mallqui told her. "At least that is where they were when I saw them."

"Did they come there in peace?" Micay asked, and he cocked his head as if there were no simple answer to the question.

"No one opposed their coming," he said with a shrug. "You see, after Atauhuallpa went south the Punas attacked us and beat us badly. So we were very weak. And the Bearded Ones had already defeated the Punas and taken control of Puna Island."

"They took Puna?" Ñupchu blurted in surprise. "How many of them are there?"

"Only about two hundred."

"You are teasing us," Micay suggested. "Who fights with them?"

"They have taken on some porters and a couple of men they have taught to speak their tongue, but no warriors. They do not need them. They have weapons, like fat blowpipes made of metal, that spit thunder and balls of lightning. They can destroy a wall or anything else that stands in their way. And the Bearded Ones wear helmets and armor made of the same metal, which repels stones and darts. Their clubs and spears cut like obsidian yet are harder than stone."

Micay heard something like satisfaction in his voice, as if he had some need to shock them. She stared back at him steadily, having heard most of these things before, and he raised his chin as if taking up the challenge.

"As I said, there are only two hundred of them, yet they have some . . . *beasts* with them who are more frightening than any warrior. They are twice the size of llamas and very fierce: they can run like the wind and kill with their feet and their teeth. Yet they let the Bearded Ones sit upon their backs and carry them wherever they wish to go."

Micay tried to imagine a giant llama with claws and fangs and a man on its back, but it was too fantastic. A sudden commotion to her right made her turn to see Machacuay crumpled over in a faint, and she nodded gratefully when Cahua signaled that she would tend to him. She looked back at Poma Mallqui, who seemed to be savoring the stunned silence his words had produced.

"What did Atauhuallpa say about this?" she asked, and his satisfaction vanished so abruptly that she understood why he had been forced to seek it here.

"He said nothing. He only listened and then told me to come here and tell the war chiefs."

"I will tell them for you," Micay promised. "I am certain they will be more moved by this news than Atauhuallpa was."

Poma Mallqui bared his teeth in a crooked smile, appearing both apologetic and grateful. "I have walked a long way to tell about what I saw, my lady. I have not seen the Bearded Ones fight, but I have seen and heard enough to make me fear them."

Micay gave him a respectful nod, noticing out of the corner of her eye that several of the women near the open side of the awning house had risen and gone out into the courtyard. She had also been aware for some time of the odor of something burning, and suddenly the smell was so strong that it stung her nostrils.

"Grass fire," Poma Mallqui exclaimed softly, and they all rose and started for the courtyard. The sky was the deep orange-red of sunset, and far to the south they could see black smoke rising in a ragged, billowing sheet.

"It is a trick Tomay and Cusi have used many times," Ñupchu murmured hopefully, though she did not look around to see if anyone agreed. Micay lifted her face to the wind and realized with a sinking feeling that it was blowing from the east. It would be in their faces if they were advancing toward the river, at their backs if they were retreating. The smoke seemed to hang in the air like an evil omen, and finally Micay had to turn her eyes away. She found Coca beside her, and when their eyes met the girl shuddered and hung her head, resting her chin on her clasped hands.

"This is my fault, my lady," she whispered abjectly, and Micay put an arm around her and drew her close.

"No, my daughter," she soothed her. "I had already forgiven you your promise before you broke it. Your love cannot hurt either of you anymore."

Coca buried her face in Micay's mantle, sobbing incoherently. Over the girl's head she saw Poma Mallqui regarding her with a tentative expression on his long face, as if he felt he might be to blame for upsetting her.

"No doubt my message can wait," he suggested, and Micay could only nod in agreement.

"We have enough enemies already. For now let us worry about the ones who are in front of us . . ."

Huanacopampa

T HE WAR CHIEFS held their council in a rough mud and stone enclosure that must have belonged to one of the royal herdsmen, because it still smelled of llamas and there was plenty of dried dung for their fires. Cusi sat next to Challchochima, Quizquiz sat by himself, and Rumiñaui sat close to the litter that held Ticci Capac. Atauhuallpa had sent his spirit brother along to inspire them, but until now it had mostly been carried in the rear. The bands and pockets of gold set into the stone caught the firelight and threw the maze of ridges and crevices around them into even deeper shadow. It seemed devious in its impenetrability, useless at a time when tricks could not save them.

Without much discussion or argument the four men quickly decided most of what was still in their power to decide. They had gathered all the warriors left to them, except for Ucumari's force on the Royal Road. There was no point in retreating any further or in trying to establish defenses among the hills where they had been driven to ground, because they did not have the strength or the supplies for either. They would simply have to fight when Huascar finally came to finish them off. No one could understand why he had already given them two days to recover from their defeat, though no doubt the scouts and raiding parties who kept the Quitos under constant harassment had told him how few they were.

When the order of battle had been determined, most of the lesser war chiefs left and Quizquiz got up and began to pace restlessly around the compound. Challcochima went to join him, leaving Cusi to feel the absence of Tomay and Quilaco. Quilaco now seemed like the fortunate one, despite the seriousness of the wound that had forced them to leave him behind in Yanamarca. If the chosen woman tending him were resourceful, he might be able to escape Huascar's revenge, perhaps even make it to Vitcos. It appeared unlikely that the rest of them would be so lucky, and Cusi wished Micay had allowed him to make her a map.

Rumiñaui was motioning to him, inviting him to come closer to Ticci Capac, but Cusi simply looked back at him and shook his head. Atauhuallpa should be here to die with us, he thought, restraining himself from saying it aloud only because he refused to accept his own death. Rumiñaui scowled at him and then made an awkward pretense of praying to the spirit brother, giving up when Quizquiz and Challcochima came back and sat down across from him.

"Bring him in," Quizquiz said curtly, and Rumiñaui drew a consenting nod from Challcochima before beckoning to a man who was squatting in the doorway of the house behind them. As the man came forward Cusi saw that his head was wrapped in red cloth and he was carrying a pair of small braziers and a long bronze tube that was blackened at one end, the headdress and implements of a Huaro yacarca, a fire reader. Cusi drew a sharp breath, smelling the scorched odor of his own clothing, and he looked down at the patches of glistening grease that covered the burns on his legs and feet. Then he picked up his shield and battle-ax and rose to his feet, startling the fire reader, who had set down the braziers and was filling them with tinder from the coca bag under his arm.

"Do you have something better than this, Cusi?" Challcochima inquired, allowing an uncharacteristic note of pleading to creep into his voice. Cusi shook his head.

"No. But I have had enough of fire."

"We must know if we still have a chance," Rumiñaui insisted.

"And what if he tells you we have none?" Cusi asked. "Do you lie down and die, or have him killed for telling you? We will know soon enough if we have a chance."

With that Cusi turned and walked out of the enclosure, leaving the fire reader in a visibly frightened state. He turned right and followed the line of the ridge back toward the tents of the Hawk Men. There were less than a thousand of them left, including the handful of survivors from Tomay's regiment. What they had encountered in the ravine was not merely an ambush but a major flanking movement by thousands of Huascar's troops. Quizquiz had seen it happening and had disengaged at Cotapampa and brought his warriors south in support, arriving just as Cusi and Challcochima were on the verge of being overrun. They had counterattacked and driven Huascar's men back out of the hills, scattering them across the plain at Huanacopampa. The Quitos had just regrouped and begun their pursuit when they saw the wall of fire sweeping toward them, pushed by a wind that had already dried out the tall grass. The Hawk Men had been in the rear at that point, but they had still lost men to the smoke and flames, and others had drowned in the desperate flight across the Cotapampa River. It was the kind of defeat that caused everyone to wonder if Huascar were indeed being guided by Huanacauri, and that made the war chiefs turn to fire readers for signs of hope.

Cusi had of course had no chance to grieve for Tomay, though his loss was with him at every moment, a hollow ache beneath his heart. It hurt most of all to have been close enough to see him killed, yet too far to be of any help. By retreating up to the ridge, he had done what he had to do, just as Tomay had said he would, but it did not make him feel any less like a comrade who had failed.

As he came up on his own camp, he was challenged by a sentry who turned out to be Huallpa. Cusi took that as a good sign, since the boy had nearly drowned crossing the river and had been unable to stand alone the last time Cusi had seen him.

"It is good to see you on your feet, my son," Cusi told him. "Huascar's hesitation has been our gain."

Huallpa coughed into his hand. "I could use another day if he will give it to us."

The high, skirling cry of a hawk suddenly sounded from the darkness to their left, and they crouched down behind their shields and stared down at the trail that zigzagged up the slope from the gully below. They saw the shapes of at least ten men, moving in a mass, and as the group ascended into the moonlight Cusi and Huallpa both recognized the captive being pushed along in their midst. His angular face was unmistakable, sticking out above all the heads around him.

"So he has finally come over to us," Cusi murmured, drawing a skeptical grunt from Huallpa. The captors were one of the squadrons Cusi had deployed as forward sentries, and their captain greeted him with a mixture of eagerness and bemusement.

"My lord . . . this man told us to bring him to you. He led a raiding party into our ambush, then held us off by himself while his companions escaped. When they were gone, he screamed as if he had been stabbed and then put down his weapons and asked for you."

"They are well trained, Cusi," Rimachi said from behind the captain. "They only beat me a little."

"He wounded four of my men," the captain protested, but Cusi simply nodded and gestured to the other warriors with his battle-ax.

"Let him go. He is my brother."

It took the warriors several moments to cut all the bonds they had used to secure Rimachi, and they stood back with their weapons raised warily when he shrugged off the last of the ropes and came forward to meet Cusi.

"Why now, Rimachi?" Cusi asked, and Rimachi glanced once at Huallpa before looking down his long nose at Cusi.

"I saw Tomay," he said brusquely.

"Alive?"

"No. Only his head . . . impaled on the point of a spear. I carried it for a while myself before I learned who it was. He had only one earplug and half a scalp, and his face was all bloody, but the Collas who killed him knew who he was. So did I when I looked. Huascar sent the head back to Cuzco to be made into a drinking cup."

Cusi's voice was harsh, once he could bring himself to speak. "So you defected. He would be gratified to know his death accomplished that much."

"I do not expect to be accepted in his place," Rimachi said with equal harshness. "But I know Huascar's plans. I can give him to you."

Cusi swallowed and cleared his throat, feeling he could laugh or weep at any moment, though he wanted to do neither. "Nothing could mean more to us," he managed. "I will take you to Quizquiz and Challcochima."

"You come, too," Rimachi said to Huallpa, who was staring at him with unmitigated suspicion and dislike. Cusi gestured for one of the other men to take the boy's place and then led the two of them back the way he had come, wondering if it was hope he felt stirring in the hollow place beneath his heart.

WHEN THE first of the enemy scouts appeared below, groping his way through the mist that shrouded the bottom of the ravine, Cusi had to swallow the urge to let out a whoop. He turned his head toward Rimachi, who was lying flat on the ground beside him, and received a disdainful smile that mocked him for not having believed sooner. Letting out a careful breath, Cusi glanced over his shoulder and nodded to Huaman Cachi, who grinned in amazement and then crept back over the ridge to take the news to Quizquiz and Challcochima. Cusi again trained his attention on the file of men passing below, counting thirty and making certain no more lagged behind. Then he whistled once, and the Hawk Men on both sides of the ravine sprang silently from their hiding places and fell on the scouts, cutting them down with ruthless efficiency. Only a few dying screams broke the dawn stillness, and then the Hawk Men backed away, leaving one man standing over each body with his weapon raised so that Cusi could count them. When he had all thirty, Cusi stood up and waved his battle-ax, and the Hawk Men began to climb back up both slopes, leaving the dead where they lay.

"Well trained," Rimachi murmured admiringly as he and Cusi went up over the ridge and began to march in the direction from which the scouts had come. According to the plan Rimachi had revealed to them the night before, the scouts would be followed at a distance by five thousand of Huascar's best warriors, led by Huascar himself. The ravine would bring them out behind the Quitos' main camp, at which point they would attack with the specific purpose of capturing or killing Quizquiz and Challchochima, thus bringing the war to a swift and glorious conclusion. It was a plan worthy of a warlord, which was why the Quito war chiefs had been reluctant to believe that Huascar had conceived it and would actually carry it out. They had needed some proof before they took the risk of diverting a large force from the front lines, and the scouts had just now provided that.

"But will he truly risk himself?" Cusi wondered aloud.

Rimachi clicked his tongue impatiently. "I *told* you, and the rest of them: He believes Huanacauri is guiding him to a certain victory, and he does not wish to share the glory with anyone else. If you had heard him speak, you would have thought he had killed Tomay with his own hands. He will come."

Cusi glanced back past his own men and saw Challcochima's warriors coming up onto the ridge, almost running in their eagerness to catch up. "His victory did seem certain," Cusi admitted, looking up at Rimachi. "Until you came. Perhaps Huanacauri was guiding both of you . . ."

Rimachi snorted derisively. "It was no god that made me feel sick to be alive. I earned that myself. Now I have betrayed everyone, including my wives and children."

"What do you mean?" Cusi asked, but Rimachi chose not to reply. They had reached the place they had scouted earlier, so Cusi had to turn away to put his men into place, reminding them that they must not be seen or heard until Huascar had marched past them into the trap. For the first time in months they obeyed his commands with real enthusiasm, smiling at each other as they unwrapped their slings and began to gather rocks.

Accompanied by Huaman Cachi, Challcochima soon brought his warriors in behind the Hawk Men, waving them down as he came forward to where Cusi and Rimachi were standing. The three of them crouched down in the space that had been left in the midst of Piqui's squadron.

"So it is happening," Challcochima blurted out, unable to contain his excitement. "I still cannot believe it."

"You should have trusted the fire reader if you could not trust me," Rimachi suggested. "Huascar's flame flickered out, did it not?"

Challcochima gave him a hard stare, then decided to ignore the taunt. "If he comes himself, we will snuff it out for good," he declared. Then he left them to go consult with his commanders.

"It was not you he doubted," Cusi said to Rimachi. "It was Huascar. And it is Huascar you have betrayed, not your wives and children."

Rimachi pretended to examine the well-worn groove in his spear thrower before looking up at Cusi. "When they brought me in, you called me your brother. Do I still have the right to ask a favor of you?"

"Of course. What do you want?"

"Find Quespi and Tusoc and our children when you get to Cuzco. Take them out of the Cañari quarter before any harm can come to them."

"You can do that yourself," Cusi told him. "Together we might be able to protect the whole quarter."

"I cannot go back to Cuzco," Rimachi said flatly. "Just promise me that you will look after my family."

"I have already lost one brother," Cusi protested, but Rimachi waved the spear thrower in front of his face to stop him.

"Promise me, Cusi. I deserve to lose them, but they do not deserve to be lost."

Cusi was aware of the silent men around him, especially Huallpa, who was regarding Rimachi through narrowed eyes. Cusi caught the boy's gaze, encouraging him to speak, but Huallpa looked down at the ground instead. Cusi sighed and nodded to Rimachi.

"You have my promise."

"Good. Let us rest now until it is time to avenge Tomay's death," Rimachi said, and they settled down in silence to wait for Huascar to appear.

THEY HAD stationed themselves at a bend in the ravine, so Cusi heard the tramp and shuffle of sandaled feet for some time before the first warriors came into his line of sight, which was greatly limited by his own desire not to be seen. The vanguard were mostly golden-eared Incas by privilege, marching four abreast at a pace that quickly took them out of view. The first litter went by so fast he almost missed it, and only after it was past did he realize that the motionless bundle of rich cloth it carried was Huanacauri. The second litter was larger and more elaborate, with a wooden canopy over the high-backed seat on which Huascar sat with a golden-headed battle-ax across his lap. The warriors around his litter were a mixture of Cañaris, Chachapoyas, and Incas, and bringing up the rear was a regiment of mitmacs from various tribes, more Incas, and a contingent of Collas. The sight of the latter brought a snarl to Cusi's face and made his heart race, anticipating revenge.

The swiftness with which they passed bespoke a confidence that bordered on blind arrogance, and Cusi soon felt a tap on his foot, indicating that the last of the column had gone around the next turning. He rose swiftly, as did the men around and behind him, because there was not much time before the vanguard came on the bodies of the scouts, which should jolt them out of their arrogance. If they were foolish enough to press on, they would find Quizquiz lying in wait ahead, but it was more likely they would have the sense to try to retreat.

Some of the Hawk Men found new hiding places along both sides of the ravine, and the rest crept up to just below the crest of the ridge, fitting stones and darts into their slings and spear throwers. Farther east, Challcochima led a large force down into the ravine and around the bend, where they could not be seen. Cusi had just dropped back down next to Rimachi when the sound of shouts and commotion echoed back down the ravine. The rear guard of Collas appeared moments later, moving fast and scanning the ridges with frantic vigilance. Cusi let them come past him, until they were almost to the bend and Huascar's litter was again visible farther down the ravine.

"Tomay Guanaco!" Cusi yelled, rising up and slinging the first stone in a single motion. Before he could hear it hit, the Hawk Men around him rose up with a roar and sent down a hail of stones and darts that thinned the Colla ranks and made them scatter in confusion. Those who tried to climb the slopes found Hawk Men waiting to finish them off, and those who continued forward were thrown back and trampled down as Challcochima's warriors came charging around the bend to join the battle. Huascar's litter made a hasty turn and proceeded in the opposite direction, leaving the rear guard to fight and die as Challcochima surged forward in pursuit and the Hawk Men ran along both ridges, hurling down stones and darts and preventing any escape from the ravine.

As Cusi drew even with the place where they had killed the scouts, he saw Huascar's litter stalled directly below with his guard trying to form a defensive circle around it. A tremendous noise ahead told him that the Cuzco vanguard had run headlong into the ambush Quizquiz had prepared for them. It was time to go down into the fighting, and Cusi wrapped his sling around his forehead again and unstrapped his battle-ax. Beside him Rimachi hurled his last dart with a force that made it sing, then tossed the spear thrower aside and pulled out the war club he had carried inside the straps of his shield. He gave Cusi a smile that was wild and reckless.

"Farewell, Cusi Huaman. Live long, my brother," he said, and before Cusi could decide whether to try to stop him, Huallpa stepped into Rimachi's path, pointing a spear at his chest.

"My mother would want you to live and come back to her," the boy said. Rimachi lowered his weapon, staring at him in astonishment. Cusi signaled Tarapaca to lead the men down while he stayed behind with Piqui and Huaman Cachi and the rest of Huallpa's squadron.

"I cannot go back," Rimachi said. "I have delivered my own people to their enemy."

"I have done that," Huallpa snarled. "You can find the courage to bear it."

Rimachi cast a seemingly helpless glance at Cusi, then suddenly came up with his war club, intending to knock the spear away. But Huallpa jerked the weapon out of the way and brought it back just as quickly, so that the flint tip touched the base of Rimachi's throat and made him recoil.

"I want you to come back with us," Huallpa said insistently. "I cannot count on having another father."

Rimachi glanced at Cusi again, appearing sincerely bewildered.

"Decide," Cusi told him. "We are losing our chance to be the first to Huascar."

Rimachi straightened up to his full height and pushed his chest out against the spear point, staring down the shaft at Huallpa. "Would you kill me yourself?" he demanded, and Huallpa faltered and drew back, aiming the spear at Rimachi's midsection.

"No," he admitted. "But I would wound you so that you could not walk to your own death."

Rimachi stared at him for another moment, then threw back his head and laughed. "You may spare me that. Come, my son," he said, stepping forward so that Huallpa had to turn with him toward the ravine, "let us go down together and put an end to the man who brought all of this upon us . . ."

CHALLCOCHIMA was the first to reach Huascar, leaping up out of the milling crowd to pull the ruler out of his litter and throw him down into the dust. The remaining members of his guard immediately tried to surrender but were cut down where they stood; only the litter bearers and one Inca commander were spared. Huascar was bound and turned over to Quizquiz for keeping, and Challcochima climbed up into the litter, carrying the golden battle-ax and the fringe he had snatched from Huascar's head. Cusi and Rimachi and all the other available golden-ears put on the white helmets and armbands Huascar's men had worn and formed themselves into a replica of the Cuzco vanguard, with Huanacauri carried like a trophy in their midst. The Hawk Men and the rest of Challcochima's warriors took places around and behind the royal litter, Challcochima pulled down the curtains around his seat, and the column marched forward out of the ravine, over the bodies of Huascar's five thousand.

The column passed through the Quito lines from behind, and though the warriors had been warned not to cheer or otherwise reveal their triumph, that did not stop them from raising their weapons and humming fiercely in approval. Cusi had taken a place beside Huanacauri's litter, and the air around the huaca seemed to vibrate with a rougher, less grateful version of that same hum, as if Huanacauri were gloating. Cusi remembered carrying the litter into the square in Tumibamba, and he wondered if this war had not begun on that very day, when the Sapa Inca and his warriors stood apart from one another for the first time. Huascar should have known not to trust a war huaca he had never served in battle.

They came down out of the hills, stopping once to change bearers, and then marched out onto the burned-over plain of Huanacopampa, where only days before they had been sent fleeing for their lives. The ash stirred up by their passage hung around them in a cloud, turning their skin gray and making it hard to breathe, and they had to step over the charred remains of shields and helmets and discarded weapons. Challcochima led them past the beginning of the fire line onto grass that had been trampled but not burned, before calling for a halt.

The hills ahead of them were completely covered with Huascar's warriors, and when the dust cleared and they could make out the royal litter in the midst of the procession, they began to cheer and wave their weapons and banners, so that the hills themselves seemed to undulate in triumph. Challcochima threw back the curtains around his seat and lifted the golden battle-ax over his head, and the warriors on the hills went into a frenzy of celebration, some of them starting down toward the plain to meet their ruler. Challcochima let out a derisive laugh and had the captured Inca commander brought to the foot of the litter. He displayed Huascar's fringe, which had been dirtied and spat on and stained with the blood of the fallen, then threw it down to the man.

"Take that to your comrades and tell them what has happened," he commanded. "Tell them they are the next to die."

While the commander made his way toward the Cuzco lines at a lurching trot, Quizquiz and Rumiñaui brought the rest of the Quito forces down from the hills, stirring up a great cloud of ash and filling the plain behind the waiting column with warriors. Soon after the commander had reached the base of the hills, the cheering within the Cuzco ranks ceased, and those who had started down came to an abrupt halt. At this the Quitos let out a roar of their own, and Challcochima jumped down from the litter and had the bearers dump it over onto its side. The column spread out and became the front ranks as the Quitos began to advance, and Ticci Capac was brought forward to march alongside Huanacauri. The warriors on the hills split and began to flee, some heading north toward the bridge at Cotapampa and some south, out of the Quitos' most likely path.

"To Cuzco!" Challcochima shouted, waving the golden battle-ax, and the warriors of Atauhuallpa swept forward across the plain, rushing to claim their final victory.

Limatambo

WHEN THE stunning news of Huascar's capture came to him, Ucumari brought his warriors back from Abancay, where they had been poised for an expected flight north. He found the sacred bridge at Corahuasi unguarded, abandoned by its defenders, and he took possession of it with gratitude, adding his own offerings to those that Micay and Cahua took to the famous shrine of Pachamama that perched on the lip of the river gorge.

His progress up the Northern Quarter Road, however, was brought to an abrupt halt at Limatambo, where a regiment of Huascar's warriors had regrouped and blocked off the narrow entrance to the valley. After several days of stubborn fighting, Ucumari's men had pushed their way into the valley, but the Cuzcos still controlled the road from behind the defenses they had erected around the buildings of the royal rest house. Ucumari had sent a request for help to Quizquiz and Challcochima, who were advancing toward Cuzco on the Western Quarter Road to the south, but he had yet to receive a reply.

Ucumari was just preparing to send a second messenger when the help he sought arrived unannounced in the form of the Hawk Men. No one saw them until they attacked, and then they seemed to be everywhere, one group swooping down from the heights above the rest house while the main column came in along the Northern Quarter Road and struck the Cuzco defenses from the rear.

Micay was standing near Ucumari when he dismissed the messenger and waved his reserves forward, and she and her women advanced toward the rest house with him, their medicine bags and carrying bundles slung over their shoulders. They were still at a distance from the fighting when they saw something remarkable happen. The Hawk Men had overrun the barricades across the road and surrounded the men defending them, pressing them into a tight knot. Seeing the hopelessness of their situation, the Cuzcos lowered their weapons and begged for mercy. To the amazement of everyone watching, the Hawk Men backed off and let them surrender, disarming them and then leading them away from the barricades. They were made to sit out in the open, under guard but unmolested. The Hawk Men did not even bother to subject them to the beatings and humiliation that captives customarily endured.

From her vantage point Micay could not tell who was more shocked by this leniency, the Cuzcos or Ucumari and his men. There was a decided hesitation on both sides, and then the Cuzcos within the rest house began to wave white cloths and display their empty hands to their attackers. When Ucumari saw that the Hawk Men were accepting the surrender and taking more prisoners, he sent out an order to his own men to do the same. They complied reluctantly, compelled by the frustration of the last days to taunt and harass the prisoners as they herded them out onto the field across the road from the rest house. Micay had an awful moment in which she was struck by the fear that they were being gathered in order to be killed. But then she saw Tarapaca taking charge of the crowd, forming the prisoners into short columns and sending them off toward Cuzco between rows of armed guards.

Cusi was waiting in the road, and he glanced past Ucumari and smiled in greeting when he saw her. She was able to see that Piqui and Huaman Cachi were with him, though the men ahead prevented her from searching out Huallpa.

"Greetings, Cusi Huaman," Ucumari said. "I am grateful for your assistance. How long have we been taking prisoners? Or is that your own policy?"

Cusi laughed. "I spoke for it," he admitted. "But Quizquiz and Challcochima have told the Incas left in Cuzco that they will not be harmed if they surrender and pledge their loyalty to Atauhuallpa. They asked for three days to decide, and we granted them as much. In the meantime we send them all the men we capture, knowing they will speak for surrender."

"So you have not entered the city?"

"We are camped just above it at Quihuipay. The Cuzcos will give us their answer the day after tomorrow."

"We should march, then," Ucumari decided, and he turned to beckon to Micay and Ñupchu. "As you see, I have brought your wife and daughter and the wife of Tomay Guanaco."

Micay went forward at Ñupchu's side, and they were followed by the wives and daughters of the men in Tomay's regiment, all of whom had joined Ñupchu in mourning without knowing for certain if their husbands and fathers were dead. They still wore their hair loose, though since they had completed the first phase of mourning they no longer smeared their faces with ashes or exhibited their grief aloud. Cusi had put his shield and battle-ax aside, and he reached out and gently stroked the head of little Suchi, who was clinging to Ñupchu's neck.

"I am sorry, Ñupchu," he murmured, tears welling up in his eyes. "We were ambushed, and I could not go to help him. He died fighting, like the warrior he was." Cusi had to stop and blink back his tears before he could look past her and address the other women. "All of your husbands died bravely, like Hawk Men. Your welfare is my responsibility now, and I will see that you and your children have everything you need."

Huaman Cachi had come up on Ñupchu's other side to comfort her, and suddenly a large man threw his shadow over all of them. Micay gasped in disbelief when she recognized Rimachi's face beneath an unfamiliar helmet.

"We avenged his death, my lady," he said to Ñupchu. "We took Huascar in return."

Ñupchu nodded and bowed in gratitude, though she was weeping too hard to speak. The men stood awkwardly for a few moments. Then Huaman Cachi let Suchi climb onto his back and coaxed Ñupchu into motion, and they all turned to join the flow of warriors moving up the road. Cusi took one of Micay's bundles and slung it over his own shoulder, then took back his shield and weapon from the warrior who had been holding them. He was walking backwards, gesturing for Cahua and Ococo to come join them, when Micay showed him the tightly rolled sheet of leather she had carried with her from Abancay.

"What is that?"

"A map to Vitcos," Micay told him. "Ucumari drew it for me in Abancay."

Ucumari shrugged his broad, sloping shoulders in response to Cusi's glance. "I could see no hope for you, after the defeat at Huanacopampa, and I expected a hard retreat to Caxamarca. I urged Micay to go immediately, but she would not leave while you were still in the field. She never stopped believing you would find a way out."

"Neither did I," Cahua declared as she and Ococo came up beside Cusi. Coca was just behind them, and Micay was relieved to see that Huallpa was with her. He looked thin and haggard, but his eyes were very bright, and he widened them in recognition when Micay smiled in greeting. A moment later Cahua realized that the man walking ahead of her was Rimachi.

"Uncle Rimachi! Are you on our side again?"

Rimachi glanced back with a pained smile on his face, but before he could reply Huallpa spoke up from behind.

"He is!" the boy said proudly. "He has even joined the Hawk Men."

Micay glanced back at him in surprise, then ahead to Rimachi, who nodded and displayed the red and black shield on his arm. Cusi simply smiled, appearing to enjoy her bewilderment at this newfound alliance.

"Were you the one who gave us Huascar's plans?" Ucumari asked.

Rimachi gave an elaborate shrug. "I was the messenger," he allowed. "But Cusi tells me it was Huanacauri's doing, and I always defer to my brother in such matters."

Cusi snorted, smothering a laugh. "We took Huanacauri along with Huascar," he said to Ucumari. "That seemed to have been his intention."

"Is it over, then?" Ucumari asked. "Is there anyone left to fight?"

Micay started, drawing a swift glance from Cusi. But she did not think this was the time or place to tell him about the Bearded Ones. She shook her head, and he turned back to Ucumari.

"Only if the Cuzcos choose to die rather than surrender," he said flatly. Then he lifted his shield to urge them onward. "They will give us their answer very soon. Let us walk swiftly, so that we will be there to hear it for ourselves . . ."

Quihuipay

I T HAD RAINED during the night and turned sharply cooler, and as day broke the lingering clouds held the chill in the air. Not long after first light, a runner came back to the Quito camp to report that a line of men and women had emerged from the Haucaypata and begun the long climb up to Quihuipay. They were unarmed and had their heads bowed like mourners, and some of them were singing what sounded like a death song.

The Quito warriors cleared the field in which they had slept and took up positions around it, standing four deep with their weapons in their hands. Ticci Capac and Huanacauri were brought out on their litters and set down at the far end of the field, where Quizquiz, Challcochima, and the other war chiefs stood waiting. Micay and the other women filled part of the space left open behind the war chiefs, sharing it with the tight, vigilant cluster of guards who surrounded the captive Huascar.

While she waited Micay curled her arms inside her mantle and hugged herself to stay warm; it did not appear that Inti was going to bless this event with his warmth and light. Micay was at least confident there would not be a general massacre, if only because the war chiefs had yet to receive any instructions from Atauhuallpa, who might want certain people kept alive for his own purposes. Both Rumiñaui and Quizquiz claimed to have been given personal instructions by Atauhuallpa: Rumiñaui's were to discredit Huascar and challenge his right to the fringe; Quizquiz had been told to stand in Atauhuallpa's place and speak with the voice of the Apu Inca, putting fear and obedience into the hearts of his subjects. Challcochima was primarily interested in establishing their authority over Cuzco and the provinces beyond, and Cusi had allied himself with that cause, arguing that they should not squander any more of their strength on pointless killing. To support his argument he had brought Micay into their meeting to recount Poma Mallqui's information about the Bearded Ones. Though the other war chiefs had not seemed overly impressed during Micay's recitation, Cusi told her later that she had helped to turn them away from a more vindictive course.

The field was still empty when a squadron of Challcochima's men came around the outside and escorted a small group of women and children into the space behind the war chiefs. They were all members of Chuqui Huipa's court, and leading them was Cori Cuillor, Challcochima's wife. Cori looked dazed and forlorn and many years older than when Micay had seen her last, and she fell into Micay's arms when they met, shaking but apparently too drained to weep.

"Will he take us back, Micay?" she moaned.

"He must," Micay assured her. "Why else would he bring you here ahead of the others?"

"Chuqui must be spared, too," Cori insisted desperately. "She has been Huascar's victim more than anyone."

One of the warriors had returned with Challcochima, and he stood staring down at the two of them for a moment, his face stern and unforgiving.

"You have not been harmed?" he asked in a tone that was half accusing and half fearful, and Micay realized that he was really asking if she had been violated. Cori shook her head.

"Only in spirit. I have suffered most from missing my husband."

"Then why did you not leave when Micay did?"

Cori glanced at Micay in mute appeal, and Micay had to suppress a surge of guilt before she could reply. "We could not both abandon Chuqui, my lord. Cusi insisted on taking me away with him. Had you come in his place, I would surely have felt compelled to stay behind."

Challcochima looked back at Cori and rubbed his chin, frowning even as he relented. "I have missed you, too," he admitted. "All the other women stayed behind with the court. Wait here and I will find you when this is over."

"I have never stopped waiting for you," Cori said. Then she looked up and held out her hands, palms up, to him. "And my lord, if you can, see that Chuqui is treated with kindness. She is innocent, and she is not well."

"We will not touch her," Challcochima said gruffly, "but we cannot do anything for her, either. Atauhuallpa will decide what happens to her."

Cori shivered as they watched him return to his place behind the litters, and Micay put an arm around her waist to steady her.

"Does Chuqui still have her weapon?" Micay whispered.

Cori's eyes widened in comprehension before she shook her head. "Her mother stole it from her. Rahua Ocllo was afraid Chuqui would use it and leave her to face Huascar alone."

The warriors suddenly began to hum, and Micay looked out through the gap between Cusi and Challcochima and saw the Cuzco Incas coming into the field. They were wearing fine cumbi-cloth garments, and gold glittered from their wrists and necks and the dangling earplugs of the men, but their faces were downcast and their eyes never left the ground. They came in their household and clan groups and stayed together in clusters as they spread out over the field and squatted down in the grass.

When they were all contained within the enclosure of warriors, Quizquiz gestured brusquely, and men stationed around the perimeter waded in among the groups and began to pull out selected members, hauling them roughly toward the front, where they were thrown down on their faces. Most of those selected appeared to be high-ranking warriors, though the high priest, Challco Yupanqui, and several other priests were also among them.

Quizquiz stepped out in front of the litters and surveyed the supplicants, an expression of utter contempt on his narrow blade of a face. His voice had a hard, metallic ring as he addressed them.

"You have acclaimed a false ruler and taken up arms against the Apu Inca, and for that you should die and be left for the vultures. But in the name of Atauhuallpa I will forgive you for your crimes and allow you to live. You must bow and make the mocha to your ruler in Caxamarca, and to his spirit brother, Ticci Capac, Foundation Prince and Lord of the World. Show me that you are ashamed of your treason and grateful for the gift of your lives!"

While the Cuzcos abased themselves, plucking hairs from their eyebrows and blowing them toward Ticci Capac, Quizquiz gave another signal, and men carrying large rocks came out and dropped them onto the backs of some of the prostrate prisoners, crushing them against the earth. A few in the crowd raised their heads at the strangled screams of the victims, and Quizquiz's men quickly moved in to beat them down. Quizquiz stood with his arms crossed on his chest, pointing with his chin at anyone who faltered in his show of deference, which brought them an immediate beating.

"That is enough," Quizquiz finally decided, and the people in front of him collapsed in an exhausted heap. He turned his back on them and beckoned to Huascar's guards. "Bring him out."

Huascar was carried out tied to a frame made of poles and straw bundles, much like the frames used to stretch and cure hides. The guards stood him upright next to Quizquiz, facing out toward the crowd. Quizquiz pointed a finger at him rudely.

"Here is the one who called himself the Sapa Inca and brought you all this trouble. Here is the one who pretended to be the son of Inti and the favorite of Huanacauri. Huanacauri gave him back to us in disgust at his presumption!"

Quizquiz lifted his hands, and the warriors began to jeer and heckle, calling out insults until the war chief signaled for silence.

"This is the man who murdered Huayna Capac's trusted kinsmen," Quizquiz went on, walking out among the prisoners on the ground, "and the brothers Atauhuallpa sent as his ambassadors. Who gave this evil man the title of Sapa Inca? Who placed the fringe on his head?"

Quizquiz motioned to his men, and two of the prisoners were jerked roughly to their feet. They were both Sun priests, and the one Micay could see most clearly was Challco Yupanqui, the high priest. They were dragged up in front of Huascar, and Quizquiz addressed himself to the high priest, prodding him in the chest with his finger.

"Was it you, Challco Yupanqui?" he demanded. "You who were silent when the real high priest, Topa Yupanqui, was murdered. Speak—tell us by what authority you gave the fringe to a murderer."

Challco Yupanqui winced and tried to back away from the prodding finger, but his captors held him fast. Quizquiz balled his hand into a fist with one knuckle extended and was about to prod the priest with that when another voice spoke out. Micay realized it was Huascar's; she could see his head moving between the slats in the frame that held him.

"Tell him," he commanded. "Tell him that I am the rightful Sapa Inca."

With Quizquiz glaring in his face, Challco Yupanqui obeyed in a quavering voice, claiming that Inti himself had commanded him to invest Huascar with the fringe. "He is the son of the Coya and the appointed Heir of his father," the man finished, but Quizquiz's derisive laugh touched off another chorus of jeers from the warriors. Rumiñaui came out past the litters, pausing to spit on the ground in front of Huascar before turning to shout at the priest.

"You are a worthless liar! Mama Cusi Rimay was the Coya when Huascar was born—his mother was nothing! She is a faithless whore who betrayed Huayna Capac's wishes in order to help her miserable son. No one has ever regarded her as the true Coya, and she was despised in Tumibamba. Who can say Huayna Capac was the father when it could have been one of many others?"

There was more jeering and then a commotion in the crowd, and Micay saw Rahua Ocllo rise and walk forward, her hands clenched into fists and her face contorted with rage. The warriors gradually fell silent as she went past Rumiñaui and Quizquiz without looking at them and strode up to Huascar.

"*You!*" she cried, and she rose up onto her toes to slap him across the face, a resounding blow that echoed out over the field. "You would not listen to anyone, and you could not feel the shame of what you did. You killed your father's brothers and cousins and then invited me to feast with you! You are a monster, and you have turned the gods against you. You have brought this punishment on yourself, but now we must suffer with you for what you alone did. I should have killed you myself before you were even born."

Rahua Ocllo stepped back, her chest heaving and her teeth bared in a snarl of hatred. Quizquiz and Rumiñaui were both grinning and motioning with their hands, urging her to slap him again.

Huascar spoke up in a voice that seemed utterly detached and emotionless. "No one asked you to speak, old woman. Nor do these rebels deserve a reply. This is a matter between myself and Atauhuallpa, and we are the only ones who can resolve it. The rest of you should keep silent."

Micay saw Cusi turn toward Huascar with an astonished smile on his face, but Challcochima strode forward angrily, pounding a fist against his own chest.

"We have already resolved it!" he declared loudly. "The only thing left to decide is the manner of your death, and you will wait for that in the Place of the Pit! That should teach you that you no longer command anyone."

"I have said all that I wish to," Huascar said in that same eerily imperturbable voice, and Quizquiz started for him but was intercepted and restrained by Rumiñaui. So Quizquiz turned and inflicted his anger on the two priests, striking them repeatedly with his fists until they hung limp and bloody in the hands of the warriors. Then he seemed to realize he had lost control of the proceedings and motioned wearily for Challcochima to take command.

"The rest of you can go back to your homes," Challcochima said to the squatting Cuzcos. "Be grateful that we have spared your lives, and be ready to answer our commands. In the name of the Apu Inca Atauhuallpa, I have spoken."

He waved a hand dismissively, and the Cuzco slowly rose and began to file out of the field with their heads still bowed. Quizquiz's men began to secure the prisoners left lying on the ground, some of whom were groaning under the rocks on their backs. Micay had to turn her eyes away when she saw a pair of warriors lift one of the rocks to waist height and let it fall a second time. When she looked up again Cusi was beside her, nodding in greeting to Cori Cuillor.

"We will be going down to the city soon," he said to Micay. "I must find Rimachi and make sure that we are the first to the Cañari quarter."

"We will find you there," Micay assured him. "Did you see what happened to Chuqui?"

"She was brought up to join her mother, if that was her I saw. She looked very ill and walked like an old person. I suspect they will be imprisoned near Huascar."

"Can you do anything to help her?" Cori Cuillor asked.

Cusi lifted his shoulders in a shrug. "We must keep her alive until we hear from Atauhuallpa. That might require the services of a healer."

"You know who to send," Micay told him. Then she put a hand on his shoulder and gave him a light shake, urging him to go. "Find Rimachi and Huallpa and take them down to Quespi. Now that they have found each other, they should not be without their wife and mother."

"Yes," Cusi agreed, and jerked his chin toward the field as he turned to go. "There are better ways to demonstrate our power, and *much* better ways to show our mercy . . ."

Cuzco

CUSI CAME OUT through the great hall attached to the Amarucancha and found Tarapaca and Piqui's squadron waiting for him outside, squatting on the sandy ground at the edge of the Haucaypata. Because of several near clashes with Quizquiz's men, who resented Cusi's protection of the Cañaris, they had insisted on accompanying Cusi to the palace. But they were also eager to hear what Atauhuallpa's messenger had said, and though Cusi was in no mood to talk to anyone, he felt he owed them some explanation: They had waited a month for this message, too.

"Atauhuallpa is not coming to Cuzco," he told them bluntly. "At least not

right away. The Bearded Ones are still on the coast, at a place near Piura called
Tangarara, and he wants to attend to their movements from Caxamarca. He
is sending his uncle, Cusi Topa Yupanqui, as his inspector."

"Is he sending anyone to the coast?" Tarapaca asked as Cusi led them
around the outside of the square, heading for the northern corner, where the
Chinchaysuyo Road began.

"If you mean warriors—no," Cusi said. Then he realized how fast he was
walking and slowed his gait, turning his head to look at the great stone dais
in the center of the square. He had performed a ceremony of mourning here,
but he had yet to celebrate an Inca victory in the place made sacred by such
celebrations. At the moment he had a strong feeling he never would.

Tarapaca politely cleared his throat, and Cusi held up a hand and shook his
head in apology.

"There is more," he admitted, "and you will hear all of it presently. You
know it is not my way to withhold things from you, but I must think about
this."

They had come to the place where the street left the square and began its
long climb up to Quihuipay, passing the Cañari quarter along the way. An old
instinct made Cusi glance to his left, toward the street that led to the Patallacta, and suddenly he knew where he should do his thinking, and with whom.
He stopped and separated the squadron into two parts, keeping Tarapaca with
him and telling Piqui to take his half of the men back.

"Tell Micay and the others I will come shortly," he said to Piqui. "Tell them
I have gone to consult with Pachacuti."

THE RETAINERS at the Patallacta gate appeared panic-stricken at the approach
of twelve armed men, and the sight of Cusi's Iñaca headband calmed them only
a little. They protested meekly that they had no more gifts to give, an allusion
to the extortion being practiced by some of the Quito warriors in the city.
Quizquiz had officially forbidden looting, but he had said nothing about solicit-
ing "gifts" from the captive population, who responded generously to the right
kind of threat.

"I have *brought* a gift," Cusi said, holding up the bag of coca leaves he had
been given in the palace. "I intend to take it to Pachacuti."

The declaration seemed to unnerve them even more and sent one of them
running off to find someone with greater authority, though Cusi was not about
to wait for anyone's approval. He left Tarapaca in charge of the men, took up
his battle-ax and the coca leaves, and began the climb up the terraced hill. He
noticed that the walkways had been swept rather carelessly and that the
buildings and gardens were beginning to show the effects of prolonged neglect.
There seemed to be no shortage of retainers, but they merely watched him from
the shadows of walls and doorways and shrank from his path if he came upon
them in the open.

He paused in the courtyard of the enclosure that had once belonged to

Otoronco Achachi, standing next to the stone seat from which Otoronco had told him the story of Pachauti's vision. He looked over at the house where he had lived while preparing himself for manhood, where he had made love to Tocto Oxica on his last night in Cuzco. He needed to think about the future, but his memories of the past held him rooted in place, filled with a nameless yearning. He was actually relieved when the head retainer, a man named Titu Amaru, came rushing in with a breathless greeting.

"My lord Cusi Huaman . . . welcome. The elders of the household have sent me to see to your wishes, my lord—and to ask you not to enter the Illapa Cancha at this time."

"Why not?" Cusi demanded.

Titu Amaru bowed apologetically while he gulped for air. "Pachacuti is grieving and cannot be disturbed. Forgive me, my lord, but that is all I can tell you."

"You are forgiven," Cusi said easily. "But I am still going to see him. You can assure the elders that I will cause no disturbance and take nothing away with me, if that is what concerns them."

"Please, my lord . . ."

"Leave me, Titu Amaru. The elders know my blood and my rank. They should have come themselves if they felt they had the authority to challenge me. You clearly do not."

The retainer fell silent, and Cusi turned and headed toward the stairs to the next level. As he climbed the steep, narrow staircase to the Illapa Cancha, he emerged into the slanting rays of the afternoon sun, which slid smoothly across the surface of the fine stone walls, giving them a golden sheen. He resisted the urge to look back over Cuzco and crossed the landing toward the open door-way of the high-walled enclosure, expecting to be accosted by a priest at any moment. But there were no priests in attendance, and he passed unhindered into the shadowy interior, the sunlight cut off above his head by the enclosure walls. He blinked to adjust his eyes, then started toward the awning house, able to make out two figures sitting side by side beneath the thatch. As he approached, he felt an immense sadness settle around him, weighing on his limbs so that it was an effort to walk.

He stopped when he was close enough to see inside, where a woman holding a golden mask in front of her face was sitting on a low platform next to Pachacuti's mummy. Cusi squatted down and placed his battle-ax and the bag of coca on the ground in front of him. The woman's long black hair hung loose on her shoulders, and the golden discs fixed into Pachacuti's eye sockets glistened with an inexplicable wetness. Cusi waited, wondering whom to address, but no sound came from behind the golden mask to guide him.

"Forgive my intrusion, Grandfather," he said finally, making the mocha to the golden-eyed bundle. "I am Cusi Huaman, the grandson of Otoronco Achachi, who brought me here to see you some twenty years ago. You blessed this battle-ax and sent me out to win fame. And when I was last in Cuzco you sent these earplugs and this headband to me, by the hand of the high priestess

Tocto Oxica. I have come to express my gratitude and to give you these coca leaves."

There was a long pause, and then a low voice issued from the golden lips of the mask, slightly muffled but definitely a woman's voice. "I know who you are and what you have done, Cusi Huaman. Your gratitude has not brought you back here in twenty years. Why do you interrupt our grieving with it now?"

Cusi lowered his eyes, shamed and stung by the scolding tone the voice had taken on. "I am sorry, but I have been away for most of those years, serving the Sapa Inca on the battlefield. When I tried to return to Cuzco I was greeted with the hostility that led to this war."

"You have had your revenge for that," the voice said in the same tone. "Have you come here to gloat over Huascar's failure?"

"No!" Cusi said, surprised into anger. "Is it for Huascar that you grieve?"

"Not for Huascar!" the voice burst out. "For the loss of the Four Quarters, the world Pachacuti made and left to his children. They have squandered their inheritance along with their honor. They call themselves Incas, but they did not even fight for Cuzco!"

"We are Incas, and we fought for Cuzco," Cusi pointed out. "I must ask for whom *you* speak, my lady."

The golden mask was lowered abruptly, and Cusi was shocked by the obvious age of the withered face behind it. The glossy blackness of her hair had led him to expect a much younger woman, and he still remembered, twenty years later, the ease with which his battle-ax had been plucked from his hands. This woman would have been old even then.

"Pachacuti is silent," she admitted, "but I know what is in his heart. He remembers the prophecy that the twelfth Sapa Inca would be the last, and he has seen it come to pass. The Incas will never again rule as they were meant to." She studied Cusi's face for a moment, and her voice softened. "I see you do not protest. Perhaps I have told you what you came to hear."

Cusi realized with a pang of reluctance that she had, and he felt the sadness around him seep into his skin. He had to clear his throat before he could speak.

"Atauhuallpa is sending an inspector to Cuzco in his place. There will be more revenge taken, more killing. I will not be asked to participate in this, but I cannot stop it, either. I am being sent out of the city, and part of me is glad to go."

"And the other part?" the woman prompted.

"The other part . . . feels like a deserter, a man who has no loyalty and no leader. I was told long ago that we had only one enemy, the one who would bring the pacha puchucay, the end of our world. I had thought Huascar was that enemy, but it could as easily be Atauhuallpa or the Bearded Ones. And the world into which I was born is already gone; squandered, as you said."

"I think you have made your choice," the woman said. "I cannot absolve you of your sense of duty; you will carry that for as long as you wear the earplugs of an Inca. But Pachacuti has no more illusions, no more hope that the Incas will find themselves. That is why he grieves in silence. Go where you must, Cusi Huaman. There will be no voice to call after you in reproach."

Tears ran down through the crevices in her cheeks, and Cusi knew that he could not speak without weeping himself. So he bowed and made the mocha and went forward in a crouch to place the bag of coca leaves at the foot of the platform. Then he retrieved his battle-ax and backed out of Pachacuti's sorrowful presence, and went to tell his wife and comrades where they were going.

CAHUA TIED the head cloth around the back of Chuqui's head and then finished combing out her hair, so that it hung down over her back like a smooth black pelt.

"There," Cahua said with satisfaction, and she came around to squat in front of Chuqui. Chuqui's dull gaze settled briefly on her face before drifting past her without recognition, and Cahua felt her satisfaction vanish in a wave of resentment. This was the third time she, her mother, and Cori Cuillor had come all the way down here, past all the unfriendly guards and the prison where the vultures perched on top of the enclosure walls and the air smelled like something dead. The third time she had washed Chuqui's face and combed the tangles out of her hair and sung to her to make her feel better. But Chuqui just sat there like a pack llama and showed no sign that she felt anything.

Cahua glanced over to where her mother and Cori Cuillor were talking to the Old Coya, who was full of questions as usual. Her mother had told her to be gentle with Chuqui and not to blame her because she would not speak. She had suffered more sadness than she could bear, and it was not her fault she was being punished along with Huascar. Still, Cahua did not see any reason why Chuqui should not talk to her, and she remembered how she had brought her father back on the battlefield at Tumibamba. Seeing that the other women were not paying any attention to her, she addressed herself to Chuqui, speaking quietly but with what she thought was the proper sternness.

"Now I am supposed to make you eat something, even though the food smells terrible and I know you will not want to. But how can I help you if you will not help yourself? We tried to bring you better food, but the guards would not let us bring it in. They think we might bring you poison, even though we told them we want to make you well. You should want to be well, too."

Chuqui's gaunt face quivered slightly, but her eyes remained blank and unheeding. Cahua cast another glance at her mother. Then she lifted Chuqui's limp hands from her lap, giving them a light shake.

"This is the last time we will visit you," Cahua went on. "We are all going away from Cuzco. Cori Cuillor is going to Collasuyo with Challchochima, and we are going with the Hawk Men to Ollantaytambo. And then we will probably go to Vitcos to see Sinchi. It could be a *very* long time before we come back to Cuzco."

The last was uttered as a threat, and though it aroused no reaction in

Chuqui, Cahua was aware that her mother was looking over at them. She gave Chuqui's hands a hard squeeze.

"Is this how you wish to be remembered, my lady?" she demanded. "You are worse than Paucar Rimay, and you do not have a wound in your head. Shame on you, Chuqui Huipa! You should have the manners to say farewell to your friends."

Cahua dropped Chuqui's hands abruptly as Micay crouched down beside her and looked into her face.

"What are you doing? Did I not tell you to be gentle?"

"I was trying to bring her back from her dream," Cahua said sullenly. "Like I did with Father."

Cori Cuillor and the Old Coya had joined them, and Rahua Ocllo clicked her tongue impatiently.

"What does it matter? She does not hear anything. She has given up and left it to me to win our release."

"She hears more than you think, my lady," Cori Cuillor said. "And she can still be hurt."

"I did not mean to hurt her," Cahua protested, trying to avoid her mother's fierce gaze. "I just wanted to say farewell."

"Your visit is not over yet," the Old Coya said, looking at Micay and Cori Cuillor rather than Cahua. "You have not told me everything you know about Atauhuallpa's message. You have not said what he plans to do with us."

Cahua felt her mother's attention shift away and saw her exchange a swift glance with Cori Cuillor before replying to the Old Coya.

"Atauhuallpa has not confided his plans to the war chiefs, my lady," Micay said. "He has said only that no harm is to come to Huascar or the members of his family."

"Surely he said more than that," Rahua Ocllo insisted. "He must have heard how I spoke to Huascar. Surely that has swayed him."

"I would assume he heard," Micay began, but she stopped short when Chuqui suddenly straightened up, her head bobbing on her neck. She blinked and squinted for several moments, as if learning to use her eyes again, then focused hazily on Cahua.

"Is he dead?" she asked in a hoarse voice, and when no one else responded, Cahua felt she had earned the right.

"Who, my lady?"

"Huascar. Is he dead?"

"No, my lady," Cahua told her. "He is in another part of this compound, with many guards around him."

Chuqui blinked some more and looked around at the other women, appearing finally to recognize the Old Coya.

"He should be dead. We should all be dead."

"No, my daughter," Rahua Ocllo said soothingly. "Atauhuallpa has commanded that we not be harmed. He knows we are innocent."

Chuqui shook her head in denial, showing the whites of her eyes. "They will come for us very soon. Micay . . . Cori . . . you must flee before you are taken with us."

"We are all safe," Rahua Ocllo said more sharply. "Especially them. You should be asking them to stay and speak for our release."

"I have prayed for release," Chuqui murmured, "but it never comes." She leaned forward toward Cahua, her face animated but oddly rigid. "Go back to Tumibamba with your mother and father, Cahua. Do not return to Cuzco until we are all dead."

"We are going to Ollantaytambo, not Tumibamba," Cahua pointed out, but Chuqui merely smiled and nodded.

"Yes, and to Quito, too . . ."

Cahua stared at her in dismay. "You must not talk about being dead, my lady," she pleaded. "You must make yourself well again."

"There is no time now," Chuqui said, her voice sinking to a whisper. "They will be coming for us soon. Very soon."

"She does not know what she is saying," Rahua Ocllo said bluntly, and Chuqui nodded to herself. Cahua turned toward her mother just as Micay thrust herself forward onto her knees, seizing Chuqui's hands and raising them to her lips.

"Chuqui, my sister," she cried. "We have come to say farewell and to thank you for your friendship. I will always remember the time we spent together in Tumibamba and Quito."

Cori Cuillor pushed in on the other side, joining her hands to theirs and speaking with the same urgency. "I will always remember how brave you were during the sickness and how kind you have always been to me."

Cahua could not think of anything to say, but she put her hands on the pile in Chuqui's lap and watched as Chuqui shuddered and then slowly came back to them, opening and closing her eyes several times before they stayed open.

"Yes . . . of course you must go," she said dazedly. "Your presence will be missed at the court, but the White Women are always needed. I will see you when it is time to begin again . . ."

Her eyelids slid down and she began to sag forward, and Micay and Cori Cuillor quickly removed their hands and held her upright while Rahua Ocllo spread a blanket out behind her. Then they carefully lowered her down onto her back and watched as she curled up on her side and went to sleep.

They all stood up, and when Cahua saw that her mother was weeping, she went to her and hugged her and began to weep herself. Cori Cuillor gathered up the few things they had been allowed to bring in with them, fumbling through her own tears, and the three of them drew back to where Rahua Ocllo was standing.

"So . . . you have had your farewell," the old woman said, her voice as dry as her eyes. "Now tell me what you know, and do not try to spare me. It is better to know the worst."

Micay kept an arm around Cahua's shoulders and looked over at Cori

Cuillor, who dabbed at her eyes with the edge of her mantle and gestured for Micay to speak.

"We truly do not know Atauhuallpa's plans for you and Huascar, my lady," Micay told her, "but many people have been put under guard in anticipation of the inspector's arrival. All of Huascar's women and children have been brought here, and his administrators and advisers and count takers are being held in the palace at Collcampata. The households that supported him have had their members rounded up and imprisoned within their household buildings, and there are warriors at all of his favorite shrines and huacas and at the Royal Archives at Puquin. It appears that everyone who ever served Huascar will be made to answer for it."

The Old Coya seemed to sag, but she waved off the hand Micay held out to her in sympathy.

"Which of the war chiefs are leaving besides your husbands?"

"Rumiñaui has been summoned back to Caxamarca," Micay reported, "and Ucumari is taking a regiment to the Western Quarter."

"So Quizquiz will be left to rule Cuzco alone," Rahua Ocllo concluded glumly. "Quizquiz and Cusi Topa Yupanqui. I know him a little, maybe well enough." She fell silent for a moment but looked up quickly when Cahua stirred. "Tell me one more thing: are the Viracochas still free?"

"I believe so," Micay said. "They have made a settlement at Tangarara, on the coast. That is all I know beyond what I told you on our last visit."

"Yes, and I am grateful. Few as they are, they are a source of hope. Perhaps they will keep Atauhuallpa in Caxamarca and distract him from his thoughts of vengeance."

"Perhaps," Micay allowed. She cleared her throat politely. "We must go now, my lady. I am sorry we cannot do more for you and Chuqui."

The Old Coya looked back at Chuqui and tears sprang up in her eyes. "I never dreamed I would need anyone's help. Not like this. How could the Coya ever come to be a prisoner in her own city?" she demanded. Then she shook herself and raised a hand over them. "But go . . . with my blessing. Go quickly, and do not look back in pity or remorse."

They bowed to her and backed away before turning to go through the enclosure gate, but at the last moment, Cahua could not keep herself from looking back over her shoulder. She saw the Old Coya standing over Chuqui with her head bowed and her hands clasped in front of her, unmoving, and suddenly she understood, with a certainty that frightened her, that there were people who bore no wounds and showed no signs of sickness, yet could never be brought back among the living.

The Yucay Valley

T HE EASTERN QUARTER road came over the pass and curved down along the lip of the gorge that opened out to the left, offering a wide view of the green valley with its winding river and the dark red-brown mountains that rose up abruptly on the other side. A land untouched by war, Cusi thought, gazing down at the crop-filled fields that covered the valley bottom and climbed halfway up the slopes of the mountains on terraced steps. Drawing Rimachi with him, he moved to the side of the road, beneath a ledge from which moss hung like a shaggy gray curtain, and waved the rest of the vanguard past. He had sent Tarapaca and five hundred warriors out in advance a full day earlier to meet any serious threat that might exist, but he was still not about to take any chances with the safety of the column behind him. So he scanned both the mountainside above and the loops in the road below before nudging Rimachi and falling in behind the men.

They had descended to the second of the loops when they saw a messenger coming up the hill at a trot, bent over beneath the Hawk Man shield on his back. The warriors stopped and waited, parting their ranks so Cusi and Rimachi could come to the front to greet the messenger. It was Huaman Cachi, running easily with a war club in his hands and a relaxed smile on his face.

"My lord," he said between breaths, "Tarapaca has sent me to tell you that we have encountered no opposition to our presence in the valley—not even a slingstone from on high. The fortress at Pisac had been abandoned by its garrison, and we are told the same is true at Ollantaytambo."

"Told by whom?" Cusi asked.

Huaman Cachi smiled again. "The people of Pisac came out to greet us with food and jars of akha. They all claim never to have had any love for Huascar, and to prove it they led us to the places where the members of the garrison were hiding. Some had tried to disguise themselves as retainers, and the people turned them over to us, too. We have all of them under guard."

"What of this Manco Inca, Huascar's brother? Was he here?"

"Some time ago," Huaman Cachi confirmed. "They say he is very young and has only a small band of warriors and women with him. They think he has gone over the Andes into the jungle. Tarapaca has sent the scouts out to see what more they can learn."

Cusi grunted, reluctant to display his satisfaction. He had no real desire to hunt down this little-known brother, but it might be necessary to do so later. In the meantime the jungle would be his prison.

"Find some shade and water at the bottom and wait for us there," he told the captain of the vanguard. "If anyone brings you akha, save some for us."

The captain laughed and led the warriors on down the road. Cusi and his companions gazed out over the gorge in silence, watching dark-winged doves swoop down toward the valley, which shimmered behind a haze of golden sunlight. Cusi could not remember when he had last seen an unbroken expanse of well-tended fields, fields that had not been abandoned or burned or trampled beneath the feet of passing warriors.

"Beautiful," Rimachi murmured. "And all at the disposal of the warlord of the Eastern Quarter."

Cusi grunted at the title, which Quizquiz had given him as a sarcastic incentive to leave Cuzco, a way of telling Cusi he could do anything he wanted as long as he did not try to interfere with the work of Atauhuallpa's inspector.

"It is mine only to count," he said dryly.

"And when you have counted all the fields and herds and retainers," Rimachi said suggestively, "and all the houses and compounds left vacant by the war, will you not have to see to their administration?"

Rimachi was looking down his nose at him, and Huaman Cachi seemed to be wearing a conspiratorial smile.

"You wish to advise me on my duties?"

"I am merely suggesting that there are probably many places to be filled here, and the warriors must be quartered somewhere. It would no doubt give them pleasure to help with the harvest."

"No doubt, but they were sent here as warriors, not mitmacs," Cusi reminded him. "We could be summoned back to Cuzco at any time, once the inspector is done there."

"But why would they need us?" Huaman Cachi interjected. "Both Quizquiz and Atauhuallpa have enough warriors to do whatever they want, and neither one would trust you to do it for them."

"Not after Catiquilla," Cusi muttered, looking from one to the other. "But what is this? Since when do you speak for the warriors, Rimachi?"

"I do not claim to be their representative," Rimachi demurred. "But they speak to me through my son, and many have come on their own to ask about the Cañari women. You were the one who put ideas into their heads, Cusi."

"How did I do that?"

"You told Tarapaca he could marry Ñupchu when she had completed her mourning. She is not the only widow we have with us, as you know."

"Tarapaca's request was a special one," Cusi argued. "Ñupchu could have gone back to Hatuncolla with Challcochima, if she had wished. I was honoring her choice as much as his."

"All the Hawk Men think they are special," Rimachi scoffed. "That is also your doing. So you should not be surprised if they expect to be rewarded accordingly."

"With what? Lands that do not belong to me and houses they would have to leave? Most of them are from the north anyway."

"But few expect to return there," Huaman Cachi said swiftly. "They think Atauhuallpa will want Tumibamba and Quito for himself, and . . ."

"And?" Cusi prompted when Huaman faltered.

"And they think he will not want you there. Or the rest of us either."

"They know your reputation," Rimachi said, laughing at Cusi's sour expression. Cusi glanced back up at the head of the trail and saw a column of women and children just coming through the pass.

"All of this is premature," he said to the other two men, adopting the forthright tone of a war chief. "First we must establish our presence in this valley and ensure the loyalty of the tribes on the other side of the mountains. Then we will make our count, which will have to include the harvest. So we *will* help with that. When all the counting cords are in order, we will send them to Cuzco along with a generous share of the harvest. The response should tell us whether we have a future here or not."

Rimachi and Huaman Cachi looked at each other and then nodded. "That is fair," Rimachi agreed. "We can wait a few more months."

"That is good of you," Cusi said sarcastically. "While you are waiting, consider that while Atauhuallpa may be pleased to have me disappear, he may also be suspicious of what I am doing out of his sight. If he ever suspects I am taking something that belongs to him or ruling in my own name rather than his, he will not hesitate to remove me. Remember that when you are tempted to begin dividing the valley up among yourselves."

"We will remember," Huaman Cachi promised, though he was smiling.

"And I will not call you the warlord of the Eastern Quarter again," Rimachi vowed. Then he also had to grin. "At least not until you are ready to claim the title . . ."

Ollantaytambo

THE WALL was fifteen feet high, composed of six huge slabs of stone set side by side, with thin vertical fillets of the same stone fit tightly between them. The smooth, even surface of the slabs had been embellished with a variety of knobs and ledges, and three of them bore carvings of pumas and stepped patterns in low relief. It was a masterful piece of Inca stonework, made more impressive by the fact that the wall had been erected on a ridge high above the place where the Patakancha and Urubamba rivers met.

After allowing the Machiguenga chieftains sufficient time to marvel at the wall, Cusi led them around it, taking them to the small, ancient shrine behind it. Micay hung back with Quespi and Rimachi; she had visited the shrine once, but it was a male preserve and she did not feel comfortable about going there again. The three of them turned toward the massive stone gateway that led out of the ceremonial area, stepping around one of the great stone slabs that had been hauled up here and shaped and smoothed, only to be left lying on its side.

"The priest told me that the new work here was initiated by Topa Inca," Rimachi said, "and was continued by Huayna Capac even after he went north. He asked me if I thought Atauhuallpa would finish what they had begun." Rimachi snorted. "I told him Atauhuallpa's representative was more interested in the repair of terrace walls and irrigation ditches."

"Then these stones will sleep here forever," Quespi concluded, running her hand along a smoothly beveled edge as they passed. They continued in silence until they were through the gate and out on the topmost terrace. The steep slope below them was ringed with terraces that curved to fit the contours of the mountainside, growing wider as they descended to the valley floor. From this height, the complex of plazas, enclosures, and thatch-roofed buildings below formed a pattern of interlocking squares and rectangles, with the thick silver ribbon of the Patakancha River running down the middle like a seam. The mountains rose up abruptly on the other side of the valley and supported other terraced structures at an even greater height, including the three-tiered palace called Pincuylluna. Micay shook her head with an awe undiminished by many viewings. The builders of this seemed to have had the defiance of belief as their primary objective.

"It is like being a bird," Quespi murmured. "Or a god."

"We could hold off an army from up here," Rimachi said with a satisfaction that precluded awe.

"Whose army do you expect to come against us?" Micay asked sharply.

Rimachi shrugged. "Anyone who might not want us to stay here. I was simply looking ahead. Does Cusi still intend to go on to Machu Picchu and Vitcos?"

Micay nodded warily. "Once he finishes meeting with the forest people and has heard from Cuzco. Why do you ask?"

"I was remembering when we saw Uritu in Cuzco, when you gave him your son. He told us about a prophecy of Incas coming to live with the Campas."

"I remember very well. You sneered at it."

"I did," Rimachi admitted. "I wanted to believe I had a home in Cuzco. I have suffered for that belief, and so have my people. That is why I look ahead now, to find a home we can defend."

"Someone is coming," Quespi interrupted. "I think it is Tarapaca."

Micay looked down and to the left and saw four men climbing the steep staircase that connected the terraces. The man in the black tunic had to be Piqui, and the one with the knit cap on his head, Tarapaca. The two smaller men behind them were probably Huaman Cachi and Huallpa, who had also been part of the honor guard accompanying the counting cords and supplies to Cuzco. Micay thought it was a good sign that no one—such as an inspector—had been sent back with them.

The three of them drifted over to the staircase to meet Tarapaca, and they were still waiting when Cusi brought the Machiguenga chieftains out through the stone gate. He was wearing a circlet of green and blue parrot feathers on his chest, partially obscuring his golden Sun shield, and he carried himself with a gravity that made him appear broad and heavy. It meant more to the forest people that he was the grandson of Otoronco Achachi than that he was the representative of Atauhuallpa, and it was a role Cusi could take on without reservation. There were times when Micay could hear the old warrior's inflections in his voice and feel the authority of his gestures, and only his small stature reminded her that she was not in the presence of Otoronco himself.

When he spotted Tarapaca coming up the stairs, however, Cusi immediately became more animated, making explanatory gestures to the chiefs as he brought them over. The terrace was barely wide enough for two people to stand abreast, so Micay, Rimachi, and Quespi moved to the other side of the staircase, bowing and adding their farewells to Cusi's as he sent the Machiguengas down. Tarapaca and his companions waited on the level below until the delegation was past, then came the rest of the way up. Cusi motioned for everyone to follow him and led them back through the gateway into an informal courtyard formed by two of the great stones that lay end to end at a right angle. Micay came to Cusi's side as they made a loose circle inside the stones; she noticed he had a pouch of some kind clasped in one hand.

"You did not linger in Cuzco," he said to Tarapaca. "How were you and the cords received?"

"None of the cords were questioned," Tarapaca reported. "And once they saw how much food we had brought they treated us like heroes. Apparently the Southern and Western Quarters are so depleted that Challcochima and Ucumari have sent back to Cuzco for supplies. So both Quizquiz and Cusi Topa Yupanqui were eager to have us stay here and expand the next planting. They even suggested that some of our men be settled on the confiscated lands for that purpose. Their only complaint was that we had not found Manco Inca and sent him back to Cuzco."

Cusi nodded with apparent satisfaction, though he was eyeing Tarapaca closely, as if he sensed he was withholding something. "What else has happened in our absence?" he asked.

Tarapaca grimaced and took a moment to respond. "Quizquiz said to tell you, my lord, that they have done to the memory of Huascar what was done to Catiquilla."

Cusi stared back at him impassively, though his voice was hollow. "How many did they kill?"

"All those who had been put under guard while we were there," Tarapaca said. "Well over a thousand. Huascar and the two Coyas and a few others were spared, but they were made to watch while the rest were killed. It was done in the Haucaypata, and then the bodies were impaled on stakes and left to rot along the Northern Quarter Road."

"The Haucaypata," Cusi repeated, as if he might not have heard correctly. "What about the households?"

"The leaders of the Lower Cuzco households were taken out and hanged, and Quizquiz let his men loot their shrines and storehouses and abuse their women." Tarapaca paused to wet his lips with his tongue. "But the Capac Ayllu household received the greatest punishment, since they were the only one from Upper Cuzco to support Huascar. Quizquiz boasted to me that he had the mummy of Topa Inca dragged through the streets at the end of a rope before it was burned and its ashes were scattered to the wind."

"The inspector encouraged this desecration," Cusi said, unable to make it a question.

Tarapaca nodded wearily. "*He* boasted about how he had gone in person to Puquin Hill, to burn the royal archives and have all of Huascar's Remembers tortured and killed. It was all done by Atauhuallpa's order."

During the long silence that followed Cusi slumped back against the stone behind him, shaking his head in dismay. Micay knew he had expected something like this, yet that could not lessen the shock of learning it had actually happened. He looked down at the pouch in his hand, which was painted with black and yellow spots to resemble jaguar fur, and then turned to Rimachi.

"What are your thoughts, my friend?" he asked quietly, and Rimachi shuddered with anger, so that his voice quivered.

"He slaughtered my people in Tumibamba, and now he slaughters Incas in the Haucaypata. I think we should settle here and forget about ever going back."

Micay followed Cusi's gaze to the others, who were nodding in agreement. He let his eyes rest on Tarapaca.

"You know how close we are to Cuzco and how many warriors Quizquiz has. Could we defy a direct order to return?"

"He could not take all of his warriors out of Cuzco," Tarapaca reckoned. "Not even half. We could hold him off indefinitely, here and at Pisac."

"What if Challcochima and Ucumari were recalled to assist him?" Cusi suggested.

When Tarapaca did not reply immediately, Rimachi broke in. "Then we retreat to Vitcos and let them try to come after us."

Cusi straightened up against the stone. "What do you know about Vitcos beyond the stories Uritu used to tell us?"

"Nothing," Rimachi admitted. "Though I also remember Otoronco Achachi's stories about how difficult it was to get there and how long the Campas held him off. The Hawk Men could do as well against anyone Atauhuallpa might send against us."

The other warriors hummed in agreement, and Cusi studied them for a moment. "Even if we assume that Vitcos is defensible, is it a place we can live? Are you ready to live in the forest?"

"I would rather remain in Pisac," Tarapaca confessed. "But if the choice is between the forest and going back to Cuzco . . ."

"The forest!" Huaman Cachi said.

"The forest," Huallpa agreed. "I would rather live in the jungle with the Shuaras than with the murderers in Cuzco."

Cusi looked at the one man who had not spoken. "Piqui?"

The captain shuffled his feet and cleared his throat before meeting Cusi's gaze. "You have always led us wisely, my lord; I would never tell you what to do."

"Your comrades would."

"That is their way," Piqui shrugged. "But we are all warriors, and we were sickened by what we saw and heard in Cuzco. So were the warriors who did it, though they pretended they felt nothing. Their hands are stained along with Atauhuallpa's."

Cusi looked down at his own hands, and Micay could tell he was remembering Catiquilla. Then he turned to her. "What do you think, my wife? Are you ready to live in the forest with our son?"

"I think we should go to Vitcos and see what kind of refuge it would offer," she told him. "Even if we are never forced to use it for that."

Cusi nodded, appearing resigned but grateful, as well. "That is what we will do, then. In my absence, Tarapaca, I would like you and Rimachi to share the command—you in Pisac and Rimachi here. Settle the men wherever you see fit, but also see that all the fields are planted."

"Most of the men have already chosen their places," Tarapaca said with a glance at Rimachi. "We will place the others where they are most needed."

"What about the women?" Rimachi asked. "They have completed their mourning."

Cusi glanced at Tarapaca and Huallpa, then at Human Cachi, who had asked for one of the Cañari ñustas. "All those who wish to marry may do so. Whatever they need for their households may be taken from the confiscated stores."

Huallpa and Huaman Cachi grinned and banged their weapons against each other's shields, and Tarapaca asked Cusi if he would preside at his marriage to Ñupchu.

"Before I leave," Cusi promised. Then he opened his hand and displayed the spotted pouch on his palm. "One of the Machiguenga sorcerers gave me this. He said it was jaguar medicine, so that I could see in the dark and would never be lost in the forest."

"You should still send for Uritu to guide you," Rimachi recommended, and Cusi looked at Micay and smiled for the first time.

"I may, though only to see him and Sinchi a little sooner." He gestured with the pouch and started them all moving toward the gate, clapping Tarapaca on the shoulder with his free hand. "And if Cuzco should ask for me while I am away, you can tell them I have gone in pursuit of the elusive Manco Inca . . ."

The Inca Trail

NOT FAR DOWNRIVER from Ollantaytambo, another valley opened out to the north, with a trail that went over the high Panticalla Pass and down into the Vilcabamba Valley. This was the most direct route to Vitcos, and the squadron of scouts traveling with Cusi's band left them and went that way, intending both to map the trail and to carry Cusi's message to Uritu. Cusi continued on the trail along the river, passing the deserted sentry post where once all travelers had been made to stop and show proof of the Sapa Inca's permission to go further. All the territory between here and Machu Picchu was considered the exclusive domain of the Inca royal family, which included the households of the past Sapa Incas.

Palatial clusters of gabled stone houses, set on banks of terraces that appeared molded to the mountainside, began to appear at regular intervals on the heights overlooking the trail. These were the first of the royal rest houses, but Cusi went by without stopping, satisfying himself with a visual inspection of their natural defenses. His scouts had visited these places long ago, with orders to reassure the inhabitants of his peaceful intentions, so he felt no compulsion to visit them in person. Besides, he had looked forward to this journey as a respite from the duty of being The Inca. He wore no insignia of rank beyond his earplugs and headband, and he carried his own weapon and a pack on his back like the other warriors.

As they continued westward, the air grew warmer and the foliage thickened, and the mountains began to shoulder in on the river from both sides, forcing the rushing water into a narrow, boulder-strewn channel flanked by overhanging cliffs. When another valley opened out to their left, they crossed the river on a rope bridge and followed the trail southward along the bank of the Cusichaca River. Even on the valley bottom the terrain was rugged and rose steeply, though the Inca trail makers had gone to great effort to provide a path level enough for litter bearers.

They soon came within sight of a hillside complex that Cusi's scouts had identified as the administrative center for the rest of the rest houses. It was called Patallacta, Terrace Town, because of the twelve tiers of terraces that ringed the hill beneath the complex, descending all the way down to the river. The scouts had found only a handful of mamacona present when they had come, and there was no one in evidence now as Cusi and his band of warriors and women made their way up through the terrace fields, though several half-harvested plots told him the abandonment was recent. The trail leveled off at the top and took them through the middle of the complex, which was remarkably large, with more than a hundred buildings clustered to form compounds along both sides of the road. The echoes of their footsteps and the sight of the empty doorways and courtyards evoked vivid memories of the ruined cities Cusi had visited on the coast, and he wondered if these rest houses were destined for the same fate. There was nothing so great it could not be lost to memory, and the Incas had already squandered much of the greatness of their past. Topa Inca had been reduced to ashes, and even Pachacuti was silent and bereft, grieving for what had been lost.

Subdued by his thoughts, Cusi entered the plaza before he recognized what it was, and then he saw the crowd of people standing off to his left. When he stopped short in surprise, drawing his shield and battle-ax in close to his body, all the people in the crowd went down on their knees, humbling themselves before him. There must have been three hundred of them, and despite their abject posture they made Cusi keenly aware that he had a total of only ten warriors with him. Piqui came up next to him, and the other men drew themselves up on both sides in front of the women and children. For a long moment no one moved. Then an old man wearing the long robe of a priest rose and came forward, bowing and gesturing profusely in deference.

"On behalf of all those who serve here, I greet you, Captain," the old man said in a sorrowful tone. "We have gathered to hear the judgment of Atauhuallpa."

"I have not come to render judgment," Cusi said, puzzled by the greeting. "Were you not told you could live here in peace?"

"Oh, yes," the priest agreed hastily. "There were warriors who came in the name of the war chief Cusi Huaman, the lord of the Eastern Quarter. But that was months ago, and since then we have heard what has happened in Cuzco. We knew the inspector would attend to us before long."

"I do not represent the inspector," Cusi told him. "And what happened in Cuzco will not affect you here."

The priest stared at him in obvious disbelief, though he also seemed reluctant to voice his doubts. "But Captain . . . we are the servants of the Sapa Inca. Of Huascar. We are as much a part of his family as those who were killed."

Cusi was tempted to glance back at Micay, just to be certain he had heard the man correctly. Was he asking to be killed?

"Huascar has no more family and no one to serve him," Cusi said bluntly. "And I am not a captain. I am Cusi Huaman, and I tell you again that you will not be harmed."

The priest bowed deeply, fluttering his hands in front of his face in apology. But when he straightened up he appeared as doubtful as ever, pained by his uncertainty. Cusi felt his patience slip away and was surprised by the anger in his own voice.

"Do you wish to be punished?" he demanded, and the priest cringed back from the force of his presence.

"No, my lord. But we cannot forsake the duty we owe to the Sapa Inca. He is the reason we live here and devote ourselves to the maintenance of the shrines and the houses and the trail. Huascar was the last to come to us, and his visit is something we will always treasure. The memory of his wisdom and his holy power is still alive in our hearts, and we could never renounce our love for him, no matter how low he has fallen. Not even if it costs us our lives."

Only astonishment kept Cusi from uttering any of the harsh rejoinders that sprang to his lips, and a moment's reflection made him realize they would have been pointless, beyond the priest's comprehension. If the man could speak with such conviction of Huascar's wisdom and holiness, there was little chance he would believe Cusi's account of the ruler's stupidity and viciousness.

"If I *were* the inspector's representative," Cusi said instead, "what you have just told me *would* cost you your lives. I tell you that to spare you the grief of learning it for yourselves."

The priest cocked his head and squinted at him. "What are you saying, my lord?"

"I am saying that Atauhuallpa has not come to Cuzco and it is unlikely either he or the inspector will come here very soon. In the meantime, I am in command, and I have no desire to take away your memories or punish you for your loyalty to the Sapa Inca. Keep the beliefs that sustain your courage and sense of honor, and keep yourselves and this place alive. I am Atauhuallpa's representative, but I am also an Inca who has never forgotten how few of us there are."

Cusi finished out of breath, frustrated by his inability to make himself understood by people so isolated and innocent. They might as well have been foreigners, speaking in mutually unintelligible tongues. Yet after a long pause the priest seemed to regard him with a new temerity, glancing curiously at Cusi's headband and then at the image on his shield.

"May I ask, my lord . . . what has brought you here?"

"We are on our way to Machu Picchu."

The old man's eyebrows rose slightly. "May I ask why?"

"Because it is holy."

"Ah!" the priest exclaimed softly, and he permitted himself a tentative smile. "In the past it has been the custom for the Incas to begin their fasting and purification here. Would you allow me to assist you, my lord?"

The notion of a thorough cleansing had an immediate and powerful appeal for Cusi, but then he hesitated, thinking of his companions. Huallpa and Huaman Cachi had brought their new wives with them, and they would surely find the required abstinence most difficult to bear. And Piqui . . . the thought of Piqui entering an Inca shrine brought his earlier exasperation into sharp focus and made him turn back to the priest with a challenging smile.

"You may assist all of us," he said, and saw the priest's eyes glide past him, no doubt noting that none of the other warriors wore earplugs and that among the women only Micay had a wife's mantle pin.

"But these are not all Incas, my lord."

"I am aware of that. But we came here from Quito together, through the war, and we will go to Machu Picchu the same way."

"But you must know, my lord, that the shrines are not open to those of common blood. I could not permit them to enter, not even at your request."

"I will not insist," Cusi assured him. "But I will not go alone either." He glanced around at the others. "We will march on."

"You must allow us to give you food and shelter for the night, my lord," the priest pleaded. "That is our duty, and we would feel derelict if you shunned our hospitality."

"You have also made it your duty to judge our worthiness," Cusi said without sympathy. "And in that you are most derelict. You should know that the world outside this valley has changed. The blood of the Incas has been spilled in anger by other Incas. It can no longer be regarded as the sole measure of worth. You will have to learn to accept that, or your presence here will become irrelevant and pointless."

The priest stared at him in outraged astonishment, but Cusi simply bowed and started off across the plaza, letting his companions fall in behind him. Micay eventually came up beside him.

"You honor your comrades greatly," she murmured, giving him a searching look. He shrugged to show he had not planned it, then nodded forcefully to show he meant it.

"These people honored Huascar," he told her. "They should do no less for the Hawk Men."

Huiñay Huayna

A S CUSI AND PIQUI led the column down onto the terrace that would take them back onto the trail to Machu Picchu, the occupants of the rest house lined the terraces above and below, murmuring farewells and holding out bunches of flowers. Their faces seemed to hover and float along with Micay as she went past, and their voices came to her in unpredictable bursts. She heard Cusi's name and her own, along with whispers about the Retainer Captain and the Little Healer and the Hawk Men of Tiahuanaco. The ground beneath her feet was strewn with soft green leaves and blossoms that seemed luminous with color, and Micay lifted her head and smiled as a shower of bright petals drifted down in front of her. Beside her Machacuay was laughing as he brushed at the bits of red and orange and gold that clung to his hair and skin, and Micay risked a glance over her shoulder to see that Cahua and Ococo had both collected an armful of flowers and were tossing them back to the children they passed.

Soon the fine stone walls and gabled buildings were behind them and there were only a few people to mark their passage, mostly farmers who turned from their work in the terrace fields to bow over their hoes and digging sticks. Then the trail went into the trees and they were alone in the cool green shadows, moving at the slow, stately pace appropriate to fast-weakened pilgrims. They were not far from Machu Picchu now, and their departure from the rest house had been timed so as to bring them to the holy city just before sunset. There they would conclude their journey with the ritual celebration of their arrival and the breaking of their fast. There she would see Amaru, Parihuana, and Fempellec again. And she would finally meet Mama Inquil, the woman who had told the rest house keepers to open both their shrines and their hearts to the travelers. She glanced sideways at Machacuay, who leaned forward as he walked, his gait light and eager.

"I am glad the mamanchic intervened for us," she said to him. "It would have been hard to come this far without a welcome."

Machacuay nodded. "I was afraid the fasting and purification would be too hard for me and make me faint. But I have not come close."

"It makes you stronger if you give yourself to it," Micay agreed. "Even the new husbands have not minded it." She looked ahead and lowered her voice. "I am not so sure, however, about my own husband. He still seems wary."

"He says less to the priests," Machacuay reported. "But perhaps he is simply tired of answering all their questions about Tiahuanaco and the other holy places he has visited."

"Perhaps," Micay allowed, though she wondered if Cusi were not being silent about other things, as well—things the priests would not think to ask him about or would not wish to. She had not forgotten his bitter comment about Huascar as they marched out of the rest house called Patallacta.

Suddenly they came out into the sunlight again, and to their right, across a deep, tree-choked gorge, they could see a waterfall tumbling hundreds of feet down the mountainside, looking like a roughly woven silver curtain against the green. The hissing rumble of its descent mingled with the more distant sound of the Urubamba River, which cut a winding path far below the terraced bluff on which Huiñay Huayna stood. The column slowed to a halt, and Micay saw Piqui nudge Cusi, pointing with his chin at the rainbow arching up out of the mist.

"Huanacauri," Piqui said reverently. Then he smiled. "I understand why the Inca took this land for himself."

Micay blinked in surprise, having never heard him offer an unsolicited opinion about anything, much less with a smile. The Retainer Captain, she thought appreciatively, noticing that Machacuay was staring at him with a fascination that seemed almost worshipful. The retainers who lived in the rest houses had stared at him in the same way, often shedding their habitual restraint to reach out and touch him.

Cusi looked up at him with a kind of bemusement, then slowly smiled and tapped his battle-ax against Piqui's shield in recognition.

"Surely it has not hurt the Inca to share it with us," he said dryly, and he cast a parting glance at the waterfall before turning to lead them back into the forest.

THE FINAL ritual of purification, conducted in a small group of buildings outside the gates of the city, proved to be the most rigorous. The five women— Micay, Coca, Huaman Cachi's wife Chuqui Llantu, Cahua, and Ococo—were crowded into a tiny bathhouse so hot and steamy that every breath was itself a prayer. They came out gasping and reeling and were taken in hand by an equal number of mamacona, who helped them bathe and wash their hair and dress themselves in the garments they had saved for their arrival. Micay was so grateful for the gentle handling by the mama who attended her that she felt compelled to introduce herself. The old woman nodded and smiled shyly.

"We know all about you, my lady. The mamanchic awaits you in the square."

"Mama Inquil?" Micay asked dazedly. The woman simply nodded again and led her on to the next phase of the ritual, which was a long session of prayers and songs to Pachamama and Mama Quilla.

Finally, walking barefoot and carrying their sandals in their hands, they were taken out to where the men were waiting. The bags and bundles they had been carrying until the fourth day of their fast, when Cusi had reluctantly agreed to accept the help of porters, were also waiting for them. Cusi put down his shield and weapon to help Micay sling her medicine bag over her shoulder.

"Apparently the mamanchic is pleased to have us carry our true burdens into her presence," he explained. "Even our shields and weapons."

They lined up in double file, the women and their husbands and the two girls in front, Machacuay and Piqui and the rest of the warriors in the rear. In Micay's enervated state the medicine bag was a heavy burden indeed, and she had to bend beneath it as she went forward at Cusi's side. A strong wind was blowing from the northeast, pushing dark clouds over the mountains, while the sun cast a golden light across the tops of the trees that lined the trail. Then there was a stone wall ahead, with open sky above it and the blunt peak of a mountain rearing up in the near distance. A wooden gate in the wall swung open, and as the mamacona led them through Micay had her first view of the holy city of Machu Picchu.

Below her, from the base of the hill on which she stood to that of the blunt peak she had glimpsed a moment before, stretched a narrow ridge of land that had been leveled and terraced to support an incredible array of walled enclosures and thatch-roofed buildings packed together in rows or multitiered clusters on both sides of a central strip of contiguous broad plazas. Patches of green that must have been gardens stood out between the shrines and houses, many of which had been built of a stone so light it appeared whitewashed. The ridge dropped off precipitously on both sides, permitting glimpses of terrace fields that seemed to hang in space and then a sheer plunge to the river, thousands of feet below. Beyond the gorge surrounding this island in the sky, the mountains rose up again on all sides, their rugged flanks covered with the hazy green of the cloud forest. A mama at one of the earlier rest houses had told Micay that the holy city stood on "the brow of Pachamama," and now she knew precisely what the woman had meant.

Awed by the sight, Micay had forgotten both her weariness and the weight on her back, but she remembered them again as she and Cusi followed the mamacona down a long staircase that descended the hill in steep, straight courses. The muscles in her legs seemed to clench and flutter by turns, and the wind whipped around her like a live thing, tugging and pushing her and blowing her hair in her face. Cusi merely grunted when she gripped the edge of his shield to maintain her balance.

To her immense relief they went only half way down before turning left onto a level walkway that ran between two ranks of tall, gabled buildings, one slightly above and one below, neither with entrances onto the walkway. They walked in the shadow of the blank stone walls for some distance before emerging into an open square wide enough to trap and hold the slanting rays of the sun. Micay could no longer feel the pull of the wind, and as they crossed the square and ascended a flight of steps to an adjoining plaza the silence seemed to thicken around them. More mamacona were waiting in the second plaza, and they fell in on both sides of the column and accompanied it up another stairway to the third and final square.

Here the silence was complete. Even the constant, muted roar of the river was cut off by the terraces and buildings that rose up on three sides. Micay was still trying to assimilate the dizzying sense of being suspended in space when suddenly she felt completely enclosed and grounded, her bare feet planted at the very center of the earth. The sensation was so startling that she was slow to notice that the terraces flanking the square were lined with people, most of them mamacona wearing solid gray, white, or blue. The mamacona who had been leading them parted, and she and Cusi came to a halt in front of a tall gray-haired woman who could only be the mamanchic, Mama Inquil. She wore silver bracelets and gold, emerald, and red shell bead necklaces over a shift and mantle of fine buff-colored vicuña, and though there were several priests among the women behind her, none stood with her as an equal.

Following Cusi's example, the members of the column squatted down and emptied their hands in order to make the mocha. Micay heard the woman's bracelets chime together as she raised her hands over them in blessing. Her voice was warm and resonant, filled with an assurance that was somehow beyond challenge or dispute.

"Greetings, my children. You were not summoned or sent here in the usual manner, but you have shown that there is reverence in your hearts, and you have borne the necessary hardships with courage and grace. Lay down your burdens now, and rise so that I may look upon you."

Micay was only too pleased to lay down her medicine bag, though she rose too quickly and came close to fainting when the blood rushed to her feet. Cusi steadied her with a hand under her elbow, and when her vision cleared she found the mamanchic regarding her with patient concern. The woman gave her a sympathetic nod, then turned her attention to Cusi, studying him in silence for a long time.

"Forgive my scrutiny, Cusi Huaman," she said at last. "I have heard many things about you, but I needed to see for myself the war chief who made us open our shrines to commoners and retainers. You are young to be a judge of who is worthy."

"I meant no disrespect, mamanchic," Cusi said politely. "But there are few of the Old Ones left to guide us, and we have had to form our own judgments about many things. I have seen what is in the hearts of my comrades, and it is no less worthy than what is in mine."

Mama Inquil gave him a bemused smile. "I understand why our priests found you so baffling. You speak like an Inca of old—like your grandfather, Ayar Inca, or your uncle, Lloque Yupanqui. But you say things they would have found shocking and outrageous."

Cusi spread his hands in a kind of shrug. "They shaped me, my lady, but the world they left me is very different from the one they knew. My uncle began to see that himself, but not soon enough to save him from a shocking and outrageous death."

The mamanchic's face tightened, and for a moment Micay was afraid Cusi had gone too far. He seemed unaware of how arrogant he sounded, and Micay was strongly tempted to apologize on his behalf, fearing that Mama Inquil might withdraw her welcome, which had seemed extraordinarily generous and forgiving. When the old woman spoke again, her voice was as cool and even as Cusi's had been.

"I knew Lloque Yupanqui, and I mourned his loss," she said. She turned to Micay. "Just as I mourned the loss of Chimpu Ocllo, who was my half sister. The deaths of those we love always seem unjust. Is that not so, Micay?"

"It is, my mother," Micay agreed, holding the woman's eyes to show her sincerity. "We have seen too many die too soon, my lady, and perhaps it has hardened us."

Mama Inquil inclined her head in a subtly acquiescent gesture, accepting the implicit apology.

"No doubt that would make the world seem empty of kindness," she allowed. Then she clasped her hands in front of her with a flash of silver. "But come, you must let us fill your hearts with the love the gods have shown us. We remember and preserve it here in the way of the Old Ones. We may even find the power to touch the angry heart of Cusi Huaman and make him as worthy as he believes himself to be."

Cusi seemed genuinely surprised by the reprimand, and Micay saw him bite back a rejoinder. Instead he crossed his arms on his chest and bowed with a deference that had not shown on his face. The mamanchic stared at him for a moment, her eyes narrowed, then motioned for them to follow and led the way toward one of the beautiful white stone buildings. The mamacona began to sing, and Micay went forward with a distinct sense of relief, grateful to be found worthy and eager to make herself whole again.

THE HOUSE Cusi had been given was in a row along the western edge of the city, and from his seat in the doorway he could see down over the hanging terraces to the winding silver cord of the Urubamba River. Lulled by the river's muted roar, he let his eyes roam aimlessly over the green canopy of the cloud forest while he thought about the dream he had had about the Bearded Ones—the second dream.

He looked up when Amaru came down the stairway at the end of the house and toward him along the narrow walkway. He was rather elegantly dressed in a tasseled red tunic and wristbands studded with pieces of shell, and when he squatted down across from Cusi he smelled freshly bathed.

"Here you are. I thought I would find you at the shrine of Illapa, where I was going myself. The priests always need warriors to assist them with the ceremonies."

"I was invited to attend," Cusi acknowledged.

"I know. All your men were there, acting as if it did not matter that you were not with them."

"Why should it? I assume there were enough without me."

"Enough that I decided to come here instead. I thought you might like to take another walk with me."

Cusi nodded and stood up with him. "Is there something in this city you have not shown me? It cannot be anything you or Sinchi Roca built."

"No, it is well before either of us," Amaru said, and he started to turn away. Then he turned back. "I must tell you . . . Mama Inquil will meet you there. She asked me to bring you."

"Did she think I would not come if she asked me directly?"

"I do not know what she thought," Amaru said with a trace of impatience. "I comply with any request she makes of me. Unlike most of the Incas we have known, she is both fair and honest. I cannot believe you do not see that."

"I do see it," Cusi told him. "And Micay tells me again every day."

Amaru cocked his head in exasperation. "Then why have you not gone to her yourself? She would accept your apology and think no more about it."

"I am sure she would," Cusi agreed. "But what if I do not have an apology to offer?"

"Then defend your conduct instead. You are famous for saying what you think and for thinking strange thoughts. You did not earn your reputation by sulking in silence."

Cusi gave him a wan smile. "You did not earn yours by serving priestesses and urging proper conduct on your brothers. But come, let us go to the mamanchic. Let us see if she truly wishes to hear what I think . . ."

THE STAIRWAY wound down to the base of a large, jutting outcrop of white rock, which provided the foundation for the buildings massed above. Below was an irregularly shaped enclosure formed by the juncture of terrace walls and other outcroppings of blank stone. One of its many sides was open, while others gave way to deep, shadowy nooks and passageways that seemed to be half tunnel, half cave. The strangeness of it put Cusi on the alert, especially since there was no one else about, not even one of the ubiquitous gatekeepers. Then his eyes were drawn to the center of the open space, where an image had been sculpted out of the white bedrock that was the floor. It was a large, slightly rounded triangle with a beaked oblong head at its apex. A condor, Cusi realized, and as he stood over it, he remembered the condors in Raurau Illa's song and Micay's dream, and the one they had seen on the way to Macas's cave. He also remembered the condor banners waved by the Chachapoyas at Cochahuaylas as they marched into the trap he had helped arrange for them. He stirred uneasily, aware of Amaru standing silently behind him.

"What sort of place is this?" he asked finally.

"It is the Place of the Condor, a place of penance. People are sent here to ponder their errors and misdeeds."

Cusi grunted. "It would seem she expects more than an apology from me."

Mama Inquil suddenly appeared from a passageway to their right, alone and dressed in plain gray garments, her face unpainted and her breast unadorned by the usual jewelry. As he bowed, Cusi noticed the dust marks on the front of her shift, evidence that she had been kneeling in prayer.

"I am grateful, my son," she said to Amaru. "I have also had a chance to speak to the man you asked to take with you, the Colla stoneworker. You may have him for a year if you will then return to see to our needs here."

"It will be my pleasure, my lady," Amaru replied. "As I was telling my brother, you have always treated me with kindness and generosity."

"You and Parihuana and Fempellec have added to our lives here," Mama Inquil told him. "You will always be welcome in our midst."

Amaru bowed again and left them. Cusi glanced down at the condor, feeling the mamanchic's eyes on him, searching but exerting no pull. He looked up at her expectantly.

"My lady?"

Mama Inquil let out a forceful sigh. "As I was praying, I wondered how you would greet me—whether you would show remorse or the stubborn defiance of injured pride. Instead, as I most feared, you greet me calmly, with conviction. It was not just that I corrected you, was it? I proved something to you."

Cusi tilted his head back, impressed by her candor. "Perhaps. I had begun to have misgivings on my way here, and you seemed to confirm them with what you said. It was not my intention to speak rudely to you, my lady, though Micay assures me I did."

"I am not accustomed to having my own words thrown back at me," Mama Inquil said dryly. "But that is not what I found rude. It was the look you gave me after I chided you for your anger. It was the look one gives a fool who is nonetheless above you in rank. It said I did not deserve to understand."

"That *is* what I felt," Cusi admitted. "You held my uncle up to me as an example, but you did not want to hear what kind of example he had actually been. Especially, you did not want to be reminded of how he had died. You compared his death to that of Chimpu Ocllo."

"I did."

"Yet you know Chimpu Ocllo died of the sickness. She was not tortured and mutilated and thrown off a cliff by Huascar's assassins."

The mamanchic winced. "No, she was not. I only meant to suggest that we have all borne grievous losses . . ."

"And I was trying to suggest that we have lost more than you could know, living here." Cusi spread his hands. "Surely that sounds arrogant, even to my own ears. But perhaps it is true, my lady."

"Perhaps it is," Mama Inquil allowed. "You said you came here with misgivings, my son. Yet you participated fully in the rites of purification. They gave you no relief?"

"*No,*" Cusi said, too loudly, so that he realized how hard he had been holding this admission back. "How could they, when the priests who administered them still profess their loyalty to Huascar? Even as they sought to purge me of my anger and doubt, they always found a way to remind me of its source. I could never forget they had passed Huascar through these same rites and pronounced him clean."

"But no priest has that power," Mama Inquil pointed out. "The Sapa Inca confesses his crimes only to Inti."

"Huascar reveled in his crimes!" Cusi retorted. "The last time he came here, my lady, he had just been at Calca, where he killed three of Atauhuallpa's ambassadors and made this war unavoidable. I was there, my lady, and I survived only because he thought it was more cruel to humiliate me instead." Cusi paused, panting for breath but unable to stop himself. "Yet when he came here, the priests could see only his wisdom and holiness. They honored the blood in his veins and ignored the blood on his hands. I wanted to ask you, in the square, if you had done the same. I wanted to know if you had questioned his worthiness and scolded *him* for the anger in his heart."

Cusi dropped to one knee, gasping, overwhelmed by the violence of his feelings. When the mamanchic did not reply, he put his hands down on the condor and went on, spewing out all the ugly, blasphemous thoughts he had been carrying inside him.

"When the priests appealed to Inti for his blessing, I could not feel his benevolence or even his concern. I could only wonder why he had allowed this to happen to the Incas. If we are his favored people, why did he take back Ninan Cuyochi and leave us Huascar and Atauhuallpa? Why did he allow his sons to commit unholy acts?"

"Go on," Mama Inquil urged quietly. "Say all of it. Cleanse yourself."

"There is no cleansing for this! The stain is on all of us, and it is irrevocable. I have seen the Incas slaughter their brothers and their friends . . . I have seen them desecrate shrines and break huacas into bits. And the Old Ones brought us to this, my lady. Their memory cannot save us now. We are alone, and in my dreams I have seen the bearded strangers scatter us before them . . ."

A comforting hand came to rest on his shoulder and he shuddered, then lurched forward on his hands and knees and vomited onto the condor stone. He heaved and retched until he was empty and his eyes ran with tears.

"Now I have desecrated this place, as well," he croaked, sitting back on his heels and wiping at his mouth.

"The condor is an eater of filth," Mama Inquil said, and she reached down to help him to his feet, displaying surprising strength. He looked at her dazedly, beginning to feel ashamed at his loss of control.

"You are not a godless man, Cusi Huaman," she told him. "I know that from what I feel, as well as what Micay has told me about you."

"But you have heard what *I* feel . . ."

"I have heard your pain and doubt. You have a right to those, as you do to your anger. You must forgive me, my son, for presuming to judge what was in your heart."

Cusi glanced down at the mess he had made and slowly shook his head, denying his right to forgive anyone.

"I must ask you to leave me now," Mama Inquil went on. "I must consider what you have told me and what it means for our future here. How soon will you go on to Vitcos?"

"As soon as I hear from my initiation brother, who is the high chief there. I hope he will come to guide us."

"We will speak again, then. You have opened your heart here, Cusi Huaman. Do not close it again. Inti is not the only god we have, nor the most venerable."

"I have heard you, my mother," Cusi said, and he bowed as he backed out of her presence. He felt rain on his head as he climbed the stairs and saw that fog had already begun to roll in over the city, as it did nearly every night. He lifted his face to the rain and welcomed the swirling blankness of the fog, knowing it would cover whatever the rain could not wash away.

WHEN THE first dart flew past Cahua lazily mistook it for a hummingbird, and Ococo, who was dozing sitting up against the trunk of a papaya tree, did not even stir. But some instinct had been alerted, and when a second dart cut through the leaves no more than a foot above her head, Cahua caught a glimpse of it and heard the sequence of its flight, from the abrupt exhalation that had launched it to the sharp click of its impact against a terrace wall somewhere behind her. She scanned the bank of flowering shrubs across from her and one level down but saw no one lurking behind the thick foliage. Then, slowly and deliberately, the hollow shaft of a blowpipe emerged from the shiny leaves and scarlet blossoms of a cantut, pointing right at her.

"Sinchi!" she cried, and her brother, still in hiding, answered her with a whoop that made Ococo start up in fright. Then Sinchi came out with the blowpipe in one hand, waving it at her and grinning his trickster's grin. He was wearing a long cotton garment that hung loosely almost to his ankles, and there were feathers plaited into the black hair that fell to his shoulders. Except for his light skin and the marked eye—and the familiar grin—he could easily have been mistaken for one of the forest Chunchos who had come to visit their father in Ollantaytambo.

She watched the way he came toward her, around the curve of the terrace and up to her level. He ignored the paths and the stairs, slipping in and out of the shrubs and jumping over the flower beds, scrambling up the vertical face of the retaining wall as if the flat, embedded stones were in fact a staircase. He was there almost before Cahua could move to meet him, and as he swept her up into an embrace she realized he was bigger than she was, and much stronger than she remembered. He also smelled like a Chuncho, a heady aroma that mingled wood smoke, crushed leaves, and damp earth, along with several sharper, ranker scents she did not truly wish to identify. He squeezed her so hard she could feel his spirit brother, hidden beneath the rough weave of his tunic, dig into her chest. But more than that, she could feel how much he had missed her, and it was a feeling that made all the others seem insignificant. This was her brother, her *twin* . . .

He finally let her go but continued to stare at her, beaming with a joy that seemed doubly strong because she could feel it from the inside. Then Sinchi noticed Ococo and drew back in surprise, glancing around the sunken garden as if to reassure himself of where he was. Before Cahua could introduce him, he leaned forward and spoke to Ococo in a language Cahua recognized as Campa, though a Campa very different from the one Ococo had been teaching her. He seemed to release the words in short bursts, catching some of them low in his throat in a way that warped the sound. Ococo did not seem to understand him at first, either, but he repeated himself and made encouraging gestures with his hands until she brightened with comprehension and said something back to him, apparently telling him her name. The two of them went back and forth with increasing rapidity, with Cahua recognizing only the place names and the Quechua words for which there were no Campa equivalents, like "mitmac" and "chosen woman."

"Speak the high speech!" Cahua demanded finally, and they jumped and looked at each other with sudden self-consciousness.

"I asked Ococo if she had ever been to Vitcos," Sinchi explained, "and she said no. I was telling her how much she would like it."

"Is it like this?" Cahua asked. Once again Sinchi glanced around at the sheltered hollow with its curving terraces and neat rows of trees and shrubs, the bottommost level lined with carefully tended plots of rare and delicate flowers and plants. He wrinkled his nose and waved his blowpipe in a vague gesture of accommodation.

"On the hill where the Incas built their compounds, it is like this. But the Campas live among the trees, with the other forest creatures and the spirits of the ancestors, and they do not keep their houses in one place forever. This is the nicest garden I have seen here, but it is very small and there is nothing to hunt."

"Except your sister," said Cahua dryly, unable to resist the temptation to make him grin again. "Who told you where to find us?" she asked, and he lifted his chin toward the tall trees that formed a windbreak along the upper rim.

"Father is above with Uncle Amaru and Uncle Uritu. Mother is with the mamanchic and has not come to greet us yet."

"We were with them all morning, visiting the holy places of Pachamama," Cahua told him, hooking her arm around his. "Come, let us go up and find her. She will not believe how big and strong you are."

"There is meat in the forest if you know how to find it," he said modestly, allowing her to lead him along the path. Then he seemed to pull back slightly as if seized by another thought. "Is it true, Cahua? Is Huallpa married to our cousin Coca, or was he just teasing me?"

Cahua laughed. "It is true. You have been away for a long time, my brother. Huaman Cachi has a wife now, too, and Tarapaca married Ñupchu. The war changed everything."

Sinchi shook his head in wonder as they went up the stairs with Ococo just behind them. He gave Cahua a searching glance. "Father is different, too . . ."

"How do you mean?" Cahua asked. He frowned and shrugged. "He seems older . . . and lonely. He told us he misses Uncle Tomay, but I think he misses more than that."

"What could he miss? We are all here with him."

"Maybe it is not a person," Sinchi murmured in a hushed tone, so that she knew he was talking about the spirits of the ancestors or something equally mysterious. She felt a kind of fond annoyance, remembering how he used to insist, when he was little, that the people who had died had just gone away somewhere and might soon return. She gave his arm a tug and they jumped up the last step together.

"You may look like a Campa," she told him with a smile, "but I am glad you are still the brother I knew . . ."

HE HAD BEEN dreaming again of the Bearded Ones, fighting with them as he had before, he and Tomay rushing at them out of ambush and forcing them to flee. The silver shirts fell and they trampled on them, dodging the fiery darts that flew from their booming metal blowpipes. Then the beasts appeared, dark shapes that quickly became huge shaggy bodies, and he could see their clawed feet ripping up the earth as they ran toward him. They had the bald, ugly heads and evil eyes of vultures, and the thunder of the blowpipes seemed to drive them into a frenzy, though they did not throw off the Bearded Ones who sat cross-legged on seats on their backs, lashing out at Cusi's men with metal spears and war clubs. Tomay had disappeared and everyone was running in terror, and fear caught Cusi and made him flee, running as fast as he had ever run yet barely staying ahead of the beasts, praying he could make it to the safety of the forest . . .

When he saw Micay leaning over him and realized he was awake and safe, he felt such immense relief he could only stare up at her blankly.

"Are you awake?" she whispered, and he managed a nod, wondering if he had cried out in his dream and awakened her. But then she went on with an urgency that had nothing to do with dreams. "Sinchi is not here. And there is a storm coming."

Cusi raised his head and heard a rolling growl of thunder, a reassuring sound since it explained the booming in his dream. He threw off his blankets and found his tunic with the help of a flash of lightning.

"I will find him," he promised, and he slipped out past the doorway curtain, which was flapping in its holder. The wind swirled up into his face, damp but surprisingly mild, and fresh with the smell of rain. Lightning lit up the flying clouds from behind, and then a jagged, blue-white bolt broke free and struck one of the nearby peaks with a crash that was immediate and resounding. Cusi jumped, feeling the exhilaration he had experienced at the beginning of his dream, before the battle turned.

He turned right along the narrow walkway in front of the house, assuming Sinchi had gone to sleep with the other Campas, who were in the guest houses on the terrace above. He did not know why Micay had not assumed this herself and simply gone back to sleep, except that she had not been prepared for the change in Sinchi and did not trust it as easily as he did.

As he came around the corner, however, he found his son curled up in a cloak at the base of a winding staircase that had been carved out of the bedrock that supported the terraces. Cusi's approach could not have been heard above the roar of wind and thunder, yet Sinchi's eyes were open and alert when Cusi squatted down next to him.

"Your mother wondered where you had gone," Cusi told him, finding they were sheltered by the rock and did not have to shout.

"I am not used to sleeping in stone houses," Sinchi said, and Cusi bared his teeth in a wistful smile, recalling that Uritu had made a similar complaint when he first had arrived in Cuzco.

"What are the other Campas doing?"

"They make tents for themselves out of blankets, inside."

"You could have done that," Cusi suggested, but the boy shook his head.

"Mother would not have liked it."

"She is not used to her son looking like a Campa," Cusi said, lifting his head as multiple shafts of lightning crackled around Huayna Picchu, the peak that rose up at the other end of the city. "Illapa," he murmured, looking back at Sinchi. "It has been a long time since we shared a storm."

"The Campas do not like them," Sinchi said ruefully. "They whisper about me because I go out to watch them alone."

"You are not alone now," Cusi assured him, rising to lead the way up the narrow steps. At the top he emerged from the shelter of the rock into a horizontal rain, the drops flying past his face and striking his bare arms like darts. A river of clouds flowed by overhead, seeming close enough to touch, and the lightning came in crashing bursts that illuminated whole sections of the city below. Sinchi let out a whoop that Cusi just heard before it was lost in the din, and then he was whooping himself, adding his own spirit to the storm by bellowing along with it. The air around them lit up with a piercing crack, and they were both dancing in place, Sinchi's long hair flailing around his head, his eyes wide and his mouth open in a howl of terrified delight. In the stark light his birthmark looked like war paint, and Cusi threw back his head and screamed out a warrior's salute to Illapa and Thunupa, a war cry that was also a kind of prayer.

Then the clouds above them seemed to collapse under the weight of the rain they carried, dropping it on their heads and drenching them in an instant. Cusi was blind for a moment, coughing and spitting water, and he suddenly remembered that Raurau Illa had lost his eyesight to lightning. So he grabbed Sinchi by the arm and pulled him toward the stairway. They groped their way down the slippery steps, lashed by the wind and rain, their hands and feet going numb with the cold. Cusi slipped on the walkway, but Sinchi kept him up, and they staggered the last few feet together, bracing themselves on the doorjamb before pushing past the sodden curtain into the room.

There was a wick burning in a bowl in one of the wall niches, and Micay quickly rose to greet them, holding an armful of towels. Cahua and Ococo were crouched at the window, peering out under the curtain at the storm.

"Where did you go?" Micay demanded, but they were both breathing too hard to speak. So she simply put the towels on the floor beside them, and Cusi and Sinchi turned their backs to the girls and stripped off their wet clothes. The sight of the gold-rimmed obsidian disc hanging against Sinchi's bare chest made Cusi remember his own spirit brother, and after removing it from his waistband he held it in his cupped palm and showed it to Sinchi. Sinchi studied it intently for a long moment, his face impassive, then smiled at Cusi and thrust out his chest to display the shining disc.

"Lloque Yupanqui's last gift," Cusi murmured, feeling a sudden loosening in his own chest. Perhaps some things could be saved and passed along.

"Hawk," Sinchi said succinctly. The two of them shivered simultaneously, which made them laugh and rub vigorously at their bodies with the towels. They wrapped themselves in blankets before turning around to face Micay and the two girls, who were sitting against the back wall. Micay was regarding them with rueful exasperation, while Cahua and Ococo were hiding their amusement behind their hands.

"So . . . you had to test yourselves in the storm," Micay concluded, glancing from one to the other. "I hope it was worth the risk."

"It was," Cusi said without hesitation, smiling when Sinchi whooped softly in agreement.

"But where had you gone?" she asked Sinchi. "I waited a long time before rousing your father."

"I was just outside," said Sinchi, toying with a wet strand of feather-plaited hair. "The Campas do not live in stone houses."

"But you are an Inca," Cahua said with an incredulous laugh. "We have always lived in stone houses!"

Sinchi hooded his eyes and let his face go blank, as if her words could not possibly apply to him. It was the Campa way of evading a potential argument, but Sinchi had not fully mastered it or was too conscious of himself in this company. Instead of a tactful withdrawal, it seemed like a pointed silence, a rebuke. Cahua appeared astonished and hurt.

"Let us all sit," Cusi suggested, nudging Sinchi with his elbow. "It is time we talked about who we are and who we wish to be."

"I am not ashamed to be an Inca," Cahua said angrily. "And I do not wish to go barefoot and live in the trees!"

Cusi caught his daughter's eye but did not reply until he had settled himself on the floor. "Your brother did not mean to insult you," he told her. "Just as you did not know you were insulting him."

"But what I said is true! He was born an Inca, just like me."

"Your Uncle Uritu was born a Campa, but he became an Inca by privilege," Cusi pointed out. "He has granted your brother the privilege of becoming a Campa."

"I must earn it," Sinchi insisted. "In the rites."

"Of course. But you should not have to earn our understanding and acceptance of your choice." Cusi glanced across at Micay. "That, we should offer freely."

Micay sighed and nodded in resignation. "I know I have been reluctant to accept the change in you, Sinchi. It does not seem that you have been away from me very long, and I keep seeing my Inca son wearing a Campa disguise."

Sinchi frowned but did not try to withdraw. "Some of the Campas see me that way, too," he admitted. "They always correct my speech and make comments about the lightness of my skin and the mark around my eye. They will never let me forget I am different."

"That is just as well," Cusi said, "because you are different. You are the son of lightning, as you saw again tonight. That will not leave you, even if there are no Incas around to remind you. Even if you come to know the gods of the sky by other names. It is a part of your spirit that you should claim, however you choose to live. The fact that you have kept your spirit brother shows you know that."

Some uneasy thought flitted across the boy's face, but he quelled it and nodded in agreement. Cahua held up the silver bracelet around her wrist to attract Cusi's attention.

"I have also kept what the high priestess gave me. And the stone from Pachamama. But Sinchi told me the shrines of Mama Quilla and Pachamama in Vitcos are empty. The mamacona left with the other Incas when Huascar was defeated."

"They did," Cusi agreed, and he gave her a challenging look. "But there is nothing to prevent you from filling them with your own holiness. The mamanchic would probably send someone to guide you, if you wished. You might even choose to invite the Campa women to join the cults . . ."

Cahua brightened with interest and exchanged an eager glance with Ococo, but Micay held up a hand to Cusi as if to slow him down.

"We have not seen Vitcos yet, and you are already recruiting for the cults. What if we do not find it a suitable place to live?"

Cusi shrugged. "It may be some time before we know where we can settle safely. But wherever we live, we will do so under our own authority. We must take the best of what we know and feel and use it to begin again."

"To begin again," Micay echoed. "We have waited a long time."

"We were not free until now. We are not really free yet. But in Vitcos we can act as if we are. No one can dispute us there."

They were all silent for a few moments, considering their freedom, and Cusi was aware of the rain drumming on the thatch overhead, a sound so constant he had failed to notice it while they were talking. He had heard that there was less rain and fog in Vitcos, and he hoped that was true.

"Will we still call ourselves Incas?" Cahua asked finally.

Cusi smiled to reassure her. "Those who wish to may." He smiled sideways at Sinchi. "Others may wish to earn another name for themselves. There are many bloods represented among the Hawk Men, and we cannot allow blood to bind or separate us as it has in the past. We must be bound by our respect for one another."

"Will you call yourself an Inca?" Cahua persisted, though she appeared more curious than resistant. Cusi reached up and touched one of his earplugs, grimacing ruefully.

"I have no choice as long as I wear these. But I truly do not know what becomes of an Inca who turns his back on Cuzco and loses his regard for Inti. We will all have to find ourselves anew."

"Let us sleep, then," Micay suggested, and, lifting her chin in Sinchi's direction, she added, "That is, if you have had enough of the storm and can bring yourself to sleep in a stone house."

Sinchi glanced from her to Cusi, grinning shyly. "Perhaps I can still remember how. We will be back in the forest soon enough."

"We will," Cusi agreed, and he let out a whoop that made them jump and turn laughing toward their beds as he rose to blow out the light.

Vitcos

SINCHI HAD promised one of his adoptive uncles he would help him cut palm leaves for his roof, so it was midmorning before he began the long climb up to the Inca settlement. The trail switched back constantly as it ascended the steep, thickly forested slope, and at several of the turnings he noted the cloth markers his father and Amaru had left to indicate possible sites of sentry posts. Halfway up, he slipped off the main path onto a game trail that would tax his legs but save him some time. As he pushed the foliage out of the way with his bow, tipping the leaves away from him even though the dew had mostly dried, he reflected that an ordinary Inca would not even have seen that the trail was there. Incas could barely tell one kind of tree from another, and two trees of the same kind were utterly indistinguishable. His father was a little better, with his scout's eye and memory for details, but he still had a tendency to look up and ahead rather than down and around to orient himself.

Though he was breathing hard in the thinning air, Sinchi heard the sounds of a commotion ahead and froze, instinctively loosening the string wrapped around the shaft of his bow. Then he heard a laugh and other sounds that only people made. He rewrapped his bowstring and crept forward noiselessly, remembering a small clearing in a thicket where the deer sometimes bedded down. They seemed to know instinctively that they were safer near the Incas, who claimed all the game on this mountain but seldom hunted for themselves. The sounds were definitely coming from the clearing, which was off to the right and not visible from the path. Sinchi could have gone by without seeing or being seen, but the forest in daylight was not a place of secrets to him, so he went to look.

He wormed his way forward on his hands and knees until he could peer upward through a gap in the tangle of leaves, stems, and vines. He saw Fempellec's face first, and then Machacuay's appeared close beside it, pressing his lips against Fempellec's cheek. They were both smiling, their eyes hooded with pleasure, and Sinchi smiled, too, touched by the affection that was so plain between them. He had always liked Machacuay, but he did not think he had ever seen Fempellec display such unguarded tenderness.

Then they sank down to his level, onto the grass, and he saw that they were both naked and that they were stroking and touching each other. Sinchi suddenly felt warm all over and did not know what to think. The Incas said this was wrong, a crime; the Campas merely shrugged and smiled into their hands whenever someone hinted at what the men did when they were away on a long hunt. These men had bodies that were soft and smooth like girls', except for the places where they were undeniably men—where Fempellec was now putting his lips, his tongue, his fingers sliding so delicately along the inside of Machacuay's thigh. Sinchi looked down at himself and saw that his tunic was standing out like a tent between his legs, and he experienced a longing he had heard the older boys talk about but had never felt in himself. He wanted to be touched like that. He could feel it inside his skin, a yearning that flowed along with the rush of blood.

He found himself thinking of Ococo, of the way she brightened when she saw him and then turned shy, waiting until no one else was paying attention before murmuring a greeting in Campa. He would be ready for the manhood rites soon, and his former playmate Huallpa was already married. Did Coca touch him like this? Sinchi was seeing things behind his eyes as well as in front of him, and the excited blur dizzied him until he nearly fell over. He was afraid he had made a noise and froze, but the couple on the other side of the thicket did not falter in their slow, rhythmic movements. Letting out a silent breath, he sank down onto his side to watch, deciding that these city men had something to teach him after all.

"WE COULD create another Quito here," Parihuana was saying as they paused in the doorway of the half-sized chamber at the eastern end of the great hall. "Much smaller, of course, but also less likely to be spoiled by anyone from the outside."

" 'Little Quito,' " Micay mused aloud, recalling Amaru's elaborate model of that city. Leaning into the chamber, she made a quick visual estimate of the floor space and the number of people who could be housed here if the need arose. The great hall was typically large in its proportions but unusual in that its roof had been built in four sections with uncovered passageways in between, and its interior space had been divided into ten separate chambers. It had been erected for ceremonial gatherings of a size that had probably never occurred here, since only a couple of the larger chambers showed signs of much use. Micay added the requisite knot to the memory cord she was making, thinking it would provide excellent temporary housing should they be forced to evacuate their people from the Yucay Valley.

"You have been very quiet, Micay," Parihuana ventured. "About whether you like Vitcos . . ."

Micay stepped back out of the doorway and looked out over the grassy meadow that had been left open at the southern end of the site, no doubt intended as a public square for those ceremonial gatherings. A mixed flock of llamas and alpacas was presently grazing out in the middle of the square under the watchful eyes of a herd boy. The grass extended right up to where the mountainside dropped off, permitting an expansive view of forested hills and valleys and the snow-capped peaks of the mountains in the distance. Vitcos was as high as Machu Picchu but seemed much less of an island in the sky, the drop to the surrounding valleys softened by the unbroken canopy of the cloud forest.

"Ococo has reminded me that Chachapoyas is like this," Micay said to Parihuana. "She likes it, and I think Cahua does, too. Obviously you and Amaru can see a home for yourselves here."

"We will have to see what the rainy season is like," Parihuana said judiciously, "but it is already warmer and less cloudy than Machu Picchu. And as we ourselves saw, it would not be easy for anyone to get here if we wanted to stop them."

Micay could only nod in agreement, remembering the hard four-day march from Machu Picchu and the many places on the trail where a handful of men could turn back an army. They had found their refuge—if they were ready to retreat from the rest of the Four Quarters.

Suddenly the llamas and alpacas lifted their heads in unison, then bolted off across the meadow, and the herd boy came running toward the hall, gesturing frantically over his shoulder at the people who had just come out of the high grass at the meadow's edge. Amaru was limping along at their head, accompanied by the old Colla stonecutter he had brought with him from Machu Picchu, but they were being prodded along at spear point by men wearing earplugs. There were perhaps ten of these men with an equal number of women trailing them at a short distance.

Piqui and Huaman Cachi suddenly appeared at Micay's side with war clubs in their hands, and three more Hawk Men came on the run from the other end of the hall.

"Is this all we have?" Micay asked.

Piqui nodded grimly. "Everyone else went with Cusi," he reported, bending to address the herd boy, who came skidding to a halt in front of them. "Cusi

Huaman and Uritu should be on their way back from the White Rock. Tell them to bring the warriors ahead as fast as possible. Go!"

Piqui straightened up and turned to Micay. "Perhaps you should also leave, my ladies. Take the passageway through the hall and then go east the way I sent the boy. We can hold these intruders off."

"But they have Amaru," Parihuana protested.

"They also have women with them," Micay observed, "and look how ragged their clothes are." She coiled the cord around her wrist and plucked the golden pin from her mantle with her other hand, letting the mantle fall to the grass behind her. "No," she decided, "I would not flee *to* Vitcos, and I certainly will not flee *from* it."

Piqui merely grunted in compliance, and he and Huaman Cachi took up positions on either side of the women, the other warriors alongside them. As the group approached, Amaru straightened up and shook his head slightly, indicating with his tight-lipped, scornful expression that he had not told his captors anything about himself. Micay held the pin down next to her leg and spoke to Parihuana out of the side of her mouth.

"Do not show that you know him," she warned, keeping her eyes on the group, which came to a halt about twenty feet away. Now she could see how young and sick and desperate they were, and out of the corner of her eyes she saw Piqui and Huaman Cachi recognize the same thing and relax slightly behind their weapons. A young man with a spear stepped forward in front of those guarding Amaru, and despite the mud and swollen insect bites on his face the resemblance to Chuqui Huipa and Huascar was plainly apparent to Micay.

"We want food and clothing," the young man snapped, gesturing at Amaru with his spear. "Quickly, or we will kill him."

"What will keep us from killing you?" Piqui shot back, brandishing his war club with a confidence that told Micay he was not bluffing. She stayed him with a gesture of her cord-wrapped hand.

"Greetings, Manco Inca," she said in a calm voice, taking his surprise as confirmation of her guess. "I am Mama Micay, the wife of the lord of the Eastern Quarter, Cusi Huaman. You are welcome to food and clothing, and I have medicines for those among you who are sick. There is no need for threats."

"Bring it to us," the man demanded as if he had not heard. "We will release him when we are safely away from here."

Micay gave an indifferent shrug. "Release him whenever you wish. He is one of Huascar's men, and my husband spared him only because he has useful skills. So you see, your threat is not only unnecessary, it is empty."

"Perhaps you would make a better captive," the young man decided, and Micay gave him a level stare before lifting her chin to indicate the warriors around her.

"You are young, Manco Inca, and I doubt you have ever proven yourself against men like these. They fought their way here from Quito, defeating the best warriors your brother could muster. I can assure you that you are no match for them."

"I am not like my brother!" he snarled, and he made a move toward her. Piqui and Huaman Cachi immediately moved to intercept him, and Amaru chose that moment to snatch a club from one of his guards and break into the open.

"Amaru!" Parihuana screamed, as several of the other guards surged toward him. Amaru cut two of them down but left himself off balance and vulnerable, and a third man was lunging with a spear when Micay saw a blur of motion in the distance and an arrow came hissing down and embedded itself in the man's shoulder. He fell with a scream that froze everyone in place except Piqui, who jumped forward and struck Manco Inca in the face with his fist, sending him sprawling to the ground, limp and unconscious. Huaman Cachi sprang to Amaru's side, driving the remaining guards back, and Micay saw Sinchi come trotting across the grass, another arrow fixed in his bow.

"I told you threats were pointless," she said to the warriors who were still on their feet. "Now lay down your weapons!"

After only a brief hesitation they did, and Piqui straightened up with Manco Inca's spear in his hand, motioning to his men to retrieve the other weapons.

"Welcome to Vitcos," Micay said dryly, and she relaxed the sweaty grip she had on her pin and turned to look for her mantle.

ONE OF THE retainers had intercepted Cusi and Uritu on the trail, telling them that the danger was past and that the captives had been taken to the large courtyard on the upper level. The warriors with them had cheered at that, but Cusi had simply gone on at the same trot, still chastising himself for not being more vigilant. When he entered the courtyard he found the captives sitting or lying on the ground with Piqui, Amaru, and the Hawk Men standing a loose guard around them. Micay was tending to one of the wounded, and Fempellec and Machacuay were helping Parihuana and a retainer woman distribute food and water to those who were able to sit up.

Cusi took Piqui and Amaru aside and got a full account of what had occurred from the moment Amaru and the stonecutter were surprised in the forest to the point at which Sinchi's arrow and Piqui's fist had ended the confrontation. Piqui's recital was typically curt and made the victory seem inevitable, but Amaru was still pulsing with the emotions aroused by his capture and escape, which he described in much more passionate terms.

"I saw my death on the point of that spear," Amaru declared, "and then Sinchi's arrow came out of nowhere to save me. You have taught him well, Uritu."

They all glanced over at Sinchi, who was sitting next to the man he had wounded, holding the bloody shaft of the arrow he had used. He was talking to the young Inca, who wore golden earplugs but was probably no more than sixteen years of age.

"I taught him nothing about hunting men," Uritu said quietly, and he left them to go join Sinchi. Cusi gave his battle-ax to one of his men and went over to where Manco Inca was sitting by himself. The food and water in front of him were untouched, and when the young man raised his head he revealed a bruised cheek and a badly swollen jaw.

"I am Cusi Huaman," Cusi told him, examining him without sympathy. "You should have accepted my wife's offer of hospitality. Have you not heard of my leniency toward those who served Huascar?"

"I have never served Huascar," Manco muttered, wincing at the movement of his jaw but still managing to sound scornful. "I also heard that Quizquiz sent you to hunt me down. Why would you show me any hospitality?"

"Why not?" Cusi demanded in return. "I am familiar with the brothers who were close to Huascar, and you were never one of them."

"So you would feed me and give me new clothes," Manco suggested bitterly, "and then send me back to Cuzco to have my throat slit in the Haucaypata. It is better to die trying to take what I need."

"You had your chance to do that," Cusi assured him, "and you will not have another. I have no desire to send you back to Cuzco, but I also have little reason to keep you alive here."

A glint of hope appeared in the young man's eyes, and he pushed himself to his feet, wobbling slightly before he caught his balance. "My mother was a full sister of Huayna Capac," he said earnestly. "Someday . . ."

"Do not promise me your favor," Cusi interrupted. "It may be as worthless later as it is now."

"I will fight for you, then," Manco offered, pushing out his chest to make himself seem larger. Cusi looked at him and laughed.

"Taking unarmed men captive is not fighting. Besides, I have hundreds of men who will fight for me and who do not need to be trained."

Manco blew air through his nose and glared at Cusi in frustration. "You are toying with me. You have no intention of letting me live."

"Not if I cannot trust you," Cusi said. "You have not offered me that."

Manco cocked his head and squinted at Cusi with pained curiosity, as if his words carried a meaning that resisted decipherment. Cusi stared back at him calmly, letting him come to his own understanding. Finally he did, nodding in a way that was both shrewd and humble.

"What must I do, my lord, to make you trust me?"

Cusi nodded in return. "Your question is itself a first step. I will answer it by telling you what I want you to do: Once your people are healed and fit to travel, I want you to take them to Machu Picchu. I want you to stay there and make yourselves useful to the mamanchic and do nothing that would attract the attention of Cuzco. Can you do that?"

"Yes," Manco agreed without hesitation, hope in his eyes again.

"You are young, and it is a solemn place," Cusi warned him sternly. "You must understand that it could be years before it is safe for you to go anywhere else, except perhaps to come here."

"I understand," Manco insisted. "I am young, my lord, but I wish to grow older."

Cusi raised an eyebrow. "You showed no evidence of that earlier."

Manco glanced at Amaru and Piqui, holding up his palms in apology. "I was desperate. We have been dying slowly in the jungle, and I did not believe anyone would help us. I did not believe there was any mercy left among the Incas."

"Now you know otherwise," Cusi said, and made a gesture of dismissal. "So eat, Manco Inca, and reassure your companions. We will talk again later."

"I am grateful, Cusi Huaman," the young man murmured, touching a hand to his mouth in deference as he bowed. He turned and scooped up the bowl and gourd he had left on the ground, lifting the gourd to his lips. But then he changed his mind, lowered the gourd without drinking, and went to join his companions. Cusi grunted softly in approval.

"Now he wants only to be alive," Amaru said skeptically, "but later he will want to be the Sapa Inca."

"Yes . . . 'someday,' " Cusi agreed. "Let him have his dream. He will need it to sustain him at Machu Picchu."

"We should train him," Piqui suggested. "Make him one of us."

"A Hawk Man?"

"We have accepted men of lesser blood," Piqui said with a shrug, and Cusi let out a loud laugh, surprised by the joke.

"He would have to be trained here, of course. Would you be willing to attend to that if you were the commander here?"

Piqui's lips widened in what might have been a smile. "I would attend to all my duties if I were the commander."

"Then the post is yours," Cusi declared, "along with the title and the commander's residence. We will celebrate with a feast before I leave for Ollantaytambo."

Amaru cleared his throat. "I have already promised to return to the valley with you, my brother. But when I have done my work there, I would like to settle here and help make this a place where everyone would want to live."

"I suspected as much," Cusi admitted. "I will try not to keep you too long in the valley. Now I must talk to my wife and my son. I doubt they expected to be heroes today."

"Mama Micay refused to flee when I asked her," Piqui said.

"And Sinchi joined the fight without being asked," Amaru added appreciatively. "No one even knew he was watching."

"He has the eyes of a Campa," Cusi said with a proud smile. "He sees everything in the forest and is never lost . . ."

THE DAY AFTER the feast, Manco Inca and his companions—still groggy from the night of celebration but all fit to travel—departed for Machu Picchu. They carried Micay's regards to Mama Inquil, and they left with renewed expressions of gratitude and loyalty, including Manco's eager promise to return for training.

The next morning, the small group that was going back to Ollantaytambo assembled in the same courtyard where the feast had been held. The group consisted of Micay and Cusi, Amaru and the Colla stonecutter, and a few of the scouts for whom land had already been reserved in the valley. Uritu was also going along to visit Rimachi, but he would join them at the bottom of the mountain.

Micay and Cusi first said their farewells to Coca, Huallpa, and Huaman Cachi, and as the five of them exchanged embraces and handshakes, they found themselves unexpectedly moved by this parting.

"It is not that you will be gone so long," Coca said tearfully. "It is that we have come so far together."

"It is time the marching ended," Cusi said, "at least for some of us."

"March back soon," Huallpa urged, "and bring more of the Hawk Men with you."

"But if you have any need of your comrades . . ." Huaman Cachi added, leaving the offer unstated when Cusi nodded and held out his shield so that Huaman Cachi and Huallpa could rap their knuckles against its hard, glossy surface. Micay shouldered her medicine bag and Cusi his carrying bundle, and they all went over to where Amaru was saying good-bye to Parihuana and Roca. Cahua and Ococo were standing with them, since they would be in Parihuana's care while Micay and Cusi were gone, and Sinchi lingered in the background, staying close to Ococo without seeming to mean to.

There were no tears of parting here. Parihuana had exacted Micay's promise that she would be back in time for the birth of Parihuana's second child, which was due in five months, so she was dry-eyed and cheerful, demonstrating her trust in their return. Micay was grateful for this, since she was still suffering pangs of anxiety about being separated from her children and did not want to betray herself with weeping. She hugged Cahua and Ococo again, reminding them to be courteous and to obey Parihuana and the other adults.

"Come back in time, Mama," Cahua said with a slight frown. "You have not trained us as midwives yet."

"I will not keep your husband any longer than I have to," Cusi said to Parihuana. "And I will not let him go near the sleeping stones at Ollantaytambo."

"He knows we need a bathhouse here," Parihuana said easily.

"And some musicians," Fempellec said as he and Machacuay came up to join them. "The Campas we had at the feast tried hard, but they made every dance sound like one of their own—or like something worse."

"That only made the dancers more creative," Micay told him. "It was a memorable feast, Fempellec, a fine beginning for the new people of Vitcos."

"Thank you, my lady," Fempellec said, taking her hand and bowing over it. "For once, we had only ourselves to please . . ."

Then Amaru wrapped him in a brief embrace and led him aside for some final words, and Micay fell in beside Machacuay as they all began to make their way toward the courtyard gate, where the scouts and the stonecutter were waiting with Piqui.

"I will look after the children while you are gone, my lady," Machacuay promised. "Though I still feel I should be going with you."

Micay smiled but shook her head. "No, my friend, you have your own life now. You are the assistant to the chief of feasts, and while Fempellec may assign you your duties, you are not his servant or anyone else's."

"It is a great gift," Machacuay said in a low, tremulous voice, sounding both grateful and daunted.

"It is only what you deserve," Micay assured him. "Whenever you doubt that, let Piqui be your example. You have come as far from Quito as he."

They had reached the gate, and Micay had spoken loudly enough for Piqui to hear. He nodded to both of them and gestured toward the fine cumbi-cloth tunic he was wearing, a gift Cusi had given him at the feast.

"Far enough to shed the darkness of our origins," he declared, and he straightened up when Cusi came up beside Micay.

"I leave Vitcos in your hands, Commander," Cusi told him. "I will send you more men as soon as they can be recruited and equipped."

"Uritu's people will help us in the meantime," Piqui said, "and I have conferred with Amaru Inca about what to build first."

"I will see you have time as well as workers. I will not make you defend Vitcos again before you are ready."

"We will always be ready," Piqui insisted. "If Cuzco demands too much from you, tell them farewell and bring the Hawk Men here."

Cusi rapped his battle-ax against his shield in reply and led them out through the gate, with everyone turning for last looks and final words of farewell. Micay waved to Cahua and Ococo and received a last reassuring smile from Parihuana before they turned the corner of the enclosure and headed for the trail that would take them down the mountain. She discovered that Sinchi had somehow gotten past her and was walking just ahead of her and Cusi, carrying his long, black bow and quiver of arrows.

"The Campas do not believe in farewells," she said when he glanced back at her. He shook his head in a swift denial. "Some of your spirit might wander off with the traveler."

"You have none to spare? Not even for your mother?"

Sinchi slowed, appearing genuinely alarmed. He cast a plaintive glance at Cusi, who smiled and shrugged and made no effort to intervene. Micay was about to tell him she was only teasing when he put his head down and walked out ahead again. He had his chin tucked into his chest and appeared to be talking to himself, arguing with his own thoughts. Micay glanced at Cusi and saw he was equally astonished.

Sinchi disappeared into the forest ahead of them and was out of sight for several moments. But he was waiting just within the cool shadows of the trees when Micay and Cusi arrived. Amaru and the others had apparently perceived his strange behavior and were lingering behind at a discreet distance. Sinchi had propped his bow against a bush, and without a word he came up to Micay and put a necklace over her head, carefully dropping it down inside her shift. Even before her fingers found the black beads, she knew what it was, and she stiffened in dismay, trying to think of how to refuse it without hurting his feelings.

"Hawk," he said softly. Then he grinned at her with what seemed like relief.

"Are you certain you want to do this?" Cusi asked when Micay could not speak. Sinchi nodded emphatically.

"I will begin preparing for the manhood rites soon, before you return. The head sorcerer told me I could not have Hawk with me during the rites. He thought I should not have it at all and offered to help me bury it where it could not hurt me. I told him I would give it to you, but I was going to keep it, hidden away somewhere."

Cusi laughed. "I was sent to the Grass Man as punishment for a similar deception."

Micay put a hand over the disc beneath her shift, feeling its shape against her breastbone. "My son . . ."

"Please, Mama, keep it for me," Sinchi pleaded. "Then I can face the head sorcerer with a clear heart and you can remember me wherever you are."

"I would do that anyway," Micay told him, but then she nodded in acquiescence. "I will keep it safe for you. It will be my gift to you when you are a man."

Sinchi grinned and hugged her forcefully, squeezing the air out of her. Then he snatched up his bow and turned to lead the way down the shaded path, tossing his feather-plaited hair away from his face as he looked back over his shoulder.

"Come, then," he commanded, and let out a joyful whoop. "The sooner you leave, the sooner you will be back to stay . . ."

Ollantaytambo

RIMACHI'S SON Topa, and another boy had discovered the fish trapped in an eddying pocket in the riverbank, just above the bridge. They had been trying unsuccessfully to kill it with stones until Uritu went over and showed them how to make a net out of reeds and willow branches. Now he was instructing them on how to cast and draw the net, making them stay on the bank while he stood knee deep in the shallows, ready to catch them if they slipped.

Cusi was watching along with Micay and Quespi and a number of other people, marveling at Uritu's patience and his knowledge of the ways of fish. When he glanced across the river, though, and saw Rimachi, Amaru, and the Colla coming through the freshly planted fields, he slipped away from the group and went toward the bridge to meet them. He was eager to hear their assessment of the quarry they had gone to inspect, which was closer than their present source and could have a significant effect on their building plans.

He was in the middle of the bridge when he saw the smoke of a signal fire rise from a nearby ridge. The first widely spaced, gray puffs told him a message was coming from Cuzco, and he halted in his tracks. A series of smaller puffs that he could not decipher followed, no doubt part of a code that Rimachi and Tarapaca had devised for their own use. Out in the fields, Rimachi and Amaru had also stopped to gaze up at the signal, and now they lurched back into motion, Amaru struggling to keep up with Rimachi's long strides.

Cusi looked down at the silver-green water rushing past beneath the bridge and experienced a moment of intense dizziness that revealed to him just how much he had been dreading this eventuality. In the months since his return, he had been a dutiful lord, sending cords and reports on the harvest and the new planting and his various construction projects. He had also sent an ample share of that harvest, along with many of the gifts he had received from the forest tribes. Other than expressions of satisfaction, the only response he had had from Quizquiz was a report that the bearded strangers had left their camp in Tangarara and were marching south along the coast, apparently on their way to meet with Atauhuallpa in Caxamarca. The report had come without any additional comment from Quizquiz, as if simply to remind him of his ties to the world outside the Eastern Quarter.

Two months had passed since that report had come to him. Could the Bearded Ones have reached Caxamarca so soon? Or had Atauhuallpa ambushed them somewhere along the way? One of Cusi's envoys to Cuzco had heard rumors that Atauhuallpa planned to capture the strangers and use them—along with Huascar and his few remaining relatives—as sacrifices in a triumphal celebration of his power. Cusi feared he would want to hold such a celebration in Cuzco, or worse, that he would summon all the war chiefs back to Caxamarca to witness the event. In either case Cusi would be compelled to attend, since a refusal would be an insult that Atauhuallpa would be equally compelled to avenge. He would send the whole army if he had to, and even Vitcos could not withstand that. Not yet.

The bridge began to vibrate beneath his feet, and he looked up to see Rimachi and Amaru and the Colla approaching.

"A message from Cuzco," Cusi said, as they stopped next to him. "What did the rest of the signal say?"

"It said Tarapaca is bringing the message himself," Rimachi told him. "It must be important."

"The Bearded Ones have been killed or captured," Amaru predicted. "Or they have fled again in their floating houses."

"Or they have set loose another sickness," Rimachi said darkly, sending a shudder down Cusi's spine.

"I had not thought of that," he confessed.

"Invisible warriors," Rimachi said with a shrug, and he started them moving toward the people gathered on the riverbank. The fish had obviously proven too large and wily for the boys' net, because Uritu was now stalking it with bow and arrow, checking the sun and his own shadow as he circled the swirling pool. Micay and the others were watching him intently, paying no attention to the men on the bridge. Uritu finally found his place and went still, holding the bow at the level of his waist and tilting the arrow downward as he gradually pulled the bowstring taut. The people around him seemed to be holding their breath. Then Uritu released the arrow and the water seemed to erupt, showering the people on the bank and throwing up a fish that thrashed in the air, gushing blood from its pierced side. Topa and the other boy let out a cry and jumped down with their net stretched out between them.

The men on the bridge had stopped to watch, and Amaru looked at Cusi and let out a long breath. "I am suddenly reminded of the end of the Carangui . . ."

"The Lake of Blood," Cusi murmured in agreement.

"It is only a fish," Rimachi said impatiently, and he started forward again. "Save your memories and predictions. Let us go hear what Tarapaca has to tell us."

THEY WAITED in the road, distracting themselves by watching Uritu teach the boys how to gut and skin the fish and then admiring the catch when Topa brought it over to show his parents. Rimachi told him to take it to the cooks, adding a promise to the other boy that he and his parents would eat with the commander that evening.

Tarapaca finally appeared around the bend in the road, leading a small column of warriors. Cusi felt Micay briefly tighten her grip on his arm before letting him go, and he nodded in acknowledgement of the fears they both shared. They had allowed themselves to believe in the possibility of a new beginning at Vitcos, gambling that the outside world would not interfere before they were ready to resist all such interference. A march to Caxamarca—back into the realm of Atauhuallpa's willfulness—seemed unimaginable. Let him send the whole army, Cusi thought with a kind of despair; we will fight them in the forest.

Tarapaca came to a halt in front of them, raising his spear to Cusi in a salute. Then he hesitated and swallowed as if the words he had to say were sticking in his throat. Cusi felt his heart sink, certain that his worst fear was about to be confirmed. Tarapaca shook himself and spoke in a flat voice.

"My lord, Quizquiz sends this message: The Bearded Ones are in Caxamarca. They came into the city one day and . . . and they took Atauhuallpa captive the next."

"Again," Cusi heard himself say amid the chorus of shocked exclamations. Micay was leaning against him, and he put an arm around her waist to steady her.

"How did it happen?" Rimachi demanded.

Tarapaca shrugged. "The messenger did not know much. Apparently the Bearded Ones had hidden themselves in the buildings around the main square, and they attacked without warning. Hundreds of Atauhuallpa's best warriors were slaughtered in the square. Quizquiz has summoned a council of the war chiefs in Cuzco."

"Did he lose his mind?" Amaru wondered aloud. "To let them set up an ambush in his own city and then fall into it . . ."

"He did the same thing in Tumibamba," Cusi reminded them, exchanging a glance with Tarapaca. "He had to show that he feared no one."

"There was no one to help him escape this time," Tarapaca said. "Everyone waited to see if he would do it again. Instead, when he was allowed to send a message to his warriors, he told them not to attempt a rescue because the Bearded Ones would kill him if they did."

Micay suddenly straightened up, looking from one to the other, her face animated. "We are free, then. He cannot command us from captivity, and no one can rule in his place while he is still alive."

The men looked at each other and slowly began to nod, Rimachi and Amaru breaking out in smiles. Cusi glanced at Tarapaca, whose expression was more wary, and at Uritu, who was regarding him impassively.

"That is true," he agreed, meeting Micay's expectant gaze. "But I must still go back for the council."

"But why?"

"Because it would be dangerous to declare our freedom this soon."

"Why do you have to declare anything?" Rimachi asked. "Simply ignore the summons. Quizquiz will not miss you enough to come after you."

"He might if I am the only one who is missing. He is a vengeful man, and if he cannot strike back at the Bearded Ones, he might choose another target. I want to be sure it is not us."

"I see your point," Micay said reluctantly. "But what if he and Challcochima ask you to go to Caxamarca? You are always the one they turn to when they cannot prevail by force."

"They can ask, but they will not persuade me. Quizquiz heard what Atauhuallpa said to me at Catiquilla, so he knows I owe him nothing now. And Challcochima knows me too well to try to influence me against my better judgment."

"Then I have only one question," Micay said. "Are you certain you do not wish to fight the Bearded Ones yourself?"

Cusi paused for a moment, thinking of his vision, of the one enemy who would destroy their way of life. But that battle had been lost long ago, when the Incas had begun to fight each other.

"Quite certain," he said to Micay. "I have fought them in my dreams—several times—and I always lost."

Micay sighed in resignation. "Then go. But take some good men with you."

"You left our other comrades in Vitcos," Tarapaca said quickly, "but I am available now."

"So am I," Amaru declared, surprising Cusi into a smile. "I want to hear for myself how this happened."

Rimachi looked down at Cusi and shook his head. "I have no desire to see Cuzco again, and I could not pretend to care about what happens to Atauhuallpa. I will watch over the valley until you return."

Cusi glanced at Uritu, who nodded before Cusi could speak.

"You do not have to ask, my brother. I have waited a long time to return what you gave me when I went to Cuzco for the first time. You opened your home to me, and now I would make you at home in Vitcos. So I will see that he remembers his promises, Micay, and I will bring him back when he is done."

"Then I have my good men," Cusi said. He put his hands on Micay's shoulders. "This is the last time I will ask you to wait for me, my wife. Nothing will keep me away, I promise you."

"I will not say farewell, then," Micay decided, and Uritu whooped in approval.

"Let us eat some fish before you leave," Rimachi suggested gruffly, and they all turned and began to walk back to Ollantaytambo.

Cuzco

THEY CAME into the city in the late afternoon, under a threatening sky that blotted out the sunset. Their progress had been slowed by the vigilance of Quizquiz's sentries, who had stopped them at every checkpoint along the way. Once they were in the streets, they could see and hear the reasons for the sentries' uneasiness: the people of Cuzco had stopped hiding and had begun to reassert their presence in highly visible ways. Shrines that had been closed or defaced had been reopened and now served as gathering places for groups of men and women who watched the column of warriors pass in stony silence, showing none of the deference that should have been accorded to the golden Sun shield on Cusi's chest. Other groups of young men roamed the streets at random, carrying staves and hoes and stone hammers in a way that made them weapons rather than tools. They regarded the warriors with unconcealed hostility, making Cusi glad he had brought an additional ten warriors along as an honor guard.

As they came into the sacred precinct around the Haucaypata, they could hear the sounds of voices and activity behind the walls of the household enclosures, and everywhere, it seemed, songs of praise were being sung to Viracocha. Obviously the Bearded Ones were again being seen as the avatars of the god, at least by those who had suffered at the hands of Atauhuallpa.

It began to rain as Cusi led his men up to the main gate of the Amarucancha, which appeared deserted except for its complement of guards. The captain in charge told him that Quizquiz had moved his quarters up to Huascar's palace on the Collcampata and that the Amarucancha was indeed empty of both provisions and servants.

"Where are Ucumari and Challcochima being quartered?" Cusi asked, and the captain again shook his head.

"Challcochima is in Andamarca with Huascar and the other prisoners. Atauhuallpa had sent for them before he was captured. Ucumari had to stay in Chincha to put down a rebellion."

"So I am the only one who is *not* missing," Cusi said with a bitter laugh as he and his companions went back out into the rain. Since Quizquiz had apparently given no thought to where they should be quartered, Cusi decided to seek shelter at the Patallacta, which was much closer than the palace on the hill. He spoke to the gatekeeper through a crack in the wooden door that blocked the entrance, explaining who he and his companions were and adding that he and his brother were both members of the Iñaca household. The man said he would check and went away before Cusi could demand entry.

Time passed and the rain intensified, and though Cusi could see a growing number of people milling around behind the door, no one answered his inquiries or moved to open the door. Finally he lost patience and knocked forcefully with his battle-ax, splintering the logs of the door and causing everyone around him to jump. A short time later the door swung inward, and he found himself facing a small crowd of angry men. Five of the household elders were in the front, and the men behind them were mostly retainers armed with sticks of wood and ceremonial staves and weapons. Among the latter Cusi recognized the fiercely gloating face of Titu Amaru.

"My lords," Cusi said politely, ignoring the angry frowns on the faces of the elders. "May we come in out of the rain?"

"No!" the head elder said emphatically. "The last time you were here you forced your way into the Illapa Cancha against our expressed wishes. We do not have to tolerate that now."

"I am a member of this household," Cusi said, "and the great-grandson of Pachacuti. I simply exercised the prerogatives of my blood and rank, and none of you tried to dissuade me. You sent a retainer instead."

"I am telling you now to go," the head elder insisted. "You will not defy us a second time."

"I have not defied you once," Amaru put in, rapping the ground with the butt of his spear. "But you tempt me greatly. I would like to see you drive us away with sticks."

"No, we will go," Cusi said. "When the Iñaca turns away its warriors, it is fit only for retainers with sticks."

With that Cusi turned his back on them and walked away. Amaru paused to spit on the ground before he followed.

"My people still have a compound here, in the eastern quarter," Uritu suggested quietly. "We would be welcome there."

"Even here you must give me a home," Cusi said, shaking his head to clear the water from his eyes. "Let us go quickly, before I forget I am no longer an enemy of those who live here . . ."

THEY WENT up to the Collcampata early the next morning, their clothing stiff and smoky from the fires over which they had been dried. By now Cusi was not surprised to find the palace guards unprepared for his coming and even more suspicious than the sentries outside the city. His honor guard was denied entry altogether, and he, Amaru, Tarapaca, and Uritu were forced to leave their weapons in an outer courtyard. He and Uritu had also brought their coca bags with them, and these were searched twice as they passed from one contingent of guards to the next, using half of the morning to reach the courtyard outside the royal residence.

After another long wait, a man who identified himself as the captain of Quizquiz's personal guard came to tell Cusi that Quizquiz was sequestered with his women and could not be disturbed. Without offering an apology, he suggested that Cusi return sometime later that day.

Cusi looked around at his companions and at the armed warriors who surrounded them on all sides, watching them as if they might transform themselves into assassins at any moment. He let out a harsh laugh, though what he felt was not amusement but the angry swelling of his presence.

"Take this message to Quizquiz," he said to the captain, who waved his hands in a gesture of futility.

"My lord, *no one* can disturb him now!"

"Then you can tell him later, when you find the courage, that Cusi Huaman came to Cuzco for the council of war chiefs and left again when no one would meet with him." Cusi leaned toward the man, making him feel the weight of his threat. "That is my message, Captain, and you can deliver it whenever you like."

Amaru grunted in approval, and the four of them turned as one and started for the courtyard gate, forcing the warriors behind them to break ranks and step aside. The captain had to run to catch up with them again.

"Wait, my lord," he pleaded. "I will tell him you are here . . ."

Even then Quizquiz did not appear in person but had the captain bring out a young Inca warrior named Yucra, who was introduced as one of Atauhuallpa's nephews. The young man seemed frail and hollow-eyed, as if he had just recovered from a serious illness, and he flinched at Cusi's first glance. This made Cusi hesitate long enough to quell his anger, and he forced himself to speak softly.

"You have something to tell us, my son?"

The young man nodded and spoke in a whisper. "I was in Caxamarca, my lord. When the Viracochas came . . ."

"The Bearded Ones," Cusi corrected. He took him by the arm and led him over to a shaded portion of the courtyard. "Come, tell us what you know."

The five of them took seats on the ground, and Cusi waved the guards away. When Yucra did not seem to know where to start, Amaru leaned forward impatiently.

"Tell us first: What was Atauhuallpa's plan?"

"His plan?" the young man repeated blankly.

"Yes. Why did he let them come into the city? What did he think they would do?"

"I do not know, my lord. He did not tell his plans to anyone. He simply told us to act like Incas . . . like men who did not know fear. Those who showed they were afraid were killed."

Cusi signaled Amaru to ease off. "Who were they, my son? And when did this happen?"

"It was the day the Viracochas arrived. Atauhuallpa was at the baths at Cunu, and some of them came to see him, carried on the backs of their warrior beasts. They came too fast for the sentries to warn anyone of their approach. Their captain had a man from the coast who spoke and interpreted for him, and this man told Atauhuallpa that the leader of the Viracochas wished to meet with him and make him his friend. Atauhuallpa said he would do so the next day, in the square." Yucra paused, and his dark-ringed eyes went wide. "Then, instead of taking Atauhuallpa's reply back to his leader, the captain turned his warrior beast and made it run in circles around the courtyard, stirring up great clouds of dust and making the most horrible noises with its metal feet. I could not stand to watch, but I could not keep myself from watching. Then the beast ran right at Atauhuallpa, as if to devour him, and it stopped only a foot away from where he sat, so close that its wind lifted the fringe on Atauhuallpa's head."

Yucra stopped for a moment, panting with fear at the memory. He finally went on in a choked voice. "Atauhuallpa did not move. He did not even blink. I was too frightened to move, though I wanted to run for my life. Some were so frightened that they cried out or fell back, and they were the ones who later died. They were all related to Atauhuallpa by blood, but he did not spare any of them."

Cusi exchanged glances with his friends, giving the young man time to compose himself, though he appeared to have suffered a fundamental loss of composure.

"And the next day?" Cusi prompted. "You went to the square?"

"We went to the square," Yucra repeated, nodding. "We started out from Cunu too early and had to stop for a while, stretched out along the road. The Viracochas must have been watching, because they sent a messenger, saying how eager they were to meet Atauhuallpa and asking him to come ahead. They did not know we were waiting only because we did not want to arrive until sunset."

"Why was that?" Cusi asked, perceiving a glimmer of a plan. "Why did Atauhuallpa want to arrive at sunset?"

"I assumed . . . anyway, it was well known that the warrior beasts were useless after dark. They lose all their fierceness and just stand in one place, or lie down." Yucra blinked and frowned. "I am no longer certain, though, if that is true."

"How many went to the square?"

"Several thousand. There were sweepers to clear the ground in front of Atauhuallpa's litter, and servants and extra bearers, and all the priests and men and women of the court. All of the earplug men and the captains and commanders of the foreign troops, too."

"Were the warriors armed?" Tarapaca asked.

Yucra showed some surprise at the question before shaking his head. "Not those in the procession. But Rumiñaui had thousands more outside the square and around the city, and *they* were all armed. The Viracochas knew they were there, too, because they had not hidden themselves."

"But the Bearded Ones *had* hidden themselves," Cusi suggested, "when you arrived at the square?"

"It was completely empty," the young man agreed, "until we filled it. I thought they must have lost their courage when they saw how many we were. Only one of them came out with the interpreter, the one who is their priest and wears a long tunic like the Chunchos do," Yacra added with a glance at Uritu. "The priest made a long speech to Atauhuallpa, who was sitting in his litter, held aloft by his bearers. I was not close enough to hear everything the interpreter said, but the priest was telling about his ruler and the high priest of their gods, who live far away on the other side of Mama Cocha. They have three high gods but one who is above the rest, though it was not clear if that one was one of the three. The interpreter did not seem to understand it either, though it was after that that he started becoming reluctant to translate the priest's words for Atauhuallpa."

Yucra paused for breath. Cusi simply waited, seeing in his eyes that he needed no prompting. He was back among the crowd in the square, living it again.

"What the priest was saying," Yucra went on, "was that their god had sent them to rule over the people of the Four Quarters and teach them the ways of the Viracochas. He was telling Atauhuallpa that he should submit to this and give up the gods of the Incas because they were false gods." He focused on Cusi for a moment, still incredulous at what he had heard. "Can you believe the madness of it? Saying that to Atauhuallpa in front of thousands of his people!"

"What did Atauhuallpa say?"

"He became very angry and did not try to disguise it. He asked the priest where he had gotten these ridiculous ideas, and the priest answered by showing him one of their huacas. I saw it when it was passed up to Atauhuallpa, and it was small and black and seemed to be coming apart at the edges. Atauhuallpa turned it over in his hands and held it to his ear, and then threw it down to the ground in disgust, saying it was weak and empty. The priest seemed to go mad then, snatching it up and shaking it at Atauhuallpa, and then running back to the great hall from which he had come, screaming and wailing the whole way. There were smiles on many of the faces around me, and we would have laughed if we had not been afraid of Atauhuallpa's anger."

Yucra smiled to himself, then blinked and saw Cusi looking back at him. The smile vanished, and he swallowed with difficulty. "That is when the Viracochas attacked. There was a great boom of thunder, and balls of fire came shooting out of the top of the tower at one end of the square, plummeting down on us and tearing holes in the crowd. Then the Viracochas came rushing out of all the buildings, shooting their blowpipes and cutting people down with their metal clubs. The warrior beasts trampled over everyone in their path, and there was no room for the people to run." He spread his hands in a frantic gesture. "We did not know what to do! The warriors were mixed in with the other people, and we had no weapons and no one to give us orders. We stood there the way Atauhuallpa had sat in front of the warrior beast, only the Viracochas did not stop, they killed and killed . . ."

The young man's eyes glazed over and he raised his hands to his ears as if he could still hear the screams of the dying. Tarapaca, who was sitting closest, reached out and put a hand on his arm to calm him.

"Did you see them capture Atauhuallpa?" Cusi asked gently.

Yucra shook his head without looking up. "I only saw his litter tip over as the bearers were cut out from under it. Then the crowd began to move and I ran with them, though there were too many really to run. The Viracochas had blocked the gate, and they drove us against the high wall along one side of the square. People were crushed to death against it and we climbed up over their backs to get to the top, fighting each other for the chance to escape. Finally there were so many people on the wall that the adobes burst apart and it collapsed, and we ran for our lives with the warrior beasts still chasing us."

The silence that followed Yucra's conclusion was unbroken until a new voice spoke, and Cusi looked up to see Quizquiz standing over them with a drinking cup in his hand.

"Have you heard enough?" Quizquiz repeated with a trace of scorn.

"No," Amaru said bluntly. "What about Rumiñaui and the warriors outside the square? What did they do?"

"Nothing," Quizquiz admitted. "They fled when they heard Atauhuallpa had been captured. At last report Rumiñaui was leading them north on the Royal Road toward Quito."

"It is the prophecy of Catiquilla," Cusi murmured. "Just as the old priest told us . . . before Atauhuallpa cut off his head."

"Then I am glad he is not alive to gloat," Quizquiz snapped. "Will you come inside or do you wish to have our council here?"

"Here," Cusi decided, and Yucra got up without a word and walked away. Quizquiz sat down in his place and gestured to the women behind him, who came forward with empty cups and jars of akha. They were all beautiful and quite young, one of them still wearing the gray and blue uniform of a chosen woman. When the women had poured and departed, Cusi and his companions waited for Quizquiz to make the traditional toast to Inti. But the war chief fixed his bloodshot eyes on his cup with a kind of angry longing and then drank deeply, ignoring the amenities. Cusi exchanged a glance with Amaru and then drank himself, making a silent toast to Catiquilla.

"I have not seen either of you in a while," Quizquiz said to Amaru and Uritu. "That must mean there are no uprisings in the east, at least. You still have not captured Manco Inca?"

"He must have perished in the jungle," Cusi said. "There is no one who would support him anyhow. No one misses Huascar, except for a few isolated priests."

"Many miss him here, as you have no doubt perceived. I told Challcochima to do away with him, but he says he must wait for the command from Atauhuallpa."

"Are you certain Atauhuallpa is still alive?" Amaru asked, and Quizquiz snorted derisively.

"He has made a pact with the Bearded Ones to ransom himself. He has promised to fill a room in Caxamarca with gold, and another with silver, in return for his freedom. The Bearded Ones will do anything for gold, so they will not kill him."

"Where will he get this gold?" Cusi asked.

"It is being sent to Caxamarca from all over the Four Quarters. I did not ask you for any because you had already sent the gold dust the Chunchos gave you."

"Why not send warriors instead?" Amaru suggested. "They can kill him at any time, and they probably will, once they have the gold. It would be better if they died defending him."

Quizquiz gave him a baleful look, his nostrils flaring like dark wings in the middle of his narrow face. "I suggested that to Challcochima, too. He said he did not want to take Huascar out of Andamarca or leave him there either, and he reminded me of Atauhuallpa's own order not to attempt a rescue, which all the men know about. He said it is only gold we are giving up, and the longer Atauhuallpa is a prisoner, the greater the chance he will escape or be freed."

"So we are all captives with him," Cusi concluded, and Quizquiz drained his cup and set it down hard on the ground in front of him.

"I do not have enough men to go myself, unless you think you can hold Cuzco while I am gone."

It was a halfhearted offer, but Cusi pretended to consider it for a moment before shaking his head. "I do not have enough men either. And Cuzco has been yours for too long for anyone to replace you now."

"You mean you do not wish to inherit the hatred they have for me," Quizquiz said sharply, hearing the veiled taunt in Cusi's refusal.

"That is also true. I want nothing I have not earned."

Quizquiz glared at him, but his indignation, too, was halfhearted, and he let it drop when Cusi stared back at him calmly.

"So, warlord . . . go back to your Hawk Men. There is nothing we can do now except hold our places. It would be very different, though, if the Bearded Ones had come here first."

They put down their cups and stood up, shaking out their limbs and rearranging their clothes. Cusi was surprised when Quizquiz held out a hand to him, but he gripped it, then watched as the war chief did the same with Amaru, Uritu, and Tarapaca.

"Very different," Quizquiz muttered. Then he grunted and turned away, leaving them to find their own way out of Cuzco.

THE HERD BOYS had seen them coming long before, and Cusi could not be certain how hostile Alco might be, so he led his whole party up to the ridge that overlooked the huaca. The sun was shining out of a clear blue sky, and a cool breeze tinged with the smell of smoke blew in their faces. Cusi halted at the top and scanned the hollow below, seeing no one at first, then the solitary figure crouched in front of the jutting stone with his back to them.

"Alco," Tarapaca said, recognizing the puma-skin mantle that covered the man's back. He put down his spear and shield and pulled out the gift bundle tucked into his waistband; Cusi put down his shield but kept his battle-ax and the coca bag under his arm.

"Wait for us here," Cusi said to the others, and he started down the slope with Tarapaca beside him. The breeze diminished and the smell of smoke became stronger as they descended, and Cusi saw there was a small offering fire burning in front of the huaca. Then he felt the stillness surround him and draw him in, soothing yet tugging on all his senses, so that a vague excitement stirred in the pit of his stomach. The crouching figure rose as they approached but kept his back turned to them. When they stopped a few feet away, he raised his arms over his head in invocation.

"What is your message, Cusi Huaman?"

"It is over," Cusi said, almost without thinking.

"What is over?" Alco demanded.

"The rule of the Incas. The life we knew when my mother first brought me here."

Alco grunted and lowered his arms, then slowly raised them again. "What is your message, Tarapaca?" he asked. The warrior made a startled movement and looked at Cusi with wide eyes. Then he concentrated on the question, frowning thoughtfully for several moments before he replied.

"There is no one left to serve except the leaders we know and trust. We owe nothing to men who live in palaces far away."

Alco lowered his arms and turned to confront them, revealing a face that had been painted in two broad vertical stripes, half black and half white. His eyes, though, were bright and piercing, and Cusi could feel the power of his presence so strongly that he experienced it as a threat. Alco glanced at the battle-ax in Cusi's hands and the golden Sun shield on his chest, and his lips curled back in disdain, cutting a pink gash through the black and white paint.

"So. Illapa has kept you alive to see the end."

"And . . . the . . . beginning," Cusi managed, feeling a sudden constriction in his throat that made it hard to speak.

"The end," Alco insisted harshly. "The pacha puchucay. So of course the Running Boy runs away from Cuzco."

Now Cusi could not speak at all, and he realized Alco was doing this to him. Fear made him tighten his grip on his battle-ax, and he saw Alco notice the movement and nod with a kind of satisfaction.

"Have you brought an offering this time?" Alco asked, and Cusi freed a hand to unsling the coca bag from around his shoulder. Tarapaca simply held out the gift bundle in his hands.

"Put them on the fire," Alco commanded, stepping aside so they could approach the stone. Cusi and Tarapaca went down on their knees before the huaca and emptied their hands so that they could make the mocha. As he straightened up, Cusi saw a memory cord lying on the ground just in front of the fire, but he went ahead anyway and dropped the coca bag onto the glowing coals. He watched it begin to smoulder, then picked up his battle-ax and stood up. Suddenly Alco was close behind him, speaking in his ear.

"Give me your weapon."

The command seemed to settle around him like a heavy net, trapping his arms against his sides and overwhelming his instinctive urge to whirl and swing the ax. The certainty that Alco meant to kill him swept through him with a rush, and he stiffened in resistance and denial, straining with his whole being to break free. Yet his fingers seemed to open of their own accord, and he felt the weapon being lifted out of his hands. Next to him, Tarapaca let out a strangled cry and fell to the ground. There was a shout from the ridge behind them, but it sounded very far away, while Alco's voice buzzed inside his head.

"Once I saved you both. Your lives belong to me."

An icy sweat broke out on Cusi's body and tears of desperation sprang up in his eyes. He could not believe he was meant to die like this, but he could do nothing to save himself. He heard running footsteps and Amaru's furious warning.

"Hurt him and you are dead!"

"Stay back!" Alco snapped, brandishing the battle-ax over Cusi's head. Then he spoke again into Cusi's ear. *"Burn the cord. Free us both."*

Cusi was released so suddenly that he stumbled forward, and for an instant all he felt was a desire to escape, to leap over the fire and let the warriors finish Alco. But then he realized, simultaneously, why Alco had been able to hold him and why he had let him go. So he stopped and lifted the bundle of cords from the ground, feeling how dry and brittle they had become with age, then dropped them into the flames that had begun to curl up around the blackened coca bag. The memory cord went up like tinder, crackling loudly as it burned. When it was gone Cusi turned to face Alco, who was holding the battle-ax across his chest, his back to the other warriors. Beyond him Cusi could see Uritu holding Amaru back.

"Do you understand now?" Alco asked quietly. Cusi stared back at him, flexing his fingers and testing his muscles one by one.

"I never hated you," Cusi said.

"No, you did not need to. You did not care about me at all, yet you had the power to ruin my life."

"As you had it over me just now. But I think you were already free before I burned the cord."

It was the first time Cusi had ever seen Alco smile, and it only served to make his painted face appear even more grotesque. He handed the battle-ax back to Cusi with a slight bow, then turned to help Tarapaca to his feet, apologizing for the force he had used on him. It was also the first time Cusi had ever heard him apologize for anything.

"This lesson was for me," Cusi said to Tarapaca. "I will tell you about it later. Lead the others back to the road, and I will catch up with you."

Amaru required some additional assurances before he would leave, but soon he and the others had disappeared over the ridge and Cusi was alone with Alco in front of the huaca. The plume of black smoke rising from the offering fire drove them back a few steps, giving them an excuse to move about and examine each other without seeming to.

"We have known each other a long time," Cusi said tentatively, "but we are still strangers."

"Raurau Illa never meant for us to be friends. He used you to test me and make me gather power. And he used me to drive you back out into the world when you wanted to withdraw from it. He was not a man given to anger, so he did not understand that the things we did to each other might come between us as men."

Cusi nodded, finding the assessment persuasive, and impressive for its lack of any lingering resentment. "Must it come between us now?"

Alco gave him a long look. "What can exist between us now? You are leaving, and it is unlikely you will ever return. I must stay here and prepare my people for the rule of the Bearded Ones."

"What do you know about them?"

"I know that more and more of them will come here and that they will treat all of us like retainers. They will also destroy our huacas."

"This one?" Cusi asked, glancing up at the stone.

"Any that cannot be hidden from their sight."

"You cannot stop them?"

"No," Alco said, clamping his jaw down around the word. "No one can stop them."

"You should leave before they destroy you, as well. Come to Vitcos. Human Cachi is already settled there, and there is land for many more—land that is well protected by the mountains and the forest. No one has claimed that the Bearded Ones can fly, and we can close the trails to anyone who has to walk."

Alco bared his teeth in a smile even less pleasant than the first. "That is indeed good fortune. But then, you have always been fortunate."

Cusi cocked his head and squinted at him. "You sound like the Alco who was ruled by his hatred and envy, but you have already shown that you are free of that. So why would you refuse me?"

"Why would you offer?" Alco shot back. "You do not owe me any favors. I did not spare you just now; I could not have killed you in this place, as you should have known."

"You saved me from the sickness," Cusi pointed out. "And you provided the weapons that helped us escape from Calca."

"The first was my duty. The second I did for Huaman Cachi."

Cusi grunted, exasperated by the man's stubbornness. He looked up at the huaca, seeking guidance, but instead found himself imagining the stone's destruction and its absence from this place. The aching sense of loss that came over him made him realize how blithely he had recommended Alco's departure. I now have the power to preserve his life, Cusi thought ruefully, but I am still showing no concern for what he feels about it.

"I do not want you to come to Vitcos when you are bereft and pathetic," he said to Alco. "I want you to come when your power is still intact and your people still have their spirit. Bring your herds, too, and those of Inti and the Sapa Inca. I do not want anything more to be squandered if it can be of use to us."

Alco stared at him impassively for another moment, then placed a fist against his chest. "I have heard you, Cusi Huaman. I will have to see what is possible for me and my people."

"Of course," Cusi agreed. "I will leave you to consider."

They bowed to each other, and then Cusi turned and squatted down facing the huaca, placing his battle-ax on the ground in front of him but keeping his hands upon it. He let himself feel the stone's powerful presence, its ancient stillness, sheltering yet aloof. He again offered his life, his new life, to Illapa, vowing to accept whatever he was given with a grateful heart. He took his hands off of the battle-ax to make the mocha for the last time, though he kept himself from murmuring a farewell.

Rising with the weapon in his hands, he nodded once to Alco and backed away from the huaca, keeping his eyes on its towering, jagged shape until he came to the end of level ground and had to turn and climb the slope. He went up over the top of the ridge without looking back, heading northeast toward the Yucay Valley and Vitcos, toward Micay and the children and their friends and comrades. Toward the life we must make for ourselves, Cusi thought, and began to run, remembering the swiftness of a boy and running with the endurance of a man.

Epilogue

THIS IS what is remembered of the last of the Incas:

The Sapa Inca Huascar, from his place of captivity in Andamarca, managed to make overtures of his own to the leader of the Spanish invaders, Francisco Pizarro. When Atauhuallpa learned of this, he secretly sent a message to his men in Andamarca, and Huascar, the Coya Chuqui Huipa, and their mother, Rahua Ocllo, were all put to death. It is said their bodies were cut to pieces and thrown into a river.

Atauhuallpa remained a captive while the ransom he had offered was collected and shared out among the Spaniards, whose number had been doubled by the arrival of Diego de Almagro and his men. Atauhuallpa was then accused by his captors of fomenting rebellion among his people, and despite his protests of innocence and his promises of more gold he was tried and sentenced to death. In return for his acceptance of Christian baptism, Don Francisco Atauhuallpa was garroted in the square in Caxamarca rather than being burned at the stake. It is said his body was later stolen from its burial place and taken to Quito.

The war chief Challcochima had earlier surrendered himself to Hernando de Soto, apparently believing Atauhuallpa had summoned him to Caxamarca. He was taken along as a captive when the Spaniards marched to Cuzco in late 1533. Also with them was their chosen successor to Atauhuallpa, a little-known half brother named Topa Huallpa Inca. When this young man died under mysterious circumstances during the march, Challcochima was suspected of having conspired to poison him. He was later accused of this crime and was burned at the stake at Sacsahuaman.

The warchief Rumiñaui had established himself as the ruler of Quito and the surrounding territories, ostensibly on behalf of his captive lord. After Atauhuallpa's execution, however, he declared his independence by murdering all of Atauhuallpa's relatives and supporters. His cruelty to the Quitos finally became so excessive that they appealed to the Spanish for relief. Pursued by Sebastian de Belalcazar, Rumiñaui laid waste to the city of Quito before fleeing into the jungles to the east, where he presumably perished.

The war chief Quizquiz briefly delayed the Spanish advance on Cuzco, then fled to the north with the warriors who remained loyal to him. He was later pursued by Almagro and the newly arrived Pedro de Alvarado, but he and his men inflicted a serious defeat on the Spaniards and escaped into the mountains.

There the war chief's unbending determination to fight to the end provoked a mutiny among his warriors, and he was assassinated by one of his own captains.

Huascar's younger brother, Manco Inca, came out of hiding when the Spaniards reached Cuzco. He presented himself as the legitimate Heir and put himself under Spanish protection. Believing his father's kingdom would be restored to him if he helped the Spanish bring order to the Four Quarters, he lent his legitimacy to their cause. When his loyalty was rewarded with insults and abuse, including confinement in irons, he became disenchanted and secretly began to organize a rebellion. In May of 1536, while Francisco Pizarro was away in Lima, Manco and his followers rose up against the Spanish in all parts of the country, with the strongest attacks aimed at Lima and Cuzco. The latter city was besieged for eight months, during which the thatched roofs of its buildings were set afire and its streets and terraces were torn up to hinder the Spanish horses. Though vastly outnumbered and under constant attack, Hernando Pizarro and a small band of Spanish soldiers and Indian allies held out in the Haucaypata and finally launched a desperate raid on the fortress of Sacsahuaman, dislodging the Inca forces and breaking the spirit of the siege. With Spanish reinforcements approaching from the south and his own troops deserting to tend their neglected fields, Manco admitted defeat and withdrew to the Yucay Valley. He maintained his opposition to Spanish rule, however, holding Ollantaytambo against them for several years before retreating to the safety of the forest settlements of Vitcos and Vilcabamba. For several more years he led periodic raids into Spanish territory, carrying a sword of Spanish steel and fighting from horseback. In 1545, during an argument over a game being played on the green at Vitcos, he was murdered by a group of renegade Spaniards to whom he had given refuge.

Manco Inca had three sons who succeeded him in turn as rulers of Vilcabamba. The first, Sayri Topa Yupanqui, cooperated with the Spanish and was given an estate in the Yucay Valley, where he died peacefully in 1560. The second son, Titu Cusi Yupanqui, retreated to the forest strongholds, where he was visited only by Spanish priests. He died unexpectedly of a mysterious illness, and the suspicions aroused by his death led to the martyrdom of one Spanish priest and the murder of a group of ambassadors who had been sent out by the new Spanish viceroy, Francisco de Toledo. The viceroy retaliated by sending out his soldiers, who fought their way through the forest to Vitcos and Vilcabamba. Manco's third son, Tupac Amaru, led the Inca resistance for six months before being defeated and forced to flee into the jungle. He was hunted down by a Spanish captain and was taken back to Cuzco, where the viceroy rejected all pleas for mercy and sentenced him to die as a rebel against the Crown.

On the day set for Tupac Amaru's execution, thousands of people poured into Cuzco, some already weeping and singing songs of mourning. The prisoner was led out to the platform that had been erected in front of the cathedral in the Plaza de Armes, and the grieving of the crowd became so loud that the black hood was removed from the prisoner's head so that he could quiet them. Tupac Amaru had been converted to the faith of the conquerors and had been baptized Don Pablo Tupac Amaru, and in his final speech to his people, he vigorously renounced the beliefs he had been taught by his father and brother. Still, the signal was given and the prisoner was made to kneel, and with a single blow of the executioner's ax, the last Inca to wear the fringe was beheaded in the square that had once been called Haucaypata. The year was 1572.

Glossary of Quechua Terms

akha: fermented beverage made from maize and water; the maize is chewed to release its sugar content.

amaru: large serpent, specifically the anaconda.

Amarucancha: palace compound of Huayna Capac in Cuzco.

ayahuasca: Vine of the Dead, a vision-inducing drug drawn from a jungle liana, *Banisteriopsis caapi;* also known as yage.

Aymara: language of the tribes around Lake Titicaca and of many of the Indian inhabitants of present-day Bolivia.

bola: weapon consisting of two or more heavy balls tied to the ends of strong cords.

charqui: freeze-dried meat.

chonta: dark wood of the chonta palm, used for bows and clubs.

Chuncho: somewhat derogatory collective term for the forest tribes east of the Andes Mountains.

chuño: freeze-dried potatoes, usually in the form of flour.

coca: leaves of the shrub *Erythroxylon coca;* a mild stimulant when chewed with lime.

conopa: small stone figurine kept in the household for luck.

Coya: full sister and wife/consort of the Sapa Inca.

cumbi: fine tapestrylike cloth produced in the House of Chosen Women and worn by the Inca nobility.

guanaco: smaller wild relative of the llama.

huaca: object, place, or person thought to have otherworldly powers; quality of aloofness or holiness.

huacacachu: psychoactive drug made from the datura plant.

Huarachicoy: Ceremony of the Loincloth, the Inca initiation rites for young men.

Huatac: Inca official endowed with the punitive powers of the Sapa Inca.

Inti Raymi: Solemn Feast of the Sun, Inca celebration of the winter solstice.

mamacona: religious women employed in a variety of devotional and practical capacities.

micho: lieutenant governor of an Inca province.

mitmac: lit. "stranger" or "outsider"; tribal groups resettled by the Incas as a matter of state policy. They maintained the dress and customs of their original homeland and did not intermarry with their new neighbors; acted as spies and auxiliary troops for the Inca provincial officials.

mocha: extreme form of deference involving the blowing of kisses and hairs from the eyebrows; paid only to huacas, images of the gods, high religious figures, and the Sapa Inca.

Mollecancha: palace compound of Huayna Capac in Tumibamba.

Napa: flawless white llama, symbol of the First Llama.

ñusta: unmarried daughter of the nobility, past the age of first menstruation; does not imply chastity.

palla: wife of Inca blood or primary wife of a blood Inca.

Quechua: language of the Incas, spoken by many of the Indian inhabitants of present-day Peru and Bolivia.

Quicuchicoy: Inca initiation rites for young women.

quinoa: Andean grain that can be grown at high altitudes.

tocapu: form of fine weaving featuring individual squares of symbols personal to the wearer.

uta: leishmaniasis, a wasting disease similar to leprosy that attacks the mucous membranes of the face.

verruga: insect-borne disease afflicting both humans and llamas in valleys above 6,000 feet in altitude.

vicuña: smaller, wild relative of the llama, greatly prized for the fineness and silkiness of its wool.

vilca: psychoactive drug made from the seeds of the vilca tree.

vizcacha: Andean rodent similar to a rabbit.

yacarca: soothsayer who uses fire to foretell the future.

yanacona: lit. "the black ones," indicating the obscurity of their origins. People consigned to a state of perpetual servitude for reasons that are not clearly known; they were not slaves and often held important posts, drawing their status from the Incas they served.

Glossary of Characters

(* denotes historical figure)

Acapana (Swift-flying Cloud Rack): Inca official; micho and governor of Chachapoyas Province.

Acari: Nazca commander.

Acunta: Chimu guide and appointed chief of Chan Chan.

Alco (Dog): tribal sorcerer; brother of Urcon; successor to Raurau Illa.

Amancay (Lily): Inca ñusta and wife; companion of Chuqui Huipa.

Amaru (Anaconda): Inca warrior and architect; brother of Cusi and Quinti Ocllo; husband of Parihuana and father of Roca.

Ancoayllu (Tough Bolas): Colla chief of Hatuncolla; father of Tomay.

Ancocoyuch: son of Huaman Chumu, Grand Chimu in Chiquitoy.

Apu Poma (Lord Puma): Inca official; micho and governor of Cañar Province; husband of Mama Cori and father of Amaru, Quinti Ocllo, and Cusi Huaman.

Aranyac (He Who Dances in a Mask): Inca teacher in the Cuzco House of Learning; lord of the Eastern Quarter.

*Atauhuallpa (Royal and Victorious Turkey Cock): son of Huayna Capac by a secondary wife; war chief and Regent of the Northern Provinces; last indigenous ruler of Inca Empire.

*Atoc (Fox): Inca war chief; half brother of Huascar.

*Auqui Toma (Encirclement Prince): Inca war chief; half brother of Huayna Capac.

Auqui Topa Inca: Regent of Cuzco in Huayna Capac's absence.

Ayar Inca (Quinoa Inca): father of Lloque Yupanqui and Mama Cori; grandfather of Cusi, Amaru, and Quinti.

Cachi (Salt): female retainer; wife of Sucso.

Cahua (Prudent)(1): chosen woman and Woman of the Sun in Caxamarca; later known as Mama Cahua.

Cahua (2): daughter of Cusi and Micay and twin sister of Sinchi.

Casca: Chachapoya rebel chief; father of Misa/Micay.

*Challcochima: Inca war chief.

*Challco Yupanqui: half brother of Huascar; high priest in Cuzco during Huascar's reign.

Chimpu Ocllo (Pure Halo): high priestess in Tumibamba; also known as the mamanchic ("our mother").

Choque Chinchay (Golden Lynx): Cañari captain of the Royal Guard; father of Rimachi.

*Chuqui Huipa (Golden Ecstatic Joy): Elder daughter of Huayna Capac and Rahua Ocllo; full sister and wife/Coya of Huascar.

Chuqui Llantu (Fleeting Shadow): Cañari ñusta; wife of Huaman Cachi.

Cisa: younger daughter of Quinti Ocllo and Quilaco Yupanqui.

Coca: elder daughter of Quinti Ocllo and Quilaco Yupanqui; wife of Huallpa.

Condor Tupac (Royal Condor): Inca micho of Chachapoyas Province.

Cori Cuillor (Golden Star): Inca ñusta; wife of Challcochima; companion to Chuqui Huipa.

Cumpi Illya (Tapestry Treasure): Cañari woman related to Rimachi.

Cusi Huaman (Joyful Hawk): Cusi Auqui (Joyful Prince) as a boy; Inca warrior and scout; son of Apu Poma and Mama Cori; brother of Amaru and Quinti Ocllo; husband of Micay and father of Cahua and Sinchi; war chief and lord of the Eastern Quarter under Atauhuallpa.

*Cusi Rimay (Joyful Speaker): full sister and first Coya of Huayna Capac; mother of Ninan Cuyochi.

Fempellec: Chimu male courtesan; chief of feasts for Apu Poma, Mama Huarcay, and Chuqui Huipa.

Hanp'atu (Toad): Callawaya healer and medicine man.

Huallpa (Turkey Cock): Chachapoya son of Quespi and adopted son of Yasca and Rimachi; brother of Yutu; husband of Coca.

Huaman Cachi (Hawk Salt): apprentice and warrior under Cusi; husband of Chuqui Llantu.

*Huaman Chumu: Grand Chimu of Chimor Province under Inca rule during reign of Huayna Capac.

*Huanca Auqui (Field Guardian Prince): half brother of Huascar and war chief under him.

Huañu (Crescent Moon): Colla warrior and scout from Hatuncolla.

*Huascar (Hummingbird): son of Huayna Capac and Rahua Ocllo; brother of Chuqui Huipa and Tocto Oxica; twelfth Sapa Inca; husband of Chuqui Huipa.

*Huayna Capac (Youthful Prince): son of Topa Inca; eleventh Sapa Inca; husband of Cusi Rimay and Rahua Ocllo (among others); father of Ninan Cuyochi, Huascar, Chuqui Huipa, Tocto Oxica, Atauhuallpa, and Manco Inca (among others).

Inca Pasac: half brother of Atauhuallpa and one of his ambassadors to Huascar.

Inca Roca: half brother of and adviser to Huascar.

Inquil (Blue Flower): chosen woman in Caxamarca.

Kirupasa (Big Frog): Shuara sorcerer and chief.

Llampu (Gentle): Cañari wife of Rimachi and mother of Topa.

Lloque Yupanqui (Esteemed Lance): Royal Rememberer and adviser to Huayna Capac; twin brother of Mama Cori; uncle of Cusi, Amaru, and Quinti Ocllo.

Macas: holy woman and keeper of a huaca in the mountains east of Tumibamba; also referred to as Pachamama and Huaca Woman.

Machacuay (Serpent): retainer attached to Micay; assistant chief of feasts at Vitcos.

Mama Amancay (Lady Lily): daughter of Huayna Capac; primary wife of Atauhuallpa.

Mama Chiclla: Inca wife in Tumibamba.

Mama Cisa: midwife in Quito.

Mama Cori (Golden Lady): twin sister of Lloque Yupanqui; Inca wife of Apu Poma and mother of Cusi, Amaru, and Quinti Ocllo; member of the Coya Rahua Ocllo's court.

Mama Huarcay: Fourth Wife of Huayna Capac; not a full sister.

Mama Inquil (Lady Blue Flower): high priestess of Machu Picchu; also referred to as mamanchic ("our mother").

Mama Pura: Quito wife of Ninan Cuyochi.

Mama Ticlla: cousin of Chimpu Ocllo and her chosen successor as high priestess of Tumibamba.

*Manco Inca: son of Huayna Capac and younger brother of Huascar; puppet ruler under the Spanish and rebel leader of the Incas of Vilcabamba.

Mayca: Inca warrior; cousin of Sutic; initiation brother of Cusi.

Mayta Yupanqui: Inca governor of Chimor Province under Huayna Capac.

Micay (Roundface): also known as Misa; chosen woman and Chachapoya ñusta; wife of Cusi Huaman and mother of Cahua and Sinchi; healer and companion to the Coya Chuqui Huipa.

*Michi (Herder): Inca war chief under Huayna Capac.

*Minchancaman: Grand Chimu of Chimor Province prior to Inca rule.

Naymlap: Chimu sorcerer and high priest of Chan Chan.

*Ninan Cuyochi (Fire Flaunter): son of Huayna Capac and his first Coya, Cusi Rimay; Inca war chief and Regent of the Northern Provinces; husband of Mama Pura.

Nofan-Nech: Chimu high priest at Huaca Urcco (El Purgatorio).

Ñupchu (Red Flower): Colla wife of Tomay Guanaco and mother of Suchi; later remarried to Tarapaca.

Ococo (Frog): Campa chosen woman from Chachapoyas and companion to Cahua (2).

*Otoronco Achachi (Grandfather Jaguar): son of Pachacuti and brother of Topa Inca; Inca war chief, Royal Inspector, lord of the Eastern Quarter, governor of Chachapoyas Province; Cusi's great-uncle and his guardian in Cuzco.

Ozcollo (Wildcat): Campa high chief of Vitcos; father of Uritu.

*Pachacuti (The World Turned Upside Down): ninth Sapa Inca and founder of the Four Quarters; father of Topa Inca and Otoronco Achachi (among others); head of the Iñaca household.

Parihuana (Flamingo): Quito chosen woman; wife of Amaru and mother of Roca.

Paucar (Gaudy): Inca warrior and scout.

Paucar Rimay (Gaudy Speaker): Inca by privilege from Cuzco; warrior injured at Piura.

Pias: Chachapoya high chief of the village of Suta.

*Pinta: Carangui war leader.

Piqui (Flea): retainer from the Quito area; captain of warriors under Cusi and commander of Vitcos.

Poma Mallqui (Puma Scion): Inca warrior and messenger from Tumbez.

Pongmassa: Chimu guide in Chan Chan.

Quespi (Crystal): Chachapoya wife of Yasca and mother of Huallpa and Yutu; later remarried to Rimachi; healer.

*Quilaco Yupanqui: Inca war chief; husband of Quinti Ocllo and father of Coca and Cisa; wounded at Yanamarca.

Quinti Ocllo (Pure Hummingbird): daughter of Apu Poma and Mama Cori and sister of Cusi and Amaru; wife of Quilaco Yupanqui and mother of Coca and Cisa.

*Quizquiz (Small Bird): Inca war chief; last ruler of Cuzco prior to Spanish occupation.

*Rahua Ocllo: full sister and Second Wife/Coya of Huayna Capac; mother of Chuqui Huipa, Huascar, and Tocto Oxica.

Raurau Illa (Flaming Lance): blind sorcerer and chief of village outside Cuzco.

Rimachi (Speaker): son of Choque Chinchay; Cañari Inca by privilege; warrior and commander of Royal Guard; husband of Llampu, Tusoc, and Quespi and father of Topa.

Roca: son of Amaru and Parihuana.

*Rumiñaui (Stone Eye): Inca war chief under Huayna Capac and Atauhuallpa.

Runtu Caya: retainer woman attached to the family of Apu Poma and Mama Cori.

Sinchi (Warlord): son of Cusi and Micay and twin brother of Cahua (2).

Sinchi Huaman (Warlord Hawk): father of Apu Poma and grandfather of Cusi, Amaru, and Quinti Ocllo.

*Sinchi Roca: half brother of Huayna Capac; famous Inca architect and mentor of Amaru.

Suchi (Fat Fish): daughter of Tomay Guanaco and Ñupchu.

Sucso (Discolored): head retainer at the Rainbow House; husband of Cachi.

Sumac Mallqui (Handsome Scion): instructor of young warriors in Cuzco and Inca war chief.

Sutic: Inca warrior; initiation brother of Cusi; cousin of Mayca.

Tarapaca (Eagle): Lupaca warrior from Cuzco; captain and commander of Pisac under Cusi; husband of Ñupchu.

Titu: Inca warrior; initiation brother of Cusi.

Titu Amaru: head retainer of the Iñaca household in Cuzco.

Titu Atauchi: sorcerer and adviser to Huayna Capac.

*****Tocto Oxica** (Maize Flower Sandal): daughter of Huayna Capac and Rahua Ocllo and full sister of Huascar and Chuqui Huipa; high priestess of the Moon on Coati Island; later married to Paullu Inca and baptized as Doña Catalina.

Tomay Guanaco (Circling Guanaco): also known as Tomay Huaraca; Colla from Hatuncolla and Inca by privilege; scout, commander, and war chief under Incas; husband of Ñupchu and father of Suchi.

Topa (Royal): Cañari son of Rimachi and Llampu.

*****Topa Colla:** Inca war chief under Huayna Capac.

Topa Poma (Royal Puma): half brother of Atauhuallpa and his ambassador to Huascar.

Topa Roca: Inca micho of Chimor Province.

*****Topa Yupanqui** (Esteemed Nobleman): high priest of the Sun under Huayna Capac.

Tusoc (Dancer): Chumpivilca chosen woman and wife of Rimachi.

*****Ucumari** (Bear): Inca war chief under Huayna Capac and Atauhuallpa.

*****Urco Colla:** Cañari high chief of Tumibamba under Huascar.

Urcon (Buck Llama): herder from the village of Raurau Illa, outside Cuzco; brother of Alco and comrade of Cusi.

Uritu (Parrot): Campa from Vitcos and Inca by privilege; commander of warriors and high chief of Vitcos.

Yahuar Huacac (Blood Weeper): half brother of Atauhuallpa and his ambassador to Huascar.

*****Yasca:** Inca war chief under Huayna Capac; husband of Quespi and father of Huallpa and Yutu.

Yucra: nephew of Atauhuallpa and witness to his capture.

Yutu (Tinamou) (1): chosen woman in Caxamarca.

Yutu (2): daughter of Quespi and Yasca; sister of Huallpa.

Glossary of the Gods

Apu Inti (Lord Sun): mature aspect of the Sun god, associated with the summer solstice and the Capac Raymi festival.

Axomama (Potato Mother): goddess of the potato crop; worshiped by Inca women.

Chuqui Illa (Burning Spear): sky god combining aspects of Inti and Illapa.

Churi Inti (Child Sun): immature aspect of the Sun god, associated with the winter solstice and the Inti Raymi festival.

Collca (Granary): the Pleiades.

Huanacauri (Rainbow): Inca war god and special patron of the warriors of Cuzco.

Huayna Punchao (Young Daylight): immature aspect of the Sun god, associated with the winter solstice and the Inti Raymi festival.

Illapa (Lightning): sky god of lightning, thunder, and rain; one of the three Inca high gods (with Inti and Viracocha).

Inti (Sun): solar deity; consort of Mama Quilla and father of the Incas; special patron of the Incas as a caste.

Inti Illapa (Sun Lightning): sky god combining aspects of Inti and Illapa.

Mama Cocha (Mother Water): Pacific Ocean.

Mama Ocllo (Pure Lady): First Mother of the Incas in the legends of the founding of Cuzco; aspect of Pachamama.

Mama Quilla (Mother or Lady Moon): Moon goddess and consort of Inti; mother of the Incas and special patroness of Inca women.

Pachamama (Earth Mother): ancient earth goddess and goddess of fertility; manifest in the earth itself; worshiped by women.

Saramama (Maize Mother): goddess of the maize crop; worshiped by Inca women.

Si: Chimu moon goddess, worshiped as high god by both men and women; special protectress against thieves.

Thunupa (Thunder): ancient Aymara sky god from region around Lake Titicaca; possibly high god of Tiahuanaco civilization.

Viracocha (Foaming Water): Inca Creator god; one of the three Inca high gods (with Inti and Illapa).

Glossary of Places

(All distances are extremely approximate)

Abancay: Inca rest house on the Royal Road to the north; site of the modern town of Abancay, 120 miles west of Cuzco.

Ambato: site of famous battle between forces of Atauhuallpa and Huascar; modern town of same name lies 75 miles south of Quito in northern Ecuador.

Ancayaco: site of battle between forces of Atauhuallpa and Huascar; north of present-day Ayacucho in south-central Peru.

Andamarca: Inca rest house where Huascar was held in captivity; south of the modern city of Jauja in south-central Peru.

Atacama Desert: great desert in the extreme southern part of the Southern Quarter; now northern Chile.

Apurle: Mochica/Chimu site in the Lambayeque Valley on the north coast of Peru; near the modern town of Motupe.

Ayaviri: capital of Cana tribe, north of Lake Titicaca; modern town of same name lies 160 miles south of Cuzco.

Calca: site of Inca pleasure villas in the Yucay Valley; modern town of same name lies 20 miles east of Cuzco.

Caxamarca: city in central highlands of Peru, now called Cajamarca; about 800 miles north of Cuzco.

Caxamarquilla: capital of Chachapoyas Province in mountainous forest region east of Marañon River; possibly site of modern town of Chachapoyas, 175 miles northeast of Cajamarca.

Chan Chan: capital of Chimu empire prior to Inca conquest; near modern city of Trujillo on the Pacific coast of Peru, 600 miles north of Lima.

Charcas Province: region of Inca control south of Lake Titicaca; now part of Bolivia, near the city of Cochabamba.

Chincha: coastal valley on the central coast of Peru; modern town of Chincha Alta lies 125 miles south of Lima.

Chiquitoy: Inca capital of Chimor Province, 15 miles north of Chan Chan on the north coast of Peru; also known as Chiquitoy Viejo.

Chucuito: capital of the Lupaca tribe, on the western shore of Lake Titicaca; the modern town of the same name lies 230 miles south of Cuzco.

Chuquiabo: city of La Paz, Bolivia; just south of Lake Titicaca.

Chuquisaca: capital of the Quillaca tribe in Charcas Province south of Lake Titicaca; near the modern town of Sucre, Bolivia.

Cinto: coastal valley on the north coast of Peru, south of Motupe; under Chimu control prior to Inca conquest.

Coaque: site on the northern coast of Ecuador, north of Manta and Guayaquil; original landing point for the Spanish under Francisco Pizarro.

Coati Island: Island of the Moon in Lake Titicaca, an Inca shrine.

Cochabamba: fertile highland valley south of Lake Titicaca; near the modern city of Cochabamba, Bolivia.

Cochahuaylas: site of battle between forces of Atauhuallpa and Huascar; in the central highlands of Peru, north of Caxamarca.

Cochisque: site of Carangui fort north of Quito; in northern highlands of Ecuador.

Collique: coastal valley on the north coast of Peru, south of Motupe; under Chimu control prior to Inca conquest.

Combapata: site on road from Cuzco to Lake Titicaca; just north of Sicuani.

Copacabana: pilgrimage center on the southwestern shore of Lake Titicaca; now part of Bolivia.

Copiapo: Inca outpost in the extreme southern part of the Southern Quarter, near the Atacama Desert; now part of Chile.

Cotapachi: Inca site in the Cochabamba Valley, south of Lake Titicaca; now part of Bolivia.

Cotapampa: site of battle between forces of Atauhuallpa and Huascar; just west of Cuzco across the Apurimac River.

Cusipampa: Inca administrative center on the Royal Road between Caxamarca and Tumibamba.

Cuzco: Inca capital in the southern highlands of Peru and the center of the Four Quarters; 1,230 miles south of Quito and some 2,000 miles north of the boundary of the Southern Quarter.

Farfan: Inca administrative center in the Jequetepeque Valley on the north coast of Peru; 30 miles north of Chan Chan.

Hatuncolla: capital of the Colla tribe, just west of Lake Titicaca; some 200 miles south of Cuzco.

Huaca Urcco: Mochica ruin known as El Purgatorio on the north coast of Peru; near the modern town of Motupe.

Huachala: site of Carangui fort north of Quito in northern highlands of Ecuador.

Huamachuco: capital of the Huamachuco tribe in the central highlands of Peru; 33 miles south of Cajamarca.

Huanacopampa: site of battle between forces of Atauhuallpa and Huascar; just southwest of Cuzco, across the Apurimac River.

Huancabamba: Inca administrative center on the Royal Road; 150 miles north of Cajamarca; near modern town of Cajas.

Huiñay Huayna: Inca rest house on the Inca trail from Ollantaytambo to Machu Picchu; in the Urubamba Valley northeast of Cuzco.

Incallacta: Inca site in the Cochabamba Valley, south of Lake Titicaca; now part of Bolivia.

Lambayeque Valley: large river valley on the north coast of Peru, north of Chan Chan; perhaps a cotton plantation under the Incas.

Latacunga: highland site 40 miles south of Quito in northern Ecuador; modern town is called La Tacunga.

Leche Valley: river valley on the north coast of Peru, just north of the Lambayeque Valley.

Limatambo: Inca rest house on the Royal Road to the north; perhaps 30 miles from Cuzco.

Lynx House: estate belonging to the cult of Mama Quilla in the mountains east of Tumibamba.

Machu Picchu: Inca religious center in the Urubamba Valley, just northeast of Cuzco.

Manta: coastal site on the north coast of Ecuador, north of Guayaquil; legendary point of departure of Viracocha after creation.

Mira Valley: Carangui stronghold north of Quito in the highlands of Ecuador; near the modern town of Ibarra.

Motupe: site on the Royal Road between Piura and Chan Chan on the north coast of Peru; modern town bears same name.

Nasakara: high point on road leading into the Cochabamba Valley, south of Lake Titicaca; now part of Bolivia.

Ollantaytambo: Inca religious-administrative center in the Yucay Valley at the juncture of the Urubamba and Patakancha rivers; now a town and tourist attraction on the way to Machu Picchu.

Pacatnamu: Mochica/Chimu shrine on the coast outside the Jequetepeque Valley on the north coast of Peru, 30 miles north of Chan Chan; renowned as an oracle in Inca times.

Pachacamac: ancient shrine on the coast just outside present-day city of Lima; most venerable oracle in the Four Quarters.

Pisac: Inca fortress–administrative center in the Yucay Valley, east of Cuzco.

Piura: site in the Piura River Valley on the north coast of Peru, south of Tumbez; under Chimu control prior to Inca conquest; modern town bears the same name.

Pomata: town on the southwestern shore of Lake Titicaca in Peru.

Puna Island: island city in the estuary of the Guayas River in southwestern Ecuador between Tumbez and Guayaquil.

Quihuipay: site just north of Cuzco where the Cuzco Incas surrendered to the forces of Atauhuallpa.

Quiquijana: site on the Royal Road south of Cuzco.

Quito: highland city in northern Ecuador; 1230 miles north of Cuzco and

160 miles north of Tumibamba; the northernmost major city of the Four Quarters and the capital of present-day Ecuador.

Rainbow House: estate in the mountains east of Tumibamba, given to Cusi by Huayna Capac.

Rimac: famous oracle shrine on the central coast of Peru; now within the expanding limits of the city of Lima.

Riobamba: site on the Royal Road between Quito and Tumibamba, capital of the Puruhua tribe; modern Ecuadorian city, 40 miles south of Quito, bears the same name.

Savapata: Inca fortress in Charcas Province, south of Lake Titicaca.

Sechura Desert: large desert on the north coast of Peru, just south of the Piura River Valley.

Sican: Mochica/Chimu site on the north coast of Peru; near the modern town of Motupe.

Sicuani: site on the Royal Road some 60 miles south of Cuzco; modern town bears the same name.

Sullana: first river valley south of Tumbez on the north coast of Peru.

Suta: village in eastern Chachapoyas Province; home of Casca and his daughter Misa.

Tangarara: site on the north coast of Peru, just north of Piura; occupied by the Spanish under Francisco Pizarro before their march to Caxamarca.

Tarabuco: Inca site in Charcas Province, south of Lake Titicaca; now part of Bolivia.

Tiahuanaco: capital of the pre-Inca Tiahuanaco culture (1000–1300 A.D.); the partially restored ruins lie 12 miles south of Lake Titicaca and 30 miles west of the city of La Paz, Bolivia.

Tipycala: Aymara name for Tiahuanaco; the Collas and Lupacas of the area claimed ancestry with the builders of the site.

Titicaca: enormous (80-mile-long) highland lake some 200 miles south of Cuzco; considered sacred by the Incas and the Aymara-speaking inhabitants of the region; the Incas had temples to the Sun and Moon on islands in the lake.

Tumbez: port city on the extreme northern coast of Peru; capital of the Tallenes but under Chimu control prior to Inca conquest.

Tumibamba: capital of the Cañari tribe in the central highlands of Ecuador; birthplace of Huayna Capac and the base for his northern campaign; now the site of the town of Cuenca, Ecuador.

Urcos: Inca site on the Royal Road about 20 miles south of Cuzco.

Vilcabamba: mountainous forest region to the northeast of Cuzco; refuge of Manco Inca and his successors after their rebellion against Spanish rule.

Vilcashuaman: Inca administrative center on the Royal Road, 150 miles northwest of Cuzco; near the modern town of Andahuaylas.

Vitcos: capital of the Campa tribe in the mountainous forest region northeast of Cuzco.

Xauxa: capital of the Huanca tribe in the central highlands of Peru; 400 miles south of Cajamarca; modern city is called Jauja.

Yanamarca: site of a battle between the forces of Atauhuallpa and Huascar; just north of the city of Xauxa (Jauja).

Yucay Valley: river valley just east of Cuzco, site of the estates and pleasure villas of the Inca royal family, as well as of Pisac and Ollantaytambo.

Zaña Valley: coastal river valley on the north coast of Peru, north of Chan Chan; now called Sana.

Glossary of Tribes

Callawayas: tribe living in the mountains northeast of Lake Titicaca; famous as itinerant healers and medicine men.

Campas: tribe living in the mountainous forest region northeast of Cuzco, with capital at Vitcos; famous as bowmen.

Canas: Aymara-speaking tribe with capital at Sicuani.

Cañaris: tribe occupying the highlands of southern Ecuador, with capital at Tumibamba; favored subjects/allies of Cuzco Incas.

Carangui: tribe occupying the highlands north of Quito with capital in the Mira Valley; fought eleven-year war against the Incas.

Caxamarcans: highland tribe occupying the region around the city of Caxamarca; allied with Chimus before conquest by Incas.

Chachapoyas: tribe occupying the mountainous forest region east of the Marañon River in northeastern Peru, with capital at Caxamarquilla; rebellious subjects of the Incas.

Chancas: highland tribe occupying the regions northwest of Cuzco; enemy of Incas who almost captured Cuzco before being defeated by Pachacuti in 1437.

Charcas: Ayamara-speaking tribe living south of Lake Titicaca with capital near Potosi; subjects of Incas.

Chimus: coastal tribe who controlled the Pacific coast from Rimac (Lima) in the south to Tumbez in the north prior to conquest by the Incas in 1460; capital at Chan Chan.

Chinchas: coastal tribe occupying the Chincha Valley, south of Lima on the Pacific coast.

Chiriguanos: also known as Guaranis; itinerant forest tribe with homeland near Pilcomayo River in Paraguay; raided Inca outposts in Cochabamba Valley in 1524 under leadership of Spaniard Aléjo García.

Collas: Aymara-speaking tribe occupying the high plains west of Lake Titicaca with capital at Hatuncolla; renowned as herders, stonemasons, and rebels against the Incas.

Huamachucos: highland tribe of central Peru with capital at Huamachuco, south of Caxamarca.

Huancas: highland tribe of central Peru with capitals at Huancabamba and Xauxa.

Huancavelicas: lowland tribe occupying the region near Guayaquil in southwestern Ecuador.

Icas: coastal tribe inhabiting the Ica Valley, south of Lima; part of the Ica-Nazca culture, 400–1000 A.D.

Incas: Quechua-speaking highland tribe that ruled the Four Quarters, extending from the Maule River (Chile) in the south to the Angasmayo River (Colombia) in the north, and from the Pacific coast in the west to the Amazon basin in the east; capital at Cuzco.

Lupacas: Aymara-speaking highland tribe inhabiting the high plain west of Lake Titicaca with capital at Chucuito; traditional enemies of the neighboring Collas before Inca conquest.

Machiguengas: forest tribe living in the cloud forest and jungles northeast of Cuzco.

Mascos: forest tribe living in the cloud forest and jungles northeast of Cuzco.

Mochicas: coastal tribe that ruled a large area of the Pacific coast from 400–800 A.D. and were the forerunners of the later Chimu empire; built monumental edifices (huacas) of adobe brick in the Moche (Chimor) Valley and other places.

Moxos: also known as Mojos; forest tribe inhabiting the jungles to the east of the Bolivian Andes.

Nazcas: coastal tribe inhabiting the Nazca Valley, south of Lima; part of the Ica-Nazca culture, 400–1000 A.D.; famous for the great line drawings allegedly meant to attract extraterrestrials.

Paltas: highland tribe of south-central Ecuador with capital near Loja.

Piros: forest tribe occupying the cloud forest and jungles east of Cuzco.

Punas: coastal tribe occupying Puna Island in the estuary of the Guayas River in southwestern Ecuador; famous for their resistance to Inca rule.

Quillacas: highland tribe occupying an area south of Cochabamba, Bolivia, with capital at Chuquisaca (Sucre).

Quitos: highland tribe of central Ecuador with capital at the city of Quito.

Rucanas: highland tribe living southwest of Cuzco; renowned as litter bearers.

Shuaras: also known as Jivaros; forest tribe of the jungles of eastern Peru and Ecuador; famous as headshrinkers.

Soras: highland tribe living southwest of Cuzco; renowned as litter bearers.

Urus: highland tribe living at the southern end of Lake Titicaca.

Yarovilcas: highland tribe of central Peru, living on the upper Marañon River near Huanuco.

About the Author

DANIEL PETERS was born in 1948 in Milwaukee, Wisconsin, and was educated at Yale University. He has lived in Vancouver, rural New Hampshire, Maryland and upper New York State, and currently lives in Tucson, Arizona, with his wife, the feminist writer Annette Kolodny.

An avid student of America's pre-Columbian civilizations, Mr. Peters is also the author of *The Luck of Huemac*, a novel about the Aztecs, and *Tikal*, a novel about the Maya.

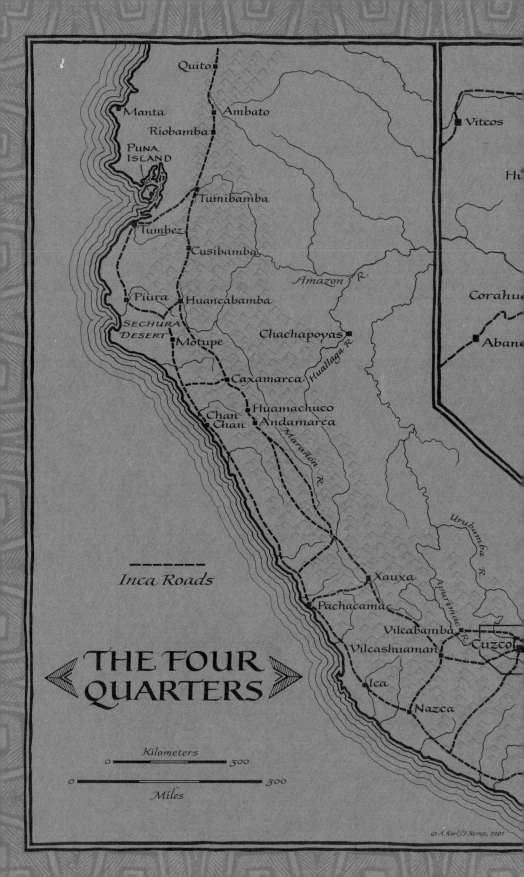

THE FOUR QUARTERS

Inca Roads

Quito
Manta
Ambato
Riobamba
PUNA ISLAND
Tumibamba
Tumbez
Cusibamba
Vitcos
Hi
Amazon R.
Corahu
Piura
Huancabamba
SECHURA DESERT
Motupe
Chachapoyas
Abane
Caxamarca
Huallaga R.
Chan Chan
Huamachuco
Andamarca
Marañón R.
Urubamba R.
Xauxa
Pachacamac
Apurimac R.
Vilcabamba
Cuzco
Vilcashuaman
Ica
Nazca

Kilometers
0   300

0   300
Miles

© A. Karl/J. Kemp, 1991